HOUSE DIVIDED

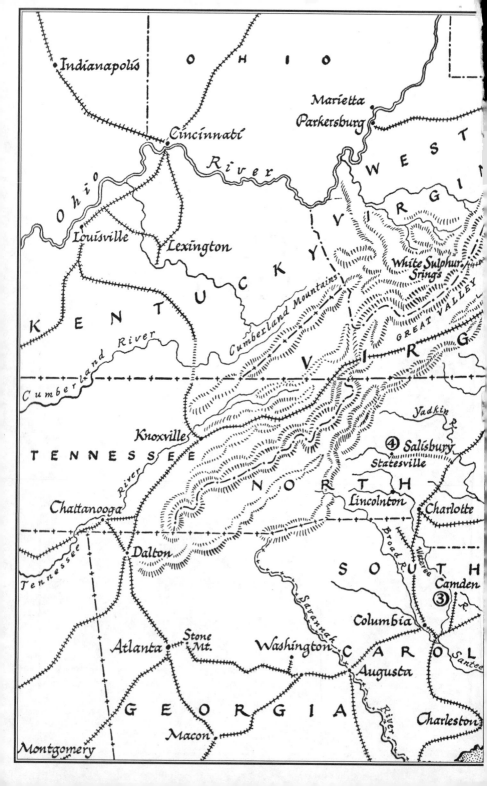

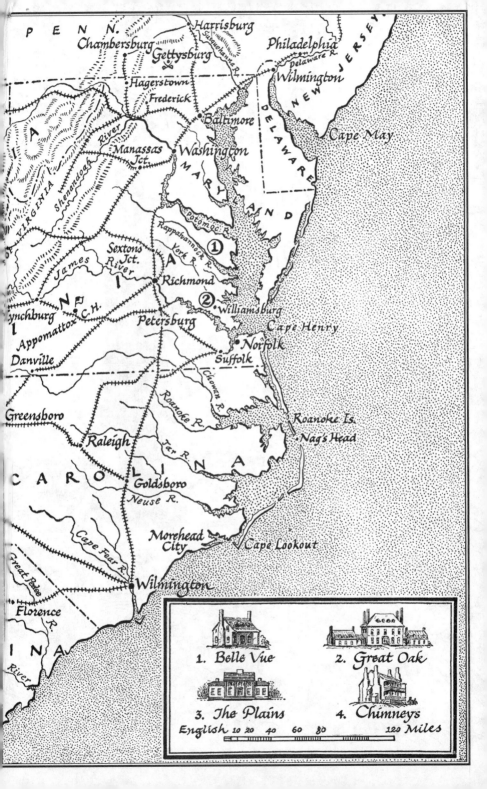

PENN.

Harrisburg
Chambersburg
Gettysburg
Philadelphia
Susquehanna R.
Delaware R.
Hagerstown
Wilmington
Frederick
NEW JERSEY
Baltimore
DELAWARE
Washington
Cape May
MARYLAND
Manassas
Jct.
Shenandoah River
Potomac R.
VIRGINIA
Rappahannock
①
York R.
Sextons
Jct.
James River
Richmond
②
Williamsburg
Lynchburg
N. C.H.
Petersburg
Cape Henry
Appomattox
Norfolk
Danville
Suffolk
Chowan R.
Roanoke R.
Greensboro
Roanoke Is.
Nag's Head
Raleigh
Tar R.
CAROLINA
Goldsboro
Neuse R.
Cape Fear R.
Morehead
City
Cape Lookout
Great Pedee River
Wilmington
Florence
River
INA

1. Belle Vue   2. Great Oak

3. The Plains   4. Chimneys

English 10 20 40 60 80 120 Miles

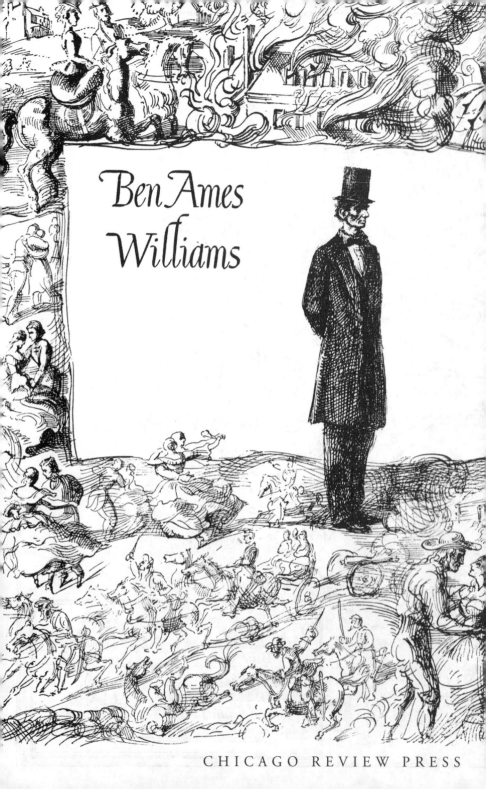

Ben Ames Williams

CHICAGO REVIEW PRESS

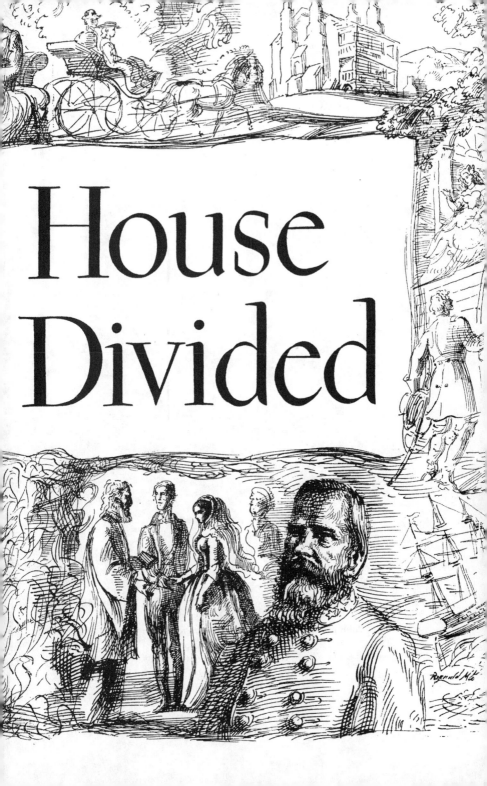

House Divided

Published in 2006 by Chicago Review Press, Incorporated
814 North Franklin Street
Chicago, Illinois 60610
ISBN-13: 978-1-55652-619-0
ISBN-10: 1-55652-619-9
5 4 3 2 1
Printed in the United States of America

To My Daughter

HOUSE
DIVIDED

Acknowledgments

WITH the completion of a work which in its finished form represents a dozen or fifteen years of preparatory thought and study, topped by about fifty-two months of concentrated labor, it is a pleasure to call a grateful roll of some of the men and women who have made helpful contributions. The list cannot be complete, since concrete information and stimulating suggestions came from many sources. For a long time before beginning to write this book, I read no Southern fiction, old or new; but I turned eagerly to every other source likely to be useful. Correspondence with two or three score librarians, historians, book dealers, and informed individuals was supplemented by an eight-thousand-mile journey which covered every locale described in these pages, and which gave me the opportunity to talk with many people. From these conversations came sometimes a phrase or a sentence, sometimes a chapter, sometimes an entirely new conception of an historic event.

At the top of the list of those whose co-operation has made this work possible must be set the names of Mrs. Williams and of my daughter, Ann. Mrs. Williams not only endured with an equal fortitude the abstractions, the depressions, and the exhilarations which are part of an author's travail; she preserved for me, often against heavy odds, a serene home where distractions were kept to a minimum. In addition, she made, with painstaking accuracy, a series of large-scale maps — of old Richmond, of the retreat from Petersburg to Appomattox Court-House, of the scene of war in Northern Virginia and around Richmond, of the Gettysburg battlefield, and of other regions — without which the difficulties of my task would have been infinitely greater.

My daughter typed from my longhand draft the first third of the manuscript; she read the entire manuscript at least three times at various stages of revision; she was able to discuss with me at any time any passage concerning which I wished her opinion; and when the text of the manuscript was completed, she, with the assistance of Miss Emily Reynolds, checked the punctuation, decided which words should be capitalized and which should not, and whether such compounds as "smoke house," "down river," "business man" and a thousand others should be printed as one word, or hyphenated, or set as two words.

My thanks go, too, to Miss Emily Reynolds, who during the months of revision typed and re-typed some three thousand pages of manuscript, always alert to detect those treacherous slips which — once the author has set them on paper — elude him as easily as an error in a problem in addition. For the enormous physical labor of producing the manuscript, a task which consumed fifteen or twenty thousand pages of white and yellow paper, a quart or so of ink, and two or three hundred pencils, my thanks go not only to my daughter and Miss Reynolds, but also to Miss Caroline Boissevain and Miss Joan Andrews, who struggled with my always difficult handwriting through the intermediate stages.

To turn to those whose help, less direct, was nevertheless continuously valuable: Through the entire period of the work I had the ready advice and counsel of Douglas Southall Freeman, who answered by return mail and with courteous helpfulness every question asked, and who during my stay in Richmond put at my disposal not only his library but masses of unpublished matter which had been collected in the course of his own tireless studies. Major Bell I. Wiley, whose extensive researches have made him an authority on the subject, was generous with help in my attempt to arrive at a cross-section of the personnel of the Army of Northern Virginia from the point of view of the social and economic position of the individual soldier.

Many passages in the book are concerned with the private life of General James Longstreet. My mother, whose uncle he was, contributed from her own recollection and from the memories of relatives and friends in Macon, Mississippi, incidents and anecdotes which helped to round out his character. The General's surviving widow, Helen Dortch Longstreet, answered many letters of searching inquiry, and out of her memory of conversations with the General provided details not to be found in any documentary or published source. For further information about Longstreet as a husband and father, I am indebted to his son, Fitz Randolph Longstreet of Gainesville, Georgia, and to his daughter, Mrs. L. L. Whelchel of Washington. For details of his military career not elsewhere available I owe thanks to Colonel Donald B. Sanger, who allowed me to read his as yet unpublished biography of the General. Katharine M. Hall of the University of Chicago libraries furnished me with the Sanger manuscript. Lionel B. Moses of Chicago loaned me the unpublished memoirs of his grandfather, Major Raphael J. Moses, who served as Commissary on General Longstreet's Staff. Through Mrs. Longstreet, James Longstreet Sibley, Sr., of Milledgeville, Georgia, gave useful answers to some questions. Henry Minor of Macon, Mississippi, searched old files of the Macon *Beacon* for information about the General.

Without the ready co-operation of librarians, this work would have engaged me for months longer than it did, and would have required more thousands of miles of travel. Miss J. M. Campbell of Lynchburg and her assistants in the Jones Memorial Library not only traced out for me every useful reference to General Longstreet's stays in Lynchburg, and to the Garland family there, but also introduced me to Miss Mary Lightfoot Garland of Richmond, who was generous in answering from her tremendous store of historical and genealogical information a thousand questions. Miss Josephine Wingfield of the Jones Memorial Library searched old newspaper files and took off for me pertinent excerpts. Mrs. Martha Adams of Lynchburg, through her wide and intimate knowledge of the city and the region, was able in five minutes to locate Mrs. Laura Landrum Crawley, who as a five-year-old child touched the sword of General Longstreet when he laid it aside while he dined at her mother's home in Concord Depot, on the day General Lee's army was paroled at Appomattox; and she was able to describe that scene in vivid and convincing detail.

Mrs. Lyman Cotten of the Library of the University of North Carolina at Chapel Hill not only answered many letters of inquiry, and provided me with books not elsewhere available, but she also filled out the history of the Williams plantation on Panther Creek in North Carolina, and guided a rapid search through some original manuscript letters in the archives of the library.

Miss Ellen Fitzsimmons and her associates of the Charleston Historical Society put into my hands newspaper files and useful books. Miss Emma Woodward of the Public Library in Wilmington, North Carolina, scanned the Wilmington *Daily Journal* for January, 1864; she provided details of life in Wilmington during the blockade-running period, and she produced photographs of Wilmington streets which made it possible to describe them as they were eighty years ago.

Mr. L. F. Ranlett, head of the Bangor Public Library, contributed to the first stages of research. Mr. Harry P. Sands of Nassau gave me valuable information about the days of the blockade-runners, when Nassau was a boom town.

A typical example of the helpfulness of librarians everywhere came from Bloomington, Illinois. In answer to the question: "What business would take a Richmond capitalist to Bloomington in May and June, 1856?" Miss Elizabeth Abraham of the Withers Public Library there sent me enough material to make a novel in itself.

Mrs. Louise F. Catterall and her associates in the Valentine Museum in Richmond allowed me to examine photographs and books which enlarged my knowledge of the history and architecture of Richmond. Mrs. Charlotte G. Russell and the staff of the Virginia State Library found every periodical, book, or document which I wished to consult. Mr. Robert C. Gooch of the Library of Congress met every request; and through the War Archives department he procured for me photostatic copies of a map of the Gettysburg battlefield on four-foot contour lines. This supplemented a map on a larger scale which was kindly loaned me by Mr. Hillory A. Tolson of the National Park Service.

Mr. R. A. McGinty of the Clemson Agricultural College at Clemson, South Carolina; Mr. F. H. Jeter of the North Carolina State College at Raleigh; Mr. W. E. Garnett of the Virginia Agricultural Station at Blacksburg; the staff of the South Carolina Agricultural Experiment Station on the highway from Camden to Columbia, and Mr. Richard L. Morton of Williamsburg, Virginia, were helpful in the study of agricultural methods of the period.

Mrs. Harold Lamb of Union Point, Georgia; Mrs. Noel McHenry Moore of Augusta, Georgia; and Mrs. Thomas Bailey of Augusta simplified my search for information about General Longstreet's convalescence there in the summer of 1864.

Mrs. Louise Haskell Daly of Cambridge, Massachusetts, presented to me her privately printed biography of her father, Alexander Cleves Haskell, who commanded the Seventh South Carolina Cavalry during the last months of the war. No book that has come into my hands so vividly describes the philosophy, the tactics, and the strategy of the Southern cavalryman. Mr. Richard M. Boykin of Pelham, New York, provided me with his memoir of his grandfather, Captain Alexander Hamilton Boykin. This book gives an invaluable cross-section of life on a plantation near Camden, South Carolina, before, during, and after the war.

Professor John N. Ware of Rome, Georgia, supplemented my information as to what General Bee really meant when he called General Jackson "Stonewall" at First Manassas.

Miss Rose MacDonald of Berryville, Virginia, located scenes which I wished to visit near that town. Miss Anne Mann of Petersburg, Virginia, helped confirm my conjecture as to the identity of Mrs. Longstreet's hostess during her stay in Petersburg. Mr. David R. Williams of Mulberry Plantation in Camden, once the home of Marv Boykin Chesnut whose *A Diary From Dixie* is an encyclopedic picture of life in the Southern circles in which she moved during the War of the Sixties, put his well-stocked library at my disposal. Mr. Randolph Williams of Richmond gave me a History of the Richmond, Fredericksburg and Potomac Railroad, and added from his own knowledge many details about the railroads which served Richmond during the War.

To Mr. and Mrs. Lovell Thompson, and to Mr. Paul Brooks, I am indebted for suggestions which helped me knit this book more closely together, eliminate many obscurities, and avoid unnecessary errors.

Special thanks in their particular field should be rendered to dealers in old books who have sought and — sometimes after months or years — have found for me rare volumes which enriched this work. A complete list would include a score of names; but from Mr. Lawrence Foster of Tuskaloosa, Alabama, and Mr. J. T. Gittman of Columbia, South Carolina, to Miss Marion Dodd of Northampton, Massachusetts, and Mr. Rudolph Gerlach of Goodspeed's in Boston, they were uniformly helpful, going far beyond routine business procedure.

For tireless work in my interest I must express my gratitude to Mrs. E. L. Gibbon of Richmond and to P. Victor Bernard of New

Orleans, who searched old newspaper files to locate requested material, and whose judgment in selecting additional useful paragraphs of which I knew nothing often fortified my investigations.

It is a matter of regret to me that of these helpful people five — Colonel Sanger, Mr. Sibley, Henry Minor, Miss Campbell, and Mrs. Daly — died before I could publicly express my appreciation.

B. A. W.

Prologue

1783 - 1809

LUCY HANKS, pulling corn, hating the weary task, moved slowly up the clearing. She wrenched off the full ears with a resentful vehemence, tossing them in little piles behind her. The bull-tongue plow that broke the land had run an erratic course to avoid stumps not yet wholly burned, so the rows were sometimes widely spaced, sometimes close together; and the hills, since the seed corn had been dropped by hand, might have one stalk or half a dozen. But the stalks were higher than a tall man's head, for the soil, not two years freed from the forest, was lavishly fruitful; and the girl as she worked had to force her way through the warp and the woof of the interwoven sword-shaped blades.

The farm lay in a deep valley walled by forested ridges that frowned against the sky; and the slope where the corn grew, slanting southerly, baked in the fine September sun. Sometimes Lucy wiped her steaming brow with her arm in a quick, angry motion; and now and then she slapped away a fly that stung her. She had been at this toil through the long afternoon, pulling the ears and piling them, her father or one of her brothers coming to gather them into shoulder baskets of split hickory and carry them away to the storage crib.

Behind the screen of laurel at the forest's border, Mike's Run descended from a cleft in the mountains to flow into Patterson's Creek. Near the laurel Lucy saw that wild turkeys had pulled down some stalks and ravished the ripe ears. Joseph Hanks, coming to load his basket, was not far away; and she called:

"Pa, the turkeys have et the most of it along here."

He came to see for himself, grumbled at the damage. "I'll lay out for them before day, put a stop to that. You git a hustle on, Lucy. Quicker we git this gethered, the less they'll steal."

3

"I'm a-hustling," she said sullenly, and he moved away. At row's end she straightened, stretching to ease tired muscles. Her heavy hair hung in disorder, her cheeks were sweat-streaked, her calico dress was torn so that a triangle hung down from shoulder line to breast.

She stood a moment, breathing deep. Then—perhaps she had heard a sound in the bushes behind her—she turned as alertly as a deer, startled at its feeding, lifts its head. The trees here pressed close, the creatures of the forest day by day patrolled the borders of the tillage. She poised in an attitude of attention, then as the branches parted recoiled a step or two; but then she was motionless again, speaking on a spent breath as though her heart came out of her with the word.

"Tony!"

A young man stepped out of the laurel, and looked warily to left and right before he came to her. She caught at her dress, lifting that torn triangle, holding it in place to hide the whiteness of her breast; her other hand tried to push her hair into some order. Down toward the cabin there were voices in the stillness of late afternoon, so when he spoke it was softly.

"Hello, Lucy."

"Oh, Tony!"

"I came as soon as I could."

"I'm a sight!" She laughed in happy embarrassment.

"I thought maybe you'd forgotten me."

"Tony, Tony, I'll never forget you!" Near-by in the concealing corn someone was moving. "Hush! That's Bess over there, coming this way. I'll tell you where to be." Whispering, eager, she gave swift directions as to time and place, her hand on his arm, her eyes toward those nearing sounds. A girl's voice called her name.

"Lucy!"

She thrust him back into the covert. "Tonight," she murmured, pressing his hand. "I'll come early as I can. Keep out of Pa's sight. Go on now!"

The laurel received him. Her sister called again, and Lucy answered and went toward her, and they moved away together, working two rows apart, talking as they worked, their voices receding down the slope toward the cabin below.

*   *   *   *   *

She had bidden him meet her where the big sycamore overhung the creek. When her brothers and sisters and Pa and Ma were all asleep in the narrow cabin, she rose from her pallet of husks to steal away; but before coming to the appointed meeting place, she paused by the deep hole in the creek to lay aside her torn work dress, to bathe in the soft waters of the stream, to braid her hair, to put on her other dress kept sweet and clean.

Tony was here before her, waiting in the darkness, in the warm shadows. She sped to him, her bare feet soundless on the turf. In his arms, her arms around his neck tugging and tender, she felt him tremble; and she whispered: "Don't be afeard, Tony. Pa's asleep."

"He might wake, come after you."

"Let him. I ain't afeard of him—only for you!" Not till then did she have his kiss, so long desired. She murmured through many kisses: "Oh, Tony, Tony, seemed like you'd never come!" Her low voice sang.

"They'll hear us talking," he warned her. Around them light began to come, for the moon was almost risen above the lofty mountain wall.

"It's too fur. Besides, Pa don't hear nothing, 'less some critter comes around. He'll sleep till first bird song."

They kissed and kissed till first hunger eased; they sat, he with his shoulders against the smooth bole of the sycamore, she drawing his arm around her, pressing his hand in both hers. "Tony, how'd you ever find us, 'way off here so fur?"

"I asked along the way. Mr. Cavett brought your letter, and he told me where you'd be. I left my horse down the creek, hidden in the woods. I watched all day yesterday for a chance to speak to you; then all today, too, till you came into the corn. I didn't want to go to the house."

"Pa talks big, but I ain't afeard of him, much."

He spoke in amused reminder: " 'Afraid,' Lucy; not 'afeard.' "

She lifted her lips to kiss his cheek. "I'm learning fast's I can, Tony. Mis' Dodsworth teaches me. It was her wrote the letter I sent by Mr. Cavett. She's going to teach me to read and write and all, so you won't be ashamed of me." Then, on sudden inspiration: "Tony, she lives up the crick three miles and she knows about you! You can go there and stay long as you like. She'll bed you and hide you and not tell Pa you're there. That's what you can do, Tony!"

"I can't stay long—two days, maybe three."

"Did you come to fetch me?"

"I will, Lucy, as soon as I can make my father understand. He's away now, so I could come without his knowing."

"Couldn't you come before? It was hard doing, waiting and waiting."

"He wouldn't let me. I told him about you, Lucy, but he said I was a young fool, and he wouldn't even talk about it. He said I'd thank him some day."

"Pa was the same," she confessed. "He heard about us some way, and he put it to me, and I told him it was so."

"Told him?"

She felt his dismay. "Why, I wouldn't lie about us, Tony! I'm not ashamed of loving you!"

"I know. Neither am I. But—he wouldn't understand."

"He don't have to, long as you and me feel the way we do." Lips seeking his.

"Was he—angry?"

She laughed a little. "He near skinned me alive. He wore out a willow switch on me, but he couldn't make me cry! I knowed you'd come back to me!"

"I couldn't come till now, Lucy. Father took me to Yorktown. He wanted to see General Lafayette. You know, my grandfather was French, but my grandmother—she was Irish—wouldn't marry him till he changed his name to Currain. She said that sounded Irish enough to suit her."

Lucy laughed fondly. "I bet she was pretty!"

"Yes, she was. I never saw her, but Father has her portrait." And he went on: "So Father took me to Yorktown with him, and we saw the English army march out and surrender, and then Father bought a place down there, near Williamsburg. The biggest house around." There was a querulous contempt in his tones. "He thinks the little house in Richmond County isn't good enough for him any more. He'd buy Stratford, or Nomini Hall, if he could. He gave the old place to my sister and her husband, so we live at Williamsburg now."

She kissed him sweetly. "What do we care? But oh, Tony, couldn't you come from there before this?"

He shook his head. "Father kept me by him, Lucy. He went to France for General Washington, to work with Mr. Jay, and took me for his secretary. We were there all last summer. He's gone to France again now with Mr. Oswald; but I broke my leg when my horse refused a fence, so I didn't have to go."

"Oh, poor leg! Is it all well again?"

"Yes. So as soon as I could ride I came to find you."

"Here I am, Tony!" About them lay the brightness of the moon, and along the creek warm night air softly flowed. Their voices murmured almost wordlessly a while, till Lucy in his arms asked: "Tony, what's your father really got against me?"

"Oh, all he thinks about now is founding a great family; so I have to marry somebody important!"

"Didn't you tell him you just wanted to marry me?"

"Yes, but he says I'm a child. Says we both are."

"I'm not, not any longer! Maybe I was, three years ago, but I'm a grown woman now. Tony, I learn real fast. Mis' Dodsworth says. He won't have to be ashamed of me."

"Your father's as bad as mine, Lucy."

"Pa says your folks think I ain't good enough for you. He says you're just—fooling with me, says you won't ever marry me. That's why he sold out and moved away up here, to get me away from you."

"We have to talk them around."

"We don't need either one of them, Tony! We don't need anyone only each other. We can get married and go off to Kentucky or somewhere."

"I wouldn't be any good in new country."

She spoke teasingly. "Oh Tony, you're always so afeard—afraid—of things. When I want anything the way I want to be married to you, I'm not afraid of anything." Her word was a whisper, her breath fragrant against his cheek. When he spoke, his voice was shaken by his heart's hard pound.

"Your hair smells like cut hay in the sun, like new-plowed ground in the spring of the year."

"I love the smell of you, too, Tony Currain!"

"Your eyes are so dark in the moonlight, as if they were black."

"They are, kind of."

"Deep, so I can't see the bottom of them."

"Awful deep, Tony. And full right to the top of loving you."

"You smell like wine just before the first sip of it. I can feel your kisses run all through me."

"Your hand on my cheek's so soft and smooth. It's smoother than mine, Tony. Mine are pretty rough and hard."

"I hate having you work so."

"I'll work both hands to the bone, taking care of you."

He was silent; and she felt the doubt, like reluctance, in his silence. "I can't just—I have to talk Father into it, Lucy."

"Your father's a long ways off! You can stand on your own hind legs! You have to, some day!"

"Suppose I did. What would we do?"

"We'd just go away and away and away."

"I haven't anything, nothing but a few things in my saddlebags."

"We don't need anything to start."

"My horse won't even carry double."

"You ride and I'll walk! Oh, Tony, if I was with you, I could walk a horse to death!"

"Lucy Hanks, little girl, big heart!" Fondness for a moment filled him, fears forgotten.

"Can't we, Tony?"

"Oh, Lucy, I'm used to easy living, servants, everything. I'd be no good to you in Kentucky."

"I'll make easy living for you. I'll be better than any twenty people taking care of you. Wouldn't it be worth it, Tony?"

"It would be if I were worth it."

"You are, you are, to me you are." Words like a song. "And I'm the one to judge, it looks to me. Maybe not, though. You'd have to do without a lot, give up a lot; but I wouldn't be giving up anything. I'd be getting everything. But I'd give you everything I've got, Tony Currain, all my life. And I'd keep learning how to give you more, how to be a fine wife for you."

"Lucy, oughtn't you to go back, in case he wakes?"

"You're always fretting so."

"I'll meet you here tomorrow night, every night, as long as I can stay."

"I don't want to let you go. There might not be any tomorrow night, ever, Tony. I don't want to ever let you go."

"I'm trying to do right for both of us."

"Don't ever go, Tony Currain! Oh, don't ever go!"

He pondered, almost persuaded. "I could go back and bring a led horse for you, and a gun, and some money; things we'd need. Oh, Lucy Hanks, I'm as crazy-headed as you are to talk so, to think so."

"Say my name some more."

"Lucy Hanks."

"Say Lucy Currain! Lucy Currain's nicer, Tony! Mistress Tony Currain."

His breath caught. "When you keep saying my name, it's like music singing inside of me."

"Tony Currain, Tony Currain, Tony Currain, Tony Currain. I'll sing it to you always."

"I'll start home tomorrow, Lucy, to fetch another horse and things."

"Not tomorrow. Don't go away tomorrow. Stay one more night."

"The sooner I start, the sooner I'll come back."

There was that singing in her voice again. "To carry me away, to marry me away. Tony Currain, Tony Currain, Tony Currain!"

"To marry you away." A singing in him, too. "We're crazy, Lucy!"

"Happy crazy, Tony Currain. So we'll always be."

*   *   *   *   *

In the wood a bird murmured in its sleep and tried a note or two of song; another answered. Lucy quickened her homeward hasting, swift on silent feet. The night was almost sped; bright moonlight paled with a hint of coming day. So late, so late! The long, rich hours had gone like seconds! Hurry, Lucy; hurry! First bird song was Pa's waking time.

The cabin door was always shut fast against night dews and vapors; when she came there it was closed, but she must open it and go in, for soon Pa would be about. She pushed the door no wider than she must in order to slip through, but Pa growled a challenge.

"Who's that?"

"Me, Pa."

"Where you been?"

"Outside a minute."

He grunted sleepily; then as his thoughts cleared he came to his feet, thrust wide the door, drew her out into the paling moonlight, stared at her in hard suspicion. "Huh! Your hair all braided smooth! And your store dress on! Where you been?" His voice roused Ma in the cabin.

"Outside, I said. What's wrong with that?"

"Damn your lying trollop's tongue! What hedge-hopper have you took up with now?"

"Take your hands off me!"

"I'll lay my hand on you so you'll know it!"

Ma came strongly to Lucy's rescue. "Now, Pa, leave the girl be! Can't she go out of your sight for once?"

"You hush up, Nannie Hanks! I'll handle this slut!"

"Leave her be, I say!"

The woman ruled him. His hand released its grip, but his eyes cast all around. Light was coming fast. Past him, following his glance, Lucy saw her footprints dark upon the dew-hung grass. Suppose he traced them, caught up with Tony before her lover could be gone. She spoke to hold him here.

"I just went to the crick to wash myself."

"Wash yourself? Middle of the night?"

"I was hot enough to smother. I couldn't sleep."

"Foolishness! Yo're always washing yourself."

Ma cried: "What if she does! It don't do anybody any hurt to keep as clean as they can."

"What you doing in your store dress?"

"I washed out my other one, left it spread on the bushes to dry." This was true, in case he went to look.

He grunted, grudgingly convinced. "This one'd be dirty again time you got the corn pulled. Go along and fetch the other. Nannie, git breakfast started. Long day ahead; but not long enough for all we've got to do."

Lucy breathed deep with relief. Pa was deceived; so Tony was away, safe away. Tony Currain, Tony Currain, Tony Currain! How many days to Williamsburg? How many days to return again, to carry her away, to marry her away!

No matter how many! While she waited, her heart would sing its song.

* * * * *

Ma was first to guess the truth; Ma, and then Bess and the other girls, and then one by one the boys. All of them knew before Pa did; but he had to know some time. On a winter night he warmed frost-burned hands at the log fire; and Lucy, helping Ma get supper ready, passed between him and the flames and so was silhouetted there. The cabin rocked with his angry shout.

"You, Lucy! What makes your belly so big?" The brief silence was tight with terror. Then he lunged, dragged the girl to him. "By God-amighty, I'll take the hide off'n you!"

Ma fought between them. "Joe Hanks, you leave her be!"

"I'll skin her alive!"

Lucy faced him, as hot with rage as he. "You tetch me and you'll never sleep and wake up again! You ever tetch me again long as you live and I'll take an axe to you!"

"Who done it?" He still gripped her arm, till Ma pushed him clear, and Lucy defied him.

"None of your business."

"Was it that Currain young one? He come sneaking up here after you?"

"I ain't a-going to tell you a thing."

"I'll beat it out of you."

"It'll be the last time you ever hit a lick at me or anyone!"

With Ma on her side, Lucy withstood his first rage; but he began thereafter to be much away from the farm, leaving the work for the boys to do. Through that winter he was gone sometimes for days on end, till spring drew near and it would soon be plowing time and planting time. Ma nagged at him to be at the tasks that needed doing, but one day he cried:

"Hush up! I ain't a-going to plant a crop for someone else to gether!"

Ma stared at him, pale in sudden fear. "Joe Hanks, what's got into you?"

"We're selling out, soon's I can find someone to buy. We're moving on."

"Oh, Joe!"

"I aim to take that hedge-cat gal of ours fur enough off so her Tom can't find her!"

"We're doing real good here!" But Ma pleaded vainly. When at last she knew herself beaten, she fought for delay. "Well, anyway, I ain't a-going a step till her baby comes; not till she's fit to travel."

"We're going the day I sell the farm! Make up your mind to it."

But he could find no buyer, and in March he put parched corn and sowbelly in a poke, thrust knife and hatchet in his sash, took down his gun. Ma challenged him. "Now Pa, where you a-going?"

"Back to Farnham Parish." There, above the Rappahannock, had been their earlier home. "I'll find someone there that wants a good farm cheap." He brushed aside her pleadings, strode away.

When he returned, Lucy's baby was three weeks old. She had named it Nancy, for her mother. Pa said grimly: "All right. Now we'll move on."

"Did you sell the place?"

He shook his head in stubborn shame. "I'll let Peter Putnam have it for the mortgage money." When Ma wept protests he jerked his head toward Lucy, sheltering the new baby in her arm's protecting circle. "Blame her, not me! We're moving on."

"Where to, Joe?"

"We'll know when we git thar! Don't ask so many questions. We'll be on our way."

*   *   *   *   *

Before they set out upon the weary journey, Lucy slipped away to Mrs. Dodsworth, had her write a letter to Tony to be sent to him by the first traveller. When they were settled on Rolling Fork in the Kentucky country, Lucy herself, remembering as much as she could of what Mrs. Dodsworth had taught her, wrote Tony where she was; and after that letter was sent, she waited bravely, singing to her baby, for Tony to come and marry her away.

During the three years of that empty waiting, more than one troop of migrating Virginians passed through Rolling Fork; and Lucy asked many questions of many men before John Maynard, come direct from Williamsburg, had any answer for her. He said Tony was married, to a girl named Sally Williber, with a big wedding and a great throng there.

Tony married? The anguish of that word brought at first its own anodyne. Before pain came, she remembered what Tony had said. So probably Sally Williber was someone important, and Tony's father had had his way.

But oh, Tony, why did you let him? Till this day Lucy had waited loyally, tending their baby, teaching herself to read and to write and to speak as Tony would wish her to, making herself worthy of him against his coming. But now he would never, never come! Through blinding tears she wrote him another letter, as much in anger as in woe, this time to curse his name, to tell him he was forever forgotten; and she found one to take that letter to him in faraway Williamsburg.

Thereafter, for help in the forgetting she had vowed, she turned to any man; and sharp-tongued neighbors spoke of her in reprobating whispers, and Ma wept for her. But Lucy laughed defiance alike at whispers and at tears.

"Pa says I'm a trollop! Well, I ain't a-going to make a liar out of Pa! He'd ought to know!"

Ma wept, and Lucy's sisters tossed angry heads, but Lucy took her chosen road; and the day came when Pa told Ma: "Nannie, there's a stink of sin and shame in this house. Get rid of it or you'll see the last of me!"

So Lucy must go. Her brother Bill and his wife offered a home for her, and for little Nancy too. Lucy warned them. "Don't look for me to change!"

Bill said steadily: "Suit yourself. But long as you want it, there's a place for you."

* * * * *

The way Lucy had with men was wanton and wild, but Henry Sparrow would not have her so. He was a dull, slow man, but he was a brave one, and he loved and chided her. "You're acting foolish, Lucy. You hadn't ought to do the way you do."

"How'd you want me to do, Henry?" Her tone held a light derision.

"Why, do decent, same as other folks."

"But Henry, I'm different from other folks!" There was more malice than pain in her words. "Ask Pa. He'll tell you so himself. He's told me often enough! And Henry—long as there's men that like their wenching, there has to be a wench for them. Don't there?"

He colored, slowly angry. "Damn it, Lucy, you just carry on the way you do to spite your Pa!"

"I carry on the way I choose to carry on. Who's going to stop me?"

"What you need's someone to take a stick to you!"

"You ever try it, Henry, you'll never take a stick to anybody else!"

"If you'd give 'em half a chance, some decent man'd marry you."

"Would you, Henry?" She was mocking him.

"I would, if you'd behave yourself!"

She laughed long. "Oh, Henry, Henry, I don't know but you would!" Then with her quizzing smile: "You don't have to marry me, Henry. No man does, if I like him! And I like you."

Henry Sparrow was hard to turn aside. "You don't fool anyone. I see through you! Nancy's father, whoever he was, and the way your Pa treated you; you're just trying to get even with them, cutting off your nose to spite your face! You're a real nice woman, Lucy, if you'd let yourself be, 'stead of acting such a fool."

"Damn you to Hell!"

"It's true. You're half crying now."

"I ain't neither! And if I am it's just because you make me so mad."

"You're mad because you know it's true."

"No such of a thing!"

"What you need is something to bring you up so short your heels dig dirt!"

"What I need is folks to let me alone! And I'd thank you to do it, too."

But Henry would not let her alone. Some way to change her, to make her settle down? He found—or thought he found—the answer. When the grand jury met he went before them, to speak to them of Lucy. He was an urgent, honest man.

"You know her, some of you. Lem Holmes. John Berry. Dave Prescott. Jim Harrod. John Haggin. You all know her. Or the ones that don't know her know all about her. She's a mocking and a by-word all around.

"But there's good in her, plenty of it; and them that know her know that, too. I want to marry her, if she'll settle down. I'd marry her and settle her down, but she won't have me. She needs someone to give her a cuffing, shake some sense into her. I want you to do it."

He was so earnest that they listened to him, astonished yet respectful too. What he proposed was a bitter, hard thing to do to any woman, and especially to a woman you wanted to marry. They told him so, but he stood his ground.

"It'll do her good. It might, anyway. One sure thing, it can't do her any harm. She's hell-bent now. She's a gone goose if someone don't stop her. It's worth a try."

He had his way with them. When Lucy heard that the grand jury had indicted her for fornication, she went to this one and to that one till she had the truth, and so to Henry Sparrow in a rage of tears.

"This is your doing! I'm a mind to kill you dead!"

"It's your own doing, Lucy. You'll have to go to court, when court sits in the spring."

"I don't have to do anything unless I've got a mind to!"

Henry Sparrow shook his head. "Yes, you do. Everybody does, one way or another, and so do you." He added mercilessly, "Only if you marry me."

"You! I'd as soon marry a hawg, after this you done to me."

"You keep on the way you been and a hawg's too good for you. But I'd marry you."

She drove him away, but all that winter he besieged her, sometimes with threats of what the court would do to her and sometimes with tenderness, ignoring alike her anger and her jeers. "I want you to marry me. I always have, since the day I saw you."

"I'd ruther go to jail any day than marry you!"

"Go to jail then, if nothing else'll do you. I'll marry you when you git out. I'll marry you whenever you say the word."

"There's plenty other women'd marry you and glad to, if it's marrying you want. Go talk to them!"

"You're the one for me. All the rest put together ain't good enough if I can't have you."

"I ain't a-going to marry anybody just to keep out of jail."

"I don't care why you do it, so you do."

"Well I ain't a-going to do it. I keep a-telling you!"

"Telling won't stop me. I'm keeping at you, Lucy, till you do."

Scorn that was half terror swept her. "You're a fine one, letting on to be sweet on me and then getting the jury to do this!"

"If I had a young one that was cutting up, I'd take a switch to it, but I'd go on loving it all the time."

"What do you want of me anyway? I'm every man's woman! Ain't you man enough to find a woman of your own?"

"I aim to see to it you're my own, soon or late."

His steady persistence made her wish to wound him, and she knew the way. "You don't have to marry me, Henry. I've told you so. And anybody'll tell you how nice I can be."

But she said this once too often. His blow spun her around and knocked her off her feet; above her he stood black with sober wrath.

"Mind your tongue. You go too far with me."

She sprang up, his death in her eyes. "If I had a gun, or anything—" Then at last she was sobbing in his arms. "Oh, Henry, I can't best you. I've tried to make you mad, and I've tried everything, but you just keep on being good and kind."

"I'll always be good to you."

"You're a good man. I wouldn't let you marry a woman like me!"

"I'll resk it." Her tears choked her. "Go on and cry, Lucy. Cry all you want. It'll do you good. You've had hard years to cry away."

"I'll be in jail!"

"You won't have to go to jail if you'll say you'll marry me. I'll give bond for a license and show the court and that's the end of it."

"I won't do it to you, Henry. Folks would always remember the way I been, always keep saying it to you."

"You can show 'em different, Lucy. We'll give bond for the license, and tell the court, and then we'll wait. I'm not a hand to hurry. We'll wait till you come and say to me, 'Henry, I can be a good wife to you.' We'll wait till you've showed them the true kind of woman you are."

So at last she surrendered. "What do we have to do?"

"You write a paper that you'll marry me, so I can show it to the court. I'll do everything after that."

"Do I write it right now?"

"There has to be someone see you do it. I'll bring someone tonight. You can write it then, for them to sign."

He brought Bob Mitchell and John Berry; and while they stood by he gave her a quill and paper. "Here's what you want to put, Lucy. I'll read it off to you." He read slowly, while she wrote: "'I do certify that I am of age, and give my approbation freely for——'"

Lucy interrupted: "How do you spell 'approbation'?" He told her, and she said: "Oh, I went and put an 's' instead of a 't'." She scratched out the word, wrote it afresh. He went on:

"'—give my approbation freely for Henry Sparrow to git out a license.'"

He paused and when she had written this much she asked: "Is that all?"

"All the main part, only 'given under my hand this day' and sign your name."

She began to write, and stopped, and looked up at him, suddenly radiant with smiling eyes; and then she finished with a stumbling, hasting pen. "Bother, I ran out of ink! There 'tis, Henry."

He took the slip of paper and read aloud, for Bob Mitchell and John Berry to hear. "'I do certify that I am of age and give my approbation freely for Henry Sparrow to git out a license this or any other day.'"

She laughed, her cheeks bright. "I put that in because it's true, Henry. You're a real good man, and I'll do anything you say, now or any time."

"Well," he said, soberly content, "I don't know as it's reg'lar, but I guess it'll do. But Lucy, you've just wrote, 'This day' and then 'Monday' and your name under. You want to put 'April 26, 1790.'"

She took the pen again. "The 'Monday' don't hardly show, anyway, except the 'day' part, after I'd dipped in the ink again." She wrote the date above, and he was satisfied; and called the others to sign, and while they did so he moved to stand beside her. Lucy caught his hand in hers. She pressed his hand to her cheek, and peace flowed into her.

* * * * *

When she was alone Lucy wrote a letter, to be sent somehow, some day, to Tony Currain, far away. She began defiantly, telling him she would wed; but when she had written: "I have to wait a year to marry Mr. Sparrow," she paused in thought a while. Suppose before the year was gone Tony's wife died? Suppose he came at last to marry her away? Her eyes shadowed, deep and wistful.

But then she shook her head. Let him come if he chose; it was too late. She was Henry Sparrow's now. She finished the letter; and when a chance offered she dispatched it by the hand of Jim Bohannon, who was returning to Virginia.

That was the end of Tony Currain. She would never think of him again.

But she did. She thought of him after her father's death. Joseph Hanks died still unrelenting; her name was not so much as mentioned in his will. She thought of him again when her little Nancy, who was Tony's daughter, married Tom Lincoln, and again when Nancy's first was born. Sarah was the first. The second was a son. Tom Lincoln and Nancy named it after Tom's father.

Lucy wrote to tell Tony Currain about that. She had long since forgiven the past, forgiven him; and now that Tony had, way out here in Kentucky, a grandson named Abraham Lincoln, it was a thing he might be glad to know.

I

Overture
1859-1862

1

MRS. ALBION was still awake when the door bell rang; but Tessie always slept soundly, so Mrs. Albion rose and went into the upper hall and called: "Tessie! Tessie!"

"Yes, ma'am, I'se a-comin'!"

Mrs. Albion, herself in darkness, saw presently below her the candle's gleam. The door bell clanged again, with an angry impatience. That must be Tony. No one else would come at this hour. Tessie, in a bright-flowered wrapper that was snug to the splitting point, appeared in the lower hall. Her tight black pigtails stiff with indignation at this midnight rousing, her candle sputtering angrily, she trudged slap-footed to the door and with her hand on the bolt challenged this midnight caller.

"Who dere?"

"Mr. Currain, you black slut! Open up!"

The servant's tone changed to appeasement. "Yassuh! Yassuh!" Looking up over her shoulder while she turned the key, she muttered a low warning. "Hit's Mistuh Currain, ma'am."

Her mistress at the stair head nodded resentful assent. "Light the gas." Then as Tessie opened the door: "Tony, what in the world?"

Tessie hooded the flickering candle against the night air, closed the door behind him, held the candle flame to the gas jet.

"Too late, Nell?" His tone was a challenge.

"Oh no," she said wearily, "I'll make myself presentable. Tell Tessie—anything you want."

She turned toward her room, wondering why he had come, puzzled and uneasy. In the hall below she heard him give his orders. "Tessie,

21

bring a bottle of the old Madeira. And carry it as if it were a sick baby! If you cloud it, I'll cut you into strips and fry the strips."

"Yassuh! Yassuh! Must be a big evenin', you going to open one o' dem last two bottles."

"Only two left? Why, damn your hide, I brought six dozen from Great Oak eight years ago. You've been at them, you black 'scallion'!"

"Nawsuh, not me!" Mrs. Albion, ready to receive him, returning to the stair head, saw him cut at Tessie sharply with his light cane; and Tessie chuckled with fright, her fat flesh shaking. "Nawsuh, I ain't never tetch 'em!"

"Lying wench! Well, if there are only two, I'll have both."

"Yassuh!"

Tessie departed, and Mrs. Albion waited while he came up the stairs. A small woman, slenderly rounded, looking less than her forty-odd years, she was beautiful not so much because of any single attribute—unless it were her loosed hair in a rich cascade across her shoulder—as from a harmony of features, voice, and manner. Anthony Currain, gaunt and bony, with a dark mustache and a spike of beard to frame his wide loose mouth, now in his fifties and a little stooped as tall men may be, bowed over her hand, then kissed her cheek. She spoke in sharp repulsion.

"Tony, I won't have you using tobacco before you come to me!"

"I didn't expect to come." In the small pleasant room where a stick of lightwood freshly laid on coals still smouldering waked into crackling flame, he walked toward the hearth to rid himself of the source of his offense. "Hot for a fire," he said.

"I find it chilly." There was a hard anger in her. He never came at such an hour as this unless he had had too much to drink, and the fumes of liquor mingled with the reek of tobacco on his breath.

"Well, I'm hot," he insisted. "I walked from Merrihay's."

"Luck with you?" She knew what his answer would be. He was always a losing gambler.

"No."

"So you're in a bad humor?" She seated herself, the bright fire between them. "They had the luck, but I see you had the brandy?"

"Did I? I hardly know. I told Tessie to bring the old Madeira."

"So late?"

"Rather I'd go?" His tone was derisive.

"Don't sulk!" She smiled lightly. "But really, Tony, coming at such an hour! Suppose you'd surprised me! If this is to become a habit, I shall have to practice discretion."

He considered her with a thoughtful eye, and the firelight touched her hair. "You know, you've grown more beautiful every year. I wonder how life would have gone for us if we had married."

"Not so well, I think," she suggested. "This way, with sometimes weeks when we do not meet, it has been easier to endure each other." Then, at Tessie's discreet knock. "Come." The servant bore the dusty bottles, each in its basket, reverently; on the laden tray were glasses, and a dish of pecans already shelled. "I'll call you if we want anything, Tessie," said Mrs. Albion.

"Yes, ma'am." Tessie departed, and he nibbled nuts to rid himself of the taste of tobacco, took one of the bottles, ceremoniously opened it.

"My father put this down in 1825," he reflected, "the year before he died; thirty, thirty-four years ago. He used to import it in the cask, let it ripen in the hot attic before old Mose bottled it." Gently, he filled the glasses, gave one to her, raised his own. "To the good years behind us, Nell."

That was a phrase faintly ominous. She watched him warily. "And to those to come," she said, and sipped the wine.

He made a grunting sound, staring at the fire. "You don't know my family, Nell," he muttered; and an icy finger touched her throat. What was in his mind?

"Of course I do," she protested. "After all, Trav's my son-in-law. And I've seen Mrs. Dewain and Mrs. Streean times enough. I don't know your other brother."

"Faunt? Faunt's the best of us, he and Cinda."

"And I know Mr. Streean," she reminded him, and smiled at the memory. "He brought you and that handsome son of his to call on me once; remember? You were horribly embarrassed."

"Damned awkward business. He asked if I knew you, and I'd have denied it; but I couldn't well say I didn't know my own brother's mother-in-law. So I said I hadn't known you were in Richmond."

"Thus damning me, once and for all."

"Why?" He looked at her in dull interest.

"But obviously, if your family and your brother's wife's mother weren't on terms! Don't be an innocent, my dear!" She added: "Darrell Streean has been a devoted caller ever since. Of course he saw the truth about you and me at once, and I suppose that made him think me fair game."

"Insulting young blackguard!"

"Oh, no woman in her forties is ever insulted by the flattery of a dashing youngster in his teens—no matter how frankly dishonorable his intentions."

"Darrell was at Merrihay's tonight," he commented. "Tried to borrow from me. He takes after his father. Worthless rascal."

"You dislike Mr. Streean?" He made a scornful sound and she said provokingly: "He calls quite often. He was here only a week ago, with three other gentlemen, discussing their eternal politics, growing noisy over their own opinions—and my brandy."

"Streean's a scoundrel—but he lacks courage to follow his bent." Tony laughed shortly. "You know, it was I who introduced him to Tilda, but it never occurred to me she'd marry him! She's had time to be sorry."

She said in a light amusement: "He and the gentlemen he brings here—well, I always air the curtains after they've gone."

He stared at the flames. Outside the quiet room a belated horseman passed at a foot pace along the dusty road. The thudding hoof beats were louder as he drew near, softer as he departed. The fire crackled, and Tony rose to step upon a spark. He filled his glass, ate a pecan meat, sat down again.

"Funny that you and I've got along all these years, Nell," he reflected. "Most people soon get their fill of me. Dislike me. Specially men." She wondered what had produced this mood in him. "Always been that way," he insisted, as though she had denied it; and he went on: "I was a spoiled young one, the first baby. After me there were two who died; and that made Papa and Mama the more tender with me. Then when I was eight Trav was born. He took some of their attention away from me, so I hated him. I remember once Mama hushed me for fear I'd wake him from his nap, and I went out and cut a hickory switch and whipped one of the nigger boys till his yells woke Trav. Old Mammy May thought it was pretty cute of me to be

so jealous of my baby brother. I'm afraid Mama agreed with her."
He said in heavy wonder at the flight of time: "That was over forty
years ago."

She thought, listening to his maundering: Why, he's an old man!
And I've had ten, yes eleven years of him! And Heavens, I'm forty-
seven myself!

"Yes, I was a despisable young one." She saw that he took a per-
verted pleasure in the fact. "After Trav, there was Cinda, and Tilda,
and Faunt. I was crowded more and more into the background, so
I raised Cain. I used to carry a riding crop and slash at every nigger
who crossed my path. They laughed and dodged my blows and kept
out of my way. Except the wenches. They didn't avoid me. I suppose
my attentions flattered them."

If talk was all he wanted, let him talk! He went on with a sour
relish.

"Oh, I was a hellion! I took up with the son of the overseer on the
next place. We used to steal whiskey from the sideboard. Papa and
old Mose kept it locked, the decanters put away, but we could pick
the lock." He filled his glass, gulped the contents, filled the glass
again. "I never told you about Tommy Williber, did I?" She shook
her head, and he said: "Papa had been married before, to a girl
named Sally Williber. When their first baby was coming there was to
be a ball—it was soon after Christmas—at a neighbor's twenty miles
away; and she and Papa set out to ride over. They were caught in a
storm of wind and cold and snow, and got lost, and finally came to a
negro's cabin and took shelter there, half-frozen. Before morning she
fell sick and lost her baby; and after that they never had another. She
was an invalid till she died. He married Mama three years afterward."
He looked at her uncertainly. "What was I saying? Oh, yes, I set out
to tell you about Tommy Williber."

"You're sleepy, Tony. Tell me in the morning." But of course he
would ignore the suggestion, would drink himself into a stupor here
where he sat. How well she knew him; the little meannesses that were
a part of him, the reasonless cruelties, the childish delight in praise and
flattery, the readiness for self-pity. Their lives touched only at a tan-
gent. He had his orbit, she had hers; and yet she knew him through
and through.

But this whining talk, this laying his secret shames open for her to see; this was something new. He seemed not to have heard her words.

"Yes, Tommy Williber," he repeated, "Papa's first wife's nephew. My cousin. He came to visit me at Great Oak, and he seemed to Sam and me—Sam was the overseer's son—a damned self-righteous little prig. Wouldn't drink, wouldn't go prowling around the quarter after dark. We hated him, he was so damned good.

"One day we went sailing. Sam had stolen a bottle of brandy, and he and I drank most of it. There was a squall coming up. Tommy wanted to turn back, but of course we refused. The squall hit us, and the next thing I remember is the field hands waking Sam and me, before day next morning. The boat had gone ashore above the landing, with us drunk and asleep."

He was silent till she prompted him. "Where was Tommy?"

"I don't know. No one ever saw him again." He nodded. "Never again." Self-pity swept him. "The worst of it was that his mother— his father was dead—his mother didn't blame me. If she had, Papa and Mama might have taken my part, but she didn't."

"Didn't Sam know what had happened?"

"He ran away. No one ever saw him again." His head drooped. "Papa died the next year. He had some trouble with his heart, took to his bed. They thought he couldn't move without help; but one day when they left him alone he got up and climbed the attic stairs. They found him dead, in his night shirt, at the head of the stairs. Mama said his shame for me had killed him."

"Why did he climb the stairs?"

"I don't know. Out of his head, probably. He must have been, because he had lighted the fire in his room before he went up to the attic, but it was a hot summer day."

"His name was Anthony, too, wasn't it?"

"Yes. I'm the third Anthony Currain. He was the first. He lived up north of the Rappahannock when there was no head right on the Northern Neck, so he bought land, thousands of acres. That's Belle Vue, where Faunt lives now. Grandpa was a friend of Washington and Lafayette. After Cornwallis surrendered, he bought Great Oak, and later Chimneys. He was always buying land. Quite a man. But Papa was not much." He laughed in ugly mirth. "Except as a stud horse. He was forty odd when he married Mama, but they had two that died and five of us that lived. He was sixty when Faunt was born. Sam and I thought that was funny."

"I suppose you would."

"So I'm the third Tony Currain." He shook his head. "There've been too many of us." Another glass of wine. "Faunt's the best of us now," he repeated, "Faunt and Cinda. Tilda's a fool, and I always hated Trav, till I persuaded Mama to send him off to Chimneys and got rid of him."

"That's where I met him," she remarked. "I set my cap for him, you know."

"You? For old Trav?" He chuckled.

"M-hm! We hadn't a penny, Enid and I. What money Mr. Albion left I spent, and after that we visited and visited till we wore our welcome thin everywhere. Enid was fifteen, but I'd practically kept her in pinafores, so I could pass for thirty easily enough; but I knew I had to hurry. We were visiting at Emmy Shandon's, and Trav was so shy and awkward that he seemed an easy catch. I led him to talk about his farming at Chimneys, and he loved it."

"Can't imagine what you'd see in Trav."

"Why, money, and position!" His mood for reminiscent confidences infected her. "I'd have got him, too, if it hadn't been for Enid. She played the adoring child, and I suppose it didn't occur to him to be afraid of her till too late. I'd persuaded him to give a party at Chimneys, and I was to play hostess for him. Enid wasn't supposed to go, but she did over a dress of mine and put up her hair and made an appearance. She was lovely, of course; and she went to his head. Even then I could have beaten her game, I suppose; but you appeared, so I let her have him."

"Thought you could marry me?"

"Oh, I never thought that."

He asked curiously: "Were you ever in love with me, Nell?"

"Enough. I needed you." She laughed lightly. "I hadn't a penny, you see."

He grinned with sudden malice in his eyes. "Speaking of pennies, Nell, reminds me why I came tonight. The turn of the cards at Merrihay's took my last one. My last penny. And—you're an expensive luxury, my dear."

The attack was so sudden that for a moment she lost her composure. "You've always Great Oak!"

"Oh, it hasn't paid its way for years." He laughed briefly. "Normally I'd go to Cinda's husband. Brett Dewain's the banker of the family, handles all the Currain money. I've had to stand up to his cross-examinations in the past. But now—well, he and Cinda are abroad, won't be back till October. No, this is final, Nell."

There was a racing panic in her; she had so long depended on him, could not easily accept this overturn of her world, sought some expedient. "If you need money, sell some negroes South."

"We Currains don't sell our people."

"You virtuous Currains!" She was frightened and angry too. "Then take Chimneys away from Trav. Enid says it's prosperous, and it's yours as much as his."

"It's Mama's, not Trav's," he corrected. "She's willed Great Oak to me, and Chimneys to Trav, and Faunt gets Belle Vue, and Cinda the Plains; but they're all Mama's as long as she lives. And she may live for years."

"You can get around her!" She fought to hold him. "I'll go to Chimneys with you." His eyes met hers in a sardonic glance that warned her his decision was made. "But I suppose you have some other plan?" He grinned. "I see." He was flicking her with a light lash, playing one of his cruel games, thinking she would weep, threaten, cajole. "You want to—want us to part, Tony?" He wished to savor her flattering supplications; but pride came to her rescue, steadied her tones. "Why, very well, if that's what you want!"

She saw that her easy assent had shaken him. From the bottle beside him he poured the last drop, tilted the glass to his lips, spilled a little, took his handkerchief, touched his chin and beard. She watched him coldly. What had he expected? She was no snivelling, love-sick child.

"What will you do?" His words were faintly blurred.

"Why, I've thought of going to Washington." She spoke as though she had long considered the question, wishing to hurt him if she could. "I hear so much politics talked by the gentlemen who call upon me. It interests me. And Washington is the place for politics."

He mumbled drowsily, his eyelids drooped with sleep; and for a long time, while Mrs. Albion watched him with level glance, he sat with bent head, his inhalations becoming audible. The fumes of brandy and of wine suddenly had overwhelmed him. Occasionally in the past she had seen him thus succumb, with little or no warning, going in an instant from a surface sobriety to sodden slumber; and sometimes she had been amused. But not tonight. She watched him with narrowed eyes, a little desperate; he had been her reliance for so long. Fear made her angry now. She spoke at last in sharp tones to rouse him.

"Yes, Tony, I'll go to Washington."

His lids opened and hurriedly closed again, as though light hurt his eyes. "Washington, eh? Well then go." He grunted and chuckled. "Joke on me! I thought you'd make a great fuss."

"Really? Why, Tony, you should know me better." She wished to provoke him to discussion, but his muttering voice trailed into silence, and his head sagged forward. The flicker of the dying fire laid shadows on his bony countenance; he looked like a bearded skull. For a while she sat where she was, her eyes on him, her thoughts casting backward. Had she sold ten years of her life to this old man?

With a quick motion at last she rose. It was high time she was rid of him. She went into the hall.

"Tessie! Tessie!"

From below came Tessie's drowsy answer. "Yes, ma'am?"

Nell had meant to bid Tessie hustle him into the street; but she hesitated, her fingernail tapping her teeth, looking back through the open door at him asleep in his chair. He was old, yes; yet if he had Chimneys he would be rich again, and lean years had taught her to value riches, and in the long run she could always manage him. She might speak to him again of Chimneys, and more urgently, in the morning. Her anger faded; she called to Tessie:

"Come help me put Mr. Currain to bed."

2

July, 1859

THE CURRAINS, through their Courdain forebears, had been Virginians for a hundred and fifty years, since in 1703 Jules Courdain immigrated from French vineyards and set himself up as a victualler, distilling the spirits which he sold, and prospered thriftily. His son Jules married Annette Harrison, and their second son they named Antoine. When he became a man that son Antoine, at behest of pretty Molly O'Hara whom he wished to wed, changed his name to Anthony, and to Currain.

In that first Anthony Currain, the wholesome blends of good peasant stock came to strong fruition. He turned to the soil, to the planting of tobacco; and he sought always more land to replace that which his ruthless cropping impoverished. Ten years after the Revolution, anticipating the decline in Virginia agriculture which would at last leave Mount Vernon a waste and reduce Thomas Jefferson in his old age to destitution, he set out to investigate the wilderness beyond the mountains. He proposed to follow the new trail through Danville and Salisbury and on southwesterly; but he turned aside to see and to admire the solid brick houses built by the Moravians who had come down from Pennsylvania to establish a religious colony at Betharaba and Salem and Bethania. When he resumed his journey, riding westward through forest broken by an occasional farm, he caught now and then glimpses from some mild eminence of a bold peak off to the north, twenty or thirty or forty miles away. Its shape reminded him of a camel with two humps, one of them jutting confidently upward against the sky; and he remembered that he had been told to look for Pilot Knob as a landmark useful to travellers hereabouts.

He rode slowly, and came into a region where farms were more numerous; and as the sun dropped down the western sky he emerged from a belt of forest into a ten-acre clearing under good cultivation. To his left, set among oaks and junipers on a low saddleback that paralleled his road, a neat and spacious house promised hospitality. He turned aside. The lane led between a grassy meadow and a garden hedged with junipers to the door.

His chance host proved to be an old acquaintance. Colonel Joseph Williams, commanding the Surry County militia, had served well through the Revolution; and Anthony Currain had met him at Yorktown. So there was a warm welcome waiting. In the cool of that first evening the two friends walked together in the garden, and Colonel Williams showed Anthony Currain the small shoots of box brought from Hanover County in Virginia to outline the garden beds.

"And these along the hedge are tree box," he said. "They will grow tall to replace the junipers by and by. And that sapling yonder will be a fine magnolia some day. Just savor the fragrance of this rose, if you please, Mr. Currain. I propose to make a pleasant garden here, with lanes and vistas, and an arbor of scuppernongs, and fruit trees well nurtured."

He was a man of many plans and projects; and he led Anthony Currain beyond the garden to a small walled enclosure. "The bricks in that wall were made on the place, sir, like the bricks in the house," he said quietly. "When I no longer sleep in the house, I shall come to sleep in this lovely spot, and my generations after me."

They leaned on the farther wall to watch a doe and two fawns in the glade below. "I call that my deer pasture, Mr. Currain," the Colonel explained. "They come to drink at the springs. We never molest them, and they seem to know themselves secure against man; yes, and against panthers, too. This is Panther Creek, but the beasts seldom approach the house."

Anthony Currain liked the remote peace and the gentle beauty of the spot, and he lingered, listening to his host's stories of the day in February 1781, when Cornwallis and his army crossed the Yadkin at the ford a mile northwest of the house. When he told his errand, Colonel Williams eagerly displayed all the beauty and the promise of this region, urging that if it was land the other wanted, here was his perfect goal.

"Fifty years from now, sir," the enthusiast predicted, "all along the Yadkin here will be strung, like beads on a rosary, scores of rich and fruitful farms. Anything a man can want this soil will produce. It's only necessary to girdle the trees and drop a few seeds. I began to build here before the Revolution, but I never found time to finish my house till after Cornwallis surrendered." He chuckled. "In fact, it's not yet finished. The walls bulge every time my family increases. And this is a land for good increase, Mr. Currain. Stay here and you'll be glad all your days."

"I had a thought to pass the mountains and see what lies beyond," Anthony Currain confessed; and after hours of talk the Colonel saw he could not be shaken.

"Ride on, then," he agreed. "But I know a place will hold you. It's a long day's ride due west, in the friendly hills. Cross at Shallow Ford and go on; but avoid the road to Wilkesboro. Mulberry Field Meeting-House, we used to call it, but they're making a town there now, and you and I have no love for towns. Ask your way to a place called Chimneys. Any man you meet will direct you. It's a great house, all of brick, with twin chimneys at the ends. Thomas Brettany came from Betharaba to build it and brought his bride there; but she and their first-born died together, and now the place is ashes in his mouth. He'd sell for the merest song."

So Anthony Currain made his farewells and rode on; and at the day's end, following many words of direction, he came up a winding drive to a great house that looked off for miles south and west: southward over the long swell of gently rolling hills, westward across fertile bottom lands and past the flank of an isolated mountain mass to where many lesser heights rose in a crescendo to the pale distant silhouette of tall peaks against the setting sun.

There he found that lonely man of whom Colonel Williams had spoken, and Thomas Brettany would sell, so Anthony Currain looked no further. He bought Chimneys and established there his younger son, and he himself went home to Great Oak and lived and died. When that younger son of his died childless, Chimneys fell back into the weak hands of the second Anthony Currain, who sold it on terms to two brothers named Higpen. They made rapacious play with the rich bottoms till in the 1830's the gold rush to placer workings in the mountains a few miles southeastward lured them away; and the discoveries around Gold Hill kept them enchanted there till they were penniless. When the second Anthony Currain died, their unpaid debt put the place back in his widow's hands, and greedy tenants worked the land till Tony—the third Anthony Currain—persuaded his mother to send Travis, his younger brother, there to take charge.

For Trav the move was promising; the prospect of freedom from Tony's many impositions was an attractive one. Two passions were strong in him: a passion for keeping good land healthy and at work, and a love for the poetry of numbers. When one of his tutors while he was still a boy introduced him to Welch's *Improved American Arithmetic,* Trav read it through as one reads a novel, hungrily; he turned back to pore over it page by page. What was alligation? Why were some fractions vulgar? What was double fellowship, the rule of three, tare, tret, cloff, suttle?

The answers led him inevitably to an exploration of the plantation ledgers; he became their custodian. But at Great Oak, Tony and a succession of sloven overseers made the crops, and Trav had only the figures to set down. At Chimneys the double responsibility would be his. He welcomed it, and since then a dozen years had failed to bring satiety.

Riding homeward in the late afternoon Travis checked his horse on a rise of ground and turned to look out across the low hills clad in pine and chestnut through which many little streams hurried to fatten the south fork of the Yadkin a few miles away. He and James Fiddler had gone toward his eastern bounds to inspect a sandy slope where a young vineyard of scuppernongs began to show fine promise; and now the overseer reined in beside him. Trav was a big man in his early forties, heavy-shouldered so that he seemed to stoop, with soft brown hair thinning a little, eyes mildly blue. He was close shaven; and even on this hot evening in early July, after a long day in the saddle, there was cleanness about him. The dust upon his garments and his boots and heavy on the brim of his soft old hat, and the sweat that darkened his shirt were superficial; the shirt had been fresh that morning, the boots scrupulously polished.

His eyes swept this his domain, and James Fiddler's too. The overseer's father had been one of the tenant farmers here, greedy and improvident; James himself had stayed on, at first to rob Trav, then to love him. Their horses cropped the dry grass, willing to pause a while; and Trav spoke without turning, contentedly. "We've made a change here, James, in these years."

"Yes."

"I remember well how it was when I came; all the old fields gone to sedge and pine. But we've put them back to work, one way or another; wheat and corn, tobacco, the orchards, and the vineyard now. All the land that's workable is working, or resting to be put to work another year." James Fiddler looked at him in a way that suggested the comradeship between these two, and Trav spoke half to himself. "And always something new to do. It's a full, rich way of life."

The other spoke of what they both knew. "I used to plan to get what I could and go away. Now I want nothing but to go on here with you."

"The place is more than me or you."

"Hard to think of Chimneys without you!"

Trav smiled contentedly. "Yes. I've set my roots here now."

He turned his horse to go on. The trail, following a meandering branch, dipped into the grateful shade of oaks undergrown with dogwood and haw and scattering redbud. The horses jogged serenely till Trav, leading, turned up hill along another trail. Then his beast sheered in protest at this departure from the homeward way, and Trav spoke chidingly and urged the horse to an easy canter, while James Fiddler dropped far enough behind to be clear of the pebbles thrown up by flying hoofs. They came over a rise and down into a cove among the hills, to a triangular clearing in the bottoms where a man with a mule on a jerk rein was plowing between freshly sprouted rows of corn while at his heels a boy of eight or nine dropped black-eyed peas in the fresh furrows. Ed Blandy had here a few well-tilled acres, a saddle-bag log house which his hands had built, and a wife and four youngsters.

He came toward them; and he and Trav spoke together like old friends of the need of rain, and why there were always more pests to eat the crops in a dry season, and how corn depleted a piece of land if you planted it year after year. Their voices were hushed by the quiet peace of the ending day. Trav saw Ed's boy waiting yonder by the flap-eared mule and said his own Peter would soon be old enough to ride the rounds with him. "Lucy—" She was his daughter, ten years old, named for his mother. "Lucy comes along sometimes, now, when I'm not going too far."

Blandy had killed a young buck deer down by the branch that morning, and he went to fetch a haunch from the spring house. With the venison hung to his saddle, Trav led James Fiddler homeward, the horses fretting because they must walk the last mile to cool off quietly. They came up past the saw mill toward the house, and when they emerged from the woods Trav saw scores of swallows and martins circling above the corn cribs, and bull bats on whickering wing high in the sky.

"A flight of weevils coming out of the old corn," he said. "Let's empty the cribs for a good brushing and scrubbing before we put the new crop in."

Fiddler assented. At the stables, Negro boys raced to take the reins, and Trav moved on alone toward the big house. He approached it from the rear, past the smithy where black Sam was still at work, a fountain of sparks rising from his ringing hammer blows; past the poultry yards where roosters scratched and geese hissed and strutting gobblers made their stiff wings scrape the ground and guineas potracked nervously and 'Phemy, the mulatto woman whose charges they were, was stuffing the young turkeys with pepper corns; past the idle windlass of the horse-powered thresher, and the shoemaker's shop; past the log house wherein wool from his own sheep was spun and woven.

This was his world, complete in itself; and he loved it. He entered the big house by a side door on the ground level, coming directly into what—before he added a separate wing—had been the kitchen. This was a low-ceiled room, its walls and ceiling half-timbered, the spaces between the timbers filled with straw and clay nogging. Always cool in summer, a deep hearth gave ample heat when heat was needed. Here were his ledgers and his letter press and all the meticulously kept farm records; here were James Fiddler's desk and his own; to this sanctuary he could always retreat when he wished to escape Enid's fretful complaints which might whine like a nagging wind through the house above. Here, except himself and James Fiddler and a servant to bring lightwood for the fireplace and to brush up the floor, no one ever came.

When Trav took off his hat, his forehead, always shaded against the sun, showed white; his cheek and chin were dark saddle brown from much exposure. He slapped dust from his trousers and his boots and disposed of the crumb of tobacco in his cheek and ascended narrow stairs into the cross hall of the floor above. A Negro with one foot gone, his knee bent back and strapped into the home-made peg he wore, came to meet him; and Trav said in a friendly tone: "Joseph, I left a haunch of venison on my saddle. Don't let it go to waste." He had accepted the gift to please Ed Blandy; but Enid did not like wild meat, and Trav avoided argument with her. The Negro's teeth shone. "Yassuh! Nawsuh!" Joseph had worked in the saw mill down by the branch till a rolling log tripped him into the saw, and after his leg healed Trav brought him into the big house to easier service. Enid objected to the tap of his peg, to his general awkwardness; she said he ought to be kept in the fields; but Trav, without answering her fretful protests, nevertheless ignored them.

Hearing their father's voice as he spoke to Joseph, Lucy and small Peter came racing through the wide transverse hall to greet him, Lucy as he stooped throwing her arms around his neck.

"Hullo, hullo!" he said happily. "But be careful, Honey, you'll get yourself dirty. I'm all horse and sweat."

"I don't care!" She kissed him, and he hugged the children close, kneeling, embracing them both. The black girl who was their nurse, with four-months-old Henrietta cradled against her shoulder, watched in dull disinterest, till Enid called angrily to her from the hall above:

"Vigil, for Heaven's sake, take that snuff stick out of your mouth! How many times do I have to tell you?" Then, without any change of tone, scolding Trav as she had scolded the nurse. "You always come home a mess! Why can't you wait till you've cleaned up, to maul the children?"

Vigil led them away, and Trav went up the stairs toward his wife, walking slowly as though suddenly tired. Enid was much younger than he. Her eyes, startlingly blue, contrasted with bright hair, and she was slim, scarce more rounded than a child. She recoiled from his proffered kiss.

"Oh, Trav, you're a sight! Boo! Smelling of horse and dust and saddle leather. Don't touch me! Now hurry and clean up, do. What made you so late?"

"We stopped by Ed Blandy's."

"Can't you keep away from that white trash?" This was an old quarrel, and it followed him as he moved away. "You won't ever go anywhere with me! I declare you'd rather go to a hog killing or a corn shucking than to a ball! but you'll talk for hours to that no-count——"

In his own room he closed the door, shutting out her words yet still hearing her voice as he began to rid himself of dusty clothes. He and the overseer had tramped through woodlands today to locate a few oaks that would make beams for a larger mill house Trav thought of building, so he was not surprised to find a tick on his right leg already well embedded; and he called Joseph to bring him a handful of penny-royal and rubbed the tick till it let go. He went down to use the outdoor shower and was bathed and dressed and downstairs again before Enid descended. Joseph brought him a frosted julep in a silver goblet and he sat at ease on the veranda, watching blue shadows flood the valley lands below, till Enid in sharp impatience summoned him. She never ceased to resent his insistence on delaying the day's heavy meal till dusk, for despite her small proportions she was always hungry. But Trav liked long days afield, and he was unwilling to come home while hours of daylight still remained. Now when he followed her into the dining room it was already so nearly dark that candles were needed; and Enid scolded Joseph because he had not lighted them. The Negro thumped away to the kitchen to fetch a spill, and Trav wished he need not be alone with Enid when she was in this humor. His thought found words.

"Enid, I wish Lucy and Peter could eat with us."

"They have their dinner at a sensible hour. Just because you choose to starve from sunrise to dusk is no reason they should! It's bad enough for me to have to go hungry. Besides, I hear enough of their chatter all day." And she added: "Mr. Lowman sent a boy with a letter from Mama today. She's coming to visit us."

He looked his slow surprise. "Why?"

"Why? Why not, for goodness' sake? Why shouldn't she?"

"Well—she hasn't been here since we were married." He tried to amend his error. "Well, that will be mighty nice for you, won't it?"

"You act as if she weren't welcome here!"

"Why—she's never come before, that's all; not since we were married. But I'm glad she's coming."

"Well, I'm not!" Even after ten years she still confused him. Let him take one side of any question and she was sure to take the other; but if he yielded she instantly seized the ground he had abandoned. It was as though she preferred argument to agreement, discord to the peace he would have chosen. "I'm not!" she repeated. "It means turning everything upside down, getting ready for her."

"I should think she'd be comfortable . . ."

"What do you know about it? As long as you're fed, and can go to sleep at dark and get up at daylight, and go off all day visiting your no-count friends, you never notice things! But every bit of silver needs cleaning, and the floors have to be waxed, and the furniture needs polishing, and I don't know what all. I'm just desperate!"

"Put the people at it."

"They don't do anything right unless I'm after them every minute. I declare, sometimes I think it would be easier to do things myself."

"Well, if you'd rather she didn't come . . ."

"Oh, I suppose you'd like to see me turn my own mother away!"

"Why, I just thought getting ready for her might be too much for you. But if you want her . . ."

"It's not what I want! Don't imagine that for a minute." Yet she began to plan, thinking aloud. They must do this and that, thus and so, to entertain her mother. "Emmy Shandon's one of her oldest friends, of course, if they'd ever be at home instead of off at the Springs or somewhere; and Clarice Pettigrew; and we'll have the Lenoirs." Forgetting him, excited by her own anticipations, she rattled names of neighbors for fifty miles around, from Happy Valley beyond the hills northwesterly to Panther Creek away to the eastward. Trav made no protest, but he dreaded the festivities she planned. With men like Ed

Blandy and the small farmers who lived between here and Martinston, he was easily comfortable. Their common devotion to the land bound them all in a close-knit fraternity. But men like Pettigrew and Shandon, leaving their places to the overseers and willing to follow a pack of hounds and a frightened fox full gallop across their own fields or across his, and to smile in amused tolerance when he protested at their trespasses; with such men he had nothing in common.

Yet he liked them, these people who all knew each other so well and laughed so easily; and sometimes he thought how pleasant it would be to be one of them, able to meet them amiably. They reminded him of his brother Faunt, who was always so completely himself, gentle and courteous and merry yet without loss of dignity. Trav in company felt awkward and conspicuous, seemed to be forever stumbling over his own feet, was as likely as not if he moved across a crowded room to trip over a rug, or to knock something off a table. If he sat down on a chair, it creaked complainingly; there had been wretched moments in his youth when chairs broke under him. Long since, in self-defense, he had put on a ponderous dignity to hide his own fears; it never occurred to him that strangers and casual acquaintances were more afraid of him than he of them.

So now, with Enid's mother coming, with Enid planning parties for her entertainment, he was afraid. He tried to believe that he dreaded merely the tax upon his time at this season when there were not hours enough in the day for him to do all he wished to do and should be doing. Every hand fit to work was busy from daylight to dark, except for the two-hour rest at midday and the weekly holiday from noon on Saturday till Monday morning. There was the corn to plow, peas to plant for feed; there was always, if you looked ahead to another season, compost to be making. That meant hauling ditch sides and swamp mud into the pens where sheep and hogs and cattle were every night collected, for even with the guano he had begun to buy and the peas he plowed under, every acre of cultivated land needed a hundred loads or so of compost each year.

And the tobacco! The plants were thriving, but they wanted the hoe at least once a week, and to be hand-weeded besides. To grow tobacco hereabouts meant constant vigilance, and needed luck in the weather too. Even Ed Blandy, when Trav began to experiment with the new yellow tobacco that men were raising on sandy soil in Caswell County, had predicted certain failure. Trav accepted the challenge; and three years ago, with tobacco at thirty-five dollars a hundred, the crops he made had brought over five thousand dollars. He hoped this year, if the price held, to do as well again.

While his thoughts ran their course, Enid talked herself into better humor; and as his attention came back to her he saw with deep and affectionate appreciation how lovely she was—and how young. He was forty-four, she only twenty-seven; sixteen when he married her. Watching the play of beauty in her eyes he remembered the moment when he first realized she was not the child he had thought her, and the heady happiness of the days that followed, and the incredulous rapture of the hour when she half prompted his blundering declaration, answering him almost before he spoke. He tasted again the bliss he had known when she came into his awkward arms, fragrant and indescribably sweet and ardent in surrender. Absorbed in his long labors here, he had bound her to what must be for her a dull and empty way of life, and tonight, watching her in the candlelight, he blamed himself for thoughtlessness, vowed that when her mother came he would do whatever she chose, would help her to a happy interlude.

Afterward, to be sure, they could settle back again into the routine that contented him.

During the sharp frenzy of Enid's many preparations for her mother's advent Trav spent long hours afield, driving himself and driving the people to do as much as possible before she came; but all too soon a letter from Mrs. Albion announced her imminent arrival. Enid said he must go to meet the stage that would bring her from the railroad. "I've thousands of last-minute things to do, Trav; and besides, I hate that long, dusty ride."

"We could start early, drive slowly. Or we could go the day before and stay over night in Martinston."

She laughed at him. "Trav Currain, I believe you're scared of being alone with Mama! Why, you used to like her! Oh, I know how she flirted with you! She'd have married you if I hadn't snatched you just in time! I expect she's just as pretty and charming as she ever was." Then in quick delight: "Honey, you're red as a brick! I declare, I wish you could see yourself! You look so funny, all blushing and embarrassed!"

He remembered Mrs. Albion as a pretty woman with a possessiveness in her manner which had in the past at once flattered and alarmed him; and he dreaded the six- or seven-mile ride home from Martinston alone with her. On his way to town to meet her he stopped to talk with Ed Blandy and with Lonn Tyler and Jeremy Blackstone and other farmers along the way, postponing as long as possible his arrival at the tavern where the stage would halt. A baking summer sun lay across the land, and Trav drove slowly, appraising with an expert eye the condition of the crops in each man's clearing, smiling at the children playing around each cabin. He overtook an occasional wagon, or a man and woman on horseback with bulging saddlebags, the woman's cotton wrap-around riding skirt whipping in the light breeze, her face hidden under her sunbonnet. Once he alighted to drink where a spout-spring came down from the mountainside, then watered his horses in the hollowed gum log which the spring fed. While they drank with cool sucking sounds he heard in the wood the log-cock's pounding tattoo, heard the drum of a grouse; and twice before he drove into the village he saw turkeys, and once a deer crossed the road a quarter-mile in front of the carriage.

At the tavern, on the long veranda shaded by an overhanging second story supported by slender brick pillars, a dozen men were awaiting the arrival of the stage. He joined them, for they were his friends. They sat along the benches or in tipped-back chairs, their voices easy in the midday heat. Judge Meynell and Miss Mary were here to take the stage when it should arrive. The Judge, high-dressed for the coming journey, was hot and sweating; but Miss Mary sat demurely, her bonnet box upon her knee, her cheeks pink with the excitement of the occasion. Trav sat down beside the Judge and they fell into talk together, and other men drew near to listen to the discussion; for Trav, as the only big planter for many a mile, and Judge Meynell, on his way now to Quarter Sessions, were men whose words were heeded. Judge Meynell was a justice of the peace and a person of authority. He and his fellow justices, sitting as the County Court, not only heard petty legal causes but they appointed the sheriff and the road overseers, and decided where bridges should replace fords, and where schools were needed, and who should stand for the Assembly. But Judge Meynell never acted against Trav's advice and counsel.

The abolitionists up North were bound to make trouble, the Judge suggested; but Trav said the politicians down in the Cotton States were quite as bad in their way. "Little boys calling names on both sides," he and Judge Meynell agreed. Except for Trav and for the Judge, who owned an old house servant, none of the men in the group on the veranda owned slaves; and when Trav said slavery was not worth getting mad about, most of them nodded. But Matt Resor, sprawling on the stoop, added a word.

"I'd admire to git my sights on one of them Republican abolitionists, all the same. Anyone says I got to have niggers pulling up to my table, marrying my gals!" He spat with listless violence.

Trav was careful not to smile. Matt was one of those individuals who never stood when he could sit, never sat when he could lie down. Most farmers hereabouts were thrifty and hard-working men; but Matt never did a lick. Trav thought any Negro who sat at Matt's table would be still hungry when he rose; and of course Matt had no daughters. Many white men were poor, but Matt was 'poor white,' a very different thing. Such men as he had nothing except their white skins of which to boast, so they hated Negroes and abolitionists with an equal venom. "Well, I doubt if it will come to anything," he said, and Matt was appeased.

Talk turned to crops and weather, and Chelmsford Lowman came over from the Post Office to wait for the mail sack the stage would bring, and at last the thudding of hoofs on the dusty road announced its coming. The four horses drawing the clumsy vehicle turned into the wide street, lumbered nearer, stopped at the tavern steps; and Trav rose to watch for Enid's mother to descend. She alighted prettily, her gray merino pelisse and soft gray hat somehow managing despite the dusty journey to make her appear immaculate; and even before he stepped forward she recognized him with a quick, welcoming smile.

He offered his hand, but she kissed him. "It's good to see you, Trav my dear." She looked at him in calm appraisal. "You're handsomer than ever! I always thought you were just about the nicest-looking man I'd ever seen."

She said this so simply that it left him unembarrassed. He handed her into the carriage, called a Negro to fetch her baggage from the boot, and turned the horses homeward. His awkward politenesses she answered pleasantly. Her trip had been a hard one, yes. "But it's worth it, to be here, and nice of you to meet me." As they left the town behind she exclaimed with delight at a trumpet flower in full bloom, and then at the laurel which clad every hillside in bright blossoms; and Trav warmed to her praise of the beauty of this region which he loved.

"Lots of flowers and flowering trees here," he assured her. "There's nothing any prettier than a fringe tree, and the redbuds and the dogwoods just make a garden out of the whole place when they're in bloom. You see a tulip tree all covered with yellow- and copper-colored blossoms and it will take your breath away; and the smell of the olive blossoms in spring is about the sweetest smell there is. We've got a strawberry tree, right by the porch, and we did have some Carolina jessamines, but Enid didn't like the smell, so I had to root them up." He added mildly: "She's not much for flowers."

He felt her eyes touch his face, and she led him to talk about Chimneys, to recount what he had done, and to recite the things he planned to do. He expected to increase his acreage in orchards and vineyards, and he explained to her why this region was good fruit country.

"We seldom get frost after mid-April, or before late October, and we have a lot of slopes that are well above the frosts that hit the bottom lands, and at the same time not high enough to get the freezes in the hills."

She asked the right questions. "Isn't it hard to farm on the steep hillsides?"

"We plow them crosswise so the rain won't run down the furrows and wash the soil away. You won't find any bad gullies on the place anywhere. There were plenty when I came, but we've thrown brush in, and planted wild honeysuckle and ground vines to catch the silt." Under her prompting he told her about the tobacco that was his special pride. "The idea is, you put in just enough guano to give the plant a good growth, but not too much. That way, when it's grown it begins to starve, and the leaves turn yellow, just like trees in a dry summer, and the flavor gets better at the same time. It needs light, sandy soil; but we've got two ridges that are good for it."

She asked for Emmy Shandon, but he had not seen these neighbors recently. "We don't have much in common," he confessed. "Mr. Shandon's not my kind. He's so stirred up about politics that he's letting his place run down."

"Aren't you interested in politics? No one thinks of anything else in Richmond."

He moved his whip in a wide gesture that embraced the scene before them. "I'm too busy with all this to bother."

"But, Trav," she urged, "if the abolitionists have their way you won't have this. You couldn't do anything without slaves."

"Maybe I could." They passed a small house, and Trav raised his hat to the man splitting lightwood by the corn crib. "That's Ed Blandy. Take him, for instance. He gets twice as much per acre out of his little patch here, with just Mrs. Blandy and his boy to help him, as I get per acre with all my people. I'd rather have white men if I could get them; but around here the white men all have their own farms, and work them." He added, quiet pride in his tones: "I know to work is sort of disreputable all over the South, because it's mostly negroes that work; but that's not true here. It's loafing that's disreputable here."

"If you raised more cotton, or if you raised rice, I expect you'd want slaves."

This was doubtless true, and he did not argue the point. "This is where our land begins," he said.

"I think I'd have known. The fields are so neat and clean."

He nodded, silent now, his eyes alert, looking for tasks that needed doing; and she did not speak for long minutes, till they came to the turning where his driveway left the road. As it topped the first rise of its winding ascent, the big house, hidden till now by a roll of the land, came into view, still well above them; and she cried: "Oh, Trav, it's beautiful! But it wasn't white before? It's brick, isn't it?"

"Yes, built of big bricks they used to make around here, nine inches long, laid up in Flemish bond. But Enid thought it would look better painted white, and we've put on a fresh coat, specially for you." He added, his eyes on the big house as they approached: "We've taken off the old tile roof, too. Mr. Brettany, the man who built the place, brought the tiles from Salem. They were shaped like shingles, a foot long, and furrowed to let the water run down. The men who made them used to mark those furrows in the soft clay with their fingers before they baked the tiles. The old roof was a mighty pretty red, but the wind got under the tiles sometimes, loosened them, drove water in, and that bothered Enid."

"It didn't bother you?"

"Well, I liked the old tiles, and the plain brick walls, but Enid thinks the paint looks nice."

His eyes were on the house, and hers too. The ascent from the road was moderate, but the horses took a foot pace, switching their tails, ears pricked, glad to come home. A clump of oaks for a moment shut off their view, but when they rounded the trees Trav saw Enid waiting on the wide westward-facing veranda. He pulled up the horses at the foot of the steps, and Enid, lovely as a child, came running to kiss her mother, and to kiss Trav too in this happy hour. She swept Mrs. Albion away upstairs, and Trav left Joseph to tend Mrs. Albion's bags while he himself went down to the cool shadowed room on the ground floor to hear James Fiddler's report of the day's activities.

When later he had changed his clothes, Joseph brought his julep out to the veranda and he sat at ease, watching the sun drop toward the distant mountains while lengthening shadows reached toward him across the cultivated bottom lands. Knowing his delight in them, Vigil fetched the children; and Lucy stood in the crook of her father's arm and Peter wriggled on his knee.

Then Enid and her mother appeared, and Enid said in a sharp tone: "Vigil!" The black girl guiltily snatched her snuff stick out of her mouth, and tried to hide it in her skirts. "I declare," Enid protested, "that worthless nigger drives me distracted. Sometimes I wish we hadn't sold Sapphira!"

Mrs. Albion, already making friends with the children, asked lightly, "Who was Sapphira?"

"Oh, she was a bright, and much too uppity." Enid added maliciously: "Of course Trav liked her!"

Trav felt Mrs. Albion's eyes rest on him for a moment, but then she said something to make the children laugh, and he thought she knew how to please people. She had changed in these years, was more attractive, not at all alarming. Her visit promised pleasantly.

3

IN THAT interval after her arrival when she and her daughter were alone together abovestairs, Mrs. Albion decided that Enid was as pretty as ever, if she only knew how to do her hair. It hung in ringlets, with a frizzed bang; but coronet braids in the current fashion were so much more becoming unless your hair was naturally curly. Enid's, though it was a delicious honey color, was as straight as a string; and people with straight hair, if they were intelligent, arranged it simply and almost severely. Enid's gown, too, was atrocious, the sort of thing you gave away quickly to your servants. Mrs. Albion thought: "But there, I mustn't blame her. It's my fault. I didn't teach her these things when she was a child. It's lucky I came."

They had a long hour together while Mrs. Albion repaired the disorders of her journey. Enid was exclamatory with welcome. "Oh, Mama, it's so wonderful to have you here! Trav and I just go on and on, year in, year out, never seeing anybody! Except, of course, he goes away on business sometimes; but he never takes me!"

Mrs. Albion marked her querulous tone for future attention. "What a pretty dress! Did Trav pick it out for you, on those trips of his?"

"Trav? Heavens, Mama, he never thinks of bringing back anything —except of course head cloths for the women and Barlow knives for the hands! Never anything for me. No, I made this over. It's one I got in Raleigh three years ago. I haven't been away from the place since! Can you imagine that? The children and the place, up at daylight, go to bed at dark; that's Trav's idea of the way to live! He never considers me!"

Mrs. Albion's eyes narrowed thoughtfully. "You talk as though you and Trav didn't get along."

"Oh, I guess he's satisfied, but it's awful for me. We just live like poor whites."

"In this lovely house? With everything you want?" The older woman's tone sharpened. "Don't be silly! You've nothing to whine about!"

"You don't know Trav!"

"I've known—other men."

"Trav isn't Tony, by miles!"

There was a hint of malice in Enid's tone, and Mrs. Albion heard it. Probably the little snip had guessed the truth about Tony long ago. Well, let her! "Whining does no good, with men," the older woman suggested. "It just makes them feel guilty, so they get mad. A man's like a cat, or a mule. Pushing and pulling and hauling makes men stubborn; but they can be gently led to do anything, if you're clever."

"I notice you never married Tony, all the same!"

"Tony? Why, Heavens, he's an old man, dear!" The best defense was always to attack. "I'm surprised you haven't been able to handle Trav. You were clever enough to make him marry you."

"I just did it to spite you! I wish I'd let you have him!"

"Well, you made your bed! It's your own fault Trav is in it." She was busy with her hair. "I never get this braid to look right. I should have kept Tessie. She was good with it, but she was a bother other ways." Tessie knew too much, for one thing; Mrs. Albion, ignoring her entreaties, had mercilessly sold her to a slave trader from Louisiana. So far away her tongue could do no harm.

"Let me try."

"Oh, I might as well learn now as later." Nell's tone became lightly casual. "By the way, speaking of Tony, I hear he's run Great Oak into debt. Trav's made Chimneys pay, hasn't he?" She was more intent than she pretended. It was for this, above all else, that she had come.

"I guess so. He used to brag about it all the time; but it bored me, so I never listen now."

"You should. Men—even husbands—like to talk about themselves and their work." Her hair suited her at last. "There, that will do.

Enid, I think Tony may decide to take Chimneys over, now that Great Oak doesn't earn its way."

"Oh, nobody will ever get Trav away from here."

"Wouldn't you like to live at Great Oak?"

Enid's eyès shone. "Of course I would! Trav's never even taken me there! I was always going to have a baby or something. It must be wonderful, people to see, things to do!"

"Someone said Mrs. Currain felt that since Trav had done so well with Chimneys he might be able to bring Great Oak back. If she wants Trav there, you ought to make him go."

"Make him? Why, Mama, no one can make Trav do anything he doesn't want to do! You can argue and argue, but it's like pounding pillows. He just grunts and does what he was going to do anyway."

Mrs. Albion smiled, sure of her powers; and she held to her design. Out of Tony's past generosity she had saved, in secret ways, a considerable sum; but now that he had cast her off, she would have to spend her savings, and money spent was gone. Yet, if Tony had Chimneys, she was sure she could recall him to her side. "You can manage Trav if you try," she urged. "But perhaps you don't really want to move to Great Oak."

"Oh, I do!"

"Maybe I can help you with Trav." Certainly Enid had no notion how to handle him. She rose, and they came downstairs, and she thought that reference to Sapphira, when they joined Trav on the veranda, was just plain silly. Sensible wives, if they suspected that their husbands had noticed one of the wenches from the quarter, pretended not to see. Enid was a fool, no doubt of that; but Trav could be managed. When they were at table—she had taken care to make herself perfection, in a low-necked lilac-colored gown with angel sleeves that did not conceal her round arms—she watched him appraisingly. Enid ignored him, chattering as though he did not exist; so Mrs. Albion sought to draw him into their conversation. She expressed some opinion, asked him directly: "Trav, don't you agree?"

Enid spoke in a quick impatience. "Oh, don't bother Trav, Mama. He doesn't like to talk when he's eating. Always thinking about his crops, I suppose."

"Well," Mrs. Albion smilingly commented, "he thinks to some purpose, I can see that." All men liked flattery. "The change in Chimneys since I first saw it is just unbelievable. Trav, does your mother ever come here?"

"No," he confessed. "She never has."

"Not even to our wedding!" Enid's tone was sharp with resentment.

"She's pretty old to travel," Trav said defensively.

"She'd be mighty pleased to see all you've done here," Mrs. Albion suggested.

"Oh, she won't come," Enid said positively. "I've never laid eyes on her. Trav goes to see her every year, but he doesn't take me. He always says it's just a business trip to Richmond; but then he goes down to Great Oak too. I think he's ashamed of me!" And as though weary of this topic: "Mama, have you sold your house in Richmond? Why are you moving to Washington?"

"Oh, Trav's not interested in my doings, Enid." Mrs. Albion held him in play. "Trav, is Great Oak as prosperous as Chimneys?"

"No." He added as though in apology: "I reckon Tony's not much of a farmer."

"Too bad you can't take charge there for a year or two, put it on its feet again. Now that Chimneys is in such splendid condition." Enid was about to speak, but the older woman caught her eye, warned her to silence. "You'd enjoy that, I expect."

"It would be a hard pull." Yet she saw the stir of interest in his eyes. Great Oak would challenge his capacities.

"I expect you like a hard pull, don't you? Is Mr. Fiddler still overseer? I remember he was here when you and Enid were married."

"Yes, he's a good man."

"Well then, with him in charge, Chimneys would go on all right." She would tell Tony, some day, how deftly she had prepared the way for him; it would amuse him to hear how she had played on Trav.

"Yes, James Fiddler could handle things," Trav reflected. Clearly, she had set him thinking, so the fight was half won.

"Could Great Oak be brought back, do you suppose?"

"Oh yes, certainly." On firm ground now, his tone was sure, and quick with interest. "Yes, it could be done. Edmund Ruffin found out years ago how to revive worn-out land. Manure did it no good, but he decided that was because the land was sour——"

"Heavens, I didn't know land could be sour—or sweet either, for that matter. What do you mean?"

"Why, sour land has too much acid in it. Some of it comes from rotting vegetation; and some plants, the roots throw off acid. Mr. Ruffin decided that lime would counteract acid, and there were plenty of marl beds—full of fossils, really lime—on Coggin's Point, where his farm was; so he dug up a lot of marl and spread it on fields where he'd been getting five or ten bushels of corn or wheat to the acre, and even the first year he doubled his yield." There was a high admiration in his tone. "I wanted Tony to try it at Great Oak, but he never would."

Enid made an impatient sound, weary of this conversation; but they ignored her. Mrs. Albion asked, in lively interest: "Do people know about Mr. Ruffin's way?"

"Oh, yes. He used to publish a farmer's magazine full of advice about using marl and about draining wet lands and about farming with machinery. Then he gave his Coggin's Point place to his son and bought a worked-out farm up on the Pamunkey. He named it Malbourne and in three years he had it producing again." Well-launched, he became eloquent. Let him talk; he would persuade himself. "Yes," he concluded. "All those old fields at Great Oak could be put back to work."

"Then it's certainly a pity to let Great Oak go downhill." But she must not press him too hard. Men hated to be hurried. "Is your mother well?"

"For her age, yes."

"Too bad you can't see more of her. Do your brothers and sisters get home more often than you?"

"Faunt does, and Cinda; but she and Brett have been abroad all this last year." He added, his thoughts still on farming: "Clayton's managing the Plains. That's their place, down near Camden. Clayton's their oldest son, and he's a good farmer. He came up here when he was eighteen and spent the summer, and I took him to see Mr. Ruffin. He wanted to learn all he could." He reflected, half to himself: "Clayton could run Great Oak, but Brett needs him at the Plains. Brett's more of a business man than a planter."

"If Clayton can't do it, perhaps you should go back to Great Oak.

The place needs you, and—you'd be with your mother. She won't live many more years."

He hesitated, shook his head. "I can't imagine leaving here." Yet there was no finality in his tone. She smiled to herself, contented with the progress she had made; and that night before she slept she wrote to Tony.

I came down for a little visit with Enid, shan't be returning to Richmond. [To reassure him, to make him understand that he was free.] I'll go from here to Lynchburg to visit Molly Rand, and on to Staunton. Sue Nicholson lives there and I haven't seen her for ten years. Then to Washington. I put my house in Mr. Freedom's hands, to sell or rent. I hope he does well with it. I'll need the little it may bring. [To keep Tony mindful of old obligations.]

Chimneys is beautiful, every field under cultivation, orchards and vineyards along the hills. Trav's done wonders here. Mr. Fiddler, the overseer, is a thoroughly competent man. Trav says he could manage everything. I suppose you won't want to take it over till the crops are made and ready for market, so that you will handle the money; but once Trav has gone back to Great Oak you could leave Mr. Fiddler in charge, wouldn't need to stay here unless you chose. Trav hates to think Great Oak has run down. He's itching to get his hands on it, I'm sure. And I suspect he's homesick, too; would like to see more of his mother. It's really lovely here, but Enid would be glad of a change. There aren't many young folks, and she's only twenty-six, and pretty as a picture. Darrell would flirt with her outrageously, the rascal! Remember me to him most kindly. [Jealousy was a useful weapon, if it were lightly used.]

Affectionately,
Nell

She did not sleep at once, wishing she had seen Chimneys before she allowed Tony even temporarily to escape her. They were used to each other; and if he had Chimneys' income at his disposal, they could be happy together. But that could be managed later; she must not hurry, must move carefully. A woman alone had to be wary and wise.

4

ED BLANDY was proud of his small farm, fifty or sixty acres of forest and bottom land in a cove cradled between wooded ridges. Along the road to Martinston there were a dozen farmers better off in land and buildings than he; but he had made his place with his own hands, seasoned every acre with his sweat. When he bought it, with money painfully earned and laboriously saved, the fields were far gone in briers and buck brush, the old log house crumbling in decay. He and his bride came there like pioneers. They made the hut briefly habitable and it served till the babies began to come; then he built a better house, two big rooms with a chimney between. The corn crib, the stable, the spring house, every fence and building on the place was a product of his axe and his splitting maul and wedges, and his hammer and his saw. He had come here, newly married, soon after Trav took over Chimneys; and Trav, riding to and from Martinston, saw the quick fruits of Ed's industry. So they came to be friends.

Ed was not unique in the locality; for this was a region of yeoman farmers, most of them in straight descent from the first pioneers who settled the mountainous northwestern corner of the state when it was still dark wilderness. Ed worked no harder than other men, but a little more wisely. He had some education; and it was all the more surely his because it had been dug out of the few books upon which he had been able to lay his hands, rather than absorbed from some dull unskillful teacher as passively as a mule absorbs blows. One of the things which after they became acquainted drew him and Trav closer was their equal liking for figures. Before his marriage and his coming from Virginia to the Martinston region, Ed had worked for a man named

Harvey Hill, a West Point graduate with a mathematical bent who after serving in Mexico resigned from the army to become a professor at Washington College in Virginia, and later at Davidson College. Professor Hill took an interest in Ed, advised him to study and make something of himself, set problems for him to do; and one summer on a vacation excursion to the mountains he rode this way to see how Ed progressed. Ed was proud to introduce him to Trav; and the three men, for each of whom a neat calculation had an almost musical harmony, relished that and subsequent encounters.

Ed and Trav were forever comparing notes and records, checking the results of their agriculture. Other farmers had good years and bad, and so did they; but to the others it was simply that times were good or times were bad. Ed—as well as Trav—could leaf through a worn and much-thumbed book of accounts and tell you just how much each year had yielded, and what crops in the long run were best, and why.

Mrs. Blandy, still pretty despite the marks left upon her by a dozen years of hard and steady work indoors and out, thought Ed was a man beyond all other men. He had taught her to read and write, but she knew she could never know as much, nor be as wise and wonderful, as he. She had proudly borne him four children and would presently bear another; she was as ready to die for him as she had been to live and toil for him through these dozen years. Since Trav was Ed's friend, so was he hers. With strangers she was shy as a wild thing, but with Trav she was at ease. So when one day in a pelt of rain, he and James Fiddler stopped at the gate and the dogs barked greeting, she bade them 'light and come in out of the wet, and she sent one of the children to fetch Ed, who was carting mud from the swamp for his compost pens. Trav said they could ride and find him, but she declared it was high time Ed came in. He would be wet to the bone as it was, in the sluicing rain. So they sat, their damp clothes steaming by the fire, and Trav talked with her, and the wide-eyed children watched and listened till Ed presently appeared. He was as wet as she had predicted, and he allowed her tender scolding to shepherd him into the other room and into dry clothes. While he changed he wondered why these two had come today. There was purpose in their manner; something sober, something almost sad. When he joined them by the fire he was sure of it, yet waited without questions to hear what Trav had to say.

It was worse than anything Ed might have imagined. Trav, like a man diving into icy water, put it at last without preamble.

"I came to say good-by, Ed. I'm leaving Chimneys tomorrow."

Ed knew from the other's manner and tone that Trav meant he was leaving for good and all, yet he refused to accept the sorrowful certainty. "Business?" he asked. He saw Mrs. Blandy watching them, knew she too was shaken, knew how much would go out of their lives if Trav no longer were their neighbor.

"No, I'm not coming back, not to stay." As though Ed's silence accused him, Trav said defensively: "Greak Oak is run down. My mother wants me to take hold of it."

"Virginia farms are mostly all cropped to death with tobacco." It was as though Ed argued against Trav's departure. "You've got Chimneys to where there ain't a plantation this end of the state can match it."

"My mother's pretty old. I don't see her much. And I can better things at Great Oak, some at least."

"Seems like you could come and go." Their voices were level, but Ed was sick with sorrow and emptiness.

"Oh, I'll be back." Trav chuckled, trying awkwardly to jest. "I'll have to keep an eye on James Fiddler here, see that he keeps things going right."

Ed looked at the overseer. James Fiddler was a good man when he had Trav to direct him. How well would he stand alone? "You'll be wanting to come back, yes."

As though Ed's thoughts were words, as though to justify himself in the face of Ed's unspoken protests, Trav explained: "Mrs. Currain wants to go." Ed for a moment hated Trav's wife; a stuck-up, conceited, lazy, useless critter too high and mighty to be civil if she rode past your door, half the time pretending not to see you tip your hat to her. "It's pretty lonesome for her here," Trav reminded him. "She'll see more people at Great Oak." See more people? Ed's jaw set. There were people enough around here, as good as she was! Yes, a sight better, too, if it came to that! But she took mighty good care not to see them.

"Likely," he admitted, his tone blank.

"My brother will live here," Trav said appeasingly. "He's older than I, a fine man. He's here now, wanted to come today to make your acquaintance; but he had a chill and it was raining. He'll be down the first good day. You and James Fiddler can tell him anything he needs to know."

"I heard he was here," Ed assented, then said frankly: "We're going to miss you, Mr. Currain. All of us. But specially Mrs. Blandy and the young ones and me."

"I never thought I'd leave here; but I reckon it's what I ought to do." Trav added honestly: "It's going to be interesting, handling Great Oak, trying to bring it back."

"Who's been farming there?"

"Why, we've needed a good overseer. We've had five different ones, the last ten-twelve years; but unless you can get someone like James Fiddler, a man had better be his own overseer."

Trav's interest in the task that awaited him at Great Oak was in his tones; he and Ed fell into long discussion of the wisest ways to proceed, James Fiddler now and then saying a word. Ed saw that the overseer was as depressed as he by Trav's prospective departure.

Mrs. Blandy, silent in the background, rocked slowly in her small chair. The baby fretted and she fed it and it slept in her arms. When Trav and James Fiddler departed Ed went out, heedless of the rain, to see them go. He came back to face her still sitting quietly; their eyes spoke without words. Ed sat down before the fire, his back to her; and after a moment she put the baby in its small bed and came to his side, her hand on his shoulder.

"It'll be some different with him gone."

Ed nodded, not turning his head. "He's a real good man. I never knew a better. Yes, he'll leave a hole."

"This brother of his prob'ly ain't much like him."

"He'll be made welcome. Everybody likes Mr. Currain. They'd go a long ways for his brother, even if he was a polecat." He added hopefully: "You can't tell. He might be real nice too."

"He's bound to be, the same blood in the both of them."

Ed nodded. "I reckon he's sickly, what Mr. Currain says; not wanting to come out in the rain." He rose. "Well, I can't set here, rain or no rain. Too much to do." He felt tired, felt strength withdrawn from him. "Never thought I'd take anything so hard."

Next day the rain was over, the sun shone. They saw the carriage pass with Trav and Enid and Vigil and the children, a wagon loaded high with bags and boxes coming behind, the horses splashing through the mud from yesterday's shower. Trav lifted his hat, and even Enid bowed to Ed's salutation. When they were gone, Ed looked at Mrs. Blandy.

"First time she ever took any notice of us," he said in a dull tone.

She came close to him to borrow comfort. "Oh Ed," she murmured sadly, "I know how you feel. I do too, kind of like I'd watched a funeral go by."

5

ENID left Chimneys with no regrets, ridiculing Trav's reluctance.
"Oh, don't be silly! I think you'd like to just stay here till you rot!"

"Well, when you work hard to make something, you—I suppose
you get to like it. Tony won't feel the way I do about the place."

"Well, neither do I," she retorted. "It's been just a prison for me.
I'll be glad to see the last of it." And in a sudden rapture at the prospect of release she forgave him even imagined grievances, clipping
him ardently, kissing him over and over. "Oh, darling, darling, I'm
so glad we're going, so grateful to you. I'll show you. Wait and see!
I'm going to love you so." But when his slow blood stirred and his
arms tightened around her she freed herself. "There, Honey, now
I've so much to do!" She had married when she was sixteen, had
borne a baby a week after her seventeenth birthday. The first years of
their marriage were a crowding succession of pregnancies, though
only three of them came to fruition. Her abounding vitality survived
the drain; but fear of having another baby taught her to curb the intemperate surrenders in which she as often as Trav had taken the
initiative. Trav was easily put off; and though she did not admit it to
herself this was one of her grievances against him, till the coldness she
pretended became real enough. Only in such happy hours as this did
her natural ardor reveal itself in brief tempestuous caresses.

She was afraid Trav would rebel at last at surrendering his beloved
Chimneys, so she hurried their departure. In Martinston while they
waited on the tavern porch for the arrival of the stage that would take
them to Statesville, men spoke to Trav, clumsily expressing their affection and respect, telling him how much he would be missed; and to

see his pleasure in their friendly words made her eager to be gone. When the stage arrived she hurried the children and herself aboard, and fretted till he joined them. Only when the last house in the village was left behind did she fill her breathless lungs. At last, at last they were on their way, out of this wretched wilderness into the beautiful, the gay, the beckoning world!

Her overflowing happiness infected the children; they laughed with her and sang with her till Trav and even Vigil, the dull-witted wench who held little Henrietta in her arms against the jolting of the stage, began to smile. She clung to Trav's arm, pressing against him, teasing him, reaching up to kiss him; and she commanded that he sing their foolish songs with them, and seduced him at last to do so, and they laughed at his deep voice unused to song, and he said he had never seen her so happy. "Like a colt let out to pasture, feeling his oats."

"Oh, I never was so happy in my life," she agreed. "Oh, darling, darling, we're going to have such fun!" She kissed him again and whispered: "You'll see, old sobersides! You just don't know how sweet I'm going to be!" She saw his dull color, his quick uneasy glance at the children; and she laughed with new delight and kissed him again.

She refused to be disturbed by the discomforts of the journey, lurching stage coaches, wretched taverns, hot and crowded cars of which the floors were stained and slippery with brown ambeer. It was dusk of a sultry summer day when they reached Richmond. Trav took them to the Atlantic Hotel, where in the past he had sometimes stayed; but the hotel had passed its best days, and their suffocating small rooms and the prospect of another long stage journey tomorrow brought Enid at last to a weary dismay. But Trav suggested that they wait over till Saturday morning and go down river on Captain Davis's steamer, the *Curtis Pack,* and she welcomed that proposal with a new delight. She looked forward to the day in Richmond; but the stifling heat and the clouds of dust stirred up from the unpaved streets by every passing hack and carriage made her head ache, till at last she surrendered and spent most of the day abed, requiring Vigil to keep a sheet of brown paper soaked in vinegar upon her brow.

But next day, though to rise in time for the half-past-six departure of the steamer was a nuisance, her spirits revived. Vigil tended the children while Trav identified the gracious houses along the river, telling old tales of Dutch Gap where Indians massacred the colonists Sir Thomas Dale had settled there; of Jordan's Point where lovely Cissy Jordan had so many beaux that she betrothed herself to two at once and was haled into court by one disappointed suitor; of Berkeley, where pretty Sarah Harrison gave bond to marry William Roscow and within two months married Dr. Blair, and, though when the ceremony was performed she refused to promise to obey, settled sedately down as the wife of the founder of the college at Williamsburg; of Westover, whence Evelyn Byrd went to England and loved Charles Mordaunt, and after her disapproving father hurried her back to Virginia refused to wed any other, and died of a broken heart; of Brandon, where a disappointed lover shot a bride on her wedding day, and the bereaved husband hung the wedding ring on the crystal chandelier, and her ghost sometimes returned to try that ring again upon her finger. "They say in damp weather you can still see where her blood stained the heart-pine floor," Trav said; and he told other tales, till Enid asked at last teasingly: "Mercy, Honey, how do you know so much about the lovely gay ladies?"

Trav colored, grinning. "Why, I was always too shy to talk to pretty girls; but I used to like to read the old stories and imagine I was the hero of them."

She laughed in delight. "Why, Trav, I declare I didn't suppose you ever read anything but that old *Farmer's Register!*"

He was glad to change the subject. "That was Mr. Ruffin's paper. Remember I was telling your mother about him? His place is on the river. I'll show you when we pass it." And he told her, as he had told Mrs. Albion, how Edmund Ruffin, taking over as a boy of nineteen the worthless acres of his Beechwood inheritance, brought them back to fine fertility.

"I don't see how you can get so worked up over a farmer!" Enid protested, bored by his enthusiasm; and Trav said seriously:

"Why, a great farmer's a great man. George Washington did about as much for the South by raising the first mules in this country as by any battle he ever won. And Mr. Ruffin, finding out how to bring back Virginia lands, has put thirty million dollars in values into the pockets of Virginia farmers." He added, thoughtfully: "He's not in-

terested in farming now. All he thinks about is politics, writing letters
to the *Enquirer,* or to the *South,* saying we ought to withdraw from
the Union and form a separate confederacy. He claims no one in Virginia has the courage to stand up for Southern rights, so he's moved
to South Carolina. They take politics more seriously down there."

He talked on, of farming, and of his grandfather who destroyed
good land by cropping it with tobacco till it would no longer yield.
"He wanted land just for the sake of making money out of it," he
explained. "He was always money-hungry." He laughed at sudden
memory. "He thought he'd make a fortune out of Moris Multicaulis.
That's a special kind of mulberry, and there was a time when everybody was either buying mulberry shoots or selling them. They used
to sell shoots at so much for each bud; and the price kept going up
till it was three or four and finally six cents per bud. The shoots were
wonderful to sprout, but the sprouts wouldn't grow up; they just kept
putting out more sprouts. And the silkworms wouldn't eat them, and
the sprouts couldn't be killed, till finally everyone had mulberry shoots
to sell and no one wanted to buy them. Papa lost a lot of money. It
was just a crazy speculation." He added, his thoughts drifting: "Then
after that excitement blew over, people got the gold fever and headed
for the mountain country down south of Chimneys. They found quite
a lot of gold, too. There was a man there, Bechler or Bechtler or some
such name, used to coin gold pieces down there for the Government."

His voice droned on, but Enid no longer heard him. Sun on the
water and the warm wind against her cheek had made her drowsy,
and even while he spoke she fell asleep. She slept past Dancing Point
and did not wake till Trav roused her to see Great Oak, the big house
on the clay bluffs above the river set well back and half-hidden by
trees; and after that she was full of eagerness. He had sent word ahead
that they were coming, so when they landed at Allen's Wharf, the
carriage and a cart for their belongings were waiting to meet them.
They came into Williamsburg by Francis Street and angled past Capitol Square; and as the horses trotted westward through the town,
Trav pointed out the court house in Market Square and the old Magazine across the way, and the college building with ugly square towers
defacing its front; and he told her of the town's great days until she
protested:

"But, Trav, all that was seventy or eighty years ago. Doesn't anything ever happen here now?"

"Well, I suppose Williamsburg has to be satisfied with having been important once."

Sudden misgivings touched her and she clung to his arm. "Trav, will your Mama like me?"

"Of course, Honey."

"Oh, I hope so."

He pressed her hand, gently reassuring. "Don't worry. You and she'll get along just fine."

Uneasy silence briefly held her. They took the Barrett's Ferry road. "Is she big and stern, Trav?"

He laughed. "About as big as a minute! She won't come much higher than your shoulder."

"You're big, and I remember Tony was tall and lanky, and Cinda's sort of big, too." Brett and Cinda had come from the Plains for their wedding, and Tony from Great Oak. I've never seen Faunt or Tilda."

"Father was tall," Trav explained. "Tony's like him. But Mama's a little bit of a thing."

They turned into an oak wood, and Enid sat breathless, watching the drive ahead. The oaks gave way to an avenue of tulip trees which passed stables and poultry yard and the overseer's house on one side, the smoke house and the corn cribs on the other. At the head of the avenue the big house was at first concealed; then as they drew near it came more and more clearly into view, till the circle of the driveway brought them to the hospitable door and the waiting welcome.

"There's Mama," Trav said. Mrs. Currain, small and exquisite and smiling, stood at the head of the steps, and at her shoulder a fat old Negro woman beaming with love and pride. "And April," Trav exclaimed. Then the carriage pulled up and he swung Enid to the ground, and her fears were forgotten. She took Mrs. Currain in her arms, and the little old lady returned her kiss with ready affection.

"Welcome to Great Oak, my dear!" she said, and held Enid at arm's length to survey her approvingly, and turned to take Trav's kiss, and to welcome Lucy and Peter. While Trav stayed a moment in talk with April, Enid and Mrs. Currain turned into the great hall, and Enid uttered a cry of delight.

"Oh, Mama, it's so big; so big, and so beautiful!"

Mrs. Currain smiled at her happiness. "My husband used to say you could drive a coach-and-four through the hall, if you could get them through the doors. Well, now, I'm glad you've come, my dears; I'm happy you're here."

Vigil at Enid's command brought the baby to be admired; and then April and Vigil took the children away and Enid went whirling through the lofty rooms, admiring everything, exclaiming and asking questions and not waiting for answers. She saw Trav watching her with content in his eyes, and called to him: "Oh, Honey, I never was so happy in my life before!"

During the summer days that followed, Enid explored everywhere, indoors and out, with a delicious secret sense of ownership; for surely, some day, all this would be Trav's, and she would be its mistress. The big house, though it needed painting, though the roof sometimes leaked, though it was shabby here and there, was a continuing wonder. The lofty arched hall with fluted pilasters, the marble mantels, the carved panelling, the wide curving stairs, the high-ceiled rooms with wall paper brought from England a hundred years before, all these were beyond superlatives. Side halls connected the central part of the house with what had once been separate wings, so that the whole structure was now full two hundred feet from one end to the other. The drawing room, its windows hung with bright damask, caught the sun all day long; and old portraits, richly shadowed, hung between the windows that reached from the floor almost to the ceiling.

Mrs. Currain was in these days as happy as Enid. "You musn't let me wear you out with so many questions, Mama," Enid warned her; and the little old lady said smilingly:

"Why, my dear, there's nothing I like so much as having you love this house. I do too, you know." She knew all there was to know about the old mansion. "Mr. Bexley built it, more than a hundred years ago. My husband's father bought it from Mrs. Bexley. She was Martha Foxhall, and my mother was a Foxhall, so we were distant cousins, so I've always felt at home here since the day Mr. Currain carried me up the steps and across the threshold." She knew the architectural features by their proper names and spoke of the hipped roof with its dormers, of pilasters and pediments and finials, and of flutings and entablatures, of modillions and rosettes and soffits, of balusters and balustrades, till Enid was lost in amused bewilderment.

"I declare, Mama, you've got me so mixed up I don't know windows from doors," she confessed. "I can hardly remember which are mantels and which are panels."

Mrs. Currain smiled at her pretty confusion. "The mantels are marble," she pointed out. "Carved in England before they were brought here. And the panels are heart-pine like the floors, cut and sawed and shaped here on the place."

"The floors are hardly worn at all," Enid commented. "Pine must be like iron."

Mrs. Currain nodded. "Yes, but of course it would burn like gunpowder. We're always afraid of fire. If one ever started, the whole house would go. That's why we never take lamps upstairs at all. Candles are so much safer."

Enid liked best of all the drawing room, so full of warm lights and rich shadows. She and Mrs. Currain received callers there, Mrs. Currain presiding at the tea table where silver and glass and eggshell china gleamed and shone; and after the stately ladies had gone she told Enid all about them, and her own words forever led her into memories. "My husband brought me home here fifty-two years ago, you know," she might say, with perhaps a smiling apology for her garrulity. "I was nineteen—he was much older, of course—so I've lived almost a lifetime here. But even when I first came the people loved to talk about the days before the Revolution, when Williamsburg was a great town." And she would drift into interminable tales, of old Mrs. Wills and other famous gossips, and of Mrs. Davis whose passion was collecting bonnets through long bedridden years, and how Decimus Ultimus Barziza came by that strange name, and of the Reverend Scervant Jones who would rather write a poem than a sermon, and of a dozen more.

Enid, though she might protest to Trav that his mother would talk her to death, yet enjoyed these hours with the older woman; and she took a sensuous delight in the big house and its noble setting. The service buildings were on the side away from the river, receding among concealing oaks. To right and left of the lawns toward the river, the gardens were enclosed in a hedge of tree box, and enriched by lush masses of bush box and with each bed framed in its own dwarf border. Now in midsummer there was not much bloom; but Mrs. Currain, to whom each plant was an old loved friend, saw with the eyes of memory and spoke of wistaria and jasmine, sweet shrub and calycanthus, mock orange and dogwood, smoke trees and lilacs, crape myrtle and Cape jessamine, roses by a hundred names, lesser blossoms by the score. Enid never tired of this talk of what had been and would be again.

On the river side, wide lawns were protected by ha-has against the incursion of the horses which grazed freely across the further levels. Solitary in the middle of the lawn which its spreading shade over a considerable space discouraged stood the huge oak tree that gave the plantation its name. The great trunk was more than twenty feet around, the lofty crown almost a hundred feet above the ground, the widest spread of the heavy branches a hundred and thirty feet from side to side. Within the trunk there was a hollow where a man could stand erect, extending upward into darkness. Lucy, although she was ten, was not too grown up to begin to make a play house in this ample cavity; and old April, who since Vigil was busy with little Henrietta made Trav's other children her special charge, helped her find furnishings for her retreat, and set one of the Negroes to make two small split bottom chairs just big enough for Lucy and Peter and to construct a tiny cradle; and she herself fabricated—out of a corn cob and some bright calico—a doll baby for Little Missy.

Enid did not interfere with Lucy's make-believe. She had her own delights, savoring every hour, never forgetting that if she were careful to keep Mrs. Currain's good will, she would some day be mistress here. Mrs. Currain was a scrupulous housekeeper. At Great Oak the bed rooms were aired daily, the mattresses put out in the sun twice each month. Every implement in the kitchen, whether it had been used or not, once a week was scrubbed and scoured. Daily, her keys at her waist, Mrs. Currain inspected her domain; she visited the dairy and the laundry, she went to the smoke house and the cupboard to measure out the day's supply of butter, sugar, lard, meal, and flour, and doled out whatever ingredients the coming meals required. Every cupboard and every outbuilding had lock and key. "The people don't think it's stealing," she told Enid. "So we keep temptation away from them." She supervised the making of starch and of soap; she oversaw the dipping of candles, and she kept the trash gang—men and women too old to labor in the fields, children too young—at work all day raking drives and paths or grooming the wide lawns and terraces. Each leaf that fell must be removed.

Enid, who except in the flurry of preparation for her mother's visit had let Trav oversee everything at Chimneys, was half astonished, half amused by Mrs. Currain's insistences. She herself did not escape the old lady's discipline, for she was expected to keep Trav's clothes in order, his buttons secure, his socks free from holes and smoothly darned. She and Mrs. Currain spent long hours together, their needles busy; and often the children were near-by, for the older woman enjoyed them, laughed at their play, relished the memories they aroused in her.

"Little Peter's so like Tony when he was a baby," she said once. "Always wanting to be the center of everything, forever shouting: 'Mama, look at me! Look at me, Mama! Look at me!' Tony would do all sorts of absurd things, jumping around like a jack-in-the-box— anything to attract attention."

Enid had seen Tony only once, years ago when he came to her wedding and devoted himself to her mother; but she had at once disliked him and she resented this comparison. "Peter's not like that usually! It's just that you laugh at him!"

"Oh, my dear, that's a grandmother's privilege, to spoil her grandchildren." But Mrs. Currain had guessed Enid's resentment. "I spoiled Tony, too," she confessed. "I shouldn't have done it; but you see my next baby died." Her eyes were on her needle. "Mr. Currain was in Richmond the night the theatre burned, and he was in the audience. The Placide stock company presented a pantomime called *The Bleeding Nun,* and fire started during the performance, and scores of people were burned to death; Governor Smith, and Sally Conyers, and the young man she was to marry, and so many of our friends. Mr. Currain was not hurt, but he came home and told me about it, and I was so horrified that my baby was born too soon and died, and the next one died too. So till Travis was born, Tony was all we had, and we spoiled him sadly." She added, smiling quickly: "But I don't mean Peter's spoiled! He just likes to be the center of things."

One day she took down from above the mantel in the library a sword in its scabbard, a long, straight, double-edged weapon, and belted it around the youngster, and laughed at Peter's delighted strutting. "It was Mr. Currain's father's," she explained. "He brought it from France when he went over with Mr. Oswald to help make the peace with England. Mr. Currain would have gone with him to be his secretary, but his horse refused a fence and threw him and broke his leg. There, look at Peter swagger!" But when Peter without permission one day helped himself to the long blade and went into the garden and slashed at a young rose bush with it, she restored it to its place of honor above the mantel and said he must not touch it again. "But you may have it when you grow up and go to war," she promised him, and she told Enid: "Travis used to love to wear the sword when he was little; yes, and after he grew up, too. I came to the door one day and caught him brandishing it, lunging and stabbing." Her voice suddenly was thoughtful. "He was surprisingly graceful, Enid, like a fencer." Then she smiled. "He saw me presently in the long mirror, and he was so embarrassed. I suppose he imagined himself fighting a duel or something."

Enid remembered Trav's confession the day they came down the river from Richmond. "He used to like to read old love stories and pretend to himself he was the hero. Peter's always imagining things, too."

"He's such a sturdy little boy." Mrs. Currain loved Peter, but she was fond of Lucy too. "I'm glad you named Lucy after me, Enid." She smiled over her needlework. "You know, it was because my name is Lucy that Mr. Currain fell in love with me." And to Enid's quick, amused question. "Well, he used to tell me—teasing me, to be sure—that his first sweetheart, years before he met me, even before I was born, was a girl named Lucy."

"Why, I declare, Mama, that's real romantic. Did he marry her?"

"No, she wasn't of a good family, so his father wouldn't let him."

"Of course not! I reckon she was a hussy."

"I'm not so sure. Mr. Currain said she was really very sweet. But her father took her away to Kentucky and they never saw each other again."

"So then he married you?"

"Not till long afterward. First he married Sally Williber. They never had any children. She was an invalid for a long time, and I never knew him till after she died. He always said he fell in love with my name before he ever saw me; always declared I reminded him of that first sweetheart."

"Weren't you jealous?"

Mrs. Currain tossed her head. "Oh, to be sure; but he never told me till long after we were married!"

Trav and Enid and the children arrived at Great Oak in early August; and late that month Tilda, Trav's sister, wrote that she and Dolly would come down from Richmond for a visit. Enid said when she heard: "I've never met Cousin Tilda. Is she as nice as Cousin Cinda?"

Mrs. Currain hesitated, smiling in a wistful way. "I ought to be ashamed of myself for saying so, but—well, no, she isn't. It's not her fault, probably. You see, Cinda was always the popular one, and Tilda couldn't help knowing it. When she was little, even old May used to hold Cinda up to her as an example."

"Who is May?"

"She nursed Tilda when she was a baby. She's dead now. June took care of Cinda, and of course old April was Trav's, and May was Tilda's."

Enid laughed. "April and May and June! Were they sisters?"

"Yes." Mrs. Currain chuckled in the way which always reminded Enid of a chipmunk's chirp. "Yes, their mother was named Calendar; and she had a January and an August too. But May was bad for Tilda. I tried to put a stop to it, but you can't do anything with nurses."

"I know," Enid agreed. "Vigil doesn't pay the least bit of attention to anything I say." She asked curiously: "Didn't Tilda hate having Cinda thrown up to her all the time?"

"If she did, she didn't let on. She's devoted to Cinda even now. I'm afraid I couldn't be as Christian as she is. Cinda's always had the best of everything. They both fell in love with Brett Dewain, you know. Tilda was only sixteen at the time, but girls that age take things hard——"

"I was only sixteen when I married Trav!"

Mrs. Currain nodded. "Then when Brett married Cinda, Tilda was sure her heart was broken, till one day Tony brought Mr. Streean home from Richmond." The old woman wandered so easily among her memories. "I wouldn't have chosen him for Tilda. His people were nobodies; but she was so grateful for his attentions that I hadn't the heart to put my foot down. Sometimes I wish I had. He was very businesslike. I never told Tilda this, and you musn't, but before he spoke to her, he came to me about a settlement. I gave them a house in Richmond and an income, and they live on Tilda's money—though of course it's his now—and he went into politics. He takes himself ever so seriously—" She broke off. "There, I shouldn't talk so about my son-in-law, but he really is tiresome!"

"Gracious, Mama, I hope you don't feel about all your in-laws the way you do about Mr. Streean!"

Mrs. Currain patted her shoulder affectionately. "Nonsense! I like you very much, my dear."

Enid looked forward to Tilda's coming, but she quickly found the other tiresome. Tilda was so absurdly ready with flattering praise. "Oh, Cousin Enid, isn't little Peter the cleverest thing?" "Mama, just look at Lucy! Isn't she sweet?" Henrietta, she insisted, was such a baby as the world had never seen before; Enid herself was the loveliest young mother in Virginia. Tilda's admiration fell without discrimination on everything and everyone, and Enid began at last to feel a choked, clogged sensation, as though she had stuffed too long on sticky sweets.

But if Tilda were wearying, her daughter was completely charming. Dolly Streean at sixteen was already a beauty, and within twenty-four hours of her arrival at Great Oak, beaux flocked around her. She introduced Enid to these youngsters as "Aunt Enid" so persistently that Enid told Trav in amused resentment:

"The little witch makes me feel a hundred years old, and she knows it, too! I believe she does it on purpose!"

Trav chuckled. "She's a lovely child!"

Enid tossed her head. "She ought to be! She practices all her pretty airs and graces in front of a mirror by the hour." Yet she liked Dolly and sought her company, at once envious and admiring.

Toward the end of August, Redford Streean and Darrell came for a few days. Enid disliked Mr. Streean at once. She thought him fat and pompous. But Darrell was a handsome youngster with a disturbing twinkle in his eye, and during his stay Enid enjoyed his teasing compliments and the audacious impropriety so often hidden in his words. The things he said were the sort you pretended not to understand, at once exciting and—since he was, after all, only a boy!—perfectly harmless; yet Trav one night remarked:

"You and Darrell have a lot of jokes between you, don't you?"

"He's loads of fun." Then in mischievous amusement: "Do you object, Honey?"

"I? Why, no." He added soberly, "Darrell's been in a good many scrapes, Enid. He's a wild youngster."

"I think he's nice." She laughed teasingly. "I declare, I believe you're jealous!"

"Oh, no. But I can see Mama is a little puzzled sometimes at the way you two go on."

She might have ignored Trav's opinion, but Enid would not risk awakening any critical thoughts in Mrs. Currain. Thereafter in the older woman's presence, her manner toward Darrell gave no slightest cause for reproach.

The Streeans were no sooner gone back to Richmond than Faunt arrived. He had ridden down from Belle Vue, stayed two or three days. Enid had not met him before, and she told Trav the night he came: "Oh, I like Faunt! I like him so much."

"He's a fine man."

"He makes me feel—I don't know; not just beautiful, but—well, good. Noble and brave and everything. He's just charming. Why isn't he married?"

"He was, twelve or fifteen years ago. He married Betty Farrington, but she died when their baby was born, and the baby died too."

"Oh, poor man! But I should think some nice girl—does he live all alone?"

"Yes, up on the Northern Neck, at Belle Vue. That was my grandfather's first place, and when Faunt and Betty were married Mama settled them there. After Betty died he built a little chapel, and she and the baby are buried in it, and he lives there alone to be near them."

"I wish we could find a nice wife for him."

"Oh, don't go bothering Faunt, Enid. He's made his life the way he wants it to be."

Trav's warning curbed her tongue, but not her eyes. She watched Faunt day by day. Once she saw him walking toward the river with the children, Peter clinging to his hand, Lucy looking up to him with serious eyes. Enid wondered what in the world he found interesting in these children of hers; and at dinner she said to him: "I hope Lucy and Peter didn't bother you."

"No, indeed. I enjoyed them."

"What ever did you find to talk about?"

"Well, we inspected Lucy's play house in the old tree, and I told her—remember, Mama?—about the time before I was born when Tony dared Trav into climbing as far as he could up into the hollow, and Trav got stuck and had to be dug out."

Trav grinned sheepishly. "I hollered like a good one. Never been so scared since."

"And I told them about the underground passage that used to run from the house to the river, and about the pit under the hearth where gold and silver could be hidden if the Indians came." He smiled at Enid reassuringly. "But I didn't frighten them. They're fine children."

"Well, naturally I think so," she assured him. As a matter of fact they often seemed to her a great nuisance; yet that Faunt should enjoy them somehow made him nicer in her eyes. When he said he must go on to Richmond and then back to Belle Vue, she made charming protests. "We're just beginning to get acquainted, Cousin Faunt! Living away off at Chimneys, I've never had a chance to know Trav's family; but I'm sure you're the nicest of them all."

He smiled and said he would come again in October for Mrs. Currain's birthday. She would be seventy-one. "Cinda and Brett have promised to be home for that," he explained, "and their children and grandchildren are coming from the Plains to meet them here, so you'll see us all together then."

For the rest of September there were no guests at Great Oak, but early in October three of Cinda's children arrived by the stage from Richmond. Enid thought Burr was like Faunt. Even at twenty he had some of his uncle's fine gentleness and strength. Vesta, two years younger, was a freckled, laughing girl whom Mrs. Currain greeted with smiling fondness.

"Well, Vesta, you're as homely as ever! And twice as many freckles!"

Vesta tossed her head, laughing; and Enid saw the affectionate bond between these two. "It's your fault for letting Mama be so ugly! If she were as beautiful as you are, maybe I'd look like you, and then I'd have broken every heart in Camden by now."

Mrs. Currain smiled. "All the looks went to your brothers!" she admitted. "But there, dear, you're nice enough to make up for it!"

Burr and young Julian—Julian was fourteen, sturdy and straight—stood smiling by; and Julian said mischievously: "Grandma, make Vesta tell you about Tommy Cloyd!"

Vesta turned as red as her freckles. "Julian Dewain, you just hush up! Don't listen to him, Grandma!"

"Of course I won't, Honey," Mrs. Currain promised. "What do men know about such things anyway? When will your mama get here, do you know?"

"I don't know exactly, but she told us she'd be here for your birthday. Clayton and Jenny and the babies will come up next week. He had to stay to tend to things till the last minute. Grandma, Kyle just declares and declares that he remembers you! He's so cute! And Janet's the fattest little thing you ever saw!"

"I do hope Cinda gets here."

Vesta hugged the little old woman, kissed her again. "Oh, darling, don't be such a fuss-budget!"

"Well, I worry, all the same," Mrs. Currain confessed. "You may say what you like, ships do get wrecked. Why, two years ago, over five hundred people were drowned when that Havana steamer sank off the Capes."

"But, darling," Vesta reminded her, "Mama and Papa aren't coming from Havana!" The charming lack of logic in this made them all laugh, and silenced Mrs. Currain's fears.

On the Thursday before the birthday, Clayton and Jenny and their children—Clayton was Cinda's oldest son—arrived. Of the grandchildren, Kyle was three, Janet a year old. Clayton and Trav from the first spent their every hour together, for Clayton too was a lover of the land. Enid thought Jenny was an astonishingly quiet young woman. Unless someone addressed her directly she seldom spoke, and Enid remarked this to Trav.

"And yet she always seems to be having a wonderful time! You can feel her being happy inside."

"She's a darling girl," Trav agreed. Enid had never heard him speak so warmly of anyone, and she looked at him in surprise. "Everybody loves Jenny. I suppose it's because you know right away that she likes you, so naturally you like her."

Enid, in an unaccustomed self-appraisal, thought that she herself seldom felt real fondness for anyone. Trav was her husband, so of course she loved him; but he bored and often irritated her. Mrs. Currain could be frightfully tiresome, and Tilda too, and Mr. Streean was common! The young people were nice enough, though Dolly, calling her "Aunt Enid" as if she were a thousand years old, sometimes made her furious. Darrell was fun, in an exciting, wicked sort of way, but of course she did not really like him. She could not think of anyone— except of course Faunt—whom she really liked; Faunt, and now Jenny. Since she and Jenny were in-laws, Currains only by marriage, outsiders in the close-knit family, it was natural that they should draw together. To be sure, Mr. Streean was an in-law too; but no one could like Mr. Streean.

On Friday, an hour before dinner, Faunt arrived. When Vesta gave him a laughing hug and a kiss, so—with a sense of daring—did Enid, and felt her cheeks suddenly hot. Lying awake that night with Trav heavily asleep beside her she remembered that kiss, and she thought that when Faunt departed she could kiss him again! Why not? After all, they were kissing cousins!

Next day Tilda and Mr. Streean and Dolly came down from Richmond, but this time Darrell was not with them. Mrs. Currain hoped they might have heard from Cinda, but they had not. Monday would be Mrs. Currain's birthday. Sunday, with everyone wondering about Cinda and bravely trying to hide any hint of concern, dragged itself away and dusk descended. Mrs. Currain delayed going to her room till long past her usual time.

"They might get here tonight," she urged, till Vesta at last hustled her away upstairs.

"They'll be here bright and early tomorrow, darling," she assured the old woman. "You wait and see. But you must go to bed and be all rested up. Come along now."

Jenny and Tilda went upstairs with them, but Enid stayed a while to watch Faunt, liking the sound of his voice, waiting to catch his eye. The men talked politics, and she heard Redford Streean declaim against the abolitionists.

"They'll do their best to elect a President next year," he predicted. "If they succeed, if a Black Republican is elected and put in command of the army and navy of the United States, the South will rise! As sure as that day strikes, so surely will we see disunion."

Clayton nodded in agreement, but Faunt doubted that anything so extreme would happen. "All this talk is just politics," he urged, and said courteously: "No offense meant, Mister Streean." Enid remembered that Mr. Streean was a politician. "But reasonable men take political talk with a grain of salt."

"Republicans aren't reasonable men!" Streean retorted. "They're all crazy abolitionists, believing their own lies! Don't you ever read their pamphlets? To hear them talk, we whip our slaves to death, brand them, cut off their ears, keep the cowhides going all day long, take their—" He looked at Enid and paused and she guessed, in a secret excitement, what he had been about to say.

Faunt smiled faintly. "Yes, they lie about us," he agreed. "But we sometimes exaggerate a little about them. Not all Yankees spend their lives selling wooden nutmegs and cheating their grandmothers." He added in sober concern: "The North has been told so many things that aren't true, and so has the South, that we're beginning to believe them. When lies are repeated often enough even wise men begin to accept them. Most of the evil we believe about the North is probably as false as most of the evil they believe about us."

"They've been slandering our peculiar institution for thirty years," Streean said harshly. "One day we will call them to account."

"Slavery isn't important," Faunt suggested. "Washington and Jefferson and Madison freed their slaves, and many lesser men. If we were let alone, we'd rid ourselves of slavery in time."

"It's important to the South."

"It's what men think and say about it that's important," Faunt corrected. "Not slavery itself."

Trav said his old neighbors in North Carolina wanted no trouble over slavery. "But they believe in it," he admitted. "They don't own slaves themselves, but I suppose most of them hope to buy a few, some day, to do some of their work for them."

"Not many men in the South do own slaves," Faunt assented. "Of course all our friends do, but there aren't many of us. A few thousands, out of millions. We can't very well expect the whole South to fight the North just so a few of us can keep our slaves. Virginia certainly never will leave the Union over slavery. I expect a good share of all the slave owners in Virginia would free their people if they could afford to."

Streean laughed harshly. "If you said that in the Cotton States you'd be tarred and feathered."

Faunt's cold eyes touched the other. "I think not," he said in icy tones; and Enid saw sudden sweat on Redford Streean's brow, and wanted to clap her hands. Clayton spoke quickly to ease the momentary tension.

"Mr. Streean didn't mean that literally, of course, Uncle Faunt; but in a way he's right. People in South Carolina feel pretty strongly about abolitionists. There've been horsewhippings, yes and shootings too. We don't want anyone preaching that doctrine down our way, or printing it."

Trav said North Carolina was much the same. "An abolitionist gets hard treatment. Professor Hedrick, at the University, said three years ago that he meant to vote for Frémont; and the Raleigh *Standard* demanded his dismissal, and the students burned him in effigy, and he was discharged."

"They let him off too easy," Streean declared. "We don't want any Republicans in the South."

Clayton said soberly: "Well, if the abolitionists elect a President next year, South Carolina—at least the men I know—will think it's the last straw." He added in strong resentment: "The negroes don't mind being slaves!"

"That's true, of course," Faunt assented. "One of my men was a good carpenter. I told him he could go hire himself out wherever he chose. He came home last summer. He'd been gone three years, worked in Chicago, Washington, New York, saved over three hundred dollars. He brought half of it to me and said he was happier at Belle Vue and wanted to stay there."

"I went North four years ago," Clayton told them. "I saw the way white people are worked in the mills in Massachusetts, and the way mine workers have to live; and Papa's written about the white miners in England. They're worse off than our slaves. But slavery's not the point. The point is, are we going to let the abolitionists tell us what we must do? We don't like taking orders!"

Trav asked: "Are you saying what you think, Clayton, or what your neighbors think?"

Clayton colored faintly, but his head rose. "I reckon if trouble comes I'll do what my neighbors do."

Trav nodded, and Faunt said: "Yes. Yes, in the long run, whatever our personal opinions, most of us will stand with our class."

When at last Enid left them to their endless talk and went upstairs, she met Vesta and Dolly, in wrappers, laden with good things pilfered from the kitchen, tiptoeing through the hall. Dolly's eyes were shining with mischief. "We were starving, Aunt Enid, so we went down the back way, and Vesta's got an apple pie and I've a sago pudding. Come help us eat them."

Enid, because she envied them their youth and their high spirits, said severely: "Mama will be distressed. She plans all the meals ahead so carefully."

But Dolly made a teasing face at her, and Vesta gaily protested: "Oh, she won't mind, really! Come on! Do!"

Enid refused, and went into her own room. Before she slept—Trav had not come upstairs—she heard delighted screams along the hall, and her door was flung open and the two girls came racing in and slammed the door and set their shoulders against it, laughing excitedly. She sat up in bed.

"What ever are you up to now?"

"It's Uncle Faunt!" Vesta cried, and Dolly—richly beautiful, her dark hair flying—amplified the tale.

"He's pretending to be a highwayman or something! He's got on a great black cloak and a big hat and boots and he came bursting into our room with a regular roar! We were eating the pie, and he caught one of us under each arm and kept kissing us and tumbling us and saying he'd take us off to jail."

Vesta broke in, and for a moment they both talked at once. "And I wiggled away—" "—and he dropped me and chased her—" "—and I tripped him up—" "—and we got away and—" Dolly came to perch on Enid's bed, still excited, cheeks bright; and Vesta peeped out of the door and exclaimed in consternation:

"Dolly, he's out here eating our pie!"

Dolly cried: "Oh the big thief! Come on!"

They raced away to rescue their booty, leaving the door wide, and Enid slipped out of bed to close it, and stayed for a moment listening to their laughing voices yonder. How astonishing that Faunt, always so dignified, should play this prank upon them! Suppose she had accepted their invitation, had joined them—in her wrapper, her hair loosed as theirs was. Heavens! How embarrassed she would have been! And Faunt too, of course! He certainly would not have dared maul her as he had these children!

She blushed at her own thoughts, and went back to bed; but she was still awake when, hours later, she heard hoof beats and the sound of wheels on the crushed oyster shells of the drive, and the summons of the bell that woke them all.

6

FOR three days the ship had been becalmed, and Cinda was in a fret and fever of impatience. September gales had driven them far off their course, the uncertain engines failed, they worked their laborious way under sails alone, and then with the Virginia shore in sight the wind died altogether. They tipped and teetered on long lazy swells, the rigging slatted idly.

"It blew hard enough when we didn't want it to," Cinda cried in sharp exasperation. "Oh, Brett Dewain, if we don't get home in time Mama's going to be so disappointed! I'm almost ready to jump overboard and swim!"

"I'll arrange something," Brett promised.

"I know I shouldn't fuss so. You always find a way." Cinda was a solid, plain woman with broad cheekbones and straight black hair; but Brett saw beauty in her, and fondness bound them close. He counselled with the Captain, and when another dawn came across a glassy sea and showed the land still distant, the longboat hit the water and a sling rigged to the yardarm deposited Cinda safely in the stern sheets. Brett dropped to a place beside her and four sailors swung the heavy oars. Before sunrise they were moving toward the sandy shore.

They landed where a creek cut the outer beach and Brett commandeered a Negro with a farm cart to carry them to Norfolk. There —with some difficulty because it was Sunday—he hired a barge to ferry them across to Newport News. When they landed, Cinda said gratefully: "I declare, Mr. Dewain, I believe you'd move mountains if I asked you to."

He thought she might be too tired to go on. "We could stay with the Lawrences, or the Groves," he suggested. "Start early in the morning."

"No, no. Mama won't sleep tonight unless we're there."

So Brett chartered a carriage from the tavern keeper and they proceeded. Before they reached Warwick Court-House, early October dark came down and there was still far to go. "But even if they're abed, Mama will be awake," Cinda declared. "Oh, Brett Dewain, I'm like a horse eager for its stable. I want to see my children. I want my mama!"

The pace seemed to her maddeningly slow: the side lamps showed only a scant restricted fan of road and roadside; the horses plodded patiently, their hoofs almost silent in the sand. When the carriage passed through Williamsburg, there was never a lighted window; but even in the dark Cinda knew the turn for Great Oak a few miles beyond. Then the big house loomed black against the stars and she did not wait for Brett to hand her down, running to tug and tug at the jangling bell before she threw open the door.

At the bell's alarm and at her eager calls the sleeping house stirred to life. While Brett lighted candles in the tall stand in the great hall, Cinda raced to meet her mother at the stair head; and then Trav and Enid appeared there, and at sight of them Cinda's questions sprang and went unanswered and forgotten as Vesta and Clayton and the others came to sweep her in their arms. Everyone trooped downstairs; and Cinda sat happy at her mother's side, her arm around Vesta, Julian at her knee, while questions and answers flew like arrows, many voices mingling. Why was Tony gone to Chimneys? How nice for Travis and Enid and the children to be here! Thus Cinda, glowing with happiness at being again with those she loved.

She would have stayed talking till dawn, but Mrs. Currain at last put a period to this hour. "There, now, back to bed for all of us. We've another day tomorrow."

"It's already tomorrow, Mama," Cinda reminded her. "It's your birthday already. Feel any older, dear?"

"Not now, Cinda; not now you've come."

"Pooh! You knew I would!"

"You always do; but I always worry, too."

Alone with Brett, even after candles were out and they lay in darkness, Cinda was unready for sleep, clinging to his hand. "Thank you, Brett Dewain, for getting me here. You've never failed me. I almost wish you would, once. You're too perfect to be true."

"Time to go to sleep, Cinda."

"I'm too happy to sleep. Travis is as quiet as ever, isn't he; doesn't have anything to say."

"You didn't give anyone a chance to say anything."

"Isn't it wonderful having him here! And wonderful having Tony so far away! Do you suppose Travis can do anything with Great Oak?"

"He can if anyone can."

"He's dear. I love Travis. And Faunt doesn't change. Nor Tilda. She's so mealy-mouthed! Some fine day I shall slap her face! I've always wanted to do something, just once, that she wouldn't say was sweet! And then Mr. Streean will call you out and you can shoot him for me. Not in the heart, Brett. His is too small a target! Nor in the head. There's nothing there to hit! I think the stomach is his vital organ. I notice it's becoming even more conspicuous!"

"I'll have to put a curb on that tongue of yours some day!"

She was thinking aloud, happy with her thoughts. "Brett Dewain, you know we have some wonderful children. Clayton's the man of the family already, and Burr's as handsome as you, and Julian's almost grown! He's taller than I am. Poor Vesta and her freckles! Why couldn't she have looked like you, and let the boys look like me? It doesn't matter so much when men are ugly."

"Enid's a pretty little thing."

"Yes; but she—well, hovers! She's always so quick to smile if you look at her. I suppose she's not very sure of herself. Stuck away in the wilderness with Travis all these years, poor young one, how could she be? We must be nice to her. Her mother's not her fault, after all."

"If we start talking about Tony and Mrs. Albion we'll never get to sleep!"

"Have you ever seen Mrs. Albion since Enid's wedding?"

"No. I'm told she has an interesting mind!" A chuckle in his tones.

"Mind indeed! The hussy! All the same, I want to see her again some day. She must have changed, to be able to keep Tony in hand for ten years! I suppose she flattered him. He always loved that. I wonder if he'll appear tomorrow—today?"

"Let's go to sleep and wake up and see."

"Oh, Brett, there's so much to talk about." He pretended to snore and she tugged at his hand. "Wake up!" He snored again. "Oh, all right! But make a shoulder for me." In his arms she too presently was sleeping.

Vesta came next morning for late breakfast with her mother—Brett was already abroad, joining Trav for an early ride around the plantation—and brought Cinda's accumulated mail and all the news from the Plains and from their friends in Camden and Columbia; and their tongues ran endlessly till Cinda, watching this daughter of hers, sensing behind Vesta's happy talk and her quick readiness for laughter some brimming well of happiness, said too casually: "Tell me about yourself, Honey. You've talked about everyone else. What have you been doing all these months?"

"Oh, the usual things."

Cinda chuckled comfortably. "Now, now, don't try to fool your old mother. Who is he?"

"Who's who?"

"Who makes your cheeks so red?"

"Oh, Mama, I'm always as red as a brick!"

"Do you want me to box your ears, darling? What have you been up to?"

"Nothing, honestly."

"Rollin Lyle?"

"Heavens, no!"

"Perry Barnwell? Tommy Cloyd? Cedric Hunter? That Hayne boy?" Watching shrewdly. "Vesta Dewain, it's Tommy Cloyd! Isn't it?"

"Oh, Mama, you're so funny."

"Well, Tommy's a nice boy. I've always liked him, and his mother's a fine woman. But how did you ever get him to the point? He swallows his tongue if a girl so much as looks at him."

"Honestly, Mama, there isn't a thing to tell. Only——"

"Only what?"

"Well, I like him, that's all. And he sort of—hangs around."

"And you like to have him sort of hang around?"

"Well—yes, I do. He's so—cunning!"

Cinda laughed delightedly. "So are you, darling."

"But, Mother, there's nothing, really!"

"Don't worry, Honey; I won't spoil it."

"Well, I wish you'd make Julian behave. He's always teasing Tommy."

"I'll put a bug in Julian's ear, never fear."

"Do you have to tell Papa?"

"Of course. I tell Brett Dewain everything." She kissed Vesta happily. "I'm glad you told me, dear—even if there isn't anything to tell!"

"There honestly isn't!"

Cinda smiled. "Except that you're happier than you've ever been in your life. You're a darling girl, Vesta."

"Mama, how do you get boys to—say things?" Vesta's tone was for a moment so forlorn that Cinda burst into pealing laughter, and Vesta indignantly protested. "Well, I don't see anything so funny about it! Tommy's all right when we're with people, but when we're alone all he can do is gulp and swallow."

Cinda wiped away tears of mirth. "Don't worry; it will happen some day, just like that! Wait and see."

When Brett returned, Vesta before she left them together kissed her mother and whispered: "Please don't tell him yet, Mama." So Cinda told Brett everything except this, all the news of their friends. Harry Eader had fought Orrin Vincent, shot him through the shoulder.

"I wish someone would kill Harry and be done with it," Cinda declared.

"A good many men have tried it."

"He's always forcing quarrels. I suppose it soothes his vanity. He's proposed to every pretty girl he's seen for thirty years and no one will have him. Let's not talk about him! It just makes me mad!" Her tone sobered. "Vesta says everyone down home thinks we'll leave the Union, Brett—and most of them want to. Old Mr. Waller is so sure there's going to be war that he's collecting fowling pieces and pistols and sabers, filling his house with them. Poor dim-witted old man! Gaines Anderson—you remember how huge he is—has married a little somebody from Alabama and she's only about four feet tall. Isn't that always the way?" She chattered tirelessly. So-and-so's baby was a boy, named after its father. So-and-so was going to marry So-and-so. "Oh, and there are dozens of letters, some for you. I've read them all, and there's nothing important. I had letters from Molly Paine and Betsy Chisholm and Lily Hammersley and Louisa Longstreet and Jenny Lamar and——"

"How are the Longstreets?" he asked. "I'd like to see him again. Haven't seen him since their wedding." Brett's home had been in Lynchburg; he was an only son, his father died when he was a child, and it was what proved to be his last visit to his mother which had taken him to Lynchburg at that time.

"Oh, fine. They were just about to move to Albuquerque when Louisa wrote. Major Longstreet's paymaster, you know. Their little girl died, so they've just three boys now. Louisa says they're crazy for a daughter. Molly Paine says she and Ranny may come to Richmond this winter. Wouldn't that be fun? And Betsy Chisholm says—but, Heavens, it's almost dinner time! Go away, Brett Dewain, while I make myself presentable."

At the big dinner table Cinda counted noses. "Sixteen of us! Not counting the three young ones upstairs! Mama, aren't you proud of your big family? Tony's a wretch not to come, and Darrell too, Tilda."

"I had a letter from Tony," Mrs. Currain explained.

"I suppose he was sick! He always makes that an excuse."

"No, he said he was very well, but there was something about a muster of the militia, and he seemed to think it important."

"Tony? For Heaven's sake!" Cinda voiced the surprise they all felt, and Mrs. Currain said crisply:

"Now, Cinda! Oh, I know you never liked Tony; but I think he's changed. His letters sound different! He seems quite happy at Chimneys, speaks of so many friendly people. I think perhaps he's found himself."

Cinda laughed. "Well, if he did, he didn't find any treasure!"

"Cinda, you're always too ready to say cutting things! I know you don't mean them, but it's ungracious of you, and unbecoming, too."

When Mrs. Currain spoke thus firmly she ruled them all, and Cinda said in quick contrition: "I'm sorry, Mama. Tony's fine when he wants to be!" Yet she could not long be repressed. "The trouble is he never wants to be! When we were little I hated the way he treated Travis; and when Tilda and I were growing up and boys began to come around he made me so mad, teasing them, really insulting them, till they just about stopped coming. It's a wonder we ever found husbands!"

Brett laughed. "You'd not have rested till you did."

"Oh I was all settled after I met you! Remember, Tilda, I told you that first night that I'd met the man I was going to marry. You did your level best to take him away from me, too, till you saw it was no use."

"Well, I still think Brett's about the nicest man I know," Tilda confessed; then added in timid haste: "Except Redford, of course!"

"Brett's all right," Cinda assented, her eyes touching his; then she added mischievously: "Except about money, forever fussing over every penny I spend!" And in a different tone, "Oh, for heaven's sake, speaking of spending, I haven't told you, Mama; but Brett's bought a house in Richmond!" This was news, provoking many questions; and Cinda gave details. "The Peterson house on Fifth Street."

"That's a lovely house," Tilda cried softly. "I'm so glad, Cinda. We'll be neighbors, won't we?"

"Yes!" Cinda laughed teasingly. "That's the only reason I hesitated!" Tilda flushed with hurt, and Cinda said: "There, there, I'm joking, darling. Of course it will be nice being near one another." She explained to her mother and to them all. "Brett made an offer for the house before we sailed, and the lawyers—they're settling the estate —accepted by mail. We heard in London. Of course it's a regular barn, those big bare rooms, so ugly and plain; but I'm going to do it over and make it all bright and cheerful. We brought a whole ship-load of things from London; none of your gloomy old mahogany, Mama, but lovely gilt mirrors and the most beautiful carved chairs, and gold cornices to go over the windows, and medallions to put on the ceilings and—oh, just wait till you see! After we're settled you must come and stay as long as you can stand us!"

"Oh, Cinda, I never go anywhere." Mrs. Currain smiled at Enid. "Not even to see Enid and Travis married. I'm too old to go visiting."

"Nonsense! You'll come visiting me if I have to carry you." Cinda saw Enid's eyes full of eagerness. "And Travis, you and Enid must come! Enid's too pretty to be tucked away down here. You too, Faunt. I expect we'll live there the year round. Clayton can run the Plains. He's like Travis, good with land, knows how to handle it. Brett Dewain never was a farmer. The only thing he can manage is money. I never know anything to do with money except spend it, but he always wants to put it to work somehow, the way Travis works with land."

"That's where the money comes from, Cinda, out of the land," Brett reminded her; and he spoke to Trav in warm praise. "You did fine things with Chimneys." Cinda saw Trav's deep pleasure. "I hope you can do as well with Great Oak."

"While Tony ruins Chimneys?" Cinda drawled, but Brett said quietly:

"Give him a chance, Cinda, since he seems to like it there."

Enid cried: "Well, he's welcome to it! I never was as glad of anything in my life as I was to leave that old hole!"

There was at this outburst a moment's silence, all of them uncomfortable for Trav's sake. Then Mrs. Currain said kindly: "Well, we're all very happy you're here at Great Oak, dear."

The talk ran on, but Cinda thereafter watched Enid with a thoughtful attention; and when presently they all rose from the table, Mrs. Currain to go for her nap, the others scattering, Cinda drew Trav away, making him walk with her toward the river. He moved beside her in silence till she said, affectionately chiding:

"Never a word to say for yourself?"

He grinned. "I'm too busy to talk much, I reckon."

She nodded. "Yes, and too busy to think of that lovely little wife of yours! The very idea of keeping her shut up at Chimneys all this time. Why, Travis, she's just a child! How old is she?"

He thought back. "She must be twenty-seven, twenty-eight this month."

"She doesn't look it! And she's never had any good times! Bring her to Richmond this winter."

"I'll be pretty busy here."

"Oh, you don't have to work all the time!" She felt the unyielding resistance in him. "Forget your farming and be nice to Enid. You'd better! I warn you!" He looked at her in surprise and she insisted:

"Oh yes, you heard me! Just because you married her didn't automatically make her middle-aged, you know." Pleadingly: "She's sort of pathetic, Travis; so anxious to be liked, and approved of, and praised."

"Why, I'm sure Enid's happy here, Cinda."

She nodded absently. Probably he was right; yet she had felt something, sensed something in Enid which disturbed her. She asked, guardedly, for this was doubtful ground: "Does she ever see her mother?"

"Mrs. Albion came to Chimneys last July, yes. She's gone to Washington to live."

"Enid might like to go visit her. Washington's very gay."

"I don't see how she can, Cinda. Mama needs someone here, and then there are the children."

Cinda pressed him no further, but that night when she and Brett were alone she asked: "Brett Dewain, does Travis know about Tony and Enid's mother?" She answered her own question. "Probably not. He says Mrs. Albion visited them last summer. I don't suppose he'd have had her in the house if he knew. And of course Enid would never guess the truth. She's such a child. Travis says Mrs. Albion's in Washington now. Why did Tony break with her?"

"I suppose she was an expensive luxury."

"I'd like to meet her again. I never met a *femme fatale*—at least not when I knew it!"

She fell drowsily silent, but Brett was willing tonight to talk. "Faunt says Darrell's gambling again. Came to him a month ago to borrow money."

"I suppose Faunt gave it to him."

"Oh, yes."

She said soberly: "Poor Tilda! But you can't expect much from Darrell, with a spineless mouse for a mother and Mr. Streean for a father. And Darrell's too handsome for his own good, of course."

"Dolly's a raving beauty, isn't she?"

"Yes—but I'm afraid she knows it." Her thoughts drifted. "We're a queer, mixed sort of family, Brett Dewain; we Currains. Three of us are pretty nice, and the other two——"

"Nice?" As though in doubt. "Let me see now, which ones——"

"Oh, you be still! You know as well as I do. I'm nice, and so are Travis and Faunt; but Tilda's an idiot, and Tony's a scoundrel. I wonder why we're so different. Why do some ancestors leave their mark on us, and not others? Faunt used to fly into rages when he was a boy, and Mama always said he got his high temper from Grandpa Currain; and that's where Travis gets his industry and his love for land, and his—oh, unshakableness, if there is such a word. Heaven knows where I get all the things in me! From you, I guess. You're a fine man, Mr. Dewain." She kissed his cheek; and after a moment, thoughtfully: "Brett, why do people like some people and not like others? Tilda's my own kid sister, and I try to be nice to her, but I never liked her. Nobody does."

"I do."

"Oh, you like everyone. That's why everyone likes you. But you know what I mean. Tilda's sort of pathetic. I've always said dreadful things to people, and she's always said nice things to them, and yet people never seem to mind what I say, but she—well, you'd think sometimes she had insulted them! You'd think it would be me they'd —avoid."

"Oh, I don't know. I've managed to stand you for twenty-five years —though it seems like more!"

"Beast! Just for that, I shan't speak another word to you tonight."

Before dinner next day Mrs. Currain ordered up the big carriage and took Cinda and Tilda, Jenny and Enid upon a round of calls. When they returned and even before they alighted, they heard Redford Streean's angry voice from indoors.

"Mercy," Cinda exclaimed, "Mr. Streean's making a speech!" The sounds came from the library, and they all turned that way. Cinda, the first to reach the door, saw Darrell. He must have come from Richmond, for he was still hot and dusty from the long ride. She heard his father cry:

"Well, if the damned abolitionists want a fight, they'll get it, mighty quick!"

Their faces were all so grave that she realized this was not mere ranting. "What is it?" she asked; and when they swung at her word she went quickly toward her husband. "Brett Dewain, what's happened?"

Redford Streean shouted, in a voice hoarse with rage: "The abolitionists have invaded Virginia to raise the niggers against us." But Brett, without replying in words, turned with a newspaper open in his hand and gave it to Cinda. She saw the headline:

INSURRECTIONARY OUTBREAK IN VIRGINIA

Below there were three lines in smaller type:

> *Seizure of the U. S. Arsenal at Harper's Ferry*
> *Governor Wise at the Scene of Action*
> *Troops Ordered from Richmond*

And while their voices went on around her, Cinda read the story below.

> The startling intelligence reached this city yesterday that an insurrectionary outbreak had occurred at Harper's Ferry Sunday, and that negroes to the number of 500, aided by 200 white men under the command of a white captain named Anderson, had seized the U. S. Arsenal at that place and captured the town itself.

There was a telegram from President Garnett of the Baltimore and Ohio reporting the outbreak, and the paper said soldiers from Jefferson County, soldiers from Richmond, marines and artillery from Washington and from Fortress Monroe were rushing to the scene. The main story was followed by short dispatches. From Frederick, Maryland: "Armed abolitionists have full possession of the United States Arsenal ... one negro killed. ..." From Baltimore: "The special train with Colonel Lee's command passed Monocacy Bridge at 11½ o'clock. ..." From Washington: "The Mayor of the city, fearing the servile insurrection may extend, has made suitable preparation to quell it. ..."

She put the newspaper down, going to her mother's side in an instinctive protectiveness. "Don't worry, Mama," she said, trying to keep her voice steady. Yet—a slave revolt? That was the nightmare that haunted one's dreams. The Negroes were so many, their masters so few.

But Mrs. Currain was undisturbed. "I'm too old to worry. Besides,

I've seen it happen before." Her word caught them all. "You children, all of you except Faunt, are old enough to remember Nat Turner."

"I do, yes," Cinda agreed. "I was terrified, couldn't sleep for weeks." Enid asked sharply: "Who's Nat Turner? What did he do?"

"Why, he was a slave." Mrs. Currain spoke as though she were explaining something to a child; as though she were telling things everyone knew. "In Southampton. He had taught himself to read, and they say he thought he was God, but I always thought it was from drinking apple brandy. I remember it was in August, the same month we had the spotted sun."

"Spotted sun, Mama? Whatever was that?"

"No one ever knew, Enid. When the sun rose that day it was all pale green, and then it turned blue, and long before dinner time it was white as silver; just a tremendous silver disc, with a hideous dark spot in the middle of it. The people were all sure it was a sign something awful was going to happen, and when Nat Turner started cutting up, they knew that was it."

"What did he do?"

"Why, he and five or six others got drunk one night and broke into the house and killed Turner's master and all his family with axes and then went around the neighborhood killing all the white folks they could find. They killed over fifty that night, mostly women and children; but as soon as one white man—old Mr. Blount, and he was chair-bound with the gout—stood up to them, that was the end of it. The soldiers soon caught them all, shot them or hanged them or cut off their heads and stuck them up on poles." She laughed in her brisk little fashion. "It was really quite exciting for a while. Everyone expected the same sort of thing would start up everywhere, so we all made perfect fools of ourselves. Boys organized militia companies, people left their farms and moved into town where they'd be safe. All over the South people acted like a lot of chickens when a hawk flies over. In North Carolina mobs kept grabbing poor negroes and whipping them till they admitted they were plotting to kill their masters and then killing them. As far away as Louisiana, silly women shivered in their beds, and the men were just as bad. The legislatures everywhere kept passing laws that slaves mustn't do this and they mustn't do that. Nat Turner could read, so they made laws that no one should teach negroes to read. It went on for years, this silly panic."

Faunt said thoughtfully: "I've wondered sometimes how many of the things we do come out of our secret fear of the negroes." He added: "I remember we used to make up games about it, when we were children. We'd make one of the negro boys play captive, and we'd make-believe torture him till he confessed, and then we'd shoot him. Not actually, of course; just a game." He looked at Trav. "You remember? Big Mill was our favorite victim. I think he used to have as much fun out of it as we did. Of course he could have handled the lot of us if he had wanted to."

"I'd outgrown games by that time," Trav reminded the other. He was ten years older than Faunt. "Mill's the best hand on the place now. I'm going to make him driver."

"But that fear's always in the back of our minds," Faunt suggested. "Remember three years ago, after the last presidential campaign, lots of people believed the Republicans had organized a slave revolt that was going to start right after Christmas. That scare went all over the South. I've heard that at least forty negroes were hanged in Tennessee. Actually, of course, the slaves didn't make the slightest trouble anywhere. Except in our minds."

Enid cried: "But maybe they just put it off till now. Maybe this is the start of it!"

Mrs. Currain said calmly: "We'll talk ourselves into hysterics. Let's eat our dinner and forget about it."

"Forget about it? Heavens, I'll not sleep a wink tonight."

"Nonsense! There's nothing to be so upset about."

At dinner and afterward Mrs. Currain refused to permit any further discussion of the news Darrell had brought; but when she went for her afternoon nap, she wanted Cinda with her. "I wouldn't admit it to the others," she confessed when they were alone. "But it does make the cold shivers run up and down my spine, Cinda. You can say what you like, the people can kill us all in our beds any time they want to."

Cinda stayed with her till at early dusk they descended to join the others. Cinda found herself watching with new attention the servants who brought the loaded supper trays and set them out on the little tables, trying to read the thoughts behind those cheerful, dark faces.

She well remembered the Nat Turner days, and the fear that for months thereafter was never quite forgotten. Now came this fresh reminder. Would she ever again feel at peace and secure with these black people always at her elbow, serving her, preparing every mouthful she ate, spying on each move she made? They were always laughing and singing and they seemed content and serene; but who could know the thoughts behind the sable masks they wore? Could a slave ever forget he was a slave, ever cease to hate his master? Not even animals submitted tamely to the dominance of man; in the gentlest horse or dog lurked always a seed of revolt. Were Negroes less spirited than horses, than mules? In sudden surrender to her secret fear she spoke to the black butler. "Uncle Josh, draw the curtains at the windows." Who knew what malevolent eyes watched them from the covert of the outer dark? To be hidden from those possible watchers was somehow to be safe.

Out of respect to Mrs. Currain's wishes, no one at supper or afterward spoke of this which was in all their minds; but that night, to Brett, Cinda said wearily:

"Oh, Brett Dewain, I'm so scared, and so confused! What does it mean?"

He was slow in replying. "Faunt and I rode into Williamsburg this afternoon," he said. "Mr. Lively at the *Gazette* office says the men who made the trouble were killed or captured this morning by the marines under Colonel Lee. The leader was a man named John Brown. Lieutenant Stuart recognized him. You probably never heard of him, but he's supposed to have murdered half a dozen men in the Kansas troubles; took them out of bed and chopped them to bits with sabres." She clung to him, and he added slowly: "Brown is a fanatic, probably insane. There can't be many men even in the North who would try to start a slave revolt—or who would think it possible to do so."

"Don't you think it's possible? I do. I never feel I know what the negroes really think of us."

He said firmly: "No, it's not possible. For one thing, even if the negroes had real grievances, they've no leaders." He added: "But—men on both sides, North and South, will be angry now; angrier than ever. Even Faunt was in a deadly rage today."

"Will this—start us all fighting?"

He hesitated. "There's no reason why it should; but of course the politicians will make a great to-do." He added in an even tone: "Faunt and I are going to Richmond tomorrow, and Clayton will go back to the Plains, in case this stirs up any trouble there."

She shivered. "I don't like being left alone."

He held her close. "You'll feel better in daylight. I wouldn't leave you if I thought there was any danger."

"Trav will be here, of course," she reflected, "and Burr and Julian."

"I'll probably go to the Plains with Clayton," he told her. "I'll send Caesar and June to Richmond and some of the people. You'll need them to help unpack the things from England. You can stay at the Arlington till the house is habitable."

She laughed in quick fondness. "Clever Brett Dewain, trying to get my mind on other things. You always know how to comfort me. And you're right, of course. If I keep busy, I won't have time for worrying."

7

RICHMOND, beautiful on rolling hills, had not yet felt the harsh touch of coming winter; but here and there the trees began to put on brighter colors, just as a woman conscious of encroaching age chooses new cosmetics and becomes more beautiful for a while before she fades. Faunt, happiest at Belle Vue, seldom came to the city; and today he found the crowded, dusty streets, with groups of men in hot discussion everywhere, disturbing and oppressive. The very air seemed to him heavy, as it may be on a sultry afternoon before a thunderstorm. Redford Streean had offered them hospitality, but at Faunt's suggestion they put up at the first hotel they came to, the Exchange on Franklin Street, two blocks down the hill from Capitol Square.

"I always get indoors as quickly as I can, whenever I come to town," Faunt confessed. "I'm jumpy as a fresh-broken colt in crowds, ready to sheer across the nearest ditch at any alarm, wall-eyed as a scared darky."

Neither Brett nor Clayton shared this feeling. "I suppose living with Cinda has made me used to crowds," Brett remarked. "She's a crowd in herself. And Clayton here is young enough to enjoy being in the middle of things."

Clayton assented. "Yes, I like it, seeing so many people, watching their faces, wondering about them."

"Strangers?" Faunt objected.

Clayton held his ground. "Yes, strangers! I like to try to guess what their—well, what they're thinking. What do they hope to make of their lives? What do they dream about? Do they think they're pretty fine fellows? No one can ever really know any man but himself, I suppose; but trying to guess about strangers seems to me mighty interesting." He stood at the window, watching the throngs on Franklin Street and up toward Capitol Square. "Look at them, ladies, gentlemen, children; some going one way and some another. Where are they going? Why?"

The older men exchanged glances and Brett crossed and touched Clayton's shoulder, a deep affection in the gesture. "Well, I can tell you where I'm going, and why." There was a chuckle in his tones. "I'm hungry. Come along, son."

In the dining room and through the hours that followed they heard the attack on Harper's Ferry discussed from every point of view. Indoors and out, till the hush of night belatedly descended, there was a clamor of excited and passionate voices in the air. By the more accurate reports it developed that the original version had been wildly exaggerated. Instead of two hundred white men and five hundred Negroes, there were only a score or so in John Brown's party. Sunday evening they seized the town, stopped the twelve-forty train, killed a Negro porter, the ticket agent, the train conductor, two or three others. Monday morning the first troops came; the rioters took refuge in the engine house. That evening Colonel Lee and a small detachment of marines arrived; at daylight Tuesday morning, after a fruitless parley between Lieutenant J. E. B. Stuart and John Brown, the engine house was stormed by marines, the raiders were all killed or captured. Now John Brown and the other survivors would be tried and hanged.

But these scant facts were the grains of wheat in a bushel of chaff; there were a thousand rumors. John Brown, the butcher of Osawatomie, had hoped to rouse the slaves to bloody insurrection; Northern abolitionists had backed him. That was the flagrant, the frightful, the unforgivable. Everywhere, in each excited group, furious voices rose.

Faunt and Brett during the evening became separated from Clayton, so when the two older men came back to their rooms they sat in talk for an hour or so. "I'll probably not sleep anyway, till Clayton comes in," Brett explained.

"That's a fine son of yours, Brett."

"Well, Cinda and I are almighty proud of him, don't hesitate to admit it. In fact, we're proud of all our children." He added: "Clayton's done a lot of living in his twenty-three years, Faunt; known all the nobler emotions—except sorrow." His tone softened on the word.

Faunt nodded, reading the other's thought. "Yes, I'd loved and lost a wife and a baby at his age." His eyes were serene. "I've lived pretty well inside myself, since; but I don't think I ever did have Clay's interest in—other people. Friends, family, yes; but outside the close immediate circle of my world, people could do as they liked for all of me." He met Brett's glance. "There's a wonderfully comforting and satisfactory peace in solitude, Brett; in living close to the earth, your daily intimates the fields and forests, the trees, the blossoms in your garden, fresh ones opening to greet you at every dawning, the birds that seem to know you, calling a musical 'God bless you' as you pass. But I begin to wonder if it isn't a selfish life. I wonder if to live so isn't to dodge your responsibilities to—well, to the human race of which you are a part."

"Except in stormy times, a man is free to do the thing that most contents him."

"I don't come close to men—or to women." Faunt, in an unaccustomed self-searching, was thinking aloud. "Oh, we have a mannered intimacy; we smile, we say good morning or good evening; we exchange what might be called opinions. But I'm careful not to challenge the opinions of others—or to intrude any possibly disturbing opinions of my own. I sometimes feel—especially when I'm with adults—like an actor, playing the part expected of him. I'm more at ease with children."

"Not many men are."

"Perhaps they're abashed at discovering in children something they themselves have lost. Children have so many gifts. They're able in fancy to create for themselves in a moment a world complete and satisfying."

"That's true. Our children as babies were forever drawing pictures, telling each other stories, making poetry. But they got over it."

"They do, yes. Why, Brett? Do we somehow stifle them, smother all those powers, reduce them to futility? I suppose my closest friend is a child, Judge Tudor's daughter, Anne. Their place runs with Belle Vue on the west, you know. She and I have pleasant hours together, meeting casually when I ride that way, talking nonsense ever so seriously—or speaking of serious things lightly, as though to pretend we're not serious." He added: "But she's growing up. I think she's fourteen now, almost a young lady, so we're not so comfortable together, not such good companions as we were two or three years ago. Why do children change?"

"Oh, we all change. Either from inside ourselves or from outside. We grow—or shrink. Or something happens to change us, some event, some force outside ourselves."

So they came back to the thought foremost in their minds. "This present event, for instance? It means changes, Brett."

Brett shook his head. "It's just a piece of outlawry, to be handled like any other outrage done by violent and lawless men."

Faunt was not so sure. "You're a man of business. Your instinct is to smooth over everything which disturbs the surface composure of the world."

"Possibly. Certainly after this, my South Carolina neighbors will be waving the bloody flag."

Faunt nodded. "I too felt at first just plain rage—till I realized that my anger was rooted in fear. As I said yesterday at Great Oak, this fear of a slave revolt lies somewhere deep in all of us in the South. I suppose basically it rests on an unadmitted sense of guilt. No man can honestly defend slavery—except perhaps upon the selfish ground that it shows a profit. In our hearts we know this; so we feel guilty, and so we fear the blacks, and so we are angry at anyone who reminds us of that fear."

Brett hesitated. "In England I was sometimes put in the position of defending slavery. Of course I was able to remind my English friends of conditions in England and Ireland, quoting their own authorities; the *North British Review,* Sir James Clarke, Douglas Jerrold. I could remind them of women and little girls in their coal mines, chained to the cars they dragged through those underground corridors; girl children put to such work at eight or nine years old, carrying coal up ladders on their backs, working twelve hours on end, day and night; no education, no religion. And the metal workers in Birmingham and Sheffield, children there too, whipped to their tasks. Children as young as seven set to lace making for as much as fourteen hours a day, living in terrible sinks and cellars, starving. Ireland's worst of all, of course. But reminding the British that their white wage slaves were treated worse than our negroes neither convinced them nor satisfied me. Yes, I know that sense of guilt, and even a little of that fear." He spoke reluctantly. "We're so quick to boast, and threaten, and utter loud defiances. Probably the noisiest among us are the most afraid."

They were still deep in talk together when Clayton presently returned. He had gone with young Jennings Wise to the Marshall Theatre to see Maggie Mitchell. "She's charming," he told them. "The whole town's wild about her. We were too late for the first piece— *Milly, the Maid with the Milking Pail*—but *Beauty and the Beast* is what we went to see. It's a sort of fairy spectacle, and Miss Mitchell sings beautifully. Then afterward we went to the Powhatan Hotel. The actors live there, some of them. Jennings Wise knows them all, and two or three of them were with us. It was a mighty interesting evening for me." He was full of talk, and Faunt saw with affectionate amusement the bright excitement in the younger man, stimulated by this new experience.

Next morning Brett had business with Mr. Haxall at the Farmers' Bank, and Clayton proposed to Faunt that they climb to the roof of the Capitol. "I always do, when I'm in Richmond," he explained. "Jenny and I came here on our honeymoon, and we went there two or three times."

Faunt agreed, glad to escape for a while from the excited talk in the streets. He found that the vantage to which Clayton led him offered an outlook far across the rolling country, with the river a silver thread winding through meadowland and forests. The city itself was spread below them, and Clayton like a proud proprietor pointed out this landmark and that: the scattering houses of Manchester across the river, Belle Isle, the waterworks dam, the slate roofs of Tredegar Iron Works under a black smoke pall. "It's mighty beautiful, isn't it, Uncle Faunt?" His eyes were shining.

"Everything but the city itself," Faunt agreed. "The world's a beautiful place, Clayton, except where men have herded together and produced their special ugliness."

The younger man laughed. "We'll never agree on that, sir. People interest me. I like them, whatever they do."

Clayton and Brett delayed a few days their departure for the Plains; and after they were gone Faunt stayed on, listening to the talk he heard. John Brown's plans had been elaborate: his store of arms was found and seized; it was said he had written out a constitution for the political community he expected to organize; he had a supply of commissions in blank to be issued to the officers of the armed force he hoped to raise among the Negroes. The *Dispatch* in an editorial Thursday morning said of the Northern abolitionists: "They have, no doubt, their agents in every Southern state, and if this lesson at Harper's Ferry is lost upon the South it cannot say in the future that it was not forewarned." It called upon "the reflecting men of the North" to "deplore such calamities and to exert their best energies in preventing their recurrence." The editorial seemed to Faunt surprisingly temperate; certainly it did not mirror the angry vehemence of the utterances he heard on every hand, where each new rumor provoked new rage. He met Redford Streean in Capitol Square and found him afire with the most recent report.

"There's an abolitionist plot started to attack the jail and free the rascals," Streean declared. "Word came from Harrisburg last night." Tilda's husband was sweating with excitement, his voice harsh. "By the Almighty, we'll know how to meet that! Unless we act, they'll set the red cock crowing all across the South!" Faunt wondered whether Streean believed his own words. "Our wives, our children helpless on lonely plantations everywhere; and the North wants to turn the blacks loose on us. Afraid to fight us themselves, they'll rouse the niggers, arm them against us. But we'll crush the egg before it hatches!"

Others, attracted by his excited tones, had paused to listen; and Faunt drew clear of the crowd, yet stayed to hear their talk. At once —and he guessed that everywhere, in many another group, the same seed began to root itself—the obvious counter measure was proposed. A rescue? Why then, act before that rescue could be attempted! A few determined men, a few lengths of stout rope, a convenient tree!

Faunt thought what they threatened was worse than what had happened. This John Brown and his band, they in themselves were nothing. Even in the North, he was sure, responsible opinion would condemn them. But to answer lawless violence with lawless violence could only provoke new violence in turn; like ripples from a chance-tossed pebble, death would be spread in all directions. Redford

Streean, talking to these men here, was dangerous; such men as he were dangerous everywhere, as dangerous as poor, crazy, blood-drunk John Brown himself.

He moved down toward the Exchange, threading his way past other groups like this which had gathered around Redford Streean; and as he approached the hotel he saw a larger crowd collected and heard a man's voice declaiming words at once familiar.

> " '. . . swell and rage and foam
> 'To be exalted with the threatening clouds;
> 'But never till tonight, never till now
> 'Did I go through a tempest dropping fire.
> 'Either there is a civil strife in Heaven
> 'Or else the world, too saucy with the Gods,
> 'Incenses them to send destruction.' "

He paused to listen, and Jennings Wise greeted him and made way so that Faunt saw the speaker, a darkly handsome little man in a fur-trimmed overcoat—for the day was chill—which seemed too big for him. But Faunt forgot this, caught by the magnetic quality of the other's voice and the extraordinary way in which, by simply changing his tone, he became another speaker.

> " 'Why, saw you anything more wonderful?' "

And again that instant change, so that it was as though they listened not to one man but to two who were met in awed, half-frightened conversation.

> " 'A common slave—you know him well by sight—
> 'Held up his left hand, which did flame and burn
> 'Like twenty torches joined, and yet his hand,
> 'Not sensible of fire, remained unscorched.' "

An angry murmur ran among his listeners, and the words evoked in Faunt's imagination the picture of a Negro with a blazing torch of lightwood racing through the darkest night, touching his torch to homes and barns and corn cribs, planting everywhere a swift-growing seed of flame. The voice was half-whispering now, hushed terror in its tones.

> " 'Against the Capitol I met a lion
> 'Who glared upon me and went surly by
> 'Without annoying me, and there were drawn
> 'Upon a heap a hundred ghostly women
> 'Transformed with their fear, who swore they saw
> 'Men all in fire walk up and down the streets.
> 'And yesterday the bird of night did sit
> 'Even at noon day upon the market place
> 'Hooting and shrieking. . . .' "

Some country man, drawn to the fringes of the little crowd, cried delightedly: "That's right! I heared a squinch owl yesterday!" Two or three men laughed, nervous tension in their tones; but the speaker laid his spell on them again, his voice this time a woman's, shaken with deep terror.

> " 'A lioness hath whelped in the streets;
> 'And graves have yawned, and yielded up their dead;
> 'Fierce fiery warriors fight upon the clouds
> 'In ranks and squadrons and right forms of war
> 'Which drizzled blood upon the Capitol.
> 'The noise of battle hurtled in the air,
> 'Horses did neigh and dying men did groan,
> 'And ghosts did shriek and squeal about the streets.' "

He paused, and now he held them all breathlessly waiting till he spoke. When he did, his tone had become natural, conversational, deprecating—and this made his words the more impressive.

"And I believe these are portentous things. Portentous to the people upon whom they descend. That was a day in Rome; but in Richmond today there are omens in the sky for any eye to read."

A stir almost of relief ran among his listeners, the tension slackened, each man spoke to his neighbor; Faunt to Jennings Wise. "That's a remarkable young man. Who is he?"

"You don't know him? I'll present you." Wise led Faunt forward. "Mr. Booth, may I present Mr. Currain, of Belle Vue. Mr. Currain is looking forward to the pleasure of witnessing one of your performances."

Booth bowed. "Your servant, Mr. Currain."

"Sir!" Faunt returned the other's greeting; and he said courteously:

"I was impressed, a moment ago, by your remarks. You are a Virginian?"

"By sympathies only. I was born in Maryland, in Harford County; but my ambition since childhood has been to become the most beloved actor in the South. Last winter, and again this, I have come to feel toward Richmond as though it were my home."

"And won our friendship," Jennings Wise graciously assented. "Mr. Booth will always find a ready welcome here."

Someone else came to grasp Booth's hand, and Faunt went thoughtfully to his room; but he found himself remembering that little man, faintly ridiculous in his big fur-trimmed coat until you heard him speak and warmed to the fire in him. Yet he was amused by his own susceptibility to the impression the other had made. The man was only an actor, after all, playing a part by rote.

Monday Faunt set out for Belle Vue. His horse, stabled during these days in Richmond, was in lively humor; and on the long gentle rise from the last houses of Richmond to the crest of the low ridge toward Mechanicsville, he let the beast work off its first zeal. They came down toward the Chickahominy at an easier pace, paused at the toll gate and went on by the many wooden bridges that leapfrogged from one patch of hard ground to the next across the wide marsh to the river itself. Faunt was in no hurry. When he reached the Old Church, he remembered that Edmund Ruffin, of whom Trav so often spoke admiringly, lived at Marlbourne not far ahead; and Ruffin these ten years and more, using the written word—for the man was no orator—had been a violent advocate of Southern independence. Curious to hear his comments on Brown's enterprise, Faunt watched for Mr. Ruffin's gateway. It was at the crest of a long hill where the road broke down to the Pamunkey bottoms, and Faunt turned aside to call upon the old gentleman.

He lodged there that night. Marlbourne was set a quarter of a mile off the highway, a compact and comfortable frame house with a wide hallway and lofty ceilings and a white-pillared double balcony that looked across the well-drained lowlands toward the trees that marked the river two or three miles away. The house was on a bold bluff perhaps a hundred feet high, with terraced walks and plantings down the steep slope to the levels below. Mr. Ruffin, a frail little man inches shorter than Faunt, with a wide mouth and curiously gentle deep-set eyes, and long spidery white hair hanging uncut below his shoulders, received him with a gracious hospitality; and these two had, that evening and next morning, long hours of talk. Faunt was the listener, prompting the other with a question now and then.

But Mr. Ruffin had little need of prompting. He was hot with words. "Harper's Ferry, sir? Why, the outrage there is but the beginning—premature, to be sure—of a campaign long prepared. This butcher from Kansas, self-blinded to the universal affection throughout the South between master and slaves, driven by his own hatred, thought he need only sound the tocsin to rouse every slave in that part of Virginia. The Northern papers justify and applaud everything about this invasion of Virginia's sacred soil except its rashness. You will see Massachusetts sending her ablest pleaders to try to avert from these murderers the doom they have earned; the prayers of Northern pulpits will go with them to their shameful graves; yes, they will be canonized as martyrs. Had Brown succeeded in setting the slaves at our throats, the North would have held a jubilee of gladness!"

Faunt thought this unlikely, and he urged: "Not responsible men, surely, sir."

"If there were men of courage, responsible men, in the North, they would have silenced the abolitionists long ago," Mr. Ruffin retorted, and he added: "The South should welcome this incursion as proof that the North is ready to support treason, murder, open insurrection, to destroy slavery. Henry Clay and his damnable compromise postponed the inevitable conflict, made our victory more difficult. Had we struck in 1850, there would be two nations on this continent now. But it is not too late. They call me a radical. Well sir, I accept that designation proudly; yes and triumphantly. For me John Brown is the answer to prayer, to the prayer of the Southern radicals that the South awake to its danger."

He planned, he said, to go at once to Harper's Ferry. "I hope the abolitionists will try a rescue," he declared. "Let every would-be rescuer be put to death like a rabid wolf. For ten years it has been my holy purpose to reveal the North in its true character; to prepare the South for independence. Now my goal is in sight. It is still necessary tu rouse the people of the South; but John Brown has given me the means. I shall take possession of the pikes with which he intended to arm the negroes and send one to be displayed as an object lesson in every state capital in the South. The way to rouse the people is to play upon their fears, spread rumors of negro bands preparing to attack their homes, fan their anger. Do you know Yancey?" Faunt did not. "He's a useful instrument, an eloquent and powerful public speaker," the old man said. "Too wordy for my taste, to be sure. I have heard him, full of liquor and obviously so, speak for four hours on end. But he is effective. I used him to start the 'League of United Southerners.' With that as a nucleus, we can move mountains! If Yancey and the League will but stiffen Alabama into a resolute demand for independence, the Cotton States will follow her." His eyes burned with a strong fire. "Yancey will control the League; the League will control Alabama; Alabama's leadership will inspire the rest. The lower South, safe against Northern invasion behind the bulwark of the Border States, will erect a new nation, to which one by one the Border States will then adhere."

Faunt, recognizing the profound sincerity in the other, saw too his unscrupulous readiness to adopt any device to serve his ends. This was a frightening old man. Was he not in his way as mad as John Brown—and more dangerous? He asked quietly: "Would that not mean war, sir, with the North?"

The other said hotly: "So be it! The South can face the prospect without fear. If Northern armies invade our soil, every Southerner of military age will leap to arms, well mounted, to meet them. Leaving our slaves to their labors, we will be free to fight. Victory will be quick and sure."

They talked, or rather Mr. Ruffin talked and Faunt listened, till late at night; and in the morning the old gentleman was reluctant to let his guest depart. He thrust into Faunt's hands four pamphlets.

"Read them, sir," he urged. "I wrote them. They have been printed by the thousands at my expense, franked out to every corner of the South by Mr. Hammond, Mr. Mason, and others. Here, for instance, is *The Influence of Slavery, or its Absence, on Manners, Morals and Intellect.* Read it! Do you realize that in the industrial North, fattened by the tariff at the expense of every farmer in the North and in the South, the farmer has been forced to a life of endless toil, of mental and economic poverty! Only in the South under slavery is the farmer still a gentleman." He added: "Then here is *The Political Economy of Slavery,* and then *African Colonization Unveiled* and finally, *Slavery and Free Labor Described and Compared.*" He laid the four, with a gesture almost affectionate, in Faunt's hand. "I'm proud of them, sir. I believe you will find them worthy of your closest attention."

When Faunt took the road again, his eyes were grave. Was it conceivable that this sincere, violent, unscrupulous old man—and others like him—could precipitate the whole nation, North and South, into terrible and bloody war? Faunt nodded grimly. Yes, for it was thus that wars were made. Passionate men obsessed with an idea could by long reiteration persuade even the calmest of their fellows to take arms, to attack, to resist, to kill, to die! Ideas were devils, men became possessed, they raced to their own destruction. Mr. Ruffin and such men as he, in the North and in the South, were springs to set in motion forces which once started no man could control.

Profound despondency rode with Faunt on his way across the rolling hills that beyond the Mattapony began to sink into a level plain. The sun was still high when he caught a first glimpse of the Rappahannock still well ahead, and the long blue line of the Northern Neck beyond. He lodged that night in Tappahannock, listening to the talk of the men in the common room, hearing a dozen opinions on the topic that filled every mind. In the morning he boarded the ferry at the end of the long pier for the half-mile crossing. From the ferry landing his road followed firm ground four or five miles along the border of a grassy marsh before he could turn toward Belle Vue; but his horse, sensing journey's end, was eager, and so when Faunt came up from the riverside to higher levels he took a straight course cross-country toward home, delighting in the spring of the muscular body between his knees, avoiding cultivated fields, threading the forest ways.

As he crossed the Tudor lands adjoining his own, he met Judge Tudor and Anne riding together, and stayed to tell them the news from Richmond and to answer the Judge's troubled questions. When he proceeded, Anne turned to ride with him a while, and he found as always pleasure in her company, conscious of her frank affection, happy because of it. Today, seeing that he was troubled, she matched her mood to his, trying to understand what it was about the violence at Harper's Ferry that so disturbed him.

"Isn't Mr. Brown just crazy, Uncle Faunt?"

He thought of Mr. Ruffin, but he said: "Yes. Violence is a part of him. He had a hand in the Kansas troubles, and one night he and some others took five helpless men from their homes and butchered them." He said apologetically: "You're young to hear such things, Anne, but I've always talked to you as though you were grown up."

"I like you to. Papa never treats me like a baby either."

"The men he killed at Harper's Ferry weren't hurting him," Faunt explained. "He even shot a negro porter off the train because the poor fellow tried to run away when they told him to halt."

"What will they do to him?"

"Bring him to orderly trial, I hope. Try him and punish him."

"Punish him how?"

"Hang him, I suppose."

"Oh, the poor old man!"

He stared straight ahead. "I'm afraid many people will feel as you do, Anne; will think of him as a poor old man—or as a hero, or a martyr." And he added: "The abolitionists in the North are already doing so. The Richmond paper yesterday quoted Henry Ward Beecher—and he's a minister—as saying that unless John Brown's act was part of a plot it was madness; but he said that even if John Brown was a plain criminal, slavery was to blame for provoking him to do what he did."

"Do they have to hang him, Uncle Faunt? Maybe if they didn't, people wouldn't be sorry for him."

"I don't know whether I can make you understand. Perhaps I don't understand myself. But it seems to me John Brown's not a fact; he's a symbol. He's all the hatred built up between North and South by years of lying, abusive talk on both sides; all that anger and hatred personified in one—well, as you say, in one poor old man. Hanging him will do no good; may do harm. But it won't be men who hang him, you know. It will be the law that he has broken. If you touch a hot stone, you will be burned. That's one kind of law. If you do murder—and John Brown is a murderer—you will be hanged. That's another kind of law."

"I see."

"But the trouble is," Faunt reflected, "people will forget the law he broke and remember only the hatred which led him to break it. That wasn't hatred of men; it was hatred of a thing, of slavery. Men in the North will recognize in their own hearts that same hatred; so they will make a hero out of old John Brown, because they feel in themselves the hatred that made him do what he did."

"I see," she repeated; and after a moment: "Do you hate slavery, Uncle Faunt?"

"I'm ashamed of it, Anne."

"Why? Our people are contented, and happy, and they love us."

He hesitated. "Well, I went to a slave auction at Davis and Deupree's in Richmond, ten or twelve years ago. They put up to be sold a woman much like Big Martha, my cook. She had a husband, a crippled little negro not good for much but the trash gang, and two children, five or six years old. The planter who owned them had died, and all his people were being sold. The auctioneer was a kindly man, and he tried to sell this woman and her family together; but no one wanted them all, since the husband wasn't worth anything, so he sold her alone. She stood there during the bidding, holding herself bravely; and her husband sat on the bench with his arms around the two children and his tears flowing. She was sold to an Alabama man, and the children and the little husband began to wail as though she were dead."

"Oh Uncle Faunt!" Anne's eyes were brimming; then in sudden proud and happy certainty she cried: "You bought her!"

He smiled, deeply pleased. "Well, yes, I did. I shouldn't have done it. We've more people at Belle Vue than we need. I had gone there not to buy, but just to see what an auction was like. But—yes, I bought her, gave the Alabama man a profit, bought her husband and children."

"Why, she's Big Martha!" she cried in sudden understanding. "She really is Big Martha!"

"Yes. Little Zeke—you know, he takes care of my horses—is her husband. And the two children are strapping great fellows now."

"I think you were wonderful to buy them."

He said gravely: "Well, that's the ugly side of slavery, Anne: selling helpless people away from their families and their homes. That's why men hate it. That's why, secretly, we Southerners are ashamed of it. That's why John Brown hated it."

Their horses moved quietly, contented side by side. After a little she asked in a low voice: "Uncle Faunt, if we fight the North over slavery, will we be fighting for something that's really wrong?"

He spoke slowly. "I don't believe Virginia will ever fight just to defend slavery, Anne. If the North tries to compel us to—free the slaves, we may fight against that compulsion. If they try to compel us, they will be trying to—well, in a way, you might say they'll be trying to enslave us, to make themselves our masters. We have a right, a duty, to fight to avoid being enslaved."

She asked haltingly: "But then if it's right for us to fight the North to keep them from making us do things, wouldn't it be right for the negroes to fight us to keep us from making them do things?"

He said, deeply troubled: "Any child can ask questions that the wisest men can't answer, Anne. I can't answer you."

She touched his arm. "I'm sorry. I didn't mean to bother you."

"You didn't bother me. It's my own doubts that bother me."

When they parted, he thought what a pity it was that men could not see problems as clearly as a child. But—could this problem be solved? To free the slaves seemed simple; yet to do so was to wash your hands, like Pilate, of the responsibility their dependence laid upon you. His people here at Belle Vue were less his servants than his masters. He served them as truly as they served him. To free them overnight would be as base as to turn out of doors a cat or a dog or a horse that was used to expect from you kindness and care, shelter and food.

So thinking he came home. The house which his grandfather had built almost a century ago had long since burned and had been replaced by a smaller structure a story and a half high, the roof extending downward over a small porch in front. To lessen the danger of another conflagration, the chimneys at either end touched the house only to serve fireplaces on the first and second floors, and there was an open space between them and the weatherboarding for five or six feet below the ridgepole. The house needed paint, it seemed to be crushed under the weight of straggling and untended vines, there was one step broken and a loose board in the porch. The yard was bare and littered, the fence had lost many palings; the ramshackle kitchen and the outbuildings were in a state as bad or worse.

Faunt, living here alone, was indifferent to his immediate surroundings; but the chapel in an oak grove a mile away, under whose flagged floor those he loved were buried, was a place of beauty and peace, surrounded by a tight fence and by well-kept flowers and shrubs. Little Zeke, the stableman, made the flowers his care, but except when Zeke needed help no other Negroes ever went to the chapel, nor any white person except Faunt himself. Each Sunday at first dawn, Faunt if he were at home walked down through the silent oaks to the revered spot and unlocked the door and knelt for a while at the altar rail. Sometimes he stayed, reading in the prayer book; sometimes he gathered from the neat garden outside a few blossoms, and filled a silver vase with water from the run that passed the gate, and brought it to set on the altar; but if he did this, he always came again at dusk that same day to remove the flowers, unwilling to let them wither in this holy shrine.

Today, happy to be at home again, his heart warmed by the welcoming smiles of the people who came to greet him, he gave his horse to a boy and went in to bathe and change. Then as always on his homecomings he turned to the chapel, as though to announce to those who dwelt there that they were no longer alone.

During the days that followed, Faunt's thoughts dwelt on John Brown. He read in the Richmond papers every comment from the North. When John Brown was convicted and sentenced, Wendell Phillips and Henry Ward Beecher said his martyrdom would inspire a million imitators; and at this the Richmond *Dispatch,* which had at first been moderate in its tone, cried out in fury:

"If the crown of martyrdom in such a career is so magnificent and glorious, why don't they come on and clasp it to their own swelling temples?" And of the abolitionists: "Brown is the first of the white-livered pack that has attempted to do anything but bark; the first who has come out of his kennel, crossed the Southern line and undertaken to bite. Now they call the hanging of this intruder martyrdom and call the blood of martyrs the seed of the church; but let them come and sow a little more seed!"

Faunt thought it might have been Redford Streean speaking. Streean and Edmund Ruffin and men like them in the South, Phillips and Beecher and their rabid ilk in the North; it was such venomous irresponsibles who would bring on bloody war. He arranged to receive the Northern papers and found in them passionate tributes to this crazy murderer with his hands still red from bloody crimes in Kansas, this man who dragged harmless strangers from their beds and chopped them to death. Emerson the philosopher said John Brown's hanging would make the gallows as glorious as the cross; even Thoreau called him an angel of light. Faunt tried to find some denial of Brown's purposes, or of his deeds; but there was none. John Brown admittedly had sought to set the Negroes loose like wolves across a peaceful countryside, to put weapons in their hands and urge them on. And it was that avowed purpose which ministers of God and men of presumably balanced minds now openly glorified.

His own pulse beat harder with a rising anger as he read. If there was that ruthless mind in the North, why then such men as old Edmund Ruffin were right. If the North wished to see in the South a carnival of murder and extermination, why then open conflict could not be long delayed.

He had occasion, as the date set for John Brown's execution approached, to remember that little man whom he had heard declaiming to the crowd outside the Exchange Hotel. Late in November Governor Wise sent troops to keep order during John Brown's execution. The Richmond *Enquirer* reported the arrival in Charleston of the Grays and of Company F. "Amongst them," wrote the correspondent, "I notice Mr. J. Wilkes Booth, a son of Junius Brutus Booth, who though not a member, as soon as he heard the tap of the drum threw down the sock and buskin and shouldered his musket and marched with the Grays to the reputed scene of deadly conflict."

When, in due course John Brown and the other prisoners were well and duly hanged, Faunt wondered how the little actor reacted to that spectacle; and when he went to Great Oak for Christmas—all the family except Tony and Darrell were there for the merry days together—he spoke to Brett of the scene in front of the Exchange which had so impressed him. "A curious man," he said. "I've thought of him more than once."

Brett nodded. "There's some quality in him, yes. I saw him start off with the Grays that day. They boarded the train on Broad Street, almost in front of the theatre. There was a crowd to see them off, and this fellow came plunging through the crowd and appealed to Lieutenant Bossieux—he was acting captain, since Captain Elliott was commanding the regiment—to take him along. Mr. Kunkel, the manager of the theatre, begged him to be sensible. Booth was supposed to play that night. Kunkel kept saying: 'What am I going to do? What am I going to do?' Booth shook him off, said: 'I don't know, and I don't give a damn!' Captain Bossieux tried to talk him out of it, too; but the crowd and some of the young gentlemen in the Grays were on his side, laughing and urging him on, so they sent for a spare uniform and took him along." He added: "George Libby—he's in the Grays, went with them—said he kept an eye on Booth at the hanging, and that he turned pale, came near fainting, took a stiff drink of whiskey before he was steady again."

"I suppose the actor's instinct made him imagine it was he who was being hung."

"Possibly. I've met the man. He makes me uncomfortable, but he's seen everywhere in Richmond, received everywhere, has a host of friends."

Faunt nodded. "I can understand that. I'm so reserved myself, so ill at ease with strangers, that I rather envy anyone who can face—yes and captivate—a crowd so masterfully. There's certainly something striking and memorable about the man."

8

WHEN TILDA came back to Richmond after her mother's birthday, Redford Streean said at once: "Tilda, Cinda's planning to put up at a hotel till her house is ready. I want you to make her stay with us."

Tilda heard him in something like consternation. Their house, one of a row a few blocks out Franklin Street from the mansion Brett and Cinda had bought, was small, and there were only two servants. Old May, who had nursed Tilda through babyhood, came to her from Great Oak when Darrell was born; but when Darrell one day needed a switching and May gave it to him, Streean in a rage sent her back to Great Oak. "No damned nigger's going to lay a hand on my son!" he declared. Now Tilda's household tasks were in the lazy hands of a fat sloven in the kitchen and a wench named Sally who since Streean bought her had borne two mulatto children, and who treated Tilda with a casual impudence at which Streean was openly amused. Once when Tilda appealed to him, he said if she couldn't manage two niggers she had better learn how, and he said it in Sally's hearing, so that Sally snickered with triumph. With Emma's greasy cooking and Sally's shiftless sweeping and dusting and the two pickaninnies forever squalling in the yard, to have Cinda and Brett here would be a nightmare.

But Tilda made no protest, her desperate thoughts seeking some escape from this necessity, while Streean pointed out that it would be to his advantage if Richmond gentlemen were constantly reminded that Brett Dewain was his brother-in-law, and that Vesta's friendship would open doors for Dolly. Tilda felt no surprise at his frankness; for she had no longer any illusions about either her husband or her son. For Darrell as a baby she had held fine hopes, and while he was a boy she could smile at the traits that offended others; but by the time he reached his middle 'teens his pranks had become vices and her only defense was to shut her eyes. Long before that, she knew Streean through and through. His father and mother had a worn-out small farm in Spottsylvania County, but he had broken every bond that tied him to them. Having made a successful marriage, and counting on Tilda's eventual inheritance of a share of the Currain fortune, Streean had never sought any gainful occupation. They lived on Tilda's modest income; but while he spent as freely as a gentleman should, Tilda at home must make many small economies.

Streean's orders were explicit, and Tilda tried to do as she was told; but when Cinda declined her hospitable urgencies and went to live at the Arlington, she felt a grateful relief, enduring Streean's anger at her failure.

"But if she won't come here, you can go to her," he said in open contempt. "At least she won't show you the door."

So when Brett sent servants from the Plains and Cinda and Vesta began to put the big house on Fifth Street in order, Tilda went there almost every day. But this was hard for her. The house, compared with their own cramped establishment, was generous and gracious, built of brick over which a coat of stucco had been subsequently laid. From Fifth Street, steps led up to a small porch with white columns and flanked on either side by a fenced and brick-paved areaway. The areaway gave entrance to the basement pantries and storage rooms. On the first floor a wide hall from front to rear opened directly upon the double portico supported by great columns. The lower level of the portico overlooked a garden with a retaining wall high above the sidewalk on the Franklin Street side; the upper level looked south and east across the rooftops of the lower city to the river and to the wooded valley downstream. Two great magnolia trees and a sycamore shaded the garden and screened the one-story brick kitchen and the brick quarters for the house servants in the farther corner of the lot. The stable was underneath the servant quarters, opening on the alley that ran from Fifth Street through to Sixth. It was reached by steps that descended from the garden level.

On the Franklin Street side of the central hall there were two large rooms, and two somewhat smaller on the other, with a graceful stair in the side hall between them. The ceilings on this and the floor above were high for coolness; but Mr. Patterson had added an upper story where the rooms, smaller and more numerous, might on a summer day be mercilessly hot.

The interior finish of the house had been of a classic severity; but Cinda changed this. "I'm sick to death of bare plaster walls," she told Tilda. "And I never want to see another piece of mahogany or veneer as long as I live! Oh, upstairs probably; but I'm going to have everything bright and cheerful downstairs!"

She had taken exact and careful measurements of rooms and doors and windows before she and Brett went to England; and as the boxes and bales and crates were unpacked, each article had a place waiting to receive it. Hand-painted canvas medallions, four to each room, one to each corner, were pasted on the ceilings of drawing room and parlor. The walls were painted to give the effect of an ornate plaster moulding framing large panels. An elaborate plaster frieze joined walls to ceiling, while in a moulded design around the drawing room chandelier, chubby little cupids seemed about to take wing out of a sea of plaster flowers and garlands.

The drawing room was Cinda's particular delight. The plain wooden mantel was replaced with one of white marble adorned with carved grapevines and carved white fruit in huge clusters. On the mantel a gilt clock under a glass bell was flanked by two gilt girandoles hung with glass prisms to match the chandelier. Above each window the workmen under Cinda's jealous eye set a heavy gilded cornice, bright and gleaming, cast in an elaborate and intricate pattern of fruit and leaves and vines. This cornice was continued to connect the two windows overlooking Franklin Street, and below it a mirror as high as the ten-foot windows filled the space between them. The mirror was framed in gilt, and its base was a low, marble-topped table with its legs concealed by a brass skirt moulded in a pattern that matched the cornices. At the windows full lace curtains hung to sweep the floor.

Tilda, watching all these changes, praised everything. "It's lovely,

Cinda," she declared. "So bright and cheerful! No one could ever be dismal and unhappy in a room like this!"

"Just wait till it's finished!" Cinda told her proudly. When the fine Brussels carpet gay with yellow flowers and charming browns and greens and blues had been laid, Tilda watched new wonders take their places. There was a carved whatnot. "And I've ever so many lovely things to put on it," Cinda promised. "I'll fill it and the corner cupboard and have treasures left over." A pianoforte on one side of the room faced a melodeon on the other. They were painted black and decorated with a bright pattern of yellow flowers and green leaves which was repeated on the tiptop table, not only on the top but down the legs. The same design adorned the card table, and the oval, marble-topped table in the center of the room. On this and on the card table, under glass bells, a cluster of wax flowers and a bowl of wax fruit enchanted the eye. The settee and the occasional chairs, of carved ebony, were upholstered in black silk brocade; the foot stools in needlepoint of beads like tapestry.

Tilda swallowed the bitter taste of gnawing envy. "I declare, Cinda, I never imagined anything could be so beautiful." Her own home seemed when she came back to it as dismal as a tomb; the dark gleam of mahogany, the severe lines of chairs and tables, the decorous mouldings, oppressed and crushed her. She returned again and again to Cinda's as a drunkard to his cups, and she was always able to exclaim at each new treasure, from the huge tapestry which exactly covered one wall of the dining room to the Derby china—dark blue bordered with gilt, pink eglantine centers—and the delicate French porcelain and all the treasures that filled the whatnot and the corner cupboard and overflowed into any corner where there was room for them. But she went home afterward to grieve and suffer wretchedly, and it was no comfort to her that Vesta refused to be enthusiastic about all this new splendor, admitting that she preferred plain old familiar things. Tilda thought Vesta was a silly young idiot with not wit enough to appreciate beauty when she saw it; and certainly the other ladies, Cinda's friends whom she met at Cinda's house, were as delightedly approving as she.

Before they all went to Great Oak for Christmas, the new house was settled; but after Christmas, Streean still drove Tilda to haunt Cinda's door. Dolly, as shrewd as her father, knew well enough that Vesta's plain, freckled countenance was a flattering foil for her own beauty; and Vesta's friendliness made it easy for them to draw together. Burr had gone back to South Carolina College at Columbia, and Julian presently was banished to the Plains. "He's entirely too young to be footloose in Richmond," Cinda told her sister. "Brett and I think of sending him to Virginia Military Institute. He's at the age to need some restraint." She smiled. "But meanwhile he likes the Plains."

In February, Vesta followed Julian southward, to meet the north-bound march of spring; but Brett and Cinda stayed on, and one day in early April, Streean spoke to Tilda.

"I'm going to Charleston to the Convention," he told her. She knew vaguely that Democratic delegates would meet there to nominate a candidate for President in the coming election, and that Streean had sought unsuccessfully to be chosen one of them; and she thought it was like him to go to Charleston even without official purpose. To force himself into the company of greater men was always his delight. "Suggest to Cinda that Dolly go as far as Camden with me, and stop for a visit at the Plains." He chuckled. "Tell her Dolly's peaked after this long winter, needs southern air. Cinda won't have any excuse to say no."

Tilda, proud of Dolly's beauty, resented his suggestion that weather could affect it; nevertheless she did as he directed. Cinda, after a momentary hesitation, said generously: "Why, of course! And you come too, Tilda!"

"Oh, Cinda, that's sweet of you!" Tilda's heart leaped with delight at the prospect. "But——"

"No 'buts' about it," Cinda laughingly insisted. "It's lovely there this time of year. I'm going down myself next week. Julian's entering North Carolina Military Institute, and I want to get him ready."

"North Carolina? I thought you said Virginia."

"I did," Cinda assented. "That's what we planned, but Julian wants to go to Charlotte, and we're letting him have his own way." She added: "Brett and I are going down next week. He's going to Charleston too. These men and their politics! But I'll stay at the Plains while he's gone, so do come, you and Dolly both."

"Won't I crowd things terribly?"

"Nonsense! There's plenty of room."

"Why—I'll see what Redford says," Tilda agreed. She was not surprised that he at first thought she should stay at home.

"Dolly'll have a better time without you," he predicted; but when Tilda repeated this to Cinda, the older sister said sharply:

"Nonsense! Besides, I won't have Dolly without you!" She laughed in a way that took any sting out of her words. "I won't take the responsibility of fighting off her beaux! Don't be absurd! Of course you're coming."

Streean in the end relented. He even sanctioned the enlargement of Tilda's wardrobe for the occasion. She and Dolly had his escort as far as Kingsville where they waited to take the Camden train; and in Camden, Vesta and Clayton met them with the carriage and they set out at once for the Plains. They crossed the Wateree at the ferry, and beyond they turned up river. The road dipped and rose as it skirted the clay and gravel slopes that rose out of the alluvial bottom lands. In the fields along their way Negroes were planting cotton, and the soft murmur of their voices, laughing together or sometimes singing, came through the still hush of evening. The horses splashed through the ford at Twenty-Five-Mile Creek and turned toward higher ground, the road winding through long-leaf pines whose green crowns glistened in the sun.

"Most of the plantations around Camden are east of the river," Vesta told them. "We're really off by ourselves here, at the edge of the sand hills, with the tackeys for nearest neighbors; but we always seem to have lots of company somehow."

The road emerged from pines into an avenue of oaks that led toward the big house, and Vesta said the quarter and most of the work buildings were down nearer the creek, hidden by the rise of ground; but she pointed out the conical peak of the screw where cotton was pressed. "We used to love to ride the mules 'round and 'round when we were little," she said. Smoke house and kitchen and the cabins of the house servants and the small building which Clayton had put up for a nursery were near the house. The house itself was of wood, painted white, squared pillars ascending from the ground to the roof, and supporting a wide veranda at the first floor level. Tilda saw azaleas still showing some bloom and exclaimed approvingly, but Vesta said the azaleas and the yellow jessamine and the japonicas were gone. "And the wistaria, of course. That great vine along the balcony railing just smothers this side of the house when it's in bloom. But the real gardens are on the other side, on terraces falling away down toward the creek."

As the carriage halted where twin flights of stairs led up to the veranda, Cinda and the babies appeared to greet them, and Tilda kissed her sister and said effusively:

"Oh, Cinda, you were sweet to ask us!"

"Don't thank me! Thank Jenny! She's mistress here now. I'm just a visitor, free to enjoy my grandchildren." She had two-year-old Janet in her arms, Kyle tagging at her knee. "Aren't they sweet, Tilda?"

"They're darlings," Tilda assured her. "Just perfectly lovely, both of them."

"Oh, fiddlesticks! They're nice enough, but they look too much like me to be beauties!" Jenny came out of the house, and heard, and smiled; and Cinda told her cheerfully: "If you wanted beautiful children, Honey, you should never have picked me as their grandmother." Tilda thought Jenny herself was no beauty. Whatever had Clayton seen in her? How did people like Cinda and Jenny manage to win such nice husbands? She felt a familiar twinge of jealous pain.

Indoors they moved through the wide hall to the south veranda, Tilda carefully admiring all she saw while envy tortured her. Was she to spend her whole life oh-ing and ah-ing over other people's possessions? Below the veranda the garden terraces descended steeply into the ravine where the creek ran. Cherry myrtle trees had been trimmed to make massive hedges, each a series of arches. The terraces curved to follow the contour of the hillside, with ivy and smilax on the slopes, and gravel walks, and Tilda saw Cherokee roses and honeysuckle in rich bloom, and the air was sweet with warmly drifting fragrances, flowing up the sunned slope to them. To Dolly's delighted ejaculations, Vesta said lightly:

"Oh, that's partly honeysuckle you smell, but it's mostly just banana shrub and sweet shrub. They're so sweet they're sickening."

She swept Dolly away, and Jenny said: "I'll show you to your room,

Aunt Tilda." On the stairs she explained: "I'm putting you in the west wing, next to Mama. Dolly'll be in with Vesta, and Vesta's inviting some friends from town, so the east wing will be noisy. I thought you'd like to be quiet, more by yourself."

The room was bright with the late sun; and Tilda said it was beautiful and she said Jenny was a dear to let her come, and to invite Dolly. "Dolly's always so popular wherever she goes. She'll have such a good time here." Because she dreaded being left alone, she kept Jenny in talk while she removed the traces of her journey. "Aren't you awfully off by yourselves here?" she asked. "Vesta said most of the plantations are across the river."

"They are," Jenny agreed. "But our land is as good as theirs, and we don't have to worry about floods, or keep up a levee, and we're high enough to be away from the vapors in the low land."

"What do you raise, rice and cotton?"

"Cotton, and corn of course, and we make some naval stores, but no rice. There are some rice fields on this side of the river down in Green Swamp, but not many."

When Tilda was ready, they came down together to supper, sandwiches and cakes and fruit conserve and tea served on the little tables in the gracious drawing room. The visit at the Plains began delightfully and Tilda watched with happy pride Dolly's charming triumphs. The big house was presently as if besieged, young men from the plantations across the river riding over every day by twos and threes and fours. Vesta had, as Jenny promised, invited some of her friends to stay with her. "Dolly and I just simply can't entertain all these nice boys all by ourselves, Aunt Tilda," she explained. So the rooms in the east wing were full; and whenever the young horsemen appeared, an appropriate number of lovely, merry girls would—after laughing, brief delays—come trooping down the wide stairs to greet them.

One morning Tilda, even from her room at the other end of the house, heard a welcome particularly vociferous; and she hurried down to discover the occasion. It was Burr who had arrived; Burr and a handsome, laughing youngster whom Cinda introduced to Tilda as Rollin Lyle.

"He's Burr's very best friend at college in Columbia," she explained;

and in the same breath demanded: "But Burr, you scamp, what are you two doing here?"

Rollin Lyle, with a twinkle in his eye, protested: "Ma'am, how can you ask—when so many charming ladies——"

"Fiddlesticks! You can't catch this cat with butter! You two have been up to something!"

Burr grinned redly, but Rollin drawled: "Why, ma'am, young gentlemen can't bury themselves in books forever; so sometimes they play a little prank. Some rascal sprinkles hellebore in a recitation room to set us all sneezing, or rolls cannon balls down the stairs at midnight to spoil our sleep—they're usually hot enough so that the proctor who tries to pick them up drops them mighty quick——"

Cinda good-humoredly interrupted. "You've been rusticated, the pair of you," she said accusingly. "Now what have you been up to? Burr, answer me!"

Burr hesitated. "Well, you see, there was a slaminade——"

Dolly cried: "Slaminade? Whatever's that, Burr?"

"Why, when one of the teachers makes himself unpopular—well, it's like a serenade, only not so musical, beating tin pans under his window, whooping and yelling, racing your horses past his house. It's all fun, but Old Bullet——"

"Who's Old Bullet?" Dolly was again the questioner.

"Judge Longstreet, the President," Rollin explained, and Tilda saw him smile at Dolly. She thought him about the nicest-looking young man she had ever seen. What a picture he and Dolly were together! "We all call him Old Bullet."

"You ought to be ashamed of yourselves!" Cinda exclaimed. "He's a perfectly charming old gentleman."

"Oh, we all like him," Rollin assured her. "Like to call on him." He smiled in faint apology. "It's fun to get him started talking about old songs, because he'll bring out his glass flute and play them for you; Indian tunes, and old Scotch ballads, and be so serious about it."

"You scamp, making fun of him!"

Burr laughed. "I'm not so sure about that, Mama. I think half the time he's making fun of us, thinking how ridiculous it is for us to come and listen to an old gentleman toot on a flute. He can be stern and serious when he wants to. This last lark, he took it seriously enough. He sent for us, one at a time, and asked if we knew who had a hand in the affair. Of course a lot of us did know—but of course none of us would tell him." He looked at his mother, briefly abashed. "So he expelled about half the college. He said legally we were accessories and accomplices."

Dolly cried in a charming indignation: "Why, that's the most ridiculous thing! Of course you wouldn't tell!" Tilda saw Cinda bite her lip, and then the young people moved away together, and Tilda said comfortingly:

"Don't be distressed, Cinda."

"Oh, I'm not distressed! I'm just trying not to let Burr see me laughing. Why do teachers take themselves and their lessons so seriously?"

"Who is that charming Mr. Lyle?"

"Rollin? His father's Randolph Lyle, and Andrew Lyle was his grandfather. His mother was Martha Pettigrew. But there, you don't know South Carolina families, of course. Mr. Lyle's brother, Rollin's uncle, is our factor in Charleston. They have enormous rice fields near Georgetown. I've heard Rollin say his father has six or seven plantations, and they make hundreds of tierces of rice every year, when the rice birds don't eat it all before the harvest."

Then Rollin would be wealthy, unless of course there were other brothers. "Have they a large family?"

"Oh, Rollin's a good catch," Cinda said dryly, "if Dolly can land him. No, just one other son."

Tilda flushed. "Well, I don't care! You're so rich you don't have to think of such things, but I do."

Cinda smiled. "There, I'm sorry. But you're so transparent. Never mind. Dolly's having a good time, isn't she?"

There could be no doubt of this, and now with Burr and Rollin here and other young men and older ones appearing every day, the big house had few quiet hours. There were always extras for dinner and for supper. Jenny met calmly each demand upon her household, and Clayton was never too much occupied with the business of the plantation to play host. So the very air was musical with laughter, and each evening old Banquo brought his fiddle and there was the whisper of light dancing feet. Tilda, observing all that passed, saw that Vesta had a devoted swain in Tommy Cloyd. He was forever at her side, or if chance parted them his eyes followed her. Tilda thought Vesta, homely as she was, would probably jump at the chance to marry this mooning, love-struck youngster. She was so full of curiosity about these two that one day she questioned Cinda. "Of course you've noticed it," she said.

"Of course," Cinda agreed. "Oh, and that reminds me, I must call on Mrs. Cloyd. We'll drive up there this morning." On the way she told Tilda something about Tommy's mother. "She's a remarkable woman," Cinda explained. "When Tommy's father died Mrs. Cloyd calmly took over the management of the plantation. It was a small place, and short of hands; and at first she used to be up at daylight, even working in the fields with her people. She gave up seeing her friends and some of them, the silly ones, turned against her; but I've always liked her. Don't be surprised at anything she does. I suppose it's sort of a defiant gesture, but she does exactly what she chooses."

Before they reached the house, Mrs. Cloyd, mounted on an unkempt marsh pony, rode up beside them. Tilda saw a tall, vigorous woman with intensely black eyes under a mass of iron-gray hair and a voice as heavy as a man's and as compelling. Mrs. Cloyd insisted that they stay to dinner, and as soon as they reached the house she shouted orders to the servants and a great scurrying began. Then she settled herself with her guests and overpowered them with conversation.

"You'll just have to let me talk," she declared. "I don't get many chances. Tommy's away half the time making sheep's eyes at your Vesta, Mrs. Dewain; so I mostly eat alone unless someone stops by. If they do, I keep them long enough to let me get some of the dammed-up words out of me."

Tilda was startled by Mrs. Cloyd's sudden burst of almost masculine laughter. What in the world could Cinda see in such a woman? And what could Cinda be thinking of, to let such a woman's son pay attention to Vesta? She suffered through the hearty dinner of boiled salt pork and fried fresh pork and bacon and potatoes and hot breads, served on the plain board table in the gallery between the house and kitchen; and driving home afterward with Cinda she spoke her mind.

"That incredible creature! However do you stand her, Cinda?"

"I'm fond of her."

"Eating as much as a man. And rubbing snuff in her gums with that stick afterward!"

"I rather like snuff myself."

"But not in company. Why, Cinda, I didn't know such people existed!" Tilda's astonishment made her forget caution. "You surely wouldn't consider letting Vesta marry the son of a woman like her."

"Nonsense! I've a high respect for her—and Vesta likes her. If Tommy has his share of her virtues, he'll turn out to be a fine man." She added: "And there's the best blood in the county, on both sides. If Vesta does marry Tommy, I won't have to apologize to anyone whose opinion I value."

Tilda bit her tongue, hurriedly made amends. "I'm sure she's wonderful, if you think so," she agreed; but a malicious satisfaction still lay in her tones. "All the same, I'm glad Tommy isn't devoting himself to Dolly."

Cinda smiled. "Why then, we're both satisfied," she assented.

The bright days sped. Jenny planned charades and amateur theatricals; and when the moon came to be full, she arranged a picnic supper at Muster Spring. Cinda protested that there were springs just as cool and spots just as beautiful in the ravine up the creek and nearer home; but Dolly and Vesta agreed with Jenny that it was always more fun to go somewhere.

So when the day came, carriages, each overflowing with lovely girls, and each with its escort of horsemen, set out on the ten-mile drive, discreetly spaced to avoid the dust. Muster Spring boiled out of the slopes of Stony Hill, a little off the Columbia road, to form a pool ten feet wide and twice as long from which the overflow ran in a chuckling stream down to Green Swamp in the valley below.

Banquo, Jenny's major-domo, had gone ahead with the wagon loaded with picnic fare to make a platform for dancing, laying smooth planed boards on levelled ground, pegging the boards in place, spreading rugs and deer skins and cushions all around. When the first carriage arrived, he and other servants had cooking places built to boil coffee; and while the feast was preparing, the young people by twos and fours went wandering through the forest, exploring the ravine below the spring, or climbing Stony Hill to where in a lofty oak a platform reached by a zigzagging stair wide enough for hoopskirts gave an outlook across the lands toward the river.

Tilda, seeing Dolly stroll away, her fingers intertwined with Vesta's, and with Tommy Cloyd and Rollin and another in attendance, sighed happily. How clever of Dolly to keep Vesta always near her! "Dolly's so friendly with everybody, isn't she?" she said to Cinda. "I like that Mr. Lyle."

"Rollin's nice." Cinda frowned, a faint line between her eyes. "But I can't say much for Mr. Eader."

"Which one is he?"

"The old man with dyed hair, trying to edge in between Rollin and Dolly." Cinda called Clayton to her side. "Clayton, did you ask Harry Eader?"

"No, Mama." He added tolerantly: "But you know how he is."

"I know he's ridiculous! Prancing around with these children. He's fifty if he's a day!"

Tilda said complacently: "It's the same wherever Dolly goes; all the men just simply make perfect fools of themselves!"

"Well, Harry Eader's no conquest to brag about," Cinda assured her. She said uneasily to Clayton: "I wish he hadn't come."

"I'll keep an eye on him," Clayton promised. He moved away and Tilda asked:

"Why don't you like Mr. Eader, Cinda?"

"Oh, dozens of reasons! He mistreats his people, for one thing. He had one old man beaten to death a few years ago because he was too sick to work. And he's forever calling someone out on some ridiculous pretext. And he usually picks on boys!"

"Heavens! I hope he doesn't quarrel with anybody over Dolly!"

Cinda looked at her sharply. "You don't hope anything of the kind and you know it and so do I! You'd be tickled to death if he did! Tilda, don't make a fool of Dolly. She's so pretty she's apt to be spoiled."

"Why, Cinda, Dolly can't help the way men act!" She said almost spitefully: "But I don't suppose men ever make idiots of themselves over Vesta, so you can't realize——"

Cinda laughed. "Now, now, Tilda, you can't make me unhappy about Vesta. She's a hag and Dolly's Cleopatra herself, if you like."

Tilda hurried to make amends. "Oh, you know I didn't mean that, Cinda! Vesta's just as sweet as she can be." She sought safety, changed the subject. "Cinda, this is a lovely spot, isn't it?"

"I've always liked it. Whenever we spent the summer at the Plains we lived in cabins up in the sand hills, five miles or so. It's healthier there during the hot weather, as long as you don't dig up the ground or plant gardens or anything. If you turn up the soil you have malaria, even in the hills. We used to move before the end of June and stay till frost; but sometimes I'd bring the children down to the spring here for picnics, and they loved it. There, things are ready. Banquo's going to blow the horn!"

When at the summons the young people came trooping back, Tilda saw Mr. Eader still contesting for Dolly's attention. Dolly was so cunning, the way she kept him and Rollin both in play. Mr. Eader, Tilda decided, was just boiling mad inside; and at something he said she saw Rollin flush and bite his lip, till Clayton maneuvered Mr. Eader away. How silly of Clayton! Things like that were just perfectly natural, when a girl as pretty as Dolly kept flirting in such a cute way with all the men.

Before they had done full justice to the heaping platters, dusk fell; and when the moon rose yellow above the great trees that walled the glade around the spring, old Banquo was already tuning his fiddle, Cass plucking and screwing at his banjo, Cato experimentally clicking the bones—dried spare ribs of some giant hog—that in his gnarled black fingers like castanets would set the beat; and suddenly Banquo in his deep baritone began to sing.

> Hush Miss Betsy, don' you cry.
> Sweetheart comin' by and by.
> When he comes he'll come in blue
> Tuh let you know his lub am true.

He bawled his invitation. "Pardners foh de fus' cotillion!" And when the set was quickly full, "For'ard fours."

So in the risen moon the dance began.

Tommy Cloyd sought Tilda as his partner. Tilda had seen Vesta send him to do his duty; she received him ungraciously. Of course you could not expect much from a boy with such a mother; and he was afraid of his own shadow, stammering and blushing if anyone spoke to him, ridiculously awkward and homely. Vesta was welcome to him! Tilda while they danced paid little attention to Tommy, watching the others. Clayton had claimed Jenny, laughingly brushing aside the youngsters who would have contested for her; and Tilda saw Cinda beset by half a dozen boys. Mr. Eader, when Dolly gave Rollin her hand, turned to Vesta in perfunctory courtesy, and Tilda thought he was furious. It just stuck out all over him.

During the hours that followed she was divided between resentment because the young men who paid her attention were so obviously serving politeness rather than their own inclination, and delight because Dolly was besought by everyone. Oh, Cinda had the Plains, and the big house in Richmond, and more money than she had any use for; she had everything in the world, all the things Tilda coveted. But at least she didn't have a wonderfully beautiful daughter like Dolly! All the same, Tilda, smiling and smiling, hated Cinda; she hated Clayton and Jenny; she hated them all, yet smiled and smiled.

She even, whenever she caught his eye, smiled on Mr. Eader, till at last as the music paused he came to her side.

"Isn't it lovely, Mr. Eader?" she cried. "These dear children, all having such a good time." He was so obviously the oldest man here; his dyed hair deceived no one, just made you realize how many wrinkles he had. All her life Tilda had been an outsider, and she recognized in him another like herself, forever struggling to become a part of the pleasant world from which he was excluded. Maliciously she taunted him. "They're so beautifully young, aren't they? Aren't they nice to let old people like us share their happy times."

She saw his thin lips draw tight, saw the hard anger in his eyes; but before he could reply the music paused, and Dolly and Rollin Lyle, Vesta and Tommy Cloyd came toward where they stood. Dolly was lovely in the moonlight, crying out happily:

"Oh Mama, isn't it wonderful? Mr. Eader, aren't we having a marvelous time?"

As always, others had followed in her train, crowding around her now. Rollin, when Dolly spoke to Mr. Eader, paused two paces off; but Mr. Eader raised his voice to a pitch that commanded attention.

"Really, Miss Dolly? I would expect you to find our Camden youths rather callow after Richmond men?"

Dolly gaily protested: "Why, goodness no, Mr. Eader. I think these boys are just sweet!" Rollin at the older man's word had turned sharply that way, his young head high, and she slipped her arm through his. "I declare, I think everyone's just too charming for words!" she cried.

But Rollin gently put her hand aside, his eye stern on the older man. "Sir," he said clearly, "whatever my years, I am old enough to have observed the sorry fact that though a man can be a man but once, he may sometimes be twice a child!"

There was an instant's hush, and Tilda felt her pulses tingle. What would Mr. Eader do? But before he could do—or say—anything, Cinda called hastily: "Clayton, tell Banquo we want a Lancers!"

She took Mr. Eader's arm, compelling him away; the fiddle began to sing and there was a quick gust of relieved voices. But Tilda saw Mr. Eader after a moment bow to Cinda and excuse himself and stalk toward where his horse was tethered and gallop away. She trembled with anticipatory certainty. If Mr. Eader was as hot-tempered as Cinda said, he would not forget that Rollin Lyle had insulted him before them all.

Cinda drew Clayton aside and spoke to him; and Clayton too went to find his horse. Then Cinda came toward Tilda, frowning with concern; and Tilda salted the wound.

"Cinda, Mr. Eader was real angry, wasn't he? Why can't men keep their tempers! Just because there's a pretty girl around!"

Cinda made an impatient gesture. "Oh hush, Tilda!" She said under her breath: "I wish to Heaven Brett Dewain were here!"

9

CLAYTON was twenty-four years old, yet now, cantering through the moonlit night to overtake Mr. Eader, he felt himself very young and uncertain; he too wished his father were here. But Brett Dewain was in Charleston, so he must master this moment alone. It would be best to come up with Mr. Eader before the other encountered anyone. Clayton pressed his horse to a good pace, and the man he followed must have heard the hoof beats, for at the crossroad Clayton saw him waiting. He came beside the other, quieted his mount.

"You left in some haste, sir," he said gravely.

"I did indeed," Mr. Eader assented. "My conversation with Mr. Lyle can more suitably be resumed in somewhat different surroundings."

Clayton hesitated; he said then almost pleadingly: "Will you permit me to request—in my father's name and in my own—that you do not pursue that conversation? Mr. Lyle is young; young men are rash. Yet they readily regret any discourtesy."

Eader laughed briefly. "I am confident, Mr. Dewain, that your father has taught you that even a young man must accept responsibility for his remarks."

"I feel justified in assuring you that Mr. Lyle will express to you his regret if he has wounded you."

"I prefer to take my own measures to make that regret sincere—and lasting."

Clayton's uncertainty ended; a calm anger gave him strength. "Sir," he said gently, "you spoke a moment ago of responsibility. I am just now concerned with my responsibility as a host. In that capacity, I request that you refrain from renewing your conversation with Mr. Lyle."

"I decline to grant your request."

"Then, sir, I must be more explicit. If there is any point in dispute between you and Mr. Lyle, it has not even the most remote connection with any word that passed tonight. Upon this I insist."

Eader's heel urged his horse a little nearer. "Mr. Dewain, is it possible that you presume to threaten me?"

Clayton's tone was level. "Sir, your horse is crowding mine."

For an instant, in the moonlight, their eyes held; then Eader drew his horse away. "I request that you explain yourself," he suggested.

Clayton now was completely composed. "You are a belligerent man, Mr. Eader. I am sure that on many subjects you and Mr. Lyle would disagree."

"Are you speaking for Mr. Lyle?"

"I am speaking for myself. If you and Mr. Lyle are to differ, it must be in such a way that no thought can arise in any mind that your difference arose when you were both my guests. Is that clear?"

"I find your remarks full of interest—but somewhat lacking in particularity."

"Then I will be more particular," said Clayton evenly. "I hope to have the pleasure, Mr. Eader, of welcoming you to my house tomorrow. I hope to see you and Mr. Lyle in friendly conversation there."

"Have you any further—particulars—to suggest?"

"Why, yes," Clayton assured him. "You will call upon us tomorrow morning, and by your manner you will make it clear that there is no shadow on your friendship with Mr. Lyle. Then tomorrow evening, if you ride to Camden, you will find Mr. Lyle in the common room at the Kershaw House. It would be natural for you to fall into a discussion of the relative advantages of rice and of cotton as crops; and you might disagree, might come to words."

Eader laughed. "You are young, Mr. Dewain. I assure you it is most unlikely that I will appear at your home—except by an emissary—tomorrow." He turned his horse to depart.

But Clayton came beside him. "And I in turn assure you, Mr. Eader," he said simply, "that if you do not do precisely as I suggest, I will shoot you down as surely as I would destroy any other vermin that annoyed me."

"When I have dealt with Mr. Lyle, sir, I will be at your service."

Clayton shook his head. "You mistake me, Mr. Eader. I did not say I will call you out. I said I will shoot you down." He held the other's eyes, saw the older man wet his lips in a sharp uncertainty. "I hope you will call upon us tomorrow, sir," he said, and this time it was he who wheeled his horse away. There was a long moment when, moving at foot pace, he held his breath, half expecting the blow of a bullet between his shoulder blades; but then he heard Mr. Eader's horse plunge into a gallop and depart, and he filled his lungs again in deep relief, and removed his hat and wiped his dripping brow.

At the spring he found Banquo and the other Negroes clearing away the traces of the picnic; the carriages and the riders had set out for home. Before they reached the Plains he overtook them. Tonight he must tell Rollin Lyle what to expect tomorrow, must bid him—for Dolly's sake—meet Mr. Eader with a friendly courtesy; and when the young ladies had gone to their rooms, he drew Rollin and Burr together, told Rollin what he had done.

Rollin said regretfully: "I'm sorry I lost my temper, Clayton; sorry to embarrass you."

Burr cried: "But damn it, Clay, he had every provocation!"

Clayton nodded. "I know. I don't blame you, Rollin. However, this affair must be handled carefully."

"You think he will come tomorrow?"

"Yes, I'm sure he will."

Rollin nodded. "I'll do my part," he said. "You can count on me."

Clayton, before going to his own room, reported to Cinda, telling her every word that had passed. "I wish Papa had been here," he confessed. "But—I did the best I could, Mama."

Cinda kissed him gratefully. "I think you did exactly right." She uttered an angry exclamation: "But the fools, the fools! Why don't men ever grow up? Yet if they did, I declare we wouldn't love them so! Clayton—must they meet?" He did not answer, and she nodded. "I know. I know. But—why hasn't someone killed Harry Eader long ago?"

Jenny, when she heard, asked only: "If Mr. Eader does not do as you require, will you kill him?"

"He will come," Clayton assured her. "He can make a virtue of it, you see. He will be playing the gentleman, protecting Dolly; will thus earn a little credit. Mr. Eader is hungry for credit in the eyes of men."

"I hope so. I hope you needn't kill him."

"There'll be no need," he promised. "There will be no need."

Yet next day he was uneasy till Mr. Eader appeared. Through the hours he stayed at the Plains, he and Rollin Lyle seemed the best of friends, each laughing in appreciation of the other's every quip, equally composed. Only, before Mr. Eader left—he declined to stay to dinner—he said meaningly to Rollin:

"Do you never ride into Camden? Of course, with so many attractions here——"

Rollin answered him readily: "Why, in fact, sir, Burr and I thought to ride in this evening. Even in Charleston, Mr. Eader, we've heard praises of the wines in Mr. Robinson's cellar at the Kershaw House."

"I know where he keeps his most choice bottles," Mr. Eader assured them. Thus politely the rendezvous was made.

Clayton rode to Camden with them. When he and Burr and Rollin reached the Kershaw House, two or three acquaintances were in the taproom, but not Mr. Eader. Clayton thought he would not be long. Someone remarked to Clayton that he seldom came to town, and with an ear for Mr. Eader's arrival, he took the chance-offered cue.

"I'm much too busy at the Plains," he said. "Cotton's a crop that requires a man's attention."

"No more than rice," Rollin suggested.

"Every man thinks his own task the most difficult," Clayton agreed. "My uncle Travis believes tobacco offers more problems than either cotton or rice."

As he spoke, the door opened, and Mr. Eader and Mr. Bellmer, a white-skinned, flabby little man, who had acted for Mr. Eader in more than one affair, came in together. Clayton's dislike of Mr. Bellmer was almost as intense as his feeling toward Mr. Eader. Nevertheless he felt himself today obliged to a surface cordiality.

"Ah, gentlemen. Will you join us, and state your pleasure?"

When they were seated—Mr. Eader across from Rollin as though already they were confronted—and full glasses had been set before them, Clayton resumed the conversation. "We were discussing," he explained, holding his tone casual, "the trials of the farmer. My uncle, Mr. Travis Currain, makes tobacco profitable at Chimneys, but he is forever protesting at the labor involved; seed beds in which every clod must be pulverized and the very soil purged by fire, seedlings to be weeded and tended through six or eight weeks, transplanting, many cultivations, buds to be pinched off, leaves and suckers to be removed, horn worms that must be culled by hand like a delicate fruit—and after the plants are grown, the harvesting, curing, stripping." He smiled. "Why, to hear him, you would suppose it to be a lifetime's work to raise a pipeful. For my part, I think the cotton planter best deserves sympathy."

"You are correct, sir," Mr. Eader assured him, as though he spoke by rote. "No other crop requires such tender and unabated care. The land must be bedded in early winter, it must be well drained, it must be plowed exactly thus and so, the crust must be harrowed—and all this before the first seed is sown. There's a winter's work in itself! Then the seeds, once sown, must be covered, and the earth scratched to permit them to germinate; and then come weeds, and plowing, and chopping and more plowing with mold-board and sweep after the turn-plow has dirted the plants. And picking and ginning, each is an art in itself! Then when one year's crop is saved it is time to start preparing for the next. Yes, cotton-planting has its difficulties." He looked for the first time at Rollin Lyle, said in a condescending tone: "Now rice is easy, by comparison; no more than a matter of letting in the water on your swamps. Yet I have heard Charleston men complain."

"I assure you, sir, there is more to rice culture than flooding the swamps," Rollin objected. "In the fall and winter, there are the ditches and the drains to clean, levees and gates to keep in repair. Then the plowing is a long muddy business, and harrowing and trenching, all before you let the water on at all. Sowing the seed is easy enough, to be sure." They were all as quietly attentive as though he spoke of matters of which they were ignorant; and the other gentlemen in the taproom, perhaps recognizing that something unusual lay behind this conversation, ceased their own talk to listen. "It's only after planting time that water helps at all," Rollin continued. "There's the sprout-flow to start the seed, but after that the hoeing must be done before the stretch-flow—the long-flow—to make the seedlings reach for air and thus outgrow the weeds; and the people have to wade through the fields and pull weeds the hoes missed. And after the stretch-flow the fields must be hoed again while the plants make their dry-growth before the lay-by, the harvest-flow. No, Mr. Eader, there's more to growing rice than flooding. The hands have work enough, you may be sure."

"Ah, yes, I see," Mr. Eader assented. "And for the hoeing the hands must wade in mud all day long, I suppose. Tell me, Mr. Lyle, is it the hard work or the wet feet that kills off your niggers so fast?"

Clayton at that word felt his nerves draw taut, felt the sudden breathless silence in the room. In that silence came Rollin's quiet reply.

"Why, Mr. Eader, I would not have expected so much solicitude from one who notoriously and cruelly abuses his people."

Mr. Eader with a violent movement thrust back his chair and stood up; and Mr. Bellmer, as though they were two manikins operated by the same spring, rose with him. Mr. Eader spoke. "Do I understand you correctly, Mr. Lyle?"

"Why, I think so," Rollin assured him. "If you understand me to express my contempt for a man who treats his negroes as you treat yours —you understand me precisely, sir."

So, for good or ill, the thing was done. Clayton knew a profound relief. From what was now to follow, Cousin Dolly's name need take no stain.

10

WHEN Brett Dewain returned from Charleston to the Plains, he was concerned because of what had happened at the Democratic Convention, and he looked forward as he always did to sharing his anxieties with Cinda. But when she and Clayton met his train, her quick embrace had in it an intensity which warned him that she too was deeply troubled; that even more than he needed her, she needed him.

"Oh, Brett Dewain," she whispered, holding him strongly. "Don't ever leave me! Don't ever leave me again!"

Meeting Clayton's eye, seeing his son's grave countenance, Brett knew this was no small matter. He led her toward the waiting carriage where they were secure against being overheard. When they were on the road, before he could ask a question, Cinda said hurriedly:

"Tell him, Clayton. I'd get it all mixed up."

She linked her hands through Brett's arm, pressing close to him; and Clayton looked at his father, hesitated, said at last:

"Well, Papa—you knew Cousin Dolly and Aunt Tilda were here?"

"I knew they were coming. I saw Mr. Streean in Charleston. He said he had put them on the train at Kingsville."

"Well," Clayton explained, "Jenny and I wanted to make it pleasant for them, so one night we had a picnic at Muster Spring." He told Brett, in quiet detail, what happened there. "So when Mr. Eader rode away in a rage, Mama sent me after him to try to—smooth things over."

Cinda whispered: "Oh I wish you'd been here, Brett Dewain!"

"I'm sure Clayton did all I could have done," he assured her; and Clayton said regretfully:

"Well, I couldn't do anything, sir, short of intervening; and I had no right to do that." He explained exactly what he did do, Brett nodding approval; and he continued: "When they met, I acted for Rollin. They used your pistols, sir." He hesitated. "Rollin is not a good shot, and he wanted to kill Mr. Eader, so he required that they sit facing each other across a table."

Brett looked his grave surprise. "Did Mr. Bellmer agree?"

"He disagreed pretty strongly at first," Clayton admitted.

Brett, feeling Cinda beside him suddenly shiver, wishing to ease her distress, spoke laughingly. "Like Congressman Potter's reply to Roger Pryor a fortnight since. Had you heard about that?" Clayton had not, and Brett explained: "They had some words on the floor of the House, and Pryor sent him a challenge, and Potter accepted and specified that they would fight with bowie knives. Pryor's second refused to let him meet Potter on those terms; and the Northern papers were amused. Their idea is that a duel arises from a mutual desire of two men to kill each other. Potter, incidentally, is a giant; and Roger Pryor is rather frail." He added: "Most Southern men sympathize with Pryor, of course."

"Well, Mr. Bellmer used pretty strong language," Clayton admitted: "Called the idea barbarous, and vulgar. I offered to discuss the point with him on any terms he chose, so he modified his language. I know he thinks of himself as a stickler for the code in every detail."

Brett nodded. "Yes. In the Martin-Scott affair twenty years ago he acted as second, and Mr. Martin fired after the word and Mr. Bellmer killed him. But I believe he has seldom acted as principal."

"He modified his language," Clayton said quietly. They had come to the ferry, and he spoke no more till they were on the road again. Brett saw the Negro ferry man watch them with furtive eyes. This affair must have made much talk among the blacks as well as whites. Once away from the ferry, Clayton continued: "I gave them their instructions."

Cinda, clinging to Brett's hand, asked in a shaking fascination: "What instructions, Clay?"

"Why, I explained that I would say: 'Ready, gentlemen? Fire! One-two-three. Hold!' They must not fire before I said the word, nor after I said 'Hold!' That's the formula." He looked at his father, and hesitated, and Brett watched this fine son of his, wishing Clayton need not have suffered this ordeal. The marks of strain were plain in the young man's eyes.

"What happened?" he asked quietly.

"Why, I think Mr. Eader's courage failed him," Clayton said slowly. "Or perhaps he lost control of himself. They sat facing each other across the table, their pistols pointed upward at arm's length. They were so close that when the pistols were levelled the muzzles would practically meet. I said: 'Ready, gentlemen?' And before I gave the word, Mr. Eader lowered his weapon and fired."

Brett felt choking rage fill his throat. "That was deliberate. Harry Eader has nerves like ice. I will kill him for that."

But Cinda's hand tightened on his arm, and Clayton said quickly: "No, Papa. You see, the bullet hit Rollin in the jaw, and he started to fall out of his chair, and Mr. Eader jumped up, and then Rollin's pistol went off. He didn't know what he was doing, but the bullet hit Mr. Eader in the heart."

For a moment no one spoke. Then Brett asked: "How is Rollin?"

"Why, he'll get well."

Cinda cried: "But the poor boy is scarred for life, the whole left side of his jaw shattered."

Brett said steadily: "Harry Eader's needed killing these thirty years, but I'm sorry it happened this way." He pressed Cinda's hand. "It was hard for you—and for Dolly."

"Dolly?" Cinda almost laughed in open anger. "Why, she was just simply gloating! Clayton and Burr brought Rollin home——"

"Burr?"

"Yes, he and Rollin were expelled from the college for some silly boyish bravado. They brought Rollin home, and Dolly insisted she would take care of him, nurse him! She was as excited as an Indian with his first scalp. I packed her and Tilda off to Richmond—sent Burr with them—so there wouldn't be too much talk about it."

"Is Rollin still here?"

"Yes. Doctor Trezevant came and patched him up, and the wound is healing. Judge Longstreet was kind enough to call, and he says Rollin can go back to college when he's well enough. Oh, Brett Dewain, why weren't you here?"

"I could have done no more than Clayton did." Then to lead her thoughts into less disturbing channels, he added: "I couldn't have prevented their meeting, and—I was watching another sort of meeting which may have even more serious consequences."

Cinda looked puzzled, but Clayton said in quick interest: "We heard that the Convention broke up."

"The Democratic party broke up," Brett corrected, "Split in two."

Cinda said impatiently: "Oh, politics!"

"This is more than politics," he told her seriously. "Mr. Yancey calls it the first step of a new revolution."

"But—what does he mean?"

"Disunion!" Brett's tone was low, his eyes stern. "Disunion." And he said wearily: "Oh, it was in the air from the first, the plot, the plan, the thought in every mind. The night before the Convention met, a crowd with a band marched up to the Charleston Hotel and demanded speeches; and after two or three fire-eating harangues, some dissenter shouted: 'Hurrah for the Star-Spangled Banner!' The crowd turned on him like so many yapping dogs, and he had to run for his life, and someone else yelled: 'Damn the old rag! Tear it down!' That set them cheering again."

Cinda asked, incredulous: "They can't do it, can they? They don't mean it, do they?"

"Yes. Yes, they mean it. The leaders do." He elaborated upon what had happened in Charleston to make her forget this tragic business here at home. "The plan may work, Cinda. With the Democratic party split, the Black Republicans may elect Seward; and then these same men who split the party will call his election the signal for that irrepressible conflict Roger Pryor is forever predicting. They've split the party to elect Seward, and they'll use Seward's election as a pretext to split the Union. They're already shouting the battle cry, declaring that Seward's election would deliver the South, bound and helpless, into the hands of her enemies. Yancey, Rhett, Pryor, all the hotheads."

Clayton said: "Judge Longstreet's one of them, sir. Ever since he came to the college he's been telling the students that we must fight the North and whip them. I heard him speak to them about John Brown, call him every name in the calendar. He's sure that if we withdraw from the Union the North won't dare do anything. If the rest of the

South won't secede he says for South Carolina to take her stand alone."
He half smiled and quoted: " 'Put her cause in the hand of God and
take her stand alone!' "

Brett chuckled. "I've heard so much oratory in the last two weeks
it's hard to talk naturally," he agreed. "But I think if Seward is elected
the South will secede." And while the horses trotted smartly homeward,
he went on: "Yancey had persuaded Alabama to instruct her delegates
that unless the platform insisted on the extension of slavery to the territories, they were to withdraw. When the Cotton States lost out on that
point, we talked to Yancey—several of us, Taylor of Louisiana, and
Slidell, and some others—urging him to keep Alabama in the Convention. We persuaded him, too; but Governor Winston insisted the instructions be followed. So Alabama and all the Cotton States withdrew
from the Convention."

Clayton said: "Papa, I couldn't understand why they didn't go ahead
and nominate Mr. Douglas anyway, even after the Gulf States withdrew."

"Why, the two-thirds rule made it difficult," Brett explained. "But
also—the South doesn't trust him." He added thoughtfully: "I was
surprised at the strength of the sentiment against him. Mr. Butler of
Massachusetts—I had a long talk with him one evening—says that
Lincoln, the Illinois man, ruined Mr. Douglas politically in the South
when he ran against him for the Senate two years ago. They had a
series of debates, and Lincoln led Mr. Douglas into saying that slavery
could be kept out of the territories by unfriendly legislation. They
call that 'The Freeport Doctrine' and it killed Douglas in the South."

"Who's Mr. Lincoln?" Cinda asked. "I never heard of him."

"He's a small-town politician out West, one of the blackest of the
Black Republicans. He's practically unknown in the South." Brett
hesitated. "As it happens, I heard him speak, three or four years ago,
in Bloomington, Illinois. I was there on business. Mr. Dwight of New
York was taking over a railroad they were building out there, the
Alton and Sangamon, taking it over to protect his investment in it. He
wanted me to put some Currain funds into it, suggested I go out and
look the situation over. Bloomington was a little town in the middle
of a real-estate boom, and a man named Fell, Jesse Fell, tried to sell me

'some land. There was a political meeting one evening, and Fell suggested we attend, so we did."

He paused, as though remembering. "This man Lincoln was one of the speakers," he said. "He's a scarecrow; an awkward, gangling, shabby, incredibly ugly man. When he stood up, I almost laughed. But his speech impressed me. In fact, he—well, frightened me. I don't remember what he said, except one thing. He said the Republicans were going to stop the spread of slavery, and that they would not see the Union broken up. He said the North wouldn't secede, and that the North wouldn't let the South secede."

Clayton laughed. "They can't stop us!"

"I remember his words," Brett admitted. "He looked tremendous, up there on the platform. He said, as if he were talking to our secessionists: 'We won't go out of the Union, and you shan't!' And the crowd went wild!"

Clayton made an angry sound, but Cinda asked uneasily: "Has he—any following?"

"No," Brett assured her. "No, Mr. Butler says he's only important because he killed Senator Douglas politically." He said thoughtfully: "Mr. Butler's an interesting man. I saw a good deal of him. Some of my business acquaintances in the North think he's a devil with horns, because he fights for shorter hours for labor in their mills. They call him names that would be shooting talk down here. He seemed to me a clear-headed man, with mighty few illusions, but I wouldn't want him for an enemy. He'd be a pretty ruthless fighter." And he added: "He believes competition between the laborer and the employer for the profits of production stimulates the employer and leads to industrial progress. He says slavery is holding back the South, because by using slave labor we get along too easily; that if we had to do without it, we'd work harder—and do better. He reminded me how many planters had gone bankrupt in the last ten or fifteen years, and I suggested that the South was being ruined by the tariff; and he retorted that the sooner we big planters were bankrupted, the sooner we'd create an industrial South and begin to share tariff benefits." Brett chuckled, said dryly: "He says that as long as we Southerners don't have to work for a living, we'll never develop our real capacities."

Cinda exclaimed: "Of all the insulting idiots! Why didn't you—slap his face, or call him out?"

"I'm afraid he wouldn't have come!" Brett told her smilingly.

Clayton asked: "Papa, is Mr. Seward as black as he's painted?"

"I doubt it," Brett told him. "Of course, he's an abolitionist; but he's a New Yorker, and his friends there won't let him make too much trouble."

Cinda said: "But you're worried, Brett Dewain."

"Yes," he admitted. "Yes, I am. Our Southern hotbloods, men like Ruffin and Roger Pryor and Rhett and Yancey, are ready to secede on any pretext—or to make one."

"Men my age have been brought up to expect secession," Clayton reminded him, and Brett saw the proud light in his son's eyes. Young men were so sure of their strength. Probably Burr felt as Clayton did. Yes, and Julian too.

"Have you heard from Julian?" he asked Cinda. The youngster had gone off to the Institute at Charlotte before he himself left for Charleston.

"Oh yes, a long letter." She smiled. "He insists he isn't the least bit homesick. That's not very flattering to us, is it?"

"Probably he's just bragging. He wouldn't admit it if he were."

"I'm not sure we did right to send him there. Major Hill doesn't sound very impressive. Julian says he's a shabby sort of man, never gets the right buttons into the right button holes, little and peaked and almost hunchbacked, always peering at you over his spectacles."

"His record is good," Brett assured her. "Trav knows him, and I looked him up. He ranked well at West Point and did fine work in Mexico. Trav likes him because he's a mathematician." They smiled together. "But he has other qualities—though perhaps Julian is too young to appreciate them." He asked: "How does Julian get along with his work?"

"He claims he's doing well. He says being a 'Newy' is rather strenuous. The older boys make their lives miserable, and even Major Hill teases them a good deal, in little ways. But Julian says he's sure he can get a 'minus demerit' every month—whatever that is. It's all in his letter." The carriage turned into the drive and she said happily: "Oh, I'm glad you're home."

Vesta and Jenny and the children met them with riotous greetings, and Brett and Clayton and Vesta went to see Rollin Lyle, still in bed, his head swathed in bandages and his jaw bound so that he could not talk. But Rollin's eyes made their apologies to Brett for what had happened, and Brett understood and reassured him. When later they were alone he told Cinda: "The youngster blames himself; but boys that age are a high-spirited lot."

"I blame Dolly," Cinda retorted. "She's an outrageous coquette, Brett Dewain—and heartless and cruel besides. She's—well, I'm afraid she's always going to make trouble wherever she goes. She's too beautiful!" She smiled at him. "You can be thankful that I'm homely as a hedge fence." He came to kiss her, and for a moment she clung to him. "Don't ever leave me," she whispered. "Don't ever leave me again."

11

CINDA was interested in anything that interested Brett. Before they went abroad he had paid little attention to political matters; but she saw that he was deeply troubled now. The morning after his return from Charleston, they heard of the dreadful tragedy at Boykin's Mill Pond the evening before, when another picnic had ended in disaster. Two or three score boys and girls put out into the pond in a big flatboat which sank under them, and twenty-four were drowned. The whole neighborhood was saddened, and Cinda and Brett, Clayton and Jenny did what they could to ease the general grief. Cinda was secretly almost grateful for this distraction which helped them all forget Mr. Eader's death, and Rollin's hurt; she hoped it would wash Brett's mind clear of political anxieties.

It did, but not for long. By the time they returned to Richmond, the Constitutional Union party had nominated John Bell of Tennessee for President, and Brett had some hope the Democracy would unite again to support him. "He's a good man," he told Cinda. "He's always stood against disunion." He added doubtfully: "But of course he voted against the repeal of the Missouri Compromise, and opposed the Lecompton constitution for Kansas, and his own party has disowned him."

"I've heard of Democrats and Republicans," she hazarded, "but I never heard of this party of his. Is it important?"

"Well, they had delegates from twenty-two states at their convention," he told her, "and their platform is equally against abolition and disunion. A lot of people would like to stand on that middle ground."

"In a fight, it's the ones in the middle that get hurt, isn't it?" Since these matters filled Brett's thoughts, she must try to understand.

He nodded soberly. "That's Virginia's danger now," he commented. "We'll be besought by both sides. We're a big state, the biggest in the Union except Texas; and we're rich and powerful. Our state bonds sell higher in New York and in London than the national obligations. So we're a prize worth playing for. The North will try to persuade us to side with her, and the South will try to win us over."

Sometimes when she heard his grave tones her heart froze with fear. "Do you seriously think—trouble is coming?"

"I don't know," he confessed. "I talked today with a number of gentlemen, Mr. Harvie and Mr. Robinson and Mr. Haxall and several others." He smiled doubtfully. "All business men, of course; and men of business are slow to believe that anything can upset the settled order of things. From their point of view, it's absurd to think of trouble when the South's as prosperous as it is now. Especially the Gulf States. Mr. Haxall spoke of a Louisiana man named Burnside who has made six million dollars in sugar; and with the huge cotton crop last year, and another big crop coming, land and slaves are worth more every day. So these gentlemen find it hard to take Yancey and Roger Pryor and old Mr. Ruffin and such men seriously."

Cinda said with some vehemence: "Well, so do I!"

Brett smiled. "By the way," he said, "Mr. Robinson's resigning." Edwin Robinson was president of the Fredericksburg railroad, in which considerable Currain funds were invested. "Mr. Daniel will take his place."

"What does Mr. Daniel think about all this?"

"Oh, he's optimistic," Brett assured her; and he caught to some extent the infection of their hopefulness. John Brown's raid had sent a wave of passionate anger across the South, awakening as it did that fear of a slave insurrection which lay dormant in every Southern mind; and most Southern states passed laws making more rigorous the restrictions on the slaves themselves and forbidding the publication or circulation even by word of mouth of abolitionist tracts. But after the legislatures had acted, fears and the anger they bred began to subside; mobs were not so ready to cowhide or to tar and feather any suspected abolitionists, nor the courts to bring them to trial. There was a proposal in North Carolina to tax slaves as property; but that was a part of the dangerously increasing pressure to take political control out of the hands of the wealthy and presumably the wise and statesmanlike and give it to the mob. Brett agreed with the men he knew best that any extension of the voting power of men with neither property nor political wisdom was a mistake. Even war, if it checked the growing power of the illiterate and irresponsible, might be a good thing.

But he could not believe that war was coming. When the Republican Convention met in Chicago, he told Cinda: "If the Republicans nominate Seward we can surely work something out."

"Will they nominate him?"

"Well, all the best men in the North seem to be for him, and a majority of the delegates."

"Then—doesn't that make it pretty sure?"

He nodded. "I think so, yes." He laughed. "But anything can happen in a place like Chicago."

"I remember you didn't like it when you were out there four years ago."

"No, I didn't," he agreed, and smiled. "They called it the Mudhole of the Prairies, and the name fitted. The streets were just a mire barely above the level of the lake; but even when I was there, they were lifting the whole city out of the mud. I stayed at the Tremont Hotel, and you had to walk down a flight of steps to get from the sidewalk to the office; but soon after I left, they put five thousand jacks under it, took twelve hundred workmen, and just lifted the hotel bodily to grade level. I told you, anything can happen in Chicago."

"If they nominate Seward we'll be all right, won't we?"

"I hope so." He laughed his own fears aside. "Oh, I'm sure we will. There's no one else who has even a possible choice. I'm not so worried as I sound."

He thought the Convention would make its nomination on the second day; and that evening he was late coming home. "I've been in Jennings Wise's office," he explained. "Waiting for news; but they've adjourned till tomorrow."

"I'll be glad when it's settled."

"It seems to be safe enough for Seward," he said, "but I want to know as soon as possible. There are some investments I will change if things go wrong."

Next day things did go wrong. When he returned from the *Enquirer* office, he was blackly despondent, and at Cinda's quick question he said soberly: "Why, they nominated that man I told you about, that Lincoln."

"Lincoln? Why—what you said—he sounds like white trash!

He nodded. "I know." He grinned mirthlessly. "I told you anything could happen in Chicago."

"But how did it happen, Brett Dewain? How could they?"

"Well, Chicago's just a crazy frontier city," he explained. "They built a special hall for this convention and named it the 'Wigwam,' as though they were a tribe of wild Indians gathering for a powwow! And Lincoln is an Illinois man, so the crowd, the local mob, was for him." Sudden scornful anger hardened his tone. "'The Rail Splitter' they call him. He's a cheap politician, a country lawyer with no background whatever." He cried, almost as though she were to blame: "What sort of nation is this, Cinda, where a man like that can be seriously considered for the Presidency?"

"You thought he made a good speech that time you heard him. Maybe he'll turn out all right."

"Oh, it's possible, of course. But—why even his nomination was just the mob's work. They packed the galleries with backwoodsmen and stinking riffraff, and the crowds shouted Seward out, shouted Lincoln in."

"Shouted him in? How do you mean?"

"Oh, they raised the roof, ten thousand of them, all bellowing his name at the top of their lungs."

She said disgustedly: "How disgraceful! I declare, Brett Dewain, it sounds just like a negro revival

"Well, it's done." His lip curled. "Democracy! The country's turned over to a damned mob."

"What do people think about it?"

"Why—everyone is just stumped. Not twenty men in Richmond ever heard of this damned Lincoln. Outside of a few politicians, I suppose I'm the only man in Virginia who ever heard him speak, ever saw him." He added strongly: "But that man hates the South. We've got to beat him, Cinda."

"Why in the world would anyone want such a man for President?"

"It was the Westerners," he told her, calmer now. "They're a poverty-stricken, uneducated, ignorant lot; so they hate anybody who has money, hate all cultivated, well-to-do people." He spoke broodingly, thinking aloud. "Lincoln wasn't nominated because he hates slavery. Seward is just as violent against slavery as he. But Seward was honest enough to condemn John Brown, and the North wouldn't stand for that. You know the North made a hero out of that murderous old lunatic! Seward was the only public man in the North with the courage to say that what John Brown did was sedition and treason. That probably cost him the nomination; that and the fact that he represents money, ease, culture, decency—all the things those Westerners despise. They nominated this country lout because he's their own kind, took him and shouted him in."

"Maybe the East won't vote for him." She tried to find some word of comfort.

"Maybe not. I suppose if we unite we can still save ourselves." He said soberly: "This wouldn't hit me so hard if I hadn't been so sure of Seward's victory."

She kissed him, teasing him as if he were a small boy. "There, there! We're all wrong sometimes, Mr. Dewain. Don't look so humble! I was even wrong myself, once. I remember it well."

Together they laughed their fears away, and during the days that followed, when the Richmond papers searched the record of the Republican nominee, they began to take hope again. Lincoln was poor white trash, the son of a shiftless squatter; he had tried keeping a store, and everyone in the South knew Yankee store keepers were a lying, cheating, penny-pinching, depraved, disreputable lot; he had won some petty political success by his skill at wrestling, boat racing, pitching horseshoes, and telling vulgar stories like any tavern loafer; he insisted that the Supreme Court should allow itself to be overruled by popular vote, that right was not right but was simply what the majority of voters at any given time believed; he stood for popular sovereignty in spite of the fact that the South, ruled by men of wealth and character, had through seventy years' dominance in national affairs made the

United States the greatest country in the world; he looked like an ape; he was uneducated, violent in his language, lacking political prestige, a dull and witless monster distinguished only by his hatred for the South—and so completely contemptible that the Republican party, by nominating him, had destroyed itself. Even Brett began to be reassured. It was incredible that such a man could be elected President of the United States.

12

ENID had counted on Cinda's promise to invite her for a visit in Richmond; had waited at first with eagerness and then with impatience and then with anger. "She's forgotten all about me, stuck off down here," she told Trav. "I suppose I have to expect to be ignored by your family!"

But this summer, soon after Lincoln's nomination, Cinda sent the promised invitation. She wrote much about their stay at the Plains, and about the babies, and about Julian going off to school, and finally about their return to Richmond.

> We're so happy in this lovely house. Vesta's here with us, of course; and Burr too. He decided not to go back to college, even if Judge Longstreet would have him; and we're just as well pleased. There's too much big talk down there about fighting the North. We'd rather have him here in Virginia where people are more sensible. He's glad to be here too; and he's suddenly interested in Barbara Pierce. She's a sweet girl, but still young enough to enjoy keeping him dangling. Brett says Burr has a head for business. They're forever talking about banks, and money at interest and things.

There was much more in like vein, for Cinda was as vocal with her pen as with her tongue; but for Enid the best part of the letter was in the last paragraph.

> So now that we're all settled down and humdrum, I want you and Enid to come for a visit. Travis too, of course, if you can drag him away. You'll be perfectly comfortable here, and I'll send Burr down

to fetch you whenever you say the word. Don't argue. Just say when you'll come.

Love
Cinda

Enid's eyes shone. "Oh, Mama, that's wonderful! Won't we have fun!"

Mrs. Currain smiled. "I'm afraid it's out of the question for me, Honey. I haven't been away from Great Oak in years, except once to the Plains to pay my respects to my first great-grandchild; and I vowed then I'd never go away again. Things were all at sixes and sevens when I got home."

"You'd enjoy it, Mama, once you made the effort. Trav will keep things running here."

Mrs. Currain shook her head. "No, I'll stay at Great Oak. But of course you must go."

Enid wanted to dance with delight, but she dutifully protested: "Darling, you know I can't leave you alone!"

"Why, the very idea!" Mrs. Currain tossed her head. "As if I couldn't take care of myself. Don't be ridiculous. Of course you must go."

So Enid made happy plans. Burr came to serve as her escort. They would travel by stage. Rising early on the morning appointed, Enid while she dressed called along the hall to Vigil to bring the baby and the older children to say good-by. A moment later she heard little Henrietta scream with pain, heard Vigil's frightened wail; and she raced to the nursery and snatched the baby from Vigil's arms, and saw blood trickling from Henrietta's eye, and herself began to weep aloud, adding her tears and cries to the child's anguished screams.

"Oh, my baby, my baby! Vigil, what did you do to her?" She was already furious, realizing instantly that now she could not possibly go to Richmond today, blaming Vigil as much for her own disappointment as for the baby's hurt. The colored girl confessed her fault, mumbling through her lamentations.

"It uz de snuff stick, ma'am. When I went to pick her up it done jab her in de eye."

"Oh, you worthless nigger!" Enid was almost screaming in her rage.

"I've told you a thousand times—" April, drawn by the outcry, plunged into the room and heard enough to understand; and she snatched Vigil, spinning her headlong. Enid, beside herself, cried: "Kill her, April! Kill her!" April caught up a stick of firewood from the iron basket by the hearth and struck at the cringing girl, and Vigil howled and raced blindly to escape, April a fury on her heels.

Then others were here. Trav had gone on his morning rounds of the plantation; but Burr appeared, and Mrs. Currain. The older woman, competent and steady, hushed Enid's passionate wrath and sent Burr full gallop to Williamsburg to fetch the doctor, and brought flax seed to poultice Hetty's eye and told Enid again to be still. "You're making a fool of yourself, child. Behave!"

Enid wept: "Oh, Hetty, darling baby!"

"Hush," Mrs. Currain insisted. "You're just making matters worse, scaring her!"

"I could kill Vigil. If I've told her once I've told her a thousand times——"

She was near hysterics; Mrs. Currain in sharp exasperation caught her shoulders, shook her. "Be quiet, Enid! Behave!"

Enid at last was still; but when the doctor came, he said Hetty's eye would need days of care. So the visit to Richmond was postponed, and Enid's disappointment led her into a violent quarrel with Trav. She demanded that he have Vigil whipped; but Trav protested:

"Now, Enid, Vigil's had a bad beating already. April chased her clear down to the quarter, pounded her senseless with that stick of firewood. It's a wonder she didn't kill her. I think she would have, if the people hadn't stopped her. Vigil's got a broken arm and a couple of broken ribs, as it is."

"It's good enough for her! Make them take a blacksnake whip and just cut her to pieces, skin her alive!"

"We don't need to turn into animals!"

"Trav Currain, don't you dare call me an animal!"

"I only said——"

"I heard what you said. I've stood a lot from you, but I don't intend to stand much more! Defending that worthless nigger against your own wife, after she's just about killed your baby, maybe made her blind for life!"

"Vigil feels as bad about it as you do, Enid. And after all, it was an accident."

Her anger fed on opposition; she was half-screaming. "You go have her whipped, you hear me! Have her whipped and then sell her south! See how she likes that!"

"No." His tone was final. "I don't have negroes whipped. And I won't sell our people off the land, out of the family."

"Did you hear what I said?"

"Yes. Everyone in the house can hear you."

"Trav Currain, are you going to do what I say, or aren't you?" He turned away, not answering. "Oh I hate you! I hate you! I just married you in the first place to spite my mother! I wish I'd died first."

He came back to plead for silence. "Don't, Enid. You upset Mama."

"Well, she ought to be upset! I want her to be upset! I'd like to see you upset just once! Vigil goes and puts your own baby's eye out, practically, and you stand up for her. I guess you think more of her than you do of me! Probably she's not the only one! That sassy Sapphira, for instance—the way you stuck up for her!"

She would have welcomed a raging anger in him. His refusal even to resent these wild accusations which she knew to be ridiculous was like oil on the fire of her fury. She felt a vengeful hatred toward him which she was sure would never die; and she was not appeased when three days later April, triumphantly established as Hetty's attendant and jealous guardian, reported that Vigil had been sent back to Chimneys.

"Mighty lucky for dat nigguh she gone, too! I ever lay eyes on her again I'll beat de haid off'n her."

Enid saw in Vigil's punishment not surrender on Trav's part but only evasion; and to realize that he had held his own unyielding way hardened her resentment. Some day, somehow, she would even the long score.

The accident to Hetty postponed, but did not in the end prevent, Enid's going to Richmond; and the manner of her going was so delightful that she forgot her original disappointment. Burr, since he had come to Great Oak only to act as her escort, returned without her; but as Hetty mended, Faunt one day appeared, and stayed the night.

He was on his way to Richmond; and Enid, since Hetty no longer needed her constant attendance, seized upon this opportunity. Mrs. Currain agreed that she could go with Faunt as well as not; Trav made no strong objection; Faunt said he would be honored to be of service.

The prospect of days and perhaps weeks in Richmond—for Enid meant to stay as long as Cinda would let her—was delight enough; but to make the daylong journey in Faunt's company was like an intoxication. He left his horse at Great Oak and they went by stage; and he was so courteously thoughtful of her comfort, so pleasantly attentive, so ready to answer her thousand questions that she was brimming with content. Seeing his amusement at her happiness she played up to it, eager to provoke his quick charming smile.

At the big house on Fifth Street, old Caesar opened the door and greeted them like a courtly host. "Marste' Faunt, you's quite a stranger," shaking Faunt's hand. "And how's you, Mistis?" Caesar for all his gray hair was big and black and muscular, sleek with abounding health. "Hopes I sees ye well. Mighty glad to see de bofe o' you."

He ushered them in, and Enid glowed under his flattering courtesy. Then Cinda and Vesta were here with their welcomes, and Cinda led Enid to the room prepared for her. Had she had a pleasant trip?

"Just wonderful, Cinda! Faunt's so thoughtful and polite; and when he smiles he's the handsomest thing you ever saw!"

"Oh, everybody goes crazy over Faunt," Cinda agreed. "But Travis is my favorite brother. Faunt is moody sometimes, but Travis is always the same."

"Well, I wish he wasn't! I wish he'd be different, once in a while. I'm real provoked with Trav, Cinda, the way he acted about Vigil. You know the terrible thing that happened?" Cinda said Burr had reported the accident; nevertheless Enid repeated every detail. "And poor little Hetty will always show it, Cinda, and maybe be blinded in that eye. Wouldn't it be awful if she was?" She had Cinda's ready sympathy. "But Trav didn't mind. He stuck up for Vigil and kept saying it was an accident. Why, he wouldn't even have her whipped the way I wanted him to! I declare I'm furious with him."

Cinda said comfortingly: "Husbands are an aggravating lot, but you'll get over it."

And in fact Enid's resentment faded in the happy pleasures of this visit. During the hours and days that followed, each new experience delighted her.

"Caesar's wonderful, isn't he! He's so courtly and dignified."

Cinda laughed. "Dignified? He's just lazy. He puts on his dignity to get out of work." Brett was with them and she spoke to him. "Remember, Mr. Dewain, the time when Vesta was a little girl, having a tea party for some of her friends, and she wanted Caesar to serve them on the low table in the nursery, and he said, ever so hoity-toity: 'I don' wait on no pine tables. Wait twell you big enough to put youah laigs unde' mahogany.'"

Brett chuckled. "And Vesta was so shocked at the indelicacy of his remarks that she wanted him whipped."

"You should have had it done! You've spoiled him for years."

"He tickles me. Just this morning I caught him wearing a shirt of mine. I tried to make him ashamed of himself, asked if he was sorry, and he said: 'Well, tell de hones' truf, I ain' sorry I stole hit, but I sho' is sorry I got cotch!'"

Enid laughed with him, but Cinda protested. "Oh you make me so mad, Brett Dewain! You think everything Caesar does is just howlingly funny." Enid, watching this comfortable give and take, recognizing the warm and tender bond between them, felt a wistful envy; they were so close, so fond. There was nothing like this between her and Trav.

Enid would have enjoyed Richmond more but for the fact that the men could talk of nothing except some convention or other that was about to be held here. She had made Faunt promise, on their way from Great Oak, to squire her everywhere. "Will you take me to Pizzini's for strawberries, Cousin Faunt? And to promenade in Capitol Square? And to see just simply everything?" He smiled and agreed; but even Faunt was at once engrossed in talk of politics, and he and Brett might be closeted for hours with other gentlemen in grave discussions which she could find no excuse for interrupting.

The day before the Convention was to meet, Tony unexpectedly appeared. Enid, remembering her own dislike for Trav's brother, was glad to see that there was no warmth in Cinda's welcome.

"Oh, hello, Tony! What brings you to town? Hankering after the fleshpots?"

"Hullo, Cinda." Enid thought Tony seemed embarrassed. "I haven't seen you for over two years, not since you and Brett went abroad."

"So you haven't! But don't try to tell me you came to see me!"

"No, as a matter of fact I came to watch the Convention."

Cinda laughed. "Really? I can't imagine you being interested in politics!"

"Well, I suppose I am. James Fiddler and Ed Blandy and Tom Shadd and all my neighbors want to know what's going on."

Enid saw Cinda's amazement. "You mean you came to find out and tell them?"

"In a way, yes." Tony laughed uneasily. "You see, Cinda, the country around Chimneys is pretty far away from everything. The people there just have little farms. No slaves." Cinda was watching him with searching eyes, and he added almost in apology: "But they come to me for my opinions, and I suppose that flatters me. Anyway, I want to be able to—answer some of their questions."

Cinda went suddenly to him and kissed him. "Why, Tony—" She hesitated, did not finish; and he said honestly:

"I know they just respect me because they respected Trav." Enid felt a puzzled wonder. Why should anyone respect Trav? He was as common as dirt! "Trav and I never got along, but they think a lot of him down there. I've tried to—" He laughed, amused at himself. "Well, I suppose I've tried to live up to Trav. And I like it there."

Cinda touched his shoulder in strong affection. "Isn't it lonely, away off in the mountains?"

He chuckled. "Lord love you, no, it's not lonely. There's lots going on. We have dance frolics; and the men get together at the tavern, or at the store, or at the mill." He met Enid's eyes. "I'm letting them have their corn ground at our mill on the place. Trav used to, so I kept it up; so there may be half a dozen men there, waiting their turn, some days. Then we do a little horse racing, and we all get together for the corn shucking and the hog killings." He smiled. "And you've never seen a real dance till you hear one of our fiddlers h'ist a tune!"

Cinda looked at Enid. "Did you and Trav do all those things?"

"Heavens, no! Trav used to spend most of his time with—" Enid

hesitated, looking at Tony; but her tone was still scornful. "With people like Ed Blandy; but of course we never went to any of their
doings." She felt in Tony and in Cinda too a withdrawal, an unspoken
criticism; and suddenly she was angry. "I don't see how you can stand
them, Tony; all that—trash!"

His eyes hardened; when he spoke there was derision in his tone.
"What do you hear from your mother?" It was as though he warned
her to curb her tongue. She felt Cinda's inquiring glance, and she
spoke quickly.

"Oh, she's fine!" Then, to appease him: "I expect I'd have liked
them too if I'd known them; but we never went to their doings. Trav
always wanted to stay at home and go to bed!" Flatteringly she added:
"I declare I just don't understand a thing about politics, Cousin Tony.
You'll have to explain it all to me." She took the first means she found
to avert his tongue from her mother. If Cinda ever guessed that Tony
and her mother—Enid shivered with terror at the thought, and her eager,
charmingly innocent questions kept Tony in play. If men liked to talk
about politics, she must learn to talk too, or at least listen; but it was all
so confusing. Apparently everybody hated that old Abe Lincoln, and
some of the Democrats were for a man named Bell, and some were for
Senator Douglas, and the Convention here in Richmond was going to
nominate Mr. Breckenridge. Tony seemed to think it a mistake to have
so many different candidates against Lincoln, and Enid protested:

"But I should think three men could beat him easier than one,
Cousin Tony."

He smiled at her innocence. "They might if they all got together.
The trouble is they won't. John Bell proposed that all three of them
withdraw and unite on someone else, but Mr. Douglas wouldn't do it.
So now they'll each beat the others—and let Lincoln win."

"Why, I think that's awfully silly, if what they want is to beat him!"

"Men do some mighty foolish things."

After the Convention finished its business Enid thought Faunt would
at last pay her some attention; but he left at once for Belle Vue. She
reminded him in pretty reproach that they had as yet done none of
the things he had promised they would do together; but he said he

must go home for a week or two. "Perhaps you'll still be here when I return."

When he departed, Tony went with him. They would go first to Great Oak, but Tony proposed to proceed from there to Washington. He said he went to see what men in the Capital thought about the campaign, but Enid suspected him of planning to call upon her mother.

Her visit had already been a long one, but she stayed on in Richmond. Faunt was gone and Brett was much too absorbed in something or other to pay her any attention, and Burr spent most of his time with his father or calling on Barbara Pierce, and Vesta had many friends, so Enid was left much alone with Cinda. She remembered Darrell. He had been amusing at Great Oak, and presumably he was in Richmond. "Do you ever see Tilda?" she asked one day, Darrell in her mind.

"Oh, yes," Cinda said. "But she and Dolly haven't dared face me since that awful business at the Plains." Enid had heard nothing of this, and her questions flew, and Cinda answered guardedly. "The less said about it, the better," she declared. "Dolly's conceited enough as it is, without having men fighting over her."

"Oh, I won't say a word," Enid vowed; but at her insistence they did go to Tilda's to call, and Enid in an itch of curiosity tried to lead Tilda and Dolly to talk about that fatal picnic at Muster Spring. Cinda's presence and her grim silence kept them silent, too; but thereafter Enid came again, alone, and easily led Dolly to tell her the story. Dolly masked her demure complacency behind many protestations.

"It was simply terrible. I think men are just perfectly ridiculous, Aunt Enid, don't you?"

Enid agreed that they certainly were. She and Dolly fell easily into a surface friendship; and Darrell, happening to come home while Enid was there, joined them, flattering Enid with easy compliments. At his suggestion they strolled over to Pizzini's for an ice, and one of Dolly's many swains joined them, so Darrell escorted Enid back to Fifth Street. She was sparkling with happiness.

"It's been just the nicest time I've had since I came to Richmond, Dal. Thank you kindly."

He bowed. "A pleasure, ma'am. Now I shall have to answer many questions about Richmond's newest belle."

Enid blushed and protested that he mustn't make fun of an old married woman, and invited him in; but he said good-by at the door.

In her room Enid found a letter from Trav suggesting that she come home; but of course that was ridiculous when she was having such a good time. "He wanted me to come back to Great Oak. But I just told him I was going to stay till he came up to get me," she confessed to Cinda. "I'm going to make him put himself out for once, if it's the last thing I do!" She added: "Of course I'll go on home if I'm too much bother to you?"

Cinda said politely that she must stay as long as she chose, and Enid stayed till at last Trav surrendered and came to fetch her. He reached Richmond on a Saturday, would stay over Sunday; and Sunday morning, as they were all about to start to church, Faunt and Tony rode up to the door. Enid, when they appeared, was nearest. She cried out a glad welcome and kissed Faunt, and then because some sense of guilt made it seem necessary to do so, she kissed Tony too. She proposed they all stay home from church, but found herself overruled; and all through the service she was furious because she had not pleaded a headache. Trav meant to take her away to Great Oak tomorrow; she would see hardly anything of Faunt at all!

She had, in fact, no moment with him alone. At dinner they were all together, and immediately afterward Mr. Streean and Tilda—having learned at church of Tony's return from Washington—came to hear what he could report. So Enid had to listen rebelliously to hours of tedious talk; but she listened most of all to Faunt, and to him her eyes constantly returned.

Tony thought Lincoln would be beaten. "Even the Republicans are ashamed of themselves for nominating him," he explained. "Charles Francis Adams of Massachusetts made a speech in Congress about the great Republican party, and the Republicans have printed the speech and spread it all over the country—but it doesn't even mention Abe Lincoln's name!" He had brought home a book prepared for use in the campaign. "This is his biography, and some of his speeches, and there's enough right in this book to make anyone vote against him. I'll read you some of the things it says."

"Oh, do you have to?" Enid protested. "I'm awfully tired of politics." But no one answered her, watching Tony as he turned the pages.

"It's written by a man named Howells—W. D. Howells. It starts off with Lincoln's ancestors." He grinned. "If he had any. They don't seem to be sure." He read: " 'It is necessary that every American should have an indisputable grandfather——' "

" 'Indisputable'?" Brett echoed, amused. "That's a modest word. Of course, I've known men who didn't even have an indisputable father, but those men weren't running for President of the United States!"

Tony went on. "This book admits there's an 'extremely embarrassing uncertainty' about Lincoln's great-grandparents, says it's 'not very profitable' to try to trace his ancestry."

Cinda uttered an incredulous exclamation. "You mean to say that book's put out by Lincoln's friends?"

"Yes."

"Heavens! If that's the best his friends can do, what will his enemies say?"

Tony chuckled. "Of course I'm just reading the funniest parts. They did dig up a grandfather for him." He read: " 'His grandfather (anterior to whom is incertitude)——' "

Their laughter checked him; but Faunt said thoughtfully: "All the same, lots of us, even our FFV's, are in the same position if the truth were known. Anterior to the grandfathers of a good many of us there is incertitude."

"Nonsense!" Cinda protested; but he shook his head.

"Not at all," he assured her. "Studying such things is one of the ways I spend my days at Belle Vue. Many of the fine Virginia families of today were founded by a grandfather or a great-grandfather like ours, by men who became big land owners simply through a superior ability to meet and master wilderness conditions. We like to think of ourselves as cavaliers, but there were mighty few aristocrats among the early settlers, even in Virginia. After all, the dandy who shone at court in London wouldn't choose to come out here and starve and freeze in a log cabin; and if he did come, unless he went to work and worked harder than his neighbors, he soon found himself left behind by the procession."

Enid watched Faunt and thought how wonderful he was. He went on: "Outside of a few families, most of the best-known Virginia names don't go back very far beyond the Revolution. The aristocrats of colonial days were usually Tories, so when the King's troops were expelled, they went along. Our grandfathers who stayed behind had to pull themselves up out of the ruck by their own boot straps."

"Well, I simply don't believe it," Cinda declared. "There's everything in having a fine inheritance. Why, Faunt, you wouldn't ride a horse that wasn't well bred!"

Faunt smiled, and Enid loved his smile, loved the way he now and then caught her eye as though to assure her she had a part in this conversation. "I value the sort of grandfathers most of us Virginians really had," he remarked. "They were men who knew how to work and win their way. I value them above the sort of grandfathers most of us like to think we had."

Redford Streean took the Lincoln biography from Tony's hands, leafing through the pages; and Brett Dewain said reasonably:

"You're overlooking the intangibles, Faunt, aren't you? Pride in our ancestry is often a source of virtue in us. We behave ourselves because we feel that to do so is expected of us, that courtesy and a sense of honor and an acceptance of responsibility are the traditions of our families. You'd better not take that away from us. A lot of us—if we were ever convinced that our grandfathers had been rascals—might readily enough turn to rascally ways ourselves."

"Yes," Faunt assented, and he smiled. "Yes, it's probably good for us to believe that Grandfather Currain, and presumably all the Courdains before him, were high-minded gentlemen!"

"Exactly!" Cinda agreed. "Because we think we're fine people, we try to behave in fine ways."

Streean looked up from the book. "Speaking of Virginia grandfathers," he said, "Lincoln had one, too. His grandfather migrated from Virginia to Kentucky and the Indians shot him."

"Too bad they didn't shoot him sooner!" Cinda's dry comment amused them all.

"His father's name was Tom Lincoln," Streean told them. "Tom married a girl named Lucy Hanks." * Enid was struck by the familiar

---

* Every reader of this work in manuscript has remarked that Lincoln's mother was not Lucy Hanks, but Nancy. But Mr. Howells, in the campaign biography they were here discussing, mistakenly said her name was Lucy.—B. A. W.

name. Her own daughter's name was Lucy, and so was Mrs. Currain's; and Enid remembered that there had been another Lucy whom Mr. Currain loved long ago, and she fell to wondering about that other Lucy. If Mr. Currain had married her, instead of letting her father take her off to Kentucky, then he would never have married Mrs. Currain; and these children of his here talking together would never have been born at all. She thought maliciously that if Tony and Tilda had never been born, no one would miss them; nor Trav, if it came to that. Cinda was rather nice, though Enid was sometimes a little afraid of her, but of them all, Faunt was the only one who would be any real loss. It was a delight just to watch him move, to see the way his head turned toward anyone who spoke, to hear his quiet voice, to see how respectfully they all attended when he said anything.

When she began to listen again, Streean was speaking. "Abe's father was a squatter, never stayed long in one place. He went from Kentucky to Indiana." He laughed at something on the page under his eye. "It says here that he wasn't much good as a hunter, never even learned to shoot. Then his father moved on to Illinois, and Abe began to split rails."

Faunt said in regretful tones: "Brett, the best men in the South have always gone into politics; but if the Government is to fall into the hands of such riffraff as this, the halls of Congress will no longer be tolerable for gentlemen." Why couldn't Trav be like Faunt, instead of sitting stupidly half-asleep, with never a word to say? Faunt added almost sadly: "And a nation dominated by such uneducated, graceless bumpkins can never command Virginia's loyalty."

"Yet Virginia will go a long way to avoid disunion," Brett predicted. Then Streean chuckled at something he read and said in amused derision:

"Here, this is worth hearing. It seems there were some bullies in his neighborhood called the Clary's Grove boys, and Lincoln got into a wrestling match with one of them, and was winning, but the other fellow's friends pitched in, so Lincoln gave up, said he couldn't fight them all. Now here's the funny part!" He read: "'This gave him a reputation for courage——'"

"Courage?" Cinda cried. "To quit just because the odds were against him! Is that what the North calls courage?"

Tony took the book from Streean. "Let me find you some of the things he's said in his speeches about slavery," he suggested. "Here." He read: " 'I hate it because of the monstrous injustice of slavery itself. I hate it because it deprives our republic of its just influence in the world, and enables our enemies to taunt us as hypocrites, causes the real friends of freedom to doubt our sincerity, forces so many really good men among ourselves into an open war with the very funda-mental principles of civil liberty.' "

There was a moment's thoughtful silence. Then Faunt commented: "Well, there's some truth in that. Our having slaves has lost us a lot of friends. And we all know slavery's wrong."

Streean took issue with him. "It's right economically, Faunt."

Trav, surprising them all, argued the point. "I don't believe so, Mister Streean," he declared. Enid realized that none of them ever addressed Streean less formally than this. Trav went on, faintly un-easy at having entered the discussion, yet standing to his guns: "When they had that fight in Congress last winter over the speakership, be-cause Mr. Sherman and a lot of other Republicans had endorsed Helper's book, I sent to New York for a copy and read it. It's full of statistics. You know I like figures. Of course the book is silly, violent, and—well, silly; but the figures are hard to get around." He hesitated, then went steadily on: "With free labor in the North and slave labor in the South, the North has gone ahead a lot faster than we have. We send North for just about everything we buy: clothes, furniture, car-riages, books. And even in farming, the North is way ahead of us. They grow more per acre than we do, a third more wheat, almost twice as many bushels of oats, twice as much rye, half again as much corn. The North's hay crop is worth more than all our cotton and tobacco and rice and hemp and hay put together. Their crops are worth more and their land is worth more. No, Mister Streean, slavery isn't economically sound." He added, embarrassed at his own lo-quacity: "Slavery may be a good thing in other ways—I don't know; but I do know it's not a good thing for the farmer."

Streean said angrily: "White men can't work in the heat, Trav. They can't stand the sun in the cotton fields; they get malaria, yellow fever, all sorts of diseases."

Trav shook his head. "You're mistaken, Mister Streean. I know not only white men but white women who work in the fields. I know some women who even hire out to do field work; and thousands of white men, brought down from the North, work on railroad building and construction and stand the heat better than negroes do."

Enid thought Trav was simply exasperating. "I suppose you'd like to see ladies picking cotton," she said sharply; and there was a moment's silence, Trav not replying. Then Faunt said:

"No, Mister Streean, it's not easy to defend slavery. Colonel Lee has emancipated his slaves. I've considered doing the same. If the whole South did it, we'd stand on firmer moral ground."

"Throw a billion dollars' worth of property away?" Streean spoke in angry challenge.

Trav said earnestly: "You'd enrich the South if you did. Not the planters, of course; but the whole South, yes." He hesitated. "Well, I'm getting into figures again," he said apologetically. "But you know mighty few of us own slaves. Only about twenty-five hundred men in the South have over a hundred slaves apiece. You're one of them, Brett, at the Plains; and we have about a hundred and thirty at Great Oak. But only about a third of the families in the South have any slaves at all."

"They're the families that matter!" Cinda protested.

"Well, we think so," Trav assented. "We think of ourselves as the South, but we're not. There aren't many of us. There aren't as many of us as there are of the kind of people we call white trash. And in between us and the white trash are people like the men who live around Chimneys, poor as dirt, owning no slaves, working hard, but with mighty little chance to get along." He flushed awkwardly. "And it's we slave owners who keep them so. They can't compete with us. If it weren't for the slaves, every white man in the South who doesn't own any negroes would be better off—and there are lots more of them than there are of us."

Enid thought Trav was ridiculous, till Faunt agreed with him. "We exaggerate our own importance. Maybe the real strength of the South lies in the ordinary little people. Individually they're not much, but there are so many more of them than there are of us."

"Perhaps that's the trouble, Faunt," Brett suggested. "There are so many of them they'll take charge and run things if we're not careful. That's the chief reason I mistrust Mr. Lincoln. He wants to let them."

"I know," Faunt agreed. "And of course he's wrong. Ordinary men aren't qualified to decide great questions."

Cinda said sharply: "Well, the politicians haven't been able to decide about slavery, and they've been arguing about it ever since I was a child! Ordinary men couldn't make any worse mess of things."

Streean spoke to Trav, returning to their difference. "If you think slaves are a losing proposition, why don't you sell them South?" His tone was almost a jeer. "There's a good market for them there."

Trav did not reply, but Faunt did. "We don't sell our people, Mister Streean."

Streean laughed. "Why not? Slaves are no different from any other cattle."

Faunt said mildly: "We don't feel so, Mister Streean. We don't even think of them as slaves. They're our people."

Enid recognized the rebuke and Streean may have felt it, too, for he retorted: "Names aren't things! Whatever you call them, they're still slaves." He spoke with a dry rancor. "If you want to quibble, there's mighty little legal difference between a black slave and a white married woman. She and her husband are one person—and he's the person! She can't own property, or bequeath it, without her husband's formal consent; she can't sue or be sued. If her husband whips her she can't testify against him unless he causes her permanent injury! You call them wives, and you call slaves people, but words don't change facts!"

Enid felt cold anger in them all, and Cinda said in a dry tone: "Well, Tilda, you'll have to be careful not to annoy that husband of yours, or he'll take a cowhide to you." She looked at Brett. "I'm glad you aren't a lawyer, Brett Dewain."

Brett smiled, spoke to Streean. "From the business point of view, I agree with you," he said generously. "We can't afford to free our slaves. Taking Great Oak and Belle Vue and Chimneys and the Plains, I suppose the Currain family has half a million dollars or more in—human assets. So abolition would be our ruin."

Streean nodded. "Of course. Even Abe Lincoln, the greatest fool alive, is willing to leave slavery where it is!"

Faunt said, after a moment: "I've done a lot of thinking, these last two weeks. We have to try to see things straight. What's happened, it seems to me, is that the frontier has seized political power, North and South. The Gulf States, the Cotton States, are in the saddle here, just as western backwoodsmen like this Lincoln have come to the top in the North. If there is trouble coming, it's because Northerners have been taught to believe they're better than we are, and because we've been taught to believe we're better than they are; and on both sides we're ready to fight to prove it."

His quiet words left them briefly silent. Tony turned the leaves of the book in his hand. "This fellow Lincoln's ready to fight too, you know," he said at last. "Here's something he said once, talking to us." He read: " 'Man for man, you are not better than we are, and there are not so many of you as there are of us. If we were fewer in numbers than you, I think that you would whip us; if we were equal, it would likely be a drawn battle; but being inferior in numbers, you will make nothing by attempting to master us.' "

After a moment Brett said quietly: "He's right, of course. Twenty million or so on their side; say six million on ours. No, if it comes to fighting, we'll be beaten."

Cinda urged: "But, Brett, it isn't just mathematics. You're as bad as Trav about figures. We can whip the North! They're all cowards. All they know is making money."

Brett said reasonably: "Well, even making money is largely an intelligent balancing of risks. They can beat us. That's a fact. No escaping it." And after a moment he added: "Unless we can defeat Lincoln." His voice hardened. "He's a nobody, the hedge-bred son of a squatter and of a woman nobody knows. To nominate such a man for President would be ridiculous if it weren't so damnable! He must be beaten!"

Tony said even the Republicans in Washington were doubtful of success. "And the Democrats think the Northwest will go against him."

Brett doubted this. "My correspondents in New York don't like Lincoln, but they say he'll carry the Northwest. That region holds a grudge against the South that goes back to Calhoun. He promised to improve navigation on the Mississippi if they'd help admit Texas to the Union, and they did help; but then Mr. Calhoun compromised on the Oregon question, and when President Polk vetoed the Great Lakes navigation bill Southern Congressmen helped sustain the veto. The Northwest thinks the South betrayed them."

Streean said cheerfully: "Well, we'll lick Old Abe if we can, Brett; but even if we don't, we'll hold control of Congress. Without Congress there's nothing he can do."

"Unless—if he's elected—the Gulf States secede," Brett reminded him. "If they do, their representatives in Congress will have to resign, and there goes our control."

Cinda rose rebelliously. "We're talking ourselves into a panic. I'm sick of it." She moved toward the door. Tilda like a shadow followed her, and Enid rose to go with them. As she reached the door, Faunt and Trav spoke both at once, and Faunt yielded.

"Sorry, Trav. Go on."

So in the hall outside the door Enid, wishing Trav had held his tongue, waited to hear what Faunt had been about to say. Trav, always interested in any point that involved mathematics, explained: "Why, I was just going to say that it's our slaves who give us our strength in Washington. They're counted as population, three-fifths of them. We only have about a third as many voters as the North, but figuring the negroes that way, it's just the same as if every Southerner voted twice. So we've always been strong in Congress. Eleven out of fifteen Presidents have been Southerners."

Tony remarked: "Lincoln says the same thing in one of his speeches. He claims that because slaves don't vote, they shouldn't be counted."

Faunt spoke again, in those deep strong tones that Enid had waited to hear. "We had a fight over that same question here in Virginia, in the Constitutional Convention ten years ago."

"Not on counting the slaves," Brett objected.

"It amounted to that. Western Virginia wanted representation on the basis of suffrage; and the Piedmont and the Tidewater wanted to base it not only on the number of voters but also on wealth, on taxes paid. Governor Wise was the only prominent eastern man who favored the suffrage basis. We in eastern Virginia called him a 'modern Jack Cade'; but probably his stand elected him governor."

Tony commented: "Lincoln will try to make us let the negroes vote—if he's elected."

Faunt said gravely: "I can't believe even he would want that."

But Tony stuck to his guns. "You read this book and you'll realize how dangerous he is. He's a nigger-lover, Faunt. He talks about black women in 'forced concubinage with their masters,' says they 'become mothers of mulattoes in spite of themselves.'" Enid realized that they did not know she was eavesdropping, and she started to move away, but she heard Tony's casual laugh. "I never had to force a wench. They're so willing they get to be nuisances. I used to send them off from Great Oak to Chimneys, Trav, so Mama wouldn't see too many mulatto babies around and start asking questions."

On his words a heavy silence fell, and Enid heard someone rise, and she turned to slip away and saw Cinda just descending the stairs. Enid's cheeks burned hot, and she tried to pass, to escape, and Cinda asked sharply:

"Whatever were you doing?"

Enid was so startled that she told the truth. "Listening to something, Faunt——" Then in dismay at her own words she pushed past Cinda and darted upward. From the landing she looked back and saw Cinda watching her with puzzled and uneasy eyes. She closed her door almost in panic, stood with her back against it, her breast rising and falling rapidly. Why had she said that? How much of betrayal was there in her tones?

But then her panic turned to defensive anger. Why should Cinda look at her like that? Hadn't she a right to like Faunt and to admire him if she wanted to? Everyone else liked and admired him; then so would she! Next morning when she and Trav, and Tony who would spend a dutiful day or two with his mother, were ready to depart for Great Oak, she urged Faunt to come with them. She felt Cinda's eyes upon her, and defiantly persisted. Why shouldn't she invite Faunt to Great Oak? Wasn't he Trav's brother? Wasn't Great Oak her home? Let Cinda be horrid if she chose!

Faunt would not come with them; but no matter, she would surely see him soon again.

13

Tony had enjoyed that discussion with Brett and Faunt and Trav and Streean, when because he was just come from Washington with that biography of Mr. Lincoln he held for a while the center of the stage. There was an intoxication in being listened to, in the fact that these men heard him respectfully; but that intoxication had led him too far, had betrayed him into the remark about Negro women at which the others, in unspoken reprobation, rose and left the room. He saw Streean look back at him in derisive amusement, and Tony damned Streean for grinning, and damned his own loose tongue. When in the past men thus made clear their distaste for something he had said or done, he had pretended he did not care; but at Chimneys he had tasted the respectful attention of his neighbors and liked its flavor. With Brett and Faunt and Trav he would be careful not to offend again.

He paid a brief visit to his mother at Great Oak and then returned to Richmond and spent Sunday with Brett and Cinda there before continuing on his homeward way. After dinner Brett said he must call on Mr. Daniel. "He's the new president of the Fredericksburg railroad," he explained to Tony. "I've put a good deal of Currain money into that road and I'm thinking of reducing our commitments there. I don't like keeping too many eggs in one basket, so I want to talk things over with him."

Tony proposed that he go with Brett. "I don't know anything about business, but I might learn." Brett hesitated, and Tony added almost humbly: "I'll not say anything. You needn't fear I'll embarrass you."

Brett assented, and they walked together the few blocks to Mr. Daniel's house on Eighth Street near Leigh. Tony, listening to the conversation between these two, felt like a novice admitted to the mysteries of the temple. After the first polite exchanges, Brett came at once to the point. "I'm inclined to think I have too much of an investment in your securities," he explained. "I bought some of the Ashland land around the hotel for our account when the railroad put it on sale six years ago, but I've disposed of most of that and put the money into the seven percent guaranteed stock; and I did the same thing with the 1857 debt certificates, and I already had some of the London bonds. But if all this talk means anything, if—trouble comes, the company may be in difficulties."

"If the company finds itself in difficulties, so will Virginia," Mr. Daniel suggested. "We're thoroughly sound, Mr. Dewain. Operating revenue was a hundred and sixty thousand dollars for the year ending last March. That reduced our London obligations, paid seven percent on all our stock, and left enough to make some needed improvements and to enlarge our equipment. We're laying rail from Fredericksburg to Acquia Creek, we've ten big locomotives and one four-wheeler, twenty-seven cars in good condition to carry passengers and mail, better than a hundred and sixty box cars and flats and stock cars, plenty of cash in the treasury. I don't know where you'll find a better risk."

Brett said soberly: "War would hit you hard. If Virginia were involved, your territory would be the battle ground."

"Nonsense! Who looks for war?"

"It may come," Brett replied. "This presidential campaign isn't just the beginning; it's the culmination of years of accumulated Northern aggression and Southern resentment. It has already destroyed the Democratic party. The South has compromised and yielded and sacrificed; but I doubt whether any concessions we make will satisfy the Republicans in the North. We may have to rely on procedures more stern than compromises and surrenders."

Mr. Daniel persisted. "I know. I know. The Republicans want to ruin us, and they've picked a good tool in this man Lincoln; a typical border ruffian, a nigger-lover, and a hater of all gentleness and ease and leisure. And the abolition rabble will follow him. But the banking interests in the North, the business men, won't let him go too far, even if he's elected. They have to have our cotton and they know it."

"You sound like some of my Charleston friends," Brett admitted. "They say if it comes to a fight, England and France will be on our side—if only to get our cotton. But I tell you they won't, not as long as we cling to slavery. The English are abolitionists too—in spite of the fact that their white laborers are worse off than our black ones."

"We're crying before we're hurt," Mr. Daniel argued. "The North hasn't hurt us yet, except with words. Lincoln's election would be a catastrophe, yes; but even if he is elected, Congress will tie his hands."

"I don't like waiting till we're helpless before we act." Brett shook his head. "I don't know just what I do think. My emotions get in the way of straight thinking. Politics is strange country to me. But this matter of business——"

So they returned to facts and figures, and Tony watched Brett, seeing the lines of strain and concern around his eyes. He thought Mr. Daniel was not so confident as he pretended; and when at last they walked home again, he suggested this to Brett.

Brett nodded. "Yes, that's true," he agreed. "There's been so much bitter, passionate talk, we're probably bound to come to blows. I wish more Southerners knew the North as I do, knew its power and capacities. They wouldn't be so ready to believe in our superiority. Nor so ready to hate Northerners. I suppose anyone who begins to be sure that he's a better man than his neighbor is just confessing his own ignorance; and probably it's out of ignorance and the feeling of superiority that goes with it that most wars arise."

When Tony went on his way to Chimneys he looked forward to that homecoming. His neighbors would have many questions; he had much to tell them. In the days after his return, at the mill and the store and the tavern, he found intent listeners for all he had to say; but he quickly realized that there was in these simple men none of that loud belligerence which he had heard in Richmond. Daily achieving by hard toil and careful husbandry a precarious security for themselves and their families, they dreaded change. To challenge the North over slavery, a matter in which they had no personal concern, was a folly they would avoid if they could. Tony, anxious only for their good opinion, readily learned to say the things they wished to hear, putting into words the thoughts they could not always clearly state themselves.

Here in these quiet mountain coves it was easy to forget, as summer slipped away, the distant tumult of the coming storm. He had a letter from Nell, who said Washington was full of corrupt lobbyists and quarrelling politicians and feverish social gaiety and absurd extravagance. She said one could not, without being ridiculous, appear twice in public in the same gown. Tony smiled understandingly and sent her money. He and Nell had had good years together; she had been completely reasonable about their parting, and to be generous, since Chimneys prospered, was easy. To give Nell money bestowed on him an illusion of magnanimity which he found pleasurable. In Washington he had made no move to get in touch with her, but now he began to regret this.

She wrote again in October to thank him, and she said everyone in Washington was sure, since Ohio and Indiana and Pennsylvania had gone for Lincoln, that he would be elected. "And the Southern Congressmen all say that means war. If that happens, I shall return to Richmond. My heart and my loyalty are there. Mr. Freedom hasn't sold my house, and I've written him not to do so."

Tony looked forward to seeing Nell again. She had known how to make him as happy as he had ever been anywhere except here at Chimneys. He might bring her here; might even, for the sake of appearances, marry her. The thought pleased him. If war did come, Chimneys with Nell would be a pleasant haven.

Martinston men so often asked his opinion that he took a conscientious interest in political developments. He went to the great rally of the Constitutional Union party in Salisbury, where Congressman Vance and half a dozen other outstanding men were the morning speakers, and there was a lavish dinner followed by a torchlight procession and more speeches at night. He heard over and over the accusation that such men as Yancey of Alabama and the hotheads of South Carolina were blazing the certain way to ruinous war; and with a developing instinct to take the popular side of any argument, he shouted as loudly as anyone against secession.

Brett, as the business man of the family, always reported to Trav and Faunt and Tony his decisions on matters of finance; and on the news of Lincoln's election he wrote Tony: "So now the uncertainty is over. I think there's no doubt that the Gulf States will secede. Faunt tells me Colonel Lee says secession is revolution; but most people seem to think peaceful secession will be permitted. I don't. I expect war. So I'm calling in what money we have out at interest, and making no new loans till we see more clearly what is likely to happen." Tony, reading this, decided to keep ample cash in hand for his own needs before turning over any plantation moneys to Brett. "Now that they've elected Lincoln, the Northern papers seem to be in a panic at what they've done," Brett continued. "They're all talking peace, all willing to let the South secede if she wants to; but my New York correspondents think Mr. Lincoln will never permit dissolution of the Union if he can help it, and I'm acting on that advice."

Tony thought Brett's fears were characteristic. Men of business were always cautious, and money was a timid thing. But the solid reality of Chimneys could not be touched by what old Abe Lincoln or any other man did far away. He for a while forgot that distant, angry world in the hilarious activities of the harvest season. For the corn shucking he invited all the neighborhood, and everyone came, men and their wives and their hosts of children. The crisp air was fragrant with the smell of meat cooking over the barbecue pits; there was fiery liquor, enough and to spare; every man with a horse was ready for a race; someone organized a mule race for the Negroes; and at dusk, the day's work done, a fiddle's squeak set every foot tapping. The night was half spent before the last of them departed, and Tony from the big house heard the people still singing, down in the quarter, till pale dawn.

The first hog killing was another saturnalia. Long before day Tony was waked by the glare of many fires, smoke columns glowing red in the dusk of morning; and he heard the whine of grindstones as the knives were sharpened. When he reached the scene he saw huge kettles coming to the boil on every fire; saw the last casks for the scalding being bedded slantwise in the ground; saw the heavy scraping tables ready, and the long racks where hot carcasses would hang to cool.

He and James Fiddler stood clear of the tumult, looking on. Into the pens where the troubled swine, as though scenting death, uneasily milled and grunted, sprang a dozen Negroes. They were naked to the waist, firelight gleaming on their sweating bodies, bright knives in their hands. With an indescribable dexterity they darted to and fro, working in pairs, catching an ear hold on each victim, driving home with a shrewd twist the long blade, then turning at once to new prey. The stuck pigs, their throats spouting a red fountain, ran at first in panic aimless flight, then slowed to a troubled walk, then stood in stupid bewilderment while their lives drained away; and at first their squeals rose in an ear-splitting crescendo to an intolerable peak of sound, then began to diminish and faded, faded, till the last beast expired. The reek of spilled blood was stifling in the morning air.

Before the last hog was dead, the first of them, dragged by strong hands to the scalding casks, were soused and soused again and thrown upon the tables for the scrape-scrape of the knives. No sooner was one borne away to be hung on the rack than on the tables another took its place. Kerchiefed old women thrust tubs under each hanging carcass; the splitters ripped each open; when the tubs brimmed with shining entrails, fresh tubs were brought. By full day the long racks were heavy with cooling carcasses. Small black boys went to and fro collecting bladders to be dried for Christmas; and by each fire a circle of Negroes squatted, frying pig tails on the blazing coals, thrusting spitted spare ribs into the flames, chewing crisp cracklin'. Every Negro was smeared head to foot with blood or grease; every black face grinned with voracious appetite that hours of gorging would not sate.

Tony went back to the big house, exhausted by the emotional impact of the scene, drained and shaken, vague terror beating like a pulse in his veins. How many hogs had died? Suppose they had been not swine but men? Suppose these lean Negroes, with their red knives, flame-sharp, piercing butter-soft flesh, turned to the butchery of men; yes, even of white men, men like him? He had seen the lust for killing in their gleaming eyes. This was hog-killing time, but suppose from all these years of angry talk came a man-killing time? Would men die as easily as these hogs? How many thousands? How many tens of thousands? The carcasses of these slain hogs would be devoured, but who would eat the carcasses of slain men? Rats? Yes, perhaps even hogs, grunting and gobbling across a stricken battlefield.

With the first snows of winter there was a time of leisure and a time for talk; and whenever two men came together this talk was of the North, of Lincoln and of what when he took office he would do South Carolina was moving toward secession; there was talk of a North Carolina convention to consider the matter. Among his neighbors Tony with all the eloquence he could command opposed it; and when Jacob Thompson of Mississippi, President Buchanan's Secretary of the Interior, came to Raleigh to urge secession, Tony damned the man.

He went from Raleigh to Richmond, on his way to Great Oak for Christmas, and found Vesta and Cinda alone in the house on Fifth Street. Brett and Burr were at the Plains, expected daily. Cinda said Brett was worn out with long anxieties. "He eats and sleeps and talks, but it's just the outside of him that does it. Even when he's here, I feel as though he were a thousand miles away. He never laughs any more."

Vesta said smilingly: "He laughed at the way Dolly acted when the Prince of Wales was here. Remember, Mama?"

"Oh, of course he does laugh sometimes," Cinda agreed. "And Dolly did make a perfect idiot of herself. So did most of Richmond, for that matter. The day the Prince came there was such a crowd waiting at the Broad Street station that the committee took him off to the hotel and no one saw anything of him but his white hat. Dolly had waited at Broad Street and she was furious! That tickled Brett. I was disgusted, but he thought she was cunning."

"Well, she was, sort of," Vesta urged. "You're too hard on Dolly, Mama. After all she's still a child."

"Child? She's eighteen! Old enough to know better! Tony, she devoured every word the newspapers printed, even before the Prince got here. She knew what kind of bed he slept on in Montreal, as if that was any of her business. When he went to St. Paul's on Sunday the place was mobbed."

"You went yourself, Mama," Vesta reminded her, and Tony saw Cinda color, and smiled, and Cinda retorted:

"Of course I did. I always do! But I didn't go to see him. I didn't care a fig about him! But Dolly tried to get in and couldn't and she hopped up and down in the vestibule trying to see over the heads of the people standing in front of her. And when the Prince left town, Dolly and a hundred other little fools swarmed into the rooms he had occupied looking for souvenirs. Dolly got the soap he had used, and she vows she's going to keep it always!"

Tony chuckled. "I'm not surprised Brett laughed at that!"

Vesta asked: "Did you hear the real scandal, Uncle Tony?" He had not, and she told him. Through the last decade many German folk had come to live in Richmond, and there were *turnvereins* and *volksgartens;* and some young blades suggested to the Prince that he elude the gentlemen of his suite and join them and sample the local lager.

"He had to climb out of his window on a ladder," Vesta explained, her eyes dancing. "Darrell told us he furnished the ladder, and the Prince climbed down and no one knew anything about it. But about four o'clock in the morning one of the watchmen met eight young gentlemen marching down Broad Street arm in arm and singing, and he challenged them, and each one said he was the Prince of Wales!" Tony laughed as Vesta went on: "So the watchman marched seven of them—Darrell slipped away—off to jail and locked them all up. There'd have been a fine to-do in the morning, but Darrell rushed off to wake Mr. Hunton, and they got Judge Crump out of bed, and he released the prisoners and tore that page out of the register at the jail. Darrell says the register had 'Prince of Wales', 'Prince of Wales', 'Prince of Wales', seven times!"

Cinda exclaimed: "Well, it's nothing to laugh at. Imagine what the Queen will think of us!"

"Oh, it probably did the Prince good," Tony suggested.

"Well, it certainly did Papa good," Vesta declared. "He thought it was a great joke."

Tony asked whether they had seen Trav, or Faunt. Cinda said Trav had come to Richmond for the Agricultural Fair, he and Enid. "Faunt was here at the same time. We tried to make things pleasant for Enid. Travis is a darling man, but I expect he's a pretty dull husband. We took them to hear Patti sing at Corinthian Hall, and to see Joseph Jefferson at the theatre, and she loved it."

Vesta said smilingly: "She thinks Uncle Faunt was just made and handed down, Uncle Tony."

Cinda shrugged. "Oh, Faunt and that sad look of his always fascinates women. If he weren't so levelheaded, he'd have as many girls

sighing after him as Jennings Wise!" Tony thought her tone was almost too casual, and he wondered why.

Next day Brett and Burr returned from the Plains, and Tony saw at
once that Cinda was right. Brett was changed, he seemed older, there
was a shadow in his eyes.

"South Carolina's going to secede," he told them, as soon as the first
greetings were over. "There's no doubt of that. Yet I think there's
already some drawing back from the final break. Yancey weakened at
the convention last spring; and Mr. Rhett, though he likes to be called
the Father of the Secession, was only seventh on the list of delegates
elected, and he had to withdraw from the race for governor. It was
actually a repudiation. There's a strong wave of sentiment for staying
in the Union, but the delegates are pledged to secede."

"Brett Dewain, I just can't believe it!" There was anguish and anger
too in Cinda's tone. "What has South Carolina to complain of, more
than the rest of us? Even if we're all going to make fools of ourselves,
why must she be the first?"

"She's been threatening so long, I suppose it's a habit," he suggested;
and he said to Tony: "We're great threateners, we Southerners. Governor Wise threatens that Virginia will secede and take the Government along with her, march into Washington and seize the archives
and the Treasury." His lips twisted in a mirthless fashion. "Of course
he admits Virginia might need a little help from Maryland!" And he
asked: "What do you think North Carolina will do?"

"Nothing," Tony assured him, gratified that Brett should seek his
opinion. "Secretary Thompson has been down there trying to persuade us, but he made no converts. We're conservative, Brett; not
easily blown to and fro by idle talk."

"Thompson talking secession?" Brett protested. "Why, he's still a
member of the Cabinet."

"They say he went to Raleigh with the President's knowledge and
approval."

Brett shook his head. "No man's approval would justify me to myself if I were he. Howell Cobb has resigned the Treasury. He's a
man of honor. I suppose Thompson and John Floyd have persuaded
themselves they needn't resign till their states secede."

They found Streean and Tilda, Dolly and Darrell at Great Oak before them. Mrs. Currain and Enid were worried about the baby. Henrietta's eye had never recovered from that injury last spring. It was still suppurating, swollen and inflamed.

"I declare I think she'd be all right if old April would let her alone," Enid told them. "April keeps the poor little eye smeared and poulticed with horrible messes she brews out of flax seed and calamus and ginseng and angelica and I don't know what all. She even hangs a conjuring necklace around baby's shoulders, made of bones out of a frog's skull and a snake's spine, and an alligator's tooth all strung on an eel's skin."

"Well, the doctor doesn't seem to do Hetty any good," Mrs. Currain reminded her. "And I'm sure April doesn't do her any harm. Of course, Hetty's teething now, too, and that makes her fussy."

"I know," Enid agreed. "April's waiting for one of the men to bring her a live rabbit so she can rub hot brains on Hetty's gums to soften them. I'm worn out arguing with her."

Cinda said reassuringly: "Well, dear, sometimes those old women do seem to cure people. Let's go see Henrietta. I've had sick babies myself!"

The day after they heard that South Carolina had seceded, Clayton arrived with Jenny and the children, and he said a delegation would go at once to Washington to arrange the details of the state's separation from the Union.

"If President Buchanan receives them," Brett commented, "it amounts to a recognition of South Carolina as an independent nation."

Tony watched Clayton. The young man said: "You've never believed in secession, Papa."

"No, son. No, I believe in the Union." Brett seemed to pick his words. "I suppose no one, even in the North, denies the legal right to secede; but if a state can secede, then the Union is just a bubble." He added quietly: "The North will fight, you know."

"Governor Pickens doesn't think so. He says he'll drink every drop of blood that's shed."

"That was a foolish thing for any man to say. Folly and politics are bedfellows, Clay."

"All the men down home think the same."

"I'm afraid most men have stopped thinking. That's what happens when you reach a conviction. You stop questioning it." And he added: "That's what comes of our Southern love of oratory, I suppose. When a man like Yancey is at his best, his audiences forget what he's saying in their delight in the wonderful way he says it. So we let ourselves be persuaded—and stop thinking."

Clayton's head was high. "Yes, Papa. But—well maybe I've caught it from them, but I think as they do."

Brett nodded. "I know. And I'll stand with you—and with them— if it comes to the pinch." He said gently: "But don't talk about it with Mama unless you must, Clay. She's worrying about you boys, of course."

"I know. Jenny's the same. She doesn't say so, but I can tell."

Brett touched his son's arm in a shy caress; and Tony thought it must be fine to have a son like Clayton, to share with someone close and dear your thoughts and hopes and fears. Nell was the only one who had ever, for any considerable time, released him from loneliness.

Faunt arrived last of them all, two days before Christmas. Tony, with a wistful envy, saw how warmly they welcomed him, with hand clasps and happy cries and cousinly kisses. Enid gave him the most generous kiss of all, and a hug to go with it, her cheeks pink, her eyes shining. She was a right pretty woman; but of course she would be. Nell was certainly handsome enough to have a pretty daughter. It would be pleasant to see Nell again. Tony was sure she would be glad to see him too.

At dinner that day of Faunt's coming, though Cinda and Brett tried to keep the talk in other channels, they came inevitably to speak of great events in process. Redford Streean was sure the whole South would follow South Carolina; but Faunt thought to do so would be a mistake.

"By seceding, South Carolina has lost any voice in national affairs," he pointed out. "And when Congress meets, the South will need voices —and votes—in Washington. Disunion has already ruined the Democratic party! The three Democratic candidates had among them almost a million votes more than Mr. Lincoln, so if the Southern Democrats hadn't seceded from the party they'd have beaten him! They seceded from the party and defeated themselves; and if now they secede from the Union they'll ruin themselves!"

After a moment Trav said: "I don't think you're right about the election, Faunt. I've gone over all the figures I could find, and Lincoln had a clear majority in all the states he carried, and he carried enough states to elect him. So it wasn't just the split-up of the Democrats that let him win. Even if you——"

Enid interrupted him in frank scorn. "Oh, Trav, don't be silly! Cousin Faunt's right, of course!" Her tone was so eloquent that everyone looked at her, and Tony almost chuckled. Why, the little hussy was infatuated with Faunt! In quick recollection of Cinda's tone when she spoke of Enid and Faunt in Richmond a few days before, he looked at her, and he saw that she was watching Enid. Cinda was no fool. Cinda too had seen.

14

CINDA in these days felt the tension tighten every hour like a thin, persistent ringing in her ears, scarcely audible yet never ceasing. To Brett this was first of all a business crisis which must be appraised and met, but to her the treasure at stake was not money but the sweet living flesh of her sons. Sometimes she had dreadful dreams in which all those she loved—Clayton, Burr, Julian, Brett who was dearer than her own life to her, all the fine brave men she knew, scores and scores of them—lay in a bloody heap of torn dismembered flesh. At such times she cried out in her sleep and woke and wept rackingly in Brett's assuring arms till drugged with tears she slept again.

To escape her own fears, she flung herself wholeheartedly into the Christmas gaiety at Great Oak. They had planned a surprise for Mrs. Currain, a grand new carriage built to order in Philadelphia at a cost of fifteen hundred dollars, lined with amber satin, the cushions covered with rich brocade, the lamps of silver. It had been sent on to Williamsburg and washed and furbished there, and when the carriage came grandly up the drive with old Thomas and young Tom his son in new livery on the box, they all ushered Mrs. Currain out to see it, and laughed with delight at her delight.

For this fine Christmas they were all at home, the big house full to overflowing. On Christmas Eve guests came from Williamsburg and from the plantations all around to watch the fireworks on the bluff toward the river. Then they trooped indoors for dancing; and laughter like a melody filled the air. Mrs. Currain in the great chair by the hearth, beautiful in black net with a white lace collar, watched them all with happy eyes till for a schottische Clayton bowed before her, laughed down her protests, and swept her to her feet. As they revolved around the floor, her wide skirts whirling with a hushed rustling of many petticoats, her color heightened delicately, and she smiled at this tall grandson so fondly that the others stopped to watch, their eyes stinging and their hearts filled with tender laughter. So these two danced at last alone, each intent upon the other, thrice and four times around the great hall; till Cinda, seeing a quick pulse pound in her mother's frail throat, made a sign to old Joshua and he hushed the musicians, and Clayton swept his grandmother to her chair and bowed before her and she fluttered her fan and smiled up at him and said in her clear sweet voice:

"Why, Mr. Dewain, I haven't enjoyed a turn so much in fifty years!"

The others came to cluster around her and Cinda drew Clayton aside to press his arm.

"You're a darling boy."

"She's wonderful, isn't she?"

"And so are you!" She saw Darrell Streean watching her in dry amusement from across the room, so the moment was half spoiled, but she turned her back on Darrell and clung to Clayton's arm; and when the music began again she kept him for her own.

But the memory of Darrell's derisive grin stayed festering in her thoughts, and that night she spoke of him to Brett. "Everything was perfect if it hadn't been for him. I wish he hadn't come. He watches the rest of us just to be critical, and he never says a word that isn't either sarcastic or vulgar. He's as bad as Tony."

"Tony's changed," Brett suggested. "I think Chimneys has been good for him."

She admitted that this might be true. "And he's nice to Mama," Cinda remembered. "For that I can forgive him almost anything. Brett, do you know she refuses to admit anything's wrong in the world? When I say that with South Carolina acting the way she is something terrible is bound to happen, she just says: 'Fiddlesticks! It's all a lot of talk. Great Oak will always be the same.' To her nothing else matters." She laughed in a breathless way. "She's a real comfort if you can believe her. I wish I could."

For once he gave her no word of reassurance, and his silence frightened her. In her trouble she spoke to him for the first time of Enid's infatuation. "I don't suppose she realizes it herself," she admitted, "but she's simply wild about Faunt. It sticks out all over her!"

He was astonished, and amused too. "You women! Always imagining things!"

"You men!" she retorted. "Always so blind! Brett Dewain, if Mama ever suspected, she'd throw Enid out of the house, bag and baggage."

But he told her she was making much out of nothing. "As far as that goes, every woman he meets falls in love with Faunt!" She held fast to this small crumb.

Next morning the little Negroes, children of the house servants, came to wake them with eager greedy cries of "Chris'mas gif" and to claim their rewards; and then there was family breakfast, and then the field hands and all the people, in best Sunday finery, flocked to the big house for a bounty of knives and kerchiefs and tobacco and sweets from Mrs. Currain's hands.

Afterward Mrs. Currain must display the new carriage in a round of calls, and Cinda and Tilda and Enid kept her company; but they were back in good season. The long table, when they came in to dinner, bore enough victuals for ten times their number, with a huge turkey at either end, a platter of blood-dripping breasts of wild ducks halfway down each side, a haunch of venison steaming brown, and a gigantic ham on which the flaked crust had cracked to expose the tender whiteness beneath; and there were sweet potatoes swimming in syrup and browned to a crisp on top, and mountains of white potatoes, and huge bowls of rice, and lesser bowls at strategic points filled with oyster dressing left over after the turkeys were stuffed full. Tony carved at one end, Trav at the other. Brett and Faunt were seated facing each other halfway down the big board, and the venison and the ham were their responsibilities. To the duck breasts those helped themselves who chose. There were few faltering appetites at that board, since any early refusal of an offering was sure to draw an anxious question from Mrs. Currain. "Don't you like it, Tilda?" "Enid darling, aren't you feeling well?" The gentle solicitudes were a spur to them all, and some great deeds were done that day.

The men, as husbands away from home are apt to do, made invidious comparisons. Thus Brett: "Cinda, why don't our turkeys ever have this flavor?"

Mrs. Currain beamed. "Perhaps it's because we pen them, Brett, and feed them bushels of scaly barks. I used to feed walnuts, but that does make the dark meat just a dight too hearty, it seems to me."

Or Faunt: "Even your ducks are better than any I can get on the Potomac, Mama." And Mrs. Currain said probably his ducks had been too long in salt water, or perhaps the feed for them was not of the proper sort. When Streean declared venison at home was always cooked too dry, Mrs. Currain said this haunch had been encased in dough that baked on, to be cracked off only in time to let the great haunch brown.

"And it must be brushed over with a mixture of pyroligneous acid and water, and kept just the right length of time before you cook it." The right length of time depended on the weather; four days, ten days —you had to learn by experience. A cool dry larder was essential. Moisture was bad. In wet weather meat should always be wiped once a day with a dry cloth. "And of course it must always be hung, and never laid on anything."

Enid said in a gorged tone that she could not imagine going to all that trouble; and Mrs. Currain said that the whole art of cooking lay in attention to such details. "Cleanliness, naturally," she admitted. "But constant attention before things are ready to cook and while they are cooking."

When at last the board was cleared, huge plum puddings wreathed in pale blue flame were set before Mrs. Currain and Cinda, and bountifully served. Trav smothered his with sauce, and Mrs. Currain said fondly: "I declare, Travis, you're as greedy as ever. I think you'd swim in caudle sauce if you could."

"We never had it at Chimneys," he explained. "I'm making up for what I missed."

"Oh, Enid, I must teach you to make it," Mrs. Currain exclaimed. "It's so simple really. You cut up butter in small pieces and put them in a sauce pan with a little cold water and a little flour and let it boil. Then stir in a glass of sherry. That will stop the boiling, and you must be careful it doesn't boil again. Then half a glass of brandy, and some sugar and grated lemon peel and nutmeg. That's all there is to it."

Cinda saw Enid's barely concealed impatience; and she said maliciously: "You must tell Enid how to make this plum pudding, too,

Mama! Tilda and I had to learn the recipe by heart when we were children."

Mrs. Currain did not wait for any urgency from Enid. "Well, some people don't care for this recipe," she admitted. "But I like a good rich pudding. It's a little more work than caudle sauce, Enid. You have to stone the raisins, and wash and pick over the currants, and of course mincing the suet takes time, because the pieces must be as small as you can get them." She looked at what was left of the puddings they had been served. "These are five-pound puddings," she said. "To make one I use a pound each of raisins and currants and suet and bread crumbs, and half a pound of flour. I mix the crumbs and flour and suet, and beat up six eggs in half a pint of milk and beat that into the mixture till——" She laughed. "Well, just keep beating till you're worn out. The longer the better. Then I stir in the raisins and the currants and a quarter of a pound of candied orange and lemon peel, cut very fine, and an ounce of cinnamon and half an ounce of powdered ginger, and a grated nutmeg and a very little salt. Then a glass of rum or brandy. I use brandy, and sometimes I use a big glass. Some people bake their puddings, but I boil mine for six hours, tied up in cloth. Don't tie them too tight, because they swell a little."

Brett laughed. "I know just how they feel, Mama. I'm beginning to swell a little myself."

So they rose, with appropriate groans, and the children at the side tables were too sleepy or too gorged to do more than slide out of their chairs and allow themselves to be led or carried away, and a torpor fell upon their elders; but somehow all the grownups were hungry enough for a late supper, and for some liveliness afterward. Cinda when at last she and Brett were alone thought there had been no blemish on that day, except that little Hetty was feverish and fretful. Even Darrell joined in the fun, and Mr. Streean was less unpleasant than usual.

She held fast to all this happiness; for—would they ever again have Christmas thus together? She put aside the question. Let it not be asked till it must be; let this gentle, kindly, friendly world of which she was a part endure while it could. Long after Brett was asleep beside her she heard at a distance in the quarter the people softly singing. They were too far away for her to hear the words; but she knew tune and words of old.

I wep' many tears
My heart bowed down,
Way-y-y in de King-DOM!

The last syllable came like the beat of a great drum, heavy with men's strong voices.

Wid er heavy head
An' er achin' heart
Way-y-y in de King-DOM!

That heavy beat of the great drum again, and then, softer and more softly, as though the voices were receding:

I prayed ter God
An' he tuck my part
Way-y-y in de King-DOM
Way-y-y in de King-DOM
Way-y-y in de King-g-g-g--dom!

"Pray to God and he'll take our part." She whispered the words in her heart, and so at last she fell asleep.

The days that followed were still happy ones. Dolly was as always a magnet for every young man in the neighborhood, and Burr had invited Tommy Cloyd up from Camden and Rollin Lyle from Charleston. Dolly when she heard Rollin was coming was delighted. "I thought he was real sweet at the Plains," she exclaimed. "And so brave." But his scarred face, when he arrived, offended her. "I can't help it, Aunt Cinda," she declared when Cinda chided her. "It just makes me sick to look at him." Cinda wished to remind her that for that scar she was in some degree responsible, but she held her tongue.

The two youngsters brought reports of mounting excitement in Camden and in Charleston. When Major Anderson seized Fort Sumter, in mid-December, his action had seemed to Rollin the first move toward war. "If I had had any say about it," he declared, "I'd have stormed the Fort that day." And he told Burr: "I went back to college for the short term and everyone there is ready to volunteer. Colonel Maxcy Gregg is raising a regiment, and Tommy and I are going to enlist as soon as we get home. You'd better come back with us and be with your friends."

Cinda said quickly: "Now Rollin, I won't have it, not such talk, not now!" Her heart was tight with pain, but she managed a light laugh. "Time enough for that later on. I won't have this Christmas spoiled." Yet that day and thereafter she sometimes surprised the young men in low-voiced discussion together, and knew she had only postponed what she could not avert. Their intent eyes, their stern young voices were proof enough that she could not long hold back the rising tide.

Nevertheless she compelled from them all a surface gaiety. Judge Tudor and Anne came after Christmas to visit the Judge's sister's family at Merry Hall, toward Yorktown; and Faunt brought them to Great Oak so that his family could know these old friends. Brett said to Cinda afterward:

"Speaking of Faunt's fatal charm, Cinda, little Miss Tudor fairly worships him."

"She's a dear child," Cinda agreed. "She reminds me of Jenny, quiet without being shy. Did you notice Julian? He was just simply stricken dumb; but of course he hadn't a chance! Darrell monopolized her." She added: "I wish he wouldn't. She's so—nice, and Darrell's a scamp! I've never trusted him."

"Tony's taking Darrell back to Chimneys with him," Brett reported. "Darrell gambles away every penny he can get and Mr. Streean's shut down on him long ago, so he borrows where he can. He tackled Tony, and Tony's going to take him in hand, straighten him out."

"Tony? Of all people!"

"Well, he at least understands. He's—he used to be a gambler too. And give Tony credit, Cinda. He's changed a lot. Maybe it will do Darrell good to be at Chimneys for a while."

"Chimneys didn't reform Tony," she declared. "It was getting rid of Mrs. Albion. Brett Dewain, do you suppose Enid knows the truth about her mother?"

"Now don't go getting a down on Enid. Her mother isn't her fault!"

"I know, but I was just thinking. If she does know, she must be simply scared to death we'll find out. I'm almost sorry for her—except when I'm furious with her for being such a fool about Faunt! If she makes a spectacle of herself over him, I'll scratch her eyes out!"

"Fierce!" he said, affectionately smiling; and they settled into silence; but before they slept she spoke again.

"Julian just tumbled head over heels when he saw Anne Tudor, didn't he? Standing straight as a ramrod to show off his uniform."

He laughed. "Give him time, Mrs. Dewain! You've Burr to marry off before you take Julian in hand." Her thoughts, when they spoke thus of their sons, rose like a great wave of terror that threatened to overwhelm them all. She clung to Brett, and understandingly he gentled her and soothed her, whispering: "There, sleep, sleep, sleep, my dear."

Cinda was happy presently to be at home again in Richmond. "I declare, I'm tired," she confessed to Brett. "I'm too old for such goings on." He had returned from an hour downtown to find her in her room, half-dressed, her hair loosed, drowsing on her couch. "I had June bring my shocking box—she thinks it's the devil's own magic—and took a full charge, and then she rubbed the back of my neck and I tried to sleep, but I kept thinking about our Christmas. I wonder if we'll ever have such a good time all together again."

"Of course!" He came to touch her head in caressing reassurance. "You know, Mrs. Dewain, you have a lovely suit of hair."

She pressed her cheek against his hand, speaking like a dream. "I kept thinking all the time: 'Enjoy this, Cinda Dewain! Drink deep this sweet cup! Remember every moment. These are memories to cherish always. For it's the last time, Cinda Dewain; it's the last, last time.'" And suddenly she drew him down, clung to him, weeping in his arms.

It seemed to her during the weeks that followed that their world rushed headlong toward destruction. By the end of January the Gulf States had followed South Carolina out of the Union. Virginia proposed a Washington conference to seek some compromise, but even while it convened, delegates from the Gulf States met in Montgomery, formed the Confederate States of America, and named Jefferson Davis their provisional President.

Yet this step led to no immediate clash of arms, and Cinda began to be hopeful. "Will the North just let them go on and set up their government, Brett Dewain? Isn't President Buchanan going to do anything?"

"He can't, very well. He'll be out of office so soon."

"Who elected Mr. Davis President?"

"Why, the states that have seceded. Except Texas. Her delegates didn't get to Montgomery till after the election."

"Delegates? You mean the delegates elected him, just decided by themselves?"

He nodded. "Yes, of course. This has all been managed from the top, Cinda. It isn't safe to let the ordinary, ignorant voters take a hand in settling serious matters. That's why Lincoln is dangerous, you know. He believes in letting a popular vote overturn the Supreme Court or the Constitution at any time. That would end government by law, if ignorant people could change laws whenever they chose."

Cinda nodded. That was true, of course. It would be ridiculous to let poor white trash and little farmers with a few acres of land try to tell such men as Brett Dewain, for instance, what he must do. If President Lincoln wanted that, he was not only a blackguard but a fool besides. "That old scarecrow! Brett, he's the ugliest man I've ever seen! In his pictures, at least!" She laughed suddenly. "Do you know who he looks like? A little?" He shook his head. "Like Tony!" she said. "That same bony look. But for goodness' sake don't tell Tony I said so."

Brett smiled. "I'm not likely to. Some day you'll talk yourself into trouble, Cinda."

"Oh, I'd never say it to anyone but you!"

In February Virginia elected delegates to a convention to consider joining the Confederacy; and though the delegates were by a large majority loyal to the Union, Brett was reluctantly convinced that eventually Virginia would secede. Early in March he went to Great Oak to discuss with Trav the business adjustments he was making in anticipation of that event; and when he returned, Enid came with him.

"I just had to come," she told Cinda. "Everything I own is in rags, and there's no really good sempstress at Great Oak or even in Williamsburg. Of course, if it isn't convenient, I can put up at a hotel."

Cinda assured her she was welcome, but she told Brett furiously: "You make me so mad! Letting her get around you! As if I hadn't troubles enough without her on my hands. I've a notion to give her a piece of my mind."

He chuckled at her wrath. "Don't! Keep every bit of that mind of yours. Even a piece is much too good for her."

Enid read them a letter from her mother. "Everybody in Washington is running around like a chicken with its head off," Mrs. Albion wrote. "Abe Lincoln's afraid to show his homely face. You know he's grown a beard, as if that would disguise him; and he sneaked into Washington, didn't dare come in on his special train, pulled a shawl over his head like a woman and crawled in before daylight Saturday morning and hid himself. They say he won't dare try to be inaugurated, because there are men waiting to shoot him with air rifles the minute he stands up on the platform. He's just like a scared old rat dodging around in alleys."

Before they heard this, Lincoln had taken office; nevertheless Cinda found in Mrs. Albion's letter a grain of hope. "Lincoln's being such a coward is some comfort, anyway. If the Northerners are all afraid, maybe they won't dare do anything."

But Brett did not agree. "I hear from New York that Lincoln is stubborn—like most ignorant men. He refuses to listen to any compromise on the question of slavery in the territories, and such a compromise is the only hope."

"Oh, it's all so foolish! What will he do?"

He shook his head. "I don't know. Try to hold Fort Sumter, I suppose."

"I had a letter from Louisa Longstreet today," she reported. "She says Major Longstreet has written Governor Moore of Alabama offering his services if they're needed. She says the Major thinks there'll be war."

"Where are they now?"

"Albuquerque. I suppose all soldiers hope there'll be war. After all, that's the only thing they know how to do!"

He smiled. "Don't be spiteful, Mrs. Dewain. Colonel Lee, for one, doesn't want trouble. He's done a lot to keep Virginia calm so far—in spite of fools like Roger Pryor."

"I feel as though I were walking along the top of a picket fence, with a pit a mile deep on either side. It would be almost a relief to fall off—or something."

The intolerable strain of waiting would have been for Cinda torment enough; but Enid made it worse. With a maddening persistence she spoke of Faunt, and always in such fond and tender tones that Cinda had to fight back her anger. The day came when she could endure no more. They were alone together and Enid sighed and said: "I declare, Cinda, I don't see how Cousin Faunt can stay at Belle Vue with all this excitement in Richmond. Don't you think he'll——"

So Cinda exploded. "Oh, for Heaven's sake, Enid, that's the twentieth time you've asked about Faunt! Why don't you get over being such a little fool?"

"Why, Cousin Cinda, whatever do you mean?"

"You know perfectly well what I mean! If you start making sheep's eyes at Faunt I'll box your ears. And Faunt will laugh at you! And Mama'll throw you head over heels out of Great Oak!"

"Why, Cousin Cinda, I think you're——" Enid began to whimper.

"Oh, stop snivelling and whining and pretending to be so innocent!"

"But, darling! Oh, Cinda dear, you just can't believe——"

Cinda's anger fed on her own realization that she was cruel and unreasonable. "Stop it! You make me perfectly furious!" She imitated the other's tone. " 'Cinda dear, when's Cousin Faunt coming?' 'Cinda dear, Cousin Faunt this!' 'Cinda darling, Cousin Faunt that!' I'm not your Cinda dear! I'd like to turn you over my knee, and I may do it too. You'd better pack up and go back to Great Oak! I simply can't stand having you around another minute." And when Enid wailed aloud, she said angrily: "There, there, stop that caterwauling! A little plain talk won't hurt you! Behave yourself and we'll get along, but right now you'd better go on home! I've too many other things on my mind to bother with you! Go on upstairs and wash your face! You're a sight!"

Enid wept and pleaded, but Cinda did not yield. Already ashamed of her outbreak, which she knew was provoked much more by her own anxieties than by anything Enid had done, she refused to relent, as though by standing her ground she could justify herself. If Enid had fought back, had answered anger with anger and hard words with hot rejoinders, she might have weakened; but Enid could only weep.

"Oh, you hate me! You hate me!" she sobbed. "And I've so wanted you all to love me! I've tried so hard!"

"Well, try a little harder," Cinda advised her, and added implacably: "Next time you come!"

So Enid went back to Great Oak. Not till she was gone did Cinda confess to Brett the reason for her abrupt departure. "I know it was mean of me, and I know I lost my temper; but she kept talking about Faunt till I couldn't stand it another minute, so I packed her out of the house, shipped her off home."

"Did you tell her why?" His eyes were twinkling.

"Yes, I did!"

"Good Lord, Cinda." He laughed in spite of himself. "That tongue of yours will be the ruin of both of us some day. What did she say?"

"Oh, played innocent, and said whatever did I mean, and called me Cinda dear, and began to cry and said she loved me so and—oh, I don't know! She said she'd tell Travis on me and I dared her to!" She grimaced helplessly. "The Devil was in me, I suppose! I'll make up with her some day, but I couldn't stand another minute of her. But I don't want to make a row that will upset Mama."

"Did she start off for Great Oak alone?"

"No, I sent Burr to see her safe home. But I told him to come right back. I don't want him out of my sight!" She dismissed Enid with a gesture. "Brett, let's send for Clayton and Jenny too. I want my children here with us, now that the whole world's likely to blow up any minute!"

"I'm going down to the Plains for a few days myself. Some things I want to attend to there. You might come along."

"What things?"

"Business."

"What business, Brett Dewain?"

"Well, Cinda, if war does come, the food will be scarce. I'm going to stock the Plains with enough to be sure you all have enough to eat, at least."

"Us? Where will you be, Brett Dewain?" Yet she knew the answer he must make.

"Every man will be needed, Cinda."

She pressed her hand quickly to her breast. "Queer," she said, in a low voice, "I felt my heart freeze, just then. It's turned into an icy block." He kissed her, and she said evenly: "If you're going to the Plains, so am I. I'll go wherever you go, Mr. Dewain. As long as I can."

15

BEFORE their departure a letter from James Petigru decided Brett to go first to Charleston. "That's where the explosion will come, if it must come," he told Cinda. "Mr. Petigru is a Union man and he thinks some of us ought to be there to try to hold back the hotheads." Brett, though he had never taken an active hand in politics, had the respect of everyone who knew him.

So to Charleston they went. The journey was long and wearying, the cars full of excited travellers; and there was a crowd at every stop to ask for news. At Nichols's Station where they entered South Carolina, a custom house had been established and their baggage was examined. Brett commented: "Here's one reason secession isn't practical, Cinda. Imagine a custom house everywhere a highway crosses a state line."

"You don't have to persuade me, Brett Dewain."

"I'm just trying my arguments on you."

They reached Charleston on Saturday. Brett suggested that since he would be much engaged, Cinda might wish to lodge with some of their friends; but she preferred to put up at a hotel.

"The Planters?" he asked.

"No, we'd know everyone there. When I can't be with you, I'd rather be alone. Let's stay at the Charleston. I like room to turn around, like the big rooms there."

He assented. In the hack that took them from the station through the streets full of red-faced, arguing men, and with elaborate uniforms everywhere, she closed her eyes. "I want to shut myself in," she confessed. "Play ostrich, hide my head in the sand."

Brett was at once caught up in many conversations. He met Judge Longstreet that first evening. Judge Longstreet was in his seventies, the youthful years when his *Georgia Scenes* made the whole South laugh now long behind him. For more than twenty years he had served as president of one or another Southern college, Emory and then Centenary and then the University of Mississippi and finally of South Carolina College; and since the days when nullification was an issue he had taken on the platform and in the press a leading stand in support of states' rights. He looked younger than his years, clean-shaven, with sad frowning eyes and a firm compressed mouth; and Brett found the old gentleman, who had so long preached the virtues of slavery and the wisdom of secession, now full of dismay at the imminent outbreak of the storm he had helped to raise.

"I fear I was wrong, Mr. Dewain," he admitted. "War in the abstract is one thing; but to think of those boys from the College going off to be shot to bits is horrifying. If cutting out my tongue would cancel some of the things I have said, I would gladly do it."

Brett tried to reassure the old gentleman. "Other tongues have said the same things," he remarked, "even if you had been silent." He added: "Mrs. Dewain had a letter from Major Longstreet's wife. He has offered his services."

"Yes, so he wrote me," the Judge assented. "He spoke of the sorrow his decision cost him: to turn his back on the Union, stand with his relatives." He asked: "Can you see any road to a settlement, sir? I've published a pamphlet, in effect recanting all I have said in the past; but I fear it had few readers. I urged above all that we refrain from aggression. Then at least we can enter the contest with clean hands, with no guilt upon our hearts."

"There is still some hope, yes," Brett told him. "But not if the Montgomery government lets the Confederacy plunge into war. The Confederacy is nothing yet but a name." He made an angry gesture. "No money in the treasury, no taxes levied—or likely to be. They begin by borrowing; but they have no one in the South who is even capable of engraving the bonds they purpose to put on the market. Their currency and their bonds must be manufactured in New York. There isn't a mill in the South that can make bank-note paper. Evans, Cogswell and Company here in Charleston hope to manufacture the bonds, but they have to find workmen and materials first." And he said strongly: "No sir, to set up a government requires much more than the decision to do so. It will be a long time before the Confederacy can make good their case in war. Delay is the best hope, delay and negotiations."

Longstreet agreed, and when Brett talked to Mr. Petigru, who had from the first stood staunchly for the Union, he found that Mr. Petigru was of the same opinion.

"I had some hope even the secession delegates would come to their senses in time," Brett admitted.

Mr. Petigru shook his heavy head. He was a massive man, broad of chest and thick-bodied, his hair long enough to touch his shoulders, with a wide mouth full at once of strength and gentleness and eyes that seemed to survey the world with understanding and compassion. He was Charleston's foremost citizen in spite of the fact that he held no public office; and he was a brilliant lawyer and a famous wit, but there was no jesting now in eyes or tone.

"No, Mr. Dewain," he said. "No, when the Convention met, it was already too late. This was all managed from Washington, on a plan predetermined. Time might have led to a settlement, so no time was permitted. Immediate, absolute, irrevocable secession was the program; and it was rushed through." He added grimly: "And now the program calls for war, to make reunion impossible, to prevent reconciliation and a reconstruction of the Union by far-seeing men of business like yourself."

Brett said a doubtful word. "I'm afraid our opinions have little weight today."

"That is true," the other admitted. "Yet delay may give time for a change. When a pot is at the boiling point it must either boil or cool off. It cannot be held at highest pitch forever. Simple delay is not much of a program, Mr. Dewain; yet to that we are reduced. Every day that passes without a shot being fired brings hope a little nearer."

Sunday Brett supped with Mr. Petigru and with John Manning, the former governor, at the Charleston Club. Half a dozen others were in the party, including Senator Wigfall and old Edmund Ruffin. Brett heard from them the most recent developments in the negotiations regarding Sumter. Three weeks before, Mr. Seward, speaking for President Lincoln, had promised Judge Campbell of Alabama that the Fort would be evacuated; and a fortnight later this pledge had been repeated, with apologies because its fulfillment had been delayed. As recently as yesterday, when the Secretary of State was again urged to carry out the promised evacuation, Mr. Seward replied by telegram:

Faith as to Sumter fully kept. Wait and see.

Senator Wigfall explained these things to Brett and asked his opinion. "Some of us think Mr. Seward's promises are a trick to delay our action. I know Mr. Petigru believes in delay. You're a man of sense. What is your view, Mr. Dewain?"

Brett hesitated. "You and I do not see eye to eye, Senator," he remarked. "No one questions that to secede was our right; but I believe it was also a mistake—and it may prove a costly one."

Edmund Ruffin exploded with a wrathful vehemence. "Costly? Why, sir, secession is the first step toward the creation of a great and powerful nation. The Confederacy, controlling the mouth of the Mississippi, will control the trade of its tremendous watershed. With its monopoly of cotton the Confederacy can confer prosperity upon the North and upon Europe, or deny them that prosperity at will. Our farmers, relieved from the necessity of paying the tribute to Northern industry which iniquitous tariffs now impose upon them, will go on to an undreamed-of prosperity. A glorious future——"

Senator Wigfall gently interrupted him. "Excuse me, sir. I asked Mr. Dewain to appraise the worth of Mr. Seward's promises. Let us hear him."

Brett answered with reluctant honesty. "Why, I suspect that when Mr. Seward presumes to speak for the President he mistakes his man."

Old Mr. Ruffin cried: "Absurd, sir! Mr. Seward is the *de facto* President of the United States! He will control every action of that ass the Black Republicans have set in the presidential chair."

"Politicians may think so," Brett admitted. "Even Mr. Seward may think so. But if I am well informed, Mr. Lincoln will make his own decisions. And I'm convinced he will never surrender any Union fortress."

"Exactly," Senator Wigfall cried. "You hear that, gentlemen? If we want the Fort—we must take it."

There was a murmur of agreement, but Brett spoke urgently. "I believe to take Sumter would be a mistake. If you take it, you will unite the North behind Mr. Lincoln. There's no real war party in the North today. The disposition there is to accept peaceably your peaceable secession. Mr. Lincoln will never be able to carry Congress and the North into war against you unless he can trick you into beginning hostilities."

The Senator chuckled. "I'm afraid, Mr. Dewain, you overrate this backwoods lawyer. You attribute to him a capacity for statesmanlike guile of which he is completely incapable. Abe Lincoln is a nobody, a second-rate politician with neither ability nor character." He added strongly: "But, sir, even if you are correct in thinking he wants war, I assure you that for us, too, war is necessary. I need not mince words in this company. As a loosely knit organization of independent states, the Confederacy cannot long survive. If it is to live, it must be unified by battle. Until we are bound together by blood, we will be a nation only in name."

There was a moment's silence, and Brett nodded in sombre understanding. It was not to defend slavery, not to demonstrate the right of secession, not to thwart the abolitionists, not to escape the tariff laws passed by the industrial North; it was simply and straightforwardly to set up a new nation that these men were bent.

Senator Wigfall added a further word. "This necessity was recognized when we met in Washington in January. It was faced and it was accepted, Mr. Dewain."

Brett asked curiously: "What was this meeting of which you speak, Senator?"

"Why, sir, fourteen senators from what are now the seceding states met on the night of January fifth. We decided to prompt the secession of our various states, to meet at Montgomery in February and form the Confederacy. Every step in our program was planned that night, and that program has been followed to the letter—except that we at first expected to name Mr. Hunter of Virginia as President, and would have done so if Virginia had followed us out of the Union."

Edmund Ruffin said quickly: "That is why we must now take

Sumter: to move Virginia. Without Virginia and the Border States, the Confederacy can never achieve respectable stature; but if we attack Sumter, Mr. Lincoln will call the North to arms, and Virginia and the others will unite with the Cotton States to resist coercion."

Brett for a while said no more, silently considering these several individuals. Senator Wigfall was a tall, powerful man with the muscular neck of a gladiator, his masses of black hair barely touched with gray, his square jaw and strong mouth not wholly hidden by the new beard beneath his dark mustache. His eyes were at once fierce and resolute. His passions, Brett thought, would never make him forget shrewd wisdom, never make him neglect the devious way that might most easily lead to the goal he sought. Edmund Ruffin, that spidery little old man with his lank white locks, was in stature no more than half the Texan's size; but in him there was an equal conviction of the justice of their cause—and an equal readiness to achieve by guile what force might not easily accomplish.

Mr. Petigru broke the brief silence: "You are wrong, gentlemen. My voice has little weight, yet I tell you, you are wrong. It is inconceivable that you can create here a new nation divided from the North by nothing but an imaginary line and an idea. You had the legal right to secede, but you were wrong to exercise that right. That you did so was a great misfortune. If you precipitate this conflict, you invite a terrible and tragic outcome."

After a moment the Senator spoke in courteous dissent. "Every man respects your opinion, Mr. Petigru, no matter how strongly he disagrees with you. But you are mistaken, sir. The Yankees will not fight. I know them well. They're cowardly rascals! We have ruled them ever since the founding of the Union, seating our Presidents in the White House, kicking and cuffing the Yankees like so many dogs. They're poltroons, sir!"

Brett replied: "If you begin war, sir, they will fight; and they will come against you with three or four men to your one."

"We'll find graves enough to bury as many men as they care to send," old Mr. Ruffin retorted; and Senator Wigfall said amiably:

"Pshaw, Mr. Dewain! As a man of business, you know that without our cotton, Northern industry will collapse. Cotton is king, sir. Cotton rules the world. To get our cotton, the North must yield. England

and France must become our allies, must fight on our side if we need them."

"I'd be sorry, even if you are right, Senator, to bring Englishmen to fight against our countrymen."

Edmund Ruffin banged his small fist upon his knee. "Absurd!" he cried in shrill tones. "I tell you, sir, I would rather see one of the English princes established as our monarch than live under the Lincoln government. That young prince who came to Richmond last October —I was pleased with him."

"The English will prefer to keep him to be their own king in due time," Brett suggested.

"No matter! One of his brothers would do!"

Brett felt his cheeks burn angrily, but before he could speak there was an interruption, a messenger with a telegram for Senator Wigfall. He read it; then looked around triumphantly.

"Well, here is the answer to our doubts. President Lincoln has sent formal notice to Governor Pickens that he proposes to provision Sumter." He came to his feet. "So! As for me, gentlemen, my course is determined. A bold stroke will swing Virginia and the Border States, will end their indecision. I shall telegraph President Davis, urging that we attack the Fort at once."

Quickly the group dissolved. Brett, observing that Edmund Ruffin rose with some difficulty, offered him an arm; but the old man put it aside.

"I am strong enough, sir," he said, his tones ringing. "I have an appointment with history. The Palmetto Guards have accepted me as one of them; have accorded me the honor of firing the opening gun. Till I have done that, Mr. Dewain, mine is the strength of ten thousand."

Brett said a sorrowful good night to Mr. Petigru and returned to Cinda, walking slowly through the crowded streets, hearing excited voices everywhere. He had no more hope of peace; the issue, finally, was joined. He told her what had happened.

"Oh, why are they such idiots?" she cried.

"Don't forget," he urged, "that however mistaken, these men are sincerely convinced that honor and loyalty—as well as self-interest—demand that the South insist upon its rights."

"But—being so sly, doing things in such devious ways, attacking Sumter to make the North attack us to make Virginia join the Confederacy!"

He said gravely: "Unless I'm wrong, this man Lincoln is as sincere as they—and as shrewd. He's tricked them into opening hostilities. Edmund Ruffin counts on firing the shot that will rally all the border states to join the Confederacy; but that first shot will also rally the North behind Mr. Lincoln. And with the North behind him, he will never let us go."

She nodded wretchedly. "There was a time when I'd have said we'd make him let us go, but I'm not so warlike as I was, Brett Dewain."

Next day Charleston hummed like a hive of angry bees. Tuesday, Roger Pryor arrived in town; and he too lodged at the Charleston Hotel where Brett and Cinda were staying. The Virginia Congressman had long been an avowed advocate of secession; and when the rumor of his presence spread, a great throng gathered in front of the hotel, solidly filling the street, shouting for him to show himself. He came out at last on the balcony at the mezzanine level, and standing between two of the tremendous columns just outside the window where Brett and Cinda were listening, he spoke to the intent and cheering crowd.

Virginia would be with them, he promised. "Give the old lady time! She's a little rheumatic!" He won their confident laughter. "But as sure as tomorrow's sun, once the first gun is fired, Virginia will be in the Southern Confederacy in an hour by a Shrewsbury clock!"

Cinda, when he was done and the crowd dispersed, clung to Brett's arm. "But at least, Brett Dewain, they haven't yet fired that shot. Perhaps they won't."

"They will," he said. "Roger Pryor and his like will keep the pressure on the Government. They'll have their way in the end."

Wednesday, Cinda was left long alone, and she kept her room, shutting her ears to the steady murmur of excited voices in the streets. Thursday Brett came to tell her that President Davis had directed General Beauregard to demand the surrender of the Fort. "They've sent a note to Major Anderson. He asked time to shape his reply; has till eight o'clock to yield."

"What if he doesn't?"

"Then the batteries will open." He added in a dry tone, "Old Mr. Ruffin will have his great hour."

He left her almost at once and when he returned it was to say that Major Anderson had declined to surrender. "But he says they'll be starved into it in a few days more."

"Will we wait?"

"They're demanding he fix an hour when he will yield the Fort. Colonel Chesnut and Captain Lee have gone out to him again—Roger Pryor went with them—and they have authority to act upon his reply."

"Then they can order the guns to fire?"

"If his answer does not satisfy them." He said in a wry tone: "And of course no answer Major Anderson can make will satisfy Mr. Pryor." He drew a deep breath. "The town's wild," he said. "People heard that Major Anderson must give his answer at eight o'clock, and everyone crowded down to the Battery to see the bombardment begin, climbed up on roof tops, jammed the wharves and the ships tied up alongside. I've just come from there." It was almost midnight. "They were still waiting. I suppose they won't have to wait much longer."

She wished him to stay with her, but he shook his head. "I have to be— I want to hear the word."

"Will you come back to me?"

"I'll come when I can."

But it was gray dawn before he returned, and already the town was shaken by the first thudding of the guns, and the streets were full of clamor and of outcry, the pound of running feet, the rumble of wagons, the shouts of jubilant men. When he came to their room, Cinda lay face down across the bed, her hands pressed to her ears. Without speaking he sat down beside her, and feeling the bed yield she turned and lay looking up at him.

"The guns have begun," she whispered. He nodded, and she asked quietly: "How many months, how many years, Brett Dewain, before they will be stilled?"

"God knows." He added: "Everyone is down along the Battery, watching the spectacle. Do you want to see? You could go up on the roof here."

She shook her head. "Oh no, no!" And she added wretchedly: "I know I'm absurd, as though shutting my eyes and ears could make any difference!" And she said, looking up at him, "Brett Dewain, I think you've changed already. There's something new in your eyes. Something serene. I think you're even happier." She smiled up at him. "I feel shy with you now, Mr. Dewain. As though you were a stranger by my bed. Yet a beloved stranger."

He leaned down to kiss her; and they went together to the window to watch the passers in the street below, and stood there hand in hand. All that day the distant guns beat upon their ears. The night came on with heavy rain clouds threateningly low. Brett went to buy the *Courier;* and when he finished with it she picked it up, and once she read a sentence or two aloud.

"Listen to this, Brett Dewain. 'A blow must be struck that will make the ears of every Republican fanatic tingle. We must transmit a heritage of rankling and undying hate to our children.'"

"I know," he agreed. "I read that. It's the way people are talking."

"'Undying hate,'" she echoed, half to herself. "Do we want our children to go through life burning with undying hate? Hate's a poison, Brett Dewain. What sort of world can be made with undying hate as a foundation?" He came to take her in his arms, and she pleaded: "Oh, Brett Dewain, can't you find some word to comfort me?"

"No one who's still sane can find any comfort in what's happening down the harbor, Cinda."

She nodded. "You'll stay with me, won't you?"

"Yes," he said. "Yes, there's nothing I can do. Yes, I'll stay with you."

All that night the cannonade continued. Rain for a while muted the sound, and Cinda slept and woke again at dawn. Brett was asleep. Well, let him sleep while he could. She went to stand at the window, looking along the almost empty streets; and day came, and the dawn clouds thinned and blew away, and the sun shone bright and clear.

When a few hours later the Fort surrendered, the street below their windows was full of triumphant shouting: The throng laughed and cheered as though to welcome a happy holiday.

16

FAUNT after that Christmas at Great Oak returned to Belle Vue, jealous of every hour of his absence, as though already this loved spot were slipping away from him. The plantation was nearer the Potomac than the Rappahannock, on the gently rolling plateau north of the low ridge which ran the length of the Northern Neck. Faunt had never diligently worked his land. He had no overseer and he let his people take their own way, only insisting that they raise corn and small grains sufficient to feed themselves and the horses and mules, the cattle and the hogs. This year he did no more than usual, but he sometimes rode for hours. Occasionally Anne Tudor joined him, though more often he was alone with his thoughts. From a modest height of land near the house he could see the Potomac and the sweep of field and forest in Maryland beyond, receding into the distance, broken by no hills or mountains worth the name; and through a notch in the ridge behind him he could see some high ground south of the Rappahannock. He sometimes walked to this hilltop to sit there for an hour at a time, finding peace and beauty and content.

Yet to him, through the newspapers or by the occasional report of some visitor, came the distant grumbling thunder of debate and discussion which gave warning of nearing storm. The Virginia Convention elected in February was by a count of delegates two to one against secession; yet for weeks they reached no decision. The seceding states sent emissaries to urge that Virginia withdraw from the Union; and Faunt read some of their speeches. Fulton Anderson of Mississippi, Henry Benning of Georgia, John Preston of South Carolina; the words of each fell into the same pattern. The Republican party was committed to the abolition of slavery, and now the Republicans had elected Lincoln and would control the national government. Therefore, since only by doing so could they keep their slaves, the Gulf States had seceded. Thus said each man, and each orator in turn offered Virginia the leadership of the Confederacy if she would but join the seceding states.

Mr. Benning's speech was in some passages so ridiculous that it made Faunt smile as he read. "Separation from the North," said Mr. Benning, "was the only thing that could prevent the abolition of slavery." And he went on to describe what abolition would mean: suffrage for the Negro, and therefore Negro government; inevitable white resistance to that Negro rule; a call from the Negroes to the general government for support against that white resistance; the extermination or expulsion of all Southern white men, and the forced mating of white women to Negroes; the descent of the whole South under black control into a howling wilderness. "And then," concluded Mr. Benning, the Republican North "will take possession of our territory and exterminate the blacks. Thus the end will be that the Yankees will walk our soil as sole lord, having exterminated both us and our slaves. That is what abolition in the Cotton States would be." He went on to picture the happy results of secession; the establishment of customs guards, supported by the army, along the frontier; domination not only of the North but of Europe by withholding cotton or exporting it as a reward for good behavior; separation of the North into fragments by fortifying Virginia's wedge of territory between Ohio and Pennsylvania . . .

Faunt at length ceased to find Mr. Benning's nonsense amusing. After all, the man was Georgia's accredited emissary to the Convention; he had been heard, and presumably with attention and respect. You could not laugh him aside. Dining that evening with Judge Tudor and Anne, Faunt read aloud some portions of the speech; till the Judge almost exploded.

"The man's either a fool or a scoundrel."

"I'd rather think him plain scoundrel," Faunt remarked. "Fools, if they have the gift of tongues, are much the more dangerous." He added reluctantly: "Mr. Anderson's speech, and Mr. Preston's, were respectable enough. Of course they both say their states seceded to prevent the abolition of slavery, but Mr. Anderson said something that struck me; that Northerners have been taught to believe we are inferior to them in morality and civilization. It occurs to me that we've been taught the same thing about the North."

"To be sure, to be sure," the Judge agreed. "And I'm afraid these long years of mutual recriminations and abuse have built up a tension only war can ease."

"I sometimes suspect," Faunt suggested, "that it's because we secretly know ourselves wrong that we defend ourselves so vehemently."

The other reluctantly assented. "Yes, I suppose that's true. Wrong about slavery, and wrong to secede. Yet perhaps it's as well to settle that point once and for all. As long as the right of secession is admitted, the Union can never be accepted as permanent."

Anne said surprisingly: "It's like a girl getting married and always thinking that if she doesn't like it she can go home to her mama. Till she gets over that idea, she never becomes a good wife."

Faunt smiled affectionately. "It's a pity, Judge Tudor, that we can't all see as clearly as Anne. Yet—didn't New York when she ratified the Constitution reserve the right to secede?"

"I believe so. And of course Massachusetts used secession as a threat in the Louisiana controversy, and again when Texas sought statehood."

"Will Mr. Lincoln use force against the seceding states?"

The Judge strongly shook his head. "No authority to do so rests in the executive. The Constitutional Convention expressly refused to grant it. President Buchanan, yes, and even the New York *Tribune* have admitted that there is no coercive power. Lincoln himself in his inaugural disclaimed such power. No, sir, there will be no coercion."

Faunt hoped the other was right. That Black Republican in the White House was not to be trusted. He would make himself a dictator if he could. But Congress would tie his hands. Certainly in Congress and in the North there was no readiness to follow Lincoln to war.

Yet suppose the South took arms? What then? The Convention in Richmond, under the leadership of Governor Letcher, still stood firm against secession; but against that firmness an outcry everywhere began to rise. Faunt decided to go to watch events at close range. The first week of April was steadily rainy, so he delayed; but the rains persisted till he would wait no longer. He went to the hidden chapel to make his farewells. Always before now he could say in his whispering good-bys: "I will return, my dear. I will return." But today he could not surely make this promise. In the times ahead, no man setting out upon a journey could be sure of journey's end.

He lingered, reluctant and sorrowing; and the rain beat hard and pitiless on the roof of rifted slabs above his head. But at last he returned to the house where Zeke had his horse ready. He rode through a downpour to Port Conway and ferried across the swollen river to Port Royal and took the river road to Fredericksburg. He would leave his horse there and travel on the cars to Richmond.

He had not realized the seriousness of this flood. Every little creek was out of its banks, and at Fredericksburg the raging river had wrecked the railroad bridge. Also, in the region around the head-waters of the Mattapony on the way to Richmond, the tracks were reported under water, with many lesser bridges gone; so he could only wait, a day and then another. But when the first cars started through to Richmond, he was aboard.

In Fredericksburg he had listened much and spoken little, weighing the rising clamor for secession; and on the cars he heard all around him voices truculent and boastful, cursing the laggard Convention and damning Governor Letcher for his stand. Faunt while he listened watched the passing scene outside the windows; the receding waters of the flood, the sedge and pine which overran the old fields, the impoverished farms, the occasional mansion dimly seen through screening woodlands. Tobacco was a crop that paid rich dividends, but it left exhausted lands. Like a vice, it gave brief feverish pleasure yet exacted a high price in the end.

Here before his eyes poverty now dwelt everywhere; and between the world of which he was a part, wealthy, mannered, leisurely, and the world inhabited by these wretched men and women whom he saw from the windows of the train there was a wide gulf. In his small house at Belle Vue he lived alone, surrounded by devoted servants. Even in that slack-kept establishment, if he wished to dine, fine damask and delicate china and gleaming silver were spread on the rich mahogany; the most delicious viands, the choicest wines were set before him. If he wished to read, his shelves were stocked with all the treasures of the world's literature, and every worth-while periodical of

the day lay there at hand. If he wished to ride abroad, his stables held
sleek-groomed horses; if he would drive, his carriage made by Mr.
Brewster of New York was ready for his use. He had—unless it was
the old loneliness, the heart-weariness of life without Betty and their
baby who died so long ago—no want he could not satisfy.

But how many were there in Virginia who lived thus graciously?
And suppose war came? Virginia would be the battle ground. The
storm about to break would destroy this fine world of which he and
his like were all a part, this Virginia. Anywhere in the Tidewater, in
the Piedmont, on the South Side, he could count on riding up to a
hospitable doorway and finding a welcome from old friends, or from
friends of old friends. But how many were they? In Richmond there
were thirty-five thousand people; but how many of those thousands
lived as he did, in soft and gentle ways? A hundred? Five hundred?
Hardly more. In all of Virginia how many? A thousand? Five thousand? Not many, certainly.

But how many hundreds of thousands were there of these others:
small planters with half a dozen or a dozen slaves, small farmers with
one or two? Probably no more than fifty thousand men in Virginia
owned any slaves at all. The rest were the yeoman farmers and the
teeming poor whites, crowded into wretched hovels, living narrow
lives, often hungry, often cold, unschooled, not even taught to read and
write. How many thousands were like these men and women he saw
today in the fields, in the doorways of their wretched homes, clustered
at the stations to see the cars go by? There were thousands of them,
certainly, to every individual like himself; and between the heights
where he dwelt and the gulf that was their world a deep chasm lay.

His eyes had never before been so fully open to the sordid poverty
of the countryside he knew so well. A day's ride west, in Fauquier,
and Loudoun, there were fertile valleys and thrifty farms; but here
in the Tidewater the land was worked out. Yet he had always thought
of the Tidewater as Virginia, and Virginia was the very flower of the
South. Colonel Lee had said, in a letter which Custis Lee quoted to
Faunt the other day, that if the Union were dissolved he would return
to Virginia and share her miseries. Loyal to the Union, he was loyal
first to Virginia; to this Virginia where atop a cauldron of men and

women lost in hopeless poverty and ignorance there floated a thin skimming of such men as he.

Was there any other place in the world today where so few lived richly, so many dwelt in abject poverty? Yet love for Virginia outweighed with Colonel Lee love for the Union; and in these shabby crowds at every station and here on the rattling, dingy train, packed with a gabbling throng, the aisle slippery with expectorated tobacco juice, a like love for Virginia shone in every eye, sounded in every voice. For Virginia, these men were ready to fight, quite possibly to die.

Was he as ready as they? Yes; no doubt of it. But he would be fighting to preserve the fine way of life which was the life he knew. For what would these others fight? For what gain?

Why, they had nothing to gain; but equally they had nothing to lose—no slaves, no property worth the name, no leisure, no gracious homes, nothing but their lives.

Yet they would offer their lives; no doubt of that. At Polecat Station someone in the car saw displayed a secession flag, and pointed it out, and hoarse shouts of high pride greeted the sight. Yes—they would fight—and die!

What impelled them to that self-immolation? What was this battle-madness which moved them all? He would fight with his class, with his own kind, to preserve the world he loved; but for what would these others fight? To preserve what? Why should they wish to preserve their world as it was? For them, would not any change be gain?

No, clearly not; for in war there was no gain for anyone. In war there was no victory; in war there was only universal sorrow, loss of loved ones, loss of loved things, loss, loss, loss. Surely, surely somehow the catastrophe would be averted. Almost he reassured himself.

But in Richmond newsboys met the train with extras. The bombardment of Sumter had begun!

Faunt bought one of the papers and took it with him. He put up at the Spottswood, which was still fresh and new, and went at once to his room, feeling as he always did in crowds oppressed and ill at ease. He tried to read the paper; but even the advertisements had a warlike flavor, offering for sale military manuals and textbooks and swords and guns and field glasses, and announcing the need for men of military education to serve as drill masters. The Convention had not yet acted, but clearly those first guns far away in South Carolina had set the pitch; the public mind was tuned for war.

Faunt laid the paper aside. For once he was not content to be alone. When he came down to the lobby, Jennings Wise crossed to greet him. Young Wise had returned from Paris and Berlin four years before, after a period of diplomatic service abroad; he had become an associate editor of the *Enquirer* in order to further his father's political career, and by so doing he had stepped into the bitter brawl of local politics. Many Tidewater men felt that Henry Wise had betrayed his class by supporting the demands of Western Virginia for the universal suffrage which would destroy the planter's dominance in state affairs; but his partial victory in that fight had lifted him to the Governor's chair, which he had yielded now to Governor Letcher. Jennings Wise, fighting his father's battles in the columns of the *Enquirer,* made a thousand enemies; but Faunt held for Governor Wise a high respect, and he liked the Governor's brilliant son. At once gallant—the fact that he remained a bachelor was a constant challenge to every belle in Richmond—and gentle, so that children loved him, Jennings Wise was also as ready as any bravo to receive a challenge or to send one. Any editor in the South had to be prepared to support his published utterances on the field of honor, so young Wise was not unique in this; but his encounters usually ended bloodlessly, and the fact that he himself more often than not received the enemy's fire and then withheld his own increased the love his friends felt for him. He was the complete pattern and perfection of the young Virginian, cultivated, courtly, recklessly brave, living by a high personal code, lending himself to no vices yet readily embracing the charming follies peculiar to his class.

It was inevitable that just now such a man should be afire with a happy intoxication, drunk with the certainty that war was imminent. "Father's convinced of it," he told Faunt. "I've tried to send him home—he has a bad cold, next door to pneumonia—but he won't be moved." Jennings Wise had been recently elected Captain of the Blues; and he said: "See here, sir, you'll want a share in the fun that's coming. If you join the Blues I'll promise you action."

Faunt smiled. "I haven't thought so far ahead. Where is your father? I'd like to pay my respects."

"At the Exchange," Jennings told him. "He'll be glad to see you. But don't forget the Blues when the time comes. If you wait too long we may not have room for you. A week from now we'll be off for Washington!" He laughed in audacious certainty. "Why sir, in sixty days our flag will fly over the White House. We'll establish the capital of the Confederacy there."

Faunt did not dissent. Youth would always nurse its dreams. Yet he found the former Governor as ready for battle as his son. When Faunt reached his room, a number of gentlemen were with the Governor, deep in conversation. There were some thoughtful suggestions that Virginia might still remain neutral; but Governor Wise, through spasms of coughing, brushed them aside.

"Ridiculous, gentlemen; ridiculous! Even assuming that that was our desire, here's the North on one side of us, the South on the other, like two dogs each eager to get at the other's throat. We're the fence between. Even if we wished to keep them apart, we couldn't do it. No, either Virginia will fight with Jeff Davis or she'll fight with Lincoln. That's certain!"

"Suppose she chose to fight with Lincoln?"

"Sir," the Governor retorted, his deep-set eyes blazing, "if Virginia did that I would renounce my loyalty to her—and so would every other honorable man—and offer my sword to the Confederacy."

The talk ran on, visitors came and went. Ex-President Tyler appeared; and Faunt and the others heard his opinion that the attack on Sumter would lead to the secession of Virginia.

"And Maryland, Kentucky, Tennessee, North Carolina—all will follow us," the former chief executive predicted. "But I believe that if we stand firm, no general war need ensue."

Governor Wise, his deeply cleft chin jutting defiantly, instantly dissented. He was a spare man, so lean that he seemed taller than he was; his cheeks were sunken, his skin yellow. There was no moderation in him, no halfway between right and wrong; and in private conversation or in public utterances his passionate certainties sometimes thinned his tones to an almost feminine slenderness. Those who did not know him might at such times suspect he was intoxicated; but actually cold water was his only potation, tobacco his only vice. As he spoke now the corners of his mouth were stained.

"No, sir!" he cried. "No sir, you are wrong. The North has gone too far to withdraw. They've been made drunk with abolitionist doctrine. Garrison and his like, this Black Republican clown from Illinois, *Uncle Tom,* Helper's book—sixty-eight Republican Congressmen, you remember, recommended that atrocious and bloodthirsty production to the attention of their followers—all these influences have moved them to maniacal frenzy. Whom the Gods would destroy they first make mad! The North had warning enough during the campaign that to elect this gangling Illinois ruffian would be taken as a declaration of war; but they persisted in their folly. They elected a sectional administration, the first this nation has ever seen. In ten Southern states Abe Lincoln got not a single vote!" He threw up his hands, his fists clenched. "The crime is on their heads!"

"There need not be war," President Tyler urged. "Mr. Lincoln is a self-confessed coward, skulking into Washington in disguise, delivering his inaugural from behind a hedge of bayonets. If the South presents a steady and united front, his fears will restrain him, and he will restrain his followers."

"He wants war," the Governor insisted. "When he sent a fleet to provision Sumter, it was a deliberate move to provoke us into action. Mark my word, that fleet will make no effort to relieve the Fort. They will allow Sumter to fall; and then Lincoln will call us aggressors and the North will follow him to war."

"The Northerners are not a warlike people," President Tyler urged. "In our last war with England, South Carolina alone furnished more soldiers than all New England; the South furnished almost twice as many as the whole North. In the Mexican war all New England sent only a thousand men. Lincoln will find few ready to take up the sword. Governor, you heard me say a month ago in the Convention that Virginia should present an ultimatum, demand guarantees. To do so now, in concert with our sister states, will still serve."

Faunt asked curiously: "Sir, what guarantees can protect us?"

The other turned to him. "Why, they are simple, Mr. Currain; and yet they are the minimum which we must have. This vulgarian from the barbaric West seeks to destroy us by guile and treachery; he gives us smiles and promises, and so he lulls us to sleep while he orders home the Pacific and the Mediterranean fleets to close our ports, and brings the nation's soldiers from their western duties to form hostile ranks along our borders, to encircle us, shut us off from the world, stifle us. He denies us any expansion of slave territory, hems us in our narrow land, proposes to destroy us. He will garrison Fort Washington and Fortress Monroe; and once that is done, a single armed vessel can close the James and the York and your own Rappahannock, Mr. Currain; can overnight shut us off from all commerce with the world.

"So we must demand, must insist—while negotiations are continued —upon the *status quo*; no more soldiers to Fortress Monroe, to Fort Washington, to Washington City, to Harper's Ferry. Our firm stand will hold Maryland, will win New Jersey; and I have high hopes of Pennsylvania, of New York. They are our natural allies against this slave-lover from the West. They like him no better than we. A bold, united South can win three or four of the free states; can recapture control of the Government." The old gentleman rose, afire with his own words. "We can recapture the control which the Cotton States by their impetuosity threw away. Publicly I can never criticize the course taken by South Carolina and the others; but to you gentlemen I can say that had they retained their representation in Congress, they could have prevented the appropriation of a single dollar to support Mr. Lincoln's warlike plans. They acted honorably—but not wisely.

"But we can still rule. The exchanges of the world, the clothing and commerce of the world, the wealth of the North, all these are based on cotton. Self-interest will be our ally. We need only stand firm, demand security, command respect. In their secret closets they will count the cost, foresee the bankruptcy which without the South and its cotton they inevitably face, and come humbly to seek again our friendship."

He finished, his voice ringing, and Faunt nodded, not in assent yet respectfully. But Governor Wise shook his head. "Sir, I cannot agree with you. This has gone beyond the point where Northern cupidity can restrain Northern aggression. Cotton is a weapon, yes; but here is a better one." He crossed the room to the corner where a musket with fixed bayonet leaned, and took it in his hands. "This, in the hands of the brave; this musket, this bayonet, these are worth all your cotton!"

Faunt asked: "Have we arms?"

"Enough," the Governor assured him. "John Floyd, before he resigned, sent a hundred thousand muskets from Northern armories to those in the South. But it is not the weapons which will bring victory to our cause; it is the men! Let our brave men march into the North and the rabble there will scatter like chickens before the hawk. Northerners have no taste for battle." A sudden passion rang in his shrill tones. "But what brave man waits for some magic to put a weapon in his hand? The man who will not fight unless he has a Minié or a percussion musket is a coward and a renegade. Let him get a spear, or a lance; let him take a lesson from John Brown, make his own sword or his knife from old iron or from a piece of carriage spring. If the enemy's gun outreaches his, why, let him reduce the distance between them. Meet him foot to foot with cold steel and strike home!"

There was a blaze of deadly energy in the Governor's eyes, and Faunt thought of Jennings Wise and of the many like him in the South, young men habitually ready to fight at a word or a sidelong look. Yes, Southern men would fight. It was their habit, almost their pastime. Not only men like the Governor's son but even the humblest farmer or the most miserable poor white was ready at a real or imagined affront to turn to the pistol, the knife, the gouging ring for satisfaction.

From what sprang this universal Southern readiness for deadly combat? Walking back to the Spottswood through the crowded streets he tried to understand. What was this South of which he was a part? What was its mind, its heart? Long after he was abed he lay wakeful, seeking an answer to that question. His thoughts returned to the paths they had followed earlier in the day. The aristocracy of wealth of which he was a part, an aristocracy based not so much upon birth as upon two or three or four generations of successful exploitation of land and slaves, founded by progenitors who had distinguished themselves primarily by an ability to face frontier conditions and master them; this aristocracy, acquiring leisure, had also acquired power and having acquired power and leisure and wealth it had created the gentle way of life which was his world.

But he and such as he were not the South; they were only a few individuals among millions. What was the distinctive characteristic of Southern men as a result of which the meanest one of them was ready to protect what he considered his honor with his life?

He arrived slowly at an understanding that contented him. Here was the significant fact. In the South, only slaves had masters. A man—a white man—no matter how abject his condition, rarely worked for hire. There were a few hired overseers, yes; but even they were masters of the slaves they directed. There were a few clerks, keepers of books, vendors of merchandise; yes, but they were in numbers insignificant. The South was not, like the North, a land of factories, where thousands of white men spent long days in monotonous toil and found sometimes even their homes and their scant leisure and the smallest details of their lives controlled and commanded by their employers. When such labor was needed in the tobacco factories here in Virginia, slaves were hired from their owners; yes, and treated with as much or with more consideration than the white serfs in Northern industry. The South was not a region of towns and crowded cities. There might be thirty-five thousand people in Richmond, but more than half of them were Negroes; and probably only New Orleans and Charleston in the whole South were more populous than Richmond. Faunt doubted whether any other city than these three had as many as five thousand white inhabitants. Southern men, whether wealthy or desperately poor, lived on the soil; and on their few starved acres and in their rude hovels or cabins, even the meanest of them were still their own masters. They admired and cultivated not wealth in any form but individual qualities: strength, no matter how that strength was used; courage, no matter how it was demonstrated; capacity, even though it were only the capacity to drink more fiery liquor than other men; valor, even though it were demonstrated only by follies committed without a count of consequences; dignity, even in rags. If you knew in your heart that no man could challenge you and make his challenge good, why then you were master of yourself and of the world.

And always you knew, too, that no matter how low your estate, that of the slave was lower. No man could call himself your master. You yourself were of the master race, free to claim your share of the general authority to which your white skin entitled you.

To such men servility was impossible, surrender inconceivable, defeat a ridiculous absurdity. From such men would the soldiers of the South be recruited; from men who were deeply sure that no man could overcome them. How could such men be beaten? True, you could kill them; but in no other way could you compel them to submission.

And hundreds of thousands of such Southern men were ready now to meet the North's challenge. Faunt felt in himself a high pride because of such men, whether great or humble, he was one. Before he slept he knew that he would go next day to Jennings Wise, to accept his part in that which was to come.

Faunt's decision would not at once be put into effect. When he came down to breakfast he saw, back toward him, a heavy-shouldered, slightly stooping, instantly familiar figure; and he moved to Trav's side, touched his brother's arm. Trav turned and their hands struck, and Faunt asked:

"What brought you to Richmond? Is Mama well?"

"Yes, yes." Around them excited voices sounded, and they drew a little aside to talk apart. "But Enid and I brought Hetty up. Her eye, the one Vigil hurt, is worse." Faunt heard the concern in Trav's slow tones. "We wanted Dr. Little to try if he can heal it."

"I'm grieved to hear that." Seeing the baby at Great Oak since the accident, the hurt eye always terribly inflamed and often swollen and so painful that Hetty was forever whimpering with misery, Faunt had felt a deep sorrow for her. He forgot now any thought of going today to Captain Wise. "Command me, Trav. Where is Enid?"

"In our rooms, with Baby. And we brought April." Trav smiled sadly. "We had to. The old woman seldom lets Hetty out of her arms." He added: "Enid's pretty upset. Baby seems to get worse all the time."

Faunt went with Trav to their rooms. Enid, seeing at first only Trav at the door, cried querulously: "Oh, so you're back, are you? Well, it's high time! Leaving me—" But then as she discovered Faunt, with an instant change of tone: "Oh, Cousin Faunt, it's so

good to see you! We're all just desperate! I don't know what to do!"
From the next room came the baby's fretful wails. "She's been like
that for days and days now. I hear her all night, can't sleep; and if I
doze off I hear her in my sleep." Her tears were brimming and she
came into his arms, her arms tightening around him. "Oh, do tell us
what to do?"

Faunt in her embrace felt a profound sadness. Once, long ago, he
had heard his own baby's weak and pitiful cries and found no way to
serve; once long ago Betty, her clasp almost strengthless, had thus
embraced him, bidding him goodby. Enid's terror and Trav's sober
grief made demands upon him which he sought to meet. He devoted
himself to them, summoning the doctor, listening with Trav to the
physician's protest that this baby should have been brought to him
long ago. Dr. Little said some hopeful words, but Faunt thought them
hollow and meaningless; yet when the doctor was gone and Enid appealed to him for comforting he echoed what the other had said. Let
her find hope if she could.

His concern for the baby and for Trav and Enid thrust from his
mind what went on outside this grieving room. All that day he kept
watch with them, ignoring the sounds that rose from the thronged
streets; the muffled voices of men coming sometimes as a deep undertone, sometimes as a harsh exultant shout; the scrape of passing feet
or the beat of hoofs; the whistles and the cries.

But in late afternoon, a sudden louder tumult raced toward them
like the sound of rain from a nearing shower, swelling as it neared to
rise at last in jubilant uproar. Faunt guessed the truth even before he
heard the beginning of the long reverberations of a hundred guns announcing Sumter's fall. With dusk there was a glare of bonfires
against the sky, and the hiss and silent flash of exploding rockets, and
for long hours every bell in Richmond rang in a steady clamor, so that
the sick baby whimpered and wailed, and Enid wept with her. There
was a swell of many voices from the street below their window like
the rumble of surf, and during the evening thousands of marching
feet came near the hotel and paused and raised a great shout, and for
a while the watchers in the upper room heard single voices as speakers
harangued the crowd, their words drowned again and again by a
clamor of exultant cheers, till at last the speakers were done and the

parade moved on to seek other orators at the Exchange or in Capitol Square.

Not till slow silence settled at last across the night-bound city could Faunt persuade Enid to try to sleep, making her lie down on the couch, covering her over.

"You're so sweet to me, Cousin Faunt," she whispered, yielding at last, smiling weakly up at him.

"Close your eyes," he urged. "Trav and I will be here, and we'll wake you if there's anything to do."

She did sleep at last, and so did Trav, sitting heavily in his chair, his head tipped forward. Faunt watched them both; and sure in his own mind of what the doctor expected, he sorrowed for them. In the world outside, hushed now since the first frenzy of delight had passed, there were many tragedies preparing; but for these two no tragedy would ever be as keen as this. When thousands died, the mind became blunted, no longer able to comprehend; but the death of a loved child was a little thing, inflicting pain not keen enough to bring its own anodyne and therefore fully felt, completely suffered.

Trav at last woke; and Faunt, so that Enid need not be disturbed, signed him to silence. Trav rose and beckoned him to the door, bade Faunt sleep a while. "I'm all right now. I'll stay awake," he said.

So Faunt left him; but before day Trav came to his door. Hetty seemed worse. Could Faunt summon the doctor from his bed? "She's stopped crying," Trav explained. "But—I guess she's unconscious, Faunt. Enid thinks she's asleep, but I don't think so. See if he can come."

Dr. Little's home was on Sixth Street, beyond Clay, seven or eight blocks away; but there were no hackney cabs abroad, so Faunt walked. The sleepy old Negro who answered his knock grumbled at this summons. "De doctah nigh sick abed his own self," he declared. "No bizness tuh go sky-hooting around dis time o' night!" But Dr. Little called from abovestairs and bade Faunt wait and quickly appeared. He was a frail little man; but there dwelt abounding energy in him, and Faunt had to hurry to keep pace with the other's brisk steps. He thought this headlong pace must weary the physician unnecessarily, so rather to slow him than because he expected an answer, he asked:

"Doctor, will the baby get better?"

The other laughed harshly. "You might as well ask who hit Billy Patterson! Better, in fact, because I could tell you the answer to that one. I was there—in the old Washington Tavern it was; they call it the Monument now—when Patterson made his disturbance. In fact I was one of those he overturned. I'd have done a little blood-letting on him, myself, but Alban Payne saved me the trouble, knocked him as senseless as a poled bullock." His sharp voice crackled and sputtered. "Will she get better? Why, God knows, Mr. Currain." He spoke more gently. "Yet I fear not. There appears to be an inflammation communicated from the injured eye socket to the brain. Frankly, sir, her death would be a mercy; since even if there is a recovery, the brain will doubtless suffer permanent injury." He coughed, in a wearying paroxysm. "However, we will do what we can."

There was, it proved, nothing he could do. Because next day was Sunday, the noisy celebration of Sumter's fall was not resumed; but since Hetty never regained consciousness, nothing could have disturbed her. It seemed to Faunt that the city hushed to let her pass in peace. She lived into that night, and Faunt stayed with Trav and Enid. Tomorrow the world he had known would begin to disintegrate under the stress and strain of war; but tomorrow was blotted out by the nearer fact that here in the silent room a little baby gently died.

17

FOR TILDA, these racing days when out of a precarious peace came war brought a secret satisfaction. All her life she had been forced to look upon the happiness of others, seeing them possess so many things that had never been and never would be hers; but now their world was collapsing. Now these others whom she so long had envied faced anxiety and loss and grievous pain.

It was Streean who opened her eyes to this. His marriage to Tilda had brought him a modest affluence, and though he never pretended to himself that she had any other attraction than her fortune, he had thought the bargain a good one. But in the first years of their life together, before Tilda trained herself to dissemble, he often saw in her eyes or heard in her voice surprise and shame. He was in those years vulnerable to even an unspoken criticism. Streean's father had been an honest, hard-working man who if he could neither read nor write was in that respect no different from the great majority of Virginia's yeoman farmers; and Streean's mother uncomplainingly accepted the tasks that life imposed. He might have been justly proud of them both; but he thought his father a dullard and his mother a draggled drudge; and when Tilda, who as a young woman had been warm-hearted and kind, suggested that they go to see his family, he raged at her. He had expected alliance with the Currain fortune and the Currain name to wipe out the memory of his humble origin; and when he realized that to Faunt and Trav and Brett and even to Tony he would always be an outsider, he blamed not himself but his birth. Convinced in his heart of their superiority, he still courted them; but their remote courtesy made him hate them too, and hate the people of their gentle world.

Thus now through March and early April Streean damned and doubly damned the Convention which for so long held out against secession, till Tilda said timidly:

"I didn't realize you hated the Union, Redford."

"Hell, I don't give a damn about the Union," he retorted. "I just want war! I want to see all your damned arrogant aristocrats brought low; shot, stabbed, their great houses burned, their women in rags!" There was a loosed venom in his tones, but he added with a greedy complacency: "And in war, my dear, a shrewd man can make his fortune." He spoke in vast condescension. "You see, Tilda, in normal times even high-minded men like your idol, Brett Dewain"—he had long since learned how to hurt her most keenly—"keep their heads where money is concerned. They're business men first and gentlemen afterward. But in war they forget business and think only of victory. Well, their infatuation is my opportunity. Two or three years of war will make you and me rich, my dear. Of course it will bankrupt your high-strutting family; but it will make us rich!"

She knew he meant to frighten and torment her; but actually his predictions filled her with a secret anticipation. If he were right—and no matter how thoroughly she despised him, she knew his shrewdness—war would ruin her brothers and Cinda, and people like them, from whose affectionate friendship she had always been debarred. She had, she told herself, tried to be friendly, never saying a critical or an unkind word; but no matter how she tried they set her apart, walled her in loneliness. It was because Redford was what he was that they gave her no meat save a pitying tolerance. How sweet then would be the hour when they were all brought low; how sweet to see Redford greater than them all!

So while that last week of peace sped away, she watched as eagerly as anyone for word from Charleston. When the newspapers by bulletins and by extras announced that the bombardment had begun, it was Dolly who brought home the news.

"I was at Aunt Cinda's," she explained, her eyes shining. "Burr came home and told us. He was real white and stern, and Vesta cried; but I think it's awfully exciting!" She twirled in a gay pirouette, arms outstretched, skirts flying. "Oh, Mama, what fun! What fun!"

"Why, Dolly," Tilda protested, "that's a terrible thing to say!"

"Oh, but Mama, imagine! All the men in lovely uniforms, so beautiful and brave."

"But, dear, so many of them will be hurt and killed! You musn't. talk so! When your own brother and your cousins and Uncle Faunt and Uncle Trav and Papa will all be getting shot!"

Dolly laughed at her. "Why, Mama, you old hypocrite! Papa and Darrell won't be soldiers any more than Uncle Tony will! You know that! And as for anything happening to anybody—you know perfectly well you always kind of enjoy it when people have troubles!"

"Dolly Streean!"

"Well, you do! So do I! Oh, of course I'll weep and sympathize just the way you will; but it's going to be fun, just the same!"

"Dolly, you hush!" Yet she wished to see Burr and Vesta, to spy out the secret terror in their eyes. "Let's walk over to Aunt Cinda's. I want to ask the children to Sunday dinner."

They found Vesta alone. "Burr just came home long enough to tell us the news," she explained. "Then he rushed off again." She said wistfully: "I wish Mama was here."

"There, dear, we'll take care of you," Tilda promised.

"Oh I'm all right," Vesta assured her. "But I know how wretched Mama will be. She's been dreading it so. Clayton and Burr and Papa will all be in the army; and maybe even Julian. He's sixteen. But I hope not. If Mama can just keep him at home——"

"Now, now, you don't need to worry, Vesta. Everyone says the North won't fight, and if they do we'll beat them easily. Why, by summer it will all be settled. I'm sure of that."

Dolly cried: "And it's going to be such fun, Vesta, with all the men in uniform, and parties and things all the time. I think it's terribly exciting!"

Vesta smiled ruefully. "I guess I don't want to be excited!'

"Oh, I do! I love it when everyone's so biggitty and dressed up and brave! Remember two years ago, when they unveiled Washington's statue and the cadets came from Lexington and drilled and paraded and everything. Honestly, I was so excited I nearly died! And then when they brought President Monroe's body home, and there were just thousands of soldiers everywhere. I just love soldiers! It's going to be wonderful—'specially for young ladies!"

"Well, I wish I were an old married woman, that's what I wish!" Vesta's face for a moment set in firm lines.

"But, darling!" Dolly protested. "You'd miss all the excitement! You know as well as I do, once you're married nobody ever looks at you!"

"I wouldn't mind a bit—if I were married," Vesta declared; and Tilda said in an approving tone:

"You're quite right, darling! I know I'll never be happy till Dolly marries and settles down! But she has so many beaux, I doubt if she'll ever really decide on one."

Vesta smiled. "Well, of course they don't besiege me the way they do Dolly. I'll probably end up an old maid!" And she added: "I think Burr's gone right now to ask Barbara Pierce. He's asked her often enough already; but this time I wouldn't be a bit surprised if she took him."

"If she has a grain of sense she will," Tilda agreed. "Burr's a wonderful young man."

"If she has a grain of sense she'll stay the way she is," Dolly insisted.

Vesta did not argue the point. Tilda said they must go; and when they left, Dolly insisted that they walk as far as the Capitol, and they did so. Dolly as always attracted every young man's eye, but though they bowed, or exchanged with her and with Tilda a courteous word, they quickly turned back to masculine company again. Dolly, finding herself for once almost ignored, turned pink with indignation, and it was she who suggested going home.

Long after she was abed, Tilda could still hear as a distant hoarse murmur the voice of the excited city. She woke to the hush of early morning and lay wondering what the day would bring; but she did not venture out till afternoon, when the thunder of cannon fire announced Sumter's fall. Then Dolly's eagerness swept aside her reluctance, and they hurried to join the excited throng on Franklin Street and Main and around the Capitol. The deafening cannon, the clanging of the bells, the shouts of joy and the bursts of song infected them all. Tilda shared the general madness, forgetting time and place, feeling herself no longer alone but one with all these others, intoxicated by this unaccustomed sense of oneness with the world in which all her life she had been an outsider. When a pack of small boys swept by, their shrill voices raising huzzas for Beauregard, hoorays for the Confederacy, damnation on old Abe Lincoln, she shouted as loud as any of them; till in the pack and press of the crowd she became confused and half frightened, and—for once overruling Dolly—she insisted that they all go home.

But the bells still rang in every steeple; and even indoors they could feel the pounding pulse of triumph which beat out the song of victory. Tilda's head began to ache; she went to bed, leaving Dolly watching from the windows the brightness against the night sky and listening to the steady and persistent peal of bells.

Still wide awake, Tilda turned and twisted helplessly. To be alone was frightening; she wished Redford were here, or Darrell. But Darrell was at Chimneys with Tony, and Redford had not come home last night or the night before. She had taught herself long ago to ignore his frequent absences.

She could not sleep, and after wakeful hours she rose and took a candle and went to Dolly's room. To find the bed empty and Dolly gone was terrifying; but while first panic still beset her she heard the street door open, heard Dolly's cautious: "Good night, sir, and thank you!" Candle in hand Tilda hurried to the stair head, called down into the darkness below:

"Dolly Streean, where have you been?" Then as Dolly, ascending, came into candlelight: "Oh, Dolly, how could you?"

For Dolly wore a discarded suit of Darrell's, a suit in the fashion that had appeared two or three years before. The double-breasted jacket reached just below her waist, the wide-topped trousers narrowed to the ankles. Her heavy hair was tucked into a Scotch cap; and even in this first moment of horrified disapproval Tilda thought how beautiful she was! The girl tugged off the cap, and her hair cascaded down around her shoulders, rippling richly in the candlelight. She threw it back from her face with a shake of her head and laughed at her mother's tone.

"Oh, I couldn't stay indoors with so much happening, Mama! And

I couldn't go out in hoops, now could I? So I just did the sensible thing!" She brushed past her mother into her own room, and Tilda followed her, crying reproachfully:

"But, Dolly, if anyone saw you——"

"Heavens, thousands of people saw me!"

"Did they know you, Dolly? The disgrace——"

"Now, Mama, don't worry! No one paid me the slightest attention. I kept the cap pulled down; and the coat was too big for me even across the front, and the trousers are almost as wide as hoops anyway! Oh, it was a lark, Mama! I even marched in the procession, helped carry a banner! But of course I was careful to keep away from the torches! There, darling, don't be cross! No one knew who I was!"

Tilda tried to hold a reprobating tone; but—Dolly was so beautiful, and so audacious! She herself would never thus have dared; yet she could wish she dared. Dolly's recklessness was like an emancipation for her too.

"Banners? Torches?" she echoed.

"Oh, it was wonderful, Mama! We marched and marched and sang *Dixie Land* and *The Bonnie Blue Flag* and cheered ourselves hoarse —only I didn't sing or cheer for fear someone would notice my voice. We stopped in front of the *Enquirer* office and Captain Wise made a speech for us. I think he's marvelous! He's so handsome, and so brave! He said Virginia would never allow that old Lincoln to crush her beloved sister states and that if the Convention didn't do something quickly the people would take action. He said we'd bring Governor Letcher and the other Unionists to their senses, and we all just cheered and cheered, and then we marched some more." She laughed softly. "But then the procession began to break up, and some men were passing a bottle around, and they offered it to me, and when I refused, my voice gave me away; so one of them escorted me home——"

"Who was he?"

"I don't know, but he was a gentleman, nice as he could be." And she cried: "Oh, it was such fun, Mama! I'll bet you wish you'd been there!"

"Nonsense! It was a perfectly scandalous thing to do! Goodness knows I've tried to bring you up properly——"

"Oh, Mama, you can't fool me! You're always meek as a mouse, but that's just because Papa scares you! You'd like to do all sorts of things, if you only dared!"

"Don't be absurd!"

"I love to be absurd, and bold, and do things I shouldn't!"

"Dolly Streean!"

"Well, I do! Didn't you, when you were my age? Flirt and carry on and everything? I'll bet you did! If you hadn't, you wouldn't be so prim and proper now!"

"I always behaved as a young lady should, I assure you."

Dolly said teasingly: "Really, Mama? Well, then you certainly missed a lot of fun!"

There was so much truth in this that Tilda, for once exasperated beyond control, slapped the girl sharply on the cheek. "Be still! You're a perfect little hussy! Go along to bed! I blush for you."

Dolly laughed, more amused than hurt. She drew Darrell's jacket snug around her slim waist. "It's becoming, isn't it, Mama? What a pity it was too dark for anyone to see me! Good night!" She sped away up the stairs.

"Good night!" Tilda's tone was still angry as she went out and shut the door. But alone in her room again she half smiled, pressed her hands to her cheeks. Oh, Dolly would break many a heart before she was done!

Vesta and Burr came to Sunday dinner; but soon afterward Burr excused himself, pleading an engagement. "I can guess who," Dolly told him laughingly; and when his color rose she cried: "There, I told you!" And in pretty wistfulness: "If you weren't my own cousin I'd never let her have you. I've always been desperately in love with you myself, you know!"

Burr was glad to escape, and Tilda said: "There, Dolly, it's too bad to tease him." And to Vesta: "He's really serious, isn't he?"

"Barbara's said she'll marry him," Vesta assented. "He told me this morning." She added: "That is, she says she will if he's going to war, and of course he is, if Virginia does."

"I'm sure Miss Pierce is very sweet," Tilda suggested. "But won't Cinda wish Burr hadn't committed himself without consulting her?"

Vesta smiled. "Oh, Mama'd never interfere. Besides, she likes Barbara."

"I think Barbara's an idiot, all the same," Dolly declared. "I certainly don't intend to go and get married for a long, long time."

Richmond was quiet all that Sunday. Next morning before Tilda was downstairs, Faunt came to seek her. She noticed, before he spoke, his sombre eyes.

"Why, Faunt," she cried, "I didn't know you were in Richmond. When did you come?"

"A day or two ago." She thought he seemed uncertain, as though he had lost count of time. "Tilda," he said, "Enid and Trav are at the Spottswood, and—Enid needs you. Hetty died this morning."

"Hetty? Oh how terrible! Whatever happened?"

"Her eye, the one Vigil injured, became inflamed. They brought her up to see Dr. Little. I happened to meet Trav. I've been with them ever since."

"But why didn't they come straight here? They should at least have sent for me!" Tilda felt herself wronged. Always, by these others, she was excluded.

"I don't think any of us thought of anything but the baby," Faunt explained. "But now—Hetty died just before day—Enid's grieving so terribly, and Trav can't comfort her. I thought if you could come to her, another woman——"

"Of course I will! Poor dear, alone with no one but you men!"

So she was with Enid all that day, and even Trav was excluded from their company. Tilda found in those long hours an exciting satisfaction, for Enid in her grief loosed her tongue from every bond. She blamed Trav completely for the baby's death. "I'll never forgive him, never!" she cried over and over. "I hate him, hate him, hate him!"

"Now, now, dear," Tilda dutifully urged. "You mustn't talk so. You're beside yourself."

"I'm not!" Enid insisted. "I mean it, every word!"

"My dear, my dear!"

"It's true! It was Trav made me bring Vigil from Chimneys, and he always stood up for her. I daren't think why! I can't let myself think why!" Tilda almost laughed. What an idiot Enid was to suggest such a thing of Trav! "I didn't ever want her in the house, but Trav was bound to have his way; and then when she jabbed poor Hetty's eye out, he stuck up for her against me! Oh I hate him, Tilda! Even if he is your brother! I could just simply kill him! If Faunt hadn't been here, I don't know what I'd have done!"

"Now Enid, you mustn't talk so! Trav doesn't mean any harm, darling!"

"Well, why can't he be like Faunt then?"

"You like Faunt, don't you?" Tilda's greedy interest quickened.

"Oh yes, yes I do! He's so gentle and kind! He's like you, Tilda; always so friendly! Cinda's hard and mean and cruel; but you and Faunt are so nice to me! I wish I'd never seen Trav! I certainly wish I'd never married him. I only flirted with him to spite Mama. She was after him herself and I thought it would be fun to take him away from her, but I wish I'd died first!"

Tilda would never forget these revelations. "Your mother's in Washington, isn't she?" Provoking Enid to say more.

"Yes, but she won't stay there if we have a war. We will, won't we, Tilda? I heard the guns and the bells. I hope Trav gets killed! But he won't fight! He'd rather stay at Great Oak and be a farmer. That's what he'll do!"

"Mr. Streean was acquainted with your mother when she lived here." Enid's tongue was loose today; Tilda wished to keep it rattling. "He thought her so attractive."

"Oh, all the men like Mama. Trav was crazy about her, and Tony——"

Enid caught herself, but Tilda understood. She knew well enough the truth about Mrs. Albion and Tony. Streean delighted in taunting her about her brothers, and Tony was an easy target. So Tilda knew the truth, and it had always amused her to think of Tony—so tall and lank—playing the amorous gallant to Mrs. Albion.

But till Enid now caught herself in mid-sentence Tilda had not been sure that Enid too knew the truth about her mother. That was worth remembering; it put a weapon in her hand which she might some day wish to use.

"I'm sure she's charming," she said innocently. "I've always wanted to meet her." She spoke of Trav again, skillfully fanning Enid's wrath; so that when Trav presently returned, Enid at sight of him cried out as though in pain and turned her face away. Tilda led him into the other room.

"You must leave Enid alone, Trav," she urged, watching the hurt in his eyes. "The poor little thing is beside herself. She blames you, I'm afraid; but of course, she doesn't know what she's saying. She'll be all right again in time; just let her be alone."

He said he had made arrangements for their return to Great Oak. "Maybe you can come with us," he suggested. "You'd be company for Enid, and it's going to be hard for Mama too."

"Oh, I can't, Trav." Then on sudden secret thought: "But Faunt could go. Where is he?"

"He's with the Governor and Governor Wise and President Tyler and some other gentlemen." Trav added: "Lincoln has called on Virginia to furnish three regiments to help recapture Sumter."

The sudden hardness in his tone caught her ear and puzzled her. "You mean Faunt's—helping them, or something?"

"He was with Governor Wise when Governor Letcher sent for Wise to help write the answer, and Wise asked Faunt's company."

"You act mad about something."

Trav's color rose; he said slowly: "Well—I suppose I am. As mad as I ever get. That blackguard in Washington asking us to fight against our sister states! If they want to secede, he has no right to stop them. If he thinks Virginia will help him——"

"It's funny to see you so upset. You're always so calm."

"Well, I've tried to be. I was for Virginia staying in the Union, but not now. There isn't a Union man left in Virginia now."

"Just because President Lincoln wants us to take sides?"

"He might as well ask me to horsewhip Enid, or you, or Cinda!" He laughed angrily. "I don't suppose that white trash even realizes he's insulted us!"

She felt a delicious excitement. "What will we do?"

"Secede. Join the Confederacy."

"Fight? I can't imagine you being a soldier.

He grinned faintly. "Neither can I. But there'll be lots to do besides fight. I can help." He added, remembering: "But I'll have to take Enid back to Great Oak first. Can you get her quieted down before we start?"

She promised to try, bidding him leave her alone with Enid for an hour. When he returned, Faunt came with him; and as they entered, Faunt was speaking, finishing something he had been saying as they came along the hall.

"—and even today at the very moment when the Governor was deciding we must fight the North, we were sitting in chairs made in the North, around a table made in the North, with our feet on a carpet made in the North. Governor Letcher wrote his answer to Lincoln with a Northern pen, in Northern ink, on Northern paper. The very paintings on the wall were done by Northern artists, and there was Northern coal in the grate and Northern fire irons on the hearth. Everything except our food comes from the North. What weapons we have were made in the North. Northern men run our railroads, work our telegraph, make our cannon. Trav, we start with empty hands."

"I know," Trav agreed. "But it's too late to think of that now. We've got to go ahead." He asked Tilda: "Is Enid asleep?"

"Yes." Tilda hid gleeful relish behind a sympathetic tone. "But Trav, she says she simply won't go back to Great Oak with you alone. I've talked and talked to her. I can't go, but she says she'll go if Faunt goes with you."

Trav looked uncertainly at his brother. "What do you think, Faunt? Can you spare a day or two?" Faunt seemed to hesitate; and Trav said humbly: "I don't know much about handling women. She might have hysterics or something, but if you're along——"

So Faunt assented. He suggested that since they would be all day on the road their departure might be delayed until morning, and Trav agreed to this. Tilda stayed that night with Enid, and Enid forgot her grief in the prospect of having Faunt near her.

"I shall persuade him to stay at Great Oak a while," she declared. "Till I can face life again."

Tilda wished she could go with them, to watch Enid and Faunt together. What a fine tumult it would make if Enid brought these two brothers to be enemies! If Trav were once aroused, what would he do?

18

OF THE Currain men, Tony was the first to put on a uniform; yet he would have said that for him to turn soldier was beyond all possibility. Since his neighbors were outspoken against secession, and because he relished the respect they had accorded him, he had taken their opinion as his own and stood for adherence to the Union. It had not occurred to him that war has an alchemy of its own; that the very men who most love peace may become, when the issue can no longer be evaded, first in war.

It was almost two years since he had come to Chimneys, and here Tony had been happier than ever before. He was the great man of the locality, accepted by his neighbors not only as a successful planter, but as one acquainted with public affairs, whose least word deserved attention. Like a drunkard become abstinent, he wished others to perceive the new virtue in him; and it was not any desire for the young man's companionship but some faint thought of impressing Darrell with his new-found importance which led him to invite the other to Chimneys.

Darrell readily accepted. "If I vanish for a while, it will give my creditors time to give up hope of collecting what I owe them." At Chimneys he delighted in the novelties of rural life. When a caravan of covered wagons set out to carry farm produce to some distant market, he went along, enjoying the nights in camp beside the road, the clannish spirit which knit the country folk in close alliance against the townsmen, the leisurely homeward journey when the vehicles were laden with molasses, sugar, coffee, spirits. He watched with a lively interest the preparations to roll Tony's tobacco crop to market.

Through the great casks a wooden spike was driven from end to end
to make an axle, and a split sapling served as shafts. A box nailed
across these shafts carried bedding and provision for the journey; and
a mule and an ox were hitched tandem to roll the squeaking and protesting casks laboriously along the muddy highways to the nearest
plank road and so to their destination. Darrell went on 'possum hunts
with the Negroes, who came home with their prey, caught alive after
the tree in which they took refuge from the hounds had been felled,
dangling like furry balls from a long split pole in which their tails
were pinched to hold them fast. He followed the Negroes and their
hounds as they ran rabbits till the little creatures took refuge in some
hollow log from which, kicking and sometimes screaming with terror
and pain, they were dragged out at the end of a forked stick twisted
into their soft hides. He hunted the wild hogs, tall, thin, hairy, snake-
headed, ferocious if they were brought to bay; he relished the hilarity
of log rollings and looked forward to the pig stickings and the corn
huskings in the fall.

This life was completely different from any he had known; but he
might have tired of it except for two things. For one, when in the
evenings they were alone, he and Tony regularly turned to cards.
Tony was a poor gambler. Darrell liked to win, and he had learned
long ago that to cheat a little now and then was not difficult. But he
was tactful, steadily praising Tony's play, approving his sagacity,
sympathizing with his ill fortune. "If the luck ever ran for you, I'd
not have a chance. Some day it will." Tony lost steadily; so Darrell
found his stay here highly profitable.

And another circumstance spiced his life here. One day in Martinston Tony introduced him to Miss Mary Meynell, Judge Meynell's
daughter. She was seventeen, an only child; and except for the rare
occasions when she had gone journeying with her father or her
mother, Martinston was the only world she knew. To her, Darrell
was a figure from another world. She listened to his talk with her
father and Tony; and she learned to know by heart his every intonation, the way he smiled, the fine lift of his head. His half-quizzical
deference filled her with delicious, frightening dreams; his easy compliments made her cheeks bright with happiness. Tony, always ready
to embrace a delusion, thought Darrell might marry her and settle

down at Chimneys and succeed in due time to the position he had himself achieved. When Darrell's devotion became so manifest that it could no longer go unremarked, he suggested this; and Darrell, though his eyes twinkled, did not deny it.

"It might happen," he asserted. "It might turn out so. But I've little to offer any girl, Uncle Tony. Judge Meynell would never consent."

"You've a great deal to offer," Tony assured him. "After all, Darrell, you're a Currain on your mother's side." Darrell smiled, and Tony added hurriedly, "I mean no aspersion on your father, but naturally we Currains have a certain pride of family; and aside from the question of family, I shan't stay at Chimneys always. It can one day be yours."

"It's rather outside the world," Darrell dryly commented.

"There's talk of a railroad to link Danville and Greensboro. That will shorten the trip to Richmond."

"Well, to be sure—" Darrell chuckled lightly. "Chimneys would not be unattractive if Miss Mary shared it."

Tony was pleased with this possibility. He even discussed it with Miss Mary's father, and found Judge Meynell as pleased as he. "Darrell seems a fine young man," the Judge agreed. "Of course, in these troubled times, no one can see very far into the future; yet it is in just such uncertain hours that young hearts turn to other young hearts most hungrily."

"Has Darrell said anything to you?"

"Not yet, though I have begun to expect it. Of course Miss Mary herself will make the decision; but I shall put no obstacle in the way."

North Carolina in February voted against calling a convention to consider the state's relationship with the Union; and to Tony this seemed to determine the state's future course. But on a Sunday in March when Darrell after dinner had ridden away to town, and Tony was lying down, Pegleg Joseph came knocking at his door. "Some gemmen tuh see you, suh."

"Eh?" Tony had been half asleep. "What's that?" Joseph repeated his message. "Who is it, man?"

"Dey's Judge Meynell, and Mistuh Lowman, and Mistuh Blandy and some othehs. Mistuh Darrell done come back wid 'em, suh."

Tony, in puzzled surprise, descended to find the group waiting on the veranda. Besides Judge Meynell and the postmaster from Martinston, Tom Shadd and Lonn Tyler and Ed Blandy were in the group. "Well, gentlemen?" Tony said inquiringly.

Judge Meynell cleared his throat. "Mr. Currain," he began, and then hesitated and looked at Ed Blandy and asked: "Will you read him Major Hill's letter, Mr. Blandy?"

Ed fumbled in his pocket. "Maybe you'd better read it, Judge."

Judge Meynell nodded and took the letter and unfolded it. "I think you know Major Hill, Mr. Currain," he suggested. "He's head of the North Carolina Military Institute at Charlotte."

"I haven't that honor," Tony admitted. "But I know my brother thinks highly of him."

"He and Mr. Blandy are old friends," Judge Meynell explained. "This letter came from him yesterday." He cleared his throat and began:

"'Dear Mr. Blandy—Do you remember the problems I used to set you; those mathematical puzzles in which it was always the Yankee who was the poltroon or the knave? If ten abolitionists conspire to shelter a runaway slave, and the Southerner who owns the negro overtakes them and thrashes two abolitionists, how many run away?'"

The Judge looked at Tony. "Major Hill and Mr. Blandy and your brother had a common interest in mathematics, I believe," he said, and read on:

"'We've a more important problem to which we must find an answer now. If Abe Lincoln says twenty times that he will not provision Sumter nor seek to hold it, and then tries to do so—as he will— how many lies has he told? When South Carolina seizes Sumter, this famous liar, like a dog with a can tied to his tail, will howl that we've attacked the North, will move to war against the Gulf States; and when that happens, North Carolina will not stand idly by. Having done our utmost to keep the peace, we will also do our utmost in war. As an old soldier, I expect to draw my sword. I would wish to have such men as you by my side. Can you not organize in your community a company? If you can, make haste. The time is short. The Yankees are dullards at arithmetic, but we will soon show them some examples in subtraction.'"

The Judge slowly refolded the letter, cleared his throat again. His gravity awoke a flutter of panic in Tony. He drew out his knife, cut a bit of tobacco, put it in his mouth. Judge Meynell, as though for permission to proceed, looked to the silent listeners before he continued.

"Sir," he said, "Major Hill's judgment may be trusted. It seems likely that within the month we will be at war."

Tony saw Darrell at one side, leaning against the railing, watching with a sardonic amusement; but these others wore solemn countenances. Judge Meynell was a fat little man with that excessive dignity which small men so often assume; Chelmsford Lowman's Adam's apple worked in his lean neck as he swallowed nervously; Ed Blandy and Tom Shadd stood shoulder to shoulder. They were steady men, as like as brothers. In that moment's silence that fell on the Judge's words the others stirred and then were still; but Lonn Tyler drawled an affirmation.

"We've made our brags. Looks like we'll have to back 'em."

Tony felt that he must speak. "But, gentlemen, we North Carolinians have stood for a peaceful settlement."

"That's true, and it is to our eternal honor," Judge Meynell assented. "But if Lincoln aims to choose his own time and make war upon the South, we must be prepared to act." He paused, and after a moment went on. "Mr. Blandy brought that letter to me. Yesterday and the day before we found almost a hundred men who will join us. This morning in Martinston we had a meeting." He cleared his throat impressively. "At that meeting, sir, relying on your loyalty and your valor, the company by unanimous vote elected you captain. We are come to receive, Captain Currain, your first orders to your men."

Tony set his teeth on that comforting morsel of tobacco, shaken by something that was half terror, half pride. He was no man of violence; he knew that well! More than once in his life he had heard from other men remarks meant to affront, and had taken refuge in a pretense that he did not hear. The knowledge of his own timorousness was in him now; the certainty that in any warlike crisis he would flinch and fail.

Yet—they were waiting for his assent. These men who knew him only at his best, these men respected him. They had chosen him now for leadership. Almost their belief in him made him believe in himself; almost, yet not quite. In another moment he would have found some word of negation; but he saw Darrell, watching him, smile and turn aside. Many men in Tony's lifetime had thus turned their backs on him in silent scorn. If he refused, so now would these men here.

By the Almighty, he would not refuse! After all, he was a Currain! He tried to speak, and choked and tried again, mumbling uncertainly, then finding words and gaining confidence from them.

"I beg you will pardon my hesitation. This great honor. This surprise. I am an old man, gentlemen. You could find a better leader. You yourself, Judge Meynell. You, Mr. Lowman. You, Mr. Blandy. I am the oldest of you all, my health uncertain." For any evasion it was Tony's long habit to offer ill health as an excuse; the word was automatic now. Yet he desired no excuse, not with Darrell listening. He spoke hurriedly, suddenly afraid they would take advantage of his reluctance. "Yet, gentlemen, if we must fight, why, then every brave man will do his utmost. Such as I am, I accept!"

He had a moment, even then, of terror. He wished he could recall the irrevocable word; but his assent brought them pressing around him, clasping his hand, thanking him as warmly as though already he had led them to glorious victory. So his fears faded. Why, this was like something out of his sweet dreams; this unsought eminence, this trust, this freely proffered loyalty! He stepped easily into the part he must hereafter play.

They stayed for some talk, of weapons, of uniforms, of all the steps which by way of preparation must now be taken. When they were gone and he and Darrell were alone Tony was still supported by pride; but Darrell, as the others rode down the hill and disappeared, said mockingly:

"Well, Captain Currain, you've had a taste of military glory. Do you find it heady wine?"

"I'll do the best I can." Tony spoke in honest humility.

"I'm sure you will."

Darrell's drawl was all derision; but Tony desperately wanted reassurance. "You know me better than the others, Darrell. Probably Faunt or Trav or Brett would doubt my fitness for this work."

"Oh surely not, Uncle Tony." The words were overly unctuous, but Tony took them at face value.

"Thank you, Darrell. If you think I can do my duty ... After all, I can face a bullet as easily as any man." He tried to laugh. "I won't say I can shoot as straight; but there will be good marksmen behind me."

"Then you'd best not get too far out front."

Tony tried to smile at the poor jest. "You'll join us, I hope. We'll need young men like you!"

Darrell shook his head. "Not I."

"Oh come now, every brave man—" Tony was suddenly deeply anxious to bind Darrell to his side. There was a cold audacity in the other which he secretly envied and admired. Darrell before he was eighteen had called out his man and downed him with a bullet in the shoulder; his encounters were almost as numerous as those of Jennings Wise—though not so harmless. He was a deadly marksman with pistol or rifle, a fine horseman. As a soldier he would be a host in himself. "Every brave man will be needed," Tony repeated. "I'm an old fellow, Darrell." There was clumsy affection in his tone. "I'll do the best I can; but I'll need men like you beside me."

Darrell smiled: "Sorry, Uncle. I'll never make a soldier. I'm no hero."

"You've met your man often enough!"

The other laughed. "I don't mind one man shooting at me, but I've no desire to face the bullets of a regiment!"

"You don't mean that seriously!"

"Oh, yes, I do."

Tony had been till now so lost in his own problem that he had closed his mind to the implications in the other's attitude; but now, striking like lightning through the confusion that beset him, came the almost incredible thought that Darrell was afraid! He himself had been afraid a while ago; he was, if he let himself face facts, frightened now. But he had thought himself alone in this secret cowardice. Even the suspicion that Darrell was a craven gave him sudden courage. He felt himself a Paladin, spoke in sharp contempt.

"Indeed! I had thought you were half Currain; but apparently you're Streean through and through!"

Darrell swung sharply toward him; and Tony, facing the other's coldly blazing eyes, for an instant regretted his word. But after a silent moment the young man grinned.

"Hard names break no bones!" he said lightly. "And I wouldn't want to call my brave Uncle Tony Currain to account! Even though he has proved himself a fool!"

Tony, emboldened by impunity, spoke with heavy dignity. "Since that is your opinion, you will no doubt be leaving Chimneys." As though he were a bystander he approved his own tone, his bearing, his stern words.

"At once," Darrell smilingly assured him. "Within the hour."

Tony hesitated, abruptly unwilling to be left alone. "It's late. Tomorrow will serve." Perhaps he could still make peace with the boy.

But Darrell shook his head. "At once," he repeated. "I've a neglected bit of business in Martinston to which I must attend." Tony thought of Miss Mary Meynell. Probably Darrell would go to say good-by. "I'll lodge at the tavern there. So, Uncle, you brave man, I bid you a fond good day!"

When Darrell was gone Tony thought the great house was intolerably empty and silent. Even Joseph, bringing his supper, seemed to make less noise than usual, and when Tony had finished eating, the quiet was like the silence of a forest filled with watching eyes of wild things. There was no murmur of voices in the kitchen, no sound of singing from the quarter behind the hill. He dared not go to bed, to the loneliness that awaited him there, so he sat a while on the veranda with his fears, hating Darrell because the young man's unconcealed amusement at his predicament today had goaded him into this folly, and hating that other man, that Lincoln, whose malignant schemings were at the root of all this turmoil. From fear and hating he passed to self-pity, and suddenly, like an erring little boy awaiting punishment, he wished Nell Albion were here. She would know how to cheer him, to reassure him, to give him again that sense of power and of capacity which had been so sweet this afternoon. He had had within the week a letter from her, announcing her imminent return to Richmond. Perhaps she was in Richmond even now.

Tony's thoughts dwelt on her; he remembered little forgotten things, intimate and warm and exciting. He stirred in his chair, and fires long smouldering awoke in him. Why, he had been a fool to let her go!

She could when she chose surrender herself as lavishly as a nigger—
though not because she loved him, to be sure; there had never been
that pretense between them. No, it was simply that she was at such
moments completely physical, as readily and gratefully compliant as an
animal. His pulse was a slow pounding in his throat; saliva filled his
mouth so that he swallowed again and again. The night breeze touching his cheek was like her hot fingers, burning. He rose with a fierce
surging movement, strode to and fro, paused, looked off into the night,
went lightly down the wide steps and slipped away through the darkness to the quarter. In the great iron fire troughs down the middle of
the street between the huts stale embers sent up heavy smoke. He kept
himself hidden in heavy shadow, his hands clasping and unclasping,
nails biting palms. In one of the shut and shuttered cabins a dog
barked, and a sleepy voice shouted for silence, and Tony heard the
thump of a thrown stick of lightwood and a dog's yelp of pain; and
then quiet came again. He moved furtively away, remembering this
wench and that one, slim dark girls rolling their eyes at him as he
rode by, whom he had seen and ignored. Well, he was paying for that
blindness now! There must be a dozen who would gladly serve if he
knew where to find them.

He went sullenly back to the house, to his brandy—and to rebellious
decision. Tomorrow he would recant, would refuse this command
they offered him, make some excuse. Damn the excuses! Let them
think of him what they wished! He would not, could not go off to
war, to battle, to death! At whatever cost he would be free.

But in the morning Ed Blandy rode up to escort him to Martinston
for a muster and a drill, and he could not shame himself in Ed's eyes;
and thereafter, caught in the hurry and stir of many preparations, he
forgot his qualms. None of them had any knowledge of military matters; and except for a few pistols and flintlocks there were no firearms.
Chelmsford Lowman received a letter from his brother in Georgia
describing the pikes which Governor Brown was having made: blades
sixteen inches long and two inches wide, with a three-inch spur on
either side, and a hollow shank a foot long to receive the staff. Long
Tom Mills, the blacksmith in Martinston, made a dozen or so of these;
and his smithy became a rallying point where men had other weapons
fashioned to their own designs, and in every house in Martinston

lamps and candles burned late as needles flew in busy improvisation by wives and daughters anxious to do their share.

Tony decided that to harden themselves for a military life, the men should sample it; so patrols were sent out to protect Martinston on every side. They were required to shelter themselves, and to prepare their own rations, and to keep guards posted all night long. Rain the first night damped their enthusiasm; Chester Freedley's nerves toward morning betrayed him into firing at some weeds swaying in the gusty wind, and his companions on picket retreated in very bad order indeed to the tavern in Martinston. The second night Pete Needles shot and killed Judge Meynell's lop-eared old mule when it failed to answer his challenge. Two nights later a picket sleeping in Chelmsford Lowman's barn set the hay on fire, so that the whole company had to turn out to fight the flames—and Mrs. Lowman drove the fire fighters, once their work was done, into headlong flight with a brush broom. Bob Grimm developed an extravagantly painful boil in an extraordinarily painful place, and everyone was sneezing from exposure and hollow-eyed for lack of sleep before news of the attack on Sumter and then of the Fort's surrender sobered them all.

Monday, the stage driver reported that Mr. Lincoln had called upon North Carolina to help crush the Confederacy; and that night Tony and Judge Meynell, Chelmsford Lowman and Jeff Whitaker—these were his lieutenants in the company organization—spent long hours in fruitless conjecture as to what would happen now. When the others said good night at last, Judge Meynell lingered; and after some empty talk, he asked, his tone overly casual:

"Captain Currain, what about your nephew? I haven't seen him in ten days."

Tony had half forgotten Darrell, had wished to forget him. He said honestly: "I regret to say that he declined to join us. He returned to Richmond."

The other's head for a moment drooped as though this word had wounded him. "I'm sorry. He was always welcome at our home."

Tony offered a lame defense. "Of course, he's a Virginian, Judge."

"True," the other assented. "His place is with Virginia troops." He seemed about to say more, but he did not. When the Judge was gone, Tony thought Darrell must have departed without a word of farewell to Miss Mary, and he felt an indignant anger at the graceless young man.

Next day they heard the answer sent by Governor Ellis to Lincoln's call for two North Carolina regiments for immediate service, and Tony mustered the company and read to them that stern note.

"'Your dispatch is received, and if genuine, which its extraordinary character leads me to doubt, I have to say in reply that I regard the levy of troops made by the Administration for the purpose of subjugating the states of the South as in violation of the constitution, and a usurpation of power. I can be no party to this wicked violation of the laws of the country, and to this war upon the liberties of a free people. You can get no troops from North Carolina.'"

Tony was surprised to find that as he read his own voice grew strong with anger. He finished and a hoarse exultant shout answered him, and he himself caught fire.

"So, men of Martinston, the issue is joined," he cried. "The treacherous villain in Washington, having goaded our sister states beyond endurance, now calls us to furnish soldiers to consummate his crime. Will we do it?" He answered his own question. "By the Almighty, no!" A hoarse shout of approval answered him. "Ought we to do it? No! No! We are Southern men, and we will fight to the death against those who make war upon the South! The Governor has given us our battle cry; resistance to this wicked lawlessness, this unrighteous war!" Seeing in their intent countenances the unanimity of their agreement with every word he said, he felt real greatness in himself, unmeasured powers. After all, he was a Currain! He had a fine heritage; he would do it honor now.

He set out that day for Raleigh, to announce to the Governor that the company was ready for orders. Major Hill had already been installed as commandant at the camp of instruction there. When Tony reported to him it was in a voice that rang with pride.

19

CINDA and Brett were still in Charleston when upon the fall of Sumter President Lincoln issued his call for troops. Brett read aloud to Cinda passages from the proclamation. "He says the laws have been opposed and their execution obstructed 'by combinations too powerful to be suppressed by the ordinary course of judicial proceedings' and wants 'the militia of the several states of the Union to the aggregate number of 75,000 in order to suppress said combinations.'" And he explained: "He says the troops will be used to recapture Sumter, 'to repossess the forts, places and property which have been seized from the Union.' And listen to this, Cinda. 'I hereby command the persons composing the combinations aforesaid to disperse and retire peaceably to their respective abodes within twenty days.'"

In sudden violence, Brett crumpled the paper and crushed it between his hands; and he laughed harshly. "'I command you to retire to your homes!' Why, damn the man, we're in our homes! It would be funny if it weren't so infuriating." He added more quietly: "You understand, Cinda, he's actually demanding that Virginia, North Carolina, Kentucky, all the border states furnish troops to fight South Carolina and the other Southern states. The War Department wants three Virginia regiments, with seven hundred and eighty men in each. Twenty-four hundred men! Why, there aren't that many men in Virginia who would fight against the Confederacy!"

"I suppose not." She spoke in a low tone, her hands clasped to stop their trembling. "Does that mean— Well, what does it mean, Brett Dewain?"

"Why, Virginia will fight with the Confederacy, not against her, of course!"

"I suppose everybody's furious."

"Furious? Every man in Charleston's trying to join some regiment or other." He laughed. "They're making a joke of it. They say when a new man wants to join up, they sprinkle water on him; and if he doesn't sizzle they decide he isn't mad enough to make a good soldier!"

She smiled with him, but she said: "I must be getting old, Brett Dewain! I hear ladies talking so big about all the things we're going to do, and they just sound like silly children to me. Do you suppose people are any more sensible in Richmond? Charleston's so tickled with itself for starting a war that I want to—well, to slap its face, if it had one! Charleston ought to have its ears boxed, if you ask me!"

He chuckled. "Treason, Cinda! If they heard, they'd talk tar and feathers."

"I can't help it! I'm sick of idiotic, chattering women talking about the 'glorious news' and how thankful and happy they are." Her own thoughts made her angry. "I'll insult someone if we stay here. Let's go to the Plains, stay a few days and go on home."

"The ladies are worse than the men, I suppose."

"I certainly hope the men aren't as bad," she agreed, and she said: "Miss Barnwell today—in a perfect fright of a hat—was sure our soldiers will just march into Washington and take over the Government. Oh, they're all the same, their tongues rattling like dried peas in a gourd! I hear more silly talk in an hour than I've heard in all my life before. According to them, Lincoln is a blasphemous fanatic, ready to turn a pack of thieves and cutthroats loose on us; but we'll kill the last man of them! Or if we don't, if they kill every man in the South, why, then Southern women will take arms against them! They can kill us all, but they can't conquer us, even after we're dead! You never heard such nonsense, Mr. Dewain. One minute they're talking about a quick and glorious victory, and the next they're going to fight to the last man and woman. Mrs. Caswell raved today till I thought she'd have apoplexy. She was red as a beet! She said if a man of her acquaintance delayed twenty-four hours in marching off to battle she'd cut him dead forever after! If I were a man and related to her I'd face any danger to escape being near her. They talk so much and so foolishly I wonder if underneath they aren't all just as scared as I am."

"Faunt thinks it's because we're afraid we do so much bragging."

"I know it! All the ladies keep saying we're going to whip the North in a month and we're going to do this and we're going to do that; but actually they're thinking: 'What if we don't?' Women make me tired! If our men can't whip the Yankees I'd rather be beaten than saved by all this female talk!"

Brett smiled at her violence; but he said thoughtfully: "The South's a woman, Cinda. In our refusal to face facts, our ignorance, our silly scorn of the enemy." He added: "Actually, of course, we've hard trouble ahead."

"Everyone seems to think England will take our side for the sake of our cotton."

"I know. 'Cotton is King.' I hear that everywhere, like a lullaby to soothe babies. But we'd better start helping ourselves, instead of counting on help from others."

"Oh, Brett Dewain, how did we ever get into such a mess?"

"The politicians," he said harshly. "The politicians. They made the war, but it's the people who will have to do the fighting."

"Our boys," she murmured, and she caught his hand. "Oh, I'm so tired of talk, talk, talk! Brett Dewain, I want to see Clayton. I want to see our boys."

When they came to the Plains, Cinda clung to her tall son there, and she played by the hour with her grandchildren. She delighted in five-year old Kyle, active as a squirrel, and in Janet, forever babbling a language of her own out of which single recognizable words burst with a surprising clarity.

The day they arrived at the plantation Tommy Cloyd rode over to say good-by. He had joined the De Kalb Rifle Guards. "And I start for Richmond tomorrow," he explained.

Brett asked smilingly: "All by yourself, Tommy?"

The youngster flushed and grinned. "No, sir, we'll be in the First South Carolina Volunteers. Colonel Gregg's regiment." He explained: "The regiment's been on Morris Island, and when orders came to go to Virginia, most of the men said they wouldn't go, because they'd just enlisted to fight for South Carolina. Only about half the regiment is going; so they're taking in some more companies, and combining some of the others, and we got our chance. Captain Boykin says we'll be the first regiment from the South in Richmond."

Cinda said teasingly: "Vesta's there, Tommy. She'll be glad to see you."

He reddened to the ears. "Yes, ma'am. I·want to see her, too."

He stayed for only a few moments, going on to say good-by to his mother before returning to join his company in Camden; and when he was gone Cinda met Clayton's eyes. "Hear that, Sonny? Your fire-eating South Carolinians mean to do their fighting as far as possible from the Yankees!"

"Well, we believe the state comes first, Mama."

Brett spoke gravely. "But, Clay, we're all in this together. If each state keeps its soldiers at home, the Yankees will gobble us up one by one. Ten thousand soldiers in South Carolina won't lick one company of Yankees in Virginia."

"There'll be plenty of South Carolinians in Virginia, sir! Tommy's regiment will be the first, but there'll be more."

"There will have to be," Brett commented. "We must have an Army of the Confederacy, not just a lot of home guards."

Cinda said protestingly: "Oh, you two! You won't settle anything by talking!" She left them, went to find Jenny and the children. Jenny was in the store room with old Banquo, measuring out what would be needed for dinner, and Cinda said: "Banquo, you old rascal, you get littler all the time. You're no bigger than a pint of cider!"

The Negro chuckled with delight. "Dass right, Missy. When de tall was give out, I no dere."

"How's that new wife of yours?"

Banquo made a contemptuous sound. "Her ain' no wife ob mine, not no moah."

"Why, Banquo, I thought she was a mighty pretty woman."

"Huh! Reck'n dass de trouble. You know what? Dat no-'count nigguh done had two children so fur, Missy, and bofe ob dem was twinses. My Paw nevah had twinses! Nor me neither, not yit! No, ma'am, I ain' gwine truck wid her no moah!"

Cinda laughed till she cried at Banquo's jealous suspicion, but when he was gone Jenny said in quiet amusement. "Perhaps she just has a talent for babies. Banquo certainly has! I see a lot of pickaninnies around the place that look like him."

"Fie on you, Jenny! Don't you know ladies never notice such things?"

"Don't they?" Jenny smiled. "I suppose that's why you never notice anything."

Cinda's eyes opened wide. "Jenny! Darling! Really?" Jenny nodded, radiant; and Cinda asked: "When?"

"August, I think."

"I'd never have guessed! But there, I should have, with Clayton looking like a cat after it's swallowed the canary!"

Jenny's eyes shadowed. "He's glad, of course. But—I wish it weren't happening just now."

"Nonsense, darling! It will take Clayton's mind off—other things."

Yet Cinda knew this was not true, and Jenny knew it too. Virginia passed the ordinance of secession; and except for Maryland's half-hearted compliance, every border state refused to assist in coercing the South. That night after they were abed, Brett said, almost gratefully: "I'm glad of one thing: slavery is no longer the issue, nor our right to secede. On those issues I'd have had a divided mind; but not on coercion! We're fighting for the right to decide for ourselves the government under which we choose to live! The North proposes to govern us against our will; we insist on the right to govern ourselves."

"Of course we do," Cinda agreed. "And I'd like to see them try and stop us!"

"Well, they'll try," he reminded her. "But—if we're not to live as free men—it's better to die."

Cinda, thinking of Burr and Julian far away, came into his arms. "Why—fight then, Mr. Dewain," she whispered. Her voice failed, she steadied it. "Will you join a South Carolina regiment?"

"I think not. After all, I'm a Virginian by birth."

"Then we'd better be getting back to Richmond. Burr must be missing us. We might stop in Charlotte to see Julian on the way." She asked the question she dreaded putting into words. "What will Clayton do?"

"He's going with his neighbors here, when the time comes."

"I haven't told you," she said, "but Jenny's having another baby in

August. I think I'll have them all come to Richmond, as soon as Clayton goes. I'll want all my family together, and it will be cooler for Jenny in Richmond, pleasanter, not so lonely."

"Fine," he assented. "The Plains will be in good hands. We're fortunate in our overseer. Mr. Fleming will stay on. He's a warlike old fellow, but Clayton and I convinced him that he's necessary here." He added: "And you can always come back here. I'm arranging to stock the Plains with things we'll need."

She asked, surprised: "Need? What do you mean? We raise almost everything, and we can always buy what we don't raise."

"I'm not so sure," he told her. "It's not easy to organize a new nation. There are so many details, and—money is one of them. The Confederacy is printing money, and borrowing money; but unless we impose heavy taxes, our money will depreciate, buy less and less."

"If that's so, won't we have taxes?"

"I doubt it. You see, taxable property is mostly slaves and land and the Constitution of the Confederacy says that direct taxes have to be proportioned to population, on the basis of a census which hasn't yet been made. So till there's a census we can't tax slaves or land." He added: "I know that's just a technicality; but the big owners of land and of slaves control the government, and they won't let any tax be laid till the census has been taken. It would be a violation of our rights, and we're great sticklers for our rights, you know."

What he said meant little to her. "I haven't the remotest notion what a direct tax is," she confessed. "But I can tell that you think we ought to have one."

He hesitated. "Well, actually I'm not sure what I think. As a man who knows something about business I know we can't run the Confederacy without taxes; but as an owner of land and slaves I'd hate to pay taxes on them." He added: "But in any case, I'm sure we must lay in supplies while we can still get them. We have the people to feed, you know."

"I wonder what they're thinking about all this. I never feel that I know what's going on inside their woolly black heads."

He chuckled. "Nothing to worry about, I'm sure; not as long as we give them food to put in their black stomachs."

In a swift passion of terror and of tenderness she clung to him. "Hold me close, please! Closer! Closer!"

"Steady, Cinda."

"Oh, I'm not going to cry! I won't cry! Brett Dewain, do you know what I wish? I wish I could have another baby for you." He kissed her hand, and she insisted, "Well, I do. Whenever I know you're troubled, I always love you most! I mean—not with just my heart. With all of me."

"I know."

"Remember when our first little Burr died, I made you have another one, just as quick as we could. Aren't you glad we have the second Burr now? He's so like you! And then the little girl after Vesta. I knew you wanted another girl, and she was dead before she was even born, and I could hardly wait to have another for you, and then she turned out to be Julian, and I could never have the little girl we wanted, no matter how we tried."

"Easy, Cinda. Don't distress yourself."

"I'm not distressing myself. I'm just remembering how much I've always loved you." She laughed richly. "Haven't you ever thought, maybe just once, way in the back of your mind, that I was an abandoned woman, the way I've carried on with you?"

"To be sure! Many a time I've been shocked and horrified."

"And delighted? Just a little?" And when he had answered: "Brett Dewain, do other married people act the way we do? I don't believe they do. You know what I think?"

"Heavens, no!"

"I think you're responsible! Oh I'm not joking; and I know what I'm talking about, too. Women talk about these things. Some of your dignified husbands would be horrified if they knew how much their feminine acquaintances know about them! Brett Dewain, why don't men—make love to their wives?"

He said thoughtfully: "Probably many men honestly believe that no —well, no respectable woman would want them to do so."

"They're the sort of men who have a lot of half-white babies on their plantations." Her tone was scornful.

He laughed. "You know, Mrs. Dewain, in spite of that blunt tongue of yours, you're in many ways a very charming woman."

"You'd better think so! Oh, you'd just better think so, Brett Dewain." She clung to him in a long embrace. "There, my darling!" Burrowing her head into his shoulder, sighing with content. "Don't ever leave me, Brett Dewain."

He held her close, not speaking, till at last she felt his arm relax and knew he slept; but she did not. Over and over in her thoughts she prayed: "Don't ever leave me! Don't ever leave me, Brett Dewain! Dear God, don't ever let this dear man go away from me!" Lying in his loosened clasp she was careful not to move lest she wake him. Let him rest, let him sleep, let him hold her always in his arms and in his heart.

They stayed at the Plains till the supplies Brett had purchased began to arrive. Day by day the wagons went off empty to Camden or to Columbia, and returned laden with barrels of dried or salted fish, hogsheads of molasses and sugar, coffee and soap, tea, whiskey. There were bolts of calicoes and of household linen, cotton cloth, clothing and shoes for the Negroes, handkerchiefs, gloves, blankets, knives. When Cinda exclaimed at quantity and variety, Brett reminded her that the Negroes were dependent on them.

"We have to take care of them, you know. They rely on us. And you and Vesta and Jenny and the babies, you may all want to come back here some day. This war may last for years, you know."

They heard that Colonel Lee had resigned from the United States Army and had been commissioned Major General in command of Virginia's troops; and the news made Brett eager to go home. Cinda proposed that Jenny and the children come to Richmond with them, and Clayton heartily approved; but Jenny insisted she would stay as long as Clayton was here.

"That won't be long," Brett warned her. "Virginia will be the battle ground. It's through Virginia that our armies must march to attack Washington—and it's through Virginia that the Northerners will come to attack us. Clayton will be in Richmond before the first of June."

But Jenny would not leave till he did, so Brett and Cinda set the day for their departure. To go by way of Charlotte would prolong their journey; nevertheless Cinda was bent upon seeing Julian. Before they left the Plains they had a telegram from him.

Dear Papa and Mama: Major Hill says cadets cannot volunteer without consent, so please telegraph permission at once. Love,
                                                                    Julian.

When Brett, having read the message, handed it to her, Cinda saw the drawn tightness of his lips, and her eyes raced along the lines.

"Oh, no, no, Brett," she cried passionately. "He mustn't. Please! No, no, no! Not Julian, Brett!" She was frantic. "Please, Brett! Please!" Entreating him. "He's just a baby!"

He hesitated, his arm around her shoulders. "I suppose all his friends are volunteering, all the boys he knows."

"Oh, Brett, please!"

"He's the only one of us who—adopted the profession of arms, Cinda. Trained officers will be needed, to command ignoramuses like me and Clayton and Burr; and he's had some training."

"Don't be ridiculous!"

He smiled. "I'd be mighty proud to take orders from Julian."

"Brett Dewain, you're a fool!"

"If I were in his place, I'd want to do this. I'd be a little ashamed if he didn't want to. And so would you, Cinda."

"Oh, I suppose so! But we're not going to let him!"

"I'd be ashamed not to let him."

"Well, I wouldn't!"

He kissed her tenderly. "You answer him, then. You write the answer. I'll send it off to town."

She looked at him in startled understanding, her lips after a moment twisting in a smile. "You clever, merciless, clever man!" she whispered. "I suppose I love you. I suppose I do. But, oh, how I hate you, too!"

He did not speak, and she crossed to the writing table; the pen scratched harshly. She came back, gave him the sheet of paper. He kissed her, then read what she had written.

Dear Julian: Tell Major Hill you have our proud and happy permission to volunteer. We love you.
                                                          Papa and Mama

"That's fine," he said, carefully casual. "That's settled, then. I'll get it off right away."

"But we'll surely stop and see him, won't we?"

"We surely will."

The journey north proved a long and wearying and sometimes terrifying ordeal. Cinda had never been at ease on the cars. Trains rushed across the countryside, balancing atop shaky timber trestles like a cat on a fence, threading miles of swamp where water moccasins and alligators and occasionally a panther or a bear might be seen, and ducks and herons rose in clouds, but no sign of human life appeared. They thundered through forests or across cultivated fields at a relentless, headlong pace that covered sometimes fifteen or twenty miles in an hour. At their best the cars were bad; but now they were packed full of troops on their way to Richmond. Brett and Cinda found themselves travelling with Wheat's Tigers and the Zouaves from New Orleans, bound north from Pensacola. The Zouaves were a tanned and muscular lot, in baggy scarlet trousers, blue sash, white gaiters, blue shirts cut low at the throat, gay embroidered jackets, their fezzes worn at every angle.

"But they're so incredibly dirty!" Cinda protested, almost shuddering. "I can't decide whether to be disgusted or terrified."

"They're hard men," Brett assented. "The officers tell me they were recruited from the slums and the prisons."

Nevertheless these were their travelling companions as far as Charlotte. The men crowded the cars, forever tramping up and down, shouting, drinking, spitting generously; and at Charlotte, like water breaking through a dam, they cascaded off the train to rush into the nearest stores and taverns seeking either loot or liquor, while their officers fought to control them. Cinda saw one giant emerge from a store with an armful of stolen shoes. A young lieutenant ordered him into ranks; and when the soldier laughed, the officer smashed him in the temple with a pistol butt, dropped him senseless. Then Brett swept Cinda to one side and away; and when they were clear of the mob she said, gasping for breath:

"Heavens! Will we make armies out of such animals?"

"Well," he reminded her, "if all the fashionable companies decide to stay at home, like our South Carolina dandies, we'll have to."

They discovered that Julian had left Charlotte with the other cadets for the camp of instruction at Raleigh. It was a day or two before they could find room on a train that would take them to Salisbury. There they waited again, in company with a regiment of Georgians of whom Cinda thought every man was drunk; and when their train pulled in, the men stampeded aboard so that every passenger car was instantly filled.

Cinda and Brett rode in the express car as far as Raleigh. They put up at Guion's Hotel, and in the happiness of seeing Julian she forgot all else a while. Julian told them Uncle Tony was in camp, Captain of the Martinston Company. "He asked for me to help drill them," he said proudly. "You can watch. I start tomorrow morning."

They went to the drill ground as he suggested; and when they arrived Julian and Tony came to meet them, Tony a little embarrassed and yet with something new in his bearing and his eyes. "We're just ready to begin," Julian explained. "Uncle Tony, will you put the men in company formation?" Tony turned away to obey and Cinda felt her heart swell to the bursting point. Julian stayed with them, talking abstractedly, his eyes upon Tony's company as the ragged and uncertain ranks took form; and he was so straight and proud. When the company was formed he went briskly toward them and began to speak, and at the sound of his clear young voice Cinda felt tears fill her eyes and overflow, and her smile was half a sob.

"You gentlemen will learn a great many things in the next few weeks," Julian told the men. "Sometimes you will think the things you are asked to learn unnecessary and absurd, and you'll find them confusing too; but if you learn one thing at a time, each succeeding step will follow naturally from the one before it. A soldier who knows his work is twice as valuable as one who does not. You must learn first the School of the Soldier. After that will come the School of the Company; but until you are soldiers, you will never be a company.

"Now the first thing you will learn is the Position of the Soldier. Put your heels on the same line, not one behind the other but side by side, and as near together as you comfortably can. That squares your shoulders. If you are knock-kneed, or if the calves of your legs are muscular, you won't be able to touch your heels together. That is not necessary; just put them as near together as possible. You are to stand as I am standing. First, place your heels."

They obeyed, stumbling and shuffling, watching their own heels and those of their neighbors, and someone said something, and a mutter of laughter ran along the ranks, and Julian said sharply: "Silence." His eye swept them and he went on:

"Your feet should be turned out equally, at less than a right angle, toes not too far apart to be comfortable." After each direction he waited while they sought to do what he required. "Your knees should be straight but not stiff. If they're stiff, you'll get tired quickly, can't hold the position. Your body should be erect on your hips, the upper part leaning just a little forward. That gives you good balance. No, no, don't throw your belly forward. Square your shoulders but keep your belly in." And as some of the men stretched their arms, he said: "If your coats are too tight, have someone let them out around the arm-pits till they're comfortable."

He looked along the uneasy line. "Now let your arms hang naturally, elbows near the body, palms a little forward, your little finger just behind the seam in your pantaloons. Face front and eyes front but not stiffly. Keep your heads up high enough so that your chin doesn't cover your stock. Look at a spot on the ground about fifteen feet in front of you." And when he was for the moment satisfied: "There, that's what we call the Position of the Soldier. Everything you learn will start from that."

Cinda whispered to Brett. "Look at Tony!" Some of the men, trying to do what Julian told them, grinned with their own embarrassment; but Tony with a completely serious countenance was wholly absorbed in these instructions, intent on exact obedience. "The poor dear, so solemn, trying so hard to do what Julian says!"

They watched with a lively interest as the drill went on, and Cinda's eyes shone with pride in this boy of hers; till at last Julian said: "Very well. Your company officers will instruct each of you individually. I know all this seems to you unnecessary. You're used to taking care of yourselves, but a man taking care of himself is very different from a soldier taking care of himself. You're no longer men; you're soldiers.

The way to be a good soldier is to learn these things. Your officers will
see that you do."

When the lesson was over, Cinda thought Julian and Tony might
have dinner with them; but Julian had duties and Tony too declined.
"I want to go off by myself and practice the Position of a Soldier," he
told them, laughing at himself yet earnest too.

So Cinda and Brett drove back to the hotel together. "This has
made Julian seem older and Tony younger," she said thoughtfully.
"Probably war changes everyone."

"I suppose all that detail is planned to produce an average," Brett reflected. "Something that is no longer an individual but just one of
many men who think alike and move alike and act alike." He smiled.
"It will need a stricter task master than Julian to do that to Southerners." And then, soberly: "Experience, perhaps."

Julian and Tony were both so busy every day that Cinda felt she and
Brett were almost an annoyance; so they decided to go on to Richmond. For the next stage of their journey Brett found a place for them
in the mail car. The car was smaller than any bed room Cinda had
ever seen, and they must share it with the agent—who offered them the
courtesies of his bottle of whiskey—but at least it was a sanctuary from
the drunken soldiery, and the bags of mail made a comfortable couch.

"And I don't mind anything, now I've seen Julian," Cinda declared.
"He's grown, Brett Dewain."

"Yes. Yes, he's a big fellow now."

"Some of the cadets seemed even younger than he." She knew he
understood her thoughts; they could always commune without spoken
word. Nevertheless she wished the shape of words as a foundation on
which to build the future. "Children grow up," she said. "We'd like
to keep them sheltered and protected; but to do so would be to rob
them of half of life itself. To hide, to hug safety, to spend nothing of
yourself—a man who did that might continue to exist for a thousand
years. But—he'd never live! To live is to strive and to venture and to
win—or to lose. To live is to assume responsibilities when you should,
to accept duty, to love. To earn your own respect and the love of those
you love is to make yourself terribly vulnerable to loss and grief; but—
it's worth it, Brett Dewain."

He pressed her hand. "Whatever happens, Julian—all of us—will be doing what we ought to do, and what we want to do. Our boys will be doing what we want them to do and what they want to do."

"I'm all right, Mr. Dewain."

"You're very wonderful."

"I'm all right," she repeated, like a promise. "My head is high. I shan't let it droop again."

After a moment Brett remarked: "I think Tony's found himself, Cinda."

"You know," she suggested, "I think maybe Tony's been our fault all the time. He was always perfectly horrid to us when we were children, but I expect we were just as mean to him as he was to us. Maybe if we'd liked him, loved him, praised him, been nice to him——"

"I remember Major Longstreet saying, when he came back from Mexico, came to Lynchburg to be married, that war was the natural element of some men who were otherwise contemptible. In normal life they were misfits, fish out of water; but in war, battle, they—magnified themselves, seemed giants, capable of miracles. Perhaps that's true of Tony."

"Perhaps," she agreed, and she said: "I suppose Major Longstreet has resigned from the army by now. Louisa wrote that he'd offered his services to Alabama, remember? Maybe we'll see them again."

"I suppose he'll command Alabama troops," Brett reflected. "But most of the fighting will be between Richmond and Washington. If he's sent to Virginia, maybe we will. I hope so. I liked him."

"He was lots of fun, always ready for any lark. But of course that was years ago. I suppose we've all changed. Yet I don't feel any older, Brett Dewain."

"You're not," he assured her. "You'll never grow old, Cinda." Then he added chuckling: "Age cannot wither nor custom stale your infinite variety."

"Heavens, I don't feel withered and stale! I hope I never do. I never will, either. Children snatch us back from growing old, don't they; children, and grandchildren." She stirred, trying to find a more comfortable position on the pile of mail bags. The agent, having emptied his bottle, was sprawled in snoring slumber here beside her. "But I'm feeling older every minute, right now."

"We can rest when we change at Weldon. We might stay over a night there."

But Cinda thought she would rather go on if she could; and when they reached Weldon and tried to eat a greasy supper in the dingy tavern she was sure of it. There would be a train some time in the night. "We'll stay out of doors in the fresh air and wait for it," she insisted.

Luck got them a place on that train; but at Petersburg, Henry, the driver of the omnibus that took passengers to Pocahontas, said the Richmond train was two hours gone. Brett proposed to hire a carriage to carry them on to Richmond, but Ragland's livery stable had none to rent.

"I might buy one," Brett suggested.

Cinda laughed. "No. No, this is beginning to be funny. Besides, the children will be meeting every train, expecting us." She had written Burr from Raleigh. "No, we'll wait for the evening train."

So they went to Powell's, where Brett had sometimes lodged when business brought him to Petersburg; and Cinda had a chance to remove some traces of her journey. "But not all," she told Brett when she rejoined him. "I didn't even try. I'm going to wait for the luxury of my own bathing room."

The Richmond train was crowded with men of a Georgia battery, and a North Carolina regiment; but room was made for Cinda. When the cars emerged at last from the deep cut above the bridge and she saw across the river the familiar roofs and needle spires, her eyes filled with weary, happy tears. "Oh, Brett Dewain," she whispered, "I'll never go away from here again."

In the station at the foot of Eighth Street Cinda from the car steps looked over the heads of the waiting crowd and discovered Burr and Vesta; and Burr was in uniform, and when she saw this, Cinda's hand tightened on Brett's arm, but her smile was steady. Vesta kissed her, and then she was in Burr's arms, and over his shoulder she saw Barbara Pierce watching them with a shy smile, and Burr swung his mother to face the girl.

"Mama, Barbara and I are going to be married right away," he said.

Cinda hugged Barbara tight to hide her jealous dismay. "Well, it's high time!" she cried. "I declare, child, I began to wonder whether you were as nice as you seemed, tormenting Burr so long!"

Barbara laughed. "Oh, it was fun!" she declared. "As long as there wasn't any hurry! But now we want to be married just as quick as we can, Mrs. Dewain."

'You young ones! Dillydally for years, and then all of a sudden you can't wait! Well, perhaps in a year or two——"

"A year?" Barbara's tone was full of consternation; but then she laughed. "There, you're mean to tease us, Mrs. Dewain! Why, we almost didn't even wait for you to come home!" She slipped her arm through Cinda's, Vesta came to Cinda's other side, and they all moved toward the waiting carriage. "Mama and Papa and I are coming to your house to supper," Barbara explained. "Mama says she can't possibly be ready for weeks and weeks; but you'll talk her into being sensible, won't you? Please?"

"Come home with us now," Cinda urged; but Barbara would not.

"No, you drop me at our house. You'll want Burr and Vesta to yourself awhile. I'll come later with Papa and Mama."

"Nonsense, Honey," Cinda protested. "I'd only have half of Burr unless you were there." But Barbara insisted, and when they had left her at her door Cinda told Burr: "She's as thoughtful as she is sweet, darling. Now, tell me all about yourself—and all about her."

But despite Barbara's thoughtfulness they had no time together before supper; for when they reached the house, it was to see a formidable figure just ringing the bell. Vesta whispered: "Heavens, Mama! It's Mrs. Brownlaw. Don't look! Let's drive on."

But Mrs. Brownlaw had seen them and uttered a glad cry and now waited on the doorstep to greet them. There was no escape; so Cinda made the best of it, but even without Vesta's warning she would have dreaded the worst. Mrs. Brownlaw was one of those assured women who thinks herself divinely appointed to manage the lives of her neighbors. As a consequence, whenever it was possible to do so, people avoided her as though she were the carrier of some offensive and infectious disease. When Cinda and the others alighted from the carriage, she protested that she mustn't bother them now, but she treated Cinda's politeness as an insistent invitation and came pushing into the hall on Cinda's very heels. She forgot her errand for a while in admiring Cinda's drawing room: the gleaming cornices over the windows, the decorated ceiling, the intricately carved mantel, the painted chairs and tables. "Oh, it's so bright and cheerful," she declared. "Such a relief from the ugly browns and whites you see in most houses." Cinda, herself happy in returning to these loved things, could not but be pleased.

Mrs. Brownlaw came at last to the reason for her call. She was organizing the ladies of Richmond to sew for the soldiers. There were secession flags to make, and regimental banners, and jackets and trousers and scarves and visors and Havelocks; there were bandages to roll and lint to scrape.

"Oh, so much to do, so much to do!" she cried, settling herself in one of the occasional chairs with all the elaborate motions of a hen about to lay an egg, talking on and on. Cinda, who had not even taken off her bonnet, waited in silence; Burr and Brett had escaped, had gone upstairs, but Vesta stayed loyally with her mother. The ordeal was a long one. Not till the bell rang again and Caesar admitted Mr. and Mrs. Pierce and Barbara did Mrs. Brownlaw rise at last.

"There, I must run," she said regretfully. "I just dropped in for a minute, my dear!" Even in the hall she would have waited to tell her story to Mrs. Pierce, but Cinda almost pushed her out of the door.

"Whew!" she exclaimed, in a sharp exasperation. "Dropped in for a minute: she's been here two hours!" She was in a high rage. "If there's one sort of person I despise more than another, it's women like her. She thinks we're going to war just so she can make a nuisance of herself. The great big—moo cow!" Vesta collapsed in helpless laughter and Cinda cried: "Stop it! I won't be laughed at!"

"Oh, Mama, if you could have seen yourself! You kept tossing little hints for her to go, and she just rolled right over them the way the tide rolls over pebbles on the beach. And you got redder and——"

"Hush, you imp! You could have distracted her, screamed, or fainted, or something!" She spoke to Mrs. Pierce apologetically. "I simply must run upstairs. That creature was here when we got home, so I'm still covered with cinders and dust from the train."

But Mrs. Pierce was so full of admiring comment on the furnishings that Cinda was delayed a further while. "Such bright lovely things make our home seem ever so dark," Mrs. Pierce declared. They lived on Leigh street, and though she and Cinda were not intimates, Cinda knew the house. Mr. Pierce had built it ten years before. It was of the Greek Revival period, with a step roof and dormers, crowded into a narrow lot, and Cinda, who relished the ample gardens that surrounded their own mansion, thought people living in such cramped houses must feel smothered and shut in. "I must do something like this to brighten up our drawing room," Mrs. Pierce decided. She had a nervously apologetic little laugh which Cinda found trying. "I do hope you won't mind my imitating you, Mrs. Dewain. They say imitation's the sincerest flattery, you know."

"So I've heard," Cinda said dryly, and wished she had not spoken. She must be nice to Barbara's mother. Probably Barbara would be like Mrs. Pierce as she grew older. Poor Burr! Mrs. Pierce nodded eagerly.

"Yes, and I think it's so true," she declared.

Burr appeared, and Cinda left him to play host and went up to her room to fume to Brett. "As if I hadn't enough on my mind without coming home to this!" But he laughed her into good humor again.

That was a fine evening. Burr and Barbara were so happy that a high merriment filled them all; they laughed easily, at little or nothing. But Cinda, even while she was outwardly as gay as the others, thought their gaiety artificial. They were like people sheltered together against an approaching storm who lift their voices to an unnaturally high pitch to drown out the rolling thunder, and try to ignore the blinding lightning flashes and the murmur of the nearing downpour.

She supported Burr and Barbara in their pleas for an early wedding, till Mrs. Pierce at last with a doubtful sigh admitted that it was just possible she might get Barbara ready some time in June. This was victory enough, so Burr and Barbara disappeared together, and the older people spoke of less personal matters. Mr. Pierce asked a question about Sumter's fall, and Brett gave him an account of that event, and Cinda added lightly:

"You'd have thought by the celebration that it was the greatest victory ever won in war. Actually, with all their shooting, not a soul was killed—except when the Yankees insisted on firing a salute to their old flag after they'd surrendered and the cannon exploded and killed some of them."

Barbara's father was one of those—most of the leading men in Richmond agreed with him—who had stood for the Union and against secession, till Lincoln's call for volunteers made all men of a single mind. He admitted this now. "Yet I wonder whether Robert Barnwell Rhett sleeps well of nights. He more than any man in the South has brought this on us."

"He and Yançey were the spokesmen," Brett assented. "But Roger Pryor and Edmund Ruffin did their share."

"Mr. Rhett won't have any qualms," Cinda predicted. "He likes to think he's somebody! He wasn't satisfied to be plain Mister Smith the way he was born. Just because he had a Rhett for a grandfather or something, down with the Smiths and up with the Rhetts! As if names meant anything!"

Brett smiled. "Seems to me I've detected in you a certain pride in the fact that you're a Currain!"

"You notice I was ready enough to change my name to Dewain, all the same!"

Mr. Pierce was an elderly man, now retired from active life; but he had been a director of the Bank of Virginia, and he remarked that the Confederacy would have trouble financing the war. "There's talk of putting an embargo on our cotton, but I'd like to see every bale shipped to England. Even half a million bales would give us ample credit there."

"They won't do it," Brett predicted. "They think King Cotton will be our best weapon, to bankrupt the North, and to force England and France to fight for us." He added: "Of course they may come to their senses, ship the cotton later."

"Later will be too late," Mr. Pierce retorted. "Lincoln hasn't a dozen ships for blockade duty today; but given a few months and the North will build ships by scores, shut our ports tight. If we're to export any quantity of cotton, it must be done before that happens."

Their talk ran on, and Cinda, across the room, trying to keep up a conversation with Mrs. Pierce, thought Brett was as bored as she. Mr. Pierce had a ponderous pomposity. His least utterance was preceded by a faint sound like a clearing of the throat, and his words held a dogmatic ring. You doubted them at your peril. Barbara's mother was in a different way equally wearisome. Just now she kept reciting the countless obstacles to Barbara's early wedding; and Cinda smothered a yawn, thinking that if she weren't so tired she would probably not be so irritated by Mrs. Pierce's deprecatory little laugh and her monotonous reiterations. Mr. Pierce was giving Brett some advice about investment, saying that gold was the only safe thing to buy in such times as these; and Cinda thought he was presumptuous to try to tell Brett anything about business. She was relieved when they said good night.

"Well!" she exclaimed. "I thought they'd never go! Come on upstairs, Brett Dewain. If I don't get out of my stays I'll scream!"

But Brett had matters of business which would keep him a while at his desk; so Cinda called Vesta into her room and they talked of Burr and Barbara, and of how well his uniform became Burr; and Cinda said:

"But if you think Burr's handsome you should see Julian!"

"Julian! Mama, you don't mean to say——"

"Oh, yes, he's volunteered with the other cadets."

"But, Mama, that infant! You shouldn't have let him!"

"Nonsense! It's what he wanted to do, and it's what we want him to do." These words must serve through the months ahead as her passport to a peaceful mind.

"But he's so young!" Vesta's eyes were full of tears. "Mama, couldn't you stop him?"

"Of course, if we had wanted to. He had to have our permission, telegraphed us."

"What did you say?"

"Why, gave it, with our blessing!"

"Mama!" Then, in sure understanding: "Didn't it almost kill you?"

Cinda nodded grimly. "Yes, it did! If your father had tried to persuade me to consent, I'd have fought him to the last gasp. But he left the decision to me. So what could I do?" Vesta came quickly to her, hugged her hard; for a moment they stayed in close embrace. Then Cinda said briskly: "And I'm all right now! Vesta, Jenny's going to have a baby this summer. August, she thinks. Isn't that fine?"

"Oh, wonderful! How is she?"

"Perfect! She'll bring the children here, as soon as Clayton goes. It will be nice having them in Richmond, won't it? It will keep us all busy. Kyle's a terror, and Janet's so active she'd wear out a monkey!"

She answered Vesta's questions till Vesta had no more to ask. "Now it's your turn, Honey," she said then. "What's been happening here while we were gone?" Vesta must have seen Tommy Cloyd; it was of him Cinda expected her to speak. But Vesta did not do so.

"Oh Heavens, everything," she declared. "Just crazy excitement all the time. When the secession vote was passed, the streets around the Mechanics' Institute were simply jammed, waiting to hear the news; and when people heard, there was a rush to haul down the Union flag on top of the Capitol. A boy climbed up the lightning rod, and it pulled loose and there he was swinging around in the air and everyone was just simply screaming! A man went to help him and slid down to the gutter; and when the rod bent clear over the boy let go, and the man caught him at the very edge of the roof, and they climbed back up to the skylight, and everybody cheered as if we'd beaten the Yankees already.

"It's been like that right along, Mama. People are just simply crazy." She laughed in sudden recollection. "And doing the silliest things! One Sunday the bells rang, and warnings were put up everywhere that a Northern warship was coming up the river with ten thousand soldiers to capture Richmond, and all our soldiers marched down to Rockett's——"

Cinda exploded. "Soldiers! I'm sick to death of them! I've seen nothing but soldiers since we started north; and a tobacco-chewing, whiskey-drinking lot they were!"

"Well, anyway," Vesta insisted, "everybody who had even a pistol loaded it; and you never heard so much brag and blow in your life. Of course it all turned out to be just talk. Burr said the Yankees didn't have ten thousand soldiers anyway, and they couldn't put more than two or three hundred of them on one little boat if they had them."

Cinda turned casually toward her dressing table, and began to loose her hair. "Speaking of soldiers, have you seen Tommy? He's in the De Kalb Rifles, came north a week or two ago with Maxcy Gregg's regiment. He came to say good-by to us."

"Oh yes, I've seen him," Vesta assented, but at first she said no more; so Cinda let her take her own time, asked in a lower tone:

"What regiment is Burr in?"

"The cavalry, the First Virginia." For a few moments neither of them spoke, till Vesta said sharply, as though rousing from deep thought: "Mama!"

Cinda, who had been facing her mirror, whirled around. "Eh? God bless us, child, you scared me! You don't need to shout! I'm right here in the same room. Go on, what are you trying to say?"

Vesta hesitated. "Mama, how do you tell a man to please hurry up and marry you?"

Cinda gave no sign of surprise. She answered calmly: "Oh, in any way you choose. With looks, with tears, with sighs, any way at all." She smiled. "Only, don't ever put it into words. If you do, the man will forever tease you about it. Why?" Her tone was matter-of-fact, robbing the question of all embarrassment. "Want to marry Tommy, do you?"

The girl nodded. "Yes. If he's going to be a soldier." Vesta hesitated. "He wrote me ahead of time that he was coming. I've just— pestered him to death ever since he got here. Oh, Mama, he's so sweet, and so sort of dumb and helpless. He needs someone to tell him he's wonderful, and to—well, love him! I wish he'd marry me and let me do it!"

Cinda tried to speak as casually as though this conversation were in no way remarkable. "Well, you'll have to be careful, I'm sure of that."

"I know. That's what I'm afraid of. But—I want to do something." And she said, half to herself: "I keep feeling I must hurry, hurry, hurry while there's time."

"Is he here in Richmond?"

"He's at Camp Pickens, yes."

"Well, if you see a lot of him, perhaps something will happen. I'll try to think what's best to do. If you can wait a little while."

"Oh, Mama—you're awfully wonderful. Of course I can wait—if it isn't too long. Please don't think I'm just silly, will you?"

"Silly? Heavens and earth, darling, I think you're the most sensible person I know! Next to myself, of course! And if you and I between us can't bring Tommy to time, I'll be much surprised."

Vesta laughed, in a sudden burst of uncontrollable amusement. "It is funny, though; you know it is! Us planning so cold-bloodedly."

Cinda tossed her head. "If more marriages were planned cold-bloodedly there wouldn't be half so much hot blood afterward!" She heard Brett moving in his study belowstairs. "There, Papa's shutting his desk, getting ready to come up. Good night, darling. Maybe he can think of something. I've never yet found a problem he couldn't solve."

Vesta rose to go, but then she stopped in sudden recollection. "Oh, Mama, I forgot the worst news. Little Hetty died while you were away."

"Hetty?" Cinda's heart was a gush of sorrow. "Oh, poor Trav! When? What happened?"

"Why, it was her eye, the one that got hurt. They brought her up to see Dr. Little, but he couldn't do anything. Aunt Tilda said poor Aunt Enid was simply frantic! Uncle Faunt went back to Great Oak with them."

"Faunt? Is he still down there?"

"No, he came back two or three days afterward. He's enlisted, Mama, in the Blues, Captain Wise's company."

Cinda pressed her hands to her temples. Faunt too? Then in relief she thought that if he had turned soldier, at least he was not at Great Oak with Enid. And of course they would all serve, all these loved men. "Then he's here?"

"No, the Blues have gone to Fredericksburg. Everyone says we're getting ready to capture Washington. Do you think we will, Mama?"

"I don't think anything about it. Let the soldiers do the fighting. Has Darrell enlisted?"

"No, he's in the Quartermaster's department! Mr. Streean too!"

Cinda smiled at Vesta's scornful tone. "Well, there really is something in family, heredity, isn't there? Of course, Darrell's half Currain; but he's half Streean too." Then Brett was at the door. "Now darling, run along. Come and have breakfast with me in the morning."

Vesta left them, and Cinda told Brett about Hetty's death. "I'd better go down to Great Oak to see how Mama is," she decided, and he agreed.

But she did not go at once. She waited, without admitting to herself what it was she waited for. In this brief interval she had time to see that already the Richmond she had known was changed. Even last winter it had been a serene, small world of its own. If you promenaded, everyone you met was at least an acquaintance, and usually a friend. Of course there were men and women, probably thousands of them, whom you never saw, or saw only as you saw cows grazing in a field, without noticing them; but now even Franklin Street and Grace Street were crowded with strangers, men with sharp greedy eyes, women dressed with an eloquent flamboyance, rough fellows in uniform and as often as not unsteady with drink. Instead of gentle voices and the musical laughter of pretty girls you heard hoarse mirth and hot argument. In spite of the fact that on the way north she had seen the cars full of unspeakable ruffians, she had thought of the soldiers who would defend the South as nice boys like Burr, and Julian, and Tommy Cloyd, and Rollin; as charming young gentlemen who would go to war gracefully, carrying even into battle the gallant graces of their kind. True, there were such men, whole companies of them, gentlemen, each with his body servant to attend him. Julian, when they saw him at Charlotte, had said he was writing Clayton to send him Elegant, and Burr would of course take January, old Joshua's grandson. Burr and Julian and Clayton too, no doubt, would go off to battle like knights with their attendant squires. But these crowded Richmond streets, full of lean and sallow and hard and vicious faces, were proof enough that the army was largely made up of poverty-ridden farmers and plain white trash! What hope of victory lay in such men? They would scatter and run at the first alarm, and you could expect nothing better. It was only gentlemen who offered their lives in selfless tribute to a cause; gentlemen like Julian and Burr and Clayton, yes and Faunt and Tony and—Brett.

It was for his decision she delayed her visit to Great Oak. She had not long to wait. Brett enlisted in the Richmond Howitzers. "I saw George Randolph," he explained. "He organized the Battery at the time of the John Brown business, and he's an enthusiast. So—it's settled."

Cinda nodded, not trusting her voice. Whatever the end was to be, the future was no longer in their hands.

20

TRAV was the last of them to put on a uniform. He had always been a deliberate man, and he was reluctant to depart from the solid certainties—the seasons, the land, the planting, the harvest—upon which his life was founded. Yet he could if he must leave Great Oak with few pangs. He loved Enid now less by heart than by habit. For a while after their marriage her pretty ardors enchanted and bewitched him, till the discomforts of her first pregnancy made her querulous and fretful. When soon after Lucy was born she again became pregnant, her rebellious complaints eventually turned his concern for her into weary resentment; and with no sense of unfairness he began to think less of Enid and more of his miraculously charming baby daughter. Peter and eventually Hetty came to multiply rather than to divide his fatherly affection; and at the same time he arrived at a settled certainty that Enid was unfair and unreasonable. In the intervals between her pregnancies it was she, not he, who refused to exercise restraint, and she was sometimes furious with him for his discretion; but whenever she found she was to have another baby it was not herself but him she blamed. Because he loved the children and she was their mother, she had from him now after a dozen years of marriage a loyalty which she herself could never have commanded; but it was only as their mother that she stood securely in his heart.

He had so long been accustomed to her reproaches that for her to blame him for Hetty's death was no surprise. In the carriage on the daylong journey from Richmond to Great Oak she sat between him and Faunt, but when she spoke it was to Faunt, and when the carriage lurched and bounced it was to Faunt she clung. At Great Oak Mrs.

Currain, tender and full of sympathy, led Enid away upstairs to see her safe abed. She herself presently joined them for supper. "The poor child's just heartbroken," she reported. "Trav, you'd better go say good night to her."

Trav obediently went to their room; but when he bent to kiss Enid's cheek, she thrust him away. "Don't! Don't touch me! I can't bear to have you touch me!"

"Want me to come to bed now, so you can go to sleep?"

"No! Heavens, no! I don't want you to come to bed at all! I don't want you in bed with me."

"Why, Enid, Mama wouldn't know what to think. We don't want to make her unhappy."

"Oh, all right!" She tossed and turned. "I'm so miserable! I wish I was dead!"

He asked awkwardly: "Want me to bring you a glass of water?"

"Don't treat me like a child!"

"I just want to make you comfortable. You must get some sleep. You'll wear yourself out."

She spoke in a low tone. "Where's Faunt?"

"Downstairs."

"I wish he'd come and say good night to me. He's so—so gentle. He understands how I feel."

Trav hesitated, but perhaps Faunt could comfort her. "Why, all right, I'll get him." He found Faunt with Mrs. Currain, gave him Enid's message, saw his mother's quick surprise, said defensively: "She's tired, wants to be made over. I'm no good at that, I guess."

Mrs. Currain spoke almost sharply. "Nonsense! We mustn't baby her. After all, she's a grown woman. I'll put a stop to this nonsense."

She went briskly up the stairs, and Faunt said reassuringly: "Enid will be all right presently, Trav. Give her a little time."

"Oh, she'll be fine by and by. But it was pretty hard for her, of course."

"It was hard for both of you."

Trav thought there was a criticism of Enid in Faunt's tone. "Well, of course I can stand things better than she can," he said defensively; and they spoke of other matters till Mrs. Currain presently joined them.

Trav slept little that night. Even though she kept as far from him as the great bed permitted, he felt Enid's cold, persisting anger. In the morning when he rose she seemed to be asleep, and he was careful not to wake her. She kept her bed that day; but after dinner, while Mrs. Currain was resting and could not interfere, she sent old April to summon Faunt.

Trav saw Faunt's reluctance. "Don't let her bother you," he said.

"Oh that's all right, Trav," Faunt assured him. "I'll go talk to her." But when he came down again he seemed troubled, and after some casual words, he said: "Trav, I'm afraid I'd better go to Richmond to-morrow. Jennings Wise suggested I join the Blues; but if I put it off too long——"

"I'd hoped you'd stay a few days," Trav admitted. "But I can understand that you're anxious to be doing something. I want to——"

Faunt shook his head: "You stay here, Trav. Mama and—your family need you, and the place needs you." He smiled without offense. "And I don't think you'd make a good soldier. You have too much— well, intelligence. You like to think things over. I believe I can take orders without stopping to ask myself whether they're wise; but you'd always need to wait, to consider."

"I've been thinking the same thing," Trav said. "But I've been figuring." Faunt smiled, and Trav grinned apologetically. "It's natural for me to go at things that way, to put them in figures. Faunt, companies and regiments can't just march off to battle. They have to have uniforms, and muskets, and powder and shot, and blankets, and tents, and food. I figure that a man will eat five pounds of food a day. For a regiment, say a thousand men, that's two tons and a half every day, seventeen tons a week, say seventy tons a month——"

Faunt nodded. "You're right, of course. And it will take a lot of plantations like Great Oak, growing corn and raising hogs, to supply an army. If every man rushed off to war, we'd all starve."

"So some of us will have to farm," Trav agreed. "What about Belle Vue? You could raise food there."

Faunt hesitated, his eyes for a moment hard with anger at his own thoughts. "It's for Belle Vue I'm fighting, Trav. I wouldn't fight for slavery. Slavery means nothing to me, nor politics, nor the cotton millionaires along the Gulf and their puppets who made this war; but

I'll fight for Belle Vue." He smiled in a dark fashion. "Oh I know it will do no good. Belle Vue itself may be a battle ground. I can't save it." His tone deepened. "But every time I kill a Yankee soldier it will be because he's been sent by that gangling ape in Washington to ravish Belle Vue."

Trav nodded, completely understanding. Every acre of Belle Vue was dear to Faunt. There, once, for a little time, he and Betty had been happy together. If Belle Vue lay in hostile hands, Faunt's heart would be drained of all those memories. "It may not happen," he said, in empty comforting.

"It will happen," Faunt insisted. "But if I can, I'll kill the ravishers. I hope Lincoln will show himself to me, on some battlefield. I'd like to send a bullet smashing into his black heart." He shook his head, his tone changed. "I didn't mean to—let go like this. But I'll do your share of the fighting, Trav. You stay here and take care of Mama and keep us fed."

Before Faunt left next morning Trav suggested that Enid be roused. "She'll want to say good-by to you." But Faunt smiled and dissented.

"No. You say good-by for me." His face became for a moment still and stern. "You must not let her weep too long."

After Faunt was gone, Trav had lonely days. His mother would listen to no word about the great events preparing. The fact that the college in Williamsburg had closed, every student and every teacher turning from class room to drill ground, she dismissed as of no consequence. When Trav reported that a battery of heavy guns was being placed near the ruins of the old church on Jamestown Island, she snorted disdainfully. When he told her that Lincoln was calling for more volunteers, "What of it?" she retorted. "Pay no attention to the ruffian!" If Trav said there were Northern war vessels in Hampton Roads, that the James River was blockaded, she laughed. "What possible difference can that make to us? I haven't been to Norfolk for twenty years."

Cinda and Brett came down from Richmond, Brett to return at once, Cinda staying a few days; but Cinda was quick to understand Mrs. Currain. "Let her alone, Travis," she advised. "If she can be happy in her way, so much the better. I'm glad Brett wasn't in uniform today. It might have upset her." After a first attempt to describe to her mother the confusion in Richmond, she did not try again; but she told Trav: "It's like a city full of crazy people, with strangers everywhere. Heaven knows where they come from. Everybody is wearing secession badges and sewing like mad. Do you know old Mrs. Brownlaw? She's in her element, running things! Outside of town there are camps and tents as far as you can see in all directions, and everyone goes out to the Fair Grounds every day to watch the drills." Clayton would reach Richmond next week, she said, bringing Jenny and the children. "He'll join his regiment there. Burr's in the cavalry. He's going to be married to Barbara Pierce in June. I haven't told Mama, and I won't till the day is set. I don't want to give her time to think up reasons why she can't come, because of course she must. Oh, and Trav, Tony organized a company at Chimneys, and he's the captain. He's a different man! And Julian and the other cadets from the Institute are training the new companies. We saw Julian drilling Tony and his men."

"How's Tilda taking it?" he asked.

"Oh, she's practically Mrs. Brownlaw's right hand. Mr. Streean and Darrell are something or other in the Quartermaster's department, supplies and things."

"That's the sort of work I could do."

But Cinda cried protestingly: "No, no, Travis. Stay as you are! It's such a comfort to have you still the same when the rest of the world is upside down! Besides, you have to stay here for Mama's sake. She'll never leave Great Oak, and she couldn't stay without you!" And in a different tone she said: "Enid seems—fine. Tilda says she was frantic when Hetty died. I wish I'd been there."

He felt, gratefully, the depth of her affection. "It was pretty hard at first."

"Enid's nicer than ever."

Trav looked at his hands. It was true that when he and Enid were with his mother, or with Cinda, Enid used toward him many little endearments; but when they were alone, her every word was edged with hatred. Yet this was something he must face alone. "Yes, she's fine," he agreed.

"She seems so fond of you."

He understood that Cinda was not deceived, but not even to Cinda could he speak critically of Enid. "She certainly is. I think we're closer together than we've ever been." He felt this was not convincing, so he said stoutly: "She's wonderful, Cinda; a wonderful woman."

Cinda touched his hand. "Of course she is, Travis. I understand."

Before Cinda returned to Richmond they heard that transports were coming with troops to reinforce Fortress Monroe, no more than forty miles away. General Butler would command there, and Cinda remembered that Brett had met Butler a year ago in Charleston and had thought he would make a dangerous enemy. She told Trav this; and when she was gone, and rumors flew to and fro like doves coming to feed in a stubble field at dawn, Trav to quiet his secret anxieties drove himself to an increased activity. He had long since discharged the overseer who under Tony had proved himself not only a fool but a rascal; he had since then tried one and another without finding any satisfactory candidate. The latest was a man named Jeff Liner, a makeshift whom Trav hoped to replace. One day Jeff came to announce that he was leaving. Trav urged that he stay to see the spring work done, but the other grinned.

"Nawsuh! I don't aim to make a crop for the Yankees to eat."

"No Yankees here yet."

"They will be, soon enough. They been up York River as fur as Gloucester Point already, and they'll be a-coming, a-marching up the roads." Jeff shook his head. "Huh-uh! Not me. I'm going to drag my foot out of here."

"Are you going to fight?"

Jeff spat. "Why, I dunno as it's yours to ask me, Mr. Currain, but I'd as lief tell you straight. This heah's a rich man's war! You all made it. Who gets licked and who don't ain't going to make a mite of difference to folks like me. Reckon you all had better go ahead and fight your own war."

Trav, remembering how often he had heard Ed Blandy and the other men he knew best at Chimneys say almost the same thing, wondered how many thousands all across the Confederacy would take this point of view. Hereabouts, and especially down towards Hampton and across the tip of the Peninsula, the general feeling was against the

Confederacy; but he thought this was not so much loyalty to the Union as an indolent willingness to accept the easy poverty and the drowsy passivity which, since tobacco devoured the fertility of the land, had become the state and the habit of the great majority.

Trav knew that the overseer was not alone in feeling as he did; and he felt in himself some of Jeff's resentment of the war. He wanted to be let alone to solve his problem here. Already he had made progress. Following the gospel according to Edmund Ruffin, using shell marl to make the soil more hospitable to fertilization, he was bringing the old fields back to bearing. To drill in the wheat in the fall and sow clover by hand in the spring, to harvest the wheat in season and let the clover grow without pasturing for a year; then to turn it under, put on marl and guano, raise a crop of corn; when the corn was cut and shocked, drill in the wheat again and begin the process all over: that was the program.

But it took time, years of time; and each year you must hold what you had won. Time, time, time was needed. Yet now, if Jeff were right, time was short. The Yankees would be here before the wheat was ripe for harvest.

Nevertheless Trav persisted. When Jeff Liner was gone, Trav took another lesson from Mr. Ruffin's teaching and decided to do without an overseer. Mr. Ruffin had found that one of his Negroes, Jem Sykes, could to this extent take a white man's place. Here at Great Oak, Big Mill, the giant who now served as driver, keeping the hands to their work, might assume an overseer's responsibilities. When Trav proposed this, Big Mill stood a little straighter; and Trav thought that given authority and responsibility a man sometimes developed character to meet it. Big Mill might be such a one; the experiment was worth trial.

On the last Sunday in May, Great Oak had visitors. Sunday was always a holiday for the people, but Trav rode away at dawn to inspect certain old fields grown up to briers and loblolly and sedge, which unless the Yankees came he meant to have the people clear this summer. On his return, the Negro boy who took his horse excitedly reported: "Mars' Tony here, Marste'. Him and all de gin'r'ls."

Trav in warm pleasure turned toward the house, and in the hall

Tony came to meet him, and Trav felt at once the change in his brother; the strong hand, the high head, the steady tone. Then Julian appeared, a tall young man grown inches since Trav last saw him; and in the drawing room two others waited. He saw Ed Blandy first, and shook his hand; and Ed said, turning respectfully to the fourth man.

"Here's another old friend, Mr. Currain."

"Major Hill!" Trav was delighted to greet again this sharp-tongued, bitter-humored little man, and Tony said:

"But it's Colonel Hill now, Trav. Commanding the First North Carolina Volunteers. That's our regiment. We're at Yorktown, rode over to pay our respects."

It was fine to see Ed Blandy again and to see Tony so changed and steady and sure, and to renew his old friendship with Colonel Hill. Trav heard from Tony the story of the Martinston company; and he said to Ed in friendly amusement: "Well, I'd never have looked for anything like that. The way you all used to talk down there, I didn't expect to see any of you in uniform."

Colonel Hill spoke strongly. "Those who best love peace fight hardest when the time comes, Mr. Currain."

"It was Colonel Hill's idea, our raising the company," Ed explained.

"Who all is in the company?"

Tony answered him, and hearing familiar names of old friends made Trav wish to see them. "I'll have to ride over to Yorktown. How long will you be there? When did you come?"

"We reached Richmond Tuesday night," Tony said. "Came to West Point by the railroad day before yesterday, came by steamboat the rest of the way."

Trav chuckled. "I expect some of your men never rode on the cars, before."

"This wasn't their first time," Tony explained. "We marched to Salisbury but we took the cars from there to Raleigh, so Julian could teach us some soldiering. As far as Raleigh the men were pretty quiet, but when we left there they knocked out the sides of the box cars, and a lot of them rode on top of the cars till we looked like a chicken coop on wheels. They yelled and hooted at every man they saw. They'd got hold of liquor, of course. But they'll be good fighters, Trav."

"Do you look for fighting soon?"

Colonel Hill answered him. "Not unless it's forced on us. We're here just to keep the Yanks where they are as long as we can. We've a line of pickets from Yorktown to the Yankee outposts at Hampton and Newport News; but if there's to be any fighting, they'll have to start it. They outnumber us five or ten to one." The Colonel chuckled. "I call that an even thing—even though you may question my arithmetic; but if General Butler is reinforced faster than we are, he may decide to try something."

Trav said apologetically: "I expect my staying at home seems to you poor business, Colonel; but I know more about farming than I do about war."

"Why, farming's the foundation of fighting, Mr. Currain. Men must eat before they can fight; and before this business is over, food will be scarcer than muskets." Colonel Hill added a warning word. "But unless the Yankees are bigger cowards and fools than I think, you'll not make many crops here."

"You think they'll come this way?"

"It's their safest road to Richmond, with their ships to control the York and the James and protect their flanks."

"I'll have to take my mother away before that happens."

"You'll have time enough." Colonel Hill spoke bitterly. "There's no sign of hurry on the part of the Yankees—and it's too late for us to hurry now. Two months ago—if Virginia and North Carolina had reached an earlier decision—we could have marched into Washington. Now it will take a long time."

Mrs. Currain joined them for dinner. Enid, she told them, was indisposed; and Trav dutifully went upstairs to show some solicitude. It was nothing, Enid assured him; her head ached, that was all. He saw that actually she was furiously angry, and as husbands will he felt guilty without knowing why. "Perhaps if you came down and ate something——"

"I certainly will not!"

"Well, I'm sorry your head aches."

"My head doesn't ache! You know that perfectly well."

"But you said——"

"Oh, don't pretend to be more stupid than you are. I simply refuse to sit at table with that white trash Ed Blandy."

"Why, Enid, Ed Blandy's a real fine——"

"That's right!" she cried. "Stick up for him! You always did! You're as bad as he is, Trav Currain! You're low! That's what's the matter with you. You're just plain low!"

He took a familiar refuge in silence, but his silence only made her more angry than before, till he escaped and rejoined the others, making himself forget Enid in good talk with them. His mother appeared to be completely unconscious of the fact that they were in uniform; when they spoke of warlike matters she seemed not to hear. He found himself wishing it were as easy for him to shut out of his world the bitter knowledge which she refused to accept.

After dinner she excused herself to rest a while. The others must take the road, and he called for his horse too, and went with them for a part of the way, proudly pointing out to Ed and to Tony work already done here, and work planned. When they said good-by at last and he turned homeward loneliness rode with him; he felt himself an outsider, excluded from the comradeship which bound them.

He planned to go soon to Yorktown to see these men and the other Martinston folk; but before he could do so, Brett one late afternoon arrived at Great Oak, his horse's feet splashing in the puddles still standing from a night and morning of rain. To him Trav and Enid gave an eager welcome; and Enid exclaimed with admiration at his uniform, his red "Garibaldi" shirt, short jacket, slouch hat. The Howitzers had reached Yorktown at noon that day; and Brett had a message from Cinda. Burr and Barbara would be married on the twentyninth of June, and Cinda insisted that Mrs. Currain and Trav and Enid come and bring the children.

"Mrs. Pierce wanted to wait longer," Brett explained. "She's one of those people who instinctively tries to put things off; but she'd promised a June wedding, and the children held her to it."

Mrs. Currain said at once that she couldn't think of going to Richmond. "Why, I wouldn't go as far from home as that for my own funeral!" They laughed with her, but Enid caught Brett's eyes with a reassuring nod, as though promising that she would manage the older woman. She began to ask him many questions. He said the Howitzers, although they had but just reached Yorktown, would move out tomorrow with the North Carolina troops to Bethel Church. Scouts had reported that the Yankees were preparing to advance from Fortress Monroe and Newport News; troops would be posted to check them.

"That's why Tony and Julian didn't come with me today," he said. "They were busy getting ready for tomorrow."

But Enid wished to hear what was happening in Richmond. Why, the ladies were sewing all day long, Brett said. Even the churches were turned into sewing circles. Everyone seemed to be sewing except Dolly. She was too busy with her beaux, counted them now not by individuals but by companies and regiments and battalions. All the Richmond belles were warlike, but Dolly was more bloodthirsty than any of them. When the Yankees occupied Alexandria and Colonel Ellsworth pulled down the Confederate flag on Mr. Jackson's hotel and Mr. Jackson shot him, Dolly said that would be a lesson to those old Yankees.

"I reminded her that it was a lesson to Mr. Jackson too," Brett told them, "since he was killed on the spot; but she said that just showed the Yankees were a lot of murderers."

Enid cried: "Of course they are!"

Brett and Trav smiled together; and Brett said Enid was as warlike as the Richmond belles who were declaring that they would not become engaged to any man until after he had fought the Yankees. But Brett was sure that Vesta would say yes to a certain young fellow, the moment he asked her.

"Tommy Cloyd?" Enid asked. "The one who was here at Christmas?"

"Yes. He was in Richmond for a while—he's in Colonel Gregg's regiment—but they're in Northern Virginia now waiting to meet the Yankees." Enid declared she couldn't imagine what Vesta saw in him, but Brett said: "Oh, I can. Tommy's a mighty fine boy."

Enid was hungry for everything he could tell her of these days in Richmond. He said that since the Confederate Government moved there from Montgomery the city grew more crowded every day. To rent a room anywhere already cost an outlandish sum, and prices rose by the hour. President Davis was living at the Spottswood. He was reported to expect a long war and a bloody one. General Beauregard, on his arrival in Richmond a few days before, had a reception equal to that of President Davis and took it modestly. There was a carriage and four waiting to carry him to the Spottswood, but he declined to ride in it, chose a simpler vehicle, refused even to make a speech to the cheering crowd. It was said that President Davis would himself assume command of the army, with Beauregard at his right hand. Meanwhile Beauregard had gone to Manassas to command the troops in Northern Virginia.

Brett had planned to return to Yorktown that night, but they persuaded him to stay till morning, and then Trav rode back with him to Yorktown. Before the march to Bethel got under way he had time to see Tony and Julian and Ed Blandy and Tom Shadd and Judge Meynell and Chelmsford Lowman and a dozen others, old loved friends. In all of them there was a change; and in all except Judge Meynell the change was a pleasing one. They stood more erectly; there was a quickness in their tones, and Trav felt in them a high anticipation.

But Judge Meynell seemed to have aged and to have saddened. Trav asked for Mrs. Meynell, for Miss Mary. They were well, the Judge said; and he put a question in his turn, a surprising question. Where was Darrell?

"Darrell?" Trav echoed. "Why, I believe he's in Richmond. You know him?"

"He was at Chimneys for some months."

"So he was. I'd forgotten."

"We had the frequent—pleasure of seeing him at our home."

"To be sure," Trav agreed. "Yes, I'm sure he is in Richmond." And he said courteously: "When you write, please give your ladies my kind remembrances. I don't think I've seen Miss Mary since one day when you and she were taking the stage. You were going to court. She was a mighty excited little Miss Somebody that day!"

The Judge made no comment. He turned back to his men, and Trav had an uneasy feeling that something was amiss; but he forgot this in watching the troops begin their march. It seemed to him they were cruelly burdened, and that their garments were ill chosen. The majority wore tremendous boots reaching to their knees or above, their heavy trousers stuffed into the boot tops. Their double-breasted coats, wadded for greater warmth, had skirts that hung around their knees. Each man shouldered a musket, and from his belt dangled a canteen, and sometimes a pistol; and most of them had at least one long-bladed knife thrust through their belts. Their knapsacks were sufficiently capacious to contain tobacco, pipes, linen and lint for bandages, soap, towels, underwear, socks, ammunition; but in addition many of them lugged a haversack or a carpet bag or a valise in their hands; and all of them had strapped to their knapsacks blankets rolled in oil cloth. A fair proportion carried kettles and frying pans. Loaded down like pack mules, they trudged away along the muddy roads through spatters of rain.

He wondered whether the men need to carry so much, and looking for a possible informant he saw Colonel Hill, mounted, sitting with another officer who was resplendent in blue pantaloons with a red cord down the seam, blue roundabout lined with crimson velvet, black cocked hat with a long drooping feather, long scabbard hanging low. Trav watched till this dazzling figure moved away, then joined Colonel Hill and asked who the other man was.

"That was Colonel Magruder, commanding here at Yorktown." Colonel Hill smiled. "A fine officer, but something of a dandy. The men are already calling him the Duke of York."

Trav remarked on the heavy loads the soldiers carried. "Some of them will be tired before night," he suggested.

The other nodded. "But they'll learn," he predicted. "A year from now they'll know that a blanket and a tin cup and a gun are all they need." He waved a careless hand. "Every man there is toting enough victuals to keep him stuffed for a week; but by tomorrow night they'll have eaten it or wasted it or lost it. If we stay a week at Bethel Church they'll be starving."

"No need of that," Trav assured him. "There's plenty to eat all around here."

"It has to be brought to them, passed out to them."

Trav cut a bit of tobacco, put it in his mouth, watched the men trudge by. "Would it help if I fetched you some supplies?"

The other man grunted. "Help? It might win a battle for us!"

Trav, riding homeward, turning this project in his mind, let his horse take its own pace; so he was late for supper and had to meet Enid's reproaches, hushed as soon as they joined Mrs. Currain. He had come to count on such relief from Enid's chidings, for in Mrs. Currain's presence she was always outwardly smiling and prettily affectionate. But only his mother could thus protect him. Even when Lucy and Peter were in the room, Enid's tongue forever flicked at Trav, so that he sometimes saw Lucy—she was twelve now, a grave, thoughtful child and his heart's delight—watching her mother with expressionless eyes. Trav had once urged Enid not to harangue him when Lucy could hear; but she retorted:

"I wouldn't, if you didn't always provoke me so."

After supper, he lost himself in plans to take supplies to the force at Bethel. The simple mathematics involved: how much corn, how much pork, how many wagons, how many mules, how many miles to travel, how long to cover the distance—these absorbed him. He listed the plantations along the way which would contribute wagons loaded with provender, prepared quotas for each to meet; and next day he wrote notes which he sent off by hand to the neighbors upon whom he meant to levy. When they answered, he tallied their replies and was sure there would be enough and to spare.

From the stores at Great Oak, he loaded two huge wagons. They were high, long-bodied vehicles with canvas covers stretched on arching bows, made years ago by Mr. Wells of Halifax Street in Petersburg and designed to carry three hogsheads of tobacco or an equivalent load. Six mules were required to draw each one. Before nightfall, the wagons were filled. He set trusted Negroes to stand guard on them through the night, and early next morning they took the road.

They picked up others on the way, and the caravan grew. The black drivers were in picnic humor, singing, laughing, calling to and fro; but each pause meant delay, and they covered only some twenty miles that day, and stopped the night at Lebanon Church. Trav heard at the tavern that there had already been some skirmishing, and that already the soldiers were short of provisions, so next day he would have preferred to push on; but the Sunday peace was not to be disturbed and he surrendered to firm custom. Monday morning, before full day, he set the wagon train in motion.

Not since his boyhood had Trav seen the lower Peninsula. The roads were strange to him; he had more than once to inquire the way, and regretted he had not asked Colonel Hill to furnish him a guide. The low rolling hills which gave variety to the turnpike from Richmond to Williamsburg here flattened out into a plain with no landmarks by which to set a course, level and without character. He led his train of wagons through Cockletown and on to Halfway House and found there some men of the Howitzers, their gun mounted on a farm wagon drawn by two horses. Go straight ahead, they told him, pointing down the road; and they bade him hurry lest he miss the fun! So he told the drivers to press forward without another halt, and he rode on at a trot. He met men on foot, white men, small farmers, hurrying northward away from the approaching fight; he met an old Negro on a laden cart, sweating with haste and with his own exertions as he belabored his philosophical mule. Fear emanated from them all alike. When Trav tried to question them they answered shortly and without pausing in their flight.

The sandy road, following the border of a wood with tilled land on his left, brought him suddenly in sight of a wall of fresh-dug earth squarely across the road, and he saw men moving to and fro beyond it. He rode on at a foot pace toward where a church stood by the road, and saw many men in uniform, and a few cannon, and then someone hailed him and Brett came vaulting over the low bank of dirt to meet him and to shake his hand.

"Trav! Where did you come from?"

Trav looked back over his shoulder along the road by which he had ridden. "Why, we've got together some supplies, corn and pork and coffee. The wagons aren't far behind me, a mile or two."

"Good man! We'll be hungry presently!" Trav felt the high excitement in the other. "We've been at it already, Trav!" Brett said. "The officers routed us out in the middle of the night, marched us off down the New Market road till a woman—Mrs. Tunnell, her name was—met us and said the Yankees were out in force and had come to her house and captured her husband; so we fell back here to our works to wait for them."

"Where's Tony?"

"His company's posted ahead, beyond the creek." Trav's eyes looked where Brett pointed. "Julian's with the cadets down in the angle opposite the church. Leave your horse here. I'll put you where you can see the whole thing!"

Trav obeyed, having no longer any will of his own. He was rather stupefied than excited, seeing all clearly yet not believing what he saw. This was some absurd make-believe. Here were a thousand men and boys grouped in a roughly oval enclosure, surrounded by banks of fresh dug earth. The road, including a fork above the church, was within the enclosure. Except for the church and a few trees beside it, the oval was all open ground; but forest walled it on the west. Below the church the road dipped into a wooded ravine, and over the tops of the trees Trav saw a bridge. Beyond, the road ascended a low plateau toward scattered houses and small buildings some distance off.

Brett introduced Trav to Major Randolph, standing by his guns below the church; and the Major, his small, narrowed eyes fixed on the road beyond the creek which his guns here commanded, acknowledged the introduction without turning his head. "Mr. Currain! Servant, sir."

Brett bade Trav stay here. "My place is over yonder. You'll be able to see everything." He hurried toward the bridge, and Trav felt himself lost and strange in these surroundings. Then Colonel Hill, mounted, coming to speak to Major Randolph, recognized Trav, and asked sharply:

"What are you doing here?"

"I've a few wagonloads of food coming along behind me, sir. I rode ahead to tell you, but if I'm in the way . . ."

"Good! No, stay." Colonel Hill seemed distracted, his eyes resting on the church near which they stood; and he was silent so long that Trav felt upon himself the burden of speech.

"It's a good many years since I've been this far down the Peninsula," he remarked.

The Colonel smiled faintly. "Yes, I too." He added: "This was my mother's church, Mr. Currain. I was baptized in it, worshipped here till I was a boy of sixteen."

Before Trav could reply, a distant shout drew their eyes, and on the low knoll across the creek Trav saw a man wave and point along the road. He looked that way and caught his breath. The road ran in the deep shade of trees that lined its eastern side; some small buildings obscured it on the right. In the shade Trav saw movement, and small gleaming shafts of light, and Major Randolph turned and spoke to Colonel Hill:

"There they are, sir."

The Colonel nodded. The men at their guns began to talk together in sharp tones; and one of them called: "What time is it, please sir, Colonel Hill?"

"Nine o'clock."

"Thank you kindly, Colonel."

Colonel Hill said, half to himself: "There's a cool lad!"

Trav tried to speak his agreement, but his lips were dry, his throat full. He was trembling with a ridiculous violence, and when he sought to speak, his teeth chattered so loudly that he was afraid someone would hear. He tried to cut a bit of tobacco from his twist, but his hands shook so that he could not open his knife; he gnawed off a piece instead.

Major Randolph spoke. "They've halted there, Colonel."

"That's the advanced post," Colonel Hill decided. "They've sighted us, but they'll wait for the main column to come up to them."

"Shall I scatter them? The Parrott gun will reach."

"Not yet." The Colonel spoke with a grim humor. "Wait till they lay a few more necks on the block."

"You will give me the word?" the Major asked. Colonel Hill nodded, and Major Randolph went himself to lay the gun. It seemed to Trav an endless time they waited. His eyes glazed with staring at those bright things yonder.

"What is it we see, Colonel?" he asked. "Those shining things."

"Their bayonets," the Colonel told him curtly. "The blades flash, even in that deep shade."

There was more waiting, till Trav felt himself suffocating, and filled his lungs, and realized that he had forgotten to breathe. Even to draw breath became at this moment a conscious act, so completely were all his functions paralyzed. Was this fear? Perhaps. His mind was not afraid, but his hands shook, his knees knocked together, his teeth were chattering. He could not even spit! The tobacco in his mouth was hardly moist, a shredded ball. He expelled it with an outblown breath, and suddenly he realized that there were many more bright blades in the shade yonder, the steel catching the morning sun. So the main column had come up to the advance.

Beside him, Colonel Hill said calmly: "Fire."

With the discharge of the Parrott gun that opened the action, Trav's senses were at once sharpened and confused. He was conscious of tremendous noises, but they merged and overlapped and lost all meaning. He saw the gunners a few paces off active at their pieces, heard their gleeful shouts; he saw the flashes and the smoke; through the smoke now and then he saw men in motion. His attention fixed itself on small things, things that were comprehensible, welcome little things which since they fitted into the world he knew brought this fantastic scene nearer reality.

It was this hunger for the familiar that led him to watch one of the cannoneers who was trying to lead down from behind the church a mule attached to a caisson which had been made by securing ammunition chests on the running gear of a common farm wagon. The chest seemed to be loaded with cannon balls, for a rolling and thumping in it alarmed the mule; the beast set stubborn heels and refused to move, and the man tugged and swore and then abandoned the struggle and tied the reins to a tree.

"Stay there, then!" he shouted furiously. "You long-eared son of a jackass! I hope the first shot takes your cranky head off!"

He began to pass the cannon balls by hand, carrying them the dozen paces to his gun; and Trav watched the mule, now calmly content, jerk at the reins till it got slack enough so that it could reach the weeds at its feet and begin serenely to graze. About that time the Yankee guns came into action, and Trav saw men fling themselves down to avoid the cannon balls, and then spring up again; and he felt rather than heard a sudden, thumping sound and turned to look.

A shot, a solid shot, striking the mule fair and full just behind the fore legs, low down, had passed clear through its body. When Trav turned, the beast was trying to rear; and from its wound poured a cascade of blood, a stream as thick as a man's leg, bright crimson, a torrent. Then the mule fell on its side and lay feebly kicking. It was incredible that so much blood could come out of one mule! Why, that mule was a barrel of blood, a bag of blood, draining and emptying now. Trav took one uncertain step toward the dying mule, and slipped and looked down and saw a brook of blood running across his boots.

A convulsion shook him. Instinctively he ran as far as the corner of the church. There he fell on his knees, and opened his mouth and saw helplessly another torrent pour like a cataract out of his open mouth. Not blood, this! It came again, but it was less; again, again, till there was only a thin bitter trickle which he tried to spit away. But it clung stickily to his lips and would not let go, hanging in nasty strings. He crawled aside and collapsed on his face there by the church, his body still tormented by fruitless retching, till all the strength went out of him, and exhaustion drugged him, and the world receded and was gone. He lay insensible, knowing neither place nor time.

It was Brett who roused him, shaking him, turning him over, lifting him into a sitting position. "Trav! Trav! What's the matter, man? Trav! Trav, wake up!" So Trav came slowly back to full consciousness again, to consciousness of jubilant voices all around him, of the smell of burned powder, of the smell of blood. His stomach again revolted; but Brett said quickly: "Here!" Raw liquor found his mouth, he spat it out; yet enough of the fire of it still stung him so that his senses cleared. "Are you hurt, Trav? What happened?"

"That mule!"

"What mule? Did it kick you?"

"It was so full of blood!"

Brett said: "Stand up! Get on your feet. You'll feel better." With Brett helping, Trav managed it. The world around him swayed and whirled and then steadied slowly into place again.

"What happened?" he mumbled.

"We licked them, sent them skedaddling!" Brett's voice rang; he laughed aloud. "They ran like sheep!" he cried. "The cavalry's chasing them now."

"Is it over?"

"All over! We licked them, sent them off with their tails between their legs! You should have seen Tony, Trav! He was grand. And Julian, the cadets, they were the steadiest men on the field!"

"I saw the blood come out of that mule, and it just scared the dog-water out of me."

Brett laughed aloud. "You weren't scared! Why, even some of the regular Numbers at one gun got sick. The blood turned your stomach, that's all."

"I didn't feel scared," Trav admitted. "But it certainly cleaned me out."

"You were excited! So was I!" Brett said honestly: "I made the worst mistake of anyone. I was Number Three on the howitzer over across the creek. My job was to puncture the powder cartridge with a priming wire—through the vent, you know. I got in too much of a hurry, stuck the primer in before the cartridge was in place, and the rammer bent the wire so I couldn't get it out. That spiked the gun and put it out of action. Oh, everyone was excited! I saw more than one of them vomiting, too. That's not being scared!"

Trav grinned weakly. "Well, if that wasn't being scared, I don't ever want to be."

"You're all right. Where are those wagons of yours? Everybody's hungry!"

"Why, they can't be far off. I'll ride back up the road, see if I can hurry them." To have something definite to do was reassuring. "I left my horse somewhere." His world was still a great confusion.

"I'll borrow a mount, go along with you," Brett decided. "Wait till I speak to Major Randolph."

They had not half a mile to go before they met the wagons. Trav wished Brett to take charge of them, proposed himself to ride homeward; but Brett insisted that he return. "You've thanks coming to you," he promised. "Colonel Hill will want to see you."

Brett was right in this prediction. When the train of wagons reached the earthworks, shouting men crowded around them; in a moment fires were going, and the fragrance of fat pork broiling in the flames began to fill the air. Trav saw in all these men and boys an equal exhilaration. Even Colonel Hill, when he came toward them with Major Randolph, showed the same unnatural stimulation. Was this what battle did to men? Did it make each individual a little more than his usual self, multiply and magnify him? It was as though all these warriors had drunk deep of some heady wine.

"You're responsible for this bounty?" Colonel Hill demanded.

"Why, Mr. Currain, this is better than another victory! You understand soldiering, sir."

Trav grinned. "I'm afraid not, Colonel. I haven't the stomach for it. Sight of blood—even a mule's blood—sickened me."

"Pah! That can happen to anyone! It takes boys with no imagination to do the fighting—did you see how gallantly my cadets handled themselves today, sir?—but older men like you and me are needed to lead and to feed them. The South needs men like you. Colonel Magruder will make a place for you as commissary—Mr. Vaughan is acting for him temporarily—if you're at liberty to serve."

"I'll have to make some arrangements first, sir," Trav confessed. "But—I doubt my own fitness. I lost my senses so completely I don't know what happened, even now."

The Colonel's eyes lighted. "Ah, it was a day of glory, sir! Yes, two days of glory, Saturday and again today. Twice Saturday we chased the Yankees across New Market Bridge, and now Captain Douthatt and his dragoons are chivvying them along the same course! Every man on the field today bore himself like a hero of legend, Mr. Currain! Major Randolph and his guns—" He pointed, and Trav saw the Major and Brett talking quietly together a little way off, thought Major Randolph alone among all these men here seemed calm and normal. "I tell you, Mr. Currain, as an artillerist, Major Randolph has no superior in any army in the world!" Trav thought with faint amusement that the Colonel in this hour of triumph was taking in a good deal of territory! "My field officers, my captains— By the way, Mr. Currain, Captain Currain and his Martinston men especially distinguished themselves. When Captain Bridges was ordered to retake our advanced position he was so excited that he forgot to tell his men to follow him, ran forward alone! Captain Currain saw the situation and led his own men forward, and Captain Bridges's company went shoulder to shoulder with them! Ah, sir, it was glorious! The Yankees were five times our numbers, and we've chased them for miles!"

Trav nodded. "That's fine, sir." He asked: "Were there many—hurt?"

"One of our fine boys, Henry Wyatt, yes. I fear for him. A few others were lightly wounded." His voice rang. "But the fields yonder are littered with Yankee dead! They must have lost three or four hundred men!" He laughed dryly. "I can't place their losses lower without accusing them of a degree of cowardice disgraceful even in a Yankee! For they were five to our one, Mr. Currain! Five to our one! Yes, in fact the odds were nearer ten to one, since not five hundred of our men even fired their pieces."

He was willing to talk endlessly. Trav had never seen him so vocal. The little man seemed taller than usual, as though inches had been added to his stature in this hour. Then Colonel Magruder appeared from the church and gave a dispatch to a rider who galloped away; and Magruder too, when he heard what Trav had done, was grateful. Trav was amused by the splendor of the other's uniform and by the Colonel's childish lisp, incongruous in such a gorgeous figure; nevertheless these profuse acknowledgments impressed him. Clearly, within this business of war, to supply the men was a task worth doing. Before he went to Richmond for Burr's wedding he had put affairs at Great Oak in such order that he could if he were needed be absent for a while.

21

FOR the four years after Sumter, the whole business of the South was war; but to each individual war wore a different aspect. To Vesta Dewain, its onset was a spur, an urgent warning: "Hurry, hurry, hurry! Hurry before it is too late!" She was twenty years old, and she had known Tommy Cloyd through most of her childhood at the Plains; but not till a year or two ago had she begun to see in him something more than a nice, awkward, stammering boy. Since then she had come to be sure that she loved him and that he loved her, and to assume that time would in some beautiful fashion presently bring them close to each other and that they would cleave together forever.

But now with the sudden roll of drums there was no more time. When Sumter fell, Vesta and Burr were alone in the house on Fifth Street, Cinda and Brett in South Carolina. Vesta wished her mother and father were here; and Burr's happiness with Barbara made her long for Tommy. She wrote him, not to say any of the things she wished to say but only because to write him somehow eased her loneliness; but before her letter had time to reach him, one from him came to her. He said his company would soon reach Richmond as a part of Colonel Gregg's regiment, and a week before Cinda and Brett returned from the Plains he arrived.

Vesta was one among hundreds of pretty girls at the station eager to welcome these valiant boys. Had not some of them been among the heroes in the bloodless victory at Sumter! Oh, war was glorious and beautiful and fine! Vesta caught the infection, she cheered and sang with the rest; but while she lent herself to the smiling confusion of that happy welcoming, her eyes sought Tommy everywhere.

When ranks were formed she discovered him, stiff and straight, visibly gulping with excitement while he awaited the command to march; and through brimming, laughing eyes, she saw his Adam's apple pump nervously up and down, and knew how he must be trembling, and loved him because he was so young and so anxious to look every inch a soldier. She tried to come near him, and when a moving file blocked her way she called: "Tommy! Tommy! Oh, Tommy Cloyd!" He did not turn his head; but she saw his ears red with pleasure, so she knew he had heard. Then the column began to move, small boys tramping proudly beside the soldiers in the dusty street, pretty girls with a skip and a run to keep the pace scurrying along the sidewalks. Vesta saw Dolly, on the arm of a tall young officer, watching the regiment pass, and Dolly introduced her escort, Lieutenant something or other.

"He's in the army at Yorktown," Dolly explained, with a flashing upward smile at the bedazzled youngster beside her. "They're going to keep the Yankees shut up in Fortress Monroe till they all die of yellow fever or something." Then, as Vesta tried to hurry on: "Don't go, darling!"

"I have to. I want to keep up. Tommy Cloyd's with them."

"You know perfectly well he'll come to call this evenin'," Dolly argued; but Vesta laughed and scurried on.

She kept up with Tommy's company all the long way to Camp Pickens, and saw the men dismiss, and when Tommy was free she captured him and kissed him and felt his shy embarrassment and said in laughing reassurance:

"Oh, Tommy! Everybody's kissing everybody! Don't be so bothered! Tommy, can you come right away home to supper?"

He could, and they set out together, Vesta's hand through his arm, her heart full of happiness. She poured out many questions.

"Was the trip hard?"

"Why, I guess so. But everybody was too excited to mind. You know the way you feel when your foot goes to sleep! I felt like that all over. I was some excited, and some scared, too."

"Pooh! I bet you're not scared!"

"Yes'm! I guess most of us are. I guess that's why everybody keeps saying how the Yankees won't fight, and how quick we'll be in Washington, and what we'll do to old Abe Lincoln when we catch him."

"I bet you will, too. The Yankee papers say they'll hang President Davis in Washington on the Fourth of July, but I'll bet you'll go and hang Lincoln instead." She asked: "Is Rollin Lyle in your regiment?"

"Yes, ma'am, in the Richland Rifles. His old company, most of them wouldn't come, so he joined the Columbia company."

"Wouldn't come? Why not, for Heaven's sake?"

"Some of our company felt the same way. They said they didn't volunteer to fight for Virginia."

"For Virginia!" She flamed with indignation. "I like that! Why, Virginia's fighting for them, Tommy! We didn't have to come into their old war. They had to get so uppity and start it, and then when they got in trouble we took their part; but if they're going to talk like that——"

He grinned appeasingly. "That was just some of them, Vesta; just making an excuse to stay home. Mama says the farmers she knows at home are beginning to say this is a rich man's war, and that the poor men will have to fight it. She told me to come and show them that that wasn't so!" He added: "Colonel Gregg promised the ones who did come that they could go home when their enlistments expire on the first of July, or I guess hardly anyone would have come at all. But I'm not going home till the fighting's over."

She squeezed his arm, said proudly: "Julian's in the Charlotte Grays."

"Julian? Golly, Vesta, he's awful young."

"He's only sixteen. But nobody in the Grays is over twenty-one, and all the cadets enlisted, practically! But I guess everybody has; everybody who is anybody."

"Jeff Major, down home, said he wasn't going to," Tommy told her. "But some of the young ladies sent him a package of petticoats, so he did." He grinned. "I guess a young man isn't going to be very popular if he doesn't."

"It's the same in Richmond. Everybody I know has enlisted—except Darrell."

"Who is he?"

"Darrell Streean, Dolly's brother. You remember Dolly. She visited me down at the Plains, last year."

He nodded. "When Rollin—" he began, then said only: "Yes, I remember her. Awfully pretty."

"He's a clerk in the Quartermaster's office," she said. "But he's just no good anyway. But all the other boys are in the army, and all the ladies are sewing like mad, making things for soldiers."

"It's the same in Camden," he agreed. "They gave us a battle flag before we left home. The young ladies made it, and they had a banquet, and Miss Betsy Beaufort made a presentation speech that sounded mighty fine, but Romer Pettigrew had written it all out for her. He's the color sergeant, so he was the one to receive the flag, and he had to make a speech back at her; and then they got married the next day, and the wedding coming right on top of the banquet that way, nobody had much chance to sleep any, those two days."

"Oh, what fun!" Her heart quickened. This talk of weddings might lead to what she wished to hear him say. "I'll bet he'll fight all the harder, remembering her at home, and knowing she's loving him and praying for him."

"I don't know," he said in a doubtful tone. "He might worry more about getting—hurt or something." He added hurriedly: "Then it was a big day when we marched to the station, everyone giving us presents and things, cakes and goodies and money too. You'd see gentlemen emptying their pockets and making the boys take the money, and all the girls were kissing everybody."

"Did they kiss you?" she asked teasingly.

"Yes, ma'am!" He grinned and wiped his mouth with his knuckles. "I guess I got kissed about a hundred times. It was real nice. But the train ride was pretty hot and noisy. We had to eat up all the things they'd given us quick, because we were so crowded you couldn't put anything anywhere; and then there'd be a new crowd at every station and the same celebration all over again. We got a chance to clean up, once; stopped by a branch out in the country clear away from everywhere. But nights you couldn't sleep. I'm so sleepy I might as well be dead."

"Poor Tommy!" She shook his arm. "But don't you dare go to sleep now!"

"No, ma'am, I'm too worked up to sleep, I guess." He grinned. "It was funny to see the men throwing things away between stations. People kept giving us so much, so we'd throw most of it out of the windows, and then the next station we'd have to take on a new load. The folks along the railroad can pick up enough things to eat right along the tracks to feed them all summer. The whole trip was like a picnic." He added soberly: "I guess they won't think drilling is so much of a picnic. None of us know very much about being soldiers, Vesta. It will take a while to learn."

Vesta was to hear him say something like this more than once during the two weeks and a little more before his regiment departed. She went almost every day to camp to watch the endless drills, and she too wondered why they were necessary. "I don't see why you can't just go start whipping Yankees," she protested. Tommy tried to answer her, but she was not satisfied until one day at camp she saw General Lee watching a dress parade. She had never seen him before, but she knew how highly he was respected and how deeply loved by all Virginia men. He was tall, strongly built, erect and finely posed, with black hair barely touched with gray, and a black mustache. Vesta thought him the handsomest man she had ever seen. If such a man as he approved all this absurd marching to and fro, why, then it must be wise and necessary.

So she argued the point with Tommy no more; but—especially after Cinda and Brett came home—they returned to one argument again and again. Tommy said learning to be a soldier took time, and that a man engaged in this arduous study ought not to think about getting married. Vesta retorted that Burr did not feel that way; that he and Barbara Pierce were to be married pretty soon.

"Well, Burr's in the cavalry," Tommy reminded her. "That's different. He already knows about riding and shooting and things. He doesn't have to learn drill and marching and all that; but I do, and I'm not very smart. It's bound to take me a long time."

"But, Tommy," Vesta urged, "just suppose—just for instance—that it was you and me, and you were just starting out to war, the way you are, and we were in love with each other." A dark wave of color swept his cheeks and she repeated reassuringly: "Oh, just for instance, I mean. But wouldn't you want us to be married right away?"

He swallowed hard. "Well, I guess it isn't so much a question what a man wants, as what he thinks he ought to do."

Thus for the time he silenced her, but she told her mother next morning, in one of those long breakfast-time talks which meant so much to both of them: "Honestly, he makes me so mad sometimes I could just slap him."

Cinda smiled. "I don't believe it! You're really proud of him for feeling that way. Tommy's such a sweet, shy youngster that it's easy to think of him as just a boy; but he's really a fine man." She laughed fondly. "Make up your mind to it, darling, you'll never be able to lead him around by the nose! He'll be the head of the family!"

"He'll never be the head of our family if he doesn't hurry!"

"I've always loved Tommy," Cinda confessed. "Now I'm learning to respect him too—and so are you."

"Oh, I suppose so! But I think he's an awful old slow poke, just the same!"

Clayton brought Jenny and the children to Richmond. He could stay a day or two, must then report to General Beauregard at Manassas to serve on the General's staff. He left on the Saturday morning train; and Vesta saw Jenny's good-by to him, Jenny's fine smile hiding those secret terrors which she must be feeling. Vesta found stinging tears in her own eyes. Suppose she herself were Jenny. Suppose she and Tommy were married, and she too was soon to have a baby. Could she give Tommy a smiling good-by kiss and let him go? She thought not; yet perhaps being married, becoming part of another as that other became part of you, somehow multiplied your strength and his.

Tommy came for supper that night. His regiment was ordered to move across the city to Camp Charleston; he had heard that they would within a day or two go in the cars to Manassas Gap. Vesta had held Tommy in her thoughts all day; she told him of that farewell she had seen. "I think she's marvelous, don't you?"

"I've always thought she was pretty wonderful," he assured her. "I didn't have to find it out now. She's been that way right along."

"If I were married," Vesta confessed, "if you and I were married, for instance, I don't see how I could bear to have you go." And when he only blushed in silence, she protested: "Tommy, whenever I say that —about you and me being married—you never say anything!"

"Well—you just said 'for instance.'"

She touched his hand, herself now as shy as he. "I keep talking about it, Tommy, to—sort of get you used to the idea."

"Oh, I know that. I mean, I know you don't mean—well, anything."

She started to speak, then hesitated; but presently his regiment would depart, and he must go with them to face what dangers she dared not even guess; and he was so slow, so slow! She could not wait. Time was too short. She said abruptly: "But I do, Tommy. I do—mean something!"

"Eh?" He gulped and swallowed hard.

"I mean everything!" He was so long silent that at last she had to speak. "Tommy, you've been in love with me for—just years and years. You know you have." He wiped his helpless brow. "Haven't you?" she demanded, and in tender impatience: "Oh, for Heaven's sake, say something!"

"Why—why, yes, ma'am, I wouldn't wonder if that's so," he admitted.

"I've been in love with you, Tommy, just as long as you've been in love with me!" She saw that he could not speak. "Do I have to—say it all, Tommy? I want you, please sir, to marry me."

"Oh, I want to marry you all right." He blurted out the words in startled haste. "I guess you know that."

"Well, then! Oh, Tommy—" She rocked with helpless, relieved laughter. "You idiot, why didn't you say so long ago?"

"Well, I guess I would have, probably, if it wasn't for the war coming this way."

"But, Tommy darling, that's all the more reason!"

He shook his head, spoke more surely. "No, Vesta. No, it's all the more reason for not—doing anything. You see, I've got to learn how to be a soldier. I couldn't be a good one if every time I went to shoot a Yankee I started thinking about you."

"Couldn't you fight all the harder if you were fighting for me?"

He found fumbling words. "I'm not very good at saying what I mean, Vesta; but—well, it looks to me as if I was different, somehow. The other men talk about killing Yankees as if it wasn't going to bother them at all, and I guess a soldier has to be that way. They talk as if Yankees were like sheep-killing dogs, that just ought to be shot.

But the chances are a lot of Yankees are pretty fine young men." She wished to interrupt, hotly to contradict, but now at last he was completely vocal, and she was caught and moved by something behind his words. "I mean, some are a bad lot, probably, but that's so everywhere. I keep thinking that in the North there must be a lot of boys like me, boys that just want to be—well, friends with folks. But they're getting ready to be soldiers, getting ready to be shot at, and to shoot at us. I've got to learn how to be that way too. But if I were married—to you, for instance—any time I set out to shoot a Yankee I'd be thinking: why, maybe he's got a wife at home that seems to him as nice and sweet as Vesta seems to me, and if I shoot him she'll cry awful." He shook his head. "I couldn't shoot straight, feeling that way. I have to learn to forget all about people loving people, their wives and their babies and their mothers and all that. I have to learn to just go ahead and try to kill people as if they were so many hogs I was slaughtering, and forget about their being young men like me. That's what it is being a soldier. That's what I have to learn. I guess wars are bad things, just on account of that. I mean because they make boys and young men learn how to kill other boys and young men without ever feeling bad about it. It's wrong, Vesta, to teach anything like that.

"But I have to learn it. And it's going to take me a long time as it is. I couldn't ever do it if—if I was married to you, if you'd ever showed me how sweet it is to have someone love you. I couldn't do it, Vesta." He was silent for a moment, said then helplessly: "Well, I guess I can't really tell you just what I do mean."

She had been when he began impatient, almost angry: while he spoke, retorts had come into her mind—and remained unspoken. Now they were forgotten. Her throat was full of proud tears and she dared not try to speak. Instead she rose and came to him, and he looked at her humbly, and she took his face between her hands and kissed his lips, once lightly, then with a fierce long pressure.

Then she could speak. "I know what you mean, Tommy. I think you're the sweetest, finest man in the world." She laughed, like a sob. "I'll promise, cross my heart, never to ask you again to marry me." And in a proud tenderness: "But if you ever ask me, Tommy, I'll marry you as quick as scat!"

He was quiet now and strong: "I will ask you, one day, Vesta. I will ask you soon."

She faced him, straight and proud. "I'll be ready, Tommy. Oh, I will be so ready, my dearest, darling man!"

When he left her she stood in the open door to watch him stride away; and she lay awake for hours in a brimming happiness, till all the sounds of the city hushed and she could hear the murmur of the river singing along the rapids not far distant. Next morning she went early to Cinda's room, eager to share her secret. "Mama, I asked Tommy to marry me," she said, all in a breath, her face transfigured; but then she hesitated, suddenly knowing that she could not tell even her mother this beautiful and sacred thing. Was this a part of marriage, then; to share with one other, and with no one else at all, that which your two hearts knew? "We talked it over," she finished calmly, "and decided to wait a while."

Cinda smiled, beckoned her near, kissed her. "They don't come any finer than Tommy, do they, dear?"

"They certainly don't!"

"It wasn't hard to talk to him, was it, when the time came?"

"Why, it just seemed to be the most natural thing in the world. I mean—well, after we got started, we weren't embarrassed or anything. He's wonderful, Mama."

Cinda nodded. "Sit down and have your coffee." Someone knocked and she called: "Come in." So Jenny joined them; and during the hour that followed they laughed together over little happy things. Vesta thought they all laughed so easily because these two somehow shared the happiness in her. I thought I loved Tommy before, she told herself; but that was nothing! I never really did till now!

She and Cinda went to Dr. Minnigerode's church that morning; and when they sang, Vesta heard her own voice as though it were a stranger's, rising strong and rich and true. Perhaps this too was one of love's miracles, this inner enrichment; or was it just her own imagination that told her she sang so well? No, for as they walked homeward Cinda spoke of it.

"You must be very happy, Vesta. I never heard you sing as beautifully as you did today."

When Tommy departed, Vesta was proud to see him go, understanding now how Jenny could be strong in the certainty of Clayton's love. Cinda went for a few days at Great Oak, and Brett was learning his duties as a member of the Howitzers; so Vesta was alone, yet without being lonely, for Tommy was always in her thoughts and Burr, training at Ashland, often came home.

"Yet I might as well stay in camp," he told Vesta, laughing at his own words. "Barbara's too busy getting ready for our wedding to bother with me, says I'm just in the way." Vesta suspected some hurt bewilderment in him. "Of course, she has to handle her mother."

"There, Honey, you leave Mrs. Pierce to Barbara!"

"Oh, of course." He added: "Barbara has a mind of her own, all right. She knows how to get her own way."

Vesta smiled. Most men failed to realize that their sweethearts would not always be sweetly submissive. Burr was clever even to suspect the truth about Barbara while he was still so desperately in love with her. Barbara was nice as she could be, of course; but in the long run she would make Burr toe the mark. There was no doubt of that.

"Never mind," she said, to comfort him. "After all, it's just that she's getting ready to marry you."

One day after Cinda's return she spoke of this conversation to her mother. "Burr really sounded so bewildered, Mama. I was awfully sorry for him."

Cinda smiled faintly. "Barbara's a quiet little mouse, but she knows exactly what she wants."

Vesta said in sudden understanding: "You have to be pretty careful to like the people your children are going to marry, don't you, Mama?"

"Of course. But thank heaven I do like Barbara."

"You know, Mama, there are some people you just love from the beginning," Vesta suggested. "Jenny, for instance. And there are others you like, but you never quite dare love them, for fear they don't love you." She added: "I like Barbara too; but sometimes I'm a little scared of her."

She and Cinda had through this month of June many hours together. Sometimes Jenny was with them, but not always. Without ever seeming to withdraw into herself, yet although they shared the same roof she lived a life of her own. "It's as though she knew we liked to be together," Vesta told Cinda once. "And wouldn't intrude."

In the city about them each day brought changes, and some of them were disturbing. Richmond was the gateway through which troops from the South moved to Yorktown, or to Manassas; and it seemed to Vesta that there were so many they must prove irresistible. But her father, when she said this, did not easily agree.

"They make a fine show," he admitted. "All the bright new uniforms, and officers on high-tailed horses galloping everywhere; but we need more men, and we need weapons. A lot of the guns we have are so old-fashioned and worn out they're not safe to shoot. The trouble is, each state wants an army of its own. Governor Brown of Georgia shipped the best muskets from the Augusta arsenal to Savannah before he turned the arsenal over to the Confederacy, and he won't let Georgia regiments take those muskets outside the state. If we had all the regiments and all the weapons in the South today up here where the fighting is going to be, we could march right to Washington before the North gets ready for war. But Alabama's keeping most of her regiments at home, and so is Louisiana and so's Mississippi, and North Carolina thinks she has to defend her coast, and South Carolina and Georgia are just as bad."

Vesta remembered what Tommy had told her. "Some of the South Carolina boys just refused to come, in Colonel Gregg's regiment." She added: "But I'm not sure there aren't too many soldiers in Richmond as it is. Those terrible Zouaves you and Mama saw on the train, for instance. Dolly and I went into Pizzini's for strawberries yesterday, and two of them had a fight right outside the door, slashing at each other with knives and spattering blood halfway across Broad Street. We were terrified!"

"They wouldn't annoy young ladies, you know."

"Well, I think they fought over one. I saw them talking to her just before they started. She was a horrible-looking creature, too!" She saw his troubled eyes and added quickly: "Oh, we had escorts, Papa; two friends of Dolly's. We weren't afraid, really."

He smiled. "Richmond's always been a quiet little city. Captain Wilkinson told me once he hadn't had to arrest a white man in four or five years on night police. The watchmen had to lock up a noisy negro in the cage now and then; but the old building was so near collapsing that anyone could break out who wanted to. But of course, Vesta, there are twice as many people here as we used to have, and all of them are excited and full of fight. I don't think I'd go anywhere alone if I were you."

"Heavens, Papa, of course not!" She laughed. "But with all the soldiers and all the excitement, I wish somebody'd hurry up and do something!"

It seemed to her in fact that anything would be better than this living at fever pitch, the streets forever full of marching soldiers and pretty girls, even the churches given over to groups of ladies sewing and chattering like so many magpies while their needles flew, everyone so sure that at any moment something wonderful would surely happen, everyone expecting each new dawn would bring confusion and disaster to the cowardly, villainous, ridiculous Yankees!

"It scares me, just to listen to them, Mama," Vesta confessed. "Every girl I see is just as silly as Dolly, just perfectly idiotic about how brave and handsome and graceful our men are, and how wonderful war is! Dolly's not the only one who's having the time of her life, you know."

"Oh, I know," Cinda assented. "I've seen women my age, old enough to know better, just talk themselves black in the face." She smiled a little. "I sometimes think that except you and me and Jenny, all the other women in the world are perfect fools."

Each day was packed full of high moments when the pulse beat hard. Drills and parades were tremendously exhilarating for a while, but even Dolly said one day: "After all, when you've seen one of them, you've seen them all!" Then, when June was a third gone, Richmond had the fine news from Bethel Church, and exulted in that victory. Since only one Southern soldier was reported killed, Vesta had no concern for her father or Julian, or for Tony; so there were no fears to mar her delight and Cinda's in the first report—five thousand Yankees put to flight by a thousand Southern soldiers, hundreds of Yankees slain. Cinda said in a great relief:

"Well there, it was time we did something! I was sick and tired of hearing about Yankees in Alexandria, and the James River blockaded, and Colonel Porterfield getting chased all over Northwestern Virginia. The Yankee newspapers have been blowing their big bazoo about capturing Richmond in thirty days! Maybe now they won't talk so big!"

Dispatches from Colonel Magruder and Colonel Hill emphasized the magnitude of this first success. The Richmond papers called Bethel Church the most remarkable victory in the history of warfare, and since it had been won by her father's Howitzers and by the North Carolina regiment in which Julian and Tony served, it was—as Vesta laughingly declared—strictly a Currain triumph!

But for them all, the tale was incomplete till after a few days Brett and Julian appeared. From them, with Brett the narrator and Julian forever interrupting, they heard the story.

"We'd been at Bethel since Friday," Brett explained. "We slept in the church. The New York Zouaves had written a lot of abuse on the walls. 'Death to Rebels' and—well, some things not to be repeated. And——"

Julian broke in. "They'd drawn a picture of a gallows and a man hanging on it, right behind the pulpit, and it said 'The Doom of Traitors' under it."

Vesta exclaimed in angry protest at this sacrilege, and Brett went on: "Parson Adams preached to us on Sunday. He was the Baptist minister in Hampton till the Federals occupied the town. A lot of Hampton people are Unionists, but he isn't, and the Yankees wouldn't let him stay there to take care of his congregation, threatened to put him in prison. So he came to us. We couldn't all get into the church, so he stood up in his buggy and preached out of doors." Brett hesitated. "I never saw a religious service anywhere that was so impressive." Vesta nodded understandingly, and he went on: "We'd been building earthworks all the time. We only had a few shovels and pickaxes, but we kept them busy. Lucky we did, too; because plenty of cannon balls and bullets hit those earthworks during the fight without doing any harm."

He told of Trav's arrival and why he came, and Cinda smilingly commented: "Trust Travis to be practical."

"Well, we were mighty grateful to him," Brett assured her. "Then pretty soon after he got there, the fight began. I was as excited as a girl at her first party." He confessed that mistake of his which put a gun out of action. "So we had to pull back behind the creek," he explained.

"But when the Yankees sent men to seize our old position we chased them away."

"Uncle Tony did that!" Julian reminded him, and Brett said:

"Yes, Tony did a fine piece of work. But the whole North Carolina regiment was wonderful! Julian and the other cadets helped stop the final Yankee attack. The Yankee who led that, a Major Winthrop, was the bravest man on their side. He came right up to our works before he was shot."

Julian said: "He was right in front of me!"

"Were you scared, darling?" Vesta asked in teasing fondness.

"Shucks, no! It wasn't so much! Colonel Magruder said it was just child's play." The boy added in a hushed tone: "I helped bury Major Winthrop afterward. He was a fine-looking man."

"That charge ended the fight," Brett said. He smiled, remembering Trav's collapse; then decided not to speak of this. But Vesta asked: "How did Uncle Trav like the battle?"

Brett hesitated. "Well, I hadn't meant to tell you, but Trav saw a mule killed by a cannon ball—a pretty unpleasant sight—and it made him sick!"

"I should think it would!" Cinda declared. "But you can't tell me Travis was scared!"

"Oh, we were all scared," Brett assured her, and Vesta nodded wisely.

"Tommy says everybody's scared, really." Her father, at some inflection in her voice, looked at her with a quizzical eye, and she felt her cheeks burn. "Well, he does!" she cried.

Cinda came to her rescue. "Were there really hundreds of Yankees killed, Brett?"

He smiled. "Not hundreds probably; but we buried eighteen, and the local people say the Yankees carted some dead men away with them."

"Well, we'll kill hundreds of them next time," Cinda predicted, and he looked at her in faint amusement, and she understood his glance. "Oh, yes," she confessed, "I'm beginning to talk as big as anyone!"

Julian returned to Yorktown to rejoin his company, but Brett stayed a few days. "I want to see Mr. Harvie," he told them.

Vesta asked: "Why, Papa?" She was puzzled by his tone. "You sound as if you thought—things might go badly."

"They may go badly for the railroads," he admitted. "And there's a lot of Currain money in securities of the Fredericksburg road. I'm going to take some of it out, put it where it's safer."

"In gold, like Mr. Pierce?" Cinda asked.

"No, not yet at least. But the Yankees have seized the Potomac Steamboat Company's steamers, and Virginia has taken over the Fredericksburg road's property, at Acquia Creek. Mr. Daniel's annual report is pretty gloomy. I suppose the road will be working for the Government."

"Won't the Government pay them?" Cinda protested.

Brett hesitated. "I'll know more after I see Mr. Harvie." But that interview gave him no reassurance. He said when he returned that the directors would meet in a few weeks to decide what should be done. "And they can only decide one way, of course; they must do whatever the Government wants. They've made surveys to see if they can lay tracks here in the city to connect with the Petersburg railroad, so that trains can run right through Richmond; but the surveyors say the grade is too severe. But Mr. Daniel says they'll cut fares, carry troops at two cents a mile and freight at half the regular rate. They'll have to accept payment in Confederate funds and notes at par; but unless the Confederacy imposes some taxes, the bonds will decline in value. And the road will wear out. They'll need fifty thousand tons of rails a year just to keep their tracks in condition; but our rail foundries in Richmond and in Atlanta can't make half that. The Yankees captured a lot of rails when they occupied Alexandria. President Marshall of the Manassas Gap Railroad tried to save them, but the Government wouldn't do anything to help him." He said soberly: "I'm afraid, even if we win the war, the roads will be bankrupted; and we don't want to lose our investment."

Vesta saw that he was not, as everyone else seemed to be, completely confident. If Papa was worried, then all the others so sure of victory were wrong!

Brett was still in Richmond the day Henry Wyatt, dead of the wound he received at Bethel, was buried from Mr. Duveau's church;

and they all went to the service. Next day Clayton came from Manassas for overnight, and Vesta had not known how much she loved this
tall brother of hers till it was time for him to leave again. Faunt's company was ordered to White Sulphur Springs. "Governor Wise is to
raise a force in the Kanawha Valley," he wrote, "and we will join him
at Charleston Kanawha. So I'll be in Western Virginia, and it's not
likely I can come for Burr's wedding. Give him and his charming
bride my most affectionate greetings, if you please." He added that
he meant to go to Belle Vue before his company moved west. "I shall
manumit as many of my people as wish to be free. I will not fight for
slavery. A man has to decide why he fights; and I want it clear in my
own mind that I'm fighting to drive the Yankees out of Virginia, and
not for any selfish reason at all."

As June advanced, Burr came home from Ashland more frequently.
On one of these occasions he heard, and told them, that Darrell
Streean had fought a duel. "A man named Judge Meynell," he ex-
plained. "He was Lieutenant of Uncle Tony's company. He called
Darrell a coward because he wasn't in uniform, and they met yesterday
morning, and Darrell shot him through the heart."

They did not know Judge Meynell, and Darrell was their kin; yet
for a—well, perhaps not a coward, but at least a civilian—to kill a
soldier was a shocking thing. Cinda, whose tongue knew no curb, exclaimed: "That's just—despicable!"

Burr said honestly: "Well, the insult was public, and seemed deliberate, or so I'm told. I don't know what else Darrell could have
done."

"He could have volunteered, for one thing!"

"He may do that now, of course."

"Will he be arrested?"

Burr shook his head. "You can't call another man a coward without
accepting the responsibility for your word." He added: "Uncle Tony's
taking the body back to Martinston. He knows Mrs. Meynell and
Miss Meynell, their daughter."

"How does Uncle Tony feel about it?" Vesta asked. "Did he like
Judge Meynell?"

"Yes, he said he was a fine man."

She felt some mystery here. "How old was he? Judge Meynell?"

"Why—I think he was forty or forty-five."

If Judge Meynell was as old as that, Miss Meynell must be a young lady; and the thought stayed in Vesta's mind till Tony, on his way from Martinston back to Yorktown, stopped for an hour at the house. Cinda was out, Jenny resting; only Vesta saw him. Alone with him, she risked the question.

"Uncle Tony—why did Judge Meynell go out of his way to quarrel with Darrell?" Tony cleared his throat uncertainly and she insisted: "Did they know each other before?"

"Yes," he admitted. "When Darrell was at Chimneys."

"I see." She hesitated, then drove ahead. "Uncle Tony—how old is Miss Meynell?"

She saw the effort with which he kept his tone casual. "Oh—seventeen, eighteen, I suppose."

"Is she—nice?"

He looked at her for an instant, and his glance became so stern that she felt like a guilty child expecting a merited rebuke. He said quietly: "Vesta, as you grow older you will learn to refrain from empty conjecture. Judge Meynell branded Darrell publicly as a coward. Darrell called him out and killed him. That's all that need be said."

Thus certainty and hot anger filled her. "I wish someone would kill Darrell!"

She saw his color rise. "I had thought of doing so myself," he admitted. "But killing him would only make talk. The best thing is to forget."

Vesta was silenced, but she did not forget. Her thoughts for a long time turned often to Miss Meynell, to this girl she had never seen, to this girl she would never know.

22

FOR Burr's wedding day, Cinda's house would be full; and Tilda offered to take any overflow. "Of course I know your place is just simply tremendous, compared to ours, but we have Darrell's room free. He's gone to North Carolina to buy supplies for the Department. And we have two rooms besides, even in our little house."

Cinda thanked her; she said politely that it was too bad Darrell couldn't be here. "But as far as rooms go, I'm sure we can manage. Nobody will want to sleep much anyway; we'll have so much visiting to do!"

When the time came, there proved to be, since the children could be tucked away anywhere, a place for everyone. Vesta had Peter and Kyle crosswise at the foot of her bed, with their heads projecting from under the covers on either side, and Lucy slept beside her. The youngsters were a long and hilarious time getting to sleep, because Lucy could not resist reaching down with her toes to tickle the little boys; and since the night proved chilly, Vesta in the morning found herself the center of a warm huddle of little bodies.

"I felt like a mother dog with her puppies," she told Cinda. "It was so sweet. I kept wishing they were all mine!"

Brett arrived from Yorktown on Thursday of that week, and at supper they made him tell his adventures since he went back to duty. He had been one of a detachment that went off to scout and to forage toward New Market Bridge.

"We're always short of food," he explained. "The Howitzers and the North Carolina men had raised a purse of two hundred dollars for Mrs. Tunnell, the woman who gave us warning the Feds were coming, the morning of the fight at Bethel; so we took her the money, and then we hunted for food. We got two cartloads of corn." He chuckled. "But our vedettes reported a big force of Yankees trying to cut us off, and we came back to Yorktown a lot faster than we went out!"

Vesta asked teasingly: "Scared, Papa?"

"Well, for men who weren't scared we certainly travelled fast," he assured her. "We threw away our baggage and hustled like good ones." But the alarm proved false, and they went back to recover the abandoned wagons, and Brett and two others begged a cold ham and some scant rashers of bacon from a house by the road.

"We're all half-starved," he said laughingly. "Not much to eat except fish and oysters; and what meat we get is so bad that there've been a lot of men sick this week from eating it. Even the water down there isn't fit to drink. And hot! My, but it's hot!"

Cinda said it was outrageous that soldiers should go hungry. "So near home, so near Richmond!"

"Well, we've seven thousand men in Yorktown," Brett reminded her. "And no one knows much yet about feeding an army."

"Nonsense," Cinda protested. "Women have been feeding men for thousands of years. They could do it."

He smiled. "It's a little more complicated than that," he suggested. "Calls for more arithmetic than cooking. It needs someone like Trav. By the way," he added, "Trav and Enid are coming tomorrow. Mama too, of course."

"Yes, Trav wrote me," she agreed.

Burr was at Barbara's for supper, but he came home soon afterward; and he and his father fell into talk of business concerns. Cinda stayed with them, smiling inwardly as her eyes rested on Burr's serious young face, thinking him so like his father. And soon now, day after tomorrow, he would marry Barbara; and after that, Cinda well knew, he would no longer be hers. To see a son marry was in some ways to lose him. Clayton had never been hers since he married Jenny. Cinda loved Jenny, as she loved Clayton; but she had never let this love deceive her. When Clayton married, she had gained a daughter, yes; but just as surely she had lost a son.

And day after tomorrow she would lose Burr. He too would go out through the door of her heart. She could never cherish him there

again. When henceforward he was hurt, it was not to her bosom but
to Barbara's he would turn.

Let him go, since go he must. Thus ran the world. For him to leave
her was a part of life! Nothing of life would she deny to him.

Trav and the others from Great Oak arrived in time for late dinner
Friday. Mrs. Currain declared she was not at all tired from the journey, but Cinda saw that her cheeks were bright with a frail excitement,
and as always when she was tired her speech had a faint Scotch burr.
Her father had been a Scot; and when she was tired Mrs. Currain's
tongue fell into the old tricks of her girlhood. After dinner, over many
protests, Cinda hustled her off to bed.

"Now you needn't fuss, Mama!" she said fondly. "There you are
and there you stay, till time to get dressed for the wedding tomorrow."

Enid had come upstairs with them, and when they left Mrs. Currain
she said: "Mama's so excited she doesn't realize how tired she is. She's
awful cute! Coming into Richmond there were camps and soldiers
and things everywhere but she just pretended not to see anything."

"I wish I could make it all vanish as easily as that," Cinda confessed.
"I hope she can have a little nap. I'll look in on her after a while."

"Maybe I'd better," Enid suggested. "She's used to me, you know."
Cinda felt an amused resentment. As if Mama wasn't used to her, her
own daughter, too! When a little later Tilda and Dolly came in, and
Dolly began to discuss the lovely gown she meant to wear to the
wedding, Cinda drew Tilda away, and they went to Mrs. Currain's
room and found her awake and happy to be with them. Yet Enid's
word still stayed in Cinda's mind, and she could not resist angling for
reassurance.

"Enid's a sweet little thing, isn't she, Mama? I'm so glad she's at
Great Oak with you."

"She couldn't be nicer to me if I were her own mother."

Tilda said: "Her own mother's living in Richmond now. Mr. Streean
says she was in Washington all winter, but she came back here in
May."

"Really? I've never met her," Mrs. Currain remarked. "Enid so
often speaks of her. It will be pleasant to make her acquaintance."

Cinda felt something like consternation; she saw amusement in

Tilda's eye and knew Tilda realized her predicament. For it was a predicament; there could be no doubt of that! Her mother would never understand why Trav's mother-in-law, living right here in Richmond, was not invited to the wedding. At least she would not understand without explanations that could not be given. For that matter, unless Enid knew the truth about her mother, she too would resent such an affront.

And the wedding was tomorrow, so whatever was to be done must be done quickly! There was only one thing to do. Cinda rose hurriedly, stooped to kiss her mother's cheek. "Mama, I hate to leave you, but I simply must go out for a little while."

Mrs. Currain said agreeably: "Why of course, Honey. I know you've a thousand things to do. I'll have a good visit with Tilda while you're gone."

Cinda left them, and told Caesar to bid Diamond bring the carriage around, and hurriedly made herself ready to go and do her duty by Mrs. Albion. Once decided on this step she began to feel a lively interest in the approaching encounter. At Trav's wedding she had thought Mrs. Albion silly and affected, but since then the woman had been for ten years, though in a fashion so discreet that almost no one guessed it, Tony's—well! Cinda knew Tony well enough to realize that only a gifted woman could have held his interest so long. Of course, it had been worth Mrs. Albion's while! Brett had sometimes amused himself and Cinda by trying to calculate how much money Tony spent on his fancy.

"Much more than you've ever spent on me, Mr. Dewain," Cinda used to say. "Perhaps I should never have married you at all; it might have been more profitable."

There could be no doubt that Mrs. Albion was an unusual woman. Would she be offended by a call at this unconventional hour? Possibly, or possibly she would be maliciously amused. Nevertheless she must be faced.

Cinda had always felt a lively curiosity about this scandal in the family, and she had long ago made Brett drive her past the house Tony had bought for his light-of-love. It was out in the country a mile or so, on Monroe Street toward the river and discreetly remote from any near neighbors; an attractive little brick house with two chimneys in the gable end and a small front porch, set back from the street with a fenced yard. Today she told Diamond where to go. "I'll point out the house when we come to it." When at her direction he pulled up at the gate, she saw his shiny black countenance clouded with disapproval. Was there anything the people did not know about white folks' doings? She felt her heart pound as she went up the walk and tugged the bell.

A neat young colored woman admitted her, said Mrs. Albion was at home, ushered her into the small drawing room. Cinda, during the few minutes she waited, approved all she saw. The little house was as attractive inside as out, with high-ceiled rooms and a delicately carved mantel, and a graceful stair with a light rail; and there was a charming raised pattern on the plaster. The furnishings were not so attractive as her own, of course; severely old-fashioned mahogany except for one straight-legged tiptop table with an inlay of white mahogany to relieve its plainness. There were no little ornaments to brighten the room, unless you counted the fresh-cut flowers in a tall vase; no pretty wax fruit with red apples and purple grapes and yellow pears making a charming spot of color; no pattern in the severe carpet; no pictures on the walls except for two steel engravings, the sort of thing Mama had at Great Oak. But at least everything was dusted, and the room was as neat as wax. Cinda had somehow expected to find in this den of iniquity a garish splendor, and when in a surprisingly short time she heard a step descending the stairs, she looked toward the door in the liveliest curiosity.

Why, Mrs. Albion was lovely, even more beautiful than Enid, yet in a gentle fashion that seemed to arise out of some inner grace. Her smile was not too cordial, her greeting was composed, her voice made you like her at once. She was so exquisitely neat that Cinda felt large and fat and clumsy; and she had an uneasy fear that at any moment she might flounder into something, knock something over. She regained her chair with as much relief as though it were a safe harbor after a stormy voyage.

Mrs. Albion seemed to find nothing surprising in this call; but Cinda, while they exchanged polite commonplaces, began to feel increasingly flurried and confused.

"I suppose you're wondering why I'm here?" she said anxiously at last.

Mrs. Albion smiled. "I think I know," she replied. Cinda was too surprised at this answer to speak. "You've suddenly realized that not to invite me to your son's wedding might hurt Enid, but you're too kindly to be willing to do that. So—you came to me."

Cinda sighed with relief. "Well, there!" she exclaimed, and she confessed: "You're right, of course."

The other said frankly: "I don't want to embarrass you, Mrs. Dewain. Of course I can't come to the wedding without some awkwardness for both of us; but I will tell Enid you invited me, and that a temporary indisposition—a headache, something of that useful sort—will make it impossible for me to come. I'm sure that will serve."

Cinda hesitated, astonished at herself. "I always knew you must be a remarkable woman," she said, and added smilingly: "I'll tell you just what happened. My mother's very fond of Enid, and when she heard you were in Richmond she said she was looking forward to meeting you. I hadn't thought of you at all. I suppose I came to throw myself on your mercy. But now—" There was a sudden honest liking in her tones. "Now I hope you will come."

Mrs. Albion's eyes softened. "I believe you do," she said gratefully. "I believe you mean that, and I don't believe you'd even allow yourself later to regret the impulse. But I will not come." She explained: "You and I are worlds apart—and we always will be. I accepted that, years ago. You owe me nothing, and I claim nothing from you. Between us we must be careful not to hurt Enid. That is all."

She rose in what was obviously polite dismissal, so Cinda too stood up. "But I'm coming to see you again," she declared. Mrs. Albion smiled. "Have you seen—Tony recently?" Cinda asked. The other did not reply. "He's changed—for the better," Cinda told her. "We're all rather proud of him. I've often thought he should have married years ago."

Mrs. Albion said quietly: "You're generous, and you mean to be kind, Mrs. Dewain. I'm glad you came. But—we both know that you will never come again."

Driving homeward, Cinda found herself for some reason close to tears. "Why, I wish to Heaven she was Tony's wife," she thought. "I really do!" And with some spiteful vehemence: "I wish to Heaven Enid was more like her!"

Clayton appeared just in time for supper, and Tony and Julian came well before noon next day. At the last possible moment, when the carriages were already at the door, here was Faunt too! There was not even time for questions; time only for quick happiness of greeting, kisses in the hall—Cinda saw that Enid clung to Faunt till he freed himself—before they must depart for St. Paul's, for the brief hush of the ceremony there.

That was perfect, to be sure. Julian and Anne Tudor—Judge Tudor was Mrs. Pierce's brother—led the half dozen couples who marched arm in arm ahead of Barbara and Burr to the chancel; and when they appeared Cinda thought Julian with Anne on his arm looked happy enough to be a bridegroom himself. Barbara wore a wide-hooped gown cut square across the shoulders and finished off with a bertha of delicate old lace, her hands almost hidden by the deep lace fall on her short gloves. Her dark hair was stiffened with bandoline and laid sleekly back and divided into many strands woven smoothly into wide braids which passed from ear to ear across her nape. Her veil was of point lace seeded with pearls, and her wreath and bouquet were of wild hyacinths. Burr stood tall and handsome in his fine new uniform, and both of them seemed to shine.

Cinda dutifully shed a tear as one always did, at weddings, but the sadness in her was too deep for tears. This was marriage, two people into one, to be one forever. Yet—how long was forever? How long would it be till a leaden ball, a solid shot, a bursting shell tore life out of that dear body that was Burr? "Forever" was—how long? A day, a week, a month, a year? In the world, in all the universe, this meeting and mating of man and woman was the epitome of everything, the whole in miniature. Life in these two was a welling spring, a spring from which other lives would flow.

Unless death intervened.

Cinda shook her head, fiercely banishing her dark thoughts. There must be no shadow on this merry hour before Burr and Barbara rode away.

The church had been crowded; so was the Pierce home afterward.

Cinda thought Anne Tudor was the loveliest person there; and Julian was forever at the girl's side. Cinda smiled to watch them, but she saw that Anne's eyes followed Faunt everywhere and hoped that for Julian no heartache was preparing. Tilda joined her, and saw her looking at Anne, and said: "Lovely, isn't she. If Darrell had known she would be here, he'd have come back from North Carolina to see her. She made a conquest, at Great Oak last Christmas." Cinda said nothing, but she was glad Darrell had not come.

Dolly, flanked as she always was by admiring beaux, shared with Barbara the center of the stage. When Barbara presently disappeared to dress for her journey, in the group around Dolly suddenly a laughing insistence rose, and Cinda saw that Dolly was being urged to do something or other, and was protesting and yet yielding too; till at last young Randolph Carter called for silence and announced that Miss Streean would recite for them a certain fable. Dolly protested: "Oh, really, I can't! It's so silly! And you've all heard it anyway!" But everyone cried that she must go on, go on; and with many reluctances she surrendered.

"Well, it goes like this." She cleared her throat in a pompous way that made them laugh, and so began.

" 'Once upon a time, when it was the custom of the beasts and birds of the United States of North America to elect a King to reign over them, it so happened that an ugly and ferocious old Orang Outang from the wilds of Illinois——' "

Her tone was so eloquently scornful that they all laughed again, and even Cinda smiled. The minx was charming; no doubt of that.

" '—from the wilds of Illinois,' " Dolly repeated, raising her voice a little to silence them, " 'who was known by the name of Old Abe, was chosen King.' "

Someone said hoarsely: "Down with him!" But Dolly hushed them with a pretty gesture and went on.

" 'This election created a great disturbance in the Southern states, for the beasts in that part of the country had imported from Africa a large number of black Monkeys, and had made slaves of them, and Old Abe had declared that this was an indignity offered to his family——' "

"Hurrah for old Abe's family!" That was young Jack Haven, one of Burr's comrades.

" 'To his family,' " Dolly patiently repeated, " 'that Monkey slavery was the sum of all villainies, and that when he became King he intended to abolish Monkey slavery throughout all his dominions. So the States lying on the Gulf of Mexico, where the beasts were very independent and ferocious, declared that no Orang Outang should be King over them, and when Old Abe heard that the Gulf States would not acknowledge him to be their King he flourished his great war-club over his head, and swore by his whiskers that he would whip them back into the Union. He accordingly collected a great army of Bloodhounds, Jackals, Vultures, and runaway Monkeys, and placed them under command of a notorious old Turkey Cock named Fuss-and-Feathers.' " Laughing hisses ran around the room, for General Scott was held to be a recreant and a traitor to the South; but Cinda did not laugh. This pseudo fable which Mr. Daniel had published in the *Examiner* last March had never seemed to her amusing. Dolly went on:

" 'At this time the Boar of Rockbridge, who was supposed to be a lineal descendant of David's Sow, and was notorious for the amount of swill that he could consume——' "

But then here was Barbara! Cinda welcomed the interruption, for certainly if Governor Letcher had been mistaken in opposing secession he had since played a valiant part. Barbara came down the stairs, and Dolly was forgotten as everyone thronged to see the bride depart.

When Burr and Barbara were gone away to the Valley where Burr would rejoin his regiment, and where Barbara would lodge with relatives at Staunton and be near him, Cinda was glad to go home, to be once more alone with her own. They were all here save Burr, all these loved men: Brett, and Clayton beside his Jenny; Julian, that infant, that child, a little silent as though still dreaming of Anne Tudor; Tony, tall and straight, a new pride in his bearing; Travis, the only one of them not yet a soldier; Faunt. Cinda thought Faunt had lost weight; he had seen more of camp life than these others. What a pity Tommy Cloyd could not have come for the wedding! Vesta had missed him so. But Tommy had taken his soldiering very seriously; he had sent word that he could not leave the camp at Manassas.

The dinner table had been extended to accommodate them all, and the talk ran to and fro; but beneath the general chorus Cinda heard

Faunt and Trav talking about the people whom Faunt had sent from Belle Vue to Great Oak. Only a half dozen of the men had been willing to accept the freedom he offered them. "Big Martha—she's been my cook and the mistress of the house for years—says she and Zeke will stay at Belle Vue, Yankees or no Yankees. Sam, their son, went with me to Western Virginia." He smiled. "Martha says if he lets anything happen to me she'll skin him alive." The Negroes who wished to do so, he said, had started for Alexandria. "I gave each one of them a mule and a bag of corn and some pork and sent them off. Those who wanted to stay with us I told to go to Great Oak."

Trav said if the Yankees got that far, it would be necessary to move everyone away to Chimneys or the Plains; and Cinda felt something tighten in her breast. Yankees come to Great Oak? Surely that could never happen! To close her mind and her heart against the dreadful thought she interrupted them, asked Faunt some empty question. The Blues had been in camp at Fredericksburg from late April till mid-June. "Mostly drilling," Faunt said, answering her. "We took time to celebrate the company's sixty-eighth anniversary; and we made a famous double-quick march to Acquia Creek, four miles in twenty-four minutes, when someone reported Yankees landing. But we've been in Western Virginia these two weeks. I'll rejoin them there."

When dinner was done they moved into the drawing room. Jenny and Clayton, since her baby was scarce a month away, went upstairs so that she might rest; but everyone else grouped around Mrs. Currain and paid affectionate court to her. Above their voices Cinda heard the door bell and she heard Caesar go to answer; and she thought resentfully that this was probably Tilda and Mrs. Streean! Surely none of their friends would intrude upon them in this hour. But when Caesar came to the door and caught Brett's eye he said:

"Major Longstreet wishes to pay his respects, suh, if you all is not too much engaged."

Brett sprang to his feet with a quick word of pleasure; and Cinda, as glad as he, followed him into the hall. She had not seen Major Longstreet since his wedding at Judge Garland's home in Lynchburg years ago. Then he was just back from Mexico; and this great brown-bearded man was not the youngster she remembered. But she cried out her welcome too, and kissed him; and his eyes twinkled.

"Well, that was worth the journey, ma'am! And I've the answer to it, from Louisa." He kissed her in turn, and she laughed.

"Mercy, how rough your cheek is! Where is Louisa, Major?"

But Brett said in quick remonstrance: "Here, here, Cinda, give him time to catch his breath before you start your questions. Major, come in."

In the drawing room, Brett made introductions all around; and Longstreet had a word for each. To Mrs. Currain: "Ma'am, now at last I can understand your daughter's charm." To Enid he gave an appreciative bow. To Vesta he said: "I perceive that beauty can be twice inherited." To Faunt: "I see you've been in the field, sir. I want to hear about that." To Tony: "Sir." To Trav: "Your servant, Mr. Currain." And finally, to Julian: "Well, young man, you were in haste to serve your country!"

"He and Tony and Brett were all at Bethel Church!" Cinda said proudly.

"Bethel? Aha!" Major Longstreet's eyes had a hint of mirth in them, but his tone was gravely congratulatory. "A great victory, gentlemen!"

Cinda had waited long enough. "Now, Major, where's Louisa?" she demanded.

"I left my family at Fort Bliss, to come on more slowly," he explained. "I expect they will visit for a while with my sisters and my mother in Macon on the way."

"Macon?"

"In Mississippi," he explained. "My sister Ann married Dr. Dent there, and my mother took all the family to Macon. Louisa will stay with them till we see a little more clearly what is to happen. But she laid an injunction on me to make my duties to you at once." He added smilingly: "I believe you were engaged with more important matters today, so I should perhaps have waited till tomorrow?"

"Nonsense," Cinda retorted. "You should have come to the wedding! And now you're here we mean to keep you. I've so many questions to ask I don't know where to begin. Tell me all about everything! How are the children?"

"Why, fine, ma'am." Fond pride dwelt in his voice. "Garland's almost a man now; thirteen, you know; a high spirit." He chuckled comfortably. "I used to think I could discipline my children as I would a regiment; but experience has taught me I was wrong. Garland and I were forever battling, so for the sake of peace I named Louisa to be the commanding officer in our family. Garland and I still operate under an armistice." There was, behind the amusement in his tones, a hint of regret, and Cinda guessed that his differences with his eldest son distressed him. He added, more cheerfully: "But Gussie and I get along fine."

"How old is he?"

"Going on eleven, but I can never best him in any argument. He had a fight one day and came home crying, and I asked why he didn't fight back, and he said through his sobs: 'How can a fellow fight when he's crying!'"

Cinda smiled. "How are the babies?"

"Don't ever call Jimmy a baby to his face," he warned her. "He's almost four, and he never lets us forget it. Mary Ann's the baby."

"She's—three or four months?"

"Six months."

"Heavens, where does the time go?" And she said: "When you write Cousin Louisa, tell her not to stay too long in Mississippi. I'm eager to see her again."

"I must write her tomorrow," he assented. "Since my arrival here I learn that her father died in New York early this month."

"Colonel Garland?" Brett asked.

"Yes. So she may wish to come on to Lynchburg, if only to be nearer me. She has many relatives there."

"Is her mother there?" Cinda asked.

"No." He shook his head. "No, Mrs. Garland died at Saratoga last summer. She was a Detroit woman, and she and the Colonel usually lived in the North. Of course Lynchburg is full of Garlands; but Colonel Garland was a strong Union man. Most officers of the old army had an ancient loyalty that died hard, till the threat of coercion killed it."

"You didn't hesitate, Major. Louisa wrote us last spring that you'd offered your services."

He smiled. "Well, Uncle Gus brought me up, you know, and he's been talking secession for years, and I couldn't fight against my relatives and my state."

"Uncle Gus? Oh, you mean Judge Longstreet."

"Yes, I lived with him after my father died, till I went to West Point."

Brett said: "I saw him in Charleston, Major. He was dreading this war, wished he could recant all the things he had said in favor of secession."

Longstreet's eyes were grave. "I owe him a great deal, but he's like most orators. They talk on till they begin to believe their own words. I'm sorry for the old gentleman."

Cinda was in no mind for serious talk today. "Well, I despise him, if you ask me!" Her tone made them smile as she hoped it would. "He expelled Burr from the college for something or other."

The big man nodded. "He wrote me the boys were a wild lot of unbroken colts, needed a curb." He added: "Yes, ma'am, I offered my services early. I'd been watching events, corresponding with my old friend Mr. Curry and at last I authorized him to tell Governor Moore I was his to command. I wrote the Governor myself, too. It was a relief to burn my bridges."

His tone suggested the pain that decision had cost him; and Cinda, to make him forget, said quickly: "What a shame Cousin Louisa and the children couldn't come on with you! Is she just as tiny and dainty and exquisite as ever?"

"Just the same." His voice was gentle. "I don't suppose she has ever in her life weighed a hundred pounds. Our journey would have worn her out." He smiled. "Yet it was lively and inspiring. It was like a long serenade. You should hear the Texas young ladies sing *The Bonny Blue Flag*. Yes, and see them, too! Their feet won't be still, they sway and dance in time with the tune, and their eyes shine and their cheeks are bright! They were at every stop to clap their pretty hands and wave their little handkerchiefs and cheer us on."

Cinda laughed. "Louisa says you've never lost your eye for a pretty face! I believe she's right!"

"I trust I never shall."

"When did you arrive in Richmond?" Brett inquired.

"Today. I called at the Government offices, then paid my respects to Mr. Lamar. Mrs. Lamar is my cousin, you know; and Mr. Lamar is Lieutenant Colonel of the Nineteenth Mississippi, but he's had an attack of vertigo, fears he cannot go to the front with his men." He added: "And from his bedside I came here."

Mrs. Currain left them to take her rest, and Vesta and Enid went upstairs with her. Clayton came down and Cinda said: "Remember Clayton, Major? He was at your wedding too; but of course he was only eleven or twelve years old, and you were much too excited to notice him."

His eyes twinkled. "I must confess that my attention that day was a little distracted." Cinda had asked her questions; now he had questions of his own. He led Julian and Tony and Brett to tell him of the affair at Bethel. "That was a fine beginning," he remarked when they were done, and turned to Faunt. "Your duty was elsewhere?"

"Yes, for a while at Fredericksburg, then Western Virginia, in General Wise's command."

"I hear there are ten thousand Yankee troops there."

"General Floyd so reported." Faunt added quietly: "We've not seen them, but Union sentiment is pretty strong. General McClellan is the Union commander."

"An able man. I know him of old."

"There's been some talk that we'll march against Parkersburg," Faunt told him. "But so far, I doubt we're strong enough. We get no volunteers, or almost none."

Longstreet nodded. "We'll have a problem in Western Virginia. In fact, we'll have many problems, in many places." His eyes were grave again.

"Few people in the South understand that," Brett suggested. "We think of war as a simple matter of fighting, and we Southerners like to fight. But war is much more than that." Cinda wished they would talk of more cheerful things. "It's food and horses and wagons and railroads and money. Even in victory, we'll be bankrupt when this is over."

Cinda, with a laughing glance at Brett, explained: "Mr. Dewain eats and sleeps and dreams money, Major." But Longstreet waited in thoughtful attention and Brett went on:

"Our finances are unsound. The Montgomery Constitution limits the taxing power, and there isn't twenty-five million in hard money in the whole Confederacy. We're borrowing, and printing money; but there'll be a limit to that."

"Money matters are beyond me," Longstreet admitted; and Cinda, fighting to make them smile, exclaimed:

"Me too! As long as there's plenty of money to spend, I don't see what difference it makes!"

Brett would not be turned aside. "The point is, we're unready for this war. We were led into it by the politicians in the newly rich Gulf States, and tricked into it by Lincoln. He's a clever politician, Major. He knew the North wouldn't fight unless we provoked them—so he teased us with lies and false promises till we took Sumter, and that raised the North against us."

"Clever people are always too clever for their own good in the end," Cinda declared. "He'll live to be sorry!"

Longstreet, watching Brett, said in a tentative tone: "We had the right to secede."

Brett colored almost angrily. "The right, yes; but sometimes it's folly to be right. I'd like to hear less talk of our rights and more of our interests; yes, and of our duties."

"Yet I see you are in uniform?" the other said in a quizzing tone.

"Oh, yes, I'm a Virginian. I believed in the Union, but when Virginia seceded—so did I."

Major Longstreet assented. "Most of us, in the end, stand with our own people." He hesitated, seemed for a moment lost in thought. "There's much to be done, much to be done," he said, more to himself than to them. "We'll need a good leader and good soldiers; and it takes time to find the leaders and to make the soldiers."

Cinda said: "Clayton's on General Beauregard's staff."

"Ah?" Longstreet spoke directly to Clayton. "I expect his army stands in need of many things."

Clayton hesitated. "Why, yes, but we're better off than we were two weeks ago. We were so short of weapons then that the General insisted no more troops be sent to him unless they could be armed. We're still short of weapons, and of powder and ball, and of food. The day the army gets a square meal is the exception."

Trav had been so silent that Cinda had forgotten he was here, but now he said strongly: "It's not food that's scarce. We may lack uniforms and tents and blankets and guns and powder and shot, but there's plenty of food. The difficulty is to put it where it's needed. I've done some figuring, and I don't believe there are carts and wagons and horses and mules enough in Virginia to feed a real army, once it gets away from the railroads. A man can't live and fight on less than five pounds of food a day, and that means five thousand pounds a day for a regiment."

Longstreet looked at him in quiet appraisal, and Cinda explained: "Trav loves adding and subtracting, Major. Figures are as sweet to him as a song."

"But he calculates to some purpose," Brett amended. "He arrived at Bethel with wagonloads of food for the men just after the fight was over."

"So?" Longstreet smiled. "That was well done." He added, speaking to Trav: "I like figures myself, Mr. Currain. As paymaster, figures were my province. We need men in the army who can add two and two. Have you thought you might be useful in some such capacity?"

"Yes, sir." Trav colored faintly. "I'm going to call on the Quartermaster Monday."

Longstreet hesitated; he seemed to think as he spoke. "I saw the Secretary today." His lips twisted in a faint smile. "Mr. Walker has zeal enough; but I fear he thinks more of form than of substance. I thought I might be useful in the Paymaster's department; but he seemed to think they had no place for me. So I went to Mr. Davis." Cinda thought his tone was sharpened by an angry memory; she wondered whether President Davis had offended him. "After a brief conversation, he decided to commission me brigadier. I'm to report to General Beauregard Monday. Mr. Currain,"—his eye was on Trav— "I'll need helpers, a staff. If you will come to Manassas with me, I'll find work for you."

There was an instant's surprised silence, everyone looking at Trav; but he said at once, as though he had expected the suggestion: "Why— thank you, sir. I will."

Cinda, listening, felt a deep astonishment. It was not like Trav to make quick decisions. Something, some intangible force, must have passed between these two men, drawing them together. Then her surprise gave way to sadness; for now Trav too would go to war.

So it was done! They were all gone, all these men who were dearest to her; gone beyond her farthest reach, gone beyond anything except her prayers. It was true they might return; but suppose only their lifeless bodies came back to her! Sumter, Bethel, these had been almost bloodless victories; but there would be blood, the blood of her husband, of her sons, of her brothers, trickling in dark rivulets through the grass roots, spreading in the dust, diluted by the rains, dried to dark flakes by the summer sun.

Because of one man! Abraham Lincoln! At the thought, hatred filled her like a choking flood, hatred of that man like an ape, that son of the meanest squatter, that sly, crafty, lying man in Washington. If they died, these men of hers, then as surely as though he pulled the trigger that sped the bullet to their hearts, he would have killed each one!

23

ENID, through the bright excitement of the wedding and the merrymaking that followed, knowing herself beautiful and admired, thought she had never been so happy. This was her first deep draught of the pleasant gaieties of which she had so often dreamed. In her early girlhood her mother, in order to appear to be as youthful as possible, kept her a child. Enid by captivating Trav took her revenge for that, but as Trav's wife she found herself condemned to an existence even narrower than as her mother's daughter. Trav was older than she by seventeen years; but also he was older than his years, slow and silent, with no gift for laughter and no keen zest for anything except the patient routine of the farmer. You could no more hurry him than you could hurry a grain of corn from germination to bearing. You could no more swerve him than you could retard the sluggish pendulum of the years. The pursuits that meant so much to him; to ride the place, to watch the people at their tasks, to pore over his records and by a study of the past anticipate the future—these meant nothing to her. In their first weeks she often kept him company on his daily rounds; but when he became engrossed in some problem of the land he was as likely as not to ride for an hour in absorbed silence, without seeming to hear her attempts at conversation. To persuade him to accept an invitation from th Pettigrews or the Shandons involved so much persistence that eventually she abandoned the effort. Those who might have been her friends, he preferred to avoid; those who were his, she scorned. Thus at Chimneys there were weeks on end when she saw no one but Trav and Mr. Fiddler and the children and the servants; and the removal to Great Oak, from which she expected so much, proved proportionately disappointing. Mrs. Currain's friends were of Mrs. Currain's generation. Enid was welcomed into their circle; but in Williamsburg as in Richmond, a wife, no matter how young and how attractive, was expected to remember that she was no longer a youthful belle.

So it was wonderful now to share these hours when under the spell of Burr's happiness and Barbara's, everyone liked everyone. Enid even took care not to distress Cinda by a too open devotion to Faunt. This was not altogether for Cinda's sake. At Great Oak after Hetty's death, when he came at her request to bid her good night, she had asked him like a weary child to kiss her; and when he did so, she clung to him, no longer like a child, till hastily he freed himself. He left Great Oak without seeing her again, and she read in that a warning. When just before the wedding he appeared at Cinda's, her kiss was more than sisterly; but after that she paid an ostentatious devotion to Trav, as though to assure herself, and Faunt, how much she loved her husband. Actually it was her delight in Faunt's presence which moved her; she was like a girl for the first time in love who becomes suddenly demonstrative toward her brothers or her father. But Trav's awkward pleasure in her tenderness touched and amused her and gave her a reassuring sense of power. Her mother was right; it was easy to manage a man by being nice to him.

But she sometimes forgot this wisdom. The evening after the wedding when Major Longstreet's arrival set the men to boring talk of the war and of the future, she went upstairs with Mrs. Currain and Vesta; and she was abed and drowsily near sleep when Trav came to her.

"Where've you been, Honey?" she murmured.

"We were—talking!"

"What about?"

Trav hesitated. "Why—Major Longstreet's going to be a brigadier general, and he wants me to serve on his staff."

"On his staff?" At first she did not understand. "What's that?"

"Oh, to help him with his work."

"What sort of work?"

"Why, the war."

She laughed in light amusement, rolling comfortably on her side. "Doesn't he realize you have a family to take care of?"

He said slowly: "Well, a lot of men with families have gone into the army."

"Oh, men like Brett, and Clayton, yes! But you're no soldier! What did he imagine you could do?"

"Keep his men supplied with food."

She laughed again. "What does he think you are, a store keeper?"

Trav began to remove his clothes. "I told him I'd do it; that is, as well as I can."

For a moment she lay still; then in abrupt comprehension, swept by a cold wave of terror, she sat up straight in bed. "Trav Currain, you didn't!"

"Yes, I did."

"But what about me?" Her voice rose. "What do you expect me to do? And your children? And your mother?"

"Well, you can help Mama take care of things at Great Oak."

"At Great Oak? You mean to leave us alone there with nothing but niggers? Why, I'd be just frightened to death!"

"Brett and Tony and Julian will be at Yorktown, right handy. You'll be all right."

"I'll not stay there alone! I can't! I won't!" Panic shook her tones.

"Why—I guess you'll have to, Enid," he said. "We'll all have to do a lot of things we don't want to do, for a while."

"I'm not going to do it! You must be crazy!" But she knew he could never be turned from any decision. "You'll just have to get a house for us here in Richmond. We'll move up here!"

"Mama wouldn't do that."

"Oh, she wouldn't, wouldn't she?" Fear sharpened anger. "But I suppose I have no choice! You expect me to stay way off down there, just because she's a cranky, unreasonable, half-witted old woman."

"You'll have to," he repeated. "There's no other way to do!"

"I won't do it! I just won't; that's all!"

He did not speak, opposing to her that solid wall of silence which she knew so well, which she could never break. She flung at him insistences which he ignored, entreaties to which he did not reply. When he turned out the lamp and came to bed she persisted till despair at her own helplessness brought her to tears, and he touched her shoulder in a fashion meant for comforting. But she cried: "Oh take your hands off me!" She let her sobs diminish to pathetic hiccoughings of grief, waiting hopefully for his word of yielding or of surrender.

But instead he began presently to snore, and new anger swept her. Very well! She would show him, somehow, that he could not treat her so. She lay wakeful for hours, planning vain revenges.

Next day was Sunday, and Major Longstreet came to dinner. Enid, because she hated him for taking Trav away, sought to charm him, asking him many questions about Mrs. Longstreet and about his family.

"You'll like Mrs. Longstreet," he assured her. "She too is a beautiful woman." Enid smiled with pleasure. "She was the daughter of the regiment at Jefferson Barracks and I was a young lieutenant. Colonel Garland thought I ought to win my spurs before proposing marriage, so I went off to Mexico and came home a brevet major."

"After having a leg shattered at Chapultepec," Brett remarked.

"Pshaw, that just gave me a long and pleasant relief from duty." Longstreet was so amiable that Enid, though she had determined to dislike him, found it hard to do so. When they left the table, she found him by her side; and he said: "I hope you'll forgive my borrowing your husband."

"Well, I was furious at first, Major; but if he's going off to war I'm glad he's going with you! Will you need him long?"

His eyes for a moment darkened. "Long? Yes. Yes, it will be a long business."

"Really? Why, everyone seems to think we'll just march up to Washington and take it as easily as we took Fort Sumter."

"In war, nothing is easy."

"Bethel was easy," she insisted. "Only one of our boys killed, and hardly anyone even hurt. And we killed hundreds of Yankees!"

There was sadness in his tone. "We will be hurt," he assured her. "Time will hurt us. Had we been ready to use our time three months ago, much might have been done; but we were not, and time is unforgiving. From now on, it will fight against us—to avenge itself for our failure to appreciate its usefulness."

She understood him only far enough to be sure he thought the war would be long and presumably dangerous; and she bit her lip, her thoughts taking a new turn. Trav might he hurt; he might even be killed.

Trav might be killed! What then? What would become of her? She remembered those desperate years of her childhood, when after her father died her mother was left almost penniless, not much better than a beggar, subsisting on the hospitality of her friends. But Enid shook her head. That would not happen to her. Even if Trav died, the Currain fortune would still remain.

And of course Trav would not be killed! He and Longstreet were talking now, and she watched him as though he were a stranger; the set of his head on his short neck, the thinning hair on his temples, the heavy brows, the strong line of his jaw, the mass of his shoulders. Mass, that was the word for him. How strong he was, how mighty in his strength! He cut a crumb of tobacco and put it in his mouth. Unlike other users—Tony, Brett, Faunt—he never spat; the tobacco seemed to be absorbed, leaving not even its flavor on his breath. There was always a cleanness about him, a clean smell like wine to her. His face as he listened to Longstreet was blank as a stone. She knew that blankness, yet knew how when she wooed him his eyes could glow. "The rivers are our worst enemies," Longstreet was saying. "They run the wrong way for us. They're highways leading deep into the South. The Mississippi cuts us in two, and the Tennessee and the Cumberland. The Rappahannock and the York and the James penetrate deep into our territory. The North will build ships, use our rivers." Trav did not even nod. She thought his very passivity attested the force of life in him. It was impossible that such a man as this could be brought to death. No, Trav would not be killed! He was a rock no chisel could scar, no axe could notch! She found herself, as she watched him, trembling with remembered ardors. Her eyes suddenly flooded. She rose and slipped away, to wait for him to come to her.

When next day Trav sent her and the children with Mrs. Currain back to Great Oak, Brett and Tony and Julian on their way to Yorktown riding escort to the carriages, Enid was between gladness and sorrow. Trav would no longer be her nightly bedfellow; she need no longer live in perpetual and nagging fear that she would have another baby. Yet she might not see him again for weeks, for months; if Major Longstreet was right, it might be years before he came home. It was even possible, since in war anything could happen, that he would be killed; and she thought if he were killed she too would die. In first loneliness she loved him to the point of ecstasy!

24

FOR Cinda that day was a time of good-bys, and good-bys were terrible and frightening; for if a loved one departed, when would he return? Clayton and Faunt left at dawn, by the northbound train. They would part at Gordonsville, Clayton proceeding to Manassas Junction, Faunt bound west to Staunton and on to rejoin General Wise and his Legion. When Mama and Enid and the children had been bestowed in the big carriage to set out for Great Oak, Brett and Tony and Julian mounted to ride with them; and Trav went to meet General Longstreet for the business of the day.

So the big house was left frighteningly empty, for only Jenny and Vesta remained; but in this hour of Clayton's departure Jenny needed her, so Cinda forgot herself till an hour before dinner Mrs. Brownlaw came wringing her hands. "Oh dear, oh dear! The most terrible thing!" She waited for no question. "I put the ladies in the church to making undergarments for our soldiers, some to cut them out and some to sew them up; and the stupid, stupid women cut them all for the right leg! I'm simply distracted to know what to do. Oh, Mrs. Dewain, what can I do?"

"Get some more material and cut it up for the other leg!"

Mrs. Brownlaw's eyes widened. "Why, my dear, that's a wonderful idea! How did you ever think of it? I declare, you're as clever as your sister! Mrs. Streean is just a tower of strength. I can always rely on her." Cinda thought anyone who relied on Tilda risked disappointment, but she did not say so. "You know, my dears," Mrs. Brownlaw told them, "we need every pair of hands in our work. There's to be a big battle at Manassas any day now!" Cinda saw Jenny, her head bowed over her needlework—she was making a shirt for Clayton, every loved stitch by hand—lean a little lower as though to hide the expression in her eyes. "Mrs. Clay has told Mrs. Davis exactly what the Yankees mean to do."

"Really?" Cinda's tone was dry. "How did Mrs. Clay know?"

"Why, Mrs. Phillips told her. Mrs. Phillips brought from Washington the complete Yankee plans. She had them sewed into her corsets. Wasn't that wonderful of her? A Federal officer gave them to her!"

"She needn't have troubled," Cinda commented. "The Northern papers come through every day and tell us all they're doing—just as our papers print everything we even wish we could do! If I were a general I'd keep my plans to myself!"

"Well, anyway, Mrs. Clay says they intend to march right down here to Richmond, so General Beauregard will have to fight them." Mrs. Brownlaw became again the organizer, the leader. "So we must all just work our fingers to the bone, mustn't we? Because there will be thousands of wounded, and we'll need yards and yards of bandages, and lots of lint and things like that. Now I want to tell you just what you can be doing. You see——"

"If there's so much to do, you shouldn't waste time on us," Cinda suggested, and Vesta coughed loudly; but Mrs. Brownlaw said:

"Oh, I must! It's the only way I can help." She talked on and on. The door bell rang and Anne Tudor came in, and they all submitted to the droning torrent of Mrs. Brownlaw's words. They must do this; they must do that. "You, Mrs. Dewain! You, Miss Dewain! And Miss Tudor, too!" Till at last she took herself away.

"Well!" said Cinda, in frank exasperation. "If there's one sort of person I despise more than another it's people who're always so sure what other people should do!"

Jenny smiled, and Vesta frankly giggled. "I declare, Mama, I thought you were going to just simply bust!"

"I had a notion to! As if we didn't have enough to do for our own menfolks!" She relented, laughing at her own wrath. "Anne, honey, I'm so glad you came in before you started home."

"We're not going home," Anne told her. "Papa's going to buy a house, or rent one, or something. He hates leaving our home, but he says sooner or later there'll be Yankee patrols on the Neck, and Yankee boats in the river; and he thought we'd better find a place to live here before Richmond was too crowded."

"Why, that's nice," Cinda said. "We'll want to see a lot of you." She smiled. "Specially Julian, my dear." She and Jenny went upstairs, leaving Anne and Vesta laughing together, Anne as pink as a rose, and Cinda said to Jenny: "That's a sweet child."

"She seems older than she is."

"I suppose that's because she's been so much alone with her father. And of course she and Faunt—" She hesitated, troubled by her own thoughts. "Faunt ought to be ashamed of himself. I suppose he thinks of her as still a baby."

She left Jenny and went to her room; and a little later Vesta came to her there. Cinda saw distress in Vesta's eyes. "Where's Anne?" she asked. "You should have kept her for dinner."

"She's gone home. Her father's alone." Vesta hesitated. "Mama, she thinks she's in love with Uncle Faunt."

"Nonsense!" Cinda pretended disbelief.

"Yes, she does. She said so." And Vesta explained: "She asked how long he'd be here, and I said he'd gone, and she looked so disappointed, and I said he only came for the wedding, and she said he needed a rest, said he looked terribly tired." Vesta smiled. "She might have been you talking about Julian, Mama. I said she liked Uncle Faunt pretty well, didn't she; and her eyes got big and she said: 'I guess you'll think I'm silly, Vesta; but I love him awfully!'"

"I hope you didn't laugh at her."

"I certainly didn't! I said we all loved Uncle Faunt, and she said that wasn't what she meant, and I said I knew, and she said she'd always love him, and I wanted to cry, but I just told her she was a darling girl, and—oh, Mama, what could I say? What could I do?"

Cinda shook her head. "Nothing, of course." She said in sharp exasperation: "I wish Faunt weren't so utterly absorbed in himself!"

"In himself?" Vesta was astonished. "I never thought that! He's so—gentle and so kind."

"Faunt's a dear man," Cinda assented. "But he's—well, he's the most important person in the world—to Faunt! For years now he's been living away off at Belle Vue, alone with his grief, petting it and coddling it, taking it out of safekeeping every morning to bathe it and brush its hair and feed it and give it its daily exercise and tell it sad stories all day and put it tenderly to bed at night!" Her own words fed her rising indignation. "Oh, we've all humored him, thought he was a romantic figure, so sad and so gallant. We've been fools and so has he. People have to let scars heal! He's just teased his wound, kept it open. He's thoroughly wrapped up in himself. He ought to be slapped. I'd like to give him a piece of my mind!"

Vesta laughed. "You're always doing that to somebody, Mama!"

"Well, he makes me simply furious!" Cinda shook her head. "The thing that happened to him is the worst thing that ever happened to anyone—he thinks! Why, land alive, other men have loved their wives and lost them without mooning around for the rest of their lives with faces a foot long!"

"Now, Mama, you know you're fond of him."

"Of course I am! What of it! I love you, too; and I love Clayton, and Burr, and Julian. But if one of you needed a good talking-to you always got it!" Her eyes darkened with her own thoughts. "This war is going to hurt and grieve thousands of people. If we all turned crybaby like Faunt, the world would be a mess."

Vesta laughed. "You always get red as a beet when you're mad! It's not a bit becoming!" So Cinda smiled, her anger gone; and then Vesta said, in a different tone: "Mama, Darrell is paying Anne some attentions." Cinda looked at her in sharp attention, and Vesta said hurriedly: "He can be—interesting, when he wants to be, you know. But she doesn't—well, I think he scares her."

"She surely doesn't like him!"

"I don't believe she knows what to think of him." Vesta asked: "Did you ever hear Uncle Tony say anything about Miss Mary Meynell. Darrell called out her father and killed him."

Cinda shook her head. "Now, now, Vesta, you're imagining things!" She thought again of Julian, with no eyes for anyone but Anne. Faunt ought to be ashamed of himself, and as for Darrell—— But she could not discuss such matters with Vesta.

That evening Tommy Cloyd unexpectedly appeared, and there was something shamefaced in his bearing. Vesta in the high happiness of seeing him did not notice this; but Cinda did, and wondered; and Vesta cried: "But Tommy, if you could come today why couldn't you have come for the wedding?"

His reply was an answer to Cinda's unspoken question as well as to Vesta's spoken one. Colonel Gregg's regiment of South Carolinians was being disbanded. "You remember some of the companies refused to come to Richmond in April," he reminded them. "Colonel Gregg promised the men who did come that when their enlistments expired— they're up now—they would be released and could go home or anywhere, and he's keeping his word." So instead of asking leave to come to the wedding he had waited to travel to Richmond with the regiment, and to face with them the angry derision which met them at every station and in Richmond when the train stopped on Broad Street to let them descend from the cars. "There was a crowd of girls and women there," Tommy said miserably. "Calling us renegades and cry-babies. Miss Dolly Streean was there. Rollin tried to speak to her and she said if there was anything she hated worse than an ugly man it was a man who was afraid."

Cinda said some angry word, and Vesta cried: "Why, Rollin got his scar fighting for her!"

"Well, plenty of ladies were calling us cowards," Tommy admitted. "I didn't think South Carolina men would back out of the army when we're going to have a battle any day, just because their time was up. Rollin and I—well, of course we enlisted for three months the same as the others, but we're going to stick to it as long as it lasts."

"What are you going to do?"

"Why, President Davis has told Colonel Gregg he can raise a new regiment. It will have the same regimental number, probably, but I don't want to be in it. Having something to be ashamed of is a bad way for a regiment to start. Rollin and I thought we might go into Boykin's Rangers. I don't know. We'll go home to South Carolina first, I guess, and see."

Tommy and Rollin departed, and Trav and General Longstreet, Trav with his commission as a captain, went off to Manassas Junction; and the days quickened with a tightening expectation. Soon or late the Yankees would march; then Beauregard must fight them. Meanwhile there was action in the Valley. Turner Ashby killed six Yankees in a fight at Romney, and Dolly, though she had never seen him, boasted of his exploit as though he were her possession. "They'd killed his brother, and he was just wild!" she cried. "Of course it was sad about his brother, but I guess he taught them a lesson they won't forget in a hurry." From the Valley too came word that Colonel Jackson had whipped the enemy in an affray at Falling Waters. Burr was with Stuart's cavalry in Jackson's command, and Vesta when they heard of that fight said:

"Oh, I hope Burr's all right!"

But Cinda exclaimed: "Stop it! After all, our men are going to be in danger for months, maybe years. We've no strength to waste in worrying."

General Wise and his Legion, far away in Western Virginia, had inconclusive skirmishes. The news of disaster at Rich Mountain—General Garnett killed, Colonel Pegram and hundreds of his men captured—came with a sickening shock; but everyone found quick reassurance in the fact that General Garnett had died gallantly, the retreat had been a stubborn one, three thousand Confederates had fought twenty thousand Yankees. The odds were a little too heavy, that was all. Seven to one was too much! Five to one was nearer an even thing. Wait a while; wait and see!

Tommy and Rollin presently returned, and Tommy had decided to enlist in a Virginia regiment. "Everyone's saying down home that they won't fight for Virginia," Tommy told Vesta and Cinda. "They claim they'll fight like a bag full of wildcats if the Yankees ever come as far as South Carolina, but till that happens they'll stay at home!" He spoke with a frank anger rare in the boy, named one after another whom they knew. "All looking for commissions, or trying to raise their own companies. Everybody wants to be an officer, but an army's got to have some privates in it! And the best way to fight for South Carolina is to fight for Virginia!"

Cinda said: "Ham Boykin called the other day. His Rangers are at Ashland, if you want to find them."

Julian was at home for that Sunday; and he said cheerfully: "If you want some fighting, you'd better join a North Carolina regiment. We're the best fighters in the army. Any Tar Heel will tell you so.

That's why they call us Tar Heels, because our heels stick to the ground and we never run away."

"I suppose yours is the best North Carolina regiment, too," Tommy said teasingly.

"Of course it's the best," Julian assured him. "And Colonel Hill's the best Colonel! We're only a six-months regiment, so we'll be disbanded in November; but there are plenty of other North Carolina regiments!" And he cried in sudden eagerness: "I know. The Fifth North Carolina went through Richmond to Manassas Thursday and Friday, and I know Colonel MacRae is still here, because Colonel Hill came up to see him today. I'll bet he'll let you go on to Manassas with him."

His enthusiasm in the end infected Tommy. "I'll talk to Rollin, see what he thinks," he promised. Vesta asked where Rollin was, and Tommy said: "Gone to call on Miss Dolly."

"I should think he'd have more pride!" Vesta flushed with anger.

"Well, he likes her pretty well." Tommy hesitated. "I'll see what he says. He really wants to be in the cavalry."

But Rollin proved ready enough to do what Tommy did; so these two saw Colonel MacRae, and persuaded him to accept them, and departed to join the regiment at Manassas; and Julian returned to Yorktown and there were no menfolk left in the house on Fifth Street. Mrs. Brownlaw's insistences set them to making garments for the soldiers; but because they did not wish to leave Jenny alone, they worked at home, and Jenny was as busy as they. Mrs. Brownlaw came one day to say that battle was near, so everyone must roll bandages or scrape lint. Already there were wounded in Richmond.

"And there will be so many more, Mrs. Dewain; hundreds and thousands of our dear men."

She spoke with such unction that when she was gone Cinda said spitefully: "The old buzzard! Just gloating over the awful things ahead! Jenny, don't pay any attention to her! Don't let her frighten you, darling."

Jenny shook her head. "I'm not frightened, Mama. Clayton's where he wants to be and where I want him to be." Cinda recognized her own thought, her own words. "So—I am not afraid."

In these days of waiting for the coming battle they had many callers.

After one influx Cinda said wearily: "Oh, why do women talk so much? Talk, talk, talk! Now they're saying the Northern soldiers are all thieves and cutthroats; but they can't be any worse than those terrible New Orleans regiments. And to hear these women talk you'd think every Southern soldier was a Paladin—whatever a Paladin is—and that every one of our men was an FFV or something, instead of just being mostly good yeomen or farmers; yes, or white trash. And I'm sick of hearing that any Southerner can whip any ten Yankees with one hand tied behind him!"

"I think they just talk to keep themselves from thinking," Vesta suggested. "And because they're scared."

"Well, so am I," Cinda admitted. "But I wouldn't let Jenny hear me say so. But why can't they be frightened decently and privately!"

The waiting tormented her till Brett had a Sunday at home and she could talk her fears away. "Oh, I'm so glad you've come. I'm sick and tired of being brave. I'm scared, Brett Dewain. If anyone says Manassas to me again, I'm going to scream!"

"You won't scream," he said surely. "Whatever happens, you'll face it."

"I can face anything but talk. At least I think I can, hope I can. And of course, I never let go to anyone but Vesta and you!"

"That's what we're here for."

"Why does it all have to happen, Brett Dewain? Why in Heaven's name didn't Lincoln let the South secede as we wanted to? He's like some brutal husband compelling an unwilling bride! Even if his armies conquer us, they'll never be able to command our hearts! Lincoln reminds me of Napoleon, tumbling poor Marie Louise in the bridal carriage! Won't men ever learn that they can't just demand to be loved?"

Brett smiled. "I'm not quite sure whether you're discussing secession or the secret of a happy marriage."

"They're the same thing, in a way; or they would be, if wives could secede. If I wanted to leave you, wouldn't you let me?"

"Not as long as I kept my strength!"

"Thank Heaven for that! Oh Brett Dewain, don't ever leave me! But I still think Lincoln's a brutal fool!"

To tell Brett her terrors was to ease them; yet he never denied the dangerous realities. Mr. Lincoln's call for four hundred thousand men, he said, was a warning the South must read. "But we're going merrily ahead, drunk with the idea that 'Cotton is King,' that we can blackmail the North and France and England into letting us have our way." His tone warmed. "And we're arguing about states' rights and about our personal rights, instead of forgetting ourselves for the general good. I hear that Colonel Myers was ready to call out General Walker over some imagined slight! Wise and Floyd out in Western Virginia are too busy quarrelling with each other to fight the enemy. We're ready to lose a battle while we argue about our personal dignity; but in the North, people are surrendering their liberties without a protest. The Northern Congress isn't in session, so President Lincoln has a free hand, and he's using it, and the Northern people let him, follow him blindly. They'll sacrifice everything to win. We must be ready to do the same."

"I wouldn't want to sacrifice everything! Not our honor, our self-respect!"

"I'm not sure that to sacrifice personal honor for the Confederacy isn't the highest valor."

"You're splitting straws! Or is it splitting hairs?" He did not smile, and as always when she saw him thus concerned she forgot her own fears. "Now, now, Mr. Dewain, you're worrying. Remember what old June's always saying. Never take any more worry into your heart than you can kick off the end of your toes!"

"All the same," he said grimly, "I'm tired of hearing men talk about what their self-respect requires!"

After Brett went back to Yorktown, Cinda kept a high head for Vesta and Jenny to see; but when she was alone, the weight of the sluggish crawling days settled crushingly upon her. The Yankees were moving at last, moving toward Manassas where Beauregard waited to receive them. The Northern papers came to town, full of exultant boasts. "On to Richmond," they said, was the battle cry. Cinda tried to be as confident as everyone around her seemed to be, but heartsick terror filled her.

Thursday of that week she heard that the Yankees had tried to cross a little creek at Manassas called Bull Run and had failed and fallen back. Was this victory? Some said yes, some said no. Some called the skirmish merely an opening gun, an overture; but Richmond held its breath for another waiting day, and another.

In church Sunday morning Cinda saw that President Davis was not there; and she guessed the truth even before she heard—or felt, rather than heard—a slow deep thunder far away. She looked at Vesta, met the girl's eyes, saw that Vesta too had heard. That must be the growl of distant battle. Yet even this certainty brought some measure of peace; for now the waiting, at least, was done. Surely nothing could be worse than waiting.

When the service ended, she and Vesta hurried home to be with Jenny; but Jenny all that long day was the brightest of them all, needing no reassurances, with a strength in her that seemed to shine. Cinda thought of the baby, now so near. Perhaps after the battle and the victory—yes, victory, surely—Clayton could come home for a while, to be here till the baby was born.

They had just finished supper when the door bell clamored. Before Caesar could answer it, Vesta raced through the hall. Cinda rose and tried to follow, but her knees failed her; yet from where she stood as the door opened she heard Dolly's cry.

"We won! We won! Oh, Vesta, we won!"

Cinda instantly was strong again, and Jenny came proudly to her feet. They met Dolly in the doorway, and Dolly kissed them all, laughing, glowing with happiness.

"We beat them, Aunt Cinda!" she cried, and she spun around the room, arms wide, skirt whirling. "We whipped them, whipped them, chased them all the way back to Washington with their tails between their legs! We won, won, won! Isn't it marvelous? Isn't it wonderful?"

Needing no prompting she rattled on. She had been at her father's office in Mechanics' Institute waiting for news. "Everybody was there! I don't mean right in Papa's office, but in the square, and in the streets, and in Mr. Walker's office; and then every so often someone would go to the Spottswood to see if Mrs. Davis had heard anything from the President, and we kept hearing that we'd won and that we'd lost and that they were still fighting and that—oh, everything!

"But just now Mr. Benjamin—I think he's wonderful—he decided to go to the hotel again, and I went with him, and sure enough Mrs. Davis had a telegram from Mr. Davis and he says it was a glorious victory and that we're chasing them back to Washington! Oh, Aunt Cinda, I'm so excited!" Abruptly she whisked toward the door. "Heavens! I'm so excited I left poor Lieutenant Parker outside, never even thought of asking him in. But I can't stay anyway! I just came by to tell you! We're going back to the Spottswood now to hear the latest news. Vesta, want to come?"

Vesta smiled at her mother. "No, I'll stay home. Nobody will really know what happened till tomorrow anyway."

"Why, we thrashed them! That's what happened!" Dolly in her delight kissed each of them again. "There! 'By! Poor Lieutenant Parker! He must think I'm just insane!" She was gone with a flurry of wide skirts; Vesta saw her run down the steps to the young officer who waited, take both his hands, cry: "Oh, was I hours? I'm so sorry!" Her clear, happy voice came back through the darkness as she and her escort moved away.

Vesta closed the door, and in the flickering gaslight the three left behind looked questioningly at one another; and Cinda thought that now they must wait again, that this time the torment would be even more poignant. She had wished to ask Dolly about losses, but no one yet could know who had lived, who—lived no more. So they must wait again!

Some time during the night rain began to fall, and a blustering wind to blow. Dawn was a dreary, lead-hued hour. Vesta and Jenny came to Cinda's room for breakfast; but at once afterward she dressed and went downstairs. Caesar, June, all the house servants moved in hushed silence. Were they sullen at this defeat for the Yankees—since it was also defeat for them? Had they thought the Yankees would march into Richmond and forthwith bring them freedom? Did they want to be free, these jolly, lazy, funny black people whom no white person could ever fully understand, could ever really know? Was it not incredible folly to expect a slave to continue of his own free will to be a slave; to expect him to serve and to protect your loved ones at home while you fought to hold him bound? How long would these black people wait before they struck? No one could read their minds.

It was easy to think them fools, but they had secret wisdoms of their own. Just now, for instance, old Caesar probably knew more than she about what had happened at Manassas. She wished to question him, yet dreaded what he might reveal, till in the end anxiety overcame her dread.

But he knew only things she might herself have guessed. White folks had come to Richmond last night, he said, to get bandages and medicines. "Seems like de Yankees kilt about a million ob us uns. De Richmond soldiers, dey jist about all got kilt, and de gin'r'ls, de hull passel ob 'em." Cinda recognized his extravagances, shut her mind to them. She would be less wretched if she did something, something; so she decided to pack baskets with food and with cordials, and send them to the trains to be carried to the wounded. Anything was better than idleness! Fill the hampers, even though to do so emptied the wine cellar and cleared the store room shelves! She threw herself into a debauch of giving, finding easement so.

Despite the driving rain, Vesta went to the Spottswood and to the *Enquirer* office seeking news. When she returned, Cinda looked at her in silent questioning, but Vesta shook her head.

"Nothing about anybody, any of our menfolk," she admitted. "President Davis is coming home tonight with General Bee's body, and some others. The bodies will lie in state in the Capitol; the high officers, that is. No one knows much yet, no names, I mean." She added in a low tone: "Everyone's very quiet. There's no—celebration, the way there was after Bethel. Dolly's the only one I've seen who seems—well, you know, happy."

Cinda made no comment; there was none to make. This had been no Bethel, no petty skirmish with one poor boy killed. Not one but many now had died.

The day dragged away; the city was drowned in rain like flooding tears. Cinda wished to meet the President's train, but Vesta dissuaded her. "It's pouring, Mama. You'd get soaked through—and there'll be such a crowd you couldn't move." So after supper these three sat for a while together, talking of everything and nothing; till at last Jenny stirred and rose.

"Well," she said, smiling at them, "I'm going to bed. We can't just sit here." She touched her forehead with her hand. "I'll sleep soundly.

The wind last night kept me awake, but now I'm tired enough to sleep."

Vesta rose to go up with her and Cinda asked: "Are you coming down again, Vesta?"

"Yes, I'll just tuck Jenny in."

Cinda, left alone, could not be still. She moved to and fro, adjusting the hangings at the windows, moving a chair from one spot to another and back again, straightening a picture. Things needed dusting. Unless you kept after servants every minute of the day nothing was done right and regularly. She was at the book shelves when she heard some faint sound behind her and turned.

Trav stood in the doorway. Cinda felt no sense of surprise. He was wet, his boots muddy, water running from them along the floor; and his face had a strange blankness like a mask.

"I came in the back way," he explained. "I waited till Caesar said Jenny had gone upstairs."

When Cinda spoke, her own voice was strange to her ears. She remembered once as a little girl looking down into a deep well, seeing her small head reflected against the sky in the dark mirror of the water far below; and when she called some word down the well, that reflected self answered like an echo. Her voice had the same hollow sound now. "You've brought Clayton home," she said; a statement, not a question.

"Yes." Trav was always so calm, yet now she was as calm as he. "But—I didn't want to upset Jenny."

"Where is he?"

"In a cart, up at the corner."

She thought in a far wonder: Why, how simple it sounds! And I don't feel anything. I must have known. "Jenny's gone to bed," she told him softly. "We'll wait till she's asleep. She didn't get much rest last night."

Trav nodded assent. He looked down at the mud on his boots, looked in distaste at his soiled garments; and she remembered that he had always been as cleanly as a cat, resenting dust and grime. War, clearly, was a muddy, dirty business; Trav would hate that part of it.

"Never mind," she said. "Water won't hurt the floor. Sit down, do." Why, this was like a polite afternoon call. She heard herself asking, in the artificial tone with which a hostess revives a lagging conversation: "Was the battle interesting?"

Trav, still standing, twisted his hat in his hands. "I didn't see much of it." He wiped his mouth. "I wasn't there Thursday, when they had the first of it. I was bringing up a wagon train with supplies. They say General Longstreet did well that day. His men were nervous, but he steadied them."

Vesta appeared in the doorway and cried in quick delight: "Oh, Uncle Trav!" She ran to embrace him.

"Easy, you'll get all wet," he warned her.

"I don't care! Oh, I'm so glad you've come! Where's Clayton?"

Cinda said quietly: "Hush, dear! Don't wake Jenny." Vesta turned to her, eyes widening. Her color drained away, and Cinda said in that same even tone: "Clayton's dead, but Jenny needs her sleep." Vesta pressed both hands over her mouth, her eyes tremendous; and Cinda added: "Uncle Travis was just telling me about the battle."

Vesta's knees gave way; she sank into a chair. Cinda in a remote satisfaction reflected that it was a good thing Vesta had changed into a simple dress with no stiffening. In her present posture, with her head thrown back and her feet extended and tears without sobs streaming down her cheeks, hoops and crinoline would have billowed upward in awkward absurdity. What strange thoughts one had!

"Go on, Travis," she directed. "About the battle."

"Why, Longstreet's brigade wasn't in it much, except the little fight Thursday," Trav explained. He sat down stiffly, choosing a haircloth chair. "Sunday we were mostly just waiting, or going ahead across the ford and then coming back again. Some time along in the afternoon the Yankees started to run. I don't know why. They had to go through Centerville, so General Longstreet took us forward to hit them as they went by. We went through some of their camps, and the kettles were still on the fire, whole quarters of beef hanging up, wagons loaded with things. I stayed there with my men to collect all that and take care of it." He added in a slow tired way: "So I didn't see any of the fighting, really."

Cinda saw Vesta, though her tears no longer flowed, trembling terribly. If the child had something to do, she would not suffer so. "Vesta, won't you go listen at Jenny's door? Perhaps she's asleep."

Vesta obediently went up the stairs, groping like one suddenly blind. Trav said: "I got permission that night to go see Clayton, Cinda. What happened to him was, he was carrying some orders, riding across a field where there was a cross fire. He was hit in the leg. I guess he didn't know it was as bad as it was, because he kept on till he got weak from bleeding and fell off his horse. I suppose someone saw him fall, but they were all hard at it, so they couldn't stop to take care of him." He looked at his hat, crushed in his hands. "Anyway, they didn't get to him till after the Yankees ran away. He was already dead."

She wondered whether the room was as cold as it seemed to her to be. "Is he alone now, Travis?" Alone, cold, in the rain.

"Two of my men are with him, and I sent Caesar out to stay with them."

She looked toward the door, wondering why Vesta did not return; and to think of the girl made her think of Tommy. "Do you know anything about the Fifth North Carolina regiment?" she asked.

"Yes, it's in Longstreet's command. But they weren't in any of the fighting."

She was glad of this much reassurance. "I'll see where Vesta is," she decided, rising.

She found Vesta in the lower hall, leaning against the newel in limp weariness; but at Cinda's coming the girl straightened. "Jenny's asleep," she said. "I looked in to make sure." She added: "I'm all right now, Mama."

Cinda, quietly efficient, directed what followed. When they brought Clayton into the library, she had a pallet already spread on the long table that had been hurriedly cleared of books and papers. She sent Travis away to bed, and she and Vesta and old June undressed Clayton and bathed him. The wound in his leg was so astonishingly small to have drained his life away! June took his uniform—she would work till dawn to clean and iron it, to clean the stale blood out of his boot and dry it—and Cinda and Vesta stayed with Clayton.

They talked a little. Once Cinda said in a dull tone: "It's funny. I don't feel anything."

"Oh, Mama!" The girl's voice broke.

"No, really I don't. But there's a pounding in my ears, as if my head were trying to explode. It's like—why, it's like having a baby. It hurts so much you stop feeling. You hear yourself scream and wonder who is doing it and why they're making such a noise. I suppose I will —feel pain after a while."

Vesta began to cry again, silent tears streaming. Cinda wondered whence came such a flood of tears. Were there as many tears dammed back in her eyes, too? It seemed impossible. Her eyes felt dry as dust. She sat like stone through the weary night.

In the morning when it was time to wake Jenny, Cinda herself took up the breakfast tray. Jenny roused at her entrance, said smilingly:

"Good morning, Mama."

Cinda, drawing open the curtains, her back toward the other, asked: "Sleep well?"

"Splendidly. I feel all made over."

Then Cinda turned, and Jenny saw her eyes, and knew; and Cinda knew she knew. Jenny's lips parted as though she would speak, but she did not. Cinda turned and brought the tray.

"Drink some coffee, Jenny."

Jenny shook her head. "I don't think I will." She said, slowly: "But I'll be fine, Mama. I really will." She turned her face to the wall. "I may sleep just a little longer, but I'll be fine, really."

Cinda tried to speak, but what was there to say? What were words? Jenny lay without movement, and Cinda felt herself an intruder. Oh, surely, surely Jenny had in this hour the right to be alone. Cinda went out and closed the door and stood looking at the blank panels. I hope she's crying, she thought. Oh, I hope she cries and cries and cries. I'd like to cry. It would feel so good to cry.

But she had no tears to shed. Was this grief? Surely not! If she were grieving, surely she could cry. What was grief? What was pain? Vesta had wept. Perhaps Vesta could tell her. But no—no one could tell another person what pain was. To try to do so was as impossible as to try to describe a color. Red was red, but how could you tell any-one what red was if he did not already know?

What strange thoughts! Why did the mind thus race and turn and seize on little unrelated things? Once at the Plains she had seen a rattlesnake, when Brett shot it through the body, strike and strike again with a blind fury at its own flank, as though to kill its own hurt. Perhaps the mind, under a grievous wounding, thus blindly seized on any thought at all.

She went slowly down the stairs. An hour later Jenny joined her, composed and strong; and Jenny's serenity and her steady tones seemed to Cinda more terrible and shaking than helpless tears. I can't stand it, she thought. If she doesn't do something, I'll make a fool of myself. She left Jenny and Vesta together and went out of doors and walked at random along Franklin Street and turned at random down Third toward Main.

In front of Judge Robertson's house at the corner of Main and Third something was happening; chairs and tables were being carried out of the house, cots and blankets were going in. A calm little woman with curious slanting eyes almost like a Chinaman's seemed to be superintending the work; and Cinda paused to watch and wonder, and the young woman saw her, spoke to her.

"You're Mrs. Dewain, aren't you?"

"Yes."

"I'm Sally Tompkins. Do you want to help?"

"Help?" Cinda did not understand. Miss Tompkins said sharply:

"Yes, help! You don't look stupid! Please don't pretend to be! There aren't enough hospitals to take care of our wounded. Judge Robertson says we can use his house. I'll need all the help I can get."

"Oh—I don't know anything about——"

"Nonsense! You've had children! These boys are just hurt children. You can at least scrub floors, wash bloody bandages." Miss Tompkins looked at her keenly. "You're in a daze. Did you lose someone?"

Cinda nodded. "Yes, my son. My oldest son."

"Dead?"

"Yes."

"These boys will be alive! Perhaps we can keep them alive—if you help!"

The younger woman's word was a challenge. Cinda met it. Under Miss Tompkins's driving insistence it seemed natural enough to be sweeping, dusting, scrubbing. She forgot that Vesta did not know where she was, relished the hard exhausting toil, the blistered hands, the sting of harsh soap, the ache of muscles not used to toil. She worked till Miss Tompkins sent her home. "Don't wear yourself out the first day. This isn't just one day's work; it will go on for years. Come back when you can."

The homeward way seemed long; Vesta's cry of anguished relief at sight of her seemed to come from far away. June's scolding tenderness was like part of a dream. Cinda was too tired to eat, too tired to do anything but sleep. Some time before morning Brett came; but not even in his arms could Cinda weep. In the morning she wished to go back to help Miss Tompkins, but he made her stay in bed. "You behave yourself," he said harshly. "No talk out of you."

He stayed with her all that week, and on Friday, since she insisted on returning to the house on Third Street, he at last permitted her to do so. She found peace there. It required no knowledge of medicine to be able to meet brave smiles with an answering smile. She could serve Clayton no more, could never bring back into her safe arms the sweet soft body of her baby, her first baby, her own; for he was dead. But what she could not do for him she could do for these others.

Sunday she and Brett went together to the service of thanksgiving at St. Paul's. President Davis and General Lee were in the hushed company; and there were wounded men among the congregation, bandaged heads, arms in slings. Outside afterwards, Mrs. Brownlaw was as voluble as ever. She had gone to Manassas to see for herself the horrors there.

"Oh, Mrs. Dewain, you've no idea!" There was a terrible relish in her tones. "Why, in Sudley church there were so many wounded men you couldn't walk without stepping on them, and just one doctor, and he did his operating on the communion table, and in the corner there was a pile, simply a pile, my dear, of arms and legs he'd cut off, and just clouds of flies swarming around them, and it was hot, and the odor! Oh, I thought I'd just expire! And, my dear——"

Brett drew Cinda away, but she said gently: "Don't worry about me, Mr. Dewain. I've seen worse things in these two days than she could possibly describe."

"I wish you'd stop that hospital work."

But she only smiled, and she was tireless in devotion till at the month's end Clayton's son was born. It was to Cinda as though her own Clayton were a baby in her arms again, and she said so, and Jenny understood.

"Why, yes, of course," she promised. " 'Clayton' he shall be."

So in Clayton's son recapturing Clayton too, Cinda's heart began to heal.

25

TRAV, at their first meeting, had felt in Longstreet something at once endearing and compelling; and through that summer and early fall of 1861, his respect and affection for the General steadily increased. They went together to Manassas, and Trav threw himself into the business of supply. When Longstreet's brigade, a few days before the battle, had its first skirmish at Blackburn's Ford, he had gone back to the Junction to fill his wagons; and though he heard the guns, the fight was over before he returned.

But Captain Goree gave Trav the story of that small affray. Goree and the General had met on the journey from Texas to Richmond, and Longstreet had won Goree as he later won Trav. The Texan saw in this first skirmish more comedy than tragedy. "There were a lot of funny things," he told Trav. "You see the opposite bank of the Run is higher than the ground on this side, so the Yanks were shooting down at us without our having any good chance to shoot back. See that tree down there?" He indicated a big sycamore a hundred yards from the Run and upstream from the Ford. "When the Yankee guns opened, one of our men ran to hide behind that tree; and pretty soon there were a dozen or so all trying to hide behind that one tree, stretched out in a line, pressing against each other. When a shell hit on one side, they'd all swing over to the other; and then a shot would hit over on that side and they'd swing back again." He laughed at the memory. "That tree looked like a big dog wagging its tail!"

Trav recognized in Captain Goree, in these hours after the fight, some of that strange exhilaration which he had seen in men at Bethel. "Scared, were they?"

"Scared as mice!" Goree agreed. "Everybody was, far as that goes. Our whole line broke, all except the Eleventh Virginia. The General saw them start to run, and he let out a bellow like a bull and rode right into them and over them, yelling for them to charge. He can make more noise than a battery in action, when he wants to." Trav already knew Longstreet's great voice. "They were more afraid of him than they were of the Yankees. He drove them like a flock of sheep, back to their line." He laughed again. "And then be damned if Early's men didn't fire into us from behind, and the General himself had to drop off his horse and lie flat to escape that fire; and he was swearing so hard the grass was charred all around him."

"Hard to imagine him really mad. He's usually so good-humored."

"Wait till you see him when something goes wrong!"

Trav had not long to wait for that occasion. On the day of the actual battle, they were not engaged; but when the enemy broke in panic flight, Longstreet was ordered forward across the Ford toward Centerville. They came up into the woods on the low bluff beyond the Run and found a few dead Yankees who had been killed in that skirmish three days before. The bodies were blackened and bloated and swollen, and when burial details were ordered to dispose of them Trav saw some men helplessly sick, and he was glad his duty did not lie that way.

Beyond the woods lay the abandoned enemy camps, and Trav paused there to begin to load his wagons with the treasure trove of supplies left behind. He was still thus engaged when Longstreet himself returned from the advance and swung off his horse and threw his hat furiously on the ground and kicked it, in a profane rage.

"Retreat! Retreat, by God!" the General cried. "We're ordered to retreat, and there in front of us, right under our guns, is the whole Yankee army broken to pieces. Why, God Almighty, a yellow dog nipping at their heels could chase them all the way to Baltimore! Yes, if you tied a tin can to his tail he'd chase them clear to New York! Why, if we'd let loose just one battery on them they never would have stopped running! But no, by God! Not us! We retreat! That's one hell of a God-damned way to win a battle!"

That was only a beginning. He rose to lurid heights. There was a certain majesty in that explosion; but Trav heard the General's anger echoed by the columns of soldiers wading back across the Ford again. These same men who three days before had themselves been frightened into panic, having seen now the flight of the enemy were bold as lions.

Trav's business, in the aftermath of battle, was to salvage the rations abandoned by the Yankees. He was thus engaged all that night, working in a pouring rain; and when next morning Longstreet asked him about supplies on hand, Trav was able to say: "Why, we've enough to feed the men for a week, sir."

"Hah! Enough for us to march into Washington and capture Lincoln and invite him to dinner?"

Trav answered seriously: "Yes, sir, but our wagons are loaded so heavily that they'd have hard going in this mud and rain."

Longstreet chuckled at his sober answer. "God bless you, man, don't look so solemn! I was joking. Where's your sense of humor?"

Trav hesitated. "Well, General, I can't laugh at any of this." He added stubbornly: "You didn't laugh when they wouldn't let you strike the Yankees yesterday."

"I did not!" The big man's voice was harsh. "When I want to do a thing that needs doing, I hate being prevented. I hate unintelligent opposition, and above everything else I hate a fool!"

Trav half smiled. "I expect you think anyone who disagrees with you is a fool."

The other laughed a great laugh. "Why, yes, of course! If I thought they weren't fools, I'd have to admit that they were right and that I was wrong; and I never admit I'm wrong—especially when I know I'm right!"

Trav, although he was wet through and mud-besmeared and weary from his long night of labor, now that his task was done wished to see Clayton and make sure the young man had taken no harm during the conflict yesterday; and Longstreet assented. Trav's way led him across a portion of the battlefield; and among the scattered bodies of the dead he saw furtive figures, plucking and pulling at spurs and boots, probing into pockets. At first the sight enraged him, until he realized who they were: wretched men and boys, the poorest of the poor, miserable folk from the tumbledown huts hidden away in sedge and pine where dwelt the whites too indolent or too debilitated by disease to make a crop on the soil long since impoverished by tobacco planters and abandoned now to any squatter. On a level below the world where men like Ed Blandy lived self-respecting lives, there were these thousands and scores of thousands who from one year's end to the next never saw their children with full stomachs. Let them plunder where they chose.

There were others at work among the dead, burial parties digging shallow ditches, collecting the scattered bodies which under the pelting rain lay sprawling everywhere, laying them in the ditches, shovelling over them a scant covering of muddy earth. They too ignored or abetted these ghoulish scavengers. Pity and horror made Trav tremble; but at Beauregard's headquarters he heard of Clayton's death, and this, since it gave him a task to do, drove what he had seen out of his mind.

He got leave to take Clayton's body home to Richmond, and it was some days before he returned to brigade headquarters. Longstreet gave him a sympathetic greeting, and asked for Cinda and for Brett, and Trav said they were steady under their grief; but while they talked a while together he remembered the day he rode to find Clayton, and the battlefield littered with drenched and pulpy bodies from which all blood had drained away to leave them white as so much wax. He spoke of it, and Longstreet nodded.

"You have to shut your eyes," he said. "Forget they were men. A surgeon can't remember it's a man who is squalling in agony under his knife and saw; nor can a soldier remember that rotting flesh was once the flesh of men like himself. Next time you see a battlefield, think of it in military terms. See how many men died where, and it will teach you something about the strength of the positions they died to capture—or to hold. There's no better way to learn what a rise of ground or a well-hidden ravine is worth in military terms than to count the dead in front of it. And study the dead—see how many were killed by musketry, how many by cannon fire. You can learn some useful lessons so."

Trav looked at him with inflamed and furious eyes. "I'll be damned if I will!" he said hoarsely. Then, regretting his own violence, he modified his tone. "Excuse me, sir. War's your business, but it's not mine. I'll be damned if I'll ever go at it that way."

Longstreet nodded. "I know how you feel; but, Currain, there are worse things in war than death and wounds. There's the ignorance and the lies and the stubborn vanity that causes those wounds and death, that causes war itself. Look at the dead, Currain. Remember them. Never as long as you live forget what war is like. Hate it with all your heart. The more you hate it, the harder you'll fight to end it!"

During the weeks that followed Trav often remembered that advice. He lived in a cold rage at the mismanagement and waste on every hand. That summer after the battle there was no lack of rations. Each company had a store tent; and each tent was full, barrels of flour, a fresh-killed beef every day, mess pork, peas, beans. But except where Trav was in control there was no one to husband these supplies, to serve out exactly what was required and no more. As often as not the store tents were left unguarded, and individual soldiers helped themselves as they chose. Trav, trying to impose some discipline in these matters, found he must move gently, managing more by persuasion than by authority. After all, no white man in the South ever admitted anyone's right to tell him what to do. An order, given as an order, was an affront. White men weren't niggers, weren't to be bossed around!

Trav spoke of this one day to Longstreet, and the General smiled. "Certainly, Currain." His tone was amiable, but his words were edged. "A Southerner thinks to ignore orders is to prove he's a brave man."

The men took what they wanted and wasted as they chose; and the fruitful summer's plenty provided supplies so lavishly that there was enough and to spare. But water was scarce. Full tank cars came daily from clear streams in the Blue Ridge Mountains, and when a car arrived and the whistle of the engine spread the news, the men seized whatever utensil was nearest and raced to the station yards to mass about the car in a disorderly mob till the tank was emptied. This distressed Trav, but Longstreet brushed aside his anxieties.

"Food and water are easily managed, by comparison with ordnance," he said. "Men can go hungry or thirsty if they have to, but an army can't fight without guns. We hadn't two hundred thousand serviceable firearms in the South three months ago, unless you count pistols and revolvers. Except for what we capture from the Yankees, all our cannon have to come from the Tredegar Iron Works in Richmond. Almost all. We haven't enough lead for bullets, so every bullet we pick up on the battlefield here is clear gain. Why, man, we'll have to save the contents of every chamber pot in the South just to keep us supplied with niter. We have to have it for our percussion caps." He chuckled. "That's one reason for not wasting water, though; I'll grant you that!"

Trav could not supply the weapons, but he did what he could to curtail the needless squandering of the rations he so painfully accumulated. When Longstreet was ordered to command the outpost, and moved brigade headquarters to Fairfax Court-House, where rolling hills began to rise out of the plains around Manassas to form a parapet a few miles short of the Potomac, Trav was glad to get away from the contagious heedlessness of discipline in the main encampment. Longstreet's task was to watch the enemy, whose army except for advanced positions which the Yankees still held had withdrawn across the Potomac. The First Virginia Cavalry was attached to the brigade for this duty, and that was Burr's regiment, so Trav looked forward to seeing him. When Colonel Stuart came to report for duty, Trav was with Longstreet, and the General introduced him to the young cavalryman.

"I haven't seen Stuart for many years, Currain," Longstreet explained. "We met in Texas, when I was commanding a party from the old Eighth Infantry, chasing Indians. The Colonel made a name for himself out there—he was a lieutenant then—by the way he manhandled his guns up and down the wildest precipices. Now General Jackson tells me that Stuart has found out how to watch a fifty-mile front with three hundred men; and General Early says Colonel Stuart did more than anyone to save the day at Manassas."

Trav remembered that it was Stuart, then a lieutenant, who had led the storming party that captured John Brown at Harper's Ferry two years ago. Colonel Stuart wore a tremendous red beard, but Trav thought he seemed astonishingly young. He had a charming way about him, laughing readily now at Longstreet's word; and Trav liked him at once.

"My nephew, Burr Dewain, is in your regiment, Colonel," he remarked. "I haven't seen him since his wedding. He rode off to report to you in the Valley. But of course I don't suppose you know him."

"On the contrary, Captain," Stuart assured him. "Everyone in the regiment knows young Dewain. I'll send him to report to you."

Burr came to headquarters that evening and he and Trav had an hour together. Barbara was fine, Burr said. When they left the Valley, marching as Jackson's flank guard to Manassas, she had returned to Richmond to be with her father and mother. "I hope to get leave for a day or two soon," Burr explained. "I want to see Mama." He added in a lower tone: "Barbara wrote me about Clayton."

Trav, knowing how close to one another these brothers had been, wished to find some word of comfort but could not. "General Longstreet says your regiment helped win the battle."

"I don't know how much we helped," Burr confessed. "We didn't hit a lick till pretty late in the day. Then we charged some New York Zouaves and broke them; but the scramble broke our formation too, and when we fell back to rally, a lot of our men did more falling back than rallying." He grinned. "I don't know whether it was horses running away or men; but we did a lot of running before we got ourselves together again."

Trav nodded sympathetically. "I'm not built for running, but if I ever get into a hot place I'll probably outrun a horse." He asked, smiling: "Did you run?"

"Well, I rallied to the rear," Burr admitted with a grin. "But I wasn't actually scared. Fighting doesn't bother me as much as the things I see when we're not fighting. We passed one place where the surgeons were cutting off arms and legs, and the surgeons were as bloody as butchers, and men were screeching and screaming, and there were swarms of flies so full of blood they couldn't fly." He added: "But I didn't mind seeing men shot to pieces in the battle; and right after it was over I drank out of a creek where the water was red with blood and really tasted of blood, and didn't even think about it."

Trav swallowed painfully. "I suppose you get used to it, but I don't think I ever will. Were you in the pursuit?"

"Yes, sir. It wasn't like what I'd expected, though. It wasn't cutting down men right and left with our sabres and all that sort of thing.

The Yankees kept on running till you caught up with them and then they held up their hands and you marched them off to the rear." He laughed at his memories. "Uncle Trav, you should have seen the roadsides and the fields toward Centerville. I guess a lot of Yankee civilians had come out from Washington expecting the battle would be a sort of picnic; because I saw great baskets of food and wine and all sorts of things, scattered along the road for miles. I saw parasols and lace shawls, and I passed one broken-down carriage with two girls in it, pretty girls, too. They didn't know whether to be scared of us or mad at the escorts who had deserted them. Someone had taken their horses. The whole thing was so funny you couldn't help laughing."

Through that summer, Trav's close daily association with Longstreet brought him a contenting satisfaction. The General was tireless, and the men of his staff were hard driven, but Trav could match him. "There's not much fuss and fury about you, Captain Currain," Longstreet said once, approvingly. "But you seem to be there or thereabouts when you're needed."

Trav one day asked: "General, do you expect we'll hold our position here?"

"No. When the Yankees show signs of being ready to attack, we'll fall back. It's too easy for them to flank us from Acquia Creek if we stay here." Longstreet's eyes twinkled. "Why? Are you taking lessons in grand strategy, Captain?"

"No, sir—I was thinking of rations."

"Ah! You're a man of one idea."

"Well, that's my job, sir. Of course there's plenty of everything now; but if we don't intend to hold this part of Virginia, we'd better clean out the corn cribs and collect the cattle and hogs. No use leaving supplies for the Yankees."

Longstreet agreed, so Trav's foraging parties were steadily at work, ranging as far as Falls Church on the hills above the Potomac. From the high ground a quarter of a mile beyond where the old red brick church stood beside the road, Trav more than once saw the lights of the enemy capital three or four miles away across the river.

He was glad his duties kept him much away from headquarters. Since there was little military activity beyond the routine drill, the dinners at headquarters were elaborate and jolly. An abundance of wine and liquor usually set someone to singing; and after dinner and through the long evenings a poker game was a reasonable certainty. On the rare occasions when Trav was at headquarters he watched these games without participating; and once at a jovial dinner Longstreet rallied him for his sobriety.

"Take your pleasure when you can, Currain! My only complaint of you is that long face of yours!" And he said, looking up and down the listening table: "You can always recognize greatness in a man by his readiness to taste the joys of life when they're offered him."

General Van Dorn said a loud "Amen to that!" A laugh ran down the board, and Longstreet cried:

"There you are, Currain; praise from Sir Herbert! Or was it Sir Herbert, gentlemen? My literary education has its deficiencies. But I tell you, Currain, even the exhausting pleasures are good for a man. The ascetic is too busy with self-discipline to get things done. Excesses don't produce greatness, to be sure; but I never knew a great man who wasn't given to excess of one sort or another. He liked the ladies too well——"

Van Dorn shouted: "No! No!"

But Longstreet repeated: "The ladies, yes; or he liked wine too well, or good fare, or gambling. Which reminds me, gentlemen . . ." So they turned to the waiting cards.

Usually some of the higher officers of the army were of the number around the table; and Trav saw that in these jovial hours Longstreet established an ascendancy over the other generals. There was something daunting in his size, his calm certainty, his firm tones. When in August business took Trav to Richmond he spoke of this to Cinda.

"Even General Johnston and General Beauregard defer to him," he told her. "I suppose it's because he's so sure of himself."

She smiled faintly. "Cousin Jeems was always a masterful man."

"We're not really related, are we?"

"Oh, no, but at his wedding he called every pretty girl 'Cousin Something-or-other', so we all began calling him 'Cousin Jeems'. Louisa says wherever they go he always manages to find lots of 'kissing cousins'!"

"That reminds me: one of Mrs. Longstreet's cousins, Colonel Garland, commands the Eleventh Virginia in Longstreet's brigade. Longstreet likes to torment Colonel Garland, calls him 'Cousin Sammy'; and the Colonel gets red around the ears." Trav smiled. "The General is always playing jokes on his regimental commanders. We had a review for Prince Jerome Napoleon one day. The First Virginia Infantry is in our brigade, and their uniforms are going to pieces. Longstreet borrowed a couple of smart regiments from other commands and put the First Virginia in with them, and then he joked Colonel Skinner because their trousers were out at the seat; but the Colonel turned the laugh on him—said his men might be a little out at the seat but that the Yankees would never see that part of them."

"Is the Prince attractive?"

"No. Pasty skin, dissipated, fat, soft, rude, ill-mannered. Major Fairfax had prepared refreshments, but the Prince declined to stay. We sent him back through the lines under a flag—and good riddance."

Trav, hoping to help her for a while to forget Clayton's death, talked so much more than was usual for him that she said smilingly: "I declare, Travis, soldiering's loosened your tongue. I never knew you to have so much to say. Did you learn that from Cousin Jeems?"

"He's quite a talker when we're alone," Trav agreed, and added with a chuckle: "Or when we've had wine or whiskey for dinner. Then he likes to talk—and to sing."

"Tony's changed, too," she reflected. "He was here last week. I wonder if Brett and Faunt will be changed. I hope Brett won't. He couldn't be improved."

"I had a letter from Tony," Trav told her. "He'd seen Mama and Enid and the children. I'm going down to Great Oak tomorrow." Tony had written suggesting that he come home for a visit when he could, that Enid missed him; but Trav did not tell Cinda this. Some undercurrent in Tony's letter had puzzled him, made him faintly uneasy.

"I'm so glad," Cinda agreed. "Be nice to Enid, Trav. It's lonely for her there."

This was so nearly what Tony had said that Trav looked at her half resentfully. "I suppose so."

Cinda hesitated as though about to say more. "Are you here on duty?" she asked.

"I came to see Colonel Northrop. He's—well, I want to try to straighten out some things."

"That sounds familiar! Everybody complains about Colonel Northrop. He's the most be-damned man in Richmond—and President Davis is damned for supporting him."

"Well, Colonel Northrop makes a lot of mistakes," Trav admitted. "I've been impressing corn and meat in front of our lines, because if we don't the Yankees will; but the Colonel has sent orders not to do that. I want to discuss it with him. We could draw all we need from the country west of us, as long as we stay where we are; and when we retreat, as we're bound to, everything there will be left for the Yankees. But Colonel Northrop insists on shipping everything up from Richmond. That not only puts too heavy a load on the railroad, but it uses up our stores here before there's any need."

"I should think he'd see that."

"I think that he will," Trav agreed. "When I tell him the situation." He added, half-embarrassed, laughing at himself: "Of course I don't know much about it; but I've been trying to figure out a system of supply and transportation, so things will come through regularly. As it is, one day there'll be plenty and to spare; and then when that's gone there'll be no rations at all for a day or so. The army eats up a million pounds a week—when we get it. That means a lot of wagons, besides the railroads." She nodded, and he said earnestly: "I think we ought to have at least four wagons, with four or maybe six horses to a wagon, to each company, and two to each battery, and about twenty-five more for making depots. That would take care of food and ammunition and headquarters and hospitals and everything." On this subject so important to him he became eloquent. "Then I think we ought to accumulate a big reserve of supplies in places where they'll be safe from capture but where they can be easily transported to the army. As it is, we just live from hand to mouth. That's all right in summer; but in winter when the roads are bad it means the men will be short of food a lot of the time. This war is just beginning, but we ought to plan ahead. I've talked about it with General

Longstreet and he sent me down to see Colonel Northrop and explain my ideas to him."

She said affectionately: "It's so like you to do your fighting with figures." And she suggested: "Mr. Streean might help you."

"He's in the Quartermaster's office, but I don't think he's in the purchasing department."

"He buys all sorts of things, Tilda says."

"He may be doing it as a speculation. Prices are rising already."

Cinda agreed. "Brett Dewain says they'll go sky-high," she commented. "He says paper money is no good. He worries as much about such things as you do about figures."

"Have you seen him lately?"

"Not since—" Her voice caught, and she did not finish. He guessed that she had not seen Brett since the days he spent here after Clayton's death.

"I expect you miss him," he suggested.

"Oh, I keep busy. At first I worked with Miss Sally Tompkins in her hospital." She hesitated. "I don't suppose I accomplished much, but it was—well, I got a lot of satisfaction out of it. But now no more wounded are coming in, so I have time to enjoy little Clayton."

"It isn't just wounds," he remarked. "Disease, too. We've thousands of men sick in the hospitals at Centerville."

She touched her brow with her hand in a gesture he had never seen before. "Battle isn't the only danger, is it? Mr. French and Dr. Laidley were killed right here in Richmond. They were making powder or something, and it exploded."

"We're hard put to it for such things." He remembered Longstreet's word. "Even for lead. We searched the battlefield for bullets, picked them up out of the grass, dug them out of trees and out of the walls of houses. The men got hundreds of pounds of lead that way, and we needed it all. Collecting rations is hard enough, but there's plenty of food if we manage properly."

Trav's interview with the Commissary General next day was completely fruitless. Colonel Northrop himself had a dyspeptic look, and Trav thought a man with no appetite could not be expected to realize how much soldiers needed to eat. When he went on to Great Oak, he was depressed by Colonel Northrop's stubborn stupidity, and his thoughts were all absorbed in his own problems; but remembering Tony's advice and Cinda's, he made a conscientious effort to content Enid. She had always seemed to him a person of mysterious moods: sometimes astonishingly gay and charming, sometimes wearyingly querulous, sometimes easily pleased, sometimes impossible to content. There were times when her eager responses enchanted him; there were others when at his least touch she shivered with distaste and drew away. She was an enigma he had long ago ceased to try to solve. If she accepted his clumsily affectionate advances, he was pleased; if she repelled them, he neither wooed her nor demanded what she did not readily bestow.

So, though he had mildly hoped for a warmer welcome, he was not surprised when this time she rebuffed him. "Don't start tumbling me! If you want to be a married man, you'd better stay home and take care of your family, instead of just coming when you feel like it, as though I were your mistress!"

She had many complaints. She said Mrs. Currain was becoming more exasperating every day. "She treats me like a child, doesn't think I can do anything right, doesn't trust me out of her sight. She won't even let me help her."

"Well, Mama's always run things here."

"Oh, of course you'd take her side!"

"Why, you know I'm on your side, Enid, if it ever comes to the point of taking sides; but Mama doesn't intend to make you unhappy."

"Well, I don't know what she intends, but I know what she does! She even interferes with the way I manage the children. She spoils them so that they're beginning to just hate me!" Her tone became maddeningly patient. "But I'll get used to it, I suppose. Your family never did like me."

"Cinda sent her love to you."

"That didn't mean anything! I know what they all think of me. I suppose that's why I'm so lonely."

"You see Brett and Tony and Julian pretty often, don't you?"

"Oh, yes, they ride over at the most heathenish hours, and Mama wears herself out taking care of them and then goes to bed with a headache and I have to play nursemaid to her! If you think seeing them is any pleasure, you're mightily mistaken. They never pay any attention to me anyway, except to ask for things. I might as well be one of the servants and go live in the quarter!"

That was ridiculous, of course, and it made him heavily angry; but when Enid was in this mood you could never change her. He thought if he stayed a day or two she might come to better humor; but she did not. He had some happy hours with the children and with his mother, and he made sure that under Big Mill's management the tasks were well done before he returned to Longstreet's headquarters.

As the summer ended, Trav's work became more difficult. Colonel Northrop forbade the impressment of supplies; and the small farmers would not sell their produce, already preferring the hard money paid by Northern agents to Confederate paper. Trav did not wholly blame them; but would not this feeling grow? General Longstreet expected years of war.

"We're giving McClellan time to build an army," he told Trav once, "while we spend our days on parades. The most powerful weapon in war, Currain, is time. Tactics is time. To act at the right time—as against the wrong time—is what wins battles and campaigns, and wars. If we give McClellan too much time, he'll build an army that can crush us."

When they were alone, the big man, who except in the jovial after-dinner hour was usually reserved, became easily vocal. They sometimes, at Longstreet's invitation, rode together, bound nowhere in particular, exploring the byways that threaded this impoverished countryside. "It's a pity and a shame to see a region worked out like this," the General one day commented. "Farmed to death and then let go to old field pine and broom sedge." Trav might have spoken, but the other went on as though forgetting he had a listener: "I've always had my greatest enjoyment in the out of doors. My work in the Indian service, when we lived for weeks with a blanket and our saddle for bedding and saw new country every day, was pure pleasure." And as their horses took their own pace he talked of hunting deer and antelope and panthers, of encampments in cool canyons after long sun-baked days upon the desert plains, of slaughtering wild cattle to feed the troops. "The cattle are wild as elephants in the Asian jungles," he declared. "And to a man on foot even more dangerous." And he laughed and recalled a day when a bull that he had wounded charged him after he dismounted to dispatch and bleed it. "There was nothing to climb but a cactus," he confessed. "I was picking its spikes out of my hide for days. If I'd had time to think I should have preferred the bull." He spoke of a buffalo hunt, the headlong chase, the spatter of shots, the choppy hump-shouldered canter of the great beasts which was so much more swift than it looked. "I was a young man then," he admitted. "Probably I wouldn't relish it now. But after this war is won I'm going to settle down to a quiet life on some peaceful farm."

"I've spent my happiest years farming."

"Then you've the stuff to make a good soldier. You like figures, you don't waste time, and you've an eye for topography. Topography is strategy, time is tactics, and figures are forces available. That's the whole essence of war."

"I'll never make a soldier. I lack—among other things—confidence in myself."

Longstreet's eyes twinkled. "That's not necessarily a fault. Of course, when you've seen more of the dull-witted, stubbornly ignorant, stupidly arrogant self-assurance of others, you'll come to respect yourself; but too much self-confidence is worse than too little. Bonham, and young Major Whiting, when they stopped me from opening fire on the stampeding enemy at Centerville, had too much self-confidence —plus too much authority."

"I know you were angry that day."

"If there's anything I hate worse than stupidity, it's opposition." The big man chuckled. "But then of course opposition always seems to me stupid." He was laughing in frank amusement at himself. "I can never do, wholeheartedly, what someone else tells me to do when I'm sure he's wrong."

"Are you always right?" Trav was smiling too.

"God bless you, no! But even when I'm wrong, I'm right, because I do better work when I think I'm right. A wise superior will never insist that I do something I think is a mistake. He'd better let me do the wrong thing and do it well."

Trav asked curiously: "Are you ambitious for higher command?"

"Of course! So is every officer worth his salt!" The big man hesitated. "And yet," he admitted, "I might fail. I'm worth more in action than in council. In action, I forget the remote and comprehend only the immediate, the thing that needs doing at once. You spoke of self-confidence. In action, under fire, I'm confident; then I know! That's my best field. In quiet planning, I might—think too much!"

The long summer days gave them many such hours together; Trav himself came to talk as freely as the other. Cinda would have been astonished at his loquacity. He confessed one day that he had dreaded war.

"Why, of course," Longstreet agreed. "So did all sensible men, and especially soldiers. Every intelligent soldier knows that the real function of an army is to make war unnecessary. No one but the politicians—who know nothing about war—wanted it. They had dreams of glory, but battle is the least part of war. We lost say two thousand men killed and wounded at Manassas; but there are ten or fifteen thousand men sick in our hospitals within a few miles of us today, and not from wounds. They're down with measles, and chicken pox, and pneumonia, and from eating the wrong things. We'll have a good many thousands killed in battle before this business is over, but two or three times as many will die wretchedly in camps or hospitals because their bowels insist on moving ten or fifteen times a day. Many a mother who wept with pride when her son marched bravely off with his fellows will learn—if she ever learns the truth—that he died of a bloody flux from drinking dirty water. Battle is a bloody business of screaming men and gushing blood and spilled guts. Of course, it's exhilarating. But for every hour of battle there's a month of stinking wretchedness. You'll see more vomit and ordure in this war than you will blood! You'll be much more annoyed by lice than by bullets." His voice was harsh and angry. "But that's not the politicians' dream picture of war!"

Trav told him about the feeling around Martinston, in the months before war came, in that time that seemed so long ago. "But when the war did begin they raised a company there."

"Oh, once war comes, everyone hurrahs for war," Longstreet assured him. "We all catch the infection. We see everyone around us cheering, so we start cheering with the rest. We're afraid we'll be suspect if we don't cheer. But the best of us still hate it. The politicians go to war for an idea; and because they insist that their ideas must prevail, ordinary men and women must send their sons away to die of diarrhea!" His eyes shadowed. "Yes, Currain, I dreaded this war just as much as you did. Perhaps even more. I had reason to dread it. The army was my profession. My fellow officers, North and South, were my friends. I could name you a hundred men fighting on the other side today; men I love like brothers. And I had a happy life, settled, secure; but if war came, I'd have to serve. I'd have to fight either against my own people, or against the flag for which I'd been ready these twenty years, as a matter of course, to die." He spoke more softly. "No, I didn't want war. When the rupture came, I hoped I need not take an active part against the flag I had always defended; so when I arrived in Richmond I asked for office duty." He roused as though from a revery, chuckled, slapped his knee. "And here I am in charge of the outposts, in sight of Washington, in the foremost line! Well, I like games. I shall play the best hand I can at this one, now it's begun!"

Trav found it hard in more festive hours to recognize the man who talked to him thus simply, and the festive hours were many. In lodgings as near the camps as possible, hundreds of wives and daughters and sweethearts spent the summer and fall, and there was a daily flood of charming feminine visitors. Two Baltimore girls, Jenny and Hetty Cary, escaped to Virginia with a smuggled consignment of drugs that were badly needed in the Richmond hospitals; and with their cousin Constance they paid a visit to Colonel Stewart's Maryland regiment in Elzey's Brigade, encamped at Fairfax Station. Invitations from General Elzey led General Longstreet and his staff to ride over for dinner. Afterward Colonel Stewart paraded his regiment; and Hetty Cary, with much merry prompting, put the soldiers through the manual of arms, and the men in steady ranks moved with the smart precision of machines, till in sudden pretty confusion the girl fled to join her sister and Miss Constance in the triangular portal of the tent which had been prepared to lodge them for the night. Colonel Stewart came after her, laughingly protesting that she could not dismiss the regiment without some grateful gesture; and Trav saw the three girls whisper together, and then Miss Hetty and Miss Constance, bravely facing the men still stiffly at attention, began to sing.

The despot's heel is on thy shore,
    Maryland, my Maryland!
His touch is on thy temple door,
    Maryland, my Maryland!
Avenge the patriotic gore
That flowed the streets of Baltimore,
And be the battle queen of yore,
    Maryland, my Maryland!

Till the first notes, there had been a stir and movement among the officers grouped around the young ladies; but now at once quiet fell upon them all. The scene seemed to Trav deeply moving. The steady ranks of soldiers, the silent officers, the sweet dusk across the plain, the lovely girls from whose lips came these liquid golden sounds, all combined to present an unimagined beauty; and when, at first by ones and twos and then all together the voices of the men took up the reiterated refrain, Trav sang with the rest, his tears streaming in a mysterious happiness. He and Longstreet, riding homeward through the night, were for a long time silent; when they spoke it was of little unimportant things. This had been an experience too deep for words.

The "Cary Invincibles" stayed in lodgings near the army for weeks. During the battle at Manassas there had been confusing difficulty in distinguishing the Confederate Stars and Bars from the Stars and Stripes. General Beauregard designed a "Battle Flag", with diagonal blue bars star-spangled, which would be more easily recognized, and the three girls made banners of the new pattern to present to their favorite generals: Hetty's to General Johnston, Jenny's to Beauregard, Constance's to General Van Dorn.

There were flags for each division, too; and that night the general officers gathered for a banquet at Longstreet's headquarters. The occasion began decorously enough, but it proceeded—as was apt to be the case when Major Fairfax furnished the food and drink—to a hilarious climax. When the potations he provided had done their work an argument arose. The South should have a song, a national anthem. *Dixie?* That was a good song, to be sure; but too frivolous! General Johnston and General Beauregard voted for *Maryland, My Maryland,* but General Van Dorn argued that the best of all possible songs was the duet from *I Puritani,* and he began to sing it to prove his point.

"Just a moment, General," Longstreet protested. "If you're going to sing for us, get up on the table where we can see you."

Van Dorn rose, somewhat unsteadily. "Why, willingly, sir," he agreed. "But a duet needs two voices. Add that fog horn of yours to my piping tones and we'll do it properly."

"I will, sir," Longstreet assured him. He came to his feet. But to climb on the table presented difficulties, and General Smith tried to help them and had to mount the table himself to pull them up; and they insisted that for that service he deserved to sing with them. The duet became a thundering trio, Longstreet's voice almost drowning out the other two. Trav saw General Johnston and General Beauregard laughing as robustly as anyone.

Such diversions were welcome, since they broke the long monotony of inaction; but though the officers could find amusement, there was grumbling among the men. Trav in the course of his duties had made many contacts with the private soldier; his long friendship with such simple men as Ed Blandy may have endowed him with some quality that made them trust him. The first fervor which had led them to enlist was long since cooled. Had they not whipped the Yankees, way back there two months ago? Well then, why not go home? Their wives were having a hard time making a crop; and someone had to get the corn in, and the firewood ready for winter. If the Yankee army made a move, it would be time enough to hustle back here and lick them again; but if a man stayed around camp doing nothing, he would just come down sick and be no good to anyone.

The steady trickle of desertions had begun even before the battle of Manassas; it continued and increased. Trav heard discussion among the ranking generals as to how this problem should be met. Certainly it would be absurd, when ranks were already so thinned by sickness that it was no longer worth while to put the men through the School of the Company, to start executing deserters after you had gone to all the trouble of bringing them back to duty. General Johnston considered drumming them out of the regiment, in public disgrace; but Longstreet advised against that. "Some of these men deserting now will turn out to be good soldiers before this business is done," he argued. "But take a man and shave his head and make him keep time to the Rogue's March up and down the brigade front and he'll be a scoundrel all his life. A man is as tender of his honor as a woman— and as worthless when it's gone."

So lesser penalties, some painful, some calculated to make the culprit ridiculous, were imposed; bucking, the barrel shirt, pack drill. But the men, with no enemy to try their mettle, began to fight among themselves. Soldiers were gouged or knifed or shot in these affrays, till at last something like a general battle developed in Major Wheat's battalion. The ringleaders were arrested and put under guard, but a few of their comrades tried to release them by force, and for that crime were court-martialled and ordered to be shot. The firing squad was drawn from their own company, and the whole army was marched out to witness the execution.

Trav closed his eyes before the volley rang; he said to General Longstreet afterward: "That was a hard thing to do."

Longstreet agreed. "A pity, yes. These are good men; but they've been loafing too long."

"Winter will be worse, won't it, sir?"

"Worse for the men, yes. Furloughs will help, of course." The General added: "And you and I will be able to see something of our families. Mrs. Longstreet plans to come on as far as Lynchburg this month; and Lynchburg's not far away."

Trav knew how much an occasional day or two with Mrs. Longstreet and the children would mean to the General, and he wished he could look forward as eagerly to seeing Enid again; but he had in fact no desire to see her, seldom thought of her at all. Except for that one occasion in August he had stayed at headquarters, absorbed in his routine tasks. Cinda, in an October letter, said he should come to Richmond more often. "And to Great Oak, to see Enid and the children." She added with an obscure irrelevance: "Mr. Streean thinks Faunt and the Blues will soon be coming home." That seemed a curious thing for Cinda to say, as though Faunt's prospective return was a reason for his seeing Enid; but Cinda often puzzled him. She was as perplexing as Enid, in a different way.

26

IF TRAV found contentment, during that quiet summer after Manassas, in the routine of military life, so did Tony. He was happier than he had ever been, revelling in an exhilarating sense of capacity and power. He had always thought of himself as a coward. To discover, as he did at Bethel, that he was in a modest way a hero, and to find that he was a leader whom men respected, was an inspiring stimulus.

The inspiration persisted. Through the weeks after Bethel, when action was replaced by what seemed aimless marching to and fro, and drill was the order of the day, men sickened from inadequate or improper food. Bob Grimm, who during those days of playing war at Martinston had been laid low by a boil that was funny to everyone but Bob, was their only battle casualty. At Bethel a musket ball smashed his elbow and he lost the arm and was discharged. But Jim Tunstill and Albert Hunt died of the measles and Rab Anderson of dysentery. Chub Welfare was the glutton of the company, and one day when no rations were available he led a hunt for bull frogs in a creek near camp. They caught a dozen or two, and proceeded to boil them whole. Tony came upon them grouped around their cooking fire, about to begin the feast.

"Those frogs might make you sick, boys," he suggested. It was no more than a suggestion, for he recognized the limitations of his authority; yet his advice, and after the first taste their own repugnance, made some of the men abstain. Chub, however, ate not only his own share but the leftovers of these others. The resulting dysentery stripped his well-padded frame of forty or fifty pounds of weight; and though he survived, he was weak as an ailing woman afterward.

Such incidents strengthened Tony's influence over his men. He set Ed Blandy and Tom Shadd to teach them how to sleep on the ground in mud or rain without needless discomfort. He sought advice from experienced campaigners and passed it on to them. They learned that to eat lightly and to drink cold water slowly and to wear a wetted handkerchief in their hats made a hot day endurable, and that clean feet in clean and well-darned socks did not blister so easily on a long march. In one of the training maneuvers which were the order of the summer, during a halt beside good running water, a fair third of Tony's company knelt along the stream to wash socks and underclothes; and while they were thus engaged Colonel Hill rode by and stopped to speak to Tony.

"Is this by your orders, Captain?"

"Well, it's not orders, sir; but the men are learning how to keep themselves clean."

"Good! Excellent! I wish all the companies were as well led." Colonel Hill added thoughtfully: "An army spends most of its time not in fighting the enemy but in fighting its own laziness and carelessness. More men will be put out of action in this war by blistered heels than by bullets." He nodded again. "Good," he repeated, and rode on.

So Tony met the test of the summer of idleness after Manassas as adequately as he had met the test of action at Bethel. When in August he had two days in Richmond, he told Cinda laughingly: "I don't know whether I'm a captain or a nurse. I inspect heels quite as carefully as I inspect muskets."

Even thus soon after Clayton's death, Cinda could smile. "I can't imagine you, somehow, peering at a soldier's feet!"

"Not only their feet," he assured her. "Their socks too, and their underwear. Why, I'm as critical of their laundry as Mama ever was of the way things were done at Great Oak. And I keep them up to the mark, too! Nat Emerson had to walk post twelve hours barefoot because he marched with a hole in his sock and got a blister. Joe Merritt cooked his dinner in a dirty frying pan, so I made him wash all the company's dishes that day." Thinking of Clayton he wished to lead her to laughter, and he spoke of the day when Chelmsford Lowman's horse was lame and he rode a little spike-tailed mule which balked at a ford. "So we put a rope on the mule's neck and the men tailed onto it to drag the mule across with Lowman still on its back. He's a tall, thin man with a big Adam's apple. The mule swerved into a pot hole below the ford and went clean under, and Lowman too; but when the men hauled them out he was still on the mule's back, with his Adam's apple working like a pump handle, spitting muddy water like a fountain. He said that dratted mule waded all the way across!"

Cinda was amused, and he told her about Chub Welfare and the bull frogs, and made her laugh again. "But I'm surprised your men get sick," she remarked. "They ought to be healthy enough—country folk."

"The country people seem to get measles and mumps and things like that more easily than men from the cities," he told her. "I don't know why, but it works out that way." He said thoughtfully: "Lots of things in this war have worked out in ways I didn't expect. For instance, there's mighty little fighting. We've had only three hours of it in four months."

"There was fighting enough at Manassas."

"I'm sorry, Cinda. Didn't mean to——"

She said gently: "It's all right, Tony. I'm all right. I can even forget, sometimes." She added, her eyes thoughtful: "I wonder if it wouldn't be wise for the whole South to forget Manassas, Tony. That victory may be the ruin of us."

"Oh, I don't think a good victory ever did anyone any harm."

"I'm not so sure! Everybody thought after the battle that the war was won. So now no one's doing anything!" She spoke scornfully: "Except parade down to Mr. Libby's tobacco factory to peep at Congressman Ely in prison there. He's one of the sights of Richmond. People would almost pay to see him, like a lion in a cage."

"Not much of a lion!" Tony reminded her. "Didn't we catch him hiding in the woods, after the battle?"

"Oh yes, he'd come out from Washington to see us beaten!"

"I hear everyone in Washington who could hire a carriage drove out to watch, brought their ladies, promised them a victory ball in Richmond." He asked: "Is it true the Yankees had thirty thousand pairs of handcuffs, to use on the Southerners they were going to capture?"

"I don't know," Cinda said wearily. "Oh, I've heard all the stories, but I wonder if they're true. Some of the Northern papers say we tied prisoners to trees and stabbed them, and stuck bayonets into them. Of course that's a lie; but probably our papers tell us just as many lies about the Yankees." She shook her head. "Have you seen Tilda? You must drop in on her, Tony. She'll be hurt if you don't."

"Oh, I will," he agreed; but her suggestion surprised him. None of them had ever cared whether Tilda were hurt or not.

It seemed to him, when he called at the house a few blocks out Franklin Street, that Tilda, who had always been as thin as a slat, began to be a little plump; and there was something sleek and complacent about her. "You're looking well, Tilda," he remarked. "I guess the war agrees with you."

"Why, you know, I think it does," she admitted. "I love having Richmond so full of our boys home to be admired and praised. I declare it seems as if half the army was trying to beau Dolly around! She's having just a wonderful time!" She asked: "Do you see much of Enid?"

"We ride over now and then, yes."

"How is she?"

There was a sharp curiosity in her tone which surprised him. "Why, the same as ever, I suppose." He smiled. "She thinks the war is just a scheme of Trav's so he could get away from home, takes it as a personal affront. But Enid's always discontented, fussing about something."

"Did—does she say anything about Faunt?"

He lighted a long cigar, careful of his tone. Obviously Tilda too had eyes to see. "Oh, she always asks the latest news about everybody," he said casually, and asked in his turn: "So Dolly's having a high time, is she? I expect you like watching her goings on."

"Of course I do," Tilda assented, and she added quickly: "Oh, I s'pose I ought not to be enjoying it all so much, and of course I'm sorry about Clayton; but really, Tony, he shouldn't have been in the army at all. Neither should you, for that matter! Nor Trav! You ought all of you to be farming. Redford says food is going to be ever so scarce this winter, and someone has to feed the soldiers, even if there isn't much glory in it."

He spoke in drawling amusement. "I suppose Mister Streean and Darrell feel they're making a sacrifice."

"Why, they are! Redford's just worked to death. Darrell's desperately in love with that sweet little Anne Tudor, but it doesn't prevent his being a wonderful business man! He's in Mississippi now seeing about sending some cotton through the lines." They heard the front door open, heard Streean in the hall, and she said quickly: "Oh dear, I shouldn't have said that! It's a secret! But of course we can't eat our old cotton, and Redford says if we can get food in exchange for it——"

Then as her husband appeared she checked in midsentence, but Streean had heard, for he said at once: "Hello, Tony. Glad to see you. Yes, we can make our cotton feed us and fight for us." He went to his desk as though to look for something there, and Tony said in surprise:

"I thought we meant to hold our cotton so the Northern mills would have to shut down."

"That's the official policy, but we have to be practical, too. Oh, that reminds me." Streean closed the desk, stuffing some papers in his pocket. "I'm about to pay my respects to an old friend of yours, Mrs. Albion. Care to come along?"

Tony waited a moment so his tone would not betray him. "Yes, I'd like to join you, yes, if I won't be intruding."

"Not at all," Streean declared. "She'll be delighted, I know."

Walking out Franklin Street to Monroe, Tony found himself at the prospect of this encounter pleasantly excited. A maid servant, not Tessie whom he remembered, admitted them. As he followed Streean into the house Tony heard a door close somewhere; and he recognized the sound. That was the side door, opening into the small garden through which a path led to the wicket gate. He himself, when he was with Nell and unexpected callers came, had sometimes slipped away through the garden. Who was Nell's—patron now? He felt an almost jealous pang.

Before she appeared, Tony heard the latch click on the wicket, and he strolled to the window that looked that way and saw not one man but two departing. Then Nell appeared. That serenity and poise which had always seemed to him so contenting was still hers; she was as beautiful as she had always been.

She greeted Tony without embarrassment, like an old friend; and he suspected she had seen his glance toward the garden, for she said at once: "I was sorry to keep you waiting, but two gentlemen were just leaving."

Streean obviously had not guessed this. "Eh? Who were they?"

"From Baltimore," she explained. "They're working with General Winder on secret service, so they preferred not to be recognized. I knew them in Washington, so they came to pay their respects."

"Winder's police, eh? Well, they'll find plenty to do here. Richmond's full of Northern agents. The New York *Herald* has just published a complete schedule of all our forces under arms, their location, their commanders. I suspect that information came out of the Adjutant General's office. General Cooper is Northern-born."

Nell smiled. "You might as reasonably suspect Ordnance, or the Commissariat,—or even your own department. There are many loose tongues in Richmond." She added, indicating a newspaper on the table. "The gentlemen who just left were discussing the destruction of Hampton."

Streean nodded. "Butler's taking revenge on helpless women and children for the licking we gave him at Bethel." Hampton was down at the tip of the Peninsula, not far from Tony's duty at Yorktown, but he had not heard this news; and he crossed to pick up the paper, the day's *Examiner*. The Federals—said the *Examiner*—had burned the town, "destroyed it not by sections but wholly, completely, fully," before they evacuated the place.

When Tony laid the paper aside and sat down, he only half listened to their conversation. In old days Nell would have taken him upstairs where the chairs were comfortable and a man could be at ease. That she did not do so now might be deliberate, to remind him of what he had cast aside; but probably it was only because Streean was here. They were speaking of the victory at Manassas, and Nell said it was a pity the Confederates had not pursued the shattered Yankee army. Streean laughed. "You sound like Mr. Benjamin, Mrs. Albion. He wants to be Secretary of War, so he's trying to curry favor with President Davis by criticizing Beauregard."

"I wasn't criticizing General Beauregard! President Davis himself was at Manassas. He could have ordered the pursuit. Since he didn't, he must take the blame."

"Not at all," Streean insisted. "Beauregard, or rather Johnston, stopped the pursuit. General Longstreet had his guns ready to open on the Yankees as they poured into Centerville; but Johnston ordered him not to do so, and after that it was too late."

"If you count on General Longstreet as a Davis partisan, you'll be disappointed," Nell assured him. "He'll never forgive President Davis for that question at their first meeting here in Richmond.

Tony asked curiously: "What question, Nell?"

The use of her first name was an inadvertence; but he saw her faint color and thought she was pleased. "Why, the General reported for duty, and President Davis asked him whether he had settled his accounts with the Federal Government. Longstreet was paymaster in Albuquerque, you know; and naturally he resented the question as impugning his personal honor. He turned red and said very stiffly: 'Sir, I come as an honorable gentleman to offer my sword to the South.'"

Tony nodded. "As if Longstreet were an embezzler. Were you there, ma'am?" This time he addressed her more formally.

Before Nell could speak, Streean answered him. "Mrs. Albion knows everything that happens in Richmond," he explained. "Her masculine acquaintance is large—and talkative." His tone became harshly derisive. "But General Longstreet didn't—as she so poetically puts it—'offer his sword.' He asked for a place in the Paymaster's department. Of course no one can blame him for wanting to handle money rather than men. After all, there's more profit in it."

Tony, to his own surprise, resented the slur. He felt his cheeks stiff. "Mister Streean, I have the honor of General Longstreet's acquaintance; and my brother is serving on his staff."

Streean laughed carelessly. "Oh, no offense, Tony."

But Tony did not smile. "Do I understand you to suggest that General Longstreet seeks personal profit from this conflict?"

"Eh?" Streean looked at him in surprise and then in understanding. "Why, God bless me, no!" He glanced at Nell and said, as though to throw the onus on her: "No, in spite of Mrs. Albion's opinion I'm sure he is wholly devoted to Mr. Davis and the Confederacy."

"It is not Mrs. Albion's opinion, but yours, sir," Tony reminded him, "about which I wish to be perfectly clear."

Streean was almost abject, his brow glistening. "I have the highest possible opinion of General Longstreet, of course."

"Then your remarks were subject to an unfortunate misconstruction."

"I regret that most sincerely."

Tony nodded, accepting these amends, thinking remotely: Why, I was angry, ready to push the matter to an issue. He looked at Nell and saw an amused twinkle in her eye, and then Streean came to his feet and mopped his wet forehead and said he must be going. Tony made no move to go with him; and Streean's departure was like flight.

So Tony was alone with Nell. Their eyes met, and they smiled together. "You've changed, Tony," she said approvingly.

"Why, yes," he assented. "Yes, I think I have."

"But—don't play the bully too often, my dear. Not all men are such cowards as Mr. Streean."

There had never been any pretense between them. "I was as surprised to hear myself as you were to hear me," he admitted. "I met General Longstreet only once, but I liked him." He asked: "Who told you about his interview with the President?"

She evaded his question. "Oh, I see a great many people." She asked curiously: "You enjoy being a soldier?"

"Yes." He hesitated. "I enjoy feeling that I'm needed, and that I'm useful."

"I believe you do."

"It's a new experience for me," he reminded her, and smiled, almost embarrassed. "I don't need to tell you that. You've known me a long time."

"I'm not sure that I ever knew you, Tony," she said gently; and he was deeply pleased. "What's happened to you?"

"Why—I suppose, come to think of it, you're responsible. You persuaded me to go to Chimneys, and I found myself the big man of the neighborhood. And I liked it."

So they fell into easy talk, of what since their parting his life had been, and hers. Tony stayed an hour or two, and when he left her, strolling back toward Fifth Street, he thought they had been as comfortable together as in the past. Yes, even more so; for in the old days there had always been an undercurrent of antagonism between them. He recognized that now, and wondered why. Perhaps in each of them there was even then a sense of guilty shame and a readiness to blame the other for their relationship. Probably Nell justified herself to herself by remembering that but for him she would be penniless. He decided to make sure, as tactfully as possible, that she did not lack for money now.

On his way back to duty Tony stopped at Great Oak and heard Enid's familiar complaints. "Trav leaves me and Mama and the children alone here, with such terrible things happening all around us."

"Nothing very bad," Tony suggested.

"Bad? I'd like to know what you call what the Yankees did at Hampton! Burned half the town! They say President Tyler's house is just ruined—the carpets all ripped up, and things broken and chopped to pieces till the house itself might just as well have been set on fire."

"General Butler's men didn't do that," Tony assured her. "We burned the town ourselves, General Magruder's orders." He had seen before he left Richmond this admission in the newspapers.

"Why, they did too! The Yankees, I mean! It said in the *Examiner* that they did it!"

"That was last Friday's paper," he corrected. "But the *Examiner* says now that General Magruder ordered the town destroyed. Union sentiment was strong there, and it was a refuge for runaway negroes and deserters. A school teacher named Raymond—he deserted from Hoffler's Creek—had turned the Female College into a boarding house for Northern officers. So we cleaned out the whole rat's nest!"

She abandoned the argument but not her anger. "Well, I don't care! With that sort of thing going on all around us, Trav had no business leaving his mother helpless here! Of course I don't matter; but he ought to think of her!"

"How is she?"

"She isn't down from her nap yet. But she's perfectly exasperating,

Tony. She's so silly, just refusing to listen to all the terrible goings on. She won't even believe Clayton's dead."

"I hope she never does believe it. She never saw him more than once or twice a year, anyway."

"I know, but her being so stubborn means I can't talk to her about anything! I'm so lonesome, Tony!"

He felt some sympathy for her. After all, it must be dull for a pretty young woman to spend day after day with no other company than his mother and the children. "Why don't you ask your mother down for a while?" But he knew even as he spoke that this was an absurd suggestion. As nice as Nell was, she would be out of place under his mother's roof, so he added: "Too bad you can't go to Richmond for a visit with her, but of course Mama can't stay here alone."

"Oh, I know! I'm just a prisoner here!" Her tone altered slightly. "Tony, when's Faunt coming home? They're all just wasting time out there in Western Virginia, not accomplishing anything!"

His sympathy gave way to a quiet anger at this pretty little idiot. "You'd better forget Faunt!"

"But why? I think he's wonderful! I just love him!" With a malicious amusement in her eyes, she added: "Why shouldn't I, I'd like to know? After all, he's my brother-in-law." He suspected she was deliberately provoking him, and did not speak, but she said lightly: "You're a fine one to pretend to be so proper!"

So she knew about him and Nell. He eyed her thoughtfully, wondering whether she had ever suggested the truth to his mother. God knows, he himself had in the past often enough given his mother hours of sorrow and shame; but he would never willingly hurt her again, nor make her grieve.

Nor should this common little nobody ever do so! He came to his feet and stood over Enid, so close to her that she had to lean back in her chair to look up at him. "Teach that tongue of yours to mind its manners, Enid," he said in icy tones. "If you ever discuss me with Mama, I'll make you regret it!"

She pressed her hand to her lips, staring up at him, seeing the anger in his eyes; and she squirmed sidewise out of the chair and backed away from him. Then they heard Mrs. Currain on the stairs, and

Enid slipped through the passage into the library as Mrs. Currain came in from the hall.

Tony, once Enid was gone, spent a pleasant hour with his mother. The routine of her days had never changed. Her morning inspections were as rigorous, her careful measuring out of the daily allowance of stores was as meticulous, her supervision of every activity about the place as exacting. She found security against the oppression of great events in her absorption in familiar little things; and Tony let her tell him every detail of her small problems and discussed them with her in perfect gravity, glad that no matter what happened around her, as long as Great Oak stood, his mother and her life would remain unchanged.

Riding back to Yorktown his thoughts returned to Enid. To protect his mother he had warned Enid to silence about himself and Nell, but for Enid as against Trav a good deal might be said. Tony knew well enough that there was a pagan in Nell, and probably in her daughter, too; and he could not imagine a man like Trav meeting that pagan halfway. These dozen years of her marriage to Trav must have been for Enid a long exasperation. Tony was sorry for her, but there was nothing he could do, except perhaps to advise Trav to come home as often as he could.

The letter he wrote Trav said little enough. Mama was fine, Enid and the children were well, Lucy was beginning to grow up, was prettier every day. Enid was devoting herself to keeping Mama happy; but probably she was pretty lonesome. He and Brett and Julian frequently rode over; but of course that was not the same for Enid as seeing her husband. It was too bad Trav was so far away.

He hoped Trav would read between the lines, and when a fortnight later he heard from Julian that Trav had been at Great Oak, it pleased him to think his letter was responsible.

The occasional crisp days of early fall reminded Tony that the six months for which his company had enlisted would presently end, and he felt a deep regret. This service, this sense of being useful, this exercise of authority bestowed without his seeking had been sweet to him; he would be sorry to see it end. But early in November the regiment of which his company was a part moved by detachments from

Yorktown to Richmond. Tony arrived there on the eighth of November, the Friday after the first election since the formation of the Confederacy; and when he called at Cinda's he found her indignant over the defeat of Mr. Macfarland, the president of the Farmers' Bank, who had been a candidate for Congress.

"It just shows what we must expect," she declared, "now that we're letting all that ragtag and bobtail vote. I don't see any sense in letting a man vote unless he has proved he amounts to something!"

Tony smiled. "You mean, unless he has made money?"

"Of course."

"Well, they're coming to it all over the South," he reminded her. "Till ten years ago, a man had to have at least a little property before he could vote in Virginia; and in North Carolina till five years ago no one could vote for state senators unless he owned fifty acres of land. But now any man who pays taxes at all can vote, and I suppose pretty soon he won't even have to pay taxes."

"Well, I think when we started the Confederacy we ought to have stopped all that. Why should white trash vote, I'd like to know." And she said hotly: "Mr. Dewain says that's the worst thing about Lincoln. He wants to let ordinary men vote and run things. That's why he's so dangerous. It's mountebanks like him who've ruined us."

"Who beat Mr. Macfarland?"

"Mr. Tyler. Oh, of course he's all right; but the *Examiner* said anybody who voted for Mr. Macfarland was just hoping to borrow money from his bank. As if he'd lend any one money just for voting for him! It makes me boil! You'd think being rich was a crime!"

"I suppose everyone voted for President Davis."

"Oh, yes—no one ran against him. But I do feel badly for Mr. Macfarland. He's such a fine man."

Tony lodged with Cinda till Tuesday when the regiment was mustered out of the Confederate service. Julian too was there, but the night before that formality he disappeared immediately after supper, leaving Tony with Cinda and Vesta and Jenny.

"Julian's gone to see Anne Tudor," Cinda told them. "He's in love with her, as much in love as a boy of sixteen can be—and that's a lot." And she asked: "Well, Tony, what will you do, now the regiment's broken up?"

"I haven't decided," he confessed. "This experience has meant a lot to me. I'm sorry it's over."

"Will the men enlist again?"

"I don't know. We'll be shipped back to North Carolina, and I'll go with them. We'll all go home to Martinston and talk it over there."

"Will you—stay with them? I mean, if they stay in the army?"

"I will if they want me. Yet I'm really too old for active soldiering. I tire too easily." He smiled. "I remember something you said to me once, Cinda. It was years ago. You wanted me to do something or other, and I said I wasn't well enough, and you said I talked like a woman in a delicate condition. You said it was a woman's privilege to plead a headache, or anything of that sort, but that when a man usurped that feminine prerogative he raised in the minds of others a doubt of his real sex! Remember?"

"You used to infuriate me," she admitted. "You were always apt to whine a little when you didn't get your own way, like a dog that limps when you scold it."

"I know. And there've been plenty of days this summer when I wanted to plead sick in order to escape duty. But I didn't." He added: "But the time will come when officers must stand up to hard marching, to hard living. I don't believe I could do it; not in a real pinch. And I don't want to fail men who trust me. So—I don't know what I'll do."

"I don't feel able to advise you." He guessed that she was not quite convinced of his sincerity.

"No. I'll have to make the decision myself." He added: "There's Chimneys to consider, too. Last spring our planting all over the South was mostly done before we—before any of the men left home; yet even this summer, food has been scarce. As long as the war lasts, the South will have to raise less cotton and tobacco and more wheat and corn. I might do more good, be more useful, if I stayed at home and helped feed the army." He hesitated. "I'll do what the men want me to do, in the end."

He did not hurry the decision. At Raleigh, when they were discharged, some Martinston men joined other North Carolina regiments; so the company as a company ceased to exist. Those who went on to

Martinston were of many minds. Chelmsford Lowman said he would stay at home. One of his sons had been in the company. had re-enlisted; another was fourteen.

"And Mrs. Lowman says the boy wants to go into the army," he told Tony. "Well, I won't stop him, but I'll stay home with her. Soldiering ain't what it's cracked up to be. I'll let the young fellows do the fighting."

Jeremy Blackstone put this same decision more vehemently. He had a small farm between Martinston and Chimneys; a wife, two little girls. "I've had my belly full," he declared. "I went to war looking for a fight. I like a good gouging as well as the next one. But all I get is my damned laigs marched off me! I've marched till I've wore my feet off pretty near up to the knees. Get up in the middle of the God-damned night to march. March to Hampton! March to Yorktown! March in parades! March in reviews! March off to Bethel! March to New Market Bridge! March back to Bethel! March to Yorktown! March off to Bethel again. Come down with chills and fever and get up and march some more. Why, if I'd marched in a straight line I'd be to the moon by now. March to Ship's Point, march to Young's Hill, march to Cockletown, march to Camp Rains, march to Bethel a couple of times for a change! Bethel! I never got so sick of a place in my born days! Jesus to Nancy, Captain, if I'd wanted to march I could have stayed home and walked the floor with a colicky young one! When I wasn't down with the chills and fever I was marching, and when I wasn't marching I was digging earthworks. I went into this shebang looking for a fight, but the nearest I came to it was laying behind some dirt while the Yankees shot bullets into it. No, sir, there ain't enough fighting in a war to suit me. I'm staying home from now on. The old woman'll give me all the war I want, right here at home!"

But not all the company were of this mind. Tom Shadd and Ed Blandy took a middle ground, and many followed them.

"I'm going to stay home the winter, anyway," Ed admitted. "I sh'd judge I'd learned what there is to soldiering, only maybe the fighting part. We didn't get much of a lesson at that. But right now. there's soldiers enough. Won't be any fighting in the mud this winter. It'll hold off long enough for me to get my compost made and spread and my planting done, so Mrs. Blandy and the young 'uns can make a crop next summer. Then if it looks to me I'm needed, I c'n sign up again."

Tom Shadd—he was a silent man, rarely speaking—nodded agreement; and so did others standing by. But Lonn Tyler dissented and with some violence.

"They'll never git me into it again," he declared, "and I know a plenty that feel the same way. This here's a planters' war! Nothing against you personally, Captain Currain; but there it is. You all want us-uns to go out and git ourselves killed so you all kin keep your slaves. Well, it's your having slaves that's the trouble with us-uns, if you ask me. A poor man working by hisself can't make a money crop. About the best he can do is raise enough to keep his family from starving to death. You rich men with your slaves that you don't have to pay no wages to, you can raise a crop and sell it for less than it costs a poor man to raise it."

He warmed to his theme. "Why, there ain't two men in a hundred in the South that owns a slave—no, nor wants to. I talked to a Virginia man and he says the planters worked the land up there to death and the poor man has to take their leavings." His voice rose. "Why, take it right in our company! You've got a flock of slaves at Chimneys, Captain Currain, and Judge Meynell he had one; but with the Judge dead there ain't another man in the company has ary a one, or is likely to! Get rid of the slaves, say I, and then a white man'd have a chance to better hisself! As it is, the big planter gits the fresh meat and the gravy, and the poor man gits sowbelly and grits and thankful to git it! Me go to war to keep things so? Not if I know myself!"

There were nods of agreement all around, and Ed Blandy—he was in many ways the best man among them—put the matter calmly. "There's sense in that, Captain Currain. The way it's been around Martinston, the heft of us had our own little places and worked them ourselves. We didn't look to get ahead much, nor we didn't; but we was satisfied to be let alone. Long as we knew that there wasn't any man around good enough to push us out of his way and make us take it, we was satisfied. Some of us'd maybe ride with the paterollers if one of your people lit out for the woods, or to help keep the free niggers in their place; but we was still our own men and didn't have to take nothing from nobody. We knowed you all was some smarter than us-uns, but we could stand up to you in a hoss race, or over a jug of corn whiskey, or in a shooting match, or in a fight if it came to that. So when you talked reasonable we'd listen, but your say-so didn't make it so."

Tony said sincerely: "I've tried to find the right thing to say to you, but I don't know what's best for you to do now. If I did, if I was sure, I'd tell you."

"I sh'd judge you would," Ed assented. "But there's no way you can be sure. You and them like you, you've always had plenty to wait on you, plenty of anything you wanted. There ain't so awful many of you all, but there's a pile of us. And it looks to me like the pile of us is doing the fighting for you all."

"We're fighting too," Tony reminded him.

"The heft of you are, certain. But, Captain, you're fighting for something that's yours and that you want to hang on to. What are we fighting for? Well, mostly to give you a hand, it looks to me. I be damned if I c'n see what we get out of it, win, lose, or draw."

Tony said thoughtfully that he supposed each man must answer the question for himself. With an unaccustomed insight he went on: "You all know my brother Travis. He's commissary on Longstreet's staff—if you call that fighting. He and my brother-in-law, Mr. Dewain, went to war because Virginia did, and for the same reason she did, because they wouldn't fight against South Carolina. My other brother is fighting because he wants to keep the Yankees out of Virginia. Two of my nephews are fighting because they're young, and all their friends are fighting. I went into it because you asked me to. My nephew Clayton, who was killed at Manassas, fought because he believed South Carolina had a right to leave the Union. But none of us really fight to defend slavery, to keep our slaves."

"All the same," Ed insisted, "if it hadn't been for you all and your slaves, there wouldn't be any fighting."

Tony knew no way to answer him. What Lonn Tyler and now Ed had said was true. Only a small minority of Southerners owned slaves; but those without slaves could not compete with those who had them. Slaves were wealth, and they bred wealth. Maybe North Carolina wasn't fighting to defend slavery, but to defend the right to secede, and to prevent coercion of seceding states; but from Ed's point of view, it all rooted in slavery. You could obscure the truth with parroted phrases, but Ed and these others found for the riddle a simple answer. Without slavery there would have been no secession, without secession there would have been no coercion, without coercion neither North Carolina nor Virginia would have gone to war.

And it was the slave states, the rich planting states where fortunes were made in a year, that had seceded; and it was to protect them against coercion that this war was being fought. But why should a North Carolina farmer with a few acres of land fight to defend the right of a Mississippi planter to make a two-hundred-thousand-dollar cotton crop with slave labor? Tony felt pretty sure there was an answer; but he did not know what that answer was.

All the homeward way from Raleigh, on the cars and then afoot, marching in straggling files the last few miles, there was much debate and no decision. Tony, however, observed that in each group the loudest talkers were all for staying at home. It was they who seized and held the floor; but when he himself questioned these same men alone they were not so positive. Thus Chelmsford Lowman, in an almost shamefaced fashion, said: "Matter of fact, Captain, I wouldn't be much good chasing Yankees. My knees are too stiff. But if they needed someone to lay in one place and rest his musket on a log and do some shooting, why, I can still bark a squirrel any time I hanker after a stew for supper, and like as not I could put a bullet into a Yankee." Jeremy Blackstone was another who wavered. "It's the God-damned marching I'm sick of! If a fight was to come my way and I didn't have to march from here to Tidewater to get into it, I might cut myself off enough for a chaw!" Even Lonn Tyler admitted that he might change his mind. "I guess I got some politician blood in me. I like to hear myself talk. But like as not I'll go making a fool of myself again before I'm through." And Ed Blandy said: "There ain't no sense to it; but if you set out to go back into it, Captain Currain, I wouldn't want to see you go alone."

Tony reflected that most men in a crowd, while ready enough to boast about their vices, were slow to admit their virtues; and, thinking back through his fifty years, he remembered how often he had heard a man confess a drunken bout, or a staggering loss at a gaming table, or an excursion to the quarter where some yellow wench was the attraction; how seldom he had heard one boast of a good and gracious action. A man advertised his vices; his virtues he concealed like crimes.

Safely back at Chimneys among familiar sights and sounds, he found himself suddenly profoundly tired of camp routine, marches and fleeting rumors and alarms. The blue cloud shadows drifting across the mountains, the rolling contours of the hills now in winter's bleak garb, the icy streams, the rich fragrance from the kitchen, the smell of wood smoke in the evening air, the far sound of Negroes singing in the quarter, the steady strong tones of James Fiddler as he made report of his stewardship; these were peace, this was home, the war was far away.

Fiddler gave him the news of the community. Little Miss Mary Meynell was dead. Somehow, when White's Creek was in flood, she had fallen off the foot bridge. No one saw her fall; her body, battered by the rocks in the steep gorge below the bridge, was found half a mile downstream.

"Happened just last week," James Fiddler said. "About the time we began to look for you all to come home."

Tony, when he heard this, felt his mouth fill with the bitter juice of wrath. One of these days Darrell would have a long score to pay. "Had she been well?" he asked guardedly, wondering how much was known.

"Why, she hadn't been herself, no; not since the Judge—died."

Tony understood that hesitation, knew the overseer was too kindly to remind him that Judge Meynell's death had been at Darrell's hand. If Darrell weren't my sister's son, Tony thought, I'd shoot him on sight.

But if he did so, people would—might—guess the truth; and that ought not to happen. Let pretty little Miss Mary rest; let her sleep. Let no tongue touch her name.

27

ENID would be thirty years old on the twenty-sixth of this September; and for weeks beforehand and afterward this fact lay always in the background of her unhappy thoughts. Life was behind her, and how miserly of the treasures it might have bestowed her life had been. Her father's death had made her childhood a desperate time when she and her mother lived on the generous hospitality of friends and must always try to please. Marriage to Trav, though in prospect it promised happiness, had robbed her of her girlhood; the only change in her estate was that instead of trying to please a succession of hostesses she had then to please a husband. By the removal to Great Oak she only exchanged one jailer for another; for instead of Trav, or in addition to Trav, she must now please Mrs. Currain and all the in-laws. Thus had run her life, years of trying to please others, never a time when she could please herself. And now she was thirty, an old woman!

She blamed Trav for all her woes. In the beginning of their marriage she had tried to be all he desired, gay and affectionate and tender, and she delighted in those moments when under her spell he forgot dignity and cast aside his years and became as merrily irresponsible as she. But then Lucy was coming, and Enid was physically wretched; and after Lucy was born Trav settled down to being a stodgy old man, caring for nothing but the land he loved, tolerant of Enid's demonstrative affection but no longer so easily won to a recaptured youthfulness. When under pretense of prudence he rebuffed her, she was hurt as a child is hurt, and she took refuge in a pretended aloofness. That he did not seek to break down the barriers she thus raised was a new grievance against him; her own fear of pregnancy helped to convince her at last that she hated him. When she rebuffed him, her self-pity was sharpened by his submissive acceptance of these rebuffs. Surely if he loved her, he would laugh away her coldness, sweep her into his arms, make her adore him! When he went back to duty she wept because he no longer loved her, and hated him the more.

Because she could find no crevice in the armor of his silence, she revenged herself upon those who loved him. She had long since discovered that they were easy victims. Cinda obviously and at last openly resented her affection for Faunt; and she told herself that Cinda's attitude was an insult not only to her but also to Faunt, and in a sort of defiance she thereafter let her liking for Faunt become more and more obvious. At the time of Hetty's death, when she clung to Faunt, she saw Tilda's avid interest, and one day at Great Oak she prodded Tony too into a self-betraying anger. So all of them—these kin-by-marriage whom she had wished to please and whose liking she coveted—thought her no better than a hussy!

Well, they deserved to be punished for their thoughts; and if they were so ready to suspect shameful things about her, she would give them reason. What she felt for Faunt no longer mattered; it was what they thought she felt. From the day of Cinda's outburst, Enid took every opportunity to provoke her. A week before that birthday which began to be in Enid's eyes so important, Cinda came for a few days at Great Oak; and one evening when Mrs. Currain had gone for her after-dinner nap Cinda turned to her knitting and Enid asked her what she was making.

"Socks," Cinda told her. "I keep my menfolks supplied. You ought to make some for Travis."

"Don't talk to me about Trav!" To criticize Trav always provoked Cinda, and that was fun.

"I like to talk about him. I think Travis is mighty fine."

"Oh, is that so? Well, I guess you wouldn't think he was so wonderful if he'd kept you shut up at Chimneys for years and years, and then here. He doesn't care a snap of his fingers about me. Why should I knit socks for him!"

She saw Cinda's rising anger under hard control. "Travis loves you dearly, Enid!"

Enid laughed. "Loves me my foot! If he loved me would he have kept Vigil nursing Hetty till she as good as killed her! Oh, I know why he did it, all right!" Her voice broke, and this was not pretense; she had always the faculty of believing her own words. "But what could I do?"

Cinda said sharply. "Hush! I won't listen to such idiotic talk! You're no longer a child, Enid! Stop acting like one!"

Enid's eyes filled. "Oh, you're all so mean to me!"

"Well, try behaving yourself sensibly for a while!"

"I've tried and tried, but I can't please you no matter what I do! I want you all to love me, but you're so cruel sometimes I just hate you! I hate Trav and you and all of you! None of you care a thing in the world about me!" She shook with sobs. "None of you except Faunt!"

Cinda made an exasperated sound and Enid buried her face in her arms and Cinda caught her and shook her so violently that her hair fell around her shoulders, and Enid screamed and then Mrs. Currain spoke from the doorway.

"Cinda! Enid! Whatever's the matter?"

Enid wept helplessly, and Cinda after a moment's hesitation said: "Nothing. Enid's working up a fit of hysterics, Mama! She's just lonesome for Trav, but I had to bring her out of it somehow!"

Mrs. Currain was not to be trifled with, so Enid took Cinda's lead. "Oh, I miss him so!" she sobbed. "I miss him so!"

"Nonsense!" Mrs. Currain exclaimed. "So do I, for the matter of that; but I don't start caterwauling like a swamp panther just because Trav had to go away on a business trip!"

"It isn't just a business trip," Enid wailed. "It's the stupid old——"

"Of course it's business!" Mrs. Currain always silenced any reference to the war. "Do you think he'd leave the place with no one here but Big Mill to run it if it weren't business? Now there!" She became swiftly tender and brusquely comforting. "Don't let me hear any more of this!"

Enid went gratefully into Mrs. Currain's arms. "Oh, you're always so sweet to me, Mama!" She clung to the little old woman, but she met Cinda's eyes in malicious triumph. "I don't know what I'd do without you!"

Cinda caught up her knitting and walked out of the room, and Mrs. Currain made a small mirthful sound. "Well, I'll tell you one thing you can do, child. Go fix your hair. You're a sight. And bathe your eyes. There, run along with you."

Enid smiled bravely. "I do love you so!" She kissed Mrs. Currain's cheek. "Be down in a minute, Honey," she promised, and fled to her room.

During the rest of Cinda's stay, Enid took care not to be alone with her again; but in the immunity of Mrs. Currain's company she spoke more than once of Faunt, poor Faunt, way off in Western Virginia goodness knew where. "I'll be so glad when he comes home, won't you, Mama?"

"Of course, my dear." Mrs. Currain ignored that reference to Western Virginia. "But Faunt's happiest at Belle Vue. He doesn't often come here, except for great occasions."

"I wish he would!" Enid declared. Cinda's needles were flying, her cheek was red; and Enid thought Cinda ought to be ashamed of her own thoughts! "I should think he'd be so lonely there," Enid urged. "Why doesn't he find some nice girl and marry again?"

Mrs. Currain made a smiling sound. "Faunt's like a boy who's been scolded," she said wisely. "He enjoys being sorry for himself!"

"Why, Mama, I think you're horrid to talk so about your own children."

"Just because they're my children doesn't make me blind, my dear." Cinda rose hurriedly and Mrs. Currain asked: "Where are you going, Honey?"

"To get some more yarn!"

Enid in secret glee thought Cinda's abrupt departure was like flight. "Well, I don't care, I think Faunt's sweet," she insisted, raising her voice so that Cinda would surely hear.

After Cinda's return to Richmond Enid missed her; for Mrs. Currain, absorbed in the daily routine of household management, was poor company. Enid's birthday was only a long week away, but of course Trav would forget it as he always did, and so would everyone else. She hoped they would. Certainly she did not want to be reminded that she was thirty years old, her life behind her, nothing remaining except to sit in a chimney corner and watch others have a good time. She studied her countenance in the mirror and was almost sure she found a gray hair, and tweaked it out to see; but her hair was so light that she could not be sure. Loneliness beset her more and more, but she put aside what companionship she might have had, avoiding Mrs. Currain, avoiding Lucy and Peter, staying much in her room. She told Mrs. Currain her head ached, but when the little old lady accepted the statement and advised a piece of brown paper soaked in vinegar and left her to herself, Enid was hurt. If Mrs. Currain really wanted her company she would have said headaches were nonsense, bidden her wash her face and come on downstairs and forget all about it. Clearly Mrs. Currain wanted her to just stay in her room, keep out of the way. If I had any place to go, Enid thought miserably, I'd go away and not stay here and bother people; but I've no place to go, no home, no nothing that's really my own!

Her birthday dawned, and Cilly brought her breakfast and Enid asked how Mrs. Currain was and Cilly said she was fine. Enid ate breakfast alone, her eyes wet with tears. Probably no one would come near her all day. She planned to stay in her room till someone at least sent to find out if she were dead! But the day was so fine that she decided to dress and go out of doors. She could walk down to the river without annoying anyone! Perhaps if she just walked into the river and waded out till the water was deep and let herself drown they would be sorry they had treated her so. Her birthday—and no one paid the slightest attention! Well, let them forget if they chose. She certainly would not remind them, not till it was too late for them to do anything about it. She decided how she would remind them. In six days, Lucy would have a birthday. Tomorrow she would suggest to Mrs. Currain that they have a little party for Lucy; and she could say casually that she had always been sorry that she and Lucy did not have the same birthdays, since they were so close together, and then Mrs. Currain would be ashamed of her own forgetfulness. The old woman liked everyone to make a fuss over her own birthdays, liked to have all the family together; but she was ready enough to forget that other people had birthdays, too.

Enid walked down across the lawns to the bluff above the river and felt utterly lonely and wretched; and when she came in to dinner she was blind to Lucy's exaggerated politeness, to Peter's feverish excitement, to the lively amusement in Mrs. Currain's eyes as she watched the children, to Uncle Josh's beaming countenance when he brought in and set before Mrs. Currain the enormous covered tureen of English plate which was only used for family gatherings and state occasions.

"Mercy, Mama; is that full, for just the four of us?" Enid protested.

"Our first oysters of the season," Mrs. Currain assented. "I always make a pig of myself the first time in the fall." Peter, stifling some mysterious mirth, almost fell out of his chair, and Lucy told him for Heaven's sake to behave, and Uncle Josh handed Mrs. Currain the ladle and lifted the silver cover, and Mrs. Currain threw up her hands in apparent dismay and exclaimed: "Law me, whatever is all this?"

For the tureen was full of parcels wrapped and ribboned; and Peter screamed with delight, and Lucy jumped up to kiss her mother, and so did Peter, and Mrs. Currain smiled at them, and Enid began to cry and to laugh at the same time, and went to kiss Mrs. Currain. "Oh, Mama, you're all so sweet to me!" And then suddenly there were steps in the hall and Brett and Tony and Julian came trooping in, broadly smiling, and Enid ran to throw herself into Brett's arms, to kiss them all; and when they came back to the table it was miraculously larger, with new places set, and the tureen had to be emptied of its treasures and Enid to exclaim over each one, and the tureen disappeared and came back converted to its proper purpose, and Peter babbled with excitement, and Lucy watched her mother proudly, and Mrs. Currain said it was all Lucy's doing.

"She and I've been conspiring for days," she confessed, and Lucy asked:

"Are you happy, Mama?"

"Oh, darling, I never was so happy in my life," Enid laughed like a sob. "I've been dreading this birthday. I'm thirty today, you know; but now I don't mind it a bit."

"I wish Papa was here," Lucy confessed. "Then it would be just perfect, wouldn't it?"

"It couldn't be nicer than it is, Honey. Not even with Papa here." Yet Enid knew this was not true. Her heart hungered for him. Oh, they were so sweet, so sweet; and they did love her, after all!

This was her hour, and there were toasts to be drunk, and speeches to be made, and a warm affection in the air; but the fine hour ended. Tony and Julian could only stay for dinner; Mrs. Currain never missed her afternoon nap; Peter had youthful business of his own. Brett would spend the night before departing at dawn for Richmond; but he went to consult with Big Mill. Only Lucy stayed by her mother's side.

"I wrote Papa to come if he could," the girl said. "But I guess he didn't get my letter or something."

"Probably he couldn't leave, Honey." Yet Enid thought guiltily that the way she had treated Trav when he was here a month ago would not make him want to come soon again. Poor Trav, it was so easy to make him miserable; but it was so easy to make him happy too! She would be a good and tender wife to him hereafter. This bright day had left her warm with drowsy content; the world was as languorously fragrant as a sun-baked meadow. She was full of good resolves.

28

ONE day in October an incident occurred which Cinda at the time and afterward found completely puzzling. Mrs. Albion came to see her. Cinda was with Vesta and Jenny in the sewing room on the second floor, and they had been trying to guess how soon Faunt and his company would return to Richmond. General Wise had been re-called in September. His Legion was in large part his own creation, composed of volunteers he had raised in Western Virginia and stiff-ened by the Blues, of which Faunt was a member, and by Captain Cary's company. But now General Wise was back in Richmond, and General Floyd, to whose command the Blues had been attached, said they were ill-disciplined and weakened by desertion. That word was an affront not only to them but to their mothers and wives and sweet-hearts here in Richmond; so everyone hoped they would come home to be welcomed by those who loved and appreciated them.

Cinda was saying she had always despised General Floyd anyway when the bell rang and Caesar came up the stairs to announce in tones eloquent of his opinion of this caller that Mrs. Albion was in the draw-ing room. Cinda did not hesitate. "Please tell her I will be down at once," she directed.

He stalked away, profound disapproval in his bearing, and Vesta asked: "Who's Mrs. Albion?"

"Enid's mother."

"Why, Mama!" Vesta's surprise was manifest. "I didn't know—" She laughed at herself. "Oh, of course I knew Aunt Enid must have a mother somewhere; but I never knew she was in Richmond. Why don't we ever see her?"

Cinda hesitated, uncertain what to say. There were some things you did not tell children, and she still thought of Vesta as a child. "I believe she lived in Washington till recently," she said evasively, and met Jenny's amused eye and felt herself red with confusion. "I must go right down."

Remembering Mrs. Albion's perfection of toilet, she went to her room, touched her hair, decided she was at least halfway presentable, and descended. She was uneasy, wondering what Mrs. Albion's errand could be. If the woman sought to establish any sort of social intimacy, what would she do? What could she do?

But once more Mrs. Albion proved herself completely understanding. "Thank you for seeing me," she said after the first polite exchanges; and then, as though she read Cinda's thoughts: "I'm sure you understand that this is not a—" she smiled. "A polite call. I come to ask your advice." Cinda was more puzzled than ever, but Mrs. Albion added: "Perhaps I should have gone to your brother-in-law, Mr. Streean; but it seemed to me possible that you might be able to suggest some more suitable person for me to see." Cinda admired her dexterity. It was as though she had said: "I am of course an outsider; but Mr. Streean is, I suspect, quite as much so. You are not, so you can help me."

Yet—what was her errand? Cinda put the question into words. "How can I help you?"

"I have a guest," Mrs. Albion explained. "A woman newly come from Washington. She has some military information which should be brought to the attention of the Secretary of War. Can you suggest how to do this?"

Cinda hesitated. "I'm afraid I know nothing of such matters."

"I thought you might be willing—without committing yourself in any way—to introduce her to the Secretary or to some gentleman who has his ear."

"Why, I'm acquainted with Mr. Benjamin," Cinda admitted. "But not—intimately." Was it possible that Mrs. Albion expected her to sponsor this unknown woman, or to sponsor Mrs. Albion herself, for that matter?

Mrs. Albion said earnestly: "I believe this is really important. My guest dined with General Dix in Washington, and he spoke of a plan to cross an army of two hundred thousand men at Leesburg and move against our flank."

"That sounds important, certainly," Cinda agreed. "But—if she just went to one of Mr. Benjamin's secretaries—" She left the suggestion unfinished, and the other, after a moment's consideration rose.

"Of course! I should have thought of that myself. Thank you for helping me."

Helping? That was absurd, and it was not in character for Mrs. Albion to say absurd things; but what possible reason lay behind her call today? "May I offer you some refreshment?"

The other smiled. "You're most kind, but this was not a social call. Thank you very much indeed."

When Mrs. Albion was gone, Vesta had many questions; but Cinda put her off in abstracted bewilderment. What in the world had Mrs. Albion sought to accomplish by this empty errand? Cinda was even more mystified when after church the following Sunday Mrs. Davis whispered to her:

"The President is grateful to you for sending that woman to tell her story. He telegraphed General Johnston at once."

Cinda stammered some polite disclaimer. "Mrs. Albion asked me what to do, and I simply suggested—" But then other ladies joined them, and she stopped in midsentence, regretting that she had used Mrs. Albion's name. Mrs. Davis would imagine they were friends.

She might in time have forgotten the incident, but Tuesday the town rang with news of a fine Confederate victory at Leesburg. A Federal force had crossed the river, had been thrown back in confusion. So Mrs. Albion's information had been true, and useful; but why in the world had the woman come to her? Would her name and Mrs. Albion's name be coupled? She was presently sure of it, for Brett, in Richmond for a day later in the week, had hardly entered the house before he asked laughingly:

"Well, Mrs. Dewain, what's this I hear about your winning a battle almost single-handed? I met Mr. Benjamin in Capitol Square, and he sent you his compliments and felicitations."

"That oily, squint-eyed man!"

He laughed. "You don't like him?"

"No! He has too much brains and not enough heart. And I don't like anyone who smiles as much as he does."

"He's an able man," Brett assured her. "But what about this exploit of yours? He says you sent him advance information of the Federal move." She told him the story, and he listened attentively. "Do you know who Mrs. Albion's woman was?" he asked, when she was done.

"No. And I didn't do anything anyway. Was the battle really as important as the papers say?"

"It was a bloody business," he assured her. "General Evans, commanding our men there, was directed to fall back if the Yankees landed in force, and when they pushed seven or eight thousand men across the river, he gave the orders to withdraw. But his men took things into their own hands, drove the Yankees head over heels down Ball's Bluff, smashed their boats, shot the swimmers in the water. I hear we took more prisoners than we had men in action. There were about fifteen hundred of us to eight thousand of them." He smiled in proud amusement: "General Evans was reprimanded for not withdrawing as ordered; but he said his orders were to withdraw before a landing in force, and that his men didn't consider five to one odds against them big enough to fit the definition."

She was more concerned with her own problem. "Brett Dewain, what do you suppose Mrs. Albion is up to?"

"I don't suppose she ever does anything without a reason."

"She puzzles me; and yet—I like her."

He said with a twinkle in his eyes: "You must take me to call on her some day."

"Not as long as I keep my wits! The lady's much too clever to be trusted with anyone's husband. Do you suppose she just wanted her name to be coupled with mine?"

"Mr. Benjamin didn't mention her. But she's done you no harm, at least. Perhaps we'll know the answer some day." He added thoughtfully: "I'm rather sorry we won that fight so easily. We've been dangerously overconfident ever since Manassas, and this will make us more so. But sooner or later the Yankees will learn how to fight, and our army is weaker every day—lots of men sick, lots of desertions, lots of enlistments running out."

"Is their army getting stronger?"

"Yes. Oh, we can still beat them, any time they risk a battle. But by next spring they'll have an army big enough to march into Richmond." He added thoughtfully: "I've been wishing our family securities were safe in Northern vaults. How'd you like to go North and deliver them to some of my friends there?"

She thought he must be joking, laughed easily. "Thank you, no! I hear terrible stories of the way ladies going through the lines are searched by the roughest sort of women, their clothes picked to pieces, bayonets run through their stays—with the ladies in them, for all I know. I wouldn't submit to that for all the gold of Ophir—wherever that is." But he did not smile, and she said: "You're really worried, aren't you? I'll go if you ask me to, but I don't want to." She hesitated. "But wouldn't it be—well, like rats leaving a sinking ship, for us to do that, Brett Dewain?"

"I don't feel so. We have to protect ourselves if we can. I'm afraid next spring may see things in bad shape here."

"They're bad already," she assured him. "Prices are scandalously high, and Tilda says they'll go higher." She added: "Tilda's enjoying herself, these days. She has a sort of 'How are the mighty fallen' look in her eye!"

"Prices are certainly high," he assented. "Mr. Fleming writes from the Plains that Osnaburg is thirty-five or forty cents a yard, wants to know what he's to do about clothes for the people. Prices are up, and scarcities are developing. That was one reason for the campaign in Western Virginia, to save the salt works at Charleston Kanawha. They produce enough salt to supply the whole South. And as time goes on, we'll be short of many things. Ice, for instance. You can't make a julep without ice—and most of our ice comes from New England."

She touched her brow in a weary way. "Brett Dewain, this war will ruin us and our children; and men like Redford Streean will be riding around in carriages!"

He shook his head. "No, I'll manage somehow, and after the war we can pick up where we left off."

"We can never be the same."

She was thinking of Clayton, and she knew he understood, for he said at once, in an unnecessarily cheerful tone: "I've seen Mama two or three times. Oh, and you should have been there for Enid's birthday party." He described that occasion, Lucy's pride and joy, and Enid's pleasure. "She was so happy it was almost pathetic," he declared. "I'm afraid she has a lonely time there with Mama. I never saw her look prettier."

"She's an exasperating hussy," Cinda retorted. "When I'm with her I get so mad I could shake her. In fact I did, last time I was there. I enjoyed it, too." He asked in some amusement what Enid had done to provoke her to such lengths. "Oh the same old thing. Mooning about Faunt. It didn't cure her, though. She took care not to be alone with me after that, but when we were with Mama it was Faunt, Faunt, Faunt till I wanted to scream!"

Brett threw back his head with a great shout of mirth. "She probably does it just to make you boil over."

"Nonsense. She's not smart enough for that!"

"Don't be too sure! Mrs. Albion's got a level head, and I suspect her daughter has too. And you're rather transparent, you know; never trouble to hide your feelings." He came toward her, smiling; and she tried to push him away.

"Stop it! I won't have you making fun of me and trying to——"

But he laughed and crushed her close and whispered: "You'll have whatever I choose!"

She was in his arms when the door bell rang; and a moment later Burr and Barbara—Burr tall and bronzed and bearded now—swept into the room; and Cinda went from Brett's arms to Burr's in a tearful happiness, kissing him, pressing close to him, eager to feel the solid flesh and bone of him. When he was away from her, she could never be sure he would return. She had learned that bitter lesson. From Clayton while he lived she had often been long separated; but because she always knew he would come back to her, he was even during their separations a real and living presence in her heart. That last time he went away, his going had seemed no different from many another time; nothing marked it, set it apart, warned her to take heed. He went as he had gone in the past; and presently he would return.

But he did not return.

So this was the lesson Cinda learned; that now, when her menfolk left her, they might not return. Thus she lost that sustaining sense that even apart from her, they were still reality. They disappeared, upon each new departure, into a smothering blur of fog and movement that clouded every outline; they became shadow figures seen dimly through a gossamer curtain. Only when they came back to her did they come back to reality as did Burr now. Here he was, flesh and blood and bone.

She looked up from his arms, looked into his face, searching for new things there; for she had learned too that none of these men came back to her unchanged. She saw change in Burr as in the others. Before he and Barbara were married, while he was still training at Ashland, he used to come home in a boy's high excitement, intensely alive, intensely vocal, hilariously amused by his belated discovery that soldiers were paid actual wages—not only for yourself, but forty cents a day for your horse! When she hoped he would soon be an officer he explained that he preferred to be a private. "I don't want to have to give orders to gentlemen, Mama."

"How about taking orders?" she asked, and he laughed and assured her no one minded taking orders as long as he knew he didn't have to.

Oh, those days had been fine and merry. Then he and Barbara were married and went away to the Valley; and after Manassas, Barbara came back to Richmond, starry-eyed with happiness and pride. Cinda, as now she welcomed Burr so fondly, realized with an abrupt sense of guilt that though Barbara had been in Richmond since late July she herself had hardly seen the girl. That was too bad! Of course Mr. Pierce was ponderous and Mrs. Pierce was even more tiresome than he, and Cinda had never been able to understand what Burr saw in Barbara; but she might at least have been nice to Barbara, if only out of politeness.

No matter. She would be more thoughtful in the future. This was no time for regrets, with Burr again at home. Watching him now as they all fell into talk together, she saw that he spoke more slowly, in a way that seemed abrupt without being so; his eyes had more depth but not so much light in them; there was a difference around his mouth. She saw too that he no longer talked freely about his personal experiences. He said: "We did this," and "We did that," but it was always in general terms, in plural terms. It was never "I did thus," "I did so."

When he and Brett became absorbed in conversation, Cinda asked Barbara a guarded question. "How is he, Barbara?"

"Oh, he's fine. He's just fine." Barbara added: "Sometimes he has bad dreams, but he's fine."

Cinda wondered about those dreams. Were they dreams of battle, dreams of danger and of death? Burr had in him no taint of the coward. She was sure of that. But perhaps they were dreams of death dealt out to others. Had Burr, this child of hers, had he killed a man, many men? Was it of such things he dreamed? She hoped he might be here long enough to forget ugly dreams.

Burr and Barbara stayed for supper, and afterward while the others listened Burr and his father talked together. They spoke of business. "The Government is letting Northerners take their property out of the Confederacy," Brett told his son. "I see no justification for that. General Butler down at Fortress Monroe makes no bones about seizing slaves as contraband; but Northern goods in the South are just as truly contraband of war as our slaves." He said he was considering sending their securities North, and Burr asked:

"Would they be safe there?"

"Yes, my friends in New York and Washington would keep them for me."

"Do you still correspond with them?"

"Yes, there's a regular mail service to the North. The letter carriers have special passports, charge a dollar or two a letter. They make a couple of trips every month, clear a thousand dollars or so on a trip. War's a profitable business for those who choose to make it so. But I'll be satisfied to keep what we have."

The talk turned at last to Burr's service. Brett remarked that the Confederacy should have more cavalry, but Burr said this was not necessarily true.

"Of course everybody wants to be in the cavalry," he admitted. "Southerners like to ride as well as they like to fight. But the farmers hate to see us come along, because we live off the country, dip into their corn cribs and all that. I've seen farmers right here in Virginia shake their fists after us and curse us for thieves. We make a lot of enemies that way." He smiled teasingly at Barbara. "But of course the ladies can't do enough for us. They pet us and praise us. No wonder we're a conceited lot!"

"What do you think of General Stuart?" Brett asked, a curious eye upon his son.

"Oh, he's wonderful; but he knows our faults." Burr smiled. "He says all we need is to be reduced to the ranks, that we all think we're cavaliers, lords of the manor! But he's as bad as we are, likes to do spectacular things. I think he'd rather astonish the Yankees than lick them. And he's always in a hurry. At Lewinsville, General Longstreet planned to send some infantry to work with us; but General Stuart couldn't wait. Of course we beat them; but if the infantry had been there, we'd have smashed them."

"Did Longstreet blame him?"

"No, you don't reprimand officers who win victories. General Longstreet recommended him for promotion. But General Stuart needs some levelheaded man—" He looked at Cinda. "Like Uncle Trav, Mama. If he had someone like Uncle Trav to hold him down, he'd be even better than he is."

"It's hard to draw the line," Brett commented. "I suppose *élan* is the soldier's great virtue."

"Yes, sir," Burr assented. "But sometimes it can be just foolishness. Dull duty is tedious; but someone has to do the drudgery." He grinned. "That will never be the cavalry, though. We're the show-offs of the army."

Brett said sympathetically: "It must be hard for Mrs. Stuart, having her husband and her brother fighting on our side and her father commanding Union cavalry. Hard for General Stuart too, of course."

"Is war easy for anyone?" Cinda asked quietly. "Even for those whose families aren't divided?" After a moment Brett came to kiss her, but they gave her no other answer.

Burr and Brett returned to duty and the sunny autumn days slipped by. There was never a finer fall; but the weather in Western Virginia, the papers said, had been wretched. Tilda called one day and reported that General Lee was back in Richmond, the Western campaign abandoned.

"He just didn't accomplish a thing," she said almost triumphantly.

"After all the talk about what wonders he was going to perform! Except that Redford says he's grown a beard!"

"Even Burr has done that," Cinda commented. "I suppose it's a nuisance in the field, trying to shave every day."

"Maybe General Lee wanted to prove he wasn't an old woman!" Tilda spoke in malicious amusement. "They call him Granny Lee now, you know. Redford says he's lost Western Virginia for us, lost it for good. They're going to make a new state out of it and call it West Virginia and join the North and fight against us."

"Speaking of fighting, how's Darrell?"

Tilda laughed, quite undisturbed. "Oh, he's just fine! He was home two weeks ago. He bought a lot of things, and Redford says we'll keep them till the prices go up and sell them and make a fortune."

"Will the Government let you?"

"Why, Redford's in the Government! Besides, everyone is doing the same thing!"

"I suppose Dolly's having the time of her life?"

"Oh, she's in a seventh heaven with all her beaux! There are always three or four of them at the house, glaring at each other. She says they're terrible! Just because she's nice to them they think she's in love with them! She made Darrell be her escort to the fancy-dress party at Mrs. Brownlaw's. She had so many beaux she couldn't decide between them, so she chose Darrell! She was lovely, too. She went as a lady of the French court, borrowing feathers and spangles from everywhere. She borrowed Vesta's pearls, you know. Vesta darling, why didn't you go?"

"I don't want any beau but Tommy."

"Nonsense! You ought to have a good time while you can. You know perfectly well a married woman in Richmond might as well be a nun!"

She talked endlessly of Dolly's triumphs, and that night before going to sleep, Cinda, needing some outlet, wrote a long letter to Brett, telling him what Tilda had said about General Lee.

I sat there like a dumb woman, listening. It seems to me everyone is being criticized right and left. Beauregard's friends criticize President Davis, the oily Mr. Benjamin criticizes Beauregard, I criticize Mr. Benjamin, everybody criticizes poor Colonel Northrop, and you criticize Mr. Memminger. I hear, by the way, that Cousin Jeems is taking sides against Mr. Davis. And Tilda criticizes General Lee, and I criticize Tilda!

But there, why shouldn't I? I never liked her, but I kept it to myself; she seemed harmless so I gave her the benefit of the doubt. But now she's beginning to be really malicious. She comes here and talks till I'm black in the face trying not to spit at her. Brags about Dolly's conquests, and sneers at decent things, in her back-handed way. Says women who are so glad their husbands are soldiers really hope they'll be killed! I almost threw her out of the house; but you can't do that to your loving relatives, now can you! She's perfectly insane about Dolly. Young Lieutenant Hammond had been making love to Dolly last spring, vowing eternal devotion and all that, and now he's gone and married Betty Pryor, and to hear Tilda talk, Mr. Streean ought to shoot Lieutenant Hammond. If it weren't for being cattish, I'd wonder whether that might not be true; Dolly promises so much, she must sometimes add performance to promise! There, I'm ashamed of myself, but Tilda would try the patience of a saint! And if I venture a word of protest, she says reproachfully that I shouldn't think hardly of her, that after all, if she can't count on her own dear sister, she can't count on anyone, can she. So then I'm ashamed of myself. She's always seemed so meek and mild it's hard to realize she's venomous as a rattlesnake!

There now I feel better! I won't even send you this, Brett Dewain. You'd just laugh me out of it, and I'm out of it already. The Catholics are right. Honest confession is good for the soul. Mine's all healed!

She tore the letter into little bits and sprinkled them on the fire, and as she did so, Vesta came in and saw her and asked curiously: "What ever are you doing, Mama?"

"Tearing up a letter I just wrote to your father. Now don't call me an idiot! I was just blowing off steam, never meant to send it anyway."

Vesta laughed and kissed her. "There, darling, I do that all the time—write long letters to Tommy and then burn them."

"Why?"

Vesta colored happily. "Because they're such letters as no modest maiden would write even to her husband! Tommy would be embarrassed to tears if he read them. But they're ever such fun to write!"

"Tommy's not much of a correspondent, is he?"

"He's working hard. He's terribly conscientious about being a soldier, you know."

"He's a nice boy," Cinda pinched the girl's cheek fondly. "Even if he is a fool!"

"He's not a fool!"

"Any man who could marry you and won't is a fool."

Vesta's eyes clouded, but then she smiled. "I'm not so sure. Maybe he's wise, because you know waiting makes me love him more every day. The way I feel about him just keeps growing like a—like a baby inside me!"

"Vesta Dewain! What a thing to say!"

"Oh, don't pretend to be shocked! I'm quite grown up, you know!" Vesta added teasingly: "Quite old enough to hear all about Uncle Tony and Mrs. Albion, for instance!" Then, seeing Cinda's quick distress: "I'm sorry. But I asked you about her the day she called on you. Remember? You wouldn't tell me, so I had to find out for myself."

"Who did tell you?"

"Aunt Tilda."

"That woman!" Cinda's voice was stern with anger. "I didn't suppose even Tilda would babble nastiness to you!"

"I needn't have asked her if you'd told me. Why didn't you?"

Cinda hesitated. "Why—for Aunt Enid's sake, Vesta. For her sake, that's one of the things none of us must ever seem to know."

Vesta said in a low tone: "There are lots of things like that, aren't there? Things that women must pretend not to know." Cinda looked at her sharply, and Vesta said gently: "I'm sorry, Mama. But—will you tell me things? Please? Because I'd rather hear them from you. I hate finding them out from other people."

"Who else has been telling you things?"

"Why—Dolly, for one. Ugly things, about men. I said I didn't believe her, and she said why did I suppose black girls like Sally, that servant in their house, have mulatto babies?"

Cinda pressed her hands to her eyes. "We Southern women!" She made a weary gesture. "Our men keep telling us how beautiful and unstained we are, and we tell ourselves our daughters are too pure and innocent to know things. It's just because we're too stupid and lazy to talk to them in simple, honest ways. We don't even talk honestly to our sons, so they learn for themselves, from vicious companions, or from the black girls. And our daughters learn for themselves—from people like Dolly!"

She spoke so furiously that Vesta was half-frightened. "Are you mad at me?"

"Heavens no, darling! But—oh, at our stupidity, at our way of thinking life's a fairy tale. And I'm mad at bragging and strutting and war and sickness and death—and at myself for being a shiftless coward so long!"

"You've never been a coward!"

"I have been where you're concerned, my darling! But not now! Never any more!"

The new bond between her and Vesta seemed to Cinda in the days that followed to give her strength to meet whatever was to come. She knew from Tony that Julian's regiment, the First North Carolina, would soon be mustered out; and she had pretended to herself that perhaps he would not enlist again. Clayton was gone, and Burr and Brett might go, but surely she might hope to keep Julian safe and secure. But as she and Vesta drew together she knew this hope was weakness; and when Julian came with his regiment to Richmond she asked steadily enough: "Have you decided what you're going to do?"

"Just about," he told her. "I want to serve under General Hill. He's a great man, Mama. Of course, lots of the men don't like him. He's pretty sarcastic sometimes. But—well, I started out with him and I'd like to go on with him. Most of the cadets feel the same way."

"Have you said anything to him about it?"

"No, he was promoted, you know. He's at Manassas now, but I've talked to Papa. I might go into the Fifth North Carolina, be with Tommy and Rollin."

She bit her lip. Julian was no longer a child; he was a young man, a soldier, and she would not have him otherwise. "Whatever you decide, we'll be proud of you!"

"Gosh, but you and Papa are wonderful."

She smiled. "So are our children."

"I miss Clayton terribly," he said, after a moment. "Even if I didn't see much of him lately, I always liked to think about him."

"Jenny says he's more with her now than he ever was," Cinda assented. "He—spends a good deal of the time with me, too, Julian." She smiled faintly. "But with me he's always just as he was when he was little. It's as if he'd never grown up. Sometimes I get him mixed up with little Clayton, can't tell which from which!" He came to kiss her in silent comforting.

But he went out presently, and she knew he had gone to see Anne, and expected he would be late returning. She went to bed, but she heard him come in, earlier than she had expected, and called to him. "How was Anne, sonny?"

"Oh just fine," he said from the doorway.

"You didn't stay long."

"No." His tone was lifeless. "No, she wasn't alone."

"Who was there?"

"Darrell." Julian hesitated, and Cinda tried to know what to say. "She wanted me to stay, but I knew he wouldn't leave as long as I was there." She found no word. "Good night," he said, and went on to his room.

Within the week he was gone again. He had arranged for assignment to the Fifth North Carolina and went north to join Tommy and Rollin. He wrote gaily of outpost duty in sight of Washington, of picketing the line of the Orange and Alexandria Railroad.

Late that month General Longstreet and Trav arrived in Richmond together and at once sought Cinda. Mrs. Longstreet was ready to come on from Lynchburg and bring the children. The General wished to find a home for her, and he asked Cinda's advice and help.

"Louisa won't be satisfied, anyway," he said. "But if you make the decision I can let you take the blame, so I'll escape her wrath."

She laughed. "You men! Brave as lions against the enemy but afraid of your womenfolk." She added thoughtfully: "But finding a place won't be easy. There are twice as many people in Richmond today as there were six months ago—even without counting the soldiers."

"Who are they all?"

"Oh, clerks and quartermasters and speculators and spies and gamblers and refugees from Maryland and Heaven knows what all. How long can you spend at this house-hunting?"

"A day or two or three," he said. The army was settling into winter quarters in Centerville; he could be spared. Cinda insisted that he, as well as Trav, lodge this night with them; and at supper and afterward they talked for hours. Cinda produced her knitting, and Trav asked: "Isn't that something new?"

"Knitting? Yes, just this summer." She smiled. "You menfolk wear out your socks so fast it keeps us all busy." She did not tell him her deeper reason. Since Clayton's death she had found her hands acquiring little betraying habits of their own. When some word or thought disturbed her, she could control her countenance and her voice, but unless she kept her fingers busy, they shook and trembled. "Knitting at least passes the time." She looked at Longstreet, in faint apology. "I hate waiting for something to happen. Battles are terrible, of course; but in some ways waiting is worse."

"Our waiting is a mistake," he commented. "Time runs against us. Our men lose interest. They fall sick, or desert, or their enlistments expire. The army's down to half its summer strength now, and the Yankees know it; but they're stronger all the time, so they're in no hurry. Before spring General McClellan will have built an army big enough to crush us."

"Will he crush us?"

He smiled. "Why, if he does, it will be done so deliberately we'll hardly feel it. I know McClellan. He'll work everything out to the last decimal point." He added seriously: "If we wait long enough, he'll crush us, yes; but if we strike him before he's ready, he'll be so distracted at the upsetting of his schedule that anything can happen."

He asked for news of Brett and the others, and she said: "Oh, Mr. Dewain is with his Howitzer Battalion down on Warwick River, near enough Great Oak so that he can see Mama and Travis's family quite often. The Howitzers have built cabins with windows and doors and floors—all the comforts of home. They're settled for the winter. Burr's with Stuart, and Julian—the Bethel Regiment was mustered out—is a Lieutenant in the Fifth North Carolina. He wanted to be under General Hill."

"Wasn't your older brother in the Bethel Regiment too?"

"He's at his plantation in North Carolina, planning to stay there, at least until the spring planting is done."

"I'm glad someone's going to raise food for us." Longstreet smiled at Trav. "If only for the peace of mind of Captain Currain here. He's as nervous as a housewife wondering what she'll give unexpected guests for dinner."

"And Faunt's still in Western Virginia," Cinda explained. "Though I don't know what in the world he's doing there. I hope he'll at least get back for Christmas."

The General and Cinda set out next day to seek quarters for his family, but to find a house in any way adequate was impossible. For those that could be had, the rental was exorbitant. "After all," Longstreet remarked, "my salary is only three hundred dollars a month. Three hundred and one, to be exact." He laughed. "The men say the dollar is our pay and the three hundred is just flattery. I'd find it more profitable to stay here and go into the room-renting business—let some of these landladies command my division!" He had hoped to find a house; but after one day's search he gave that up. "We'll have to take rooms somewhere."

But this decision made their task at first no easier. Every regular boarding house was full—too full to receive Mrs. Longstreet and four children—and even those private homes which had space to spare had already, either for kindness or for cash, taken folk to lodge. "I'm not sure Louisa hadn't best stay on in Lynchburg," the General reflected, thoroughly discouraged.

"I won't hear of that till we've turned the last stone," Cinda declared. "There must be something."

Luck helped them. The third day, on a matter of military business, Longstreet called upon General Gorgas, chief of ordnance; and he came striding back to Fifth Street to find Cinda. "General Gorgas tells me he's been living at the Arlington House, right down here at the corner of Main and Sixth, but he's going to move to the Armory, and we can have his rooms. Come along and inspect them with me. I'll need your opinion, to report to Louisa."

"Why, of course!" she exclaimed. "I was stupid not to think of it, right under our noses." The Arlington was only two blocks away, substantial and comfortable, set a little back from the street, facing on Main Street and with a pleasantly shady garden on the Sixth Street side. "I stayed there myself two years ago while the workmen were doing this house over and moving the furniture. It's very nice, and some pleasant people live there. Come, we'll go right down."

They met at first with disappointment; the quarters General Gorgas had occupied were not large enough to accommodate Longstreet's family; but there was a corner room looking diagonally across Main Street toward the Second Baptist Church which would serve as a parlor, and two bedrooms across the hall. One of these would do for the three boys, the other had space for the baby's crib beside the double bed.

Yet Cinda said doubtfully: "You'll be crowded. I wouldn't dare commit Cousin Louisa to this."

"Beggars—and generals—can't be choosers!" he said cheerfully. "But we'll let her decide. I'll send for her to come and see for herself."

Cinda felt his longing to have his family near; so she assented. "That's it!" she agreed. "And when she comes, you let me handle her. If she acts too uppity, I'll tell her a thing or two."

So, early in December Mrs. Longstreet arrived in Richmond; and to Cinda's relief the other said the rooms would do. "Of course they're not perfect," she admitted, linking her hand through her husband's arm. "But I'm tired of living with relatives! They're so obviously being patient and long-suffering about the children! I'd rather be with Jeems!" She looked up at him with an impish smile. "He doesn't mind the little scamps!"

Cinda laughed. "I'd forgotten how tiny you are, Louisa, till I saw you two together! You look like a reticule hanging on his arm! When will you fetch the children?"

"I'll want time to get new curtains, a new rug, a comfortable chair for the General. You won't know the place when I've fixed it up." Next day they went to Bulkley's on Eagle Square, and to Habliston's, and to John Regnault to look at carpets and rugs and curtain goods, and Mrs. Longstreet bought with a lavish prodigality and a disregard of prices which startled Cinda.

"After all," she protested, "it's not a house you're furnishing."

"Oh, I like nice things around me," the other insisted, and wrinkled her small nose in mischievous delight. "And Jeems likes me to have what I like!"

Cinda laughed. "You're a spoiled little hussy, if you ask me."

"I'm not, really. I spoil him terribly." Their shopping was done, they were back at Cinda's, weary and glad to rest. "I'm just coming to Richmond to please him. You know how husbands are, just babies if we're not around to tell them they're wonderful; and of course he loves having the children where he can see them. He's just wrapped up in Baby, and ridiculously proud of the boys!"

They had a long hour together, and Mrs. Longstreet, with little prompting, talked of many things. She spoke of their years in Texas and New Mexico; and Cinda thought it must have been hard to be buried alive so far away.

"Mercy, no!" the other assured her. "After all, all our closest friends were there, and we were very gay, making our own good times." Her eyes saddened. "It was a terrible wrench for the General to resign. Most of the officers he knew best were Union men. The army's just a big family, you know. All the older men more or less know each other. Most of them were in Mexico together. And the General—oh, he's gay, and likes a pretty face, and loves to play poker and loves a good time—but underneath all that he's the most conscientious man I know." She said seriously: "He's absolutely immovable about what he thinks is right and what he thinks is wrong. When he had to decide whether to go against the Union or against his state, there were nights he didn't sleep. I used to wake and see him sitting by the window in the dark, just thinking, and sometimes he'd be down on his knees, praying." She said with a choke in her voice: "It was really touching, Cousin Cinda, to see that great, big, bearded, strong man in his night shirt, praying."

Cinda said gently: "You love him as I love Brett Dewain."

"Oh, I get furious with him sometimes; but other times just thinking about him makes me so happy I cry! He's so gentle, and really humble, and—nice." She laughed. "When you've been married to a man thirteen years, you come to know him pretty well, don't you?"

"Is there anything on earth more fun than being happily married? I suppose not. And yet men can be awfully exasperating!"

"I've been separated from Jeems so long I sha'n't mind what he does for a while."

"Wasn't it wretchedly hot in Mississippi all summer?"

"Not for me!" Mrs. Longstreet laughed. "After all, I'd been in Texas and New Mexico for years; and I like hot weather, anyway. Sometimes I'm just frozen in Lynchburg. I stay with Mrs. Garland, on Garland Hill, and you can see huge mountains all around to the north and east, and cold mornings they're covered with snow. It makes my teeth chatter just to look at them!" Cinda laughed with her. There was something quizzical and amusing in the other's piquant countenance; the upward slanting brows, the curving lips that seemed about to smile, the suggestion of a dimple in her cheeks, the gently mirthful eyes. "And besides, I like the General's kinfolks better than. I like my own."

"His mother's dead, isn't she?"

"Yes, she died a few years ago. But his brother Bill has a charming home just north of Macon, and there are five sisters. All except Ann have married since they moved to Macon. We stayed with Sister Maria. She married a Mr. Dismukes. He likes his juleps and his toddies as well as Jeems does, such a jolly man. Sister Maria scolds him, but he was mighty nice to us. And we visited around—Sister Eliza and Sister Sarah and all of them." She added honestly: "But of course we were so far away. I know I shall enjoy being right here in the middle of things. I hear Richmond's very gay."

"It is now," Cinda assented. "There was a while, with the hospitals full of wounded men, when people wore long faces." She was glad she had her knitting. To keep her fingers busy was curiously steadying. "But now there are charades and tableaux and amateur theatricals and parties, dancing, singing, almost every night."

"I love parties."

Cinda smiled faintly. "They're not for you and me, Honey. When a girl marries in Richmond she pays her bridal calls, and maybe goes to a few dances; but then she puts away her pretties and stays at home. It's the unmarrieds who have all the gay times."

"I declare! It wasn't like that in the old army! It was we wives who ruled the roost."

"Well, you'll find the quiet set is pleasant company," Cinda assured her. "We have our good times all to ourselves."

The other laughed, her eyes on Cinda's clicking needles. "And you all sit around and knit, I suppose. I refuse to be pushed into your old quiet set! Why don't we all rebel at these bossy little Miss Somebodies?"

Cinda smiled. "Oh, I like things as they are. I call on whom I choose, and I needn't be agreeable unless I wish; needn't flatter stupid men nor flirt with nice ones; needn't go to balls and spend an evening hopping and panting. It's really most agreeable when we older people get together at Mrs. Ives's or Mrs. Macfarland's, or—oh a dozen others. You'll meet the most interesting men in Richmond at Mrs. Stanard's. Don't worry, Louisa. You'll find plenty of people to see, and things to do."

"Well, it doesn't sound very exciting." Mrs. Longstreet laughed. "But there, darling; you can teach me to knit, and we'll pretend we're two old ladies in the chimney corner together!"

When she had seen her purchases installed in the rooms at the Arlington and the new curtains fitted and hung, she departed for Lynchburg to bring the children. It happened that Brett came to Richmond next day, and Cinda told him of Mrs. Longstreet's arrival, and she said: "Cousin Louisa's just as nice as ever, but she's changed more than I expected. Have I grown old and ugly, Brett Dewain?"

"Well, let me see." He looked at her appraisingly, his head on one side, and she laughed and said:

"Beast! You should answer quickly! Of course I never was as pretty in my best days as she is even now. She's lovely, but she's—well, older."

"You haven't seen her for twelve or thirteen years," he reminded her. "And she's had six children, you know."

"Well, so have I. Though I've only three left." Her throat contracted as it always did when she thought of Clayton, and she turned to find her knitting, made the needles fly. "Her complexion isn't what it used to be!"

"You evidently studied her pretty carefully."

"Oh, we spent hours together. I suppose we'll see a lot of them."

"I hope so."

"Travis thinks the world of him, you know. And he likes Travis, too. You can see that. Travis seems a boy beside him, though he's actually older. Cousin Jeems is—well, I don't know how to put it, but he seems to be inside himself, somehow."

He nodded. "I know. Something happens to men in command. They acquire a quality—it's not arrogance, but it's a sort of, well, confidence, perhaps. An officer, a man who has once sent men he loves to their death, acquires a maturity that no civilian ever achieves. Boys become men——"

Cinda smiled. "While ordinarily, men never get over being boys?"

"I suppose not. So the General seems older than Trav, though Trav has always seemed to you and me a pretty staid old man himself. Probably no man who has commanded other men in battle is ever quite a boy again."

"Yet Cousin Jeems is full of fun," she reminded him. "There's always a twinkle in his eyes. He's always joking; and Travis says that at headquarters he cuts up scandalously."

"Oh, he's fine," Brett agreed.

The fine December days were like Indian summer. Mrs. Longstreet brought the children on from Lynchburg and settled at the Arlington. Cinda thought Garland, the eldest boy, less attractive than the others; and clearly he and his father were not on the best of terms. Mary Ann, like all babies, was perfection. Tommy Cloyd and Rollin Lyle had some days in Richmond, and Vesta was happy with Tommy, and furious at Rollin because he paid Dolly such humble adoration.

"I gave him a piece of my mind," she told Cinda. "But you just can't talk any sense into him, Mama. I reckon he just really does love Dolly, and he'll go on loving her till he dies; and she wouldn't marry him if he was the last man alive! She says his scar just makes her shiver!"

Dolly was becoming the sensation of Richmond. At least three duels, it was said, had been fought because of her. She was seen everywhere, always surrounded by beaux. Burr came home on leave and once while he and Barbara were at Cinda's, Dolly appeared, with a dazzled youngster from Burr's own squadron; and she kissed Burr prettily, and protested that she hadn't seen him for simply ages, and wasn't the cavalry wonderful, and oh how she wished she was a man so she could help whip the Yankees. "I'll bet you've killed just dozens of them, Burr! I envy you so."

He looked at her with level eyes. "Don't be a fool, Dolly!"

"But, Burr, I mean it! It must be just simply marvelous!"

He made a harsh sound. "Did you ever smell the body of a dead man whom you'd killed three days before, who'd been lying in the sun?" Giving her no time to answer, he came strongly to his feet, strode toward the door. Behind him she cried prettily:

"Why, Burr Dewain, I think you're real mean to talk to me that way! Isn't he, Aunt Cinda?"

But he was gone, leaving Barbara here; and he did not return till Dolly and her escort had departed. Cinda suspected that the dreadful question he had put to Dolly came out of his own experience; but she knew if this were true he would never tell her so. When he came back, Cinda saw that he was contrite; and she made an opportunity to be alone with him, asked gently:

"Weren't you a little hard on Dolly, Burr?"

"I suppose I was," he admitted. "But—that sort of talk—" He made a heavy, hopeless gesture. "Dolly needs someone to be hard on her!" he said, his anger returning. "She's—well, she goes out of her way to tease men and torment them; brings them to a simmer, and then when they're ready to boil, she pushes them to the back of the stove! And I don't mean just flirting! She does a lot of harm! I wish she weren't my cousin! I ought not to talk about her this way, even to you; but there's plenty of talk about her, when men have had too much to drink. I've heard things said—well, I had to pretend not to hear them, or else call the man out."

Cinda, angry at Dolly for his sake, advised him to shut his ears. "Dolly's not worth fighting over. Let Darrell protect her."

When Burr had returned to duty, Barbara shyly told Cinda their baby would be born in June; and Cinda laughed in quick happiness. "But there, I should have guessed by the way Burr strutted around while he was at home!"

It was on a Monday morning two days before Christmas that

Faunt at last returned. Vesta heard that the Blues were coming, the hour their train would arrive; and she and Cinda were in the eager waiting throng. When the train ground to a stop a happy welcome arose; but instantly this was hushed in puzzled mystification. For at the car windows and on the platforms appeared not the handsome young faces that were expected, but the countenances of weary-eyed and haggard men. The bright new uniforms were faded and tattered, the men were long-haired ragamuffins with untrimmed beards. But that momentary silence broke in a great universal sigh, like a sob of tenderness; and then as the men of the Blues began to descend the steps, this brief sadness gave way to a valorous new clamor of ardent voices, everyone determined that these heroes should never be allowed to guess that first dismay. Here were beloved warriors, now at last returned.

Faunt was as changed as his comrades. He who had always been slender was emaciated now. He had worn a small mustache; now it was lost in a heavy beard above which deep hollows pitted his sunken cheeks. When Cinda and Vesta were able to claim him, his arms embracing them were hard as wires; but his very voice was tired. Cinda felt as though a weary son had come home to her.

Yet it was astonishing to see how quickly, under Caesar's ministrations and in Burr's clothes—Brett's were too free about the middle, Burr's too broad at the shoulders; but Burr's would serve—Faunt came back to an outward normality. Vesta had a thousand questions, naming place after place. Were you there? Were you there? The Cauley? Carnifex Ferry? Hawk's Nest? Scary Creek?

"Yes," Faunt said, and smiled. "They might have named Scary Creek after me, that day. It was my first fight, seemed pretty alarming. But later on, we all got so we didn't care."

"Became brave?" Vesta asked.

"No, just footsore, half-sick, half-fed, half-drowned by rain, half-stifled by mud."

There were other questions, other answers. "We were at cross purposes, much of the time," he said. "General Floyd wouldn't agree with General Wise, General Wise wouldn't agree with General Floyd; and whenever we were about to really accomplish something, orders would come from Richmond for us to withdraw, 'to avoid rashness'."

He said grimly: "As if war were a game you could play without risk! There was a woman, Mrs. Tyree. Her husband kept a public house on the turnpike. She took no sauce from the Yankees, knocked one marauder out with a piece of stovewood, took another man's gun away from him and threatened to shoot him; and when some Yankees came and said they meant to burn her house, she locked herself in and told them to go ahead and burn it if they wanted to. If the army had been as rash as that old woman, we might have done some miracles. As it was, we just frittered away time and lives."

"Whose fault was it?"

"Why—largely the weather, I think. It's all mountains and mud out there; and it wore you out to march in the mud and rain. We marched in it and ate in it—when we had anything to eat—and slept in it. There were nights it rained so hard that the men said if you lay down you'd drown. And the men were half sick—or wholly sick— much of the time: coughs and sneezes, fever, measles." He shook his head. "I don't see how they stood it."

Cinda asked with a tender smile: "Where were you?"

He understood her, chuckled. "Oh, I was there too, of course; but— you forget yourself in admiring your comrades. I suppose that's what keeps you going."

"Do you like General Wise?"

"Yes. Floyd's a horse-faced, sulky man with not much military capacity; but General Wise is a fine man, and intelligent, and he has a sense of humor. He told a battery to open fire one day and the gunners said they had no target, and he said never mind a target, to go ahead and make some noise anyway. When things are ticklish, he just squares that big dimpled chin of his and bulls ahead—and gets somewhere."

Vesta asked: "What about General Lee? Mr. Daniel has written some horrid things about him in the *Enquirer.*"

"I think he's the best man in Virginia," Faunt said thoughtfully. "But it's true he didn't do well out there. He was too—considerate, too polite. If he'd just told Floyd and Wise and the others what to do, and then made them do it, we might have given the Yankees trouble. It's possible that General Lee isn't—well, sufficiently firm for high command."

"Do the Blues like Jennings Wise as much as we do in Richmond?"

Faunt smiled. "Are you one of his adorers, Vesta? I thought there was something about Tommy Cloyd."

"There is!" she assured him, nodding happily. "There's a great deal about Tommy! But Jennings Wise has been my dream hero for years, ever since I was a girl."

"He's a fine leader, yes," Faunt assured her. He added: "I hear he'll soon be promoted to colonel."

"Oh, wonderful!" she cried; and she asked what the Blues would do now, and he thought they would stay a while in Richmond, to rest and refit. He hoped to go to Belle Vue.

"All that country between the Potomac and the Rappahannock is Yankee ground, any time they want to take it of course," he explained. "But they haven't taken it yet."

Cinda said understandingly: "You'll hate to see Belle Vue in Yankee hands."

His cheek for a moment darkened with anger. "Yes, I shall hate that, Cinda."

When they knew Faunt's return was imminent, Cinda had delayed their departure for Great Oak, so that he could go down with them. Tony reached Richmond Monday night, and next morning he and Faunt rode escort to the carriages in which Cinda and Vesta and Jenny and the children made the all-day journey from Richmond. Tilda and Redford Streean and Dolly were not long behind them. Darrell, they said, was not coming; and Cinda was so glad that she even welcomed Mr. Streean.

Trav appeared at dusk; and everyone but Enid and Dolly was downstairs when he arrived, and they all gave him a happy welcome. "I began to be afraid you wouldn't get here, Travis," his mother confessed.

"I almost didn't," he admitted. "We went to collect some food and forage around Dranesville, took every wagon we could get together. General Stuart had a hundred and fifty of his cavalry out in front of us, and some guns, and four regiments of infantry; but the Federals stretched a wire across the road, and threw the cavalry into confusion and ambushed us. Stuart sent word to us to start the wagons back to our lines, and then he attacked the Yanks to hold them long enough for us to get away. It was a bad scramble. We saved the wagons, but we lost some men." Before Cinda could ask the question, he told her: "Burr was there, but he's all right. He and Julian came to Richmond with us. Julian wanted to see Miss Tudor, and Burr will stay with Barbara tonight, but he and Julian will start early, be here for dinner tomorrow. General Longstreet sent you his love, Cinda."

"How are they all?"

"Fine," Trav said proudly. "It's wonderful to see the way his men like him. He's so—human. It was cold the other night, and he sent a drink out to the headquarters sentries, said to the orderly: 'Tell the boys I distinctly saw one of them wink at me when I came in just now.' Little things like that make them ready to do anything for him. He goes out of his way to amuse them, keeps them interested. He's put me at work organizing some theatricals now."

They laughed together at the thought of Trav attempting such a task; but he said plans were well along. "We're going to have the First Regiment's band for an orchestra, and Mr. Hamilton and Mr. Warwick will be the managers. They both know about such things, so I've made them responsible." He asked: "Where's Enid?"

"Upstairs," Mrs. Currain said; so he went to find her. Dolly presently appeared, and Vesta told her Trav's newest assignment, and Dolly said eagerly:

"Wonderful! Why don't we have some theatricals ourselves, this evening?" She looked around, tallying them off. "Of course we haven't many gentlemen, but I can dress up in some of Julian's clothes and be the hero."

Vesta laughingly declared Dolly would never be able to look like a man. "I'll be the hero, and you can be the heroine."

"And I'll be the villain," Faunt suggested, smiling. They fell into a lively discussion of this proposal, but by the time Trav and Enid appeared it was clear to them all that the project presented too many difficulties. Instead, after supper, they arranged a happy riot of hurriedly planned charades, and turned from them to rowdy children's games in which under Dolly's pretty urgencies even Mrs. Currain joined. They played "My Lady's Garden". While two or three of the people, with fiddle and banjo and rattling bones, set the tune, the players formed a slowly marching circle around a prisoner in the middle, singing together the familiar words.

> Do please let me out! I'se in dis lady's gyarden!
> Do please let me out! I'se in dis lady's gyarden!
> De gate is locked and de walls is high!
> Oh do let me out! I'se in dis lady's gyarden!
> De gate is locked and de key is los'
> I mus' and I will git out ob here
> I'll break my neck tuh git out ob here
> Please do let me out ob dis here lady's gyarden!

On the last "gyarden" each prisoner in turn made a dash for freedom; and there were shouts and laughter and gay tussles. Trav, trying to dodge free, plunging bull-like between Tilda and Dolly, brought them both down atop him in a heap. Faunt, when his time came, slipped through a narrow opening as easily as an eel. Trav's Lucy— she was thirteen now, almost a young lady,—could never long be kept captive. When Dolly tried to elude Brett, he caught her and claimed a robust kiss for forfeit and got it; and Cinda made a mental note to call him to account for that! Dolly was badly enough spoiled already! Enid, prisoner after Dolly, made a feint to dart past Tony; but at the last moment she spun toward Faunt, and seemed to lose her balance and so fell into his arms and clung to him and cried: "Oh Heavens, you caught me! Well, then I must pay forfeit too!" She kissed Faunt with a rowdy gusto which made them all laugh; and Cinda felt Vesta's questioning eyes upon her, and lest Vesta read her thoughts she laughed with the others; but she saw Faunt's glance follow Enid as the game went on, and she had to assure herself with a certain violence that Faunt would never drift into a sordid involvement with Trav's wife! She knew her fears were absurd; yet Enid was a lushly provocative little thing, flushed and panting now in this ridiculous game, her eyes forever meeting Faunt's with that melting readiness for surrender which could turn the steadiest masculine heads. Even Brett was capering like a spring lamb, just because he had kissed Dolly! Men were all idiots when a pretty woman made eyes at them!

Next morning she lay late abed, listening to the little Negroes racing through the halls crying "Chris'mus gif'" at every door; till booted feet came thumping toward her room and a voice she knew called: "Christmas gift, Mama," and here was Julian. Burr a moment later joined them; and the bright day began and ran its course, and left them all weary with merrymaking and ready for early sleep.

After Christmas, Cinda had expected to return to Richmond with Vesta and Jenny and the children, with the men to keep them company on the road; but Faunt said he would stay at Great Oak for two or three weeks longer.

"General Wise has been appointed to command at Roanoke Island," he explained. "The Blues will come down river and go through the Albemarle Canal by barge; and I'll meet them in Norfolk, go on with them from there."

Cinda said at once that she too would stay on a little longer. Not even to Brett did she admit her reason: but she would not leave Faunt here with Enid alone.

29

December, 1861–January, 1862

WHEN Trav came to Great Oak for Christmas, it was his first visit since August, and he had many bright anticipations. It would be fine to see Lucy and Peter and his mother and the others; and even Enid after this long separation might be glad to see him, as tenderly affectionate as when she chose she knew how to be. He took time in Richmond to load himself with presents for them all, including handkerchiefs and Barlow knives for the Negroes, and candies for the little Negro children who would come clamoring through the halls on Christmas morning. But the gift that pleased him most was for Enid. From the captain of a vessel which had evaded the still haphazard blockade, running into New Berne with a cargo of luxuries, Trav bought at an exorbitant price a delicate cameo exquisitely carved, rimmed with small diamonds and hung from a slender golden chain.

When he arrived everyone welcomed him with hand clasps and kisses; but when he went up to his room and would have taken Enid in his arms, she set her hands against his chest. "No, no, Trav! I hate being mussed when you're all dusty and horsy from the road. You know that!"

He laughed to hide his hurt and went to bathe and change, and she sat before the mirror, talking idly over her shoulder, trying some new arrangement of her hair. When he was dressed, the cameo in his pocket, hiding his eagerness behind a casual tone, he said: "Oh, by the way, Enid, I've a surprise for you."

"Really?" She yawned a little, rising to go downstairs. "What?"

"Shut your eyes!"

"Oh, don't be childish, Trav."

He was heavily jocular. "You can't have it till you do." But she turned away toward the door, her wide skirts swinging indolently, so he surrendered. "Why—here, then!" He followed her, forced to hurry. "Here, Enid." She turned, her hand on the door knob, and he met her eyes and saw the hard distaste in them; nevertheless he persisted, touching her shoulder. "Here!"

Thus he laid the cameo in her hands. The small stones sparkled in the candlelight, and he waited for her delighted gratitude.

She looked at the jewel for a moment, turned it over in her palm, turned it back again. "Pretty," she said idly. "April will love it." And she crossed to drop it in the littered china tray under her mirror.

Trav for a moment did not move. Was this all? He caught her shoulders, drew her toward him. "Enid! Dear! Oh—I wish—Enid——"

"Don't!" she said. "You hurt my arms!" She twitched away, crossing toward the door again; and her eye fell on the litter of his belongings, clothes hastily laid aside, the open valise half unpacked. Trav was normally as neat as a cat, but he had hurried. She made a sound of distaste. "What a mess! I suppose you must stay. The house is so full there's no room for you anywhere else. But I've grown used to having the bed to myself. I'll not sleep a wink."

He tried clumsy tenderness. "I'll put you to sleep."

"Please don't bring your camp vulgarities home to me. Come. Supper must be ready."

So they went down to the others; and Trav as they came to the foot of the stairs saw her pause and put on beauty like a garment. Her eyes cleared of sullen shadows, her sudden smile was radiant. During the hours that followed, in the gay charades, the merry games, he watched her in wonder and in longing, her arms so slender and so fair, her shoulders warmly gleaming; her bright hair became prettily disordered, her cheeks were hot. How beautiful she was when she was happy, teasing Brett, evading Tony's grasp, laughing up at Faunt. Not even Dolly could compare with her. When they all at last went upstairs and he closed their door and they were alone she swung to him with welcoming arms. "Oh, Trav, wasn't it fun? Wasn't it fun?" Her lips pressed his with an eager hunger, and his pulse leaped in triumphant answer. He had forgotten how bewitching she could be; he took unquestioningly this enchanting hour.

Thus the Christmas at home with her and with his children was a blissful time. Enid, for some reason he did not question, gave him a lavish affection; it was bitter hard the day after Christmas to say good-by, but her kisses went with them, and his memories.

They were all day on the road to Richmond. Trav went next morning to the Arlington to call upon General Longstreet and discuss their return to Centerville. He found the General, his great bulk sprawled on the floor, engaged in a hilarious tussle with little Jimmy. Mary Ann, just a year old, watched and squealed with delight at their mock battle. Jimmy's outcries of pretended pain sometimes alarmed her, so that her eyes widened and she waited warily; but when she saw them laugh together again, she crowed and gurgled and crawled around them on slapping palms and thumping knees. Garland and Gussie, pretending to be too mature for such infantile sport yet obviously wishing their dignity permitted them to take a hand, sat by as grinning spectators.

When Trav came in, Mrs. Longstreet greeted him; and the General called: "Hello there, Captain! A rescue here! I'm outnumbered!" He rolled on his back, swinging Jimmy up in the air, shaking him till he bubbled and squealed with delight. The baby with a gleeful scream got a hand grip on his beard and pulled hard, and he shouted: "Ha! A flank attack!" He tucked Jimmy in the curl of one arm, drew the little girl into the other. "Envelop the enemy! That's tactics, Captain!"

Their laughing struggles redoubled, and Gussie could no longer stay out of it. He threw himself across the General's legs, and immediately found himself encircled by those legs and held fast. They were a rolling, squirming tangle on the floor; and Mrs. Longstreet, through her laughter, protested.

"Do stop it, Jeems! If they play too hard they'll all be crying in a minute."

Mary Ann escaped her captor and at a galloping crawl raced for safety at her mother's feet. The General, Jimmy under one arm and Gus riding him as though he were a horse, galloped after her on hands and knees, and caught her and rolled her over, and buried his beard in her small belly with great growls and buttings till she was in a hysteria of delight, and Mrs. Longstreet cried:

"There now, Jeems, you've made her wet herself!" She swept the baby away, delivered her to black arms for attendance. "And it's time Jimmy had his supper! That's enough play. Stop it, both of you! Stop it, Jimmy! Gussie, stop!" But as Longstreet came to his feet Gussie clung to the skirts of the General's coat till a button went flying; and Mrs. Longstreet cried: "There, Gussie, I declare you've pulled a button off!"

"Well, I don't care!" Gussie retorted. "I don't like that old gray coat. I liked his blue coat better anyway!"

General Longstreet roared in mock wrath: "Aha! A Union man in the family!" He swept Gussie up in his arms, swung him into the air, held him high. "Well, this is what we do to little Yankees!" And he shook the youngster to and fro till Gussie was weak with laughter, then set him down with a clap on the shoulder. "There, Yank, be off with you!"

Mrs. Longstreet shepherded them away; and Longstreet met Trav's eye. "Gussie's always said that," he confessed. "Since I gave up the blue for the gray. It still gives me a twinge."

Trav nodded, and Mrs. Longstreet came back to demand the General's coat so that the button could be replaced, and Trav saw her eye meet her husband's in tender reassurance. "He didn't mean it, Jeems! He's just a baby." Impulsively she kissed him and departed. "Better comb your beard, my dear!"

Trav smiled at the big man's disordered hair and whiskers, the sweat upon his brow. "They gave you a battle, General."

"Surprising how youngsters will wear a man down," the other agreed, still panting. "Men our age can stand up to quiet endurances better than boys; but for a dash, a quick effort, I'll take the young man every time."

"My children are a quiet pair," Trav reflected. "I don't think Peter and I have ever had a rough-and-tumble."

"Try it, Captain," Longstreet advised. "He'll welcome it. It brings you into his world. You know, we're so much bigger than children that they're awed by our size—just as you and I would be awed among a race of giants. But when you get down on the floor with them, they meet you on even terms."

"Lucy and I are pretty good friends," Trav said. "She's old enough so we seem to find lots of things to talk about."

"There's nothing like a daughter," the other agreed. "But as they grow up they turn to their mother. It's sons who need a father most." He added reminiscently: "My father died when I was twelve. Uncle Gus brought me up, did a lot for me. He even moved to Alabama in order to get me a West Point appointment." The big man chuckled. "I was never a student, though; second from the bottom. But I did well enough outside the class room."

As he spoke, Mrs. Longstreet reappeared; and she commented smilingly: "His successes were chiefly among the ladies, Captain. The other cadets voted him the handsomest man in West Point——"

"And that was before I grew a beard, too," Longstreet pointed out. "You know, when they nicknamed General Stuart 'Beauty' it was because he wasn't one! He was short on chin. He grew a beard on the theory that any change would be an improvement!" He added in pretended complacency with a teasing glance at Mrs. Longstreet: "I grew mine in order not to break too many hearts."

"He's still the most conceited man I know," she told Trav. "Here, put on your coat, Jeems."

"But my dear," Longstreet reminded her as he obeyed, "having won you, I have a right to be."

"Won me?" she laughed. "It was the other way around!" And to Trav: "Why, Captain, when he went off to the Mexican wars he was desperately in love with my hated rival; but before he came home I managed to marry her off to someone else—and caught him on the rebound!" Trav felt, behind their jesting, the strong love between these two. They talked to him, but actually they talked through him to each other. Their pretended accusations were actually tendernesses, as surely as though in secret night they whispered happy ardors; and Trav recognized this, and loved them both—and envied them. Between him and Enid there were never such scenes as this, never these affectionate railleries.

Longstreet carried on the play, answering her boast. "It's true you disposed of the rival you knew about, my dear; but I had another string to my bow!" He spoke to Trav. "The very charming daughter of the Mexican gentleman with whom I stayed to recuperate from the wound I took there." He said in exaggerated remorse: "I'm afraid I played fast and loose with her. She was devoted to me, and I made a thousand promises to return and marry her."

Mrs. Longstreet smiled. "You've discovered before this what a braggart he is, I'm sure, Captain."

"To tell the truth is not bragging, ma'am," Longstreet assured her. "She loved me, and if you had disappointed me I might be a hidalgo in Mexico today. But of course I had disposed of your most ardent suitors, so that when I came home to ask your hand you had no one else to whom to turn." He laughed. "Remember 'Lys Grant, Louisa?"

"The lieutenant with the big epaulettes? Of course."

Longstreet told Trav: "Lieutenant Grant came to me and asked me to give him a chance at Louisa. He said I could have any girl for the asking—that was true, to be sure—so wouldn't I please leave Louisa for him! But I didn't trust that young fellow! He never knows when he's licked! So I took him out to the Dent place and turned him over to Cousin Julia and she married him." He added, to Mrs. Longstreet: "By the way, Louisa, he has a command now, out west. I hope I don't have to fight him. You can knock 'Lys over, but he won't stay down."

"Cousin Julia's had a hard life with him," she declared. "He drinks terribly."

Longstreet winked at Trav. "When a man drinks too much you'll usually find he has an extravagant wife."

"Why, Jeems, do you think I'm extravagant?"

"You mean to suggest I'm a drinking man?" His tone pretended astonishment, and they laughed together, and he said in open tenderness: "My dear, whatever you spend is less than I'd like to give you." He laughed: "But speaking of intemperance, Captain, a toddy?"

"Now none of that, Jeems," Mrs. Longstreet protested. "First thing I know you'll both be singing."

"But, Louisa, this is purely medicinal! A touch of sore throat coming on. Eh, Captain?" He winked largely, and Trav was about to assent when Mrs. Longstreet said briskly:

"If you've a sort throat, I'll soon fix that. Some of your mother's salve, well rubbed in!" She rose, determined in her movements; and

Longstreet protested in sudden dismay that his throat was not sore, but she made him lie down on the couch and open his coat and shirt to bare his chest, standing over him with a small round tin box. "There, hold your old beard out of the way," she directed, and scooped up one small finger full of salve and began to rub it into his chest; and he squirmed and said it was too cold, and she told him it was always too hot or too cold to suit him and threatened that unless he lay still he should have a mouthful of it. Trav, sitting across the room, watched in a high amusement; she was so small, the man she mauled so huge. While she rubbed, she talked over her shoulder to Trav.

"This is a famous salve, for colds, or sprains, or burns, or small cuts. The General's mother invented it. She was a Maryland girl and a wonderful woman. She brought up nine children all alone after her husband died, saw them all married and raising families. Most of them were daughters, to be sure; but she always said she'd never have raised them if it hadn't been for this salve. The General's sister 'Liza makes it for the whole family now." She added: "I think she's improved the flavor, don't you, General?" And when he was about to speak she thrust her finger into his mouth so that he sat up with a great sputter and swept her down beside him.

Trav left them laughing together. He had enjoyed this hour without envy, despite his wistful realization that in the deep affection between these two lay something he had missed. He and Enid had hours of anger and they had hours of passion, but never of shared and tender mirthfulness.

He had thought to return at once to Centerville, but General Longstreet wished a few days more with his children; so Trav was still at Cinda's when two or three days after Christmas she came from Great Oak, and brought Enid with her. "Faunt's there with Mama," Cinda explained. "So this is Enid's chance for a little vacation. We'll have a party for her, charades and things."

Trav thought there was some pretense in Cinda's vivacity; and Enid seemed almost sulky. When they were alone he asked her: "Didn't you want to come?"

"Of course not! I despise travelling in cold, rainy weather." The fine autumn days had in December given way to snow and rain. "And even Great Oak's fun with Faunt there. But Cinda just dragged me away."

Yet she enjoyed as much as anyone the party Cinda arranged. Tommy and Rollin had gone home to spend Christmas leaves; but they appeared at dusk, an hour or two before the first guests were to arrive, so Vesta's happiness was complete. Rollin had time to answer Cinda's questions about the great Charleston fire which had struck the city early in December. "They say it burned over about six hundred acres," he explained. "From Hazel Street on Cooper River to Tradd Street on Ashley River, and uptown, both sides of Broad Street. It looked for a while as if it would burn out, but then the wind shifted and blew a gale and brought it back so fast people didn't have time to save much before their houses caught. Even when they got furniture out into the streets, there weren't carts enough to carry it away." He spoke of people they knew. This one's house had been burned, that one's escaped with slight damage, a third's was out of the track of the flames. Cinda trembled as she listened.

"There's nothing that frightens me any worse than a fire," she confessed. "There's so little you can do."

Vesta, with Rollin, asked: "Was it fun being at home?"

"Grand," he said, smiling. "Like old times. We had the whole neighborhood for an oyster roast on the beach, hot whiskey punch and oysters by the barrel and terrapin and palmetto cabbage and wine." He laughed. "We ate till we couldn't breathe and then danced ourselves hungry again when the moon rose."

Cinda remembered another picnic at Muster Springs; and Vesta's thoughts must have run with hers, for the girl said quickly: "You and Tommy got here just in time, Rollin. We're having a party."

He hesitated. "I wanted to make a call or two," he said doubtfully; but Vesta laughed at him.

"Dolly'll be here, you know. You'd better stay."

So Rollin grinned and grew red and stayed; and presently the General and Mrs. Longstreet arrived, and then Tilda and Redford Streean, and—after an interval during which Cinda saw Rollin watch the door—Dolly, with two young officers in her train. For Julian's sake, Cinda had asked Anne Tudor. Moxley Sorrel of Longstreet's staff, and Theodore Hamilton of the First Virginia joined the company. Mr. Hamilton had brought from Centerville funds donated by the officers of Longstreet's division with which to buy some scenery and costumes for the theatrical entertainment which Trav was to arrange. There were half a dozen others, so that the big house was brimming with gay voices and bright laughter.

Charades were the order of the evening. To present the first, Cinda chose the General, Captain Sorrel, Dolly and Enid for the principals; and Trav was drafted for a silent part.

"The word's 'industrial'," Cinda explained when she gave them their roles. "So this is an Inn, for the the first syllable. You'll be the Inn Keeper, Travis. You don't have to do anything; just be a surly old bear behind the table there. Dolly's the Barmaid, and the General's the Traveller, and he comes in all dusty and thirsty and demands a drink——"

"That won't be play-acting, ma'am!"

"Hush! And it's all pantomime, you know, so don't bellow! And Dolly serves him, and then he says he has no money to pay; so then Trav and you and Dolly just throw him out, and that will be the scene. Now let's start——"

Trav hoped he would be able to do his part. Dolly in cap and apron was a bewitching maid servant; the General a satisfactorily travel-stained wayfarer in hat and greatcoat, stamping in to take his seat at the small table and thumping for service and then visibly softening under Dolly's sprightly smiles. He ogled her and twirled his mustache till the spectators were hilarious and even Trav could no longer keep from grinning. When the General had drained the beaker that Dolly brought him, he rose and fumbled in his pockets and then with an eloquent gesture declared them empty; but before Trav could recognize his cue and do his part, Dolly caught the General's arms and rose on tiptoe, plainly assuring him that another form of payment would be welcome. He accepted the challenge, swept his beard aside and bussed her soundly, to loud applause.

Then Cinda hustled them off through the wide doors; and Trav protested: "But I thought I was supposed to——"

"Oh, you were," Cinda laughingly agreed. "But this little minx had her own ideas!"

"I thought it was nicer that way," Dolly said demurely. "Did you mind, General?"

"My dear young lady, I'm only sorry we couldn't repeat the performance! An encore, Cinda?"

"You men!" Cinda protested. "Every last one of you turns flighty at a pretty smile. Go sit with Cousin Louisa, Jeems! She'll give you a wigging!"

For the second syllable, Dolly and Vesta and Anne Tudor and Enid—Trav thought Enid seemed as young and as beautiful as they—elaborately flicked clouds of imaginary dust off every chair and table and mantel; for the third and fourth syllables combined, the scene was a court room, Longstreet the sober judge, young Hamilton the prisoner on trial. Streean and Trav were opposing counsel, and Dolly was the accusing witness. Pantomime can be more eloquent than words; Dolly with a pretty impudence made the crime of which the defendant was accused so manifest that Trav felt an uneasy embarrassment; but Longstreet, never at a loss, played his part as well as she. He bullied counsel, he sympathized with the witness, and he damned the scoundrelly prisoner—and all in pantomime—till the audience rocked with laughter. Trav, who had seen him in many moods, thought he was a dozen men in one; stout commander, devoted husband, adoring father, gamester, lover of fun—and now even an actor! He saw Mrs. Longstreet's amused affection in her eyes.

The long evening never lagged, and when her roles offered the opportunity Enid was as audacious and as charming as Dolly. Trav, watching her happiness, was happy too; and alone with him at last she was still rapturous. "Oh, Trav, I don't think I ever did have such a good time in all my life!" She kissed him, laughing richly. "You were so cute, acting all over the place! You're really sweet, you know." That night even in her sleep she clung to him, uttering in her dreams little happy sounds.

The President's New Year's reception in the White House on Clay Street seemed to Trav a dreary occasion, but Enid enjoyed it; and when next day Mr. Hamilton took her and Trav behind the scenes at the Richmond Theatre—which most people still called the Marshall—she was delighted. Trav too found this glimpse of a new world curious and interesting. In one of the plays, *The Log Fort,* muskets were fired on the stage; and a wad struck Trav's knee as he stood with Enid in the wings, and smouldered till he set his foot on it. He would remember this, for in the small hours that night he was awakened by a tumult in the town, and saw a glare against the sky, and dressed and followed the beacon of the flames to the corner of Seventh and Broad to find the theatre all afire and already beyond saving. But a saddler's shop next door had caught; and the little establishment of Mrs. Jackson, who made mantuas, was burning; and so was Davidson's Hotel; and embers flying in the updraft from the flames set roofs ablaze in the nearer neighborhood. Thus though the main battle was already lost there were many small skirmishes to be fought. Trav lent a hand in this, till all that could be done had been done. In the gray dawn he heard Mr. Dalton, the stage manager, furiously assert that the fire had been set; that Mr. Crone, the night watchman, had seen a Negro climb out of an alley window a while before the first flames appeared, had tried unsuccessfully to halt him. Trav suggested that a musket wad might have been responsible; and Mr. Dalton dissented so violently that Trav suspected him of guilty fears that this might be true.

Not only the building but the scenery, costumes, properties, musical instruments, all were gone. This made it impossible for Trav and Mr. Hamilton to buy the theatrical supplies they had hoped to secure; so next day they returned to headquarters in Centerville. Trav left Enid in Richmond. She would go down to Great Oak when next Brett, or some other to escort her, went that way.

Through the first weeks of the new year, Trav's duties were light. Supplies, in spite of Colonel Northrop's many inadequacies as Commissary General, accumulated faster than they were consumed; for so many soldiers were in hospitals, either in camp or in Richmond, that the army was no more than half an army. Sickness was not the only toll. Most of the men had enlisted for twelve months, and in April and May those enlistments would expire. Congress offered a bounty and a sixty-day furlough to every man who would promise to re-enlist, and as early as January there were many furloughs granted; but from their furloughs an alarming number of soldiers failed to return. General Longstreet told Trav that to put an adequate force in the field for the spring campaign, conscription would be necessary.

"The army's melting away like snow under a spring sun," he declared. "The men take the furlough, but they don't come back."

"They all want to go home," Trav agreed. "They hate winter quarters, and eating their own cooking, and having nothing to do but huddle around their fires and scratch themselves. But no one's going to like conscription, General."

"No one likes war!" Longstreet retorted. "But once you're in one, it's lick or get licked. Next spring McClellan will throw a hundred thousand men at us; and if things keep on the way we're going, we won't have ten thousand soldiers to meet him. Why, Currain, by the middle of May the enlistments of a hundred and fifty of our regiments will have expired. That means that just about the time fighting starts, we'll be trying to recruit new regiments and reorganize the army." And, remembering Trav's word, he exploded. "Want to go home? Of course they do! We all want that! But the way to win a war is to want to win it, to want victory more than you want anything else!"

"Do you want conscription, General?"

"You're damned right I do! I want to win this war, and I want anything that will help win it!"

But to supply men was not Trav's province, nor Longstreet's; so at division headquarters January was a lighthearted time. General Johnston's headquarters were at the hotel near-by, and Colonel Lamar came in late November and spent much of the winter there as an unofficial liaison between General Johnston and President Davis. Colonel Lamar had been a student at Emory College when Judge Longstreet, the General's uncle, was its president; and he married Judge Longstreet's daughter, so he and General Longstreet were not only long friends, but in this fashion kin. The Colonel, after a distinguished career which included more than one term in Congress, had with the outbreak of the war received a regimental command. Persistent illness disqualified him for active duty; but his eagerness to be of use led him to undertake to work for a better understanding between President Davis and the commanding generals.

Trav quickly learned to feel for the amiable and valiant invalid a strong affection, and Colonel Lamar sometimes confided to Trav his perplexities. "General Johnston and Cousin James are a stiff-necked and rebellious generation," he admitted, smiling at his own words. "Cousin James will never forgive President Davis for asking him, when he offered his services, whether he had settled his accounts as a Union paymaster before resigning. Mr. Davis is sometimes lacking in tact, but he meant no offense; and for the sake of victory, personal grievances should be forgotten." And he added: "I hope to be able to persuade Cousin James and General Johnston to like President Davis a little better."

But he did not succeed. No one could fail to respond to his charm, and General Johnston proposed to recommend him for promotion to brigadier, and General Longstreet never concealed his own pleasure in Mr. Lamar's company. "But he will never lead me to any fondness for Jeff Davis," he told Trav, with an amiable vehemence.

"I remember you said one day you'd do anything that would help win the war. Doesn't that include——"

Longstreet laughed cheerfully. "I can obey a man without liking him." And he asked in an amused tone: "By the way, how well do you agree with Colonel Northrop nowadays, Currain?" Colonel Northrop's unfitness for the responsibilities that President Davis had put in his hands was so manifest that Trav never thought of him without reddening anger.

There was in these weeks of idleness time for pleasure and Longstreet organized a club to jump horses, with a forfeit for each fall to be paid into a fund for jolly dinners. The General himself, though he weighed well over two hundred, was a fine horseman; and his big bay, a thoroughbred, was the best jumper in the army. So he paid no forfeits; but only Peyton Manning, who was so small that two Mannings would hardly have made one Longstreet, had an equally clean slate. Beverly Johnston, an older brother of General Johnston, a choleric and excessively bibulous individual six inches under six feet but as fat as he was short, one day tried a jump and took a bad fall, bloodying his own nose and breaking his mount's knees; and the jumping club came thereafter under General Johnston's displeasure.

But General Longstreet liked dinners and easily found occasions. Toward the end of January a heavy snow fell; and Moxley Sorrel and Peyton Manning designed a sleigh, fixing a box on saplings bent to serve as runners, contriving a harness so that their two horses could be hitched tandem with a Negro boy mounted on each as a postilion.

When the first ride in this rude vehicle was attempted, everyone at headquarters turned out to watch; and during the preliminary banter Trav saw Longstreet draw one of the postilions aside and speak to him. So Trav was not surprised, when the sleigh started off, to see the horses leap from a trot into a headlong run. The sleigh raced away, and everyone mounted to follow and see the sequel.

The sequel was that the sleigh overturned, Sorrel and Manning were spilled into the drifts, and the General ordered an evening of wine and song at the expense of the discomfited adventurers. Longstreet's part as the instigator of the runaway was not suspected. Trav thought he would presently, to point the jest, avow it. The dinner was hilarious, and Trav, as usual the soberest among them, watched the others and thought how surely strong drink led men to show their true selves. Peyton Manning, no matter how much he drank, was always courteous and considerate, as was Osman Latrobe. Moxley Sorrel easily became overbearing; he lost his temper readily. Fairfax played the clown, and though others found him amusing, Trav did not. Walton in his cups became sarcastic and supercilious. Longstreet forgot his heavy dignity, and he might romp like a boy.

That evening there came a tragic interruption to their merriment. The fun had reached its height. The General and half a dozen others, on their feet, with their arms across one another's shoulders, their heads together while they produced a labored harmony, were singing *Lorena* when an orderly appeared at the door.

Trav went to meet him. The orderly had a telegram for General Longstreet; and when the song was done, Trav delivered it. As the General read the scrawled message, Trav saw his smile fade, saw his lips set, saw his cheek harden. Longstreet handed him the telegram.

"Please arrange for a special engine, a special train," the General directed in a low tone, completely sober now. "I hope you will go with me."

Trav read the dispatch.

> *Mary Ann dangerously sick. Can you come home*
> *Louisa*

30

CINDA was at the Arlington with Mrs. Longstreet when the General and Trav arrived. The baby was desperately ill, and after the telegram was sent little Jimmy too had sickened. Despite all they could do, Mary Ann died late at night on the twenty-fifth of January, and Jimmy died early the next day.

Cinda came home to Vesta and to Jenny and to Jenny's babies with terror cold in her breast; for there was scarlet fever everywhere in Richmond and the Longstreet children were not the first it took, and would not be the last. To Vesta she confessed her fears.

"I wouldn't let Jenny know, but I'm frightened! Suppose Kyle got sick, or Janet, or little Clayton!"

"They won't, Mama!"

"I don't see how I could stand it! And yet of course I could. So many sorrows in the world, so many frightened, grieving people!" She added thoughtfully: "Yet I wonder if we're not brought closer together by our sorrows, Vesta. There's comfort in knowing you're one of many, all hurt and bewildered and weeping."

"It gives me—" Vesta hesitated. "Well, having those babies die makes me want Tommy awfully; makes me want to have babies for him."

"I know, darling." Then, remembering when her own babies died, Cinda added: "Whenever we're frightened we always turn, if we can, to love."

Upon Trav fell the sombre business of arranging that double funeral. He asked Cinda's advice and she sent him to Mr. Davies, the stone cutter on Main Street between Eighth and Ninth. Mr. Davies pointed out that continued cold and snow had forged a frosty armor on the ground, so that no graves could be dug; but he had a vault in Hollywood where the little bodies could rest until a later day. Trav reported to Cinda and she agreed to this.

The vault was in the hillside on the right of the main drive, not far from the entrance, faced with stone and flanked by stone walls and fronting on a stone-flagged areaway. The day was wet with cold rain that made the occasion more dreadful; the stones were dripping bleakly, touched with ice; the low portal of the vault through which even by stooping a man could only with difficulty pass was like the entrance to the den of some loathsome, carrion-eating animal. Cinda shuddered and shivered as she watched one small coffin and then the other disappear into this black hole, and she looked toward the General and Mrs. Longstreet. Their two sons stood beside them; and Cinda saw Gussie suddenly sneeze, and a hard hand clutched her heart.

That night both Gus and Garland were feverish, and the fight to save them, this new and desperate struggle, left Mrs. Longstreet and the General no time for empty grief. Gussie died a short week after the other two, and went to lie in the same dark vault; but Garland was still dangerously ill, and to Cinda this seemed almost a blessing. Before he was safe, time might begin to heal these wounds.

"But I cannot stay in Richmond," Mrs. Longstreet told Cinda, when Garland was surely on the mend. "Oh, I know I'm unreasonable— but I can't! Jeems says he'll take me to Lynchburg. I can't stay alone here in these empty rooms with just Garland. I'd be hearing their voices all the time."

Cinda made no effort to dissuade her. Probably Cousin Louisa's decision was a wise one. But till Garland was well enough to travel, Mrs. Longstreet could not go to Lynchburg; and till he could see her settled there the General stayed here by her side.

Yet Cinda saw that he was greatly changed. His eyes that once had been so ready to twinkle were shadowed now; his tongue once so quick to jest was slow and heavy. He seemed remote and far away, sometimes failing to hear what was said to him as though he were become a little deaf. He seldom spoke directly of this triple tragedy; but once when Cinda had been with Mrs. Longstreet and came to say good night to him, the General asked:

"How is she?"

"As steady as can be."

He nodded heavily. "We've had other babies die," he said in a low tone. "But they went one at a time. This—" His lips twisted in half-mirth. "I remember once in Mexico a Mexican fired at me around the corner of a house and missed. Next time, I was ready for him, but we both missed. Then I remembered Uncle Gus telling me once that at close quarters you should always use buckshot; so I took my knife and split a bullet into three slugs, and the next time we exchanged shots he fell." He said quietly: "God used buckshot on Louisa and me this time—and every slug struck home." His broad shoulders moved as though to settle themselves under a heavy burden. "I wish I could be at home with Louisa for a while."

"Can't you, till winter ends?"

He shook his head. "No. I've already stayed too long. There's much to do, and there'll be no time to do it in the spring. The Yankees will be at us, then." His jaw set. "And half the army's sick or home on furlough, and half those on furlough have overstayed their leave. And as if that weren't enough, soon now each company will be electing new officers; and that means the good men, the good disciplinarians will be thrown out, the army will become a mob. No, I must go back." She saw his face harden in grim lines.

She spoke to Trav of the change in him, and Trav agreed. "I can't realize he's the same man who played that prank on Sorrel and Manning." She asked what he meant, and he told her about the sleigh ride and the runaway, and added: "Why, Cinda, the night the telegram came saying Mary Ann was sick, at the very moment when the telegram came he was singing with some of the other officers, singing *Lorena*. I don't suppose he'll ever sing again."

"I think he'll really be glad to get back to the army, glad to have work to do."

"The men will be glad to see him," Trav agreed. He had gone twice to camp during this interval. "A lot of them asked for him—Old Pete, they call him—when I was in Centerville Monday."

"Why do they call him that?"

"It's a West Point nickname, I think. They've picked it up. Yes, he'll be better off with work to do."

The day before the General and Mrs. Longstreet would depart for Lynchburg came news of the loss of Fort Henry in the West; and Longstreet told Trav and Cinda: "It was Grant who took Fort Henry. That man is the stubbornest fighter in the North, the most to be feared." He added in grave tones: "Perhaps this defeat will wake the South to its danger. We're still celebrating Manassas; but McClellan's army is stronger every day, and the Yankee fleets are ready to pick their spot to hit our coasts."

Faunt was in General Wise's garrison on Roanoke Island, and Cinda spoke of this. "Will they attack there, do you suppose?"

"Probably, yes," he assented. "Roanoke's the key to the whole North Carolina coast, and Wise's force is inadequate. Burnside will gobble him up—unless Wise is reinforced."

From that day, Cinda was concerned for Faunt's sake. There were presently rumors of fighting at Roanoke; and then the news of the island's fall, of the surrender of the little force there and the death of Jennings Wise sent a sobering shock and a wave of grief through every home in Richmond.

She had at first no news of Faunt. Presumably—if he were alive— he had been included in the surrender and was a prisoner. But late one night the door bell roused them all. Cinda was the first downstairs. It was Brett. Faunt was at Great Oak, he said; and Cinda cried: "Oh, thank God!"

"But he's hurt, and he's sick," Brett warned her. "A bullet through the fleshy part of his shoulder, another in his side; and both wounds are inflamed. He came afoot along the outer beach from Nag's Head to Norfolk; days without shelter, and without food. He's coughing badly, and feverish." Cinda's quick imagination pictured Enid hovering over Faunt, sitting with him all day long. "I'm going to take a surgeon down to probe for the bullet in his side."

"We'll get Dr. Little. I'm going back with you!"

"I thought you'd want to," he agreed.

At Great Oak, when he had removed the bullet from Faunt's body, Dr. Little said there was no immediate danger; but Faunt would need constant attention, and Cinda decided to stay on. Enid protested that this was not necessary. "Mama and I, with April to help us, can do everything," she declared; but Cinda insisted on remaining.

Brett rode off to his post on Warwick River, and next morning before leaving for Richmond, Dr. Little assured them Faunt was better, needing only their tender care. Sleep had rested him, his color was good, and Cinda had never seen him so full of many words. A high indignation colored all he said—indignation against General Huger and against Mr. Benjamin for their failure to reinforce the island.

"The politicians will ruin us before they're done," he declared.

"Everything's politics in Richmond," Cinda agreed. "Politics and gambling. There are gaming houses everywhere, running all night long. And the place just smells of politicians. At the President's receptions I can hardly breathe for the smell of tobacco and rum they carry with them. Of course," she added, "all the riffraff has gone into politics. The best men are in the army. The rest are just in politics so they won't have to risk their necks!"

He said thoughtfully: "You ladies—I don't mean you, of course— but the ladies are to blame for that. Politics used to be the profession of gentlemen; but now if a man's not in uniform ladies call him shameful names, so they've made politics disreputable, left it to such men as Mr. Benjamin, who don't mind what names they're called. He and the Government betrayed Roanoke as truly as if they'd shot us all."

"Maybe they couldn't help you. Or maybe they didn't know you needed help."

"Know? Why General Wise told them, over and over, right up to the last minute! He was sick at Nag's Head, sick in bed, but he still directed the defense; and five days before the attack he sent Dick Wise to Huger to tell him the situation." His color rose as he spoke, and Cinda was concerned.

"Ought you to talk so much, Faunt?"

Enid answered her. "Oh, he likes to talk. He says it rests him to get it out of his system." She said to him: "Tell her how you got away, Cousin Faunt."

He obeyed so readily that Cinda thought it was true he found easement in many words. "Why, the Yankees made their landing Thursday, in a howling northeast storm. They landed on the west side, at Ashby's. One of the Yankee steamers towed about a hundred boats full of men in a line along the shore, and the boats cut loose and hit the shore all abreast, forty or fifty men in each boat. We weren't there when they landed. We crossed from Nag's Head that morning, and landed on the upper end of the island and marched down the western side. We could see the Yankee ships, but the troops were already ashore. That night Captain Wise took twenty of us to see what they were doing; and they'd gone into camp, thousands of them. They knew there was no hurry!" His tone was harsh, his eyes blazing.

"Tell her how you got away," Enid insisted. "It was perfectly amazing, Cousin Cinda. You just can't believe it."

"It's hard to believe it myself," Faunt agreed, "now that I'm here and warm and well fed and comfortable." He explained: "The fighting came next day, Cinda. The causeway crosses a marsh, and we held the causeway and hoped the Yankees couldn't come through the marsh without getting bogged down; but they did, and flanked us. It was a Massachusetts regiment. Captain Wise had forgotten his overcoat, so he had a red blanket wrapped around him, and we made him take it off. He got a bullet through his sword arm; but he bandaged it and kept on fighting till a ball struck him in the body. By that time, we knew we had to get out of there; so we carried him in a blanket up the east side of the island through the woods, and put him into a boat to take him over to Nag's Head. I was in the boat with Captain Wise, and some New York troops came along the shore and let off a volley at us. That's when I was hit. The bullet knocked me out of the boat, and the boat had to surrender."

"And he swam clear to the outer beach," Enid cried. "Bleeding all the time."

Faunt said quietly: "Why, the water was cold enough to stop the bleeding, and I didn't have to swim all the way. It was shallow enough so I could wade some of the time. I don't know why the Yankees didn't come after me—unless they were satisfied with having caught Captain Wise. Anyway, I made it. They sent gunboats later to bombard headquarters in the hotel at Nag's Head; but General Wise's men carried him away up the beach, and got a carriage——"

"I wish you'd tell about what you did, Cousin Faunt," Enid urged. "We don't care about General Wise."

"Well, a few of us just walked to Norfolk," he said mildly.

Enid exclaimed in a pretty exasperation: "You're the most provoking man! Tell her all about it, the way you told me."

Cinda could imagine that scene, Enid plying him with many questions. "How far is it from Nag's Head to Norfolk, Faunt?" she asked.

"I don't know. A long way." He hesitated, his eyes shadowed by the memory of that ordeal. "It was still storming. The hotel at Nag's Head is on a sand spit between the ocean and the Sound. Sometimes the spit is miles wide, and sometimes it's so narrow a storm tide blows right across it; and there are sand hills fifty or a hundred feet high all along. They're all just sand except one they call Kill Devil Hill. That has grass to hold it down, but the other hills keep moving a few feet at a time, this way and that, when the wind blows the sand around. The outer beach is as hard as a floor, and we tried to stay on that; but each high tide drove us up into the soft sand, and that was hard walking, like pulling your feet out of glue at every step. Where the spit was narrow, the wind drove the water right across it, and sometimes we waded knee-deep, trying to follow what road there was. I never saw so many wild fowl in my life, millions of swans and geese and brant and ducks blown in by the storm. They'd rise in front of us and circle and settle down behind us in any lee they could find."

"Were you all day on the way?"

"All day?" He chuckled grimly. "More like four or five days. I don't know. I lost count of time. We kept walking all night, feeling for the road with our feet. We had to keep going or freeze." Cinda remembered how, long ago, she and Brett, in haste to come to Great Oak for her mother's birthday, had landed on those outer beaches; but that day had been warm and clear. The wind must rip and scourge the beaches when a gale blew! "But as we came near Norfolk some people met us, and I told them I wanted to reach here, and they found a fishing boat and brought me home."

"He got here in the middle of the night," Enid supplemented. "Just simply exhausted, wet, and cold, and that horrible bullet in him. I declare, Cousin Faunt, I don't see how you ever did it!"

"Well, you can do anything you have to." His voice faltered, and

Cinda saw that he was tired, and he began to cough in a way that distressed her.

"I'm sure you shouldn't talk any more, Faunt. Sleep a while. I'll be near you if you want anything."

Enid said quickly: "Oh, I'll stay with him. April and Mama and I take turns. We never leave him alone."

"I'll take my turn too."

"I don't need anyone, really," Faunt protested. "I'll be all right in a day or two. Stay and talk to me."

But Cinda insisted that he rest. She was soon glad she had done so; for that evening he was certainly not so well, and during the night, when she took her turn at his bedside, he sometimes muttered in his sleep. Next day he was delirious, and they fought to ease him with cold compresses on chest and brow.

But that was Cinda's last day at his side, for at dusk Trav rode up to the door. Cinda was with Faunt when she heard Trav's voice in the lower hall, heard Enid's resentful question, "Trav Currain, what are you doing here?" She could not hear Trav's reply, but that he should have come at all alarmed her and she slipped out into the hall, in time to hear Enid say: "Well, what of it? You could have sent word. You didn't have to come rushing down here yourself."

Then Enid heard Cinda on the stairs behind her, and turned and Cinda brushed past her. "What is it, Travis?" she asked.

Trav said: "Why, Kyle's down with scarlet fever, Cinda."

Cinda set her teeth to keep them from chattering, an uncontrollable terror turned her cold. Scarlet fever! The Longstreet children! Faunt or no Faunt, she must go!

She would not wait for morning, and Enid speeded their departure with a zeal which seemed to Cinda eloquent. Enid was glad to get rid of her, to have Faunt to herself. No matter, she must go. An hour after Trav's arrival they set out, the carriage lurching and rocking on the rutted, frostbound highway. Trav rode with her, his led horse following.

"I wish I could be in two places at once," she confessed. "Faunt's awfully sick, Travis."

"Well, Enid says she and Mama can take care of him."

"I know. And I must be with Kyle." She asked fearfully: "Do you think he's—as sick as the Longstreet children were?"

"I don't think so; but Vesta said you'd want to be there. Jenny didn't want to send for you, said they could manage."

"Jenny's wonderful. As strong as a rock. As steady—as you are."

He did not answer, and they were silent for a long time while the horses climbed the winding road through the woods that would bring them to the Richmond pike at Six-Mile Ordinary. Trav asked at last in a low tone: "Cinda, have you noticed the way Enid is with me?"

She was for a moment too surprised to speak. "Why—how, Travis? What do you mean?" Perhaps the darkness, the silence, the monotonous hoof beats of the horses, the hissing of the wheels in the soft sand of the road had worked some spell upon him, loosed his tongue.

"She was mad at me for coming tonight," he said. "She hasn't been the same to me since Hetty died." He hesitated. "Except when we were all here at Christmas, and the night we did the charades at your house. That night she was the way she used to be. I thought she was all right again. But tonight—well, she hasn't any use for me now!"

Cinda put a guard on her tongue, and impulsively she clasped his hand and pressed it. For him to speak thus frankly to her was proof enough of the depth of his unhappiness. "We're all upset nowadays, Travis. You must allow for that." Rage at Enid mingled with her tenderness for him, yet she must not criticize Enid. "I'm sure you're imagining things. Enid loves you; but of course she's young enough to want excitement, pleasure, gay times."

"She certainly does," he agreed. "You can see the difference, just in the way she looks. She's just—beautiful, when she's enjoying herself."

Cinda said thoughtfully: "And it's lonely for her, with you away. You might bring her to Richmond, make a home for her there. Mama'd be all right alone. She lives in a world of her own anyway."

"Do you think Mama's mind is failing, Cinda?"

"Of course not!"

"I mean, the way she is about the war?"

"It's just her way of refusing to worry." Cinda returned to the point. "Why don't you do that, Travis? It might make all the difference in the world to Enid."

"Well, I'll see." He hesitated. "I may be back at Great Oak soon.

The General thinks the Federals may land an army on the Peninsula, and we'd have to move down here to meet them."

Cinda at his words forgot Enid in this new concern. If there was to be fighting on the Peninsula, it might sweep over Great Oak like a storm tide. What would her mother do? She wished to ask Trav, but he knew the answer no more clearly than she did. He was silent now, and she thought presently that he was asleep, but she did not sleep. Anxiety for her mother and fear for little Kyle were her companions as the carriage lumbered through the night.

Before they came to Richmond, dawn broke through a stormy sky, and rain presently spattered them. At home Cinda hurried to the room where Kyle lay. He seemed to her not so desperately ill as the Longstreet children had been. "But I mustn't let myself think so," she thought. "I must be ready for anything."

She had need of all her resolution, for not only was Kyle ill, but Janet had a cold, snuffles, a running nose; and little Clayton was fretful. Before the week ended they were all hot with fever; and Cinda gave herself so completely to their care that outside events scarce touched her. She heard Fort Donelson had surrendered, to that same General Grant whom Longstreet considered so dangerous; but the war was far away, the sick children were here. Her universe was all contained within these walls.

Brett was at home for the dreary, rain-drenched day when Mr. Davis was inaugurated as permanent President of the Confederacy, and to feel Brett's arms around her was strength and reassurance; but presidents and politics alike were meaningless and of no account. These sick children were more than all the world.

Not till March brought the first signs of spring were the babies safely on the mend. When she was sure of this, Cinda thought in a great thankfulness that nothing could shake her now.

31

UNTIL Faunt came home to Great Oak wounded and ill, Enid would have said her affection for him was no more than a natural fondness for the nicest of her kinfolks; and she would have believed herself sincere. If in the past she had pretended more than this, it was rather to plague Cinda and Tony for being so ready to think ill of her than from any deep and genuine emotion. But while she tended Faunt, pretense began to become reality. She was glad when Kyle's illness drew Cinda back to Richmond, for thereafter Faunt was hers alone. Through the weeks that followed she spent herself in a fierce and jealous devotion, enlisting old April's help only when she must, resenting even his mother's visits to his bedside. Faunt was her charge, and she would not willingly share him with anyone; for surely he was not so dear to any of them as to her. None of them realized as she did his charm, his courage, his gentleness, his strength. Had they not let him dwell all these years alone with his grief while they lived their heedless happy lives?

When he was at his worst she slept, if she slept at all, upon a sofa in his room; when he was better, she went no farther away than the small dressing room next to his, where April had set up a narrow cot bed. Under the long strain she who had always been slender became thin, her eyes were deeply shadowed, her cheeks hollowed, her skin acquired a pale translucency. Mrs. Currain, increasingly withdrawn within herself and increasingly blind to all that went on around her, did not observe this; but April fumed and scolded, and she was forever bringing Enid broth to drink and glasses of fresh milk and cups of steaming tea, till Enid protested:

440

"I declare, April, you treat me as if I were a nursing mother! Stop it! Let me alone! I'll ask for what I want."

"Missy, you don' know what you want!" April protested in a kindly anger. She had long since included Enid in her loyalty to Trav and to all who belonged to him. "But I does! Hit's high time Marste' Trav come home tuh tek care o' you."

Trav? If there was one thing Enid was completely sure she did not want, it was for Trav to come home. "Oh, you—" she floundered for words, hating this fat black woman sweating from the kitchen. "Leave me alone! For Heaven's sake go wash your face!"

April grunted indignantly. "What I want to th'ow wateh in mah face foh? I ain't no house afiah!" She stumped away in sullen hurt.

Brett too, on his frequent visits, saw Enid's weariness and urged her to let April take a heavier share of the burden, but she told him gently: "I'm not tired. Really and truly I'm not. I love doing things for him."

This was profoundly true. Every least act performed in Faunt's service was richly satisfying. To sit beside him while he was delirious, to hear him speak to his Betty who died so long ago, to lean close and catch his half-uttered sentences and piece out the sense of them; this was to share his inmost heart. Oh, he was fine and gallant and tender. He spoke no bitter word except when, remembering in his delirium Belle Vue and all that he had treasured there, trying to sit up in bed, trying to get to his feet, he raged at the war makers, at all men of the North and above all, at Lincoln. In these ravings, furious and blasphemous, Abraham Lincoln was so often the target that Enid came to think of Lincoln as an inhuman and grotesque monster with blood-dripping jaws, mouthing and gobbling and whining over the torn flesh of a still living woman who was the South.

She had not thought Faunt capable of such outright and uncurbed ferocity. Sometimes he shouted in his insensate fury; and then she rose and went to him, beautiful and tender in the candlelight; and at her touch and her gentle words he quickly quieted. Sometimes in these hours he called her Betty, and so ardently that her eyes swam with tears. Sometimes, thinking she was Betty, he clung feverishly to her hand; sometimes he kissed it. Sometimes, to appease him, she must hold him in her arms, kiss his wasted cheek and his hot burning brow. At such moments there was a tenderness in her deeper than any physical passion. He was never in her thoughts her lover or her beloved, but her babe, helpless and dependent. Though April made sullen protest at this indelicacy, Enid bathed him. She dressed the suppurating wound in his side which drained for a long time. She assuaged with cold packs the fever which devoured him; and all these intimacies were profoundly contenting. She loved his clean smooth skin, the wiry muscles of arms and legs, the ridged flesh on his flanks; she found a still rapture in brushing his hair, in trimming his light beard, in washing his long, thin hands, in cutting and cleaning his nails. And in thus serving him she surrendered herself as completely as though she lay in his arms, denying him nothing, wholly at his disposal, her only law his need.

When Faunt began to mend, his fever broke in a sweat that left him frighteningly weak. This weakness made him seem at first worse instead of better. April said he would recover, but Enid refused to believe, and stormed at her; and when she herself saw that April was right, she realized for the first time that she would be sorry to see him get well. While he lay ill and helpless, he was hers; sound and whole again, he would escape from her.

So she prolonged his convalescence as much as possible, refusing to let him move. "Your wound is still open, Cousin Faunt. You mustn't. I won't let you." He smiled at her pretty insistence, and his smile was sunshine, warming her; she kept him a prisoner of tenderness, watching to see him smile again.

The fact that his strength was slow in returning helped her keep him in bed; but by the end of February he was able occasionally to sit up in the great chair in his room. At first, five minutes of this exhausted him; but he was presently well enough to go for a drive with Enid and his mother in the fine carriage that had been Mrs. Currain's Christmas present a year and more ago, and that was her delight and pride. He could walk across the lawns toward the river; and since Lucy and Peter were alike devoted to him and were apt to trail along, Enid no longer had him wholly to herself. She tried bidding April keep the children away, but he asked for them; so on these strolls together she accepted their company, even though this meant that they, not she, had most of his attention. He told them endless, fearfully fascinating stories. They loved to hear of the old Negro woman at Belle

Vue who had known how to brew in the still and secret night the dreadful African poison which took six months to kill its victim.

"No one knows what she puts in it," he declared. "Not just frogs' heads, and stewed snakes, and lizards' tails and ordinary things like that, but awful secret things. And whoever takes the poison has the worst stomach ache you can imagine, and he has bad dreams and wakes up screaming in the night, and he thinks someone is shooting arrows through him, and after months and months, he dies!"

Peter delighted in these grisly terrors, but Lucy declared she didn't believe a word. "I guess if there was any such poison, white folks would know about it. I guess we're smarter than the people!"

He wagged his head, arguing the point with her. "When horses have knots in their manes in the morning, white folks think it's just accident; but it's really where witches have made stirrups to go night-riding. The people know that."

"There isn't any such thing as witches!"

"Then why are some horses that are locked in their stalls all night sweaty in the morning, if it wasn't witches who rode them?" And Faunt insisted: "Why, you don't even know what it means when a hen crows like a rooster."

"I don't believe a hen ever did!"

"They do sometimes, and it's always bad luck! Ask April! She'll tell you."

Lucy refused to be shaken. "Everything's bad luck for someone. You can call anything a bad sign if you want to."

Faunt seemed to enjoy her skepticism as much as he did Peter's delighted terror; but not all his talk with them was of these dreadful mysteries. He taught them to soak in vinegar the balls full of powdery black dust that dropped from the oak trees, and thus make a satisfying ink. He showed them the miracle of making fire with a bit of punk and a sun glass, and how to make a cat saddle—four hands clasping four wrists in a square—to carry someone hurt or weary. He and Enid carried Peter thus from the bluff to the house, and Enid was deeply moved by this contact of his hands and hers; because he was so charming with the children, she loved him more and more. If he, instead of Trav, were their father, how different her life would be!

Early in March, Brett and the Howitzers left their camp on Mulberry Island and marched to King's Mill Wharf to take the steamer to City Point. They were ordered to Suffolk, and Brett would no longer be able to come to Great Oak as often as in the past. Enid welcomed his departure, since now she would have Faunt more completely to herself; but Faunt as he grew stronger began to fret at long inaction. One day they heard guns far away down the river, and again the day after; and though he was himself too weak to ride, he sent Big Mill to Williamsburg for information. Thus they heard the great deeds the *Merrimac* had done against the Yankee warships at Newport News, and Faunt's eyes glowed.

He began to speak of returning to duty. The Blues, after their surrender at Roanoke, had been paroled and sent to Richmond to await exchange; but till they were free to serve again a skeleton company was recruited and drilled in camp near the Richmond Reservoir. Faunt wrote Lieutenant Colonel Richardson, commanding the regiment, to report that he was on the way to recovery and would rejoin the company as soon as his strength sufficiently returned.

A few days after the *Merrimac's* exploit, an hour before dinner, Brett and Tony rode up to the door. Faunt and Enid and Mrs. Currain were all downstairs to meet them; and Faunt asked what brought them, but they made no direct reply. Brett said Trav was on their heels. "He stopped to talk to Big Mill," he explained.

"Mill's better than any overseer we ever had," Mrs. Currain assured them. "He's been giving the hogs poke root mash, so we never have a sick hog now; and his kitchen garden is splendid. I don't know about the field crops, but he put in his hot beds six weeks ago, and everything, cabbage, egg plant, lettuce, cucumbers, tomato plants, they're just thriving, all the seedlings. He's got the boys transplanting already. We'll have enough broad beans to feed the whole place, and everything else imaginable; not just potatoes and cabbages, but sea kale, and rape, and chives, and horse radish, and leeks, and I don't know what all."

Brett laughed at her enthusiasm. "I declare, Mama, you talk about vegetables as greedily as if you were a rabbit."

"Well, we need vegetables," the old woman insisted. "I feed the people plenty of molasses and vegetables, and that's the reason we never have typhoid fever. It's eating nothing but fats and greases that makes people have the fever." As was always the case when she was a little excited, a Highland burr crept into her speech, relic of her childhood long ago. "There! There's Travis now."

They heard the hoof beats, and Trav came in; and he kissed his mother and turned to Enid, and she gave him her cold lips, and then it was time for dinner. Enid noticed that Brett's face was lumpy and swollen and asked why.

"Mosquitoes," he said cheerfully. "Over around Suffolk they don't just sting you! They bite a piece out of you and fly up in a tree and eat it before your eyes!" He asked Trav: "Are they bad where you are?"

Trav nodded. "Yes, and flies." Tony said flies kept him awake of nights, and Trav said seriously: "I keep slapping them till I've killed the ones hanging around me. It does seem to thin them out."

Brett laughed. "In our huts, if you kill one, ten others come to the funeral feast."

Mrs. Currain spoke chidingly. "You're all forgetting what you were taught as children. Pennyroyal! It's just as good to keep mosquitoes away as it is to make ticks let go." She rose to go up for her nap. "Try it and see," she advised them.

After she was gone, Trav explained to Faunt why he and the others had come. He had met Brett in Richmond on recruiting service, found Tony there too.

"And Faunt, I thought we'd better talk things over," he said soberly. "You see, General Longstreet thinks McClellan will try to move up the Peninsula to Richmond; and McClellan can use the rivers to outflank any line we try to hold on the lower Peninsula, so the General thinks we'll have to fall back. That means the place here will be in Yankee hands." He hesitated. "It may not happen, but I thought we ought to decide what to do about Mama if it does."

Enid watched Faunt and saw him white with anger at the thought of this that might come upon them. He said in a low tone: "Mama will have to go to Richmond."

"I suppose so," Trav agreed. "But what about the people?"

Faunt hesitated, and Brett said: "They'll have to be moved, or they'll be taken as contraband of war. We'd better send them to Chimneys and the Plains."

Tony said there were more hands at Chimneys now than he could profitably use, and Brett said slowly: "We don't need them at the Plains, either; but we have to take care of them. They're used to trusting us. If you don't need them at Chimneys, Tony, we'll send them all to the Plains. I stocked up with supplies a year ago; enough, with what they can raise, to feed them all for a while at least."

"Mill wants to stay here," Trav said. They were sitting in the drawing room, Enid near Faunt and watching him. "He says they'll all want to stay. They don't want to leave their homes."

Faunt said in a harsh tone, "None of us want to leave our homes, Trav." His hands, still thin and white from his long illness, clenched. "That damned ape!" he whispered. "That damned black Republican baboon!"

After a moment Tony said slowly: "It's all right to blame Lincoln. He's an easy target. But it was people like your South Carolina neighbors, Brett, as much as the abolitionists in the North, who started all this."

Enid, remembering how Faunt in his delirium had raged at Lincoln, expected an explosion; and Brett must have seen Faunt's color rise for he spoke quickly: "It's too late now to argue how this began, too late to think about it. Once you're in a war, it's too late to think about who got you into it." But he suggested that the hazard at Great Oak might not be so immediate as Trav feared. "I'm not so sure the Yankees can force their way up the James," he urged. "We have seven or eight guns on Mulberry Island, and the Day's Point battery on the south side of the river has seventeen. Then there are the guns on Jamestown Island. And don't forget the *Merrimac!* She's already taught them one lesson! I saw that business!"

"Saw it?" Faunt spoke in quickened attention. "I'd have given a lot to see that. Where were you?"

"General Randolph had sent me to Norfolk with dispatches," Brett explained. "Everyone knew what was going to happen, and we all rode out to Sewell's Point to watch. The *Merrimac*—she's been rechristened the *Virginia,* but people stick to the old name—came out past Craney's Island; and all the Yankee transports and tugs slipped anchor and scurried to get away. She headed for Newport News to attack their warships, so we were too far away to see much; but we could see the smoke and hear the guns, and those who had glasses could see and could tell us what was happening. She rammed the *Cumberland* and sank her, and then drove the *Congress* aground, and sank some transports tied to the wharves. The *Minnesota* went aground, too. When the *Merrimac* finally anchored for the night, right off the Point, we could see the *Congress* burning." Faunt uttered an exclamation of satisfaction, and Brett said. "Yes, everyone felt that way, Faunt. We had a real celebration that night, and everyone was sure she'd go on next day and sink every ship in sight; but next day the Yankees had this craft they call the *Monitor*. She mostly stayed in shallow water where we couldn't get at her to ram her; and our guns didn't hurt her any more than hers hurt us." He added: "But one thing's sure; the Yankees can't send ordinary gunboats or transports up the James River as long as we've got the *Merrimac* waiting for them."

Trav said after a moment: "There was a celebration in Richmond, too, till you'd think we'd won the war. Of course, if we'd sunk the Yankee fleet, we could have steamed up the Potomac and bombarded Washington; but as it is—well, Brett, it seems to me we're just where we were before. And even if they can't force the James, the Yankees can land as large an army as they need to march up past here to Richmond."

Faunt asked: "Can't we stop them?"

Trav hesitated. "I don't know, Faunt. We'll try. General Johnston has already drawn back below the Rappahannock, getting ready to move down here if he has to."

"Ah! Then the Yankees are at Belle Vue." Faunt's tone was expressionless; but Enid knew how heavy was this long-expected blow.

"Oh, Trav, how could you!" she cried furiously. "To hurt him so!"

They looked at her in surprise; but Trav said stubbornly: "Well, it's true. We've left no troops north of the Rappahannock. We started on the ninth, moving stores back from Centerville, destroying what we couldn't move. I hated seeing all the rations wasted."

"You make me so mad! Can't you ever think of anything but things to eat?"

"Well, rations are my job."

"You and your old job!" For Faunt's sake, Enid was too angry to remember the others listening. "If you amounted to anything you'd help fight, instead of being just a teamster!"

A moment's silence fell upon her words; then Brett spoke, returning to the problem they must face. "Well, I take it we'll move the people to Chimneys and the Plains. Tony, you're the only one of us free to attend to that. Will you do it?" Tony nodded assent, and Brett said: "And we might as well make up our minds that sooner or later Mama will have to go to Richmond."

Trav said: "The General will warn me in plenty of time."

Brett asked: "How is he?"

"Why, he's changed since the children died. He used to be full of fun. He's different now. There's no more singing, no more poker games at headquarters; just drill, drill, drill. He's the only general who drills the whole division as a unit."

Faunt said bitterly: "I suppose it was Mr. Benjamin's idea to give up Northern Virginia. Just as he betrayed Roanoke."

Brett answered him. "I'm not sure of that, Faunt. I hear that Colonel Randolph will be Secretary of War in Mr. Benjamin's place, but Mr. Benjamin will be Secretary of State."

"Secretary of State!" Faunt's color rose. "I'd help pull the rope to hang him!"

"I never liked Mr. Benjamin," Brett agreed. "He's too calm to suit me, smiles too much." He laughed. "Cinda hates him. But George Randolph—well, there's no one any better, for my taste; and General Lee is back from South Carolina. He's been fortifying Charleston; but now he'll be a sort of military assistant to President Davis. With Colonel Randolph and him in charge, things should go better."

Brett left that night, but Trav stayed to help Tony start the people on the long journey to Chimneys and the Plains. Not all would go. Uncle Josh, April, old Thomas the Coachman and young Tom his son, Cilly and the other house servants, and Viry who was the queen of the kitchen; all these aristocrats of the plantation and their underlings would for the present remain. Big Mill would stay; and so would those old people who preferred to live out their lives in their small cabins here. But most of the hands, including those who had come from Belle Vue, were in the long caravan which presently set out to travel afoot to

Richmond, where they would be herded into cars to continue their journey. They went for the most part with light hearts, men and women and children in picnic humor as they began this great adventure.

When they were gone, Trav and Tony departing with them, Enid had Faunt to herself again. He was presently able to mount and ride a little, and a little more each day. Enid rode with him, beautiful and bright; but—soon now he would go back to duty, and these blissful hours would end. How empty her life then would be; how empty and how intolerable!

Once, but for his demeanor which warned her to silence, she would have spoken her heart. The day had been hot and still, and they delayed till the sun set before they rode abroad. They took the Barrett's Ferry road toward the Chickahominy and turned off by a fishing trail through the swamp to come out on a low bluff above the grass marsh and the curlew ground. A flock of white herons rose in squawking alarm, their wings drifting snowflakes in the twilight; and Enid heard the silver whistle of circling yellowlegs and the "cre-e-ek" of a snipe. It was already dark enough so that a great star shone pale in the western sky, and she asked what it was. "Jupiter," he said. "It's been the evening star for three or four nights now."

They sat their horses, silent in the thickening dusk, and Enid's pulses pounded faster, and her thoughts found words. "Oh, Faunt, please don't ever go away from here."

She hardly knew she had spoken till his dark eye turned to her in long regard. After a moment he said simply: "It's hard to leave a spot like this."

"To leave me, Faunt?" Her voice was a whispered prayer.

"To leave Great Oak and Mama and those fine children of yours." Then in casual affection: "Yes, and you too, of course, Enid. You've been mighty good to me."

"I loved taking care of you; you so hurt and ill."

"You ladies are like angels tending our sick, wounded men."

"I couldn't do it for anyone but you."

He looked at her, in his eyes something monitory which she could not fail to heed. "I'll always be grateful to you and Mama. You couldn't have been kinder to me if I'd been Trav."

His reminder was enough to silence her; but that night, tossing on her sleepless bed, pounding at her pillows with her small clenched hands, in a sweat of longing, she hated him as much as she loved him. For he would ride away, perhaps never to return; ride away and leave her desolate. What then? What then for her?

Why, a lifetime married to Trav.

Before she slept she knew that if this were all that remained for her in life, she would rather die. She set her teeth. Yes, die!

And soon, soon to tell Trav so.

32

LATE in March, Julian and Tommy Cloyd came to Richmond together. Vesta, clinging to Tommy in the rapture of welcome, saw over
his shoulder a delighted pride in Julian's eyes. She turned, her arm
linked in Tommy's. "Julian," she demanded, "what are you so excited about?"

"I? What makes you think I'm excited?"

"I can tell! Now don't be provoking! What is it, Julian?"

"Well, don't look at me!" he protested. "You could see, yourself, if
you weren't blind!"

Vesta saw Tommy red and grinning, and she cried in a fine exasperation: "Oh, you're a pair, you two! What is it?"

"Look at his collar!" Julian told her. "Look at his sleeve!"

So she did, and so at last she saw the two short lateral bars on either
side of his collar, the braid in a Hungarian knot on his sleeve; and in
a rush of happiness she rose on tiptoes to kiss him, and Julian proudly
explained: "Lieutenant Potter died of scarlet fever just before we fell
back to the line of Rappahannock, so Tommy's company had to elect
a new lieutenant, and they elected Tommy!"

Vesta kissed Tommy again, in a proud delight. "But of course you
should have been a captain or something long ago," she declared. She
was thinking happily: "Surely he will know he's a good soldier now!"
After supper, after Julian had gone to Anne Tudor, she and Tommy
went for a walk and an hour or two alone. This was a warm spring
night and the whispering song of the river drew them down to the
path above the canal and along past the woody lower slopes of
Gamble's Hill. For a while their talk was nothing; but Vesta felt her

heart beat harder, and she planned what she wished to say, till at last a moment's silence gave her courage.

"Tommy," she said, careful to keep her tones steady, "you know, I haven't seen you since General Longstreet's babies died. Three of them died in a week, and they've only one left. And Tommy, when they died, I knew I couldn't wait any longer for us to be married. Please!"

He was puzzled. "That was mighty sad for him, all right; but I don't see what it has to do with us, Vesta."

Her cheeks burned, but her head was high. "I know it's no way for a lady to talk," she confessed. "But—they were so sweet, and they're dead, and I want children of my own, quick, to fill their places." His embarrassed silence gave her courage. "There, I know I'm awful to talk so, but—I've felt married to you for a long time, now."

"I sort of feel married to you," he admitted.

"Well, married people can talk about having babies! Oh I know probably lots of them don't; but Mama says people would be happier, specially married people, if they didn't pretend not to know things. Mama's pretty wise and wonderful, Tommy."

"I guess she is, all right."

"Darling, you're shocked! But Tommy, you and I aren't going to be just dumb, silly idiots, wearing blindfolds all our lives. You might as well realize right now that I love you just as much as you love me. All ways, Tommy. All ways and always."

He said slowly: "I don't know much about—being married, Vesta. But I know I want to be married to you some day, and be together all our lives."

"Well there!" Triumph made her heart pound. "That's settled! Tommy, let's get married tomorrow!"

"Golly, Vesta, I can't! I have to take the morning train. It leaves about daylight."

"Well, you can come back!"

"Not right away. I oughtn't to have come this time. I have a lot to learn, to be a good officer."

"Tommy Cloyd, you've been in the army almost a year! If you haven't learned how to be a good soldier yet, you never will."

"I guess maybe I never will," he admitted. "I've tried, Vesta. I mean, I've memorized Hardee's *Tactics* from start to finish. I can recite it by the hour, all the commands and everything. But I don't—well, I don't feel as if I knew how to—order men around!"

"Oh, Tommy, all that hasn't anything to do with you and me."

"Not with both of us, I know," he assented. "But it has a lot to do with me. I thought if I learned everything in Hardee I'd get so I did things just automatically, even in the fighting. But—well, we've been in two or three skirmishes, and I've had chances to shoot men. I could have—killed them, too. I'm a pretty good shot. But I kept remembering their wives and their sweethearts." He said unhappily: "I can't help feeling so; but I know that's not the way to win battles and war."

"I don't care who wins the battles! I like you the way you are. I love you the way you are!"

"I thought for a while maybe the other men in the company felt the same way; thought maybe they were just pretending to be so—bloodthirsty. But I guess they're not. They'd have shown it by now, if they were."

"You haven't been in any big fights yet."

"Well, we're going to be, pretty soon. We heard on the train that McClellan's landing an army at Fortress Monroe." He said quickly: "It isn't that I'm afraid, Vesta!"

"I know you're not, idiot!"

"I'm not afraid of being killed, I mean."

She turned with a quick movement to hold him fiercely close, and sharp anguish twisted her heart. "Tommy, Tommy, Tommy!"

"But I'm afraid of killing someone," he admitted. Though she was in his arms, she felt that he was still far away from her, his thoughts his own. "I've seen a man killed," he said. "A cavalry picket, scouting, ran into us one day. There were only five of them, and they came out of the woods right in front of us. We had fallen out to rest. They saw us and galloped away, but some of our men shot at them, and one of the Yankees fell out of his saddle. We buried him. He was no older than Julian, Vesta—not old enough to shave. His face wasn't touched. He had black hair. He was such a nice-looking boy!"

"Darling, darling!"

"I'd hate having to think I'd killed him." He repeated in a sudden passion: "I'd hate it, Vesta!"

Feeling his loneliness, feeling the trouble in him, full of tenderness she urged: "Tommy, when can we be married?"

"I don't know."

"I want us to be married."

"So do I want us to!"

She became cheerfully matter-of-fact. "Well, then, I'm not going to wait any longer. Papa knows Mr. Randolph, the new Secretary of War. I'll make Papa see him and arrange a furlough for you. Mama and I will have everything ready beforehand. You just leave it all to me, Tommy. You don't have to think about anything at all. When you get your furlough, you come right here!" She laughed warmly. "I'll be all dressed and ready, darling. I'll give you time to wash your face and hands, and then off we'll go!" Looking up at him. "Now don't start gulping and stammering. It's high time I made up your mind for you!"

He half surrendered. "Well—but Vesta, I'll want my mother here."

"I'll have Mama write to her tomorrow, invite her to come and stay with us. Then she'll be ready whenever you are; and I'll be ready, Tommy. Oh, my darling, I'll be so ready!" She caught his hand. "Come on, Tommy! Let's hurry home and tell Mama right now!"

Vesta from that day was in a bright fever of haste, but there were still delays; for the army was on the move, and Tommy was needed with his men. Day by day, troops on their way to meet McClellan's army marched through Richmond; and day and night the very air muttered with the tramp of feet, the roll of drums, the brassy music of the bands. Vesta and Cinda went down to Main Street to watch some of Longstreet's men march past, and one band played *The Girl I Left Behind Me,* and hundreds of pretty girls acknowledged that compliment with tender laughter and with much waving of small parasols and lacy handkerchiefs. The day was perfection, every garden bright with spring flowers as though in gala dress for the occasion. Longstreet himself rode by, cantering to overtake the head of his column. When Vesta and Cinda turned up the hill toward home, the cavalry were passing along Franklin Street, General Stuart's great red beard glowing in the sun; and they saw Burr among the troopers behind him.

Day by day the pageantry continued: men afoot, prancing horses, rumbling cannon on their iron-wheeled carriages. Sometimes word was sent ahead that a regiment was hungry; and then pantries were stripped, meals ready to be eaten were snatched off the tables, baskets were filled and borne out to await the brief halt of the men. On one such occasion Vesta had a glimpse of Tommy, and a moment's word with him; and Julian stopped for a kiss from them all before he hurried on. Uncle Trav stayed overnight, disturbed by the news of Shiloh—that was Longstreet's friend, 'Lys Grant, again—but Vesta had never heard of the place! What was Shiloh to her? The fears in all those about her she refused to heed.

Yet there was a whisper of panic in Richmond in these days. The fall of Roanoke Island had shaken that certainty of Southern invincibility which had been born on the field of Manassas. Grant at Fort Henry and at Donelson and then at Shiloh had proved that even Southern armies could be beaten. Now McClellan had another great army at Fortress Monroe, and to meet him all Virginia north of Richmond had been stripped of troops. Those who professed to be well informed were spreading rumors of coming disaster, and many who could do so slipped away. Barbara's father and mother had heard that the government archives were being packed for shipment to Columbia, and they departed to Raleigh to stay there till the danger passed. Barbara, her baby not two months away, refused to go so far from Burr, and Cinda welcomed her to the big house on Fifth Street.

"But I hope I can behave myself while she's here," she confessed to Vesta. "That little Miss Somebody is as meek as melted butter, but she always seems to get her own way somehow. Maybe it's because she knows exactly what she wants."

Vesta laughed at her. "You were so ostentatiously glad to have her, I thought you overdid it."

"I noticed you weren't over cordial."

"I used to like her lots," Vesta reflected. "I still do, I think. But there's something about her sort of—well, I don't know what. As though she were on guard, afraid of us, afraid Burr'll go on loving us or something. But I'll be as nice to her as I know how."

"Girls change, sometimes, when their first baby is coming," Cinda agreed. "But Barbara always—bothered me! I wonder why it is we like some people the minute we see them. Those Cary girls, for instance."

Vesta smiled. "Oh everybody likes them." Constance Cary and her cousins, Hetty and Jenny, had come to Richmond before Christmas, living at first at Mrs. Clifton's on Fourteenth Street; and their residence there made the dreary old lodging house a magnet for every gallant officer in town, till they moved to Mrs. Clarke's at Fourth and Franklin, only a few doors away. The three girls and Vesta were already friends, drawn together by a shared activity. The Ladies' Defense Association had been organized on the ninth of April, with Mrs. Clopton as president, to raise funds and material with which to build another ironclad like the *Merrimac*, which everyone now tried to remember to call the *Virginia;* and girls of Vesta's age were active workers on the committees appointed to solicit subscriptions. The project, as an outlet for feminine patriotism, was instantly popular; and the contributions poured in—money, jewelry, plate, treasured old pieces of furniture and sets of rare china. Old iron was needed, too, and the grillwork of many a portico, and many a fence, and every pot and kettle that could be spared, were collected by pretty volunteers. The machinery in some of the tobacco factories which now lay idle was broken up and carted away to the Tredegar Iron Works to be converted into usable metal. Before Vesta's wedding day, the new ironclad was well begun.

In spite of Cinda's feeling about Barbara, Burr's wife fitted easily into the Fifth Street household. Mrs. Cloyd came north from Camden, and Vesta drew close to Tommy's mother, leading her to talk of Tommy's father, dead long ago, and of Tommy's babyhood, and of Mrs. Cloyd's activities since her husband's death while she played a man's part in the management of the plantation.

"It's eighteen years since I've gone this long without climbing on a horse," Mrs. Cloyd said. "I'm having so much fun eating breakfast in bed I don't even mind losing Tommy. Specially to you, my dear."

Vesta loved her; her heart was big enough in these days to embrace the world.

They had to wait till Tommy could get leave, so they were not married until the last Saturday in April. Mrs. Currain refused to leave

Great Oak, and Enid insisted on staying there to keep her company. Streean was away, professedly on business, and so was Darrell. The Howitzers had gone from Suffolk to North Carolina, so Brett came only for the last two days before the wedding; and he and Tony, and when they arrived Friday afternoon Trav and Faunt, were apt to draw aside in grave discussion. But the younger men—Burr and Julian, Rollin who would be Tommy's groomsman, and of course Tommy— were merry enough so that Vesta need not heed those serious older faces.

She and Tommy would go to the McAltee place in Goochland for a few fine days together. When after the ceremony Vesta went to dress for her departure, Cinda sent every other from the room so that they could be briefly alone; and when Vesta was ready Cinda kissed her, and she said huskily:

"There, darling; be happy. You and Tommy are the finest people I know." And in a different tone: "Honey, I'm sorry to be down-to-earth, but I want you to know our plans. Travis says General Johnston will probably give up the Yorktown line and fall back to the Chickahominy; so we must bring Mama to Richmond right away. Tilda and I are going down Monday with Tony and Travis to get her, and to save what things we can."

"Oh, Mama!" Vesta felt a shock of sorrow. "Leaving Great Oak will just about kill Grandma!"

"We can stand anything we must stand, Vesta, and so can she. Don't let it spoil these days for you, my dear. When Tommy has to return to duty, you stay here and wait for us." She hugged Vesta hard. "Be happy, darling," she repeated. "Make Tommy happy. I'm very proud of my new son."

Vesta when she and Tommy rode away looked back and saw proudly Cinda's smile and her eyes not dimmed by tears. "Oh, Tommy," she whispered, "aren't mothers wonderful?" She came close beside him, her hand in his; and her heart was big with dreams.

33

THESE weeks of winter and early spring while he watched the slow disintegration of the army had been for Trav a troubled time. Clearly the army was weaker every day. Disease was the immediate and deadly foe. In some companies a score of men had died, and as many more were so weakened by dysentery or by kindred ills that they had been sent home to recover. Wet and cold and filth and inadequate or improper food reduced the strength of the men to such a point that sickness ran among them like a forest fire; and boredom was in its way almost as bad as sickness. To escape the monotony of their days they turned to any diversion, from snowballing to cock-fighting to gambling to drinking.

With warmer weather, flies and mosquitoes tormented sick and well alike; and chiggers and fleas were always with them. But worse than any discomfort for Trav was his growing certainty that they must presently abandon or destroy the mountains of stores accumulated behind the lines at Centerville and at Manassas. His mathematical mind reduced the situation to figures, and in mid-February, when the General, after the death of his children and after taking Mrs. Longstreet and Garland to Lynchburg, returned to headquarters, Trav put the problem before him.

"Colonel Northrop is setting us an impossible task, sir. He's sending supplies on here faster than we use them. General Johnston wanted to keep a million and a half pounds of rations on hand; but today the army has over three million pounds—three and a quarter million, actually—and two million pounds of meat curing, and tremendous herds of cattle waiting for slaughter. When we fall back, we can drive the herds. It will strip weight off them, but that can't be helped. But we can't move much over a quarter of a million pounds a day by the railroad. It would take us twenty-two days to get all this surplus eaten up or moved away, and once we decide to move we won't stay here that long."

Longstreet, in a tone dull with grief, agreed with this careful calculation. "Figures mean a lot to you," he commented. "To me too. But war's a wasteful business, Currain. And it's better to have too much than too little."

This was small comfort; and when in early March the withdrawal began, Trav's fears were realized. The precious stores were destroyed or left to fall into enemy hands; for the Yankee scouts pressed close on the heels of the retreating troops, deceived only briefly by the empty defenses armed with dummy cannon which were left to frighten them.

General Longstreet's command was the first to move, marching by the Warrenton pike to Culpeper. The teamsters over whom Trav had supervision seemed to use an extraordinary ingenuity in getting into trouble. They took wrong roads, and in trying to correct their mistakes they involved the columns in hideous confusion. Before his trains were safely across the North Fork of the Rappahannock, he had worn himself ragged, battling against the stupidity and the casual indifference of men to whom it seemed to be a point of personal honor not to submit to command. Trav said that night: "They're stubborn as so many mules, General! They won't move till they choose, they loaf, they fall out to rest, they stop at any excuse or at none; and they're so ignorant and at the same time so sure of their own wisdom that sometimes I'd like to take a blacksnake to them!"

The General nodded, his eyes dark. "The foot soldiers are as bad," he said. "They can't bear to leave behind any of their possessions, so they load themselves down. Knapsacks, muskets, frying pans, coffee pots, haversacks, chickens and turkeys and pigs spitted on their bayonets; and half of them tote a bag full of God knows what trash. So after a mile or two, they begin to lag. I've ordered the mounted officers to follow our columns instead of leading them, to herd the stragglers along."

Trav cut a bit of tobacco; he mopped his brow. "Well, we've come this far, somehow. The last of our wagons are safely across the river. Will you have the bridge burned?"

"Not till we must. It's easier to defend one bridge than miles of shallow, easily forded stream. We'll leave the bridge as bait. Perhaps the Yankees will try to force it."

While Longstreet's headquarters were at Culpeper, Trav, on his way to Great Oak to consult with his brothers about removing the Negroes before the Yankees came, stopped in Richmond. Martial law had been proclaimed there, and passports were necessary. At the passport office at Ninth and Broad Street, and in the Commissary General's office and wherever business led him, Trav found an infuriating disorder and a slovenly confusion. He met Redford Streean, who insisted on taking him home for supper, and Trav spoke of the things he had seen that day.

"Why, the government offices aren't even clean!" he said harshly. "Filthy pallets and beds piled into every empty room; the glass at the hydrant smelling of stale whiskey so badly I couldn't drink from it; no towel by the washstand."

"The clerks have to sleep somewhere," Streean reminded him. "And we work under such pressure that only liquor keeps us going. Every apothecary in Richmond is selling brandy on forged prescriptions."

"It all makes things worse for the army."

"It's the spies that hurt the army," Streean retorted. "Too many passports to the North are being issued, too many enemies allowed to depart, too many mail carriers come and go. Every one of them takes information north, and they have plenty to tell. When General Johnston criticizes President Davis, they know it and carry the word." He added: "But Johnston won't be long in command."

Trav had heard enough of the distrust between General Johnston and the President so that this prediction did not surprise him. "Who will take his place?"

"Lee, probably; old Granny Lee. Oh, they'll make Johnston fight a battle first. You know he gets wounded in every battle. Probably that's why he prefers a retreat to battle. But Davis will make him face the music once, at least. If he'll be considerate enough to get himself killed, it will save removing him."

Trav colored with resentment. He was enough of a soldier to be loyal to his commanding officer. "I judge you'd be glad to see him go."

"He's too ready to criticize the supply services. First he says we don't send him enough; then that we send too much; then that what we send costs too much! Why, damn it, everything costs more in war!"

"Maybe too many men are trying to profit from the army's needs." Trav's slow anger for a moment had its head. "A few courts martial, a few fusillades would put an end to that!"

Streean chuckled. "I didn't know you were so bloody-minded." His smile was lightly mocking. "After all, you soldiers have the glory of serving in the field; but we who stay at home and do the army's chores—well, surely we're entitled to some reward!"

Trav was glad to get away from Richmond, from greedy scheming, from disorder and confusion, from jealousy and knavery, from bungling and selfishness. He and Brett and Tony went to Great Oak, and the day he returned to Culpeper, Longstreet sent for him.

"Currain," he said, "I've always talked to you more frankly than to anyone else, because I've observed that you don't repeat what I say."

Trav wondered what was coming. "Yes, sir."

"General McClellan is preparing to attack us." Longstreet spoke only to put his own thoughts in order. "He may come down on Manassas, he may hit us in flank at Fredericksburg, he may make a landing near Urbana and cross our rear, or he may land his army at Fortress Monroe. But he must first and always defend Washington! If he lands an army at Fortress Monroe, Johnston can advance to the Potomac and force McClellan to meet him there. Yet there is another possibility: a strike north from the Valley, threatening to take Washington in the rear. That move will call McClelland's army to meet it, will disorganize his plans." His eyes at his own words began to blaze. "McClellan's a deliberate man. If he's made to hurry, it will upset him."

He seemed to expect some word, so Trav said: "I don't like to hurry myself. It upsets me."

Longstreet, if he heard, did not comment. He went on as though

Trav had not spoken. "Currain, sometimes, even within the rigid framework of a soldier's duty, there comes an opportunity to act. General Johnston and General Smith have gone to Richmond. That leaves me in command here. If I try what I propose and fail, I'll be court-martialled; but if I succeeed, it will dislocate all McClellan's plans. Knowing how deliberate he is, I see no risk—to the South, that is— and a chance of great gain. The risk is to me personally; but I'll take that risk, on the chance that to do so will serve the South."

He paused, and after a moment he asked: "What do you think? Should I be bold?" But before Trav could reply, he said quickly: "Never mind. I must make the decision." So Trav held his tongue; and after a moment Longstreet nodded.

"I'll give you a note to say that you will explain my views. Go to the Valley, find General Jackson. Tell him I propose, if he agrees, to lead a detachment of the army to join him for a quick strike at the force in front of him. Tell him why I suggest this. Bring me his answer." He turned to the table beside him, wrote hurriedly. "Here, this is all you will need," he said. "Go as soon as you can."

"Yes, sir."

Longstreet gave Trav the scribbled note unsealed, and fifteen minutes later Trav rode away. He had never seen General Jackson, knew little about him except that at Manassas he had turned a reproachful epithet into an honorable nickname. On that desperate field, General Bee, hard-pressed, sent to Jackson for help; but Jackson did not respond and General Bee, seeing the other's troops still motionless, cried: "Look at Jackson, still standing there like a damned stone wall!" Yet it was on that stone wall that Bee's driven regiments rallied, and the battle was won, and now Bee was dead; but he would be immortal because of that angry outburst that gave Jackson his sobriquet.

Trav had an impression that since then Jackson had made mistakes, had lost some minor engagements; but if Longstreet thought well of him, so did Trav. Jackson was reported now to be at Swift Run Gap. Trav went by rail to Orange Court-House, took horse from there and rode up the well-farmed valley of the Rapidan through Burtonville and on. Toward dusk he came down the long grade into Stanardsville; but as he drew nearer the mountains there were not so many farms, and ahead the tangled hills were dark with forest, so he lodged at Stanardsville that night, and was early on his way. Two miles or so beyond the town, while the heights on either side of the Gap rose high and higher ahead of him and he began to dread the long ascent, the road dipped into still another deep valley. He descended, then settled to the steady climb. More than once he had to breathe his horse before at last he reached the divide, and through the notch where the road cleft the forest he saw the blue reaches of the Valley far below.

The descent was easier; he came down to a crossroad, and saw dust to the north and turned that way. When by and by he overtook a marching column, he spoke to the mounted officer.

"The General?" the other echoed. "Why, sitting back there on the fence, watching us pass."

Trav turned back toward the man indicated; he rode near and dismounted, and secured his horse to the fence. The General, intent upon the troops in the road, had not yet looked toward him. Trav had unconsciously expected to see Jackson wear a visible dignity and grandeur. Instead, here was a shabby, dusty, bearded man with a dingy cap pulled low over his eyes, and wearing the biggest cavalry boots, presumably on the biggest pair of feet, that Trav had ever seen. The General perched on the fence with knees drawn up, heels on a rail; he was sucking at a lemon, his eyes upon the marching men.

Trav approached, saluted, stood waiting. When Jackson looked toward him in silent inquiry, he said, surprised to find himself suddenly hoarse: "Captain Currain, sir, of General Longstreet's staff, with a message from General Longstreet."

Jackson said softly: "Deliver your message."

Trav remembered the letter he carried; he produced it. The General turned it in one hand. The lemon was in the other. "Not sealed," he commented in a toneless voice that suggested disapproval. He fumbled the letter open, still with one hand, and read it slowly. Then he put the lemon into his mouth to free his hands and slowly tore the letter into little bits. A strong breeze was blowing; he tossed them into the air.

"Deliver your verbal message, Captain."

Trav, speaking by rote, repeated Longstreet's every word. The other did not interrupt till Trav was done; then he asked:

"You memorized that?"

"No, sir. I remembered it—the sense of it."

The General sucked hard at his lemon, looked at it reproachfully. "General Longstreet proposes to come to the Valley himself?"

" 'To lead a detachment' were his words."

The lemon again. "He ranks me," General Jackson remarked, as though thinking aloud. "But my men are used to me." He sat for a long time, head bowed, eyes shadowed; and Trav shifted his weight from one foot to the other, uneasy at this silence, till at last the General's shoulders lifted a little and he spoke.

"Tell General Longstreet you gave me his message, Captain."

Trav hesitated. "Is that all, sir?"

The other's head turned, and Trav under the impact of that glance felt his cheek burn. Jackson did not speak. Trav hurriedly saluted.

"Yes, sir," he said. He went to his horse and mounted, finding himself absurdly clumsy, hoping the other was not watching. As he passed where Jackson sat, he ventured a sidewise glance. The General was absorbed once more in watching the marching men who filled the road.

When Trav came back to Culpeper he saw eagerness in Longstreet's eyes, saw that eagerness fade as he reported Jackson's reply. The General nodded.

"He was unwilling to be ranked in his own territory," he commented. "In his place, I would no doubt feel as he does." After a moment he added: "If I were there and our strike failed, the blame would have been mine; but General Jackson would not fear blame for what he thought a promising move. Evidently he did not agree with my suggestion." He shook his head. "It is a pity, all the same. The Valley is our sally port. Through it we can hit them where they're tender. Well, another time, another time."

Of this matter, for the moment, no more was said. Longstreet had lost his old readiness for speech. To casual conversation he listened sometimes so inattentively that Trav thought Cinda was right in believing him a little deaf. When he did speak, however, in direction to his own officers, or in response to a question from General Johnston, it was firmly and positively. He seemed always completely sure of his own mind. One day Trav referred to this.

"Why, yes," Longstreet agreed. "That is true. I am sure of myself."

A faint hint of the old twinkle showed in his eyes. "A man, a man in authority, should be sure of himself. There's no advantage in knowing a thing unless you know you know it. I've been told that I am slow; but I believe in taking time to make up my mind. Once a man forms an opinion, it's hard for him to change it. It becomes his property, and his instinct is to defend it, not to question it and test it. So the wise man is slow to make up his mind because he knows that once he has done so it will be hard for him to change." He almost smiled. "Take McClellan now. He's decided to attack Richmond by the way of the Peninsula. If we make a move to threaten Washington, Lincoln will order McClellan to change his plans; and McClellan will be as distracted as a chicken with its neck wrung, making up his mind all over again." He said after a moment: "And we should try to do just that. Certainly we should do something! The longer we delay, the greater the odds against us."

The odds were already heavy enough. Regiments and companies were below their full strength; many furloughed men had not returned to duty; the hospitals were crowded, and there was a shortage of weapons so acute that even now, after almost a year of war, to arm some regiments with pikes instead of guns was seriously proposed. When the dark news of Shiloh came, Longstreet commented:

"That's 'Lys Grant again. If he were in McClellan's place he'd be in Richmond before summer. McClellan has a hundred thousand men on the Peninsula right now, and Magruder hasn't twenty thousand to hold him."

Magruder cried for reinforcements, and orders came for Longstreet to start his division toward the Peninsula. As the march began, Longstreet himself went with General Johnston and General Smith to Richmond to meet the President in council; and on the move Trav stayed one night at Cinda's. He found her troubled by the dangers in the wind and angry at the fa\hearts who were ready to despair.

"People are scurrying away, pretending it's just to escape the hot term," she told him. "But if you ask me, they're just plain scared, running off to hide in the mountains, or going south." She laughed shortly. "But I'm a fine one to talk! I'm scared myself! The only way I can get to sleep at night is to start thinking how I hate and de-

spise Abe Lincoln. It's like counting sheep! I get so mad I forget to
be scared."

"Faunt goes into a rage at the thought of him."

"How is he?"

"Well, he's pretty shaky. Tony tried to stand up for Lincoln, and
Faunt got pretty red, but Brett quieted him down."

"What in the world got into Tony?" She was suddenly as flushed
as Faunt had been that day at Great Oak. "If he ever tried that here,
I'd order him out of the house."

"Oh, he just said something about South Carolina secessionists being
as bad as Massachusetts abolitionists."

She nodded reluctantly. "Seceding was idiotic, of course; but that
white trash in Washington had no right to try to stop us." She added:
"Trav, Mr. Fleming writes from the Plains that someone is setting
fire to houses and corn cribs and barns around Camden."

"The negroes?"

"Mr. Fleming says not; says it's the sand hill tackeys. Speaking of
white trash made me think of it. No, Mr. Fleming says our people at
the Plains would fight for us, if we gave them guns."

Trav laughed grimly. "We haven't enough guns for our soldiers."

"We don't dare arm the negroes anyway. Travis, why should they
be loyal while we fight to keep them slaves?"

"I suppose it's their nature to—love their masters. Like dogs."

"I wish I could believe that! But anyway it's not the negroes who've
set the red cock crowing in the barns. Mr. Fleming says the tackeys
are excited by all the talk about conscription, claiming they'll be made
to fight the war while we get the benefit. The newspapers down there
are stirring up poor against rich, printing editorials about us riding
around in carriages while the wives of poor soldiers trudge along on
foot! Why shouldn't people use carriages if they have them, I'd like to
know?"

"Well, I'd rather see the horses hitched to my wagons," Trav admitted, and added jestingly: "But I'll let you and Mama keep your
carriages a while."

He rode away next day, following his trains toward Yorktown.
Longstreet that evening rejoined his division on the march, and Trav,

knowing the big man better every day, thought something had angered him. He was not surprised when at the first opportunity the General unburdened himself. He had been present when President Davis, General Lee, George Randolph, General Johnston, and General Smith discussed the situation confronting the Confederacy. Johnston thought the Peninsula indefensible; he wished to fall back to Richmond, stand on the defensive. "He'd abandon Norfolk, sink the *Merrimac,* open the James River to McClellan's gunboats, wait, wait, wait, let McClellan play his own game." Longstreet's tone was bitter.

Trav, thinking of his mother at Great Oak, asked: "Will they do that?"

"Not yet, at least. General Lee was for a delaying action on the Yorktown line to give us more time; and President Davis agreed with him." Trav nodded with relief at this postponement of the inevitable, and Longstreet added: "I like Lee. Johnston had his back hair up like an angry dog—he and Davis will never work together—but General Lee gentled him, calmed him."

"Did you offer any suggestion?"

Longstreet made a harsh sound. "I said nothing till an opinion was asked; then remarked that McClellan was deliberate, careful, slow. Before I could go on, President Davis interrupted me to praise McClellan to the skies. Obviously he wanted no proposal from me, so I made none." He added strongly: "Yet if we reinforced Jackson and threatened Washington, Lincoln would whistle McClellan home. The whole spring campaign against us would collapse."

Trav made no comment, and Longstreet repeated: "Yes, I was impressed by General Lee. His present position, keeping peace between President Davis and General Johnston, is a difficult one; but I believe he feels that with time to get ready we can beat McClellan here! I'd like to see him in command." His heavy fist clenched. "By the Almighty, Currain, it would be a satisfaction to have a leader who expected and sought victories." After a moment he added thoughtfully: "It's true Lee did nothing in Western Virginia; but in Mexico he knew how to find a way to win battles. I don't believe he has forgotten. I feel great, controlled strength in Lee. And—President Davis believes in him." The big man said with a strong vehemence: "We need a head, Currain. We need men and arms, of course; but the conscription act will surely pass, this week. That will keep in the army the men we have, and bring many more. It will end this whole question of twelve-months men going home when their terms expire. Yes, we'll manage for men. But, Currain, most of all we need a head! General Lee says every man in the South should be compelled to grow food or to fight! I tell you, General Lee is a man!"

When they were settled in their new position on the Yorktown line, Trav's duties gave him leisure for daily rides to Great Oak. He made the most of these opportunities for the week or ten days before Vesta's wedding. Faunt worried him. A persistent cough was presumably a relic of his illness; but also Faunt was more easily disturbed than Trav had ever seen him. When Trav spoke of the confusion in the encampment at Yorktown, where company and regimental elections were just now being held, Faunt said bitterly:

"You can be sure they won't elect good men. They want officers who ask favors, instead of giving orders." He seemed to quote. " 'Officers who can remember, sir, that they are addressing not slaves but gentlemen!' " Trav, seeing the other's burning eyes, tried to turn the talk to harmless things, but Faunt persisted. "Oh, I've seen them. The Blues, the new company, came down the end of March. The men I know best haven't been exchanged yet, but I've ridden over to see them. They're at Gloucester Point now. I'd like to be with them, but I'm weak as a kitten still. But Trav, they say the elections are ruining the army. New officers are no good, and the ones who are defeated resign and go home, so it's a loss both ways."

"Conscription will bring them back," Trav suggested; but Faunt said harshly:

"The Government can't conscript gentlemen!" A bit of coughing silenced him, and Trav watched him with concern.

On these frequent homecomings Trav delighted in the children. Peter was ten years old, a lively boy tremendously excited by great events preparing, hearing every day the sporadic cannonade at Yorktown, riding abroad to watch the soldiers marching or in their camps. Lucy was no longer a child, now at thirteen already wearing a sweet maturity, grave and quiet yet holding toward her father an unreserved affection which she did not hesitate to show. Trav found happiness with them, and with Faunt, too, but not with Enid. She made her distaste for his presence pitilessly clear. Once or twice he sought to win her to tenderness, but she met his affectionate advances with contempt. "For Heaven's sake don't try to be playful, Trav. You remind me of a capering elephant!"

His mother, in another way, equally defeated him. Trav wished to persuade Mrs. Currain to go to Richmond for Vesta's wedding; since, if she went, Cinda would keep her there and thus avoid the wrench that a forced departure from Great Oak would be. But Mrs. Currain could not be persuaded.

"I'm much too settled in my ways to go visiting," she declared. "Let Vesta bring her young man here to see me after they're married."

She was immovable, and when the time came, she stayed at Great Oak, and Enid in some baffling petulance elected to stay with her. The shift of the army from Northern Virginia to the Peninsula had brought Burr and Julian and Rollin and Tommy Cloyd to the camps between Williamsburg and Yorktown; and Trav and Faunt joined them for the ride to Richmond; and Burr was pleased because the First Virginia Cavalry had elected Fitz Lee colonel. "He's as good as Stuart," he said confidently. "They're always together whenever they can be." He laughed. "At West Point Colonel Lee always signed his name F. Lee, so they called him 'The Flea', and the nickname fits him. I expect he'll keep us jumping." And Burr added: "He's a great beau, too. They say he has a pocketful of rings ladies have given him."

"That's once when electing officers worked well, then," Trav suggested, and Burr agreed.

"Yes, there's no one any better than Fitz Lee."

They were all in festive humor that day, sharing Tommy's happiness, laughing at remembered incidents of the winter which had now yielded to the seductions of the flooding spring; and Julian was the most voluble of them all. "Winter seemed pretty hard at the time," he admitted. "But up north we could keep our huts clean, at least. When we came down here they put us in huts where some Louisiana men had spent the winter, and next day we were all scratching!" He laughed. "The Louisiana trash used to have louse races and bet on the winner. They'd put their vermin on pieces of canvas and the first one over the edge took the money. They had one race where each man put his louse on a tin plate, and one man heated his plate, so he won all the bets. We burned down the huts to get rid of the lice, as soon as the weather cleared, but I still itch!"

"I've found a few on myself," Burr admitted. "But don't tell Mama. She'd be scandalized!"

"Gosh, I won't tell anyone," Julian assured him. "I'm not bragging about it!" He told them about the famous battle of the frogs. A young officer, in the nervous hours of the night, heard splashing in the river, and thought the Yanks were coming. He ordered his men to open fire, and sent for reinforcements, and staged a lively skirmish till older heads checked the firing and a Yankee called derisively through the darkness: "Well, Rebs, how many frogs did ye kill with all that shootin'?"

Julian told them too how Colonel McKinney, who had been a professor at the academy in Charlotte, one day walked along the top of the wall of sandbags at Dam No. 2 in defiance of Yankee sharpshooters till a bullet crashed into his head. "You feel kind of naked," Julian declared, "with the Yankee balloons up in the air all day looking right down at you, seeing every move you make."

They found Brett and Tony in Richmond before them, and after the first hubbub of their arrival quieted, Brett drew Trav aside to speak of Great Oak, and Faunt and Tony followed them. "We'll hold Yorktown till McClellan is ready to attack," Trav said. "But he's getting siege guns into position, and we'll withdraw before he can use them. General Longstreet promises to let me know in time to get Mama away; but if we want to take anything out of the house we ought to do it now."

The big house was full of treasures that could not be left behind, and they made their plans to save what could be moved. Brett, since the Howitzers were now on duty in North Carolina and he must rejoin them, could not go to Great Oak; but Tony and Faunt would ride down Monday morning, and presumably Cinda and Tilda would want to go with them. These four would begin sorting and packing while Trav at Longstreet's headquarters waited to warn them when the army's retreat was to begin.

Next day, after the wedding, Brett left at once; and Sunday morning Trav and the younger men, Burr and Julian and Rollin, rode back to Yorktown. Not till they reached there did Trav hear that New Orleans had fallen. This word that the most populous city in the South had surrendered without resistance, this concrete demonstration of Northern power, was ominous and frightening. If one city fell, would not others topple, too? Might not the whole structure of the Confederacy be as easily overturned?

Monday he rode over to Great Oak for dinner, and his sisters and Faunt and Tony, after an early start from Richmond, reached there as soon as he. They too had heard of the loss of New Orleans. "Mrs. Randolph told us, after church yesterday," Cinda explained. "It's the worst news of all, isn't it, Travis? If the North can control the Mississippi they'll cut the Confederacy in two."

"It's bad, yes," he admitted. "But we've troubles closer home."

"I should say we have, right here at Great Oak," Tilda agreed. "But New Orleans was terrible. Trav, you know Mrs. Preston. They had lots of property in New Orleans." There was something almost greedy in Tilda's tones. "She says they're ruined! Just paupers!"

Enid had pleaded a headache and stayed in her room, and at dinner Mrs. Currain was gay with delight in this gathering of all her children around her. "I don't know when we've been together," she declared. "Just ourselves! Not even an in-law! Of course I'm fond of Enid and Brett, and Redford Streean, too, Tilda; but it's nice for once to just have my own children—and grandchildren of course." For Lucy and Peter were here. "I declare I don't know when I've been so pleased as having you all come and surprise me this way."

When she left them for that after-dinner nap which she never missed, Tony said wonderingly: "She didn't ask why we were here, why we were so solemn."

Cinda pressed her eyes with her finger tips as though to deaden pain. "So many old people have died, these last months, this last winter. Of broken hearts, perhaps, from seeing the sorrow all around. Maybe part of Mama, the part that can be hurt, has died. Do you notice how often she has that little burr, as though she were a girl again? I hope she never does realize what's going on."

During the crowded days that followed, Mrs. Currain wore a protective blindness, moving to and fro upon her morning routine without appearing conscious of the turmoil all around her. Enid still kept to her room; and Trav was too deeply absorbed to mark this and wonder at it. Till the army prepared to retreat he could use some of his wagons for transport; and at the big house Cinda and Tilda fell into a sort of frenzy that was half heartbreak, directing Uncle Josh and old Thomas and his son and Big Mill while they stowed in the wagons bureaus and armoires and wardrobes, pictures stripped from the walls, books from the shelves, silver and china packed with jealous care.

Before dinner on Tuesday the first train of wagons started for Richmond in Tony's charge. Everything was to be taken to Cinda's, where there was ample storage room. Tilda suggested that she would be glad to have and to use some of the furniture and china. "I know you won't want it, Cinda. Mahogany and walnut wouldn't go with your lovely things. But I'd like it."

Cinda said curtly: "After all, Mama isn't dead yet, Tilda!"

"Why, Cinda, I just thought——"

"I know what you thought! But as long as Mama's alive we won't start dividing up her things!"

Tilda bit her lip to hide the hurt, and Trav said, trying to reassure her: "Cinda's upset, Tilda. Don't let her make you unhappy." Tilda turned away, and Cinda tried to justify herself.

"She infuriates me, Travis, poking and prying everywhere, like a greedy little boy looking for goodies! Fondling everything like a miser!" She watched the wagons departing and caught her breath with a sound like a sob. "Oh, Travis, I'd like to get my fingers into Abe Lincoln's beard! I wonder if he knows how we hate him!"

Next day at Faunt's reminder the wine closet under the slope of the roof, where the sun's rays helped ripen the contents of casks and barrels, was emptied of its treasure. Old cognac, fine Madeira, peach brandy laid away sixty years before, apple brandy, hundreds of bottles of golden sherry, jugs and demijohns and kegs of gin and whiskey, all found their place; and packed in among the kegs and bottles went kitchen ware, feather beds, barrels of flour and salt meat and fish, beef, pickles, vinegar, jellies and jams, a full hundred hickory-smoked hams, sheets and table linen. The last of the furniture was lashed securely in the wagons; the caravan departed; the task was done.

That evening at headquarters Longstreet took Trav aside. "Currain, this is for your ear alone," he said. "I promised you due warning. General Johnston has decided to evacuate the lines here on Friday night." He added: "Ewell has finally been sent to the Valley; but it's too late for a diversion there. A month ago, yes; but now McClellan is ready to strike, so we'll retreat again."

Trav thought it best to ride back to Great Oak that night, to tell them this decision. He felt some concern, for now that the army was to move, his wagons would be needed. When he reached Great Oak, everyone was abed, but he roused the house; and to his relief he found that Tony had returned, that the wagons had halted for the night at Six-Mile Ordinary.

"You'll have to put whatever you have left into farm carts, or load it on mules," Trav told them. "I'll need all the army wagons tomorrow and next day." He spoke in quiet authority, shaping his plans as he shaped his words. "Mama and all of you must leave here tomorrow night at the latest."

Cinda protested: "But, Travis, you said Friday. We've still two days."

"Go tomorrow," Trav insisted. "The Yankees will be on our heels as soon as they know we're moving. I'll check over my books and papers tonight and pack what I want, in case I'm not able to come again."

Enid had not come down, but when Cinda and the others went back upstairs, Cinda called over the rail that Enid wished Trav to say good-by to her before he left, and he promised to do so. He spent hours at his desk in the plantation office, a small building a little apart from the house toward the south gardens, sorting out ledgers he wished to save and letters that should be preserved, and burning the rest. Before he finished, he was stupefied with fatigue, and he forgot Enid's request; but when he walked around the house to where Big Mill had kept watch beside his waiting horse, he saw a light in Enid's window and remembered.

Surely she must have gone to sleep long ago. The night was well spent, dawn not far away. Yet the thought of seeing her, even though only for a moment, was good, so he bade Mill wait a little longer and went indoors and softly up the stairs. If she were asleep he would not wake her, so his hand on the knob was light; but when he opened the door she was awake, lying in bed with a candle burning beside her.

He shut the door and came to the bedside. She said lightly: "Well, you were long enough! You knew I wanted to see you."

"I was busy till just now." He spoke in dull weariness. "I've got to go along."

"Where? Why?"

"Back to headquarters. To get our trains ready to move."

"You and your trains! I suppose the children and I can manage for ourselves, for all you care."

"Tony's here, and Faunt will be. They'll take care of you."

"Where do you expect us to go?" Her tone was cold as ice.

He had not considered this question, but there was only one present answer. "To Cinda's, I suppose, at least for the time being."

"I'm a little tired of being an unwelcome visitor!"

"Why, Cinda's glad to have you. And she has lots of room. Or you can go to Chimneys if you'd rather. Tony'll not mind."

She looked up at him with hot eyes. "I'll never go back there!"

He was too tired to think clearly, wished only to appease her. "There's no one but the overseer at the Plains, but I guess you could go there."

She said in a remote and empty tone: "You're a strange man, Trav. Doesn't it ever occur to you that you should have made a home for your wife and children a long time ago? After all, we've been married fourteen years, you and I."

"You've always had a home, Enid."

"At Chimneys? With no friends, no contact with people of my own kind? Or here, where I've been just an unpaid companion to your mother? And now you want me to be a visitor in your sister's house! You've never thought of me—except to turn to me as a hog turns to the trough."

"Well, what do you want me to do?"

"Nothing. I don't want you to do anything, Trav."

He shook his head in dull bewilderment. "Then I don't see what we're talking about."

She smiled. "I'm just coming to that, Trav. I've decided that I'm tired of being just your breeding wench. I'm going to leave you. That's what we're talking about. I'm never going to live with you again."

Either this was nonsense, or he was too tired to comprehend. "I don't know what you mean."

"I mean I'm going away."

"Away? Why, you've nowhere to go."

This seemed to him obvious; but at his word she sat up in bed with a movement so swift and sudden that the coverings fell away from her white shoulders and her bright hair caught the candlelight. "So?" she whispered furiously. "So?" Her hot words came in a torrent. "You think I'm a slave? You think that if I run away, you can have me fetched back and whipped and put in chains under lock and key?" Her voice rose in anger and scorn. "That's like you—you dull, un-thinking, blind lump of a man!" Rage choked her. "Oh, why can't you be gallant and gentle and fine like Faunt?"

He asked in new bewilderment: "What's Faunt got to do with it?" She lay down again, not answering, watching him with suddenly wary eyes; and when she did not speak he tried to find words. "I'm too tired to think straight, I guess. I'm sorry you're upset."

"Oh, I'm not upset."

"Well, what I'm trying to say— Well, I know the way you feel about me. Probably I'm not a very good husband. But I can't help being the way I am."

"Well, I can help living with you."

"I don't see how you can help it, Enid. After all, we're married."

"I won't stay married any longer. I'd rather be dead!" Her voice suddenly was shrill. "Dead, do you hear?"

"Well—you're not dead, Enid."

"No, and I'm not going to kill myself, either!"

"I don't see what you can do!" This was not complacency on his part; it was simply a confession. After all, what could she do?

She laughed. "Do? Why, I told you. I can leave you, darling. Women aren't as helpless as you think. Mama had nothing, after Papa died; but she's managed to get along."

"I thought she had your father's estate."

She laughed. "He had no more estate than a grasshopper! But

Mama's clever! She's ever so much cleverer than you, for that matter!
All you know is how to raise corn and tobacco and wheat and hogs;
and even then you turn the money over to Brett because you don't
know enough to take care of it! But my mother has made a home and
a fortune for herself." She hesitated and he thought she was about to
say something else, but she only said: "I'll go live with her. She'll be
glad to have me."

"She's mighty nice," he agreed. "I always liked her."

"Then why didn't you take care of her, instead of making her—instead of just leaving her without a penny to her name?"

He shook his head, ignoring that question. "If you did go to live
with her—" He hesitated. "Enid, are you talking about being di-
vorced? It doesn't seem as though I could let you do that."

"Let me?" Her word was lightly derisive. "How could you prevent
me, Trav?"

"Well, I don't know; but I don't think you can. I'm not a lawyer,
but I don't think you can."

She said, in an almost friendly tone: "And of course it would be a
disgrace to the Currains if I did, wouldn't it? But I won't disgrace
you, unless you feel disgraced by my leaving you."

"What about Lucy and Peter?"

"You can get Vigil back to take care of them. You always thought
she was so wonderful!" His eyes struck her like a blow and she added
hastily: "Oh, I just mean with the children, of course! You can do as
you choose with the children, darling." The endearing word was a
lash across his cheek. "They hate me as much as I hate them." And
she said in a casual, reflective tone: "I may decide to help in the hospitals." She smiled. "Wouldn't that be fun, Trav? If you get shot, if
a cannon ball cuts off your leg or something, I might even take care
of you! I liked taking care of Faunt. If you were hurt badly enough
I might even like you!"

"Well, I reckon they'll need all the help they can get in the hospitals,
when fighting starts."

"Of course, dear." He heard the mocking in her tones. "So you'd be
proud of me, instead of feeling disgraced, wouldn't you? So it's all
settled."

He considered this, his thoughts plodding. Settled? For her to leave him, for him to see her no more? Yet if she went away she would be no farther from him than for months past she had been. And how could he keep her if she wished to go? "I reckon I can't stop you," he admitted.

"No, you can't stop me, Trav."

Let her go. Let her go. He had had so many hurts from her. Let her go. "I'll see you don't want for money."

"Of course you will, darling! After all, you wouldn't like your wife to be a beggar on the streets of Richmond. Would you?"

He rose slowly. "Well, all right. I have to go back to headquarters." He hesitated, felt his own inadequacy. Some men in such an hour as this would know what to say, what to do; but for the life of him he could think of nothing that seemed worth saying, or doing. "Well, good-by," he said.

"Good-by."

"I reckon you don't want me to kiss you."

"I reckon I don't," she drawled.

He turned away, but from the hall he heard her chiding voice. "Trav, you forgot to close the door." When he came back to do so, she spoke again. "I won't make it too pointed, of course," she promised. "I'll go to Cinda's first; and after a few days I'll tell her I'm going to visit Mama, and then I'll just stay on at Mama's."

"Have you told Mrs. Albion what you're going to do?"

"Oh no, darling." She smiled in derisive amusement. "You're the very first to know!"

This time, when he went out, he latched the door.

34

TILDA came to Great Oak with a lively anticipation. If the big house were to be abandoned to Yankee occupancy, if she and Cinda and her brothers were to remove from it everything they wished to preserve, then many coveted things might fall to her share. The house in Richmond that had been her wedding present was furnished with makeshifts, for Streean thought there were better ways to spend money than for gewgaws; but Great Oak was full of beautiful things, and Cinda already had more than she needed. So Tilda expected a lavish bounty; and when Cinda flatly rejected her suggestion that some of the furniture be sent to her house she was miserable with despair.

But Cinda, to her delight, relented. Thursday morning, after Enid and old April and the children had been sent off in Mrs. Currain's second-best carriage to Richmond, Cinda said frankly: "Tilda, I was horrid to say what I did to you. I mean about Mama's things. When we get home you pick out what you want. They might as well be used, till we can open up Great Oak again."

Tilda was confident that temporary possession would become permanent. Probably Mama would not live much longer. She was already in her dotage, ridiculously pretending that all this turmoil was no more than an incident of spring housecleaning. Redford said the war would last for years, and that before it was over they would be wealthy. And before it was over, Mama would certainly be dead; and even if Enid and Trav came back to live at Great Oak, Tilda meant to hold fast to everything on which now she could lay her hands.

She was greedily happy as a bee in a newly discovered garden; and her happiness—which she hid behind a doleful countenance—was accented by Cinda's sadness at this disruption of everything in their lives which had seemed so settled and secure. Cinda, Tony, Faunt, Trav and Enid, they had always had so much more than she. Now they were losing and she was gaining. Let them grieve! She was as busy as a terrier, trotting through the empty rooms, nosing into every closet and cupboard. Trav had said they should all start for Richmond this evening, but she delayed them, insisting that there was still so much to do.

"We're sure to overlook something if we hurry," she argued; and since there was a threat of rain that might be avoided by delay she prevailed upon Cinda to wait till Friday and make the journey by daylight. Mrs. Currain, although she had accepted the suggestion of a visit to Richmond calmly enough, that morning developed an unsuspected obstinacy. Faunt had not yet returned and she said they must wait for him. Also, Trav would surely ride over to see her depart. Probably he would come for dinner, and Faunt would be here by that time, so they had better all stay and have dinner here.

Tilda welcomed the further delay, since she was by no means satisfied that she had investigated every nook and corner; and Tony was willing to humor his mother. So Cinda was overborne and they stayed on. Faunt did arrive for dinner, but not Trav. "I've been over to see him, and he was too busy to come, Mama," Faunt explained; but when after dinner Mrs. Currain insisted on her nap, he told the others: "Trav thinks you've gone. He won't be over. The withdrawal will begin tonight; but Trav had to get all the sick and the wounded off to Richmond first, and see the ordnance and rations loaded, and put all the division's baggage on the road before the army moves." He said the Richmond Turnpike was deep with mud. "And it will be worse tomorrow. We ought to get started as soon as we can."

Mrs. Currain was slow in waking, and Cinda while they waited gave way briefly to tears. She and Tilda were alone, Tony and Faunt belowstairs. "I'd almost rather stay," she confessed. "It's like pulling up our roots, Tilda."

Tilda saw, laid with Cinda's cloak and bonnet, two bundles; one was small, one was long and wrapped in oilcloth. "What are those?" she asked, jealously curious.

"The little bundle's an old rag doll I had when I was a baby. I couldn't bear to leave it." Cinda's eyes were streaming. "The long thing is Papa's sword. Mama wants me to give it to Travis, because he used to love to play with it when he was a little boy."

"Why, Cinda! Then she knows what's happening!"

"Of course she does!" Cinda spoke through sobs. "Letting on that she doesn't is just her way of being brave. Oh, she's so darling. I could blubber like a baby!"

Tilda pretended a sadness she did not feel. "So could I! Every little thing reminds me of so many things I'd forgotten." From the window she saw in the early twilight of this cloudy, threatening day the fine new carriage draw up to the door. Old Thomas was on the box, young Tom beside him. From the quarter some of the people, carrying bundles or leading mules laden with their small belongings, came toward the big house. "The carriage is ready," she said.

Cinda decided to wake Mrs. Currain. She dried her eyes, splashed her face, went to her mother's room. Tilda picked up the packet which Cinda had said was a doll, and turned it in her hand, wanting to laugh. How ridiculous for a woman Cinda's age to be so sentimental! She too had had dolls, when she was a girl; and she remembered seeing one of them, a ridiculous thing made out of a corn cob, in the chest of drawers in the attic, and she decided to go and get it. She could be as sentimental as Cinda, if it came to that!

It was dark enough so that she took a candle when she climbed the attic stairs. The drawer in which she remembered seeing the doll, when she tried to open it, stuck; she tugged and jerked and could not move it. So she drew out the next drawer above and laid it on the floor and lifted the candle to peer in through this opening for the doll she sought.

When she did so, she saw that two boards, one thinner than the other, ran from side to side across the rear end of this drawer. They were an inch or so apart; and the space between them looked as though it might have been designed as a hiding place. At full stretch of her arm she was able to slide her fingers down into this crevice, and touched something, and managed to lay hold on it and draw it out.

It was a packet wrapped in yellowed paper and tied with a string. Tilda in the liveliest curiosity knelt on the floor, set the candle beside her, and untied the knot. Within were half a dozen folded sheets of paper of varying sizes. Tilda unfolded the uppermost. There was a date at the top, 1781. The letter itself was written in a different hand, yet despite an occasional misspelled word it was easy enough to read.

Dear Tony, Mrs. Dodsworth is writing this for me. Mr. Cavett is going to Virginia, so I will send these few lines by him to carry to you if he can. Tony, Pa moved to Mike's Run, it is a little dreen runs into Patterson crick Mr. Cavett will tell you where. Tony, I guess you have forgot the little girl that loved you but she didn't forget you. She still loves only you, Tony. If you want to fetch her, Mr. Cavett will tell you where to come. Pa says he will shoot you sure, so come careful. I don't want him to hurt you but if you don't come I will die pretty soon I guess. Ma says I am prettier but thin as a shadder. We been here since summer now since two weeks after the last time I saw you. Pa fetched me away on account of you. Come soon as you can to your Lucy.

Lucey Hanks

The signature was scrawled in an uncertain hand. Tilda before she finished was breathless with a heart-shaking excitement. Without waiting to fold that letter she opened the next. This too had a date, 1784; the body of the letter again was in a different hand.

Tony, dear husband, because you are, for me anyway, because we said so to each other is all that matters. Tony, Pa is going west taking us. He don't even speak to me because I stand up to him. He's got the misry in his jynts. Tony, our baby is sweet, a little girl. Tony, you don't know about her because I couldn't send word and I thought you'd surely come before now. I don't know where we're going this time only west but Mrs. Dodsworth says she'll send you this letter. She's writing it because I can't write good yet. I'll send word first chance where we go to, so you can come and fetch your baby and your Lucy. Tony I have named her Nancy after Ma. Pa don't know for sure it's yours. He says he's going to kill whoever it was if he finds out but I will never tell him. Pa is a hard man and worse since he got the misry but I am as hard as he is when I git mad and I do.

Your loving wife, Lucey Currain

This time, too, the signature was a laborious scrawl. Tilda snatched up the third letter. It was short, her greedy eyes read it at a glance; but then Trav called from belowstairs, a shouted summons. "Tilda!"

She had forgotten the waiting carriage, her mother and the others ready to set out for Richmond. If Trav were here, he had come to tell them they must hurry away; but they must wait to hear these letters! She wanted to watch their faces as they listened to this fine morsel of scandal from her father's youth. She caught up all the letters and the candle, and scrambled to her feet. On the way down the attic stairs she made such haste that the candle blew out, but there was light enough. From the stair head she saw them all in the hall below, Trav and Tony and Faunt, Cinda and her mother, dressed for their journey. Candles flickered in the tall stand there.

She ran down the stairs, crying out in her excitement, panting, scarce able to speak. "Listen! Look!" She waved the sheaf of letters. "I found these in that old chest of drawers in the attic. Mama! Cinda! I can't believe—— The most horrible thing! I——"

Cinda grasped her arm. "Tilda, we're starting!"

"But we can't!" Tilda cried. "We can't till you hear! Listen! Let me read! They're letters to Papa from some wretched girl named Lucy."

"Lucy?" Mrs. Currain echoed the word; and she seemed for a moment to lose her balance, seemed about to fall. Trav caught her arm, and holding fast to him she sat down in the tall chair beside the candle stand, nervously adjusting her bonnet and her shawl. Her frail old hands were shaking. "Named Lucy," she repeated.

"Lucy, yes," Tilda exclaimed. "Some nasty hussy! Oh, Mama——"

Trav said urgently: "Tilda, you have to get to the pike before the trains."

But Mrs. Currain leaned back in the big chair. "Letters? From someone named Lucy?" Her voice was soft. "We can wait. Read them to us, Tilda."

The candles beside the old woman's chair gave light enough. Tilda pressed close, fumbling with the sheets of paper in her hands, and began to read.

35

MRS. CURRAIN meant to listen, but at once the words Tilda read awoke so many memories. These were letters from a girl named Lucy to that Anthony Currain whom she herself had married—how long ago? They were married in eighteen hundred and seven, and this was eighteen hundred and sixty-two. How long ago was it?

Travis could tell her instantly the answer to that question. He was always quick at figures. Yet figures meant so little. To these children of hers, who would always be children to her though they were now in their middle years, eighteen hundred and seven was a long time ago; but not to her. Why, she could still smell the Cape jessamine that had been in bloom outside the door of the church the day she and Anthony were married. This girl who wrote the letter which Tilda now was reading called him Tony, but she herself had always called him Anthony, or Mr. Currain. She could hear even now the merry voices and the laughter of their wedding party; she could see the little dust of snuff that Anthony always seemed to have on his waistcoat, and the silver knob on the cane he carried; she could taste the wine in which she toasted him with the others, after they had all toasted the bride and before she and Anthony stood smiling while their joint healths were drunk. Was that long ago? Why, how absurd! No, it was yesterday!

She remembered herself and Anthony in the carriage with Moses proudly on the box. Moses was a fine-looking darky. As soon as she was mistress here, she made him leave the stables and come into the house as her butler. But of course he was dead many a year ago, and now Uncle Josh was in his place. She and Anthony came to Great Oak in the fine carriage, and Anthony lifted her in his arms to carry her across the threshold into this very hall.

Her eyes turned all around; she looked once more, knowing this would be the last time, at the familiar scene. She had never seen anywhere such a wide, high-ceiled hall as this. "Big enough," Anthony told her on that happy wedding day, "big enough so Moses could drive the carriage in one door and out the other, if the doors were as wide and high as the hall." The hall ran clear through the house. Once Anthony had told her that this huge old mansion was in its design a big brother of the "dog-run" cabins of the Carolina mountains. There, humble men built a one-room shanty, and by and by as their families grew larger they built another room, with a narrow passage between the two through which if he chose a dog might run. Here at Great Oak and elsewhere across the South, as men prospered, those small cabins became larger units at first of two rooms and then of four or more; the passage was roofed over to serve as a hall; second stories were added, and attics, and stairs were set in the passage to reach those upper rooms—and so, by and by, you had such a noble house as this here at Great Oak, where she had lived so long, had known such happiness and sorrow, such anguish and such bliss, such peace and pain.

Yet sitting here tonight, half-listening to Tilda's trembling words, watching the others, she thought happiness had outweighed all else. Anthony was not always happy, to be sure; there were days when he did not smile, when his thoughts seemed to be haunted by irrevocable sorrow and she had to cheer him as she could. When things went well, he was merry enough, tender or teasing, ardent or gay; but when sadness came to them he brooded and grieved. Yet on the whole they were happy, living the rich and serene life which went with these great homes, calling upon their friends, receiving callers in their turn, visited and visiting, loving each other, loving their children.

Probably they were as happy as two people could be, when a man of forty-two married a girl of nineteen. Travis, like his father, had married a girl much younger than himself; and Mrs. Currain was not so blind as she pretended to be to the friction between him and Enid. That was probably inevitable when husband and wife were a generation apart. Yet somehow she had never thought of Anthony as old, not even in those last days before he died, when he kept his bed, immersed in sorrow and shame for Tony's sake after Tommy Williber was drowned. No, Anthony never seemed old to her. He was in most ways, in his easy gaiety and his easy despair, in his heedless happiness and his sudden depressions, in his lack of foresight and his remorse for the past, more boy than man, as unstable and as charming as a child.

Yes, this big old house had been all her life a happy place for her; this familiar home which was now as empty as a blown egg, as an oyster's rifled shell. Everything that was easily portable was gone out of it. This great chair in which she sat was so old, the upholstery so worn, that it would be left behind; and the candle stand beside it was like a tree, too tall for any ordinary home. Through the door diagonally opposite, Mrs. Currain could see faded window hangings not worth taking down, the corner of the heavy oak table which would have needed the strength of four men to move. Here and there through the house other things had been left, to be defiled perhaps by Yankee hands; but almost everything was gone.

Though she had armed herself against grief by pretending not to understand the activity of the last few days, that armor was pretense and nothing more. Of all that was happening and of every detail of her familiar surroundings here, Mrs. Currain was in this hour acutely conscious; and of all this which she loved she took farewell. She would always think of this house as the hearth in the room which was her life; the hearth on which glowed a warm fire of familiar tenderness. It was true that beyond the fireglow lay waiting shadows; but one could look only at the fire, and turn one's back upon the shadows and forget that they were there.

This was her home; here grouped around her were her children. She watched them, scarce hearing for a while Tilda's excited words.

"I haven't read all these letters yet," Tilda explained as she began. She spoke with haste, catching her breath. "I went up to the attic to get an old doll I had when I was a baby. I knew it was in that big chest of drawers. You know, Mama; the one with the glass drawer pulls and the broken leg. I accidentally pulled one of the drawers clear out, and these letters were in the back end of the drawer below, in a secret place, tucked away where no one would ever see them, tied together with a piece of string."

Mrs. Currain remembered that she had not used that chest of drawers since before Anthony died. Once it had been his wardrobe, had
held his linen; but some of the glass handles were cracked, and when
the leg was broken, Anthony bought a new chest and had the old one
put away in the attic.

Tilda's voice ran on. "The first letter was written sometime in
seventeen eighty-one. How old was Papa then, Mama?"

Mrs. Currain had no need to speak, for Travis answered. "He was
born in seventeen sixty-five. He'd have been sixteen in 'eighty-one."

"Well, anyway," Tilda repeated, "this is the first letter." She held
the paper nearer her eyes, peering at the sometimes faded ink. Mrs.
Currain thought Tilda, despite her pretense of shocked dismay, was
happy as she read. The old woman listened with only half her mind.
The letter was to someone called "Dear Tony." That must have been
Anthony. Something about Mike's Run, and Patterson Creek, and a
man named Cavett, and Tilda was saying the letter was badly spelled,
and something about a little girl who loved Tony, but whose Papa
would shoot Tony, but who would die if Tony didn't come to her
pretty soon. Tilda was giggling as she read, in a silly, embarrassed
way, and the letter was signed Lucy Hanks, and as Tilda finished,
Faunt took it from Tilda's hands and looked at it and said Lucy was
spelled L-u-c-e-y, and Tony said in a puzzled tone that the name was
vaguely familiar, that he had heard of a girl named Lucy Hanks somewhere, and Tilda began to read another letter.

"This one is marked seventeen eighty-four," she said; and Mrs.
Currain came back from her memories to listen.

" 'Tony, dear husband, because you are, for me anyway, because we
said so to each other is all that matters. Tony, Pa is going west taking
us. He don't even speak to me because I stand up to him. He's got
the misry in his jynts.' " Tilda's exaggerated mispronunciation made
the spelling clear. " 'Tony, our baby is sweet——' "

Cinda cried in quick protest: "Baby?" She came protectingly to her
mother's side. "Mama, don't you believe a word of it!"

Mrs. Currain smiled reassuringly. "Oh, that was long ago, Cinda,
before I ever knew him. Why I wasn't even born, in seventeen eighty-
four. And your father told me about this girl. He used to say, to tease

me, that he fell in love with me because my name was Lucy; that his first sweetheart had been a girl named Lucy."

Cinda protested: "But did he tell you she'd had a baby?"

"Not in words," Mrs. Currain admitted. Memories for a moment swept her away, little moments came back to her. "But I was sure she had, from—well, from the way he spoke of her." Travis, concern in his tones, urged again that they start their journey and wait till they came to Richmond to read the other letters; but Mrs. Currain said: "No, we're all together here, and there's no knowing when we'll be together again. Go on, Tilda."

She heard Tilda repeat that phrase Cinda had interrupted. " 'Tony, our baby is sweet, a little girl.' " Her thoughts drifted back through the years, returned again when Tilda read: " 'I have named her Nancy after Ma.' " That made Mrs. Currain wince with unconquerable pain; for when her own little girl was born—her third baby, the one before Travis, the one who died when she was four months old—Anthony had insisted that they name her Nancy. Probably that was why he was so wretched and blamed himself so bitterly when that baby died.

Through Mrs. Currain's memories came Tilda's dramatic cry: "And this time she signed the letter: 'Your loving wife, Lucy Currain.' "

Mrs. Currain felt all their eyes turn questioningly upon her. She said serenely: "They were never married. I'm sure of that. He would have told me."

Cinda by her mother's side stirred in protective impatience. "Go on, Tilda. Finish."

"Well, this next one, she wrote herself," Tilda explained. "It's a terrible scrawl, but it's short." She read: " 'Tony, husband, see I can write good now.' She spells it r-i-t-e," Tilda added, and went on: " 'Pa brung us to Kentucky in Nelson County here a month now. Mister Booth come with us is going back to Virginny will take this so please be sartin and come here soon to yore Lucy.' " Tilda added: "Lucy's L-u-c-e-y. Her spelling is just ridiculous, with no capital letters at all. or they're in the wrong places. Look at it!"

Cinda took the letter, but Mrs. Currain said gently: "Poor child. Your father never went to Kentucky."

Tilda echoed: " 'Poor child' indeed! If you think she deserves sympathy just listen to this next one! I was reading it when you called me.

It was written in seventeen eighty-seven; I guess it was Papa who put the dates on them. She wrote it herself, and she'd learned a little about spelling by that time, but not much. Just listen!" No one interrupted her and she read rapidly, pausing now and then to puzzle over words.

"'Well, Tony, Mister Maynard came from Virginny—'" Her emphatic mispronunciation was eloquent. "'Came from Virginny says you got married to a put on lady with fine airs . . .'"

Tilda looked at her mother with questioning eyes, and Mrs. Currain said gently: "She means Sally Williber. Seventeen eighty-seven? Yes, that's the year they were married."

"I knew she didn't mean you, Mama," Tilda agreed, and repeated: "'To a put on lady with fine airs so this is a curse on you Tony from her who loved you. First off I had an idy—' She spells 'idea' that way, i-d-y. 'An idy to drownd myself but I ain't one to cry over a no good dog. If you come now I would let Pa shoot you and laugh only to waste good powder and shot on a pore stink skunk like you. Well I've got your hedge baby Nancy and she'll have plenty of brothers and sisters I'll get the same way I got her because I can find plenty of men to—'" Tilda blushed. "I can't read some of this! It's horrible." Yet Mrs. Currain thought her eyes skimmed the lines with an avid eagerness before she continued. "She says: 'If I've got the name I'll have the game. I set out to drownd Nancy but she's so cute I couldn't but if she ever shows any signs of you I'll drownd her like a sick kitty. You'll not be the only man with me from now on, and every last one of them I'll tell them to spit on the ground and step on it, and that's for you. I hope you rot and—' Oh, I can't! Here, Trav, you read it."

So Trav took the letter, and found her place and read in flat, expressionless tones: "'I hope you rot and scab over and your children put you out to starve. I'll put a witch curse on you the rest of your life.'" He paused, looking at the letter in his hands. "That's enough, No need of reading what she says at the end."

Mrs. Currain nodded understandingly. "Poor Anthony. I can see now that he never forgot this bitter, heartbroken letter. When our son died—the baby after you, Tony—and then our daughter two years after that, he told me there was a curse on him. This must be what he meant. But when Trav was born and then you, Cinda, he cheered up wonderfully. I suppose he thought the old curse had been lifted."

Tilda, already scanning another letter in her hand, cried out in dismay. "Oh, this one is even worse. I can't—here, Trav!"

She thrust the sheet of paper at Trav, yet Mrs. Currain thought Tilda was reluctant at thus surrendering the limelight. Cinda urged: "Let's just tear them all up and forget about them, Mama!" Trav was scanning the yellowed sheet in his hand. "Is it awful, Travis?"

"Why, yes," he admitted. "I can't help feeling sorry for her, but there's no sense in reading it."

Mrs. Currain said calmly: "Give them to me, Travis." He obeyed her. "There are two more," she commented, added in a faint teasing chuckle: "I'll read them myself, make sure there's nothing here you children shouldn't hear." She added in a low tone, her head tipped back and resting against the tall chair: "I remember the day your father died. We thought he was asleep, and left him alone, and then found him dead at the head of the attic stairs. He had lighted the fire in his room. I suppose he tried to go up and get these letters and burn them before he died, but climbing the stairs was too much for him. He must have kept them hidden away all those years."

They did not speak and she began to puzzle out the letter in her hand. Her husband had written at the top the year, 1790. There was no salutation.

"Well, Tony, the grand jury presented me for fornikation I told you Id pay you off and I done it. Pa disoned me sez he cut me out of his will long ago account of you, but theres good men in the world in spite of you mister Sparrow is a good man and aims to marry me and Ill let him I signed the sertificut to marry him so there wont be any more bastuds like your Nancy after all. I aint gethered enny yet but it want for lack of trying but I have to wait a year to marry mister Sparrow and I hope you lay awake nites swetting wundering what I'm doing Nancy takes after you only shes reel sweet and good, only shes dark complected like you and lanky and gray eyes like you and a bulgy forrid."

Mrs. Currain's eyes closed. "Dark complected like you and lanky and gray eyes like you and a bulgy forrid." The words brought to life that Anthony who had been her husband; through her closed lids she seemed to see him. He too was dark and tall, as dark and tall as Tony;

and both Tony and Tilda had inherited that slightly protuberant forehead.

Cinda touched her hand. "Mama, don't—hurt yourself so! Let's just tear them up!"

"Oh, I'm all right." Mrs. Currain finished the letter at a glance.

"Shes six years old now. I never put your name on her nobuddy knows it here Pa nor enny of us ever named you. You aint worth a name only a bad one."

The letter was signed: 'Lucey Hanks the Fornikater.' Mrs. Currain handed it to Cinda. "It won't hurt any of you to read it," she said. There was one letter more; she looked at it absently. The date "1809," in her dead husband's hand, was nineteen years later than the letter she had just read. "No reason you shouldn't read all of them," she repeated. "You're adults. And—he was your father, and this baby of his was your sister, in a left-handed fashion."

Cinda asked wonderingly: "Do you believe all this, Mama?"

"Yes," Mrs. Currain assured them. "Your father was no saint. And he was—well, a weakling, in many ways. I always knew that, no matter how much I loved him." She smiled a little. "This other Lucy seems to have been a high-headed, strong-willed young woman. If he'd had the courage to marry her, she might have made a man out of him."

While the others, grouping in the candlelight, puzzled out among them the letter she had just read to herself, she scanned the last one of all.

"Well Tony I guess I've got over hating you so I thought Id rite you a few lines to tell you youve got two grandchildren out here in Kentucky."

Her eyes, at that word, closed again. Grandchildren? Swarming thoughts flew like darting swallows through her mind. Grandchildren? Then Anthony's daughter, that "dark-complected" Nancy, had had children; and she herself was their step-grandmother, just as she was grandmother to Trav's children, and to Cinda's, and to Tilda's. She groped through degrees of kinship. Were they cousins, half-cousins, step-cousins? No matter; they were all blood kin. Anthony was the link that bound them all together, for "dark-complected" Nancy Hanks was half-sister to Cinda and Tilda, to Tony and Travis and Faunt.

Mrs. Currain nodded and read another line, two lines.

"Nancy got married to Tom Lincoln here two years ago."

Tom Lincoln? Mrs. Currain paused again. In these terrible months, this year just past, she had heard more than she admitted of the talk around her. Lincoln? This man whom they all hated so bitterly was named Lincoln. But not Tom Lincoln. She was glad of that. The man they hated was not Tom Lincoln. It was Abraham Lincoln they abhorred. Reassured, her eyes returned to the letter.

"Tom worked with Joe my brother carpentering and got to know her that way. They live an all day walk from here so I don't see her much. She waited longer than most to git married. Nobody wanted her. She's kind of bony and not much to look at, and she don't laugh for days on end, only other times shes full of jokes and fun. She was second choice for Tom. He wanted Sarah Bush, but Sarah married Dan Johnson so he took up with Nancy to show Sarah she werent the only one but they named their first one Sarah all the same, and Marm Peggy Walters come by last week one day and said shed helped Nancy have her second. She says its as ugly a young one as she ever did see, all black and scrawny. They named it Abraham after Toms father. I married Mister Sparrow like I told you. Weve a houseful now.

"Lucy Sparrow"

Mrs. Currain noted absently that this girl had learned to spell, even while she read the last three lines again, stunned by the impact of that name. Abraham? Why, then the baby's name was Abraham Lincoln! Abraham Lincoln!

She came slowly to comprehension, touched with sharp terror. Abraham Lincoln, born to a bony, dark-complected somebody who married Tom Lincoln when he turned to second-best; Abraham Lincoln whom these children of hers held responsible for all their present griefs; that Abraham Lincoln was her dead husband's grandson!

What would these her children do when they knew? What would this knowledge do to them? To Tony, all his life so dissolute and shameful in his ways, till in these late years he had somehow acquired a belated manhood; to Trav, so steady and dependable; to Cinda, so admirably strong and wise, so sharp of tongue to hide her tender heart; to Tilda, affectedly humble yet rotted with a canker of envy she could not wholly hide; to Faunt, so gentle, so fine, and yet with a strain of self-pity and an egotistic and sentimental weakness long since recognized.

What would this knowledge do to them? An overwhelming billow of fear for them swept Mrs. Currain's strength away. The letter slipped from her limp fingers to the floor, and Faunt stooped and picked it up and began to read it. The others gathered around him, reading over his shoulders. She might bid them stop and thus protect them against this revelation; but—they were grown men and women, not children dependent on her tender guardianship.

Let them read, let them know. It was too late, now, to snatch the truth away.

After a moment, breaking through her weary thoughts, came their sudden stir, their sharp and startled words. Cinda was first to speak. "Abraham! Abraham Lincoln! Oh, Travis!" How like Cinda in that first anguish to cry out Travis' name! These two had always been closest joined of any of her children.

Then Tilda: "Heavens and earth! Mama, how terrible!" Yet even in that moment Mrs. Currain thought there was malicious joy in Tilda's tone.

Then Faunt, in a hoarse voice: "Great God Almighty!" Such rage in him that his words seemed to sear the air.

Then Trav, steady as always, turning as always to the solace of figures. "Eighteen-nine, this letter says. That would make him fifty-one now. Does anyone know how old he is? Tony, remember that book you had about Lincoln, before he was elected? Did it say—wait! It said his mother's name was Lucy, Lucy Hanks. Not Nancy. Not if the book was right."

Tony laughed, and Mrs. Currain thought his sudden empty mirth was like the derisive laughter of the old, shameful Tony. "Probably they didn't know who his mother was—any more than they knew who his grandfather was!" His eye went mockingly from one to another.

Faunt tried to speak; then as though his mouth was full of bitterness, he spat, stepping toward the hearth. Cinda appealed to Mrs. Currain.

"Mama, you don't believe it, do you?"

Mrs. Currain nodded. "Yes. I remember so many little things your father told me. Yes, I'm sure it's true."

Tilda cried: "We mustn't ever tell anyone!"

Faunt moved purposefully, and they watched him. With a rancorous deliberation he collected all the letters and he tore them in small bits, and crumpled them in a mass and laid them on the bare hearth. Then he wrenched a candle from the tall stand and touched the flame to the fragments; and with the candle end he stirred the bits of paper till they were all burning, the hot candle grease hissing and spitting as it dripped into the little blaze they made. No one spoke. When the last flame died, Faunt ground the black ashes to dust under his foot, then flung the still burning candle violently into the fireplace. It broke, the two halves held together by the wick rolling toward him in a crippled, uneven fashion like a man with a broken leg trying to crawl to safety. He kicked it furiously away. Mrs. Currain thought: Why, he's like a small boy in a temper!

Tony laughed again, and Faunt turned toward him with death in his eyes; but Mrs. Currain said quietly: "That will do. We should start for Richmond."

She rose and drew her cloak around her; and under the familiar compulsion they followed her. Outside the door old Thomas waited by the carriage, young Tom standing at the horses' heads; and along the driveway those of the people who had not yet been sent away were gathered, ready to follow the carriage. Their eyeballs shone white in the glare of the torches made of lightwood splinters.

Mrs. Currain felt a surge of affection for these old friends. They would follow their white folks, preferring bondage to the freedom the Yankees might bring. They led a few mules; their small belongings were packed on the backs of the animals or in bundles ready to be swung over their own shoulders.

Big Mill had the horses, Trav's and Faunt's and Tony's. Trav paused at the foot of the steps, and when he spoke Mrs. Currain thought she understood.

"I wish you'd started off for Richmond this morning," he said. She supposed he meant that to have done so would have saved them from this revelation; but when he went on, she realized she was wrong, for he explained. "The whole army's on the move tonight. All the roads from Yorktown to Williamsburg are filled, and wagons were wheel-to-wheel in town, even on those wide streets, when I came through. They'll have to go single file on the stage road to Richmond, and if the carriage gets into that line it can't go any faster than they do." He considered alternatives. "We might try Barrett's Ferry; but I think we can take the back road, hit the stage road at Six-Mile Ordinary and maybe be ahead of the trains." He appealed to his brothers. "What do you think?"

Tony said carelessly: "Whatever you say!" Mrs. Currain felt a sharp pain stab her heart, for his voice held a tone she recognized. Faunt went to his horse and from the saddlebags ripped a small flask. She saw him tip it, drain it, hurl it splinteringly against the wall beside the door; and she thought again that he was like a small boy in a tantrum! The thought was almost comforting. Childish tempers quickly ran their course; Faunt would presently be himself again.

But Tony? When he spoke just now she had been reminded of the old, evil Tony who had brought her so much sorrow in the past. "Help me, Travis," she said, and Trav handed her into the carriage; Tilda and Cinda took their places with her.

Trav told old Thomas: "Follow along after me." The Negro assented, and Trav mounted, and Tony and Faunt too. Big Mill swung his great bulk atop his mule. Through the open front door of the great house Mrs. Currain saw the candles still burning in the hall, and she called out of the carriage window that someone must make sure they were extinguished. Faunt answered her.

"I'll tend to it," he said curtly. His horse reared under his hard hand upon the reins; he dismounted, strode into the lighted hall.

The carriage lumbered down the drive; the Negroes, mounted or afoot, swung in behind. The horses and mules moved slowly through the darkness; and Mrs. Currain heard the doleful murmur of the people, heard a thin high wail of grief like a dirge rise from their mournful hearts at this departure that might be forever.

As they came from the drive to the road, Trav spoke through the carriage window. "All right, Mama?"

She saw some long object held crosswise in his hand, and she guessed it was his father's sword which she had bidden Cinda give him. Till that moment she had not accepted the departure as finality; but when she spoke her voice was steady. "Certainly, Travis."

They began to ascend the winding road which Trav hoped would bring them to the Richmond pike ahead of the crawling trains. The horses moved at a foot pace, for the ruts were deep, the road muddy. The heavy carriage lurched and tipped and swayed.

As they climbed, Mrs. Currain became conscious of a ruddy brightness among the upper branches of the trees ahead; and she heard excited, wondering voices from behind them where the people followed, and heard pounding hoof beats as a horseman galloped up the hill to overtake them. Then Faunt was here, leaning down from the saddle to speak to her in accents thick and drunken.

"Look back, Mama!" he said hoarsely. "There's a beginning at wiping out this shame!"

She had already guessed the truth, but she obeyed him. Down behind them toward the river, hidden by the trees which mercifully shut off her vision, some great conflagration was growing like a weed. She saw the waxing glare of it, and the sparks soaring upward, and the tongue-tips of high-leaping flames. She had looked back not because Faunt bade her, but only to say farewell, and she felt no surprise at what he had done, nor any sadness. The resinous old heart-pine of floors and walls would burn swiftly and fiercely till they were consumed; and she nodded almost in approval. It was as well, perhaps, that the old house was gone; so many memories, some bright, some dark, all alike gone in the purging flame.

II

Advance to Gettysburg
1862 - 1863

1

TRAV that evening had ridden over from headquarters on a nervous, highly bred hunter named Whitefoot; but when he mounted to guide his mother's carriage toward the Richmond pike, he found that Mill had saddled Nig. The stallion was a tremendous animal, five-gaited, tireless, combining enormous vitality with the disposition of a gallant dog. In the old quiet days at Great Oak and before that at Chimneys, Trav had used Nig often; but through these months since he joined Longstreet's staff, the stallion had stayed at Great Oak where the Negroes gave him proper exercise. But of course, now that Great Oak was being abandoned, Nig could not be left behind; and Trav was glad to feel the great horse under him and grateful to Big Mill for thinking of this change without direction. The black man, given responsibility, had risen to meet it in so many ways.

Trav settled in his saddle for the long hours ahead; and Nig's barrel was strong and proud between his knees. The road was soft, for there had been spring rains aplenty; and a light mist wetted his face. His father's sword, wrapped in oilcloth, lay across his saddle, but it had better be kept dry against the rain, so he handed it into the carriage to Cinda. She and Tilda and his mother were silent figures there, as still as images carved from a block of wood. It was as though some sudden spell had been laid upon them. What was the old Bible story of Lot's wife doomed by a backward glance at Sodom? Or was it Gomorrah? Doomed because she looked back at the city that had been her home.

Well, he would not look back. He rode with head bowed, so that his hat brim was some protection against the pelt of thin mist like fine rain; but by and by he heard a horse at a gallop behind him, and

Faunt's hoarse voice roused him to the knowledge that some brightness had paled the blackness of the night. So he turned in his saddle; he did look back. Through the wet curtain of the night the far glare tinted half the sky. The house at Greak Oak, except for the chimneys, was all of wood. Unless rain came to damp the fire, dawn would leave only the chimneys standing; around their solid bases the hot embers would cool into a gray muck of ash and mud.

He felt no emotion, not sadness, not blame for Faunt, nothing. He rode on, alone in the van. Faunt must have dropped back with Tony, somewhere behind the carriage. Near Trav, other hoof beats echoed those of Nig. That was Big Mill, close at his heels, ready for command. Perhaps he should send this loyal man back to Great Oak to see what might be saved from the burning house; but he dismissed the thought. There was nothing of the past that could be saved, not now. The past was gone.

And Enid was gone. Enid had torn herself loose from him, leaving such a wound as a great branch leaves when sudden wind whips it from the parent trunk. Enid was gone, and Great Oak was gone. Something else was gone, too. Trav had never consciously taken thought upon his heritage. From childhood he had felt himself to be, as a matter of course, one of the elect; yet it had not occurred to him to be proud of his inheritance of courage, honor, wisdom, strength. In fact it had never occurred to him to be proud at all—nor to be humble. He was part of a stable and settled order. A phrase touched his thoughts: divine right, the divine right of kings. He smiled in sudden gruff amusement at himself; for he too had accepted his position in the world as a right. If not divinely bestowed, it was at least bestowed by something outside himself; he was a beneficiary of the deeds of others, and he had accepted those benefits—of which Great Oak, now vanishing in flames, had been the outward symbol. Pride in the fact that he was a Currain, that Currain blood ran in his veins; this pride had been a part of him.

He had not realized how large a part till now, now that he knew tnat there was Currain blood in Abraham Lincoln too. Trav's lips twisted at the thought. His father, like a young tom turkey on the prowl, lightiy dandling a hedge wench named Lucy Hanks in some hidden thicket or some moonlit meadow, had fathered Abraham Lincoln's mother. Trav had never shared in the traffic with Negro women, in the casual and wayward sportings to which some men lent themselves. This was not because of any virtuous abstemiousness. It arose in part from the fastidious personal cleanliness which had always been his habit, in part from a shy reluctance which had sometimes provoked the smiles of other men. There had been times when he wished he might boldly do as they did; but despite these furtive desires he had lived like an anchorite. Even in marriage he had been half-embarrassed by Enid's ardor, by her eager yieldings. Passion was a mystery in which he participated almost apologetically. He could not imagine himself dallying with some white trash girl—as his father had dallied long ago with Lucy Hanks.

But his father had had no such scruple, so there was Currain blood in Abraham Lincoln. If there had never been an Anthony Currain, there would never have been an Abraham Lincoln. But it was Lincoln who had let loose this flood of war upon the South. Hence it was Anthony Currain, by that old heedless passion, who had let loose these terrors across the land. Trav was accustomed to accept blame—when blame was his due—without evasion. So, for all the Currains, for Tony and Faunt, for Cinda and Tilda, for the second generation too, he accepted in his thoughts now the guilt of this catastrophe. Lincoln personified the forces which sought to destroy the South; and for Lincoln, a Currain was responsible. Thus every Currain owed the South a heavy reparation; every Currain must strive his utmost to pay at least a part of the debt.

Well, he would try. As much of the debt as lay in his power to repay, he would repay. Between his knees he felt the muscles of his mount slide and tense and relax; felt Nig's strength held in careful bonds yet ready at a touch to be let loose. Was there something like that in him, too? Had he capacities till now restrained? Energy unused?

He did not know; but certainly the way to great deeds began with the nearest tasks. His thoughts returned to the present. Till now he had let Nig set the pace. The big stallion went at a striding walk; but his tossing head, his almost mincing gait as he chose firm footing on the muddy road, testified his readiness to answer any challenge. Now Trav loosed the reins a little; Nig's walk was still a walk, but it became a fast walk, fast enough so that Big Mill's mule had to go to a slow trot to keep his place, and a gap opened between them and the carriage, till old Thomas on the box set his horses briefly to a trot that closed the gap again.

When they came to the turnpike, they found it filled with wagons, the noses of horses and mules touching the tailboards of the vehicles in front. Trav bade old Thomas wait while he himself halted one of the wagons and questioned the driver. The man spoke profanely. He had been since an hour before dark coming this short way from Williamsburg. The road was soft, every set of wheels that passed cut deeper ruts, teams were forever getting mired.

Trav nodded. These teams and wagons that made up the army's trains were his responsibility, so Faunt and Tony must see his mother and the others safe in Richmond. He returned to speak to them.

"I'll leave you to take care of Mama," he said. "The wagons will churn the road to pieces, but you're ahead of most of them. I'll make a place in the line for you." Faunt sat his horse in silence, but Tony laughed at nothing. "I'll send Big Mill with you, in case the carriage gets stuck in the mud." Trav waited for questions but none came, so he went to speak to Cinda. "Faunt and Tony will go on with you," he explained. "I'll have to help keep the trains moving."

"We'll be all right." She added softly: "I think Mama's asleep."

"No, I'm awake," said Mrs. Currain.

"Warm enough?" Trav asked. "Keeping dry?"

"Don't be concerned for me, Sonny."

Trav's heart warmed at that endearing diminutive. He had not heard it from her lips for many years. But Tilda protested: "Trav, you ought to take care of us. Faunt's crazy, and Tony's useless!"

Mrs. Currain hushed her. "No, Tilda. Do your work, Travis. We'll be fine."

"I'll come to Richmond when I can," he said; and he swung Nig and stopped a wagon on the road and kept it waiting till a gap opened between it and the wagon ahead. Into this gap the carriage turned and slowly moved away. The people from Great Oak followed as they could, in the roadside ditches and in the fields. Trav spoke to Big Mill.

"Take care of them, Mill," he directed. "Stay with them all the way."

"Ain' you gwine need me, suh?"

"They may need you worse than I do." Tilda was right. Faunt and Tony tonight were not responsible; but Big Mill would do what he was told. "You can come back and find me."

When Big Mill had splashed away to overtake them, Trav rode back toward Williamsburg. There were many crossroads, and he passed houses with lighted windows; and around occasional bonfires hissing in the rain that was as thin as dew, men were gathered to warm themselves and to set their garments steaming. Trav found a mired wagon and stopped to see it freed and then set men to cut brush and poles and throw them into the muddy pit where it had bogged, so that following wagons could pass without being trapped. When he rode on his thoughts wandered, weariness upon him like a drug. To keep awake he took refuge in absurd calculations. How many wagons made an army? There were say sixty thousand men in this army that was now upon the move. If there were a hundred men to a company that meant six hundred companies. A wagon to every company was six hundred wagons. But that was not all; there might be, altogether, twelve or fourteen four- and six-horse wagons to each regiment, for ammunition and hospital equipment and to serve as ambulances. Then you had to count on say twenty-five wagons per division for depot purposes. Say at a guess fifteen wagons per regiment, say seventy for each brigade, say four hundred for each division. His thoughts swam in a bewildering maze of figures. Suppose the army had fifteen hundred wagons. Average four horses to a wagon and each wagon was not less than thirty-five feet over all. Three wagons per hundred feet of road would be a hundred and fifty to a mile; a hundred and fifty-eight, to be exact, assuming there was no space between them. Then fifteen hundred wagons would stretch ten miles.

And that took no account of guns and gun teams, nor of marching men. Why, if this army were stretched out along the stage road, its head—allowing for the inevitable gaps in the line—would be at New Kent Court House before the last man left Williamsburg.

His figures were mere estimates. Some day he must make measurements, make a more accurate count of the army's wagons. Trav liked definiteness, precision. Uncertainty always annoyed him.

At the first gray of dawn he came to the Frog Pond tavern, on the edge of Williamsburg; and he was heavy with weariness, drunk with sleep, soaked and mud-splattered, nodding on his horse. He must rest. He stabled Nig to be fed and groomed and went indoors. The fat old tavern keeper greeted him in a high excitement.

"By Jucks, Mr. Currain, a sad day, a sad day indeed, sir. What are we coming to? I hear the Yankee scoundrels have burned Great Oak to the ground." His brow was beaded with a sweat of fear.

Trav was too tired to clear the Yankees of that crime. "Yes, the house burned."

"A woeful thing, by Jucks! Yes, and worse will happen. What has come upon us, sir?"

"Sleep has come upon me," Trav said dryly. "I'm hungry and sleepy."

"Hot biscuits? Coffee? A warm bed? Instantly, Mr. Currain."

"Have you a room? Then send the coffee there. Let someone take my clothes to dry. Wake me when they're ready. If they're not dry by ten o'clock, wake me anyway."

It was to the splashing shuffle of marching feet, the cries of teamsters that he fell asleep. He slept, he thought, for no more than an instant; then someone was shaking him, a black face met his opening eyes.

"Yas suh, ten o'clock, suh! Heah's you' clo'es! Dey's dry as I could git 'em, suh!"

There was a pot of steaming coffee on the table. Trav dressed, still full of sleep; he sipped the scalding liquid. Now he must find the General, see where lay the greatest need for him. Last night seemed long ago; he put all thought of it aside, descended, sent for his horse.

With the stable boy who brought Nig came another Negro, a slim man, something dapper about him, something familiar about the garments he wore. The whites of his eyes gleamed with terror and his lips were gray.

"Please suh, Mr. Currain?"

Trav recognized the man as young Julian's body servant. His name was Elegant. He was a Currain Negro from the Plains, who had gone with Julian to the Military Institute at Charlotte, who had served the youngster since. The boy—or the man, for he was twice Julian's age—had always worn Clayton's discarded clothes, and worn them with an air, as though to live up to his name. Cinda used to laugh at his struttings, to say: "Elegant his name and elegant his nature."

"Where's your master?" Trav demanded. "Why aren't you with him?"

"Please suh, Miss Vesta's heah."

"Here? Where?" Trav was startled. Williamsburg was no place for Vesta, with Yankees coming.

"At Mistuh Taylor's house."

Trav asked no questions. There was no time for questions now. He swung into the saddle, bade Elegant follow him. The Taylor house was on Francis Street opposite Capitol Square, at the other end of town. He turned his horse and threaded his way through a swearing pack of soldiers who were trying to free a great gun that had bogged in the deep mud. At any other time, Elegant's frantic efforts to avoid soiling his garments in this quagmire they crossed would have made Trav smile, but not now. Vesta ought to be safe and secure in Richmond, not here in the path of war. He tried to guess why she was here, but guesses were a waste of time. At least the Taylors would give her shelter. She and Jenny Taylor were old friends; Mrs. Taylor and Cinda and Tilda had been girls together.

Elegant, despite the mud, held his place at Trav's stirrup; and Trav asked: "How'd you find me?"

Elegant grinned up at him. "I heerd tell Nig was heah, and I knowed you wouldn't go to let nobody ride him only you." He added querulously, "I aimed to wake you up befoah now, but dey'uns 'lowed you needed sleep moah dan you needed me!"

At the Taylor house Trav dismounted, gave Elegant the reins. "Keep him quiet," he directed. Nig seemed to have caught the excitement that filled the air today. He moved on tiptoe, with short, springy steps; his head was high, a fleck of foam showed at his nostrils, his ears pricked alertly. Trav left Elegant to gentle him and went toward the door.

His coming had been seen, for before he reached it the door swung wide and Vesta ran to meet him, throwing herself into his arms, kissing him, with tears of smiling welcome in her eyes. "Oh Uncle Trav,

Uncle Trav!" She clung to him in a warm tenderness that touched
and pleased him. He had always been fond of Vesta, liking her friendliness and her lack of all affectation; but till today he had never
thought her beautiful. It seemed to him now that her cheeks were
filled out, her lips bright, her eyes astonishingly clear; he thought of
a ripe apple, rosily tinted, full to bursting of sweet white meat.

"You look mighty happy, Vesta!"

"Oh I've never been so happy in my life, Uncle Trav! Tommy's so
wonderful! And now seeing you!" She took his arm, leading him
toward the house, and Mrs. Taylor and Jenny appeared to greet him.
Not till he had made his bows to them was there a chance for questions.

Vesta said she and Tommy had stopped at the house in Richmond
and learned that Cinda and the others were still at Great Oak. "And I
wanted to be with Tommy as long as I could," Vesta confessed, her
cheeks bright. "So I thought I'd come down with him and then go
home with Mama."

On the way, they heard retreat was ordered; but it was too late for
Tommy to take Vesta back to Richmond. His duty was here. So they
pressed on against the stream of traffic, and they were long upon the
road and it had been past dark last night before they came to Williamsburg. Julian had promised, the day of the wedding, to meet
Tommy at the tavern on his return; and he was there waiting
Tommy's coming.

"And when he saw me he was furious," Vesta confessed. "He just
gave me the dickens! I was an awful nuisance, I know. Julian had
orders, so he and Tommy couldn't take time to ride out to Great Oak
with me; but I made Julian wait till Tommy could eat some supper,
and that let me be with Tommy a little longer. He's so wonderful!"
Jenny Taylor laughed teasingly, and Vesta blushed to the eyes, but she
insisted: "You wait till you're married, Jenny. You won't think it's so
funny!"

"Me oh my!" Jenny tossed her head. "A body'd think no one had
ever been newly married before. Brand-new husbands are like brand-
new babies, darling! They're all wonderful."

"Well, I don't care, they're not as grand as Tommy," Vesta declared.
Trav saw she relished this teasing. It was a part of her brimming hap-

piness. But then her eyes shadowed. "Then Julian and Tommy had to go, but Julian left Elegant to take me out to Great Oak; and when we got there the house was all afire!"

Trav nodded. "I know, yes."

"And I couldn't find anybody except a frightened old negro, and he said you were all gone. So I came back here, and Jenny and Mrs. Taylor took me in. How did the house catch fire, Uncle Trav?"

He did not tell her; some things she need never know. "Some raiding Yankees after we left, perhaps. Or poor whites. Or rascal negroes." He was trying to decide what she was now to do; but he could think of nothing better than for her to stay here. It was impossible to send her away to Richmond along that road that was like a river of men and wagons plodding through hopeless mud. If she stayed here she would be safe enough. The Yankees would not harm women.

And he must find General Longstreet, report, do whatever he could do. "I wish you were in Richmond with your mother," he confessed.

Mrs. Taylor said quietly, "She can stay with us. We shall stay, Yankees or no Yankees!"

"There'll be a chance to come to Richmond somehow, after the army's gone." Trav added a smiling warning. "Stay indoors out of sight."

Vesta laughed. "No old Yankee would stop for a second look at me."

"More fools they," Trav declared, hiding his concern. Mrs. Taylor urged that he eat dinner here, but he shook his head. "I'll tell Cinda where you are, Vesta," he promised. "You stay till we can send for you."

"Mama mustn't worry about me!"

"Well, she will, till she has you home again," he reminded her, and saw her penitent regret. "But no one's going to blame you for wanting to be with Tommy. Shall I tell Elegant to stay with you?"

"Oh no, Julian will need him." She hesitated. "Uncle Trav, is the army really retreating?"

He nodded. "Yes, we'll all be gone by tonight, or tomorrow anyway. Unless the mud gets too bad. But the mud will hold back the Yankees too."

"There won't be any fighting here, will there?"

"No. General McClellan's a slow man, likes to take his time. We'll be away before he knows we're gone."

Trav left them, told Elegant to find his way back to Julian, and himself came presently to where—just beyond the town—General Longstreet and Moxley Sorrel and Captain Goree and some others of the staff had drawn aside to watch the men plod by, and to listen to a distant rattle of musketry in the army's rear.

Longstreet, intent on those distant sounds, gave Trav a brief nod; Trav heard from Captain Goree the state of affairs. Longstreet's division had begun their withdrawal before midnight last night. Hill's men, in Yorktown, were to spike what guns must be abandoned, to start as soon as the roads were clear, to bring up the rear. Stuart's cavalry would follow as a screen. From the first, the movement had been dreadfully slow. The roads were soft from many rains, and so narrow that when a gun stuck in the mud, or a wagon bogged down, or even when a trace broke and had to be repaired, the whole column stalled.

"We've been an hour sometimes in making a mile," Captain Goree declared. "With good going, we'd have been well beyond Williamsburg by now. But those shots, that firing—well, it sounds as though the Yanks had come up with Stuart's men."

General Longstreet turned his horse, and they followed him back toward the distant musketry as far as the earthwork called Fort Magruder, the pivot of the defensive line which General Magruder had built across the Peninsula here at its narrowest point. Longstreet halted there again, and Trav, watching him, trying to read his mind, saw him study the works. Captain Goree at Trav's side said in a low tone: "Till an hour ago it looked as though there'd be no pursuit. Of course they may be just the Yank cavalry feeling us."

Longstreet, as though seeing Trav for the first time, beckoned; and Trav went to his side. The General said quietly: "My men will be through Williamsburg by dark, Captain. Find places where they can bivouac. Do what you can for them."

"Very well, sir." Trav swung Nig back toward the town, his thoughts engaged with the task of making the men as comfortable as possible. They had been served out three days' rations yesterday, pork and corn meal to be cooked before the start in preparation for this march. Probably most of them had already devoured this provision, but that could not be helped. The depot wagons and the baggage, everything except the ammunition carts, were already on the road to Richmond. If it rained tonight, if this thin spit became a downpour, they would suffer. He found beyond the town a field bordered by trees that would offer them some shelter, set details to bring drinking water and to gather firewood. He did not see the General again till dark when Longstreet's last brigade was making camp in the field he had chosen; but there had been more firing to the rear, and the rumble of cannon as well as musketry.

The General was as calm as he always was when action pressed. "I'm taking Anderson's brigade, and Pryor's, back to hold Fort Magruder," he told Trav. "McLaw's men and Kershaw's stopped the Yankee infantry there; but they're to continue the withdrawal tonight. Magruder's men and then Smith's division and then General Hill's. We will follow at daylight—or hold the enemy till the army gets away. Let your trains start as soon as Hill's men clear the road." He waited for no questions, turned at once to move the two brigades.

In the early dark the men, cursing their luck, countermarched back into the town. Trav, when they were gone, remembered Vesta. Longstreet would hold the enemy tomorrow for as long as seemed necessary; but to do that meant fighting just beyond the town, and the fight might flow into Williamsburg itself. If he could get Vesta away, he had best do so. Since she had ridden down from Richmond with Tommy, her horse was presumably in the Taylor stable. An escort for her? He wished Big Mill were here; but since he was not, some other way must be found.

Toward eight o'clock, heavy rain began to fall; and this steady pelting increased his uneasiness. Tomorrow and for days to come both armies would be floundering in a sea of mud. He was more and more sure that Vesta should be sent on her way in time to escape the welter and confusion he foresaw. He himself might go with her; yes, all the way to Richmond if necessary. After all, he need not suppose that he carried the whole army on his shoulders. No man was indispensable; if a man fell, his place was always filled.

But there was no one except him to escort Vesta. Tommy and Julian were fighters; their duty held them here. He would have no part in any fighting; and he thought of his own passive part with a sudden brief contempt. He could not fight—but he could see Vesta on the road to Richmond. He remembered Big Mill, who would be returning to find him, whom they would surely meet on the way, who could take Vesta on.

So, his decision made, he gave orders to his men to resume their withdrawal in the morning when Hill's trains had cleared the road, then returned to find Vesta at the Taylor house. When he proposed that she start at once for Richmond, she hesitated, and Mrs. Taylor and Jenny protested that she must not go. But Vesta, her eyes on Trav, nodded grave assent.

"I'll be all right! I've made enough trouble, without staying behind in the Yankee lines." She asked Trav: "Do you know where Tommy is, Uncle Trav?"

"He's in the Fifth North Carolina, isn't he? General Hill's command?" She nodded. "They were the last to leave the works at Yorktown," he said. "But they bivouacked in a field beyond town. They're to march at daylight."

"Do you think I could see him?"

"Why, yes. We can find him and Julian on our way."

She laughed in rich happiness. "Then I'll surely come with you. I won't mind a wetting if I can see Tommy. Give me time to change."

So presently, wearing one of Mr. Taylor's heavy capes over her riding habit, she was ready. Side by side she and Trav rode through the town, through driving rain, past huddled soldiers and hissing fires, to the fields beyond, where Hill's division was encamped.

Trav hailed a soldier and asked the man to find Tommy; and Tommy and Julian presently came splashing across the sodden turf to join them. Where an oak gave some shelter from the rain, Vesta in Tommy's arms drew Mr. Taylor's great cape to cover them both; and Julian, like any brother, scolded Vesta for this whole imprudence till Trav drew him away.

"Let those two have a little while together, Julian. We can't stop long, Vesta and I."

"The army can't bother with ladies, Uncle Trav."

Trav smiled in the darkness at this boy so much the soldier. "I'll look out for her."

"What happened to Great Oak?" Julian asked. "Elegant told me the house burned last night."

"Yes, soon after we left." The phrases now came naturally to his lips. "Rascally negroes, perhaps; or poor whites; or maybe a Yankee patrol."

"The Yankees are all behind us!"

"They might have come by boat. It doesn't matter. The place is gone, anyway. We'll not stop the Yankees short of the Chicka-hominy."

Would they stop the enemy short of Richmond itself? He did not know.

"We'll never stop them if we don't fight them." Julian's tone was hot and angry. "I don't like retreats! If we weren't going to fight, why did we come down here anyway?"

Trav looked toward where Tommy and Vesta were one shadow by the great tree's bole. Before morning she must be far away. "The generals do the best they can," he said mildly. He had Nig and Vesta's horse on lead. "It's time for us to go."

At that parting Tommy said gratefully: "I'm mighty sorry I made you so much trouble, sir. We didn't know there'd be this retreat, or I'd have made Vesta stay in Richmond."

"It's all right, Tommy. I'll take care of her."

Vesta hugged Tommy hard; she kissed him hard and fiercely. "And you take care of yourself, Tommy," she cried, turned to her brother. "You take care of him, Julian! You hear me?" A kiss for him too.

"I'm not as mad at you as I let on to be, Sis," Julian assured her, re-lenting. "But stay home where you belong, after this."

Tommy gave her a hand up; she leaned far down for his kiss. "And here's another for your Mama," he said and drew her down again; and Julian laughed and sang:

> "'A pretty girl who gets a kiss
> 'And runs and tells her mother
> 'Does what she shouldn't do
> 'And don't deserve another.'"

Tommy retorted: "She gets it, all the same!" and almost pulled Vesta out of the saddle, and they were all for a moment very merry, and then they were no longer laughing. Trav mounted; and Nig, head tossing, tried the reins, eager to be gone. Tommy and Julian walked beside them to the road; Tommy had her lips yet once again, this time in grave tenderness.

Then she and Trav moved on through the night, past drenched campfires where they smelled wet embers and wood smoke, past laboring wagons making use of these night hours when the roads were clear of marching men. Trav stopped now and then to direct the work of some group of teamsters struggling with a wagon that had lurched into a pit, or patching broken harnesses; but unless he was needed he pressed steadily on, Vesta's horse plodding on Nig's heels. Now and then he spoke to her; her answer was always brisk and cheery and undaunted. A fine girl—and a happy one. Once he asked: "Are you wet through?"

"No, the cape keeps me dry. I'm all right."

"Chilled? I might have bought you a drop of brandy at Burnt Ordinary, or at White Hall tavern, but I didn't think of doing so."

She laughed bravely in the night and the rain. "Nonsense, Uncle Trav! I'm fine."

They rode all night, groping through the rain and darkness, along a road upon which even in the darkness there was movement; the sluggish crawling wagons, the teamsters half asleep, the plodding weary horses, all dimly seen with eyes accustomed to the dark. Trav had slept three or four hours in the morning, but that was long ago; sleep and fatigue lay heavy on him now. He thought of stopping at the tavern at New Kent Court House; but when they came there the recess under the veranda was full of men sheltering from the rain, with a bonfire burning beside the road, and he heard loud voices and singing in the common room, so he did not pause.

But dawn caught them while they were still far short of Bottom's Bridge, and he saw that Vesta's shoulders drooped with weariness. They must rest a while; and at the next house, a mean small cabin built of logs, with an open shed behind, they stopped. A bent old man and his wife welcomed them to a roaring fire, to hot bread and bitter coffee, salt pork and molasses.

Vesta ate greedily. "Oh Uncle Trav, did anything ever taste so good!" Trav was as hungry as she. While they ate, the dim-eyed old man asked Trav many questions; and when he heard the Yankees were coming he took down a flintlock from pegs against the wall and drew the load and loaded the piece again.

"Reckon if they come this way I might as well take a hand," he said.

When they could eat no more, the woman mothered Vesta, hung her cape and riding skirt before the fire, took shoes and stockings to dry, put the girl to bed under many coverlets. "You sleep a spell, ma'am, and you'll feel a sight better," she urged.

"May I, Uncle Trav?"

Trav nodded. His own eyes were closing. "I'll lie down a minute myself." He appealed to the woman. "If I may?"

"Why, Lord love you, sartain! And Jim'll give your horses a bite till yo're fit to go on."

Trav suddenly remembered Big Mill, who would surely be on the road this morning, returning toward Williamsburg, and who might pass unknowing; but Mill would recognize Nig. "Yes, give the horses a nose bag if you can," he agreed. "But keep mine in plain sight from the road. My boy will be coming from Richmond looking for me, and he'll know the horse."

"I sh'd think he would," the oldster agreed. "If he'd ever see him. I'll keep an eye on 'em, see to't no one don't take a notion to go off with them. Don't worry yourself. You lay down and rest a spell."

So to the sound of wagons monotonously passing Trav fell asleep. He woke at the sound of a familiar voice. Big Mill was here. Trav swung his feet to the floor.

"They been a-fighting," the woman told him; and Trav felt the rumble of the distant guns. Vesta was still asleep. He stepped outside to speak to Mill. The carriage was safe in Richmond, the Negro reported. Mrs. Currain, all of them had stood the journey well. "So I cotch me some sleep, and I come along looking to find you."

"I'm glad you came. I need you. When Miss Vesta wakes up, you take her home. Wake her in time so you can reach Richmond before dusk. I'm going back to Williamsburg."

"Yas suh!" But Trav heard the reluctance in the word, felt the other's loyal wish to stay with him.

"When she's safe, you come and find me again," he directed. "I'll be somewhere with the trains."

He left his grateful thanks with the old man and woman who had given them hospitality. It was near noon when he started to retrace his way, Nig splashing through shallows in the low ground among the swamps. Ahead of him, still far away but louder every time he topped a rise, he heard the growl of battle. Where a fork turned aside toward Diascund Bridge he saw men and wagons taking that way; and he asked a question. This was the vanguard of Magruder's men; they would bivouac at the bridge. Troops and wagons filled the road toward Barhamsville, and there he met General Smith's advance. The army was a serpent, its tail—Longstreet's division—still looking back at the enemy. It moved like a serpent with a broken back, thrashing awkwardly, crawling with a terrible slowness toward a doubtful safety—where?

Was this defeat? How far would they retreat? Where would they stand? Extended thus, the army was helplessly vulnerable. Suppose the Yankees landed a force from transports in the York River to strike this half-paralyzed serpent from the side, to crush its head, to cut off its tail; what could prevent catastrophe? How could this long line of men and wagons be organized again, thrown into battle order, set to face the enemy?

But that was not his province. Strategy, tactics, combat; these were not for him. His province was to keep the wagons moving, to provide somehow rations and supplies for these weary, stumbling men.

Somewhere ahead, said the distant guns, men like these men were fighting: Longstreet's men, the men Trav knew. They fought to hold back the enemy while these others escaped. The General had said dawn would see the division on the road again; but the cannons' voices gave the lie to that hope. Somehow they had been compelled to stand in battle—while their fellows marched away.

Trav remembered with a slow satisfaction that Vesta's Tommy, and young Julian, were not engaged in that ever nearer battle. They were to resume their march this morning while Longstreet's division brought up the rear. Before long now he should meet Hill's men, following General Smith's division. He began to watch as he pushed on along the slowly crawling columns. The road now was incredibly deep with mud. Once Trav saw a horse so badly mired that a two-horse team had to be unhitched to drag the frantic creature, plunging body-deep in bottomless muck, to solid footing; and once he saw a pair of mules surging through soupy mud so deep that when they fell with a great splash the thin muddy water actually closed over them, so that they disappeared from view for an instant before they scrambled to their feet again. The road and the ditches and the sedge fields on either side were alive with myriads of small green frogs. Nig's hard hooves crushed them to nothingness.

Trav watched for Tommy or Rollin or Julian; and now and then, seeing the face of an acquaintance among the passing troops, he asked a question. The Fifth North Carolina regiment? Hill's division? Heads shook. No one knew.

After a while the road became almost deserted. Where then was Hill's division? It should have been close upon the heels of these regiments he had passed. A rising anxiousness beset him. The battle rumble yonder was a persisting irritation, irksome as a buzzing fly. From among the riders he met he picked out another familiar countenance, once more put his question, this time had his answer.

"Hill? Oh, he went back. The Yankees hit us at the crack of dawn. The Fifth North Carolina countermarched into town again. They were resting on the college campus waiting for orders, when we passed there."

Trav thanked him and pressed on; and Nig fretted at the bit, and to ease him Trav loosed the reins and went at a canter. Short of town he met more wagons, of Hill's division; but though his mind automatically took note of this, his thoughts still cast ahead.

When he came into town, the thunder of the guns was loud and near; but there was no regiment resting on the campus of the college. Trav's lip tightened as he rode more slowly on. At the edge of town he saw a throng of men gathered, and heard wretched, groaning cries; and over the heads of the crowd he saw that here were Federal wounded laid on the grass beside the road to await attention. One man, rolling back and forth, screamed some agonized appeal; and a tall Confederate in the uniform of a Louisiana Tiger stepped forward and raised his musket butt over the head of the tormented man.

"Out o' yore mis'ry?" he cried. "Why sartain!" The gun butt crashed splinteringly down. In the sudden silence the killer challenged the other wounded. "Any more o' you damned Yanks want to be accommodated?" Then at the universal murmur of anger from his own comrades he backed hastily into the crowd.

Trav, riding on, thought he understood the impulse which had prompted that brutality; the age-old impulse of the pack to kill a crippled member. Animals were pitiless to the hurt, and war made men into animals, and this was war. Ahead of him the sound of firing dwindled, and the great guns presently fell silent. There was only the spatter of musketry as dusk came down. He wished for news of Tommy and Julian, but he must find the General, get his orders for the night and the morrow. Inquiries led him to a house beyond the town where he saw riderless horses held by orderlies, and a considerable group of men. He dismounted, looping Nig's reins over his arm, and found Captain Goree and put his questions.

"The General? He's inside with General Johnston and General Hill." Trav heard in the other's voice that quick excitement, that semi-intoxication which he had heard in other voices after the skirmish at Big Bethel and after Manassas. "Captain, we taught them a lesson today."

"Fighting all day?"

"All morning!" Captain Goree's voice rang. "Longstreet's a great man, Currain. I was beside him all through it. As calm as a checker player. You'd have thought he was born on a battlefield." And he explained: "They came at us hard, but we stopped them, and when they backed off he threw us at them, led the men himself. We chased them back on their reserves, and he sent Stuart to keep them running as long as they would run—like a dog chasing a cat." He laughed. "That gave them all they wanted."

"I heard guns till an hour ago," Trav suggested.

"Oh yes," Captain Goree agreed. "That was Hill's division. We'd used up most of our ammunition, and your wagons were on beyond town; so the General called on General Hill to stand by and be ready to help us if we needed help. All we wanted was to hold for the day.

General Johnston was here, but he said he couldn't improve on what Longstreet was doing. But General Hill wasn't satisfied to let well enough alone. He wanted a taste of glory too—so he tried an attack north of the Fort and bungled it, got the Fifth North Carolina shot to pieces."

Trav felt a cold hand on his heart. "Where is that regiment now?"

But before the other could reply, there was a stir on the veranda of the house in front of which they stood. The door opened; the generals emerged. It was full dark, but in silhouette against the light from the hall Trav recognized General Johnston, the burly form of Longstreet, the stooped figure of General Hill.

After a last word to the others, Johnston mounted; the men of his staff followed him as he rode away. General Longstreet came toward where Trav and the others of his staff now gathered. "We resume the withdrawal," he told them quietly. "The honors of the day go with us. The Yankees will not be in a hurry to tread on our heels again. We move first. General Hill's division will take the rear." He sent men to transmit his orders to the brigade commanders.

Trav spoke to him. "General, our trains are on the road, so there's no work for me just now. But my nephew and the husband of my niece were in the Fifth North Carolina. I hear that regiment was hurt. May I take time to inquire for them?"

Longstreet's voice softened. "Certainly, Captain. I should not have given permission for that move on our left. I blame myself for yielding to persuasion. General Hill yonder can tell you where to find the regiment." He hesitated. "Perhaps you can help them move their wounded to shelter in the town."

Trav thanked him. General Hill was giving directions to the men of his staff, standing at the foot of the veranda steps; the house door was still open and Trav saw the haggard lines in his old friend's countenance. When the other was free, Trav spoke to him.

General Hill echoed Trav's word. "The Fifth North Carolina? Mr. Currain, the slaughter of that regiment was the most terrible thing I ever saw—and their valor was beyond praise."

"Where are they?"

"I'll ride with you," the General decided. So they mounted and turned back toward the enemy, toward Fort Magruder. The road was

full of ambulances, lurching through the mud, floundering in the darkness. From each one came the groans, the sudden cries of suffering
men. Just before they reached Fort Magruder the General turned
aside, pointed to men grouped about bright fires ahead. "There they
are, what's left of them. I dread facing Colonel McRae."

Yet he rode forward; and Colonel McRae, with a heavy beard and
level frowning brows, faced them across the fire by which he was
standing. Trav saw that the Colonel's eyes were wet, tear stains upon
his cheeks. The man saluted, and General Hill looked beyond him at
the small groups silent by the fires. Trav thought they were no more
than a company.

General Hill said gently: "Colonel, General Longstreet's division
will lead the withdrawal. As soon as his last brigades have passed,
put your regiment upon the road. You will lead my division."

Colonel McRae swung to look around. "My regiment?" he echoed;
said with half a sob: "General, I took four hundred and fifteen men
into the action. There are not a hundred of us left able to walk without help"

"The wounded will be cared for by the townspeople," General Hill
told him. Colonel McRae did not speak; and after a moment Hill
turned his horse away.

Trav dismounted, introduced himself. "I came to inquire after two
of your men, Colonel," he explained. "Kinfolk of mine. Lieutenant
Cloyd, Lieutenant Dewain."

Colonel McRae shook his head, spoke in sober sorrow. "We have
not called the roll, Captain."

But from the shadows beyond the fire a young man stepped forward,
spoke to Trav. "Captain Currain, I'm Rollin Lyle. Lieutenant Cloyd
was my friend."

Trav recognized the youngster. "I remember you, sir." Yet he noted
the past tense, and his heart slowed its beat.

Rollin looked to Colonel McRae as though for permission to speak.
The Colonel nodded, and Rollin said: "Tommy—Lieutenant Cloyd—
led us across the plowed field. He carried no weapon, not even a pistol." His voice caught. "He never wanted to kill anyone. But he led
us, calling back to us to come on. We had to wheel and double-time
in order to take our place in the advance. At first we were beyond

musket range, but then the fire of the Yankee battery reached us." The young man's voice was steady now, steady as ice. "Lieutenant Cloyd was all right till the battery fired their last round, just before they drew back into the redoubt. That was close range. That last round of grape riddled him." The low tone suddenly was bitter. "Tore half his side away."

Trav swallowed dryness. "Killed him?"

Rollin almost laughed. "Killed him? God, yes! His insides spilled out in the mud."

Trav remembered Vesta, so full of happiness, something within her rich and sweet and warm; Vesta whom he had left asleep in that humble cabin hours ago. His throat burned with a swelling rage, at war, at death.

But Tommy was dead, no help for him. What of Julian? "You knew Julian Dewain too?"

"Yes, sir."

"Is he—alive?"

"He was alive at the fence, sir. Then we got orders to withdraw. I haven't seen him since. They were firing at us as we went back across the plowed ground."

Trav nodded. "Have you seen Julian's boy? Elegant was his name."

"He was with us at the fence, sir. He'd been shot in the face, but he followed Julian all the way. I saw them there. But they didn't come back."

Half to himself, Trav muttered: "I must find them."

Young Rollin Lyle said proudly: "Tommy is here. I carried him in my arms when we were ordered to withdraw."

That was something; but—Julian might be lying wounded in the night, wounded and dying. Tommy was past help, but there might be help for Julian. Colonel McRae spoke in heavy tones. "We've parties out collecting the wounded, Captain."

"May I borrow Mr. Lyle long enough to show me the field, Colonel?"

Colonel McRae looked toward the road, where in darkness marching men trudged through the mud. "We'll not move for a while, an hour or more," he assented. "But don't get him killed. I've lost men enough today."

Trav turned to Rollin; but the young man hesitated. "Tommy's body's under the trees over here, sir. Can't he be taken somewhere?"

"When we come back," Trav agreed. "Time enough then. Will you show me the way?"

So Rollin led him floundering through a thicket and across a ravine, stumbling in the darkness till they reached a fence which served to guide them and thus came out into an open field. Ahead and to their left, smoking torches moved here and there; the night silence was broken by gasps and groans and sudden screams of unbearable pain as wounded men were lifted and moved. Trav hesitated; but Rollin strode diagonally to their left across the open, and they came to plowed ground where their feet sank ankle-deep in sticky mud; and they passed two men helping between them a third, whose leg dangled, who whimpered like a fretful child, from whose leg as it swung came the faint sound of grating bones. The men paused, panting; Trav drew close to peer into the hurt man's face. This was not Julian.

"I wish we had a torch," he said.

One of the men laughed. "Be glad you can't see all there is to see," he retorted.

Trav and Rollin stumbled on. "This was the way we came." Rollin spoke in dull tones, heavy with weariness. "Out of the woods back there, and out into the field here, and then to the left. The fence is ahead, against the woods."

From somewhere off that way a musket shot sounded; then a shouted command. "Stop that shooting! Let them pick up their wounded!" That was a Yankee voice, the accent and the intonation strange. So the enemy was there, watching from the wood.

They met other men, laboriously carrying groaning human burdens back across the field. Ahead of them someone threw a torch aside to have both hands free for the duty they must do; and Trav picked up the still blazing splinter and thereafter they could see their way. Dead men lay here and there. Any one of them might be Julian, so at each one Trav held the torch near to see and to make sure. In the sudden light, black beetles came tumbling awkwardly out of open wounds to scuttle into darkness and wait till the light was gone to resume their gluttony. Trav looked upon them in a cold stillness, feeling none of that physical weakness which had beset him at Big Bethel, full rather of a black and terrible wrath.

But he did not find Julian among them, and Rollin led him steadily forward.

So they came to the rail fence. A shallow ditch ran along its face. "I saw Julian here," Rollin said. "The guns were close, yonder by the redoubt, lined up across the road. Tommy was killed just this side of the road." His voice was remote and calm. "The Twenty-Fourth Virginia was on our left. We lay down along the fence here; and when we got orders to retire they ran along the fence into the woods, into cover. But we had to go back across the open field. I picked up Tommy and carried him."

Trav moved along the fence, stepping over and around the bodies scattered here. When it was necessary he turned one till the face could be seen. The faces were curiously alike in their blankness, with open mouths, half-open eyes. There were faces bearded and beardless, faces of boys and of men, faces sometimes shattered by the impact of a heavy ball. Trav searched painstakingly. If Julian were here he must be found.

Once he thought his search had ended. They came to a Negro sitting with his shoulders against the fence and with a white man cradled in his arms. But the Negro was not Elegant, and the young man in his arms had a thin beard, and both were dead.

"That's Bob Crawford," Rollin said mildly. "He was in our company."

They went the length of the fence and back again; but Julian was not here. Perhaps earlier searchers had found him, helped him away. That chance remained; but certainly he was not here. Trav turned uncertainly to look at Rollin.

"We might as well go back."

So they retraced their course, yet still Trav turned aside to look at every dark form they passed, holding the torch to every countenance, making sure and sure. There were men whose arms or whose legs had been shot away, men whose faces were smashed to pulp, men who lay in dark pools of blood that had spilled out of them, men who showed to the casual glance no wounds at all. They came to one man who was still alive, whose eyes were open, who looked up at them with the eyes of a trapped animal, his teeth bared in a snarl, a thin blood-trickle from his mouth.

"We can carry him," said Trav.

But when they raised him to a sitting posture, the man coughed, and out of his mouth came a huge gush of blood; and when they laid him down again he twitched and twitched, his head jerking up, falling limply back, jerking up off the ground again. His feet began to kick and jerk harder and harder, then more and more weakly. Then head and feet were still. So he died.

So he was dead, as Tommy was dead. Perhaps Julian, too. They had been so much alive, so short a time ago.

In a convulsion like that of the man who had just died, Trav threw his head far back. He looked up. The clouds were breaking. He saw a calm and distant star, watching with no pity.

His teeth grated.

This war. This blood-spilling, this bowel-spilling war! This war made by a man named Lincoln.

By a man named Lincoln, in whom ran Currain blood.

Trav's jaws clamped shut. Blindly, stumbling across the muddy field, he strode away. He forgot Rollin on his heels, forgot all else in deadly rage and blinding pain.

2

TILDA thought that interminable journey to Richmond would never be done. The heavy carriage lurched and swayed and jolted till her bones ached. Cinda and Mrs. Currain seemed to relax, but Tilda could not do this. She sat tensely braced, and each shock was like a blow. The others were silent as though they slept; but when sometimes a torch, or the light from a blazing fire beside the road illumined their faces, she saw their eyes were open, fixed and shining glassily.

She herself was full of words she did not speak, of thoughts that were all ejaculations. The revelation in those letters laid on her no burden of grief or guilt. It woke instead a sort of triumph. She delighted in the consternation of these others, her mother, Cinda, her brothers; but that their distress and shame were also hers she easily ignored. True, she was as much a Currain as any of them; but since she married Redford Streean they had forgotten this, had let her live in mean and tawdry semi-poverty, had left her no part in their lives except to envy and to covet. They had never accepted Redford as one of them; he was always "Mister Streean" to them all. Oh, they had held their heads so high!

Well, their heads would be lower now! Redford Streean might be mean and base as in her heart she knew him to be, but at least he was not the uncle of Abraham Lincoln, that ogre from the North who had provoked this war and death and ruin. The cream of the jest was that the war that left her brothers and sisters paupers would not ruin Redford Streean. While they saw their world collapse he would find ways to erect a fortune, which she would share. One day, when these others were penniless, she would be rich! She imagined herself playing the kindly benefactress to them all.

She recognized the likelihood that even in their rags they might be contemptuous of Redford's wealth, but if they were, if they persisted in their hoity-toity ways, she could soon enough bring them to terms. This knowledge of their father's shameful crime was a weapon in her hands. If they held themselves too high, she would know how to bring them low!

Through the night the carriage made slow progress; but now and then wagons ahead of them pulled off the road to wait for dawn, and insensibly the flowing stream of travel on the roads began to thin. With daylight, they were able to proceed more steadily; there were no longer so many maddening delays. They stopped at New Kent Court House so that old Thomas could bait the horses while the Negroes who still followed them in a straggling band cleaned the carriage of accumulated mud. Faunt and Tony arranged for a private room in the tavern, and they all went in for long enough to eat sparingly, to relax their wearied muscles. Tilda was full of words, but the tavern keeper hovered near with questions about what was happening at Williamsburg; and Faunt kept him in play, so that they had no moment together and alone.

When they came out, the carriage was halfway clean, and they pushed on. At the house on Fifth Street, Tilda did not stay, did not even go indoors. "Mama's so tired you'll want to put her right to bed," she told Cinda. "And I must see if the children are all right. I'll come first thing in the morning."

Cinda did not protest, and Tilda hurried homeward; but halfway there her pace lagged. Should she tell Redford Streean this incredible thing that had happened? She itched to do so, to share his hilarious and derisive mirth; but if she told him, it was herself he would deride! A sense of his own inferiority was a canker in the man, a sore that steadily tormented him; and certainly he had no love for her. The fact that she was a Currain gave her some importance in his eyes; but if he knew the truth, her only ascendancy over him would vanish forever.

More than that, he would delight to spread the tale abroad; and if he did that, if he betrayed the Currain shame, what of Dolly? Tilda's pride in Dolly was tempered by misgivings. She had always assured herself—and others—that it was the right of every pretty girl to flirt and coquet as she chose, until she married and went into that semi-retirement which was the lot of even the most charming young matrons. She had never admitted even to herself any real concern over the child's pretty follies; but secretly she sometimes wished Dolly would marry and settle down into the safe world of wives. If this scandal were spread abroad, the Currains would be laughed at; and if Dolly ever thought people were laughing at her, she was capable of anything.

So Dolly must never know, and therefore Redford Streean must never know. "If I can't tell someone, I shall simply burst." Tilda spoke half aloud, talking to herself. "But I just can't tell a soul!" Yet it would be fun, now and then, to remind Cinda and the others of the truth. "When they start putting on airs!"

She walked slowly till she remembered that Redford Streean was gone to Raleigh, or to Wilmington, or somewhere down south on what he said was government business. She suspected his departure had been prompted by fear that Richmond would be abandoned to the Yankees. Better men than he had fled, during these weeks just gone. But at any rate, he would not be at home; she need not face him. And of course Darrell too was away.

So she hurried her halting steps. The door was bolted. She rang, and presently rang again. It was Emma who answered, her greasy black countenance sweat-dappled, her apron soiled, her short pigtails in twists of dirty paper. Tilda promised herself that some day she would have a butler as dignified and as courtly as Cinda's Caesar. Redford might even buy Caesar himself, when Brett and Cinda became so poor they had to sell their people. To be sure, Caesar, who felt himself privileged to show his feelings, had never concealed his contempt for Redford. Well, if they bought him, they would take all that out of him, with a whip if necessary.

Tilda vented her envious anger on Emma. "What are you doing, answering the bell? Where's Sally?" Sally, for all her impudence, was a comely young woman. That was why her babies were lighter-hued than she, that was why Redford had her in the house. But at least, in Dolly's discarded finery, she kept herself presentable!

Emma snorted. "She up wid Mis' Dolly!" The fat black woman shook with obscene mirth. "Mis' Dolly gittin' fixed up tuh kill, lak she'd slep' her last!"

Tilda knew the phrase. She had heard it herself, many a year ago, on the morning of the day she was to wed Redford Streean. Her old May, sister of Trav's April and Cinda's June, had greeted her thus that morning when she brought the waiter with Tilda's breakfast. "Well, Honey, you's slep' you' last!" But the phrase was for brides, and Dolly was not a bride; not unless a great deal had happened in these days of Tilda's absence! Yet a great deal might have happened! Tilda turned and ran up the stairs to Dolly's room.

When she opened the door she saw Sally watching in critical appraisal while Dolly revolved slowly in front of the long mirror, inspecting herself with a lively appreciation. Dolly looked over her shoulder at her mother, and Tilda thought how beautiful she was in that posture, her shoulder so sweetly rounded and so warmly white against the dark masses of her hair. She saw too that the girl's eyes were unnaturally bright, with some charming excitement, and her color was high.

"Why, Mama," Dolly cried, prettily surprised, "I didn't think you'd get here today."

"We just this minute did," Tilda told her. "I walked from Aunt Cinda's." She sat down limply, and Dolly twirled twice around before the mirror.

"Isn't this pretty, Mama?"

"Lovely," Tilda assented. "Who's the lucky young man you're going to bewitch?"

"Captain Pew. He'll be here any minute."

"Captain Pew? Whoever is he? I can't keep all your beaux straight, Honey."

"Oh, he's a blockade-runner or something. Papa says I must be nice to him, and he's simply enchanting, so handsome and so dangerous-looking."

"Papa? Is he home?"

"Oh yes, he came back as soon as he heard about the Yankees getting New Orleans. He had a lot of sugar he wanted to sell if the price went up, and it did, and he made heaps of money; but he was furious because he didn't have salt too!" Tilda felt a quick pride in Redford's cleverness; but if he were in Richmond he would be here presently, and she dreaded facing him with this secret in her thoughts. If he guessed she was hiding anything he would be sure to bully it out of her. Dolly, intent upon the mirror, said casually: "Everyone says we'll just have to let the Yankees have Richmond. Mrs. Davis is gone, and all the men in the Government. Did you see any Yankee soldiers?"

"No." Tilda hesitated, itching to tell Dolly the whole story; but she dared not. Yet there was one thing she could tell. "But Great Oak's burned down, Dolly!"

"Oh Mama, honestly?" To Tilda's surprise the girl's eyes filled with tears. "Really and truly, Mama?" It was as though she pleaded for a denial of this bitter word.

"Yes, really and truly!" Tilda told her sharply. "But I don't know why you have to start snivelling!"

"But it was so heavenly there!" Dolly whimpered. "I used to pretend to myself I'd live there some day."

"Nonsense! You never would! You can be sure of that!" Tilda relaxed in her chair, groaning. "I declare, I'm just exhausted. We travelled all last night and all day today. The roads were crowded, and so muddy."

Dolly's quick tears as quickly dried; she made sure the traces were removed. "All the same," she declared, "I'll get even with those old Yankees somehow! See if I don't."

Tilda did not understand. "Get even with them? What for?"

"Why, for burning Great Oak."

"Oh Uncle Faunt did that. After we left, he set it on fire."

"Uncle Faunt?" Dolly whirled to face her, her eyes blank with astonishment. "For Heaven's sake, why?"

Tilda wished she had been more cautious, hurried to cover her indiscretion. "He simply couldn't bear to let the Yankees have it. We could see the fire against the sky for miles. Uncle Faunt felt terribly." This much at least she could tell. "Of course, we all did; but you know, he takes things hard."

Dolly stared at her, but before she could speak the door bell rang, and the girl cried: "Oh that's Captain Pew! Mama, tell him I'll be right down, will you?" She laughed in a pleasant excitement. "Do hurry, won't you. He hates being kept waiting. And he has a fearful temper anyway!"

Tilda started to say: "Let Sally tell him!" But if she did, like as not Sally would refuse, and Dolly would say she needed Sally to help with the last touches of her preparations. Besides, Tilda was curious to see this new beau of whose temper even Dolly spoke respectfully. A bossy man with a temper might be just the husband for Dolly! She rose to obey. A mirror warned her that she was dishevelled from her journey; but he would have no eyes for her, not if he expected Dolly! From the stair head she saw Emma lumbering toward the door, and she warned the fat old woman away with a hiss and a fierce gesture, and waited till Emma had disappeared before she opened the door.

Her first emotion was a sharp surprise; for Captain Pew was not the charming boy she had expected to see. He was old enough to be Dolly's father, thirty-five if he was a day. Yet it was true that he was a mighty handsome man, though since dusk was falling it was too dark here in the hall to see him clearly. "Good evening, Captain Pew," she said quickly. "I'm Dolly's mother. Do come in! She'll be right down."

He bowed. "Ma'am, I would have thought you Miss Dolly herself if you had not told me!"

Why, he was nice—in spite of that teasing twinkle in his eye. "Absurd man!" She heard her own words with astonishment. She was simpering like a girl, under his silly compliment. "All cats are gray in the dark! Light the gas, do."

He drew a match and the fumes stung Tilda's nose. In the sudden flare of the gas she saw that he was as handsome as he had seemed in semi-dark, tall and slender yet clearly very strong, with a clean-shaven chin and a delightfully sharp mustache and strange, disturbing eyes. No wonder he had swept Dolly off her feet. Perhaps old Emma was right! "There, come in and rest yourself. Dolly won't be long."

She had a few minutes with him in the drawing room. His deep voice was exciting, his grave courtesy faintly frightening. Tilda felt in him something deliciously disturbing. No wonder Dolly had lost her head! In Captain Pew the girl might meet just the master she needed. Tilda was laughing and chatting as gaily as a girl when Dolly, with a prettily apologetic cry of welcome, appeared like a radiant picture in the door.

3

To TONY, the tale the letters told was a jest of which he was the butt; and when he laughed—his mother and Cinda and the others heard more than once that night his jeering mirth—it was at his own folly in allowing himself during these last two or three years to be proud. Trav and Faunt and Cinda, yes and his mother too, had often in the past reminded him that he was a Currain, as though this fact imposed upon him some obligation, as though when he acted in any way except decorously and uprightly he was betraying his heritage.

Ha! Heritage? A fine heritage to be sure, from a father who had gone prowling after every pretty wench he saw. His own thoughts amused Tony more and more. He wondered how many little bastards that father of his had sired, to grow up and to breed in their turn a second generation. Why, there might be dozens, scores, maybe hundreds of white trash, in the North and in the South, in whom ran the famous Currain blood! How many were there who, if they knew the truth, could call him Uncle; could say Uncle or Aunt to Faunt and Trav, to Cinda and Tilda?

And one of them was nephew Abraham! Abraham Currain Lincoln! He remembered all the names Lincoln had been called. Scoundrel, blackguard, gorilla, nigger-lover; yes, Lincoln was all those things. But also, nephew Abraham was clever, clever enough to get himself elected President of the United States. Why, the Currains ought to be proud of their kin! If a Currain were going to be a scoundrel, he should at least be a successful one! Scoundrel, blackguard, gorilla, nigger-lover! Tony laughed under his breath. He himself had been thought a scoundrel and a blackguard in his day. And as for nigger-lovers—well, he would match his own get of little pickaninnies against all his father's bastards, in numbers if not in color. The quarter at Chimneys was full of them, born to wenches whom he had sent on from Great Oak in his unregenerate younger days. Some of them were grown now, and had children of their own, bright mulattoes, their blackness diluted with the famous Currain blood!

Yet Faunt and Trav and Cinda would not be amused, as he was, by this revelation. Tilda might be, but not the others. This would jolt Trav out of his smug complacency; no doubt of it. Faunt? Why, Faunt had already set the torch to Great Oak, as though to lay his father's house in ashes could somehow destroy his father's grandson up there in Washington.

Yes, Faunt would take this even harder than Trav. This would go a long way to destroy, in his own mind, that image of himself which Faunt had created; that gallant cavalier, that man of sorrows, that brave and noble gentleman whom Faunt imagined himself to be. Faunt would never be the same man again, not now.

Cinda? Of Cinda Tony was not so sure. Somewhere in this sister of his there was a rocklike foundation of character which Tony secretly respected. A good sister, blaming him when he deserved it, praising him when praise was his due; a good daughter, affectionate and patient no matter how unreasonable Mama might be; a good wife to Brett Dewain; a good mother. Yes, Cinda was a fine woman! She, and perhaps Trav, were strong. You could not be sure what changes might be made in them by this discovery.

As the journey to Richmond dragged on, Tony forgot his amusement and began to be sorry for himself. He had learned in these two or three years to think of himself as a good man, capable of doing his just part in the world; and he had relished that feeling. But now he knew this belief had been an illusion. He was actually what till so short a time ago he had seemed to be: the depraved and rascally product of his father's depraved and rascally Currain blood. To imagine that he was anything else had been just the weakness of his middle years, marking the onset of senility.

Yet he could grieve for that lost illusion and for that lost, admirable self. In this grief, wishing to be comforted, his thoughts turned to Nell Albion, who for so many years had found ways to content and reassure him. When the carriage with his mother and his sisters and the little train of Negroes with led horses and riding laden mules came to the house on Fifth Street, he was hungry for Nell, eager to go to her. Cinda bade them in; but Tilda hurried away, and there were the people and the animals to be lodged somewhere, so he and Faunt did not accept Cinda's invitation. They turned the people over to Caesar for disposal; and then the two brothers faced each other, a question in their eyes.

"I don't want to hear a lot of empty talk," Tony said. "I'll not go in. There's a lady upon whom I propose to call."

Faunt nodded harshly. "Talk? No, no talk," he said, and licked fevered lips.

"Come along with me," Tony suggested. He was suddenly amused at the notion of introducing Faunt to Nell. Faunt must have known, for years, the truth about Tony's relations with her. In derisive challenge, he added: "I'm going to call on Mrs. Albion."

This was an invitation which Faunt in the past would never have accepted; but now he hesitated only for an instant, then turned his horse. "Very well," he said.

When they reached Mrs. Albion's discreetly retired little house, once to Tony so familiar, she was not alone. They left their horses at the rail, and a Negro maid whom Tony did not know admitted them. Mrs. Albion showed no surprise at their coming. She greeted Faunt easily, and she introduced them to the two gentlemen already here. "Mr. Berry; Mr. Mosby." Mosby was in uniform, a small man with sandy hair and a level eye which Tony thought somehow disquieting. Mr. Berry was even smaller than Mosby, aggressively erect. Mrs. Albion said agreeably: "We were about to have a small supper. I hope you will join us."

"By all means!" Tony agreed. "We're just from the road, and hungry." He looked at Faunt. "And I, at least, would be heartened by a tot of brandy."

"Of course." Mrs. Albion brought decanter and glasses from the side table. They drank, and the Negress served them; and when they began to eat, Mrs. Albion, like a good hostess leading the conversation, broke the momentary silence.

"Mr. Berry has a newspaper in Western Virginia," she explained, and Mr. Berry took his cue.

"I came to watch the flight from Richmond," the editor said with pompous scorn. "Our so-called statesmen, with New Orleans lost and McClellan rampaging up the Peninsula, find discretion the better part of valor."

"Oh yes, of course, New Orleans." Tony had forgotten that disaster; he felt no interest in it now.

"Yes sir, lost," Mr. Berry repeated. "Surrendered by a traitor. General Lovell, gentlemen, would be the better for a little hanging."

Tony smiled at the small man's vehemence. "You take a low view of the situation, sir."

"I do," Mr. Berry agreed. "The loss of New Orleans cuts the Confederacy in half. Sooner or later, Yankee gunboats will patrol the whole Mississippi. This has been the winter of our discontent, gentlemen. The enemy is in Florida and on the Carolina coast; he has broken into Tennessee; yes and into Mississippi. Much of Virginia is in his hands. Since the glorious beginning which we made at Manassas last July, our fortunes have steadily declined." He hesitated; and his words left them all for a moment soberly silent. The little editor, as though his own words frightened him, paused and then went on: "And now our statesmen play the poltroon, dodging out of Richmond, sending away the archives, shivering in dread of new disasters. It is time, gentlemen, that the public took a hand. Let us demand that courage and wisdom and steadfastness be elevated to our high places to guide and direct us."

Mosby said quietly: "To be at the bottom of the ladder means that our next step can only be upward."

Tony saw Faunt's eyes turn toward the soldier, and he himself was struck by something in the man's tone. Mosby seemed no more than a boy, yet there was force in him.

"Not if Richmond falls," Mr. Berry insisted. "Not if Richmond falls, John."

Faunt remarked: "My brother and I have just come from Williamsburg, Mr. Mosby. The army was in full retreat, the roads for miles jammed with their wagons."

"Ah?" The other's brows knitted. "I have been these five days with Mrs. Mosby and my children; so I had not known the situation there. But I expect to take the road that way at midnight." He smiled. "I had counted on an hour or two of sleep before pushing on; but my old friend Mr. Berry assured me I would find more refreshment in calling upon the most brilliant woman in Richmond." He bowed to Mrs. Albion. "I find he spoke the truth."

"What is your service?" Faunt inquired.

"First Virginia Cavalry."

"Ah? My nephew, Burr Dewain, is in the First Virginia."

"I have not the pleasure of his acquaintance."

Faunt was not in uniform, and Tony saw the unspoken question in Mosby's eyes. So did Faunt, for he said: "I was with General Wise at Roanoke. I managed to get clear of the surrender of his forces; but I took some hurts there. I am only just now ready for duty again."

Mrs. Albion said, in a tone which caught Tony's ear: "I believe you would all be the better for a glass of wine." She brought it, and Tony observed that she served Faunt first, and that as she served the others she turned to look back at Faunt. Tony watched her with a slow stir of anger. She was like every other woman, instantly attracted to this brother of his. Her liking was plain in her smile, in her voice, in her eyes. He damned his own folly in bringing Faunt here. This was a thing he should have expected, this tenderness in her. Luckily Faunt never seemed to suspect that women yearned over him.

"General Wise?" Mosby repeated. "Did he not propose, when he was in Western Virginia, to add a company of partisan rangers to his brigade? I think I heard something of the sort, last summer."

"I don't know." Faunt had drained his wine glass, and Mrs. Albion refilled it. Faunt and this sandy-haired young cavalryman were too absorbed in each other to notice her; but Tony saw that little Mr. Berry watched her shrewdly. "I was in Jennings Wise's company," Faunt said.

Mosby smiled. "You should ride with Stuart. He likes men of your pattern." He sang under his breath: " 'If you want to catch the Devil—jine the cavalry.' "

"To catch the Devil?" Faunt echoed in a thoughtful tone, and Tony saw a leaping flame in his eyes; but then Faunt commented: "Every Southerner likes the cavalry, Mr. Mosby; but it's infantry that wins the battles."

Mosby's tone hardened. "Battles are won not on the battlefield, but far behind the armies," he corrected. "Just now, for example, the place to save Richmond is not on the Peninsula; it is in the Valley." He added reflectively: "To beat the Yankees it might even be well to let them have Richmond. The farther they advance, the more vulnerable they become. Fifty good men behind their lines, well led, could cut the hamstrings of their army."

"I suppose your fifty men would be cavalry."

"Not as you use the word, no," Mosby replied. "I'd have no heavy columns of troopers with sabres flashing, banners flying. Oh no! No! That is a stirring spectacle, but it's ineffective. The cavalry's proper arm is the revolving pistol, or the carbine, or both! The sabre is for reviews, for parades, but not for work!" The little man stood up; he began to pace to and fro, his words rang. Faunt's eyes followed him, his head turning from side to side as the other moved back and forth across the room. "No, not your sort of cavalry, sir," Mosby insisted. "Just fifty brave men, good horsemen, armed with carbines and pistols. Such a force could raise havoc behind the enemy lines. Tell me, sir—" Mosby's voice sharpened with his own enthusiasm. "How will McClellan protect fifty miles of railroad against such a force? He must be in superior strength at every point, for he can never know where the blow will fall. And by superior strength, I mean he must be two, three, four to one; for if he uses infantry, a surprise attack by fifty men will scatter five times their number of foot soldiers, and if they are mounted, so much the better! You know horses, sir. Horses at a stand will not wait to receive a charge, no matter how brave their riders. Remember, there are no good horsemen in the North. You charge a troop of a hundred mounted men with your fifty, and their horses will turn and run, stampede! Then you overtake them, one by one, their riders helpless; you raise your pistol!" He snapped his fingers sharply six times. "Six shots, six Yankees down! As simple as that, sir!"

He laughed, and there was a lift to his laughter; Tony felt his own heart stir at the sound. Faunt gulped his wine; his cheek was flushed, his voice thick. " 'If you want to kill the Devil—jine the cavalry!' "

Mosby's eyes shone. "Yes sir! There's the fun!"

Faunt nodded. "Kill the Devil, yes!" Tony grinned. Faunt, Faunt of all men, was drunk! The others saw it, too, for Mrs. Albion crossed to stand by Faunt's chair.

"You're very tired," she said in a low tone. "You must rest." Under her caressing hand Faunt's head bowed like that of a contented dog. It was as though these two were alone.

After an uncomfortable moment, Mosby abruptly rose. "I must be gone," he said. "Mr. Berry, we must make our duties."

He bowed to Mrs. Albion; and she left Faunt and went with her departing guests into the hall. Tony stayed watching his brother. Yes, by God, Faunt was drunk! Faunt the cavalier, the very perfect gentle knight, was drunk, slouching in drunken slumber.

In the hall Mosby was saying: "Mrs. Albion, I like that man! He'll make a deadly fighter. If he asks for me, tell him I'll be with Stuart before noon tomorrow." He chuckled. "I'll be pistolling the Yankees! Tell him that!"

Tony heard Mosby's fingers snap again, and Mr. Berry's laughing voice. "Hear him talk of butchering the Yankees! Yes, and he's done it, too. But a year ago you couldn't have found in all Virginia a stouter Union man than John Mosby."

"That, I'll hazard, was before Virginia seceded," Mrs. Albion suggested; and their voices faded toward the door. Tony rose to wake Faunt, to take him to Cinda's or to some discreet lodging for the night. Then he could return to Nell. His hand was on Faunt's shoulder when Mrs. Albion spoke from the doorway.

"Let him sleep, let him rest. Your brother is deadly tired, he's sick, he's had some shocking blow. Let him rest, Tony."

Tony nodded. "I will, yes. I'll see him home to bed, then come back to you."

Her eyes flashed to him in quick inquiry; she gave him a long appraisal, looked from him to Faunt. "You are changed—again, Tony. Like your old self. What has happened?"

"My old self, yes," he assented. "I'll come back to you, when I have taken him home."

She looked down at Faunt for a long silent moment. "Poor—gentleman," she whispered.

"I'll see him safe, come back. I need you, Nell."

Mrs. Albion faced him quietly. "No, Tony. No. We can't retrace old paths." Then, dismissing Tony from her thoughts as she had dismissed him from her life, she touched Faunt's drooping shoulders, his bent head. "I will keep him here, to sleep, to rest, till he is healed again."

"Him?" Her word struck Tony like a blow. He had been so sure that he could turn to her.

"Why not?" she challenged gently.

He hesitated. "Why, I need you! My world's upside down tonight." Half-minded to tell her the truth, he nevertheless held back the word. If he did, she might laugh, make sport of him; and he would not face her laughter. "I've always turned to you, Nell. We were close so long."

"He needs me more than you do now."

Her tenderness to Faunt was a lash that stung and cut. Tony struck with words meant to hurt her. "No, Nell! I'll not let you get your damned hands on him!"

She smiled, wise and serene. "Poor Tony!"

He was slow to accept defeat; he pleaded, he threatened, he tried every means—and could not move her. When at last he accepted dismissal, leaving Faunt still stupidly asleep there in her chair, he bolted from the house, mounted his horse at the rail and put the beast to a gallop through the silent and deserted streets. There was a desolation and a fury in him. He felt himself lost and alone; and self-pity alternated with hard unheeding rage. Nell had cast him out! Melted by tenderness for Faunt, turned by that tenderness to wax that flowed through Tony's fingers, she had escaped him at the moment when he thought to seize her.

So he was alone.

He let his horse go without direction, lifting it to utmost speed, racing headlong out of the city along random ways, till after miles the beast slowed at last to an exhausted walk. He tried to urge it into a run again, wrenching at the reins, kicking its ribs, wishing for spurs. He dismounted to find a stick and beat the horse with a brutal violence, venting on the dumb animal all the passion in him. He mounted and brought it to a stumbling run again. When at last it collapsed, its legs giving way, its great heart broken, Tony fell with it; but beyond some slight bruises he escaped hurt. He freed himself, and tried to jerk the horse to its feet; but it could not rise.

There was night and silence all around him, and Tony had not heeded the course they took, did not know where he was. He sat down under a tree beside the road to wait for dawn.

4

May, 1862

CINDA, when she came home that night, racked and weary as much from her own thoughts as from the discomfort of the long journey, was conscious of no wish but one: that Brett Dewain were here. As the carriage made its way through the familiar streets she hoped he would be at the house, hoped he would open the door and come to take her into the secure haven of his arms; but she knew this was unlikely. He had had leave for Vesta's wedding, could hardly have come home again so soon.

But at least Vesta would be here; and Cinda was reassured by this certainty, for Vesta was strong and steady and fine. She thought wearily that she would have a houseful, with Jenny and Barbara and Enid, and the children, and now her mother too. Tonight would be a problem. Where would Faunt and Tony sleep, for instance? Which room should be her mother's? Which had Enid pre-empted? She was too tired to decide, but Vesta's level head would come to her rescue.

They reached the house and Tilda scurried away while Cinda and Mrs. Currain went indoors. In the hall, under the bright gaslight, Cinda thought Enid had a sullen look; and Barbara, with her baby coming so soon, was naturally pale; but Jenny was serene and comforting. It was good to come home again to familiar surroundings, to the cheerful drawing room with its beautiful gilt cornices and its bright colors. The tall mirror between the windows told her how bedraggled she was and she turned away, sat down on the low carved seat. "Where's Vesta?" she asked.

"I thought she would come with you."

"With us?" Cinda was surprised, and alarmed too. "No, of course not. Where is she?"

Jenny said reassuringly. "Now Mama, don't worry about Vesta! You never saw anyone so happy! When they found you weren't here, she decided to ride down to Williamsburg with Tommy and come home with you."

"We didn't see her." Cinda remembered the long weary miles, the crowded roads; and she pressed her hands against her eyes, wishing her thoughts would clear.

"There, I'm sure she's all right," Jenny insisted, and she added: "We didn't know when you would get here, but Granny's room is all ready." She explained each arrangement she had made, and her quiet words helped Cinda lay hold on comforting routine. To think of these familiar details was to shut out, at least for tonight, the troubling world. Vesta was all right, of course. If she did not meet Travis, she had friends in Williamsburg to whom she could turn.

Where to put Faunt and Tony was a problem; but Faunt was always considerate and thoughtful, and he would foresee this, and take Tony elsewhere, and thus give her time to settle the household into an orderly groove again. So she was not surprised that her brothers did not come for supper, did not reappear at all; and somehow presently the rest of them were all abed.

Cinda was so tired she slept as her head touched the pillow, and she did not wake till June came smilingly with morning coffee. June was full of talk, needing no prompting questions; and Cinda, sipping her coffee while the old woman brushed and brushed her hair, relaxed contentedly. June had a wonderful gift for telling her just the things she wished to know. Miss Vesta when she came back from Goochland was the happiest-looking bride anybody ever saw; Mister Cloyd, you couldn't touch him with a ten-foot pole, he was stepping so high and proud. Miss Barbara was poorly, for her baby was going to be a buster. It would be a boy for sure, she carried it so high! Miss Enid had been mighty nice, not making no trouble at all for nobody. The children got along together just like so many kittens in a basket. The gentlemen never did come back last night. There was a mighty lot of scared white folks in Richmond, and a pile of them were going away to some place or other for fear the Yankees were coming. So-and-so had gone, and So-and-so, and So-and-so. An expressive sniff made clear June's opinion of these craven departures. Mrs. Currain was just fine this morning, chipper as a jay bird. June had fixed her breakfast the way she liked it, taken the waiter up to her. Yes indeed, everything was fine!

Under June's soothing tongue and the smooth strokes of the brush Cinda's troubles paled and faded. When Brett came home, she would tell him the tale of the letters, then dismiss it from her mind. If a thing could not be helped, it was necessary to forget it. She thought of Clayton, dead now almost a year, dead because of this war which Abraham Lincoln, fruit of her father's stale and ancient sin, had forced upon the South. The sins of the fathers were visited upon the children, yes; but why could they not have been visited upon the children alone, instead of upon the children's children? Upon her child; her Clayton?

She shook her head, shut her eyes. There was no profit in thought upon this matter. She must armor herself against such reflections. So must they all.

She need have, she reflected, no concern for her mother. Mrs. Currain had walled herself against the impact of these troubled days. But Tony? Faunt? Tilda? Trav? What would this knowledge do to them? Tony was a weakling; or at least he had been, all his life till within a year or two. There was no knowing what he would do now. Faunt was a brave and gentle man; yet at the first impact of this revelation he had gone for a while a little mad, gulping brandy, setting fire to the dear old house that had meant so much to all of them. Yet surely he would rally his courage and his steadfastness to withstand this cruel hurt. Tilda? Tilda did not matter. As for Travis, he was a rock, a great rock in a weary land. Cinda had no fear for him.

June was still prattling, her voice a gentling monotone; but Cinda stirred. "June, ask Miss Jenny to come have breakfast with me." So her day began, but for a while there was no strength in her. "I wish it were Sunday," she told Jenny. "I feel more like going to church than like managing and planning."

But an hour with Jenny made her strong again. They spoke of Vesta, but Tommy would of course have seen her safe with friends in

Williamsburg. Faunt and Tony would be coming presently. She dressed at last and she and Jenny came downstairs together. Cinda expected Mrs. Currain would ask where her sons were; but the old woman betrayed no curiosity. She seemed to accept her establishment here in Cinda's home as perfectly normal. She enjoyed the children, she smiled at Enid's pretty attentions, she patted Jenny's hand in gentle affection. There was a great chair in her room and she held court there, mistress of the moment, of herself, and of them all. Barbara was with them for a while; and Mrs. Currain told Cinda afterward with a brisk, approving nod: "I like Burr's little wife. She's a sweet child." Cinda did not argue the point. If Mrs. Currain liked Barbara, probably she herself was wrong.

Toward dusk Big Mill brought Vesta home, and they heard the tale of her adventures, and smiled as they listened. She described Julian's brotherly wrath at her for being in the way when men had work to do, and Elegant's consternation when they found Great Oak all ablaze, and Mrs. Taylor's protests at her departure, and the ludicrous figure she cut in Mr. Taylor's cape, and how a stream of water ran off the brim of her hat when she leaned down to kiss Tommy good-by and splashed in his face, and Uncle Trav's solicitude as they rode through the night, and the humble people who gave them shelter, and Big Mill's obvious impatience to get her home so that he could go back to Trav.

"I expect he's started already," she guessed. "Just as soon as he could get a fresh mule."

Cinda, listening to Vesta's happy tones, thought youth was so brave, so confident, so sure, flinging a gay challenge in the face of destiny. Human beings were like small dogs barking their defiance at a huge mastiff that paid them no slightest heed, that brushed them aside— yes, and sometimes stamped out their small lives—in a remote and complete indifference. Oh, youth was frighteningly brave, knowing so little of the dangers in the way.

She thought Vesta knew no fear. Tilda brought next day news of the fight at Williamsburg, and of the repulse of the Yankees. "There, that's my Tommy!" Vesta cried proudly, when she heard; and Cinda looked at her in wonder. Was it possible that the girl did not know the fruits of battle? But Vesta caught that glance, came swiftly to her mother's side, kissed her and whispered: "Darling, don't look at me like that! Of course I'm worried, but I won't cry before I'm hurt!"

Cinda smiled and pressed her hand; and asked Tilda: "Then our army is still in Williamsburg?" Perhaps to abandon Great Oak had not been necessary after all.

"Oh no! Everyone says we could stay there as long as we like, but General Johnston is so stubborn. He's decided to retreat, and so he's bound to do it, no matter how often the army proves we don't have to. No, we beat them, but the army's coming on toward Richmond." Tilda asked for Faunt and Tony.

"Tony has Chimneys to attend to," Cinda reminded her. Let them assume that he had gone. "And Faunt was well enough to return to duty." She did not know where they were, but she would not tell Tilda so.

"Tony ought to have taken Mama to Chimneys," Tilda suggested. "No telling what's going to happen here. Redford says we'll give up Richmond, let the Yankees have it. Besides, you know how Mama hates hot weather, and summer here can be awful."

Cinda reflected that there was wisdom in this. "But of course Mama wouldn't go," she reminded them. "It's a wonder we ever got her to come this far."

Vesta said: "But Mama, it really would be wonderful for her. I wish we'd thought of it before Uncle Tony left. Uncle Trav says it's nearly always cool there."

Cinda nodded, entangled in her own white lie. She had as good as said that Tony was gone to Chimneys, could not now confess he was presumably still in Richmond. She wondered where he was. Probably he had turned to old haunts, the gaming table, the bottle. Perhaps Faunt was with him; but there was no profit in conjecture.

Before Tilda left she drew Cinda aside. "Has Mama said anything about those awful letters?"

"No. None of us need talk about them."

"Well, I certainly won't tell a soul; but oh Cinda, isn't it terrible? Aren't you dying of shame?"

"I'm not going to worry about something Papa did thirty years before I was born!"

"But don't you realize—" Tilda spoke in a horrified whisper. "Lincoln's actually our nephew, Cinda. That wretched brat of papa's was our half-sister."

"What of it? If you go back far enough, everyone in the world is cousins or something!"

Tilda cried flatteringly: "I think you're wonderful, the way you always make the best of things. But Faunt was terribly upset, and Heaven knows what Tony will do!"

Cinda saw that Tilda really enjoyed the situation, and of course Redford Streean would exult if he knew. She hoped Tilda had wit enough never to tell him.

Cinda slept ill that night, with haunted dreams. Two of her sons were with the army at Williamsburg, and Tommy too; and Tommy since he married Vesta was become her son. Vesta and Barbara betrayed none of the anxiety they must feel, and she hoped she had been able to hide her fears as well as they. How long must they all have terror for a bedfellow? There would be other battles, through the months and years. This time—please God—Burr and Julian and Vesta's Tommy had come safely through the deadly storm; but this was only a beginning. Yes, hardly even a beginning. The army was in retreat toward Richmond; the Yankees would press after them. Lincoln's blackguards would fight to capture Richmond, and her sons must fight to prevent them, fight while they lived.

How long? How long?

She found herself wondering about this Lincoln, whom every Southerner abhorred. What sort of man was it who would bring wounds and death to sow sorrow across his native land, and to scatter seeds of hatred which would never die? Did Lincoln in his secret heart exult in the horrors which he thrust upon them all? Did he, like a miser, count his crimes and revel in the tally? Was he wholly inhuman?

Or was he, conceivably, a man like other men, caught up in forces he could not control, hating all this yet driven by some mistaken conviction of the rightness of his course?

No, that was not possible! No man, if he were honest, could believe it right to force the South like an unwilling bride to return to a union she loathed. There must be some intermediate truth that was believable, but Cinda's weary thoughts found no answer to the dark enigma. They blurred and lost themselves in restless sleep.

She was awake, Wednesday morning, at first dawn; and she lay with half-open eyes, staring at nothing, waiting for June to come to her. She could hear, presently, small sounds in the house, light hasting footsteps as the children in their play ran to and fro, the whisper of one of the black nurses hushing her charge so grownups could sleep. Cinda always relished this quiet morning hour alone. To be thus wakeful gave her time to set her thoughts in order and to store up energy against the confused and pressing problems of each day. June would come soon. The old woman always brought hot coffee, then helped Cinda halfway through the process of dressing for the day, then fetched her breakfast. Breakfast was always on the same waiter, of black enamel gay with a pattern of green leaves and yellow flowers, which June extravagantly admired. It occurred to Cinda by and by that June today was later than usual; but when the old woman appeared, the delay was forgotten in Cinda's surprise at the fact that instead of the usual cup of coffee June this morning brought a complete breakfast, hot bread, bacon, jam, coffee, a heaping plenty.

And there was another surprise. Cinda smiled. "Why, June, you've gone and given my special waiter to someone else this morning! Did you give it to Mama?"

"Ma'am?" June was drawing the curtains, keeping her back turned to her mistress; and Cinda watched her in a closer attention, struck by something in her tone.

"And you didn't bring my early coffee." June still did not turn, and Cinda forced herself to speak lightly. "What's upset you, June? Have you and Caesar been having one of your battles?"

"Eat yo' breakfast, Honey," June urged. "How come you ask so many questions?" Her tone was almost normal; almost, but not quite.

Cinda felt her heart pound; she spoke evenly. "June."

"Yes, ma'am."

"Don't treat me like a baby. What's happened?"

After a moment, the old woman came to her; and Cinda saw tears on June's black cheeks, and she thought abstractedly that tears on dark skin looked like drops of ink. Then June drew her close, cradling

Cinda's head against her bosom, rocking to and fro, crooning over and over: "Don' you cry, Honey Chile! My baby, my little ol' Miss Cindy, please ma'am, don' you go carryin' on!"

It was sweet and richly assuaging to be held so; and for a moment Cinda let herself go, and her own eyes filled. With others, she must wear a brave front; but with June she need never pretend. Ever since she was a baby, she had always been able to weep out her woes on this black bosom.

Then she freed herself, gently, trying to laugh. "Why June, here we are both of us crying like silly women!" There was no gulf between them now; no question of mistress and slave. They were two who had loved each other long. "What's happened, June? Tell me."

She had at first to draw out the truth with many questions; but once well started, June told all she knew. One of Mr. Frisbie's Negroes had come to Richmond in the night from Williamsburg. His name was Sam—June as a narrator had one failing: she never omitted any least detail—and he rode Mr. Frisbie's roan hunter and led three of Mr. Frisbie's horses; because Mr. Frisbie was in the cavalry and wanted them safe away from the Yankees. Mr. Frisbie had told Sam to start early Monday morning, but the armies were fighting so near the Frisbie place that Sam and the other people crowded into the smoke house, and into the cellar of the big house to be out of the way of the bullets. The fighting stopped along toward dark, and Sam got his courage up and went to the stables. It was by that time late at night. While he was saddling the roan, he heard someone crying, right outside the stable door, in the dark shadows; and he took the lantern to see who it was, and it was Elegant, Mister Julian's body servant.

June said it had been hard for Sam to get much out of Elegant for a while. Cinda by this time was listening without questions, feeling no longer any emotion at all, allowing the old woman's words to flow over her, herself withdrawn in passive submission. Elegant was hurt half to death, June said. "And serve dat wuthless niggah right if he uz kilt daid!" she commented, her grief for a moment giving way to indignation.

Because Elegant had lost Mister Julian. He told Sam that the regiment marched up to a rail fence, miles and miles; and Yankees behind the fence were shooting at them with a hundred cannons. Elegant said he was so scared he tried to hide behind Mister Julian; and he tried to get his young master to run away into the woods and hide, but he couldn't. He couldn't do anything but follow along, trying to keep Mister Julian between him and the Yankee bullets. "'Stead of gittin' in front where he belonged to be," June angrily declared. "So's he cud stop de bullets and do some good!"

He said—according to Sam and now to June—that just about everybody in the regiment was killed before some of them reached the fence. He said—Cinda felt the hard clutch at her heart, yet knew no pain—that bullets hit Lieutenant Cloyd and just ripped him open the way you rip a catfish up the belly; and Elegant saw him fall and ran across to him, and some bullets hit Elegant while he was kneeling by the shattered body. But he ran back to Mister Julian, and they got to the fence and lay down there till someone said they had to go back across the field. Elegant didn't know much about what happened after that. He said he tried to stand up, and fell down, and Mister Julian got him on his shoulders piggyback to carry him. The next thing he knew it was dark, and he was in some woods somewhere, and Mister Julian wasn't anywhere around. Elegant crawled as far as he could, looking for Mister Julian all over the place, and never did find him.

"Sam went and fotch Mistuh Frisbie's old Sarah," June explained, "And dey laid Elegant in de hay mow tuh tek keer ob him de best dey could, and Sam tuk de hosses an' put out fo' Richmond de way Mistuh Frisbie tolt him to. An' soon as he git shet ob de hosses heah, he come along at daylight dis mawnin' an' tolt us."

And though Cinda harried her with many questions, that was all the old woman knew.

So Vesta's Tommy was dead. Julian? Not to know whether he lived or died was almost worse than knowing he was dead. Cinda was in some obscure way grateful that she could turn her thoughts on Vesta; on Vesta, so young and brave and sure. There was nothing she could do about Julian; but she could cherish Vesta, muster strength and offer it to Vesta as a staff and stay. To think of Vesta, to think only of Vesta; this would help her put thought of Julian into the deep background of her mind.

But oh, why could not Brett be here? Why could not he and she be together now, if only for an hour? Clayton was dead, and Vesta's Tommy—as dear to Cinda, since Vesta loved him, as her own son— and now Julian! Yes, and perhaps Burr too! Burr had been in that battling. Till he came home, till some word of his safety reached them, Cinda must live in a helpless dread. So must Barbara.

Cinda roused herself. Vesta and Barbara were her charge. While she dressed, while she fortified herself to go to them, she thought of Travis. He might do something; she did not know what.

He might at least bring her news of Julian.

Her little baby.

She found herself wondering absently what that kinsman in Washington, that Abraham Lincoln, would feel if he knew the grief and the pain he had brought to them all today. But probably if he knew the truth about his mother's birth, he had long since learned to curse the name of Currain. Lucy Hanks in one of her angry letters had called down a long damnation on Anthony Currain who had wronged her so shamefully. Had she perhaps, while this Abraham Lincoln was still a baby, taught him to repeat those curses parrotlike, taught him long hatred at her knee?

But what did it matter? Clayton was dead, and Tommy. And Julian? Cinda had seen poor shattered wounded in Miss Sally Tompkins' hospital; men so witless from suffering that they forgot their own names; men whose faces were lacerated beyond recognition. Julian might be dead; or he might be alive, groaning his life away in some secret thicket, dying alone; or he might be like one of those senseless ones, his mind forever shattered, his sweet face so marred that only loving eyes could recognize him.

She pressed her hands hard to her temple. She must put such thoughts away.

She opened her door, and from the open door of Vesta's room along the hall, the room which for the present Vesta shared with Barbara, she heard their sudden laughter at something that amused them there. June, at Cinda's shoulder, heard that bright laughter too, and broke into wrenching sobs. Cinda thrust the old woman gently back into the room and closed the door upon her. She went on to face Vesta and her task alone.

5

THAT Sunday evening when Tony brought his brother to her house, Mrs. Albion was within a week of being fifty years old; but never in her life had she felt a passionate and self-forgetting attachment for any man. She married while she was still emotionally a child, and she had with her young husband a few jolly years. When he died and left her still a careless young woman, the pinch of encroaching poverty taught her the importance of having enough money so that money did not matter. Her attempt to marry Travis Currain because he was wealthy failed as much because of her own overeagerness as because of Enid's spiteful interference; she turned to Tony in a greedy desperation.

Ten years as Tony's mistress taught her that men are lonely, simple, eager for friendliness, grateful for an audience, hungry for a sympathetic and approving and interested listener. She cultivated the art of listening; and thus she acquired a constantly widening circle of masculine friends. She liked men; not any one man in particular but men in general. She understood that by her relationship with Tony she was from the world of sheltered and respectable womankind forever excluded; and this, after a while, ceased to provoke in her any bitterness. There was another feminine world the doors of which were open to her, but for this other world she had no inclination. The result was that though she knew many men, she had few women acquaintances—and no women friends.

Her relationship with Tony came to be, at least in her own mind, regularized by its very persistence. She thought of herself as secure in a pseudo wifehood which provided all the rewards of marriage except respectability, while it imposed none of the obligations. During this period, there was a change in her. The men who learned to enjoy her company were apt to be persons of some intellectual capacity. Attracted at first by the provocative irregularity which was tacitly associated with her establishment, they found her a pleasant and gracious woman, and a good listener, and came again and again. She had the gift of silence. Their conversations among themselves in her company —for since men are instinctively conventional, no one but Tony and Darrell ever called upon her except with a companion—dealt with business, with politics, with subjects essentially masculine, and of which few women had any real understanding. She bolstered what her listening taught her by wide and thoughtful reading. She began to have opinions, and sometimes, if she were asked to do so, to express them. The men who knew her found her opinions worth hearing.

These years of settled and orderly living had another result. She was naturally as healthy as an animal, and freedom from anxieties preserved in her a sleek and contenting beauty. This was not, of course, the fresh loveliness of youth, but the richness of maturity. Her hair lost none of its lustre, her countenance showed no betraying lines, her throat was a smooth column. No one would have mistaken her for a girl; she was a woman. But no man, meeting her for the first time, ever stopped to ask himself: "I wonder how old she is."

When Tony cast her aside, she knew only a momentary panic which took the form of contriving that the profitable North Carolina plantation should pass into his hands. She was quite sure that she could when she chose go back to him; and always there lay in the background of her thoughts the fear of poverty. Against poverty she must insure herself. It was to do so that with the approach of hostilities between North and South she decided to capitalize upon her wide acquaintance among men of importance in the Confederacy. By returning to Richmond she would be in a position to learn many things of value to the Northern generals.

She sought to make sure beforehand that for her services she should be adequately paid; but when she tried to make a bargain she was met by a complacent Northern confidence in early victory. She returned to Richmond as it were on speculation; but a week after

Manassas an emissary, a Baltimore man posing as one of General Winder's detectives charged with policing Richmond, came secretly to enlist her services for the North. Since then she had contributed more than once to the flood of information which funnelled into the Richmond clearing house of the Union Secret Service.

She recognized the risk she ran. Early in April, not a month before she first saw Faunt, two men named Lewis and Scully had been convicted as spies and sentenced to be hanged; and on the day set for their execution a great throng of curious and morbid people trooped out Broad and Grace and Franklin Streets to the Fair Grounds to watch their execution. It was true that at the last moment the men were reprieved to give evidence against Timothy Webster; and the crowd, which had been once disappointed, expecting another reprieve, did not trouble to go to the Fair Grounds on the day set for his death. But Webster was well and duly hanged, so Nell knew that it was a deadly and dangerous game she played. It was because she might some day need a friendly witness to her loyalty that she had gone to Cinda with the information which led to the famous Confederate victory at Leesburg; and once or twice afterward, for a like reason, she played a double game, till she thought herself secure.

To open new sources of information and to increase her value to the North—and hence her earnings—she widened her pleasant hospitality. Her reputation as a charming and brilliant woman spread, and her pleasant little suppers acquired a limited fame. There were many men, officers in the army or members of the Government, whose homes were far away and who were glad to spend an evening thus amiably. She was such a receptive listener that their tongues forgot discretion, and her task was made absurdly easy. If a regiment moved through Richmond to the Peninsula, in this spring of 1862, the movement was recorded on a bulletin board outside the Provost Marshal's office where anyone who chose could read. Espionage was in fact so simple that its rewards were few; but Mrs. Albion discovered other profitable activities. Such men as Redford Streean were already shipping cotton and tobacco through the lines, trading ostensibly for supplies badly needed in the Confederacy, but plucking out a fat plum for themselves from every pie. She shared their plans and their profits. She had no troubling scruples, felt herself under no obligation to the

South. She went her calm and careful way without bitterness, but equally without any sense of guilt at all. She was at once cool and bold, completely mistress of herself, doing nothing without a reason, and nothing recklessly. It was her habit to appraise the men she met, to try to foresee how they might be useful to her; she saw them only as they affected her and her activities.

But from the first moment, Faunt, whether because she was at a vulnerable age when any chance acquaintance might have awakened her, or because his haggard eyes and his weariness aroused in her a maternal tenderness, or because between them some mysterious emotional current passed, made her forget herself. To watch him sitting here in her drawing room with tortured misery in his eyes roused in her emotions she had never known. She felt all her senses sharpened and demanding. She heard him speak and hungered for his next word; she filled her eyes with him, her glance touching his every feature, his image engraving itself upon her heart beyond forgetting. She felt or seemed to feel an electric emanation from him which set off in her veins an answering vibration. To bring him brandy, to fill his glass with wine, to see him eat the food she provided was rich content. But content was not assuagement. She longed to touch his hand, his cheek, his brow; and when this longing became unbearable she yielded to it. That under her touch he relaxed, surrendering to long fatigue, drowning in sudden sleep, filled her with a fierce proud passion. When Mosby and the little editor departed, she resented Tony's staying. Tony's desire to be alone with her woke in her an icy anger; when Tony was gone and she was alone with Faunt she found herself trembling, breathless as a girl.

Faunt still slept, leaning back in his chair. She came to stand beside him, touching his shoulder with one finger as though to assure herself of his actual presence here. Here was where he belonged; here he should stay. He must stay and stay and stay; stay till he was rested and well and strong again. The Negro maid came to the door and saw her mistress and saw Faunt, and her eyes widened in stammering surprise.

"Who dat, ma'am? I herd de gemmun go."

Mrs. Albion brushed the question aside. "See if his horse is at the gate, Milly."

The woman drew the curtain aside to peep out of the window. "Yes, ma'am, hit shore is."

"The gentleman is ill. We must keep him here, take care of him. Wake Rufus." The Negro slept in the shed at the foot of the garden. "Tell him to take care of the horse." Her voice tightened warningly. "Tell him if anyone ever finds out the gentleman is here, I'll sell both of you South."

"Yes, ma'am." Milly's promise had the emphasis of terror.

"Tell Rufus, then come back to me."

Between them they put Faunt, still stupid with drink and with fatigue, to bed. Milly grumbled at this indelicacy. "You go on 'bout your bizness, ma'am. I'll 'tend to him." But Nell said curtly: "He's hurt and sick, Milly; and I'm no child." When they removed his shirt and she discovered Faunt's deep scars she whispered pitying tenderness, and Milly muttered:

"Hm! De gemmun sho' ain' got no fat on him, is he? Dem ribs stick out lak a skellykin. Poah as a picked chicken. Hm-m!" Her black hands were as gentle as Mrs. Albion's. Faunt lay limp under their ministrations.

They put him in the room next Nell's own; and when their task was done Nell sent the other away. "I'll leave my door open, in case he calls," she said.

"He ain' gwine call nobody, woah out de way he is." Milly chuckled in sly amusement. "No, ma'am, he ain' gwine to be no botheh tuh you at all!" Then, seeing how still and tense her mistress was: "Ma'am, you come let Milly bresh down youh hair. You all upset you own se'f, ma'am."

Nell submitted to the other's attendance, and when she was ready for the night, Milly tucked her in, soothed her with comforting endearments. But when Milly was gone, Nell rose and drew a match and lighted a candle and went to the other room; and she stood for a long time by the bed where Faunt lay, looking down at him till her eyes were swimming and she felt her heart's thudding pound. The bed was wide. She set the candle on the stand and lay down with him, her head pillowed beside his, watching his still face with tireless eyes. Once sudden terror seized her; for he slept so soundly that he seemed not to breathe at all. She rose on one elbow to lean above him, and held her cheek near his lips till she felt the soft warmth of his breath. She stayed there in a brooding wonder at him, and at herself; yet more and more completely she forgot herself in thoughts of this dear, weary man.

Back in her own bed she lay awake, feeling a slow amazement at this thing which had come to her; at this incredible and overwhelming flood in which it was bliss to drown. Why, she had never seen this man until tonight; she had not heard him speak a dozen times. How was he different from other men? By what magic did he reveal to her these things she had never known before?

"These things I've never known before." She was to use these words more than once during the days that followed, telling Faunt over and over that which words could never tell, feeling always that he was far away from her, feeling always in him remoteness, ironic amusement, an indifferent tolerance. Too wise to demand of him more than he could give her, she shut her mind to this understanding, refused to acknowledge it to herself, took care never to challenge him. "You've taught me things I've never known before." They laughed at the phrase together, but she took care not to oppress him even with her gratefulness, giving much and demanding nothing.

During these days she denied herself to everyone, so they were completely undisturbed. It was good to see strength come back to him, to see his cheeks fill out again, to see his eyes clear, to see his rare smile. When he decided at last upon departure she did not urge him to stay; nor did she exact from him any pledge or promise. Yet at the last she said:

"I think we've found something we will never lose, Faunt; you and I."

He smiled a little. "There are so many things in our lives which we think we'll never lose."

"There's a shadow in your eyes, my dear; but sometimes I've seen your eyes without that shadow."

"I'll come back," he told her. "When I need to banish it again."

When he was gone, she counted up the days. There had been nine of them, since that night he came. She would have given all the years of her life for those nine days.

6

FAUNT had lived too long in a world of which he was the only
resident, thinking of himself as a lonely figure upon whom life had
laid a cloak of sadness which he could never cast aside. The onset of
the war was an addition in kind to that old wrong inflicted upon him
by the fates when his loved ones died. Just as death then had robbed
him of his wife and of his child, so now war robbed him of Belle Vue,
and shattered forever his ordered way of life. It was in the temper of
the flagellant, who lays a scourge of thorns across his own shoulders
and relishes pain, that he suffered the long misery of service in the Wise
brigade in Western Virginia; the wounds he took at Roanoke and
the ordeal of that terrible plodding journey up the beaches to Norfolk
produced in him a sort of holy rapture. He found a mournful pleasure
in thinking of himself as the chosen target of all the cruel gods, upon
whom they delighted to heap most grievous wrongs.

To be told that from his father's loins had sprung, in a second
generation, that monster in the White House was the culminating
blow. Wrongs he could have continued with a meek patience to endure; but this was worse than an injury, it was an insult. His first
exploding spleen gave way to reckless anger. His world was gone, the
very foundation of his life withdrawn. So be it. Then Great Oak, the
old house which was a part of the flesh and blood, the bone and sinew
of each one of them, that too should go. In that first hour of knowledge he set it all aflame, room by room, smashing every movable thing
into kindling to feed the waxing fires. He made a thorough business
of it, starting in the east wing, then in the lower floors; he retreated

before the flames as they advanced; and when the task was done, sated with destruction as a vulture may be sated with carrion, he rode to overtake his mother's carriage.

It was as much his own passions as the long tedium of the journey to Richmond which brought him near exhaustion. In Richmond he wished to escape from his mother, from Cinda, from them all; when Tony suggested they go to Mrs. Albion's, he agreed. In this hour of his own shame, to call upon the base and degraded woman who had been Tony's mistress suited his mood. After all, who was he that he should hesitate to consort with feminine depravity; who was he to feel a righteous scorn of any man or woman?

Who was he? Why, he was a kinsman of that murderous and ape-like creature in Washington; that gluttonous beast hungry for tender flesh, thirsty for blood. His thoughts dramatized this hour in resounding phrases. Mrs. Albion would doubtless prove to be a tawdry, tinsel creature; a shiny serpent of a woman as abhorrent to any honest man as her life had been, fit company for such a man as he now felt himself to be.

But after a first mild surprise to find she was not the sorry drab he had expected, he forgot her in listening to the words of that sandy-haired young cavalryman named Mosby. To be a soldier in battle, one among many; that in itself could never again content Faunt. He wished to deal out many deaths, and to know his victims. In his thoughts that were blurred by wine and by weariness, he imagined himself in the role Mosby described, pursuing a host of fleeing Yankees, pistolling them one by one till he came up at last to the leader of them, headlong in flight like the rest; and this leader was Lincoln, gaunt and long-armed and grotesquely tall, more like an animal than a man. Faunt in his thoughts that turned insensibly to dreams sent heavy bullets smashing into the enemy's back; and each thudding impact was as delicious as a kiss. From sleep which brought such dreams, he did not wish to wake.

When at last he did return to sensibility, the room in which he lay was dark; but he could see the oblong of a door obliquely illumined by the flickering light of an unseen candle. As his wits cleared, he became conscious that someone sat near him, near his bedside. He turned his head on the pillow to look that way and saw the figure of a woman, dim in the half-dark. At his movement she stirred, bowing toward him; he heard her voice.

"Are you awake at last?"

He recognized her voice. This was Mrs. Albion; so he and Tony must have stayed on here in her house. Why not? Why should he not do what he chose? "Yes, yes, I am awake," he said. A sense of time returned to him. "Where is Tony?" Her head moved in denial, as though she said she did not know. "It must be late, near morning," he reflected. Then, realizing that someone had removed his clothes, realizing more completely his condition, he lay trying to remember what had happened. "I must have slept," he said.

"Yes, slept the clock around." Her voice was husky and low.

"You serve a heady wine." The fumes still confused him.

"You were very tired."

"Where is Tony?" He repeated the question.

After a moment she said: "I sent him away. I do not know."

She did not know. Well, there were things he did not know. "Who put me to bed? Tony?"

"Milly and I."

He considered himself in dispassionate contempt. He had come here with Tony, to the home of this woman; he had drunk himself into a stupor; he had lain here in sodden sleep for—how long? The clock around, she said. Through the night, then, and the day, and into another night. He, Faunt Currain, who had lived all his life so proudly, had slept the clock around in this woman's bed. He grinned in sudden realization. He, Faunt Currain, kinsman of Lincoln. Since that other was true, these depths had no terrors for him now. He could descend no lower.

"You have been too kind to me, more than I deserved." He spoke in gracious irony. She and her servant had put him to bed; but this woman was no doubt beyond embarrassment, inured to shameless intimacies.

She rose. "Rest a little longer. I will bring you something. You must be hungry." She moved toward the door, her figure for a moment silhouetted against the candlelight in the hall outside the room where he lay. He saw with approval that she moved gracefully, and her head was proud and high. Something in her quiet dignity pleased him.

When she returned—alone, bringing a waiter laden with all he could desire—he had not moved. It was pleasant to lie relaxed and submissive, pleasant to be waited upon; pleasant to know without knowing how he knew that there dwelt in this handsome woman a readiness for rich surrender. Why should there not? Surely such a woman was past all scruples long ago. And—why should he not seize that which was so surely in his grasp? What right had he to scruples now? Below the pit in which he dwelt there was no deeper degradation. Like a man who having done one murder more easily kills again, Faunt felt himself released from long bondage to the standards he had so recently held high. While he ate sparingly, while she watched him and foresaw his wants, while they talked together—surprisingly at ease—he let his thoughts and his eyes appraise her. She must of course be older than she seemed; yes, years older than he. What was that whimsical advice old Ben Franklin had given someone or other; to take as your first mistress a woman older than yourself? Faunt's own thoughts amused him; there was a sardonic mirth in the simplest word he said.

Yet their words for a while were commonplace enough. Was he feeling more rested?

"Yes. Yes, I slept away fatigue."

"You were very tired."

"We had been on the road from Great Oak all the night before and all that day. We moved my mother to Richmond, could not leave her to fall into Yankee hands."

"No."

He added: "And in the last confusion, the house caught fire and burned. We could see the fire behind us as we came away."

"I felt that there was more than physical exhaustion to tire you so. The old house burning would have been an added grief to you."

"Oh no. Better see it burn than leave it for the Yankees to debauch."

She looked at him with wise eyes. "If you felt so, perhaps you put the torch to it yourself."

He smiled. "Perhaps indeed I did."

"Coffee?" She filled his cup again. "Tony has told me the beauty of Great Oak."

That she should speak of Tony thus simply and straightforwardly impressed him. She must know he knew the truth. This woman had strength in her. To cover his own thoughts he spoke of the man he had met here when he first came to her house.

"Mr. Mosby is a striking person."

"Mr. Berry brought him. I had not met him before."

"His idea of pistolling Yankees, that is a sport which would appeal to me."

Her eyes for a moment clouded, as though she gave this possibility more consideration than his casual remark on its surface deserved. "I know nothing of such matters," she said.

He smiled. "I think you know more than you admit." He was comfortable and at ease with her, sure of some strong bond between them. "I think you have a gift for listening. Perhaps that's why the little editor—what was his name?"

"Mr. Berry."

"Perhaps that's why he admires you. A woman, to be considered brilliant by men, need only hold up a mirror in which they can see themselves reflected."

She said in a low tone: "No woman is complete except as the mirror of some man."

He smiled. "I have also heard it said that no man is complete unless he is nourished by some woman's love."

Her eyes met his. "Tony has told me that you are incomplete. Alone."

He felt a momentary anger at this intrusion into his heart, and with an instinct to give wound for wound, he said: "You've known Tony a long time?"

She answered simply: "I think there is nothing you do not know about Tony and me." He felt himself reproved. She rose to take away the waiter with the soiled dishes; and when she reached the door he was afraid she would not return.

"But all that is past," he said, wishing to placate her.

"Past, yes," she assented. She set the waiter on a table outside the door, returned to stand beside him. "Milly has cleaned your garments. They are in the wardrobe there. The bathing room is across the hall. If you wish to sleep, do. If you wish to find me, I will be near."

He looked up at her, relishing this moment; he smiled in a quizzical way. "Why should I wish to—find you?"

After a moment she said: "I hope you will."

"I must go back to—my mother, the others."

"Must you? You need not." She held his eyes a moment longer, then moved away.

Faunt did not at once arise from where he lay. Her eyes and her tone, more than her words—and her words were open enough—left no doubt in him. Then—why scruple? Who was he to hold himself so high? For a moment, despair swept through him like hot desert winds; but—to remember her, the rich sheen of her heavy hair, her deep warm tones, the poise of her head, was comfort and assuagement. Half in self-scorn, half in hunger, he dressed and went to her.

Into the days that followed, the world outside did not once intrude. Faunt accepted this insulation without question. Here in Nell's house was a world complete enough; here were forgetfulness, and comrade- ship, and friendliness. "You're such a woman as I have never known," he told her once; and she smiled in his arms and said, as she was to say during those days so many times: "You've made me know things I've never known before." He asked for nothing she did not provide; and it came about that he sometimes tested her resources, leading her to talk about herself, wondering always at her completeness and her lucid honesty and her level self-appraisal. Once he said: "You and my sister Cinda would like each other," and she said: "We do," and told him of the day Cinda came to invite her to Burr's wedding; and after a moment's hesitation she told him too how she went to Cinda for advice when she had that information from the North which led to the Confederate success at Leesburg.

"You did the South a service," he remarked.

"A woman can do so little. I will always do what I can."

Sometimes he wished these days need never end; but at other times he felt himself debased by this association, and sharp spurs of uneasy restlessness more and more beset him. He asked once where his horse was, and she told him. He remarked once that his disappearance must have caused his mother and Cinda worry and concern. To this—he had learned that she never argued against manifest truth—she offered no reply. Eventually he asked a question about the retreat from Williamsburg; and she told him of the fighting there when Longstreet turned back the first pursuit. "Now the army is on the Chickahominy," she said. "And—Norfolk has been abandoned to the Yankees. We destroyed the *Merrimac*—the *Virginia*—so that it need not fall into their hands."

"That's sorry news."

"We are in straits," she assented. "People say Richmond will be abandoned without a fight. The tobacco in the warehouses here is to be burned to keep it out of enemy hands."

"You never leave the house, yet you know all that is happening."

"Milly and Rufus are good listeners."

He smiled. "Well taught by you," he remarked; and for a while they spoke of themselves and of no one else at all.

But next morning he referred again to the fighting at Williamsburg. "Burr and Julian, and Vesta's brand-new husband must have been there."

His words were a question. For a moment she did not speak; then she said: "Burr is at home with a slight wound. No one knows what happened to Julian; he has not been found. Lieutenant Cloyd was killed."

Sorrow swept him, and then shame; for in her grief, since Brett was away at Suffolk, Cinda must have wished for him. He had failed her, and it would be hard to face her now. "Do they know anything at all about Julian?"

"I only know what Rufus has heard from the negroes; but Julian's body was not found, or not recognized if it was found."

He might discover the truth, and thus make amends to Cinda. If he went to Williamsburg it would mean slipping through the Yankee lines; but that could be managed. When he told Nell he must leave her, he said no word of his intention. "It's high time I went back to duty," he explained, and spoke of Mosby. "I shall find him," he said. "Offer my services."

Faunt left her house an hour before day. He went at a foot pace, and to avoid any chance encounter he circled the fringe of the still sleeping city, leaving the cemetery on his left as he descended to cross Shockoe

Creek and thread his way through lanes and bypaths to the Williamsburg road. In the shadowed dusk of dawn he was mysteriously uneasy, with a disturbing feeling that he had forgotten something. Was it possible that this sense of loss was no more than missing Nell? How much of himself had he left behind with her?

Day began to come, and the stir of waking filled the air. The smell of smoke from new-lit fires, the dewed fragrance of the meadows, the barking of dogs let out of doors to greet the day, the crack of an axe on kindling welcomed the coming sun. The morning chorus of the birds had sung him out of Richmond. Now, having offered up their melodious orisons, they were hushed, busy with their breakfasting. Faunt saw men in door yards along his road, beginning their day's tasks. A horseman overtook and passed him, riding at a canter, giving him the greeting of a lifted hand. The dust kicked up by the cantering horse rose in little puffs which joined to make a small cloud that hung heavy in the still air till it settled slowly back to earth again; and another rider came up from behind at an easy trot that was not much faster than a walk. Abreast, they exchanged glances, and Faunt recognized Burr; and Burr cried out in surprise:

"Uncle Faunt! Why—what—where in the world have you been?"

"Good morning, Burr." Faunt did not answer the question. "I heard you were wounded."

"Just a scratch." Burr's eyes shadowed. "You know about Julian and Tommy?"

"Yes. How's Cinda? And Vesta?"

"Mama's fine. Yes, and Vesta, too." There was some reservation in the boy's tone. "Papa was home Sunday, and Uncle Tony. Granny's going down to Chimneys with Tony. They leave today."

Faunt felt a swift relief in the knowledge that his mother would be far away. He asked: "Have you heard anything definite about Julian?"

"No sir." Burr said in an inquiring tone: "None of us knew where you were."

Faunt thought Tony could have told them, but he must have held his tongue; yet Faunt recognized the fact that sooner or later he would need to make some explanation. "I went to Belle Vue," he said. "Did your regiment have hard fighting at Williamsburg?"

"No sir, nothing serious. When the retreat began, we went up toward Eltham's Landing, on the York River, to watch for transports moving to hit our flank." Their horses were side by side, with tossing heads; the risen sun, still low above trees ahead, struck full in their eyes. "Colonel Lee sent a patrol, a dozen of us, down along the river to report to General Stuart. The Yankees had got on Stuart's rear, so he had to circle and retreat up the river beach. We had a little excitement." Sorry memory dulled his tones. "That night, Williamsburg was just one big hospital. Bruton Church and the college and most of the homes were full of wounded. I had a little cut in my leg, just a nick from a sabre. It didn't bother me as long as we were skirmishing; but at dark it began to stiffen up, so I went to the church—the doctors were working there—to have it bandaged."

His voice caught; he coughed, cleared his throat, went on. "Uncle Trav came in while I was there, he and Rollin Lyle. You see, sir, a lot of bullets hit Tommy; a whole charge of canister or grape at pretty close range. They didn't think Vesta ought to see him, so they came to ask Mr. Ambler if he could be buried there. They'd taken him to Mr. Taylor's house, wrapped in blankets, and Rollin and Uncle Trav washed him, and Uncle Trav got someone to make a coffin. So we buried him there, just before sunrise. Mr. Ambler read the service." He added: "We couldn't bring him to Richmond."

Faunt nodded. "No, I suppose not. The army needed everything with wheels." He asked: "You couldn't find Julian?"

"No sir. Rollin and Tommy and he were in the Fifth Carolina. They were all shot to pieces, the whole regiment. No one knows what happened to Julian."

For a while neither spoke, moving quietly along the dusty road. Then Faunt asked: "Do you know a man named Mosby, in your regiment?"

"Only by sight. He was adjutant until we elected Colonel Lee; but then Mr. Mosby resigned his commission. General Stuart thinks he's about the best scout we have. Do you know him?"

"We have met," Faunt assented, thinking Mosby might go with him through the Yankee lines to make some search for Julian. "He's almost persuaded me I ought to 'jine the cavalry!' "

"You ought to," Burr agreed. "Why don't you?" But Faunt did

not reply. Remembering how he first met Mosby made him think of Nell and he forgot Burr for a while, living over his rich days with her till stale guilt came bitter on his tongue. But then he shook his head in hard defiance. Before he met Nell there had been that other shame to blacken all his world and all his life. What right had he to pride?

Self-scorn gave way to returning rage. Vesta's Tommy was dead, and Julian was lost, and these crimes were Lincoln's doing, and Lincoln was his own father's grandson! That was a shame only blood could wash away. Faunt's throat swelled, and there was a lust in him, a deadly lust to kill and kill.

7

TRAV, while the army moved by stages to Barhamsville and then to New Kent Court House and finally to Long Bridge across the Chickahominy, was too much engaged with his own duties to go to Richmond; but at the week's end, leaving camp early Sunday morning, he rode the twenty miles to town.

When he reached the house on Fifth Street and saw these familiar faces, tragedy had left its mark on each. Vesta was pale, her skin almost transparent, and her freckles more than ordinarily conspicuous. They would have been ludicrous if they were not so pitiful. But Vesta herself, as though to ward off sympathy, spoke in tart accents, completely unlike her accustomed tone. Watching her, Trav felt tenderness in him like an insupportable burden; he fought down a resurgence of that storm of rage at war and at all the bloody works of man which had swept upon him on the night-shrouded battlefield at Williamsburg.

All of them that day at Cinda's were like actors in a play; they spoke as though by rote, and there was a false note in everything they said. This was particularly true of Vesta. She was quick with sarcastic comment, meant to sting and bruise. It was as though to hurt others somehow dulled her own pain. Thus when Brett who had been at home since Friday said politely: "I'm told General Longstreet did fine work at Williamsburg," she laughed in light scorn.

"Fine work? All he did was to succeed in running away."

For a moment no one spoke, but then Trav said: "Why, yes, I believe he did well. I wasn't there till after the fighting ended; but the

Yankees had enough so they let us march off without trying to stop us. Of course the mud was terrible; so we couldn't move faster than a crawl, and neither could they."

"How is Cousin Jeems?"

This was Cinda, but Vesta added her bitter question. "Out of breath from running?"

Trav said gently: "Well, Cinda, he's never been as—jolly as he used to be, not since the babies died. His temper is pretty short. Of course he always had a rough tongue, but he's even more that way now. On the retreat, General Rains planted some shells in the roads where they would explode if the Yankees stepped on them, but General Longstreet reprimanded him for doing it."

"Why?" Cinda asked. "That sounds sensible to me."

Trav looked at Vesta, afraid she would speak. "General Longstreet considered it an improper form of warfare," he said, and Vesta laughed, but Trav went on: "And General Rains resented the reproof. There's been quite an argument about it. I believe it's been carried up to Secretary Randolph. Longstreet isn't very tactful, you know. When he thinks a thing needs saying, he says it. He's more that way now than he used to be." He added loyally: "But he's a great commander on the field. The Yankees found that out."

Vesta rose and left the room, and their eyes followed her, and Brett crossed to Cinda, and Cinda said: "She'll be all right soon. Give her a little time."

"Has she let go at all?"

"Not yet."

Brett nodded, and he asked Trav what General Johnston planned to do, and Trav did not know. As the dinner hour approached, Enid came downstairs to join them; and Trav rose in awkward uncertainty, but she crossed to offer him her cheek, light amusement in her eyes. Jenny and Mrs. Currain appeared, and Burr and Barbara, and Vesta last of all; and Brett put his arm around her shoulders to hold her for a moment close, and she said in sharp protest: "Don't, Papa! I felt all my ribs crack!"

"You're a fine young woman, my dear."

"That's no reason to break me in two!"

At dinner they discussed the destruction of the *Merrimac* by her own commander. Brett thought he must have acted under orders. "He'd not have done it otherwise."

Trav doubted this. "I can't believe he was ordered to do it. It leaves the James River open to the Yankees to come up and shell Richmond any time they choose. President Davis wouldn't do that."

Vesta said dryly: "Well, you know the ladies are building a new gunboat, so perhaps the Government decided it didn't need two!"

Cinda tried to laugh. "Yes, isn't it ridiculous? Ladies all over the South giving money and brooches and rings and kettles and clock weights, churches giving their bells, and all to build more gunboats for our own men to blow up!"

"Like children destroying their toys!" Vesta commented. "And now Mrs. Judge Clopton is calling another meeting to tell us we must work harder than ever!"

Brett said cheerfully: "Oh well, it lets you ladies blow off steam!" They thrashed this topic and winnowed it, talking like people who were afraid of silence. Trav saw the tension which bound them, the tight-drawn nerves, the wariness in every word and glance. They were all so near tears that they dared not venture on any mention of Tommy or of Julian at all.

Toward dusk the door bell rang, and Tony appeared. Trav saw the marks of dissipation on him, sunken cheeks, inflamed eyes, sagging lids; but his tone when he spoke was light and jesting. He had come to say good-by, he said; he was leaving for Danville on the morning train, going back to Chimneys.

"We've been wondering where you and Faunt were," Cinda said carefully; and Tony laughed.

"Oh, we parted at the door when we left you here. Am I my brother's keeper?" Vesta slipped silently away, so Cinda and Brett and Trav and Tony were left alone; and Tony said: "I took a ride in the country, felt the need of some good fresh air." He looked toward the door. "What's the matter with Vesta?"

Brett answered him. "Tommy was killed at Williamsburg. And we don't know what happened to Julian."

"Ha! That nephew of ours in Washington—" He checked himself and looked at Cinda. "Told Brett, have you?" She nodded, and he said: "That nephew of ours has a lot to answer for. A disgrace to the family!"

His tone was jocose, and for a moment no one spoke, and Trav held his anger hard. Then Cinda abruptly turned the conversation. "Tony, I think you might take Mama to Chimneys, if we can persuade her to go. And I think we can. She's been so—passive, since she came here, with no mind of her own. Tilda and I have discussed it." She appealed to Trav for his opinion. "She'd be cooler there, Travis; and safer, if Richmond's given up; and I think the house full of children tires her here."

"It's cooler there, yes," he agreed. "What do you think, Tony?"

Tony made a casual gesture. "Let Mama decide. After all, Chimneys is her property, not mine."

"I think she'll go," Cinda repeated. "She really has changed tremendously. She'll go if we suggest it. I'll ask her."

When they put the question to Mrs. Currain she did not at once reply; and Trav said: "You've never been there, Mama; but it's mighty fine country, the mountains off against the sky, and the nearer hills, and the rich bottom lands. Wonderful to watch, toward sunset; and the house is high, catches the breeze."

"Your father always said it was beautiful," Mrs. Currain commented. "But he never took me there." She fell silent, smiling at some thought of her own; and when Cinda spoke in gentle persuasion she seemed not to hear. Trav thought she appeared to fail a little and a little more during their every separation. All last winter and this spring, so many old people had faded and died, not from any apparent outward ill but as though their hearts were broken and they had no longer any wish to live. Sometimes grief for a son dead in battle or of disease might be the cause; yet he thought there was a deeper wound. To men and women who had been for three or four score years loyal citizens of the Union, it was a bitter thing to put that loyalty aside. Watching his mother now, her pale cheek, her frail hands, her lowered eyes, he thought of one after another among his acquaintances and friends, old people who a year ago had been happy and well and who now were gone.

Cinda finished whatever she was saying, and to which he paid no more heed than his mother seemed to pay, and Mrs. Currain said composedly: "I think I'll like it, yes. Tony, it's a long time since you and I have had a good visit together."

Thus easily the matter was decided, and it seemed to Trav his mother's surrender of her will to theirs was eloquent. Certainly she had changed greatly in these weeks just gone. Cinda took her to begin to make ready for the journey, and Tony said Mr. Fiddler had persuaded him that Chimneys this year should be put into food crops, corn and beans and hogs, and Trav and Brett agreed that this was wise. They talked, some constraint on each one, for an idle while.

Before he rode back to Long Bridge, Trav had a moment with Enid alone; a moment of his seeking. She had gone to her room. He followed her, knocked, and at her summons opened the door.

"Oh, you, Trav?" She spoke in light surprise. "I didn't expect you to come to me."

"I'm just leaving."

"Well—why not just go?" He saw mockery in her eyes.

"Have you called on your mother?" She had said she would go to Mrs. Albion's, stay on there.

"I called, yes; but she was not at home." Enid's color rose angrily. "Or at least, I was told she was not at home; yet I'm almost sure I saw someone looking through the curtains as the carriage stopped at her door."

Trav said awkwardly: "Enid, I wish you wouldn't do anything—I mean, go to visit her—for the present."

She laughed. "I suppose you think your wish is my law."

"Well, Cinda and all of them are terribly hurt and sad just now. I hope you can— Well, I hope you won't do anything to make them more unhappy."

"Cinda'd be glad to be rid of me, I'm sure." She asked: "Trav, have you seen Faunt? No one seems to know where he is at all."

"No, I haven't seen him. But Faunt's all right."

"He'll surely come home before long." Enid spoke half to herself; then she said with a quick smile, almost affectionately: "All right, Trav, just to please you I'll stay here quiet as a mouse. At least, for a while."

With her promise to reassure him, he returned to headquarters. That week, Yankee gunboats came up the James River as far as Drewry's Bluffs; and though the batteries there prevented their further passage, General Johnston ordered Longstreet's divisions to move nearer Richmond. They marched by the one road that led from Long Bridge westward, and when they came to a maze of many crossroads that ranged confusingly through a region of scrub oak and pine and worn-out farms, Longstreet kept his staff busy seeking out their best course, extending his advance toward the river till he was in position to bolster the defense there against any new venture of the Yankee gunboats.

When the division had gone into bivouac, he summoned Trav. "Captain," he said, "unless we are to abandon Richmond, we must soon make a stand. This country is all woods and swamps and cart tracks. If we're to fight here we'll have to know our way around. Get maps, and find guides who know the region."

Trav expected no difficulty in carrying out these instructions. He went to Richmond, to the War Department; but there was no detailed map of the countryside immediately around Richmond, and as far as he could discover no effort was afoot to have maps drawn. The Department was in confusion, since great masses of papers and documents had been sent away to Columbia beyond the reach of the Yankees, and Trav's impression was that everyone was much more interested in leaving Richmond than in defending it. Certainly there were no maps; and he felt an angry incredulity at this discovery. He had always been a humble man, thinking of himself as slow and plodding and dull of wit; but men in authority were presumed to have wisdom and foresight.

Since there were no maps, Trav turned to a search for guides who knew their way among the many little roads that threaded these swamps and forests. Across the countryside between Longstreet's encampment and the James, he found wretchedly poor and hopelessly indolent white people living in miserable cabins, so listless and apathetic that they were ignorant of the roads even in their own immediate neighborhod. They knew the way to the nearest crossroads, or the path to the nearest branch; but of the world beyond their immediate horizons they knew nothing. It seemed to Trav beyond belief that within a dozen miles of the Richmond he knew, the Richmond of ease and intelligence and gentleness and leisure, there could be this lightless world where dwelt men and women like animals, friendly enough, hospitable enough, courteous enough, but with no virtues to set them higher than a friendly, welcoming dog.

Because of their ignorance, Trav was forced to explore for himself; and he made a rough map of the region south of the Williamsburg Turnpike, tracing three or four roads which ran parallel from the pike south and southeastward and which he thought might be useful in any further retreat toward Richmond, indicating crossroads between them, pacing off distances or estimating them. This was a region without conspicuous landmarks, a flat, faintly rolling plateau except where it broke down toward the river. On the plateau, each old field gone to sedge and pines was exactly like every other, each patch of woodland was cut from the same pattern as its neighbor. The roads themselves were indistinguishable one from another, and crossroads were few, and the roads meandered so aimlessly that it was impossible to remember every turn or to keep clear in your mind the directions to which they tended. Some of the roads seemed to have names; but not even people who lived upon the roads agreed on what these names were. Any one of the more or less parallel thoroughfares might be called the Charles City Road, or the Darbytown Road, or the New Market Road, depending on your informant. Any road that set out in a generally northwesterly direction would eventually, unless it dwindled to cart tracks and disappeared, come at last to the Williamsburg Turnpike and so to Richmond; but beyond that knowledge there was little of which you could be sure.

When Trav reported to Longstreet, he spoke of the dark ignorance he had encountered. "Whole families, General: men and women and children who don't know anything outside their own door yards, and don't want to!"

Longstreet nodded. "Of course! Half the people in the South live such lives as that, Currain. Slavery's partly responsible. The meanest white man looks down on the slave, and that makes him feel sufficiently superior so that he loses all ambition. The besetting sin of us Southerners is complacency. What the average Southerner calls thinking is just assuring himself he's a better man than any Northerner, justifying what he has done and finding high moral ground for what he plans to do. And complacency is just plain dry rot. You think it astonishing to find these people ignorant of their own neighborhood; but what about the lazy stupidity of the War Department? Any soldier could have foreseen a year ago that we might some day have to defend Richmond and fight battles hereabouts." Trav thought the big man's words fell like rocks, with crushing weight. That slight deafness which he had sometimes suspected in the other nowadays grew more marked; and when Longstreet talked there was a hard, bludgeoning quality in his heavy tones. "Yet the War Department has not even troubled to map the roads, much less the hills, the swamps, the bridges, here within ten miles of Richmond." Anger deepened his voice. "Why, by the Almighty, Currain, I'll take any wager you can offer that McClellan knows right now more about the country around us here than any general in the Confederate Army!"

Trav produced the crude map he had made. "This at least shows the roads we may want to use," he explained. "These roads"—his finger traced them—"all lead to the Williamsburg pike and on to Richmond."

Longstreet studied the map with approval. "How did you get the distances?"

"Paced some, guessed at some. I think they're fairly accurate."

"You have more talents than appear on the surface, Captain. I'm glad to have this, but we may never need it. We're to move again. The works along the James have been improved till they can stop any gunboats that try to reach Richmond, so I suggested to General Johnston that we shift our weight northward and cross to the north side of the Chickahominy. There we will be in a position to strike McClellan's flank when he tries to pass the river."

Trav nodded. "I'll be glad to move," he admitted. "I've seen all I want to of these people down here. Once we get north of the turnpike there are bigger plantations. We'll find gentlemen who know what lies beyond the nearest hill."

Longstreet had proposed that they place themselves astride the Chickahominy in its upper reaches, but although General Johnston drew his forces nearer Richmond he did not go that far. Longstreet's divisions camped at the Fairfield race course, just off the Nine Mile Road and two or three miles northeast of the city. Longstreet lodged at the Spottswood, and Trav could have gone to Cinda's; but Enid was there, and Cinda would expect him and Enid to share the same room, so he stayed in camp.

But he rode into town for Sunday dinner and found Brett there. The Howitzer company had been withdrawn from Suffolk to Petersburg. Brett urged Cinda to take all the household to the Plains.

"For Richmond may be given up," he said. "The President's family is gone, and George Randolph has sent his family away; and Mr. Memminger has a special train waiting, ready to start at a moment's notice with what specie there is in the Treasury. I wish you'd go, take Jenny and Barbara, Vesta, Enid, the children. I'd like to feel you're all safe away from here."

Cinda shook her head. "No. No, Brett Dewain, I won't leave Richmond. Not till I'm sure about Julian. I can't!" And she cried in sudden passion: "I can't! Do you hear? I can't, that's all!"

So Brett abandoned the point and they talked of other things. Trav thought Vesta's first anguish had begun to abate, for her tongue had lost its edge. Enid asked whether Trav had seen Faunt, but he had not, nor had Brett. Before they sat down to dinner, Burr arrived, dusty from the road. He reported some skirmishing along the Chickahominy, and an occasional affray between outposts; but McClellan seemed to be entrenching, and Burr thought no early attack on Richmond was probable.

Trav said Longstreet agreed with this opinion. "He thinks McClellan won't attack us as long as we keep retreating; says there's no reason why he should."

"What does he think we ought to do?" Brett asked.

"Well, I don't always understand his terms," Trav admitted. "He talks about a defensive offensive, or an offensive defensive. I don't know the difference, but I think he means we ought to pick a good place and stand our ground till McClellan attacks us."

Cinda rose with a protesting word. "Oh, war, war, war! Can we talk of nothing else! Please, let's not even mention it at dinner. Come!"

So at the table they avoided this that filled all their minds. After-ward Burr and his father and Trav were for a while alone, and when they were at ease, Burr gave them news of Faunt. "He's joined the cavalry. He's in our regiment." Burr hesitated. "Papa, he's changed."

Brett glanced at Trav. "How, son?"

"Well, he and I and a man named Mosby in our regiment went through the lines to Williamsburg to try to find out something about Julian. Mrs. Taylor took us in. We stayed in the house in the day-time; but at night, every night, we went to that field where Tommy was killed. Uncle Faunt made us open every grave there, to look for Julian. The dead men weren't buried very deep. It was a terrible place. No one goes near it now except the pigs rooting up the bodies. Sometimes they hadn't left much of a man. The ladies in Williams burg tried to make the negroes—clean things up, but they can't keep them at it." He met his father's eyes. "Papa, I don't believe Julian is there. I just won't believe he's—in a place like that."

Trav saw sweat beads on Brett's brow. "I'm sorry you went there, Burr," Brett said.

"Well, anyway, we didn't find Julian." Burr continued: "But it's awful to see a man like Uncle Faunt kneel down beside something the hogs have rooted up and chewed at, and scrape the dirt off to see what color the man's hair was, or how big he was, or something. It isn't decent, Papa! The worst of it was, he didn't seem to mind doing it! And then one rainy evening we were out there just after dark, and we heard someone coming, so we slipped into the woods and hid. It was two Yankee soldiers. They had some bottles of whiskey or wine or something, and they were drunk already. They came along past us, and they said something about the smell of that field, and laughed; and Uncle Faunt stepped out and shot both of them." For a moment no one spoke, and Burr repeated: "He shot both of them, Papa. They didn't even have guns. They fell, but one of them was still alive, and Uncle Faunt shot him three more times."

Brett said after a moment: "I'm sorry you saw that."

"I could see his face," Burr said. "He didn't—well, he didn't even look like Uncle Faunt!"

Brett sent him away. "Go to your Barbara, son. Forget all that if you can." When they were alone, he looked at Trav, and looked away again and for a while neither of them spoke. Then Brett said: "Trav, Cinda told me about those old letters."

"I know."

"That's what's wrong with Faunt," Brett suggested. Trav thought this might well be true. Brett added: "You and Cinda are level-minded people. You know that it doesn't matter. But Faunt has lived so much alone. It matters to him."

Trav tried to find words to express what he wished to say. "Faunt and I aren't much alike," he said. "But I've been mad myself, once or twice, thinking about all that; madder than I've ever been before. If it can make me as mad as it does, I suppose it's worse for Faunt."

Brett said in sure tones: "You're all right, and Cinda's all right. Tony may go smash, unless being back at Chimneys cures him. Tilda won't much care. But Faunt—" he hesitated. "I wish Burr hadn't seen that."

After a moment Trav asked: "Brett, what can have happened to Julian?"

Brett said hopelessly: "I don't know. I've written some friends of mine in Washington. He may possibly be in a Yankee hospital somewhere. The Yankees took good care of our wounded at Williamsburg, you know; took just as good care of them as of their own. Perhaps some day we'll hear."

"Cinda can't have any peace till she knows something."

"She ought to go to the Plains. Richmond's on the edge of panic right now. Any least thing may make people here lose their heads, go plain crazy. Not even Congress has had the courage to stay. President Davis—" Brett smiled grimly. "Well, you know that old proverb: 'The Devil was sick, the Devil a saint would be.' The President was baptized last Tuesday morning, and confirmed that same day. As soon as people knew that, every departing train was crowded, and the stores sold every trunk they had in stock." He added: "I'm not sure Cinda could get away now even if she would go."

"General Longstreet thinks we'll fight for Richmond."

"Well—if we're going to fight we'll have to do it soon."

Trav wished to see Enid before he returned to headquarters; but when he asked for her, Cinda said she had gone out. "She's gone to see Dolly," Cinda told him. "They seem to enjoy each other." At dusk, since Enid had not returned, Trav rode back to camp.

Through the fortnight since Williamsburg, in addition to his map making, Trav had been busy with the problem of supply. Even here in the very suburbs of Richmond it was astonishingly hard to feed the men. The government issue of rations was scanty; and to buy corn or meal or meat meant paying enormous prices. Once Trav exploded to the General. "I'm beginning to think every man in the commissary is either a speculator for his own profit or a half-witted fool!" he declared.

Longstreet chuckled. "Don't often see you lose your temper, Captain."

"Sorry, sir."

"Oh, I don't blame you. It's good for a man to get mad once in a while."

Trav grinned. "You take your own medicine, don't you?"

The General nodded. "Yes, when I run into stupidity, I get hopping mad. It's a good thing I find myself doing stupid things now and then, or I'd have less patience than I have."

Trav saw he was in a mood for talk. "Does that happen often?"

"Often enough. Two weeks ago, for instance, I thought General Johnston was stupid to fall back this far, let McClellan come on to the river, repair the railroad bridge, build new bridges. I thought we ought to meet him in the lowlands along the river. But if we'd camped in the swamps, half the army would be down sick by now. As it is, McClellan's losing men as fast as if we fought him. If he waits long enough, his whole army'll be in the hospital."

"Our men don't like the waiting," Trav suggested.

"Time's fighting on our side, though," Longstreet insisted. "You know Jackson's hammering the Yankees in the Valley. I've always thought action there was the best defense of Richmond. Jackson has nothing but second-raters in front of him: Frémont, Shields, Banks, not one of them worth their salt. Let him sweep them back to the Potomac, and Lincoln will call McClellan to defend Washington." As so many times before, he repeated: "The Valley is our sally port. A stroke there will always relieve any pressure upon us here."

But there was no immediate sign that he was right. McClellan day by day consolidated his position; his balloons hung high above his lines so that the observers in them could overlook all of Richmond. The next Sunday when Trav rode in for dinner at Cinda's, Dolly and Tilda were there; and Dolly prettily demanded that he get rid of the balloons.

"I just can't stick my nose out of the house for thinking of those old Yankees watching every single thing I do!"

Trav said he doubted that McClellan's men were very much interested in even the most charming young belles. "It's soldiers, regiments, guns they're watching for."

"Well, just the same, I think it's impudent of them, and too rude for words."

Dolly's merry nonsense made even Vesta smile. Trav thought Vesta looked badly, but she was become her gentle self again. Something in her expression reminded him of that rich rapture of fulfillment which she had worn like a visible beauty in Williamsburg, the night before Tommy was killed. Watching her and Dolly now he wondered why he should like Vesta so much, like Dolly not at all. There was something about Dolly, despite her charming ways, which was deliberately provocative, yet unrewarding. She was all promise, no performance. Vesta was not so prodigal of promises, yet you could count on her. Dolly was more like Enid. She had Enid's thin mouth, and no matter how bright her lips, when she was not smiling they set in a hard line.

Longstreet seemed to be wrong about the probable effect of Jackson's work in the Valley, for on Tuesday they heard that General McDowell had marched from Fredericksburg, presumably to unite with McClellan's right and increase the threat to Richmond. Johnston began a slow regrouping of his forces to meet this danger, and he called his generals into conference; but Longstreet came back from that council of war in a quiet satisfaction.

"It turns out I was right after all," he told Trav next morning. "Stuart says McDowell·has countermarched back to Fredericksburg, so Jackson has frightened Washington, and McDowell is recalled to guard the capital."

"Will we just go on waiting?"

"For the present, yes. I ventured to suggest that we could maneuver McClellan out of his position at Beaver Dam Creek and strike him when he moved; but General Johnston says he has the wrong officer for the work there."

But the waiting was almost done. Thursday there was a skirmishing reconnaissance along the borders of White Oak Swamp, and Friday Trav heard scattered and spasmodic firing in that direction; but he was more attentive to the stormy, darkening sky. With the weather-wise eye of the farmer he foresaw a downpour. Longstreet went to headquarters for another council; and he had not returned when toward five o'clock, out of a still and ominous hush and under the pall of early darkness cast by a curtain of black clouds, there rose a hurrying wind and rain. The wind became a gale so strong that tents and shelters were swept away, and the bowed tops were ripped off the wagons in ribbons of shredded canvas. The strength of the wind and the bludgeoning of the rain made it impossible for men to walk or stand. They huddled in every lee while the storm-dusk turned to the darkness of night. The wind presently blew itself away, but the rain fell in a drowning sheet that churned the earth to soup into which, even though they were motionless, the heavy-laden wagons seemed visibly to settle.

With the first break in the wind, though the rain still fell, Longstreet returned and gathered his brigade commanders and gave orders for a move at dawn. "General Hill has felt out the Yankee positions on this side of the Chickahominy," he said. "We'll break them before reinforcements can reach them, roll up the reinforcements as they come in." His tone was calm and sure. "Hill will open the attack, and we'll cross to the Williamsburg road and go in to support him." There were detailed instructions to be given, preparations to be made. Since the wagons would not be needed at the scene of the prospective action, Trav had nothing immediate to do; but when the others had gone he asked doubtfully:

"General, how long a march must the men make? The whole country will be flooded tomorrow."

"Not long; an hour or two." Longstreet added in a high confidence: "And this storm and the flood will be worth two divisions to us. It will raise the river, wreck McClellan's bridges, cut his army in half.

We'll crush the half that lies south of the river, then turn on the other half whenever we choose."

"You think we'll beat them?"

Longstreet's eyes blazed. "Currain, we'll pitchfork the Yankees into the swamp with our bayonets as easily as tossing hay!" He added contemptuously: "General Smith is better at discovering obstacles than expedients." General Smith would command the Confederate left, Longstreet the right. "But our task is so simple it's hard to see how even he can go wrong."

At first light the men fell in, and Trav heard the company officers checking each man's supply of ammunition. Most of the regiments now had cartridges and had been taught how to bite them open and ram them home. He heard too the repeated admonitions. "Take your time, aim low, pick your target. It's better to wound a Yankee than to kill him, because then it will take two men to carry him off the field and you'll put three men out of action instead of only one. Pick off the officers, don't stop to plunder, don't stop to help your own wounded. If you straggle you'll be shot as cowards. Do your duty." The men answered with a derisive jocularity, and Trav thought this was their way of concealing from themselves as well as from their fellows the teeth-chattering apprehension which even the bravest might justly feel.

When the division extended itself along the road to the east, the men plodded and floundered through heavy mud; and their march presently was halted by flood waters in Gillies Creek. A wagon was manhandled into the deepest water and planks were laid across it from bank to bank to form a foot bridge. Trav thought time might have been saved by bidding the men wade, holding their muskets and their cartridge boxes over their heads. While they went slowly, single file, across the rude bridge, a messenger said General Huger's division was behind them with a longer march to make and wished to pass. So when they were across, they drew off the road to let this force go by and take the lead. General Huger came to speak to General Longstreet, and Trav heard Huger ask the date of Longstreet's commission; and in a rising impatience at so much delay he resented this discussion of rank at such a time.

The long morning of sluggish advance and endless waiting was his first experience of that terrible suspense which precedes the hour of battle. Here were thousands of mud-spattered men trudging through mire like so many flies caught in a sticky pool of molasses, pushing on to come at other men and kill them. He hated this vast futility, this squandering of strength and effort; and his hatred took the form of wrathful haste. Since the thing must be done, let it be done, and quickly!

When the road was clear of Huger's men they pushed on, and took a crossroad that turned south to intersect the Williamsburg pike which would lead them toward the enemy position. They passed the disused tracks of the York River railroad; and just beyond, Longstreet paused at a house set on a low eminence. The road below them was for a while filled with marching men who moved and paused and moved again while the morning slipped away. When at last a signal gun sounded to the eastward, a stir of relief ran through the group, and Trav felt his own pulse beat and pound. Now at last action would put a period to the intolerable strain of these tedious hours.

That first gun, like a pitch pipe that sets the key, touched off the hoarse chorus of cannon fire and then of musketry which opened the battle. When Longstreet swung his mount to go nearer, they followed him. Trav rode Nig, and the big horse, exulting in his strength, bounded ahead so violently that for half a mile Trav could not check him. When he had gentled the beast to a more moderate gait the others came up, and the General called jocosely:

"Your horse knows the first law of the soldier, Captain: to march to the sound of the guns. Hold him hard, or he'll carry you up to the cannon's mouth."

They halted again on a swell of ground that was high enough to let them overlook the wooded lowlands of the swamp ahead. Clouds of smoke rose from among the trees to drift away to the southward on the cool northwest wind. Not far away a battery was firing, and volleys of musketry flung at them a spatter of half-muffled sound, and Trav heard the shrill shouts of men like hounds on a hot track. Nig stood with pricked ears, staring off in that direction. His head was high, he mouthed the bit; and Trav felt the beast's excitement. He himself was trembling, and when Nig sidled to and fro, it was as much under Trav's restless hand as from the horse's own impulse.

Beside the pike below them, troops in reserve stood in ordered ranks; and every man's eyes turned to the sounds of battle not a quarter-mile away. Trav watched Longstreet and wondered how he could sit so impassively. Perhaps by some sixth sense the General had learned to feel even at this distance the pulse of the conflict, to comprehend it as a whole. Messengers came to report, to receive orders, to gallop away again. Under Trav's hand Nig sidled toward the General; and Longstreet looked at Nig and smiled faintly.

"Your horse wants to take a hand in that business, Captain."

Trav said: "I believe you can tell, even from here, how it goes."

The other nodded. "It goes well. We're driving them. Some of our troops are catching a little flanking fire, and green regiments are as sensitive as a virgin about their flanks; but they'll steady down."

His attention returned to the battle sounds, and Trav watched the road and saw a trickle of litter-bearers there; and ambulances were coming from the rear to receive the wounded and carry them away. Among the ambulances a handsome carriage appeared, and Trav wondered what madman chose such a day and such a road to drive for pleasure, and went down to halt the carriage and turn it back; but before he reached the road the vehicle pulled up to receive a freight of hurt men. Their blood stained the silk upholstery, and Nig snorted at the smell of it; and Trav saw that the carriage was driven by a white-haired old gentleman with the fine blue eyes of a child. Trav stayed there, watching the bloody fruits of battle drift back along the road. He saw a man with a hole torn through his cheeks so that his teeth were redly visible, and he saw a man with an arm gone above the elbow who gripped the stump with his other hand while blood leaked through his fingers, and he saw a man who bent double as he walked and cradled his body in his arms, and his arms were crimson with a bright cascade. This man for some strange reason stopped and loosed his trousers and squatted down and then fell sidewise and could not rise again, scrabbling at the grass with weak fingers. Trav felt the rising pound and throb of his own pulse like the beat of a nearing drum. His heart drove his blood so hard that a red blur dulled his vision; the grass, the trees, the very sky were fogged with this red haze. He narrowed his eyes the better to see; he looked toward the woods yonder with a surge of hate; hate of battle, hate of the enemy, hate of war. His hand was hard on the reins; and Nig resented it, tugging, tossing his head. Trav with a furious wrench flung the horse back up the rise of ground, checked Nig at Longstreet's side.

"General, can't I do anything?" he demanded.

Longstreet looked at him calmly; his voice was gentle. "I've heard you say you were not a soldier, Captain."

"I know. But——"

Trav's head swung again; there was something new in those sounds yonder. For a moment neither man spoke.

Then Longstreet said quietly: "Seems to be some confusion off there. By this time Rains should be advancing, past the enemy's left." He nodded in decision. "Very well, Currain, go tell General Rains to make his move."

Trav wheeled Nig, stopping to ask no questions, not knowing where he was to go and not caring. He loosed Nig, gave the horse its head. Nig took a fence like a bird soaring, and Trav felt his hat whisk away and did not care. Nig bore him without guidance across the road and across the sodden field toward the dark border of the wood. Scattering wounded men were limping painfully toward the rear; and Trav saw one of them go down under a bullet stroke. Every joint and muscle in the man seemed to let go in an instant. He fell as though he had been slammed violently to earth; his body seemed to bounce up from the solid ground before it lay still. Nig leaped over the limp form, racing on. Ahead, the battle sounds were a shouting welcome, a clangorous summons, a high inspiring challenge. Trav rode to the fight as a lover hastes to his mistress, grudging each moment till he comes to her ardent arms.

8

THROUGH that tormented month after she knew of Tommy's death and Julian's vanishing, Cinda was grateful because her house and her hands were so full. The house, even with Mrs. Currain gone, was crammed to overflowing. To accommodate everyone required not only management but a willingness on all their parts to accept some inconvenience. Jenny and little Janet slept in one great bed, the baby in his small crib beside them; and Cinda gave Enid too a room to herself. "Trav may sometimes be here," she pointed out, and wondered at Enid's faint smile. Lucy, almost a young lady, slept with Vesta; and when Cinda asked Vesta whether the child was a trouble Vesta said gently:

"Oh no, Mama. She's a sweet little thing, ever so thoughtful and considerate." She added honestly: "And—she's nice to cuddle up to when I lie awake at night."

Cinda made no comment, not trusting her own voice, grateful because Vesta, since she knew she would one day bear Tommy's child, was no longer bitter with grief. They told no one else, though Cinda thought Barbara guessed the truth, and of course old June knew without being told.

Barbara, like Enid, had a room of her own; and Burr, whenever he could, rode into Richmond if only for an hour. He went with Stuart toward Fredericksburg to keep an eye upon McDowell, till McDowell's army drew back toward Washington. Then the cavalry returned to be at hand if they were needed here and he came almost every day.

Once Faunt came with him. Cinda had heard from Brett what Burr reported about their search for Julian, and about Faunt's needless killing of those drunken Yankees, so she was not surprised to see a troubling difference in her brother. She tried to lead him to talk of those letters Tilda had found, thinking that to speak of them might ease him; but he laughed and said they were of no importance.

"Tilda always was a Paul Pry," he reminded Cinda. "Dragging into the light things better left hidden."

"It was all so long ago," she urged. It was not like Faunt to speak unkindly of Tilda—or of anyone. "None of us need be distressed about it."

"Certainly not," he agreed. "We've all thought too much about pride of family, pride of blood; but I've learned that one man's blood is as red as another's—and flows as easily." He grinned in a crooked fashion. "And vermin infest the garments of a Currain as readily as though he were the lowest white trash."

She recognized the rancor in him; but that too, like Vesta's grief, like the agony of her own thoughts of Julian, must be left to healing time. Men and women had an astonishing resilience, an astonishing capacity for endurance. Last summer when Clayton was killed she had thought life could inflict upon her no keener pain; but this uncertainty about Julian was infinitely more tormenting. There were hours when she felt she would rather know he was dead than spend every waking hour in wretched conjecture. She resented the empty hopes Brett held out for her to grasp, resented sympathy from any quarter. While Faunt was still here Anne Tudor came to ask whether there was any news of Julian. "He was so sweet, Mrs. Currain," she said. "I was ever so fond of him."

Cinda bit her lip to hold back an angry word. If Anne had been fond of Julian why had she not let him see her fondness? But then Faunt drawled: "Being sweet is no armor against bullets, Anne."

So Cinda was instantly Anne's partisan, furious at Faunt for that wounding word; and she saw Anne look at him with wide, bewildered eyes. When the girl was gone, she said reproachfully:

"You shouldn't hurt that child, Faunt. She's devoted to you."

"To me?" He laughed harshly. "The sooner she forgets all about me, the better."

"It's not like you to—hurt anyone."

"Not like me?" His face set in hard lines. "What am I like, Cinda?

Who am I? Does anyone know? Do I myself know—of what I may be capable?"

She laid aside her knitting, unable to sit still, and rose and went to the mantel to touch the prisms dangling from the girandole and set them tinkling; she turned to look at the gay hues of the artificial flowers under their glass bell on the card table. In spite of the glass which protected them, they were a little dusty. Vesta or Jenny must attend to that; the flowers were too delicate for awkward black hands.

She had been silent too long; she must say something. "Men make themselves what they choose, Faunt."

"Without benefit of ancestors?" Derisive mirth rang in his tones. "Why, then, so will I, Cinda. So will I!" His laugh was frightening, and she left him, and went up to her room to be alone. When a little later, ashamed of her own flight, sure she could somehow help him, she came down again, he was gone.

During that month of May, more and more troops passed through Richmond, keeping as much as possible on the cross streets to avoid being seen from the Yankee balloons which every day hung in the distant sky. On the last Thursday in the month, Brett's company of Howitzers marched up from Petersburg; and Mr. Hutcheson had a welcoming feast prepared for them at Mayo's Warehouse, and Vesta and Dolly went to help serve them. Afterward they moved out to the Williams farm east of the city and went into camp there; but Brett returned to spend the night at home. He said Johnston would attack McClellan tomorrow or the next day. "That's why we're here," he explained.

Cinda closed her eyes, pressed the lids tight shut, opened them again and as though to clear her vision shook her head. "I can't— Don't talk about it, please. Oh I know there will be many battles. When they come, I can stand them. But—I don't want to fight them before-hand."

He came to hold her close and hard. "We'll get along, Cinda."

"Oh yes." She hesitated, spoke at random. "I keep busy. That helps. It's a problem just to keep our table supplied. Prices go up every day. Any meat at all is fifty cents the pound, and butter is more than that, and tea costs two dollars a pound—if you can get it. General Winder has ordered that prices shan't go up, but that just means there's nothing sold in the regular stores. I hunt out hideous little hole-and-corner places and pay whatever they ask and feel like a spy." She added: "I hate letting them impose on me, but we have to eat."

He nodded grimly. "Richmond is full of greedy people getting rich on our necessities. Every fancy man in the South is here to make his fortune, selling blockade goods, running gambling hells to milk the soldiers, turning any dishonest penny he can."

"They're just scum," she assented. "But at least the Richmond we know, the people we know are fine." She added: "Except perhaps Redford Streean, and people like Captain Pew!"

"Who is he?"

"Dolly's latest beau. He's a blockade-runner. Tilda loves to come and boast about how he keeps them supplied with tea and coffee and all the things that are so high. Gloating over me. I'd like to slap her."

He chuckled approvingly. "That sounds more like you."

"If it weren't for the babies I just wouldn't pay the high prices," she declared. "I don't feel respectable doing it. I'd rather go hungry!"

"Oh it hasn't come to that yet," he assured her.

Next morning Brett rose early to return to his guns. Before dinner Enid came home in a high excitement to say there would be a battle tomorrow.

"I stopped at Dolly's," she explained. "And Captain Pew came while I was there, and he says Secretary Randolph says we'll attack at daylight. General Johnston's going to surprise the Yankees and just smash them." Cinda asked in a dry tone how he could surprise them if all Richmond knew his plans; and Enid confessed she didn't know. "Captain Pew says some Yankee cavalry actually rode into Richmond last night, so I suppose they do know, really."

"There are plenty of Union sympathizers to tell them," Cinda agreed. "And none of us have learned to keep our tongues still. We're all just a lot of prattling children."

"Captain Pew says he'll get a carriage and take Dolly and me out to see them fight," Enid told her, and she asked: "Do you s'pose Vesta'd like to go? You know, to sort of take her mind off herself?"

"You can ask her," Cinda said curtly. Enid would always be a fool.

She hoped Brett would come home again that night, but when after dinner the storm broke she knew he would not. No one would face this gale and this deluge unless he must. The rain would make the roads muddy tomorrow. Would that prevent their fighting? Certainly the guns could not be moved, so perhaps Brett need have no share in the conflict after all. She nursed this hope like a prayer.

Next morning Captain Pew and Dolly came in the carriage to pick Enid up; but Cinda and Vesta and the others stayed indoors, and Cinda listened for the first dreadful clamor of the guns. As the hours passed she found herself whispering: "Why don't they begin? Why don't they begin?" Let them begin, the sooner to be done with their bloody business, so those who lived might come home to her again.

They were at dinner when a distant mutter and grumble at last set the windows rattling; and for a little they were silent, listening. Then Cinda led them into talk again; led them to talk of anything at all so that their voices might distract the ear and make it possible to ignore those distant sounds that were like the growl of a carnivorous beast slavering over the flesh he rends and tears. When, hours later, Tilda rushed into the house to say that cartloads of wounded were coming into town and that their help was needed, Cinda welcomed the summons. "Mrs. Brownlaw wants just everyone," Tilda declared. "They' say we're giving the Yankees a wonderful thrashing; but hundreds of poor hurt boys are already here."

Cinda said she would go and so would Vesta. Barbara could not, and Jenny would stay with her. Tilda said Mayo's Warehouse would be used as a hospital; she bade them go there, then hurried away to enlist others in this cause. Cinda waited to collect cloth to serve for bandages while June filled two hampers with such things as the men might relish; she added a bottle of brandy and two bottles of wine. Then they set out.

During the hours that followed—they stayed till late that night when Brett came to find them and to fetch them home—Cinda lost herself in serving. A year ago after Clayton's death she had tended wounded men compassionately and prayerfully, as though by comforting them she helped Clayton too; but that experience had been terrible and sickening. This was not. Then she had suffered with the suffering men. Now, without sharing their suffering, she comprehended it the more completely and found ways to ease it. She stayed the seeping blood that welled from open wounds and never knew that her own hands and arms were smeared. She cleansed men whose hurts had made them soil themselves with no more repugnance than she felt in changing little Clayton. She forgot herself in bestowing herself upon these hurt ones. To attend to their needs ceased to be an ordeal and a sacrifice. Their wounds were no longer hideous and revolting; their agonies no longer a lash laid across her own flesh. She could draw together the edges of a wound with no more feeling than if it had been a rent in Brett's coat which she mended.

She was unconscious of this difference, unconscious of any strain or any fatigue until she rose from where she had been kneeling beside a boy whose jaw was shot away, whose whole face was a wound, and turned to find Brett here beside her. Seeing him whole and unhurt and as he had always been was an unbearable relief, so that her knees gave way and but for his supporting hands she would have fallen. He held her for a moment, steadying her.

"Jenny told me where you were," he said. "You've done enough for tonight. I brought the carriage. Where is Vesta?"

She looked along the shadowed length of the warehouse. The huge place was lighted only by lanterns set on the floor or held in hand. The surgeons were busy, the air a murmur of many blended cries and groans.

"She's here somewhere," she said emptily.

They found Vesta sitting on the floor beside a man whose hand she held in both her own. She was leaning back against the wall, and her eyes were closed; but there was light enough from a lantern somewhere near so that they saw the glazed eyes of the man whose hand she held. Cinda went to her and knelt and loosed her grip on the dead man's hand. Vesta's eyes opened and she saw her mother; but at once, remembering, she caught the man's hand again.

"No, no, Mama," she cried softly. "I promised to stay with him. He wanted me to stay with him."

"He's not here any more, darling," Cinda whispered. "He doesn't need you now."

Vesta looked at the dead boy and saw that this was true; and Brett said: "We'll go home, now, dear."

"Do I have to, Papa? He wanted me to stay." Vesta looked along the floor where lay these dozens of hurt men. "There are so many. So many."

"You're tired, tonight. Tomorrow." Brett spoke firmly. "I'm taking you both home now."

At home they found Jenny waiting. "Enid's just gone upstairs," she said. "She was full of talk. Barbara's asleep long ago." She looked at Vesta and at Cinda in full understanding. "Vesta, I'll go up with you."

So these two went up the stairs together, and Brett and Cinda followed; and he helped Cinda remove the dark stains of her labors, asking no questions, gentle as a woman. When she was in bed, he turned out the gas and came beside her and she asked:

"Have you seen Burr?"

"No, but the cavalry was not engaged. Nor were we. And Trav's work doesn't take him into the fighting."

"Did we beat them?" She was too tired to care, yet the question was like a duty.

"I think so. Some say General Huger was late; that if he had been on time we'd have won a great victory. I don't know much about it. We waited at our camp all day, were never ordered to move at all. The loads of wounded came past us." And he said: "Sleep now, Cinda. You're tired as tired can be."

Cinda meant to go early to the hospital next morning; but she slept till June woke her. She looked for Brett's head on the pillow beside her own, but he was not there. "He done gone befoah day," June told her. "He tolt me not tuh wake you up nohow, but I 'lowed you'd want to git up time foh chu'ch."

"Oh, is it Sunday?"

"Sho is."

Cinda lay still. She heard guns. So they were fighting again. "Is Miss Vesta awake?"

"No, ma'am. Don't look like she eveh gwine tuh wake up."

"Let her sleep while she can." Cinda took the coffee June had brought. With coffee a dollar and a half a pound, she ought to give

it up. To be sure, they could afford it. Thank Heaven they had plenty
of money. But to charge so much for coffee was plain robbery.

She had little appetite for breakfast, was glad when Jenny came to
her. They went to St. Paul's together. When they walked homeward
along Grace Street there was no longer any roll of guns to the eastward,
so the battle was done; but there remained the wounded, and Cinda
would have gone to them had not Vesta, awake at last, insisted she
would go if her mother did. So Cinda stayed at home, but next day.
Tilda came again to summon them. Cinda spent most of that day on
her knees with a pail of soapy water and a filthy rag, scrubbing and
wringing and scrubbing again, fetching fresh water when that in the
pail was more grimy than the floor, finding refreshment in this menial
task, glad to be busy, to be at work, to be worn out and sweating with
fatigue, to feel her bruised knees ache and her soap-burned hands dry
and parched.

When she and Vesta went home at last, she wanted nothing so much
as rest and sleep; but Trav had brought General Longstreet for supper,
and she mustered strength to make them welcome.

"Just give me time to freshen up," she said. When she came down
again, Brett was at the door, and sight of him made her forget weariness awhile.

The men fell into talk of these events just done, and she saw that
Longstreet was pleased with Trav. "This brother of yours, Cousin
Cinda, has been hiding his light under a bushel!" he said. "Have you
heard of his behavior Saturday?"

Trav's face was brick-red with embarrassment, and Enid cried:
"Why, General, has Trav disgraced himself? It's your fault for expecting him to be anything but a farmer!"

The General said almost roughly: "If he's a farmer, I wish I had
more farmers like him in my command." Enid was silenced, and
Longstreet added with a relenting chuckle: "He's assured me more
than once that he would never make a soldier; but at the hottest of it
Saturday I saw him itching to take a hand. Just then our work along
the Williamsburg road was out of joint. General Rains seemed be-
hindhand with his move. To give Captain Currain some outlet for his
eagerness, I sent him to ask Rains to take up his share of the contention." He smiled in his beard. "Captain Currain rode a great black

war horse that scented the battle afar off; and I suppose the horse must be blamed for the master's disobedience. Instead of finding General Rains, as I had ordered, Captain Currain rode into the thick of it."

Trav said honestly: "I didn't know where I was going, sir."

"You went where help was needed," Longstreet assured him, and he told the others: "There had been heavy work. Half the officers and many men were down, dead, or wounded and drowning in the flood waters through which they had made their battle. Anderson's brigade and Garland's—General Garland is Louisa's cousin, you know, Cousin Cinda—were in confusion. Captain Currain joined Micah Jenkins and lent his weight to the struggle there." His tone became serious enough. "Colonel Jenkins reports that he was as good as another regiment. He led a column through the Yankee abatis, that great horse of his thrashing down every obstacle. They overran everything in their way till Captain Currain brought the men who followed him up to the line of the railroad. Between them they swept every Yankee out of the woods south of the embankment." He smiled at Trav. "Yes, Captain; if I had a few more farmers like you I could march into Washington this summer."

Trav grinned, miserable under praise; but Enid protested: "Why, General, I declare I think you're telling fairy tales! I just can't imagine Trav being so bloodthirsty!"

"Bloodthirsty?" the General smiled. "I don't know as to that. Were you armed, Captain?"

Trav hesitated. "I don't think so, sir. Not unless I picked up a weapon somewhere. I've never worn side arms."

Longstreet threw back his head in a great laugh. "Don't think so?" he echoed. "Don't you know, Captain?"

"No, sir, I'm afraid not." Trav said slowly: "I was pretty excited, and I'd seen our wounded, and I hated the whole business, and Nig did really run away with me. I don't remember much about it. I remember smashing through some down timber, and up to a redoubt. There were two houses exactly alike, not very big, but they stuck up in the air. We went on into the woods, into another abatis." He grinned faintly. "Poor Nig is full of splinters. Big Mill has been picking them out of his hide, putting salve on his hurts, ever since." He said slowly: "I don't think I did anything. I think it was mostly just that Nig broke a path through the brush, and some of the men followed us along."

"Put it any way you choose," Longstreet assented in an amused tone. "But I'd like more officers of your cut, Captain."

Trav colored, and Enid drawled teasingly: "Why, Trav, think of you turning out to be a soldier!" Cinda looked toward her in slow anger, and after a moment Brett spoke.

"General, I've heard it said we missed an opportunity yesterday?"

Longstreet made a harsh sound. "Yes. Of course. Saturday evening General Johnston was hit. A shell fragment knocked him off his horse, so General Smith took over the command. I saw him at one o'clock Sunday morning. My men were up to the railroad, the Yankees behind it, General Smith on their flank. I urged an attack at dawn, with his guns to break their line and my men to catch them off balance and thrust them back into the river. But Sedgwick had punished General Smith severely the day before; so he was full of fears but not of fight. He left me to make the battle alone." His voice hardened with anger. "Opportunity? Yes, sir, it was tossed away! But now General Smith has reported sick, left the army." He laughed scornfully. "His departure strengthens us as much as if we'd won a victory."

"I hear General Lee has been given the command. What do you think of him?"

Longstreet hesitated. "Well, he's a staff man, and line officers always distrust staff in command; but despite his inexperience in field work, I have high hopes of Lee. Certainly he can do no worse than General Smith." He stirred. "Well, Captain, we must return to headquarters."

Trav rose; but he said gravely: "May I report back at daylight, General? It's some time since I've seen my—children."

Enid protested in quick dismay: "Oh Trav, you can't stay here!"

There was a moment's silence; but when Trav did not speak, Longstreet said: "Very well, Captain. I'll expect you in the morning."

He turned to Cinda to bid her good night. At the same time Enid came to Trav's side, and whispered to him; but Trav said, loud enough so that they all heard: "I will stay here."

Enid recoiled, and without a word darted away and up the stairs. For an awkward moment no one moved. Then Cinda said quietly:

"Good night, Cousin Jeems. Come whenever you can."

When the General was gone, Trav turned to Cinda. "Which is our room?" he asked. She told him. "I think I'll go along up," he said.

Cinda and Brett were left alone; and Brett, looking after Trav, asked curiously: "What's all that, do you suppose?"

She shook her head. "But Brett, there's a change in Travis."

"How do you mean?"

"I don't know, but you heard what Cousin Jeems said about the battle, and you saw the way Travis silenced Enid. He never did that before. He's changed, Brett. He's not the same."

9

ENID, having decided to leave Trav and having told him so, was at once terrified at her own daring and delighted with her newly asserted freedom. Words were not deeds, to decide was not to act, intention was not performance; but she forgot this. There were times when she wished to share with someone her determined jubilation. Dolly might have understood, and she and Dolly were congenial. When the other had no beaux in train they were much together; and in fact Dolly sometimes invited Enid's presence even under those circumstances, especially if Captain Pew were to be her escort.

"He's such a rascal, really," she told Enid in a gay pretense of terror. "If I were ever quite alone with him I just don't know what he'd do!"

Enid agreed that Captain Pew was a wickedly charming man. He paid her polite compliments in a way which sent cold shivers down her spine; and he was obviously wild about Dolly. "I expect you'll marry him some day," she predicted; and Dolly laughed and tossed her head, and said:

"Oh perhaps, but not for a long time. It's such fun to make him do his tricks, like a great dangerous lion who may just gobble you up at a bite any minute, and yet never quite does so."

But Enid knew Dolly's wayward tongue too well to confide in her; and also there lay in the back of her mind a doubt, which she refused to admit, of the finality of her action. For one thing, she was no longer sure of her love for Faunt. It had been easy enough, during those weeks when she tended him so devotedly, to imagine that he was all the world to her; but now when she rarely saw him there were hours and even days when she forgot him. For another thing, she was sufficiently levelheaded to know that Faunt would never love her. And also, always, something in her yearned for Trav. That night at Great Oak .when she cast him out, his submission was an affront; and after he was gone she lay in a drench of sad and desolated tears. Surely, surely if he loved her he would not so tamely let her go. Since then she had prodded him with a barbed tongue, not because she wished to wound him, but because she sought to rouse him to some violence of word and deed, to shatter that invulnerable surface he wore, to make his eyes upon her blaze and burn. He ignored her gibes, so he did not care; and Faunt would never love her, so she wept in loneliness and despair.

But if these high and mighty Currains had no use for her, she could always go to her mother. She had never been in Mrs. Albion's pleasant little house; but one day, in Mr. Ezekiel's shop on Main Street—his shelves were well laden with blockade goods, with moiré, and brocades, and cassimeres, and with shawls and scarves, though all at prices that dismayed her—she had to wait for attention, and she saw a book lying on the counter, a Richmond Directory published six years before and ragged from many handlings. She picked it up in idle curiosity. Its first forty or fifty pages were full of advertisements. She studied them and felt that instant awakening of unsuspected desires, that greedy eagerness to possess objects whose very existence has been unsuspected which they were designed to arouse. At the end of the advertisements began pages of names and addresses; she turnéd the first page, and on the second, as so often happens, a familiar name seemed to leap out of the mass of type on the page and catch her eye ... Akins, Albert, Albert, Albion!

Thus she learned the street on which her mother lived. But she did not wish anyone to know when she went there; so, instead of asking Cinda for the carriage, she walked as far as the Spottswood and took a hackney cab and at her mother's door bade the driver wait for her.

The Negress who answered her ring said Mrs. Albion was not at home and Enid was almost relieved; for at the last moment she had felt her courage fail. After all, it was years since she had seen her mother or sought to see her; and there might be no welcome for her now. In the cab again she looked back and glimpsed some movement at an upper window, so probably her mother had been at home after all! To think that this door too was closed against her made her both wistful and angry. Next time she would insist on being admitted!

But she did not go again till after Julian's disappearance. Trav asked her to do nothing that might distress Cinda. She promised, but to defy him might at least shake him out of his stolidity, so she repeated her venture. This time, so Trav would be sure to know, she asked Cinda if she could use the carriage. "I want to call on Mama," she explained. "I haven't seen her for so long. I really should."

"Take the carriage, certainly," Cinda agreed. "Use it whenever you wish. It will be nice for you to see something of her, now you're so near."

But this time, too, Enid was told that her mother was not at home. Remembering her former suspicions, she gave her name and asked when Mrs. Albion would return; and when the Negress seemed to her evasive, she said she would come in and wait. To her intense indignation, the girl shut the door in her face. With Cinda's coachman watching, Enid could do nothing but depart.

Not till a third attempt, late in May, did she succeed. This time the maid ushered her into the drawing room, and Enid while she waited had time to decide that her mother's things were sombre and ugly after the cheerful brightness of Cinda's home. When Nell appeared, Enid thought with a resentful surprise that she was as beautiful as ever, with fresh cheeks and clear eyes and a smooth round throat as firm as a girl's. Sometimes her own mirror testified that her fair hair was losing its sheen; sometimes turning her head this way and that, she detected a treacherous fulness under her chin. Certainly no one, seeing them together, would guess this woman was old enough to be her mother; and because Enid was furious at this realization she embraced Mrs. Albion with extravagant affection, and Nell said:

"I'm so glad to see you, darling. Milly said you came a week ago, and I hated missing you."

"She slammed the door in my face," Enid declared. "She needs a good whipping, Mama!"

Nell said in friendly apology: "It's my fault, dear. With so many strangers in town, a woman alone has to be careful. I've told her under no circumstances to admit anyone unless I am at home; and she knows I mean what I say." She added affectionately: "Of course I didn't mean you, darling; but I didn't expect you. After all, this is the first time, isn't it?"

"The third," Enid assured her, still indignant. "Last week, and once before that."

"I mean when you've been in Richmond before," Nell explained; and Enid, feeling herself put on the defensive, said:

"Oh I've always meant to; but we've come to Richmond so seldom, and there's always so much to do." She cried flatteringly: "You look so well, Mama. You look so happy!"

Nell smiled. "I am, darling." She nodded, with a little chuckle of a laugh, as though at some secret of her own. "I don't suppose there's a happier woman in Richmond than I."

"Living here all by yourself? Really?"

"I have Milly, and Rufus. They take care of me."

"They certainly do! No one would ever guess you were in your fifties!"

The older woman smiled as though she felt the dart. "You've not taken care of yourself, have you, darling? It's too bad very blonde people fade quickly. They're so lovely when they're young."

Enid's angry color rose; then she laughed disarmingly. "There, we're acting like two cats, Mama! I'm sorry." She needed her mother, would not risk a quarrel. "Your house is lovely, isn't it?"

"I've always liked it."

"Can we go all over it? I want to see just everything."

"Of course."

Enid heard faint curiosity in the other's tone, as though her mother were beginning to wonder why she had come; and when they rose she linked arms. "Oh Mama, I've missed you. I've wanted you so many times. Now that I'm living in Richmond, I want us to see each other often, to be—good friends."

"You plan to live in Richmond?" Nell had led the way into the dining room; and while they moved from room to room, between Enid's cries of admiration at all she saw, question and answer went back and forth between them.

"Yes. We had to leave Great Oak. The Yankees came and burned it down." She knew Faunt had set fire to the big house. Nothing he did could ever be anything but right in her eyes; yet others might blame him, and after all it was easy to accuse the Yankees. "So the children and I are living at Cinda's. Of course Travis is never there, at least not for very long." And as they came upstairs: "Oh Mama, what a charming room!"

"I use it for a sitting room. The drawing room is too formal, when I'm alone."

Enid's nose wrinkled daintily. "Do you smoke cigars when you're alone?" Her tone was teasing. "Or is it Cousin Tony?"

Mrs. Albion smiled. "I haven't seen Tony for some time; but I have many friends, you know." She led the way out into the upper hall again. "And here's my room." Enid went to and fro, handling everything, admiring everything. Her mother showed her another bedroom, immaculate, obviously unused. "And that's all," she said.

"It's really just a tiny house, isn't it?" Enid commented. It was certainly so small that she could never bring the children here; but then she had no intention of doing so. They could be left at Cinda's. "Where does Milly sleep?"

"Off the kitchen; and Rufus has his place in the yard."

Enid turned back into that pleasant room, not too feminine, where she had smelled the faint persisting odor of cigars. "I like this best of all, Mama," she declared, and sat down. "The fireplace, and the lovely pictures. Everything's just perfect. No wonder you spend most of your time up here." Her eyes twinkled. "With your cigar-smoking callers."

"You're a malicious little somebody, aren't you?" Nell said smilingly.

"I'm not really," Enid assured her. "Of course—" She hesitated, a little startled at her own temerity; but she meant to confide in her mother, to draw close to her. "Of course I've known about you and Uncle Tony. Almost from the first. But I never blamed you."

"You're ever so kind." Nell's tone was droll.

"I really admired you, your courage, doing what you wanted to do."

"Thank you, darling."

"I've always loved you just awfully, and thought you were simply wonderful, and envied you."

"Envy? You've had everything anyone could want!"

Enid laughed. "With Trav? Really, Mama!" Then, leaning suddenly forward: "Mama, do you know what I'd like? I want to come and visit you, so we can get really to know each other. We've been separated so long. Really, Mama, I think that's a wonderful idea. Let's just the two of us, be together for a while!"

Nell smiled. "That's hardly practical, is it, darling?"

"I don't see why not. You've a room for me, a beautiful room. I'd like to just not see anybody else but you for a while. I've missed you, all these years. Couldn't we, please?"

"You've your children, you know."

"They can stay with Cinda. She loves having them there. And I don't mean forever." She did, yet dared not yet say so. "I just mean— to visit for a while. Like two girls. You don't seem any older than I do, really."

"Nonsense, darling. As you reminded me, I'm in my fifties."

Enid recognized the bite in her mother's tone; and she pleaded: "Please don't be—don't hold that against me. I was just teasing. Don't you think it would be sort of nice to get to really know each other again?"

"I'm used to having my house to myself, Enid."

"Oh, I wouldn't do anything to change it."

"You're very persistent, aren't you!"

"I want it so much, Mama."

The older woman smiled. "It would never do, Enid. You were always an exasperating child. Oh, perhaps it was my fault. I kept you dressed like a child long after you thought of yourself as grown up. I was—we were desperately poor, you know. I hoped to seem young and attractive, to make a good marriage." Enid started to speak, but her mother said quickly: "No, don't deny it. If we're to be—friends, let's start with honesty. Yes, I was trying to find a husband. I had hopes of Trav till you decided to take him away from me. You were young and lovely, and you took him."

"I wish I hadn't!"

"You're a little late in repentance, my dear. So I took second-bests —without benefit of clergy. This is not a confession of a life of shame, darling. I've been, in my way, a highly moral woman. But I've learned to consider others, to try to please them."

She looked at her daughter through level eyes. "You've never learned those lessons," she said remotely. "I doubt you've ever con‚ sidered others, or ever tried to please anyone but yourself. I know you pretty well, Enid—even from afar off. You're a querulous, dissatisfied, self-centered person. You think of yourself as owing nobody anything. You think others ought to spend their time taking care of you." She laughed briefly. "I don't think we'd be congenial, darling."

Enid bit her lip. "No one has ever talked to me like that."

"Probably not. You see, Enid, if there were fewer wives in the world and more mistresses, more women would take the trouble to learn to play fair. When wife and husband are at odds, the wife need only weep to bring the poor man to heel; but when a man's mistress becomes an annoyance or a bore, he simply leaves her. There's a great deal more to the relationship between man and woman than—the unmentionables, darling!"

Enid after a moment spoke in an appeasing tone. "I can see I used to be the way you say; but I've grown up, this last year, Mama."

"Have you? I'm glad." Nell's eyes shadowed; her own thoughts filled them, and Enid saw a new beauty in her mother's face. "I've changed too, this last year, Enid. I used to consider every action, test everything I proposed to do by its probable effect on my life. Till—very recently. But I've learned something this last year—" She smiled. "This last month, in fact. Something I never knew. Something wonderful."

"You sound almost as if you'd fallen in love with someone."

"Do I? I'm a little too old for that, don't you think?"

Enid was puzzled by the quizzical note in the other's voice. "I know you're still mad at me for saying that about how old you are. But Mama, I've fallen in love myself. That's why I thought——"

"With that good, stolid, substantial husband of yours, I hope."

Enid shook her head, almost with violence. "No, Mama! I hate him! I've told Trav I—well, I don't want to be married to him any more. I'll hate him as long as I live. I don't know anything about getting a divorce, and probably I can't do that, but I'm not going to live with him any more. I'm going to leave him." She rose quickly, came to her mother's side. "Mama, that's why I want to come here and live with you."

"Nonsense, Enid!" Nell's tone was sharp. "You're an old married woman, with children. You can't leave your husband."

"Well, I'm going to. If you'll help me." Enid's eyes filled; she forgot all discretion. "Oh Mama, I hate him so. I never knew how much I hated Trav till I met Faunt."

Her mother was still seated, Enid standing in front of her. Nell had been looking up at her as she spoke. When Enid uttered Faunt's name, Nell's head dropped, not sharply but with an almost ponderous motion. She seemed to look down at her hands in her lap, and there was a long silence before she spoke.

"Faunt?" she repeated. "Isn't he Trav's brother?" She did not look up.

"Yes. Oh Mama, he's so gentle and sweet and brave and fine. When he was wounded, he came to Great Oak; and he was terribly sick, and I took care of him, and when he was better we used to ride together, and walk down across the lawn toward the river, and—oh just talk for hours and hours."

"I suppose you think he's in love with you?" Mrs. Albion watched her folded hands.

"I'm sure he is. Oh, of course he doesn't know it. He'd never let himself know it, not with me married to Trav. He's wonderful, Mama."

Nell, after a moment more, rose; she touched Enid's arm. "Darling, I'm glad you told me. But you're married; you must remember that. Only by being a good wife to Trav can you hope for self-respect and happiness."

Enid said angrily: "Oh, for Heaven's sake, don't preach to me! I know too much about you! You're a fine one to talk."

"If Faunt even suspected how you feel, you would never see him again." Nell's tone was flat and lifeless.

"I don't believe it. If I went to him—if I just told him— Mama, I know he's in love with me. I simply know it!" Nell did not speak, and Enid urged: "Look, Mama, let me come live with you, and then maybe Faunt could come here. We could ask someone to bring him. I could see him sometimes. I'd promise not to make any scandal or anything. Unless we—well, we could go away somewhere, never let anyone——"

Nell, with a swift explosive motion, slapped her hard, one cheek and then the other. She boxed Enid's ears, slapping her with both hands. Enid cried out and dodged away and backed into a chair and fell limply into it, her cheeks stinging red from the blows, angry, hurt, bewildered. Nell leaned over her as though to strike again; but then she caught herself, drew back, half smiled.

"There, darling! I had to bring you to your senses, that's all. I haven't boxed your ears since you were a baby, have I? But you were talking nonsense, you know!"

Enid, in a wave of self-pity, wailed: "Oh Mama—I thought you'd understand me!"

"I understand that you're an idiot."

"I thought you'd help me. I thought you could tell me what to do. I want to——"

"Enid, listen!" Nell hesitated, seemed to choose her words. "If you've botched your life, try to mend it; but don't expect me to take your part! I like Trav! He's miles too good for you! And as for coming to live with me—" She laughed, throwing back her head, mysteriously amused to the point of hysteria. "Living with me! Talking to me about your beloved Faunt! Why, my dear child—" She leaned suddenly nearer, no longer laughing, her eyes burning, her lips tight, deep furious furrows between her brows. "Enid, if you ever come to my door again I'll take a blacksnake whip and slash your soft shoulders to the bone!"

She stayed leaning over her daughter, hovering like a hawk about to swoop; and Enid was shaken with such terror as she had never known. When her mother, silent-footed as a cat, turned and went into the hall, Enid slipped out of her chair to peep after her. She saw Nell go to her own room, disappear; and fearful for life itself, Enid glided down the stairs, softly opened the outer door, closed it ever so gently behind her. The carriage at the gate was safety. She reached it so swiftly that the coachman dozing on the high seat did not wake till her weight tipped the carriage.

He looked around with some muttered word of apology and Enid said desperately: "Hurry! Go on! I stayed too long. I should have been home hours ago." And as he lifted the reins, "Hurry! Hurry! Do!"

Enid came home in a sweat of fear so overwhelming that she did not stop to wonder what had roused her mother to that rage so violent it was almost obscene. Never greatly curious about the emotions of others, she was not now. Beyond a lasting certainty that she would never dare go to her mother again, she did not attempt to understand, surrendering to self-pity, because she had been abandoned by the one who should have been her surest friend.

But she soon began to forget, and the fact that she seldom saw Trav made forgetting easy. She enjoyed Dolly, found Captain Pew a fascinating man, wishing Faunt would come more often to Cinda's, accepted the routine of life under this comfortable roof. Not till that evening when General Longstreet and Trav stayed for supper did anything disturb her easy acceptance of the contenting present.

Her first concern was faint. In the drawing room she became conscious of a puzzling difference in Trav. There had always been a solid strength in him against which she could make no impression; but that strength had been inert and passive. This which she felt in him was new. It was aggressive; it thrust out at her, in the stroke of his eye when his glance met hers, in the deeper tones his voice held. Her first uneasy awareness led her to torment him, as one experimentally teases a sleeping animal. When Longstreet praised him, she laughed mockingly, sure that since by the presence of others she was protected she could do this safely. She had no fear till Trav said he would stay the night.

Then in sudden panic she came to him and whispered: "You can't, Trav. There's no room. You can't sleep with me!" But when he told her, loudly enough so that they all heard, that he would stay, she fled headlong up the stairs to her room and shut the door. She sought to lock it, but there was no key; she sought somehow to barricade it against his entrance. She tried to roll the armoire from its place by the wall; but her utmost strength was not enough to move the heavy piece. She was still panting and straining when without knocking Trav opened the door and came in and closed the door behind him.

She retreated to the farthest corner of the room. She tried to speak, but her lips were dry. Trav, without looking at her, laid aside his coat; he pulled off his boots and began calmly to remove his clothes. She recaptured some grain of courage.

"Trav—you can't!" He did not answer; and she insisted. "Trav!" When he was still silent she edged sideways past the foot of the bed toward the door. Her instinct was for flight, and she had almost reached the door when with a quick movement he stepped into her path. Then at last he spoke.

"Undress, Enid."

"I told you, Trav!" She was stammering. "I t-told you at Great' Oak!" Her voice rose in the beginnings of hysteria; yet there was a secret intoxication in seeing him thus stern, commanding.

He said heavily: "I'll have no more of that sort of talk. I was too tired, that night, to care one way or another. But not now! Whether you like it or not, you're going to do as I say."

She tried to laugh, to deride him. "You think so?"

"Hush! Do you want everyone to hear?"

"I——"

"I don't want to hurt you, Enid; but if you disturb the house, I will."

"Trav, I told you——"

He set his hands on her upper arms in a grip so hard she stifled a cry of pain; yet pain and terror mingled with another emotion, a deep stir of ecstasy. He held her so firmly that it was as though he lifted her off the floor. Dry sobs shook her, but she was too frightened to weep. With his face close to her, stern and white, he said hoarsely: "You told me what you meant to do, but I am not going to let you do it."

"You can't stop me!" She twisted, frantic to be free; but with a violence of which she had not supposed even his strength capable, he thrust her toward the bed; he forced her down, held her there. When she would have screamed, his hand crushed her mouth, held her lips, muffled her cry; she felt her teeth cut her lips, tasted her own blood. Still holding her helpless, his face near hers seeming to her terrified eyes tremendous, he spoke hoarse words like blows.

"I've let you go your way too long," he said. "I won't allow that now. For myself I don't much care." In a scrupulous honesty he added: "I suppose I loved you, still do. Probably, if you choose, you can make me love you again.

"But I won't let you hinder me again, nor humiliate me. And I won't let you spoil the lives of our children, and I won't let you bring any new sorrow to my mother or to those in this house who have too much sorrow now. From now on you're going to do—to behave exactly as I bid you."

Because she lay quiet, his hand relaxed its pressure on her mouth. Through his fingers she spoke. "You can't make me——"

She had been about to say he could not make her love him; but he said: "Be still. I'm not discussing what you will do. I'm giving you orders, Enid."

"Suppose I——"

"Suppose nothing! You will do what I tell you to do."

"You shan't talk to me so!" She tried to pretend the anger she should feel, tried to hide even from herself her deep triumphant repossession. "I'll do what I——"

"What you do is for me to decide. If I choose, I can turn you into the street in the clothes you wear. Or without them! If I choose I can take a whip and strip the skin from your back as though you were a negro wench! If I choose——"

"You wouldn't dare!"

"Dare?" He repeated the word. "Dare? Why, Enid—" His voice changed. It took on the hollow tone of a man muttering in delirium. "I have seen men walk with high heads into the mouths of cannon ready to fire. Saturday I saw three men, side by side, go forward toward levelled guns; and the head of one of them was blown away and the clothes of another were set on fire by the blast of the guns. But the man whose clothes were burning and the other man went on, and leaped upon the Yankees who served the guns, and killed them any way they could. Don't talk to me about daring. I know now what men dare to do."

"Not to ladies!"

He laughed, almost mirthfully. "To ladies? Why, a woman's flesh can be ripped to shreds as easily as a man's. Listen to me, Enid. From now on—oh you can be as you like when we're alone—but from now on when others are with us, you are my wife, and you will remember it in every look and word and act." His tone softened almost wistfully. "I have great need of you. Perhaps, if you wish we may still be happy together. But whether you wish it or not, you'll do what I tell you. I will not let you leave me. We're married, and we'll stay married."

He released her and stood looking down at her; and she had never loved him as much as now. "You can't want to keep me when you know I just hate and despise you."

"I'll keep you, no matter what you want!"

She remembered something she had heard Cinda say. "You're as bad as the North, trying to hold onto the South."

Something swept across his face and for a moment he did not speak; then as though her word helped him understand himself he said gravely: "I suppose I am. I suppose I'm like Mr. Lincoln. If I'd been President when the South seceded, I would not have let the Southern states go." He nodded, almost peacefully. "Yes, Enid. I will not let you go."

And as though the matter were settled for good and all, he began to make ready for sleep. He said to her: "Undress. Get to bed."

She obeyed him, trembling with what she told herself was hatred; and when they were abed and without further word or act, without any move to seize the fruits of victory, he fell heavily asleep beside her, she was sure of it. She lay long awake, nursing her hatred, planning treacherous betrayals. He had beaten her; she was his. Yet now he did not want her! Well, even the defeated may in small ways take their long revenge. Today was his, but the future was hers! Because he did not take what in this hour she longed to yield, she would never forgive him. She wept herself to sleep with lonely tears.

10

N**ELL ALBION** in these weeks of late spring and early summer
felt youth in her renewed: its passions, its delights like wine, its frantic
disappointments, its heights and its valleys, its alternations between
ebullient hours when all the world was fair and other shadowed intervals when it seemed the sun would never shine again. When Faunt
was absent, she dreamed of his return; when he came she lost herself
completely in the rapture of delighting him, of devising every means for
his content. It was just after his departures that her spirits reached their
lowest ebb, when she remembered or thought she remembered ways
in which she had failed him and groaned with vain regrets; but as
each passing day brought nearer the hope of his return her heart rose
again, and her life reached its peak when he did at last appear.

From the first she had told him: "Send me a note when you are
coming, Faunt, so that I will be alone." When he smiled and accused
her of wishing to conceal their friendship she said: "Yes; yes I do, my
dear. I don't want anyone to share even the knowledge that we know
each other, and certainly I want none to share our hours together. But
there's another reason, a practical reason. I've always had many callers.
So send me word. Then if gentlemen are here when you wish to come
to me, I can get rid of them." So Enid's proposal that she come for a
visit seemed to Nell only amusing; but when her daughter spoke
Faunt's name she was no longer amused. Even after Enid's panic-
stricken flight, she paced to and fro for a long time, struggling for
composure, fighting down a thousand jealous imaginings. At first she
thought she and Faunt would laugh together at Enid's folly; but then

she decided he must never know. Men were so easily susceptible to flattering admiration, and Enid was lovely, and above all, Enid was young! If Faunt suspected Enid's devotion, his curiosity would be aroused; he would look upon Enid thereafter with a more acute attention, thinking always: "She is in love with me. This charming young woman adores me." Against such a thought no man would shut his mind.

Nell remembered that Faunt would see Enid whenever he went to the house on Fifth Street, and she wished he need never go there; and when she knew he had been there before he came to her she watched him with a searching eye, wondering if he and Enid had had any moment alone, wondering what word might have passed between them, wondering whether there was any change in him. Once or twice she led him to speak of Enid. When his word was kindly Nell ached with jealous anguish, and when he laughed at Enid's follies Nell feared this was pretense to hide an emotion he was unwilling to avow. The thought of Enid forever shadowed, as far as anything could shadow, their hours together.

But she let nothing else interfere with these hours. Since McClellan's army was at the city's gates, every crumb of information she could collect was at least potentially important, and she kept in touch with her regular sources and maintained her contacts with the invading army; but she was always prepared to put these matters aside if a note from Faunt announced his prospective arrival.

He came to her not so often as she wished; but after the two days of fighting at the end of May, when General Johnston's wound brought Lee to the command of the army, he was with her from late at night till dawn. During that battle Stuart's men had been used chiefly as couriers.

"And after the fighting, we were busy protecting the booty the army captured," Faunt explained. "A mob of authorized looters with passports from the Provost Marshal came to steal everything they could use or sell. Even Sunday night they were on hand, and again Monday morning. There were so many of them that the Yankees thought they were our regiments and opened fire. That scattered them finally; but as soon as they dared they were back like so many turkey buzzards around a carcass."

She nodded. "The things they stole are already for sale in the stores on Main Street: the oranges and lemons and all the supplies from General Casey's headquarters. And blankets and uniforms . . ."

"They were like a plague of locusts." Faunt's voice was hard with angry contempt. "I felt like laying a riding crop across their backs. Their pillaging cleaned out almost everything before the day was over." He added, in a different tone: "But General Lee commands now. He will teach this army to be an army."

"I hear the men don't like the work he makes them do."

"They'll come to it. He knows how to handle men. General Johnston could never get along with President Davis; but Lee will be able to. The army's a division stronger, with him in command."

She had no scruple against using even Faunt as a source of information. "Some gentlemen who called yesterday say General Lee knows more about the use of a spade than a gun," she suggested. "They believe he'll be even more cautious than General Johnston."

Faunt disagreed. "I know him only slightly; but men who do know him say that for plain cold-blooded courage he can't be beat. Tact and intelligence and the calculating brain of the engineer, that and the readiness to strike hard and daringly, that's Lee. They tell me McClellan is always deliberate. He will make a mistake if he waits too long to attack Lee."

A few days later Nell reported this opinion to a man who came late one night for a secret hour with her. This man was expected. Milly had long since gone to bed, and Nell locked the door from dining room to kitchen so that Milly could not by any chance come into the front part of the house. She herself at the appointed hour waited in the darkened hall, the front door ajar. When her visitor arrived, she led him upstairs to her small sitting room, where opaque curtains would prevent the escape of any beam of light, and they sat with a single candle between them.

This was a lean man with a mustache like a black wire across his upper lip. He wore beneath his military cape a blue uniform, and when she saw this Nell asked scornfully:

"Still cautious, Captain Mason?"

He smiled. "Why, I value my neck, Mrs. Albion. There is a distinction, you know, between a scout and a spy." He spoke with the accent of a Southerner.

"You might pass freely anywhere," she reminded him. "Your tongue would never betray you; but that uniform risks compromising me."

Captain Mason said with a twinkle in his eye: "As between you and me, I prefer you should be the one to be compromised. The Rebs would not hang a lady." He leaned forward and placed quietly on the table between them a little pile of gold pieces that gleamed in the candlelight. "You put me off last week," he remarked.

"I was engaged." Faunt had been here.

"You have something tonight?"

"Several things." She spoke in an even tone, as though quoting a memorized lesson. "General Lee's headquarters, in case you have some bold men to go seize him, are at——"

He shook his head. "We will do nothing to—remove General Lee. General McClellan was glad to see him succeed Johnston, welcomes the notion of fighting a battle of spades. With Lee in command, everything will now be done in an orderly manner, by the book."

"He is mistaken in his estimate of General Lee." Nell's tones were precise. "Lee will know how to manage President Davis, and he is winning the generals. When he called them in council he listened to them, but he told them nothing. When the earthworks he is building are strong enough to protect Richmond, he will man them with a part of his army and thus release the rest for a movement against your flank."

Captain Mason smiled. "Do you pretend to read his mind? Or does he confide in you?"

"Make no mistake about General Lee, Captain," she urged. "He will take his time, capture the imagination of the soldiers, then act. One of them, slightly wounded at Seven Pines, heard that others hurt no worse than he had applied for furloughs and received them, and he decided that he should have one. He went to General Lee; and Lee said: 'You fought on after your wound. We can't spare such men as you, my friend.' The man told the story delightedly. The soldiers see him every day among them; they're learning to trust him. I assure you he is a firm and a daring man."

"We're more interested in information than in opinions, Mrs. Albion."

She shrugged. "Sometimes opinions shed more light than information. For instance, Lee has asked Davis to reinforce Jackson with troops from Georgia and South Carolina, so that Jackson can march down the Valley and threaten Washington. That is 'information.' But my 'opinion' is that the Southern states will refuse to send those troops. They will stand on their sovereign rights as independent states, will insist that they are not subject to command by the President."

"I know," he assented, and smiled. "Your sovereign states will ruin your Confederacy. General Lee will never be able to make an army as long as each state insists her troops be allowed to serve together."

She asked: "Did you know that even with the men he had, Jackson has shattered your armies in the Valley?"

Captain Mason was startled. "That's impossible!"

"News reached here this morning. Jackson is in pursuit. Tonight's rain will mire your army in front of Richmond. I believe—but to be sure, this again is 'opinion,' Captain—that Lee will himself send Jackson reinforcements, send them direct from here to sweep the Valley clean."

"Will you know if this is done?"

"Of course."

After a moment he rose. "Any further information?"

Nell smiled. "Not even an opinion, Captain."

He said: "I'll come again, probably on Thursday, to see if any move to the Valley has begun."

Nell said: "If you see light in these windows, come again the night after, and the next, as usual." If Faunt were here Thursday night, or any other night, her door would be barred against the world.

"I may come in the daytime."

"Not in that uniform, I hope."

"Hardly."

"If you do," she suggested, "call yourself—" She hesitated, smiling. "Mr. Overcautious would not do, would it? Call yourself Mr. Overgood."

Nell had predicted that Lee would send men to the Valley, and

Wednesday she watched eight regiments entrain and knew her guess had been a good one. Early Thursday morning she had a breathless moment with Faunt, who flung from his horse at her gate and came for a swift embrace. Stuart and a thousand men were riding out the Brooke Turnpike; he stayed only an instant, hurried to take his place in the ranks. Watching from the window to see him mount, she saw another horseman pass; and her heart turned cold, for she recognized Captain Mason. The two men saluted, Captain Mason rode on, Faunt galloped away. But Nell was not surprised when an hour later, while she was at breakfast, the door bell rang and Milly said Mr. Overgood was calling.

Faunt was gone, the coast clear; so Nell received him. Captain Mason did not speak of the man he had seen leaving her door at dawn, so neither did she. She was eager to be rid of him. "You will want to get out of Richmond at once," she said. "I have the information you need. This time it is information; not just opinion. Yesterday eight regiments went by train, bound for Lynchburg and the Valley." Stuart's movement, which Faunt had confided to her, might be a part of the same design. "And Stuart left by the Brooke Turnpike with a thousand men. Probably he will join Jackson too." She added in a dry tone: "And if you want another of my opinions, I believe that when Jackson has struck his blow, he will bring his whole force back here to attack McClellan."

He was as anxious to be gone as she to have him go. When she was alone, her thoughts could follow Faunt. It might be weeks before she saw him; she disciplined herself to endless waiting. But Sunday morning at first light she heard a horse moving at a walk through the street in front of the house, and when the hoof beats stopped she sped through the sitting room to look out the front window. Faunt, dusty and worn, moving as stiffly as an old and weary man, was already coming up the walk toward the door. Still in her night garments, her feet bare, her heavy hair in a braid between her shoulders, she darted down the stair to fling the door wide, to sweep him into her arms.

He laughed in a shaky happiness. "Careful, Nell. I'm filthy."

"I don't care! Oh, I don't care! Darling, darling, are you all right?"

"Dead tired. Dirty. Sleepy. But I'm all right, yes. Nothing that a day or two here won't mend."

A day or two? Her heart leaped with delight because she was to have him for that day or two. "Wherever have you been?"

He chuckled. "Riding around McClellan's whole army." So her guess had been mistaken. Stuart had not gone to the Valley after all. Captain Mason would damn her for that misinformation. But no matter. Nothing mattered, since Faunt was here. "My horse is done," he said. "Can Rufus——"

"Oh yes, yes. Come, my dear. I'm so glad to get you home."

He was too near exhaustion to climb the stairs. Nell and Milly helped him; Nell bathed him clean, and bade him sleep and sleep, and he slept the day away. But he woke rested, and so full of conversation that she thought he was still half drunk with the excitement of his ride with Stuart. He talked for hours, while she listened, and watched him with proud shining eyes. She thought he should forget, rest, think of other things; but he laughed.

"I don't need any more rest," he assured her. "I'm not tired now. We were thirty-six hours in the saddle Friday and Saturday, and I rode all night last night to get back to you; but I'm all right now." He added with a quick, happy chuckle: "And I never want to forget it as long as I live. Oh Nell, we made fools of them! Scattered every Yankee squadron we saw! Killed I don't know how many, and lost just one man ourselves. You remember Mr. Mosby? He was here the night I met you." She nodded, and Faunt said: "The whole thing was his idea. He came back from a scout and told General Stuart the Yankees had nothing but pickets all the way from their army back to their base at White House. That was enough for Stuart." He described the attack on Tunstall Station. "Some of us went ahead with Mosby to cut the railroad there, and Stuart and the rest followed. We hit one of their wagon trains and burned it, and captured a lot of sutler's wagons and had a feast." There was a constant chuckling mirth in his tones that made her heart warm. "Oh it was a lark, Nell! A regular picnic!"

"You might all have been captured, killed!"

"Not with Stuart leading. The Yankees closed in behind us; but he knew they would, so instead of going back we went on south. The river was high, so we had to build a bridge to cross; but the Yanks were so bewildered by that time that they didn't even try to stop us."

He was free to stay with her till Tuesday before he must report for duty again. Tuesday night after Faunt was gone, Captain Mason came to her; and Nell after the happiness of these two days with Faunt was only amused by his ill humor. To watch his chagrin she began to tell him about that ride of Stuart's men; but he said angrily:

"Don't you suppose we know all that now? The time to tell me this was a week ago. Then we'd have been ready, could have bagged them all." Bagged them all? The thought that any word of hers might have brought harm to Faunt sent a chill wind of terror blowing in her heart. She must be careful, careful, careful; must always be sure that nothing she revealed to them could directly threaten him. "You said they were going to the Valley!" the Yankee reminded her.

"I told you that was only an opinion—and you don't trust opinions." She added: "But no one knew the truth except Stuart, and perhaps General Lee. I told you Lee was bold." And she added, remembering something Faunt had said: "Besides, not even Stuart knew he would ride clear around you, till he decided it was the easy way home."

"I know all that," he told her curtly.

"You know what he did, but I know why he did it," she assured him. "General Lee sent Stuart, not just to annoy you and destroy your trains, but to find out how far your right extended, and how strongly it was posted. I know that to be true." She added shrewdly: "But here is another of those opinions of which you are so suspicious. I believe General Lee plans to bring Jackson down around your right by the road Stuart took."

"Jackson's in the Valley."

"He needn't stay there. I'm not just guessing, Captain. General Lee wrote Jackson a letter today. There may have been orders in it. And Lee himself rode out to see your position along Beaver Dam Creek and the high ground where it rises, and he's already sending cars west to be ready to bring Jackson's army on."

"You don't know why he's sending cars west. You're doing a lot of guessing!"

"Tell General McClellan what I've told you."

"He'd think I was a fool."

She smiled. "If General McClellan's mind is as firmly closed as yours, Captain, General Lee will roll you all up in a ball whenever he's ready."

He rose to depart. "I'll give him your facts," he promised. "That Stuart's real purpose was to scout our right; that Lee has made a personal inspection of the ground there; that railroad cars are being sent west. That's all you really know."

"That's the A B C of it," she assented. "You and General McClellan can take my little alphabet and spell out any words you choose."

11

TRAV'S conduct that day at Seven Pines, though Longstreet was apt to say with a twinkle in his eyes that it was Trav's horse and not Trav himself that deserved the credit, nevertheless created a new bond between him and the General. Trav himself did not at once suspect this. Longstreet's commendation at Cinda's seemed to him only politeness. But during the days that followed he realized that there was a change in the attitude of his fellows toward him. On the day of the fight, while he was sitting Nig near General Longstreet, General Stuart came to join them; and at his side rode a blond young giant who carried enough weapons to equip a dozen men: a rifle slung over his shoulder, a carbine hung at his pommel, two revolvers thrust in his sash and another in a holster, an enormous sabre on his left thigh and a heavy hunting knife on his right. Trav was too absorbed at the time to give this man more than a glance; but Tuesday morning at Longstreet's headquarters he saw the same man again, among a group of officers; and the man came toward him and Trav found himself the target of a guttural flood of hearty German syllables. Captain Sorrel introduced the stranger: Heros von Borcke, a German officer come to solicit the privilege of serving the Confederacy.

"He saw you leading that column through the abatis Saturday," Sorrel explained. "And he's expressing his admiration"—the Captain smiled faintly—"and his surprise that you were unarmed. As you see, he believes in going prepared for anything."

Von Borcke spoke for himself, thrusting into Trav's hand a heavy revolver of curious design, with nine cylinders and a short barrel below the round barrel which received the balls from the cylinder. "He wants you to take it," Sorrel interpreted.

Trav stared at the piece in some perplexity. It was marked "Col. Le Mat's Patent." The loading lever was on the right side; the trigger guard had an ornamental spur, like a second trigger, projecting downward. "I never saw anything like this," Trav protested. "What is it?"

"It's a grapeshot revolver," Sorrel explained; and as von Borcke started to speak, Sorrel paused to listen, nodded, went on: "He says he got it in London. I know General Gorgas ordered five thousand of them for the army last August, and the navy's getting some, too. They're being made in Paris and sent to London for inspection. General Stuart has the mate to this one." And he laughed and said: "Fill that lower barrel with buckshot and you can kill enough Yankees for a mess."

"I wouldn't know what to do with it," Trav protested; but von Borcke was urgent, removing the holster from his own belt, pressing it into Trav's hands, taking the revolver back again to show its operation. The hammer in normal position struck the nipples that fired the chambers in the cylinder; but the head of the hammer could be depressed so that it would strike another nipple which discharged the buckshot barrel. The German explained this in a volley of words and with repeated demonstrations, and Sorrel urged:

"Take it, Currain. Give him that pleasure." Von Borcke spoke again, and Sorrel told Trav: "He says he has nine extra packs of cartridges to fit it, and he'll turn them over to you. It's forty-two caliber, the buckshot barrel fifty caliber, so it has to have special cartridges."

So Trav belted on the holster, and jammed the weapon home, and von Borcke bestowed an approving buffet between Trav's shoulders, and Trav grinned and felt completely ridiculous and yet secretly pleased.

Von Borcke was not the only one from whom he had an approving word. Longstreet one day remarked: "Currain, I shall mention your gallantry in my report of the fight the other day."

"Oh no," Trav protested. "Of course I know your kindness, sir, but——"

Longstreet frowned. "You are mistaken, Captain. I do not bestow praise out of kindness. I have just signed orders authorizing certain regiments to inscribe Williamsburg and Seven Pines upon streamers for their battle flags; but only regiments which behaved creditably are to have that honor. I assure you"—his tone lightened in kindness— "I have the friendliest feeling for you; but if I praise your conduct on the battlefield it will be because you have deserved that praise. Military honors are not lightly won, not lightly given."

Trav was not introspective, but the cordial praise of men whose opinion he respected led him to some self-examination. Certainly that intoxicating madness which had filled him on the field of battle was new to his experience. In fact the weeks since Tilda found those letters at Great Oak had been colored by many emotions he had never felt before. At first, when close upon that stunning knowledge of his kinship with Lincoln came Tommy Cloyd's death and Julian's vanishing, he felt above all else hatred of war and of this Lincoln who was responsible. Yet with that habit of seeing both sides of a question, that trait natural to the mathematician of looking for a balance, an equation, he had begun to understand that men did what seemed to them their duty; just as the South would not submit to Northern rule, and just as Virginia would not assist in crushing her Southern sisters, and just as he himself had been unhappy till he found some contenting task to do, so the North and Lincoln himself were under a compulsion they could not escape.

His decision to insist that Enid abandon her intent to leave him was somehow a part of this understanding. What she wished to do would place him in a position he could not tamely accept. His thoughts were not completely clear; he only knew that to let her go was to play a weakling's part; and this discovery gave him a new understanding of himself. He could—and did—compel Enid to submit to his will.

But clearly she could not stay on indefinitely at Cinda's, so he must make a home for her and for the children. The general flight from Richmond which was precipitated by the approach of McClellan's army should help him to find a house that could be bought or rented. He could understand, even though he did not share, the general panic. Since Manassas, the months had seen an almost unbroken succession of Confederate disasters. In the West and South, and at New Orleans.

and along the seaboard Federal armies were everywhere firmly established. Western Virginia beyond the Valley was largely in Yankee hands, and northern Virginia too. Norfolk was abandoned, and Suffolk; McDowell at Fredericksburg was only a few days' march away; McClellan was at Richmond's very door. So fainthearts accepted the certainty of disaster, and the city, which had been swollen to the bursting point, with even humble lodgings everywhere at a premium, was no longer crowded. Trav thought he could find a house for sale at a figure not beyond all reason; and when he went for a Sunday dinner at Cinda's he had this in his mind.

Brett was at home, and Burr. Faunt, Burr said, was on a patrol toward Fredericksburg. "I don't see much of him."

"We rarely see him here," Cinda assented, and Trav saw her look toward Brett, trouble in her eyes. Brett and Burr began to discuss what General Lee might now be planning, what McClellan's next move would be; and Trav watched Cinda's knitting needles and guessed a little of the strain which this waiting for the inevitably approaching battle imposed on her. The enemy was so near that if the wind served, a single cannon shot anywhere along the lines might be heard here in the city. Whenever that happened, each woman's heart must beat harder at the thought: 'Perhaps that shot struck him.' It was only when they had their menfolk here under their eyes—Barbara yonder never looked at anyone except her young husband—that they were free from fear. Only Vesta and Jenny seemed at peace; for they could not be hurt more deeply by the future than they had been by the past.

The two men, absorbed in their conjectures, talked on till Vesta cried: "Oh I wish you'd stop it, both of you! It's bad enough having to live with it without talking about it all the time!"

Brett said: "I'm sorry, Honey. We were just thinking aloud."

"Well, I wish you'd think to yourselves! Can't you see how it bothers Mama and Barbara?"

Cinda said gently: "Since we can think of nothing else, we might as well talk about it." Yet pain tore words from her. "But oh, why couldn't the North have just let us go?"

Enid spoke. "Trav says if he'd been in old Lincoln's place he wouldn't have let us go either."

Trav saw all of them turn to look at him in startled wonder; and under the weight of their eyes he felt his cheek burn with anger at Enid for thus distressing them. Cinda asked him: "Really, Travis?"

"I expect he did what he thought he must," he confessed. "Most men do."

For a moment there was silence. Then Brett said thoughtfully: "I heard Lincoln make a speech once, out in Illinois, five or six years ago. I've told you, Cinda. He said—he told the South—" Brett hesitated. "I remember his words. He's an impressive speaker. He said: 'We won't leave the Union, and you shan't!'" And he added: "I know what Trav means. Lincoln did what he thought he had to. A lot of Virginia men loved the Union, but we thought we had to go with our state. He did what he thought he had to, and so did we."

Trav spoke thoughtfully. "Longstreet says to stick with the South was hard even for General Lee. Lee is aging fast. His beard's quite gray."

Cinda said: "Really? His hair and mustache weren't gray at all, last year."

"They are now."

Burr commented, almost sulkily: "It's lucky not many of us feel as you do, Uncle Trav."

There was an uncomfortable hush; then Cinda spoke to her son. "You know, Burr, it didn't prevent Uncle Travis from fighting as hard as anyone."

Burr colored, spoke in quick apology: "I'm sorry, sir."

Trav said affectionately: "It's all right, Burr. The trouble with me is I think too much. Probably it's a mistake. To think means asking yourself questions, and that's always unsettling. I used to be sure of some things, but there's not much I'm sure of now."

Burr nodded slowly. "I know what you mean. That's one good thing about being a soldier. You learn to stop thinking and just do what you're told."

At Caesar's summons they rose to go to the table, and as they moved into the dining room, Vesta came to Trav's side and kissed him and said softly: "I love you very much, Uncle Trav. Some ways, you're like my Tommy." There was no sadness in her tone. "I know the way you meant that."

Trav saw Enid watching them. Probably she would use that tongue of hers to poison them all against him if she could. Certainly he must make a home for her, if only to keep her apart from them. When after dinner he and Cinda and Brett were alone, he spoke of this intention.

"She can stay here, Travis," Cinda assured him.

"I don't want to impose on you."

"Oh, with a family as big as mine, two or three more don't matter."

But he persisted, and they discussed possibilities and it was Brett who said: "See here, Trav; Barbara's father and mother don't intend to come back to Richmond. Mr. Pierce told us before they left. They might be willing to rent their Clay Street house, or even to sell it."

Cinda agreed. "Because they're not well-to-do, of course; and with prices so high——"

Trav said thoughtfully: "I can ask Burr to ask Barbara what she thinks."

"You needn't hurry, Travis. Enid and the children are welcome here as long as you'd like to have them stay; and Barbara's baby is coming so soon, I wouldn't bother her now."

So they agreed the matter could wait.

Burr was away on that great ride with Stuart when Barbara's baby was born. Trav came to Fifth Street for Sunday dinner to hear that the baby, a boy, was already two days old. He brought them the first news of Stuart's exploit. "And they had only one man killed, Captain Latane," he said. "So Burr is safe." Cinda hurried upstairs to tell Barbara, and late that afternoon Burr, hot and tired and dusty, rode up to the door; and when he had seen his son and his Barbara he came down to tell them the tale of his great adventure. Before he was done, Dolly arrived, her eyes big with bright excitement.

"Oh I think General Stuart's just simply wonderful," she cried. "Richmond's gone crazy over him! There's nobody like him in the whole world!" She added wistfully: "Not since poor General Ashby was killed."

Enid asked teasingly: "Not even Captain Pew?"

Dolly tossed her head. "Heavens no! Captain Pew just scares the life out of me; he's so big and fierce and cruel. But gracious knows I don't care a fig about him."

Burr said: "You'd never have been afraid of Turner Ashby, Dolly."

"Oh Burr, did you know him? What was he like? Was he wonderfully handsome?"

Burr smiled. "I don't know, honestly. He always wore gray clothes, and his jacket was too big for him, and too long, and his boots were especially high, and he was probably as fine a rider as you'd find in Virginia, but—well, you didn't notice whether he was handsome or not. He was so gentle and so modest."

"Like Cousin Faunt?" Enid asked, and Burr hesitated and said uncertainly:

"Why, no. You can't help noticing Uncle Faunt." Trav was watching Enid, struck by something in her tone when she spoke of his brother. "But you didn't notice Turner Ashby, except in a fight. He would shout 'Follow me!' and go racing ahead; and his men always said he grew a foot taller in a charge."

"The poor darling!" Dolly's eyes were brimming. "I never met him, but I loved him all the same!"

"But he wasn't as good as General Stuart," Burr assured her. "He didn't command men; he just led them. General Ashby's men could follow him if they chose, but they didn't have to! But General Stuart's men know they have to follow him!"

"I'd follow him anywhere!" Dolly vowed. "So would every girl in Richmond!"

Burr smiled. "Forgetting Turner Ashby already?"

"Why, of course!" Dolly admitted, her eyes twinkling. "After all, poor General Ashby's gone; and you know how it is: out of sight, out of mind!" Vesta rose quietly and slipped away; and Burr looked at Dolly in black anger, and Dolly said contritely: "Oh I'm sorry! I forgot. Vesta's so wonderful you never remember about Tommy at all."

Trav, riding back to headquarters, thought it a pity such a light-witted little featherhead as Dolly could hurt people so.

The day after Stuart and his men returned from their ride around McClellan, Longstreet was summoned to council with General Lee. When he returned for supper with his staff, Trav guessed that some decision had been reached, some movement planned; but it was not till two days later that he and Longstreet had an hour alone. Then Longstreet said with a twinkle in his eyes: "Captain Currain—and by the way, I have recommended your promotion—" Trav looked at him in surprise and gratification. "I don't believe you're a man much inclined to fretful fears."

Trav hesitated. "Why—if it's a question of something I should be doing, I worry about it, I suppose."

The other shook his head, brushing the remark aside, and Trav saw that he had not expected any answer. "If you have felt any doubts about General Lee's capacities," Longstreet said, "you can dismiss them."

"I've seen your respect for him growing every day, sir."

Longstreet nodded. "When he first called all his general officers into council I thought it a mistake," he admitted. "It's always a mistake to let too many men know your plans. But General Lee listened a great deal and said nothing at all. He has the gift of listening, and the gift of patience."

"Is patience a good thing?"

"Certainly. The greatest general is the one who realizes at the right time that to do anything but wait is wrong. To act just for the sake of acting is the worst possible tactical mistake. General Lee will not act until his army is ready for work." His eyes began to shine. "But he's ready now. I suggested to him day before yesterday that Stuart's ride showed McClellan's right to be in the air. I proposed that Jackson come secretly from the Valley, pass around McClellan's right, and hit him flank and rear. He said he had considered reinforcing Jackson to drive north and threaten Washington. You remember I once advocated that move. But now he has decided to deal with McClellan here. He told me he had written Jackson a week ago to be prepared to move to help us here, and had written him again the day I saw him, giving orders for the move to strike McClellan's flank, the very move I proposed."

Trav smiled. "So you think he's right."

Longstreet chuckled. "Of course. When a man agrees with you, you're bound to praise his wisdom." He added: "But General Lee is open to suggestions, too. He had planned for Jackson to strike McClellan's lines of communication, with our forces ready to attack from this quarter; but I suggested that we leave our fortified line here to protect Richmond, cross the Chickahominy and hit McClellan's flank along Beaver Dam Creek while Jackson cut his lines of supply. General Lee showed his greatness by accepting that amendment." He lifted his left hand, the fingers extended, and made a sweeping motion which reminded Trav of the way a man cradling wheat swings his scythe. "With Jackson to cut his army off from its roots, we'll sweep him back against the Chickahominy and destroy him!"

Trav's pulse quickened at the prospect, and he felt a quiet pride because Longstreet had confided in him; but when on Sunday he went again to Cinda's he found that all Richmond knew the battle hour was near. Enid asked him at dinner if it were true. "Dolly says so," she declared, and when he did not answer she said lightly: "Oh, it's no secret! Dolly says Cousin Tilda and Mrs. Brownlaw are busy getting the hospitals ready to take care of the wounded."

Trav did not answer her, and Vesta as though she saw his embarrassment said reassuringly: "No one can keep secrets in Richmond, Uncle Trav. Not even General Lee." And to her mother: "Mrs. Lee is here, Mama. Norvell Caskie told me. They've been at Marlbourne, Mr. Ruffin's place, since the Yankees came to White House." Trav had not thought of Mr. Ruffin for a long time; he wondered where the old man would go, since the nearness of the Yankees drove him away from his farm on the Pamunkey. "General Lee sent Major Mason with a flag to bring them to Richmond. Norvell says General McClellan treated them with perfect courtesy. Norvell and Agnes Lee are devoted, you know." Vesta smiled at Trav. "And of course as soon as General Lee brought his family to Richmond, everyone knew there was going to be a battle out near Marlbourne somewhere."

Brett smiled and said no man could keep a secret from women. "He can burn his papers, but he can't burn his thoughts—or his actions—and they read actions and thoughts at a glance."

"That reminds me," Cinda remarked. "I had letters from Mama and Tony. I made spills out of them. Matches are so expensive I use every scrap of paper. But Mama says the trip was comfortable, and that Tony's as jolly as can be."

"Jolly? I can't imagine Tony jolly," Enid protested.

Cinda caught Trav's eye. "Travis, Tony said some of the Martinston men have deserted. They hide out in the hills near their farms whenever anyone comes to look for them."

"Did he speak of Ed Blandy?"

"No. Or if he did I don't remember."

Trav said thoughtfully: "Most of those men have wives and children and no way to get enough to eat except to make a crop on their little farms. I can understand that some of them might think they ought to go home and take care of their families." He saw Enid watching him with narrowed eyes. "I had a lot of friends among those farmers."

Enid laughed. "So I suppose you think it's all right for them to desert?"

"Well, even some of the officers who were defeated for reelection last April left the army and haven't come back. So I don't much blame the men." His tone was even, but he was thinking that he must get Enid away to a home of her own as soon as possible. There was mischief in that tongue of hers.

After dinner he made an opportunity to ask Cinda about the Pierce house, and Cinda promised to discuss the question with Barbara. "And Brett will write to Mr. Pierce, I'm sure."

Brett nodded. "I'll write today," he promised; and then as though amused at his own precipitancy: "Not that there's any hurry. By this time next week, Richmond may be in Yankee hands."

Trav shook his head. "No," he said strongly. "No. We'll beat them." He felt even as he spoke a resurgence of the tremendous lust for violence which had driven him on that day at Seven Pines.

Perhaps Cinda saw this, for before he left the house that day she brought him his father's sword, that long blade, double-edged toward the tip, straight and heavy in his hand, which had hung above the mantel at Great Oak and which he had given her to keep dry that night when the carriage took the road to Richmond. She gave it to him now with no ceremony; she even smiled.

"If you're going to go galloping into battle all the time, Travis, you ought at least to be armed."

He took it awkwardly. "I wouldn't know what to do with this, I'm afraid. I've got a revolver, too. But even General Longstreet doesn't wear a revolver or a sword, not very often, Cinda."

"Take it," she insisted; and her eyes met his in grave affection. "Wear it, Travis. You never know."

12

ENID had never been long afraid of Trav; for no matter how she might provoke him, he could always be melted into good humor again. It amused her to know that a touch of her hand, a sudden ardent kiss, a provocation ever so lightly given could awaken in him a lumbering and awkward passion to which she need only lend herself, no matter how remotely, in order to leave him perfectly appeased. Even that night at Cinda's, though she was frightened for a while, terror gave way to yearning surrender, till his quick slumbers made her hate him. She lay dreaming of a thousand ways to do him injury, and in the weeks that followed she watched for opportunities. To tell them all that he, in Lincoln's place, would have sought to crush the South, and to see Burr's young anger gave her a delicious pleasure; and when Trav made excuses for those worthless friends of his who had deserted from the army, she reported what he said to Dolly and to Tilda. Tilda would tell Mrs. Brownlaw, and Mrs. Brownlaw's tongue was never still.

She sought ways to make those who loved Trav doubt him, and at the same time she tried to waken in him resentment against them. Whenever he came to the house she reported to him, in tones of exaggerated patience, little imagined slights. Cinda had said so and so. "Of course I know she didn't mean it the way it sounded; but Cinda has never liked me." Barbara, Jenny, Vesta: of each in turn she made complaint. "I know they mean to be kind, but . . ." She recited little differences among the children, in which Peter and Lucy were always the sufferers. "Cinda is so fond of Kyle. She just thinks he's perfect. But if Peter does the least little thing she's forever nagging at him."

Or, knowing his love for his daughter: "Lucy just worships Vesta. She's so cute about it. But Vesta treats her like a baby, till sometimes Lucy slips away by herself and just cries and cries."

When she saw that if she laughed at Trav or mocked him these others took his side, she changed her tactics and began to defend him when he needed no defender. If he came to the house begrimed from a day in the mud during that rainy month of June she would apologize to Cinda. "You mustn't scold him, Cinda. He's working so hard he just doesn't think of anything else, poor dear." And if Cinda retorted that she had no thought of blaming Trav: "Oh I know how you love to keep things neat and spotless. Please forgive him, do."

She went almost every day to be with Dolly. Captain Pew was gone to Wilmington to rejoin his ship and set off for another adventure through the blockading squadrons; and under General Lee's more exacting discipline every soldier was with his regiment awaiting orders, so Dolly had not so many beaux in attendance and she welcomed Enid's company. They could go together where Dolly, who like many gay and charming belles had few girl friends, could not discreetly go alone.

Early in the morning of the last Thursday in June, Dolly came to the house in feverish excitement. Cinda and Vesta had breakfasted and were already gone when she arrived, but she found Enid and Jenny together, and she cried: "Enid, Jenny, get your bonnets on. Hurry! Hurry!" And before they could speak: "They're going to fight today. The soldiers have been marching through town and out the Mechanicsville Turnpike since daylight, and General Jackson's coming——"

Jenny asked, smiling at her eagerness: "How ever do you always know everything that's going to happen, Dolly?"

"Oh everybody knows it," Dolly assured her. "Mrs. Brownlaw told Mama. General Lee has just been waiting for the rain to be over; and when he saw the rainbow yesterday he decided to fight them today. If we go to the Capitol and get up on top of it we can see it all. So do hurry and come on, before the best places are all taken."

"I'll stay here," Jenny decided. "I've so much to do. But Enid, there's no reason you shouldn't go."

"I should say not!" Enid retorted. "I'd just like to see anyone keep me from going." She hushed with a caught breath, for as she spoke they heard a distant cannon. They all listened for an instant; and then Dolly caught Enid's arm.

"Come on, come on!" she urged. "Hurry, or we'll miss everything."

So Enid made haste and in a moment she was ready. At the corner of Grace Street they paused in some uncertainty, for the gunfire was off to the eastward. "But the soldiers all went out the Mechanicsville pike," Dolly protested, as though this confusion were a personal slight. "They haven't had time to go back in that direction! Never mind! Come on! We'll go to the Capitol anyway."

"We'll never be able to get up on top," Enid objected. "Everybody in Richmond will be there."

"Oh they'll make room for us!" Dolly was supremely confident of her beauty's power, and they hurried on. Grace Street was already full of people. At the Capitol, as Dolly had predicted, her smiles opened a path for them. They panted up the steep stairs, gasping for breath in the hushed airless heat, to elbow their way out on the small platform set atop the ridgepole. The place was already crowded, and everyone was looking off across the valley of Shockoe Creek toward the slowly rising ground that rose to the ridge beyond which lay the valley of the Chickahominy. Dolly's eager thrusting brought them to the rail. Two or three miles away in the cultivated fields along the roads that led northeasterly Enid saw dark masses and some movement of mounted men, no larger than insects at this distance; and she knew those masses were soldiers waiting to advance. Dolly, full of questions, asked why they didn't go on and start fighting, and a gentleman from the Quartermaster's department who knew Dolly's father explained that they were waiting for Jackson.

"He was at Ashland last night. They won't move till he gets behind the Yankee flank."

Someone else reported that Powell Hill had marched to the Meadow Bridges to cross and join Jackson and roll up the Yankee flank. All the gentlemen here appeared to be informed as to Lee's every plan, and each knew exactly what should be done. Little gusts of argument arose and blew themselves out and rose again as the sun climbed higher, and the hot forenoon drew tediously on.

But Dolly tired of this long waiting, and before the morning was half gone she was ready to abandon their fruitless vigil here. "We'll go where we can really see something," she declared; and Enid was equally weary of baking in the sun high above the city.

"Yes, let's," she agreed. "Can't we find a shady place somewhere, Dolly? I'm panting like a hen on a hot day."

So they descended to the Square again and Dolly said they must go out to the hills north of town. "I've been on picnics out at Mitchell's Spring," she remembered. "And I know we can see from up on Academy Hill above the spring."

They hurried back to Second Street, and before they passed Shockoe Cemetery they were part of a flowing stream of men and women all bent the same way, trooping down to cross the creek and climb the winding road beyond. Because everyone else seemed to be doing so, they climbed Mansfield Hill, and found a throng there before them. Trees along the crest gave a grateful shade; and since Dolly always attracted many polite attentions a gentleman asked the privilege of spreading his coat for them to sit upon. They heard sudden guns off beyond the Meadow Bridges, and Dolly cried triumphantly:

"There! Hear that! There's Jackson now!"

"Jackson?" A dozen faces turned toward them, a dozen voices repeated the name; and someone said politely:

"Why, Miss Dolly, General Jackson's a hundred miles away." Enid thought enviously that everyone knew Dolly.

"That's what the poor Yankees think," the girl retorted. "But they're going to be surprised. General Jackson's going around the head of Beaver Dam Creek and get in behind them." A group of listeners gathered, as much to see Dolly's flashing smile and the charming color in her cheeks as to hear what she said.

Then nearer cannon sounded, two shots, and half a dozen; and then there began the steady roar and beat and pound of many guns. They watched with straining eyes; but the fighting was in the valley beyond the ridge, and from where they were they could see nothing. Dolly was exasperated. "Why don't they come over and fight where we can watch them!" she protested; but no one even smiled, forgetting her while they listened to the steady clamor of the cannon and the sharper sound of distant musketry.

They could hear the firing and see the smoke, but that was all; and

Enid was hot and bored. After all, there was nothing to see; and the guns could be heard just as well from Cinda's house, or from anywhere in the city. She said as much to Dolly, but Dolly declared she just couldn't bear to go away and leave those poor dear boys yonder to fight the Yankees all alone. Enid told her she was an idiot; and Dolly retorted that Enid might go whenever she chose.

But more and more spectators kept arriving, and there began to be a dreadful fascination in that monotonous and unending chorus of conflict; so Enid stayed, and the sun slipped quietly down the western sky, and evening shadows extended themselves from the foot of every tree far down the hillsides. Each patch of woodland became a dark and darker blot against the lighter hue of the cultivated ground, and windows in distant houses caught the last flame of the sun and flashed it back at them. Then dusk and dark began to come; and as the darkness thickened an occasional shell, bursting high above the ridge which lay between them and the battle, gleamed for an instant against the shadowed sky northeasterly whence night came racing toward them.

The spectacle acquired, even for Enid, an awful beauty. Around her she heard the stir of many feet as newcomers who till now had been content to perch on the Capitol or on the roofs of buildings in the city came to the hills for a better view. "Why, it's just like fireworks, isn't it!" Dolly cried in a bright delight. Against the curtain of the night there was the steady burst of shells; burning fuses traced fine lines of fire in interlacing arcs across the sky; the steady flashes from cannons and muskets, not actually seen, nevertheless kept up a flickering dance of light above the valley yonder, as though a thunderstorm played there beyond the ridge.

The spectacle continued till long after dark. Enid was ravenously hungry before the firing dwindled and died away and Dolly was at last ready to turn homeward. The watchers from the hilltops went stumbling through the dark back toward the city, and on the road up over Shockoe Hill many others joined them; for all along these crests beyond the creek there had been hundreds of spectators. Enid was too hungry to talk, but Dolly chattered steadily, and all around them in the night there were the sober tones of men, women's voices edged and shrill with excitement, the exclamations and ejaculations of children. Once or twice Enid heard women sobbing quietly; and she supposed they were fearful for the fate of husbands or lovers or sons who had a part in the battle. But she herself was much more anxious for supper than for news of Trav, or for that matter of anyone.

Unless it were Faunt. Her thoughts for a while dwelt with him. She wondered why he so seldom came to Cinda's, why she had not been able to renew that pleasant and comradely relationship which had made his convalescence at Great Oak such happiness for her. Of course there could never be any substance to those dreams she once had treasured; but her thoughts were her own, so she let them run till even in the darkness she felt her cheeks burn hot, and rubbed them fiercely, and came back to the present again.

In the moving throng she and Dolly became separated, but Dolly could take care of herself. At home Enid found Jenny and Lucy and Peter anxious for her return. "We waited supper," Jenny said. "I knew you'd be starved, so we're having a heartier supper than usual."

"I was too excited to come home to dinner," Enid declared. "We've been out on the hills beyond the creek. It was wonderful!" Peter asked some question, but she put him off. "For Heaven's sake don't pester me till I've had something to eat!"

"I thought we'd eat in the dining room," Jenny said. "Mama and Vesta came home for dinner, but Mrs. Brownlaw sent for them when the ambulances began to bring the wounded."

Peter, as soon as they were seated, renewed his questions, and Lucy too, so Enid began to tell them the little she had seen, enjoying their wonder and their eagerness. It was not often that they thus hung upon her every word. Trav was their hero, and this was more than ever true since he became a soldier; but tonight the things she had seen and done magnified her in their eyes. She told them every detail she could remember, and Peter asked at last: "Are they going to fight some more tomorrow, Mama?"

"Oh I'm sure they will. And this time I'm going to get some place where I can see."

"Can I go with you?" he pleaded, and even Lucy, usually reserved, begged to go. "Can't we all go, Mama? We can take some lunch with us, so you won't get so hungry."

It would be exciting and delightful to take these babies with her. "Well, I'll think about it."

Jenny suggested that to take them might not be wise. "Tilda says General Lee ordered even President Davis off the battlefield today."

"Really? What did Mr. Davis do?"

"Why, he obeyed! After all, when soldiers are busy fighting, they don't want civilians in the way."

Peter, seeing his hopes endangered, urged: "Mama, we won't be under foot, honestly. Can't we go, please?"

Enid put off decision. "There, we'll see. It's bed time for both of you." She sent them away upstairs.

Before Cinda and Vesta came wearily home, tney had a grain of news; for a soldier on his way to the hospital with a bullet in his arm stopped with a note from Brett. Brett wrote that the Howitzers had been in reserve all day and were now at a blacksmith shop somewhere near the lines awaiting orders. He said Stuart, and therefore Burr, were away to the northeast guarding Jackson's flank. He had seen Trav once during the day, a little before sunset, riding with Longstreet.

But after that they heard no more from any of their menfolk for a while. Through the days of steady battle, when a rising tide of victory woke jubilation that mingled with stricken grief for those who died, Cinda and Vesta were seldom at home. They came only when exhaustion drove them, to sleep, to fill hampers with Madeira and sherry and brandy, to set the people preparing food in all the bounty that was possible. Enid protested that it was ridiculous to wear themselves out.

"There are plenty to help without you," she urged. "I can't walk along Franklin Street without bumping into ladies carrying waiters full of food. You're all just working like so many niggers. Whatever do you find to do?"

Cinda said quietly: "There's really plenty to do, Enid, even if it's only mopping bloody floors."

Enid shivered. "Br-r-r! Just thinking of it makes me sick. Honestly, Cousin Cinda, I don't see how you stand it!"

Cinda's eyes shadowed. "I heard today that once when the cannon fire was specially bad General Lee asked General Jackson if his men could stand it; and General Jackson said his men could stand anything. I suppose that's the only answer, really. You can stand anything, if you want to."

Enid said indignantly: "Well, maybe, but I don't even want to."

Cinda nodded. "That's all right, dear. I'm glad you can be here with Jenny and Barbara."

Sunday and Monday the occasional sound of distant guns and the dust clouds that marked marching columns told Richmond that the battle was moving southward toward the James River. Monday at noon a boy came to the house with another note from Brett. McClellan was in retreat. The Howitzer company had crossed and recrossed the Chickahominy and marched south, passing within two or three miles of Richmond to take the Darbytown road and intercept McClellan's army and destroy it. Brett added a postscript: Trav was all right.

Cinda and Vesta came home a few minutes after the young messenger had gone. Enid resented as an indictment of her inactivity their weariness, the redness of their sleep-hungry eyes, their hoarse voices, their stony countenances; but if they chose to make idiots of themselves it was certainly not her fault! She was being sensible, that was all. Besides, her children needed her; and to prove this, she made a great to-do over the fact that Peter seemed to be coming down with a cold. With a certain elaboration she put him to bed and kept him there.

Late Tuesday morning an ambulance stopped at the door. Caesar answered the ring, and summoned Enid and Jenny. "Hit's Mistuh Trav," he explained. "Dey done fotch him home."

They ran together into the street, and Enid peered into the ambulance and saw Trav lying there with closed eyes, his cheek drained white. "Oh, is he dead?" she cried, woeful with mysterious grief. It was terrible to see him so helpless and so still.

The driver, a tall, raw-boned, slow-spoken man, said: "Yas'm. So fur, anyways; but I reckon he might come to life again."

"But we can't take care of him!" Enid protested, weeping with fear and woe. "We can't do anything! You must take him to the hospital!"

Jenny touched Enid's arm in reassurance, and the driver explained: "I done that. Had a load of 'em like him. But a lady there knowed him, and she said to bring him here, said she was Mis' Dewain, said to tell you she'd come quick as she could git a doctor to come along with her."

Enid wrung her hands, helpless with tears, but Jenny took command. Caesar and the driver carried Trav indoors. The task was an awkward one, because Trav clasped in his two hands his naked sword, for half its length a bloody smear; and when Jenny tried to take it from him, his fingers tightened so that the hilt could not be freed. The driver of the ambulance drawled:

"Be a mite keerful, ma'am. I took a fancy to that sword myself, but seems like he don't aim to let go his holt of it at all."

The sword was bloody, and there was a dark stain of blood on Trav's coat. Dust had settled on it and had become a reddish mud which as the blood clotted was overlaid with dust again; but when they moved him, in the center of this dusty patch a spot of brighter crimson slowly spread. At the driver's advice they laid him on the floor in the hall, and the children came on tiptoe and Peter asked in a whisper:

"Mama, is Papa dead?"

"Oh for Heaven's sake!" Enid cried, hysterical with bewildering compassion and tenderness and fear. "I don't know!" She began to sob in a deep, retching fashion. "Jenny, can't we do something? Can't we get a doctor?"

"Mama will bring someone. You go lie down, dear. June and I will take care of him." She spoke to Lucy. "Lucy, take your Mama upstairs and put her to bed."

Enid submitted, and Lucy led her sweetly away, mothering her in loving kindness, and she brought a cold compress to lay across Enid's eyes. "There, Mama, you'll feel better soon. Rest now and be ready, so you can take care of Papa."

Enid said wretchedly: "Oh Lucy, he's going to die." He mustn't die! "I don't know what to do, Lucy," she wailed. "I don't know how to take care of hurt people!"

"You took awful good care of Uncle Faunt!"

Enid shook her head. Taking care of Faunt had been beautiful and contenting, like a noble adventure, but she always knew he would get well. Trav was surely going to die! And Faunt after all was only her brother-in-law; Trav was her husband! An hour ago she would have said she wished him dead; but not now, not if he were really going to die!

13

WHEN the battle came to the very threshold of Richmond, the flood of wounded poured into the city in a crimson torrent. Cinda welcomed the toil this imposed upon her. To be tired to the point of exhaustion helped her forget the terrible and endless and futile wondering about Julian. Was he alive? Was he dead? Was his body rotting in some shallow, unmarked grave? How had he died? Had death come with a merciful quickness; or had he perhaps lain long hours on the night-cloaked battlefield, too weak to cry out for help, conscious yet mute, seeing rescuers near and unable to summon them? What did a boy think about when he lay dying a tormented death alone? How long did suffering endure before the approaching end eased and dulled his pain?

She worked at first under Miss Tompkins in the big house at the corner of Third and Main, only three blocks from home. When the wounded began to arrive, there were already some sick men there, brought from the camps outside the city. To make room for the newcomers whose needs were more acute, these sick were moved, hidden away in nooks and corners where they were sometimes forgotten. One day Cinda, passing the dark doorway of a closet, heard from inside a feverish mumbling. She brought a candle and lighted it, and found a boy no older than Julian, who seemed to have been laid on the bare floor there and forgotten. His eyes were swollen shut and gummed with scabs of wax and his ears were running, and they must be abscessed, because even in his delirium he cried out with pain.

She called the nearest surgeon, who said the boy was dying. "Measles and pneumonia. No chance for him at all."

"If I took him away, took care of him?"

"Oh, possibly. But there's only the slimmest hope for him; and there are so many who can be helped, Mrs. Dewain."

"I know, but I want to help him." Cinda wished to take him home, but with the children there she dared not. Their lives were precious too. She arranged with Dr. Gwathmey's wife to move him to the Soldiers' Home on Clay Street. There, if he must die, he could at least die in decency; for there ladies from near-by homes made it their duty and their happiness to keep everything immaculate, beds draped with fresh linen, curtains at the windows, the floors mopped, flies screened away.

One day she and Vesta were summoned in haste to help convert a public warehouse on Eighth Street to hospital uses. When they reached the warehouse, fifty or sixty wounded men had already been brought in, but there was no one in charge and the ladies who like them had answered this call were milling confusedly, uncertain how to begin. For lack of beds, the men, some groaning and twisting with pain, some stoically silent, some too weak to move, lay helter-skelter where the ambulance drivers had deposited them before returning toward the battlefields.

Cinda, thus thrown on her own resources, took command. Since there was no one else to give orders, she did so. She sent messengers to bring mattresses, clean water, bandages, blankets, food, wine. She bade them summon any surgeons who could come, and a desperate hour or two of confused effort began to bring some order and system out of the original chaos. When a new train of laden ambulances arrived, she went out to direct the work of bringing in the men.

It was thus she discovered Trav. When she recognized him, senseless in the ambulance, her throat constricted with grief and terror; but he, at least, need not lie with these others on wretched pallets, smothered by swarms of flies attracted by the blood smell, helplessly waiting for easement or for death. She sent the ambulance to Fifth Street. Enid was there, and Jenny; and Jenny was a rock, a firm foundation. Jenny would know what to do.

She wished to go with him, but she could not be spared. When she had seen the ambulance lurch away, she turned back inside, and a hurt man coughed and a thin line of blood trickled from the corner of his mouth. She lifted his head and shoulders and turned his head side-wise to let his throat clear itself of the blood that was strangling him; but when he coughed again a great burst of blood, as though his coughing had opened some fountain in his body, poured out of his mouth, and he died.

She laid him down almost roughly. It was the living who had need of her. Moving to her tasks she passed near Vesta and spoke to her.

"I just saw Uncle Travis. He's hurt. I sent him home."

"Oh Mama—shouldn't we go?"

"Jenny and Enid will take care of him. One of us can take a surgeon to the house when there's time."

"Now, Mama?"

"Not now. Travis wouldn't want that." She tried to persuade her-self she meant this; but when a little later she saw Vesta and Dr. Lit-tle go toward the door she did not interfere.

She was so busy that time lost its meaning, so she did not know how long it was till Vesta returned. Cinda was kneeling beside a man with a shattered jaw—she was thinking of Rollin Lyle, whose jaw had been broken by a pistol ball once upon a time, so long ago—feeding sips of brandy through the torn wound that was his mouth, hoping the fiery liquor would dull his pain. She saw someone's feet pause beside her, and looked up, and it was Vesta, and the girl said steadily:

"We saw Uncle Travis. The bullet went right through him. Dr. Little passed a silk handkerchief in through the hole in front and out the back. He has almost stopped bleeding. Dr. Little says he has to be kept quiet and"—her voice caught—"and prayed for."

Cinda nodded, returning to her task. "Jenny can do that." She added: "And Enid, of course." She dared not let herself feel pain.

The steady flow of wounded from the bloody slopes of Malvern Hill never slacked all the long day, and at dusk it had not ceased; but Vesta was bowed with fatigue, and Cinda herself could do no more. At home she found Trav on a pallet on the floor in the drawing room, with Enid and old June beside him.

"I wanted them to carry him upstairs, Cousin Cinda," Enid said, more like a complaint than an apology. "But Dr. Little said he shouldn't be moved."

"It's all right," Cinda assured her. "He can stay here. Where's Jenny?"

"She's asleep. She told me to wake her at midnight and she'd take my place."

Cinda brushed her hand across her eyes and old June's arms enfolded her. "You come along, Honey. I'm gwine put you tuh bed!"

"How is he?" These old Negro women came to know so many mysteries.

"Mistuh Trav?" June tossed her head in cheerful reassurance. "He's jes' fine. On'y way de Yankees kin kill him is cut off his haid wid a axe. No, ma'am, don' you fret you'se'f account o' him. You come along to bed 'foah I gits out o' patience wid you."

Cinda through the days that followed thought Richmond was half hospital, half charnel house. At home Trav lay in a muttering delirium; fever seared his flesh away, his cheeks sank, deep hollows formed behind his eyes. His wound was suppurating, and Dr. Little called it laudable pus; but he was become so thin, so frail, so pitiful. In the hospitals, men tossed and groaned under clouds of greedy flies which at any movement of their victim rose sluggishly, heavy with their gorging, and at once settled back to the feast again. The stench of mortifying flesh hung everywhere, and gangrene and erysipelas came to stalk like scavengers among the crowded cots. The hospitals were a horror so awful that to enter them deadened the senses; and there were so many wounded that even stores were filled with cots. Passers-by could look in through the wide windows and watch the busy surgeons and the suffering men; and every such window was jammed with small boys peering at the spectacle in morbid fascination. Now that the fighting was over for a while, there were no longer the trains of ambulances, from which came the groans and sometimes the screams of men tortured by the jolting vehicles; but instead there were the hearses and the carts loaded with coffins, trundling toward Hollywood. The humble dead went unattended, but muffled drums might accompany an officer to the waiting grave.

Tilda came one day to the warehouse where Cinda was at work; and she was full of petulant indignation at the horror of these funerals. "Mrs. Brownlaw is simply furious," she declared. "She's trying to make someone do something about it. There aren't enough grave diggers, and they don't work fast enough." A morbid relish crept into her tones. "Why, half the time, Cinda, the carts just dump the coffins on the ground and they lie there all day, or even overnight, till the grave diggers get ready to bury them; and sometimes the bodies swell up and burst the coffins before they're buried."

Cinda, kneeling beside a man whose leg was gangrenous, loosening the bandages so that the surgeon could sprinkle lead sulphate on the discolored stump, said in a low tone: "Please, Tilda, don't. You disturb the men." She was glad when Tilda moved away. The surgeon was not yet ready here, so she waited to help him when he came. Luckily the man was delirious, so he could not have heard what Tilda said. With a leg as bad as his was, he himself would soon be in one of those rough wooden boxes.

Sunday she surrendered to fatigue, stayed all day abed. The children came to her; Kyle and Peter, and then Lucy. Lucy was making a scrapbook of pictures cut from newspapers. "So my children can see what the war was like, Aunt Cinda," she explained. "Don't you want to look at it?"

Cinda forced herself to do so, and Peter came to see the pictures with her; and he was always impatient to turn the next page, and the next, lifting the edges of each one to peer at what was to come; till suddenly he snatched the book away and threw it on the floor and cried in boyish fury:

"That's him! That's old Abe!"

He jumped up and down on the open scrapbook, and Lucy ran around the bed to rescue it, and their voices rose in violence and anger, and Cinda was too tired to interfere. Even the children hated Lincoln. Well, should they not? Was it not he who had riddled and shattered and maimed and slain all these hundreds and thousands?

"Hush, Peter," she said at last. "You needn't look at the pictures unless you want to; but you musn't tear Lucy's book."

So Peter, still angry, stalked out of the room, and Lucy came to perch upon the bed again, turning page by page; and Cinda pretended to look and to listen and she spoke approving words.

But she was thinking of little Peter, and of his rage at the sight of that sketch of Abraham Lincoln; and Peter's wrath made her remember how angry Faunt had been that night at Great Oak. She had never before realized how like each other in temper were these two, Peter and Faunt. The same blood ran in them—as it did in Lincoln. Had President Lincoln too his moments of unbridled rage?

She turned back the pages of Lucy's scrapbook to look at that rough-drawn face again, trying to appraise and to understand the man himself, the person whose likeness was there portrayed; and she remembered her remark long ago to Brett that Tony looked a little like Lincoln. Make Tony's hair black, instead of dark brown now heavily touched with gray, give him a beard like Lincoln's instead of that little spike of whisker which he wore; change his mouth a little—yes, it would be easy to point up the resemblance. Of course there was no hint of strength in Tony's countenance; Abraham Lincoln, whatever his vices, looked like a man.

She sent Lucy away at last, wishing to sleep; and her eyes were closed when something made her open them and she saw Brett standing in the door. At first it was hard to believe that this was he, till he smiled and came toward her and sat down on the bed beside her and touched her hand.

"Well, Mrs. Dewain," he said in a low tone.

"Well, Mr. Dewain."

He kissed her; her limp arms rose to draw him for a moment close. "Too bad I woke you," he said.

"I wasn't asleep. Just—resting."

He said: "Burr is fine, and Faunt. I haven't seen them, but Burr sent word. They're watching the enemy at Harrison's Landing. Our company is back in camp." And he said: "How does Trav seem?"

"He hasn't taken any food, but Dr. Little thinks he will—recover. And so does June."

"I brought Cousin Jeems to dinner."

"Oh I must come down." But she did not move.

"I'll bring him up. You're old enough friends to receive him in undress. He'll tell you about Trav."

She nodded in submission, but she did not wish to hear how Trav got his wound. Why must men always relive these terrors in talk, talk, talk! Why must she be forced to listen to them? But when

Brett returned with Longstreet, it was good to see Cousin Jeems. He bowed over her hand and kissed her fingertips, not gallantly but with a gentleness that was somehow comforting. She had never thought of him as a gentle, tender man; yet there was a woman's tenderness in him now. He seemed to her now more like an abashed small boy than like the god of battles. She suspected in faint amusement that he was embarrassed at being in her bedroom. Men were so easily embarrassed, so amazingly modest in these little ways.

She asked for Cousin Louisa. He said Mrs. Longstreet was with her family, on Garland Hill in Lynchburg. She inquired for little Garland. Oh he was fine, and no longer so little. He was fourteen, and beginning to distress his mother with talk about being old enough to become a soldier.

"Oh no," said Cinda quickly. "Not the children, Cousin Jeems." Yet Julian was—had been—no more than a child. She asked: "Will Louisa come back to Richmond to be near you, now that the Yankees are gone?"

"I'm afraid not," he said. "Not Richmond." Cinda understood him. Cousin Louisa would not wish to return here where her children died. Cinda found it hard to realize that it was so short a time, only four or five months, since that dreadful tragedy. She saw the shadow in his eyes, and said, to distract him:

"You've won a splendid victory, Cousin Jeems."

"It should have been more complete," he said, his brow clouding. "McClellan's army might have been destroyed; but Huger, Magruder, yes and even Jackson, each did less than they might have done." He added: "Richmond is made safe, it's true; but—our loss was heavy. I fear our loss was heavier even than McClellan's."

"I know. I've seen them, hundreds of them, in the hospitals."

"McClellan escaped us," he repeated. "We were too slow. We might have cut his army in half even as late as Monday afternoon; but Jackson and Huger left me to make the battle alone." Cinda closed her eyes, tried to close her ears to his words; she wished to hear no more of battles—she had seen their fruit. "It was that day Captain Currain took his hurt," he said. "General Lee and President Davis and I were together, and a few shells came near us. I sent Captain Currain to ask Colonel Jenkins to push his sharpshooters forward and silence that battery. He rode that fine black stallion of his." He added: "By the way, tell him I have his horse safe, and that big revolver Von Borcke gave him, still in his saddle holster, and the scabbard of his sword."

"His sword was in his hands when they brought him home."

General Longstreet nodded, and at his own thoughts his eyes began to burn. "Colonel Jenkins obeyed orders," he said. "But Captain Currain saw some trouble where the Alabama regiments, next to Colonel Jenkins's men, had found a battery in an open field. They charged the battery and brought the issue to hand-to-hand fighting; and Captain Currain went to help them. He blooded that long sword of his more than once, and even after a musket ball struck him he still held his seat. When the Alabamans were driven back they brought him off with them. In the edge of the wood he did finally slip off his horse. He was senseless, but even then he would not loose his sword."

Cinda said with reluctant understanding: "You men love war, don't you. I can hear that in your voice." She half smiled. "You'd rather be on the battlefield than with Cousin Louisa."

"A soldier's wife learns to understand and forgive this other passion."

"I don't believe it," she declared. "These wives so ready to forgive their husbands' other loves don't care a fig for their husbands, really." Somehow she must turn the talk along a more pleasant path. "And Cousin Louisa worships you."

"Exactly! So she forgives me."

"I suppose she's had to learn to forgive a lot of things. She says you've always had a sharp eye for a lovely face."

"Certainly! Every wife is flattered when her husband admires beauty. It's a compliment to her—since she is still his first choice."

She was grateful for his willingness to meet her in light laughter. "I'm not sure you're wrong. Of course we relish any flattery. One day in the hospital I was giving a great bearded man a drink of water, and when I took the cup away and thought him helpless, he drew me down and kissed me roundly. I liked it, I declare—the scamp!"

"You Richmond ladies have been like goddesses to the men. In the hospitals this morning I heard your praises everywhere."

Weariness swept over her again. "I'm worn out. Some of them can go on and on, but I must rest sometimes. I'm so tired I just fall across

my bed and sleep till someone wakes me. I suppose that's how it feels
to die." She closed her eyes, her senses for a moment swimming; and
Brett stirred, as though to take Longstreet away, but without opening
her eyes she said: "No, don't go. Sit a while. I'll go to sleep while you
talk."

So they stayed, and she heard their talk turn again to the battlefield;
and Longstreet spoke of Hood's Texans and their charge at Gaines'
Mill and how fine a feat of arms it was. "No soldiers in the world
could equal it," he declared; and Brett agreed, and Longstreet said
gravely: "If the war could be won quickly, by courage and dash, we
would be easy victors."

Brett assented. "But we can't stand up to the waiting and the waiting," he suggested. "Show us the enemy and we're ready to spring at
his throat; but unless there is a battle in prospect, our men grumble
and loaf and fall sick and drift away to their homes. If we must wait
too often, with the North growing stronger all the time . . ."

General Longstreet interrupted. "We will wait no longer now.
We've a leader, sir! I'll give you a prediction. General Lee, between
now and frost, will drive every Yankee out of Virginia. Wait and
see."

While they talked, the windows shadowed with coming dusk, and
Cinda drifted into treacherous sleep and did not wake till June came
with her breakfast in the morning. Cinda's first question was for
Brett; but June said he had ridden away last night, refusing to let
June rouse her. "But he say he be back any day," June promised, and
before Cinda could grieve that he was gone June added that Trav was
better. His fever had broken in the night. "He be all right f'om now
on, ef'n he don't sweat his peth away," she predicted. When Cinda
went to him Trav knew her and his surroundings and himself again.

Vesta joined them. Cinda, clear-eyed and rested after her day in
bed, saw that Vesta was drawn and tired, and she remembered that the
girl was entering the third month of her pregnancy. She must not
again face the ordeal of the hospital; but Cinda knew that if she herself went back to that duty, so would Vesta, too. So she stayed that
day at home, making Trav's need of her a pretext; and before the day
ended she had what seemed an inspiration. Vesta had once spoken of

her wish to go to visit Tommy's mother, and Cinda reminded her of this.

"You didn't want to go as long as leaving Richmond would seem like running away," she remembered. "But Richmond's in no danger now, and if you don't go now, you can't go later."

Vesta seemed to welcome the suggestion; and Jenny when she heard said that she too was anxious to go back to the Plains. Big Mame, who had been Vesta's handmaiden since her babyhood, could go with them. "She's as strong as any two men," Cinda pointed out. "You couldn't have a better escort."

"I hate to go," Vesta protested. "Poor people can't get away from Richmond even if they want to. They just have to stay here and suffer, while people like us go away where it's cool, and where there's plenty to eat, and everything."

Cinda laughed lightly. "You won't be cool at the Plains, darling. It's hot as Tophet there in July. And even if it were cool—your being hot in Richmond won't make those who have to stay here any cooler."

Jenny would take the children; and Barbara, when she heard their plan, announced her intent to travel with them as far as Weldon, and thence to Raleigh to join her father and mother. Cinda guiltily realized that she would be glad to have Barbara go. It would be hard on Burr, for he could seldom take time to make the journey to Raleigh; but if Barbara were gone, when he came to Richmond they would have him to themselves. She made only polite protests, and Vesta laughed at her afterward.

"You know perfectly well you're glad she's going, Mama."

"Why, Vesta, I'm very fond of Barbara."

"All the same, darling, I hear that mother-in-law tone in your voice whenever you're being specially careful to be nice to her."

"Nothing of the kind," Cinda insisted, and hoped her cheeks were not so red as they felt. "Of course, she's the cleverest little Miss Somebody I ever saw. The way she gets around Enid is a caution. Enid's completely outdone every day of her life, and she doesn't even know it. I love Barbara for that if for nothing else."

Vesta laughed affectionately. "Poor Mama! And with Jenny and me gone you'll be left with no one but Aunt Enid. When's Granny coming back from Chimneys?" Cinda did not know. "Well, if you get too desperate you can send for me." Vesta added mischievously: "Besides, maybe Burr won't let Barbara go."

"He won't have any say about it."

"Why, she certainly wouldn't go without telling him."

Cinda laughed at herself. "I can't decide whether I'm more anxious to see him put his foot down for once or to have her go!" She shook her head. "But Barbara'll manage it. Wait and see."

That same day, Caesar came to Cinda with word that Dr. McCaw was calling. Cinda went down in a puzzled wonder. Dr. McCaw was of a distinguished family. His father had been one of many who behaved with conspicuous heroism at the dreadful theatre fire fifty years before, which was still vivid in the memory of older people in Richmond. Dr. McCaw himself had selected the site of Chimborazo Hospital, on the heights above the river toward Rockett's, and it was he who devised the flexible arrangement of small buildings, easily and quickly constructed, which had proved so admirable. Cinda knew him by reputation and through occasional social contacts, but she could not guess why he had come today.

He said, when she greeted him, that Dr. Little had asked him to stop in and see Major Currain.

"Why, you're very kind, Doctor," Cinda told him gratefully. "We're sure he's taken a turn for the better. He knew me this morning. Won't you come upstairs?"

But Dr. McCaw's glance at Trav was so completely perfunctory that she suspected this was not his only errand; and when they came down he confessed it. "I'm sure he will recover," he said. "Since he's lived this long. But Mrs. Dewain, there's something else." He waited for no question. "I spoke to Dr. Little yesterday about our need for matrons in the wards at Chimborazo Hospital. He says you have the capacity to do that work."

"Heavens!" Cinda protested. "I'm not good for anything but scrubbing floors and washing bandages, and not much good at that." She added honestly: "I just haven't the courage for it, Dr. McCaw, nor the strength. It wears me out."

"Have you ever seen the hospital? It's the largest in Richmond."

"No. I've only worked in places nearer my home."

He persuaded her to go with him to inspect the institution of which he was the head. It had been begun the year before: a sprawling establishment consisting of many separate buildings, almost exactly alike. Each was a hundred feet long and thirty feet wide, one story high, built of rough boards and painted white. They were regularly spaced, with streets and alleys between them. Each ward held two or three score beds; but the beds were no more than wooden boxes set on legs to lift them a little above the floor, with sacks stuffed with sawdust or with straw or shucks to serve as mattresses.

When Dr. McCaw and Cinda came into one of these wards, a Negro man, by courtesy called a nurse, was attempting to straighten the legs and arms of a dead soldier, giggling with nervous amusement at the refusal of stiffening limbs to do what he wished. At the doctor's sharp word he called another Negro and they carried the dead man away. The coarse sacking that had served as a sheet was stained, and the mattress below it was discolored with old traces left by other men now dead; but the soiled bed was hardly empty before from an ambulance at the door two men carried in a wounded man and laid him there.

Cinda had seen too many such incidents to be surprised; but she was half-stifled by the sour heat in this rude hut, and by the stench of the place. The small windows let in not enough light or air. "That sort of thing doesn't have to happen," she protested. "Not now, when there aren't so many wounded coming in."

"This is one of the wards with no matron," he said quietly, and he added: "Dr. Little told me how you organized the public warehouse, when wounded men had to be put there." She did not speak; and he said: "Come, I want you to see the rest."

Beyond the wards there were tents for convalescents, and Cinda said approvingly: "They can be comfortable here, and even cool."

"It's the best hospital location in Richmond," Dr. McCaw declared, and he smiled faintly. "I helped select it, so I'm bound to think so; but it's on high ground, well drained, as cool as any place can be, and as healthy. We have good water, and ice houses, and a bakery." He introduced her to Mrs. Minge, the chief matron. "But we need a matron for every ward," he repeated. "And Dr. Little believes you would be a good one."

Cinda still shrank from the challenge. "Oh Doctor, I can't even manage my own household as I'd like to."

"None of us do as well as we'd like to," he said gently. "We don't know how. We know it's wrong to frighten men when they're sick or hurt." He smiled in a sad way. "Although too many doctors put on pompous airs and ominous expressions to conceal their own ignorance, and scare patients to death who would have recovered if they hadn't been frightened. We know it's wrong to frighten people, and we know that if we don't do a man harm he may get well by himself, no matter how badly he's hurt. But beyond that we're pretty ignorant. We don't even know how best to treat our sick, and we butcher the wounded!" In a sort of indignation, more as if he were thinking aloud than as though he were speaking to her: "We put on hot poultices to make wounds suppurate, but I've seen wounds that didn't show pus heal mighty handsomely. We think quick amputation is the only chance for a man with a shattered joint; but every time I see an orderly carry away an arm or a leg I've cut off, I wonder whether the man who owned it wouldn't be justified in shooting me for a hopeless fool. We deplete for pneumonia, but the men die. I've been trying a sustaining treatment, brandy, opium; and sometimes men get better. None of us know much about medicine beyond blue mass and opium. We cut and we bandage and we drip water on the bandages and men get gangrene and erysipelas and die." He said harshly: "Why, we're blind fools groping in the dark. We can't even cure diarrhea—and whatever else is the matter with a man when he's brought here, he always has diarrhea. So Mrs. Dewain, you know as much as anyone."

"But I don't know anything," Cinda insisted. "Except that I hate blood and smells and dirt and flies. I couldn't do it, Doctor."

"If you could keep men clean and keep the flies from tormenting them, they could at least die in decency!"

Cinda, with no confidence that she could be of use, nevertheless in the end consented to try; and next day, since it was at least two miles from Fifth Street to the hospital, Diamond brought the carriage around an hour after sun and drove her out to begin her duties. She dreaded this beginning, but she found so much to be done that within an hour she forgot herself completely. It would have been easy to waste her strength on sweeping, scrubbing, washing; but it was her head Dr. McCaw wanted, not her hands. The nurses assigned to her ward were Negroes, and till she came they had been left to do as they chose. She drove them to a frantic industry, and before the day was done the floors were clean, and fresh straw had been spread in every box bed, and some of the bedding that was most in need of it had been washed and hung to dry. She saw not only the ward scrubbed but the kitchen; and between the steady drive of routine she had time to talk with some of the wounded men and learn their needs and their wants and try to meet them. She came home that night exhausted, yet content too.

"But I'm not sure just what I'm to do," she told Vesta, laughing at herself. "I promised one man he should have some soup tomorrow, the sort of soup his mother used to make. Sour soup, he calls it. You boil buttermilk and corn meal and the yellows of eggs and put dumplings in it, and seasoning. Doesn't that sound horrible? But I promised to try."

She was to find in those first days that the most baffling of her problems involved finding foods the men would eat. Her sour soup was a failure. The buttermilk resolved itself into a thin whey full of hard curds. "It don't taste nat'ral and it don't look nat'ral," the man who had asked for it admitted. "But I'll eat it if my stummick holds out."

At home she made even Jenny laugh at the tales she told. "They're all poor people," she explained, "and they've never had enough to eat in their lives, but they're suspicious of anything new, don't want to eat anything they're not used to. I made cook put some parsley in the chicken broth today, and half the men wouldn't touch it with those weeds floating around in it! One of them said he didn't like soup anyway. He said: 'I never was much of a hand for drinks, ma'am.'" She added: "I don't suppose half the men ate as much as they should, today, but I'll make them before I'm through, if I have to rub it down their throats like forcemeat balls."

She put herself under a saving discipline, coming home every day at the same hour. Jenny and Vesta were ready to start for the Plains; but Barbara wished to see Burr before she left. Vesta still thought Burr might refuse to let Barbara go, but Cinda was sure Barbara would have her way. She hoped to witness this trial of strength between them, but when Burr came home an hour after dark Friday, Barbara was in her room. Cinda and Vesta greeted him in the hall and after their kisses he asked where Barbara was. Their answer sent him at full leap up the stairs, and Vesta said in a droll tone:

"Well there, Mama! We won't see the fireworks after all!"

If there were fireworks behind Barbara's closed door, no outsider witnessed them. She and Burr presently came down arm in arm, and Cinda thought Burr was a little white and strained. Barbara said at once: "Mama Cinda, I really don't think I ought to go to Raleigh. Poor Burr will miss me so."

But Burr valiantly protested: "Not a bit of it, darlin'. It will be a lot easier for me knowing you're safe and comfortable. I won't have to worry about you."

So they had a lively little argument, Barbara demurring, Burr insisting that she go; till at last he surrendered. "Well, if you're really sure that's what you want me to do. But I'm only going because you make me, Burr, really I am."

"I know, Honey; but it's the sensible thing to do."

She kissed him fondly. "I'm going to miss you just awfully. Please darling, mayn't I stay here where I'll be near you?"

But Burr smiled and said with a bold authority: "Silence in the ranks. Obey your commanding officer, young woman, or I'll have you bucked!"

Vesta looked at Cinda with a knowing amusement in her eye. "What does that mean, Burr? Bucked?"

"Hands tied together around your ankles and a stick through your knees."

Barbara shivered. "That sounds terrible. All right, darling, I'll do it. But it's just because you say I must."

They had some talk of plans. Burr thought he could get leave to escort Barbara to Raleigh. His command was about to move to Atlee's Station; but there was no immediate prospect of early action, and he could be spared. They would start south on Monday. Sunday, Brett came home, and he took advantage of the opportunity to send by Burr's hand a letter to Mr. Pierce, asking whether he would be willing to sell or rent the Clay Street house to Trav.

"I'd meant to write him before now," he confessed to Trav, not yet strong enough to come downstairs. "But it slipped my mind. Burr can bring his answer." Trav was not sure the purchase would be wise, but Brett advised it. "Confederate finances are already shaky. Prices are rising, and that means the value of money is falling. To keep money is to see it slip through your fingers like sand; but real property can't get away. The house is a good one, the land will always be there. Yes, you should buy."

So Trav assented and Brett drafted a letter to Mr. Pierce; and next morning they departed, Vesta and Jenny and Burr and Barbara, Big Mame and the nurses and the children. Trav and Cinda agreed not to mention the prospective purchase to Enid till it was decided; but before the week was out Burr returned, and he said Mr. Pierce would sell the house. Cinda, at home when Burr arrived, took him to Trav's room to report this. Enid was at Dolly's, and when they heard her voice in the hall downstairs Cinda said: "Come, Burr, we'll let Uncle Travis have her all to himself when he tells her the news."

But Trav made them stay, and Cinda saw with affectionate amusement his misgivings; and she said reassuringly: "Don't worry, Travis. She'll be delighted." She called to Enid to come and join them. "Travis has something to tell you, Honey."

Cinda was right. When she heard, Enid was so happy that she danced around the room, and she said Trav must hurry and get well so they could move quick, and when Cinda smiled at her exuberance she cried: "But Cousin Cinda, don't you realize it will be a home of my own! Chimneys was way off from everywhere, and Great Oak was Mama's, but this will be my own, my own, my own!" Not even Trav's reminder that there were details still to be attended to could dampen her delight.

Next morning Burr rode away, and Cinda's days were full, and at night she was so weary she went at once to sleep. Sunday she hoped Brett would come, but he did not; so out of her loneliness she wrote Vesta a long letter, telling all the talk of the day. "Everybody here is furious at General Pope. He's the Yankee general in northern Virginia, and he says everyone who wants to stay in their homes there must take the oath of allegiance to the Union or else be sent into our lines and they'll be shot if they try to go home again. Everyone seems to think that's outrageous, though for the life of me I can't see why!" Cinda liked to take the unpopular side of any question. "If people mean to behave themselves, why shouldn't they promise to? And if they don't, why shouldn't General Pope arrest them? But there, I sound like Trav! Enid says when General Butler down in New Orleans issued his order that ladies who insulted his men would be treated like women of the streets, Trav said no lady would insult even a Yankee, and that Butler was just warning women who weren't ladies to act as if they were! Of course I don't believe Trav ever said it. Enid's an awful little liar. But I told her I agreed with him. I didn't really, but I knew she was trying to make me criticize Trav and I wouldn't give her the satisfaction. And in a way I do agree with Trav too. I certainly haven't any sympathy with women who insult even Yankees! But for Heaven's sake don't tell any of your friends I talk like this or they'd never speak to me again! I don't really mean it; yet in a way I do, too. Is it possible that I'm beginning to see two sides to some questions? I must be getting old! Don't ever lose your prejudices, darling. They're what keep us young!"

Late in July Redford Streean brought Mrs. Currain home from Chimneys. Cinda had not expected her till cooler weather, but Streean explained: "I dropped in on Tony, and she decided to come on with me so no one would have to go and fetch her later on."

Cinda was half sorry. It would not be easy for her mother to maintain in Richmond that protective pretense that there was nothing wrong with the world. When Mrs. Currain found Trav abed, she said briskly: "Well, Sonny Lad, it's high time I did come home! I fear ye've been eating something you shouldn't."

That soft burr in her tones had become more marked. Enid started to tell her the truth; but Cinda spoke quickly: "You just take charge of him, Mama. He needs you to make him behave!"

She tried to lead Mrs. Currain to speak of Chimneys, and of Tony; but although the older woman talked with no apparent reservations, yet there was a hint of reticence, a suggestion of things unsaid. Chimneys was beautiful, there was plenty of everything, the house was well kept and well managed.

"Managed by Tony?" Cinda asked.

"Why, I'm sure I don't know. You surely don't think I'd inquire into the workings of another person's household?"

Cinda almost smiled. It was impossible to imagine her mother allowing any detail of Tony's establishment to escape her notice; but she did not press the point. How was Tony, she asked; and her mother said Tony was well, very well indeed, always so happy, always in good humor. Clearly, Mrs. Currain's seeming frankness was pretense. Just as at Great Oak and at Richmond the old woman had shut her eyes to what went on around her, so at Chimneys there was something which she had been determined not to see.

Before that week ended, Cinda was relieved for a while from her labors at the hospital. So many of the wounded had died or had reached convalescence that the patients in her ward could be absorbed by other wards. "But there will be more battles," Dr. McCaw warned her. "We shall want you then."

Cinda promised to serve when that time came, but she was glad to be free to spend long hours with her mother. Mrs. Currain's refusal to speak more frankly about Tony sharpened her curiosity; and it was in the hope Streean might let fall an explanation that she invited him and Tilda to Sunday dinner. But her carefully casual inquiries elicited nothing new. He said Chimneys was prospering, that Tony was in fine fettle; but this was no more than Mrs. Currain had already said.

Of himself and his projects, however, Streean talked readily enough. He had hoped Brett would be here today. "I want to advise him to grow all the cotton he can at the Plains," he told Cinda; and when she said in surprise that she thought there was already a great store of cotton in the South, he agreed that this was true. "But there will be a market for it presently," he promised. "This war will not be over in one year, or in five; and to finance the war, we must use our cotton and tobacco to establish credit." Cinda had heard Brett say the same thing months ago. "The North needs our cotton," Streean reminded her. "And we need many things from the North."

"But surely we won't sell cotton to the North and fight her at the same time?"

"Business men continue to be men of business, even in wartime," he assured her. "On this last trip of mine I made contact with some New Orleans cotton brokers and some bankers. If we can send them the cotton, they will guarantee to dispose of it at a fat profit to all concerned. Tell Brett so."

"Will the North let us sell them cotton? Even if we wanted to?"

Streean chuckled. "Of course. There are business men in the North as well as in the South. When this trade is once organized we can get everything we need; clothing, food, medicines, lead, steel."

"You mean to say the North will sell us lead to make into bullets to kill their own men?"

"If we give them a profit, yes."

If there was a profit to be made in any such way as Streean proposed, he would take care to get his share of it. "What do you hear from Darrell?"

"He's in North Carolina," Streean told her. "Trying to buy cloth for uniforms. North Carolina makes more than her troops need, but she won't sell any of it. I saw him in Statesville. He thought of going to Chimneys for a visit with Tony."

Tony had said there were deserters in the country around Martinston. Darrell, so careful to stay out of the army, would find kindred spirits among them. "Tony says some of his neighbors are deserters," she remarked.

"Oh there are just as many skulkers right here in Richmond as in North Carolina," Streean assured her. "The streets here are full of them: young men who have dodged conscription, or hired substitutes. No one goes into the army unless he's made to." Cinda was about to speak, but he added: "Except, of course, gentlemen!"

She thought there was derision in his tone; yet it was hard to take exception to a tone of voice. "I suppose Darrell might be conscripted," she suggested.

"Not as long as he stays where he is! A Virginia man can't be conscripted in North Carolina, you know. And of course Darrell has a detail to the Quartermaster's Department, anyway."

"I should think he'd want to—do his part."

Tilda protested: "Well, I don't! I certainly don't want the poor boy getting killed. All these women so anxious for their men to go and be heroes ought to see what we see in the hospitals, oughtn't they, Cinda?"

Cinda was so angry that she did not trust herself to speak. After

dinner Streean went to talk with Trav, and Tilda and Dolly disappeared with Enid. Cinda took Mrs. Currain to have her nap, and she
herself relaxed in the big chair in her mother's cool, darkened room,
trying to keep bitterness out of her thoughts, reminding herself that
Streean had always been a scoundrel, and Tilda a fool. When she
heard the stir of their departure she descended to bid them a polite
good-by; then sat for a while with Trav. He was on the high road to
recovery, propped with pillows. His color was good, and she remarked
this.

"That's because I'm mad," he admitted. "Streean always upsets
me."

It was better for him not to excite himself. A book lay on his knees.
"What were you reading?" she asked.

"Hardee's *Infantry Tactics*." He colored in amused embarrassment.
"It was Tommy Cloyd's, has his name in it. I saw it on Vesta's table
here beside the bed, looked into it, discovered how many things I don't
know."

"I believe you're really turning into a soldier."

"Well, I seem to get into trouble whenever there's trouble anywhere
around; so I ought to know something about what I'm doing."

"It will be a long time before you'll be able to—ride and fight
again."

"Dr. Little says two months." Trav's jaw set stubbornly. "But I
don't think it will be that long." Yet for the present he was satisfied
to rest, to let his strength return.

Early in August a letter came from Vesta.

Dearest Mama—I meant to write you ages ago, but we've been busy
as two bees. Jenny found everything at sixes and sevens, and I put
off going to Mrs. Cloyd till Jenny didn't need me, but I've been there
since Sunday and I'm just back. She's wonderful, Mama; as wonderful as you, though of course in a different way. I told her about Bruton
churchyard and how lovely it is in that corner where they buried
Tommy; and some day she and I are going there together.

There's so much to tell you I don't know where to begin. I wish
you were all here with us. The things we have to eat would make
your mouth water. I hadn't realized how much we were doing without
in Richmond till I came here and sat down day after day to tables

just loaded with all sorts of pork roasts and sausage and bacon and things, and wonderful hams, and beef and mutton and chickens and turkeys and guinea hens, and all the eggs and milk and things we can eat. I really feel guilty, when you all are just half-starving by comparison.

But I must start at the beginning. There was trouble the minute we got here, because Samson—you don't remember him, I guess; but he'd been brought into the house since Jenny went to Richmond. Jenny says he bullied old Banquo into it, to get out of field work. Well, the day we got here he had stolen Banquo's keys, and got into the sideboard and he'd drunk bottles and bottles of wine and he was chasing all the house servants around with a carving knife, and when we drove up to the door they were screaming and running everywhere. I was terrified, but Jenny just walked up to him and told him to give her the knife and he did and she locked him up in the smoke house to sober off. I wanted her to have him taken to the calaboose, but she said he'd be all right, and he's been like a mouse ever since.

But poor Mr. Freeman is too old to run things here, Jenny says. The people can't take care of themselves. There was plenty of corn, but they've wasted so much that Mr. Freeman says they'll run out before the new crop is ripe. So Jenny thinks she'll stay and manage here. She says for Papa not to worry. She says she can run the place just fine, and Mrs. Cloyd is going to help her.

This was startling, and Cinda forgot the letter for a moment. To think of Jenny and the children so far away, alone on the great plantation with Negroes for her only protection, alarmed her. No one could know how soon the people would rise against their masters, like this Samson of whom Vesta had written. Yet Jenny had known how to handle him; and Cinda had a high respect for Jenny. All the same, she must not stay at the Plains alone. Brett would insist that she rejoin them here. Having thus shifted the burden from her shoulders to Brett's she read on.

Everybody here acts as if the war were none of their business. Or at least, they seem to want to do their fighting as far away from it as possible. People keep saying the Yankees are bound to capture Richmond. Lots of men have come back here from there saying it's no use, but if they'd stayed there and helped fight I guess we'd have gobbled up McClellan's whole army. Everybody's bragging about the sword factory in Columbia, and about Professor Le Conte's powder factory. To hear them talk you'd think it was their powder and swords that won the battles. They say the Yankees are just fighting to make money, and then they start bragging about how much money they're all making. Mrs. Cloyd says everyone makes money out of cotton except the people who grow it. Some ladies in Columbia have started a Wayside Hospital to take care of the wounded soldiers when they have to wait to change trains there. You wouldn't believe how many young men are at home here talking about getting commissions or places in the government departments or something. Mrs. Cloyd's perfectly disgusted with them.

I want to tell you about Mrs. Cloyd, Mama; and yet there's nothing to tell, really, except that she's wonderful. It's all little things, but they're beautiful little things, and all put together they're awfully important. There was only one big thing. One night while I was there we talked for hours; and she's so wise, and so good, and finally I went to bed, but I wasn't sleepy, and the moon was shining and some of Mrs. Cloyd's negroes began to sing. I think maybe they were having a religious meeting, because they sang hymn tunes; and I listened, and all of a sudden I found myself crying. I was just bawling! Even next morning my pillow was all soggy with tears. I cried and cried, and I just loved it. I kept on crying like a greedy little child who can't get enough of something good to eat. It was the first time I'd cried since Tommy died, Mama. I hadn't even cried when I was alone; not till that night. I wasn't crying for sadness, or loneliness, or anything. I was just simply crying, and I loved it, and I cried myself into the most wonderful sleep. It was like a long delicious bath when you're hot and tired and dusty. I woke up feeling all washed and clean and fresh and bright, the way the country looks when it rains all night after a hot day, and then in the morning the sun comes out and all the dust has been washed off the leaves and they're all so shining and bright and beautiful, and drops of water still on the leaves are sparkling in the sun. That's the way I felt.

So I want you to know that I'm all washed clean and fresh and new inside and out, Mama. And my baby, bless his heart! When will his darling heart begin to beat, Mama? But anyway, I'm fine and my darling baby is fine.

I feel as though there would never be anything wrong with the world again, Mama. I even know that Julian is all right! You wait and see. Please believe me, Mama. I'm so sure, I just can't be wrong.

Cinda as she read found her own eyes streaming. She wiped away tears and read on, but when she had finished she let the tears flow as they would. She had thought of Julian almost every waking moment of these weeks since his vanishing; but she had thought of him in mangled misery and in death and in shameful corruption. Now for the first time, under the spell of Vesta's faith, she thought of him as alive and beautiful and strong.

Cinda was to remember that first moment of hope and faith. Tuesday morning Mrs. Randolph came to appeal to her. There were in Richmond thousands of Yankee prisoners not yet paroled or exchanged, and many Yankee wounded. "And not all our ladies are willing to help them," Mrs. Randolph explained. "They say we shouldn't bother with the Yankees! Could you possibly come and do a little to make them more comfortable? They're so wretched and so far from home."

Cinda agreed, but she wondered what her own reaction would be to this contact with even suffering enemies. To her surprise she found they drew from her as keen a sympathy as her own kind. They too were men—or boys—in pain and loneliness and need. Cinda worked under the direction of a Massachusetts surgeon, a Dr. Murfin who had come through the lines to tend the Northern wounded here. While she was adjusting a tin cup with a string hanging over the edge so that it would drip cool water on the bandages of a hurt man, Dr. Murfin came to her side.

"I want to change his bandages, Mrs. Dewain," he said.

So she coiled up the wet string and hung it over the handle of the cup; but the wounded man asked curiously: "Dewain? Is that your name, ma'am?"

"Yes," she told him. "Why?"

"Well, it's an unusual name," he said. "But I've heard it before." She felt a quick thrust under her heart, as though a baby had turned in her womb. "One night at Williamsburg," he added.

"Tell me." She spoke quickly, her voice hoarse.

"It was one of your men," he explained. Dr. Murfin twitched the bandage off the wound, and the man winced and pressed his lips tight. Then he went on, carefully, as though steadying himself against new hurt. "This boy had tried to carry a wounded negro away from the fence in front of our lines, and a bullet hit him, and he crawled to the edge of the woods, dragging the darky after him. When the fight was over, we started gathering up the wounded, yours and ours; and when we came to him he was out of his head. He kept saying: 'Mama, it's Julian! Mama, here I am!'"

Cinda felt herself falling. She caught at Dr. Murfin's arm, dropped to her knees; but on her knees she crawled along the side of the cot, clinging to it, clinging to this hurt stranger's hand.

"Go on," she whispered. "Go on."

"I helped carry him back to where they were fixing up the wounded," he told her. "He kept saying 'Mama' and then he'd say over and over, 'Julian Dewain,' 'Julian Dewain.'"

She gripped him hard and shook him so fiercely that he gasped with pain; and at his whistling cry she came a little to her senses. "Oh I'm sorry, sorry! I wouldn't hurt you. But where is he? Where is he?"

"I don't know. I helped carry him to where the surgeons were working, but I never saw him again." He asked in a hushed tone: "Do you know him?"

"He was my baby, my youngest son. Was he— Oh was he badly hurt?"

"I don't know, ma'am. His leg was all covered with blood.

Dr. Murfin helped her to her feet, and she turned beseechingly to him. "Where is he?" she begged. "Doesn't anyone know?"

He said reluctantly: "Why, Mrs. Dewain, some of your wounded were taken to Williamsburg, and some were put aboard our vessels in the river, sent back to Washington." His voice became very gentle. "But—that was weeks ago."

She understood him. "You think he's dead?"

He said honestly: "If he recovered, there's been time for him to let you know."

For a moment she was silent; but then those sure words in Vesta's letter flooded into her mind. She shook her head. "No, no, he's alive," she said confidently. "He may have been sick, may still be too sick to know anything. But he's alive! I'm sure of it!" She turned away, abandoning this task here, forgetting it; she hurried homeward, strong and certain in this hour.

14

TRAV took his wound on the thirteenth of June, but it was not till mid-August that he was strong enough to venture out of doors; and for a long time after his eventual recovery was assured he could not even attempt the stairs. But this confinement had its rewards, and among them were long contenting hours with the children. He delighted in Lucy's grave questions, her youthful reflections upon the manners and customs of the world as she observed them, her frank affection for him; and he was sometimes astonished by what seemed to him her unusual maturity of mind and her shrewd estimates of others. She despised Dolly and hated Darrell, and she was sorry for Aunt Tilda. "It must be just awful for her to have that sort of husband, and children like that." She felt an almost maternal tenderness toward General Longstreet. "He's so awkward and shy and embarrassed all the time, and pretends to be so sure of himself so people won't guess it." It had never occurred to Trav that Longstreet was shy, yet he decided that Lucy might be right. Certainly Longstreet never let others see the aspects of his character which he revealed to Trav. His silence, his apparent deafness, his positive way of talking might all be a part of the trait Lucy saw in him. There could be no doubt that Lucy had a level head. She was a mighty sweet girl.

Trav was not so much at ease with his son, discovering in Peter an almost frightening precocity. Peter was exuberantly glad that they were going to live on Clay Street. Enid's gladness, so overwhelming that it banished Trav's last remaining doubts of the wisdom of the purchase, was easy to understand, since Clay Street was one of the most attractive in Richmond. The gracious homes set close to the street were backed by well-tended gardens, so from earliest spring until the approach of winter there were flowers everywhere; rose bushes supported by frames or by the house walls to which they clung, japonicas, Cape jessamine, azaleas, and not only shrubs and vines but every conceivable perennial and annual. The White House of the Confederacy, the home that had been provided for President Davis, stood at the end of Clay Street overlooking the ravine of Shockoe Creek. Senator Semmes and Judge Campbell lived almost directly opposite; and these two houses and President Davis's residence were the centers of much of Richmond's gaiety. Enid felt that by moving into this neighborhood they would become a part of that lively and gracious world.

But Trav discovered that Peter's pleasure sprang from other considerations; and since Trav asked the right questions and betrayed no disapproval, Peter confided to him that down in the ravine along the creek, almost under the back doors of the fine houses on Clay Street, there was a magic valley called Butchertown, in which dwelt a remarkably brave and adventurous and fearless lot of boys who were just about the best fighters that you could find anywhere around. Peter's admiration for these paragons was profound. Five Butchertown boys could whip ten hill boys any time, he declared; and best of all, the Butchertown boys were his friends. He had won admittance to their fraternity by the fact that he had secretly pored over Tommy Cloyd's copy of Hardee's *Tactics* till he knew many passages by heart, and since the Butchertown boys delighted in playing war games, they called him the Cadet and let him teach them all he knew.

Trav said: "That's real interesting, Son. Matter of fact I've been studying that book myself, so you and I were learning the same things. But how did these boys find out you could teach them?"

"Well, you see," Peter explained, "when we came from Great Oak to live at Aunt Cinda's, I didn't know any boys, and I went all around town sort of exploring, and one day I saw six or seven boys down by the creek playing with sticks for guns and pretending to be soldiers, and they saw me and started to chase me, but I didn't run away. Boys won't chase you if you don't run away, you know."

"Like strange dogs," Trav suggested. "If they see you're not afraid they don't bite you."

Peter nodded absently. "Yes sir. So we got to talking, and I told them they were doing their drill all wrong. So they started to tease me and threatened to paddle me and said I was too big for my britches. So I said I could show them. So I taught them the Manual of Arms, and how to give orders——"

"Teach me," Trav suggested. "I've never known how to do it right."

"Why, you say 'Support', sort of quiet, and then you say 'ARMS' as loud as you can. 'Attention SQUAD'. 'Shoulder ARMS'. 'Present ARMS'. Like that."

"I see."

"I knew I oughtn't to teach them all that till they learned the Position of the Soldier," Peter admitted. "But I thought it would be more interesting for them, and it was." He sighed happily. "So now they let me play with them all the time. It's going to be just wonderful living right near where they live."

"But Son," Trav suggested, "you'll be one of the hill boys, won't you? Living up on Clay Street?"

"Oh golly, no," Peter protested. "The Butchertown boys fight the hill boys all the time, and throw rocks at them and chase them. No sir, I'd rather side with my friends."

Trav thought with mild amusement that here in miniature was an age-old conflict between loyalty to class and loyalty to friends. Enid might not approve of Peter's choice of companions, but that was a question for time to solve. Certainly, even if she knew about it, it would not dim her happiness now. From the first she had been fairly intoxicated with anticipations. "I declare," she told Trav, "if you kept me living with your kin like a poor relation much longer I'd just go crazy! Cinda never lets me forget it, nor Mama."

"Why, they're glad to have you here!"

"Oh, you always say that, but you just don't know! I didn't want you to be mad at her just on account of me, so I never said anything about it; but Cinda actually ordered me out of the house once, when I came up from Great Oak to visit her."

Trav protested: "Now Enid, Cinda wouldn't—" Then he caught himself as Cinda herself knocked on the door and came in; and to his distress Enid said at once:

"Cousin Cinda, Trav and I were just laughing about the time you couldn't stand me a moment longer and sent me home to Great Oak! Remember?"

Trav looked at Cinda, sure of her denial; but she hesitated, so he knew what Enid had said was true. "Oh I just lost my temper." Cinda spoke too casually. "Musn't hold that against me, Enid. My tongue and my temper, between them, keep me in hot water all the time."

Enid laughed and kissed her and protested: "Why, you know I don't hold it against you a bit! We were just laughing about it, that's all." She did not enlarge upon her victory, but Trav felt a troubling resentment. No matter what Enid had done or might do, Cinda should keep her temper in control. He and she had always been close and understanding, and probably Enid sometimes seemed to her mighty provoking; but in any open break between his sister and his wife, he must stand on Enid's side. He found comfort in the fact that Enid presently would have a home of her own. Once the small irritations of daily contact were removed, she and Cinda would be better friends.

The house on Clay Street was built of brick in the Greek Revival style, two stories and a basement at the ground level, with the kitchen and quarters for the house servants and a stable in the yard behind. Except for personal belongings and the contents of wardrobes and bureaus, Trav bought from Mr. Pierce both house and furnishings. Judge Tudor was Mrs. Pierce's brother, and she had asked the Judge and Anne to select the things she wished to keep and remove them to their own house on Twelfth Street for storage. Enid was impatient for this process to be completed and she went to watch Anne and her father there, jealously scrutinizing everything they took, and sometimes protesting to Trav, till he reminded her that the house was not yet hers.

"I can't help it," she declared. "I feel as though it's mine already. I just hate to see them take anything away."

It was while Anne and her father were still thus engaged that Cinda had that first word of Julian. When she came home she hurried to Trav's room. "Oh Travis," she cried, "Julian's alive!" Before he could speak she added: "At least, I'm sure he is! I know he is! I found a

Yankee soldier who saw him that night after the fighting was over."
She told the story while tears without sobs poured out of her. But for
proof that Julian still lived, she had only her inner sureness; and when
Trav realized this he thought to warn her was the truest kindness.

"Don't count too much on this, Cinda," he said gently. "You know
Brett has had inquiries made in the Northern hospitals; and we've
been exchanging prisoners right along. Julian would have sent some
word."

She shook her head. "No, no, he's alive! I'm sure of it." And she
said proudly: "He was trying to save Elegant, Travis; trying to carry
him away. Even after he was shot he dragged Elegant off into the
woods. And he called to me, Travis! He called to me!"

"Perhaps that Yankee doctor can find out what happened to him,"
Trav suggested. "And General Longstreet might be able to help."

"I'll send for Brett Dewain," she decided. "He will know what to
do." She rose at once, too eager to delay, and hurried down the stairs.
When he was alone, Trav's face settled into sorrowful lines. It was
too bad, too bad. The first hurt of Julian's loss had begun a little to
heal; but now that wound was open again. The agony when this
hope failed would be worse than the first agony of despair.

Before she returned, Faunt came for a few minutes with Trav.
Faunt was lean and brown and his eye was clear, and Trav thought
he had never seen the other look so well; yet there was something
frightening in this brother of his. It occurred to him that Faunt was
like Stonewall Jackson, that warrior about whom so many legends
began to arise. At Malvern Hill Jackson had ordered a charge, and
the officer who received the order protested that if the men tried to
charge they would all be killed. Jackson, so the story ran, said grimly:
"Have no concern on that point, sir. I always carry away my wounded
and bury my dead!" Jackson had an inhuman and ferocious determination, at once bold in attack and tenacious of the fruits of victory. It
was said of him that in an advance, he might outrun his wagon trains
by miles; but if he were withdrawing, he would fight to save a wheel-
barrow. There was a tale about a Yankee officer who performed some
deed of gallantry so conspicuous that Jackson's soldiers held their fire;
but he reproached them for doing so. "The brave Yankees are the ones
it is most important for us to kill," he said. "Shoot the brave ones. The

cowards will run away." He drove his own men and the enemy and himself. "Hit those people, smash them, scatter them, kill them." That was Jackson's way. Ewell, serving under him in the Valley, thought he was insane; and there were others who agreed. Trav once spoke of this to Longstreet, and the General said calmly:

"Ordinary men usually think a genius is crazy. Most of the world's great deeds have been done by men whose fellows thought them mad."

If Jackson were insane, it was with a deadly frenzy; and Trav today felt this same restrained and murderous fury in Faunt, behind his gentle tones, behind his faint smile. More than any of them Faunt had been hurt by the shameful knowledge that no matter how diluted, his blood and Lincoln's were the same.

Faunt's stay was brief. "I haven't five minutes," he said. "A friend of mine has gone to see General Lee with some information." General Lee's military home, where when he was in Richmond he made his headquarters, was on Franklin Street just around the corner from Cinda's and down the hill toward Capitol Square. "We're leaving at once." Trav asked what the information was, and Faunt said: "Why, Mosby, one of Stuart's scouts, was captured at Little Beaver Dam station two or three weeks ago. The Yankees had him in Old Capitol Prison for ten days, but Stuart arranged for him to be exchanged and I came down and met the exchange boat at the Rip Raps an hour ago. Mosby saw General Burnside's army from North Carolina on transports at Fortress Monroe, and picked up some talk. They're on their way to Acquia Creek to reinforce Pope. That means Pope plans to move this way. I expect Lee will hit him before Burnside gets there." He added: "You'll soon be fit again. Hurry and come back to us."

Trav told Faunt that Julian might be alive, and Faunt's eyes softened. "The fine dear lad," he whispered; and for a moment Trav could recognize the old Faunt whom it was so easy to love.

"Cinda's gone to send word to Brett," Trav explained. "She'll be back soon. She'll want to see you, and so will Enid." He said in diffident affection, "You've neglected us lately, you know." But Faunt, coloring a little, said he could not stay.

Brett, at Cinda's summons, came home that night; and he and Cinda next morning went to see again the Northern soldier who remembered

Julian; and at Brett's request Dr. Murfin said he would try to get from Washington some more definite word. But Brett when they were alone told Trav honestly:

"He thinks it's hopeless, and I'm afraid it is. If Julian died, they might never have known his name. I'm writing to my old friend Mr. Gilby in Washington. He may be able to find out something."

The slow days dragged away; and Trav thought Cinda was more tormented by the waiting now than by her hopelessness before this grain of promise came. General Longstreet, whose headquarters were now in Richmond, came frequently to sit a while with Trav. The big man was lonely; for Mrs. Longstreet stayed on in Lynchburg, and he could not leave his duties to go to her there. He said she was working in the hospitals. It had not occurred to Trav that there were hospitals elsewhere than in Richmond; yet he realized this must be so. Probably everywhere in the South there were sick or wounded men, as though a plague had swept the land.

Longstreet said half McClellan's army had already been shipped away to Northern Virginia. "Jackson has gone to keep an eye on Pope," he said, "and I expect we'll follow soon." He said Trav would be missed. "In fact I thought I might need your services a few days since," he confessed, smiling in his beard. "Are you familiar with the code?"

Trav grinned. "Afraid not, General. Have you been calling someone out?"

Longstreet chuckled. "No! On the contrary." And he explained: "Powell Hill. One of his staff wrote some pieces in the *Examiner* praising the work of Hill's division so extravagantly you'd have thought no one else did anything worth doing during those days while we were pushing McClellan down to Harrison's Landing. I finally wrote a note to the *Whig* flatly contradicting these articles, had Moxley Sorrel sign it as my Adjutant General. Then Hill refused to receive Sorrel, when I sent him to Hill on an official errand, so I assumed full responsibility, and General Hill's language became so insubordinate that I sent Major Sorrel, in full panoply of sword and sash, to put him under arrest. After that Hill demanded that I meet him. I was perfectly agreeable to doing so; but General Lee cooled hot tempers on both sides, and sent General Hill off to reinforce Jackson."

Trav could imagine the lively excitement this affair had caused throughout the army; and he suspected that General Hill might have had good reason to feel himself affronted. Longstreet had many virtues, but tact was not among them. If he thought it right to reprove General Hill he would make no effort to soften his language in order to spare the other's feelings.

"I suppose he felt his honor demanded a meeting," he suggested.

Longstreet nodded. "That's the Southern idea of the way to prove one's courage, to call someone to mortal combat. We've no respect for moral courage, but only for physical bravery. We applaud a physically brave man as a hero, even though he may also be a wretch of the basest sort." And he added thoughtfully: "Take Light Horse Harry Lee. His name's a synonym for gallantry and valor and all the manly virtues. He was a fine partisan commander, and his military fame carried him to high place in civil and political life; but when he was not a soldier he was a speculator, greedy for gain, impractical, weak, lacking in principle. He was bankrupted by his follies, spent his last five years outside his own country, caused grief and loss to his friends and to his family; but he'll always be one of Virginia's heroes because of his soldierly successes, and everyone forgets his weaknesses."

"I've always thought of him as a great man," Trav admitted. "He was General Lee's father."

"Yes. They say ministers' sons turn out badly. Perhaps the opposite is true. Certainly, whatever his father was, General Lee is as good as he is great. But I was only referring to the South's blind admiration for physical courage. If General Hill had bravely accepted my rebuke, he would have been called a coward; so he challenged me. If I had had the courage to refuse to exchange shots with him, I would have been laughed at as a craven."

"Did you request his transfer to Jackson's command?"

Longstreet looked at Trav in frank astonishment. "I? God bless you, no! There's not a better general officer in our ranks than Powell Hill; none I'd rather have for the work ahead." He added with a chuckle: "And I was at fault, in some respects, and I've told him so. I am not at home in a controversy, Major. By the way, your promotion has come through." Trav colored with quick pleasure; and the other went on: "Once involved in any wordy contention I'm apt to speak more strongly than I mean. I'll never learn to follow old Ben Franklin's advice. Remember his warning? Don't ever let it appear that you know more than the other fellow. It just makes him angry. But I forget that. If a man seems to me wrong I tell him so. General Lee knows how to persuade men so pleasingly that when they accept his idea they think it their own." He smiled. "But once I begin to say a thing, I over-say it. There's a lesson you might teach me, Major; your gift of silence. Teach me to hold my tongue."

In these hours together Trav's affection for the big man grew and ripened. When Longstreet took his division north to Gordonsville, Trav resented his own weakness which would for weary weeks make it impossible for him to return to the field. Enid felt an equal resentment, because he was still too weak to move to the house on Clay Street, now ready for their occupancy. He had not yet gone downtairs, and though he was up and dressed almost every day he had lost so much flesh that his garments hung like loose bags on his wasted frame. Enid day by day urged him to hurry and get well; and she occupied this time of waiting by selecting new curtains, new linens, new rugs, new china and glassware at prices that Trav thought extravagantly high. Dolly helped her, and once Captain Pew brought a shipload of blockade goods to Richmond and gave Enid first choice. Cinda bade her take what she wanted of the things from Great Oak; and Enid wondered covetously whether Mrs. Currain would let her have Uncle Josh as butler. He and Old Thomas and Young Tom were established, with the other house servants from Great Oak, in quarters Brett had rented for them behind the ruins of the Mayborough house on Leigh Street, which had burned down last winter and had not been rebuilt. But though Enid suggested to Trav this possibility he would not let her propose it to his mother. When Mrs. Currain took the air it was in her own fine carriage, with Old Thomas holding the reins; and Uncle Josh reported to her every day. Trav would not deprive her of these friends. April was to go with them to Clay Street, and Trav thought Big Mill might serve as butler; but Enid said he smelled of the stables. Trav suggested bringing some of the people from Chimneys, and when Enid agreed to this, he welcomed the prospect of re-visiting that long-familiar, well-beloved spot.

But he must wait till he was strong again. He managed his first trip down the stairs, and another and another; and then one day came the great word that Julian was alive. Burr was at home that day, and it happened that Anne Tudor too was there when Dr. Murfin called. He said Julian was in Carver Hospital in Washington.

"He's alive," the surgeon said. "But he's still so weak he has barely strength to talk." Trav saw Cinda white and trembling as she waited on the doctor's words. "But unless something more goes wrong, he will recover," he said, and he added frankly: "It's a wonder he survived, Mrs. Dewain. I know you want the truth. He lost a great deal of blood before the hemorrhage was controlled."

Trav saw that Cinda could not speak, so he asked: "Why did they carry him to Washington?"

"He was thought to be one of our own men. I suppose his uniform was stained. At any rate, he was taken aboard our transports."

Cinda said in a low tone: "I'm going to him."

"He's far too weak to make a journey."

"I'll take care of him till he can come home."

Burr spoke doubtfully. "Mama, you can't go, can you? None of us can go with you, and you can't go alone." Trav wished he himself were not so nearly helpless. "And Papa won't let you go by yourself, Mama."

"I shan't ask him," Cinda said inflexibly. "I shan't wait to ask him."

Anne Tudor crossed to touch Cinda's shoulder. "I'll go with you, Mrs. Dewain. I won't be any protection, but I'll be company. I'd like to, really. I'm awfully fond of Julian."

"There's no need of any of you going," Dr. Murfin urged. "When he's well enough to travel, he'll be exchanged."

"Thank you," Cinda said, ignoring his warning. "You've been very kind." To Anne: "I'm glad you want to go, darling; but will your father let you?"

"Come home with me while I ask him."

Cinda rose. "Yes. Burr, will you escort us?" Trav recognized in her a driving insistence that nothing could curb; and Burr seemed to feel this too. Dr. Murfin tried again to protest.

"I really must explain to you, Mrs. Dewain——"

She shook her head. "No, please, it doesn't matter. You've been most kind; but I must do this, really." She and Anne moved into the hall; but Burr turned to the Northerner for a word and a handclasp.

"Thank you," he said. "You can see what this means to her—to all of us."

He followed them, and the outer door closed. Dr. Murfin hesitated, and Trav said: "Stay a moment more, Doctor," and as the other seated himself, he said: "My sister has had a long waiting. She will wait no more."

"I think you ought to warn her, to prepare her for a shock," the doctor said gently; and for a moment his face twisted in hard anger. "I can bear wounds, sickness, death, Mr. Currain. I can face these things steadily enough; but the maimed and mutilated men make me sick with rage at this whole bloody business."

"Julian is—maimed?" Trav asked.

The other nodded grimly. He fumbled in his pocket, drew out a letter, read some paragraphs. " 'The hunt for your man narrowed down to those wounded from Yorktown who were still alive but were also still too sick to talk. I thought I'd covered the field; but the word came to me this morning, and I saw the boy this afternoon. The wound——' "

Trav was confused by the medical terminology which followed, but he could understand that the blood supply in Julian's leg had somehow been injured or destroyed, so that gangrene set in. There had been a series of amputations, complicated by the fact that Julian developed measles and then pneumonia. The terrible details piled one upon another till Trav could bear no more; he interrupted.

"Doctor, has he any leg left?"

"Not even a stump, I'm afraid. Currain, it's one of God's miracles he's alive at all."

"I'll not tell his mother all that," Trav decided. "It's just as well she shouldn't know." He added appreciatively: "Someone must have worked hard and long to keep him alive." His eyes for a moment closed in a nausea of horror. "Several amputations?" He had heard men scream, in the hospital tents, when they fought against the hands that held them motionless while saw bit bone.

Dr. Murfin said gently: "We have chloroform in the North, of course. So he was insensible."

Trav nodded, and after a moment the other rose to go. Trav went with him to the door; he turned then and found the stairs, so frighteningly steep and high. He went slowly up to his room and wished to go to bed; but when Cinda returned she might need him, so he waited, sitting with his eyes closed, thinking of the fine boy lying among strangers far away.

They were kindly strangers, to be sure; for most men in their hearts were kind. Most men caught in this shame and horror that billowed across the world were helpless, doing what they must, borne to and fro by forces beyond their control. It was true that one man had let loose this bloody tide across the land. One man, if he had held his hand, could have prevented all this; yet perhaps that great man was as helpless as the least of them. It was easy to damn Abraham Lincoln; yet it must have seemed to Lincoln that he could do no other than he did.

Perhaps war was a disease, which just as smallpox sweeps a city sometimes swept a nation. War was a disease of the human heart, changing the heart's beat and pulse and all its functioning, making gentle men into murderers, entering into the hearts of men to turn them mad. Diseases came from none knew where; men were stricken or not; they lived or they died. It was so with war, the worst disease of all.

When Cinda and Burr returned, Cinda went to pack, but Burr reported to Trav that Judge Tudor made no objection to Anne's going. "I think he's really relieved," Burr said in a puzzled tone. "I don't know why, exactly. He says Anne may stay on in Washington with a friend of his. He wants her to take some documents to put in safekeeping; and that reminded me that Mama has some securities Papa's been worried about. She'll take them to Mr. Gilby to keep for us."

They would leave next morning, and without military passes. To secure passports meant delay. "Judge Tudor says Mr. Randolph doesn't issue passports any more, that General Winder handles them," Burr explained. "And he and his plug-uglies are pretty arrogant. Anyway, Mama doesn't want to wait for all that; and I'm sure General Stuart will let me and Uncle Faunt see them through the lines."

"Anne will enjoy seeing Faunt," Trav remarked.

Burr hesitated. "Judge Tudor asked how Uncle Faunt was. He says he saw him at a distance a few days ago, says he believes Uncle Faunt is often in Richmond. I think maybe he resents Uncle Faunt's not calling on them. It wasn't anything he said, just the way he said it." He added: "Anyway, we'll slip Mama and Anne through the lines."

When Cinda and Anne were gone, Mrs. Currain and Trav and Enid and the children were left in sole possession of the house on Fifth Street. Trav was touched to see his mother at once assume the direction of the household. She trotted about the house as merrily as a cricket. Caesar under her commands sometimes forgot his lofty dignity; and even June, though at first she sulked because Cinda had left her behind, soon fell under the brisk old woman's spell. But a few days after Cinda's departure, Enid insisted Trav was well enough to move to the house on Clay Street. Trav thought they should stay here till Cinda's return; but Enid reminded him that that might be a long time.

"And I can't stand it any longer," she declared. "I've always hated being just a visitor here anyway, and now Mama's so uppity I just won't endure it another day."

So Trav yielded. The house on Clay Street, which he entered for the first time that day, was larger than he had expected; and he had to go from room to room with Enid while she showed him what she had done and told him what she planned to do. She was radiant with happy pride, and Trav thought she had never been so beautiful.

"I never realized how much this would mean to you, Honey," he confessed, "or I'd have done something about it long ago."

She kissed him with an ungrudging ardor. "It's wonderful, darling." She laughed in a husky way. "You're an awful old slow poke, but this makes up for everything!" During the next days, watching her happiness, Trav grew swiftly stronger.

A week after Cinda and Anne departed Brett came to hear from Trav what had happened. "Mama just says Cinda's gone to visit the Gilbys in Washington. Did she have word of Julian?"

"Yes. He's in a hospital in Washington, Brett." Trav told him of

Julian's long ordeal, and Brett listened with the sweat of shared pain on his brow.

"But he's alive," he said at last. "So nothing else matters. I'll see Dr. Murfin tomorrow." His voice was sober with concern. "There should be a letter from Cinda soon, if she reached Washington."

Trav, to distract the other man, asked what the Howitzers had been doing. Brett said they had gone with some infantry on a scout into Prince George County. "The Yankee patrols had been making a nuisance of themselves, and we thought we might get a chance at McClellan's transports in the river; but they were gunboats instead of transports, so we didn't accomplish anything." He added: "Our company hasn't seen much of the war yet. We've only lost two men killed in sixteen months."

"Captain Stanard?"

"Yes, and now George Carlton."

"I didn't know him. Is the company still at Petersburg?"

"We came to Richmond this morning. The talk is we'll go north, to Gordonsville or somewhere in a day or two." He said soberly: "I wish I were with Cinda."

"She'll be all right. She rises to emergencies, you know."

Brett stayed a while in talk, as though talk eased him; and next day he came again. This time he brought young Peter home with him, and the boy was pale with excitement. "I met him stumbling along in the crowd on Broad Street," Brett explained. His tone was light, and he rested a reassuring hand on the youngster's shoulder; but his eyes met Trav's gravely. "He'd been out to Camp Lee to see them shoot some deserters."

Trav felt the words like a shocking blow. The thought of this son of his, this baby, goggling at such a spectacle was hard to accept without dismay. Before he could speak, Peter himself cried: "And I wiggled through the crowd and got right up close, Papa. When the bullets hit them, little puffs of dust came out, like when someone's beating a carpet. But it's more interesting when they hang people."

Trav could not meet Brett's eyes. "Is that so? I've never seen that."

"I'll take you some time," Peter promised. "They hung a man yesterday, in the gully back of the Almshouse. There were hundreds and hundreds of people there. A man prayed with him for a long time, sitting on his coffin in the cart, and then they hung him, and he kept kicking and squirming so they had to pull down on his legs to make his neck snap. The handkerchief fell off his face so you could see the faces he was making. They'll hang somebody else pretty soon, probably. It's awfully exciting, Papa. The crowd hoots and hollers, and women laugh and yell."

"Well, next time, you tell me," Trav suggested. He added: "But I wouldn't tell Mama, if I were you. It might make her unhappy."

After the youngster left them, he looked at Brett in an uncertain way. "I didn't know just what to say," he admitted. "But I hate the thought of his—seeing that sort of thing."

"Richmond's full of criminals," Brett commented. "Scoundrels from all over the South, and the North too, I suppose. Castle Thunder and Castle Lightning never have an empty cell—and it's mostly soldiers locked up there. Being a soldier makes a thief out of a man in short order, of course. War has a lot to answer for besides its bloody battles—and what it does to children like Peter is as bad as anything."

"They play soldiers," Trav told him. "Peter seems to have memorized Hardee's *Tactics*. He's the drill master of his crowd." It occurred to him later that this fact gave him a cue; so when he next talked to Peter it was to suggest to the youngster that being an officer meant much more than just knowing how to give orders. "Unless you're the right kind of boy, or man, your men won't readily obey your orders; so you have to be sure you behave like an officer in other ways, even when you're not drilling them." He added suggestively: "I suppose your boy friends in Butchertown go to all the hangings too?"

"Yes sirree! They never miss one."

"Do you ever see any gentlemen there?" Trav inquired.

"Why, no, sir," Peter decided, after a moment; and there was manifest disappointment in his tone.

"I suppose not," Trav agreed. "So probably I'd better not go to one with you. I'm an officer, so I have to be careful how I behave." He did not labor the point, but he hoped Peter would understand.

Late in August, with no word from Cinda, Brett and the Howitzers departed. Next day Trav had a caller: James Fiddler, who at Chimneys had been for so many years his friend and his right hand. Trav welcomed him warmly. The overseer said in affectionate concern that Trav was looking thin and pale, and Trav laughed and retorted:

"You'd not think so if you had seen me a month ago. By comparison, I'm as big as a horse now, and twice as strong." He began to ask eager questions about his old friends in Martinston. Ed Blandy? Ed was in the army, in South Carolina, Fiddler thought. Jeremy Blackstone? Jeremy was at home, hiding from the provost men; and so were Nat Emerson, and Joe Merritt, and Alex Spain.

"Deserters?" Trav asked.

"Why, they came home on furlough and stayed. Someone has to make a crop to feed their families, Mr. Currain."

"I know." Trav spoke other names. "Chelmsford Lowman? Bob Grimm?"

"Bob's in the army—with only one arm." Lonn Tyler, Fiddler said, was still a soldier too; and Jim Tunstill's oldest boy, young Jim. "Jim died of measles, you know." Trav had not known this. As though defensively, Fiddler added: "The ones that have sons old enough to work their farms, they're mostly away in the fighting somewhere."

Trav began to suspect that there was some sorrow in James Fiddler, but he hesitated to ask any direct question. "You haven't gone and got married yet, have you?" he hazarded.

Fiddler shook his head. "No. No, I don't know as I'm ever likely to." He hesitated. "I've gone on the notion that I was needed at Chimneys, Mr. Currain. I never looked to leave there. You and me put a lot of ourselves into that place." He seemed about to say more, then asked emptily: "How'd you do at Great Oak?"

So Trav recited what he had done and what he had planned. "But we couldn't stay there after the Yankees came, so they'll reap what we sowed." And he tried to prompt the other to say what was in his mind. "Must be a change for you to come to Richmond this way. I don't remember you ever did before."

"Why, no, I never did, Mr. Currain." So after a moment the truth at last came out. "I kind of had to, now. I'm going into the fighting; but I couldn't come away and leave Chimneys without I let you know."

Trav said understandingly: "It was the same with me. I thought at first I could let other folks do the fighting, but I had to get into it by and by."

"Well, I could have stayed," Fiddler admitted. "I kind of felt like if I stayed there I'd be working for you; but it got so I couldn't take no more."

So Trav guessed a part of the truth. "You and Mr. Currain?" he asked. "I thought you all liked him there."

"He's changed, sir. He's changed mightily," said Fiddler. He said this much and no more; but this was more eloquent than many words. Trav felt no surprise. They were all changed since that night at Great Oak when Tilda found the letters from poor Lucy Hanks. He himself certainly was not the same man. The old Trav could never have used violence toward Enid, could never have compelled her submission and obedience; the old Trav could never have known that stormy madness which had driven him at Seven Pines and on that day by the Charles River Road when—cutting and thrusting till his bright blade was one red smear—he had stabbed and slain. Yes, he was changed. They were all changed—and Tony too.

He would not question James Fiddler, would question no one about his brother. He must go to Chimneys, to see for himself. Enid wanted some of the Negroes brought to Richmond; here was pretext enough.

"You'll be missed there," he told James Fiddler courteously. "But the South needs good men, and you'll be a good man at any job you take in hand."

Of Tony they said no more than this, and Fiddler presently said good-by; but as soon as he felt fit to do so, Trav set out upon that journey. It would be good to go back to Chimneys again, no matter what he found.

15

To TONY, Tilda's discovery that night at Great Oak was a mocking jest—of which he was the butt. Into that weariness and that slowing of the blood which came to him in his early fifties, his life at Chimneys had brought rest and peace and a content he had never known; the respectful liking of the men who were his neighbors awoke pride in himself and in his heritage. But these men had trusted him because he was Trav's brother, Anthony Currain's son, finely bred, a gentleman. Now the name of Currain, if the truth were known, would be accursed in every corner of the South; so the name became a stigma, something of which to be ashamed, and the pride he had learned to feel was an illusion.

At first he laughed to hide his pain, and like a boy hungry for comforting he turned to Nell. When she dismissed him, for lack of any other target for his cruel anger he rode his horse to death; and he turned then to the bottle and the gaming table till his fury spent itself and he could laugh again. The suggestion that he take his mother home to Chimneys amused him, and on the journey he led her to long talk of his father whose old sins now returned to haunt them all. The fact that she spoke of that other Anthony Currain with an unchanged fondness seemed to him to point the jest.

At Martinston and at Chimneys there was a welcome for him. In Martinston this was a little guarded, a little wary; but James Fiddler was unstintedly glad of his return, and Tony spoke to the overseer of this reticence in the manner of the men in the village. "Nat Emerson saw me talking with Chelmsford Lowman and dodged away out of sight," he said. "And when I asked Lowman why, he said maybe it wasn't Nat I'd seen. And Joe Merritt was full of questions about why I'd come. You'd think I was a horse thief they were watching."

Fiddler told him the explanation. "They were afraid you'd turn them over to the conscript officers. Nat Emerson and several of the men in your old company are hiding out around here."

"Deserters?"

"Well, in a way, yes. Anyway, they're staying home long enough to make a crop. If they don't feed their families, no one will."

Tony laughed. "Why, good for them!" he said cheerfully. "They've nothing to fear from me. I'd not fight—nor send any other man to fight." He felt Fiddler's eye on him, clapped the other's shoulder. "That sounds like treason to you, eh?"

"No," Fiddler said. "No, I don't blame the men." Yet his tone held an undercurrent of disapproval; and Tony said in a sardonic tone:

"If you're feeling warlike, I'd not want to tie you down here, Fiddler."

The overseer hesitated. "The South will need all the food we can raise, sir," he remarked. "You and I can do more here than we could do in the army."

"To be sure, to be sure," Tony assented. "And the enrolling officers won't touch you here. The law allows one white man exempt for every twenty slaves on the place. That will cover both of us."

Fiddler nodded. "I know. The folks here say the planters made that law so they and their sons wouldn't be conscripted. Planter's war, poor man's fight." And he added thoughtfully: "Even clear off down here, we know Richmond's full of details and exempts. The men on furlough see them on the streets there and bring the stories home."

They were in the office, that comfortable ground-floor room with timbers showing in the plastered walls, and Tony had a bottle near his hand. He filled his glass again, emptying the bottle, and rolled the brandy in the glass and savored it across his tongue; he hiccoughed amiably and called for Joseph, and Pegleg came tapping along the hall, to take the empty bottle and bring a fresh one. When he was gone Tony looked after him, and he said to Fiddler:

"That wench of Joseph's is good enough for a one-legged man; but she's a slut around the house. Chewing that damned snuff stick, dribbling down her chin."

"Vigil was always in the house," Fiddler reminded him.

"I know, I know," Tony said heedlessly. "But send her to the fields. Mama likes house servants to be tidy."

"I'll speak to Maria," Fiddler assented. Maria ruled the kitchen and the house; an incredibly old and withered woman with the hoarse voice of a man. She had among the people the name of knowing many a dark secret, and she held them in the bonds of deadly fear. Joseph no less than the others yielded to her authority. Tony nodded inattentively, his head drooping in alcoholic drowsiness, and the overseer presently left him alone.

During the first weeks after his return to Chimneys Tony usually rode with Fiddler every morning, listening to the other's reports and his proposals; but after dinner when his mother went for her nap he was likely to sit on the shaded veranda with a julep beside him, or the brandy bottle, till he fell asleep; and if as was her habit she went early to bed he sometimes rode to Martinston to sit tippling in the tavern there. His horse brought him home at any hour of the night, and Joseph, sleeping in the chair in the hall till his master returned, waked by the sound of hoof beats, was always ready to meet him, to catch him as he slid off his horse, to help him up the wide steps to the veranda and so to bed.

The lame man had accepted Vigil's banishing without protest. He gave Tony the unquestioning loyalty of a fine dog, accepting abuse or casual blows with a cheerful grin. To replace Vigil, Maria brought into the house a woman whose tight-kinked hair was already streaked with gray, a saddle-brown mulatto. She immediately proved her worth. The big house thereafter was immaculately kept, and the change, even to Tony's uncritical eye, was welcome. When Tony questioned her, she said her work had been to manage the poultry yards, till Mr. Fiddler put her in charge in the loom house, receiving the wool when the sheep were sheared and carrying it through the intervening processes and seeing it woven at last into blankets or into closer stuff fit for fabrication.

He had never noticed her in these occupations, but now he was puzzled by something vaguely familiar. "What's your name?"

" 'Phemy."

He poured a finger of brandy into his glass and looked up at her again, and memories came more clearly. "Weren't you at Great Oak, ten, twenty years ago?"

He caught an amused gleam in her eyes as she answered him. " 'Sho wuz! Twell you done packed me off tuh Chimbleys, befoah I come to mah time."

So Tony remembered, and his thoughts turned back to sultry nights scented with the fragrance of woodland blossoms and turbulent with barbaric lusts. Yes, he remembered now. That saddle-brown skin of 'Phemy's like stained old leather now had seemed in those days the warm hue of dulled gold. While his thoughts cast backward she stood waiting, and he wondered where she had acquired that dignity she wore. He wondered too whence came that diluted blood of hers, not altogether black. Probably from his own father, who had been so profligate in sprinkling the Currain blood under any hedge row; from that father in whom he had been for a while so weak as to take pride.

He nodded at his own conjecture, sure of that which could never by any chance be proved. 'Phemy—he would have wagered on it—'Phemy was his father's daughter, a half sister to that Nancy Hanks who mothered Abraham Lincoln. Yes, and she was his own half sister, too. He laughed in a mockery of mirth. Well—he remembered a phrase his mother sometimes used—well, so mote it be!

He saw that something like intimacy developed between his mother and 'Phemy. When Mrs. Currain went for her nap after dinner every day she took 'Phemy with her. "Nobody can rub the aches out of my old bones as 'Phemy can," she explained. "You're fortunate to have her in the house, Tony. She and Maria and Joseph work well together."

"She's a superior nigger," he agreed. His mother's eyes dropped in that fashion which he had learned long ago to recognize as reproof. None of this uppity family of his ever spoke of the people as niggers; but facts weren't changed by the names you gave them, and a nigger was a nigger. Yes and niggers were all right in their place, better than white folks, in certain secret ways.

"Her mother was one of my mother's people," Mrs. Currain said. "And her grandmother, too. Her mother and grandmother came to Great Oak with me when I married your father."

"Were they black?" Tony asked, watching her quizzically.

She answered simply. "Yes. Black." That was a lesson Southern women learned, to ignore the fact that black wenches on their plantations sometimes had mulatto babies. He felt a brief sympathy for this frail little woman who had borne him; yet why could she not, as he must, face the truth; yes, and avow it? She must know 'Phemy was her husband's daughter; know it or guess it. He wondered sometimes how much 'Phemy had told her, in those hours they spent together. Women, even though their skins were of different colors, were closer to one another than men could ever be. But whatever 'Phemy dared tell her, Mrs. Currain would never admit she knew.

'Phemy proved her capacities, as the days passed, in many ways. It was she, informed through those mysterious channels which white folks could never understand, who forewarned Tony the day Redford Streean alighted from the stage in Martinston. An hour before Streean's carriage drove up the hill, Tony knew he was on the road, and told his mother; and Mrs. Currain said politely: "How nice of him to call."

Tony chuckled, for he was nowadays easily amused. "Now Mama, you don't like Streean any better than I do."

"But I always remember he's Tilda's husband," she assured him. "After all, he's one of the family." That made Tony shout with easy laughter at this family of which she was so proud.

Streean when he arrived spoke approvingly of the fine crops in the well-tended fields. "There's a fortune in those bottoms down there," he told Tony. "People next winter will pay any price for food—wheat and corn and sweet potatoes, beef and cattle and hogs."

Tony said Chimneys would be hard put to it to raise food enough for its own needs. "We're overstocked with niggers. A lot of the hands from Great Oak and Belle Vue were sent here. There's not enough work to keep them all busy, so they're hungry all the time. If we got rid of forty or fifty we'd be better off."

"Sell some of them," Streean advised.

Tony, secretly enjoying the pose, said severely: "The Currains don't sell their people, Streean."

'Phemy brought them fresh juleps, and Streean watched her come and go. "That's one who would fetch a good price if she were twenty years younger,' he commented. "She must have been a handsome wench."

"She was born at Great Oak," Tony said; and he was about to add that she was probably one of his father's bastards, but that was no business of Streean's.

It developed that Streean had come here not to pay a casual call but on business. He proposed to enlist Tony as a partner. With the authority of the Quartermaster's department he could impress farm products at the set price, ship them to Richmond in government-controlled railroad cars, or on the Quartermaster's wagons, and then dispose of them to greedy private buyers. He opened to Tony unsuspected vistas.

"A man's a fool not to fill his purse when he can," he urged. "You and I can work together. When your crop is made, hold it. I'll arrange for shipment to Richmond, and we'll share what it brings."

Tony had always an appetite for money. The machinery of the proposed transaction confused him, but the prospect of gain was attractive; and Streean, as though seeing this, spoke again of the high prices some of the surplus Negroes would bring. "Better sell them," he advised. "Put the money to work, or put it into things that can't get away. Some men buy diamonds. They're small, easily hidden, always saleable."

"I wouldn't know where to buy diamonds if I had the money."

"Oh, they're on the market all the time," Streean assured him. "Refugees from northern Virginia, coming to Richmond, are selling everything they've got for money to live on." He laughed. "Or to subscribe to Confederate loans that will never be paid. Your high-minded gentry will be paupers before this war ends, Tony, and so will you, unless you use your wits." And he said: "I can help you get rid of these niggers. I'll have Darrell arrange it, and I'll put the money into something safe for you, or I'll make it work for you." Tony in the end found himself persuaded to halfhearted assent.

When Streean departed, Mrs. Currain returned with him to Richmond. From something in her eyes, a sort of patient sadness, Tony suspected that during her stay here she had seen more than she acknowledged; but he brushed the thought aside, nursing the golden dreams Streean had awakened.

He delayed telling James Fiddler his intention to sell some slaves. The overseer's manner had begun to make Tony uncomfortable. There was an aloofness in Fiddler's tones like that uncomplaining silence which Tony detected in his mother. He told himself that his adventures among the wenches on the place had encroached on Fiddler's preserves and that the man resented it, and the thought aroused in Tony a tolerant contempt, and gave him courage to speak at last of this transaction Streean had proposed.

"Fiddler, these niggers from Great Oak and Belle Vue will eat us out of house and home."

The overseer said reluctantly: "Why, we don't need them, that's a fact."

"I'm thinking of selling them."

Fiddler looked at him in surprise. "I only remember one negro ever being sold off the place," he suggested. " 'Phemy's daughter, five or six years ago."

Tony looked at him in surprise. "Trav sold her? What was the matter with her?"

"Mrs. Currain wouldn't have her in the house. She took care of the children when they were little; but she taught herself to read, and to speak well, and got pretty impudent, and Mrs. Currain had a lot of trouble with her. So Mr. Currain sold her to the Pettigrews."

" 'Phemy's daughter?" Tony felt a stir of interest. "Is she black or yellow?"

Fiddler hesitated. "A bright," he said slowly.

"How old is she?"

"I don't know."

"Oh, damn it, give a guess!" Tony was trying to remember how long ago it was that he had sent 'Phemy from Great Oak to Chimneys. Twenty years? Yes, perhaps a little more.

"Why, she was about fifteen. She must be twenty, now; maybe a little more."

Fiddler's words seemed to Tony confirmation of his own conjecture. "Where is she now?"

"At the Pettigrew place. Captain Pettigrew was killed at Manassas, and his sons are in the army. Mrs. Pettigrew lives in Raleigh. There's not even an overseer there now. I hear the people there do as they please."

Tony was immensely curious to see this bright mulatto who was 'Phemy's daughter, but he asked Fiddler nothing more. 'Phemy would answer his questions. After dinner that day, when she brought his julep to the veranda, he asked casually: " 'Phemy, haven't you any children?"

She looked at him in quiet attention. "Yassuh, I got six."

"Who's your man?"

"Long Johnnie wuz, twell he cut his hand at a slaughtering, sticking a ole hawg, an' it mortified."

"Good children, are they?"

"Yassuh, de heft of 'em." Her answer invited a question, and he asked it, and she explained: "All only Sapphira. She got too uppity, wouldn't have nothin' t'do wid her little brothe's and siste's 'count dey 'uz black and she 'uz white as anybody."

"She's not on the place here, is she?"

"Naw suh. Misteh Currain done sold her to de Pettigrews. She high and mighty now, livin' in de big house, bossin' de place lak she 'uz white folks."

'Phemy's tone was sharp with scorn, yet Tony thought he caught in it a note of pride. "A no-good nigger?" he suggested, grinning at her. He was not surprised to see her expression change.

"All she needed 'uz someone to take a stick of firewood to her," 'Phemy assured him. "She didn't try her tricks on her ma."

"Good around the house?"

"If she 'uz around dis house, she'd better be." Their eyes met, as though she read his thought, and after a moment's silence, in a lower tone, humble and almost pleading, she said: "Yassuh, she'd be a mighty help tuh me."

Tony next morning, telling no one his errand, rode away; and before noon his horse turned into the driveway that led to the Pettigrew house. The fields, except for patches planted here and there to garden stuff, were neglected and gone to weeds and sedge; but the driveway seemed to have been freshly raked, the flower beds were clean, there was a trash gang diligent at work.

A black-skinned youngster came running to take his horse, looking at him and then at the closed door of the house in obvious excitement. Tony stripped off his gloves, slapped the dust off his trouser legs, and climbed the steps. At his tug at the knob, a bell jangled somewhere in the silent house, and the door presently was opened by an aged Negro with a white fringe around his poll and the courteous demeanor of his kind. Beyond him the wide hall was in order, the house was spotless clean. The old man bobbed and bade Tony good morning.

"It's Mister Currain, Uncle," Tony said amiably. "Tell Mrs. Pettigrew I wished to pay my respects."

"Please suh," the old man said regretfully. "De fambly is all away f'om home. Won't you step in an' rest youhse'f f'om de heat o' de day?"

Tony nodded, moved into the hall. "Will they be returning today?"

The butler was about to reply, but from the library at one side someone said: "Bring the gentleman a julep, Uncle Merry."

Tony turned at the word, and he felt a quick pulse pound in his throat. He had been prepared to see a bright mulatto wench; he saw instead a young woman who despite her plain black dress of a servant was certainly richly beautiful, who might well have been white, and who said simply: "I am Mis' Pettigrew's housekeeper, Mr. Currain. Will you make you'self easy? I know Mis' Pettigrew would want you to refresh you'self befoah you ride away."

Tony wished to laugh aloud. Why, the wench put on as many airs as if she were the lady of the house. By God, she might have been! She was a lot more handsome than most ladies, and as composed, and as well spoken. He had seen white women with darker skins, with hair as black. Clearly she ruled the old butler; yes, and to judge by appearances she ruled the other people around the place! Now how did she manage that? What weapons did she use? There were a thousand questions to which he wished to find answers.

"Is your mistress at the Springs?"

"In Raleigh, sir."

Uncle Merry came with the julep, and Tony took it. "Thank you, Uncle. I'll rest on the veranda while I drink this." He moved past

Sapphira toward the open doors at the rear of the wide hall. Would she have the impudence to follow him? If she did, what then?

But she did not. He sat at ease, surveying the sloping and well-tended lawns, catching glimpses of a little stream at the foot of the slope, shaping in his thoughts the letter he would write to Mrs. Pettigrew. "—the daughter of my housekeeper—" "—to reunite this girl with her mother—" "—sold by my brother at his wife's insistence; but his home is now in Richmond, so perhaps you will let me bring the girl back to Chimneys—" "—assures me she will be useful, has many household accomplishments; so I am prepared—" When he finished the julep Uncle Merry showed him to the door. Sapphira, to his disappointment, did not reappear.

Mrs. Pettigrew's reply to his letter was all he had hoped for. Sapphira had many valuable qualities, yes. "But I'm afraid she makes life miserable for poor old Uncle Merry. I've thought of selling her, but you know one hates to do that. However, since it is to return to her former home—" She would write to Sapphira, tell the girl her decision.

Tony, after some thought as to procedure, sent Joseph and 'Phemy in one of the farm carts to bring Sapphira to Chimneys. Let 'Phemy take her down a bit; let the girl learn her place. There was time enough. "Put her where she will be of the most use to you, 'Phemy," he directed. "You know best what she can do."

He bade them delay their departure till he and the overseer were gone; and he led James Fiddler on a longer ride than usual that day, careful not to return to the house till the cart should have had time to go and come. When they did ride up the hill, Darrell and another man were sitting on the veranda.

Tony had completely forgotten, in his new interest during these last few days, his arrangement with Streean. To see Darrell relaxed and at his ease here made him for a moment awkward with surprise; but Darrell rose to greet him, smiling amiably enough.

"Well, Uncle Tony! It's been a long time since you tossed me off this same veranda."

Tony smiled emptily to hide his thoughts; but he remembered that day long ago when the Martinston men came to ask him to lead them to war. Judge Meynell was their spokesman, and now Judge Meynell was dead at Darrell's hand, and little Miss Mary had been killed by Darrell as surely as though his bullet pierced her breast.

Darrell was introducing him to the stranger. "Mr. Pudrick; my uncle, Mr. Currain."

Mr. Pudrick was a plump little man with an oily brow and an oily smile and an ice-blue eye. "Servant, Mr. Currain!"

Tony bowed, hiding his instant dislike. "I see you've been made welcome." There were juleps on the table where they had been sitting.

"Yes," Darrell assented. "Pegleg took care of us." Tony hoped 'Phemy would be wise enough to keep Sapphira out of Darrell's sight. "We've been so well entertained we've almost forgotten hunger," Darrell assured him.

"James Fiddler and I were delayed today," Tony apologized. Joseph brought a frosty glass for him; and Tony said: "Tell 'Phemy we will have dinner in half an hour, Joseph."

Mr. Pudrick, when they were seated, said at once: "I'm a business man, Mr. Currain, so I'll come to the point. Mr. Streean says his father and you have discussed throwing a bit of business my way."

Tony stared into his mint-topped glass, thinking uncomfortably of James Fiddler and what the overseer would say to this upon which he had decided. He roused in himself anger to smother his sense of guilt. Fiddler was nothing but an overseer. The niggers were not his property. It was true, they were not Tony's either; but he could act for the family. Yes, and in the family interest, too. If Fiddler were sensible he would see this, see the wisdom of selling off some surplus slaves. He nodded.

"Why—yes, Mr. Pudrick, to be sure."

"I'm a business man and a busy man, Mr. Currain." The slave dealer's tone was a mixture of humility and insistence. "Can we set about our business this evening? I should take the road back to Raleigh tomorrow."

Tony drank deep. The cool fragrance of the mint, and the tingling sweetness soothed his nerves, uneasy after a morning's abstinence. "Presently, presently," he said in an irritable tone. Fiddler would scowl and frown; Brett and Trav and Faunt would disapprove. But with this man Lincoln bent on ruining the South, niggers would be worthless presently. "What's a good hand worth, Mr. Pudrick?"

"What we can get for them, sir."

"I'm selling to you, at your risk."

"Then I will protect myself on the price."

Tony drank again. He shouted over his shoulder for Joseph, bade him summon Fiddler. When the overseer appeared, Tony said harshly:

"Mr. Fiddler, how many people have we here from Belle Vue and Great Oak?"

Fiddler looked from Tony to Darrell, who nodded in casual greeting, and then to the slave dealer; and he wetted his lips. "I'd have to tally the lot, Mr. Currain."

"Well, damn it, man, do it then. Get them all together, with their families." He spoke to Pudrick. "You can have a look at them after dinner." Fiddler moved away, and Tony said angrily: "But you'll have to get them off the place tonight. I'll not have them snivelling around in the morning."

"That's the way I like to do business, Mr. Currain. If we do business, I'll have the whole coffle of niggers on the road by sundown."

Joseph said dinner was served. When the meal was done, unwilling to face Mr. Fiddler, Tony said: "Pudrick, I don't propose to bargain with you. You'll not pick and choose. You must take all or none. Look 'em over, come back and show me your money, and I'll say yes or no."

The slave dealer glanced at Darrell, who said in an amiable drawl: "Pudrick will give you a draft on Richmond, Uncle Tony. I'll take him to Richmond to see it honored." His eyes twinkled. "Unless you insist my visit here be prolonged."

Tony felt a befuddlement he would not avow. Matters of business were strange to him; it was a relief to leave all that in Darrell's hands. Doubtless this young man had his father's wisdom in such matters. He nodded: "Take Pudrick down to the quarter, then," he directed. "I suppose you'll find Fiddler there."

When they rose, he went to his room. The quarter was out of sight from the house, but he stood for a moment at the window, watching them go that way. Fiddler would wear a reproachful look for days. Well, let him! Tony turned in angry defiance to the brandy bottle on the table beside the bed. An eye-opener in the morning, a night cap every night: that was any gentleman's habit. But sometimes Tony's eyes were hard to open, sometimes his sleep was tardy; so Joseph knew enough to keep a full bottle by the bed. It was full now, but before Darrell and Pudrick came back it was half empty.

Tony went uncertainly to meet them. Liquor seemed to take hold of him more quickly than it had used to. Certainly he had not drunk enough to make him thus stumble-footed, to blur his eyes so that these two men moved in a red haze. The figures Pudrick quoted—so many hands, so many women young enough to make themselves useful, so many children of working age, so many other children too young to count—were meaningless to him.

"Take 'em all or none," he said thickly. "I'm a man of heart! Won't break up families. Don't leave any old ones here that we'll have to look out for. Take 'em all or none."

Pudrick flattered him. "You're the sort of man it's a pleasure to meet, Mr. Currain. Take 'em all or none, you say. Well, here's my price." He handed Tony a slip of paper. "Take it or leave it."

Tony blinked, trying to read the figures Pudrick had written, trying to seem wise and shrewd; but he was so benumbed that the bit of paper slipped out of his hand. Darrell picked it up, and Tony demanded: "How's it sound to you, Darrell?"

"Seems fair to me, Uncle Tony."

"Huh!" Why was his vision clouded? It could not be the little brandy he had drunk. Maybe a touch of malaria, left over from those weeks on the Peninsula last year when he was playing soldier. "Done," he muttered, and scowled at Pudrick. "Now get the niggers off the place! They don't belong at Chimneys, anyway, this lot. My brothers unloaded 'em on me." Sudden puny anger filled him. "Get 'em out of my sight, damn it! Don't sit there gawping like a catfish! Get 'em away from here!" The effort exhausted him; his head drooped. It was mighty comfortable to close your eyes, shut out the wavering and formless world.

He woke in his own bed, in the dimness of drawn shades through which sunlight came peering to affront his eyes. So it was daylight. Joseph must have put him to bed. His wandering eyes found the bottle within reach; and a gulp from it ran through his shaking body. A wonderful thing, a drink of brandy when you woke! He lay enjoying this pleasant relaxing ease, this passive recovery. Another drop or two would complete the process.

When he rose, shouting for Joseph, he was sufficiently restored to be almost jovial. Joseph brought coffee; Tony flavored it with a spoonful more of brandy. "Those gentlemen gone, are they?" he demanded.

"Yassuh!" Tony saw the whites of the Negro's eyes.

"What time is it?"

"Sun two hours high."

"Well, damn it, hustle my breakfast. Get my horse, too. Tell Fiddler I'll be right along."

"Yassuh, he heah waitin'."

Waiting? For Fiddler to be waiting was outside the normal pattern. The overseer always found things to do till Tony was ready to join him, or till Tony decided not to ride that day. "Waiting?" He repeated the word aloud.

"In de office, suh. I git you some breakfus'." Joseph stumped away.

Tony dressed slowly, and he ate slowly; he put off as long as possible going down to the cool pleasant room on the ground level where the plantation books were kept. But in the end, fortified by another glass of brandy, his head high as became that of a master going to meet his underling, Tony went to face James Fiddler.

The overseer was at the desk; he rose when Tony appeared. Tony yawned with some elaboration. "Slept late and I'm still sleepy," he commented. "Kept you waiting, I'm afraid."

Fiddler nodded. "I just wanted to hand you these things," he explained. "This is the duplicate bill of sale you signed last night. Mr. Darrell left it for you. He said to tell you he'd return in a few weeks to make an accounting."

"Put it where such things go," Tony directed. "We ought to be on our way."

"I must have a word with you, Mr. Currain."

"Eh?" Tony's anger stirred. "Well, damn it, go ahead." He sat down, slapping at his boots with his riding crop. "Go on, out with it, man."

James Fiddler hesitated. "I've been all my life at Chimneys, Mr.

Currain. Born here. Grew up here. My father and mother are buried here."

"You've told me so before. Don't repeat yourself!"

"I've decided to go into the army, Mr. Currain."

"The army? Good God, what for?" And Tony urged, suddenly alarmed: "See here, Chimneys can't go on without you. You're needed here." His eyes narrowed. "The enrolling officers won't touch you, Fiddler. You're exempt. Both of us are. One white man for twenty slaves!"

"I prefer the army, Mr. Currain."

Tony understood the other's tone, and a venomous rancor filled him. He tipped back his head, said in a jeering drawl: "Why, I thought you were devoted to Chimneys!"

The other bit his lip, seemed to grope for words. "It can't do any good talking about it, Mr. Currain."

"Go on, talk about it," Tony challenged. "Don't pretend it's because you love the South. It's because you don't like me. Come, out with it!"

"Why—well, sir, we've never sold slaves from Chimneys, not in my time here."

"How about that wench of 'Phemy's?"

"That was to please Mrs. Currain."

"I've brought her back. I suppose you know."

Fiddler looked absently at his right hand, looking into the palm, then closing the hand and looking at the knuckles. "Yes, sir," he assented.

Tony was furious, yet the overseer's tone was so mild it was hard to find cause for offense. Prod the man a little; prod him into speech and then slash your riding crop across his face, teach him his place. "Come, come," he drawled. "You'd have stayed here with Trav." Fiddler did not answer. "Wouldn't you?"

"Yes, sir."

"All right then, what's the matter with me? Speak up!"

Fiddler answered in a low tone, almost gently. "Something has changed you, Mr. Currain. You've gone to pieces." His own thoughts warmed his words. "You're drunk most of the time, prowling around the quarter like an old goat, bringing your wenching——"

Tony scrambled to his feet with lifted hand. "Why, God damn you, Fiddler, are you——"

Then James Fiddler's eyes met his like a blow, cutting off his word; and Tony hushed, and Fiddler asked very gently: "What did you say, Mr. Currain?"

Tony felt a trickle of fear along his spine, and his knees turned to wax. You did not with impunity God damn a white man; not even an overseer.

"I said 'God damn it.'" His voice shook.

"Really? Is it possible that I misunderstood you?"

"I'm sorry if—what I said—could be misunderstood." Tony sat down hurriedly, for to be seated offered some security. He even dropped the riding crop. Let Fiddler see that he was helpless, unarmed. He wished Fiddler would step back a little, would not stand so threateningly near.

He was relieved to see the battle light fade in the other's eye. The overseer looked at the ledgers on the desk, the letter press on its stand in the corner, all the familiar objects here. "Is there anything you want to ask me, Mr. Currain?" Tony hastily shook his head. God almighty, no, no questions. Let the man go!

So he shook his head, and Fiddler nodded. "Then I'll bid you good-by," he said.

When the other was gone, it was some time before Tony risked rising and going quietly upstairs. Through the open front door he saw his horse at the hitch rail there; but he would not ride today. Fiddler might bushwhack him on some woodland trail. He called Joseph. "I've sent the overseer to Martinston," he said. "Let me know when he's gone."

He stayed in his room till Joseph came to say Fiddler had ridden away. At once then, he felt loneliness press down on him. He would miss James Fiddler. It was something, among so many dark faces, to have a white man around. Self-pity swept him, and a profound sense of loss. Now there was no friend near to whom he might turn; no friend except that familiar bottle.

But he found reassurance in the bottle, and at length inspiration too. He shouted for Joseph, bade the Negro send 'Phemy. When she came, speaking curtly to remind himself that despite the fright James Fiddler had given him he was still master, he said:

"'Phemy, I'm getting tired of that peg leg of Joseph's thumping around me all the time. It makes me nervous. That girl of yours, can she wait on table?"

"Yassuh." He saw the spark in 'Phemy's dark eye. You couldn't fool a nigger. They always knew. But what difference did that make? They were his, body and soul, the lot of them. They knew that, too. They did what they were told.

"Good," he said. "Keep Joseph out of my sight, then. Send that girl of yours in here. Let her wait on me."

16

DARRELL, though his detail to the Quartermaster's department protected him against conscription, seldom appeared in Richmond. To do so was to invite hostile glances from every pretty girl he met, jeering outcries from small boys on the streets, an occasional slur from men. To enter the army would have silenced his critics, but he had no intention of doing so; there were so many less dangerous and more profitable ventures to which he might turn. He and his father were partners, united by a common greed. If their business affairs required on Darrell's part an occasional trip to Richmond, he came without ostentation and seldom showed himself in public places.

Mr. Pudrick's purchase of surplus slaves at Chimneys involved such a trip. The whole transaction, since Darrell did not trust the slave dealer and meant to deceive his father, was devious and involved. Field hands were worth from fifteen hundred to two thousand dollars, and other Negroes in proportion; but the price which Tony drunkenly agreed to accept was calculated on a basis of twelve hundred and fifty dollars for an able-bodied hand, and the total was just under fifty thousand dollars. By the bill of sale which Darrell drew, the slaves became not Pudrick's property but his. In Raleigh he sold the slaves to Pudrick for sixty-five thousand dollars; but, not satisfied with this, he required Mr. Pudrick to accept a bill of sale at sixty thousand, to give him a draft on the Farmer's Bank in Richmond for that sum, and pay the difference in currency. The dealer said resentfully:

"If your father finds out you're lining your own pocket at his expense, he'll take it out of your hide."

"If he finds it out I'll perforate yours," Darrell pleasantly assured him.

"That's a game two can play," said chubby little Mr. Pudrick, a cold light in his blue eyes.

Darrell chuckled. "Now, now; there's enough for all of us. No need to fight over the carcass, man."

The draft, when Pudrick handed it to him, was payable to Streean; and Darrell grinned when he saw this, but he accepted it. In Richmond he made Streean agree to divide the difference between the amount of the draft and the fifty thousand due Tony.

"Don't be small about it, Papa," Darrell smilingly warned the older man. "After all, you've undertaken to turn Uncle Tony's money into diamonds for him. You can make a profit there and charge him a commission besides." He added cheerfully: "And I may meet highwaymen before I can deliver the stones to Uncle Tony; so it's not a bad bargain, take it all in all."

Streean laughed. "Darrell, my boy, you're too grasping! I'll keep his stones in safekeeping here till he can come for them, and thus avoid the hazards of the road."

Darrell stayed a week or two in Richmond. The city was jubilant over the overwhelming defeat of the Yankees in two or three days of heavy fighting on the familiar ground at Manassas. The change in the public temper since April and May, when even government officials were fleeing from the threatened city, was complete. Then McClellan's great army had been at Richmond's very gate; now there were only scattered and inconsiderable forces left anywhere on the Peninsula, and the last Yankees in northern Virginia were racing headlong, a shattered mob, back to the Potomac and to Washington. With a ready optimism Richmond forgot its fears, and just as a year before after First Manassas, so now again everyone was sure the war was won and independence near. Those who in April and May had fled came trooping back, the streets were full of brawling soldiers and of those who preyed upon them, the gambling houses were at full blast again. Everyone seemed to know that Lee would march into Maryland, the people there would flock to join his ranks, Washington must fall. Before the year's end the North would be prostrate.

Dolly was as exuberant as anyone; but Darrell and his father were not so well pleased at the prospective early end to the war. Darrell said frankly: "Hope the Yankees don't quit yet, Papa. Every month the war lasts is money in our pockets."

Streean scowled. "You talk too much, Darrell. Think what you like, but keep such thoughts to yourself."

Tilda said chidingly: "Yes, dear! You musn't talk so, when so many of our men have been killed, and everyone's so sad and grieving."

Darrell laughed in open derision. "You don't fool anyone, Mama. You know darned well you enjoy it!"

"Why, Darrell, what a thing to say!" She bridled indignantly.

"Oh I've seen through you since I was a boy. You hate the lot of them, from Aunt Cinda down! I don't blame you, either, the way they've treated you."

"You're simply horrid." She appealed to her husband. "Redford, don't let him say these dreadful things!"

Streean made an irritated gesture. "Oh hush, Tilda. That damned family of yours has always treated us like dirt and you know it. I'd like to see them get their deserts—and so would you."

Tilda made a helpless sound; and Darrell drawled: "If they keep on being heroes, there won't be many of them left. Clayton and Julian and that husband of Vesta's——"

"Oh, dear little Julian is alive," Tilda reminded him. "In a hospital in Washington. Cinda's gone to be with him."

"I know. Anne Tudor went with her, damn it! I called to pay my respects to her the other day." Darrell grinned. "Her father seemed delighted to report she was not at home." He rose, yawning. "This house smells," he said. "I'm going out to get some air."

He had when he left the house no particular goal in mind. For a while he walked aimlessly—and his thoughts moved at random too. They touched this recent business of the slaves from Chimneys, and remembering Tony made him think of Nell Albion. He had not seen her for years; he had been then a reckless youngster, had thought of her as an old woman to whom—for the fun of annoying Uncle Tony—he had paid some flattering attention. Yet she had been, in a mature way, sufficiently attractive so that he sometimes forgot she was old enough to be his mother. Probably by this time she had become a draggled drab or a silly old woman trying with paint and powder to seem younger than she was. It would be amusing to watch her antics. Doubtless she was lonely enough to welcome any visitor.

So he was surprised, on being admitted, to find that Nell was not alone. When the door opened, he heard masculine voices in the drawing room; he gave his name, and a moment later she came into the hall to greet him.

"Why, Dal!" she cried, in frank pleasure. "I haven't seen you for ever so long."

She looked younger than he remembered, and she was beautiful, no doubt of that; richly beautiful, her cheek and throat smooth, her hair warm and heavy about her face, her eyes the eager eyes of a happy girl. "Too long," he echoed; and clapped his hand to his brow in pretended despair. "Heavens, what a fool I've been!"

She laughed easily. "Same charming Dal, aren't you? Come in and meet these gentlemen." He followed her, and she said: "Congressman Means, and Captain Pew, this is Mr. Streean."

Darrell bowed with a cold formality to a fat little man with a dyed mustache and a small pointed beard, on whose bald brow veins crawled like worms in the gutter after rain, and to a tall calm man with a steady eye. The tall man said easily: "I believe I have the honor of your sister's friendship."

Darrell stared at him in sudden anger. For any man to speak of Dolly in this house was an affront to her; and Darrell was on the point of stiff rejoinder; but something in the Captain's manner made him decide he did not wish to quarrel with Captain Pew.

"Ah, indeed?"

"Yes, Miss Dolly has sometimes given me the pleasure of her company."

Darrell thought Dolly must be even cleverer than he had supposed if she could keep such a man as this one dangling. Nell crossed to the couch. "Sit down, do, gentlemen," she urged; and she told Darrell: "Mr. Means has just announced to us that General Lee is about to invade Maryland."

Darrell caught the faint amusement in her tone, and he looked at the fat little man. "Ah, Mr. Means. Then you have the General's confidence?"

Means flushed, and Nell explained: "Congress has assembled, you know, Darrell. Mr. Means——"

Darrell grinned. "Ah, they've come out of their holes again, have they?" There was something daunting about Captain Pew, but to Mr. Means, obviously, you could say what you chose. "I thought Mc-Clellan's army made you all run so fast and far you'd never find your way back."

Mr. Means harumphed with embarrassment, but Captain Pew said mildly: "I presume, Mr. Streean, you helped drive the enemy away from Richmond?"

Darrell felt the impact of that question. "I'm detailed to the Quartermaster's department," he explained, damning himself for his own apologetic tone. If Captain Pew took Mr. Means's quarrels upon himself, then the fat man was no longer fair game; yet he ventured a counter question. "What is your service, sir?"

Nell said quickly: "Captain Pew commands a blockade-runner, Dal."

Darrell's interest quickened, and Captain Pew smiled and said: "So both of us are profitably occupied, Mr. Streean." There was now a certain affability in his tone.

"Your duty carries the greater risk," Darrell suggested, suddenly eager to be on friendly terms with this man.

"There's little risk." Captain Pew seemed not at all reluctant to talk about himself. "The blockading squadron is kind enough to carry lights at each masthead, so it's easy enough to avoid the enemy ships. At Nassau they cruise off Abaco Light; so we approach by the Tongue of Ocean, or keep clear of the reefs around Eleuthera and come in from the east. Either way needs daylight and a man at the masthead to look out for coral heads; but there's two or three fathoms of water, and we draw less than eleven feet, so it's just a matter of taking care."

Darrell knew nothing of reefs and fathoms, but he nodded wisely, and Nell said: "I suppose New Providence is a lovely island."

Captain Pew smiled. "I don't know. From the sea it just looks like a flat desert of scrub brush and some sandy beaches. Of course it's hot in summer, a hurricane a year ago, and yellow fever every year, more or less. It's been bad this year."

Nell shivered. "I wouldn't care for that."

"The town is beautiful, in a way," the Captain said thoughtfully,

"The houses are mostly white, sometimes even the roofs; and so are the roads and streets, and everyone dresses in white clothes." He smiled. "It's hard on the eyes, with the sun glaring down; but of course there's lots of shade, banana and orange trees, and laurel. And the black faces. The negro women wear bright colors, the brightest they can find. They look like walking rainbows. And there are millions of humming birds and butterflies and flowers, so there's color enough. The flowers mostly open in the evening, so nights smell sweet."

Darrell smiled. "Enough to make a man turn poet."

Captain Pew seemed faintly embarrassed at this remark; he said casually: "Well, I'm only there on business, just long enough to move cargo and start for Wilmington. Coming into Wilmington's as simple as entering Nassau. We've the choice of two channels, New Inlet or over the western bar. We can come up or down the coast within a biscuit's toss of the breakers, too close inshore for them to follow us, and slip in as we choose."

"Doesn't sound easy to me," Darrell admitted. "But I'm not a seafarer."

Captain Pew smiled. "The Yankee skippers might as well be landsmen. They stay on post where they're easily seen and dodged, when the same number of vessels cruising out in the Gulf Stream could hedge us in completely."

Nell said thoughtfully: "The Northerners might welcome that suggestion, Captain." She made a laughing gesture. "But they would doubtless ignore it, just as General McClellan refused to believe Jackson was coming till it was too late to save himself."

Captain Pew remarked: "I had not heard that McClellan was informed beforehand."

"He must have been," she reminded him composedly. "Half Richmond knew it, and Richmond is full of spies."

Darrell asked the Captain: "You spoke of profit in your enterprises?"

"To be sure. Even the common sailors are paid a hundred dollars gold, every month. Yes, sometimes more. And bounties."

"Captains in proportion?"

"Five thousand gold," Pew assured him. "And the captain can usually bring back a private venture in luxury goods on which his profit is substantial." He added: "Of course the big gains go to the owners and to the Nassau merchants. They need only take title to the cotton we carry off to them, ship it in a neutral bottom to England, and take their commissions. And the owner—" He laughed. "Well, if his ship makes three successful voyages before she is captured, he has made his fortune."

Little Mr. Means cleared his throat. "Ah-hum!" Having caught their attention he said pompously: "All these private profits should accrue to the Confederate Treasury. Governor Vance assures me that as soon as he is inaugurated he proposes to urge the purchase by North Carolina of a blockade-runner. The Confederacy too has made a beginning in that direction. In fact I may say that vessels are now being purchased in England for this trade."

"Of course, the trade is just starting," Captain Pew told them. "But there will soon be a swarm of ships under private ownership. I contemplate the purchase of another myself. It excites my cupidity to see so many neglected opportunities." He spoke to Darrell. "When you arrived, we were discussing the possibility that Mr. Means and Mrs. Albion might participate in my new venture."

Darrell looked at Mr. Means, who colored in some embarrassment. "Ah-hum!" The little man cleared his throat again. "As a public man I advocate what seems to me the proper policy; yet if my counsel is ignored, I may surely take advantage of the opportunity left open."

"Exactly," the Captain assented. "And I will try to make our mutual investment a profitable one."

Darrell leaned forward. "See here, sir, my father and I have some funds to invest. Perhaps——"

Captain Pew showed what Darrell acknowledged was a natural reluctance to admit too many to share the prospective profits; but Darrell argued that the risk would also be divided. With success, the enterprise might be enlarged: more vessels, more profits. The Captain yielded a little and a little more; Darrell, intoxicated by these successes, forgot his first impression that Captain Pew was a daunting and a dangerous man. He felt he had met the other on his own ground and won a victory. Nell from the first was mildly on his side; Mr. Means was chiefly concerned with keeping his own participation secret. It might be misunderstood. Nell, smiling a little, agreed that this was true.

"For a member of Congress to profit from the straits in which the Confederacy finds herself—yes, you are right, Mr. Means. Perhaps you would care to let one of us take over your share?"

"Ah-hum!" The fat man chuckled. "Not necessary, Mrs. Albion; not necessary at all. Scruples need never be carried to extremes." He rose. "So it may be considered settled. Now I must say good night. Certain matters——"

He looked expectantly at Captain Pew, but the Captain did not stir. Mr. Means might have sat down again, but Nell had risen to go with him to the door. Captain Pew, when he and Darrell were alone, speaking quietly under cover of the voices in the hall, inquired: "You are not leaving, Mr. Streean?"

Darrell smiled. "Nor you, Captain?"

The Captain chuckled and drew a gold coin from his pocket. "Leave it to chance?" Darrell nodded; the coin spun.

"Heads," said Darrell.

Captain Pew glanced at the coin in his palm; he shrugged, surrendering. As he dropped the gold piece in his pocket, the front door closed, and Nell rejoined them. Captain Pew came to his feet. "I too must go," he confessed. He spoke to Darrell. "You and your father and I can discuss details tomorrow."

Darrell nodded as casually as possible, hoping his manner suggested that this was after all only one among his many ventures; he was anxious to impress this cold-eyed man who made him feel like a child.

When Nell returned from seeing the Captain to the door, Darrell said quizzically: "So we're rid of them."

"Captain Pew doesn't usually leave the field so easily."

He nodded, laughed. "Dolly may discover that, one day."

"I can see that she might find him fascinating," Nell commented. "Of course he's a scoundrel; but at least he makes no secret of it."

"That reminds me," he drawled, "I saw Uncle Tony recently."

Her eyes met his in warning. "He and I are old friends, you know."

"When did you see him?"

"A few weeks ago."

Darrell laughed. "I hadn't seen him in years. Shocking old sot. Let's not speak of him. He's changed. You've not, you know; or if you have, I wish all changes were so enchanting." She smiled, and he said: "I used to think of you as an old woman; attractive, something of the coquette perhaps, but—well, old."

"I'm older now, by—how many years is it?"

"You seem no older than I."

"Perhaps it is you who have aged." Her eyes considered him. "I seem to see the ravages of—time, is it, Dal?"

"What have you been doing with yourself?" he insisted.

"Why, I've been—busy, and happy."

"Busy?"

"The hospitals," she reminded him. "And for a time I worked for Mr. Memminger. The Confederacy is printing so many bonds, so much currency that the Treasury keeps a room full of ladies signing bills and bonds all day long."

He grinned. "Working in a money factory? Did you bring home an occasional sample of your product?"

She said: "I gave up the work. There were so many whose need of employment was greater than mine, who have no other income, ladies driven from their homes in northern Virginia, refugees."

Darrell nodded indifferently. "So you've been busy. But the happiness?" At this question, he thought there was concern in her eyes, and felt a lively curiosity. As an experiment he rose. "See here, Nell, this is an embarrassingly formal room. I remember a much pleasanter little nest upstairs."

"I no longer receive there."

Darrell smiled teasingly down at her. "Your discretion does you credit, Nell; but isn't it suspicious?"

"Suspicious?"

"That little room was not sacrosanct in Uncle Tony's—reign. Has he a successor?"

"You used to be a nice boy, Dal," she said quietly, "but you were always impudent. That could be forgiven—in a boy."

He eyed her shrewdly. "Those roses in your cheeks, that sparkle in your eye!" And then in delighted astonishment: "Why, God bless me, you're blushing! I'd not believe it of you, Nell!"

For a moment she did not speak. Then she said evenly: "Good night, Darrell."

"Oh come now—" Her eyes held his; he tried to laugh, shook his head. "I'm not going so soon." He sat down again, defiantly, as though to stay forever. "Nell, listen."

She rose, moved toward the mantel where a bell pull hung. He saw her intent, leaped after her; but she turned swiftly to face him.

And there was, from nowhere, a small double-barrelled Deringer in her hand, levelled at him fair.

He stopped in his tracks, but he laughed in quick amusement. "Why, Nell, you look dangerous!"

She nodded. "I am, Dal. Be sure of that." With her left hand, the little weapon steady, she reached behind her to the bell pull. He spoke in sudden anger.

"A little late, these scruples, Nell!"

For a moment then he knew fright, for there was death in her eyes; but then steps sounded on the stair. As Milly appeared in the door the pistol hid itself in the folds of Nell's skirt.

"Good night, Mr. Streean," she said.

He bowed, choking with rage. "Good night, ma'am."

Outside the house he turned to look back. Certainly Uncle Tony had a successor. Some day he would make it his pleasure to know a little more about that successor who had made her so happy and so beautiful. It occurred to him suddenly that the successor might be Captain Pew, and, thinking of the Captain, he remembered their conversation; so when he came home and found Redford Streean still at his desk, he spoke of the blockader.

"I've seen him dancing attendance on Dolly," Streean agreed, and Darrell said dryly:

"I wouldn't take him for a dancing man; but he has an interesting proposal in hand." He related their conversation. "I suggested he talk with you."

"It sounds interesting," Streean agreed. "I'll suggest he come here so he and I can talk privately."

"Privately?" Darrell laughed. "With Dolly around?"

"You'll have to see she's not at home when he comes." When

Darrell objected that he wished a voice in whatever arrangement was made, Streean said: "I won't settle anything without you. Make Dolly take you to see Enid's new house. Trav has bought a place on Clay Street. Dolly and Enid seem to like each other."

Darrell reluctantly agreed, and next day he and Tilda and Dolly went to call on Enid, and she delighted in showing him everything, leading him happily here and there, explaining this and that. He amused himself by paying her many compliments, at which she bridled like a girl. Women never realized that their charms faded. She had always had an eager ear for his faintly veiled audacities, so phrased that for a woman to appear to understand them was half surrender. If it had been worth the trouble, he would have made her his mistress long ago, as her mother had been Uncle Tony's; but it was certainly not worth the trouble now. Besides, Uncle Trav had a quality that Darrell recognized and respected. In the role of a betrayed husband he might be dangerous. Darrell asked Enid where Trav was.

"Oh he's gone to Chimneys to see Tony." They had finished their inspection of the new house, were back in the drawing room with Dolly and Tilda; and Enid cried: "That reminds me, Tilda. Clarice Pettigrew called this morning. You know we used to be neighbors at Chimneys. Mr. Pettigrew was killed at Manassas last year, and one of her sons is in a hospital here, and dying, she thinks."

"There are hundreds of poor boys here now," Tilda agreed. "It's terrible to see them, Enid."

"Well, I certainly don't intend to see them," Enid declared. "It would make me sick. Clarice was just out of her mind. I think that's why she called, really. She just had to have someone to talk to. We never saw much of each other at Chimneys. They were very gay, always off gallivanting somewhere; and of course Trav never wanted to go anywhere, as long as he could spend his days with white trash and niggers. Oh, that's what I started to tell you. I had a nurse for the children for a while, a bright mulatto named Sapphira, and she was just wickedly beautiful, and Trav was always—well, I made him sell her to Mr. Pettigrew. Clarice says Tony has bought her back again. You know how Tony is, and I'll just bet Trav told him about her. He—" She broke off, clapped both hands over her mouth. "Heavens, I shouldn't say such things! I forgot you were here, Darrell."

Darrell said in a gravely reassuring tone: "I didn't hear a word, Cousin Enid. She's beautiful, eh?"

"Oh, beautiful as sin, really." She went on: "And now Trav's at Chimneys. He said he wouldn't be gone long, but if that girl's there——"

Darrell saw his mother listening avidly. She would spread this whisper, and it would run along busy feminine tongues as swiftly as a telegram along a wire. Enid knew this as well as he. Uncle Trav ought to take a riding crop to her, teach her discretion. "What's the girl's name?" he asked. "I was at Chimneys recently, may have seen her."

"Sapphira," Enid told him; and Dolly laughed teasingly.

"You're awfully interested, Darrell, it seems to me."

"Just wondered if I'd seen her." If this wench was a house servant, Uncle Tony had kept her out of sight. "I'll probably drop in at Chimneys again before long, Cousin Enid; see if she's all you say."

After their participation in Captain Pew's ventures had been arranged, Darrell proposed to his father that he return to Chimneys and take Uncle Tony the proceeds of that sale of slaves; but Streean wished him to sail with Captain Pew on the next trip to Nassau. "I'd like to go myself," the older man explained. "One of us ought to keep an eye on the Captain. He's——" He smiled. "Well, Captain Pew doesn't seem to me entirely devoid of self-interest, Darrell. But I've too many irons in the fire, so you'd best go."

Darrell assented. Uncle Tony could wait, and that unknown Sapphira.

17

TRAV had already decided that when he was strong enough he would go to Chimneys to bring back house servants for Enid; but James Fiddler's word made him hurry his departure. As a result, the journey exhausted him, and the jostling stage awoke a ferocious pain in the region where the ball had pierced his body. When he arrived at Martinston he was so near collapse that he put up at Pete Loury's tavern, intending to go on to Chimneys next day, when he would be rested.

But in the morning, though rebellious at his own weakness, he felt unable to move. He was troubled too by something in the tavern keeper's manner, and by the actions of the servants at the inn. The Negro who carried his bag to his room had scuttled away, and in the morning no one came to him till he heard shuffling footsteps in the hall outside the door and called, and a Negro girl with broom and dustpan looked in.

He asked her to summon her master, and when Pete Loury came to the door Trav saw in his eyes an embarrassed uncertainty.

"Mawnin', Mister Currain," Pete said awkwardly. "Right smart of a mawnin', now ain't it?" The sun was streaming through the windows.

"Well, I don't feel so smart myself," Trav confessed. "I got a hole through me, here a while back, that a mouse could crawl through; and the trip didn't do me any good. I'm going to lie abed today, if it won't be too much of a bother to you."

"Sho, no trouble at all," Pete assured him. "Yankees too much for you, wuz they?"

"Why, they laid me low for two months. Pete, I'd be obliged if you'd send word to Mr. Currain at Chimneys that I'm here. I'll be able to go on tomorrow, if he could send the carriage in for me."

"I'll do that, to be shore. And I'll have old Miranda fix you up a real nice mess of breakfast."

He turned, almost with relief, to depart; and Trav said: "Come back when you have time; let me hear the news."

"Well, we git our news mostly when the stage comes. I did heah they's some new fighting up't Manassas Junction."

"I know. I heard that yesterday. But I mean the news around here, Pete. I've been away a long time."

The tavern keeper hesitated. "Well, ain't much happens heah, but I'll be back."

A Negro presently brought a loaded tray, and Trav, devouring bacon and grits and coffee, hot bread and dark molasses, felt his strength return. When Pete at last appeared, he asked questions; and Pete, at first cautiously, told him of this man and of that one, living furtively on their scattered farms and ready at the approach of authority to vanish into the wooded highlands.

Trav said understandingly: "I can see being in the army might come hard on some."

"Why, I sh'd jedge it's all right for them that likes it," Pete admitted. "You-uns that looks to git something out of it, or to hang on to what you got, you might look at it different; but they ain't a thing in it for the likes of us around heah, only laying in camp to git sick and die off, or gitting theyselves kilt by the Yankees." Pete himself was an old man, dried and lean and frail. "It wouldn't suit me," he said frankly. "And I don't know as I'd blame a man if it didn't suit him."

"It didn't suit me," Trav admitted. "I never thought to do any fighting. I set out to rustle up corn and hog meat for the army to eat, all such." Unconsciously, as always when he met these old friends, he fitted his speech to the other's pattern. "But if you get nigh enough to it, soon or late you're bound to take a hand."

"I dunno," Pete reflected. "Used to be I liked a good gouging as well as the next one; but I neveh did have no stummick for cuttin' and shootin' folks. It's too gol-blamed permanent."

Trav nodded, and his own thoughts made his anger rise. "I hate the whole business the way you hate a rattler. I just want to kill it, kill it dead."

"Well," the tavern keeper commented, "I reck'n theah's enough of you all that feel the same way to keep it going long as yo're a mind to. But the thing is, it comes on a lot of folks that don't feel the way you do. Law says a white man with twenty slaves don't have to go in the army less'n he's a mind to; but that don't let out anybody around heah. Ain't none of us got any twenty slaves. So we-uns do the fighting and you-uns set on the verandy all cool and comfo'table and watch youh people sweat." He seemed to remember that his word might give offense, for he said apologetically: "Leastways that's the talk I heah." He spat accurately at the white china spittoon beside the bed. "Men come home on furlough and tell't Richmond's full o' young sprigs that's got details, or bought themselves out of fighting or something. They ain't nobody got details around heah."

Trav would not willingly agree, but he could not honestly dissent. What Pete was saying was true enough. As the law stood, no man of means or influence need fight unless he chose; but the poor man had no choice. "I saw James Fiddler in Richmond," he said. "He'll be missed at Chimneys. I didn't think he'd ever leave."

The innkeeper looked at him in a sidelong fashion. "That young Mr. Streean—youh nephew, ain't he?" Trav nodded. "Him and a man named Pudrick come along a while back and bought a lot of the people. Pudrick let on they'd been bought cheap. Did some bragging. I sh'd jedge Jim Fiddler didn't hold with selling them."

Trav held his eyes steady, hid his astonishment. The overseer had not told him this, and Pete's disclosure shocked and angered him; but he would not say any word critical of Tony. "Chimneys had more people than were needed there," he said.

Pete nodded. "I jedge the place c'n git along with what's left," he assented. He rose. "Well, you rest yourself. I sent a boy to Chimneys to tell Mr. Currain yo're here."

Trav, left alone, lay for a while in thought of this which Tony had done; and he slept and woke when a bountiful dinner appeared. He drowsed again till he heard a horseman gallop into town, and excited voices below; and not long after, Chelmsford Lowman came to his door.

The postmaster's manner was hearty enough. "Heard you was here," he said. "But Pete said you was wore out. But here's some news will make you perk up. Word just come from Sal'sbury that General Lee give the Yanks another going over last Friday and Sat'day, up at Manassas, same as we did last summer. Busted 'em wide open till there ain't what you could call an army left." He laughed in a rich content. "Looks like it's bad luck for the Yanks to come down Richmond way. You'd think they'd learn."

Trav had heard yesterday first rumors of the opening of that battle; he asked many questions now, unwilling to accept too easily this word of glorious victory. So often rumor coupled with the easy optimism of the South to exaggerate successes. But Lowman knew enough to make it certain that this had been an overwhelming defeat for Pope's army. "A signal victory," General Lee called it; and Lee was a man who weighed his words.

Trav felt a deep impatience to be back with the army again, to do his share of these great deeds; but first he must see Tony. Next morning he was strong enough to move; and in the late forenoon the carriage drew up at the tavern door, and Tony came to welcome him.

This was an affable and cheerful Tony, readier to laugh than Trav had ever known him to be. During the drive back to Chimneys, Tony's monotonous good humor began to be disturbing. To Trav's relief, for he dreaded questioning his brother, Tony volunteered the statement that James Fiddler was gone. "More fool he," he said with a chuckle. "But he was bound to don the dreadful panoply of war." Trav suspected that Tony had had no small amount to drink this morning. "I tried to make him see his folly; yes, and his disloyalty, too. He's as much of a deserter as any of these white trash fellows hiding out around here."

"You'll miss him."

"Oh I think not." Tony's persistent laughter was increasingly irritating. "I'm a pretty good farmer myself, Trav. Enjoy it, you know. Mighty interesting. And profitable, too. By the way, I've done the sensible thing, sold off all the surplus people." Trav felt the other's sidelong glance, kept his own eyes upon the road. Ed Blandy's cabin was just around the next bend, still hidden by the pine wood. "They were eating us up like a swarm of locusts," Tony declared. "Bound to make trouble. Not enough work to keep them busy, and the ones that were working were quarreling with the ones who weren't. Niggers have to be busy, Trav. Keep them busy. Then they're happy." This clipped way of speech, these ejaculatory sentences were something new. So was this loquacity, and the empty laughter. "Should have consulted you all, no doubt, but you were off to the wars. Seemed best to act in your interests."

"It's all in the family," Trav assented. "You're in charge here." Each of them—Faunt at Belle Vue, Brett at the Plains, he himself here at Chimneys and later at Great Oak—had always acted on his own decisions. It was true they never sold slaves, but Tony's deed was done past mending, and recriminations were folly.

"Might have discussed it with Mama while she was here," Tony admitted. "I did talk with Redford Streean. He agreed it was wise to get a price for them while we can. Didn't want to bother Mama. She's aged fast."

They came to Ed Blandy's house. "I'll stop a minute," Trav decided, "if you don't mind waiting. Come in with me?"

But Tony declined to do so. "I haven't the pleasure of the lady's acquaintance." A faint derision in his tone made Trav's ears burn.

He had from Mrs. Blandy and from the children a shy welcome. They were none of them, except the new baby who crowed and gurgled on the wide bed in absorbed contemplation of his own toes, at ease; but this did not surprise Trav. Mrs. Blandy said Ed was fine, the last she heard. He and Tom Shadd were together in the Eleventh North Carolina, stationed at Camp Rains, near Wilmington. Trav did not know this regiment; and she said the Colonel was an Englishman and that Ed thought he worked them awful hard. Ed said Colonel Leventhorpe had the loudest voice he'd ever heard; and Trav chuckled.

"I'll match General Longstreet against him, Mrs. Blandy. The General can wake a mule up half a mile away without raising his voice above a whisper."

They laughed together at that, and the children too, all of them for the moment forgetting to be afraid of Trav. He said the corn looked good, and she said she and the children had worked as hard as they knew how, and Trav told her to remember him to Ed when she could, and she promised to do so. He returned to the waiting carriage, refreshed by this brief interlude. People like Mrs. Blandy made you feel as good as a deep draft of buttermilk cold from the spring house. She was somehow like Cinda; and Trav, back in the carriage, thinking of Cinda, said:

"By the way, Tony, did you know Cinda had word of Julian?"

"No. Streean told me he was missing after Williamsburg."

"Well, he's alive," Trav said. "Or at least he was, the latest news she had. He's in a hospital in Washington. She went to bring him home."

Tony chuckled. "Washington? Maybe she'll call on that nephew of ours, Trav."

Trav looked at his brother in regretful comprehension. The revelation of his kinship to Lincoln had not awakened in him any sense of personal humiliation. If his father's seed were somehow the source from which this war sprang, why then he would do his best to exterminate the dreadful weed; but he felt, beyond this obligation, no burden of shame upon himself. Tony, from his tone, did. Trav asked gently: "You're worrying about that, are you?"

Tony laughed. Why must he always laugh? "Worry? No! Damned clever fellow, that son of a bastard! He's fooled the Yankees, got to be President! Trouble is, he's out to get even with his grandpa's family. We'll all be no better than beggars before he's through with us; but I'm going to show the laddie boy I'm as clever as he is. He won't beggar me!"

Trav, not knowing what to say, said nothing, and Tony flicked the horses idly with the whip, but presently Trav's silence seemed to oppress him. "New Governor coming in, in a few days now."

Trav accepted the lead. "Colonel Vance. Yes, I know. He had a big majority."

"Of course. We're against this damned war, down here, you know. And so's Zeb Vance. He was against secession."

"Not after Lincoln called on North Carolina to furnish troops."

Tony chuckled. "Oh, no one dared say what he thought after that.

Vance volunteered, Colonel of the Twenty-sixth. Sure. But everyone knows where he really stands. Even the Philadelphia papers said his election was a Union victory. They sent soldiers into the country to keep deserters from going to the polls and voting for him; but he won anyway. We don't like Jeff Davis down here, sending Virginia men to impress our guns and the cloth from our mills. Governor Vance will show them that North Carolina is still a sovereign state, boss in her own borders."

"We'll never beat the North if every Confederate state takes that attitude."

"We'll take care of ourselves."

Trav said soberly: "I think maybe you're wrong about North Carolina, Tony. She's sent over sixty thousand volunteers already."

Tony laughed. "Yes, but half of them have deserted and come home."

Trav hesitated, but before he could speak the big house came into view, and a moment later they turned up the drive. The familiar sweep of cultivated lowlands, the rolling wooded hills, the distant mountains made his pulse quicken with content, and he felt strength flow into him. Next day he rode for an hour, the day after he rode with Tony till dinner time; and all he saw was good. The plantation was in order, every field well tended. It was true that for this season's crops James Fiddler was largely responsible; but Tony would be able to go on. He could manage—if he would. Perhaps Big Mill might come on here to act as driver, to keep the hands at their work. Certainly the gigantic Negro had accepted responsibility at Great Oak and met it well.

Trav waited for an opportunity to suggest this to Tony; but Tony always breakfasted alone in his room, and by the time he appeared he was a little fuddled. Trav, like any other man, took his thimbleful of brandy before his morning coffee, his juleps and his Madeira when he chose, his quiet glass at bed time; but Tony obviously drank from morning till night. He even carried a flask in his saddlebags; and either he drank a great deal or what he drank affected him more than it should. It was no injustice to say that he was drunk much of the time. At night, more than once, Trav, rather than let 'Phemy see Tony limber-legged, helped him to bed.

'Phemy was a newcomer in the house, but Trav admitted to himself that she was an improvement on Joseph. The peg-legged Negro had been willing, but he was inept; the house was now spotless, and always in perfect order, and this had not been true in Joseph's time. On his first day at Chimneys, Trav asked for Joseph, and found him now in charge of the saw mill where with power from a singing little mountain stream logs were converted into posts and rails and boards for the plantation's many needs. Joseph was happy in his new work; he had always had an accurate eye to decide just how each log should be sawed, slabbed here, slabbed there, planked or quartered, cut into posts, riven into rails. In his two-legged days Joseph could tell at a glance how to get the largest amount of usable material out of a log. He had on his return to the mill calmly assumed command.

So Joseph was all right, and 'Phemy kept the house immaculate. Trav in the past had seldom seen her; but it seemed to him now that behind her dignity and the efficient way in which she foresaw all his needs and Tony's, there was something rancorous and angry, something almost malevolent! He remembered that daughter of hers who was even lighter in color than 'Phemy, and who had nursed the children till Enid insisted he get rid of her. Perhaps 'Phemy had blamed him for selling the girl. He tried to take toward her a kindly tone, suggested there was more work here than she could manage alone.

'Phemy said firmly: "No, thank'ee. I gits along." Curiously, when he spoke to old Maria who still ruled the kitchen, suggesting 'Phemy needed help, she used almost exactly the same words.

"Dat high yaller! Huh, she gwine git along!"

'Phemy's almost arrogant composure puzzled Trav. She was as easy in her manner as though she were the lady of the house; but once, returning with Tony from one of their rides, coming up the path past the quarter and toward the loom house, Trav heard what was unmistakably 'Phemy's voice, shrill with anger.

"Don' you go let dat old goat line you, you heah me! You do an' I'll——"

Then there was a sudden silence, as though the riders had been seen; and Tony beside Trav laughed in that reasonless way of his and lifted his horse to a canter till they came to the house and dismounted there.

So 'Phemy was not always so composed. Trav wondered what had prompted the outburst he overheard; and after she had served their supper that evening, Trav asked Tony some questions about her. Tony chuckled into his glass.

"'Phemy? Her mother was one of the Coyby niggers, came to Great Oak when Mama and Papa were married. She's one of Papa's other bastards, I suppose."

Trav felt his cheeks stiff with anger. "You take all that too hard, Tony."

Tony grinned at him, wagging his head. "Too hard? I'm surprised at you, Trav. Papa and Mama brought me up to think that blood, family was everything. If I took a cut at some nigger wench with a riding switch, Mama used to say that that was no way for a Currain to behave!"

"A man's name doesn't matter. It's what he does."

Tony nodded sagely. "A Currain by any other name would smell as sweet. To be sure."

"Any man makes mistakes. They don't count. It's the fine things he does, the good things."

Tony drained his glass. "So you'd remember only the good. But what did someone say, Trav?—the evil that men do lives after them! Hence, obviously, all the little bastards in the world!"

Trav yielded to sudden anger. "Tony, you drink too much! For God's sake, man, have some self-respect!"

Tony's eyebrows rose in owlish derision. "Self-respect? To be sure. Am I not one of the noble Currains?"

Trav bit his lip. There was no profit in this. Perhaps by talk of other things he could bring Tony back to a saner mood. He began to speak of the need for an overseer or a driver here. It was true that all the good white men were fighting; but Big Mill— He spoke at length, as persuasively as possible; he thought Tony was listening, even though his eyes were closed, till the other presently began to snore.

Trav left him asleep at the table. He went out to the veranda and sat a while, trying to solve this problem. When he came wearily indoors at last, Tony was no longer in his chair. 'Phemy, presumably, had put him to bed.

Next morning, Sunday, the hands were idle; but since Tony did not appear, Trav took a horse and rode far. His strength was almost completely restored; he relished the fine rhythm of the saddle, exulting in his own returning vigor. He came home hot and dusty, and used the shower and came down to the veranda. 'Phemy brought him a julep; before it was done Tony joined him.

Trav saw at once that there was an unnatural excitement in the other; but Tony's laugh was as persistent as ever. "Afraid I dozed off in the middle of your discourse last night, Trav. You were as long-winded as the Reverend What's-his-name, used to hold forth at Bruton Church when I was a boy. Sorry, but I never could stand being preached to." He lifted his glass, let the spicy drink trickle through the ice into his mouth, finished the julep at one long draught, tossed the glass heedlessly over the veranda rail. "Come along, old Slow-and-steady! Dinner time. I saw you off for an early ride this morning. You must be starved."

Trav set his half-empty glass aside and followed Tony through the hall to the dining room; but in the doorway he stopped dead still. A woman stood in the further corner of the room, fear in her eyes. Trav recognized her; 'Phemy's bright mulatto daughter whom he had sold to the Pettigrews long ago.

Tony went to her, took her hand, said amiably: "Come, come, child! Nothing to be afraid of. It's just your Uncle Trav!"

The Negress looked at Trav, her eyes blank with terror. Trav saw with a cold precision and with complete understanding that her dress was fine, and there were jewels in her ears. Her obvious fright reminded him that for this moment she was not to blame. Then he saw 'Phemy in the door that led to the gallery and the kitchen, watching them.

But 'Phemy was not to blame, nor the girl. This was Tony's doing. Trav, still in the doorway, looked at his brother; and Tony, teetering a little, laughed and said:

"This pretty niece of yours presides at my table, Trav, when I wish particularly to grace the board."

Trav turned quietly away. In his room, cold with anger and yet with pity too, he packed his bag and descended the stairs. As he went toward the front door to call for a horse, to ride to Martinston, to put this place forever behind him, he heard Tony laughing in the dining room.

18

ANNE TUDOR, in this summer of 1862, was just past seventeen years old. Judge Tudor had married late in life, and he was forty-three when Anne was born. Anne's mother died soon after the baby's coming, so Anne was an only child; and Judge Tudor in his first grief retired from public life and preferred to stay thereafter at the plantation on the Northern Neck. The fact that when Anne was a year old Fauntleroy Currain, who was the Judge's next-door neighbor, suffered an even worse bereavement, losing both wife and child, drew the Judge and Faunt together.

As a child Anne found Uncle Faunt a jolly and companionable playmate and an understanding friend; and when she came into her 'teens her heart went out to him in the lavish and demonstrative affection of which only girls at that age, not yet schooled in conventional inhibitions, are capable.

Since neither Faunt nor her father ever treated her as a child, it was not till with the outbreak of the war her father decided to move to Richmond that she realized her own youth, and began to suspect that her devotion to Faunt might seem to older people amusing. She clung to it, as though to prove to them and to herself that she was old enough to know her own heart; yet she came to know in Richmond many boys and girls of her own age. Julian was one of them; she liked him, even while this liking seemed to her disloyalty to Faunt. That she seldom saw Faunt and that when she did he seemed almost unconscious of her presence only strengthened her determination to prove her constancy.

When she volunteered to go with Cinda to Washington, she took her father's consent for granted; but after Cinda and Burr had left them he asked her: "Are you surprised that I'm letting you go, Anne?"

"Why, Papa, you always have let me make up my own mind."

"I know." He looked at her thoughtfully. "How old are you?"

"Seventeen, idiot!" Her tone was tenderly affectionate. "You know that as well as I do!"

He smiled, and for a moment he did not speak, and when he did it was carefully. "Anne, I don't want to distress you. But may I just tell you what is in my mind?"

"Why, of course, Papa." She could not guess what was to come.

"I'm sorry your mother isn't alive." She waited, her eyes wide and still. "But you and I have always talked man to man." He hesitated, then went on: "Anne, war changes people. Sometimes men whom you never respected before become valiant warriors and splendid gentlemen; but sometimes the reverse is true. War is—well, it's like strong drink. Some men it magnifies, some it debases."

She knew no way to help him to what he wished to say.

"Sometimes fine men, the finest men, change for the worse," he said regretfully. "Anne, you've always liked and admired Uncle Faunt. But he is changed, Anne. Perhaps by the war, or by his wound and his long illness. I know no other explanation. But believe me, he is changed; changed in ways you can't know. And if you did know, you wouldn't fully understand. And he's often in Richmond. If you stayed here, you would see him." His eyes met hers fairly. "Anne, I'm glad you're not to see Uncle Faunt for a while. That's why I'm glad you're going with Mrs. Dewain."

Anne almost smiled; he was so humble, awkwardly floundering, loving her. She had no faintest idea what he meant. She knew men did disgraceful things, but she did not know what those things were, nor did she wish to know. Uncle Faunt's sins, whatever they were, did not matter now. Nothing mattered except to make her father happy. She came to him, kissing him.

"Why, Papa, I'm surprised at you, making up romances for your daughter just like a gossipy old lady. Of course I've always liked Uncle Faunt; but good gracious, Papa, I'd never go falling in love with him!" In her heart some voice protested at this betrayal, but she

hushed it. "Don't you worry, silly old darling! The minute I'm falling in love with anyone you'll be the first one I'll tell. I'll tell you before the young man even begins to suspect it himself. You wait and
see!"

She found pretty ways to make him forget his fears; but when she
was abed that night, her departure all prepared, she tried to understand
what he had said. His words still had for her no clear meaning; she
only knew that for some reason her father was critical of Uncle Faunt.
Yet surely Uncle Faunt had never done anything he shouldn't; he was
too gentle and sweet and wise and brave and fine!

When early next morning the carriage with Burr and Cinda stopped
at the door she hugged her father hard; she kissed him, bade him not
worry, and went swiftly down the steps to join them. Burr's pass and
the deference that she and Cinda commanded easily overcame any
obstacles General Winder's men might have put in their way. The all-
day journey to Gordonsville seemed to her interminable; for Longstreet's brigades were hurrying to join Jackson there, so the cars were
crammed with troops and the roads she saw from the windows were
full of regiments on the march, and of crawling wagons and great
guns.

"Burr," she said once, "I didn't know an army was all spraddled out
like this. I thought an army was soldiers in nice straight lines like the
drills at the Fair Grounds."

Burr laughed. "No, this is what an army looks like, Anne; men and
wagons and guns and ambulances scattered for miles. The army that
wins battles is the one that gets them un-scattered, gets them all together at the right time."

They talked together in the easy forgetfulness of youth, till Anne
saw Cinda's still eyes and remembered their errand, and fell silent.
But Cinda, as though she guessed Anne's thought, became thereafter
so valiantly merry that when at last they reached Gordonsville and left
the train, Anne squeezed her arm and whispered that she was wonderful.

Burr had left his horse at High Fields, the Forgy home, halfway between Gordonsville and Louisa Court House; and there they were
made as welcome as old friends. Mrs. Forgy said General Lee's head-

quarters were at Orange Court House. Pope's army was concentrated between the Rapidan and the Rappahannock, thirty miles or so northeastward. Stuart had ridden off along the plank road toward Chancellorsville a week ago; but she did not know where he was now.

Burr decided to leave Anne and Cinda here while he went on to find Fitz Lee's brigade. The wait for his return seemed a long one, though on Sunday Major Forgy rode down from Orange Court House with half a dozen brother officers for dinner, and Anne was radiant under their gentle gallantries. Not till late Sunday evening did Burr return, and Faunt came with him. Burr had found General Fitz Lee close by, at Louisa Court House; but he was to move tomorrow through Verdiersville toward Raccoon Ford.

"And if we join him there tomorrow night, he's sure he can arrange something," he promised.

Mrs. Forgy would have put her carriage at their service, but at Burr's suggestion they had brought their habits and were prepared to ride; and Faunt and Burr thought this the wiser plan.

"The carriage will make you keep to the roads," Faunt explained. "Mounted, you can go where you choose." Cinda reminded him that they each had a trunk, and he said the trunks might follow in a farm cart. "But the less you take with you the better," he warned them. "You'll be able to buy anything you need, even in Alexandria. Better leave here whatever you can manage without."

"Not even Anne's little trunk?" Cinda urged. Burr said the trunk could be packed on a mule, and eventually, with some contriving, they managed to cram indispensables into it and into saddlebags. Their hoops would be secured behind their saddles.

That night they made their preparations, and at first sun next morning they set out. Anne, when Faunt joined them, had felt faintly guilty, because it was to make sure she should not see Uncle Faunt for a while that her father had consented to her coming. To appease her own conscience she assumed toward him a mature and aloof dignity; but she was a little hurt to find that on the road he seemed to avoid her, riding most often with Cinda while Burr kept her company.

They went through Louisa, and Anne thought it was a charming little town, the old court house with its small flanking buildings, the comfortable brick houses. Beyond, their road followed gently rolling high ground where they had to pass Fitz Lee's plodding wagon trains; and from an occasional rise they could see through summer haze the bold mass of the Blue Ridge that seemed very far away. "But on a clear day you'd think it wasn't five miles off," Burr assured her. The way swung more northerly, through a region of small farms and tumble-down houses; and to Anne's question Burr explained that the more extensive and substantial places lay to the west, near Boswell Tavern and Gordonsville and Orange. The road began to cross a succession of ridges and deep valleys in which ran bold bright streams, and once she saw what Burr said was an iron furnace a little above the ford they passed. The creeks were headwaters of the North Anna river; one of them, a fair twenty feet wide, was the river itself. The deep valleys were cool and pleasant, and from each ridge they saw the distant mountains marching with them miles away.

When the wagon trains were behind them they had a free road, since Fitz Lee's main body was well ahead; and they took an easy gait staying far enough behind the cavalry that the dust the column raised had time to settle. On one height where there was a church on their right, a large house a little off the road on the left promised hospitality; and they were cordially received and rested and went on. A high cone-shaped hill, still well ahead and a little to the left of their course, seemed to spy upon their approach. "It keeps peeking at us over the tree tops," Anne said laughingly. "Like some old maid peeping out of her window around the blind."

Burr smiled. "That's Clark's Mountain," he said. "And I wouldn't be surprised if someone were watching us. General Jackson probably has a signal station there." The lofty hill had at first seemed far away; but it came nearer, and as they approached its shape seemed to change. No longer a cone, it became a ridge, highest in the center, tapering off to lower ground at either end.

At the crossing of the plank road, a cavalry patrol to which Burr spoke said Stuart had been close to capture that morning near Verdiersville, when a force of Union cavalry surprised him and a few members of his staff at dawn before their horses were bridled.

"General Stuart had to jump his horse over the fence," Burr reported, when he came back to them. "He lost his hat and cloak. That fine hat of his is his pride."

"Don't we all know it!" Cinda agreed, her tone sharp. "Whenever he comes to church, he makes a point of arriving ten minutes late and marching down the aisle to a front seat and swinging that plumed hat against his knees! I'm glad he's lost it!"

Burr smiled. "He's getting a lot of quizzing about it today. He'll be at Raccoon Ford by the time we get there."

Well before sunset, they arrived at General Stuart's headquarters; and he lodged them that night in the farm house on whose veranda he himself would sleep. Anne, though she had seen him riding at the head of his men like a figure out of dreams, had never met him face to face. His great red-brown beard and his huge mustache made him seem enormously full of dignity; but she saw the twinkle in his eyes when he bowed over her hand, the teasing smile with which he said they were his prisoners.

"Pass you through the lines?" he protested, when he heard their desire. "Hardly! If you're the loyal hearts you pretend to be, we'll never willingly lose you; and if you're disloyal, you'd tell all our secrets to General Pope!"

Anne looked uncertainly at Cinda; but Cinda gave him a dry answer. "You'll find you've caught a tartar, General! You'll presently be ready to take any risk to be rid of us."

"Threats?" He frowned elaborately. "I assure you, I'm never afraid —of ladies."

"But when you see the Yankees," she reminded him, "you run so fast you lose your hat."

For an instant in his flashing eye Anne caught a glimpse of the warrior; but then he smiled again. "That debt, Madame," he assured her, "I shall collect one day from General Pope."

Supper was a laughing time, with Anne and Cinda the belles of the occasion and a dozen young officers paying them many compliments. General Stuart turned to a desk and began to write one letter after another, but half his attention was still with them; for presently, without turning, he shouted: "Bob!" On that signal three Negroes appeared: a sleek mulatto with a guitar, and two others inky black. Bob, the mulatto, strummed and sang *Listen to the Mocking Bird,* and one of the others began to whistle an accompaniment, embroidering the air with so many lively flourishes that Anne thought even a mocking bird would have been abashed by the superior excellence of this performance. The whistling Negro seemed to fill the room with bird notes, and Stuart even while he wrote joined in the singing; and at last he called: "Bob, let's have a breakdown!" The mulatto abandoned his guitar for rattling bones, the whistler set the tune, and the third Negro, while Stuart and the other gentlemen kept time with clapping hands, danced heel and toe, faster and faster, his steps an infinite variety, his eyes rolling, sweat beginning to glisten upon his black face, till Anne thought he must collapse in helpless exhaustion. He finished his dance with a bound that took him through the door, and the others vanished with him.

There were other songs thereafter, led by a man named Sweeney with a banjo; and they all sang together, Stuart and his men, Anne and Cinda. They sang *The Dew is on the Blossom* and *Evelyn* and Stuart's ear caught Anne's sweet tones and he invited her to sing for them. *Lorena,* he suggested. She protested that *Lorena* was a man's song, for a man to sing; and he said they would all sing it with her. So she began, but as she sang he signalled the others one by one to silence, so that at last she sang alone.

> It matters little now, Lorena,
>   The past is the eternal past,
> Our heads will soon lie low, Lorena,
>   Life's tide is ebbing out so fast;
> But there's a future. Oh! Thank God!
>   Of life this is so small a part
> 'Tis dust to dust beneath the sod,
>   But there, up there, 'tis heart to heart.

When she finished there was a moment's silence, and no one smiled till Cinda said briskly: "Well, I should think in plain politeness someone should ask me to sing." So they laughed, and General Stuart said she must and she asked:

"Do you know *The Four Marys,* General?" He did not; and she said: "It's an old Scotch song my mother used to sing when we were babies." Anne met Faunt's eyes across the room. Burr was not in the company tonight, was with his own men; but Faunt was attached to

Stuart's headquarters as an aide and scout. "She still sings it, some-times," Cinda told them; and she began, so softly as to impose a silent listening upon them all, and Stuart came near her to hear every word while Sweeney with the lightest touch woke faint chords from his banjo.

> Yest're'en there were four Marys,
> This nicht there'll be but three.
> There was Mary Seaton, and Mary Beaton,
> And Mary Carmichael and me.

The song ran its wistful course; and when it was done, in the mo-ment's hush, Cinda bade them all good night. In their room Anne said happily: "Oh wasn't that fun, Aunt Cinda! And I loved it when you sang." She laughed. "I declare, if war's like this I think I like it." And then in quick regret. "I'm sorry, ma'am. Please."

Cinda touched her hand. "There, darling. It was fun, even for me; but I hope we can go on tomorrow."

Stuart left them next day, moving his headquarters nearer the Ford; but they waited where they were. "We'll follow along when the way is clear for us," Faunt promised, and early Wednesday morning they set out. Faunt was detailed by Stuart, and Burr by Fitz Lee, to see them safely on their way; and since the horses lent them by Mrs. Forgy had been sent back, they were offered an ambulance for transportation. But they both preferred to ride, if mounts could be provided; so new horses were found.

Stuart, Burr said, had crossed the Ford and would push on toward Stevensburg and Brandy Station. They might find roads less crowded if they flanked his march. So after they crossed the Rapidan, their horses splashing through the wide shallows, they turned aside; but they encountered columns of infantry on the move and Burr and Faunt agreed they should rejoin Stuart.

"It's hard to overtake and pass infantry," Burr explained. "Even on horseback! Of course if you meet them they'll make room; but when you're overtaking them, they don't hear you coming, and you have to keep shouting to them to clear the road, and they pretend not to hear and make it as hard for you as they can. They don't like the cavalry anyway."

So they took lanes and byroads, with the mass of Pony Mountain on their right; and they crossed an easy, well-farmed plain. The mountains to the west were in clear fine view today, and nearer, lesser hills bounded the gently rolling valley. They heard presently the distant spatter of pistol shots and the heavier sound of guns as Stuart somewhere north of them herded the Yankee cavalry back across the Rappahannock; and when they came opposite the bold northern end of Pony Mountain, Faunt and Burr agreed they might turn east to Stevensburg. Stuart's patrols would be between them and the Rappahannock, and Jackson's men at Culpeper were filling all the roads that way.

They lodged at Stevensburg that night and next morning rode on toward Brandy Station, and Burr made Anne look back to see Clark's Mountain still watching them around the northern shoulder of Pony Mountain. Leaving Brandy, they followed a slowly ascending byway over rolling hillocks, and kept to the road behind Yew Hills and heard the muffled sounds of the fight at Beverly's Ford beyond those wooded heights; and Anne felt herself part of mysterious events, tremendous and dramatic. Burr and Faunt were forever looking that way, listening always to the sound of distant skirmishing; and once Cinda spoke to Burr, said gently:

"I'm sorry we're keeping you out of all that, Burr. Sorry for your sake. I know you wish you were in it."

"It's all right, Mama."

Anne asked: "What's happening, Burr? Can you tell?"

"We're feeling for their flank, trying to get around it," he explained. "If we can do that, we might hit the railroad behind them, cut their line of supplies." He added: "They captured some of General Stuart's dispatches at Verdiersville, so Pope knows we hoped to trap him between the Rapidan and the Rappahannock. So he's retreating along the railroad, and we're trying to slow him down so he'll have to fight."

During these long daylight hours in the saddle Anne watched Faunt, wondering and wondering. Her father was right. There was surely a change in him. Yet she thought it a good change. He seemed younger, stronger, more alive. He had used to shave his cheeks, but he was letting all his beard grow now; yet that did not account for the difference. Once or twice when the chance of the road left him beside her, almost timidly she asked him questions. "Uncle Faunt, why are so many of these country roads like ditches or creek beds, sunk below the level of the fields? Sometimes I can hardly see out."

"I've never thought," he said. "I suppose it's because every rain really turns the roads into ditches, especially if they're on a slope; and the water washes the dirt away, and nobody troubles to haul it back again."

She nodded, seeing the logic of the suggestion. "It really is only on the hills that they're sunk down," she agreed. "And they're sort of built up, at the bottom of the hills, where the road levels off."

He did not comment, but she led him into talk, trying to understand why her father doubted him. "Are you always with General Stuart, Uncle Faunt?"

"Why, often, yes," he said. "I usually report to him."

"What do you report?"

"Some of us serve as scouts, Anne."

"What is that?" she persisted. "What do you do?"

"Oh, we work by ones and twos, slipping through the lines, dodging the Yankee pickets, hiding near their camps, trying to find out what they're up to." Under her prompting, he told her more and more of his duty. "Why, we work as we can. We usually keep hidden in the daytime, sleep in the woods somewhere, travel at night when we're not so apt to run into an enemy picket. Their fires show us where they are, so we can slip around them." And he explained: "It's important to keep the Yankees from knowing we're near them, so we try not to leave a trail. If we have to cross a muddy road, we dismount and back our horses across, and walk backward ourselves. When we find an enemy encampment we crawl up as close as we can and find out how many there are and where they come from and where they're going to, and take word back to the General."

"You like it, don't you?"

"Yes. Yes, I do. It's like playing a game—hide-and-seek, or Indians, or something like that. I like being cleverer than the Yankees. And it's interesting to know what's happening, or what's going to happen. The men in the ranks never know."

She said innocently, "I'm glad you don't have to do any fighting."

He laughed, and something in that laughter frightened her. "No, fighting isn't our job," he agreed. "We don't fight unless we must. Our task is to hurt the Yankees all we can—and not let them hurt us."

There were pleasant houses north of Brandy and beyond, and at one of these they were made welcome for the night; and when next morning they rode on, almost at once another man joined them. He was sandy-haired, with curiously steady eyes and a forward thrust of his head, and Uncle Faunt introduced him as Mr. Mosby. Anne guessed that he brought some message from General Stuart; for after he had spoken apart to Faunt and Burr they quickened their pace, riding on more rapidly. There was today no whisper of battle in the air, no faintest pinpricks of sound from distant guns. Their road that for a while had run among tilled fields dipped into tangled woodland. After the wide openness of the gently rolling levels from the Rapidan north, to plunge into this forest maze where the eye could see no farther than the next turning was oppressive and smothering. Anne was glad they rode more rapidly, eager to burst out of this blind meandering into open land again.

They pushed on and came down through the forest to a narrow stream. Burr said this was the Rappahannock, Waterloo Bridge, and Cinda asked:

"Then isn't this the road to Warrenton? Brett and I have visited up here. I've heard of Waterloo."

"Yes." Anne saw Burr's eyes shine. "We've slipped around the Yankee flank," he said exultantly. "Stuart's gone on to Warrenton ahead of us with a strong force, to hit the railroad behind Pope."

The bridge rattled under the hoofs of their horses; and when they emerged from the shadowed depths of the forest Anne realized that the sky was dark with angry clouds. Cinda asked: "Will we reach to Warrenton before it rains?"

"We may not," Burr admitted. "We'll have to keep scouting ahead to make sure we don't run into trouble."

Anne was interested in their procedure. From the river to Warrenton the road was all up hill and down across a series of ridges, so that it might be half a mile from one ridge down into the valley and up to the ridge beyond. Faunt and Mosby rode well ahead of Burr and

Anne and Cinda. When these three reached each crest, they saw the two scouts on the next ridge in silhouette against the sky, waiting to signal them on. Then they let their horses haste down the slopes into the valleys and up toward another vantage; but Burr always checked them short of the summit while he rode ahead to make sure that at least as far as the next ridge the road was clear.

Cinda was forever looking back over her shoulder to where black and menacing storm clouds that had been piled above the bulwark of the mountains now raced to overtake them. Those angry clouds were shot through with fitful lightning glares, and sometimes Anne saw outlined for an instant against the blackness of the clouds the naked lancing flame of the flash itself. There was an electric tension in the air. Thunder murmured behind them like the bass chords of the song of distant battle, and it came nearer. The storm moved faster than they. It sent night ahead, and when they were still a mile or two short of Warrenton they rode in darkness broken only by the spasmodic flickering of lightning, while the thunder like galloping hoof beats trod upon their heels. The hiss and whisper and rising roar of pelting rain rushed to overtake them; the first drops struck singly, then the pressing downpour. As though satisfied that its prey was seized and helpless, the storm ceased its growling; rain brought the blackness of unrelieved night and Anne felt icy threads of water trickle from cheek and throat down inside her collar, over her shoulders and her bosom.

The horses with bowed heads moved at a plodding walk, and Uncle Faunt and Mr. Mosby waited to ride with Anne and Cinda through black and sluicing rain across the last level and up into the town. Anne saw the dark mass of a large building dim against the night sky, and Burr said: "There's the court house." Mosby led them aside to the wide steps of Norris Tavern, and the men were quick to help them to the ground and up the steps and so to shelter.

Cinda thought they must have a room, but Burr said regretfully: "I think you'd better get as dry as you can at the fire here, Mama. You'll want supper; but you'll have to go on tonight. This damned rain—sorry, Mama. This rain will make it unpleasant, but Uncle Faunt's gone to find a carriage to take you to Centerville."

"We'll never get to Centerville tonight!"

"No, but you can't stay here. The rain will give Stuart a fine chance to surprise the Yankees. He's going to hit them at Catlett's Station; but he'll come back this way, and they'll be chasing him. There's likely to be fighting right here in Warrenton before daylight, so you'd better be away."

A brilliant hissing flash lighted the window, and close on its heels came the thunder crash. "I'm a coward in a thunderstorm," Cinda confessed.

Burr said apologetically: "I wish we could have managed better. You'll probably get wet; but we'll stay near you till we see you meet a Yankee picket. They'll treat you all right."

"I'm too scared of this thunder and lightning to be afraid of anything else," Cinda assured him; and Anne wished she could say as much. She rather liked the deafening bombardment from the skies; but the thought that presently she and Cinda would be prisoners of the Yankees was a terrifying one. "But of course we'll do what you say," Cinda promised, and Burr nodded and smiled proudly.

"I'm not worried about your being afraid," he said.

When Faunt returned, he had been unable to find a carriage. "But we've got a cart with a cover to keep off the rain," he said. "And a negro to drive it. The Yankees won't be moving in this wet, so there's no hurry. Mr. Mosby and Burr and I will ride a piece with you." He added quietly: "If we suddenly disappear don't be surprised. We'll be near you till you're safe in Yankee hands."

"Will that be safe for you?" Cinda asked.

"Oh, Mr. Mosby and I are as much at home behind the Yankee lines as behind our own."

When they had supped, the cart was ready, and Burr and Faunt helped them in. Anne set her teeth to keep them from chattering, for she was determined not to let Faunt see her terror; but once they were on the road, she took Cinda's hand in the darkness and clung to it. "You may not be scared, but I'm just frightened to death, Aunt Cinda."

"So am I," Cinda admitted. Lightning was almost constant, the flickering glares briefly revealing the muddy ruts and the road like a brook bed deep in water. "I don't mind the flashes so much, but when it thunders I want to pull a feather bed over my head and scream!"

"Oh, I love the storm," Anne declared. "It's the Yankees I'm afraid of."

Cinda chuckled. "That's fine. You be scared of them and I'll be scared of the lightning. Then we can reassure each other."

The cart lurched on through blackness constantly dispelled and constantly returning, the driver swaying on his seat above them, the wheels sluicing through mud. The canvas cover leaked little drips and streams of water which they could not avoid. Once or twice Burr or Faunt came with a splashing of hoof beats to speak to them through the open rear end of the cart; but usually their escorts rode ahead, singly, an interval between. Time dragged wearily on, till Anne surrendered to exhaustion and lay down, her head on Cinda's knees; and despite the uproar of the storm she slept.

She was waked by sudden light across her eyes, and sat up to face a lantern's glare and a bearded countenance dimly seen, and to hear a harsh question:

"Who are you?"

Anne's heart raced and she pressed her hands to her lips, but Cinda said calmly: "A Southern mother on her way to see her wounded son in hospital in Washington."

"Slipping through the lines in the dead of night, in this rain?"

"I'm going to my son."

"M-m! Who's this?" He peered at Anne. She thought hopefully that his voice was not unkind.

Cinda's hesitation was only momentary. "My son's betrothed," she said. Anne was so astonished that she was instantly wide awake. Aunt Cinda was clever, to think of that answer so quickly. She would play her part. The lantern light fell on her face again and after a moment's scrutiny the questioner said courteously:

"Your son is to be congratulated, madame." Why, he was real nice, for a Yankee! "But I must send you to headquarters at Centerville. If you're what you say you are, you'll be passed on to Alexandria, and I trust to Washington."

He moved away; and in the lantern's light, Anne saw horsemen on the road. She thought them Faunt and Burr and Mr. Mosby; but then she realized that when the Yankees approached these guardians would have moved aside into the concealing darkness. Probably they were still near, listening; and she bit her lip to keep from crying out to them. Then their questioner called orders. "Morrison! Frame! Conduct these ladies . . ."

So the cart proceeded on its way. Anne whispered a question: "Where are Burr and the others?"

"They saw the lantern and the campfire ahead, and slipped off into the woods. This was what they expected, you know. We're all right, dear."

The horsemen who were their escort were dark figures in the darkness behind the cart, and Anne thought she ought to be afraid; but she was more sleepy than frightened. She lay down again and slept again, and it was broad daylight when she woke to find that they were plodding into Centerville. There were many soldiers here, in blue uniforms soaked through by the night's rain; and while Anne and Cinda waited for the commanding officer to be ready to see them, someone brought them tin cups of coffee and cold hard bread and hot fried bacon. Anne thought Yankees were not at all what she had expected them to be.

But she was not so sure when Aunt Cinda had to face a new and more rigid interrogation, and when all their possessions were thoroughly searched. These Yankees were polite enough, to be sure; but they were frighteningly stern. "I'll send you on to Union Mills," the officer at last decided. "You can get aboard a train there, but you must promise to report yourselves to the Provost Marshal in Alexandria."

"Certainly," Cinda assented. "It's to Alexandria we want to go."

Their own cart would take them the few miles to Union Mills. On the way they found themselves a part of a throng of refugees, afoot or driving wagons laden with household goods. The skies cleared and the sun made that journey easier; and Anne said apologetically: "I wasn't much company for you last night, sleeping all the time."

"I'm glad you did," Cinda told her. "The road comes across the fields where the battle of Manassas was fought last year." Anne remembered that Clayton had died in that battle. "There were signs enough of the fighting. I'm glad you didn't have to see them. It was just about light enough to see, when we crossed Bull Run."

Anne said nothing, but she clasped Cinda's hand in both hers and held it fast.

At the railroad, after some waiting, a train appeared; and an empty cattle car returning to Alexandria for supplies for Pope's army and which still bore plentiful traces of its recent occupants received them and their small trunk and as many of the other refugees as could crowd in. Anne was desperately weary. Her habit was still damp and she felt dirty and draggled and miserable; but Cinda was so serene that Anne took heart from her, enduring the lingering wretchedness of the journey.

It was dusk when they reached Alexandria. In the confusion there, except to order them all out of the cattle car so that it could be loaded again, no one seemed to notice them. Soldiers and teamsters were everywhere busy at their tasks; but Cinda found a Negro to carry Anne's small trunk on his shoulders and led the way through the crowds into the half-darkness of the dimly lighted streets.

Anne asked: "What are we going to do now, Aunt Cinda?"

"Polly Mason will take us in."

"Oh I know Dr. Mason. Papa and I used to come to Alexandria sometimes. They live on Fairfax Street, don't they?"

"Yes, just off Queen."

"In a high narrow brick house with carving above the windows," Anne remembered.

Cinda, the Negro following, found her way down Queen Street to Fairfax. Dr. Mason's house was at first glance dark, but a faint light showed through the drawn curtains; and Cinda tugged at the bell and an old Negro cautiously opened the door and Cinda recognized him and said in a great relief: "It's Mrs. Dewain, Uncle Ned. I haven't seen you for years."

The old man's teeth showed in a delighted grin; he bowed low. "Yes ma'am. Yes ma'am. I'm pleased tuh see y'all." His glance at Anne included her in this welcome; and then Mrs. Mason, hearing Cinda's voice, came into the hall.

Anne forgot her weariness in the gladness of this sanctuary; yet she saw at once that the house was not as she remembered it. The floors were bare, the book shelves empty, and sheets covered much of the furniture. Mrs. Mason was older than Aunt Cinda, a slender little woman with burning eyes. Her sister, Mrs. Linwood, lived here with her; and Anne thought they were so much alike they might have been one person. Their conversation was an antiphony. If one began a sentence, the other finished it; Anne as she listened was forever turning from one to the other to follow the successive phrases.

But their hospitality was generous and unstinted. Anne and Cinda were hurried away upstairs to be rid of their damp clothes, and warm wrappers were found for them. Uncle Ned brought the little trunk, and Cinda asked: "Where are our hoops? The boy had them too." Uncle Ned, as stiffly as though he felt himself at fault, said there were no hoops, and Anne and Cinda were tired enough to laugh themselves halfway to hysterics at this mishap. Neither of the sisters could supply the deficiency, for they were both smaller than Cinda, larger than Anne; but Mrs. Mason said:

"Never you mind, Cinda. You can manage over Sunday." Her sister finished for her. "And you can buy what you need first thing Monday morning."

"Are there things to buy? Our Richmond stores are empty."

"Oh dear me, yes," Mrs. Linwood assured her; and this time it was Mrs. Mason who completed the remark. "We can buy anything at all; but that can't keep us happy, with our men all gone to war."

Uncle Ned brought waiters loaded down with good things, and Anne's young appetite did them justice. Cinda said the Yankees clearly were not starving them; but the two sisters in a sort of duologue insisted that the Yankees were hateful as could be. That was why the house was so bare, all the nice things hidden away, the silver and the best china buried under the cellar floor, the best furniture in the attic. Cinda asked whether the Yankees had actually taken anything. No, but they were sure to try to, one of these days! It was frightful, never knowing what moment would bring disaster. A body could not sleep of nights! Why, even the first day the Yankees came they just butchered poor Mr. Jackson, down at the Marshall House. But didn't he shoot Colonel Ellsworth, Cinda inquired; and the sisters said of course he did. The Yankee had pulled down Mr. Jackson's flag, so what else would you expect him to do? And Dr. Mason had to hide in the attic for days till a pass could be got to send him through the line. Did the Yankees come hunting for him? No, but they might have! Oh it was horrible to know that at any hour of the day or night the scoundrels might batter down the door, break into the house, into your very bed rooms, anywhere. One dare not prepare for the night for fear of what might happen before dawn. Had any soldiers actually come into the house? No, but there was nothing to stop them if they chose to do so! Were not some of the officers gentlemen? Gentlemen? Why, one did not even notice their existence! If it was necessary to step outside your own door, you simply pretended not to see them.

When she and Cinda were at last alone, Anne asked wonderingly: "But Aunt Cinda—why do they talk that way? After all, the Yankees haven't bothered them."

"They're afraid, darling," Cinda told her. "Just two frightened little old ladies, talking to keep their courage up."

"But they—" Anne laughed a little. "They talk so biggity, too!"

"Even men do that," Cinda assured her. "They brag the loudest when they're afraid."

"You'd think they'd be used to it by this time. The Yankees have been in Alexandria over a year now."

Cinda pressed her hands to her eyes, hard; she shook her head, as though to clear her vision. "Men get used to things," she assented. "But women aren't—adaptable, Anne." And she added thoughtfully: "Southern men may forgive the North, some day, for this war. The best of them will. But Southern women will always keep the old wounds open." She smiled sadly: "The South is very feminine, you know; so quick to boast, so proud of victories, so sure each victory is decisive, so eager to believe what she hopes is true."

Anne asked thoughtfully: "Aunt Cinda, do you think the North will beat us?"

Cinda laughed. "Heavens, that's for men to worry about. Let's go to sleep now, child."

The long Sunday in that half-furnished house behind drawn shades seemed to Anne a weary time; and when on Monday she and Cinda went to the Provost Marshal's office it was through streets shadowed by an almost determined gloom. For a year and a half no lover of the

South had dared to speak in public here an honest word; so the older people kept to their homes and it was only young children, jealously attended by their black guardians, who freely moved abroad.

At the Provost Marshal's they met a disarming courtesy. Cinda told the officer who they were—Anne found it amusing to be introduced again as Julian's betrothed—and their errand.

"To Washington?" he echoed. "Then I'm sure you will wish to take the oath of allegiance?" Yet his tone was mild, and Cinda smiled.

"No, thank you. I believe even the Northern custom is to accord courtesy to those who go through the lines to help the wounded. That is our only purpose. I'm sure you would not expect us to swear falsely, even for the boy Miss Tudor and I both love."

"H-m! Well, frankly, madame, I expect nothing; but I must require you, for your own protection, to report yourselves when you reach Washington."

"You take so many precautions as almost to suggest some doubt of your own strength."

The other colored. "I assure you—" he began stiffly; but then he laughed. "There, I suppose it amuses you to—twit us."

Cinda said quietly: "Nothing about this war amuses me. My eldest son and my son-in-law have already been killed; my youngest son has been insensible in one of your hospitals since May. So nothing amuses me now, Captain."

The officer hesitated, and Anne thought he was about to say some sympathetic word; but he only nodded and wrote a permission for them to go by one of the steamers that several times every day passed between Alexandria and Washington. Next morning, waiting to go aboard, seeing on the wharves great piles of stores, shells, guns, pontoons, all the tremendous variety of supplies needed by a great army, Anne felt the oppression of dismay. Surely there was enough here to crush the South. From the steamer they were to take, huge guns were slung ashore; the horses that would draw them were led off the gangplank. All along the wharves other craft were unloading or waiting to unload; and Anne, watching, held fast to Cinda's steady arm. When at last, their passes checked, they went aboard and the paddle wheels began to slap the water, it was a relief to leave all that evidence of Northern strength behind.

They landed at the wharf at the foot of Sixth Street to find a whisper of foreboding excitement in the throng there, and to meet more than one suspicious challenge. Anne pressed close to Cinda, and when they were presently in a hackney cab she said admiringly:

"Aunt Cinda, I just don't see how you do it! You don't get excited or anything, and you seem to manage so wonderfully."

But Cinda was silent, watching the scenes through which they passed, the crowded streets, the uniforms everywhere, the laden wagons crawling toward the wharves; and Anne thought it was as though an overwhelming flood moved sluggishly and ponderously on and on to destroy the South and all the fine gentle folk she loved.

The cab deposited them at Mr. Gilby's door. Cinda thought the fare exorbitant and said so; but the driver said reasonably: "Some'd charge you more, ma'am." She had brought gold currency to meet their expenses on the journey; and she paid him and climbed the steps and rang the bell, and a Negro butler admitted them to what seemed to Anne a richly beautiful house, with Nottingham lace curtains at every window, marble-topped tables, walnut chairs and sofas upholstered in glistening hair cloth, ingrain carpets, bric-a-brac wherever there was room for it. Daniel Gilby had for years been Brett's good friend, and when Mrs. Gilby came swooping down to welcome them, she embraced them both.

"We've been expecting you, Cinda," she declared. "Dan wrote Brett as soon as he found Julian, and I knew you'd come. Dan has seen the poor boy. He's been terribly sick of course; but he's getting better, and he's going to be all right."

Cinda confessed that Mr. Gilby's letter had not reached them. "A Northern doctor, Dr. Murfin, brought me word he was alive. Anne and I started next day. I want to go to him at once."

Mrs. Gilby nodded easily. "Dan will be home for dinner, and I'm sure he can arrange it, though Mr. Stanton is horribly unreasonable about things sometimes. But we'll see when Dan comes." She had a lively tongue; and as she chattered on, Anne wondered that Aunt Cinda could listen so patiently. Mrs. Gilby said Washington had been very quiet since Congress adjourned, and Anne, remembering the crowded streets thronged with men, civilians in stovepipe hats and high boots, ladies in vast swaying hoops, soldiers in every fantastic variety of uniform, marching regiments, trundling wagons plowing through the mud, wondered what it had been like before. "Of course it's different now, with so many new regiments coming in all the time and marching off to Virginia," Mrs. Gilby confessed, and then in quick apology: "I shouldn't talk of such things, Cinda; but we can't pretend to ignore them, can we?"

"No, we can't ignore them," Cinda agreed. She seemed undisturbed by Mrs. Gilby's volubility; but it was a relief to Anne when Mr. Gilby presently appeared. She liked him at once; a chubby, bald little man, clean shaven, beaming with good will. Cinda wished to go to Julian on the instant; but Mr. Gilby seemed doubtful.

"There's some excitement in town today," he explained. "Pope's telegraph has been cut, and there's a report that your cavalry has raided the railroad and destroyed our supply depot at Manassas Junction. All sorts of rumors are flying around. So officials won't have much time for us."

"I promised to report to the Provost Marshal," Cinda remembered.

"Well, we'll do that first. His office is in the Gwin house. Then we'll have to get a permission from the Surgeon General." He hesitated. "I don't know your—hopes."

"To see Julian, first; after that, when he can travel, to take him home."

"Well, we'll see, we'll see." Yet Anne felt the doubts in him. "I wrote you his condition."

"I didn't get your letter. I know he's been very ill, ever since May." Cinda said almost humbly: "I haven't thought of anything but coming to him."

"H-m!" Anne saw his deep distress, saw his sidelong glance at Mrs. Gilby. "H-m! I see. I see." He touched his chin with his finger. "Ah, yes, I see," he repeated in a deep uncertainty.

Cinda spoke evenly. "Tell me about him," she said. "Since he's alive, I can bear anything, I think."

"Oh, he's all right," he assured her hurriedly. "That is, he will be. There may be a little deafness. He had measles, and his ears were abscessed, you know."

"No, I don't know anything."

"And pneumonia. And—er—well, I'm no doctor. The terminology escapes me."

"He was wounded, I know," Cinda prompted.

"Oh yes, yes, wounded to be sure. They tell me it's miraculous that he's alive at all. They think early amputation best, but in his case there was no broken bone, just a heavy hemorrhage; so they delayed."

Anne saw Cinda's color drain away; and Mrs. Gilby, more understanding than Anne had expected, suddenly rose and came to take Cinda in her arms, and she said impatiently to her husband: "Oh for Heaven's sake stop being tactful! Tell her!" Then, not waiting for him to speak, "They cut his leg off, Cinda; cut it off right at the hip." Cinda seemed to grow smaller in her arms. "But he's alive, dear," Mrs. Gilby added. "After all, nothing else matters. He's alive."

Cinda lifted her head again. "I must see him," she whispered.

"To be sure," Mr. Gilby agreed. "To be sure. We'll arrange that, of course; just as soon as we can."

It was to be a long and torturing time before Cinda saw Julian. At the Provost Marshal's that afternoon they had to wait for hours, jostled and hustled by the crowd, till too late to see the Surgeon General; and next day the flood of rumors from Pope's army occupied every official mind and so excited the city that Mr. Gilby insisted they stay indoors. "Washington's full of rascals, blacklegs, bummers, gamblers, sutlers, camp followers, adventurers of every scoundrelly sort; and most of them will be drunk today, waiting for news from Pope." Thursday was worse, with reports of a Union disaster; and distant cannon could be faintly heard. Mr. Gilby said people were scurrying into Maryland, frightened by the report that Pope was beaten, that General Lee was already approaching the Chain Bridge with two hundred thousand men. Friday the guns were louder and the panic grew; Saturday was a sullen angry day when the air shook with distant cannonading.

For those days they could not hope to meet the Surgeon General. Late Saturday afternoon Mr. Gilby came home, and Anne thought he was divided between sympathy and triumph. It was hard to remember that he was a Yankee; he was so friendly and kind. "There's a War Department bulletin," he told them. "It says we've won a great and dreadful battle; but there are thousands of our men wounded and the call is out for every surgeon and every nurse who can be spared. They're leaving the Maryland Avenue depot by trainloads, and hundreds are waiting all the way from Willard's to the Surgeon General's office for carriages and ambulances and anything else that will take them off to the battlefield. Long Bridge is jammed—hacks, wagons, everything." He added regretfully: "I don't know when you will be able to see Julian, Mrs. Dewain. Every hospital's in confusion now."

Cinda had in these days learned patience, and she nodded in submission; but Anne, when they were alone that night, asked pitifully: "Aunt Cinda, do you think they really beat us?"

Cinda looked at her almost in surprise. "Why—I hadn't thought about it, Anne. I hadn't even wondered. I suppose it's true, if the War Department says so." She pressed her hands to her eyes. "All those cannons, all those men we saw—how could General Lee hope to beat them all?"

So Anne had her night of tears; but next day the truth reached Washington, at first in a trickling whisper, and then in a widening flood. At nightfall on Sunday Mr. Gilby came home haggard and worn.

"Pope's army is destroyed," he said. "Stragglers are pouring into the city. It's as bad as it was last year after Bull Run. Some people think Washington is lost." His jaw set; he looked at his wife. "But I'll be damned if I'll run away."

Mrs. Gilby came to his side; she kissed him. "We're not the kind that run away, my dear." Anne wondered how she could have been so blind to the goodness in this woman; and to see Mr. Gilby's despair made her forget for a while her gladness at the South's great victory.

Cinda and Anne, not venturing out of doors, saw through Mr. Gilby's eyes the frantic days that followed. Politeness kept Anne from open rejoicing, but she was full of secret triumph. Mr. Gilby said the Union army, what was left of it, was a mob; Pope was relieved of command; McClellan would try to defend Washington. Stanton was preparing to send away the government archives, and there was a steamer ready to take the President to safety.

Monday afternoon when a terrific thunder shower joined its uproar to the blast of gunfire which seemed to come from just across the river, the streets were full of people scrambling like frightened sheep away from the coming danger. Everything that had wheels had joined the procession, and drivers swore and fought for room to move, and wheels locked, and crippled carriages were toppled on their sides in the mud to make way for those still fit to travel. From the windows they could watch the rout, and Mr. Gilby cursed the cowardly soldiers. There were drunken men everywhere in the mob. "Most of them are nurses," he said furiously. "They've guzzled all the liquor meant for the wounded." He was so angry that Cinda said tactfully:

"It was like this in Richmond last May. Not so bad, perhaps; but even Mrs. Davis went away."

"Well!" Mrs. Gilby spitefully commented. "If Mrs. Lincoln went away no one would think anything about it. Hardly a month that she doesn't go gallivanting off to New York to let herself go in some extravagance. That woman!" Her tone was so eloquent that Anne smiled.

"I never thought of him as married," she admitted. "He's so homely."

"My dear child, compared with that wife of his, he's an Apollo! But the airs she puts on! You'd think it was her who was President, instead of him. She spends every cent she can lay hands on, and tells the newspapers every stitch she buys! And vain! All any man who wants public office has to do is pay her a compliment and she'll ding away at Mr. Lincoln till he gives in, poor thing!"

Cinda, at the window watching the rabble in the street outside, asked without turning: "Is he as despisable as she is?"

"Well, lots of people think he's a fool to let her make such an idiot of herself. But she's so sickening that people are sorry for him."

Mr. Gilby said, with some mirth in his tone: "You mustn't take everything Mrs. Gilby says too literally, Mrs. Dewain. Washington ladies can't speak of Mrs. Lincoln without getting mad; but I expect she has some good qualities."

"Well!" Mrs. Gilby exclaimed. "If she has, I'd certainly like to know what they are!"

Cinda nodded toward the passing throng. "Will Mr. Lincoln run away from Washington?"

Mr. Gilby after a momentary reflection shook his head. "No. No, I'm sure he won't. No, that man is no coward."

"We think he is, in the South." Cinda came away from the window. "In fact we believe everything bad about him."

"I know. There are men here too who think of him contemptuously. He does make many blunders, but he seems to me to learn from them. The men around him learn nothing, but he learns."

"Do you know him?" Cinda asked. Anne wondered at her tone, at something almost hopeful in it.

"Why, everybody knows him, at least by sight. I've had a little business with him, yes; but of course he doesn't know me."

"I believe you think well of him."

"Compared with what the rest of Washington thinks of him, yes I do. He's probably the only man in Washington tonight who doesn't believe the Union is lost."

"Do you believe it's lost?"

He looked at her in brief hesitation, but then he clapped fist into palm. "No!" he said. "No! The Union's too great and good a thing to be destroyed! No, and as long as Abraham Lincoln lives it never will be!"

Each day he came home with rising confidence. McClellan had the army again in hand. General Lee invaded Maryland; but on Friday this new army of McClellan's marched away to meet the Southern hosts. Cinda and Anne saw some regiments pass the house; and Mrs. Gilby, watching with them, said sorrowfully: "Oh dear, they don't look the way they did before, with their uniforms all spick-and-span, and their guns all clean and everything. Just see them! Lots of them even in their shirt sleeves! Even the officers look shabby!"

Cinda said thoughtfully. "They look more like our men now. Perhaps they'll fight now as our men do."

The army marched away, but that other army of the wounded stayed behind. Cinda pleaded to see Julian; but Mr. Gilby advised waiting. "Washington is scared," he reminded her. "There are plenty of Southern sympathizers in town, but they're keeping out of sight. I suppose the Provost Marshal has forgotten you're here. If you went to him for any favor now, he might lock you up." Later, to Anne, he said urgently: "Persuade Mrs. Dewain to wait, can you? I don't want to tell her, but they've moved Julian to make room for our wounded; and I can't find out where he is. So don't let her insist, till I find him."

Anne did as he asked, and Cinda waited with reluctant patience; and then one day when a fresh flood of wounded poured into the city, the news from Antietam set Washington into a riot of joy to match the despair that had swept the city two weeks before. Lee was whipped, the rebel army was driven back into Virginia, Washington and the Union and the North were saved.

Just as Cinda and Anne had refrained from exulting, so now Mr. and Mrs. Gilby tried to conceal their happiness; but Cinda said how relieved and how proud they must be. "And I'm almost glad myself," she admitted. "Because now perhaps I can see Julian."

"Of course, of course," Mr. Gilby agreed; but Anne heard evasion in his tones and knew Julian was not yet found. She saw doubt in Cinda's eyes too; and she was not surprised next morning—Mrs. Gilby had gone to market and Mr. Gilby was away from the house—when Cinda appeared in shawl and bonnet.

"Anne," she said, "I'm going out. I'll be back soon."

"I'll go with you, Aunt Cinda."

"No, dear, you stay here."

But Anne caught her arm. "Aunt Cinda, what are you going to do?"

Cinda hesitated; but then she said frankly: "I'm going to find Dr. Hammond. He's the Surgeon General, and Mrs. Gilby says he's a fine man. He will help us if he can."

"Mr. Gilby has tried his best."

Cinda said grimly, "Men are too polite to accomplish anything. I'm tired of—politely waiting. I want my boy!"

"Well, if you're going, I'm going with you," Anne insisted. "I may not be of any help, but I won't hinder. Please?"

So Cinda consented, and Anne hurried to make ready. When they set out, Cinda walked so fast that Anne panted to keep pace with her; and she felt the driving insistence in the other which now at last, weary of delays, broke all bonds.

Anne had misgivings; and at the Surgeon General's office, hearing Aunt Cinda's sharp tongue let loose upon those who tried to put her off, she expected arrest or any other catastrophe. Cinda, determined to see the Surgeon General, refused to be put off, till at last she learned what she wished to know and returned to Anne triumphant.

"He's at the hospital in Armory Square," she said.

"Julian?"

"No, no. Dr. Hammond. He's operating there. Come."

So they set off again, and on the way Cinda, suddenly guileful, stopped to buy a basket and stuff it with good things; fruit, a bottle of sherry, a cold roast fowl.

"This will get us into the hospital," she promised Anne.

There was a sentry at the door who tried to bar their way, demanding passes. "I'm taking these to my son," Cinda explained.

"Gotta have a pass all the same."

"The leg my boy left at the Antietam is my pass," Cinda retorted. "Where were you that day?"

"It's no use, ma'am," the man said sullenly; and when Cinda would have entered he laid his bayoneted gun across the door. She faced him with high head.

"If you touch me, I'll have you shot!" she cried.

"I can't let you pass, or I'd be shot anyway, ma'am."

"Oh—go wash your face," Cinda said curtly. "You're in no fit condition to talk to ladies!" She thrust his musket aside so briskly that in his surprise, caught off balance, he stumbled down the steps and their way was clear. Anne, scurrying after Cinda into the hospital, saw him start after them and then stop and come to attention as an officer approached. Then Cinda whipped aside from the main hall into the first corridor, and they were not pursued.

The corridor they entered was short. Around the first corner an open door revealed benches where capes and bonnets were laid, and there were mops and brooms leaning in a corner. Cinda uttered an exclamation of satisfaction. "Ladies working in the hospital leave their things here," she told Anne. "Quick. Take off your bonnet. Take a broom or something." She set the example, and Anne in helpless mirth that was near hysteria obeyed. "Stop laughing," Cinda told her crisply. "Now we look as though we belonged here. Come on."

Anne followed her; and thereafter, asking directions in an authoritative tone—"I've a message for Dr. Hammond. Where is he, please?"

—Cinda presently reached her goal. A nurse, a hoarse man with whis-key on his breath, pointed to the door from which he had just emerged.

"He's in there. I've been helping him. But don't bother him now," he advised, and grinned in a terrifying way at Anne. "Or he'll cut your gizzard out!" His arms to the elbow were spotted and streaked with half-dried blood.

The door he indicated was screened with semi-transparent gauze; but since the hall where they stood was dark, while a skylight illumi-nated the operating room, they could see clearly enough the group in-side. There were three men in black frock coats and two others in shirt sleeves with stained hands; and on an oilcloth table lay another man whose face was hidden by a white cloth. Anne caught a sick-sweet smell in the air.

But even in that first glance she was sure of Dr. Hammond, he tow-ered above the others so commandingly. Tall and broad shouldered, with a huge dark beard that rested on his chest, he stood facing them across the table where the hurt man lay.

"Get that bandage off," he said; and something strong and sure in his voice warmed Anne through and through. The bandage, darkly hideous, came away with little sticking sounds, and Dr. Hammond shifted a cigar from his hand to his mouth and turned back his cuffs over his coat sleeves and bent to inspect the swollen and discolored arm thus exposed. He took from a basin a wet cloth and mopped at the arm and the cloth slipped from his hand and fell to the floor. He picked it up and wetted it and squeezed it dry and scrubbed at the dried blood and pus around the wound and tossed the cloth into the basin again, and muttered something. He removed the cigar from his mouth and said curtly to the other men:

"This should have been taken off on the battlefield. Wiseman is right: 'Cut off the limb quickly, while the patient is heated and in mettle.' If we did, we'd save half the men who die. Too late for this lad, I'm afraid. We'll see."

The two men in frock coats nodded respectfully. Dr. Hammond replaced his cigar, opened a mahogany box on the table beside him, took out a slender knife, tried its edge on his thumb and then stropped it lightly on his palm. "Ready?" he asked.

One of the other doctors said hurriedly: "Oh, just a minute." He took needle and thread from the box in which instruments were kept, touched thumb and finger to his tongue, twisted the thread to a point, threaded the needle and thrust it in his lapel to be in readiness. Then he picked up a hooked steel instrument and a length of string. Dr. Hammond nodded and lifted that dark arm that no longer looked like an arm at all and with a keen blade drew a circle clear around it, near the shoulder.

Anne saw the quick oozing blood, and then a spurt, and then the doctor was busy with that length of string, tying knots. She tried to look away and could not. The grate of the saw seemed to rip through her spine. When one of the men in shirt sleeves threw the severed arm aside, she saw it fall upon a heap of other arms and legs in a corner of the room, a heap out of which drained an almost colorless liquid streaked with pink, spreading across the floor.

A moment later Dr. Hammond wiped his hands on a towel already soiled and turned away. "You gentlemen can stitch the flap," he said, and relighted his half-smoked cigar and came toward the door where Anne and Cinda stood. He saw them and stopped in surprise.

"Well, ladies, what is it?" His voice was crisp, impatient.

Through the now open door, Anne could see more clearly; and she felt her knees give way . . . and then she was lying on the floor, and Aunt Cinda was fanning her, and Dr. Hammond's voice was fading into distance, to the beat of his departing footsteps. She tried to sit up, and with Aunt Cinda's help she managed it, and asked a question, and Aunt Cinda said wearily:

"Well—we may as well go home."

Anne, once on her feet, was able to walk. Aunt Cinda found the room where they had discarded their bonnets. In the open air Anne's senses returned, and she began to shiver, and she whispered: "Oh Aunt Cinda, wasn't it terrible?"

"I shouldn't have taken you. Yes, it's terrible." Cinda's voice was remote and calm.

"I should think they could at least keep things clean!"

"Clean?" Cinda looked at her in honest surprise. "Why—I've never seen an operating room as clean as that, Honey. Compared with that, our hospitals are—pig pens! They didn't even have any flies there!"

Anne felt ridiculously young and ignorant; and Cinda said gravely: "Cutting people to bits isn't clean work, you know, Anne."

"But all those horrible—arms and legs—on the floor!"

Cinda said drily: "They had chloroform. I've seen surgeons doing amputations on men who screamed and fought and had to be tied down—and other hurt men lying in the same room, listening and watching while they waited their turn."

Anne shivered piteously. "Did you find out where Julian is?"

Cinda shook her head. "No. Mr. Gilby had already seen Doctor Hammond. The doctor is too busy now, with so many men here from the last battle. He can't even try to help us."

"So we have to wait?"

"Yes, wait," Cinda wearily agreed.

They had reached Washington on the twenty-sixth of August. It was a month lacking only five days before their waiting ended. To receive the terrible flood of wounded from the second battle at Manassas—Second Bull Run, Mr. Gilby called it—and then from the battle on the hill between Antietam Creek and the Potomac, the Washington hospitals had been cleared. Convalescents were sent north to other cities, and patients who could be moved were shifted to make room for those in greater need. Under the pressure of the times, registrations were neglected, records vanished; and it was only after days of tireless inquiry that Mr. Gilby traced Julian. He heard, late one Saturday night, that some Confederate wounded had been put into a warehouse in Georgetown. Since other such hopes had proved groundless, he said nothing to Cinda, but drove to Georgetown to see if Julian were there. Before he came home, the household had retired; but at breakfast he told Cinda that Julian was found, and at once they went off to Georgetown together.

Anne would have gone, but Mr. Gilby said there were sights she should not see, and Mrs. Gilby stayed at home with her. At dinner time Mr. Gilby returned alone; and he was in a flurry of exhaustion, flinging up his hands in despair. To Anne's eager questions he said wearily: "Julian? Oh yes, he's right enough, glad to see his Mama. He'd begun to think she was never coming. She stayed with him, wouldn't leave him, says she won't leave him there. It's a filthy place, damp, full of stinks, full of vermin, food miserable; and it seems I'm to get him out of there." He laughed helplessly. "Mrs. Dewain knows her mind, Miss Anne; but untangling Washington red tape is hard enough on week days, let alone Sundays." He was under Cinda's orders to take back clean sheets, blankets, a mattress, a hamper of food. "And she swears she'll stay with Julian till she can bring him here."

"Well, why not?" Mrs. Gilby cried. "I think that's sensible."

"Why not?" He laughed helplessly. "Oh, Dr. Hammond's willing enough. He gave me permission as soon as I finally found him. But after all, Julian's a prisoner." He looked at Anne. "It seems your Government has been pretty severe with some of General Pope's officers, in retaliation for one of Pope's proclamations. The windbag! I'm glad Lee whipped him! But at any rate, Provost Marshal Doster says Stanton's orders are to accept no parole, and Julian can't be released without one. I'm going to find Dr. Hammond again as soon as I've had a bite, and see if he can do anything."

Mrs. Gilby packed the things Cinda wanted and he loaded them into the carriage and set off. At dusk they heard the carriage at the door, and Anne ran to the window to look out; and she cried: "Oh, Mrs. Gilby, they've brought him! They've brought him!" She hurried to fling wide the door, and saw Cinda and Mr. Gilby and the strapping Negro coachman supporting between them—someone Anne was sure she had never seen before. This was not Julian! This was a tall, thin, pale man with a thin beard of a straw-red color. He had only one leg, and that hung as limp as a rope; and his garments were rags and he was hatless, his hair hanging to his shoulders.

But when they carried him up the steps, the light from the gas chandelier fell on his face and she saw his lips part in a smile and he said in a hoarse, weak voice: "Howdy, Miss Anne. Mama said you were here."

So this was Julian after all! Anne's eyes flooded, and she could see no more; but Julian seemed to sag, and the big Negro picked him up in tender arms and asked Mrs. Gilby: "Where you gwine put him, ma'am?"

Julian was borne away upstairs, and Cinda and Mrs. Gilby and all the household for an hour were busy in his service; but Anne stayed with Mr. Gilby. He told her in a chuckling triumph: "I found Doctor Hammond. He soon settled it, ordered Julian moved here in my custody. I thought Stanton might find out he was here and have him arrested; but Dr. Hammond said Stanton would never learn where Julian was from him, and if I let the cat out of the bag I'd be responsible! So! Now we'll soon have the youngster well again."

Julian in the days that followed came quickly back to some measure of strength. Before Anne saw him a second time, that absurd thin beard was shaved off and his hair cut to a proper length; and clean, in a clean bed, he seemed to gain by the hour. Cinda smilingly declared she would never have known him. "I declare, Anne, he's grown at least three inches since May!" she cried proudly. "Isn't that wonderful?"

Julian laughed and said: "Why, I had to do something to kill time, Mama. There was nothing to do but lie abed. Besides, with only one leg I'm going to need a long one!"

Anne saw Cinda's lips white. "Of course. That's sensible," she agreed; but her voice shook, and he said in sternly tender warning:

"Don't cry over me, Mama."

"No, darling."

"I'll be as good with one leg as with two, as soon as I learn how to use crutches."

"Of course! I'll get you some."

He laughed. "We had a song in the hospital, to keep us from feeling sorry for ourselves." And he sang a lively jig:

> " 'Felix was you drunk?
> 'Felix was you mad?
> 'What did you do
> 'With the leg that you had?' "

Then, seeing his mother's eyes fill, he said apologetically: "I guess it wasn't much of a song, but it cheered us up. You know, right at first."

Anne cried: "I think it's a beautiful song! Teach me all of it, will you, Julian?"

"I certainly will. Come on!" He began to sing again, repeating that verse. Cinda rose, her face convulsed; but they looked at her with pleading in their eyes, and sang in defiant chorus:

> " 'What did you do
> 'With the leg that you had?' "

Cinda stamped her foot, her tears suddenly streaming. "Oh you idiots!" Then, smiling through tears: "Darlings!" She almost ran from the room. Anne wished to follow her, but Julian caught Anne's hand.

"No! Second verse! She'll be all right. Sing!"

So they sang till they laughed till they cried, and when Cinda returned they taught her that song together.

Julian was eager to be out of doors. Fine days, he and Anne spent together in the garden behind the house; and as he became used to his crutches they went farther afield. They saw the unfinished Capitol, and the shabby mansion set in unkempt grounds where the President lived and where the air was hideous with a sickening odor that came from decaying refuse in a near-by ditch; and they saw the Monument that looked in its uncompleted state like a factory chimney with the top broken off. No one challenged them. Legless men were not rare in Washington. This tall boy and the lovely girl beside him attracted many glances, not because he was crippled, but because there was the bright beauty of youth upon them both. Mr. Gilby somehow acquired for Julian a faded Confederate uniform, and Julian wore it without insignia; and there were so many paroled Confederates in Washington that he went unhindered. One day they had their daguerreotypes taken by Mr. Whitehurst; once Julian bought Anne a little flower pin at Mr. Hood's jewelry store.

In these happy hours, Anne forgot to wonder how soon they could depart, but she knew that Cinda was trying to secure the necessary permission. Then one day when Cinda returned to the house after a morning's absence, Anne saw in her eyes some profound emotion. She sprang to the older woman's side.

"Aunt Cinda? What is it?"

"Why—we're going home." Cinda spoke in a hushed voice, like a whisper.

"Really, Aunt Cinda?" Anne was breathless with delight; and Julian struggled up from his chair.

Cinda nodded. "Yes. We'll get our passes this afternoon, leave tomorrow."

Julian cried: "Grand, Mama! Grand! How did you do it? Did you have any trouble?"

Cinda nodded slowly. "Yes. Yes, a great deal of trouble. But it's ended now." She spoke like a person asleep, and she opened her hand and extended it to them. A rectangular white card lay in her palm. They peered at it, their heads together. Anne saw a few lines written in a small neat script, and Julian read the signature aloud.

"'A. Lincoln'?" His tone was a question, and Cinda nodded again, in that strange abstraction, and Julian asked: "Mama, did you see him?"

"Yes," said Cinda. "Yes. I saw Abraham Lincoln." She turned away, holding the card between her two hands, and walked quietly along the hall and up the stairs.

19

THE Howitzers left Richmond on the twenty-sixth of August. Brett had no word from Cinda. He wrote Vesta at the Plains that her mother was gone to Washington, and he asked Tilda to stop in as often as possible at Fifth Street, where Mrs. Currain, alone with the servants, was happily content; but there was no more he could do.

Four or five days of marching brought the Howitzers to Rapidan Station, where they heard the news of Lee's great victory at Manassas. On the fourth of September, pushing on toward the Potomac, they camped within two or three miles of that battlefield, and Brett and some others rode over to see the terrain. Brett would all his life regret having done this. The Yankee dead had lain unburied for days under the broiling sun, and the swollen, bursting bodies, covered with maggots, were sometimes so many that from a distance the ground seemed solidly carpeted with blue uniforms. The Confederates had buried their own dead and collected their wounded; but since the Confederate surgeons had inadequate facilities and insufficient medical supplies even for their own men, hundreds of wounded Federals still lay where they had fallen. An ambulance train sent from Washington was just beginning to collect those Northern wounded who had survived four or five days of hunger and thirst and pain.

Sunday at dusk the Howitzers moved into Maryland. They crossed the Potomac at White's Ford. The water was sometimes more than belly deep for the horses, but a sandy island in midstream gave a chance to halt and rest. Before Brett reached the farther shore night had fallen; but a fine moon almost at the full shone across the water and silhouetted the dark figures of men and horses and woke reflected gleams from gun barrels and from the metal in harness or bridle. Brett paused to watch and to listen to the shouts and curses of the drivers, the splash of plunging horses, the clank and rattle of accouterments.

While he waited, he heard his name called, and answered, and Faunt rode up from the water's edge to join him; so Brett had his first news of Anne and Cinda. "We saw them halted by a Yankee picket," Faunt said. "And one of our men who lives in Alexandria slipped into town last Sunday to see his family and brought word that they stayed a day or two at Dr. Mason's house there, and then went on to Washington."

Faunt and Brett had only a few minutes together. Stuart had crossed into Maryland at this same ford two days before; but Faunt, weakened by a severe attack of dysentery, had stayed two days in Leesburg to recruit his strength. He spoke of that great victory at Manassas.

"I rode over the battlefield," Brett told him. "It was horrible. The Yankees hadn't been buried. You could smell them for miles."

Faunt laughed shortly. "Remember what Catherine de Medici says in that book by Dumas? 'A dead enemy always smells sweet!'"

Brett looked at the other in the moonlight. "I haven't read much Dumas." His tone must have betrayed his distaste, for Faunt said a curt good-by and rode away.

In Frederick, two or three days later, Brett saw Burr for a heartening hour, and heard the story of the ball which Stuart and von Borcke had organized Monday night at the Academy at Urbana. "When the fun was at its peak," Burr explained, "the Yankees attacked our pickets and the officers had to leave their pretty partners and gallop off and take a hand. But after the Yankees were driven away, they went back and danced till daylight. Then the ambulances came along and turned the Academy into a hospital, and the young ladies in their party dresses took care of our wounded. That's quite a mixture of fun and fighting, Papa."

Brett asked whether many Marylanders were enlisting to fight with the Confederates. "I expect that's one of the things Lee hoped for," he suggested.

"They were certainly glad to see us here in Frederick," Burr said. "But I don't think very many have enlisted. No."

From Frederick the Howitzers toiled up the pass across South Mountain, the horses straining with cracking sinews as they breasted the steep grade; then with wheels braked hard they came briskly down to Hagerstown. Thence new orders sent them back across the Potomac at Williamsport and so to Shepherdstown. They lay idle there during the bitter day of fighting at Sharpsburg, and they heard there of Jackson's fine capture of Harper's Ferry. Three or four days later, temporarily under Stuart's command, they crossed into Maryland again to fight a skirmish near Williamsport; but by that time Lee had completed his withdrawal into Virginia, and McClellan did not pursue.

A week after Sharpsburg, the Howitzers were in camp two miles from Martinsburg when at dusk Brett saw a man on a great black horse accompanied by a gigantic Negro passing along the road toward town. He recognized Trav, and at his shout Trav swung Nig that way and dismounted and the two men clasped hands.

Trav had intended to push on to Martinsburg. "I'm told General Longstreet is there," he explained. "But I'll spread my bed near yours tonight and go on tomorrow." It was hours before they slept. Big Mill somehow found a chicken for their supper, and they ate and drank and talked; but most of all they talked. Brett was hungry for any word of Cinda and of Julian; but Trav could tell him little except that Cinda and Anne were at Mr. Gilby's in Washington.

"There've been two letters from Cinda. Vesta brought one over Friday evening. I left Richmond Saturday." This was Wednesday.

"Vesta's home?" Brett asked eagerly.

"Yes. Jenny stayed at the Plains."

"I knew she was going to. How's Julian? When is Cinda bringing him home?"

So Trav explained that Cinda when she wrote had not yet seen Julian. "They emptied the Washington hospitals to make room for wounded from Manassas. All the Confederate wounded were moved, but no records were kept, and Cinda hasn't found out where Julian is."

Brett swore. "She must be half-crazy!"

"Her letter sounded sort of—desperately calm," Trav admitted. He had to answer many questions, till Brett reluctantly accepted the fact that the other actually could tell him nothing; so at last they came to talk of other things. "I spent a few days at Chimneys," Trav said. "James Fiddler, my old overseer there, came to Richmond to say he'd left Tony. I judged there was something wrong, so I went down." He paused, went on: "Tony has sold off some of the people, Brett. Chimneys was overstocked, and those we sent there from Great Oak had little to do. At any rate, he sold them."

"Well, that was probably good business." Brett laughed in grim amusement. "We hear Lincoln's going to set them free, anyway. Not that that will make any difference to them; but they'll be worth less and less from now on. All the same, I wish Tony hadn't sold them."

"Tony's a lost man, Brett." Trav hesitated, then went on: "He's taken a negress into the house as his mistress, a bright mulatto girl named Sapphira. He tried to seat her at the table with me."

Brett felt the other's sorrow. "Tony was lost long ago, Trav. He had his little time, captaining that Martinston company; but he was lost before that."

"He'd begun to have some self-respect. I suppose this Lincoln business knocked it out of him."

"When were you down there?"

"I got back to Richmond on the ninth. We'd had the news of Manassas at Martinston. Richmond was still drunk with triumph, talking about hundreds of Yankees killed and captured, and hundreds of muskets and guns taken, and mountains of stores. People thought Lee's army was marching into Maryland like conquerors, to seize Harrisburg and Baltimore and Washington."

Brett said drily: "The army might have done better if President Davis hadn't announced two months ago that we were going to carry the war into Northern territory. Well, maybe time will teach us not to brag too soon. How long were you in Richmond?"

"Two weeks or so. I'm not strong yet, and seeing the way things are at Chimneys took a lot out of me. I stayed in bed a few days. Vesta got there the Saturday after I did." He smiled. "She was furious because Cinda hadn't waited so they could both go to Washington. She showed me Cinda's letter, and one from Burr. Have you seen Burr since Sharpsburg?"

"Yes, he came through without a scratch. At Boonsboro and again at Sharpsburg, when we retreated, Fitz Lee's men relieved the pickets. At Sharpsburg that meant extending the brigade along the whole line of battle, dismounting his men to stand to while the army crossed the Potomac behind them. For hours McClellan had nothing in front of him but that thin line of pickets; but they pulled back at dawn with no trouble."

"That must have seemed like a long night!"

Brett chuckled. "Yes, even Burr admits it." He asked: "How's Enid, and your mother?"

"Oh Mama's happy as a cow in clover, managing the house to suit herself." Trav did not speak of Enid. He seldom did unless he must, so Brett was not surprised. "Tilda's bragging about Streean's speculations," Trav added, and he said thoughtfully: "You know, Brett, she brags so much about how clever he is that I think she's a little ashamed of him." Brett did not comment, and Trav said: "Streean apparently had a lot of salt that he'd bought cheap, and he sold it at a dollar and a quarter a pound just two days before General Loring drove the Yankees away from the Kanawha salt mines and the price fell to five or ten cents." He added: "By the way, Dolly says Tony has gone into partnership with Streean, bought shares in a blockade-runner."

"Probably they'll make money," Brett said. "Streean seems to have a knack that way, and no conscience to hinder." He asked: "Had Richmond heard about Sharpsburg before you left?"

"Only through the Northern papers. The Philadelphia *Inquirer* claimed a victory and said Longstreet was wounded and Jackson a prisoner. Everybody assured everybody else that it was just a Yankee lie; but when we started for Gordonsville we began to meet trains full of wounded, and to hear some of the truth."

"We weren't there," Brett said. "We've hardly fired a gun." Big Mill added a few sticks to the dying fire and Brett stared into the new flames. "We camped one night at Gainesville and I rode over to look at the Manassas battlefield. The Yankee dead hadn't been buried. I'll swear you could have smelled them ten miles down the road." He set his jaw hard. "Lots of wounded still there."

"Ours?"

"Theirs mostly. We buried our dead, but we couldn't wait to bury the Yankees." He added in a lower tone: "But we left our dead to rot on the field at Sharpsburg." He wiped his brow. "There were hogs getting fat on the bodies at Manassas, Trav. I'd like to take some of the damned politicians who made this war and show them a week-old battlefield."

Trav asked: "What went wrong at Sharpsburg, Brett?"

Brett looked around to be sure no one was within hearing. "I think General Lee asked too much of the men," he said. "Half the army was worn out on the march from Manassas. They say Jackson gave orders to shoot stragglers, but a lot of men simply couldn't stand the pace. I doubt if we had thirty thousand men at Sharpsburg when the battle opened, and McClellan had three times that. Lee and Jackson are alike. They want to fight—and to Hell with the odds! But it's death on the men." After a moment he added: "I hear Longstreet didn't want to fight at Sharpsburg, but he did the work of a thousand men once they got at it. Give him my compliments when you see him."

The army lay inactive for a while. There was a drought in the Valley, all but the larger stream beds dry; and once or twice troops had to be moved to a better supply. But food and forage were plentiful, and the men complained of too much beef to eat rather than of too little; and there was time to bring from Richmond and Staunton new uniforms, guns, munitions. There was time, too, for Trav and Brett more than once to see each other. When next Trav rode out from Martinsburg, Brett asked at once:

"How's Cousin Jeems?"

"Fine," Trav smiled. "He wasn't out of bed when I got to headquarters, the day I came; but Captain Goree and I waked him. He's a sight in his night shirt, Brett. I noticed he was limping and he swore at himself for being such a damned fool that he wore a loose boot and blistered his heel and had to fight at Sharpsburg in carpet slippers."

"Any of your friends hurt?"

"Major Sorrel got a shaking up from a shell burst. He tried to settle down and play invalid in someone's home over in Shepherdstown where there were a couple of pretty daughters, but the Yankees shelled him out. Walton got a bullet through the shoulder, nothing serious." He laughed at a sudden memory. "Major Fairfax rode a big stallion named Saltron, and a round shot struck it fairly in the rump and the Major came back swearing mad because the Yankees shot Saltron in the butt! Longstreet told him to be thankful he didn't get shot in the butt himself!"

Brett chuckled. "How does the General feel about things?"

"He says the army will soon be better than ever; and he believes there never lived as fine a commander as Lee."

"That's probably true," Brett agreed, "unless Lee's too fond of a fight. He certainly shouldn't have fought at Sharpsburg. With the river behind us we'd have lost the whole army if they'd beaten us."

"He didn't plan to fight there," Trav said. "But a copy of one of his orders fell into McClellan's hands, so McClellan knew where we were and what we meant to do. It was a near thing whether he wouldn't cut the army in two; but the fight at South Mountain gave Lee time to reconcentrate."

"I wish I could share Longstreet's confidence in our eventual victory."

"He doesn't believe we should ever invade the North," Trav explained. "He says to win the war the North must invade the South, and that whenever she does so we can smash her armies just as we did McClellan and Pope this summer. His point is that we don't have to conquer the North. They have to conquer us."

During the fortnight that followed, Brett began to believe Longstreet's optimism was justified. Sharpsburg was surely a defeat; but this did not act or look or sound like a beaten army. Not only were the men better fed every day, and better equipped, but as soldiers who had straggled under the hard march into Maryland returned to duty, each company and regiment filled its thinned ranks. The army that had put a scant forty thousand exhausted and barefoot men into battle at Sharpsburg presently counted sixty-five thousand soldiers, rested and fit to fight again.

Brett saw these things proudly, but he longed for some word from Cinda. In mid-October a chance came to go to Richmond. McClellan one day pushed out from Shepherdstown to feel for Lee's army, and

Lee himself barely escaped an encounter with Yankee cavalry on the road from Kearneysville to Smithfield. Two Parrott guns of the Howitzers were in action near Charlestown. A cannon ball tore Lieutenant Carter's cravat without seriously wounding him, Burley Brown was killed, and Captain Ben Smith lost a foot.

When Brett heard this he asked for and received permission to make the journey home with Captain Smith. They reached Richmond Monday afternoon. When they left the train, one of General Winder's sentries officiously insisted that the wounded man could not be taken to his own home but must go to a hospital. Brett, seeking an over-ruling authority, went to George Randolph, who had been the first commander of the Howitzers and who was now Secretary of War. Brett was shocked at the other's appearance. Randolph was younger than he, but the Secretary had lost weight so that his pale face was netted with a fine mesh of wrinkles and his small eyes seemed to have receded into their sockets.

He greeted Brett with a warmth which suggested he would have preferred service in the field to this desk assignment; and he asked many questions about the fortunes of his old command.

"It's on account of one of the men, Ben Smith, that I came to you," Brett said; and he related his experience with the sentry.

Secretary Randolph made a hopeless gesture. "All authority is being taken out of my hands," he said. "General Winder is the Czar of Richmond. My office can't even issue passports now. But by God I'll see Ben Smith settled in his own house or resign!"

So Brett, satisfied that Captain Smith's fortunes were in good hands, hurried home to Fifth Street. He found Vesta there, but no news from Cinda. Trying not to let Vesta see his disappointment, he asked questions about the Plains, and about Jenny and the children. Vesta said Camden was full of refugees from the islands along the coast, who had fled when the Yankees threatened landings there. "And they say lots of their negroes steal boats and row off to join the Yankees; so the rice planters are moving their people to plantations back from the coast. I expect Rollin's father's rice swamps are all abandoned." She spoke of what had been happening in Richmond. Mrs. Lee and her daughters had gone to Hickory Hill, the Wickham place, when General Lee went north with the army; now they were at Warren County

Springs in North Carolina. Richmond was as crowded as ever. Everyone just laughed at President Lincoln's proclamation about freeing all the slaves on the first of January. "Why, Papa, the people don't want to be free!" Vesta declared. "They wouldn't know what to do with themselves if they were."

Brett nodded. "I hear the price of slaves has gone up since the proclamation. Of course that's partly because money's worth less." Vesta said she didn't understand such things, and he smiled. "It's a question of how you put it. You say two thousand dollars will buy a slave, but I say that a slave will buy two thousand dollars."

She brushed aside this puzzling quibble. Richmond was a sad city, she said, since Sharpsburg. There were thousands of sick and wounded in the hospitals. Yellow fever had been bad at Wilmington, and Darrell had gone blockade running with Dolly's Captain Pew, and maybe he would catch it! Prices of everything were simply terrible. Sixteen dollars for a barrel of flour! "Oh and did you know Congress has raised your pay, Papa? Privates get four dollars more a month now. Don't you feel rich? Just think, you can almost buy a barrel of flour with your next month's salary."

They laughed together, and Brett said: "All the same, for a lot of our soldiers that extra four dollars is pretty important. Their families at home have to live on their pay."

"Well, I wish President Davis would do something about the old speculators' putting prices up. They charge two dollars and a half for a pound of coffee, and you can't get any, even for that. We've been toasting corn meal and making our coffee out of that."

"Probably better for you," he said smilingly.

"Oh, I always did hate things that were good for me! Now there, I've told you everything I know and you haven't told me anything. How are Burr and Uncle Faunt and Uncle Trav?"

So he told her about Stuart's bold raid into Maryland. "Burr and Faunt were both along, of course. But now the whole army's resting and skylarking. 'Specially the cavalry. Stuart's headquarters are at old Colonel Dandridge's place, the Bower, near Shepherdstown; and it's one of the most charming houses in the Valley. They have dancing every night, charades, theatricals, plenty of pretty girls. You know how the girls love the cavalry; and of course the cavalry loves pretty girls. Every day is Ladies' Day there."

"I guess they didn't take ladies on that ride into Maryland."

"No, but there was a fine evening of dancing to welcome the heroes home; and now they have parties every evening. There's a German, von Borcke, serving with Stuart. He's a giant, but a great dancer and a great hand for entertainments. He and Colonel Brien put on a silhouette show the other night, von Borcke playing sick and Colonel Brien playing doctor, pretending to reach down von Borcke's throat and pull out things he had eaten, antlers, a whole cabbage, a pair of boots, I don't know what all. Von Borcke had stuffed his stomach with pillows. He was supposed to have indigestion."

"It sounds perfectly disgusting," Vesta declared; but her eyes were twinkling.

"They say it was funny to see," Brett assured her. "Then another time von Borcke dressed up as a girl. He weighs two hundred and fifty, stands about six feet two; and he put on about twenty petticoats over his hoops, and some false braids, and simpered around on Colonel Brien's arm. Von Borcke's a clown; but he's a hard fighter. Stuart likes him."

They talked late, and Brett slept next morning till the sun was high. After dinner he called upon Captain Smith, whom he had brought home to Richmond; and he stopped to see Enid and the children, to tell them Trav was well. Brett had always liked Enid. She was so young, and so anxious to please them all; and so often the things she did or said which Cinda resented seemed to him a pitiful sort of defiance of Cinda's dislike. No matter how much he loved Cinda he was not blind to her faults; and her long fondness for Trav made it inevitable that she should be critical of Trav's wife.

He spent half an hour with Enid and Lucy and Peter; and when he came home, Cinda was there!

In the first moment of reunion, Brett's gladness was so great, and hers, that they could only cling together in a silent rapture; but while he still held Cinda close, he saw beyond her a tall young man whom for a moment he scarce recognized. Here was Julian, now overtopping Brett himself by an inch or so!

Julian was balanced on his crutches, one trouser leg tucked up and pinned; and Brett wished to weep. But—no tears now; no laments, no sympathy! Then what should he say? What word could he find to reassure this fine boy looking at him so happily, yet with a secret terror in his eyes. Brett guessed Julian's dread of vain condolences; and he had a saving inspiration. Someone, somewhere, on some occasion, had devised the pattern for a jest; and the pattern caught the army's fancy. Did a man appear in unusually high boots? "Come out of those cisterns! I see your head a-rarin up!" Or in a top hat? "Come down out of that steeple! I see your legs a-hanging down!" Or to a man who waxed his mustache: "Take them mice out of your mouth! I see their tails a-sticking out!" So Brett's first word now, to his maimed son, was jocose. "Come down off those stepladders! I see you up there!"

He felt Cinda stiffen in his arm's circle, and look up at him in hurt surprise; but Julian understood, and grinned delightedly. "Don't shoot, Papa! I'll come down!"

There were long fine hours of good talk together, with every word a sweetmeat to be savored to the utmost. Anne Tudor had gone home to her father. "She knew we'd want just ourselves here, the darling," said Cinda. "She's been so sweet, Brett. Hasn't she, Julian?" Julian nodded happily. Vesta and Brett made Cinda begin at the beginning, but under their questions she forever harked back or skipped ahead. When she spoke of their journey from Warrenton to Centerville, Brett said:

"The battle was fought right along that road, a few days afterward." He was glad they had passed that way before the battle and not afterward, to see—as he had seen—those fields littered with hideous carrion.

"I know. After we got to Mr. Gilby's, we could hear the guns, and then the wounded came pouring into Washington and the place was crazy with panic, people running away as fast and as far as they could go."

Julian laughed. "That was the best medicine we had, in the hospitals, Papa; I mean where there were Southerners together. To hear how scared the Yanks were."

"Anne and I just had to stay indoors," Cinda told them. "There were frightened people and drunken soldiers everywhere. But Brett

Dewain, McClellan must be a great man! Inside a week he'd made an army again. I saw them march out H Street. Their uniforms weren't pretty any more, but—they looked like soldiers! It scared me to see them! When the news of the fight on the Antietam came, I wasn't surprised."

"The Yankees will learn to fight, give them time."

"Oh, and the North has so many, and so much! When we left here, Anne and I saw wagons and guns with our own army; and we thought there were millions of them; but the North has a railroad train full of things for every wagon in our army."

Vesta urged: "Go on and tell us about finding Julian, Mama." She laughed fondly. "He's a lot more important than the war."

So Cinda described that Georgetown warehouse and it's crawling infestations. "But I've seen worse, right here in Richmond, for our own men." She spoke of Dr. Hammond, the Surgeon General. "I wish we had someone like him. He's a great-hearted man, besides being a great doctor. He let us take Julian out of that horrible place to Mr. Gilby's, even when Mr. Stanton's orders were against it. Then when Julian was well enough to travel, Mr. Gilby and I went to see Mr. Stanton. He's terrible and cruel. He's a little man. I think little men are all natural bullies. They have to make up somehow for being small, so they love to be bossy. There were lots of people waiting to see him. I don't know how many. Twenty or thirty. He came march-ing in and looked at us and said, 'Two minutes each.' Five of us were ladies, so we went first. Even the Yankees are courteous. The first poor woman whispered something, and Mr. Stanton fairly shouted at her: 'Speak up, madam! No secrets here!' By the time my turn came I was too mad to be frightened. He glared at Mr. Gilby and said: 'Step aside! We have no use for advocates!' So poor Mr. Gilby retreated and I said: 'Mr. Secretary, I want a passport to take my wounded son to Richmond. A pass for myself, my son, and his betrothed.'" She smiled at Julian. "We always called Anne that. It saved explanations."

Julian's color rose; he laughed happily. "I'll try to prove you weren't fibbing, Mama."

Brett said quickly: "Go on, Cinda."

She nodded. "So Mr. Stanton said: 'To Richmond? Then you're a rebel?' I told him I was a Virginian. He said: 'Your son's a rebel!' I said Julian had only one leg, and I said: 'So you needn't be afraid of him.' He said: 'Afraid? Madam, you're wasting your time and mine. Good day.' I was frightened enough by then to—beg. I said: 'Mr. Stanton, my oldest son was killed a year ago. This one almost died—' But he interrupted me." She hesitated. "I think he's a little crazy! He said: 'Madam, my son, who was not a rebel, died three months ago, an infant. I have no tears to shed when a rebel dies. Good day!'" She laughed, a little breathlessly. "And the sentry came across from the door and took me by the arm. They threw me out, Brett Dewain!" Brett looked thoughtfully at his clenched fist; but she smiled and touched his hand. "There, my dear; I didn't mind. From a man like him, insolence was really a compliment."

He nodded. "Yet—you did bring Julian home."

"Yes."

"How?"

Julian answered quickly. "She went to Mr. Lincoln, Papa. He gave her a pass."

Brett looked at Cinda in tender understanding. He could guess what it must have meant to her to entreat the man she hated so. He asked in his thoughts a thousand questions; but Vesta put at least one of those questions into words, and Cinda answered her.

"What's he like?" she echoed thoughtfully. "Why, I suppose he's even uglier than his pictures, Vesta; so tall, so awkward, long arms like an ape's arms. His legs don't seem to work right. He—sort of staggers. And—when he said good-by to me he hung to the door frame with one hand, exactly like a tremendous monkey, as though he could have curled up his legs and still hung there." She laughed. "He's perfectly ridiculous, Vesta, really!"

"But Mama, how did you get to see him at all?"

"Dr. Hammond took me. Dr. Hammond doesn't like Mr. Stanton any better than I do. He was really wonderful. He took me to—the President—and said I had a disabled son who would never fight again——"

Julian laughed. "A lot he knows!"

Brett met the boy's eyes and smiled; and Cinda went on: "So Mr. Lincoln asked who I was, and I told him, and he asked whether Julian and I would take the oath, and I said we were Virginians, and

—Well, Mr. Lincoln said he guessed Julian would do the Union less harm in Richmond than in Washington, and he wrote a pass and told me not to show it to Mr. Stanton, and that night we took the steamer with prisoners coming back to be exchanged." She met Brett's eyes. "When we came up the river, I saw the black chimneys of Great Oak. The house is all gone. But—here we are. Oh it's good to be home!"

Vesta had questions still, and Cinda answered her; but Brett felt evasion in her answers. Lincoln? Why, he was thus and he was so— and always her word suggested a grotesque man, almost inhuman. Yet, knowing her better than these others knew her, he understood that she held something hidden, something of which she was perhaps not herself aware. He knew too that when the time came she would tell him more than she told them; so he asked no questions at all. It was enough that she was here, that Julian was alive, at home.

Brett wished no outsider to intrude upon this hour; but before supper Redford Streean and Tilda and Dolly appeared. Dolly had heard that Julian was here; they came to welcome him home, and Dolly was never more lovely than when she kissed him, gently as an angel. "Oh Honey, it's wonderful to see you!" Tilda struck a mistaken note. "You poor dear darling!" Julian looked at her in flashing anger; and Streean must have seen this, for his greeting was bluff and hearty. Brett thought Streean had the politician's quick adaptability when he wished to please.

Dolly said Rollin Lyle would be mighty glad to hear Julian was home. "He asked about you every time he came to the house." So Julian pinned her with questions about his old regiment. "Why, just about all of them got killed at Williamsburg," Dolly told him, and Brett thought pain must crush Vesta at that word, and looked at her and saw a fine light in her eyes and knew she was unshaken. "And then a lot more of them got shot or something in the fighting around Richmond." Julian asked for names, and Dolly remembered a Lieutenant Jones. "But then they stayed near here till—oh I guess it was the end of August, or maybe September. Anyway, I haven't seen Rollin since."

Cinda asked how he was. "He came to the house once or twice, during the summer, Julian," she explained. "But I was working in the hospital and was never here; and Vesta and Jenny had gone. Enid saw him. She said he looked sick, Dolly."

Dolly said lightly: "Oh I guess he had malaria or something for a while, but I don't really know how he looked. I never can bear to look at him. He's a sight."

There was a moment's silence; and Brett said thoughtfully: "I think he's in Hill's division, Cinda. They say Hill's fight at South Mountain saved our army. By the way, General Garland was killed there. He's Mrs. Longstreet's cousin, remember."

Dolly wanted to hear the tale of Julian's adventures; and Cinda and Tilda went up to see Mrs. Currain, and Streean suggested that he and Brett withdraw to the study. "You're a business man," he explained. "I'd like to hear your views on the state of things."

Brett, leading the way into the other room, confessed that he had given little thought to business for a long time now; that the war was the only business of the day. Streean said war was largely a matter of business, and Brett agreed. Streean thought it a pity there were not more business men in the Government, and he added: "I think the best contribution any of us can make to a sound management of public affairs is to keep our own business in order. A nation of level-headed men whose own lives are well managed would be a sound nation." Brett guessed what was coming. "I took the liberty, for instance," Streean went on, "of advising Tony to sell the surplus slaves at Chimneys." He added hurriedly: "Too large a proportion of Currain money is tied up in slaves. Of course since President Lincoln said he proposes to free them, the going price has risen; but that's largely a defiant gesture, the sort of thing Southerners like to do." Brett knew this was true. "I hope you'll pardon my advising Tony to sell."

"Tony had the disposal of the people. He was in charge at Chimneys."

Streean cleared his throat, and his eyes narrowed thoughtfully. "The slaves he sold were from Great Oak and from Belle Vue. And of course all Currain funds are handled by you."

"The people were in Tony's hands."

The other smiled. "But the proceeds are in mine, and I have Tony's authority to reinvest it. I assume he agrees with me that it should be invested for the common interest of all of you." Brett did not speak, and Streean went on: "So I'd welcome your opinion, Brett. For my part, I abhor idle money. To put this sum to work involves choosing among many alternatives, ranging from conservative and only mildly profitable to bold and immensely lucrative. I've seized some opportunities myself. For instance, a small speculation in salt . . ." Brett thought Streean almost smirked with satisfaction. "Well, it turned out well. I sold out before we recaptured the salt works in Kanąwha. Just now I'm taking some shares in a blockade-runner. The profit there is so great that after two or three voyages each dollar is clear gain."

Brett held his tone mild. "I'd be inclined to leave the question in Tony's hands—and the money too. After all, selling the people was his venture, not ours. I shouldn't care to profit by it."

Streean cleared his throat again, and his eyes flickered uneasily. "I see. Well, very well. But by the way, there's something in the wind which might affect your plans at the Plains. I know you agree that cotton is our great asset."

"It might have been."

"It will be," Streean assured him. "I can tell you, for instance, that a European loan will be floated by Mr. Slidell, using our cotton as security, the cotton to be delivered after the war. That will go far to finance our foreign purchases." Brett thought no wise European investor would rely too much upon a promise to deliver after Confederate victory; but he did not say so, and Streean went on: "However, something more immediate, and nearer home, is being arranged which will provide a market for our cotton. Some of us have been buying cotton in anticipation. The price in the North and in Europe is soaring, you know."

"You say something is being arranged?"

"Exactly. Do you know Mr. Foulkes?" Brett shook his head. "Mr. Dunnock?"

"No."

"Well, the proposal is to trade, or to sanction trade, in cotton with the Yankees. We have it and they want it; and they have many things that we want, so the trade will be to our advantage and to theirs. Mr. Foulkes proposes to trade cotton for bread and meat. Mr. Northrop, the Commissary General, favors that. Mr. Randolph would add blankets and shoes to the list." Streean smiled. "Everyone is proceeding very cautiously, sticking one toe into the water to see if it is too hot a venture. So far, not much has been done, though Mr. Benjamin has given some permissions to sell cotton at our ports, and to send it into Mexico; and some Mobile business men have been granted licenses to trade with the Yankees in New Orleans."

"For private profit?"

"For the public good—and for private profit too, of course. Muzzle not the ox, you know. The men who conduct the transactions are entitled to be rewarded for their services." Streean leaned forward, pressing home his point. "Brett, in another year our cotton will be going into Northern markets in great quantities." He leaned back. "So here's the point. The Plains should raise all the cotton it can."

Brett said slowly: "I'm afraid the whole idea sticks in my craw, Mister Streean."

"If the Government approves, doesn't that overrule private scruples?"

"Well, governments, in what they consider the defense of their own interests, can do many things which in a private citizen, for his own interest, would be reprehensible."

"Do you conceive it your duty to surrender all your capital to the Confederacy?" Streean's tone was a challenge.

"Certainly not! I conserve our capital in every possible way."

"Exactly. But—remember the parable of the talents, Brett? To bury a talent, to refrain from putting your capital to work to the best advantage, is a business crime. I'd rather lose it in a wise risk."

"There's a distinction," Brett said; he rose to end this conversation. "I prefer not to profit from the extremity of my neighbors, of Virginia, of the Confederacy."

Streean shrugged. "Then why not be consistent? If you won't use your possessions, give them away; give them to the Confederacy."

"I see no need for that," Brett assured him; and rose, and they went back to the others again.

Brett was glad when that day was done, when he and Cinda were at last alone. She said she had delivered to Mr. Gilby those securities which Brett had wished her to take North. "I was terrified that I'd be searched," she confessed. "We hear so many stories, and my petticoats were stiff with crackly papers. But the night we got there I put everything in Mr. Gilby's hands. They're in Riggs' Bank. Mr. Gilby will take care of them for you; he promised, if there was another such scare as Washington had in September, to send them to New York."

She talked on and on, as though afraid of even a moment's silence. "Mr. Gilby thinks Mr. Lincoln's proclamation about freeing the slaves was timed to keep England and France from recognizing the Confederacy. He says for a while England shipped surplus cotton to New England, but now she's running short, and mills are shutting down in England, and idle men are rioting; but not even men out of work and with their families hungry want to support slavery. The whole world hates us for having slaves, Brett Dewain."

He nodded sorrowfully. "And Lincoln is shrewd enough to know that, so he turns this into a war against slavery and thus puts us in the wrong." He thought to speak of Lincoln might lead her to say more about that man; but she continued to cling to generalities, describing things seen in Washington. Mrs. Gilby had told her this, had told her that. Many Washington women worked in the hospitals just as Richmond ladies did.

"But they're better planners than we are," she said. "A Miss Dix, a spinster lady older than I, bosses all the women who do the work. They have men nurses, mostly. The women just help. Mr. Olmsted —the same man who wrote that lying book about his trip through the South a few years ago—runs the Sanitary Commission; and Mrs. Gilby says he's wonderful! He's almost an invalid himself, but he manages things marvelously. And Mrs. Gilby says a Miss Barton went right on the battlefield at Manassas to give the wounded men things to eat, and she went to the battle on the Antietam, too."

"People won't know what you mean if you call it that here, Cinda," he suggested. "The North likes to name battles after streams; Bull Run and Antietam Creek. But we usually name them after the nearest town. Their Bull Run is our Manassas, and their Antietam is our Sharpsburg."

But he seldom interrupted, let her talk. When she began to repeat some of the things Mrs. Gilby had said about Mrs. Lincoln's extravagances, her ugliness, her ridiculous costumes, her pretentious airs, her moods and tempers, her almost insane grief when Willie Lincoln died last spring, he expected her to go on to speak of her meeting with the President. But it was not till they were at last abed, in darkness, that she came to that which was foremost in both their minds. She had been silent for a moment, and he was about to speak when she said:

"Brett Dewain, I saw President Lincoln."

He kept his tone casual. "I've often thought I'd like to see that man again. I saw him once, years ago, out in Illinois."

"Dr. Hammond took me to him." Her voice was low. "The President sees people at noon, but there is always a crowd then; and Doctor Hammond wanted me to see him alone. Doctor Hammond hates Mr. Stanton. That was one reason he helped me, I'm sure; just because Mr. Stanton would not."

She paused, and Brett waited. "We went early," she said. "Dr. Hammond had made an appointment. There were people waiting, all sorts of people, men and women, poor people and rich people, just waiting. When we went in, Mr. Lincoln was saying good-by to an old gentleman and a pretty girl, and the girl was laughing up at him and he was smiling. Then he turned to us, and he was still smiling; but then the smile just seemed to drain out of his face and leave gray sadness and sorrow." Her hand found Brett's. "Brett Dewain, I never saw such sadness in a man's eyes."

Brett, lest he break the spell, neither moved nor spoke.

"Oh, he's ugly," she said, more to herself than to him. "He's ugly, yes. His mouth is ugly, and his cheeks are ugly, and his beard and his hair; and sometimes his left eyebrow cocks up and he looks like an ugly old owl, as though he wanted to smile and wouldn't. His mouth, when he isn't smiling, looks as though he never smiled. It's heavy as lead. There's a wart or something on his cheek. He has the biggest ears I ever saw. Tony really does look like him, a little."

He felt perplexity in her. "What puzzles you, Cinda?"

"Well, I know he's ugly. But I never looked at a man who made me —well, who filled me with such calm happiness. Except you, of course."

"Why?" he asked.

"Happiness isn't the word," she admitted. "I don't know the word. I felt warm. I felt safe. Brett Dewain, I felt safe. I trusted him."

"What happened, Cinda? Tell me all about it."

She filled her lungs, lying here beside him. "Well, Dr. Hammond introduced me. He said I had come from Richmond to get Julian. He said Julian had been nearer dying than any man he ever saw who lived. He said Julian's leg was gone at the thigh. He said Mr. Stanton would not let me take Julian home. Mr. Lincoln's eyebrow cocked a little at that. He was almost sitting on the table or the desk or whatever it was, leaning back on it, bracing his hands on it, with his shoulders hunched up. He said Mr. Stanton was a strict man. Then Dr. Hammond left me alone with him. He looked at me. I didn't say anything."

Brett ventured to chuckle. "A remarkable man, Cinda, if he silenced you."

"Well, he did," she said. "I just stood there and waited. After a while he said he expected Mr. Stanton wanted me to take the oath. I didn't answer. It wasn't a question. He asked if Julian was my only son, and I said: 'No, I've a boy who rides with Stuart.' He said: 'Then your boy makes us a lot of trouble.' I said: 'He tries to.' I told him about Clayton. He wiped his forehead with his hand, and nodded as though he were very tired. Then he said: 'So you wouldn't take the oath for Mr. Stanton?' I told him we were Virginians. He nodded at that, too. Then he said something I'll never forget."

Brett waited, and she went on: "He spoke very softly. He said: 'Some men fight for themselves; but some fight for a cause, and some fight for a scruple, with nothing to gain and all to lose. I regret they decided as they did; but I honor them for their decision.'" And she added: "I think he meant all of us in the South."

"He's a good man."

"He said another thing." Cinda seemed not to have heard. "He said: 'My grandfathers were Virginians.' I wanted to tell him I was a Currain, to see if he knew the name, but I dared not. He turned and leaned over his desk and wrote on a card: 'Pass the bearer and her party, unmolested, by Government transport, to Fortress Monroe and Richmond.' He signed it—of course we had to get the military passes afterward—and gave it to me and said, 'Don't show this to Mr. Stanton,' and smiled, and it was like sunshine coming into the room. Then he let me out by the side door, holding to the lintel with one hand, watching me go away. He was still standing there watching me when I met Dr. Hammond where the passage turned."

Brett, in the hushed darkness, said quietly: "You'll remember him, won't you, my dear?"

"Yes. But I'll always wish I'd told him that my name was Currain before I was married."

"Why?"

"To see if he knows."

"He wouldn't have told you."

"I could have guessed, by the way he took it."

After a moment Brett asked: "Do you still—blame him as bitterly?"

"Oh Brett Dewain, Brett Dewain," she whispered. "Is he right? Are we all wrong?"

20

CINDA'S journey to Washington won Julian back from the shadows, and to that extent it brought her happiness; but also it awakened in her a doubt the seeds of which had been sowed long ago. Before Brett left at month's end to return to duty she confessed this to him. "I suppose I've known, with the sensible part of me, that the South wasn't perfect; that there always is some right on both sides of any question. But it was so simple and easy to just blame the North, and Mr. Lincoln, and never doubt ourselves at all." She shook her head. "But now I can never do that again. I'll never be able to forget that sad, sad man in Washington. He's my kin, Brett Dewain; and you know, though I wouldn't say this to anyone but you, I'm proud of it." And she cried wearily: "But oh, it was so much easier never to question, just to be sure we were right and that they were wrong!"

Brett said proudly: "If you were any other woman but yourself, you'd still do that, shut your eyes, plunge straight ahead like a blindered horse. Thinking hurts, Cinda. It's a lot easier never to think at all, if you can manage not to."

"Other women seem to manage it. Yes, and men too. Why can't I?"

He smiled and kissed her. "Because—it's just possible that I've suggested this to you before—because you're unique among women, Mrs. Dewain."

She laughed and clung to him and cried: "Oh, I hate to have you go again. I need you so! I need you so!"

Yet he must go; and she sometimes thought, after he was gone, that she was stronger without him. Because she had to be strong, because she could not surrender to the weakness of her own doubts and fears, she did not. Yet occasionally she envied her mother, who could shut away the world. It must be bliss not to know the world was all gone wrong; but it was a bliss Cinda could not grant herself. The simple business of managing the house and of supplying the table gave her more than one perplexed and frightening hour. Caesar might do her marketing in normal times, but not now. When she told him to buy a barrel of flour and gave him sixteen dollars to pay for it, he came home to report that the price was twenty dollars; when she herself went next day incredulously to question this absurdity, she had to pay twenty-four dollars—and thank the merchant for the privilege of purchase. For such an indispensable as salt the price fluctuated maddeningly. One day the stores were asking seventy-five cents a pound, but the City Council would sell a pound per month per person for five cents. In a sudden panic lest this source of supply disappear, Cinda bought twenty pounds more at seventy-five cents in a store on Main Street. A fortnight later Tilda told her that buyers had paid a dollar and thirty cents a pound at auction, and Cinda vowed she would never pay so much. When suddenly the price dropped to thirty-five cents a pound, she hurried to buy fifty pounds. They would have salt enough at least!

"I know I'm silly," she wrote Brett, describing these erratic purchases. "But the thought of not being able to buy things when you want them just terrifies me, and I go perfectly insane. I suppose everyone else does the same. Probably most people, people like us, have enough salt in their store rooms right now to last them for years; but we keep buying more! Why are we all such fools, Brett Dewain? Probably there'd be plenty for everyone if some of us—me, for instance—didn't behave like pigs! They're asking forty dollars for a barrel of flour now, and I hesitated to pay half that a month ago. What's going to happen to us? Are we all mad? You can't buy shoes at any price, really! Fifty dollars a pair for boots—and none to be had. Shirts are twelve dollars! People on the streets are actually ragged—except the negroes! They have their Sunday clothes, clothes we gave them. I wish I had back some of the things I've given June! And of course the speculators and the quartermasters and the commissaries are as slick as hogs! Redford Streean—but I mustn't get started on him!"

Streean and Tilda and Dolly were in fact a steady irritation. She never saw them without a surge of anger. About the time Captain Pew and Darrell returned from their adventure through the blockade, Tony came to Richmond; and he seemed to Cinda as offensively complacent as Streean.

"We live on the fat of the land at Chimneys," he assured her. "You know, once they build the Danville railroad through to Greensboro, Chimneys will be a valuable property."

"Are they going to build the railroad?"

"Streean thinks so. He says General Lee believes the Yankees will cut the Weldon Railroad, sooner or later; and when that happens, every bite Richmond eats will have to come through from Danville. When that road's built, I'll be able to get a price for whatever I raise."

He had come to Richmond on business, he said. "Streean and I are in partnership." He put on an elaborately mysterious manner, then could not resist boasting. "We've bought a steamer to run the blockade."

"Oh Tony," she pleaded, "don't try to make money out of all this!"

"Why not?" He chuckled. "If that nephew of ours in Washington is bent on ruining the South, I'll show him there's at least one of his uncles as smart as he."

She hesitated. "I saw him in Washington, Tony. He let me bring Julian home."

"Ha! Tell him who you were, did you?"

"Of course not!"

"Good! I wouldn't give that baboon the satisfaction of knowing we're kin!"

Cinda expected Tony would lodge with them, but he declined. "No, Tilda's putting me up. Streean and I have a lot of things to discuss, another venture." She let him go; but next day Mrs. Currain suggested that it would be nice if Tony and Tilda came to Sunday dinner, and Cinda went to suggest this.

She found Streean at home, but no one else. "They've gone to Enid's, Captain Pew and Darrell, Dolly and Tilda, Tony, the lot of them." He bade her sit down and wait and said they would soon return. She spoke of Tony's big talk of business, and Streean chuckled.

"His real business here is buying dresses," he told her. "Dolly and Tilda are advising him." And to her astonished question he said Tony was apparently in love. "Playing King Cophetua to some beggar maid, I suspect," he said. "Certainly he's buying a regular trousseau."

Something in his tone frightened Cinda. He spoke with a malicious enjoyment, as though he could tell more if he chose. Because she was afraid of what he might tell if she questioned him, she refrained from doing so; instead she referred to that new enterprise about which Tony had been so mysterious.

Streean was not at all reticent. There was a plan to trade cotton with the North for salt, a bale of cotton for ten sacks of salt. Governor Pettus of Mississippi had persuaded President Davis to agree. They were both Mississippi men. "President Davis hopes to get twenty sacks of salt for a bale of cotton," he said. "Of course he won't get that much. He'll get ten sacks, and the men who handle the business will get the difference. Tony and I mean to take a hand in that trade."

"Isn't that—it sounds wrong."

"It's good for the Confederacy," he assured her. "We'll get not only salt but meat and shoes and blankets, and we need them! The Yankees will give us anything except arms and ammunition, if we'll give them cotton. They'll allow fifty cents a pound for cotton." He smiled. "And of course there'll be a fifty percent profit for the handlers."

"I'm glad we don't raise cotton at the Plains now." Distaste was in her tone.

"Oh it's perfectly respectable," Streean retorted. She saw that he wished to provoke her, and held herself in hand. "Why, even Governor Vance of North Carolina is buying cotton, and the state plans to go into the trade," he declared.

"I suppose the Jews are all in it." She spoke contemptuously.

"If they are, that just proves it's good business!" he assured her. "Most of us hate the Jews because they're cleverer than we are. You're too sentimental, Cinda. So is Brett. He's missing a real opportunity."

She could no longer conceal her angry scorn. "I don't believe Brett considers the death agony of the South his 'opportunity'."

"You think the Confederacy is dead? Or dying?" His tone was one of mock concern.

She flushed. "Of course not! But—the vultures are watching their chance."

Streean looked at her for a moment with eyes unmasked, and she saw in them his long hatred. "Calling names won't keep you all from ending up as paupers, Cinda. Then you'll learn to sing a different tune."

"I suppose there are many who feel as you do." She tried to be fair to him. After all, he was Tilda's husband.

He nodded, good-humored again. "I didn't make this war," he reminded her. "It was made by men full of lofty notions, living with their heads in the air, ready to fight for a high-sounding word. Well, that's their privilege! Practical men, even politicians, would like to end this war now. Governor Vance, for instance, says North Carolina is ready to reconstruct the Union. But people like you and Brett take a high ground, and talk of death as preferable to surrender. Well, that's your privilege, too. As for me, I don't take sides. Settle it between you. But I'll look out for myself while you're deciding." And he said calmly: "It's women like you who keep the war going, Cinda."

"I won't quarrel with you," she said wearily, but she was thinking: Is he right? Is it true? Are we women, already mourning for our lost ones, urging those we love to go on and on? "Perhaps the women are the only patriots left," she suggested: "The women and the army."

"The army?" He smiled. "The officers, perhaps, yes; and the sons and husbands of you women. They don't dare face you if they refuse to fight! But they're not the army! There's not one of you aristocrats—" Cinda thought he almost snarled the word. "Not one of you out of every ten men left in the army. You've bought substitutes, or retired to your plantations with your twenty slaves per man, or got yourself details——"

"Like you and Darrell?" she suggested.

"Exactly," he agreed. "Oh, a year ago last spring you all volunteered for three months or for six; but last spring the whole army was dissolving, so you passed the conscription law to make poor men fight, and to make it easy for rich men to avoid fighting. Poor men can't get out of the army legally; but do you know how many of them have deserted? And how many more would desert if they dared? And how many have been shot for trying it? Go out to Camp Lee some day and see a few of them shot! Ask Tony about his neighbors at Chimneys—poor fellows skulking in the woods, afraid to show their faces, cultivating their fields by moonlight so their families won't starve, hiding from the conscription officers." And he cried: "Why, not ten percent of the men in or out of the army would vote to go on fighting if they had their say! Why should they? Why should eighty or ninety percent of the men in the South fight so the rest of you can keep your slaves?"

Cinda rose. "I'll not wait for the others."

"Forgive my plain speaking, Cinda; but you might as well face facts."

"I'm afraid I can't," she admitted; yet she knew there was truth in what he said, a sufficient weight of truth to silence her. She gave him the invitation to dinner. "Mama wants you all," she explained, and hurried to escape before Tilda and the others returned.

For that dinner on Sunday Tilda asked whether Captain Pew might be included. "He and Darrell and Dolly and Enid have such good times together." Cinda consented, a little curious to meet the Captain; and since not to do so would be a slight, she asked Enid too. At dinner, Captain Pew proved to be an interesting and an easy conversationalist. Cinda thought there was certainly danger in the man, but Dolly was not unique in enjoying playing with fire. The Captain delighted Mrs. Currain, making her smile again and again, and he paid Cinda a courteous deference which could not fail to please her.

Tilda as usual had news for them, news that brought tears to Vesta's eyes. General Lee's daughter Anne had died in late October, at Warren County Springs. Vesta said sorrowfully: "I think she was closer to General Lee than any of the other girls. Agnes is sort of stiff and offish, and Mildred is too clever for her own good, always saying bright things that hurt people's feelings. But everyone just loved Anne."

"Mrs. Lee and Agnes are coming to stay with the Caskies," Tilda said. "You know Norvell Caskie and Agnes are devoted."

"Is Mary coming?" Vesta asked.

"She's visiting now at Cedar Grove, Dr. Stuart's place. They've put Mildred in boarding school in Raleigh."

Vesta nodded and the talk drifted casually. Enid said something about what fun she and Captain Pew and Darrell and Dolly had had together last Thursday, and Cinda gathered that they had all been at the house on Clay Street not only then but on other occasions. After they were gone she spoke of this to Vesta.

"I wish Enid would behave herself. She shouldn't be cutting up with Dolly when Trav's away."

"I expect she's pretty lonesome," Vesta said forgivingly. "After all, she doesn't know many people, even in the quiet set. And of course Dolly's sort of an outsider too."

"That's her father's fault. Everyone despises him."

Vesta said reluctantly: "Well, it's not all Mr. Streean's fault. Dolly does sort of make a little fool of herself sometimes."

Through the weeks that followed, Cinda came to realize that her uneasiness about Enid was not without some foundation. Before Captain Pew and Darrell left Richmond she heard from some of her friends who were among Enid's neighbors an occasional remark about what gay little groups seemed to gather in the house on Clay Street. Mrs. Brownlaw one day spoke more forthrightly.

"That sister-in-law of yours, Mrs. Travis Currain, had better mind her p's and q's," she declared.

Cinda was accustomed to Mrs. Brownlaw's sometimes slanderous tongue. That energetic woman, as the work in which she had been an officious pioneer became better organized, found herself more and more excluded from the position of dominance which she had sought to seize. Mrs. Minge, Miss Sally Tompkins, Miss Pettigrew, Miss Mason, and others not so vociferous as she, had by their abilities acquired a leadership they did not seek. Mrs. Brownlaw, no longer able to dominate the volunteer work in the hospitals, had come to Cinda today to enlist her help in caring for the refugees fleeing to Richmond from Fredericksburg, where General Burnside, who had succeeded McClellan as the Union commander, seemed about to precipitate a battle. She explained that she had gone first to Enid, and had been rebuffed. "She says, if you please, she's much too busy to think of taking strangers into her home," Mrs. Brownlaw declared. "As far as I can discover she hasn't a thing to do except act like a belle of twenty, when she must be forty if she's a day!" And she added, watching Cinda: "She says her husband wouldn't approve; says Mr. Currain thinks we've brought our troubles on ourselves——"

Cinda protested: "Oh, now, Mrs. Brownlaw, I'm sure Enid didn't say quite that!"

"Well, perhaps not exactly; but she says he stands up for that dreadful nigger-lover in Washington!"

To argue with Mrs. Brownlaw was useless. She had the irritating habit of not hearing what you said; and even when she seemed to listen it was with poorly concealed impatience, while she waited for her turn to speak. "Just what do you want me to do?" Cinda asked.

"Why, the Yankees have threatened to bombard Fredericksburg, you know; so everyone who has anywhere to go is leaving. Last night's train was just crowded with poor women and children—yes and negroes too—all of them weeping and wailing; and we must take care of them somehow; as long as we can, at least! Heaven knows we may be driven out of our own homes any day, with the Yankees, just hundreds of thousands of them, coming at us from all directions."

Cinda felt a resentful irritation at this babbling woman; yet there were many in Richmond as fearful as she. Last spring the enemy had been almost at the gates. General Lee and his men had driven them out of Virginia, and on the rising tide of success had marched into Maryland, and everyone thought victory was near and certain. But Sharpsburg, no matter how loyally you pretended it had been a victory, had forced Lee to retreat; and now Burnside had marched deep into Virginia again, and General Lee seemed unwilling to fight him. When early in November a deep snow blanketed the northern part of the state, everyone had hoped winter would lock the armies in mud and give them all a respite until spring; but since then the weather had been fine enough and now there was again a secret sense of danger in every Richmond home.

"I don't see how I can do anything, take anyone in," Cinda confessed. With Julian at home and still needing watchful care, she had not even returned to her service in the hospital. "My son and Mr. Dewain may come home at any time, and we're crowded as it is. But I'll do anything I can—except take strangers here."

She held to that decision, though in the days that followed more and more of these refugees came to Richmond. Once the train that brought them away from their homes was fired upon by the Yankees.

Yet Fredericksburg had not been bombarded; probably it would not be. They fled from their own fears; but Cinda thought they might quite as well have stayed at home. Certainly there was danger here in Richmond too. A plague of smallpox began to sweep the city, and the disease this year seemed to be particularly fatal. Dr. Brock proposed to vaccinate healthy children and save the scabs with which to immunize adults; and Mrs. Brownlaw was busy persuading parents to allow their children to be used for this purpose. Cinda was glad Jenny's children and Barbara's baby were far away, so that she need not refuse Mrs. Brownlaw's insistences.

The problem of housing the increasing throng of refugees was a daily burden. Some could find temporary lodging in the hospitals which were almost empty now. But it became daily more certain that unless winter came to make any movement by the armies impossible, there would be a battle presently on the Rappahannock yonder. The first Sunday in December was a day of bitter cold, and Cinda found ice in the pitcher in her bed room when she rose that morning; but at once the cold moderated, and Thursday's train from the North brought word that the shelling of Fredericksburg had at last begun. That night was soft and warm. Next day Richmond heard that the Yankees had crossed the river. There followed rumors, each more frightening than the last, of battle, of victory, of defeat. Saturday afternoon Tilda came in a flutter of excitement, half fear and half anticipation, with a report that President Davis had gone to Mississippi! She thought it was shameful for him to run away when the Yankees might come bursting into Richmond any minute! Cinda said flatly:

"I don't believe he's gone, Tilda. You mustn't credit everything you hear. Or if he has gone, be sure he went for a good reason. Anyway, babbling all sorts of wild tales can't help."

Sunday morning, the fourteenth of December, was like a day in spring, warm and fair and beautiful; and Cinda's spirits rose. Surely on such a day there could be no great wrong anywhere in the world. She and Julian went to church. Mrs. Currain no longer stirred out of the house, and Vesta, whose baby was a short two months away, now stayed secluded; so they went alone. At the church gate Cinda saw Mrs. Davis the center of a group of ladies; and she joined them and heard the news of battle the day before.

This had been a bloody repulse for the Yankees, but a day of tragedy too. General Cobb was dead, General Hood desperately wounded, none knew how many others hurt or slain. Cinda at her prayers that day whispered: "Dear God, must we always wait and wait, never knowing when the word we fear will come? It wouldn't be so hard if it weren't for the waiting and the waiting. Please, God, don't make us wait longer than we must. I can stand anything, anything, once I know it. But to wait and wait and not to know——"

Yet from that waiting for news of her dear ones there was no quick escape. That day and the next the wounded began to arrive; and to drown her own terrors Cinda returned to her work at Chimborazo Hospital. Tuesday afternoon Julian came on his crutches the long way to find her there with word that Brett and the others were safe.

"Mr. Barksdale, on General Longstreet's staff, came with a trainload of wounded and brought you a letter from Trav," he said. "I opened it, Mama. Do you mind?"

"Of course not, darling." She snatched the letter.

"They're all right," he told her. "Papa, and Burr, and Uncle Faunt."

Cinda's eyes raced along the lines. "He's seen them all," she whispered. "He's seen them all."

So for that time the shadow and the terror passed. There would be other battles, other waitings; but of them Cinda refused to think, not now, not till she must. General Lee reported that Burnside's army had withdrawn again to the hills beyond the Rappahannock, and winter came to bring what passed for peace. They could taste security awhile.

Saturday night Trav came home, and he stopped at Cinda's before going to Clay Street. He said that Brett and the others hoped to be here for Christmas. He was sure there would be no more fighting for a time. "They put General Burnside in command in McClellan's place," he reminded Cinda. "But we beat them terribly. The soldiers say Burnside is burned not only on the sides, but all over now." They laughed together, the quick nervous laughter that marks release from strain; and he added: "He won't try anything till his scars heal. General Longstreet has gone to Lynchburg for Christmas." He stood hat in hand, and he turned now toward the door. Julian asked some eager question; but Trav said he must go home. "I'm anxious to see the children." Cinda noticed that he did not speak of Enid. "Maybe we can come to dinner tomorrow."

"Do!" she agreed, shivering at the cold blast when the door was opened. "We'll try to keep you warm."

Next day at dinner and afterward, no one mentioned the battle till Mrs. Currain had gone for her nap. Vesta went with her; but Lucy and Peter stayed hanging on Trav's words, and Julian pressed him to long talk. Trav spoke at first with obvious reluctance. "Why, Julian, it wasn't a battle; it was just slaughter. Our men were in a sunken road behind a wall, and the Yankees kept marching up to us across an open field and we shot them down. It was horrible!"

Enid protested: "I declare, Trav, I think you just hate to have us kill Yankees!"

Cinda looked at her, and Trav said: "Well, this was so easy, like butchering hogs. General Longstreet said that as long as our ammunition held out, a bird couldn't have flown across that slope the poor fellows tried to climb. I had to just stand and watch and not do anything, and that made it worse. All those lines of men in blue marching toward us, and then our muskets and our cannon playing on them, and when the smoke cleared, most of them would be lying there, or crawling, or squirming, or screaming. And they weren't blue any longer. They were so near us you could see through your glasses the red blots on their uniforms, and red pools of blood on the ground." His face twisted with a sort of pain. "And during the night, our men went out and stripped the shoes and uniforms off the dead men, so next day they were white instead of blue or red. It made me sick."

Enid said provokingly: "I suppose you'd have felt all right if they'd been ours." He turned his eyes toward her in a heavy way, and Cinda thought Enid watched him with a puzzling eagerness, but when he spoke it was to them all.

"The hard part of it was the waiting," he said. The waiting? She knew that torment. To busy her fingers would steady her, so she crossed to get her knitting. Trav's eyes followed her movement, and she thought he understood, for he said: "I ought not to tell you about these things. They sound worse, put in words. At the time, you're so excited you don't really feel it till afterward; but sitting here listening to me talk about it, you all can't understand that. So it seems to you really worse than it seemed to us in the middle of it. But I said the hardest part was waiting, waiting for each new attack to get near enough so we'd start to kill them. You here at home have to wait too; so you can understand how hard that is."

Cinda, her eyes on her knitting, said yes, they knew. Even Julian said: "I know it's bad just before the shooting starts."

"We'd had weeks of it, really," .Trav reminded them. "Waiting for the shooting to start. I think everybody hated that, except General Longstreet. He never seems to be bothered. Even General Lee gets upset, gets angry at little things. When his head begins to twitch in a jerky little way, they say that's a sign he's mad inside, apt to let off at anyone who comes near him.

"And I suppose it was harder on him than on anyone. He must have blamed himself for going into Maryland in such a hurry. You know our men were worn out before the fight at Sharpsburg. I don't think he expected the Yankees could put an army together again so quickly after he smashed them at Manassas. He probably thought he could march right to Baltimore or Philadelphia before they were ready to meet him. It turned out he was wrong, and he must realize that. The strain shows on him. His hair is almost white now, and his beard too."

"I was in Washington when Sharpsburg was fought," Cinda reminded him. "After Manassas they were in a panic there; and of course lots of people here thought the war would be all over by this time."

"Well, it's a long way from over," Trav admitted. "The Northern army will be stronger than ever in the spring." He added quickly: "But so will we. We got stronger every day after the army fell back into Virginia. Stragglers and deserters came back, or were brought back." Cinda, remembering Streean's assertion that most men in the army fought only because they were made to, closed her eyes. "There was time to rest, and we had plenty to eat, plenty of everything except shoes."

"Are you still handling the commissary?" she asked.

"No, Major Moses does that now. He's better at it than I was. No, I'm just an aide. General Longstreet seems to like to keep me with him." He grinned. "He wouldn't even let me ride Nig during the battle last week. He said Nig would get me into trouble. He said I'd better stay afoot so he could keep an eye on me."

"Good for him! I shall thank him for that."

"We'd been at Fredericksburg quite a while," he went on. "We'd stayed in the Valley till the Yankees showed signs of moving, but early last month we fell back to Culpeper, keeping between them and Richmond, waiting to see what McClellan would try to do. Then they put Burnside in his place. General Longstreet thought it was as good as a victory for us when they took McClellan out. He thinks McClellan is the best general the North has—unless it's General Grant."

"How do Cousin Jeems and General Lee get along?" Cinda asked.

"Oh, fine," Trav assured her. "General Longstreet is wonderful, and General Lee knows it. Longstreet was perfect, in this fight last week; never excited, always doing the right thing. The men like him. He doesn't baby them, but he's always taking care of them; little things like teaching them to boil their meat instead of frying it, for instance. They're a lot healthier since he set them to doing that. And teaching them to rake away the ashes from their cooking fires so they can sleep on the warm ground where the fire was. He's stern when he should be, and severe when he should be; but they know he's fair. Lee and he are as close as brothers. You can see it whenever they're together. Longstreet never says 'Yes' to Lee when he should say 'No,' and Lee nearly always takes his advice." He added thoughtfully: "Longstreet likes to let the Yankees do the attacking. Jackson and Lee always want to attack. Maybe it's because I like him, but I think Longstreet's right. We don't have to whip the Yankees. They have to whip us."

"They can't!" Julian said proudly. "They never can."

Trav went on, weary with remembrance: "So we had a month of waiting. The worst part of that was seeing the poor people leave their homes in Fredericksburg. General Longstreet said that was the saddest thing he's seen in the war. It was pretty bad, old men and women and children plodding along through the mud and the rain."

"Most of them came to Richmond," Cinda said.

He nodded. "We were pretty nervous till Jackson got there," he said. "For fear the Yankees would attack. But after that we felt better.

Everyone was sure we'd beat them." He laughed. "There was a lot of skylarking. When it snowed, the men would have regular battles with snowballs. One day General Hood's whole division turned out to try to lick General McLaws' division. They fought all over General Stuart's headquarters. It wasn't all a joke either. There were a couple of broken legs, and a snowball hit one man in the eye and knocked it out." His voice suddenly was husky. "I tell you it was sort of wonderful! Most of those men were barefoot in the snow, and they were sleeping nights right on the ground. Some of them hadn't even blankets."

Julian laughed delightedly. "I'll bet if General Burnside had seen that snowball battle he wouldn't have dared attack us!" And he said: "Uncle Trav, I've never been to Fredericksburg. What does it look like?"

"Why, it's a gray little town sloping up from the river to low hills. The slopes are mostly cleared land, and there's level ground along the river, but there were woods on the hills where we were." He seemed to recall a series of pictures, his eyes shadowed. "The fog hung in the valley every morning, enough to hide the town; but we could see across above it to the hills where the Yankee guns were. The day they laid their bridges across the river they bombarded the town. Everybody knew they were going to, and not all the townspeople had left, so all morning they were climbing up to where we were, men and women and children, toting everything they could carry. The fog was still too thick to see; but after a while a cloud of dust and smoke began to drift up through the fog, where the shells had knocked houses down, or set them on fire. When the fog finally lifted, we could see houses burning."

He hesitated, and they waited silently till he went on: "They laid their bridges that day and commenced to cross."

Julian asked: "Couldn't you stop them?"

"General Lee wanted them to cross and attack us where we were," Trav explained. "He was sure we could beat them. We watched them crossing all next day. We could see wagon trains and artillery coming down to the river on the other side, and long columns of infantry, and their bands were playing and the flags flying. It was a wonderful, terrible thing to see. They came across and deployed along the railroad in the low ground, and dug ditches, and put their batteries in place. There were so many of them it didn't seem possible we could beat them. But there wasn't even any artillery fire that day, except to check ranges. We just waited."

"And next day they attacked you?" Julian prompted.

"Yes. There was some fighting off to our right. I didn't see that—it was mostly in some woods on General Jackson's front. But the worst part was in the fields above the town. The Yankees would come out of town and form in some low ground and start toward us. They'd have about a quarter of a mile to come, up hill all the way. Our men were behind a high stone wall, in a road that runs along just where the hill begins to get steeper. The road was wide enough and the wall was high enough so that when a man stepped back across the road from the wall to load his gun he was safe, couldn't be hit by shots from the attacking regiments. They'd let the Yankees come close enough so they couldn't miss, and then shoot them." He wiped his eyes with his hand as though to shut out the sight. "Next day there must have been three or four thousand Yankees lying dead in a place about three hundred yards one way and half a mile the other."

Julian asked in a hushed tone: "Where were you?"

"With General Longstreet, on one of the hills a little back and to one side. Telegraph Hill they call it. General Lee was there with us most of the time. We could see the whole thing through our glasses."

Julian had more questions. "What happened after you beat them?"

Trav answered reluctantly: "Why, nothing, except the truce to bury the dead Yankees. That night after the battle there were the most gorgeous Northern lights I've ever seen, and the men said the skies were setting off fireworks to help us celebrate; but someone said that couldn't be, because they were Northern lights, so they wouldn't help the South celebrate. That made the men laugh; but everyone was so strung up it didn't take much to make us laugh. But we didn't laugh next day, watching the Yankees try to bury all the men we'd killed. It had turned bitter cold in the night, so they had to rip the bodies loose from the frozen ground. We'd see two men pulling at a dead man's arms to pull him loose. And they couldn't dig real graves. They put two or three hundred bodies into an ice house owned by a man named Wallace and just left them there to stay frozen till spring." He clenched his fists. "Let's not talk any more about it, Julian."

Enid said with mock seriousness: "Yes, Julian, it hurts Uncle Trav's feelings. He's so soft-hearted! And he says it didn't amount to anything, really; didn't accomplish anything."

Cinda thought angrily that Enid seemed to go out of her way to demean Trav in their eyes. Trav spoke evenly. "I didn't say quite that, Enid. We killed two or three of them for every one of us they killed; but they can afford that. They've plenty of men. We didn't lose. That's something. But we didn't gain."

Cinda exploded. "Nobody ever seems to gain, Trav! It's just more and more men killed, our men and theirs, and nothing settled."

He nodded. "I'd like to know some way to end it, Cinda."

"The North won't give up," Julian reminded him. "And neither will we."

"I would," Trav said harshly. "I'd give up! Nothing's worth the things I've seen."

"Didn't you get a chance at them at all, yourself, Uncle Trav?"

"No. No, I stayed there on Telegraph Hill, out of range of all but their biggest guns. One shell hit the parapet near General Lee, but it didn't explode. The only real danger was when two of our own guns burst, right beside us; but no one was hurt."

Enid rose impatiently. "I'm sick of hearing about it," she declared. "Mama must be awake. I'll go have a little visit with her." Julian thought he might take a walk; and Peter and Lucy departed with him. Cinda saw Trav's eyes follow her tall son, and she said:

"He's all right, Travis." She smiled. "He's very much in love with Anne Tudor. He'll probably leave the children at your house and go on to see her now. You know she went to Washington with me. He's in love with her—and she with him, I'm sure."

"You haven't told me about that," he reminded her. "Washington."

Her eyes for a moment rested on her knitting, and she heard Vesta and Enid laughing with her mother in her room upstairs. She said in a low tone:

"Travis, I saw President Lincoln." Her eyes rose to meet his and she said gravely: "He's kind, Travis, and gentle. And he's the saddest man I've ever seen."

Trav's jaw set. "He let loose this thing on us."

"I know." She hesitated. "Yet, I think he's doing what he thinks he should."

After a moment he nodded. "We're all just—chips floating on a strong river," he said slowly. "I suppose all men are, Cinda. Yet we keep thinking we decide things." He shook his head. "All any of us can do is—go where we're swept. Go where we have to go."

"And try to survive, to live." Her voice was no more than a whisper.

"Why?" he challenged angrily. Then: "Oh you're right, of course! We hang on to life as though it were precious; but the thought of dying doesn't frighten me. I think sometimes I'm so tired it would be like a rest to die."

After a moment she smiled deeply. "Men may feel like that, but women treasure life," she said. "We hate death and fight it. In the hospitals, at the sick bed, everywhere we meet death, we fight it. We give life, Travis. Perhaps that's why we value it so highly."

He urged: "Men give life too, Cinda. We share that giving."

She shook her head. "Not quite. You—toss a penny to a beggar, and perhaps you have a moment's pride in your moment of generosity. But it takes a woman a long time to give something that a casual bullet, fired at random by a stranger, in a moment takes away."

"Cinda, is there any answer?"

"Just to go on being men and women. Not trying to understand."

He said grimly: "I wish I didn't know how to think. I envy—fools."

She laughed at him in tender affection. "When you talk like that, you've no need to envy them, Travis. You are one."

In the end none of the others were able to come for Christmas. "So you and Julian are our only menfolks for this time, Travis," Cinda said smilingly. "And Julian thinks of no one but Anne. You'll have to let us all share you." She said he and Enid must come for dinner on Christmas day, and he agreed. Vesta reminded her that she should ask Aunt Tilda's family too; and Cinda reluctantly did so.

But as though to make up for the absence of loved ones, they made that dinner a merry time, laughing easily. Redford Streean remarked that in another week, by President Lincoln's proclamation, old Caesar and June and all the people would be no longer slave but free; and

Vesta cried: "Heavens, I hope someone's warned them. They won't know what to do!"

Julian laughed. "I suppose old Lincoln expects they'll all come running out of their cabins throwing their chains in all directions and yelling, 'Bless de Lawd and Marse Lincoln! We's free!' and start for Washington to give him a hug and a kiss for thanks!"

Streean drawled: "After a few thousand have embraced their deliverer, he'll wish he'd left them where they were."

"We're living in a fools' Paradise," Julian declared with a lively chuckle. "Next Wednesday you'll have to start doing the cooking, Mama; but you don't act worried! Lucy, how'll you like picking cotton? Aunt Enid, I can just see you dipping candles, and making soap, and doing your own washing. Peter, you'll be on the trash gang!"

Since they were hungry for laughter, they rang many absurd changes on this theme, and at their own jesting laughed themselves to tears. To laugh helped them forget how much they missed the absent ones.

Then Christmas was gone, and the papers said Stuart was off on another raid into the enemy territory behind Burnside's army; so they knew Burr and Faunt rode with death again. Death went from door to door in Richmond too, for smallpox was worse all the time. Trav must return to duty, and he took the northbound train. Upon them all the loneliness and the terror and the waiting settled down again. Cinda turned back to the hospital with a deep sense of peace. It was a blessing to have some task to do.

21

FAUNT suffered from the rigors of that fall and winter. The cavalry had hard service. An epidemic of sore tongue and greasy heel among the horses put many men afoot. These dismounted horsemen were called "Company Q"; and the derision of their mates was so galling that horse stealing became a commonplace and no man left his mount unguarded.

Because the ranks were thinned every man had double duty. When in late October the Northern army began the slow sidling movement that would take them down the valley of the Rappahannock to Fredericksburg, Lee moved with them and Stuart was his flank guard and his rear guard. For a month there were horsemen on every road from the Blue Ridge to Warrenton. The easy hills, the scattered woodlands, the cultivated fields all felt the beat of hoofs and heard the thin rattle of scattered musketry or pistol shots, and the ring of steel on steel as sabres crossed, and the occasional deeper challenge of the guns. Around every turn of the road lay the chance of a skirmish, an affair of patrols, a charge or a flight.

Long days in the saddle stripped away what little flesh Faunt had accumulated since the illness following the wound he took at Roanoke. He might have shirked, but no man could be spared, nor spare himself. Stuart, though his baby daughter sickened and died in Lynchburg, held to his duty. His men saw him every day, bold and valiant, singing them to their work. Faunt loved this man who, no matter what his grief, remembered the Biblical injunction to rend his heart but not his garments. Private griefs had no place in war. When after the little girl died Mrs. Stuart and their small son came to Culpeper for brief days with the General, Faunt' made three-year-old Jemmie his particular charge.

When Burnside threw his men into the scythe of fire on the slope above Fredericksburg, Faunt watched those blue-clad men go down like grain before the reaper till he was sated with the sight of dead enemies and torpid as a gorged snake. After the battle, the victorious army prepared for a cheerful Christmas. Mrs. Stuart came again with Jemmie, to be near her husband for this holiday. Hampton's horsemen went foraging in Loudoun County and brought home a trove of hams, chickens, turkeys; and von Borcke planned for minstrels at the feast.

But Faunt had no heart for this prospective merriment. To see Mrs. Stuart and the General so close and tender woke old hurting memories in him. Belle Vue, though behind the enemy lines, was not far away. His thoughts dwelt on a lonely chapel hidden in the forest there; and two or three days before Christmas he went to Stuart to request a leave.

"My home was down on the Northern Neck. May I go scouting that way, see what the Yankees are about?"

There would be Yankee patrols foraging down the Neck, and Yankee gunboats in the lower river, so this was such an adventure as Stuart himself would have relished. "Take half a dozen men, if you like," he agreed.

Half a dozen was too many, and Faunt said so. "I might take Mosby, if he cares to go."

But Stuart could not spare them both at once, so Faunt went alone, riding far down river before he sought to make the crossing. On a dark and rainy night he found a ferryman willing to risk setting him and his horse over to the enemy side; and he landed undetected and before dawn was across the height of land and near Belle Vue. The woodlands gave him secure hiding for the daylight hours. Six men together would have been in danger of discovery; but the Yankees, secure in their numbers, thought it unnecessary to take precautions against a man alone.

He drew near Belle Vue without any dangerous encounter, and left his horse in a thicket, and went to the chapel to be for a while with the two he loved. What he found there turned him sick with a poison of rage; for a party of Yankees had at some time camped near the spot. Much of the fence had been taken for firewood, so that hogs since then had rooted where they chose among the flowers and shrubs. The chapel door had been burst open, it hung now by one shattered hinge; and horses, haltered to the altar rail, had defiled the sacred place.

Faunt, in his first desperate anguish, tried to clean away the traces men and beasts had left; but the task was almost hopeless. When dusk fell, he abandoned the attempt and slipped through the trees to spy on the house. Horses were secured to the palings there, and he saw lighted windows, and heard loud drunken voices and then the crash of breaking wood as someone shattered a chair and threw the pieces on the fire. He watched for a while, tallying as accurately as possible the numbers of this patrol. If by and by they slept soundly enough, he might creep near and make sure some of them never woke again.

But till they slept, any attack was vanity and folly; and Faunt, despite the storm of anger in him, was neither vain nor a fool. He slipped away to where his horse was tethered, and took his blanket and chose a spot among the oaks near the chapel and lay down to sleep awhile.

He had had no deep sleep for days, and sleep now betrayed him. It bound him fast till the night was almost gone. At dawn someone nudged his back, and he looked up over his shoulder at a blue-clad soldier, and saw two others, with ready muskets, standing by.

Said the first, whose toe had roused him: "Wake up, Johnny! You've got company."

Faunt was already wide awake, but he grunted drowsily. "Oh, let me alone," he grumbled, and rolled over from his right to his left side, as though to go back to sleep again. By this movement his right hand was freed. Of his two pistols, one was rolled in his hat that served as a pillow; but the other lay ready by his knee, and under the blanket his hand closed on it there and softly cocked it. He had rolled to face the man who waked him. Another Yankee stood beyond that man. The third Yankee was behind Faunt, but he could be risked.

The three men laughed at his sleepiness; and the one who had spoken leaned down to twitch Faunt's blanket away. As the blanket came clear of his right arm, Faunt shot, past this man's thigh, the Yankee just beyond. Instantly he jammed his revolver into the belly of the man leaning down over him and fired again. As the dead man fell, Faunt rolled over far enough so that, somewhat shielded by the Yankee's body, he faced the third soldier, who till now had been behind him. At him Faunt threw a shot. The man in panic turned to run, and Faunt scrambled to his knees for careful aim and with a second shot rolled that man over like a rabbit hit by a throw-stick.

Then Faunt was on his feet, and he caught up his other pistol. Two of these enemies, though they had mortal hurts, still lived. He took a moment to remedy that, then ran to his horse, tightened the girths, adjusted the bridle. The shots would bring others from the house. He mounted, and waited, still in cover, till he saw a dozen blue coats, afoot, running toward him. He spurred his horse, shouting as though to comrades on his heels: "Follow me! Follow me!" The Yankees scattered, and as he rode through them he fired three calm shots, saw one man fall. Too bad not to do more, but it was a mistake to empty both your guns. Wild bullets nicked the trees beside him as he raced away.

Half a mile from the house he pulled aside through scrub oak and in a dense copse drew up to reload his weapons. One was empty now, the other had one chamber discharged. They were Colt revolvers which he had taken from a dead Yankee, and a stock that could be fitted to either one for long-range work hung at his saddle. He had found them to his taste, throwing a heavy ball, with a notch in the hammer to serve as a rear sight for careful aim, contentingly accurate up to forty or fifty yards, deadly at close range, and sufficiently heavy to be used as a club if a foe were met hand to hand. Faunt, since he was in no haste, drew the wedge which released the barrel of the empty weapon and removed barrel and cylinder. With a straight twig and a bit of oily cloth he wiped out burned powder grains and blew through the chambers of the cylinder and picked the nipples clean. Then he reassembled the weapon and reloaded, ramming the conical balls firmly home. As he capped the nipples he heard the furious pursuit go by, and judged by the sound that the whole patrol had passed; so when he had reloaded the discharged chamber in the other weapon he rode back toward Belle Vue.

From cover he made sure that unless someone was ambushed in the house itself the place was deserted. He zigzagged into the open to draw fire, but no shot challenged him. These men he hated would desecrate his home no more. He dismounted; and he left the little house burning when he rode away.

His horse went lame, so he stayed all day hidden in the forests along the high ground toward the Rappahannock; and that night one of Judge Tudor's Negroes in a leaky skiff set him across the wide river. He took saddle and gear with him in the skiff, left the lame horse behind. There were friends enough across the river who would give him a fresh mount. The Negro who ferried him over said Mrs. Murtrees was at her place, and he carried Faunt's saddle and bridle and blanket that far. Mrs. Murtrees, in the dead of night, aroused at Faunt's summons, and made him welcome.

"A horse?" she echoed. "Why, of course. I've my two carriage horses, but I never use the carriage now. Take both, or either one."

Faunt thanked her and said one would serve. She insisted that he stay to eat something hurriedly prepared; and he was glad to face a warm fire, shivering.

"Are you sick?" she asked in friendly solicitude. "You've a chill."

"Oh no. I was cold, but I'm warm now."

"Stay till morning. Rest. You're certainly tired."

He shook his head. "I must go back," he said.

When he left that house he rode, or meant to ride, toward Fredericksburg; but the darkness was confusing, and weariness made him nod in the saddle, and the horse he rode could not know from its own experience where he wished to go. So at dawn Faunt could see no familiar landmarks. His teeth were chattering, his head ached, he was enormously thirsty, his back gnawed with pain, and the world swam before his eyes. There was somewhere a steady pounding in him, and he was burning hot, and all the world was strange.

He could never remember where he went that day, or where he slept that night, if he did sleep. It was only by reckoning backward that he could afterward calculate how many days and nights were thus lost to him forever, lost in a fog of delirium. He remembered men who tried to speak to him and whom he brushed aside; and he remembered Negroes staring at him with loose jaws, the whites of their eyes showing their fright. Then one fine sunny day his senses briefly cleared, and he saw on the ground about his horse's feet white bones and scattered skulls and rags of faded uniforms. From low rain-washed mounds a skeleton hand here and there protruded, or a foot from which the shoe had been stripped and the flesh eaten or rotted away. He nodded in heavy understanding. Men here had been buried wholesale, in shallow trenches no deeper than a plow would dig, so this had been a battlefield; but he did not recognize his surroundings till he turned his horse up a near-by hill for a wider view.

Then he knew, for yonder was the Capitol, yonder was Richmond. So yonder was Nell, and rest and peace. Gratefully he turned his horse that way.

Dark had fallen when he rode into Richmond through a wet pelt of snow. At Nell's gate he slid from his horse and fell and rose and stumbled to her door. When it opened to him, his eyes were closed; he mumbled drowsily: "'I am dying, Egypt, dying—'" Then surrendering to oblivion, he toppled forward, prone across the sill.

Thereafter, on the thread of passing days were strung like beads stray moments of half-consciousness, and in each one there was Nell. Faunt saw her face close above him, hovering over him in tender caring; he saw her by candlelight sitting the night through at his bedside; he saw her at first sun and at dusk. Each glimpse of her was like a lullaby, bidding him close his eyes and rest again; and he obeyed, and slept and slept, till at one dawning the clouds were gone. He had been awake a while, in that halfway state between sleep and waking, between sensibility and delirium. Then the clouds thinned and vanished and she was there, asleep in the chair so near him, absurdly small in the warm quilted robe, the heavy braids of her hair burnished by the dawn sun through the window. He watched her till under the caress of his eyes she murmured in her sleep, and then her eyes opened and met his; and she rose and came quickly to him and touched his brow, tenderly yet remotely too, so that he understood she thought him still as he had been for—how long? So he spoke.

"I'm all right, Nell. I'm myself again."

In flooding gratefulness she fell on her knees beside his bed, head buried in her arms, sobbing and sobbing; and he gentled her and soothed her with his hand upon her hand, and saw that hand of his and wondered at it. For it was like a bag of creaking bones, like one of those skeleton hands he had seen on the battle ground in the brief interval of his delirium when he knew where he was and found his way to her. That must have been somewhere toward Gaines's Mill. He remembered a bridge across which his horse had brought him toward the city, guessed he had followed the New Bridge road. But how had he come there from the Murtrees plantation on the Rappahannock? General Stuart must think him lost; must think the Yankees had him.

Nell brushed her eyes free of tears and smiled. "Oh my darling, you've been so sick, so long!"

"I remember coming to your door."

She laughed in rich tenderness. "Milly opened to you, and you frightened her into a fit; said you were dying, Egypt, dying. You thought Milly was me! I'm not complimented!"

"How long ago?"

"No questions. You're still so weak. We'll make you strong again, Milly and I. Sleep till your breakfast's ready. Poor Faunt! You're thin as a picked bird! Sleep again a while."

"What's the matter with me?"

"You've had the smallpox, darling."

He tried to rise. "Smallpox? Who took care of me?"

"Milly and I."

"You?"

"Milly's had it, Faunt; and I was vaccinated two months ago, when the epidemic here began."

He relaxed, grinned weakly, touched his cheek with an exploring finger. "Smallpox, eh? I'm glad I grew this beard."

"You didn't break out badly, Faunt. It turned in. That's why you were so sick. So don't worry, vain man. It will hardly show. Now sleep!" She fled away.

He grew stronger, but he coughed a great deal, a light cough that wearied him. She was with him every hour. Now and again, after supper, he heard the door bell ring; and Milly came to summon Nell to a whispered moment in the hall. But she always returned at once to him, answering his questions with light evasions. "No one I wanted to see; not when I've you here."

Then one evening after dinner he fell asleep; and when he woke he heard the rumble of a man's voice somewhere at a distance, and out of nowhere, with the shock of a bullet, came a disturbing memory. When she returned to him he watched her with a new attention.

"You had a caller," he said.

"I often do, you know, my dear." Then as though she felt the impact of the thoughts he did not utter, she said frankly: "This time I had two, in fact. They wished to rent my house. There are no houses left in Richmond, you know." She smiled. "They offered me seventeen hundred dollars a month. That was a temptation—to a business woman like me."

"Are you a business woman?" His tone was even, but his thoughts were hard.

"A woman alone in the world has to be, darling." She smiled. "And every one in Richmond is in business now. Even Mr. Randolph, since he resigned as Secretary of War, has gone into partnership with Mr. Myers, helping men who don't want to be conscripted into the army, getting details for them or finding them substitutes. Lawyers are growing rich by keeping men out of the army. Substitutes are worth two or three thousand dollars. Everything is business, money, profit now."

"I haven't been in Richmond for so long——'

"I know. Oh my dear, I know." She came to kiss him quickly. "Haven't I tallied off the days?"

He wished to question her, yet not to seem to do so. "And I don't know anything that has happened since before Christmas; nothing at all."

"Nothing has happened, nothing that matters." She considered. "General Stuart made another ride behind Burnside's army, went within a few miles of Washington. Too bad you missed that. And let me see, what else is there? The negroes here didn't pay any attention to Lincoln's proclamation saying they were free; but in Norfolk where the Yankees are, thousands of them marched in a parade, and even the Yankees had trouble making them behave. President Davis told Congress that if the proclamation leads to a slave insurrection, he'll have every Yankee officer we capture hung as high as John Brown; and there's talk that in the next battle there'll be no prisoners taken on either side." He watched her eyes, listened to the tones of her voice, thinking his own wary thoughts. "Now what else?" she wondered. "Do you know—of course you don't—General Bragg won a great victory in Tennessee; but like most of our victories it led to nothing. All the talk here is that the North is ready for peace, or that England and France will take our side; but the Northern armies are still in Virginia, opposite Fredericksburg and at Norfolk and Suffolk. Two weeks ago they started from Suffolk toward Petersburg; but then they turned around and went back. They could have marched right into Petersburg if they had come on. I hear that some spy told them they could take the city if they chose; but perhaps they didn't believe it! General Lee is in Richmond now. Maybe that frightened them."

Faunt found in her words the opening he had wished for, said quietly: "Speaking of spies, I saw one hanged, last summer."

"Really? What happened?" He could discover in her no suggestion of guilty fear, nothing but surprise and interest.

"Why, it was just before we smashed Pope. I had taken a message from Stuart to General Longstreet, and while I was with him the column halted. He was on the march to join Jackson, and he rode ahead to see what the trouble was. They told him an order to halt had come from Lee, and he asked who brought the order. The courier was just riding away. Longstreet said to fetch him back, and two or three of us overhauled him." His eye was steady on her. "The message from Lee was forged. Longstreet said to hang the man. Major Sorrel called together a drumhead court-martial, and the fellow admitted he was a Northern spy. He was spinning on a halter rope within ten minutes after we caught him."

She nodded. "I suppose so. Poor man."

"He said his name was Mason. Captain Mason. I had a feeling I'd seen him somewhere before."

"Really?"

"I finally remembered where it was." He watched her, yet he was ashamed of his own thoughts. "It was one morning last June, the morning Stuart started on his ride around McClellan. I was to go with Stuart, but I stopped here for a moment; and as I left, a horseman was just passing. We exchanged salutes, and I had an absurd moment of jealousy, thinking he might be coming to you. I think it was that same man."

Her eyes were wide with astonishment. "Why, I remember. I saw him meet you. He did come back afterward, too." She smiled. "Your jealousy wasn't as absurd as you suppose. I think he was a little in love with me." If there lay guilt in her, she must be desperately wondering whether the dead man had by any word betrayed her; but if she were frightened she gave no sign. "But his name wasn't Mason. It was Captain Overgood. Or at least he said it was. He called several times, with one of General Winder's men. His home was in Baltimore. Did he remember you?"

The question was natural enough; if she had not asked it, that would have been strange. "No. At least he didn't say so. I could have testified to having seen him in Richmond; but since he admitted his guilt there was no need."

"I wish I'd known he was a spy! I might have prevented the harm he must have done before you caught him."

Faunt hesitated, sure now that his doubts of her were groundless; for no one could play a part as perfectly as this. So he was glad; but also he was ashamed, and he sought forgiveness through confession. "Nell, I'll have to tell you. Since that day, thinking about it, about his being here, I've—well, I've suspected you."

"I see." For a moment she did not speak, and sadness touched her tone. "Yes, I see. You naturally would." She met his eyes steadily. "After all, I'm not what anyone would call a—reputable woman. I've no illusions about that, and neither have you." He tried to speak, but she shook her head. "No, don't protest! We both know it's true. But—well, do you still suspect me?"

"Not since I'm with you here again. Not now."

"Sure?"

"Completely sure, Nell."

She said in a low tone: "If you had said 'Yes', I think I should have died." She laughed in a breathless way, came to her knees beside him. "Oh Faunt, Faunt, half of me dies anyway, unless you're here." He kissed her hands, saw her eyes proud with tenderness. "Don't get well too soon, my darling," she pleaded. "As long as you're sick I can keep you here."

"I'm better every day."

"Get better! Do get better, please. Yes." She laughed richly. "Oh my dear, my dear, I want you strong! I want you strong!"

The days slipped heedlessly away. When he felt fit to do so he began to get up for a few moments and for longer every day. That persistent small cough did not yield, and she was concerned; but he hushed her fears.

"What I need is the saddle again, the open air." He laughed. "Riding in cold and rain, sleeping on the frozen ground. Then I'll be rid of it."

He was presently strong enough to begin to think of going back to duty; but General Stuart must long since have given him up, and there was no action in the north to call for his services. The armies lay quiet, the guns hushed by winter's cold. He need not hasten his return. If she had sought to hold him he might have fretted at any hint of restraint; but when he spoke of his eventual departure she put no hindrance in the way. "Your horse is fat and sleek and ready," she told him. "Go when you think you must, but stay as long as you're glad to stay." She held him by tenderness, by laughter, by quiet talk. They were lovers, but also they were congenial friends, meeting in a companionship of minds in which he delighted; and they talked not only of themselves but of the world of which they were a part. How was the army to be kept up to strength when exemptions from conscription could be had by anyone who would pay for them, when every enrolling officer could be bribed, when any unscrupulous surgeon could say the decisive word that would provide immunity, when the conscription law itself offered a dozen invitations to escape? How was the problem of soaring prices to be solved? Today a week's supply of food for a small family—the same items that would have cost only six dollars and a half in 1860—would cost almost seventy dollars. Nell thought the flood of paper money was as much responsible as any real shortage, but Faunt argued that the speculators were largely to blame.

"Oh I know it's the fashion to call them extortioners," Nell agreed. "But when prices keep going up, you're bound to have speculation. That's just human nature." And when he laughingly declared she must be a speculator herself, she said frankly: "Why of course! Everyone is, whether they know it or not. When they refuse to buy something because it's too high, it's because they're hoping you can buy it cheaper later on. That's speculation. Look at these prices in the *Dispatch* today. Bacon used to be a short bit a pound; now it's a dollar. Sugar's up from eight cents to a dollar fifteen. Salt's fifty times what it was. Why, if you knew prices were going to keep on going up like that, wouldn't you buy all you could today, so that you needn't buy them at higher prices later? Well, that's speculation!" She smiled affectionately. "And it's simple common sense too, my darling!"

"I wouldn't buy to hold for high prices."

"Oh yes you would. That's what we all do. You'd buy things before you wanted them, and hold them to use them later. That's just as bad as holding them to sell them later. I bought four barrels of flour when it was twelve dollars, and it's a hundred dollars a barrel now. I've no notion of selling. I'd rather have the flour than the paper money."

"I've seen the time when our soldiers would have liked to have that flour."

"Then Colonel Northrop should have bought it for them when I bought mine." She added honestly: "Of course, rising prices are hard on poor people. I've always bought flour by the barrel, because it's cheaper to buy that way; and women who have to buy by the pound pay more than I do. That's one of the ways money makes money, Faunt."

He smiled at her seriousness. "You sound like my brother-in-law, Mr. Dewain. He's a great believer in keeping money at work."

"Of course. So am I. So is every sensible person. Cotton is worth seventy-five cents a pound in the North now, and our own Government is buying it cheap and sending it through the lines to sell it at a profit. The blockade-runners buy cheap in Nassau and bring things here and sell them at such high prices that a ship pays for itself sometimes in a voyage."

"You sound envious!" He chuckled at her tone.

She laughed. "I am! I like making money, my dear."

Faunt enjoyed these days so much that he might have stayed or indefinitely; but an intrusion precipitated his departure. On a Sunday evening in early February they were at supper together, and something had made them laugh aloud just before the doorbell rang and hushed them to a whispering silence. Milly went through the hall below to answer the bell and they heard a man's voice ask for Mrs. Albion, heard Milly answer: "She ain' tuh home." Then they heard the negress in sudden protest repeat: "She ain' tuh home, suh!"

The man laughed lightly. "Hush your lying mouth, Milly! I heard her laughing. Yes, I know she has company; but I'll join them."

Faunt knew Darrell's voice. Nell whispered: "Go to your room, Faunt. I'll get rid of him."

But Darrell's foot was already on the stair; and Faunt smiled in thin cold rage at this intrusion. "I'll not hide," he said. Then Darrell appeared in the open door. His head was high, he was laughing; but he saw Faunt and stopped dead still.

"Well, by all the gods!" he cried. He laughed again. "By all the naughty little heathen gods!"

Faunt stepped lightly toward him, hungry to get his grip on that arrogant young throat; but Nell's hand on his arm checked him, and Darrell laughed once more, and bowed profoundly.

"I apologize," he said. "Oh I apologize from the bottom of my heart for forcing myself upon you! But the harm is done. I am here. What possible amends——"

Faunt said thickly: "Get out."

But Nell's hand tightened on his arm, and Darrell urged: "Need I? After all, Mrs. Albion and I have a long friendship. My esteem for her is the highest possible." He spoke to her. "I'm leaving for New Orleans tomorrow, Nell, on business for my father. I thought you might permit me to call, *pour prendre congé*. It may be months before I can pay my respects to you again."

Nell hesitated; she said to Faunt, appeasingly: "I've known him for years, actually."

Faunt was still angry; but to quarrel with Darrell, short of killing him, would do no good, and might do much harm. Darrell, watching them shrewdly, said: "And you too are her friend, Uncle Faunt, I'm sure. Our admiration for her is a new bond between us, sir."

"Have supper with us?" Nell suggested. She met Faunt's eye, appealing to him to yield, and he surrendered. The harm was done, his secret known. Make the best of it. When they were seated, Darrell said courteously:

"I didn't know you were in Richmond, Uncle Faunt."

"I'm returning to duty tomorrow." Faunt was surprised by his own words. Why need he go? The reason was obscure; yet he could not stay hiding here with Nell now that Darrell knew.

"Dolly saw Aunt Cinda at church today," Darrell reported. "But she didn't speak of having seen you." Faunt hesitated and Darrell chuckled and added: "Aunt Cinda didn't mention anything, in fact, except her new grandchild. Dolly went to admire it this afternoon, says it's a marvelous baby, looks just like Vesta."

Vesta? Faunt felt a quick gladness for her, and a deep wonder too. It seemed to him that years had passed since that night at Williamsburg when Vesta's Tommy died. Was it really so short a time, this eternity since his own fine and gentle life had shattered into ugly shards? For a while he did not listen to Darrell and to Nell. He was remembering that night at Great Oak when Tilda read those letters by the light from the tall candle stand. He felt again the sick and furious despair, the madness of that moment when he put the old house to the torch. That madness had been a part of his life since then; a life of secret ambush and treachery and any ruthlessness to kill, kill, kill. His only respite came in these intervals of fine content which he had spent with Nell.

He remembered, as though it were a stranger whom he recalled, himself as he had been till that night last spring. In a brief instant of limpid clarity he was that other man again; he saw through the eyes of the man he then had been, the man he had now become. To think of Vesta, and of her brave love for Tommy Cloyd, come now at last to sweet fulfillment, filled him with despair and shame.

In self-defense he tried to attend to what Nell and Darrell were saying, to forget himself in listening to them; but during the hour that followed he said little, till at last Darrell rose to go.

"If you were anyone else, sir, I'd sit you out," the young man said smilingly. "A moment alone with Mrs. Albion is worth a long vigil. But I give way to your years." He said good night. "I expect to be in New Orleans for a while, Mrs. Albion; but I hope you'll tell Milly to admit me when I call again." To Faunt: "I'll tell no one you're in town, sir; leave to you the happiness of surprising them."

Nell went down with him to the door, and while she was gone Faunt moved restlessly to and fro. He met her as she returned and she said understandingly: "I'm sorry."

"No help for it. And no harm, I'm sure."

"He loves mischief." Her tone was concerned.

"He's a bold young man," Faunt assented. "But he knows the wisdom of discretion, too. And he values his skin, as all these skulking bombproofs do."

"But you must go." It was not even a question, and he was grateful to her for understanding.

"Yes. Not because of him; but I must go. I should have gone before."

"I wish you needn't. I hate that cough of yours."

He smiled. "I'll be over it with the first fine days of spring."

She looked at him long. "Will you go tonight?" she asked, shaken and still. Faunt came to her, drew her gently close.

"Not till tomorrow, Nell, no," he said, as though in comforting. "Not till tomorrow."

Next morning she bade him good-by. "Be bold, be brave, be careful," she told him. "And—come when you can." His horse was at the gate. When he was mounted he looked back, saw her standing in the open door, raised his hat to her as he rode away.

His puzzled thoughts rode with him. Why had Darrell's coming made him sure that he must stay no longer? Why, because Darrell knew or surely guessed the truth about him and Nell, must he now leave her? Because of Vesta and that baby of hers; that babbling baby whose father, months ago, the worms had eaten? What had that baby to do with him; or for that matter what had dead Tommy Cloyd to do with him? Tommy Cloyd was no more now than a rack of bare bones, like those Faunt had seen naked to the rain on the hill above Gaines' Mill in the interval of his delirium. Why consider Tommy Cloyd? Or his baby? Or Vesta? What had she to do with him? She was not alone in having lost a husband and borne a son! What was this urgency which made him turn from Nell and all her breathless ardors and her soft assuagements; to hasten back to the fierce hot surcease of hard battle hours?

He found no answer. He wished to ride directly out of Richmond, to thrust his horse along the northward road, to put all the dream-soft ways of peace behind. But Darrell might tell Cinda he was here. He must show himself to her. Yet to force himself to Cinda's door was a braver thing and harder than a headlong gallop into blazing cannon fire.

Old Caesar opened to him, welcomed him, would tend his horse; Faunt went alone into the hall. The house seemed empty till he heard voices abovestairs; and he climbed those stairs and came to the door of the room where Vesta lay pale and smiling in her great bed, her head turned toward those who clustered with tender cries about the crib-side. Standing in the doorway unperceived, Faunt watched them: Cinda and old June beaming together, and Tilda and Dolly, and Enid. Then Vesta saw him and cried out in happy greeting. "Oh Uncle Faunt!" Her arms reached out to him, and he went to her; but when he was about to kiss her lips, in a bitter revulsion he remembered Nell and kissed her fingertips instead. Enid clasped him, with too generous kisses, so that he was uneasy and embarrassed. As she released him he saw her quick glance at Cinda. Dolly's kiss was as ardent as Enid's. What was this thing in some women and not in others—this abandonment, this offering of surrender? How easily it was recognized, how hard to put a name to it! Listening to their happy greetings and their eager questions, he thought it easy to put each in her proper category. Cinda and Vesta, though Vesta had been Tommy's wife for only a short week, were wives. They had lost themselves in their love for fine men, and in losing themselves they had found something greater than they lost, something rich and strong and beautiful. Tilda was a wife too; but not as they were. They had bestowed; Tilda had given nothing, had envied everything. For that matter, so was Enid a wife; but neither she nor Tilda had earned this fine estate of wifehood which made Cinda and Vesta, otherwise so plain, in fact so beautiful.

He turned back to Vesta; he dutifully admired the baby; he tried to say to Vesta what his heart wished her to know. But from the others, except Cinda, he was anxious to escape. "I must see Mama for a moment. Where is she?"

"Downstairs," Cinda said. "Going up and down stairs is hard for her nowadays, so we've fixed a room for her down there." Enid would have come down with them, but Cinda said: "No, you all stay here. Seeing too many people at once tires her." She closed the door upon them. "I want you to myself, Faunt, for a moment," she confessed. "Are you well? You look ill."

"I have been, for a month," he assented. "I've been staying with some friends in Ashland; just came down for an hour here before returning to duty." He damned himself for that lie, and to hush her questions, questioned her. "I haven't seen you since July, but I know you brought Julian home. Where is he?"

"He's somewhere with Anne Tudor," she said. Anne Tudor? That clear-eyed, lovely child who had ridden with them to Warrenton last summer, asking dear questions, hanging on his words. He had told her tales to delight her then, just as the Moor of Venice, that Negro not so black at heart as he, had bewitched poor Desdemona.

"Julian's fond of her?" he asked.

"He's in love with her." Cinda added gravely, "Faunt, I think she'd be in love with him if she weren't still so fond of you."

"You brought him home from Washington?" He spoke any word at all to lead her on to other matters.

"Yes. President Lincoln gave him back to me." His eyes at that name struck hers like a blow, his anger leaping; but she said quietly: "I know how you've felt toward him, toward Mr. Lincoln, Faunt. But I saw him. He's a strange, sad, tender man."

Faunt said grimly: "Let him be what you like."

"I'm—I could be proud to call him kin."

He heard the entreaty in her tones, and his jaw set in sullen defiance. He shook his head. "You think of him what you choose, Cinda. Let me do the same."

"Your thoughts are poison, Faunt."

"They're mine. Let's go to Mama."

When they came to her room, Mrs. Currain sat in a low chair, and Trav's Lucy and young Peter were with her. Mrs. Currain was singing to them an old song Faunt remembered.

Oh little did ma mither think
The night she cradled me
That I wad die so far fra' hame,
And hang on a gallows tree.

They'll tie a napkin 'round ma e'en
An' they'll no let me see to dee—

Then she saw them there in the doorway and broke off the song, and Faunt went to kiss her dry brow, and she said in bright pleasure:

"Dear Faunt! Ma ain lad!" She smiled, with misted eyes. "Eh but I was the proud one the day I named ye. Fauntleroy! *Enfant de le Roi.* The King's son!" But then, her head on one side, scanning his countenance: "Eh, you've been sick, Laddie."

"I'm well now, Mama."

"Are you then? Come let me look at you." He leaned nearer and she said smilingly: "Nae, nae; on your knees then. I'm wee and sma' and old to see you so high in the sky. Come doon to me!"

So he knelt, and she took his face in her hands and looked into his eyes, and he remembered how she used to do this long ago when he was small, shaking his head to and fro with her hands in loving chiding, saying, "Have ye been a good lad, Faunt? Tell me true now." He had never been able to deceive her then. Could he today?

She was smiling, but her smile passed; her eyes searched his long. He felt a thrust of panic in him, and wished to escape this scrutiny and could not; and she whispered: "Ye've changed, Lad." And after a moment she repeated: "Aye, ye have changed." She released him, but for a moment he did not rise, and she wagged her head and whispered sorrowfully: "Aye, ye've changed sore."

Faunt stood up. "It's this beard!" He found his breath short, coughed. Cinda said quietly:

"We've all changed, Mama. These are changing times."

"It's ne'er the times that change; it's the people that live in them." The old head nodded. "There's a wide ditch to every run, and a high fence too, or so your father used to say; but you can size a man by the way he takes the high fence." Her arm circled Lucy who stood now beside her; and she began to sing:

" 'Oh they lookit up, they lookit down
' 'Tween the bowsters and the wa'
'And there they got a bonny lad bairn
'But its life it was awa'.' "

Cinda said wonderingly: "I've never heard that verse, Mama."

Mrs. Currain cocked her head; her eye had a slant of mirth. "There's mony anither," she retorted; and she sang:

" 'The Prince's bed it was sae soft,
'The sheets they were sae fine—' "

Cinda spoke in tender protest. "Shame, Mama! Such songs for children's ears! Or for mine either! I'm surprised at you!"

Mrs. Currain seemed small in her chair; she looked up at Faunt. "Aye, Lad," she repeated, as though Cinda had not spoken. "Aye, ye're sore changed."

Faunt swung miserably toward the door. He heard Cinda behind him, on his heels, catching him in the hall. "Faunt! Please! Don't mind her!"

"She's right," he said thickly. "She's right, Cinda! God help me, yes. I'm—sore changed!"

"Faunt dear!"

He said: "She's changed too, Cinda. I never heard the old way of talk on her tongue so plain before."

"She's older every day," Cinda assented. "It comes back on her. Faunt, will you stay——"

He shook his head, caught up his hat, went strongly toward the door. Caesar had put a black boy to hold his horse there. "Good-by, Cinda." He dared not linger, did not trust his voice. She kissed him; he swung into the saddle. As Nell had done, Cinda stood in the door to watch him ride away.

He meant to put this place and these dear loved ones all behind him; but chance led him to encounter Anne Tudor and Julian. Riding out Grace Street to take the Brooke Turnpike, he saw them a block ahead, strolling slowly. Julian's crutches told Faunt even at a distance who they were, and his first thought was to turn aside, to avoid them. But then he remembered Cinda's word: "—if she weren't still so fond of you." That might be mended. At a foot pace he overtook them, and when they turned he called:

"Why, hello there! Anne! Julian! Is that ever you?" He laughed. "Well, Julian, the Yankees gave you a pruning, didn't they?" Julian grinned; but Anne, whose eyes at first sight of Faunt had flooded with delight, now sobered in puzzlement; and Faunt saw this, and marked their silences. "Eh? Cat got your tongues?"

"Hello, Uncle Faunt." Julian was at ease, but Faunt felt Anne watching him, and he spoke to her in rude teasing.

"Anne, it was hardly worth that long trip to Washington to bring back three-quarters of a sweetheart, was it?"

She flushed with angry tears; but Julian touched her arm. "He's funning, Anne."

"It's not funny!" she cried.

Faunt threw back his head and laughed aloud. "Ho! If you're sweet on a one-legged man you'll have to learn to laugh at things—eh Julian? Won't she?"

Julian still managed to grin. "Yes sir. That's so, all right!" And to Anne, pleading with her to smile: "Remember our song, Anne? 'Johnny, were you drunk? Johnny, were you——' "

"Stop it!" Anne was watching Faunt with the wounded eyes of a child who has been inexplicably slapped by someone loved and trusted; and Faunt's heart twisted with pain. Yet it was this he had intended; he drove home the hurt.

"Didn't even leave you enough of a stump to strap a wooden leg to, did they, youngster? You'll have to turn centaur, join the cavalry. That one leg of yours is long enough to wrap clear around a horse!" By Julian's pale cheek, by Anne's tragic eyes he knew he had done enough, had said enough. She would turn to Julian now. With a sharp twitch on the reins, heels driven home, he made his horse bound, and reined it to a trot; and as he rode away he sang over his shoulder:

> " 'If you want to kiss the girls,
>   'If you want to raise Hell,
>   'If you want to have a high time—
>   'Jine the cavalry.' "

From a trot to a rack, from a rack to a lope; hurry, my friend! Hurry to leave them far behind before your heart breaks. Oh, you left a hurt back there—but that hurt will heal. This hurt in him—this was past healing. With cruel jests he had thrown something long dear to him aside forever. But if Cinda were right, then perhaps what he did was well done. He nodded, grateful for one tally on the credit side, and rode on to the wars.

22

TRAV'S Christmas at home brought him no content. When in October he departed to rejoin the army, Enid had seemed happy in their new home, and of course he wanted her to be happy; but beyond insisting that they present to the world a surface concord, he wanted nothing else from her. That on this Christmas leave she appeared to take pleasure in discrediting him to Cinda and the others did not surprise him; but sometimes when they were alone she seemed to wish to provoke him beyond endurance. She told him Captain Pew and Darrell were often at the house.

"But of course Dolly's always with them, and usually Tilda. I know you wouldn't want me to get myself talked about."

"I know you won't."

"Captain Pew has no eyes for anyone but Dolly, though to be sure he does say gallant things, just to be polite. And Darrell's so amusing. I know you don't mind." He did not answer, feeling her eyes upon him. "If you do, I won't let them come again."

"No, I don't mind."

"I certainly can't imagine your being jealous."

"I'm not."

"They're really the only intimate friends I have, outside of your family. And of course Vesta and Cinda have their own friends." He had an uncomfortable feeling that something was expected of him, but he did not know what it was.

In talk with Lucy, he might forget Enid till he felt the thrust of her eyes and looked across the room to where she sat watching them. She contrived to make him feel guilty because he enjoyed Lucy's company.

If he tried to include Enid in their conversation, asking her opinion on this point or that, she smiled patiently and said: "Really, I'm sure you and Lucy know best. I don't want to interfere."

Even Lucy resented her attitude. "Oh Mama, what do you act that way for?" Once she cried: "Mama, what's the matter with you, moping all the time when Papa's home? You have fun enough with Cousin Darrell and Captain Pew."

Enid protested, too humbly: "Lucy, don't be silly! You mustn't ever speak of such men in the same breath with your father, dear!"

Trav sometimes thought Lucy tried in her childish way to make up to him for Enid's manner, and he loved her for it. They drew close; but between him and Peter there was a barrier hard to define. The boy was seldom at home, disappearing early, coming home late; and to Trav's questions he gave evasive answers. Yes, he sometimes still drilled the boys in Butchertown, but that wasn't much fun in winter. Oh yes, they had snow fights sometimes, when there was any snow. Oh, they didn't do much of anything, just sort of fooled around. Jim Pedersen had a cave all fixed up with a stove made out of old iron, dug into the side hill above the creek, and that was fun. No, probably Trav had better not go there to see it. Jim didn't want too many people knowing where it was.

Trav thought he recognized the signs. To this war, boys, and boys grown up to be men, had at first reacted with an equal martial ardor; but in most cases that soon gave way to an easy liberty and license. For a hungry soldier to accept the gift of a good dinner, freely proffered, was one thing; but the next step was to ask for it, the next to forage for it, the next to steal it. No hen roost or pig pen or orchard or corn field anywhere near an army encampment was safe from marauders; and from stealing food to stealing other things was a short and easy step. Last summer in northern Virginia, by the testimony of Virginians themselves, Southern soldiers had done more damage than the Yankees. Fences were torn down, and doors and even walls were ripped off outhouses and farm buildings to be used as firewood, and gardens were not only robbed but trampled heedlessly. Not a fortnight ago a group of citizens of Fredericksburg had come to Longstreet's headquarters to complain that Confederate soldiers were wandering through the half-ruined town, stealing from abandoned houses everything they could carry away; and Trav himself had been sent to post guards in the town. Thieving soldiers caught and convicted were forever facing court-martial, but their punishments were usually more ludicrous than painful: to ride a mule facing backward with a placard announcing their offense hung around their neck; to stand for hours a day, similarly labelled, on a barrel in the busiest part of camp; to forfeit their meager and now almost worthless pay.

Peter's evasions made Trav sure that the boy was ashamed of some of the things he did, but Trav knew the futility of empty chiding. He tried remembering or inventing youthful peccadilloes of his own and relating them; till Peter laughed and forgot to be afraid and told Trav enough to confirm his conjecture. Trav was careful to take these confessions lightly, to put his reprobations rather as friendly advice than as reproofs.

But Enid might, if she would, help keep Peter in hand. He risked a mild suggestion that it was too bad for Peter to roam the town like a stray colt.

"Why, I do what I can, Trav," she said. "But a boy needs a father."

She eluded him and baffled him and made his days wretched. It was a relief to come back to headquarters at Hamilton's Crossing, where the army lay in winter quarters along the Mine Road on the southward slope of the hills.

When General Longstreet returned from Lynchburg, Trav saw that these few days at home had been a tonic for the big man. Mrs. Longstreet was well, he said; and Garland's voice was changing. The General chuckled fondly. "Funny to hear him crack and squeak! He's a fine boy! Mighty good to his mother. Louisa says he's her beau. He's taller than she is now, of course; and she doesn't seem much older than he." He added: "Louisa's coming for a visit, presently, if things seem quiet here."

Trav shared the other's pleasure in this prospect, for the winter days were weary ones, snow and bitter cold and dreary rain. There was rain the day Fitz Lee's brigade of cavalry paraded in review; rain so hard that Lee and Longstreet and Stuart and their staffs were well drenched, and a man could not see fifty yards through the downpour. Trav met Burr afterward and Burr was furious. "Up before daylight and march fifteen miles and then march back again for a damned show no one could see, and not worth seeing. But General Stuart's vanity had to be fed somehow, I suppose!"

Trav said appeasingly: "Take away General Stuart's vanity and he wouldn't be the great leader he is, Burr."

Burr was too wet and tired and angry to be reasonable. "Let him have a one-man parade all by himself, then! The rest of us don't enjoy showing off in the rain."

Ten days later Mrs. Longstreet came for that promised visit. She stayed at Forest Hill, the Hamilton place. John Marye, whose own Brampton stood on that hill above Fredericksburg against which in December Burnside had thrown his men in bloody, vain assaults, had married Jane Hamilton; and since the battle they lived at Forest Hill, and Mrs. Maria Page was usually there with them. The house was a quarter of a mile south of Mine Road, a little more than a mile from headquarters at the Crossing; so Longstreet was able to ride over every evening, to spend the night there and return next morning. He took Trav with him for Sunday dinner. The house was set on a bold south-ward-facing shoulder of the ridge that ran between Mine Road and the river, with a fine outlook across the valley white now with winter snows. Trav found Mrs. Longstreet even more charming than in the past; there was a gentleness in her which grief had warmed and nurtured. Her devotion to the General and his to her were manifest; and Trav thought that the year-old scars of that triple tragedy when their three children died within a week began at last to heal.

She said Lynchburg was full of refugees, and she told them laughingly of an incident in Mr. Kimble's church. "He announced from the pulpit one Sunday that the congregation didn't like refugees crowding into their pews, and asked all the strangers in church to take seats up in the gallery. They did, and then he read off the hymn, and the last two lines of the first stanza were:

> " 'Haste, my soul; oh, haste away
> 'To seats prepared above.'

"That made everyone laugh, and since then the wardens always try to seat refugees with the congregation, but they prefer the seats prepared above!"

After she was gone back to Lynchburg, while they waited to see what General Burnside would attempt, some of Longstreet's old joviality returned. There was again an occasional poker game at headquarters, and someone organized amateur theatricals. The army itself was in a mood for frolicking. When snow fell, mock battles were fought; and regiments that faced enemy fire unflinchingly, dodged and faltered under the white bombardment of flying missiles. Longstreet, watching one of these affrays, spoke of this.

"But it's natural enough, Currain. You can see a snowball. If bullets were visible, no regiment could ever be brought to charge."

Trav sometimes felt his heart warm with pride in these ragged men who were the army. He had seen Richmond full of "bombproofs," young men who by influence or by purchase had secured some easy detail and an exemption from the conscription, and who endured no hardship except contemptuous glances. Here in winter quarters the few officers and men who had means could achieve a minimum of comfort; but they were few among the many. The soldiers huddled in their huts, two might share a single blanket, and in that snow battle he had seen many who were barefoot, with neither socks nor shoes. Their rations were plain corn bread and meat, but the meat was tough and stringy and sometimes it had begun to rot, and corn bread became deadly monotonous, and there was frequently not enough in the daily ration to satisfy a man. Except for the North Carolina regiments, most of the soldiers were inadequately clad. Body lice were a universal affliction from which not even officers could keep themselves free. Yet these hungry, cold, dirty, miserable men were ready at the least pretext for a jest or a frolic—or for a battle and wounds and death. Trav had learned at Chimneys to like and to respect the simple men who were his neighbors there; now that feeling grew stronger, like an enriching flood, filling him with love and faith. Men of the class of which he was a part had always distrusted the poor whites and even the small farmers, opposing any political change which gave their votes new weight. Jefferson Davis had been elected provisional and then permanent President of the Confederacy not by the vote of the people but by the vote of the states, each state casting one vote. The people were not trusted to make any important decision at the polls. Trav knew all the arguments in support of this point of view. Let all the people vote? Why, that was ridiculous! Half of them were poor whites who could neither read nor write. Two-thirds of them did not own any slaves at all. No one except ignorant demagogues—like Lincoln, for instance—wanted to give such men any voice in affairs. Was it not obvious that with the extension of the suffrage, the demagogue replaced the statesman in public office? No gentleman would demean himself by pandering to an illiterate and unthinking majority; so the stature of men in public office must steadily decline. Even in Virginia, the good old days when none but gentlemen could aspire to political preferment were ended; and any nobody or the son of a nobody might be elected Governor, or sent to Congress. The state, yes and the whole South, was sinking into a slough of democracy. Trav had heard the phrase often enough. Governor Letcher was the son of a butcher; down in Georgia Governor Brown was a cracker from the red hills; in Mississippi Governor Pettus had made his office as common as the public rooms in a tavern. To be a successful politician one need only learn how to befool the ignorant; then the voters were easily led, as a blindfolded horse can be led from a burning stable. The nimble tongue was the key to victory. An unthinking audience forgot the speaker's matter in his manner, cared less for what he said than for the way he said it. To let ignorant men vote was to deliver power into the hands of the unscrupulous. The plain man was not fit for the suffrage. Trav had heard that assertion, in a thousand forms, a thousand times.

Yet watching these plain men who made up the Army of Northern Virginia while their betters skulked in safe details at home, seeing them every day through the weeks after Fredericksburg when no suffering could long subdue their high spirits or dim their silent valor, Trav thought they wore a certain grandeur. Lincoln was right! If the meanest men were capable of these greatnesses, then they were capable of having sound opinions, and of expressing them at the polls.

Longstreet, he found, agreed with him. "After all," the General reminded Trav, "that's the theory behind the old Union: the idea that the majority is entitled to rule. The Confederacy doesn't accept it. We don't admit that because the North outnumbers the South it has a right to decide what the South shall do. When we seceded, we repudiated the rule of the majority and drew our swords. It's as though we said: 'There are more of you, to be sure; but we're the better men.' "

"Suppose we lose this war?"

For a moment the other's eyes were shadowed. Then he said: "Why, we've appealed to the God of Battles. If He decides against us, we should accept that decision."

During this interval of idleness Trav listened to long talk among his fellows on the staff about the lessons learned during the summer's campaign. For one basic weakness in the Southern soldier there was no remedy. He would follow a gallant leader anywhere, but he must be led, not sent. For a commander who failed to meet this requirement, the men had a scornful phrase. "Swap him for a brush pile, and set him on fire." When a regiment faltered at Blackburn's Ford in the first major skirmish of the war, someone asked the men derisively: "Why did you run? Why didn't you hide behind the trees?" A soldier retorted: "There weren't enough trees for the officers."

Yes, these men must be led. But the consequence of that fact was that too many good officers were killed, or so badly wounded that their services were lost forever; and the South had not enough first-rate officers to waste them needlessly. Already, even among the generals, the list of losses was a long one. Maxcy Gregg and Tom Cobb had died a month ago at Fredericksburg, and there had been many others. Suppose Longstreet were killed, or Jackson, or even General Lee. Lee had risked his life at Fredericksburg, making a dangerous reconnaissance within easy range of the Yankee lines.

Yet could an officer send his men where he himself would not go? The question led to hot debate, and no conclusion.

There were other arguments. Was the Parrott gun as good as the Whitworth? Would breech-loading rifles, if you could get enough of them, shoot as far and as hard as a muzzle-loader with the bullet well rammed home? Certainly to be rid of the ramrod would make for rapid fire; and it would save casualties, since most men shot in the arm were hit while loading. A musket well charged with buckshot was deadly at fifty yards. Yes, but a good marksman could sometimes kill at five times that range with a rifle. Thus the conflicting views. The long hours of talk covered every aspect of battle and of camp;

and Trav wondered how men equally well-informed could so com-pletely disagree.

When in January General Lee went to Richmond, Longstreet was left the ranking officer in the field. At once, as though to take ad-vantage of Lee's absence, Burnside in the camps across the river began to stir; and General Jackson came to Longstreet's headquarters and the two drew apart in talk together. When Jackson rode away it was with something resentful in his bearing; and Trav wondered what had happened. That afternoon, riding with Longstreet and General Alex-ander to inspect the defensive works along the high ground upstream, he took advantage of a moment when he and Longstreet were alone to speak of the incident.

"We thought there might be some movement planned," he ex-plained. "Major Moses began to worry about rations."

Longstreet shook his head. "No, we will not move. General Jack-son thinks Burnside will try another crossing below us; but mud and swamplands won't let him go far that way. Jackson wished to march down river to be ready for him, and I declined to consent." He added reflectively: "Jackson's genius is for battle. Idleness distresses him. But my decision was to stay where we are; and, whether I'm right or wrong, it was my responsibility to decide. When the enemy attacks it will be by the upper fords."

Trav could read into the other's words more than they said. Gen-eral Jackson must have asserted his right to use, in Lee's absence, his own judgment; and it had taken courage to remind him that neither the authority nor the responsibility was his. But Longstreet had cour-age to spare, and a stubborn strength. Right or wrong, he would al-ways have an opinion, would always hold to it.

Before Lee returned, the staff knew by whispered rumor of this small clash between the two commanders; and when Lee's opinion accorded with that of Longstreet they felt a loyal pride. When a day or two later Burnside did try to move down river, and mired his wagons and his guns as Longstreet had predicted, in their eyes Long-street's prestige grew.

The General, during these weeks of winter, directed the construction of defensive positions all the way to United States Ford; and General Jackson came one day to see these works, and complimented Longstreet on his use of the traverse to protect men against a cross fire. Longstreet disclaimed the credit

"It was General Alexander's suggestion," he explained. He said to Trav afterward: "Jackson's a fine man, Currain."

"I can see there's a lot of sense in that way of building entrenchments."

"Oh, that was nothing. He just took that way of telling me he understood my insistence the other day; of conceding that I was right and he was wrong." He added: "I'm glad he spoke. Jackson and I are General Lee's two arms; he has a genius one way, and I another. But it's necessary for us to agree. When generals quarrel, their armies lose the fighting edge."

In mid-February, General Longstreet was ordered to proceed to Richmond. Burnside, over across the river, had been relieved from command and replaced by Hooker; but the Yankees were active in North Carolina and were threatening to move from Norfolk to Suffolk and on toward Petersburg. Trav's old friend, General Harvey Hill, had been sent south a month ago to be ready to meet them. Pickett and then Hood followed him; and General Longstreet, since these divisions were drawn from the First Corps, went to take command.

When they boarded the cars, he and Trav were together. "I've telegraphed Mrs. Longstreet to meet me in Richmond," he told Trav. "I'll be some time in Petersburg, and I can have her near me there."

"Stay with us, as long as you're in Richmond," Trav proposed. Enid might not relish unannounced guests, but she must welcome them. "Cinda will want you, but so do we; and we've plenty of room. Garland must come too!"

"Very glad to do so," Longstreet agreed. "At least till Louisa can find quarters for us in Petersburg."

"Do you look for any action down there, sir?"

"I think not," the General told him. "General Pryor has had some small contention along the Blackwater, but I doubt there's any strong Yankee force there." He chuckled. "President Lincoln will keep Washington covered as carefully as a lady draws her shades before she disrobes. No, the North tried the Peninsula last year and had a bad licking. They'll waste no serious effort down here. Our movement is largely to simplify the task of supplying the army. Everything has to go to the Rappahannock on a single line of railroad; but at Petersburg, we can feed our divisions from North Carolina."

Trav had been troubled for months by the army's lack of proper food. A scrap of bacon, a little flour and rice, some miserable beef; that was the fare. Men were down with scurvy, and stragglers scoured the countryside like half-starved dogs. "Food's short in Richmond too," he suggested. "The railroad could bring more than it does, if rations were to be had. We may be able to collect enough to send some to Hamilton's Crossing."

Longstreet nodded. "The first step to victory is to feed our men. If we can help a little in that direction, this movement is worth while."

In Richmond, Trav saw proudly the fine welcome that greeted Longstreet's appearance. While the General was at the War Department he went to tell Enid that the Longstreets would be their guests. He was prepared for objections, but to his surprise Enid cried delightedly:

"Oh, that's wonderful! I like him so much. Remember how jolly he was the night we did charades at Cinda's? We must have a party for him!"

Trav said the General would be in no mood for parties. Then Lucy heard her father's voice and came running downstairs to throw herself into his arms, and Trav hugged her close, and over her shoulder he said to Enid:

"Mrs. Longstreet will join him here." He smiled at Lucy. "And Garland's coming," he told the girl. "Remember him? He'll be a beau for you."

He left them to decide which rooms these guests should have; and on the way back to the War Department he stopped at Cinda's, and admired Vesta's little Tommy; but he thought his mother was changed. "Is she well, Cinda?" he asked, when he could.

"Why, I think so," Cinda assured him. "But of course she's older all the time." She spoke softly: "She's—drifting away into a world of her own, Travis."

He told her the Longstreets would be his guests and Enid's; and she said: "I hope Enid can find something to give them to eat. But there, she and Dolly are together all the time, and I suppose Mr. Streean can get her anything she wants."

Her words suggested a criticism of Enid, but Trav shut his ears. He asked for news of Brett and the others, and she said he had missed Brett by a day. "He was here almost a week, trying to get a pardon for some poor man who had been sentenced to be shot as a deserter, and who probably wasn't guilty. Brett found witnesses and papers and things and got a pardon for the man; but he had to hurry back to camp because the man was supposed to be shot day after tomorrow." She said Burr had not been in Richmond recently, but Faunt had stopped for a moment about two weeks ago. "By the way," she asked, "do you ever hear from Tony?"

"No. Why?"

"He isn't married, is he?"

Trav, remembering the last time he saw Tony, remembering that shameful moment in the dining room at Chimneys, said: "I doubt it. Why do you ask?"

"He was buying dress materials and finery here in Richmond a while ago. He took Dolly to advise him and to—try things on; but he was very mysterious about it, just laughed at questions."

Trav thought in a sombre anger that Sapphira looked not unlike Dolly. She was quite as beautiful, with the same dark hair; and her skin was only faintly darker. But for Tony to use Dolly in this fashion was unspeakable. However, Cinda need never know Sapphira existed. "Well," he said lightly, "that's interesting. Perhaps he's playing Prince to some Martinston Cinderella. No, I haven't heard from him since I was down there."

When he left her, snow had begun to fall, a northwest wind driving the small, hard flakes like sleet into his face. He found General Longstreet, and a hackney cab took them to the house on Clay Street. The snow by that time came in clouds and flurries, and the wind was strong to buffet them. Trav thought of the soldiers in camp on the heights above Fredericksburg, sharing thin blankets, half-frozen, half-starved, ill-shod; and when he came indoors he was not surprised to hear the General say:

"Gives you a damned guilty feeling, doesn't it, Currain, to be warm and comfortable, and to remember our men on the march?"

Trav nodded. "But to make ourselves uncomfortable won't help them, General!" It was his part to play the host; and it was pleasant to see the other relax and take his ease, to see Enid so prettily excited that her flushed cheeks and her laughing eyes and her hair lustrous from long brushing made her lovely as a girl again.

Dolly, she told them, had meant to come for supper; but this storm would keep everyone indoors. Longstreet said it was just as well. "With Lucy here, and you, Mrs. Currain, another beauty would be too much for one man's eyes!"

Lucy, sitting by Trav's side, squeezed his arm in shy delight, and Peter put many questions to the big man. "Did you ever shoot anybody, General Longstreet?"

"Not for a long time, youngster."

"I'm going to shoot a hundred Yankees some day."

Longstreet chuckled. "Be sure they don't shoot back."

"I wouldn't be scared!"

The big man asked teasingly: "Hardened to blood already? How old are you, young man?"

"I'm eleven! But I've seen them shoot a lot of old deserters out at Camp Lee, and I saw them hang that nigger woman up back of the almshouse for killing the baby, and I'm going out to see them shoot John Broderick Monday!"

"Hello!" Longstreet looked at Trav in disturbed surprise; and Enid said hastily:

"Peter's awfully morbid, General! I declare I don't know what I'm going to do with him! Peter, it's time you went to bed. Now you march, young man."

Against Peter's protests she led him from the room, and Trav said awkwardly to his daughter: "Honey, why don't you go to bed too?" When he and Longstreet were alone, he said: "That's the hardest part of all this, for me: not being with my son. I hate to think of him goggling at public executions."

"There are worse things than death in war, Currain." The big man stared at the fire, and when he spoke it was in dry anger. "I touched some of them today. I went to Colonel Northrop, told him our army was short of food. His only answer was that he'd foreseen they would be!" Longstreet's heavy fist thumped his knee. "That pepper doctor seems to feel that if he has expected disaster, he's done his full duty toward averting it." He was silent for a moment, grumbling in his beard. "Currain, President Davis will ruin us all unless he learns to admit his own mistakes. Northrop should have been discarded long ago. You're worth a dozen of him." Trav had no high opinion of Mr. Northrop, and he thought honestly that this was probably true. "The army will do its best," Longstreet said. "And its best is better than any other troops in the world can equal; but behind the army there's corruption, inadequacy, laziness, greed, desertion, skulking. Currain, not one Southern man in ten has his whole heart in this war. If we had as many soldiers as we have exempts and extortioners—I could put together a full division of them from the men I saw on the streets right here in Richmond today—we could march to New York!"

Trav smiled at this extravagance; yet there was truth in it too. "I know there seem to be plenty of able-bodied young men in the departments."

"Rats gnawing at the roots of our strength." The General's anger rose. "Damn it, soldiers must eat; and it's only bad management that keeps them from it. Why, even here in Richmond tonight many a mother had to put her babies to bed hungry; yet there's food enough for every baby, yes and every soldier, within two hundred miles of us as we sit here." He came to his feet. Trav did not speak, and after a moment the other's wrath ended in harsh laughter. "There, I've talked too much, thought too much. In wartime no man should ever think at all, or he'll go stark raving crazy. He'd be better off if he did, too! I'm worn weary, Major. Shall we go to bed?"

The General next day insisted on tramping off to St. Paul's. Enid stayed at home, but Trav went with him, plodding through packed snow inches deep. Not many others faced the blizzard that day, but Cinda was at church; and President Davis was in his usual pew, and the President and General Longstreet talked a moment together. Others, after the service, crowded to speak to the General; and that evening, despite the continuing storm, there were callers at the house on Clay Street. General Pickett's division was at Drewry's Bluff, and General Hood's had passed through Richmond a day or two before; and these two officers came to pay their respects. Trav often wondered at Longstreet's cordiality toward Pickett. He himself, though faintly ashamed of his own feeling, disliked the other for his effeminate mannerisms, his long hair in careful curls around his shoulders, the cloud of scent which emanated from his hair and beard. Pickett was stupid, too; slow of wit and short of memory. Whenever Longstreet gave him an order, it was in elaborate detail and with many explanations.

General Hood, on the other hand, Trav liked and admired. The tall young man, with fair hair and a tremendous beard the color of marsh grass after frost has touched it, had blue eyes in which a profound sadness seemed to dwell; but there was no better fighter in the army, and in camp he was a fine companion, with an easy laughter and a merry tongue.

Tonight he was as shy and ill at ease as an awkward boy till Enid presently retired; but then he was himself again. The march to Richmond had been a hard one, he said. "There was no bottom to the roads at all, and a man's feet picked up so much mud he might as well have had on a ball and chain. One boy died, trying to keep up. He was bound he wouldn't straggle, so he marched till he fell dead." General Hood had halted his men outside Richmond and given them time to wash the mud off their clothes, to scrape their boots and polish their muskets. "And I thought they'd better march through Richmond after dark," he explained, and smiled. "Then they wouldn't break ranks to buy liquor or candy. But I forgot about the theatre!"

He told the hilarious tale. The Texans came opposite the theatre on Broad Street just as the audience was gathering; and some laughing soldier yelled: "Let's go to the show, boys!" That started an instant rush for the entrance. The officers good-humoredly abandoned the attempt to keep formation, and in five minutes the auditorium was filled with bearded men, their muskets held between their knees, the muzzles rising above their heads like a thicket of leafless saplings. Some effort was made to persuade them to leave, but they had come to stay.

"Hardly a man of them had ever been in a theatre before," Hood explained. "The performance was *The Virginia Cavalier,* and they sat there with their jaws hanging, taking it all in, till they forgot it wasn't real." Mirth rumbled in his tones. "The last scene was a Yankee breastwork and it was supposed to be captured by our men. Well, the boys in the seats couldn't stand the excitement, and when the fighting on the stage got real hot, someone yelled: 'Drive 'em, boys!' And at that the whole brigade swarmed out of their seats and charged the stage!"

He laughed, a great guffaw, and they laughed with him. "I'd give a fat cut of Texas beef to have been there," he confessed. "The orchestra dived out of sight under the stage, and what ladies were in the theatre began to scream and faint on the bosoms of their bombproof beaux. The manager, Mr. Ogden, saw the thing start, and he turned out the gas; and of course that stopped them. After they quieted down, the gas came on again, and Mr. Ogden came out and made a nice speech, said it was the best compliment his actors had ever had, and if they'd keep their seats, the show would go on." He said again: "I wish I'd been there," and Longstreet agreed with him, and Trav chuckled; but he thought Pickett's mirth was touched with fastidious distaste. Probably even the imagined odor of all those sweaty, unwashed bodies offended Pickett. No doubt it was to defend himself against such contacts that he perfumed himself so heavily.

Longstreet may have had the same thought, for he said to Pickett: "I trust your men behaved themselves, General."

"The men, yes sir," General Pickett assured him. "But we had a charmingly hospitable welcome from the ladies, plenty to eat and to drink, and some of the officers let it go to their heads. I've put four of my Colonels under arrest and preferred charges of drunkenness against them."

Longstreet chuckled in a good-humored way. "Yes, yes, you have to do that, of course. They court-martialled General Van Dorn for drunkenness out west. Acquitted him, naturally; but if Van Dorn had an opportunity to drink too much and didn't do it, he's changed since that first summer at Centerville. Be sure you return your officers to duty as soon as we need them, General."

Hood and Pickett presently rose to say good night. Longstreet would have had them stay. "You'll find no spot as comfortable at this hour," he urged.

Hood smiled. "I'd rather be in Hell," he said, and chuckled at his own jest, and looked at Trav in laughing apology. "Not actually, Mr.

Currain, to be sure; but they tell me the gambling hells here in Richmond are as near Paradise as a soldier requires, with good cigars, good eatables, good drinkables, and a game if you want it. I mean to see for myself."

"I've heard it's true," Longstreet agreed, "but I never investigated."

"The gentleman waiting to escort us makes many promises," General Hood told him. "I once spent an evening in the palace Jim and Alf Monteiro run; but the stakes there were too high for me. That's where the extortioners lose the money they bleed out of the rest of us; there and at Merrihay's. But if we play, it will be at Johnnie Worsham's. He's respected in spite of his calling, and he'll give a soldier his last dollar as readily as he'll win it back from him!"

When they were gone, Trav and Longstreet sat late, in comfortable talk together. Longstreet had business next day with President Davis. The army needed men, and there were scores of thousands in the militia of the several states. "A hundred thousand at least," Longstreet told Trav that night before they went upstairs. "General Lee thinks the number will run as high as a hundred and fifty thousand, and nine-tenths of them are fit for service in the army. But the states keep them at home, won't let us have them. General Lee asked me to put the case to Mr. Davis, see if he can't beat some sense and decency into the state governments."

Next day while Longstreet went to deliver this message, Trav met the train upon which Mrs. Longstreet and Garland arrived. He thought Mrs. Longstreet looked badly, pale, with shadowed circles under her eyes. She asked where the General was, fretting because he was not here; she complained of the cold and the snow. Trav saw Garland pat her hand in reassurance; and she laughed and said: "I know, Sonny. I'm all right. Just let me fuss a little if I want to."

At home Enid and Lucy—Lucy with a shy glance backward to where Peter had taken Garland in charge—led her away upstairs. When Longstreet arrived, the boys had departed on some business of their own, and the ladies had not yet come down. Longstreet's scowl was evidence enough that his conference with President Davis had led nowhere; and to Trav's questioning glance he said:

"No, no encouragement. President Davis says the states are too

jealous of their rights to let him call their militia." He added thoughtfully: "He says the Confederacy was founded on the theory of states'
rights, and that we may yet founder on it. If we do we'll die of a
theory!" And he asked: "Did Louisa come?" At Trav's word the big
man bounded up the stairs three steps at a time, eager as a boy.

But when he and Mrs. Longstreet presently appeared again he was
subdued and silent. Mrs. Longstreet on the other hand was unnaturally animated. The General watched her with bewildered eyes, but
she never looked at her husband; and Trav recognized the signs.
Something was amiss between them. When, after supper, he and the
General were alone, he thought the other might confide in him; and
he was not surprised when Longstreet said Mrs. Longstreet wished to
take a house in Richmond.

"I told her that couldn't be managed," he explained. "Any house at
all rents here for two or three thousand a year, and a general's salary
won't stand that. And even at that price there are no houses to be
had!" He added: "But I'd like her nearer me, anyway. I'll see if
Major Moses can't find a place for us in Petersburg."

This might have been the source of their difference. "He'll find
something if there's anything to find," Trav agreed. "Major Moses
could find a side of beef in a cageful of lions."

They stayed in Richmond till Tuesday, the General busy at the War
Department; but Trav was glad when they took train for Petersburg.
After the first pleasant excitement when for a while Enid seemed as
beautiful and as charming as she had used to be, so that when they
were alone together he had to remind himself that there was a gulf
between them, she had begun again to dart at him words that stung
like persistent insects. If Mrs. Longstreet admired their home: "Trav
always thought I was silly to want one, but I hate living with in-
laws, no matter how nice they are. Of course Trav's Mama was as
nice as she could be to me, in her way. At least I'm sure she meant
to be."

Or if the General spoke of the young men exempted from military
duty who filled the Richmond streets, she might say: "Yes, isn't it terrible? But Trav says he doesn't blame farmers for deserting when
everyone else is dodging the enrolling officers." Longstreet remarked
once that he preferred to keep his military plans to himself until time

to put them into execution; and she said smilingly: "You'd better! Don't even tell Trav. He talks in his sleep, terribly!"

The General laughed. "Not everyone shares your husband's couch, you know," he reminded her; and Mrs. Longstreet said in an exasperated tone:

"Jeems! I declare, sometimes your vulgarity is beyond endurance!"

Enid delivered all her shafts from behind a pretense of amusement at Trav's eccentric ways. When Longstreet once spoke of how Trav charged into the thickest fire at Seven Pines and again at Frayser's Farm, Enid laughed and explained: "I expect he was mad! You know he has a frightful temper. It wouldn't surprise me a bit if he just wrung my neck someday."

This was so profoundly untrue that when they were alone Trav said coldly: "It might be a good thing if I did wring your neck, Enid."

She looked at him with mocking eyes, her head on one side. "Really, Honey, I wish you would! Anything would be better than just treating me like—furniture!"

She made him miserable, and Trav found small comfort in the fact that Mrs. Longstreet harassed the General too. He had developed a heavy cold; and she was sure it resulted from his folly in going to church through the storm on Sunday. She wished to put him to bed and rub his chest with that famous salve, and she was furious because he refused to accept her ministrations, and accused him of catching cold deliberately to worry her. When on Tuesday he insisted, despite his indisposition, on proceeding to Petersburg, she was so angry that she would not kiss him good-by.

On the train, Longstreet filled his lungs with a deep sigh. "I'm glad women don't command the enemy armies, Currain. We'd never be able to guess what they'd do next." Trav said nothing, since to agree would seem a criticism of Mrs. Longstreet; and the General may have feared his remark might be thus interpreted, for he added: "Their health has so much to do with their spirits." He coughed, not because of his cold but in a heavy masculine embarrassment. "Between ourselves, Currain, Louisa suspects that she's in a family way, and that upsets her and she takes it out on me."

Trav thought how absurd it was, and how appealing, that this man who could dominate a battlefield should be so helpless against the tyranny of a woman not half his size. He was uncertain what to say to the General's confidence, so he said nothing; and after a moment the other added:

"It's just over a year ago that our babies died. I'd begun to forget; but she'll never forget. She doesn't want any more children. At least, that's her feeling now. So she's wretched and rebellious, and angry at me." Trav remembered that Enid had always raged at him when she knew a baby was coming. There were some wild animals among whom the female, at such times, drove the male away, as though to protect their unborn against the sire. Probably this reaction among women was a vestigial trace of that ancient instinct, a remembered defense against the possessive jealousy of the male. Longstreet said in a confused distress: "I never loved her as much as now, but she seems almost to hate the sight of me."

"She'll be glad to be settled in her own home," Trav suggested; and the General said in some relief:

"Yes. Yes, give a woman a house to fuss over and she's happy as can be."

Longstreet's cold grew worse instead of better, and for several days after they reached Petersburg he kept his bed; but this did not hinder his direction of affairs. His command embraced North Carolina, where there was some enemy activity in the eastern counties; and he sent Trav off to Goldsboro to see General Hill, who had gone there a week or two before, and get his report of the situation.

He found the General, always irascible, in a mood of more than usual exasperation. "Major," Hill demanded, after the first greeting, "what poison's loose in your old neighborhood?" And to Trav's surprised question: "Why, damn it, sir, that whole region—yes, all the mountain country—is a hotbed of armed treason!" He fumbled among papers on his desk. "Here's a letter from Governor Vance about the latest trouble. Yadkinville's not far from your old home, is it?"

"Not far, no sir."

"Hah! Colonel Joyce sent fourteen good men to round up some of the deserters and conscripts there the other day. The rascals took shelter in the school house. They killed Mr. West, the justice, and John

Williams, and drove off the Colonel's men and escaped. Oh, I believe some of them were killed and wounded, but the rest got clean away. They headed for Tennessee. What have you to say for those old neighbors of yours, Major?"

Trav hesitated: "I've known there was—feeling there."

"Feeling! By God sir, that's a nest of traitors! That whole section. The entire population is banded together to hide the fugitives. An enrolling officer takes his life in his hands if he shows himself there. And if Colonel Joyce's prisoners are brought to trial, Judge Pearson will hold the conscription act unconstitutional and turn them loose!"

"Well, you know, General, that affair at Laurel Valley in December left an angry feeling all through the mountains."

"I know, I know! Governor Vance sent me a copy of Mr. Merrimon's report. I suppose Colonel Keith acted beyond what was necessary. According to Mr. Merrimon, he dragged unresisting men from their homes, whipped some of their women, took thirteen or the men off and shot them without a pretense of trial. But Major Currain, something has to be done to meet this plague of desertion, or we'll have no army left. These men who were shot had forcibly seized the country town, looted it, stole all the salt in the place. That was plain brigandry."

"I suppose they needed the salt to cure their hog meat."

General Hill looked at him sharply. "By God, I believe you sympathize with the rascals!"

"I sympathize with hungry men, and hungry women and children."

The other after a moment nodded grudgingly. "I know, I know! Yes, there's much suffering on those little farms with the men away; but we've got to suffer if we're to lick the Yankees."

Trav brought him to the point. "That's one reason General Longstreet sent me to you. The army's half starved. Is there a chance to collect provisions here?"

General Hill said this could be done. "There's plenty of bacon and pork and corn in all the coastal counties, Hyde and Tyrrel particularly; and we've forage to spare." He thought cavalry might come from the Rappahannock to rest and graze their horses and at the same time to collect a vast quantity of stores.

While they were talking, Trav remembered what Mrs. Blandy had told him, and he asked: "By the way, General, is the Eleventh North Carolina in your command?"

"Yes, of course. There's not a better regiment in the army. Colonel Leventhorpe served in the British army, and he had time to give his men some real work on the parade ground before they ever heard an enemy musket. It's a pleasure to watch them. Why?"

"Two Martinston men are in that regiment. You remember Ed Blandy. He and Tom Shadd. I'd like to see them."

"Blandy? God bless me, I didn't know that. But they're not here today. Off toward Kinston keeping an eye on the Yankees. Can you ride out to see your friends?" Trav felt he should take the first train back to Petersburg, but he wrote Ed a note which General Hill promised to forward.

Back in Petersburg, Trav found General Longstreet recovered and himself again.

"I think I'll go see General Hill myself," the General decided, when he heard Trav's report; and he said with a lively satisfaction: "But Currain, I've found a place for Louisa to live. To satisfy Louisa I had Doctor Jimmie Dunn come in and physic this damned cold of mine, and he says Mrs. Dunn will be glad to have another lady in the house. They live on Sycamore near Wythe; and they have plenty of room for refugees like us." He was in a high good humor at the solving of this problem. "I'll take the morning train for Goldsboro and see Harvey Hill, and you go fetch Louisa and Garland down from Richmond, see her established here. I'll be gone four or five days, long enough for her to get settled and to get over blaming me for not finding a house for her."

So Trav had another night at home. He found Lucy and Garland the best of friends; but Mrs. Longstreet seemed glad of the prospective move to Petersburg, and Enid gave him no peace. She was disappointed with some of the furnishings of the Clay Street house. "Everything's dark and dull," she said. "I want to do over the drawing room, make it all bright and cheerful like Cinda's."

"You can't buy anything in the Richmond stores."

"Captain Pew says he can get me just anything I want in Nassau."

Trav was weary of the virtues of Captain Pew. "He'd better use his cargo space to bring back some of the things the army needs!"

"Oh you! All you think about is your old army! Can't you think about us once in a while?" She added: "Besides, I've already told him what I want, and he's already gone to Wilmington. He didn't know for sure what he'd have to pay, but I said you'd pay him when he got back."

Trav looked at her with bleak eyes. "You should have consulted me."

"I never know when you'll be home." She was watching him expectantly; but of course he must accept this obligation she had thrust upon him. Yet probably these purchases of hers would amount to a staggering sum. Nevertheless he must meet Captain Pew's account when it should be presented. He nodded absently.

"But don't spend any more unnecessary money without my permission," he warned her; and she said he was ever so good to her and came to kiss him gratefully.

Before he left for Petersburg, she said he ought to do something about Peter. "He's simply beyond me, Trav; just doesn't pay the slightest attention to anything I say. I wish you'd talk to him."

Trav did talk to Peter, groping awkwardly. "I count on you, you know, son, to take care of Mama when I'm away."

"Oh Papa," the youngster protested. "She doesn't want me around! She just sends me to bed or something!"

"If you tried very hard to be nice to her——"

"That wouldn't do any good! You're always nice to her, Papa; but she's awful mean to you!"

Trav almost nodded, but a sense of danger touched him and he checked himself. "Oh no, son! You don't understand us, that's all. Grown people say things jokingly that aren't meant the way they sound to you. No, Peter, Mama's as nice to me as she can be. You try being nice to her and see what happens." For Peter or Lucy to side with him against Enid would be a tragedy.

When Trav escorted Mrs. Longstreet to Petersburg, concern over Enid's extravagance went with him; and a few days later a chance remark from Captain Blackford, the Judge Advocate attached to Longstreet's staff, caught his attention. Captain Blackford was a Lynchburg man; and, reading a letter from home, he exclaimed: "Hullo! Here's a windfall! I bought some tobacco early in February and my father's just sold it at fourteen thousand dollars profit."

Those who heard him spoke in cheerful envy, and Trav later made an opportunity to refer to the subject again. "I used to send my bright tobacco from Chimneys to the Lynchburg market; but a year's crop wouldn't bring half that."

"Oh, this is just speculation," Blackford explained. "With prices rising every day it's like finding money."

"I can raise tobacco, but I don't know anything about trading in it."

"Let my father make some money for you," the Captain proposed; and Trav, with an exciting sense of his own temerity, gave Blackford fifteen hundred dollars, enough to margin a purchase of four thousand pounds at a dollar and ten cents a pound. When his purchases presently sold at a dollar and sixty-five cents, the twenty-two-hundred-dollar profit gave him an intoxicating satisfaction; and at Captain Blackford's advice he reinvested his original capital and a thousand dollars of his gains.

"Father made over ten thousand dollars in one week for John Minor and Staige Davis," the Captain told him. "And of course, the more you invest the more you make."

This first success, and the prospect of further gains, gave Trav as far as money was concerned an easier mind.

Trav had little comfort from his trips to Richmond, nor were these weeks a time of content in Petersburg. Mrs. Longstreet was by no means well, so the General was distracted; and except when military business demanded his attention he stayed much with her. Sometimes he seemed half-drugged with weariness, and his temper was sluggish; yet he could rouse to hard anger too. The strain of administering an independent command, where the inadequacy of their means was a continual problem, one day woke him to an almost pettish outburst.

"Damn it, we're in a hopeless struggle, Currain!" he cried. "Everybody is forever wanting more, more of this and more of that! Whiting wants another brigade at Wilmington, Hill wants more men and more guns." He grunted. "He burst his guns by putting too much powder in them, and then asks for more powder with which to burst more guns. Ransom, Elzey, they all wanted more! French—" He thrust irritably at a letter on his desk, quoted in a piping voice: "'I am having chills or I would come and see you.' French is always having chills! But even he wants more!

"Why, God damn it to a blistering Hell, I'm as bad as any of them! I want more men, if I'm to do anything. Hood and Pickett are here for defense only; I can't move them away from the railroad for fear General Lee will want them. He's another who is condemned always to want more, more men! If he does, he'll want them in a hurry. Each of us wants more! And there's not enough of anything, not enough men, not enough horses, not enough food, not enough guns, not enough powder and ball and shell. The Confederacy will die of 'not enough', Currain, with all of us forever whining for more!"

"We're getting more food, at least, General."

Longstreet grudgingly assented. "Yes. Yes. And that's what we're here for."

"No move against Suffolk?"

"Not seriously, no. General Lee says he doesn't see how we can accomplish anything there, and neither do I." Trav was surprised, since the preparations for an advance went on day by day; but as though reading his thoughts Longstreet explained: "No, whatever we pretend to do in that direction is just pretense. Perhaps we can fool the Yankees into expecting us to attack them, so they'll stay in their lines and let our wagons range as they choose. The Yankees like to play tricks, and tricksters are always easily tricked. No, I won't lose a man or fire a gun unless we must." He scowled at Trav. "I know you've a still tongue, Currain. Keep it so. If even our own men expect some great stroke by us, the Yankees will expect it too."

Trav nodded, half understanding. He heard complaints enough against this long inaction; but if others were discontented he found comfort in the steady collection of supplies from all the territory where their wagons were free to go. He and Major Walton worked with Major Moses at that task, while General Longstreet made a great show of military activity. He sent General Hill to threaten New Berne and to make gestures toward the North Carolina town of Washington; he moved the forces here in hand toward Suffolk and established his lines along the Nansemond. But while the enemy lay behind his fortification waiting for the assaults that never came, the wagon trains were busy, foraging undisturbed through the coastal counties.

Yet Trav, despite what he knew of the other's mind, was distressed by General Longstreet's inertia. He sometimes thought that if Mrs. Longstreet had not been so near, the big man's energies would have been more actively directed against the enemy. Yet this may not have been the only reason. The cold the General had taken in Richmond had not completely left him; he coughed a great deal, in a hacking, weary way. Certainly either ill health or worry over Mrs. Longstreet weakened him. Something of his firm command of men was lost. Major Sorrel showed Trav one day a letter from General French.

"Just see this, Currain," he said. "I wrote General French some instructions, in General Longstreet's name. Here's his reply. Listen." And he read: "'In answer to the general's kind inquiry if it will be agreeable to me to resume the responsibilities of the river batteries and their protection, I reply it will not be.'" Sorrel crumpled the letter angrily. "Sarcastic insolence! I thought the General would order him under arrest; but when he read it he just grunted, made no comment at all. What's wrong with him?" He added, almost apologetically: "Yet I suppose he's accomplishing the important thing, collecting enough supplies to feed the army for a while." He laughed in hot scorn. "Though Colonel Northrop's men from Richmond make it as hard for us as possible. Major Moses says he could buy bacon for twelve and a half cents when he began; but now commissary agents from Richmond are paying a dollar, and we have to meet their price. And most of what they buy they'll charge to the Government at twice that, and pocket the difference." He shook his head. "I don't suppose we could take Suffolk anyway, without some protection from the Navy on our river flank. And we couldn't spare men to leave a garrison there if we took it. But I can't understand the General's inaction."

"Like Jackson last June," Trav reminded him. "For a few days after he came from the Valley he didn't have any driving energy. If he'd come up in time, that day at Frayser's Farm, we'd have cut McClellan in two."

Sorrel nodded. "I know. Every man is better on some days than on others. But I never expected to see General Longstreet take this insolence from French—or let George Pickett ride off to Chuckatuck every night to shake his perfumed locks at his lady there—or let that burlesque duel between Major Belo and Captain Cussons go as far as it did. Has he said anything to you?"

Trav evaded a direct reply. "After all," he reminded the other, "anything he did here would cost men and ammunition; and we've neither men nor ammunition to spare. And of course, he's always been against attacking except defensively. You know how often he says that we don't have to beat the North, that we just have to keep them from beating us."

"I know," Sorrel agreed. "And at least he's kept us busy enough so that the men are keen and in good spirits, and we've collected God knows how much pork and corn." He spoke more cheerfully. "Maybe this loafing has been good for us. Spring's here. We'll have fighting enough now before long."

He was right. On the twenty-ninth of April a message came from General Lee. The enemy had crossed the Rappahannock. It was time for the army to unite again, to rise and once more hurl the Yankees back.

23

JULIAN would be eighteen in September, and Anne Tudor was a few months younger; so as such things go in normal times, Julian was a boy, Anne a young woman. But boys in battle and in the hurting aftermath of battle become men more quickly. Through weeks of desperate sickness Julian came back to life again, and he thought his youth as irrevocably gone as that leg the surgeons had removed. The fact that his hearing was at first impaired added to this feeling; there was a hush all around him, as though people walked on careful tiptoe, and talked in whispers. Anne's was the only voice which he heard clearly and without any effort. One day while they were still in Washington he asked her: "Anne, do you talk louder when you're talking to me?"

"No, Julian. Why?"

"Well, I hear you all right; but I can hardly hear the others at all, not even Mama."

For this and for other reasons he was happiest with Anne. With her he could jest at his own hurt and feel no pain in her nor in himself. When he was with his mother or his father or with any other of those by whom he was beloved, he was always conscious of the anguished sorrow in their hearts. No matter how bravely they hid it, he knew it was there. They treated him like a cripple, forever offering him a helping hand, steadying him on his crutches; and even their unspoken solicitude brought him so near tears of self pity that he hated it. But Anne never offered to help him; if he fell, she laughed at his awkwardness and let him get up again. She did not seem to be sorry for him at all, and that was wonderful. Julian did not want to go through life nagged by perpetual sympathy.

Next to Anne, his father and Burr came nearest to understanding this; but even with them, to treat him as casually as he desired was an obvious effort. Anne made no effort. She was—without trying—just what he wished her most to be.

He was much with her, turning to her at every opportunity. They talked together hour on hour. That was a long and cold and snowy winter in Richmond, so fine days were rare, but if the day were fair she was likely to suggest that they take a walk. At first these were not long excursions; perhaps no more than around the block. Later they began to go the few blocks to Capitol Square, where on good days there might be many gentlemen gathered in groups discussing the latest news from General Lee, or the scandalously high prices, or the chance for a profit in blockading, or how much So-and-so won at Monteiro's last night, or whether the expedition against Charleston which the Yankees were preparing would succeed, or whether President Davis would ever be able to persuade the courts to accept the suspension of the writ of habeas corpus. Capitol Square was always a popular gathering place for gentlemen, or for ladies with wide skirts swaying to their leisurely promenade, or for nurses with their charges; and sometimes the Battalion Band played lively airs, and on sunny days the scene was almost gay.

Through the last months of that winter Julian and Anne avoided the residential streets; for smallpox was widespread and it was sad to see many houses fly the white flag of pestilence. Little Andrew Pizzini, the confectioner on Broad Street between Eighth and Ninth, came to know the two young people and to welcome them; and long before the season opened he promised they should have the first strawberries that appeared. As spring days began to come and the flood waters in the river roared across the rapids, they more and more often turned that way to follow the path along the canal and watch for first spring flowers in the woods on the hillside above, or by the waterside; and canal boats might pass below them, setting out for Lynchburg or dispatched by one of the hospitals to trade for food among the farms along the way.

Anne insisted that unless it were actually raining or snowing Julian should walk somewhere every day; so even on dull days she remembered errands she must do and took him with her; and sometimes they stopped idly at one of the auction rooms, where dresses, fine lace, silverware, jewels, oil portraits, furniture, a thousand family treasures were put up for sale. These were the possessions of refugees from the Virginia counties now occupied by the Yankees, being sold to provide their owners with money to buy, at steadily rising prices, the bare necessities of life. At first Anne and Julian laughed at the haggling bidders forever alert to seize on any bargain, till they came to despise the sleek complacent folk grown suddenly rich through speculation who paid casually any price at all for some object to which they took a fancy, and decided not to enter these establishments again. But one day they met Mrs. Harrison, whose home on the Northern Neck had been only twenty miles or so from Faunt's and from Judge Tudor's, so that she and Anne were old friends. She was a lively, merry woman as old as Cinda; and Julian thought there was something feverish in her gaiety. Anne was particularly nice to her, saying reproachfully: "We've missed you. You know, you never come to see us."

"Oh I'm much too busy," Mrs. Harrison assured her; and she told Julian, with laughter in her tones: "You see, I've a family to support. Not my own, to be sure; but little Betsy Annabel's husband was killed last summer. He and my boys rode with Stuart. So Betsy and her baby and I have a nice room together, and Judge Tudor persuaded Colonel Northrop to make me a clerk." She added gaily: "I wanted to help sign money, but all those places were filled months ago and there were a hundred applicants for every vacancy." They were moving slowly along Main Street, and she talked as they walked. "I had to pass a horrible examination in arithmetic, vulgar fractions, tare and tret, all sorts of silly things. Heaven knows how I did it! So now I earn a hundred and twenty-five dollars a month. Isn't that remarkable, Mr. Dewain?"

"I should think so. I never earned a penny in my life."

"But our day's work's done at three o'clock," Mrs. Harrison explained. "So—" They were opposite the doors of an auction room, and she cried: "Oh, let's go in!"

Anne protested. "No, no. I don't like them."

"Oh, this is Mr. Lehman's," Mrs. Harrison insisted. "You'll like him." And somehow she hustled them through the doors. The room was already crowded; and except for gas jets over the auctioneer's platform it was dimly lighted. They chose a corner where Julian could rest against the wall, and Mrs. Harrison and Anne flanked him. This auction seemed to Julian much like any other: an old man with a sing-song voice indifferently parroting the bids; another man at a desk beside him keeping the records. "That's Mr. Lehman at the desk," Mrs. Harrison whispered. "He's a good man."

Julian thought Mr. Lehman did not look the part; and it saddened him to see the things that one by one were put up and sold, sometimes for little, sometimes for much. They were a miscellany of household articles—china, silver, plate, pictures, furniture; but when presently a silver coffee service was put up, Anne exclaimed:

"Why, Mrs. Harrison, that's yours!"

Mrs. Harrison nodded, for once not smiling; and they did not speak till the bidding ended and the auctioneer said: "Sold! To Mr. Streean!"

Julian felt his cheeks tight with anger and shame that his uncle should be a bidder here; but Mrs. Harrison said: "Splendid! Now I must run." They went out with her; and she told Anne: "Mr. Lehman gets the best prices for things! He's really wonderful. If the bidding doesn't suit him he nods to one of his men to buy things in himself, and then he sells them over again another day, and gives you credit for the highest price they bring."

Anne said sympathetically: "You must hate selling your things!"

The older woman laughed, shook her head. "As a matter of fact, I don't! I've been the slave of things all my life! I didn't own them, they owned me. When the war started, every soldier on the march loaded himself down with enough things to break the back of an elephant; but now they've learned to get along with mighty little, and so have I! I never felt really free in my life; but I didn't know I was a slave until I began to get rid of—things!"

They laughed with her; but when they parted Julian saw her face, as she turned away and need no longer wear for their benefit that gallant smile, shadowed with bitter pain. Anne saw it too. "Major Harrison was killed at Sharpsburg, you know," she told Julian. "She has two boys in Burr's regiment. They had such a lovely home."

"She seems cheerful about it."

"She's wonderful! But what little she earns must buy food for her and Mrs. Annabel and a baby and pay the rent of their one room besides. So I suppose she's selling everything she owns. She was cheerful with us, but she'll cry into her pillow tonight, you know."

As Julian grew stronger, their strolls extended. They liked the promenade along the canal toward Hollywood, where they could overlook the river and the tumbling rapids above the railroad bridge; and sometimes they climbed the steep hillside above the canal, laughing together at Julian's struggles with his crutches, and found a vantage from which they could look back toward the city. The needle spires of the churches sharply pierced the sky, and the Capitol rose in a bold mass above the lesser buildings all around it, and the bulk of Mr. Libby's warehouse where Yankee prisoners were confined frowned by the river front, and they could see the soldiers on Belle Isle in the river just below them guarding other prisoners there. Sometimes Julian told her about his own days as a prisoner in Washington when he lay helpless and ill and alone; till Anne saw pain in his eyes and silenced him.

"Stop it!" she said. "You're just making yourself miserable."

"Well, why shouldn't I? So much I want to do, but a one-legged man can't do anything."

"Nonsense! Oh of course there are lots of things you can't do. But there are lots of things you can! Concentrate on them. You can't run faster nor walk farther than other men, but you can learn to think straighter and truer. You can do a lot more, if you just forget the things you can't do, than some of these silly ninnies who think they can do anything in the world when really they can't do anything well at all!" He smiled, loving her earnestness; and she insisted: "Besides, there's no better fun than trying to do things, even when you're pretty sure you can't. And anyway, no one ever knows what he can do till he tries."

He asked lightly: "What do you want me to try?"

"Well, you can learn to do things with your head. Papa would be just as good a lawyer or a judge if he didn't have any legs at all! We can read some of his law books together; and when we're tired of reading we can take walks."

They came to spend many a rainy afternoon in Judge Tudor's library; and they walked by the hour. Julian was increasingly at home on his crutches, and he accustomed himself to the curious glances of strangers, and to the kindly and voluble sympathy of chance-met acquaintances. Anne helped. She kept her quick tongue playing, talking so steadily and so gaily and so brightly that he forgot himself in his delight in her.

She talked of many things in her childhood and in the present; of her quiet years with her father when they seldom saw anyone but Faunt, of the delights of their occasional trips to Richmond when she and Judge Tudor stayed grandly at a hotel or perhaps visited his sister, Barbara's mother. She told him some of the tales Faunt had told her, of his scouting behind the enemy lines. She spoke of Faunt so often and with such frank affection that Julian knew how much the older man meant to her; so on that day when Faunt overtook them on Grace Street and mocked Julian so cruelly, he forgot his own hurt in hers. When Faunt had ridden away, Anne stared after him with streaming eyes, between anger and grief.

"Oh he's mean; he's mean!" she cried.

Not for Faunt's sake but because he knew how it wounded her to see her idol shattered, Julian spoke in his uncle's defense. "He was just joking, Anne. Trying to be funny."

"No he wasn't! He was being mean on purpose!"

Julian suspected that this was true. Uncle Faunt was too wise to be so witless without intent; and with some faint glimmering of the truth he said honestly: "I guess maybe he did do it on purpose, Anne. He's too considerate to talk that way without knowing how it will sound. Maybe he thought it would be good for me to make a joke of it."

She would not so easily be appeased. "No, Julian! He wasn't joking! He was just trying to hurt your feelings!" Her tears were dry, but sorrow blended with hurt anger in her tones. "I've always thought he was so wonderful. Oh I wish he hadn't acted that way!" They moved on more slowly, silent together; till presently she laughed and tossed her head. "There, I won't let it make us blue. Let's not even think about him any more."

Julian told no one about that incident. His mother, or his father, would be made angry; and somehow he felt sure that there was an explanation if he could guess it. Early in March Burr came home for two days; and Julian and he were much together, and Julian asked:

"Burr, do you see Uncle Faunt right along?"

Burr hesitated. "No. No, he's with Mosby now. Mosby has a partisan band operating behind the Yankee lines, raiding the railroads, attacking wagon trains, cutting up Yankee patrols. They're making General Hooker plenty of trouble."

"I expect Uncle Faunt is good at that sort of thing."

"You haven't seen him for a long time, have you?"

"Just once, a month ago, on the street for a minute. His beard changes him, doesn't it?"

Burr nodded, his eyes abstracted. "Uncle Faunt doesn't—well, all he wants to do now is kill Yankees. Mosby's partisans get together for raids whenever Mosby sends them word; but in between times they never see Uncle Faunt. He just goes off by himself somewhere, works alone."

Julian asked wonderingly: "Works at what?"

But the other shook his head. "I don't know. Doing the enemy all the harm he can, I suppose."

Burr said no more than this in words, but his tone was so eloquent of disapproval that Julian thought it was remotely possible Uncle Faunt had meant to be as cruel as he seemed. But since Faunt never came to Richmond, or at least never came to Fifth Street, Julian presently forgot him in nearer things. He was acquiring the knack of walking with one crutch instead of two; and he was puzzling to devise some harness—a strap around his waist, or the sort of thing women wore—to which in default of any useful stump an artificial leg could be attached.

Late in February, Rollin Lyle came one day to the house on Fifth Street. He had gone without a scratch through South Mountain and Sharpsburg and his regiment had a fine month along the Opequon, recuperating after that campaign into Maryland. "And at Fredericksburg we weren't really engaged at all," Rollin explained, "but I got a shell fragment through my shoulder, and it didn't want to heal. So I've been down home since before Christmas."

"I'll bet that was fun."

"In a way, it was," Rollin agreed. "Papa's there. He was too old, so they wouldn't take him in the army; so he's raising all the food he can, managing all the plantations. He had to move away from the coast, because so many of the people went off to the Yankees; so he moved the rest of them to Fallow Fields, up the Peedee River in North Carolina. It's healthier there. He had twenty-eight negroes die last year, working the rice, and twenty-two of them were task hands. Mama likes it better at Fallow Fields, but it wasn't the same as being at our real home."

When Vesta and Cinda appeared, they greeted Rollin delightedly. Cinda asked whether he had visited Camden.

"Yes, I came around by Columbia," he said. "I've been eight days coming from there—four days waiting for floods to run off, and four days on the cars." But he had ridden from Columbia to the Plains to see Jenny and the children. Kyle and Janet were both riding, he reported; little Clayton was walking and talking a little. Jenny seemed well, and she was busy, and as fine and as beautiful as she had always been. Managing the Plains certainly agreed with her, and Mrs. Cloyd said no man could do it better. Jenny and Mrs. Cloyd saw a lot of each other.

After supper Rollin went to call on Dolly, and Vesta and Cinda agreed that his long devotion to Dolly was his only flaw; but Julian said Dolly was an awfully pretty girl. "And Rollin, once he likes a person, is mighty loyal." Rollin had promised to return to spend the night; and Julian waited up for him. When he came, Rollin reported that Dolly had had another caller, a Captain Pew.

"I think he's a friend of Mr. Streean," he said. "He's a blockade runner. He was still there when I left. Dolly seems fond of him." Julian almost smiled at his tone.

After Rollin left Richmond to rejoin his regiment along the Rappahannock, Julian's rich hours and days with Anne continued. She was her father's housekeeper, and when bad weather kept them indoors, Julian might sit with a law book on his knee while she puzzled over her accounts. In March she was scandalized to have to pay thirty-two dollars for a barrel of flour. "Papa says he's a mind to move South," she told Julian. "He says he's just sick and tired of paying through the nose to these old extortioners!"

But she was to be glad she had bought that barrel when she did, for a few days later the Government seized all the flour in the city's warehouses. "I expect lots of people just simply haven't got any at all," Anne declared, and Julian found that this was true. Even Aunt Enid borrowed from his mother, and she was furious at the Government's tyranny.

"There's going to be trouble, you wait and see," Enid predicted. "The warehouses are just simply full of flour and we can't get any! People won't stand it." The day one of the warehouses burned, she came to repay the borrowed flour and to say triumphantly: "What did I tell you? Someone set that warehouse on fire! I'm just as sure as I can be." Cinda said she need not have hurried to repay the borrowed flour, but Enid said Captain Pew had brought her a barrel from Nassau. "He and Dolly came to supper last night. He just got back day before yesterday." She was in the liveliest humor, her eyes sparkling. "Julian, that's what you ought to do, go blockading! You don't need two legs to do that, and Captain Pew makes heaps and heaps of money. He told us last night he took a load of cotton that he paid forty-three thousand dollars for, and traded it in Nassau for Yankee goods and some lead from England, and he got some gold besides, and put that in the bank at Nassau; and he sold the things he brought back for almost a million dollars! So you see!"

Julian grinned. "Sounds like a made-up story to me."

"Well, it isn't! Why, one of the sailors on his ship bought six gallons of gin in Nassau for twenty-five dollars and sold it in Wilmington for nine hundred dollars." She laughed in sudden amusement. "Dolly just declares she's going to get a little ship and go blockading herself and make a fortune! She could, too. Anybody can! Of course some people think it's wrong; but Trav says if people didn't buy blockade goods there wouldn't be any blockade-runners, so he says you can't blame them!"

Cinda protested: "That doesn't sound like Travis, Enid. You must have misunderstood him."

"Well, of course I never know what he really means," Enid conceded. "But I know what he said! I know it's true, too. I mean about blockaders making all that money."

When she was gone, Julian whistled. "Golly, Mama, how do you stand her? How does Uncle Trav stand her?" But Cinda did not reply.

A winter's snow melted fast; and Friday morning Anne stopped on her way to do some household errands and insisted that Julian go with her. It was still slippery enough so that he took two crutches, and he was to be glad he had done so. They were in Smithers's dry goods store on Main Street when they felt rather than heard, a muffled, jarring explosion. They. hurried out of doors and saw people running down toward the river and heard far thin screams; and as fast as Julian could manage they followed the crowd till they were caught in a press of pushing people and Julian found it hard to hold his footing. Anne suddenly stopped and held his arm.

"There, we won't go any farther," she declared. "I won't have you jostled so."

He knew a quick delight at her solicitude. "I'm all right. Let's go see what happened."

"I don't care what happened. You'll fall down."

"I'll get up again."

"In this crowd? Julian Dewain, don't be an idiot! Here, get into this doorway so people won't bump into you." And as he yielded: "I declare, you can be the most exasperating man!"

His happiness overshadowed any curiosity about the explosion which had set this hurrying crowd in motion; but presently an ambulance passed them, and another, and the news of what had happened spread from mouth to mouth. Something ignited the powder in the cartridge factory on Brown's Island and blew the sides out of the flimsy wooden building so that the roof fell in. The workers were almost all young girls and women; and many of them—no one yet knew how many—were torn by the blast, or crushed, or burned.

Julian and Anne went home knowing no more than this; but the Saturday *Whig* said at least thirty girls had been killed. Sunday,

Julian and Cinda and Vesta met Anne and her father at the church gates. Julian had not seen the *Whig,* but Anne had.

"And one poor girl, Miss Burley, has simply vanished," she told him. "Nobody knows what happened to her. I guess she was just blown to bits." She said pitifully: "Oh Julian, they were all so poor! Think of having to work in that dreadful place to make a living! I'm so sorry for them."

He nodded, thinking she had never been so beautiful. "But do you know something, Anne?"

"What?"

"I'm sorry for them, of course; but I enjoyed the excitement that day."

Her eyes widened in bewilderment. "Why, Julian?"

"It was such fun having you boss me around and take care of me."

Her color rose. "Why, I think that's horrid!" she declared, and turned to go into the church; but from the top step she looked back at him with a shy quick smile.

When he took his seat he could see her sitting beside her father a few rows nearer the pulpit, see the curve of her cheek past the border of her bonnet. To watch her was so absorbing that he paid little attention to the service. Until today, his thoughts had not cast ahead. To be with Anne as often and as long as possible had filled him with unquestioning content. But after this day there began to be a change in the rhythm of his pulse. They went together, he in respect to a gallant and a valiant man and she to keep him company, to Major Pelham's funeral; and the measured tramp of many feet and the slow beat of the Dead March woke in him a hasting and an urgency. He seemed to hear a whisper: "Hurry, hurry!" Thereafter, when he could not be with her, this frantic sense of haste grew stronger. Thursday snow began again to fall; and by morning it was eight inches deep. He dreaded a day without seeing her; but presently she came with a laughing challenge.

"Julian," she cried, "General Hood's Texans are marching down Main Street and having a snowball fight, right in the street. Come watch the fun!"

He hesitated. Snow lay deep in the streets, and the very air was a scour of wind-blown flakes. "I don't know whether I can, Anne."

"Oh you can do anything you want to do!"

So he went with her, and they laughed together at his difficulties. To swing his foot forward, supported on his crutches, was easy enough unless he tried to take too long a step; but when that one foot was firmly planted, he had to lift his crutches high and swing them wide or they caught in the heavy, clogging quicksand of the snow. He was soon panting and breathless; but Anne gave him no respite, teasing him for his slowness, urging him on.

There were half a dozen blocks to go. Hood's men had started north to meet the threat of that Yankee thrust in which the brave Pelham had been killed; but now the Yankees were repulsed and they were returning to their camp across Mayo's Bridge. Before Anne and Julian came to the corner where the Texans turned down toward the bridge, he was shaking with fatigue and his pulse hit hard. Anne's hand slipped through his arm and she asked softly:

"All right, Julian?"

"Fine."

"I wasn't just being mean, making you hurry. It's good for you to do hard things. Isn't it?"

"You bet. You just keep after me."

Then his eyes turned to the line of marching men. These Texans had won fame at Gaines' Mill and had kept that fame untarnished. The laughing warriors trudged through the heavy snow, and they made a frolic of their march. Snowballs were flying up and down the column, and sometimes the men broke ranks for a sudden furious skirmish. They yelled shrill challenges and bold defiances and shouted in hot triumph; and the crowd along the sidewalks laughed and cheered.

Then one of them saw Julian and levelled a pointing finger and sang:

> " 'Johnny, was you drunk?
> 'Johnny, was you mad?' "

Julian grinned delightedly. The rough derision of the song made a joke of his hurt; and it told him he was one with them and had their love and loyal comradeship.

> " 'What did you do
> 'With the leg that you had?' "

There were five, and ten, and then twenty voices singing; and Julian joined with them and went on with them; and Anne, looking up at him in fine and tender pride through smiling tears, sang with him.

> " 'I was chasing me a Yankee
> 'To make him cry and beg.
> 'Along came a cannon ball
> 'And stole away my leg.' "

The Texans shouted their delight; and a tall young fellow in the ranks scooped up a handful of the soft snow and flung it over Anne, and she laughed with them and brushed the snow away and stood proudly close by Julian's side as the last of the column passed.

They went homeward more slowly, happy together, speaking little. At the house on Fifth Street, Anne came in for a while, and she and Vesta discussed housekeeping problems. Since Cinda was so much at the hospital, Vesta managed this house as Anne did her father's. Flour was thirty-eight dollars the barrel, and prices of all kinds of foodstuffs went higher every day. "I suppose we'd be sensible to go to the Plains," Vesta admitted. "But—well, it's like running away. The poor people can't run away from Richmond. It doesn't help them any for us to stay; but they have to stand it, and if they can, so can we."

Anne said sympathetically: "I don't see how they stand it. Specially having their children hungry."

"Uncle Trav says some women down in Salisbury, not far from Chimneys, just broke into the stores and helped themselves," Vesta told her. "They went in and offered government prices for flour and bacon and salt and things; and when the storekeepers wouldn't sell, the women just took them! There were hundreds of women, and they had hatchets, and no one dared try to stop them and lots of people cheered. And he says some women did the same thing at Boon Hill when they couldn't buy corn."

Anne tossed her head. "I've been mad enough sometimes to take a hatchet myself!" she declared. "And I'm not even hungry!"

Thursday morning Anne came early to the house to take Julian with her to market. "I want to go before everything's sold," she explained. "And it's such a beautiful morning, I didn't even wait to have breakfast."

Julian gladly agreed. The elms and the occasional sycamores along Franklin Street were gay with spring's first tender greenery, already casting some shade; the sun was at once brighter and kinder than on a summer day. The two young people crossed Franklin Street, intending to go on down Fifth; but from the middle of the crossing they could look down to Capitol Square, four blocks away; and even from this distance they saw an astonishing number of people gathered there, clustering around the base of the Bell Tower and standing or moving to and fro on the slopes beyond. They stopped to watch, and Anne wondered why so many people should be there so early, and Julian proposed that they go that way and see.

They came down to the corner of Ninth Street, just across from the Square, and paused to watch and to speculate upon this surprising assembly. Hundreds of people were already here, and each moment the number grew as individuals and groups joined the thickening throng. The crowd was disturbingly silent, and almost frighteningly motionless; it was as though these hundreds were listening and waiting for something they all foresaw.

"And they're almost all women," Anne pointed out. "Julian, let's ask someone what's happening."

Julian might have objected, but Anne led the way across toward the gates, and he followed her. The crowd was massed beyond the Bell Tower and in the lower part of the Square, and they came to its fringes and Anne spoke to a neatly dressed young girl with hollow cheeks and sunken eyes.

"What is it? Some celebration?"

The girl looked at her with an angry laugh. "Celebration?" She extended one hand, and Julian saw her arm was thin and almost fleshless. "Do I look as if I had anything to celebrate?"

From the center of the clotting throng a woman's voice rose in a sudden, hoarse, vehement harangue. Anne asked: "What's she saying?"

The girl's face was stony and expressionless. "She says her name's Mary Jackson. She's a huckster in the market. She says we have a right to live, and we're going to."

The crowd began to move, and the girl moved with them. Anne called after her: "What are they going to do?"

The girl looked over her shoulder. "Get bread!" she said. "Get bread and eat it!"

The mass of people, as though by a single impulse, flowed down the slope toward the foot of the Square; it flowed through the gates into Bank Street like a whirlpool draining from the fringes toward the center, and Anne and Julian were sucked into it. Julian had brought only one crutch today. Anne kept close on his other side. They were caught in the clot of people pressing toward the gate, and Julian saw frightening faces all around him. The countenances of these women—there were few men in the crowd—were white and strained, their eyes burned, their lips twisted with unuttered whisperings. Their garments were ragged and faded, and from the throng, even in the fresh morning air, a stale, sour odor rose. Where had they come from? He would not have believed such people existed. What folly on his part had let Anne become entangled in this hideous mob?

He tried to hold his position, to let the women pass and thus extricate Anne and himself; but the current swept them on as gravel is rolled along the bottom of a rushing stream. They were carried through the gate and across Bank Street and on down the hill across Main Street, and still on.

The hush was like the hush of a storm about to break; Julian and Anne lost any independent volition. They were entrapped by the cohesive force inherent in this union of many minds driven by a single impulse to a single end.

On Cary Street this mass of people, meeting hundreds of men and women swarming up from the lower part of the city, doubled or trebled its numbers. At the same time its structure loosened, as the women and the increasing number of men who now composed the mob spread along the street. Julian and Anne were able to escape the onward pressure, to stand aside as spectators; and Anne said softly:

"But if they want bread, Julian, they won't get it here. These stores are all extortioners."

Julian whispered: "Look!" A woman had produced a hatchet, she smashed in the window of a store. As though this had been a signal, a hoarse cry and the crash of breaking glass sounded all along Cary

Street, and violence swelled like the roar of a storm-scourged tide. There were drays and country carts and wagons caught in the milling mob. The drivers sought to whip their horses and force a way out; but desperate women snatched at the reins and bridles, and drivers in sudden panic jumped to the ground and lost themselves in the crowd. Cary Street was jammed for as far as Julian and Anne could see; and the clamor of many shrill, greedy, hungry, hysterical voices had a high and terrible resonance like the vibration of a taut wire about to break.

The two young people stood still, too intent to move, while stores were broken open and looted and wagons and carts piled high. A woman shuffled past them with her arms full of cavalry boots. A cart, so laden with brooms, bonnets, dresses, cloaks, and shoes that it seemed likely to collapse, was guarded by men and women who tried to force a way along the street with their loot. A man with a roll of cotton cloth like a baby in his arms sidled along the walls, and a woman with a tanned cowhide under her arm and a hatchet in her hand brandished her weapon to clear a path through the swirling masses of shouting men and screaming women and wet-lipped Negroes and excited children.

"They're not after food," Anne said. Yet Julian saw that most of the people had seized what foodstuffs they could find; sacks of corn or meal, loaves of bread, slabs of meat. Hunger was the spring which drove the mob; the looting was no more than incidental. A sudden new stir ran along the street, a movement of the whole mass, and Julian touched Anne's arm.

"They're moving," he said. "We'd better get out of their way."

The crowd, having emptied the stores along Cary Street, flowed back up Ninth toward Main. Julian and Anne, in the mob's path, tried to keep ahead of the pack; but they were overtaken. Someone brushed Julian so roughly that he fell and could not rise for the press of others thrusting by, and Anne fought to protect him, elbowing aside the hurrying stream, frightened by the staring eyes, the open mouths, the blank heedless faces.

Then an enormously fat woman, sweating profusely though the day was chill, her sleazy black dress torn down the side, saw Anne's plight and paused to help her, shouldering aside the crowd.

"Get him up on that leg of his, darlin'," she said cheerfully. "Get him into the door yonder, out of their way." Anne, sobbing her thanks, helped Julian to the haven of the doorway; and their benefactor said: "There! Now have some sense, young ones. Stay where you are!" She hurried away.

They waited where they were for the crowd to pass; and Anne, sure Julian must be hurt, was full of sweet solicitudes. He reassured her as he could. "Not hurt a bit, honestly! Bumped my knee when I fell, but that's all."

"Honest, Julian?" She searched his eyes, she caught his hands. One of the knuckles on his right hand was barked. "Oh look!"

He laughed. "Guess someone stepped on it. It's nothing." He sucked at it to clean the small hurt.

"Are you really and truly all right?"

"Well," he drawled teasingly, "I might pretend, if you'll make over me!"

She colored. "Don't! There's nothing funny about it!"

The stream of passers-by had thinned, and they could go on. Looking along Main Street they saw the mob at work again, smashing windows, breaking doors. Then the City Battalion marched down from Capitol Square, escorting a carriage with Governor Letcher and Mayor Mayo. The soldiers forced a way into the throng, and Governor Letcher shouted for silence and got a grudging attention; and Julian and Anne saw Mayor Mayo stand up in the carriage and read something, and heard snatches of Governor Letcher's words.

"—disperse! —five minutes—order to fire!"

Anne whispered pityingly: "Oh, Julian, they can't shoot these poor women!"

"We'd better get away from here before anything happens."

"No, no, look. There's President Davis, on that dray!"

They were near enough to hear most of what Mr. Davis said. "Disperse and go to your homes, I beg of you. Do not force our own soldiers to turn upon our citizens the weapons that should be let loose only against the enemy!"

A woman screamed, like an animal in pain: "We want bread for our children!"

"I would share my last loaf with my suffering people!" he cried.

Someone beyond him shouted in derision and threw a loaf of bread which hit him in the head and staggered him and fell at his feet. He picked it up, held it high. "You see! You've plenty of bread, enough to throw it at people!"

A quick relenting laugh ran through the crowd, and the tension of the moment eased. President Davis had their ear, and he talked a little longer, till the packed press began to loosen. From the borders of the throng, first individuals and then groups and clusters moved reluctantly away.

Julian and Anne went slowly homeward, sobered by what they had seen. "I didn't know there were so many poor people, Julian. Oh, I've seen little cabins and miserable farms tucked away in the pine woods up home, of course; but I always thought they were just shiftless old poor whites too lazy to work. But people like us—Papa, and you, and all the men I know—we don't do any work either! Do you suppose there are lots of real poor people like these everywhere?"

"I suppose so," he admitted. "If you stop to think of it."

"If it's hard for us to get enough to eat, even when we have plenty of money to pay for it, it must be just hopeless for them!"

"President Davis said the Yankees were to blame," he reminded her.

"I guess the war's to blame, whoever started it."

"Well, old Abe Lincoln started it."

"I guess so. But Julian, do you suppose women like these cared anything about—oh, all the big words, secession, and coercion, and slavery and things?" She hesitated. "Papa says the trouble comes from letting ignorant people vote, because they elect bad men to office and then the bad men make the trouble."

"I don't know much about things like that, Anne."

"I don't either." After a moment she asked thoughtfully: "Julian, is it just people like us who want to fight the Yankees?"

"People like us didn't even want to secede. Not till Abe Lincoln tried to make us fight against the South."

"I know," she assented. "General Lee didn't want to secede even then. Papa told me so. But Julian, even if everybody like us wants to fight, there aren't many of us. And all those thousands of poor women on Cary Street today, I guess they'd like to see the war stop."

Cinda and Vesta, when the two young people came home to tell what they had seen, were as disturbed as they; but then Tilda and Dolly appeared, and Tilda was furious. "It was just outrageous!" she declared. "I don't know why the soldiers didn't shoot them all, show them their places." She said General Elzey and General Winder wanted to bring troops into the city to keep the peace. "I think they ought to do it, or we'll all be murdered in our beds! The Yankees probably sent spies to start the whole thing anyway. Southerners wouldn't behave like that unless someone egged them on."

Next day there were still angry crowds abroad, and at noon the City Battalion marched down Main Street again to drive the women away. There would be other lesser disturbances, and Colonel Rhett's command was kept ready to meet any new emergency. Even a week after the riot, two battalions of soldiers were marched into the city to keep the peace. At Cinda's insistence, Julian stayed indoors. "After all, Son," she reminded him, "you might have been badly hurt if Anne hadn't been there to take care of you. You'd better not risk getting caught in a crowd again."

Until she said this it had not occurred to Julian to be ashamed of his own inadequacy; but for a while he no longer went to seek Anne, till she came one day to demand his company. "I guess you'll think I'm just haunting you, but if you never offer to be my escort, I have to come and make you, don't I?"

Julian went with her, but he was so silent that Anne watched him with troubled eyes. General Wise had just driven a small Yankee force out of Williamsburg, and she said if the big house at Great Oak had not burned they could go back there. Julian reminded her half the bridges were gone, so no carriage could make the journey, and Anne retorted that it was high time he began to ride again, and he said he guessed he never could, and she cried in a burst of tender anger:

"Of course you could!" When his face set, she pleaded: "Don't be mad at me; but you can do anything if you try, Julian! You make me just simply furious!"

He shook his head. "I'm not much use, Anne. I can't even go downtown without you to take care of me!"

Her eyes flashed at him, widening in a way that made his heart leap. "Julian Dewain, you're just perfectly ridiculous! Besides, I love taking care of you!"

Her tenderness was wonderful; but with a boy's instinct to nurse his woe, he put it away from him and said remotely: "We don't see so many women on the street corners now. Maybe they're getting more to eat."

She hesitated as though resentful because he avoided the issue; but then she accepted his cue. "Things are cheaper," she agreed. "I got a pound and a half of bacon yesterday for three dollars, only two dollars a pound. They say there's lots of bacon and flour coming from North Carolina, but Papa says General Lee wrote to Colonel Northrop yesterday that the army is just starving. He says the men get just barely enough to keep them alive!"

"Aunt Tilda came for dinner Sunday," he said. "She bragged that Mr. Streean has just made a lot of money buying bacon in North Carolina for forty cents and selling it for a dollar here."

"Oh, who does he sell it to? I'd like to buy some as cheap as that."

"To the stores. They buy up all they can get from the cheating quartermasters, and sell it for what they can get." He said grimly: "That's why there isn't any for the army."

"Oh!" She looked at him in quick apology. "I never thought of that. I declare I just won't ever buy any more!" Yet then she added honestly: "But I suppose I will, Julian. Papa says breakfast just isn't breakfast without bacon, and what little we use doesn't matter anyway, do you think?"

"Oh, Anne, I didn't mean you!" They laughed together at the absurdity of supposing that he could blame her for anything.

So their hours together were resumed, but now and then some sorry thing happened to remind Julian of his lameness. They were on Main Street the day Mr. Dixon, clerk of the House of Representatives, was killed in an interchange of pistol fire with a man named Ford whom he had discharged. The shots were fired on Bank Street, parallel to Main and half a block away; but one wild bullet came down through the intersecting street and wounded a man not a dozen paces ahead of Anne and Julian. When he heard the thud of that bullet and heard the man's cry, Julian tried to step in front of Anne to shield her;

but his crutch tripped her so that she fell to one knee, and when he tried to catch her arm to break her fall he lost his balance and came down fairly on top of her. The mishap seemed to Anne completely ludicrous and she would have laughed and forgotten it; and Julian, angry and shamed and hurt, made himself laugh with her.

But thereafter, in bitter humiliation he stayed more and more indoors. He sometimes sat for hours at a time with his grandmother. Mrs. Currain, though she appeared happy enough, wearing always a quiet little smile, seemed to be smaller every day, shrinking to nothing in her black bombazine with the white lace collar. In her quiet room Julian found a sort of sanctuary; and Anne came daily, taking her welcome for granted, saying a few polite words to Vesta, or to Cinda if she were at home, and then serenely joining Julian and Mrs. Currain. She began to lead him back to confidence again. When Yankee gunboats came up the river to bombard the fortifications at Drewry's Bluff, they went the long way out to the heights above Rockett's by Chimborazo Hospital and joined the throng watching that spectacle. It was late afternoon of a brilliant day, and the sun set grandly, dipping among scattered purple clouds and sending long light lances to pierce the smoke of battle. As dusk fell, the flash of shell bursts pricked the night with points of light; and the crowd of watchers stayed till full darkness ended the affray.

Soon afterward the tacit truce which winter's mud imposed came to an end. General Hooker led his army across the Rappahannock, and Lee moved to throw himself in the enemy's path. Saturday Anne brought a rumor that Yankee cavalry had cut the railroad between Richmond and Lee's army; Sunday they were at Ashland, not twenty miles away.

Anne came after dinner that day to the house on Fifth Street. Since Lee would soon fight the Yankees, a new flood of wounded must be expected; and Cinda and Vesta had gone to help with the necessary preparations. Julian and Mrs. Currain were together when Anne arrived, and Julian stood up to greet her, and Anne kissed Mrs. Currain's wrinkled cheek, and the old woman's smile was for a moment no mere emptiness but warm with a gentle affection.

"I always feel better when you come to see me, child," she said.

"I always feel better when I see you," Anne assured her. Mrs. Currain nodded, and Anne told Julian about the Yankee cavalry so near the city. "And the telegraph line to General Lee has been cut, so no one knows what's happening. Everybody's pretty worried, Julian."

Mrs. Currain began to sing softly to herself, so softly they scarce heard her.

> . . . and Mary Seaton
> And Mary Carmichael and me.

"If General Longstreet was with him he'd be all right," Julian said. "And Hood and those Texas men. Remember the snowball fight?"

"Wasn't that fun?" They laughed together. "And they sang to you." Then she hushed, realizing that Mrs. Currain was singing.

> But for a' that she could say or do
> The babe it wad not dee.

Anne whispered: "Sit down, Julian." She sat beside him, and the quavering old voice sang whisperingly:

> " 'She rolled it in her apron
> 'And set it on the sea.
> ' "Gae sink ye, swim ye, bonny babe.
> 'Ye'se get nae mair o' me." ' "

> " 'The Prince's bed it was sae soft
> 'The sheets they were sae fine,
> 'That out of it she could not be—' "

Julian protested: "Grandma!" But Anne caught his hand to hush him. "I never heard her sing that verse," he said, his cheek red.

"It's all right. I don't mind."

> I wish I could lie in my ain kirkyard
> Aneath the auld rowan tree,
> Where we pu'd the gowans and strung the rowans,
> My brithers and sisters and me.

"What are gowans?" he whispered; Anne shook her head. Her hand was fast on his, and the old voice was a thin sweet sound in the hushed room.

Eh, little did ma mither think
The night she cradled me,
That I wad die so far fra' hame
And hang on a gallows tree.

They'll tie a napkin round ma e'en,
An' they'll no let me see to dee
And they'll not let on to ma faither and mither
That I'm awa' with the sea.

She finished, and in the hush her eyes that had rested on nothing turned and found them. After a moment Anne said softly: "Such a sad little song."

"Ma father tell't me when I was a lass," said Mrs. Currain, and her eyes were far away. "Some said it was a song sung by Mary the Queen, the night before they struck off her head; but ma mither wad tell me 'twas a court lady in some far land that drowned her ill-got babe, and by the law her head had to fall; and when it tumbled down, the King wha loved her picked the puir head up by the ears and kissed the lips still trembling."

Julian laughed uneasily. "Granny, that's no fairy tale for children."

Mrs. Currain made a little chirping, mirthful sound. "Ma father tell't to me, and I was a wee one," she said. "All the harm came, he said—and he said it was a lesson best learned young—all the harm came from not marrying when you should, and that I was to remember it, and tell my bairns." She nodded. "I did so," she assured them. Her head moved slowly. "But there was one that forgot, and trouble came of it, and the sorry change in a fine lad, to be sure."

She drifted away into her own thoughts for a little; but then her eyes cleared again, and rested quietly upon them. "So 'tis best," she said. "So 'tis best to marry when you should." She nodded firmly. "For a lass without a husband is a flower without a stem. For it ever takes two to make a whole one, to be sure; and there is no complete one by himself alone." Her faint words blurred, her head nodded. "Aye, to keep away from trouble and loneliness and incompletion, ever marry when you should."

She smiled at them, and nodded again, and drowsily closed her eyes and seemed to drop into the light sleep of age.

After a moment Anne came to stand in front of Julian, her eyes on his, grave and still. He grasped the arms of his chair to rise, but she put her hands on his shoulders.

"No, don't," she said. She took his face in her hands and bent down to him and kissed him and looked into his eyes and said: "Julian, we've waited long enough. Too long. Please."

She kissed him again, and his arms reached up to her; and they heard a chuckle of approval from the doorway. Old June stood there beaming upon them, a waiter in her hand.

"Fotched Ole Miss a cup o' hot milk," she said.

Anne laughed richly and looked at Mrs. Currain. "She's asleep."

June came in to set the waiter on the small table by Mrs. Currain's knee. She was watching the young people as she came, and only when she had set down the tray did she look at Mrs. Currain. Then she was for an instant completely still, her gaze fixed on the little old woman sleeping so soundly; and then she turned in calm compulsion.

"Now you all go on along out o' heah," she said. With a rough tenderness she helped Julian to his feet. "You go on 'tending to dat biz'ness you wuz up to. I'm gwine tek care ob Ole Miss."

She thrust them into the hall, closed the door, shut them out. Julian said, puzzled and curious: "What did she do that for?"

Anne looked at the closed door for a long thoughtful moment. When she turned to him her eyes were streaming, but she did not speak. With no word, reaching up to kiss him, she came into his arms.

24

ENID enjoyed the excitement of those early days of May, when Yankee cavalry came so near Richmond that sometimes the spatter of gunfire could be heard. Sunday, though she and the children went to church, it was more to hear the latest news than to heed the remarks of Dr. Minnigerode. The minister's heavy German accent always awoke in her more mirth than reverence. Dolly and Tilda were at church; and Dolly, who always seemed to know things more quickly than most people, said the enemy horsemen had cut the railroad at Trevilian Station. Enid and Lucy and Peter dined that day at Tilda's; and though after dinner Tilda went for a round of the hospitals to oversee preparations for the expected battle, and the children went home, Enid stayed on. Dolly as usual had callers, each of whom brought a new rumor. A man named Davis had killed his horse by riding eighteen miles from Ashland to say the Yankees were there, so the City guard had been turned out to prepare to defend Richmond. Then a boy from Hanover rode in to report that six thousand Yankee horsemen were not far away, and Enid decided she had better go home; but she stopped at Cinda's to make sure they had heard the news.

She found old June and Caesar there in charge of an empty house, and both were weeping. Mrs. Currain had died as gently as a baby goes to sleep, and when she heard this, Enid, infected by their grief, wept with them. Julian had walked home with Anne, and Cinda and Vesta were still at the hospital; so Enid stayed to do what she could.

Not that there was anything for her to do. June, with the steady hands which had served her white folks all their lives and in so many ways, had already bathed the old woman and dressed her. "She done tole me many's de time de dress and de stockings and de little slippers wid de silver heels." So when Enid saw her, Mrs. Currain seemed peacefully asleep, a small sheeted figure in the smoothed bed. Enid went into the garden and cut spring flowers to set on the table by the bed in the room with its drawn blinds; and she sat with the dead woman, her thoughts drifting in a dreary wretchedness, feeling dreadfully alone. Trav's little mother had been uniformly affectionate and kind to her, kinder than any of the others. Enid remembered those long days of companionship at Great Oak with a tender sorrow; days when Mrs. Currain talked endlessly of household matters, and of her husband, and of her children and grandchildren. How fond she had been of Lucy, how amused at Peter! At the time, Enid had sometimes been bored to the point of intolerance, but memories now were wistful. Mrs. Currain had never made her feel an outsider, had never been critical. Enid was sure the old woman had never shared Cinda's insulting thoughts about her and Faunt.

But now this dear, kind, friend was dead; and there was no one left upon whose love Enid could rely. Faunt she never saw, Cinda hated her, her own mother had shut the door in her face, Trav no longer loved her. There had been a time when she thought she despised Trav, and after that hour of brutal violence when he mastered her and then ignored her, she persuaded herself she hated him; yet when he was hurt and near death she knew she loved him, and in the new house her rapture would have been complete if he had seemed to share it. But he was cold and stern, and he went away to the army again, and at Christmas he had kept himself remote from her. She tried to wake in him again that anger which even when she was herself the target made her pulses leap. Surely a blow would have been preferable to his stony calm, his heavy stare. She thought miserably:

"Why, I'd rather he'd just kill me and be done with it than ignore me the way he does."

But, though she wished to do so, reciting at length the delights of her hours with Captain Pew and Darrell, she could not even rouse him to a show of jealousy. Trav no longer loved her; that was sure. Mrs. Currain was the only person who had shown her any fondness. And now Mrs. Currain was dead, and she was left friendless and alone.

Enid tried to guess what the next few days would bring. This was Sunday, and if another big battle, and another flood of wounded, were imminent, Mrs. Currain had better be buried quickly. After the fighting around Richmond last summer, there were so many soldiers dying in the hospitals that graves could not be dug fast enough to receive the dead. Julian would probably be the only man of the family here for the funeral; Julian and Redford Streean. Trav was in Petersburg with Longstreet, and Tony could not be summoned from Chimneys in time, and Brett and Faunt and Burr were with Lee's army in the north. And certainly Mrs. Currain's funeral could not be delayed.

When Cinda and Vesta returned, when there had been a little time for them to comprehend what had happened, Enid suggested this. Vesta made some wretched sound, and Cinda after a moment asked where Julian was. Enid told her he had gone home with Anne. "And June says they didn't know Mama was dead," she explained.

"Then he'll probably stay to supper," Cinda reflected. "But I think I'd like him here. On your way home, Enid, won't you stop by Judge Tudor's and tell him?"

Enid colored, feeling herself dismissed and denied even the right to weep for Mrs. Currain, who had been so kind to her; but she submitted to Cinda's will.

Mrs. Currain was buried on Tuesday, and Trav as it happened was in Richmond for his mother's funeral. By that time everyone knew that Lee and Jackson had met Hooker at a place called Chancellorsville, and driven him headlong back across the Rappahannock; that Jackson was wounded. Enemy cavalry still hovered around Richmond, but for those who loved her all these things were forgotten while in a driving rain Mrs. Currain was borne out to Hollywood Cemetery and laid there at last to rest.

Because of the rain, Enid stayed in the carriage. "It won't help for all of us to catch our deaths," she declared. But Trav and the children and the others stood by the grave; and afterward, driving home, Enid rated Trav roundly for that folly. He ignored her, did not speak till at home he had changed to dry clothes. Then he said:

"General Longstreet will be here tonight, Enid. I told him to come straight to the house. He'll be late. He's not leaving Petersburg till seven o'clock. Have his room ready and I'll wait up for him."

She had wanted tonight to have Trav to herself; for she knew his grief, and wished to cherish and comfort him. "Oh Trav, anyone would think this was a hotel!"

"We've room enough."

"Is Mrs. Longstreet coming with him?"

"No, she'll stay in Petersburg. She hasn't been well. He's worried about her."

"What's the matter with her?"

"Well, she's going to have a baby, and she's had to keep to her bed most of the time, can't eat much of anything."

"Really?" She forgot her resentment at the prospective intrusion, asking many questions; but Trav could tell her provokingly little. When General Longstreet arrived she appealed to him, amused at his reluctance to discuss this which was to her, or to any woman, at once so absorbing and so commonplace. "I expect she has a hard time," she suggested. "She's so little and you're so big." It was fun to torment the big man with these embarrassing indelicacies.

"She keeps remembering our three who died," he said. "Keeps reminding me. And she's sure she and the baby will both die this time. She hasn't been able to sleep. I've sat up all night with her, a good many times."

Enid envied little Mrs. Longstreet, who could make this giant of a man so miserable. He would unflinchingly face a storm of bullets, or send a thousand men to death, but he was sick with terror now. She had often wished Trav would worry about her, but he never did. Perhaps that was because she had never been sick enough to frighten him. Even when she lost her unborn babies, she was soon as healthy as ever.

But for that matter, Mrs. Longstreet was healthy enough! After all, she had had six children and had come to no harm. Enid wondered whether if she were to have another baby and pretend to suffer terribly, she might wake in Trav an equal solicitude; but during the few days he was at home he ignored the cajolements she so sweetly proffered.

During those days she understood, from overheard talk between Trav and the General, that Longstreet and President Davis were at odds. The President wanted Longstreet and his men to go at once to join Lee; but Longstreet thought it wiser to stay in Richmond till the city was safe from marauding Yankee cavalry. Lee in the end supported him, writing that he need not hurry to rejoin, that his troops might better be used to protect the railroads, and to punish the enemy cavalry for the damage they had done. Military matters had little interest for Enid; but when the two men sat late in long talk she sat with them, listening idly.

"Hooker's beaten," the General said, on one occasion. "There's no fight left in him. Our real danger now is in the West. Unless we do something there, 'Lys Grant will have Vicksburg; and if he gets it, the Yankees will control the whole line of the Mississippi, slice off the western end of the Confederacy. If that happens, our defeat only waits on time. We'll bleed to death as surely as a man with only one leg, left untended on the battlefield."

Trav whittled a bit of tobacco and put it in his cheek. "I've never been in the western country, west of Chimneys," he said. "Would it hurt us so much to lose the West?"

Longstreet laughed grimly. "You Virginians think only of Virginia. Hood's Texans are the best soldiers in the army. General Lee would like to have a dozen Texas regiments; but he'll get none if Texas men have to stay at home to fight their own war."

"What can we do about it?"

The General said strongly: "If I were in authority, I'd send Hood and Pickett to help Bragg crush Rosecrans and march on Cincinnati. That would draw Grant off." He shook his head. "I talked myself hoarse to Secretary Seddon today, urging just that; but it was no use. The Government thinks Virginia is the Confederacy." He made an angry sound. "I hear a lot more talk about the money to be made by sending cotton to the Federals along the Mississippi than about sending men to drive them away."

Trav nodded. "I judge a good many men are making money out of the war."

When the railroad to the north was safe, the first trickle of wounded came, and then a flood of them. Hood's and Pickett's divisions went to rejoin Lee; and Federal captives by the thousands arrived to be packed into any buildings that could be made to serve as a prison. A week after Mrs. Currain died, Longstreet and Trav departed; and toward dusk that Sunday, like a hammer blow, the news of Jackson's death struck Richmond.

Late Monday afternoon his body arrived from Guiney's Station, and tolling bells greeted the train as it rolled slowly down Broad Street. Enid, drawn to the spot more by curiosity than by grief, nevertheless caught the infection and found herself sobbing with the sobbing crowd. Neither able to move nor wishing to, she stood with streaming eyes while the procession formed to escort the hearse to 'the Capitol, where in the governor's mansion it would lie in state. General Elzey and his staff led the march; the Public Guard and a North Carolina regiment followed, and then the band, and another regiment, and the hearse with nodding black plumes and drawn by two white horses. General Jackson's staff rode escort, and behind came city dignitaries. The reversed arms of the soldiers stirred Enid to a new flood of tears; the measured notes of the dirge as the band passed shook her like hard buffeting blows. Till sundown tolling church bells kept time to the sorrowing pulse beat of the city and of the whole Confederacy.

Late that night Trav and General Longstreet returned and roused them. The General would be a pall bearer; and next morning Enid and the children watched at the corner of Grace Street and Second as the ceremonial *cortège* passed. They had a vantage from which they could see the head of the procession come up Second Street and turn directly in front of them to file away toward the Capitol; and as the military escort passed, Peter's hand clenched on his mother's, and she felt him tremble. Two regiments of Pickett's men were headed by General Pickett and his staff. Then came an artillery company, and a company of cavalry, and then the Public Guard. Behind the hearse, a groom led General Jackson's horse, the General's boots crossed on the empty saddle; behind the hearse followed the General's staff officers, and behind them General Longstreet and the others who would serve as pall bearers. On their heels came what soldiers of the Stonewall Brigade were in Richmond, convalescents from the hospitals, men on crutches, men with an arm gone or a leg. The day was baking hot, the street was like an oven. Except for the muffled notes of the Dead March, the thud of hoofs, and the tramp of many feet, there was no sound. Behind President Davis in his carriage the heads of departments followed on foot, Mr. Benjamin and Mr. Seddon leading. Behind the long files of departmental clerks came the Governor, and scores of minor dignitaries, trailing down at last to city officials and Benevolent Societies and finally to a trudging line of humble individuals, men and women who thus dumbly evidenced their grief.

Long before the end, Enid was hot and weary, and twice she proposed departure. "There, Peter, that's really all!" But he and Lucy were bound to stay till the procession was past, and bound to fall in with those who followed it, and to file through the Great Hall of Congress where the body lay in state for all to see. She could not resist going with them, but the infection of this universal mourning left her weak and drained, and it was a relief next day to know that the General's body had been taken away to Lexington. When Dolly came to the house that morning Enid said so.

"After all, he's not the only man who's been killed in the war," she exclaimed. "I'm glad they don't make so much fuss about all of them!"

"Oh but he was a general," Dolly protested. "I just love generals! Did you hear—" Then she caught herself, looking quickly at Lucy; and Enid, understanding, sent the young girl away.

"Hear what?" she asked then.

"About poor General Van Dorn?"

"Who is he?"

"Don't you remember, he was in the army here in Virginia the first summer. He was terribly handsome, and they say he had dozens of affairs! A man named Dr. Peters shot him! They say Mrs. Peters was in love with General Van Dorn. I think that's terrible, being killed by some old jealous husband!"

"Why, Dolly," Enid laughed, "young ladies like you aren't supposed to know such things."

"Oh—figs! Of course we know! Didn't you know such things when you were my age? Lots of wives fall in love with other men besides their husbands!" She cried laughingly: "You don't need to be so prim and proper! I used to see the way you watched Uncle Faunt all the time."

Enid's cheek crimsoned. "Why, Dolly Streean!"

"Oh you did! You know you did! Mama saw it too. And the way you used to kiss him on the least excuse! I bet you were just pining for him! I bet you still are!"

"Nonsense! I haven't laid eyes on him for months."

"Honest? Cross your heart and hope to die?"

"Of course. Why?"

"Well, I know he comes to Richmond to see somebody!"

"Really?" Enid had not thought of Faunt for a long time; but suddenly she felt herself wronged. "You mean to tell me——"

"Oh I don't mean to tell you anything; but I do know he's been here! Captain Pew met him once, and other gentlemen have told me they'd seen him. So Mama and I thought maybe you and he——"

"Why, how perfectly horrid!" Yet Enid found the suggestion exciting. Her unsuccessful wooing of Trav during his few days at home had wakened in her longings she could not rouse in him; when he was gone, they turned to bitter anger. If he no longer desired her, then she owed him no loyalty! If he chose to go off to the army and stay away months on end, must she, because he left her alone, remain alone? Perhaps if he thought he had lost her . . .

During the days that followed, her thoughts led her more and more to Dolly, as though the girl, so easily enchanting to every man, knew a secret which she might discover. Besides, it was fun to go to the Streean home. Tilda's household was brightened by Dolly's gaiety and by the affluence war had brought.

Enid went there the day after fire destroyed the machine shops and the boring mills and pattern shops of the Tredegar Iron Works, where so much of the Confederate artillery was manufactured. Tilda was sure Yankee spies had set the fire. "Because Richmond's full of them, you know. Like old Miss Van Lew. She doesn't even pretend not to hate the Confederacy. If I were President Davis I'd send her North where she belongs."

"I thought spies were hung," Enid protested; and Tilda said:

"No, just the men. There was one named Webster, right in the War Department. He and his wife were both convicted. He'd killed some people too, they say. Anyway, they decided to hang him, but they sent Mrs. Webster through the lines to Washington." And Tilda said spitefully: "But I think women spies are the worst, making love to the soldiers, and getting all they can out of them. I'd hang the ladies as quick as I would the men. Of course Miss Van Lew probably isn't really a spy, because everyone knows she hates us, so they watch her all the time; but I'd get rid of her all the same."

They were still discussing Miss Van Lew and other known or suspected Union sympathizers in Richmond when Dolly and her father arrived together. Dolly was beautifully excited because she had met General Lee.

"He's so handsome he just looks like God!" she declared. "I was with Mrs. Brownlaw, Mama. You know she's Mrs. Lee's forty-second cousin or something, always bragging about 'my Cousin Robert.' She saw him coming along Broad Street and sort of ran to meet him, and he bowed, and she practically patted him and told him his beard made him look older than he was—it's all gray, you know—and he smiled and she said if she were Cousin Mary—that's Mrs. Lee, you know— she'd make him get rid of it the moment the war was over." Dolly drew a great breath of awe. "And then he looked so stern and sad, and he said: 'Mrs. Brownlaw'—I noticed he didn't call her Cousin! 'Mrs. Brownlaw, when the war is over they may take my beard, and my head with it if they choose!' "

Enid asked: "But did you actually meet him, Dolly?"

"Yes I did! Mrs. Brownlaw named him to me, and he bowed and paid me some compliment, and the blood was pounding in my ears so I couldn't even hear him, and I just stood there with my mouth open, and he walked away. Oh, he's so wonderful!"

Streean said, as though he were in the inner councils: "General Lee came with Stuart to see Mr. Seddon. Secretary Seddon wants him to send Pickett's division to Mississippi to try to save Vicksburg; but General Lee says it's a question of defending either Virginia or Mississippi; and Lee's a Virginian, so to him Virginia comes first." And he added, like an oracle: "That's the trouble with the South. Every state is more anxious to keep its troops at home than to send soldiers to Lee. Two years ago, when twenty thousand well-armed men would have been enough, with the army we had, to capture Washington, there were a hundred and fifty thousand state troops not even in the field. Georgia, Louisiana, the Carolinas, Texas, all of them kept their men— and their weapons—at home. And in spite of conscription it's almost as bad today. Lee has seventy-five thousand men, but the states could send him that many more, easily enough. He beat Hooker with fifty thousand, and Hooker had three times his force. He could take Washington and Philadelphia in a month if the states would give him their militia."

He spoke so strongly that no one heard the front door open till Darrell from the hall called in derisive approval: "Hear! Hear! Get up on your platform, Pa! Never heard such eloquence." As he came into the room, Tilda and Dolly ran to welcome him, and he took their kisses and challenged Enid. "No kiss for your handsome nephew?" She laughed and went to him. She had always liked this audacious youngster. She kissed his cheek and said:

"There!"

"Hold on!" he protested. "If it's worth doing, it's worth doing well!" His arms swept her close, his lips found hers not resisting.

When she freed herself, Dolly whispered in her ear: "That's the way you kiss Uncle Faunt!" She and Dolly laughed together, but Enid felt her pulses thud. She listened while Darrell answered his father's questions, something about sending cotton to New Orleans. He spoke of Mr. Clark and Mr. Ford in Mobile, of Governor Pettus, of Mr. Josephs; he said a certain Mr. Ranney had refused to carry the cotton on his railroad till General Pemberton threatened to seize the railroad if he refused.

"I arranged the authorization to the General from President Davis," Streean explained. "I trust the agreed amount of salt was delivered in exchange?"

"Oh yes. Minus our commission, of course." Darrell said he had gone three times to New Orleans, had collected cotton in Mississippi and Alabama and seen it on its way to Yankee hands. "I'll go over the accounts with you later; but we haven't wasted our time, be sure of that."

"We'll have to share the profits with others," Streean reminded him. "We're not the only ones in this business now. The Secretary has Mr. Crenshaw operating. The Government's going to buy five thousand bales of cotton for him to handle. Davenport and Company of Mobile raised Cain over the thousand bales General Buckner let you ship, because they weren't allowed to ship any; and there's an import and export company being formed in Savannah to get into the trade."

"We've skimmed the cream," Darrell said. "The fun's almost over. Georgia's practically taken herself out of the Confederacy, and North Carolina's climbing on her high horse too. Harvey Hill wants more conscripts, and Governor Vance refuses to call them away from their crops."

"I saw a letter from General Hill today. Something about 'organized factions.' What's he talking about?"

Darrell smiled. "Did you ever hear of a red and white cord?"

"No. What about it?"

Darrell's eyes met Enid's and she thought how nice he was, and how wickedly handsome. And he certainly was no longer a boy; there was a wise maturity about him. After all, he was not so very much younger than she, a few years, not enough to matter. He went into the hall and returned with a cane in his hand. "Ever see a man do this?" he asked, and tapped three times on the toe of his right foot.

"No," Streean admitted.

"Well," Darrell explained, "if business takes you to Alabama and a man catches your eye and does that, and you say to him: 'I dreamed the boys are coming home,' he'll be your friend."

Dolly cried delightedly: "Oh Darrell, that's simply thrilling. I love secrets. Go on."

He grinned, shook his head. "Can't tell you, Sis. After you know a thing, it's no longer a secret."

Sally, the Negro maid, came with languorously swaying hips to set out small tables for the supper trays, and Enid exclaimed: "Heavens, I didn't realize it was so late! I'll have to run." But Tilda said of course she must stay, and Enid protested that she couldn't go home through dark streets, and Darrell promised to escort her, and she stayed. When the supper—cups of real coffee, hot biscuits of white flour, toasted sandwiches, and sugar and cream—had been set before them, Darrell said: "But I'll tell you all this much. There's a Peace Society in Alabama and Georgia."

"Tom Watts spoke of it last year," Streean assented. "But he was pretty vague about it."

"It's still vague; but it's growing. All the small farmers hate the conscription, and they hate the impressment laws. The officers take their wagons and horses and beef cattle and supplies at government prices and then sell them at a profit." Streean smiled, and Darrell said: "Oh I know we approve, but the farmers hate it all the same; and they hate the tax-in-kind." He threw Enid one of those quick glances which made her pulses quicken. "They say the rich people don't pay taxes, and that this whole tax-in-kind comes on the farmers."

Streean laughed. "The moral is: Don't be a farmer!"

Darrell grinned. "I don't know much about morals." Enid colored under his eyes, as though his word were meant for her alone. "What people call morals are usually just reasons why you mustn't do what you want to do. By the way, Mama, speaking of morals, I stopped at Chimneys. Uncle Tony's spruced up till you wouldn't know him. He has a pretty bright mulatto wench——"

Tilda cried out indignantly: "Darrell! Hush! How can you say such a thing before Dolly and Aunt Enid! I'm ashamed of you!"

But Dolly laughed and elaborately put her hands over her ears. "Go on, Dal! I promise not to hear a word. Enid, don't you dare listen." Enid smilingly covered her ears, too; but she thought that bright must be Sapphira, whom Tony had bought back from Mrs. Pettigrew.

Streean said drily: "Don't worry, Tilda. If it were true, Darrell would have stayed on at Chimneys."

"I didn't see her," Darrell admitted. "Uncle Tony kept her out of sight. I couldn't stop then, so I'm going back. Richmond's no place for me anyway, with even the Public Guard playing at soldiering."

"You might as well stay here," Streean told him. "Details are easily arranged, and a lot of clever clerks are getting rich by helping their friends get hold of government supplies." He added frankly: "I prefer less risk, so I keep inside the law; but risk never frightened you."

The talk ran on till Enid at last said she must go. Darrell, as he had promised, walked to Clay Street with her. The moon was fine, the night was still and warm, and he was a gay companion. At her door he paused for a word or two, and, half-frightened by her own daring, she invited him in. "Peter and Lucy will want to hear all about your adventures."

But he said laughingly that some of his adventures were not for youthful ears. "And the night's too fine to go indoors. I shall take a stroll through the town."

She wished he would suggest she keep him company on that stroll; but of course even if he suggested such a thing she must refuse. "Well then, good night," she said. "It's nice to have you home again."

"You made my welcome perfect," he assured her, and lightly kissed her lips; and before she could speak he turned away.

She was left by that kiss in a turmoil and a shaking storm. She moved toward the door, and paused, and pressed her hands to her hot cheeks, and listened to his receding footsteps, and laughed to herself in a breathless way. "Thank goodness he didn't come in!" she whispered. "What's the matter with me?" The door, since in these days more and more marauders prowled the Richmond streets, was locked and on the chain. She had to ring to be admitted to the sanctuary of her home.

She hoped Darrell would call upon her next day, but he did not; and she warned herself not to be an idiot. Why should he? She was old enough to be his mother! Yet she looked forward, half in fear and half in longing, to their next encounter. Once or twice, hoping for some word of his movements, she spoke of him to Dolly; and when a week and then ten days had passed, she came at last to a direct question. "Where's Darrell keeping himself? I haven't seen him since he got home?"

"Oh, he spends most of his time in bed, sleeps all day and prowls the town all night. He saw Uncle Faunt for a minute, the day after he came home. Did you?"

"No! Why should I?"

"Neither did Aunt Cinda," Dolly said. "I know because I asked her. Where do you suppose he goes?"

"Why should I suppose anything about it?"

Dolly smiled. "I'm sure I don't know, darling," she drawled. "Oh, Aunt Cinda says Julian and Anne Tudor are going to be married next week or the week after."

"I know, yes. I should think they'd at least wait till Grandma Currain was cold!"

"Well, I think Anne's silly, if you ask me," Dolly declared. "I certainly wouldn't marry a man with only one leg. I won't marry anyone till after the war's over so I can be sure who's still all in one piece."

"You're a cold-blooded little thing!" Enid laughed in spite of herself. "You shouldn't talk so."

"I don't, except to you."

"Anne used to be crazy about Faunt."

"I know, but I guess she's sorry for Julian; and of course Uncle Faunt will never marry anyone."

Enid said maliciously: "Neither will Captain Pew!"

Dolly laughed. "He'll marry me if I want him to."

"Has he ever asked you?" Enid challenged; and seeing Dolly hesitate, she insisted: "Tell the truth, now! No fibs! Has he ever actually said: 'Miss Dolly, please ma'am, will you do me the very great honor to marry me?'"

"Heavens, he'd never do that! I can't imagine it. But—if I ever decide to—I'll just be 'specially sweet to him some day, and he won't be able to stand it, and he'll just sweep me up in his arms and carry me away to a preacher and marry me."

"You know, some ways"—Enid was almost sorry for the girl, so young, so sure of her powers—"you're just a baby, Dolly. Don't try to make too much of a fool of Captain Pew."

Dolly's eyes narrowed. "Thank you, ma'am, for the advice. I'll give you some in return. Don't you make too much of a fool of yourself over Darrell!"

"Over Darrell?" Enid felt her cheeks hot. "Dolly, you're an idiot!"

Dolly laughed. "There, darling; let's not quarrel. But I assure you, Darrell's quite as dangerous as Captain Pew!"

Enid could not forget that conversation, but she did not see Darrell till he called one Sunday evening after Lucy and Peter had gone early to bed. The door bell rang, and old April let him in; and even in the first moment Enid thought he had drunk more than he should. She said, for April to hear, that this was a mighty strange time to call.

"I came to say good-by," he told her. "I'm off for Chimneys in the morning."

"Why, you're nice to come!" April was still in the hall, within hearing; and Enid said to her: "I'll let Mister Streean out, April. You needn't wait 'up." She heard April move toward the rear of the house, and the old woman would go out to her own quarters in the yard. Except for Lucy and Peter, doubtless already asleep, she and Darrell would be alone in the house.

"I'm going to help Uncle Tony with his agricultural pursuits," said Darrell, and sat down. Enid heard the back door close. April was gone.

"I declare," she told him, "you never do stay any time at all in Richmond. You haven't been near me since you came home!"

He met her eyes. "I'm not proper company for a respectable young matron whose husband is away at the wars."

"Why, you old silly! We're kin!" There was enough impropriety in being thus alone with him to make her heart beat faster.

"Husband away at the wars," he repeated, suddenly lugubrious. "Everybody's away to the wars, everybody but me." Then in a livelier tone: "Did you hear the latest? We're going to whip the Yankees this summer. Taylor Whiting wanted to wager today that General Stuart will be in Philadelphia in two weeks. Guess General Lee'd trade Philadelphia for Vicksburg any old day."

She was amused by the faint thickness in his speech. "Darrell, why don't you stay in Richmond?"

"Don't like the weather," he declared. "These warm, hazy days make me sleepy. Red sun through the haze looks like blood. Even the moon is red-blurred—blood on the moon."

"It's more like fall than summer, isn't it?"

He blinked at her appraisingly. "You're not looking well, Aunt Enid."

"Nonsense! I'm perfectly well."

"You have a dusty, late summer look about you, instead of the be-dewed freshness of spring." He shook his head as though in reproach. "Why, Aunt Enid, you look older than your mother!"

That word was like the awakening shock of cold water dashed into her face. She had not seen her mother for months, and she said so, almost angrily.

"Really?" he commented. "She's a handsome woman, Aunt Enid. She looks younger than when I first met her; and that was long ago, when I was still a boy."

"For Heaven's sake stop calling me 'Aunt Enid.' I'm not so very much older than you, actually!"

"You look old," he said severely. "But to be sure, your mother's drunk a fresh draft of the elixir of youth. Perhaps that's what you need, Aunt Enid!"

"Stop it!" Curiosity drove her. "Whatever are you talking about? About Mama!"

"Why, your mama is in love!" Enid was silent in blank astonishment. "And it's mighty becoming to her. To love works a miracle on a woman." His voice was dreamy. "Remember how homely Vesta was till she fell in love with Tommy Cloyd? Remember so many plain young women suddenly become radiant? When I see someone who was never worth a glance before, and who suddenly delights the eye, I say to myself: 'Aha, Miss'—or 'Madame' as the case may be—'you've lost your heart.'"

"I don't believe it. I mean about Mama!"

"I assure you, it's true."

"How do you know?"

"Well, it's a discreditable confession," he admitted. "But I spied on her. It's a long story."

"Go on, tell me!"

He watched her, and now there was shrewd calculation in his eyes. "Well, it goes back to last February," he explained. "I've been an admirer of your charming mother for a long time, and before departing for New Orleans I went to pay my most decorous respects. I was told that she was not at home, but I forced my way in and found her *tête-à-tête* with a gentleman. I may say that he resented my conduct, and quite justly, too; but I made my peace with them and left him in possession of the field."

"Oh that doesn't mean a thing! Mama always had a lot of callers."

"But they didn't stay till dawn," he drawled, and there was suddenly a turbulence in her; and somewhere in the back of her mind a whisper sounded. "As this caller did," said Darrell. "For I rode away, but I returned quietly afoot and watched to see him go."

"Who was it?" She found it hard to shape the words.

He smiled. "I shouldn't speak of matters so indelicate to a happy married woman pining for her husband away at the wars."

"Besides," she argued, "that was months ago."

"Ah yes, so it was. But do you remember the night I brought you home, a few days since?"

"Not particularly!" She tried to speak casually; but her cheeks burned, and he laughed, leaning suddenly forward.

"Ah Enid, blushing? That's confession!" He mimicked her tone: " 'Not particularly,' says she; as if to stand with breathless parted lips under a young man's kiss, to stand as still as a lovely image in the moonlight while he walks away, to stand with all her pulses beating the drums of longing for him to turn back to her—as if this happened to her every moonlit night of her life! As it should, to be sure, to one so beautiful."

"I stood to watch the moon!"

"Because you wanted me to come back!"

"Don't be ridiculous! Go on. What happened that night?"

"I wanted to turn back," he said, gravely now. "But I dared not. When our lips touched, some magic touched us both, and I was afraid of it. For the girl I kissed was no girl but a wife. She was another's, his property, his captive, his possession. She dared do nothing except as that other bade, dared not obey her heart but only that other's commands."

He paused, and through her thoughts came tumbling images and phrases, people and scenes: Trav bruising her lips with his hard hands; little Mrs. Longstreet who could rule her husband, though he was master of his tens of thousands; that Mrs. Peters who loved General Van Dorn, and her husband who loved her enough to kill her lover; Faunt upon whom when he lay hurt and sick and helpless she lavished such tenderness; Faunt who now came secretly to Richmond but never to her; this charming boy whose deep tones made her tremble now; Trav whom she hated, because he no longer loved her; this audacious boy whose teasing, thrilling voice ran on; Trav who when he was angry so deeply stirred her blood; Trav who if he heard Darrell now would surely rage and strike and kill.

"So I knew it was useless to turn back," said Darrell sadly. "For the lovely woman I had kissed was a bond slave, not free to love. But my blood was hot and surging, and the moon was fine, and I remembered a charming woman——"

He paused. She said in a strained voice: "Go on."

"I went to her, to your mother," he said. "This time too, her door was closed to me; so again, as once before, I watched the house till dawn. The same gentleman came out and rode away. To make triply sure, I called on your mother that evening. Her beauty was my answer. Yes, she is in love."

"Who was it?" Her voice was a flat challenge.

He shook his head. "What does that matter? It is only the transforming miracle that matters; not the agent. She is in love, so she is beautiful. The recipe is as old as man and woman, Enid."

"Tell me who it was."

"Why should I?"

"I want you to."

His head tipped to one side, and now there was a reckless challenge in his eyes. "How badly do you want to know?" She did not speak. "Suppose I tell you?"

She leaned back in her chair, her hands along the arms, her eyes full on his. Bond slave? To Trav? Who thought all he had to do was just lay down the law! Who did not love her! Who would never love her more! Loneliness and longing and hot desire welled up in her; and Darrell, seeing her thoughts in her eyes, suddenly laughed and came to his feet and leaned down, his eyes plunged deep in hers.

"Come, come," he urged, still smiling. "Cat got your tongue? Speak up! What if I do?"

She said huskily: "Tell me and see."

25

CINDA during this winter and spring had achieved peace of mind and heart. "I think it began in Washington," she told Brett, when in April he had two days at home. "The day I saw President Lincoln. I don't know just why. And having Julian at home, and Vesta. And I no longer worry about Burr. He seems to be invulnerable."

Brett pretended hurt. "How about me? Don't you worry about me?"

"Oh I can't imagine anything happening to you. You're so much a part of me."

"Soldiers are like that," he reflected. "No man ever really expects death for himself. Except once in a while—and then it happens. Lieutenant Jim Utz in our company told me the night before the fighting at Fredericksburg that he would be killed next day, and he was."

"Were you in danger that day?"

"No." He smiled. "Except the danger of collapsing from exhaustion on the march to get there. We were on the move all night, and I'd swear the mud was waist-deep every foot of the way. The horses bogged down, and half the time we pulled the guns by hand." He laughed. "It was all a lot of trouble for nothing, too. Our little naval howitzers aren't worth much against the Yankee guns. We haven't the range. I don't believe we've killed a Yankee yet; but we make as much smoke and as much noise as any one. And you ought to hear us holler!"

She said wonderingly: "How do you stand the hard life, Brett

Dewain? You always liked to be comfortable, but you make a joke now of things that sound terrible to me."

"I suppose that's the answer," he admitted. "We do joke about it. Some of the jokes are pretty rough. Last winter, one bitter cold night, some joker passed the word that the sentries must blow through the touchholes of our pieces to be sure they were clear. Of course when a man put his mouth to the cold iron, his lips stuck to it, and they all had sore, swollen, bleeding mouths; but every sentry passed the word along till they were all fooled. That amused the whole company, even the ones who got hurt."

"It doesn't sound funny to me."

He chuckled. "Well, when your teeth are chattering with cold, any excuse to laugh will help you stop."

He made her laugh with him. His days at home were as heartening as the coming of spring after a bitter winter. She would not see him again for months; but after Chancellorsville he wrote that he was safe and well, and so was Burr. "The poor damned Yankees got hurt hard," he said. "I don't mind battles, but I hate battlefields the day after. Shells had set the woods on fire, and a lot of wounded Yankees were burned where they lay. Rain finally put the fire out, but in a way the rain was worse than the fire, for then the wounded froze. We've found some who crawled to the little brooks to get a drink and the rain raised the brooks and the men hadn't strength to get away, so they drowned. Maybe there's glory on a battlefield while the guns are going, but there's none next day. I'll never see a buzzard again without shuddering, or eat a bite of hog meat without nausea. Oh, I suppose I will. When you're hungry enough you'll eat anything. And anyway, it's probably almost as bad to be eaten alive by lice and fleas as to be eaten dead by hogs and buzzards. God forgive me for writing thus to you, my dear."

"Write as you please, write what helps you," she replied. Trav was just then in Richmond with General Longstreet; he would take her letter to Brett. "If writing so helps you, do. It does not hurt me. Words sink into me like pebbles into a dark pool, leaving only a moment's ripple. I'm almost happy, Brett Dewain; though it's in a strange still way. I never knew how much strength there was in human beings till now, seeing the wounded. I think working with them helps me more than it helps them."

General Longstreet called next day to pay his respects; and she saw the trouble in him and found the root of it. "Louisa always took her babies hard," he admitted. "But this is the worst time she's had."

Cinda smiled in friendly understanding. "And you husbands always blame yourselves, of course. When is it to be, Cousin Jeems?"

"October."

"Then she'll be feeling better from now on; and you know she'll really be better without you, too. When our husbands are with us, we wives always want a lot of sympathy. When Brett's here, if things look black I just kick my heels and scream so he'll have to comfort me; but with him away I have to behave myself."

"Louisa doesn't complain," he said loyally. "I wish she would. It's her being so brave and cheerful when she feels so ill that makes it hard for me."

"She'll be fine. You wait and see!"

After he and Trav were gone, the May days dragged away. General Jackson's death left heavy sadness in every heart, and Brett wrote: "They say any man can be replaced, but I doubt if he can be." But Jackson was dead, and they must go on without him. They faced the steady struggle to find food. The Government tried to fix prices at a level below the current market, but the only result was that speculators refused to sell. Far away on the Mississippi, Vicksburg still held out; and up along the Rappahannock in early June Lee's army, proud in its strength, began to move. To Maryland? To Pennsylvania? Last year to invade Maryland had meant disaster; but last year the army was already exhausted by a hard summer of fighting. Now the soldiers had had a winter's rest; they had tasted victory at Chancellorsville. To such an army anything was possible, and hopes and prayers commingled. Judge Tudor called one day and confessed his own confusion.

"I try to preserve an even mind," he admitted, smiling at his own weakness. "But hope is always gnawing at common sense. Just now, if I let myself, I'd be expecting Lee to capture Washington, destroy the government buildings, destroy the city as completely as old Carthage, root out the Yankees denning there, send them scurrying, show foreign nations the helplessness of the North. I'd be assuring everyone that Grant's army is about to be destroyed, that Vicksburg is safe. I almost believe these things, because I hope them; yet I know that at the first reverse the whole house of hopes will collapse and I'll be twittering and wringing my hands like a despairing old woman."

"We all go through the same cycle," Cinda agreed. "After First Manassas we were sure the war was won, and we were sure again after Second Manassas, when our army marched into Maryland, and now we're sure again after Chancellorsville."

"The philosophers have never decided," he suggested, "whether the pessimist or the optimist is more completely wrong; but mighty few of us can keep from being either the one or the other."

Julian and Anne were married on the ninth of June, at St. Paul's Church, with only the family and closest friends attending. Cinda had hoped Brett at least could be there, but he wrote from Spottsylvania Court House that the Howitzers were marching toward Culpeper. Trav was with Longstreet and could not leave, nor could Burr come, though he wrote hopefully that this summer might end the war. "If the cavalry can capture enough horses from the enemy to replace our worn-out mounts. We've done it before, and I guess we can again."

Cinda missed her menfolks, but their absence could not mar her happiness for Julian and for Anne. Anne on her wedding day was even lovelier than Dolly; Julian, tall and fair, wore a shining splendor.

They would live, at least for the present, with Judge Tudor. He proposed to lodge for a while at the Spottswood and leave them in possession. Everyone went with them from the church to the house and stayed for a merry hour. Walking back to Fifth Street with Vesta afterward, Cinda said contentedly: "Anne's so lovely. And Julian—I didn't even notice his crutch. I was surprised at myself, but it's true."

"Of course it's true," Vesta said quietly. "What do legs matter? He's alive."

It was unusual for Vesta to refer even thus indirectly to her own loss. This day of Anne's happiness must have been a racking time for her; yet any word of tenderness might loose a flood of torturing tears. "Yes, of course," Cinda agreed, carefully casual.

Vesta smiled, understanding the other's thought. "It's all right, Mama. It didn't bother me, really. I was so glad for them." And she added: "Being married's wonderful. I'm going to marry again some day, Mama. I know Tommy'd want little Tommy to have a papa and some brothers and sisters."

"Of course." Cinda, to hide her profound gratefulness, smiled and asked lightly: "Anyone in mind?"

Vesta laughed, tossed her head. "Oh I'm beginning to sit up and take notice!" But Cinda knew the jesting was only meant to comfort her. It would be a long time before Vesta's heart was healed.

"Enid looked unusually pretty today," she remarked.

"She certainly did. And she looked happy. Maybe that's why she was so pretty. She usually has a sort of complaining look."

"She has mighty little to complain of!"

Vesta smiled. "I'm not so sure. You'll never admit it, of course, but Uncle Trav must be pretty trying sometimes." She said thoughtfully, "Aunt Enid always makes me think of a child trying to make friends with grownups, and always getting snubbed and told to run away and play."

"I'm sure I'm always perfectly nice to her. A lot nicer than she deserves!"

Vesta laughed. "There, Honey. I wasn't being critical! I know you mean to be."

They heard next day that there had been a great fight of cavalry at Brandy Station, with thousands on both sides engaged. The papers said Stuart had been shamefully surprised; but he drove the Yankees back and won the victory, and everyone damned the papers, for Stuart could do no wrong. Burr must have been in that hard fighting, but Cinda was sure no harm would come to him. The army moved on toward the Valley, and General Ewell drove the enemy out of Winchester. The day the Government decided that able-bodied clerks must volunteer or be conscripted, Dolly came to report that Darrell had gone to Chimneys.

"He meant to go two or three weeks ago," she explained. "But he kept putting it off, but now he's gone." She laughed. "I guess he thought if they were making even the clerks fight, they might get him too."

Vesta asked: "Don't they make men fight in North Carolina?"

"Oh no, not if they don't want to. Governor Vance won't let them."

"They ought to be made to!"

"Well, Papa says Georgia and North Carolina and all the states have a right to keep their men at home if they want to."

Cinda met Vesta's eyes. "I wonder if the Confederacy can ever win if everybody's so particular about their rights."

"Well, people do have rights, you know," Dolly reminded her. "But Captain Pew says President Davis wants to boss everything. He's trying to make all the blockade-runners just bring in nothing but old guns and things. As if anybody'd take such terrible risks if they couldn't make money out of it!"

"How is the gallant Captain?" Cinda asked. "I haven't seen him for long time."

"Oh he's wonderful! He wants to take me to Nassau on one of his trips, and I'm crazy to go; but Mama says I can't till Darrell will go along, and Darrell just says maybe, some time."

"I think your mother's quite right."

"Oh, I suppose so, but it would be awfully thrilling, just the same."

That victory which Ewell won at Winchester proved to have been a splendid one, with thousands of Yankee prisoners taken, hundreds of the enemy killed, Milroy's army driven headlong back across the Potomac. Just after noon on Saturday, the twentieth of June, a bundle of Northern papers came through the lines with the news that the vanguard of Lee's army had entered Pennsylvania. Till long after dark that night Capitol Square and all the streets in the heart of the city were thronged with jubilant crowds. Surely, this time, the tide of final victory was on the flood!

26

G ENERAL LONGSTREET, when on the ninth of May he and Trav left Richmond to rejoin Lee's army, wished he need not go so far from Louisa. Last year, months of active campaigning had helped him forget his grief for his babies; and at Christmas in Lynchburg he found that Louisa too had learned to laugh again. They were so happy together that she was easily persuaded to come and be with him for a while in January at Hamilton's Crossing. The orders that sent him to Petersburg, where he counted on having her and Garland near him, were welcome; but when she came to meet him in Richmond, she told him in resentful terror that she was to have another baby.

He tried to give her comfort and reassurance, but his own fears would not down. Perhaps Death was not done with him. Perhaps now Louisa was to die. She was so little that it had always seemed to him a miracle, a part of the miraculous of which she was a concentrate, that she could bear his children at all. During her first pregnancy, like any young father, he was half frantic with fears he would not let her see. That was Garland, and then there was Gus, and then Dent who lived only a few months. Harriet died in her first summer, and Jimmie and Mary Ann died when Gus did, last year. He and Louisa had had six children, but now five of them were gone, dead and gone; and another was coming, and Louisa this time was more miserable than she had ever been.

Yet she had still to endure the hot summer that was coming, and all the long months till October. During his stay in Petersburg and at Franklin, she had made a valorous jest of her own weakness. When he came to her, she gave him a gay and tender welcome; but he knew that when he was away she kept her bed, husbanding her strength in order to be able to meet him thus smilingly; that after he left her she might be days recuperating. In loving solicitude he urged her to stay abed even while he was there, but she laughed and told him:

"Indeed I will not! No man likes to come home to an ailing wife, Jeems. Don't worry about me! You've quite enough on your mind."

He wished the seat of this war could somehow be transferred to the South Side so that he might do his duty and still be near her; and he tried to devise some worth-while stroke that might be dealt the Yankees at Suffolk during these months of early spring, while snow and rain and mud still held in restraint the hosts of the enemy along the Rappahannock. But he was too much the soldier to waste men in an enterprise that could only succeed at heavy cost, and that would yield at best a prize which could not be held.

He accepted the certainty that sooner or later he must leave her; but he dreaded the moment and welcomed each delay. When General Lee advised him that Hooker was moving and that it was time for the First Corps to rejoin the army, Longstreet was glad that his foraging wagons, too precious to be abandoned, were widely scattered. To collect them would keep him near her a few days more. For the same unacknowledged reason he managed the withdrawal from Franklin with utmost care, persuading himself that not to do so was to invite pursuit and disaster. As his men moved, sappers notched every tree along the roadside; the rear guard with a few axe strokes dropped these trees across the roads. Even when it was clear that there would be no pursuit, he did not relax his precautions; for these obstructions would prove obstacles to any Yankee attack on Petersburg—where he must leave Louisa. When word came that Lee and Jackson had smashed Hooker's army at Chancellorsville, he knew he need not hurry, he could take his time, could stay near her another day, another day.

For when he left it might be forever; he might never see her face again.

But at last there were no more delays which he could justify even to himself. Reluctantly he went as far as Richmond. President Davis urged him to rejoin Lee at once; but the Yankee cavalry was on the move all about the Capital. They might even make a foray toward Petersburg and Louisa. His military duty would be served by making Richmond, and therefore Petersburg, secure against them. He said so to President Davis, and a letter next day from General Lee supported his decision. Longstreet loved the man for that letter.

But presently the blue-clad raiders withdrew; the way to Fredericksburg was open; he must go. On the cars with only Trav for company he sat for a long time silent. The noises of the train, jolting and swaying along the worn and ill-laid rails, helped shut out the world. But Currain was a man you could talk to. Longstreet's own sadness led him at last to speech.

"I hate leaving Louisa," he confessed; and since Trav merely nodded, he drifted into reminiscence of their years together and of his youth before he met her. "I was young for my age," he said, remembering. "I went to West Point as a boy from the country, shy, ignorant of city ways. When I landed in New York a couple of street urchins pounced on me with a long tale of woe about a dead father and a sick mother. I'd have divided my money with them if a policeman hadn't come along and sent them scampering." His own words made him smile. "And at Jefferson Barracks I wasn't much wiser; just a country bumpkin. Someone organized some dramatics and planned to put on *Othello* and cast me as Desdemona, because I was the only lieutenant who blushed easily; but I was six inches taller than the man who was Othello, so that wouldn't do. 'Lys Grant played Desdemona.

"When I knew I wanted to marry Louisa, Colonel Garland said I must first win a promotion or two; so off I went to Mexico. Colonel Garland and I both took wounds there, but he came home before me. When I returned, I telegraphed for permission to pay my addresses to Louisa and he replied: 'With all my heart!' So we were married, and we've had happy years. After I became paymaster I could be at the post, live at home. That's the sort of work I wanted in this war, and for the same reason. I like being with my family, Currain." He added grimly: "Though there's not much family left now; just Garland and Louisa."

At his own words, old pain clamped like an iron band around his heart and silenced him. The train stopped and started, started and stopped, jolting slowly northward. Trav said: "I could almost walk faster than this train. We've made less than eight miles in the last hour."

It was typical of Currain to think in figures—and also it was characteristic that he should listen without comment and speak afterward of something entirely unrelated to what had just been said. Talking to him was like talking to yourself, like bouncing a ball against a wall. That pretty little wife of his must sometimes find his unresponsive silence irritating.

As they approached their destination and from the car windows saw the rude camps, the parked guns, the wagons slowly moving and the ragged soldiers, the General's thoughts swung back to this business of war. He remembered his talk with Secretary Seddon; his proposal that he go west and take Hood and Pickett to help Bragg. That was good strategy. The Confederacy had in this conflict one advantage; it held the interior lines. Its forces, even on the ill-managed, badly equipped, poorly supplied Southern railroads, could be shifted from east to west and from west to east more rapidly than Northern armies could be moved. Now that Hooker was shaken by defeat, it would be a long time before the Yankees again offered battle. If during this lull Bragg were reinforced, he could crush Rosecrans and march on Cincinnati. Then Washington would call Grant away from Vicksburg. 'Lys Grant would not want to come, true. Secretary Seddon had said so, and he was right. But Lincoln would make Grant let go his death hold on Vicksburg in order to save Cincinnati. Lincoln would never risk losing the West.

Longstreet, contemplating these strategic possibilities, felt his blood begin to stir again. He must forget Louisa if he could. The war was his task.

Yet she was so little and so weak, so tender and so brave!

No matter! Here was his work to do. The train stopped at Hamilton Crossing. He rose and shook his great shoulders and settled his hat on his head.

He reported to General Lee and though he saw the marks of fatigue on the older man, Lee's welcome was as warm as always. They clasped hands, and Longstreet said: "You've had heavy work, General."

Lee nodded gravely. "Yes, a severe affair."

"A great victory."

"I would trade that victory to have General Jackson back again."

Longstreet was surprised at the other's anxious tone. "Secretary Seddon said he stood the amputation well." His word was a question.

Lee shook his head. "I've a message from Hunter McGuire today. Jackson's recovery is very doubtful." Longstreet's throat filled with such a gush of grief that he could not speak; and after a moment Lee added: "And we have had heavy losses. The organizations are badly broken up. There is much to do, much to do."

Next day Jackson died; and sorrow hushed voices in the camps and around the cooking fires and damped even the pride of recent victory. Longstreet and Trav and some others went to Richmond for the ceremonial funeral march; and on the return journey Longstreet fell to thinking of the difference between himself and Jackson. Jackson as a general had qualities which he himself could never emulate; a driving force, a lancelike velocity. "Stonewall" they had called him, ever since First Manassas; but actually his genius was not defense but attack. That could be a weakness. After Fredericksburg, if Lee had not forbidden, Jackson would have thrown his men against the shattered Federals along the river; but such an attack would have cost the South as many men as Burnside had wasted in attacking the sunken road. No, Jackson was not a stone wall; he was a hammer, a lance, a thrusting sword. "He was better than I at rapid movement, at quick and headlong assaults," Longstreet thought. "I'm slow, ponderous. I can hit just as hard, but not as quickly."

His quiet thoughts perceived a deeper difference between them. Jackson was a man about whom legends gathered. Everything he did was marked and noted and told and retold. During the fighting around Richmond he personally supervised the process of cleaning up a battlefield, directing men as they buried the dead, and removed the wounded. Someone asked why. "Because I must presently march my men across this field and I do not wish them to see disturbing sights." His shabby dress, the sorry nag he rode, his habit for a while after First Manassas of holding up his hand to ease the pain in the finger he had lost there, his insistence when gentlemen called on him upon collecting their hats and putting them away, his ferocity in battle, his kindness in camp, his profound religious feeling, his flashes of humor, his care of his men on the one hand and his orders to shoot stragglers on the other—every smallest trait was observed and remembered and reported as mortals might chronicle the actions of one of the lesser gods come down to earth.

Longstreet thought no one would ever repeat anecdotes about him, not as they did about Jackson. Without envy, he wondered what was this quality which made one man a picturesque and memorable figure, while another—no matter what great deeds he might perform—never heard his name on the tongues of men? To be sure there were men like Stuart who courted such notice. Stuart loved the spectacular exploit, he delighted in holding the center of the stage; but Jackson never sought to be conspicuous. He sought only to do his great works, and did them; he never seemed to think of himself but only of his work.

So it was not by intention that Jackson had become a legend, but by performance; and Longstreet knew that nothing he himself might ever do would win him an equal fame. Men would remember him as a silent, somewhat forbidding person of whom they were a little afraid and whom therefore they easily disliked. They would credit him with strength and stubborn persistence, but that was all. Even if he wished to do so, he could not change himself. Jackson was one man; he was another. Nevertheless, there was useful work which he could do.

Back in camp, thinking thus to distract General Lee and help him forget grief for Jackson, Longstreet spoke of his proposal to Secretary Seddon to send a force west, and pointed out its possibilities.

"Yes, even its necessity, General," he urged. "If we do not relieve the pressure, Grant will have Vicksburg, and the whole line of the Mississippi. If he can lop off the western states, the Confederacy will be as much weakened as a man who loses a leg." It was not necessary to elaborate the point, for General Lee knew better than he every aspect of the South's problems; but Longstreet did so, anxious to hold the other's attention.

"The thing would be worth doing, and doubtless could be done," Lee said at last. "But I need Hood and Pickett. I need you, General." He smiled a little, sadly. "I need you more than ever now."

Let him not think of Jackson. Longstreet urged: "Our most pressing task is to save Vicksburg."

"It's true," the other assented. "To lose the Mississippi would hurt us sadly; but to lose Virginia would hurt us worse." Lee was for a moment silent. "My own loyalty is to Virginia above all; but if Virginia falls, so does the Confederacy. I am sure of that."

"Isn't Virginia safe for the present, General?"

"I want those people a little farther away."

"You can't drive them. They're secure behind the Rappahannock. Neither they nor we can force and maintain a crossing."

"We must not waste the summer," General Lee reflected, and Longstreet saw that his attention now was all upon matters of strategy. "Our problem is how best to use it. The western venture has virtues; but there may be a nearer way that is less hazardous." Longstreet looked at him, already guessing what was in his mind; and General Lee said quietly: "Those people would abandon everything else if we were to threaten Washington." He added: "It's hard to provision our army where we are, General; but there are fat lands within our reach."

So these two, as men will, turned from a shared grief to the solace of work. Fat lands? That meant invasion of the North. Longstreet's instinct was to urge the defensive; but a thrust north through the sally port of the Valley might be the best defensive.

"Invade the North?" He reflected. "Draw them to battle on ground of our choosing? Fight another Fredericksburg, but this time on terrain where we can follow up a victory?" He said with a deep certainty: "Give me a position where they must attack, and I will give you another Fredericksburg."

"We can't march away and leave those people here with the road to Richmond open," Lee reminded him. "But if General Hooker waits to see what we will do, he leaves the initiative to us. We will use it."

So once more they would invade the North; and there was a challenging promise in the thought. But when Longstreet was alone, he remembered an army of barefoot men hurrying into Maryland last September; an army from which sheer exhaustion stole hundreds day by day; an army whose thinned ranks faced twice or thrice its numbers on the hills at Sharpsburg, and which held its ground there only because not to do so was to die. If they were to thrust north again, then let there be no haste, keep the men unwearied, maneuver the enemy into a position where he must attack, and where when he faltered there would be room to drive and scatter him.

Longstreet was sure General Lee agreed with this design; but Lee had an eager heart for battle, and that fighting heart might betray him. So before any move was made, they must talk a while. They must talk here in Virginia, calmly and thoughtfully. They must make their decisions here while the blood still ran slowly and the mind was clear. Then, their tactics predetermined, they would be safe against betrayal by the hot lust for battle. When they moved, their heads must all be cool, their plans already formed, their design to seek another Fredericksburg and then a chase and a great shattering.

But first there was much to do. Jackson was dead; Jackson and his cool head and his hot heart were gone. That meant reorganization. General Lee shaped the army into three corps instead of two. Ewell would have one of them; it was his due. When Lee spoke of Powell Hill, Longstreet urged that as surely as Ewell deserved the Second Corps, so did Harvey Hill, rather than Powell Hill, deserve the Third.

"He's never gone wrong, General," he urged. "He began well at Bethel, Seven Pines was his battle, he held off half McClellan's army at South Mountain, he had the hardest contention at Sharpsburg." He added in a lighter tone: "He's General Jackson's brother-in-law, and he has some of Jackson's fighting qualities."

But Harvey Hill was in North Carolina with hard work to do there, so Powell Hill was the choice. Well, General Lee had the right to choose his tools; but Powell Hill would need watching. Longstreet remembered the episode after Seven Pines when he and Hill came near the absurdity of a duel; but this memory did not influence him now. Hill had always been a good fighting man, a good leader for brigade or division; but Longstreet did not consider him fit for corps command. He lacked the quality of patience, the ability to wait before he struck. That June day when he crossed the Meadow Bridges to march against Mechanicsville, if he had waited for Jackson how much more might have been accomplished! Hill was likely to act before he thought, as for instance when he sent that ridiculous challenge after the Seven Days; but once in a fight, no one fought his men harder or

better. The Seven Days had established his reputation, Second Manassas and then Sharpsburg enhanced it. All the same, that impatience
of his might one day embroil them all in battle not of Lee's choosing.
Longstreet was uneasy about Powell Hill.

The commanding general must choose his tools; but Longstreet
watched for opportunities to clarify in both their minds the calm decision that when they invaded the North, their tactics must be defensive. There was time enough before the army moved. He and General
Lee discussed the preliminary maneuvers, the problem of slipping
away from Hooker's front without leaving open the road to Richmond.

General Lee's plan was designed to play on Hooker's fears and on
the timidity of Lincoln; for above all, the North must hold Washington. Already there was good ground for hoping England would
recognize the Confederacy. She was sending a dozen or fifteen new
regiments to Canada, and some Confederate Congressmen believed
that a promise by the South to emancipate the slaves would remove
the last bar to English recognition. Certainly the capture of Washington would swing the balance, so Lincoln would never risk losing
Washington; and even a distant threat would lead him to call Hooker
back to a defensive position.

So Lee's first move would be to shift one corps, or perhaps two,
westward as far as Culpeper. If the weakening of the force in front of
him tempted Hooker to try an advance, he would need two or three
days to bridge the Rappahannock. That would give them time enough
to march back from Culpeper and meet him. If he stayed passive
where he was, then a movement toward Warrenton, threatening his
flank and rear, would force him to withdraw; and each mile he withdrew would give them that much more freedom. One day Lee showed
Longstreet a map, drawn in the utmost detail and with the name of
every farmer marked beside his homestead, of the Pennsylvania region
far north of Washington and east of the mountains. General Jackson,
Lee explained, had had that map prepared; and he said that if Hooker
fell back toward the Potomac they could cross into the Valley and let
one corps mask Winchester and push on toward Chambersburg. The
rest of the army would follow and reduce Winchester, and behind the
screen of the Blue Ridge, with cavalry to hold the Gaps, race northward and pour out into these Pennsylvania farm lands toward the

Susquehanna. Somewhere on enemy soil in that York-Harrisburg-Chambersburg triangle, the armies would meet in the battle that might isolate Washington or lead to its capture. To do this would bring England to recognize the Confederacy. That would end the war.

They came to details. Which corps would lead the way? "Let Ewell lead," Longstreet advised. "Leave Powell Hill at Fredericksburg. If he were in the van he would attack the first enemy he met, involve us all."

So Ewell was sent for, and in that conference Longstreet found the opportunity to emphasize the point which he considered so important: the folly of offensive battle on enemy soil. "For if we propose to make offensive battle, we can cross the Rappahannock and make it here," he pointed out. "There is no need to make a wearying march into Pennsylvania in order to attack General Hooker, when we might as readily hit him where he stands."

Before they parted, he was satisfied that both Lee and Ewell agreed. When Lee rose to bid them good day, Longstreet saw him wince, and asked a question; and Lee said almost brusquely: "Nothing! Nothing! A little pleurisy, a touch of rheumatism. It will be gone with the first hot days."

Longstreet nodded. "Summer will march northward with us." Outside, he and General Ewell separated, each to set in motion the first detachments of his command.

To withdraw from Hooker's front was a gingerly procedure. Longstreet told Moxley Sorrel, as they sat their horses watching McLaws's division prepare to move: "It's like trying to get out of the room where a baby is sleeping. We'll go tiptoe, very carefully, ready to hurry back if the sleeper wakes." His own words made him think of Louisa; for sometimes when he was with her she fell lightly asleep, and he took care not to wake her when he slipped away. "A ticklish business," he repeated. "The Yankee cavalry is better than it was. Hooker knows more about what we're doing than we know about him."

For a day or two the Yankees seemed unsuspecting. Then a demonstration opposite Fredericksburg—a pontoon bridge thrown across the river and the seizing of a bridgehead—made the Confederates wait a day to see whether this was serious; but Hooker did no more than feint, and the cautious sidling was resumed. Stuart's headquarters were at Culpeper; Ewell's corps and Longstreet's would join him there. They marched westerly along the Rappahannock, and crossed the Rapidan and made bivouac on the rolling plain south of Culpeper toward Pony Mountain.

June was not yet settled into summer heat and the meadows were still green and there was bloom in every garden. West and north the Blue Ridge received the morning sun, and on its flanks all day as the sun marched the shadow patterns changed. What seemed to be a flat wall acquired depth and perspective; long slopes and ridges, dark ravines, deep valleys took shape and form and then receded into invisibility again as easily as a wild animal, by becoming motionless, loses itself against the forest tapestry. As the sun drew westward all the eastern slopes acquired a deep and deeper blue, till purple pools of night lay along the lower ranges. At sunset the summit ridges drew a knife line against the pearly iridescence of the deep caverns of the sky beyond, and night came down with stars to match the little bivouac fires that dotted all the plain.

Off to the eastward an uneasy Hooker drew back a little from Fredericksburg. General Lee, when he was sure of the other's inactivity, left Hamilton's Crossing and came to establish his headquarters near Longstreet's. He was in good spirits. While they waited for Hooker to withdraw a little farther, he would review the cavalry. "Stuart invited me for a grand spectacle on Friday," he explained. "I could not go; but we'll ride over and see them tomorrow. It will please him."

"It won't please the men," Longstreet remarked. "And it will take pounds off the horses. The Friday affair was full panoply. The squadrons did the march-past at a walk, and then at a trot, gallop, charge. The ladies were delighted, and Stuart, too. He plays war like a game for boys. But for the horses and the men, that Friday affair was as much work as a skirmish."

General Lee smiled. "We'll keep them at a foot pace this time," he said. "But I'll be glad to see what force I have in hand."

The review was a splendid pageant, eight or ten thousand men and horses ranked across the plain in a double line a fair three miles long. Lee led a score or so of officers at a canter along the front; then he halted his horse while the squadrons marched past at a sober walk, the horses proud with tossing heads. Longstreet's own pulse quickened as he watched. It was true, as he had said, that Stuart played war like a game; but he played it well. He could be forgiven a fine pride in these men. When the review was over, Longstreet sent Trav with a message of congratulation.

"And ask General Stuart to give me someone competent to act as a guide through the Yankee lines," he directed. "I want to send a scout toward Washington."

When Trav returned from that mission, he brought Burr and Faunt. "You remember these gentlemen, General," he said. "My brother Faunt, and my nephew Burr, Cinda's son. He's one of Stuart's men, in Fitz Lee's brigade."

Longstreet thought he would not have recognized Faunt, drawn and thin, with a spot of color on the high cheekbones above his beard, and burning eyes shadowed as though by persisting pain. It was hard to believe that Faunt and Trav were brothers, the one so obviously consumed by an inner flame, the other except under the spur of hot contention so completely phlegmatic. How often brothers were thus different! And Burr, their nephew, was unlike either of them; a lean young fellow, easy in his saddle and lithe as a whip stock, yet with a laughing gentleness in him. He was the sort of gallant youngster whom the wrong kind of wife would easily rule. The General greeted them, asked Burr: "Where's your father?"

"The Howitzers are camped half a mile north of Culpeper on the Fauquier road," Burr explained. "I'm riding over to see him."

Longstreet chuckled. "The Howitzers? The little guns with the big noise?"

"They keep hoping for bigger guns, sir."

Trav said: "General, I gave your request to General Stuart. He referred me to Major Mosby, and the Major says my brother here is the man you want."

Longstreet looked at Faunt, and as though the look were a question, Faunt answered: "Most of my work is done behind the Yankee lines, General."

Longstreet nodded, and he thought any Yankee who met Faunt might regret it. "I've a scout," he explained. "A man named Harrison.

Secretary Seddon sent him to me at Suffolk, and he was useful there. He knows Washington and the country north of the Potomac, but he's not familiar with northern Virginia. Will you see him across the Potomac?"

"Yes sir."

Longstreet hesitated. Faunt looked like a man who might forget other business if he saw a chance to hit the enemy. "Keep him out of trouble," he suggested. "See him safe and secretly across the river."

"Yes sir," Faunt repeated.

Longstreet asked Trav to summon Harrison. The scout was in civilian dress—a mild, bearded, inconspicuous man. Longstreet had already supplied him with gold and given him instructions. "Harrison, this is Mr. Currain," he said. "He will put you across the Potomac. When you've anything to report, come to me."

"Where will I find you, General?"

"At headquarters of the First Corps, Mr. Harrison. You'll find me there." It was best to trust no one more than you must. He saw Faunt watching the spy, and he asked Harrison: "Have you a horse?"

"A mule."

Faunt said quietly: "We can start when you're ready, Mr. Harrison."

When they were gone, Longstreet invited Burr to stay and mess with them, and he spoke of the fine display the cavalry had made that morning. Burr said proudly: "We did it better three days ago. Much more of a spectacle. General Stuart enjoys such things."

"The rest of you?"

"Well, we like to please the General."

"There's a fine spirit in the cavalry," Longstreet agreed; and when they dined he led Burr into easy talk of the jollity with which Stuart liked to surround himself.

"It's not all laughing and dancing and singing, sir," Burr reminded him. "General Stuart is a fighter too. We think he deserved more credit than he will ever get for Chancellorsville. General Jackson started it, but most of the fighting was done under Stuart after he had to take over the command."

"General Jackson's death overshadowed everything on that field," Longstreet reminded him; and Burr nodded.

"We were at Orange Court-House when he died," he said. "We had a chance to rest our horses there, and get some fresh ones; and we had some good times." He laughed, remembering an incident. "Captain Scheibert was with us. He's a Prussian, an artist, a fat little man, wears a short jacket and white trousers too tight for him; and he's forever getting into ridiculous trouble. One day he sat down on a fresh oil painting and transferred the portrait of a lady to the seat of those white pants of his and came back to headquarters fairly whooping at the joke on himself. He keeps us laughing most of the time."

Laughter and Stuart went together; but the day after the review the laugh was at Stuart's expense. His headquarters were on Fleetwood Hill, between Brandy Station and the river; and the Yankee cavalry, divided into two powerful columns, crossed the river and struck him hard converging blows. There was an all-day battle on the slopes and levels around Fleetwood Hill, with twenty thousand horsemen hotly engaged, and for a while Stuart was in serious trouble. At the first heavy onslaught one of his brigades was badly broken, and the Yankees got on Stuart's rear and threatened to inflict upon him a major defeat.

But the end of that hard-fought day saw the enemy cavalry draw back across the river again, so though there were losses, the screen along the Rappahannock was restored. Longstreet thought Stuart would be a better soldier if the Yankees had now taught him to respect them; yet the fact that the enemy cavalry fought so well was disquieting. When the Yankees learned their work, their advantage in numbers would begin to tell.

The day after that great cavalry battle, General Ewell's Corps proceeded toward the Valley. Longstreet was with General Lee when Ewell came for a last word; and Lee repeated the broad outline of his plan.

"If Winchester is strongly held, leave it for us, General," he said. "You move on, cross the river, march into Maryland." He added quietly: "And on into Pennsylvania. General Longstreet will stay east of the Blue Ridge for a while." He met Longstreet's eyes. "To hold off those people till Hill can pass in his rear. So you leave Winchester for us, keep your men in hand, keep them fresh. We'll follow you."

Ewell rode away; and for almost a week Longstreet and Lee remained at Culpeper. On the fifteenth, Longstreet led his divisions
northward, following the valley roads while the Rappahannock ceased
to be a river and became no more than a shallow creek, easily forded
at any crossing. After the halt for a nooning, Longstreet called Major
Currain to ride with him. Ahead, the dome of Cobbler's Mountain began now and then to show itself, and Longstreet's thoughts
drifted.

"What's a sugarloaf, Currain?" he asked, and seeing Trav's surprise, he nodded toward the height ahead. "That mountain—any
mountain shaped like that is apt to be named Sugarloaf; but it looks
much more the way a pile of sugar might look if you poured it
through a funnel. What is a sugarloaf, anyway?"

Trav did not know. Another mountain with a double top appeared
on the left ahead, as Cobbler's was on the right. "Now that one,"
Longstreet suggested jocosely, "looks like the rear end of a horse
going away from us at an angle. I wonder what its name is?"

"Saddleback, probably," Trav suggested, and Longstreet agreed.

"Always the obvious," he assented. "And why not? I wonder if the
world wouldn't be a happier place if we all of us always did the
obvious. What a lot of trouble we would avoid so."

They made a fair twenty miles that day, and when they halted for
the night the two heights stood like sentinels guarding the morrow's
road to Markham and beyond. Stuart's men were off to the east toward the Bull Run Mountains, on guard against any enemy thrust
against the flank of the moving columns. Next morning a courier
brought a dispatch from General Lee, still at Culpeper. Ewell had
stormed Winchester, had won a substantial success; but Longstreet,
remembering Lee's instructions to leave a defended Winchester behind and push on, found that action blamable. If Ewell were going
to precipitate battle on his own initiative, he was as dangerous as Hill.
The fact that he himself had been sure Ewell would keep a cool head,
and that he had told Lee so, made him uncomfortable. He spoke of
this to Sorrel.

"I hate to be proved wrong," he admitted. "General Lee may twit
me about that a little. But of course Ewell will be forgiven. It's easy
to forgive a victory."

"It sounds like the sort of thing Jackson might have done," Sorrel suggested; and Longstreet nodded.

"Ewell learned his work under Jackson. Perhaps he learned it well."

They marched through Markham and up the valley of Goose Creek, climbing easily toward Ashby's Gap. The ascent for a while was gentle, and there were many small farms, the houses usually set well away from the road. From some of them, when the column approached, children came in a headlong race to the roadside to perch on the fences and watch the regiments pass, or perhaps to march for a while beside the men, stretching their small legs to keep the pace. The bolder ones might beg the privilege of carrying a soldier's musket for a while; they asked a thousand questions; their searching eyes missed no detail. When the road ran near the clear winding creek, these youthful volunteers filled canteens, or fetched pails of water for the thirsty men. Between the children and the soldiers there was a quick and affectionate communion, an easy intercourse.

Longstreet, bound to keep his men fresh for the work that lay ahead, did not hurry them. He put the First Corps in position along the eastern slopes of the Blue Ridge, guarding Ashby's Gap and Snicker's. His orders from Lee were to remain east of the Ridge, but he had discretion. When a courier from Stuart reported that Major Mosby had seen the Yankee army moving north to cover Washington, Longstreet thought it time to send Pickett's division through the Gaps into the Valley.

General Lee had come on to Markham, and Longstreet sent him a dispatch reporting he had done this. Lee replied in a tone puzzlingly uncertain. He remarked that to operate east of the mountains might have confused Hooker. "But as you have turned off to the Valley, and I understand all the trains have taken that route, I hope it is for the best."

This was so near a reproof that Longstreet half resented it; but General Lee was in constant pain from his pleurisy and from the rheumatism which he could not shake off, and probably he was worried because he had so little news of Hooker.

"Just as I am worried about Louisa, not hearing from her," Longstreet reflected; but next day a letter from her overtook him. It was

almost two weeks old; but like all her letters it was affectionate and
cheerful. She was taking the best care of herself, she said; she was
resting every day. He must never worry. "Have me in your heart,"
she wrote, "but not on your mind. We know you'll beat the old
Yankees any time they meet you." She gave him some crumbs of
news. "There's been a fine rain to break the drouth, and everyone's
boasting about their gardens. Prices are terrible; but somehow we
manage. Everybody seems to be getting rich by speculating."

There was a postcript. "I must never keep anything from you, because if I did you'd worry; so I'll 'fess up that I had a bad time a week
ago, the same thing. Even Dr. Dunn was worried, but I'm fine now."

That disturbed him for a while, till his work drove thoughts of
Louisa into the background of his mind. Friday, General Lee broke
up his headquarters at Markham and rode through Ashby's Gap and
down into the Valley; and on Saturday, Longstreet was perplexed by
a dispatch from headquarters directing him to be ready to move toward the Potomac.

"But we're ready now," he told Moxley Sorrel. "What am I expected to do? General Lee saw the disposition of McLaws's division at
Ashby's. Possibly he thinks we should pass through the Gaps and cross
the Shenandoah." Till Powell Hill was up, the Gaps should be held;
but these orders seemed to mean that Lee felt Longstreet could now
leave his post.

Very well, he would move across the Shenandoah. He gave orders
for the march. The ascent was easy, by a grade seldom steep enough
to weary the men; and from the crest they saw the waiting beauty of
the Valley, as inviting as the blue of the sea on a hot summer's day.
The way down was long and tortuous, winding through forest that
seldom permitted any distant outlook; but at the foot of the Ridge
they came to wide levels and to frequent farms and pushed on across
the tilled lands and down to the ford, and so made their bivouac on
the rising ground beyond the sparkling stream.

The mountains were like a wall between them and the enemy, but
next day Stuart sent word that Yankee cavalry in force was pressing
him toward the Gap; so McLaws's division had to climb back up that
steep winding road to be ready to hold the Gap if Stuart were pushed
too far. But by the time they were in position Stuart sent word that

the Yankees were withdrawing, that he was harrying them through Upperville toward Aldie. McLaws's men had that hard day's march to no purpose; but Longstreet, though he regretted the waste of good shoe leather, knew this would not daunt the men. A soldier soon learned to accept the changing minds of his commanders.

General Lee had made his new headquarters a little beyond Berryville, on the west side of the Charlestown road; and Monday when the Gap was secure and McLaws was bringing his division back down the mountain to the ford, Longstreet had a dispatch from the commanding general enclosing an open letter to be forwarded to Stuart. In this open letter General Lee bade Stuart move northward and take position on Ewell's flank in Pennsylvania; and his covering dispatch to Longstreet said Stuart might in his discretion go through Hopewell Gap and pass Hooker's rear, turning north between the Federal army and Washington.

Longstreet was troubled by this discretionary order. Stuart's proper place was between this army and the enemy, and Stuart of course knew this; but still smarting under the sting of that surprise at Brandy Station, he would be in a mood to do something spectacular. Acting as a flank guard was dull work, and it would be like Stuart to elect that risky alternative of a ride around the enemy.

Longstreet tried to dismiss his misgivings. Stuart was too good a soldier to get out of touch with the commanding general. Lee's letter indicated that the northward movement was to be resumed, and Tuesday evening the expected orders came: the First Corps was to move through Berryville and Martinsburg toward the Potomac at Williamsport.

Pickett's division was at Millwood, McLaws's men lay between Millwood and the river, Hood at Snicker's Gap could pass through and march to Berryville and take his place in the advance. Longstreet gave orders to move at dawn on Wednesday; and when McLaws led his men through Millwood and followed Pickett toward Berryville, the plodding foot soldiers filling the road for miles as they filed northward across the low rolling hills, Longstreet mounted and rode with his staff to overtake Pickett and come to the head of the column.

There was a deep reluctance in him, and a sadness at this setting out; and he wondered why. Perhaps it was because every mile took him farther from Louisa. Moxley Sorrel rode beside him, and Major Goree, and these two were talking cheerfully of nothing; and Longstreet wondered almost resentfully if they had no families to whom their thoughts turned as his did to Louisa. Then he remembered that Goree's Texas home was far away, and Sorrel's too; so a few miles more made little difference to them. But a man like Currain, with a wife and children in Richmond, could share his own homesick longing; and beyond Berryville Longstreet called Trav to his side.

"This is one of those times I'd as soon forget I'm a soldier," he confessed. "So let's not talk business. You'll always be a civilian at heart. Even when you fight, you're less like a soldier than like a drunken man in a brawl."

"I'm no great shakes as a talker, either, General."

"Yes, but you can listen. Let's ride ahead." Longstreet touched his horse to a trot, and Trav followed and the rest of the staff kept pace behind. But the narrow road, honeysuckle like a hedge along the fences on either side, was crowded, and it was always hard to pass marching infantry; so Longstreet turned into a byway, clear of the column and of the sluggish dust clouds stirred up by so many tramping feet.

"The men have their own dust to eat," he suggested. "Let's not make it harder for them by adding ours. We'll ride through Charlestown and be ahead of them at Kearneysville." Trav followed his lead without comment, and Longstreet welcomed that silence, thinking how ready with conversation some of the others on the staff would have been. A wise general chose his staff not only for their capacities but for their qualities. Fairfax was a clown, loving meat and drink and lusty pleasures, ready when the wine flowed to make an ass of himself. Well, there were hours when a man wanted to play the fool, and in such hours Fairfax was a jolly companion. Longstreet remembered one occasion when both of them were in their cups and he rode Fairfax like a horse around the mess table, and Fairfax played his part to perfection, bucking and neighing like an unbroken colt. Walton drank as heavily as anyone; but liquor edged his tongue with sarcastic barbs and set his temper on a hair trigger. Latrobe and Peyton Manning were gentlemen by instinct and breeding, unfailingly kindly in word and act, prompt for any duty and equally ready for the gentler pleasures. Sorrel was probably the ablest of them all, certainly the one best fitted for command; but he was a little too ready to urge his own opinions, and easily critical. Goree and Longstreet had in common many friends in Texas, and there was a strong affection between them. Goree was a diligent and intelligent and trustworthy officer; but if he had a fault it was too ready a tongue. For instance, he would never have ridden here beside Longstreet mile after mile, as Currain was doing now, with never a word. To be with Currain was like being alone: you could keep your thoughts to yourself or let them find words as you chose, sure that Currain would do more listening than talking.

Longstreet's eyes swept approvingly across the pleasant fertile fields that ran with the road; and at last he spoke. "This is fine country, Currain. Some day I'm going to quit the army and find a smooth bit of turf under a shady tree and just sit there for the rest of my life!"

"I'd probably plow up the turf and plant something."

The big man nodded, only half hearing. "Yes, some day I'll turn civilian." And after a moment he said thoughtfully. "You know, Currain, army life is strange. Here are thousands of us in closest companionship day after day, and yet each one of us is always alone. Have you ever noticed, at headquarters or in camp, how often a man draws apart by himself? There's a difference between comradeship and friendship, isn't there? You can be comrades with a stranger. Friends, even when they're apart, are still friends; but comrades, after the hot moment of action is passed, are no longer comrades." He nodded over his shoulder. "These gentlemen here, and the soldiers on the road yonder, are all knit together in a military comradeship; yes, and close knit too. But separate them and they're individuals again." Currain made an assenting sound and Longstreet added: "It may be an armor we put on. If we loved our comrades too much, we could not endure it when they die."

"I guess that's so."

"Whatever the reason, the thing is true. If you doubt it, Currain, watch them in their leisure. At work, or at table, or at some jest together, they're laughing and genial; but the moment nothing any longer holds them together, see how quickly each withdraws himself into silence, into another room, another place. Men value their privacy; they like to be alone."

"I like to run into people I know," Trav said. "Get news of friends and kin. I've got some friends in the Eleventh North Carolina that I want to look up when the army draws together again." He added as though this made a difference: "But of course, they were my friends before the war."

An elderly gentleman rode out from a great house they passed and saluted them, introducing himself. "Thomas Paynton, General." Any march brought such incidents as this. The gentlemen of the neighborhood were apt to ride a few miles with you, seeking what information you cared to give them, volunteering information that was often useful. Trav dropped back to let Mr. Paynton ride by the General's side, and their talk was random till Longstreet remembered that in Charlestown, now not far ahead, John Brown had been hanged, and spoke of it.

"Yes," Mr. Paynton agreed. "Yes, I talked with that man, after his capture." And he explained: "He came to my home during my absence to try to work on my negroes. They saw in him only an old man with a long beard who wanted to give them pikes with which to kill their white folks. Of course they were frightened, so they never spoke of it till after he was safe in jail; but then my old Andrew saw the maniac and recognized him and told me. I was sufficiently curious so that I went to see Brown before he was hanged, told him Andrew recognized him. Brown admitted it without any evidence of shame. He said I need never fear my negroes, that he could not move them at all, that they were completely loyal."

"I had not known that Brown tried to excite the people."

"Oh yes. He was in the neighborhood for some time before he turned to actual violence; visited many plantations hereabouts. When he found he could not enlist any black men as his recruits, he decided they were afraid to rise, that a bold stroke might give them their cue."

"He knew as little about the black people as any other abolitionist," Longstreet commented. "I've sometimes thought it must puzzle those ignorant fanatics up North, if they have enough intelligence to be puzzled, to see millions of slaves loyally protecting our women and children and our homes while we march off to war. You know, if there were even one slave insurrection anywhere in the South, every soldier in Lee's army would desert and go home to protect his family, and the war would be over."

"Of course," Mr. Paynton agreed. "And if there were even a grain of truth in the lies preached by men like Garrison and Beecher and Emerson, the slaves would have butchered us long ago. But I suppose there were liars on both sides. Massachusetts at one end of the country, and South Carolina and Alabama at the other, equally ignorant, fed us lies for thirty years. Lies and abuse, flung back and forth by ignorant men, were bound to lead to battle in the end."

"Lies are the tools of politicians." Longstreet spoke sternly. "Good tools, too; because you can never catch up with a lie. And a lie is usually more interesting than the truth, so it's listened to more readily. The politicians feed us lies till they persuade us we believe things we really don't believe at all. It's their talk, poured into our ears or thrown at us by the newspapers, that brought us into this war. People will always be easily led to war as long as they believe what they hear and what they read, instead of thinking for themselves. And of course the lie most easily believed is that they're better than other men. The abolitionists think they're better than we are, and we think we're better than they are. So we're all fighting to prove it."

Mr. Paynton amended that. "The abolitionists never could have done it without the Republicans to help. I suppose the worst insult you can throw at a Southerner for the next hundred years will be to call him a Republican."

The next hundred years? Yes, that was the question: not what was best and wisest for today, but for tomorrow, for the years to come. Suppose the Confederacy established itself; suppose the Union fell. Was that, after all, conceivable? Longstreet at his own thoughts shook his head. No, it was not. Any victory the South won would be only temporary. Inevitably the force of a common language, common interests, blood ties, a shared heritage, would draw North and South together again.

But then this war, these battles, all were a bloody futility. He fell into an abstracted silence; and when Mr. Paynton presently, as though feeling himself dismissed, said good-by and turned homeward, Longstreet rode alone. The countryside was increasingly familiar. Bunker

Hill, where after Sharpsburg he had spent some weeks, was off to the west not far away. From the Shenandoah there was a rising swell of ground to the rolling plateau along which ran the Valley pike, with the masses of North Mountain paralleling the road to the westward. In the pastured lands beside the road, bone-gray ledges frequently broke the sod. Sometimes these ledges might extend for long distances, set on edge so that slanting slabs like toppling grave stones rose two or three feet above the green turf.

Off there to the westward, as the road he followed approached its junction with that which his men had taken, he saw a low cloud of dust stirred up by thousands of tramping feet; and his thoughts returned to his present problems. The army was a serpent stretched to its utmost length along many miles of road, with South Mountain to guard the flank toward the enemy; but they would presently enter Yankee territory. Then they must draw more closely together. They would have to live off the country; and as for fighting, they carried no more than enough artillery ammunition for one great battle. The soldiers could replenish their cartridge boxes from the wagons, but unless they won a battle and captured powder and shells and solid shot and canister and grape, the great guns would become useless baggage.

General Lee hoped this northward thrust would draw the enemy army out of his beloved Virginia. He hoped to fight a defensive battle where victory might earn a rich reward. He hoped at the worst to keep the fighting north of the Potomac till summer waned.

But suppose instead of victory they met defeat, or fought a drawn battle. What then? A strong uneasiness made Longstreet lift his horse to a trot. At Kearneysville he found Garnett's brigade, with Colonel Hunton for this day at its head, and he heard that General Lee was gone toward Martinsburg and pushed on to rejoin the commanding general. The rolling levels gave way to many little hills, and from the crest of each he could see behind him the line of marching men, the guns, the wagons of his First Corps on the move, crawling steadily northward along the undulating road. Above them hung the dust, and Longstreet thought the dust seemed to dull the sun, and he glanced upward. The sun was in fact obscured, but not by the dust. A thin mist of cloud, scored by barely perceptible lines, was drawn like a veil across the western sky. That promised rain tonight, or tomorrow.

Suppose, somewhere up there in Pennsylvania where they now were bent, they met a shattering disaster, and rains raised the river to flood stage behind them. What then?

This road they followed, this region they traversed, woke sombre thoughts. Hagerstown was not far away. Last September he had been at Hagerstown when a messenger brought word that McClellan was fighting to cross the South Mountain and strike their scattered forces. Then came the desperately hurried concentration and that bitter day of death at Sharpsburg. Longstreet looked off that way. South Mountain was a dim shadow in this increasing haze, but he could make out the notch of the gap through which McClellan came. The ford where after that bloody day at Sharpsburg this army crossed back into Virginia to lick its wounds was only a few miles to the eastward. Probably a crow could fly from here to last September's battlefield in five minutes, ten at the most. Longstreet remembered the dead who strewed that field, and the nightlong cries of wounded as they died; and he wondered whether those dead men might not just now feel the pound of marching feet as this army passed, and rouse from their shallow graves, and—what was that shuddering line he had read somewhere?—come to squeak and gibber at old comrades, and to call derisive greetings to living men who would soon be dead as they.

He set his jaw, forcing himself to forget that disastrous field so near the line of march they followed now. Last September Lee had only thirty or forty thousand men to face McClellan's hundred thousand, but now Lee led twice that many seasoned veterans toward Pennsylvania. The issue must be different this year.

He pushed through Martinsburg and on along the Valley pike. The road, a crushed limestone macadam, had once been hard and smooth; but for two years the tides of war had scoured it, the wheels of cannons and caissons and supply trains and the hoofs of horses and the feet of traveling men had beaten it and broken it. The damage they did, frost and snow and rain extended; so now it was in many places impassable for vehicles. At such spots the breaks had been by-passed, wagons and guns turning off into the fields; and when the ruts they cut became too deep, they took new ways. Every fence rail for miles had been burned for camp fires, and the highway, bordered by the scallops of the many turnouts like so much rude embroidery, was marked by the skeletons of wagons wrecked and abandoned, by the decayed carcasses of horses or of mules.

Longstreet continued on this highway till, a few miles beyond Martinsburg, he found Lee's bivouac where a singing creek flowed into a great bend of the Potomac. Its music was sweet in the hush of the evening, and the hamlet, not surprisingly, was called Falling Waters. Longstreet spoke to the commanding general. Had the warm day helped those persistent rheumatic twinges? Yes, they were better, Lee assured him. Yes, all went well.

Next morning they woke to a drenching rain. The day began in sobering fashion. With a hard task ahead, the men must be kept strictly in hand, and though General Lee usually dealt lightly with offenders, this was not a time for mercy. So at dawn there was one execution in Pickett's division, and there were four in that of General Rodes. Longstreet from his tent heard the spatter of those fusillades. The sound was muffled. Probably the poor devils had been marched down to some glade among the willows by the river, where the steep banks would stop any bullets that went astray; and Longstreet imagined the squads with levelled muskets, the men about to die, the condemned and their executioners alike drenched by the steady rain and the drip from sodden trees.

When they had breakfasted they mounted, and at eleven o'clock they reached the ford at Williamsport. The Potomac, though it was here a wide and shallow stream, had long ago cut for itself a steep-sloped valley; and the road descended sharply to the narrow bottoms choked with willows, and crossed them to the waterside. Pickett's division was in the lead, and although the hard rain had already soaked them through and through, nevertheless the men, preparing to wade across, stripped off their trousers. As he approached the other bank Longstreet saw a group of ladies, looking under their umbrellas like an overnight growth of strangely tinted mushrooms, waiting to welcome General Lee into Maryland. Then one of the trouserless soldiers called in shrill warning:

"Shet yore eyes, ladies! Here we come!"

Pickett turned to hush the man with a stern word; then, splashing back to his place at Longstreet's side, he said with a chuckle: "That's

Red Wheatley of the First Virginia. He's the regimental clown, keeps the men in good humor on the hardest march."

Longstreet had looked around to identify the jester, a brick-faced stalwart whose hat was all brim and no crown, his flaming hair plastered down by the steady rain. "He needs a new hat," he commented, in mild amusement.

"He claims he likes that one," Pickett explained. "Says he's afraid that red hair of his will catch fire if he keeps it dry!"

When they rode up from the ford, General Lee spoke to the waiting ladies with a gentle courtesy. Longstreet thought one of them, so small she seemed like a child, was no bigger than Louisa. Last night a courier had brought Lee dispatches from Richmond; but there was nothing from Mrs. Longstreet, and Longstreet wished he had some word. This was her fifth month; and during her pregnancies her worst times came with an inexorable regularity. She would be feeling badly through the days just ahead.

Pickett's men took the road that followed the valley of Conococheague Creek toward Greencastle, but Longstreet rode with General Lee to a roadside grove beyond the last houses of Williamsport. While they were at mess, a youngster brought a basket of raspberries as a present for General Lee. The boy was the age Gus would have been if he were still alive, and Longstreet made friends with him, at ease as he had always been with children. He called Trav to discuss in serious tones whether they could not use this young man on the staff, and the boy grinned and squirmed delightedly.

Next morning General Lee rode on through Hagerstown toward Chambersburg, but Longstreet stayed to bring up the rear. When at last he turned his back on the Potomac he was conscious of a quickening of all his faculties, an intensified perceptiveness. He felt too a profound uneasiness. They were surrounded by a wall of hostile silence behind which any disaster might be preparing. Hooker was presumably almost directly south of them, for they had moved northwest into the Valley, then northeast to the Potomac. Washington itself was off to the southeast, so they were deep in enemy territory, and Longstreet felt like a blindfolded man, or like one who tries to cross a strange room in darkness, expecting at any moment to stumble over the furniture.

No doubt their own cavalry now guarded their flank and rear, and General Lee must know from Stuart's reports where Hooker's army was; yet Longstreet could not be sure. This morning when they parted, Lee had certainly been in an angry humor, jerking his head in that nervous, sidewise fashion which always meant that his temper was under hard control. Longstreet had suggested that they detach men to establish signalling stations along the mountain on their flank. "They could give us early intelligence of any enemy approach," he pointed out. But General Lee shook his head.

"No, no. Stuart will let us know. He's watching them. I think Hooker has gone to sleep." And he repeated: "If those people had moved, Stuart would let me know." Longstreet thought that repetition sounded as though Lee wished to reassure himself.

This was another weary day of mud and rain, so that even when they rode out of low rolling hills into a wide and fruitful valley, they could see only near-by farms and fields. South Mountain to the east, though its ramparts could not be far away, was screened by the steady downpour. Longstreet, remembering that day last fall when McClellan had come over the mountains to threaten flank and rear, wished to be ready for any such move by Hooker now, so he stayed near the rear; and long before dark began to fall, a few miles short of Greencastle, he ordered the headquarters tents pitched and halted for the night.

Rain, two days of rain, with its threat of rising water in the river behind them, gave him troubled dreams; but when he woke it was no longer raining, and the tone of the wind and the feel of the air gave cheering promise of better weather. He was at breakfast when Moxley Sorrel brought a stranger to meet him. "Lieutenant Colonel Fremantle of the Coldstream Guards," Sorrel explained. "He has letters of introduction from Secretary Seddon." Sorrel added smilingly: "He's been trying to catch us up for days."

Longstreet, eager in this clearing weather to push on, gave the Englishman only an inattentive welcome; and when breakfast was done he took the saddle. Greencastle seemed to be a modestly comfortable town, with pleasant brick houses and an air of thrifty well-being. Cer-

tainly it was set in fine farming country, through which it was contenting now to ride. He and the staff were somewhat ahead of the column
of the First Corps when they came into Chambersburg. The few citizens
on the streets watched them with masked eyes; the solid and substantial houses and business buildings, closed and shuttered, seemed to
wear sullen and forbidding aspect.

The road by which they entered the town descended to a public
square that was not a square at all but a diamond, with uneven sides.
There Longstreet pulled up his horse, and Moxley Sorrel brought one
of the civilians who had watched their arrival to answer the General's
questions.

The man was willing enough to talk. Longstreet inquired about
roads. This pike by which they had come, the man said, led on to
Harrisburg. The highway that crossed the square was the turnpike
from Pittsburgh to Baltimore. If they turned east toward Baltimore,
six miles would bring them to Fayetteville and then to a little village
named Greenwood two miles farther on, and then over the mountains
to Cashtown sixteen miles away. Gettysburg was twenty-four miles
eastward along the pike; and another fifty miles or so beyond Gettysburg lay Baltimore. Longstreet asked the man his name and his business.

"Jacob Hoke," he said. "Merchant."

"Have you seen General Lee?"

"Yes sir. He and General Hill got here yesterday afternoon. They
had a council of war right here in the Diamond. Then he rode out
the Baltimore pike, so I guess that's where you're bound."

"The less guessing you do, Mr. Hoke, and the less talking, the safer
you will be. Where is General Lee now?"

"He camped out in Messersmith's Woods. Shetter's Woods, they
used to call it, till George Messersmith bought it. It's a picnic grove."

Sorrel approached to say General Lee had left an aide here with
orders. Longstreet's corps was to proceed without a halt out the Harrisburg Turnpike and camp well beyond the town. "We turn off the
pike after we pass a Mennonite church," Sorrel explained. "There's
good water in a creek, and good camping ground."

General Pickett was already leading his division into the square.
"You had better leave guides for General McLaws and General Hood,"

Longstreet directed. "Tell them General Lee wants no halt in the town." He called Major Moses, and as the officer approached Longstreet spoke again to the civilian who had answered his questions. "Mr. Hoke, this is Major Moses, in charge of our commissary. I trust you will help him meet some of our needs."

Mr. Hoke promised to do so, and Longstreet nodded in dismissal and turned his horse to join General Pickett and rode on through the town. Beyond the Diamond and the tight-shuttered stores they came into a neighborhood of comfortable homes. A few women watched them pass, and Longstreet saw one buxom matron with a Union flag, pinned by the upper corners, spread across her ample bosom. He was not surprised when from the ranks behind him a jocose soldier shouted:

"Look out thar, ma'am! Show us Virginny men breastworks with a Yankee flag on 'em and we'll storm 'em every time!"

A shout of laughter from the ranks applauded the jest, and the woman fled indoors. Longstreet said to Pickett in a mild amusement: "General, that sounds like your red-headed man again."

"That's Wheatley, yes," General Pickett agreed. "But you can't blame the men for answering sauce with sauce."

Longstreet smiled in his beard. "Sauce for the goose, sauce for the gander, eh?"

A little beyond, as the street ascended at an easy grade toward the outskirts of town, a pretty girl standing under a cherry tree beside the fence that enclosed a well-tended lawn called: "Won't you shoot off the bands a little, please, sirs?" General Pickett doffed his hat and bowed low and passed an order along to the first band in the column. The band began to play and Pickett reined his horse toward where the girl stood and pulled down a branch of the cherry tree and plucked a handful of the ripe fruit and sat a moment in laughing talk with her, eating the cherries, before he put his horse to a canter to overtake them.

The road that led them out of town had climbed so gradually that Longstreet was surprised, when the last houses had been left behind, to find himself upon a crest with a wide outlook. To the east, beyond rich rolling farmlands, rose South Mountain like a wall; to the northwest at some distance he saw another conspicuous height of land.

When the road dipped abruptly into a valley he pulled up his horse. The creek which had carved that valley meandered toward him from the east, its course easily traced by the willows and the thickets along its banks, and crossed the road ahead and then swung southward; the hill on that side dropped off more sharply.

While the General's eye swept this suddenly unfolded panorama, Pickett's men filed off the road to bivouac along the creek. Longstreet chose a pleasant clump of trees where his own headquarters tents would be pitched. Then he asked Major Currain to find someone to show them the way to General Lee's headquarters; and Trav brought the farmer on whose land Pickett's division was making camp.

"This is Mr. Long, General," he explained. "He's concerned about the damage we may do to his standing crops."

The farmer seemed resigned to loss. "Guess't can't be helped," he said. "If you'll keep your men away from my barns and my family, I won't complain." He went with them to point out a byway that would take them across to the Baltimore pike. "You hit the pike and turn back towards town and you'll see General Lee's tents."

The ride proved longer than Longstreet had expected, a fair three miles. When they arrived, General Lee was dictating an order; and Longstreet waited till he was done, then made his report.

"Pickett's division is going into camp, General. I left guides to lead McLaws and Hood to the bivouac, and ordered no halt in the town."

Lee nodded approval. "Keep your men in their camps, General. No one is to go into Chambersburg except on business. We must give the citizens no cause to complain of us. See to it that your men behave themselves as soldiers should. We will stay here till tomorrow, possibly longer."

Longstreet wished to ask whether there was news from Stuart; but Lee seemed abstracted, so he refrained. He rode back to his own headquarters, scanning this Pennsylvania countryside. The small farms appeared to be fruitful and prosperous, but there were none of those handsome houses and vast estates which were a part of the Southern scene. He reflected that where everyone shared a general prosperity, classes must tend to disappear; but would not that put an end to aspiration, to ambition? Was not a caste system the mark of a healthy society? Certainly every Southerner believed so.

Or at least every Southern planter believed so, every Southerner of family and cultivation. It was possible that the poor man or the yeoman farmer or the mechanic might disagree. Longstreet shook his head. No matter. His business was not to reform society. His business was war.

At headquarters Major Moses was waiting Longstreet's return. "Well, General," the Major reported, "your Mr. Hoke is a spendthrift with words. He could talk the legs off a stove!"

Longstreet smiled. "You met your match?" The Commissary had a lively tongue.

"In more ways than one, yes sir. To hear Mr. Hoke, there's hardly a dry crust of bread left in Chambersburg." And the Major explained: "The local people began to move off toward Harrisburg a week ago Monday; took their wagons, horses, cattle, carriages, everything they could carry or transport. Some of Milroy's fugitives from Winchester came through that day, and our cavalry got here the day after."

"Had we any trouble with the civilians?"

"No sir." Moses laughed. "One of our troopers fell off his horse and the jar set off his carbine. He thought the shot had come from a house, and went raging up to bang on the door. The man who lived there, a man named Brand, put on his wife's clothes and ran off and hid to save his neck. After that, General Jenkins required all arms to be surrendered."

"When did General Ewell get here?"

"Tuesday. But by that time the Chambersburg people had cleaned out the freight warehouse full of government stores; bacon, bread, beans, flour, everything. Damn their eyes! We could have used those stores. Rodes's division came in Wednesday morning. Mr. Hoke says over ten thousand men passed through here that day."

"I suppose Mr. Hoke sent the news to Harrisburg."

"He denies it, but of course someone did." And Moses added: "General Ewell was travelling in his carriage. He put up at the Franklin Hotel, raised a flag over the court house, seized all the liquor in town, and requisitioned clothing and saddles and bridles and feed, and as much bread and molasses and salt and flour as they could supply. He paid for everything, of course, though the people here didn't think much of our money. But some good trader bought up all he could get at five cents on the dollar and then sold it for twenty-five cents to the local tanner; and the tanner used it to buy the hides of the beef cattle that Ewell's corps slaughtered."

Longstreet smiled. "You'll get no change out of these Dutchmen, Major. They're pretty sharp." He asked: "When did General Ewell leave?"

"Yesterday. He went toward Harrisburg, but General Early took the Baltimore pike."

"No resistance?"

"Nothing but casual skirmishing. Mr. Hoke compliments us on the good behavior of our men. He says a man named Strite was killed by some stragglers a few miles south of town; but that was the only real violence."

Longstreet nodded. "Be sure you give no unnecessary offense in your work."

Colonel Fremantle joined them at mess that day, and Longstreet drew the Englishman into conversation. Fremantle said he had entered the Confederacy through Mexico and Texas some three months before. "I travelled from Brownsville to San Antonio in a wagon driven by a jolly gentleman named Sargent——"

"Sargent?" Longstreet echoed in surprise. "A fat fellow with a gift for mule talk?"

"Yes. Though he was outshone in the latter respect by his companion, Judge Hyde. You know Mr. Sargent?"

"Hyde too, eh? Yes, I know them both. I served for several years in that country." Longstreet smiled. "I expect your English judges are a little more careful of their dignity, Colonel."

"Yes, perhaps they are," the other agreed. "I understand that Judge Hyde is a member of your Texas parliament; but he seemed to make our mules his particular charge."

"I'll wager you heard some language from those two."

"From Mr. Sargent, at least. If he thought a mule needed discipline, he called on the Judge to administer the cudgelling; but he himself produced the language without any assistance!"

"You must have heard some words new to you?"

"Yes sir, I did." Fremantle added: "Yet I have observed that most of your cultivated gentlemen speak very much as Englishmen do."

"Well, many of them were taught by English tutors, or studied in England, or travelled there."

"But not the ladies?"

"No, most of our ladies spent their childhood in the care of negro nurses," Longstreet explained. "That has influenced their way of speaking." He asked whether Texas had been hard hit by the war.

"I think not," the Englishman told him. "Texans were sending a lot of cotton into Mexico, to be shipped to New England or to England from Mexican ports, and the trade was profitable." He smiled. "One of my compatriots had an amusing experience. He purchased some cotton in Texas and hired waggoners to haul it to the border; but drouth stopped them, no water for their animals. Then a Confederate agent seized the cotton, gave an order on the Cotton Bureau in payment, and seized the mules and wagons too, and pushed on to Brownsville. When a mule died of thirst, he impressed another from some farmer along the way, so he left a trail of dead mules behind him. He crossed the cotton by the ferry to Matamoras as Confederate government property; but my compatriot was there to meet him with a claim which the Mexicans recognized, so his cotton was transported at no cost to him." He added: "Your friend, Judge Hyde, seemed to relish the story. He says the Confederate agents down there are an arrogant and offensive lot, and he was glad to see them—as he put it—cut down to size!"

Fremantle under the General's prompting described each step of his journey through the Southern states. He had met General Magruder in Texas, and General Scurry. "An unfortunate name for a soldier," he commented. He had travelled by wagon, on horseback, by stage and rail and steamer; had been taken for a spy in Mississippi; had heard Grant's guns pounding Vicksburg.

"I found at General Johnston's headquarters," he remarked, "the opinion that rather than yield, the South would prefer to become subjects of our Queen. In fact, I heard one man say he would rather be the subject of the French Emperor or of the Emperor of Japan or of the Devil himself than return to the Union! General Johnston assured me that nine Southerners out of ten would choose to serve the Queen rather than submit to the North."

Longstreet grunted scornfully. "Joe Johnston is a fine commander; but if he said that, he's a damned fool! This is a family quarrel, Colonel; and you know what happens to any outsider who mixes in a family quarrel."

Fremantle had come by way of Chattanooga, and when the Colonel spoke of this, Longstreet said thoughtfully: "I believe this army should be there today. A victory there and a march toward Ohio would relieve Vicksburg."

"I had the impression," Fremantle remarked, "that General Bragg's soldiers at Chattanooga felt no love for him. He executes a great many deserters. One was shot in Wartrace while I was there." But Longstreet made no comment. This was a subject on which the less said the better.

When Sorrel reported that Hood and McLaws were going into bivouac along Conococheague Creek, Longstreet went again to General Lee, and they had some talk together. Lee said Ewell was at Carlisle, on the way to Harrisburg; Early's division was near York.

Longstreet ventured the question which held first place in his thoughts. "Stuart?"

General Lee did not reply; his head moved in fretful fashion. "We will rest here tomorrow," he said. He had outspread on his table the map Longstreet had seen once before, and Longstreet bent over it. His eye followed the Baltimore turnpike eastward to Gettysburg, where many roads converged.

"This town, Gettysburg, is like a magnet," he commented.

"Early was there yesterday, but he moved on this morning."

"No enemy there?"

"A few militia."

Longstreet nodded. The question about Stuart—he put it in another form. "Where is Hooker?"

Lee's head twitched, but his voice was calm. "Ten days ago he was moving slowly toward the Potomac. He has a pontoon bridge at Edward's Ferry, but if he had crossed the Potomac, Stuart would have let us know. Hooker will come by forced marches when he comes. He'll be strung out over miles of roads. We will concentrate and meet the head of his columns and roll him up like a ribbon." There was a sudden deeper note in his voice, a hoarseness and a hunger. "To strike those people hard could end the war this summer, General!"

Longstreet hesitated. Here was the danger, that Lee's high heart would plunge them into offensive battle. "We need not beat Hooker. He must beat us. We can let him break himself against us."

"He has waited too long," Lee said surely. "He has lost the campaign. Before Hooker's advance reaches Frederick, Stuart will let us know. Then we can concentrate to crush him."

Longstreet did not express his anxiety, but he rode back to his own headquarters with a troubled mind. Ewell had been in Pennsylvania since Tuesday or Wednesday, and today was Saturday; and Hooker must have known their movements long ago, must be hurrying to meet them. Even if he were laggard, Lincoln would have spurred him on. Hooker himself might have preferred to cross the mountains and strike their communications; but to do so would have been to let Lee intervene between him and Washington, and Lincoln would not risk that.

No, Hooker must be moving north. Was it possible that Lee trusted Stuart too far? His habit of reliance on his commanders and on his army made him heedless of odds. Just now his army was scattered as it had been before Sharpsburg; but to divide your forces in the face of the enemy was perilous. At Sharpsburg it had brought them to the threshold of disaster. It was true that at Second Manassas and again at Chancellorsville the maneuver had led to fine success; but some day it must prove a losing gamble. Stuart or no Stuart, Hooker was surely coming, and coming fast. To lie idle here while the enemy hosts streamed northward was a procedure full of peril.

Longstreet woke to a fine morning; and lying relaxed and half awake he remembered it was Sunday, and thought of Louisa, and wondered whether she would feel well enough to go to church today. Unless General Lee issued new orders, this would be for all of them a day of rest. He himself felt no need of rest; but he had ridden while his men marched, and their feet must be bruised and weary. Let them rest while they could.

Like many men, he was apt to be short-tempered till he had had a bite of breakfast. Major Moses, though he was an admirable commissary, began each day in such a cheerful frame of mind that Longstreet sometimes found him rather trying. This morning even from his tent he could hear the Major laughing as he told the others of the staff something about Colonel Fairfax. ". . . still asleep, with his bottle on one side and his Bible on the other," he reported. "I looked in on him, but he hadn't even had his first six drinks, much less his bath; and he was snoring like the wind." Longstreet rolled to his feet and pulled on his clothes, wishing Major Moses would at least once in a while wake with a headache that would blunt the edge of his good humor. But a cup of coffee put him in a better frame of mind.

"This sure enough coffee's a treat, Major," he said approvingly, "after all the make-believes."

"I expect to locate some more today," the other promised. "I'm going to search ever cellar and pantry in Chambersburg till I do." Colonel Fremantle, who shared his tent, would go into town with him. "The Colonel here hasn't taken his boots off since he joined us," Moses jocosely declared. "So I let him share my tent but not my bed. He's afraid the Yankees will catch him in his socks! If he's to die it will be with his boots on!"

Fremantle smiled. "These boots are still so wet I can't get them off," he said. "And if I did, I couldn't get them on again; so on they stay."

Longstreet gave Major Moses an official requisition, and the two departed. Then orders came from Lee to move Hood's division and McLaws's to a new location on the Baltimore pike toward Fayetteville; and Longstreet called Sorrel to ride with him to where these two divisions lay and gave the necessary orders. To avoid the town the men would march across the fields. The engineers must take down fences and replace them again when the last regiments and the last guns and wagons had passed through the gaps. While Sorrel put the engineers to work, Longstreet rode on to find General Pickett, whose brigades would for the present stay where they were. The other divisions were already breaking camp; the fields along the creek were a swarm of activity. As Longstreet joined Pickett, someone near-by whooped:

"Look yonder, boys! That sure looks like a mice!" Longstreet recognized the voice, and he saw Red Wheatley's flaming red hair; and as one of Hood's regiments fell in, Wheatley shouted: "Hey, boys! If you ketch up with any bluebellies, shoot 'em in the haid. Don't go bloodying up their clothes! I need me a new pair of pants!"

Their grins answered him. Such a man, with his lively laughing tongue, was worth a regiment of gloomy faces. Longstreet and Pickett found a vantage on the hilltop to watch the other divisions begin their march. A scattering of curious civilians had gathered there; and the rolling fields and meadows to the eastward were alive with masses of men and long trains of wagons. The sound of fife and drum and an occasional bugle call came up to the watchers on the hill, and now and then they heard the voice of an officer giving some routine command. One of the regiments began to sing; and others joined in the song. Longstreet caught the murmur of distant voices, but his ears were not sufficiently keen to identify the tune. He saw, off to the north, thin columns of smoke rising and shredding in the light breeze, and asked a question, and Pickett said detachments were destroying the railroad. Longstreet could picture the men cheerfully at their work, ripping up rails and ties, laying the ties in piles and the rails across them, so that when the ties burned the red hot rails would bend in the middle from their own weight and become useless strips of iron. Soldiers relished such a task. Men were like boys, delighting in an orgy of destruction.

When the two divisions were well on their way, Longstreet directed the removal of his own headquarters to the vicinity of Fayetteville, to be near their new bivouac. There at supper time Fremantle rejoined them. "But Major Moses has had no success," he reported. "He's found nothing but whiskey and sugar and molasses; but he's scratching at every door in town like a terrier at rat holes."

After supper Longstreet spent an hour with General Lee; and once while they talked he saw Lee's lips compress, as though at a twinge of pain. Longstreet asked: "Are you more comfortable, General?"

"Yes, yes. My discomfort is nothing. I should never complain. Mrs. Lee suffers so much more severely than I. She can only move on crutches now. She's gone to Hickory Hill to be with Rooney." General Lee's son had been wounded at Brandy Station. "Robert's there, and I suppose the girls are too. I hope Mrs. Lee will go to the Hot Springs when Rooney is improved."

Longstreet nodded sympathetically. "I'm concerned for Mrs. Longstreet," he remarked. "She hasn't been well since winter." And he said, half smiling: "No matter what our responsibilities in the field, we can never long forget our families." Returning to his tent a little later he thought this preoccupation with their beloved ones was a bond between them; he could measure the depth of General Lee's anxiety by his own.

Longstreet was asleep when Major Fairfax and Moxley Sorrel roused him, knocking on his tent pole. "Here's Harrison, your scout, General," Sorrel reported. "His news is so important that Fairfax and I decided you ought to hear it at once." Longstreet was instantly awake. "Harrison came to our outposts," Sorrel explained. "They didn't know him, so they sent him under guard to me." He called Harrison in, and the General said graciously:

"Well, Mr. Harrison, I'm glad to see you."

"Glad to get here," Harrison replied. "I didn't fancy travelling with that escort you gave me. Just about as soon sleep with a rattlesnake. He don't even rattle before he strikes. He'd rather knife a Yankee picket than sneak by him, any time."

Longstreet remembered that brother of Currain's with the hot flame in his eyes. "Never mind. Let's have your report."

Harrison nodded. "I went to Washington, looked around, kept my eyes open. Didn't get anything till day before yesterday. Then I found out Hooker's army was crossing the Potomac."

"Day before yesterday? Friday?"

"Yes sir. And that General Hooker——"

"How did you find out?"

"I make a business of finding out things, General."

"Where is his army now?"

"There's two corps at Frederick and another one near there and two more toward South Mountain." South Mountain? That might mean Hooker intended to cross the Blue Ridge. Longstreet's thoughts were racing. Unless Lee already knew these things, Stuart had failed; but if Lee knew, this army would not be idle here. So Lee did not know. Harrison added: "And General Hooker's been relieved by General Meade."

Longstreet's attention quickened. "Sure?"

"Yes sir. Colonel Hardie brought the order from Washington to Frederick at two o'clock this morning."

Longstreet, remembering the map, felt a sharp doubt. "Frederick? You couldn't have come all the way from Frederick today."

"Not all the way, no, General. No, I was heading for you, to report that Hooker had crossed the river. My horse went lame short of Emmitsburg, and I picked up the news from the Yankees there. They'd had a dispatch from Frederick. I found a stable someone had forgotten to lock and borrowed a good-looking horse and crossed Monterey Pass and came on through Waynesboro. I hurried, but I got here."

Longstreet grunted. The feat was barely possible; yet Harrison's news was so disturbing that he was reluctant to believe. "How did you know where to find us?"

"The Yanks at Emmitsburg knew where you were."

Longstreet nodded, accepting this. The army was in enemy country; their every move would of course be reported to the enemy. "Major Fairfax," he directed, "take this man to General Lee. Say I have found him reliable. No, wait. I'll give you a note."

Sorrel handed him a pad of paper, and he wrote: "This scout has served me well. If he is right about Meade, you've again given those people a new commander. I suppose if we move east, they must follow us." He might make that suggestion stronger; but Lee would weigh it. He folded the paper and handed it to Fairfax. "Report back to me what the General says."

Fairfax and Harrison departed, and Sorrel, always easily vocal, was eager to discuss the scout's report; but Longstreet withdrew into his own thoughts. To move east of the mountains would be a threat to Baltimore and Washington, would certainly compel Meade to meet them. Meade would be reluctant, he was not so bold as Hooker; but Lincoln had driven Burnside into disaster at Fredericksburg and Hooker into catastrophe at Chancellorsville, and he would do the same to Meade. That man Lincoln was the South's best general. From McDowell to Hooker, every Union commander in the east had been defeated as much by Lincoln's uneasiness about Washington, or by his impatience for victory, as by Lee's army.

Yes, Meade, no matter what he wished to do, would have to find them and attack. If defensive ground were well chosen they could inflict upon the Yankees another Fredericksburg; and when the enemy was broken they could strike him in his flight.

When Fairfax returned, Longstreet asked: "Well sir?"

"General Lee heard him," Fairfax reported. "Then he sent Harrison outside and asked me your opinion of the man. I said you thought well of him, and he told me to bring him back to you. That's all."

Longstreet was struck by the other's tone. "You sound tired." Fairfax was always tired on Sunday, after bibulous Saturday nights. "Go along to bed." Fairfax departed, and Longstreet called Harrison and made him repeat every detail of his report. Then a messenger from General Lee asked that Harrison be sent to him again. Longstreet put the scout this time in Sorrel's charge; he lay awake, waiting, sure that Lee would before he slept make some decision.

He was right. When Sorrel returned, he said: "General Lee has decided to concentrate on Cashtown. He's sending for Imboden, and for Robertson's cavalry to hurry and join us, and sending couriers to recall Ewell to Cashtown. Hill will move tomorrow. We'll follow next day."

Longstreet for a moment did not speak, weighing this, approving. Lee's decision to concentrate east of the mountains was sound. Here was a great victory in the making. He filled his lungs in deep content. "Good! Good!" In the prospect of present action, he felt all the tension in him ease and relax. He was never so completely master of himself as in the pitch and heat of hard contention. Somewhere on the eastern slopes of South Mountain they would find a position with a good field of fire, and wait for Meade to drive his men up to be slaughtered. Over there at Cashtown they would give Meade another Fredericksburg. "Good!" he said for the third time. Sorrel was waiting for orders, but there was no hurry. "Since we don't move tomorrow, we'll not disturb McLaws and Hood tonight. Good night." He was quickly asleep, undisturbed by dreams.

The cloudy dawn brought a frowning threat of storm, and rain presently began to fall. When Longstreet went to the commanding general he saw an extraordinary discomposure in the other's eyes. Lee dropped the tent flaps so that they could not be observed; and while they talked he paced restlessly up and down, and once he ran his fingers through his hair.

Yet his tone was calm enough. "I've just now sent off another dispatch to Ewell," he said. "He should have it by noon or soon after." He frowned at his own thoughts. "We need cavalry badly, General. It's most embarrassing. Robertson should have been here no later than yesterday, and I don't know what Imboden can be doing! What mounted strength we have is all with Ewell. We're even using artillery horses for our foraging."

Longstreet noticed that he did not speak of Stuart; yet Stuart must be foremost in Lee's mind. "We can manage," he said hearteningly. "We don't have to find Meade. He must find us. Lincoln will demand that. We need only select a good position and wait for his attack and shatter him." His own confidence was in his tones.

"Meade will make no mistakes," Lee commented. "Neither must we. If we do, he will take advantage of them."

"The mistake will be made in Washington." Longstreet was calm with confidence. This was Monday. By tomorrow night the army would be all in hand east of the mountains, with time to select a strong position there. Before the week was gone, the clash would surely come. It could have but one outcome.

"In Washington. Yes, perhaps," said Lee. "But if those people ever give a commanding general his head, he may cause us trouble."

They decided the details of the coming movement. Pickett must stay here to guard the rear till Imboden arrived. Since Robertson was not yet up, Law's brigade had better stand at New Guilford as a flank guard. Hood and McLaws would move toward Cashtown tomorrow morning, following Hill's corps when the road was clear. To be without cavalry was annoying; yet cavalry would not help them cross South Mountain, and horsemen would not be seriously needed until they came out into the plains of Pennsylvania. Surely by that time Stuart would appear.

Longstreet drew the necessary orders for his divisional commanders. Then, rather than be inactive, he called Goree and rode into Chambersburg, watching the few townspeople on the street, wondering what these stolid Germans thought of their enemy visitors. "Ewell stripped the town," he remarked. "Even Major Moses has had trouble finding anything worth a requisition."

"He unearthed some velveteen that will make good trousers," Goree told him. "He promised me a piece, at least enough to patch the seat of the pair I'm wearing."

They stopped for a moment at the Franklin Hotel, where General Ewell at first had made his headquarters. The proprietor said Ewell only stayed one night, then moved out to the grove by the Mennonite church on the Harrisburg Turnpike. Probably General Ewell found the hotel beds held too many small tenants. Every soldier in the army had become reconciled to sharing his garments and his bedding with insect pests, but at least in your own bed and your own blankets, your bedmates were your familiars.

They rode idly through the town; but the streets were almost empty, civilians avoided conversation, most buildings were closed. Longstreet took the pike toward where Pickett's division was in camp along the creek; he went from Pickett back to McLaws and to Hood, informing each one of the situation as it stood, and of tomorrow's plan. It was always particularly important to make sure Pickett understood his orders. He was a fighter, but that was a matter of heart, not brains; he always needed careful direction. Before they came back to headquarters, the shadows were long.

Longstreet was roused, sometime in the night, by the rumble of many wagons and guns, coming from the direction of Chambersburg and going out the Gettysburg pike. When soon after breakfast he joined the commanding general, the wagons were still passing; and he asked whose they were.

"They're part of Ewell's," Lee explained. "I told him unless he found good roads east of the Mountain he could send his wagons this way; so he ordered part of them back through Chambersburg."

"Then they'll be ahead of us today. We've only one road over the mountain."

"We haven't far to go," General Lee reminded him. "If we're in Cashtown tomorrow night, with the army concentrated, I will be content."

Longstreet nodded. There was time enough. Mistakes could be corrected long before Meade's army was up. When General Lee was ready they mounted, proceeding at a foot pace, overtaking and passing the lumbering wagons and the trundling guns. Colonel Fremantle rode with Major Fairfax, till Longstreet called the Englishman and introduced him to the commanding general and himself dropped back. Riding now behind the other he saw that General Lee, usually completely easy in the saddle, today was tense, as though braced against any painful twist or jolt. A pity! Lee had enough to think about without that damned rheumatism.

They passed McLaws's division and Hood's, waiting in the fields beside the road; and Longstreet directed the divisional commanders to be ready to follow Ewell's trains, and himself went on. The road crossed easy rolls of ground, dipping into hollows, rising to low heights. Short of Fayetteville another road entered this one from the north, and along the sides of that road men were sprawled at ease. General Lee paused to ask a question, and Longstreet heard the answer. This was Anderson's division of Hill's corps, and they too were waiting for the road. General Lee said they had better precede McLaws and Hood; and Longstreet, fuming a little at this new hindrance, sent Sorrel back with that order.

When they rode up the hill into Fayetteville, the flanks of South Mountain began to converge upon them. It was as though those heights formed a funnel with only one outlet, through which this army must flow. The pass they were soon to climb seemed from this point of view not particularly formidable. The folds of the hills compelled the road to a winding course; but to ascend to the divide appeared to be easy enough.

Yet the column moved so slowly that at Greenwood, a little cluster of a half a dozen houses only seven or eight miles from their starting point, General Lee called a halt. "We need go no farther today," he said. "Cashtown is just over the mountain, and Ewell can't reach there before tomorrow afternoon. We'll keep the men rested and fresh for the work ahead."

The road was still jammed, and when the tents were pitched Longstreet sent Major Currain to investigate the situation. Currain after an hour returned with a discouraging report. Not only were the wagons clogging the pike and the pass, but Johnson's division of

Ewell's corps, after retracing its way from Carlisle to Shippensburg, was coming south by a country road that skirted the base of the mountain, and they would enter the turnpike a little ahead of this bivouac. So the congestion on the single road over the mountain would for a while grow worse and worse.

Longstreet reported this to Lee, and the commanding general said regretfully: "Well, Ewell has complicated things for us, but tomorrow will clear up the situation."

Longstreet spoke in grumbling anger: "With Anderson coming in by that road behind us, and Johnson ahead, it will be tomorrow afternoon before McLaws and Hood can make a start at all."

Lee smiled affectionately. "The old War Horse scents the battle afar off. Never mind, General, your corps will be up in good time."

That evening General Hill rode back to report that Heth had pushed Pettigrew's brigade on from Cashtown toward Gettysburg and encountered enemy cavalry. Longstreet was with Lee when Hill arrived. At Hill's word, Lee shook his head.

"I find it hard to credit that!" He turned to Longstreet. "Your scout said those people were no nearer than Emmitsburg." Longstreet reminded him that Emmitsburg was only a short march away, so Meade might easily have not only cavalry but infantry in Gettysburg; but Lee was still incredulous. "I doubt it," he repeated. "He only took command Sunday. He would need a day or two, at least, to gather the reins."

Longstreet turned to the map on the table, and Hill said: "Heth met no infantry, though one of his staff thought he heard their drums."

"No infantry, certainly," Lee insisted. "Cavalry, perhaps; an outpost, a scouting squadron. But certainly not infantry."

After Hill was gone, Longstreet, studying the map, said thoughtfully: "Meade will find a concentration at Gettysburg very tempting, General. He has almost as many roads of approach as he has corps to use them. But even if he concentrates there, he must still come to us at Cashtown."

"We will see, we will see." Lee's head twitched impatiently. "We will see tomorrow. Tonight there is nothing to be done."

The day had been windy with scattered clouds, and next morning the promise of clearing weather was fulfilled. Longstreet, early awake, saw Anderson's division passing. Once Anderson was gone and Johnson had filed in from that byway ahead, then and not till then McLaws and Hood could move. He rode back to find them and explain this long delay. When he returned to headquarters, Lee was waiting for him, asked pleasantly: "Well, General?"

"My men are ready whenever the road is clear."

"I've sent word to Imboden to come on and relieve Pickett in Chambersburg today," Lee told him. "Direct Pickett to follow us as soon as Imboden is up. Imboden will guard the passes and gather what supplies he can find. I hear there are some hundreds of barrels of flour at Shippensburg, and I told him to investigate. Headquarters will be at Cashtown tonight. Imboden can park his wagons in the pass between here and Cashtown, after Pickett has moved through."

"I told my divisions to cross the pass and camp on the east side of the mountains tonight, no matter how late they had to march to get there."

"Exactly. Tell Pickett to expect Imboden today. Then you and I will ride on."

It was almost noon before they set out. As they rode, Longstreet saw the other now and then ease himself in the saddle, as though he were in pain; but the fine day, the warming sun would work a cure. They went at a walk; and though because the road was all ups and downs it was hard to be sure, Longstreet thought there was for a while more descent than climb. After a time they found themselves following a sparkling little stream which came singing to meet them, chuckling through the forest, dancing over sun-flecked shallows; and presently below the road they saw the charred ruins of a considerable group of buildings. A few skeins of smoke still rising indicated that they had been recently burned. General Lee pulled up his horse.

"An iron furnace, apparently," he commented. "Forge, rolling mill, stables." He spoke to one of his staff. "Major Taylor, find somebody to tell you how this fire happened. One of those men yonder, perhaps."

He pointed to where a little group of civilians stood watching the passing troops; and Major Taylor rode toward them to inquire, and presently returned. "General Early's men burned the furnace a few days ago," he reported.

"I forbade any unnecessary destruction of property."

"The furnace belonged to Congressman Thaddeus Stevens," the Major explained. "You know he is one of the bitterest enemies of the South." He added appeasingly: "After all, General, there's been plenty of malicious destruction in Virginia; and you remember the Federals burned Mr. Bell's furnace in Tennessee."

"We need not follow a bad example." Lee spoke sternly. Taylor fell back, and Lee said to Longstreet: "Yet I think we have done as little damage as those people could expect."

"I heard no complaints in Chambersburg," Longstreet agreed.

They pushed on, and the road and the dwindling stream still kept company as the gorge narrowed more and more; but the grade was not severe. A mile beyond the furnace, Colonel Fremantle brought his horse beside Longstreet's.

"A compliment for you, General," he said. "The soldiers we're passing want to know who you are; and when they hear your name they watch you out of sight."

Longstreet was pleased. "They're Ewell's men," he explained. "My own men know me." Then he saw General Lee, a little ahead, pull up his horse, and Longstreet paused at his side.

"Do you hear that, General?" Lee asked.

Longstreet listened, shook his head. "My hearing is somewhat impaired."

"I hear guns." Lee made an exasperated gesture. "What does it mean?"

"Powell Hill must have struck the enemy."

"I warned him not to involve us." Lee fell silent, listening. Just ahead of where they stood, the road crossed the stream; and the men wading through the shallows or leaping across the narrow trickle at a stride, made some noise. Longstreet called to them to halt and be still. Lee said thoughtfully: "If that's just skirmishing, it's of no consequence; but if those people are by any possible chance here in front of us, we must fight them. I'll ride on and see for myself."

"I'll wait to make sure of the situation behind us, let my men understand that they may be needed."

"Join me when you can," Lee directed; and he pushed on. Longstreet summoned Moxley Sorrel.

"You and Major Currain go back," he directed. "Tell McLaws and Hood to waste no time. As soon as McLaws is moving, send Major Currain to report to me; and you go on to General Hood and ask him to push his men."

Sorrel wheeled his horse, calling Major Currain's name, and Longstreet went slowly on; but he paused often, anxious for word that his divisions were in motion. Once he pulled up his horse to let some guns pass. They were three-inch rifles, and he spoke to one of the men.

"That looks like a Yankee gun." The man looked up, and Longstreet exclaimed in recognition: "Dewain!"

Brett laughed in quick pleasure. "General! Yes sir, this is one of the guns we captured at Winchester." And he added: "Here's something curious. This piece was taken from Company D, First Virginia Artillery. That's a Western Virginia company; but we're Company D of the real First Virginia!"

Longstreet chuckled. "Most of our guns were furnished by the Yankees. If they didn't supply us, I don't know how we'd manage. You're in Ewell's corps, aren't you? You stole our road from us back there."

"Yes sir, we countermarched to Shippensburg day before yesterday, camped at Scotland last night, came on to Fayetteville this morning. Is Trav with you?"

"I sent him back with orders. He'll be up presently."

Brett went on to overtake his guns, and Longstreet more slowly followed him. He judged the summit was not far ahead. Once over the divide, wagons and guns would make quick time. The ascent of the pass from this side was surprisingly easy. He wondered whether the road dropped more steeply beyond.

It was an hour after General Lee left him—though he had come no more than a mile or so—before Longstreet heard the rumble of those distant guns. Fairfax and Moses had heard them long before, and the others of the staff, and had told him so; but now the distant sound made him impatient. He went on more rapidly, finding the last pitch steeper than the approach had been, and so came to the summit. He paused there, looking down and out across the level Pennsylvania farm lands, spread below him like the sea and faintly tinted blue. Battle sounds were now clear even to his ears; but he could see no smoke rising, nor any sign to mark the scene of the distant conflict. Probably it was hidden behind that spur of the mountain here near at hand which closed his view.

He saw an ambulance climbing the steep road that led up to where he stood. It must be coming from the battle yonder. The marching men descending toward Cashtown swerved to let the ambulance pass; and when the driver at the summit pulled up to breathe his horses, Longstreet moved nearer to question the hurt men.

They were of Heth's division, Hill's corps; and one of them, grinning with the pain of a shattered foot, explained what had happened.

"The General said we'd go to Gettysburg to get ourselves some shoes," he told Longstreet. "But the Yankees got there first." He looked at his bloody foot. "A hell of a lot of good a pair of shoes will do me now!"

"Was the enemy in force?"

"It felt like it to me." The man added proudly: "But we're giving them what-for!"

Longstreet turned away, and his jaw set. This was Powell Hill, forgetting his orders, plunging prematurely into battle. At such an hour as this, there should be no mistakes to complicate Lee's task! Hill's orders had been absolute: he must not precipitate an engagement. But he had done so! And Ewell, sliding his damned trains into the road back there, had clogged the turnpike for God knows how long! This army was out of hand. Lee no longer had it in control. The army commanded him, not he the army; not now!

Longstreet sat his restless horse, waiting for word from the rear, listening to the distant guns; and up the road, against the flow of marching men and rumbling wagons, came an increasing stream of wounded. Hill had found hard contention, that was clear. Then Currain appeared, on that great black stallion of his, breasting the last pitch at a smart trot, and Longstreet swung to meet him.

Trav reported that McLaws was on the road. "The turnpike was not clear for him till four o'clock. We told him to keep well closed up."

That was good as far as it went, but in what was to come every man would be needed. Law, back at New Guilford, had better come on. Longstreet scrawled a note. "Take this to General Law," he directéd. "I'll go on, join General Lee." Then, remembering: "No, I'll have Fairfax take that dispatch. Your brother-in-law, Mr. Dewain, is not far ahead of us. You'll want a word with him. You come with me."

The descent was steep and tortuous, the road winding dizzily downward; and they had to hold their horses hard against a fall. When they overtook Brett, Trav stopped only for a moment. As he came up with Longstreet again, someone called: "Howdy, Major Currain." Longstreet saw Trav swing down from his horse to greet a man with a healed stump where his left hand should have been, but whose right arm now was wrapped in a soiled and bloody rag. Trav gripped the man's good shoulder, spoke to him warmly; and Longstreet asked: "Who's this, Major?"

"Bob Grimm, General," Trav explained. "An old neighbor of mine in Martinston. He lost one hand at Williamsburg, but he volunteered again."

"I could shoot as straight with one hand as with two," Grimm said calmly. "But I dunno as I'd be much good with none at all."

Longstreet looked at the wounded arm. The bones were certainly broken; the arm would have to go. "We hate to lose men like you, Grimm. What command?"

"Eleventh North Carolina, sir. Pettigrew's brigade, Heth's division."

"You found the bluebellies?"

"Yes sir. Our brigade went to Gettysburg yesterday, but the Yanks were there, so we drew back four-five miles and camped; but today the whole division went on. The Yanks were on some high ground this side of town. We piled into 'em, but they gave us some trouble, sir. Colonel Leventhorpe was hurt, and I think they nabbed him; and I saw Major Ross killed."

Longstreet's teeth gritted. Damn Hill and his headlong folly! Trav asked: "Any Martinston men with you, Bob?"

"Yes sir, Ed Blandy, Lonn Tyler, Tom Shadd. They——"

But Longstreet, in a fierce impatience, wheeled his horse. "Come along, Currain." He spurred away.

They had paused in a deep gorge cut by a trickling little stream; but as they went on, the horses labored up a steep and rocky climb to another crest, then settled back on their haunches and cautiously began the last precipitous descent. When they came to more level ground, the mountain behind them, Longstreet loosed the reins, lifting his mount to a gallop. That great black beast which Currain rode held to a single-foot, yet easily kept pace.

They passed half a dozen houses, and Longstreet wondered whether this inconsiderable hamlet was Cashtown; but he did not pause to inquire. The road, now almost exactly straight, led eastward across softly undulating farm lands. Ripe wheat in some of the fields had already been cradled and bound; and Longstreet's eye noted more than one position ideal for defensive battle. Place this army along one of these low ridges overlooking the smooth reaped fields; then the assaulting enemy would have no cover, the guns would have a perfect field of fire. Another Fredericksburg!

Lee could not take position here till he had extricated Hill from that contention ahead; but to discover this terrain so suited to their plans was reassuring. Longstreet checked Hero to a trot. The heat, even thus late in the day, was oppressive; and certainly there was no need for haste, no necessity to kill their horses. No matter how the battle went today, he could not help till his First Corps reached the field. But as he rode he memorized the countryside; and from each rise of ground he studied the drift of smoke and dust above the battle that was nearer all the time. Presently he saw over intervening groves and low ridges the wooded crest of what seemed to be a lofty hill, somewhat south of the smoke of the guns. Such a hill might play an important part in any battle near its base.

His attention turned from the terrain to the increasing number of wounded men filing along the road. They were almost universally pale beneath the sweaty grime that covered their faces, nursing a hurt arm, or limping and faltering, or with heads swathed in a soiled rag of bandage, or with open wounds in cheeks and jaws where dust had dulled the raw red of torn flesh. Some, finding themselves too weak to walk, sat by the roadside, or sprawled on the ground; and no matter what cheerful pretense they made, nor what jest they called to passing comrades, their helplessness was plain.

The wounded men wore an almost identical expression. Their eyes were unnaturally wide open, as though something pulled their eyebrows upward; their nostrils were dilated, their lips drawn away from their teeth, their teeth exposed in a grimace like a snarl, and deep lines curved from nostrils downward to frame mouth-corners. Longstreet had seen on many a battlefield that same characteristic grimace. It was as though each hurt man were listening, his mouth a little open, for some sound that would announce the onset of new agony.

These were the flesh-and-blood debris of battle, but suddenly to one side he saw material wreckage; a dismounted gun and a wrecked limber. Here, back of a cross road, batteries had been placed to play on the shallow valley ahead, where scattering single trees marked the track of a meandering little brook. Beyond the cross road and nearer the battle, a building on the right seemed to be a tavern. On the left of the pike stood two or three houses, and an orchard ran down to the stream side. Under the apple trees surgeons were at work among the wounded, and Longstreet heard a man scream, and felt his throat fill with pity. But he turned his eyes away. A soldier must ignore such sights and sounds, must never remember that he too might presently lie writhing in torment under the surgeon's probe, screaming to the rasping grate of saw on bone.

Along the gentle slope to the right of the road, scattered singly and by twos and threes all the way from the cross road down to the brook, lay lifeless bodies. Theirs was the nondescript garb which with most Confederate soldiers passed for a uniform. Longstreet's accustomed eye read the story. A Confederate line of battle, formed among some trees a little off the road, had advanced down that slope and across the brook and into tangled woods beyond. A single dead man meant that a bullet had found its mark. Where two or three lay close together, an enemy shell had torn a gap in the advancing ranks. The Confederate advance to strike the enemy had been a costly one; to that the dead could testify.

As he and Trav crossed the bridge, Longstreet discovered the first blue-clad bodies, almost hidden in bullet-riddled underbrush in the wood that fringed the brook; and up the slope beyond there were more. At one point a broken line of them extended from the road southward past a small house to another patch of woods. The Yankee flank had rested on the road; for here lay many dead, and groaning wounded had propped themselves against the fence posts and with dulled eyes watched the riders pass. They had that same expression, with wide eyes and open mouths and lips drawn upward, like men listening. He saw one, a boy with a mop of curly black hair, who had died as he sat against the fence and slumped to one side.

A little farther on he checked his horse to look more closely at traces that marked the scene of bitter battle. A Yankee regiment, or perhaps two, had crossed the road to charge what seemed to be a railroad cut, a hundred yards to the north. To do so they had had to climb two fences, one on either side of the road; and the fences were a windrow of blue uniforms. The Confederates in the railroad cut were marksmen, that was clear; for from the road to the cut scores of Yankees, dead or helplessly wounded, lay sprawled in the trampled grass. He saw beyond the railroad cut what looked like a Confederate line of battle, fronting some heavy woods; but these men were lying down, so they too were dead or disabled. A single volley from among the trees had obliterated a regiment of Southerners. Oh, this had been a bloody day.

He rode up a slight rise past a large orchard on his right and came to shallow defensive works extending right and left of the road: fence rails, logs, cut trees, the sort of works men threw up in haste. Probably the Yankees, driven from the line of the brook back yonder, had tried to rally here. Beyond the works the road dipped gently down, and a little below him a byway lined with trees led up to a grove on his right; but for a moment he paid it no attention.

For along the pike by which he and Trav had come, he saw the first houses of the town of Gettysburg.

Sometimes in early spring along a woodland stream the new opening leaves form a semi-transparent screen, destroying perspective so that the eye is unable to explore the depths beyond. Longstreet saw the town through a similarly confusing screen of dust and smoke. But that was always true where men were fighting. Battles were never seen in depth but always flat, as though they were painted on a wall. Dust was heavy and clung to the earth, while the hot smoke rose, so the screen through which now he had to look was of a tawny color at its base, a pale blue where it met the sky.

Between him and the town, and north of the town, and in the town itself there was fighting; he heard the thump of guns and bursting shells, the clatter of musketry. South of the town, low hills rose a little higher than the spot where he stood; and that nearest the town was marked by the white stones of a cemetery. Blue-clad soldiers were trickling up toward the cemetery, sometimes running, sometimes dodging and crawling, sometimes pausing to take cover and to turn their pieces on the town from which they had been driven. Small smoke puffs showed briefly when they fired; there was smoke along the crest of the slope above them, and below them smoke and dust obscured the town.

Where Longstreet stood, the sun was behind him. His shadow and the shadows of the men of his staff, pressing close around him, extended down the slope below where he had paused; and the sun added a blood-red tint to the tawny blue of the dust and smoke yonder. He looked at his watch. It was not yet five o'clock. Time enough to push those scampering Yankees out of the cemetery where they were taking refuge, to thrust them toward the lower ground south of that height, to keep them running. Never let them rally. Meade's army was coming up from the south. Roll these beaten men back into his columns as one rolls a ball into a group of tenpins. Throw the whole advance into confusion.

General Lee must be somewhere near. To the right of the road, near a building with a bell tower which might be either a church or a school, a group of officers sat their horses; and Longstreet and his staff, following that line of shallow defensive works, rode through the grove to join them. As they approached, General Lee lifted his hand in absent greeting, then fixed his eyes again upon the battle yonder. General Hill was near Lee, but he moved his horse to meet Longstreet. Longstreet saw that the other was pale, and he remembered that it was Hill who had precipitated this unwanted engagement.

"Why, General," he said in ironic sympathy, "you look badly."

"I've been sick all day."

"Well, you've opened battle," Longstreet commented. "That should cure you!" Hill knew as well as he did that to avoid battle had been Lee's insistent order.

Hill made an unhappy, defensive gesture. "General Lee assured me yesterday that the enemy was no nearer than Emmitsburg. Today

General Heth wished to go into Gettysburg and seize some shoes for his men, and since General Lee was sure no enemy was near, I saw no objection; but I warned Heth not to accept battle."

Longstreet grunted. "Well, he accepted it." Through his glasses he studied the town yonder. "You've driven them, I see," he said, more generously.

"Yes, finally. They held us at first. Rodes came in on their flank, but he got into trouble, too. Iverson's men were slaughtered. But then Gordon came up to hit their flank again, and they broke." He added honestly: "But they fought harder than I've ever seen them fight before."

General Lee, for a better view, rode south along the low ridge, past that big building with a belfry on top and past a house and across another road and out into a projecting clump of trees whence he could look east and south across the open fields. Longstreet, following him, picturing in his mind the map of the region, judged this was the Hagerstown road which they had crossed. The town was now directly east of them. South of that cemetery where the broken Yankees were rallying, the ground sloped gently downward for almost a mile before pitching steeply up to the wooded peak Longstreet had seen as he came on from Cashtown. With his memory of the map to supplement his sight, Longstreet followed the line of the Emmitsburg pike from the town southwest through the rolling levels between where they stood and that wooded hill. By the map, another road, leading to Taneytown, ran straight south from Gettysburg; and the Baltimore pike angled away southeastward. The Taneytown road must be east of that wooded peak. Meade with the rest of his army would come hurrying up those roads tonight. Unless the Yankees were driven out of that cemetery over yonder before dark, Meade would take position with the hills to anchor his flanks, and think himself well placed.

And in fact he would be well placed, on high ground and with these intervening fields and meadows neatly squared by fences to give a perfect field of fire for almost a mile in front of him. Across this well-farmed countryside, no force could move to attack him without being seen. In wooded country, or even in a land of rolling hills, a column could frequently surprise the enemy, as Jackson had surprised

Hooker's flank at Chancellorsville; but here no surprise was possible. To attack Meade, once he was in place over yonder, would be an undertaking as hopeless as Burnside's attack at Fredericksburg.

So it was vital to seize those heights south of the town tonight. Then Meade would find no natural fortress waiting to give him sanctuary, and they could crush him tomorrow. The tactical necessities of the situation clear in his mind, Longstreet went to join the commanding general.

Lee was looking toward the town. He said in a troubled tone: "General, I'm like a man with a bandage over his eyes. We seem to have blundered into the whole Federal army. I can't think what has happened to Stuart."

So Stuart, so badly needed here, was off on one of his showy rides. Longstreet held his tone even. "Is there no report from him?"

"Nothing! Not for a week past! Can he have met with some disaster?"

Hill, precipitating battle; Ewell, jamming the roads with his trains; Stuart, electing to make a skylarking raid when he should be attending to his business: these men between them had betrayed Lee into a battle he did not wish to fight. Longstreet felt a hard anger, but he spoke reassuringly. "You need not fear for Stuart, General. No doubt he saw some fine opportunity and seized it."

"I don't know what's in front of us," Lee confessed. "Prisoners say Meade's whole army is coming, and that there are at least two corps already here. Of course we've hurt them badly; and I've sent word to Ewell to seize that hill south of town at once, if practicable." That was a matter of course, the necessary move to capitalize the day's success; but the way to carry a position was to carry it, not waste time wondering whether you could. "If practicable." Had not Lee used those same words in his orders to Stuart? And where was Stuart? Lee added, thinking aloud: "I hadn't intended battle here, so far from base; but we can't forage with those people right in front of us, and we can't retreat without discouraging the men. They've tasted success. Their blood is up. We must fight!"

This was the hour which Longstreet a month ago in Virginia had foreseen; the hour when in the presence of the enemy General Lee's valorous heart would urge him into a battle that should not be fought.

He spoke as calmly as though he and General Lee were still at Hamilton's Crossing, planning this campaign. "If Ewell seizes the cemetery, Meade will have no defensible position over yonder. But even if Ewell does not consolidate his gains tonight, the position is a trap for Meade. With his flanks strong, he will think himself secure; but if we move around his left between him and Washington, then he must come and attack us on ground of our choice."

Lee made an impatient gesture. "If he's there tomorrow I will attack him." General Hill joined them, and Lee repeated: "If Ewell doesn't move them tonight, we'll hit them as early as practicable tomorrow."

In Virginia a month ago Longstreet had thought Lee completely agreed that their tactics should be to provoke attack, not to deliver it. "If he's there tomorrow it will be because he wants us to attack him," he protested.

General Lee shook his head, watching toward the town, waiting for the clangor of Ewell's move. Except for that negative gesture he did not reply. Major Taylor returned with word that Ewell's orders to attack had been delivered; but time passed and still Ewell did not strike. Moxley Sorrel came on a panting horse to report that Hood had begun his march.

"I waited to see him start," he said. "He's closing up on McLaws."

"They'll be needed here tomorrow," Longstreet told him. "Hill and Ewell have broken the enemy, but that's only a beginning. Send circular orders to all column commanders to come on as fast as they can without exhausting their men."

Sorrel dismounted to draft these orders, and Longstreet rejoined Lee still hopefully waiting for Ewell to attack the hill above the town. Ewell had had his orders now for fully half an hour. By all the Gods of battle, why did he not move? A messenger reported an enemy force near Fairfield, a few miles to their right rear; and Lee directed Hill to send General Anderson to guard that quarter. Carriers came and went, and the sun slipped down the sky. Scattered musketry rattled along the borders of the town where sharpshooters were making steady practice; but Ewell sent no men driving up the hill against the beaten enemy.

A rider brought Lee a dispatch, and the commanding general read it and uttered an exclamation of relief. "At last!" He spoke to Long-street. "Here's word from Stuart," he said. "He's at Carlisle." And to the courier: "Go tell him to make haste. We will need him here tomorrow."

The man galloped away, and Longstreet saw again that nervous twitching movement of neck and head which testified to General Lee's smothered anger. Well, he was rightly angry! Stuart had gone rampaging off none knew where and left them to blunder blindly into this battle; and Hill had against orders permitted Heth to precipitate the fight; and now Ewell ignored Lee's orders to seize that hill over there and crown today's success. Yes, Lee had reason to be angry!

The precious moments dragged and dragged away. The group of officers sat like statues, their still hopeful eyes fixed on the town, their ears tuned to catch the first murmur of rising battle when Ewell advanced. Their horses with tossing heads won enough slack to reach down for a mouthful of grass. At an occasional sprinkle of shots or the solitary thud of a single gun they lifted their heads, their ears pricked, they were for an instant as attentive as the men. But each time they returned to their grazing, knowing as well as their masters that this casual and spasmodic firing was not battle.

Longstreet saw sunset shadows reach from the wood behind them across the tilled lands toward the town. The town was still in sun-light, but the shadows touched the houses, moved up their sides, flowed over the rooftops. A church spire like a golden needle held the sun for an instant; then it too was drowned by the rising flood of coming night. Ewell had not moved.

General Lee at last turned his horse. "It is too late," he said re-signedly. "I must go to Ewell, find out why he did not strike." He rode back across the Hagerstown road and past the school building and on to where beside the Chambersburg pike his headquarters tents were pitched. Longstreet and the others went with him, and Long-street swore under his breath in steady rage. As they reached the turn-pike, Johnson's division, coming from Chambersburg, filed off into the fields north of the road. "Perhaps Ewell was waiting for Johnson," Lee reflected, watching the men pass. "Well, he has waited too long. It will be dark before Johnson is up."

With two or three of his staff, he rode toward the town, and Long. street's eye followed him till in the deepening dusk Lee's tall form was lost to view. There were hundreds of dead men and hurt men, wreckage of today's battle, scattered across the meadows; and those whose business this was moved among the wounded men, deciding which ones must be left to die, which must face the ordeal of the knife and saw. Sometimes when clumsy hands touched a sufferer, his scream of pain sounded thinly through the night; and as darkness hushed the last firing, beneath the low hum and tramp and rumble of turning wheels and marching men, there began to sound a droning, moaning undertone made up of faint cries for water, and sobs of pain. Here and there lanterns gleamed like fireflies, moving to and fro.

Longstreet waited till full dark meant the day's work was surely done. When he turned to ride back toward Cashtown, Dr. Cullen, one of the surgeons on his staff, joined him and said triumphantly that the day had given them a fine success.

Longstreet grunted. "I'd rather not have fought at all than fail to do what more we had a chance to do." Dr. Cullen fell back, and Longstreet rode alone.

His thoughts were heavy. They could not retreat. Lee was right. To countermarch this army back to Cashtown or to Chambersburg would be as hurtful as defeat. The men would yield to discouragement, the North would take heart. But surely Lee would not attack Meade in that strong position yonder. No army, outnumbered as they would be tomorrow, could successfully assault the line Meade would draw tonight: masses of infantry in every wood and behind every fence and wall, guns posted on the high ground at the cemetery and on the hills to the south to throw a cross fire through the ranks of the attackers.

But Lee need not attack! The most promising maneuvre was to move to cut Meade's lines of supply, just as Jackson had cut Pope's last summer at Manassas. Then Meade must come to them, as Pope had come to Jackson. Then Meade must make his battle where they chose. Lee when he said a while ago he would attack tomorrow had spoken in heat and anger. After a night of quiet thought he would see more clearly.

Longstreet, with Sorrel and Manning and Currain and Goree and the others riding quietly behind him, returned along the Cashtown road. It was almost ten o'clock before they met McLaws, leading his division. He and Longstreet and the others drew off the road to let the soldiers pass, and Longstreet said approvingly:

"You've wasted no time, General."

"No, sir. We've done a dozen miles over the pass in less than six hours."

"Will your men be ready for work tomorrow?"

"Anything you ask of them, General."

"There's a big creek a little ahead of you. You'll find good camping ground just beyond. Move your men before day, General. You'll have about three miles more to do in the morning."

McLaws assented and went on, and Fairfax reported that the headquarters tents were pitched not far ahead. Before they reached the spot, Longstreet met General Barksdale with his brigade; and the Mississippian drew up to speak to him.

"I've a letter from home, General. I was down there in January, you know; spent a day or two in Macon, met your kinfolks."

"Ah. What's the Macon news?"

Barksdale laughed. "Well, Mr. Ferris is still apologizing for defending Beast Butler."

"What was that? I seldom hear from my sisters."

"Oh, he wrote an editorial in the *Beacon* about what he called the 'simulated' indignation against Butler. He said he had no sympathy with ladies who so far forgot their modesty as to insult strangers in the streets of their city. He meant well, but you never know what people will read into what you write. As an editor I can sympathize with him." Barksdale had for years edited the Columbus *Democrat*. "Poor Ferris has been explaining ever since." And he added: "Noxubee County's mighty proud of you, General. They expect great things from the First Corps in this campaign."

"There's a Macon youngster in the Ninth Alabama," Longstreet remarked. "A sharpshooter, Peter Minor, just a boy. He made himself known to me in Chambersburg. We're all a long way from home, General."

"General Semmes, too," Barksdale reminded him. "His home's just

across the Tombigbee from Columbus. But we're here for good reason, General." Though he and Longstreet were the same age, Barksdale's hair was white; but his eye held a proud youthful fire. He had
studied law in Columbus, not far from Macon, and settled there; and
he went to Congress and served till war broke out. He was a violent
pro-slavery man; for in Mississippi everyone grew cotton, and unless
you owned slaves you were nobody. Barksdale, as Colonel of the
Thirteenth Mississippi, had done well at First Manassas; at Malvern
Hill last year he had won General Lee's commendation by seizing the
regimental colors and leading a desperate assault under heavy fire.
His promotion to brigadier came soon afterward; he was a proved
man.

"For good reason, yes," Longstreet agreed. "Give your men what
rest you can, General. They'll have work to do."

Barksdale rode on and Longstreet continued to where his tents were
pitched. McLaws was up; Hood would be here in due season. There
was no more he could do tonight. At supper he paid little attention to
the lively talk around him. These men had no misgivings; tomorrow's
battle was in their minds already won. Tom Goree, that Texan whom
Longstreet had met on his way to Richmond two years ago and whom
he had kept since then by his side, was jubilant over today's success;
but little Peyton Manning suggested that the initial victory was rather
the result of good fortune than of good management.

"I'll take the luck," Goree retorted. "If God has decided to come
down and take a proper view of the situation, we'll win the war
tomorrow."

The discussion ran on till someone asked Major Currain's opinion.
Longstreet listened for the answer.

"Well," Currain said, "I asked a man in Chambersburg, a minister,
Mr. Schenck, how long the war would last. He said it would last as
long as we kept on fighting, ten years, or twenty. He said that even
in Chambersburg there were plenty of able-bodied young men not
yet in the Union army. He said the North would raise a new army to
replace any army we destroyed. He said the North can raise bigger
armies than we can, feed them better, give them better guns." He
paused, but no one spoke, and he added: "Mr. Schenck had travelled
in the South, and he said he hadn't seen in the South any countryside

as generally prosperous as this. He said all we had to do was look around us here to see how much stronger the North was than we are."

There was an almost resentful silence, but Longstreet thought what that minister said was true. In the South there were great plantations, and there were little two-room mountain cabins and the miserable hovels of the poor whites; but there were nowhere such fields and barns and well-kept and comfortable small farms as these he had seen in Pennsylvania. Every man here knew this. Their silence was an admission. Then Colonel Manning broke that silence with a laugh.

"It doesn't matter how many men they have; it's the kind of men they are. As for their guns, the more they have, the more we'll take away from them."

Longstreet thought contempt for the enemy was the great weakness of the Southerner, just as his confidence in himself was his great strength. Colonel Fremantle asked him a question. "Are you as confident as these gentlemen, General?"

He was not, but he would not by admitting his own doubts plant doubt in the minds of these men who followed him. Besides, though Ewell had missed his chance tonight, if at dawn he stormed that hill south of town, these optimists might be proved right. Ewell was a fighter when the mood was on him, and big things might be done tomorrow.

"To be sure, to be sure," he said easily. He went to his tent and lay down, though not at once to sleep. Better not think now of the morrow, for at night every shadow was black. He put anxieties aside, forcing his thoughts to General Barksdale and to that little town in Mississippi where his sisters and his brother lived. Louisa had enjoyed her stay there two years ago. When the fighting was done, he must go back to see them all again; perhaps he could buy some land and settle there and turn planter.

He lay long awake, hearing on the road near his tent the steady march of weary men. The bright moon was a blessing, for stumbling through dark night was hard work. They were McLaws's men, or perhaps Hoods's. Well, they were here, and by noon tomorrow Law might be here; and Pickett tomorrow afternoon. Once he had the First Corps in hand, he could face anything.

Longstreet woke to the stir of men near his tent, and the stroke of axes and the crackle of fires. When he stepped out into the moonlight it was a little after three o'clock. Probably Law was just about starting from New Guilford.

Moxley Sorrel spoke to him. "Hood is up, General. Law should be here this afternoon."

"Perhaps by noon," Longstreet suggested. New Guilford must be twenty miles away over the Mountain, and any pace better than two miles an hour for a long march was fast work; but Law would come fast. "He will push hard. Where is Hood?"

"In bivouac this side of the creek. He said he would move at three o'clock."

"Three o'clock? It's three o'clock now. He must be filling the road. I told McLaws to march before day. Direct him to let Hood pass, then follow." And he asked: "Are those our wagons on the road here now?"

"No, General; they're the last of Ewell's. They went into park at dusk to rest the horses and give our divisions the road. Our trains are coming behind them."

Longstreet remembered all those roads that converged on Gettysburg, thinking that on each road men and wagons, their own and the enemy's, were hurrying to the town where presently they would collide. An army was a sprawling thing. His First Corps counted twenty thousand men, eighty guns, well over a thousand wagons. You might sit in one spot for a day and a half or two days and watch the First Corps pass, with its tramping feet of men and its thudding hoof beats of the horses, and its bands and its bright flags flying. There were many flags, since each regiment and each brigade had its own; for the South was a Confederacy of sovereign states which fought as allies.

Herein lay a difference between this army and Meade's. The Northerners fought under one flag, the Southerners under many. Was that perhaps a source of weakness? Could a confederacy ever be so closely knit as a union? He brushed aside the doubt. That was a matter for the politicians. He was a soldier.

It was still dark when they breakfasted, but moon and stars were bright; and as they rode toward Gettysburg, day broke fast ahead of them. They overtook and passed regiments of McLaws's division already on the march; and the sun rose, glaring in their eyes, red and angry. A hot day dawning, and hot work to be done.

At a little after five in the morning, Longstreet topped the rising ground and saw again the town beyond and turned aside to the squat little house with a broken paling around the yard where Lee had established his headquarters. The tents were pitched among trees beside the house. General Lee greeted him.

"Ah, General, good morning. Where are your men?"

"Close behind me."

"Good! Those people are still on the hill above the town." Lee looked that way. "But I don't see any force on the ridge south of the cemetery. I've asked Captain Johnston to inspect the ground on our right, and General Pendleton has gone that way, too. I sent Major Venable to Ewell to ask whether he can seize the cemetery this morning." He added: "Ewell and Early and Rodes were all against an attack there last night, but their views may have changed. I told Major Venable to make it clear that the question is whether to move all our forces around to our right."

Then General Lee was still considering a move around Meade's flank to maneuver him out of that natural fortress yonder. Thinking he read the other's mind, Longstreet nodded. "Exactly. And even if we can't see them, Meade must have poured men into the position south of the cemetery all night long. They may be behind the swell of ground out of our sight. The light's still poor, and the sun's against us."

Lee said regretfully: "We're still in doubt as to the force over there, but Ewell captured a dispatch that gave us some information. General Sykes's Fifth Corps camped four miles east of Gettysburg last night, and apparently the Twelfth Corps is already on the ground. I wish Stuart were here to tell us what we have to face."

"Meade had at least two corps here yesterday?" Lee had said so, last evening.

"Three, or so our prisoners tell us. The Third Corps came on the field at sunset."

"And now the Fifth and the Twelfth. That's five Corps you can be sure of. Probably more. Meade is a careful man. After what Ewell and

Hill did to him yesterday, he would not be over there now unless he were in force."

"I hope Ewell can hit them this morning."

"If he doesn't see the way clear," Longstreet said surely, "we need only maneuver to the right to call Meade to ground of our own choosing." He did not elaborate the point. Before their northward march began, now almost a month ago, he had urged that in any engagement their role should be defensive; and Lee's silence then had seemed consent, as it did now. Yesterday the commanding general had said he would attack today, but clearly the night had brought wisdom. Lee was himself again, the game was in their hands.

They mounted and rode to that jut of trees from which they had watched the dying battle yesterday, and Lee levelled his glasses on the town and the cemetery and the low ridge to the south of it. Longstreet joined him in that long scrutiny. As the sun in their faces burned the dew away, a faint dawn mist thinned across the fields. The morning was a breathless hush, the silence a pressure and a burden; yet the air itself seemed to beat like a pulse, as though it matched the rhythmic respirations of the thousands of men gathered in this neatly ordered countryside, as though the world were a pig's bladder such as children inflate to use as toys, and which filled and emptied as these hosts of men inhaled and exhaled. Longstreet was as conscious of these thousands all around him as though they were massed here under his eyes; his pulse kept time to theirs, he breathed when they breathed.

He and General Lee looked past a house and across fields on some of which the wheat had already been cut to a rise of ground a mile away. The fields in their front bore no wounds of war. Yesterday's fighting had been west and north of the town and in its streets, not here. A few single trees dotted the fields between them and the town, and a house and a small orchard lay off to their right, and other houses and other orchards along the Emmitsburg road beyond. Longstreet saw a few cows grazing; but in these open pastures cows need wear no bells, so there was not even that small sound. A hundred and fifty or two hundred thousand men in battle harness waited here within a two- or three-mile radius; but except that he could see a few batteries in position, and a few blue uniforms over yonder, the scene was as peaceful as a Sunday morning.

General Hill joined them, and General Heth, his head bandaged because of a wound received the day before. Then Hood rode through the trees to report to Longstreet. "My men are moving into the fields behind us here," he said. "McLaws is on our heels."

Longstreet nodded. "Good!" He heard Moxley Sorrel call to someone, and turned and saw Colonel Fremantle and a fat little man in soiled white pants and a short jacket, perched in a tree for a better view. Sorrel advised Colonel Fremantle to come down; but the Englishman said he was comfortable where he was. Longstreet asked Sorrel about the other man.

"That's Captain Scheibert," Sorrel explained. "He's the Prussian young Dewain told us about, the one who took an impression of a wet painting on his pants."

Longstreet smiled faintly. He turned his horse, riding back along the Hagerstown road and across the fields behind the wood till he saw Hood's men filing off the Chambersburg pike. Yesterday the Yankees had been driven back up that slope along which the men now were marching; and Longstreet saw a few unburied dead, each the focus for a swarm of flies buzzing in the sun. The leaders of the advancing column sometimes swerved to avoid them. He sought McLaws and bade him place his men beyond Hood's, conveniently ready to move.

When Longstreet returned to the commanding general, Lee was sitting alone on a log at the edge of the trees, and Longstreet dismounted and joined him. Lee said, his controlled tones suggesting his impatience: "Venable has not yet returned. Nor Captain Johnston. Nor General Pendleton."

"McLaws is coming up," Longstreet told him. "I think Law will be here by noon, Pickett this afternoon."

Lee made no comment. Longstreet's eyes swept the gently undulating levels which lay between him and the enemy position; but there was nothing to see, nothing to hear except the occasional bark of a skirmisher's rifle. Major Currain requested permission to go and exchange a word with Brett Dewain, and Longstreet gave it. Hood approached, and sat down on the log, and selected a dead stick and produced his knife and began to whittle aimlessly. A man whittled as a woman knitted, to ease taut nerves. Longstreet too opened his knife, tried it on his thumb, picked up a twig from the ground and sharpened it to a needle point with careful strokes of the keen blade. It was not yet eight o'clock, but already the sun was baking hot, the shade was grateful.

Lee rose and walked away, and Hood said quietly: "General, he's going to attack. He told General Hill if we don't whip Meade he'll whip us."

"Attack?" Longstreet spoke in gruff incredulity. "If we'd wanted to attack, we could have done that in Virginia, without marching God knows how many hundred miles!"

Hood did not reply, and Longstreet watched Lee, a little way off, his coat buttoned to his chin despite the increasing heat, his hands clasped behind him, walking to and fro with bowed head. Sorrel came up beside them and asked in a sprightly tone: "Well, General, how does it look?"

Longstreet grunted, not answering. Sorrel was as talkative as a woman, but this was no time for talk. If Hood was right, Lee's blood was up! That fighting heart, that instinct to plunge headlong at the enemy had him in command.

But if Lee ordered an attack, a thousand men would die today in these fields beyond which Meade was waiting! Yes and die vainly! Longstreet lifted his glasses to study the ground yonder. The cemetery was somewhat higher than the spot where he sat. He watched Yankee skirmishers come toward the Emmitsburg road and lie down in the wheat. Meade was organizing his position to crush the assault he expected, and General Lee could see those movements over there plainly enough. Surely Hood was wrong!

Longstreet heard a step and lowered his glasses and saw General Lee approaching. He rose, and as they met, Lee said firmly: "General, if Ewell meant to attack, Major Venable would have come to tell us; so presumably General Ewell sees no good prospect. We must strike them from this side." Before Longstreet could protest, he added: "I will show you the position. We can see better if we ride a little to the south."

He turned his horse and Longstreet followed, gnawing at his mustache. When they mounted, so did the others. They rode southward through an orchard, the ground descending a little and then rising to another orchard which projected from the border of the woods almost exactly west of the cemetery. Lee paused and Longstreet drew up beside him and they dismounted.

Lee pointed south across the cultivated fields. "See down there where the Emmitsburg road crosses that knoll?" Longstreet's eye turned that way, and Lee explained: "I mean that ground twenty or thirty feet higher than we are here. Look between the two houses and beyond." There was a house in an orchard a quarter-mile southeast, and another a little west of south, twice or thrice as far away. They framed between them fields and meadows that sloped gently upward to where on the higher ground fences marked the road. "If we had some guns on that knoll we could hurt those people over there," Lee said. "You had better prepare to seize it."

Longstreet's cheeks were stiff with angry blood. "You wish to attack?"

"Yes. If we don't hit them, they will hit us." So Hood was right! "Their left is anchored on that rise, in the trees around the house you can just see past the right side of the nearer orchard. Move your men to the right till you're beyond their flank; then throw your right across the road and strike up the road toward the town. If you give us that knoll to place our guns, we can hammer them from both sides; you from there and General Ewell from the town. We'll crack them like a nut!"

Longstreet held his voice steady. "If you win a victory here, sir, what fruits will you gather?"

Lee smiled affectionately. "Let's get the victory first, my old War Horse! Once we shake the tree, the fruits will fall into our lap."

Longstreet tried to speak; but he was choking at once with the certainty that to attack was wrong and with humiliation. General Lee knew his opinion, knew he was opposed to an assault. To be even thus gently overruled had not happened to him before. The confidence in him which Lee had always shown made this rebuff the more painful.

But he reminded himself that General Lee had had trying days. To constant pain and the responsibilities of command had been added the burden of the errors of others. But for Stuart's absence, Lee would have known Meade's movements; but for Hill, there would have been no battle yesterday; but for Ewell's sluggishness last night, Meade would be today in full retreat from that natural redoubt yonder. Stuart, Hill, and Ewell had among them thrown the army into this sorry position. No wonder General Lee wore less than his usual serenity, saw less clearly than usual.

So Longstreet's resentment gave way to affectionate understanding; but his anger was to rise to full flood again. For a moment after General Lee had explained his desires, Longstreet did not speak; and Lee, with that characteristic nervous sidewise twitch of his head which was always a mark of irritation, turned toward where the other officers were gathered. Longstreet saw him, with a map spread open in his hands, give some direction to McLaws. That was a new humiliation! Any orders for McLaws should be given through the commander of the First Corps. Longstreet strode toward them.

"Place your divisions here, General," Lee was saying to McLaws, drawing a line with his finger across the map. "Can you do it without being seen by the enemy?"

The line Lee had drawn crossed the Emmitsburg road at the spot where the commanding general himself had said the enemy flank was anchored; but his own orders to Longstreet had been to move beyond that flank before crossing the road. So not only was General Lee wrong to give direct orders to McLaws; his tactics were mistaken.

"I can take a few skirmishers and reconnoiter," McLaws suggested; but Longstreet interrupted.

"General McLaws, I do not wish you to leave your division." With a blunt forefinger he drew a line on the map that General Lee still held, a line parallel with the road. "And your division should be here!" His plan was clear in his own mind; he would throw Hood across the road beyond McLaws, and place McLaws in position to strike the Yankees in front as Hood rolled up their flank.

Lee said quietly: "I wish the division placed across the road, not along it, General Longstreet. I wish you to advance up the Emmitsburg road, toward the cemetery."

There was an instant's silence, while Longstreet held his temper hard in check. Surely General Lee could trust him with the tactical handling of his men! For Lee to give a direct order to McLaws was an affront, and Longstreet's anger bade him resign on the spot and instantly; but loyal second thought reminded him that this was out of the question. There was no man Lee could put in his place; he could not desert his post in the face of the enemy.

And this was even more profoundly true if General Lee were today so far from being himself that he could thus confuse his own intent. Certainly too this was no time for disputing and discussion. Longstreet called Moxley Sorrel. "Send for Colonel Alexander," he directed. As Sorrel hurried away, Longstreet's pulses quieted. An officer rode up to General Lee with some report; and Lee explained to Longstreet: "This is Captain Johnston, General. He has been looking to our right." And to the officer: "What did you find, Captain?"

"We rode over to that low wooded hill yonder," the Captain said, and pointed. "The farmers call it Little Round Top, and the higher hill south of it is Round Top. The lower hill is all big boulders, no place for a horse unless he wants a broken leg; so we turned south and circled back."

"Did you encounter the enemy?"

"No, sir, no sign of them. We saw three or four troopers at a distance, but they didn't see us."

"Are there roads over those rocky heights?"

"No sir. They're impassable."

"Thank you, Captain." Lee turned to Longstreet. "General, those hills will guard your right as you advance up the road. Guide your left by the road."

As he spoke, Colonel Alexander rode up and dismounted, saluting them. Longstreet asked: "Where are your guns, Colonel?"

"A mile from here, beside the stream called Willoughby Run, down behind this ridge."

"Bring them up," Longstreet directed. "General Lee wishes us to throw our right beyond the enemy's flank, to wheel and attack up the Emmitsburg road and seize that high ground yonder." He pointed out to Colonel Alexander the vantage Lee had indicated. "Have your guns ready to go into action, but keep them behind the woods where they can't be seen by enemy signal stations on those wooded hills. As soon as we seize the knoll, throw your guns forward to that position. Let me know when you are ready, if you please."

When Alexander was gone, Lee said approvingly: "That was well done, General! Now I must ride over and see General Ewell." He raised his hat in friendly salutation, and departed.

When the other was gone, Longstreet saw McLaws and Hood watching him, and he knew what they were thinking, and knew they understood what he must have felt a little while ago. Because it was McLaws who had been the innocent instrument of his humiliation, Longstreet spoke harshly. "Well, General McLaws, you have your orders!"

"Very well, sir." McLaws mounted and rode away along the border of the wood. Longstreet sat down again; and Hood asked, the question suggesting his surprise at this inaction:

"Do we move at once, General?"

"Not yet. I don't want to attack without Pickett. I never like to go into battle with one boot off." Longstreet added: "General Lee is a little nervous this morning."

He regretted that word as soon as it was spoken. What he had said was true, but there were times when the truth should not be uttered. Hood knew as well as he that to try to throw Meade out of that position over there would cost heavily and profit little. When he himself spoke to Colonel Alexander a moment ago, he had seen the surprise in the artilleryman's eyes. Alexander had a quick eye for terrain; he knew that such an attack must be expensive and of doubtful issue. These two were as sure as he that Lee was wrong.

Nevertheless he should not have said what he did, and he was glad Hood made no reply. Hood was like Major Currain; he knew how to hold his tongue. He had come on to Virginia with his Texans, a young man just turned thirty, a year ago last fall; and during that first winter of the war he welded his regiment and then his brigade into a fine fighting unit.

Hood could hold his tongue, and he could get fine work out of his men; and Pickett, too, for all his perfumed ringlets and his lovesick sighing for that lady down below Petersburg, could be relied upon. Longstreet had known Pickett for twenty years: at West Point, in

Texas and New Mexico, in old Mexico, and now in this army. A little slow of understanding, so that it was always safer to give him a written than a spoken order, nevertheless he was one whom no battle task would ever daunt. That he was not only valorous but firm he had proved at San Juan when the British threatened to land forces there. He retorted that if a landing were attempted he would open fire, and the British abandoned their design. Pickett might neglect routine military duties to make his devotions to the lady of his choice; but when battle offered he was of a direct and single mind. Thus far no great military opportunity had been afforded him, but when it came he would seize it.

In his mood just now Longstreet thought that of his divisional commanders McLaws was the least effective, if for no other reason than that his health was precarious. But as his resentment of the incident of a few minutes ago began to pass, Longstreet gave McLaws more credit. Certainly the other was a gentle and a courteous man, completely unselfish in his relationship with his brother officers. Yes, and he had a fine self-possession on the field. His highest achievement thus far had been the seizure of Maryland Heights and the emplacement of cannon there, when he shared with General Jackson the success won at Harper's Ferry. His men were always well in hand. On that terrible march into Maryland last year, though for two days they had no water to drink, none straggled. At Sharpsburg McLaws did well; at Marye's Hill above Fredericksburg, his was the close direction of the defense which worked among the enemy such slaughter. Longstreet, calmer now, nodded contentedly. With three such men to handle the divisions, the First Corps could be relied upon.

The minutes drifted by. Colonel Alexander came to report that he had found a way to bring his guns into position unobserved by the enemy. "One of my men knows this ground, General," he said. "Lieutenant Wentz. He lived as a boy in a house down there on the other side of the Emmitsburg road." He pointed toward the knoll a mile or more to the southward, which they meant to seize. "You can just see the roof. There's a peach orchard all around the house. The Lieutenant's parents still live there, but he's lived in Virginia for years. You might care to question him. He's here with me."

Longstreet welcomed the opportunity. If he were to direct this attack, he should appraise at close range the tactical features of the ground: the woods, whether they were open or thickets; the fences, rail or stone; the farm houses, the swales, the marshy runs, the ravines that might give shelter to attacking troops or serve as obstacles to an advance. But he did not wish to leave this spot; for Lee would presently return, and they could then inspect the ground together. In the meantime, Colonel Alexander's man might contribute useful information. He said agreeably to the young Lieutenant: "Well, sir, Colonel Alexander tells me this was your boyhood home."

"Yes sir." Wentz, though he was no boy but a man of thirty or so, was flushed and excited, and Longstreet led him into talk that would put him at his ease.

"But you preferred Virginia?"

"Why, I was apprenticed to Mr. Ziegler in Gettysburg, making carriages," the Lieutenant explained. "But about ten years ago I decided to set up for myself and I moved to Martinsburg."

"And prospered, I'm sure," Longstreet smiled. "From carriage making to service in the artillery was a natural step. Our gun carriages are just a little stouter than your sort, that's all."

"Yes sir," Wentz assented. "I was in the Martinsburg Blues, and when the war began most of us went into the army."

Longstreet nodded and came to questions. He pointed across the rolling fields. "How deep is the valley behind that rise over there?"

"Fairly deep, sir. The ground breaks off pretty sharply toward Rock Creek. Folks around here call that Cemetery Ridge, over there. That's Evergreen Cemetery you see. It's not much of a ridge except at the cemetery, and when it gets to the Round Tops."

"You mean those rocky hills?"

"Yes sir. And this along here is Seminary Ridge, named after the seminary up by the Chambersburg road; but they call it Warfield Ridge when you get down beyond the run by Mr. Warfield's farm."

"Our maps show several roads leading up from the south."

"Yes sir. There's the Baltimore pike beyond the ridge, and the road from Taneytown comes up east of the Round Tops and along the ridge. You can see the Yankees placing guns over there along the Taneytown road. This is the Emmitsburg road right in front of us."

"Then there may be enemy troops we can't see, down behind that ridge opposite us?"

"Yes sir." Longstreet thought Meade would know how to make the most of that natural screen, shifting his troops to any threatened point unseen and secure. Lieutenant Wentz added: "I talked with Mr. Warfield this morning, General. His house is down here on a lane this side of the Emmitsburg road, not far from my father's. I wanted to ask him to tell my family to move out. He says the Yankee line hooks around through the cemetery and over Culp's Hill. You can see the top of Culp's Hill there. So their right flank is only about half a mile back from the ridge opposite you here."

Longstreet's eyes swung to the right. "Is that your father's house I can see?"

"No sir, that's Mr. Sherfy's. Father's house is almost behind Mr. Sherfy's from here." Whatever embarrassment had at first curbed the Lieutenant's tongue, he was full of talk now. "Then as you come up the road toward town there's Mr. Smith's house, and Mr. Klingel's and Mr. Rogers's. You can see them. Then the Codori place. You can't see it from here. It's behind the Bliss house and the orchard, and down behind the knoll. Codori's is the last house till you get almost to the cemetery."

Longstreet nodded dismissal, and the Lieutenant and Colonel Alexander moved away. Longstreet let his eyes drift across these fields, considering the tactical features. Some of the meadows had not been mowed, and he thought it was a pretty careless farmer who would let his hay stand this long; all the goodness was dried out of it by now. The wheat, where it was not yet reaped, and the tall meadow grasses gave good cover for skirmishers and sharpshooters between the lines.

Toward eleven o'clock, Lee came riding through the orchard; and Longstreet rose to meet him. "Ah, General," Lee exclaimed, with a little angry twitch of his head. "Still here? Are your men deployed?"

"The guns are up," Longstreet told him. "And McLaws is ready to march and so is Hood; but Pickett is not here."

Lee brushed his beard with his hand. "Ewell is firmly opposed to attack on his front," he said. "But he will make a demonstration when you attack. Anderson will extend General Hill's front here toward the right. Let McLaws take position beyond Anderson, Hood on McLaws's right. They must sweep up the road and roll up the enemy flank." He pointed. "Give me that high ground along the road there, General." His tone was kindly, but it was insistent, too. "It is time to move."

Longstreet was himself so sure that a maneuver to the right would draw Meade to battle on their own terms that he had hoped till this moment for a change of plan; but now Lee's orders permitted no question. The attack would commit them; it held great risk and no compensating prospect of great gain. But it must be made.

Well, if it were to be made, every man would be needed. "Law will surely be up within the hour, General," he suggested.

"I think you had better go to work with the force in hand."

"We will need Law," Longstreet urged. "We will need every man."

Lee spoke in reluctant consent. "Very well, your attack can wait on Law; but let McLaws and Hood move into place. Captain Johnston has found a way to bring your divisions into position without being seen by those people over there. I will let him guide McLaws, and Hood can follow."

Without waiting for a reply, Lee rode toward the right; and Longstreet mounted, but his jaw set in sullen anger. So Captain Johnston was to direct McLaws's division! Very well, he would ride with Hood! He knew himself to be as unreasonable as a sulking small boy; yet damn it, Lee was wrong! This attack was wrong! If Lee were bent on it, he himself would obey orders; but Lee need expect no more.

When he emerged from the orchard on the slopes where Hood's men were waiting, a messenger reported that Law was here. Captain Johnston had reached McLaws, for that division was already moving into the road that led toward Fairfield and Hagerstown. The road angled away from the prospective battlefield; but if General Lee wished Johnston to take them that way, that was Lee's affair. Longstreet said to Hood: "Follow McLaws, General." Hood turned to give the necessary orders, and Longstreet sat his horse, hearing behind him the murmuring voices of the men of his staff. The slopes below were alive with movement. There were wagons in park, and ambulances, and guns held in reserve, and hospital tents; and through this orderly disorder the two divisions of the First Corps marched southward to enter the road and oblique away southwesterly. Thousands of men filed across the already trampled meadows in two columns that extended at first halfway to the Chambersburg pike, that grew shorter as they came to the road and entered it. McLaws's division counted say seven thousand men, Hood's a few more; so there were fourteen or fifteen thousand men in motion here under Longstreet's eye.

They were marching to battle, and to useless battle, too; and hundreds of these men would die before the sun set tonight. Longstreet's throat ached with grief and anger and humiliation. It was Lee's province to decide, his to obey with a whole and willing heart; but he remembered something he had said to Major Currain long ago, that when he was told to do a thing he knew should not be done, his effectiveness was gone. Probably Lee knew this. Probably that was why Lee had put Captain Johnston to direct McLaws. Now Captain Johnston was leading these men miles away from their eventual destination, wearying them with needless marching. He would bring them already footsore to the battlefield! Oh, wrong, wrong, wrong!

A messenger from General Pendleton suggested that Longstreet come and see the ground over which the assault would be made. Longstreet followed the messenger, riding through the fields beside the road so that he need not hinder the marching men. The road the men took led them away southwesterly, the enemy lay to the east. Probably Captain Johnston, remembering how at Chancellorsville General Jackson took his men by a wide detour to strike Hooker's flank, dreamed of guiding a like maneuvre today; but Jackson had marched through screening forests. In this open farm land with only an occasional fringe of trees for cover, no such surprise was possible. Long before they came into position they would be seen.

Well, the plan was General Lee's, not his. He and the messenger who was his guide descended to cross a shallow stream and went on for a mile or more over rolling ground to where the road crossed a low hill. It was within minutes of noon when he joined General Pendleton. Beyond, the road the men were following dipped into the ravine of a large creek, and Longstreet saw that at the creek the head of McLaws's column was turning left along a lane that swung back southeasterly to lead directly toward Round Top, three or four miles away. He could see the lofty hill, but the column in the lane down there was fifty or sixty feet below him; the men would not be visible to any enemy watcher on that distant height, not yet.

General Pendleton pointed off to the southeast where they could look over the tops of the trees to higher ground beyond. "The Emmitsburg road is there, just beyond the woods," he said. Longstreet levelled his glasses, and General Pendleton added: "I saw enemy cavalry there this morning, and an infantry column moved up the road with their artillery and trains."

Longstreet lowered his glasses in scornful amusement. It must be two miles, perhaps more, from where they stood to the Emmitsburg road. A survey from this distance might be General Pendleton's idea of reconnaissance, but it was not his. Colonel Alexander joined them and Longstreet asked: "Where are your guns, Colonel?"

Alexander pointed toward the woods, a mile and a half away to the east. "In those trees, General. The road is just beyond."

Longstreet turned to Pendleton. "You had better go with Colonel Alexander and show him what you can," he directed; and he himself rode back along the column of marching men till he encountered General Lee. As they met, an aide reported to General Lee that the enemy was extending his left toward the Round Tops.

"Those people might have saved themselves the trouble," Lee said cheerfully. "General Longstreet will have them out of there before night."

Longstreet knew this was Lee's way of praising him, and his heart warmed. Off toward the front there was some scattered outpost fire. The small sounds came faintly to Longstreet's ears, and his blood began to stir. This was Lee's battle, not his; yet he would know how to fight it when the time came. A halt came back along the line, and in impatience at this new delay he left General Lee and rode across the fields to investigate. McLaws cantered to meet him.

"General," McLaws reported, "if we follow that lane any farther we'll come under enemy observation."

So Captain Johnston had botched his job, and all this marching had been wasted. "Well, what do you propose to do?"

"We might countermarch to that ravine"—McLaws pointed back

along the road by which they had come—"and follow it south through the woods till we can turn east without being seen."

What McLaws proposed meant that the column must retrace its steps, meant a wasted hour. That was Captain Johnston's fault, and it was General Lee's fault for putting Captain Johnston to guide the column; but time enough had been wasted! "Do so. Let General Hood take the lead," Longstreet said curtly. "Be quick, but don't exhaust your men. From now on, I'll direct the march."

McLaws rode away, and Longstreet found Hood and gave him his orders. As a consequence of Captain Johnston's blunder, fifteen thousand men must march two or three unnecessary miles in blistering heat before they went into battle; but he would see to it no more strength was wasted! When Hood's column, returning by the way they had come, at last reached the sheltering ravine, Longstreet directed them to follow the stream down through the woods. Then with Sorrel and the others of the staff he pushed ahead through grateful shade and out into the blazing sun again. They followed the shallow branch till Longstreet saw a school house on the other side, and a lane leading up the slope toward a point of trees that widened into a belt of woodland.

He waited at the waterside till Hood joined him. "Cross your men here, General," he directed. "Send scouts ahead of you to make sure those woods up there are clear. Oblique your men to the right behind the woods and move them through to the road in battle front. McLaws will come in on your left. General Hill has extended his line this way. McLaws will make contact and pivot on him, and you on McLaws. You are to cross the road and wheel toward the town, guiding your left by the road."

The movement was clear in his mind. General Hill's corps was the fence, lapping the Union right; his own divisions were the swinging gate that would throw the Union flank into disorder. Second Manassas was the model for the maneuver. There Jackson had been the wall that received the enemy attack, while he himself swung against their flank. True, there was a difference. At Second Manassas, Jackson had first cut the Union line of supply. He himself had proposed to Lee to do the same thing here, but Lee overruled him. Well, perhaps Lee was right! Certainly the position today offered great possibilities. His pulse quickened to the coming hour.

Hood's scouts went up past the school house; the head of Hood's column splashed through the shallow brook. The men were dripping with sweat. As they waded the little stream, without checking their steady pace, they scooped up water in their palms and drank. Wounded men would suffer terribly from thirst today. Any wound in any weather made a man thirsty, but in this heat thirst would be keenest torture.

Longstreet rode up along the lane to the point of trees where Hood's men, screened by the rising ground and by the woods on its crest from enemy observation, were obliquing to the right; and he found that short of the highest ground the lane forked. Hood's men were taking the right fork, which went through thick woodland and over a slight rise before dipping at an angle toward the road again. The other fork bore left to pass a house and then to turn even more to the left into another wood lot. This lane too was screened by trees. Good! The men might move into position without showing themselves.

He returned to the streamside as the head of McLaws's column, doubling on Hood's, approached the crossing. Hood's column was nearest the brook, McLaws's men on the right of Hood's; but this was awkward, since when they deployed McLaws must form on Hood's left, not on his right. McLaws might halt his column here till Hood's last brigades were past, then cross Hood's rear; but that would leave a gap on Hood's left for half an hour or more before McLaws reached his proper position, and gaps were dangerous. The alternative was to halt Hood, and let McLaws pass through him here. Then their columns, proceeding side by side to where the lane forked, and opening like jaws to right and left, would come into battle front almost simultaneously.

He sent Sorrel to direct Hood to wait, and himself spoke to General Kershaw, whose brigade led McLaws's division. Kershaw was a South Carolina man, a good friend of Cousin Cinda and of Brett Dewain, whose plantation was down near Camden somewhere. After serving as a delegate from Kershaw County in the South Carolina convention which passed the ordinance of secession, Kershaw was elected Colonel of the Second Regiment. He was on Morris Island during the bombardment of Sumter; his regiment won its spurs in Bonham's brigade at First Manassas, and as brigadier he had since then distinguished himself at Harper's Ferry, at Sharpsburg, at Fredericksburg, and at Chancellorsville. His place in the van of McLaws's column was well earned.

Longstreet explained the situation. "I'm halting Hood's brigades to let you pass through them. Follow the lane to the fork, and then take the left fork through the woods till you can see the Emmitsburg road. Deploy under cover there and make contact with Hood on your right."

Kershaw said crisply: "Very well, sir." He led his men across the creek. Longstreet reflected that by giving Kershaw orders directly, instead of through McLaws, he had done exactly the thing which when General Lee did it he had resented; but McLaws, never jealous of his prerogatives, would take no offense.

Nor, damn his own hide, should he himself have taken offense at Lee! That was sheer childish petulance. Here was a battle to be fought; nothing else mattered! He brushed aside his ill humor in a rising haste for action, watching the regiments pass, seeing how the heat and their long march had drained strength out of even these hardened veterans. For almost three hours they had been plodding clear around Robin Hood's barn, along roads miles away from where they should have been.

But now at last the brigades were coming into position. Barksdale passed with a salute and a word of greeting. Hood's men along the stream were taking the chance to rest and to drink the warm brook water while McLaws went through them. General Pendleton rode down from the higher ground toward the enemy and eased his horse through the column and spoke to Longstreet.

"General, the enemy has extended his flank a little farther south. It rests now at a four corners due east of you here. He's thrown some men into a peach orchard, has a battery there and some infantry."

"Will McLaws be beyond his flank, if he follows that lane to the left through the woods?"

"Oh yes."

"You've directed Colonel Alexander where to place his guns?"

"Yes, General."

"Good."

Pendleton rode away; and McLaws came to join Longstreet. Longstreet asked: "How are you going in, General?"

"I'll wait and see what's on my front."

"General Pendleton says you will have nothing in front of you. I told Kershaw to take your leading brigade along this lane through the woods up there and form on Hood. Meade's flank is anchored in a peach orchard, but when you reach the road you will be south of them."

"Then I'll cross the road and wheel to the left and attack."

Longstreet nodded. The little sounds of distant shots came pricking through the shimmering heat of midafternoon, as sharpshooters or skirmishers thought they saw a target. But of course no one could shoot straight at long range on a day like this, when the hot air rose from the sunned earth in waves that distorted vision. Colonel Fremantle and two or three others rode up from the south and Longstreet greeted the Englishman amiably.

"Well, Colonel, have you scouted the enemy position for us?"

"No sir. We went to find a farm where we could buy some feed for our horses, robbed a cherry tree or two, bathed in the stream down there. What's going to happen, General?"

"We propose to roll their flank up the road toward the cemetery." Longstreet with action near was in high good humor. "Go back where you were this morning and you can count them like sheep as we drive them by!"

Fremantle laughed and moved away, and Longstreet rode with the column advancing toward the front, picturing in his mind the field of battle still hidden beyond the woods. Powell Hill's corps on his left confronted the enemy along a line drawn parallel with the Emmitsburg road. His own men would cross the road and swing into action on a front perpendicular to the road. It was thus Lee had designed the attack: McLaws the hinge, Hood the swinging gate. Longstreet remembered that hour at Second Manassas when as Pope's line of battle faltered in front of Jackson his own corps swung crushingly against the enemy flank. That might well be the story of this day!

In a rising and confident exhilaration, his doubts of the morning and his anger alike forgotten, Sorrel by his side, the officers of his staff following close, Longstreet cantered up past the schoolhouse. There he called to Trav.

"Currain, go to General McLaws, keep me informed. I will see Hood's brigades across the road."

He turned to the right along the lane Hood's men had followed. The lane was full of them, pressing slowly forward as the regiments in front made room. To his left he saw through the fringe of trees an orchard, and as he continued there were open fields just across a wall within ten feet of him. Where the lane presently bore more to the right, he kept straight ahead, then picked his way through the woods till he saw the road a hundred yards ahead across an open field.

He halted there in the cover of the trees. Northward toward the town a belt of pasture and tillage bordered the road as far as he could see. The road itself came toward him along the crest of that rising ground which General Lee had pointed out this morning from their vantage two miles northward. The worst heat of the day was past, for it was after three o'clock; but even here in the forest shade, men gasped and panted and wiped their dripping brows. Longstreet took off his hat to let what airs there were cool his forehead. From where he stood, the ground rose slightly toward the road; but beyond, it seemed to descend again, and he could see the tops of apple trees in orderly rows half a mile away down the gentle slope. To his left, not far away across the road, rose a low wooded hill; and beyond the apple trees the Round Tops were bold against the sky. Somewhere off to the north, Yankee skirmishers were posted on this side of the road, for he heard the occasional bark of a musket; and once at a sharp report he saw a crow, flying high toward Round Top, tower and veer away to the north on quickened wing.

General Hood came to report that his men were well closed up in the fringe of the trees on this side of the road. "A lane leads from our front straight toward Round Top," he explained. "We can file into that, or we can cross the road in line of battle."

"File into the lane," Longstreet directed. "Put scouts ahead and skirmishers on your left flank. There's nothing in front of you. Meade's flank is half a mile north of us, extending along the road to that peach orchard you see yonder. When your brigades are across the road, left face and you'll be in line of battle on Meade's left rear. Use skirmishers, and close support in strength, and hit them hard."

Hood wheeled his horse away, and Major Currain on Nig came bursting through the thickets. "Sir, General McLaws reports that the enemy on his front is in great strength. He says they extend well to his right."

"He must be mistaken," Longstreet protested. General Pendleton had reported that the enemy flank now rested in the peach orchard; but that was only the anchor of his line, could not be strongly held. "Tell him to attack at once."

Trav raced away, and Longstreet rode to the right to watch Hood's advance. Down below the road a spatter of skirmishing fire told him Hood was already visible to the enemy. Currain returned with an insistent message from McLaws; the force in front of his division was strong and well placed; Colonel Alexander's guns would have to break the enemy before a direct attack was feasible. "He wants you to come and see for yourself, sir," Trav explained.

Longstreet's anger of the morning returned. If the reconnaissance by General Pendleton and Captain Johnston had been faulty, his was not the blame. General Lee had believed them, had believed the enemy flank was on that high ground half a mile north of the peach orchard, and in that belief had given his orders for the tactical development of the battle. Well, they were wrong, so General Lee was wrong. It was true the enemy had, since Lee's orders were given, reached down the road to the peach orchard; but Pendleton must have reported that to the commanding general, and Lee had sent no new orders. McLaws must do as General Lee had directed.

"Tell him to advance," Longstreet insisted. "Tell him to cross the road and wheel to the left as General Lee directed."

As Trav went to carry this order for a third time to McLaws, Moxley Sorrel brought a message from Hood, whose skirmishers had begun to develop the Yankee position. Sorrel said the enemy flank, instead of being up there in the peach orchard as McLaws thought, was refused. The peach orchard was the angle of a salient; their line drew a concave curve from the orchard to the foot of Round Top, with that low tree-clad hill below the road as a strong point midway of the curve. Hood believed, and Sorrel agreed, that to attack up the road would be to accept enemy fire on flank and rear.

"Hood is wrong, Sorrel," Longstreet said calmly; but his own words did not persuade him. Hood could be trusted not to be wrong! But damn it, he must be. He had to be! Longstreet found himself with two divisions committed to battle—to a battle which was to be fought against his judgment and advice—on the assumption that Meade's flank was in the air; but instead, Meade's left was solidly posted, anchored against Round Top and bolstered by that low hill here below the road and by the guns in the peach orchard half a mile to the north.

Well, no matter; he must attack. It was almost four o'clock. Lee was somewhere two or three miles away. There was no time to report this changed situation. Lee's orders, overruling his suggestion of a maneuvre to the right, gave Longstreet no discretion. He was nothing but Lee's instrument, to see Lee's orders obeyed.

"Hood is wrong, Sorrel," he repeated. "Tell him to drive north, his left to guide on the road."

Sorrel bit his lip. "General Hood says if there is any other way the attack can be made, any other way at all, it would be better than this." And he said urgently: "Also, General Law's scouts report Meade's trains, almost unguarded, just south of Round Top. A move to the right would bring us on them, and on Meade's flank and rear."

Longstreet almost smiled at the irony of this suggestion. He had proposed this morning exactly the same thing; yes and last night too. But General Lee would not listen. Well, it was too late to renew that argument now. From the peach orchard, enemy guns began an irregular fire on Hood's brigades.

"Say to General Hood," Longstreet directed in a flat tone, "that General Lee's orders are to attack up the Emmitsburg road."

He felt Sorrel's surprise and wonder as the other departed to bear this message. Longstreet turned to go to McLaws, riding out of the corner of the woods and across an open field where a few scattering trees along a fence to his right gave him some slight concealment from the enemy in the peach orchard. He and the little knot of horsemen who followed him made an attractive target for any alert Yankee gunner; but in his present mood he did not greatly care. Before he had gone far, a horseman came in haste to overtake him. This was Captain Hamilton of Hood's staff.

"General Hood has now completely developed the enemy line, sir," Captain Hamilton reported. "He fears an attack as ordered can accomplish nothing and requests permission to move to his right as offering better work."

Longstreet did not check his horse. "General Lee's orders, Captain," he said in even tones, "are to attack up the road."

He rode on, his head bowed now in a deep depression. The fact that first McLaws and now Hood asked the plan of attack be changed was proof enough it was unsound; but he himself had urged as strongly as he could this march to the right which Hood now proposed, and Lee had overruled him. Not even Lee, the kindliest of men, would forgive a third insistence.

He had to meet one more appeal when Colonel Sellers of Hood's staff came with a third urgent message. Longstreet gnawed at his mustache, but he was in no doubt what his reply would be. Without having seen the enemy position, relying on the reconnaissance of General Pendleton and Captain Johnston, Lee had ordered this attack; and he had refused to consider the very maneuver which Longstreet last night and this morning, and Law and Hood now on the field itself advised.

Then there was no more to be said; the responsibility was Lee's. When Colonel Sellers was done, without checking his horse, without looking at the Colonel, Longstreet spoke slow words like bludgeons. "Please repeat to General Hood that General Lee's orders are to attack up the Emmitsburg road."

Colonel Sellers at that harsh reply wheeled his horse and galloped off; and Longstreet's anger mounted. By God, Hood must attack, whether he thought it wise or not! He too turned, and he lifted his horse to a run and followed Colonel Sellers, taking one fence and then another by the road, and so came down to where Hood was waiting. He saw Sellers speak to Hood as he approached; and then both men turned to face him, and Hood began to speak.

But Longstreet interrupted, in a chiding tone that was almost derisive. "Now, General, you know we must obey the orders of General Lee."

Hood met his eyes in a long glance; and Longstreet thought, as he had often thought before, that there never was a man in whose eyes such sadness dwelt as in the eyes of Hood. Then Hood turned his horse without a word and cantered forward to ride ahead of his men toward the enemy position.

There was a mounting clamor of great guns from the peach orchard half a mile away, shot and shell striking here among Hood's regiments. As they pushed northward along the slope parallel with the road, infantry opened on them from a patch of woods diagonally to their right and ahead. The rising clang of battle steadied Longstreet's pulses. He spurred his horse to come up with Hood. Under that fire from the cover of the trees yonder, the men instinctively changed front a little, quartering down the slope to face the enemy; and Long-street swung with them, matching his horse's pace to that of the men on foot. The bursts of shells swept the lines with flying fragments, and he took off his hat to fan the smoke away, shutting his eyes to the sight of hurt men and dead men on the ground. He had no need to look at them to know what he would see: blood trails on the broken grass where a man had dragged himself to the half-shelter of some tree or boulder; helpless men with palms upraised toward the enemy as though to stop the next bullet pelting toward them; men with arms shot away running to the rear, their soundless mouths open so that they seemed to scream even though their screams could not be heard; dead men . . . Why did so many men die on their backs, but with a knee pulled up, so that they appeared to lie at ease, their sightless eyes staring at the sky? Why did a man shot through the belly always try to move his bowels? How absurdly symmetrical were the dust puffs thrown up by the hoofs of a riderless horse! Why did a horse with a dead man dragging by one foot from the stirrup always gallop at full speed, like a dog with a tin can tied to its tail? Why were the eyes of a wounded man surrounded by white skin, as though tears of pain had washed the dust and sweaty grime away?

No matter; such thoughts were better not thought, such sights were better not seen. In camp he might consider the health of his men, their comfort, and even their amusement; but not on the battlefield. With that detachment which combat always brought him, he reflected that the general, like the surgeon, must forget that the instruments he used were flesh and blood. Even civilians armored themselves against this realization. They said that Lee drove McClellan away from Richmond, that Jackson cut Pope's communications at Manassas, that Longstreet smashed Burnside's attack at Fredericksburg; but this was just a protective simplification. It was not Lee who harried McClellan from Mechanicsville to the James. It was sixty or seventy thousand nameless men, hustling into flight a hundred thousand other nameless men; and a good many of them died in the process.

But by thinking of battle in terms of generals, the civilian shut his mind to the agonies of individuals; and as long as he never visited a battlefield, he could continue to do so. Longstreet wondered whether, if politicians were set to the task of cleaning up the debris of battle, hurrying to bury the dead men before maggots and beetles and rats and foxes and hogs devoured them, moving bodies which had swollen and burst after a day in the sun, they would be quite so ready to lead a people to war.

Yet he was as bad as any civilian, shutting his eyes to the sights about him. And like any civilian, he too thought in names; McLaws, Hood, Pickett. But McLaws was not one man. He was four brigades, he was seven thousand men, he was a mass. Hood was a few more bayonets than McLaws; Pickett not so many. As for the brigade commanders, Law, Anderson, Robertson, Benning; each was not a man but a brigade. Kershaw, Semmes, Barksdale, Wofford; they were each a brigade. Each name was a symbol for say fifteen hundred men; each commander multiplied himself fifteen hundred times.

Then there were the regiments, but Longstreet was not concerned with regiments. His weapons were divisions, or sometimes brigades. In his work, regiments were nothing. For that matter, brigades were nothing. This fight just now begun would cost in killed and wounded enough individuals to make up a brigade; yes, perhaps enough to make two brigades, for the position in front of him was a strong one. Yet victory would be well worth that price, if you did not think of brigades as men. You must think of a brigade as a broom with which to sweep the enemy aside. If in the process that broom lost some straws, no matter; the urgent, the necessary thing was to get the job of sweeping done. Just as those surgeons whom he had seen working on the wounded yesterday must close their ears to cries of agony, so must a commanding officer shut his eyes to death.

In this abstracted mood, Longstreet rode forward into the storm of fire, till Fairfax and Moxley Sorrel came up beside him and Fairfax cried: "Go back, General! We'll do this!" So Longstreet checked his horse, remembering that it was not his business to face those guns ahead. He reined in, pausing to survey the ground. Along this slope below the road there was a vista of open fields as far as an orchard, beyond which there seemed to be a fairly deep ravine; beyond that ravine lay the peach orchard that was their goal, wreathed now in smoke from the batteries emplaced among the trees. Down to their right a larger orchard covered the face of that low wooded hill; and by the signs there were Yankee skirmishers in that orchard, and masses of Yankee infantry in the wood on the hill.

Well, Hood must make his own battle. Sorrel said Hood's right was going astray; so Longstreet rode back and up the slope till he could look down to the low ground toward the Round Tops. Hood had made his move with two brigades: Robertson's here on the left guiding by the road, Law on the right; the others in reserve. Sorrel's report was correct. Law's men were pressing into the forest along the foot of the Round Tops; and smoke drifting upward from among the trees said they were meeting brisk contention on those hidden slopes. Well, if the enemy was there he must be fought. Law must clear his flanks before he went ahead. But Law's drift to the right while Robertson pushed straight ahead thinned the center of Hood's line of battle. If it were drawn too thin it would break. That must not happen.

"Fairfax! Sorrel!" Longstreet spoke calmly. "Repair the line there!"

The two staff officers raced away to bring Hood's support brigades to the point of danger. Longstreet stayed where he was, scanning the enemy front now clearly outlined by their fire. Robertson was in that first small orchard now, but he was checked. From the low rocky hill on his right and rear, flanking fire was punishing his men, and the cannonade from the peach orchard was heavier all the time. That peach orchard was the anchor and the angle of Meade's front. Smash in that angle and you would split the enemy line and shatter it; but Hood's advance was meeting sheets of fire, was held in hard and growing battle. Worse, as Robertson's regiments instinctively swung to face the fire from the wood on their flank, between his left and the road a gap began to open.

McLaws must fill that gap, but McLaws had not yet moved. Goree came to report that Law had cleared the lower slopes of the Round Top; he was pressing across the dip between the two peaks toward the lesser height. In the center, the support brigades were fighting their way into the woods on that low hill which threatened to split the line; so Robertson's flank would presently be clear. Longstreet nodded; he was not needed here. Hood would bring his brigades to effective focus now.

"I'm going to hurry McLaws," he said. He rode at a canter back across the road and circled to the north. Kershaw was waiting behind Alexander's busy guns. The batteries were under heavy fire from the enemy not half a mile away; and Longstreet saw men down, horses kicking in their death throes, guns dismounted. Lieutenant Wentz, whom Colonel Alexander had brought to Longstreet that morning, had drawn back from his position and was hastily knotting a handkerchief about his forearm. Longstreet pulled up his horse.

"Hurt, Lieutenant?"

"A scratch, nothing."

"What's between the Round Tops and that rocky little hill on Hood's flank?"

"Low land, a brook. Boggy ground. A lot of big rocks."

"Whose peach orchard is that, where the guns are?"

"Mr. Sherfy's. That's his house west of the road." Longstreet saw a two-storied house with a chimney at one end and three large trees shading it at the other. Probably there was a Yankee sharpshooter in every window; and the Yankee batteries in the orchard, screened by the trees and by their own smoke, were being well served. "My father's house is east of the road, just across the lane from the peach orchard," Lieutenant Wentz explained. "You can see it as the smoke shifts."

"Your people still there?"

"I expect so. My father's a hard man to move."

Longstreet chuckled. "We must move him," he said. Those houses were at the apex of the angle. Well, they would smash that angle, and doubtless the houses too.

Longstreet found McLaws and General Barksdale together. Below them in the fringe of trees Barksdale's brigade was waiting. Longstreet had come to order McLaws instantly to advance; but he saw at once that the other had been right not to move. The massed fire of the enemy batteries was too heavy for infantry to face. Alexander's guns were off to the right at longer range; but guns along this front would give converging fire against the Yankees in the orchard. His first word to McLaws was sharp.

"Why haven't you a battery here?"

"It would draw fire on Barksdale's men."

"Place a battery here," Longstreet said curtly.

McLaws gave the order, and guns in reserve came quickly into position. Their fire at once drew fire; and solid shot and shell tore through the trees where Barksdale's brigade lay at ease. Barksdale said urgently to McLaws: "Let me go in, General." McLaws made some answer, and Barksdale appealed to Longstreet. "Let me go, General. I can take those guns in five minutes."

Longstreet looked at him absently. Barksdale's men were Mississippians; and Longstreet thought it possible that some of his own kinfolk might be here in Barksdale's regiments. Perhaps in a few minutes some of them would die; but not yet! Barksdale must not throw a thousand or fifteen hundred men into that furnace blast of fire.

"Wait," he said quietly. "We're all going in presently."

Yet waiting was costly too. As shells rained into the fringe of trees he heard cries of pain; and hurt men stumbled or crawled past them to the rear. Damn those Yankee guns! Were they invulnerable? Off there below the road Hood was fighting himself out, fighting the battle alone; but if McLaws went forward now his men would be slaughtered! The ground over which Barksdale's men here must advance rose a little toward the orchard; and there were fences and stone walls that would delay them and hold them under point-blank fire.

Currain reined up beside him. "I went to find you, sir," he said, "to say that General McLaws asked your presence here. Now General

Hood is wounded. He has been carried from the field. Sorrel reported to General Law and Law took command, and he asks for help."

So! Hood gone! What Hood could do with his men Longstreet knew; but could Law do as much with them, or less, or more? Law was young, a South Carolinian, a graduate of the Military Academy in Charleston and in later years a lawyer. He was a lean man with a conspicuous brow and bold yet sombre eyes, who chose to keep a line of whisker that continued the line of his mustache down to the small spade beard under his chin, but left cheeks and chin bare except for a small tuft attached to his lower lip. A man who took such pains with the pattern of his beard confessed a certain vanity, and vanity suggested a lack of self-confidence. It was as though Law sought to persuade himself that he was a better man than he believed himself to be.

But Law had done some fine fighting since that day at Manassas when as lieutenant colonel he took the bullet through the elbow which had made his left arm stiff and awkward ever since. He had lived up to his opportunities and a little more, not only at Boonsboro, but again at Fredericksburg. His recent marriage had not distracted his attention from the business at hand. Longstreet nodded, accepting General Law, reminding himself to bear in mind that Law, who a moment ago had been a brigade of some two thousand men, was now a division of seven thousand muskets, and to be used accordingly.

These reflections had been instantaneous. Before Currain could quiet his panting horse, General Law rode up to them at full gallop.

"General, we're held!" he reported, and he turned to point across the smoke-shrouded field. "Our right is on that lower peak, our left has drifted into those woods beyond the road." Longstreet nodded, understanding that Law spoke now not of his brigade, but of the division. If Law's left was in the wood, that gap which he himself had seen beginning to open, between Robertson's brigade and the road, was now become dangerously wide. Law added: "I ventured to suggest to General Kershaw that he cross the road and wheel so that his right will touch my left."

Longstreet nodded again. Law was right; Kershaw's brigade must fill that gap, and at once. No more delay! If those guns yonder in the peach orchard could not be silenced, they must be carried and their fire quenched with blood.

Well, if it must be done, these men could do it. "Tell General Kershaw we will cease fire and then give him three slow guns as a signal to advance. I will allow you time to return to your division. Speak to him on your way."

Law galloped off, and Barksdale asked eagerly: "May I go in now, General?"

"Wait," Longstreet insisted. "General Law must have time to get back to his command." He spoke to McLaws. "These walls and fences in the way will make trouble for horses. Dismount all officers." Kershaw's move would draw the enemy fire, give Barksdale a brief opportunity, reduce the murderous storm which he must face.

When he was sure Law had had time to reach his division, Longstreet turned to Peyton Manning. "Tell Colonel Alexander to cease firing," he directed. "Then he is to give three slow guns. Kershaw will pass through the batteries. When the guns are clear, Alexander will resume fire." Manning sped away, and Barksdale in his impatience whirled his horse and rode down through the trees toward his men. Longstreet spoke to McLaws. "Warn General Barksdale to keep his ranks well closed and aligned. He must not let those walls and fences break his formations. And see to it that he dismounts."

McLaws would manage here. Longstreet himself went to watch Kershaw's move. As he reached Kershaw, Alexander's guns were suddenly hushed; then one, and a second, and a third spoke singly. Longstreet dismounted, and as Kershaw's regiments filtered through the guns, he walked with General Kershaw as far as the road. The men vaulted over the fences and walls; and beyond the road they formed and went steadily on, ignoring the grape and canister that tore their lines. Longstreet summoned General Semmes to bring his brigade on a left oblique to fill the gap between Kershaw's left and Barksdale's right. Semmes and Barksdale were neighbors down in Mississippi; or at least Barksdale had said that Semmes lived just across the Alabama line from Columbus. Well, they would march side by side in good neighborly fashion here today.

Barksdale's drums up the road yonder were beating the assembly; and Longstreet returned to where an orderly held his horse and rode back to watch Barksdale's charge. The enemy fire was concentrated now on Kershaw and on Semmes; so Barksdale's regiments as they formed front of battle had a respite from punishment. Longstreet spoke to McLaws.

"Very well," he said. "Let Barksdale go."

The Mississippians had been pent till they were taut for action; they were off at a bound. Wofford's brigade came on behind them, and Longstreet, dismounting again, went with Wofford toward the road. It was impossible to see through the smoke and dust, but his ears quickly caught a sudden sharp difference in the tumult before him, and his pulse lifted in a great exhilaration. By God, Barksdale had already overrun that damned battery! Now the guns were silent, the smoke thinned and he could see. The Yankees were broken; the angle of their line was ruptured, swinging back in fragments.

Oh, drive them, drive them now! Never let them rally, never let them stand! Send Wofford on! Send word to Powell Hill on the left that it was time for his men to take a hand! Bring up the guns! He spoke quickly to the first messengers at hand, and they raced away to convey his orders. Farm buildings stood beside the lane that led toward the peach orchard. He paused in front of the house. "I'll be here, or near here, if you wish to find me," he told McLaws. "You have them now! Go on!"

Alexander's guns, blanketed by the advance of the infantry, had been briefly silent; but now with the Yankee line broken, Alexander could rush them forward into closer action. Since some apple trees behind the house obscured his view that way, Longstreet rode down along the lane a few paces more till he could see clearly in that direction. Yonder by the guns there was an orderly milling of men and plunging horses. Alexander had not waited for orders to seize his opportunity. Limber to the front!

Longstreet's eye swept the ground over which the batteries must advance to reach the peach orchard, and he saw a rail fence in their path. Beyond the fence, Major Fairfax and a few men were herding a flock of Yankee prisoners at a trot across the road. Longstreet loosed that great voice that could be heard above the roar of battle:

"Fairfax! Get that damned fence away!"

Fairfax heard and drove the prisoners to the task. A gate with stone posts was too narrow for guns to pass; but the men attacked the fence beside the gate, and under their hands it disappeared as chalk marks on a blackboard vanish under the stroke of a wet rag.

Then they scattered, for here came the guns, Alexander with his sword drawn leading them: six batteries, twenty-four guns, six horses to a gun, the guns bouncing and careening behind the limbers, caissons following at the gallop. The gap in the fence was wide enough; but the leading gun on this side swerved close to one of those stone posts, and a man on foot, running swift as a hound beside his gun, was crowded against the post. The washer hook plucked at him, and something like an unfurling pink ribbon came out of him and dragged him off his feet and on till the ribbon parted and he rolled over and over along the ground.

Longstreet averted his eyes. Forget the man, watch the grand spectacle of those racing guns; three or four hundred horses, five or six hundred men, the batteries as perfectly in formation as though on the drill ground, the drivers riding three to a gun and urging their mounts with whip and spur. Oh that was a splendid and a glorious spectacle, if you could forget the man whose entrails had been drawn out of him.

As the head of the column reached the orchard yonder, Longstreet saw Colonel Alexander wheel; his sword hand swept up and to the right. Action front! The first battery whirled, each gun team swinging in perfect pattern. Before they were full halted, the men were at the pintle hooks; before the caissons had passed Longstreet's vantage here, the first guns yonder were already firing. The others as they arrived took station to pour upon the stubbornly retreating enemy a flood of fire.

The man whom the washer hook had disembowelled no longer moved. Longstreet's eyes touched him, then turned to scan the battle. The fight was rolling along the road and moving off down the slope below. Lee had wanted that high ground north of the peach orchard. Well, it was his; they had it, they would hold it.

But success had opened opportunity. They could do much more, could tumble half Meade's broken line northward toward the cemetery, could jam the other half back against the Round Tops, could cut his whole damned army in two and shatter it! Bring in Hill's corps! General Lee was doubtless with Hill, a mile or so to the north. He would see to the work there; but Anderson's division of Hill's corps was close by. Longstreet, hot with battle passion, mounted and rode to Anderson.

"Throw Wilcox at them, General!" he said crisply. "Let him sweep those bluebellies off Barksdale's flank."

General Wilcox was with Anderson. He wore an old straw hat and a short jacket, more like a comfortable farmer than a soldier. His side whiskers were bristling, his heavy mustache hid the line of his mouth which always suggested that he tasted something bitter. He was an old West Pointer, a soldier ever since his graduation; and despite his bucolic garb he was a skillful and a bold leader. If he had a weakness, it lay in the fact that he saw obstacles as clearly as he saw opportunities; and now before General Anderson could reply he said, pointing toward the road: "That apple orchard will force me to the left!" But he went with General Anderson toward his brigade.

Longstreet, watching them move away, heard his name called, and turned and saw General Pickett. He felt a fine satisfaction. Now the whole First Corps was again in hand. He said warmly:

"Ah, General, I'm glad to see you!" Remembering even in this moment Pickett's infatuation for that lady in Petersburg, he asked with a twinkle in his eye: "How's Miss Sally?"

"Excellently well, General."

"Splendid. Where is your division?"

"The head is up," Pickett told him. "The division is stretched out along the road. We left Chambersburg soon after midnight."

Longstreet nodded. "Then you'll be ready for work tomorrow." He turned his attention to the field again.

To keep clear of that orchard in his path, Wilcox was moving by the left flank. Once past the obstacle, he bore to the right up slightly rising ground toward the road. Skirmish fire met him, but the brigade pushed on and the Yankee skirmishers withdrew. Infantry in line of battle in the road, protecting a battery there, held for a moment while most of the guns were hustled off and then gave way; and Wilcox and his men pressed across the road and down descending slopes beyond.

Off to the left, Perry's brigade came in on Wilcox's flank, meeting heavy fire as they crossed each roll of the ground on the way to the road. General Anderson, again at Longstreet's side, said Colonel Lang today commanded Perry's brigade. Well, whoever led them, they were keeping the battle firm.

"Who is that coming in beyond Perry?"

"Wright."

Longstreet nodded with satisfaction. There was a fighting man, Ranse Wright! With no military training he had enlisted as a private. His regiment elected him Colonel, and before the war was a year old he won a general's star. Longstreet sometimes thought Ranse Wright looked like Sam Hood, with the same sad and gentle eyes. His men would go anywhere he led them, following him with a blind adoration; for he had the gift of being liked, and with it the cool head and the shrewd eye which made him a fine tactician.

Longstreet saw that Wright and the others were exploiting to the utmost the success already achieved. That outthrust Yankee salient which had been anchored on the peach orchard was all collapsing. Wilcox and Perry and Wright would pierce Meade's line at its very center, isolate his whole left wing from his right. Powell Hill need only send forward support for Anderson's men and the enemy would be broken and shattered. There was still time enough for great work to be done today.

The situation was wholly favorable; the rest lay with General Hill. Longstreet left Anderson and rode back to the house where he had stood to watch the guns go forward. McLaws was there to make report.

"Kershaw had trouble," he said. "His men got too far to the right and were badly raked; and then an enemy column came at him across that wheat field down there. It became a mêlée for a while. General Semmes took a mortal wound." He added quietly: "Meade is pouring fresh troops into the field."

"Anderson's brigades have cut Meade's center," Longstreet told him. He listened, impatiently watching toward the ridge a mile away. "Hill should be helping Anderson widen that break," he grumbled. "Yes, and Ewell should be hitting the right to pin the Yankees in front of him. Why the hell don't they move? If they'll take a hand, we'll rip Meade in two!"

Below them the heavy battle rang; and over on the slopes of the ridge increasing musket fire said Anderson's brigades were meeting reinforcements; but Hill sent no help to Anderson, and there was no stroke by Ewell. McLaws said quietly: "Barksdale was shot, down beyond the peach orchard. He cannot live."

Poor Barksdale, who had been so eager to plunge into this fray! Well, there would be tears for him down in Mississippi when they had the news. But though Barksdale was dead, or soon would be, yet now he was immortal too. His Mississippi men had swept the enemy away in the first hard push of their charge. Longstreet felt a moment's sorrow for Barksdale, and for all the others who had fallen; but with it as he watched the battle came a deeper sadness.

For the chance for a great victory was passing, and every moment made it less. Wilcox and Perry and Wright, after their steady thrust through the broken enemy and up the ridge yonder to cut Meade's center, now were checked and under increasing pressure; but Hill did nothing to support them. As Longstreet saw the opportunity depart, he groaned aloud. Oh, this battle had gone badly! Hill was at fault, Hill and Ewell. If they had struck even half an hour ago, how different the tally now!

They were at fault, but—and in his heart he knew it—so was he. In his sullen surprise at finding himself facing not the Yankee flank but a well-placed defensive line, he had blundered like a novice. Hood's fine brigades had made their battle alone. They were fought to a standstill while the weight of artillery at the angle still held McLaws passive; their momentum was lost before McLaws moved, and McLaws in turn was checked before Anderson went in.

Yet though the battle had been poorly managed—and for this Longstreet knew himself to blame—it had been won! Thirteen brigades had broken the Union line, had pierced the Union center. This was no credit to him, to be sure; but it was high credit to the men. No soldiers ever fought better than these men of his had fought today.

But while thirteen brigades broke Meade's center and rolled his line back to right and left, twice that many Confederate brigades stayed passive spectators. Longstreet, trying to forget that his own battle had been badly managed, damned Ewell's inactivity, and Hill's. But he could not forget. Why, he had been as clumsy as McClellan at Sharpsburg, fighting his battle a little at a time as McClellan had done on the hill between the Potomac and Antietam Creek. He should have held Hood in hand till he himself had fully surveyed the field, then massed guns against that angle by the peach orchard and thrown all his force against that salient in an overwhelming flood.

Angry at his own errors, he spurred his horse forward. Down there in a wheat field below the road a Yankee battery was still at work. He crossed the road and overtook Wofford and called him on; and he rode in the van to sweep that battery away! This grand First Corps which was his pride had been glorious today, but he had failed them. There was a moment, riding toward those enemy guns, when he would have welcomed the blow of a bullet in his heart. Barksdale and Semmes had died in glory. Well, so would he! No man could ask a finer fate!

But the gunners broke and fled; and Moxley Sorrel touched his arm. "This field is ours, General," he urged. "The field is ours; but the sun's gone. There's no more to do today."

Longstreet filled his lungs, and calm returned to him. What Sorrel said was true. The sun had set, the roar of battle was diminishing. "See how the work goes on our left," he directed. He himself rode toward the right. Goree reported that Kershaw's men were short of ammunition. Well, they would not need much more. Meade might fight back tonight, but Longstreet doubted it; the Yankees had been too badly hurt today.

There was still heavy musket fire on the slopes of the little Round Top, and he sent Major Currain for a report from that quarter. A reaction from these high hours began to possess him. He felt sleepy, and small details caught and held his dulled eyes. There were a great many dead and wounded men along the stone wall beside which he rode. Stone walls raised the devil with an attack; they were hard to carry, easy to defend. One man behind a stone wall was as strong as five men in the open; and this field where they had fought today was all stone walls and boulders and houses and woods and fences and orchards. Such ground made for deadly fighting.

He heard a sudden storm of musketry to the north. New reinforcements must be hitting Wilcox. Let Peyton Manning go and see what could be done for him. At the word Manning whirled his horse so eagerly that he almost trampled a wounded man who had propped himself against a tree. Longstreet rode slowly toward the lane that led up to the peach orchard. He passed a dead man from whom blood had flowed down an eroded bank in a wavering line that reached twenty or thirty feet from where the man lay. How much blood was there in a man? Why did it not splash around inside of him audibly when he walked? Yonder a Negro moved from one still figure to the next, probably a servant looking for his master's body. There would be many such seekers on this field tonight. In the woods, among the rocks, how many dead men would escape that search, would never be found; yes and living men, too, who had not strength to cry out and thus attract attention? As Longstreet reached the lane, someone screamed; and he saw a man with a dangling leg just being lifted into an ambulance, saw the pink-white end of a projecting bone. The ambulance jolted away, the man babbling in a vise of intolerable pain.

Back at the house on the lane he found Sorrel and McLaws and General Law; and Major Currain came to report, and Colonel Manning presently appeared, carrying saddle and bridle because his horse had been killed under him. It was dark enough now so that against the sky, as the last shells went whirling toward the enemy, the burning fuses could be seen. Longstreet roused himself from the slaked listlessness which held him and sent Sorrel to report to General Lee.

"Tell him we have that height he wanted for his guns," he directed. "Say that I will stay here, in case Meade makes a night move."

To his divisional commanders he gave instructions. "Hold your positions and correct your lines. We may be ordered to attack in the morning. Have that in mind." To General Law he added: "Reconnoiter to your right, around those hills, General." Even now the best hope lay in that move to the right which he had urged upon the commanding general, and upon which Hood and Law when they saw the ground agreed.

Colonel Alexander came for orders. "Place your guns with an eye to work tomorrow," Longstreet directed. "General Lee will want you in position to pound the cemetery." He remembered Lieutenant Wentz. "Did that lieutenant of yours find his family at home?"

Alexander said: "His father, yes. The rest had moved to safety.

When we seized the orchard, Wentz hustled his father down cellar out of harm's way. We've a battery in his yard." Alexander added in an amused tone: "The old man was sitting in his own kitchen smoking his pipe when the Lieutenant got to him. Several of our shells had hit his house, but fortunately he wasn't hurt."

Longstreet said approvingly: "Well, Colonel, the Yankees around that house under your fire were hurt, thoroughly. A good day's work."

When Alexander was gone, Longstreet asked the losses of the day. McLaws thought his strength had been reduced by at least two thousand bayonets; Law said Hood's division now under his command had lost as many or more. So four thousand men had paid in blood for that high ground on which General Lee wished to place his guns. Four thousand men? A heavy price. The whole army lost not many more than that at Fredericksburg! Four thousand? Yes, and Anderson's brigades had losses, too.

Major Currain requested permission to go seek Brett Dewain and find out how he had fared. Moxley Sorrel returned, and when he dismounted Longstreet saw some awkwardness in his movements. "Hurt?" he asked.

"A shell fragment hit my right arm, bruised it a bit; nothing serious." Sorrel made his report. "General Lee congratulates you on your success and says you have accomplished what he hoped. He requests that you renew the attack in the morning."

"He knows Pickett is here?"

"Yes sir."

Longstreet nodded. Colonel Fremantle had come with Sorrel. "Well, Colonel," Longstreet asked, "had you a good view?"

"Yes, but a distant one."

"The enemy was not where we had been told he would be. We had to fight him where we found him."

"General Lee was right under my tree," said the Englishman. "I was interested to see that he sent only one message. Apparently he leaves all details to his commanders." He added smilingly: "I understand your staff objects to the way you exposed yourself!"

Longstreet grunted. Major Fairfax joined them, exasperated because he had spent most of his time marching prisoners to the rear. "Like a damned mule driver," he declared, and they laughed, glad to find an excuse for mirth. Currain came back and to Longstreet's question answered that Dewain was all right.

"The Howitzers were up near the Seminary, had only two or three casualties. A shell burst near them and frightened Brett's horse, and it ran away with all his belongings. He chased it, but it galloped right through our battle down below the road here, and he had to let it go." He came near Longstreet, said in an interested tone: "General, here's a curious thing. I passed where they were sorting over the muskets picked up on the battlefield, seeing how many of them could be used; and I talked with the lieutenant in charge. They had seventeen hundred and sixty-three muskets there, and they'd picked out four hundred and twelve——"

Longstreet made an amused sound. "Figures will be the death of you, Currain." The Major was a simple man, always easily predictable except when sudden storming lust for action swept him out of himself.

"Yes sir; but here's the strange thing, General. Three hundred and four of those muskets were still loaded, and the lieutenant said at least half of them had more than one charge, sometimes four or five. One had nine charges that they drew and counted, and another was loaded right to the muzzle, solidly. I don't see how that could happen, sir."

"Easily enough," Longstreet assured him. "Men in battle get excited." His tone was jocular. "I seem to remember an occasion when you were a little stirred up yourself; though to good purpose, to be sure. What happens is that excited men forget to cap the nipples. They snap their pieces and ram home another load without noticing that there was no shot." He himself was usually completely calm in battle, or thought he was; but then he never carried a weapon, had not done so since his days as a young officer. "I remember an affair in Mexico when I kept snapping my pistol through several hours of action and never thought to load it till next day. Young soldiers lose their heads." He rose. "There, I see a bite of supper ready."

Over their supper, talk drifted wearily. The night seemed cool after the blistering day, but it was still hot enough so that no tents were needed, nor blankets. Longstreet sent Currain to ask the farmer near whose house they were preparing to bivouac whether they could take a few armfuls of hay from his barn, and Trav returned with this permission. "Mr. Warfield says as long as you don't sleep in the barn and like as not set fire to it, he won't complain." An orderly carried an armful of hay into the orchard across the road from the cooking fire, and Longstreet told Currain to ask Dr. Cullen about General Hood, and so lay down, half-listening to the talk back by the fire. The younger men of the staff discussed the day's work, their voices now argumentative and eager, now hushed with sorrow for friends hurt or dead. None of them were satisfied with what had been accomplished; and Longstreet understood their discontent. They had done what Lee asked of them; but the First Corps was used to doing more than was asked. Colonel Manning blamed inadequate reconnaissance.

"General Pendleton said he'd surveyed the ground, but if he did, either it was from a long way off or else he had poor eyes. I don't believe he came within a half a mile of the road. The Yankee prisoners say they had pickets out last night almost to Fairfield, and General Wilcox found Yankee outposts in the woods north of us here when he moved down this way today. If General Pendleton came this far, he would have run into them."

Fairfax said: "Speaking of General Wilcox, he's in a damned bad humor tonight! He got right into the Yankee lines over there on the ridge, and sent for help; and his messenger found General Anderson in a ravine back in the woods, sprawling on the ground with all his staff around him as calm as if there wasn't a Yankee within fifty miles!" He laughed. "I suppose they kept in the shade for fear they'd get a touch of sun."

"Did General Anderson send help?" Manning asked.

"No. General Wilcox repulsed three attacks by Yankee reinforcements and then gave up, pulled his men back. He says with support he could have broken the Yankee front; but no support came, and they were hitting him from three sides."

Longstreet would remember that against Anderson; yet even if Anderson failed, Hill—without waiting to be asked—should have sent fresh brigades to strengthen Wilcox. But it was too late now to correct mistakes. The day was done; afterthought never won a battle.

The voices died, the men drifted into sleep. Longstreet, his head pillowed on his folded hat laid atop his spyglasses, felt in his ear the hard pound of his heart not yet slowed to normal beat from the swift tattoo of battle rhythm. His blood was still too hot for sleep. Not till he heard Colonel Alexander begin to put his guns into position for to-morrow's work did he drowse a little, and he woke at first light and sat up and rubbed his eyes.

Tom Goree, seeing him awake, reported that Hood would probably lose an arm, but should recover. Well, Hood fought with his head and with his dauntless heart; not with his arms. When breakfast fires were lighted, Longstreet got to his feet, stiff with dawn chill; but a hot drink would set him right again. Sorrel brought the reports of Law's scouts. There were enemy forces facing Law and massed behind the Round Tops; but south of those rocky hills the way to Meade's rear was still open and of easy access. If Pickett and his fresh men were sent around Meade's flank to hit the enemy trains behind the Round Tops, would not Meade's whole line be dislocated? Dawn melted into day and Alexander came to report his guns in position, with the Washington Artillery to add to their weight of fire.

"I had twenty of them in a bad spot," he confessed. "I placed them after dark, but this morning I saw they would be under enfilade from the cemetery hill above the town. Luckily the Yankees couldn't see them in the morning mist, and they're better placed now."

"Get some breakfast while you can," Longstreet directed. "As soon as Pickett is ready, we'll go to work."

Guns opened off north of the town, and he heard heavy musket fire; so Ewell was already engaged. Too bad Ewell had not been as energetic yesterday. While he ate, Longstreet reflected on yesterday's battle. The Yankees, give them credit, had done disquietingly well. With their line broken and their center pierced, they had recoiled, to be sure; but down in that wheat field below the peach orchard they had fought as tenaciously as cats. He remembered General Hill's re-mark day before yesterday, that the Yankees had never fought as hard as they did that day. This might be because they were defending their own territory, for every dog is a hero in his own yard.

But whatever the cause, their new prowess was all the more reason for seeking to defeat them by wit rather than weight, by maneuvre rather than assault. Perhaps General Lee would sanction that move to the right which Pickett's coming made so feasible.

As Longstreet finished breakfast, the commanding general with three or four of his staff and General Hill rode toward them through the orchard. Longstreet rose, and with a word of friendly greeting, Lee said: "Well, General, from the position you won yesterday we can hurt those people today."

Longstreet repeated the report brought by General Law's scouts. "They found good opportunity to send Pickett around Meade's flank," he suggested, and pointed to the rocky heights that marked the southern end of the enemy line.

Lee shook his head; but before he could speak, General Pendleton rode up from the peach orchard. "I can see no room for improvement in the gun positions, sir," he reported. Lee turned to scan the field. From the crossroads at the orchard the road ascended slightly to that knoll, yesterday their objective, which was now in Confederate hands. The batteries there, withdrawn a little west of the road to avoid an enfilade, were not much more than a mile from the cemetery on the hill above the town.

Lee said to Pendleton: "Then you will want to arrange the Third Corps artillery." Pendleton rode away, and Lee turned back to Longstreet. "General, if you advance your corps to that low point of the ridge over there, you will break their center."

Longstreet waited to speak calmly. "To go there, sir, we must accept the fire of the enemy massed here on our front. As we advance, they will be on our flank and rear. My divisions are weaker by four or five thousand bayonets than they were yesterday morning; and if we move as you direct, Meade's left will pour down and crush us."

Lee through his glasses studied the enemy position. "Is his left strongly held?"

"We took prisoners from twenty-five brigades in the action yesterday. There are at least a dozen brigades in front of us this morning." And since Lee did not immediately comment, Longstreet said strongly: "General Law can hold them on our right, and General McLaws can hold them here; but if Law and McLaws attack as you direct, Meade's left will be let loose behind us."

Lee yielded the point. "We cannot strip our right as long as their left is strongly held. That is true." He urged in firm insistence: "Yet their center is weak. We will break it. If McLaws's and Hood's divisions must stay here, you may have some brigades from the Third

Corps; and Pickett's men are fresh." He turned to include General Hill in his instructions, pointing across the road northeastward. "That spot where the trees are thinnest, that little clump of trees to the right of the cemetery hill, that is the spot to hit. Place your men, but keep them hidden behind the trees on our ridge here till they move. Let Heth's division form on Pickett's left, with two of Pender's in close support. Pickett will have farther to go than they, so they must time themselves to hit those people all together."

His tone was positive, and General Hill at once departed to make these arrangements; but Longstreet said flatly:

"General, you give me at best fifteen thousand men. I don't believe any fifteen thousand men who ever carried a musket can march half a mile through converging artillery fire from front and flanks, and through the musketry of the defenders, up to the saddle of that ridge."

"Wright took his brigade there yesterday," Lee insisted. "If one brigade can do it, fifteen thousand men can certainly do it."

"Ranse Wright can take his men anywhere men can go," Longstreet conceded. "But he was driving troops already broken. Also, since he was not supported, he had to withdraw." Bitterness over that failure to support his battle yesterday was in his tones. "But today the enemy line is re-established, with guns placed to enfilade an attack. The condition has changed, to our disadvantage."

Other officers had drawn near, listening; and Colonel Long of Lee's staff spoke to Longstreet. "General, the guns on the hill on your right front can be silenced."

Lee added: "And I'll give you Anderson's division if you need it, General."

Longstreet's pride responded to the implicit compliment; for although the attack would be delivered by a force made up of only three of his brigades and nine or ten of Hill's, he was to command. Nevertheless he said honestly: "I do not believe it can be done, sir."

Lee's head twitched in a rising irritation; but his tone was mild. "Anything is possible to this army, General! The enemy is there, and I am going to strike him."

Longstreet did not reply; there was no more to be said. He saw Pickett a few paces off, waiting for orders, and at his nod Pickett joined them. Longstreet explained what was to be done. He pointed out the tactical features of the field, turned to ask General Lee: "What point, exactly, do you wish to strike?" Lee indicated again that clump of trees a little south of the cemetery, and Longstreet said to Pickett: "I suggest you form your men behind the ridge, behind the guns. Heth's division will be on your left." He asked Lee: "Will Heth command his men?" General Heth had taken a head wound in the battle he precipitated two days ago, and which had embroiled them all.

"No, General Pettigrew will handle Heth's division."

Well, Pettigrew was as good a man as Heth. Except for the inevitable confusion that must result from the shift of command, the division would do as well under one leader as the other. Longstreet continued his instructions to Pickett. "And two brigades of Pender's division will support Pettigrew. How long will you need to put your men in position?"

"They will be ready at ten o'clock."

General Lee had moved aside to listen to the sounds of Ewell's fight, two miles northeast. Longstreet called Colonel Alexander. "You must rearrange your guns, Colonel," he directed. "Draw back the batteries on the left. You will want to deliver converging fire on the ridge just south of the cemetery. Make sure your guns do not blanket each other."

Alexander and Pickett rode away together. As Longstreet rejoined Lee, the commanding general received a salute from General Wofford and said courteously:

"Well, sir, you made a good battle yesterday."

Wofford flushed with pleasure. "Thank you, General. We came close to the crest of the ridge."

"Do you think you can do it again today?"

The other spoke doubtfully. "My advance yesterday was a pursuit; but the ground over there is difficult, and they have had all night to make themselves secure."

Longstreet saw General Lee's impatience at this new remonstrance. Wofford, feeling himself dismissed, rode away; and Lee spoke to Longstreet. "I've sent word to Ewell that you will be ready at ten; but I fear his battle will have worn itself out before that."

"Pickett will be ready at ten," Longstreet corrected. "But we must wait for the guns to break a way for us. Colonel Long is of opinion we can silence the enemy batteries on the hill over there. I hope he is right. I presume the Third Corps artillery will smother the guns in the cemetery."

"General Pendleton will see to that," Lee assured him. "Shall we ride along your front?"

So Longstreet mounted, and as they rode, Lee spoke of the failure of Ewell's battle the day before. General Johnston's division and General Early had made a gallant and partially successful assault; but Early, finding his right in the air, had to retire.

"General Rodes was to have supported Early," Lee explained, "but he was not prepared in time."

"What was General Hill doing all afternoon?"

"He left Anderson's division to help you. The others were inactive."

Longstreet bit back a sardonic word. Inactive? Yes, Hill was inactive yesterday, and Ewell too! Unless they did their part today, Pickett's men would be slaughtered. But surely they would do their part today; General Lee would see to that. True, he had sent forward no support when support was needed yesterday; but perhaps from his position Lee had been unable to follow the action on the right. Today the assault on the Yankee center would be directly under his eye; he would be able to watch every move, to send forward supporting columns at the proper time.

They rode at first to the right, and General Lee stopped to speak to McLaws; but Longstreet went on to tell General Law the day's plan. "When Pickett moves, you must make a hard push to pin the enemy in front of you," he directed. "Keep them off Pickett's flank."

Law said soberly: "General, for me to send my men at them is madness. The enemy is above us, behind two lines of breastworks. His upper line can fire over the lower at our assaulting troops. Also they've massed infantry on our right rear, so I've had to refuse my right a little. If we advance they will encircle our flank."

Longstreet was about to remind Law that to magnify difficulties was not the road to success; but he was himself sure this day's work offered no promise, so Law could not be blamed. "Make what pressure you can," he insisted. "But keep your right secure." Meade must not be permitted to find any open road around Law to this army's trains. "When Pickett advances, you and McLaws must somehow keep them off his flank." Law's prominent eyes were more prominent than usual today, but most men of nervous temperament were a little wide-eyed in the hour before battle. Longstreet said hearteningly: "We will feel no anxiety with you here, General."

He rejoined General Lee, but he did not repeat what Law had told him. Since Lee meant to attack, to raise new objections would be useless. They returned past the farm buildings near which he had spent the night and continued northward. Alexander had rearranged his batteries to extend for about three-quarters of a mile in an irregular line from the peach orchard down through lower ground and past a house and along the front of another orchard and up to the corner of a large mass of woodland. Longstreet thought those guns could concentrate their fire on the spot Lee wished to strike.

He and General Lee paused behind the left-hand batteries, and Longstreet studied the terrain across which the assault must be delivered. Till they moved, Pickett's men could wait here in the woods behind the guns. To the right, in a shallow ravine, a little brook rose to trickle back through the trees and go on to the west. The regiments could form in that sheltered swale; but to reach the road they would have to pass through the line of batteries and across an open field. The ground between here and the road was not sufficiently undulating to hide them from observation, nor to protect them from artillery fire; but just this side of the road there was a knoll, and beyond it Longstreet saw the roof and the upper part of a house and barn. When the men got that far, the knoll and the house and the barn would give them temporary shelter.

But to reach the house they must march half a mile through intense and concentrated fire; and to reach the house was nothing. They must go on another two or three hundred yards, up gently rising ground and with no least protection, before they came to grips with the enemy.

So these green and gently rolling fields would presently be littered with dead men, men of his corps, men who would have died in a futile and a hopeless undertaking. He turned away, unwilling to look longer upon those meadows where today so many men must die.

General Lee turned with him and they rode side by side, not speaking. Longstreet saw that the other was white with weariness; and he felt a sudden tenderness, and a sympathetic comprehension. In these two days the commanding general had lost a fourth of his infantry, and with nothing gained. From the day this army crossed the Potomac, one thing and then another had gone wrong: Stuart had left Lee blind, Hill threw him into battle, Ewell halted at the moment when victory was in his hands. There must be in General Lee today a welling sorrow which made cool judgment impossible. Pride too was at stake; pride in his own victorious career, pride in his army. That he might fail to crush those people whose armies he had so often shattered must be for Lee unthinkable; even to maneuver must seem to the commanding general a confession of inadequacy. There was the enemy, waiting to be struck. Well, he would strike them!

Yes, and perhaps Lee was right to try this last throw of the dice. It could hardly bring victory; it would be costly; but it would shake Meade and make him even more cautious than his habit, and so give them a respite and a chance to retreat. Longstreet thought with a sudden clarity that this battle they were to fight today was actually a rear guard action. Win or lose, Lee must retreat. He had not strength enough to exploit victory. Tonight, even if they broke the Union center and shattered the force in front of them, their own army would be reduced in strength, its ammunition spent. A week ago it had seemed possible to deal such a blow that the war's end would be in sight; now, after two days of fruitless and exhausting battle, there was nothing to hope for but escape back to Virginia, back to long and desperate defense.

Yet General Lee had certainly not entertained this thought. He must be telling himself this morning that if they could split Meade's center and roll back its flanks they would open the gates to Baltimore and Washington. But that was an illusion. If they were victors today they would have say fifty thousand men fit for battle; but they would be encumbered with their own wounded, and with thousands of prisoners, and they would have little or no remaining ammunition except what they might capture from the enemy. Their army would be almost as badly crippled by victory as by defeat.

Longstreet shook his head, thrusting the truth away. No matter. He would do as much as he was able to do. His attention returned to the present task. The battle on Ewell's front seemed to be slackening; but behind them to the southward sudden firing suggested that Meade was feeling for Law's flank. Well, Law must meet that move in the best way he could.

They paused where Ranse Wright's brigade was taking position; and Lee spoke to General Wright. "General," he suggested, "tell General Longstreet what you learned when you went over to find those people yesterday. We expect to follow your example in a little while now."

"Why, it's easy to go over there from here," Wright explained. "There's a ravine down in the swale beyond the road that offers a chance to correct your lines. But the ground north of here offers no good place to pause. General Posey could not even cross the road yesterday. That's what let the enemy in on my left. We were right in their guns, but we had to withdraw; and to come back is harder than to go there." He added, harshly to hide his sorrow: "My brigade lost seven hundred men yesterday, General. You can see our dead lying out there in the sun to mark the line we took."

Lee did not speak, and Longstreet said in a kindly tone: "Thank you, sir. I will tell Pickett to use that swale of which you speak." As they rode on, he spoke to Lee. "Pettigrew must guard Pickett's left, General."

Lee nodded absently and they turned back through the trees to come out behind the crest of the ridge. There, hidden from the enemy, regiments and brigades were moving into position. Longstreet paused to speak to brigade commanders, directing that the regimental officers be led through the woods to see the task before them and to note their guide points. Toward the front there rose a sudden clamor of guns. He sent Moxley Sorrel to see what was happening, and Sorrel reported that enemy skirmishers had tried to seize a house and farm this side of the road on Pettigrew's front. The Third Corps artillery was battering the house to drive them away.

"We may need those shells later," Longstreet commented. Alexander's guns, he noticed approvingly, were silent. Colonel Alexander would use his ammunition only for a worth-while end.

Turning southward again they passed Pickett's brigades lying in the shade, and the men without command rose and took off their hats and stood while Lee rode by. "Well, General," Lee commented, "those Virginians of Pickett's will do anything men can do."

General Hill joined them and they returned through the trees to the front toward the enemy, and paused behind Alexander's batteries. Longstreet could see skirmishers, thrown forward to protect the guns, lying in the tall grass in the blazing sun. It was even hotter today than it had been yesterday. The firing on Ewell's front and on Law's had died away. The house the Federal skirmishers had tried to occupy was burning cheerfully; flames ate their way through the roof and blossomed from the windows, and smoke billowed briskly upward. The enemy skirmishers had fallen back nearer the road, and an occasional smoke puff marked their positions, but these scattering shots came at long intervals. There was a pressing quiet in the still and stifling air.

Well, this quiet would not last. Longstreet imagined the interweaving pattern of shot and shell and canister and grape which presently would scour those fields. Then General Hill, as though driven by an uncontrollable longing, said urgently: "General Lee, let me throw my whole corps into this assault."

Lee shook his head. "No, no, General. We must keep something in reserve."

Longstreet marked the word, and he understood. Lee knew well enough that against them lay heavy odds. He would not have ordered this desperate venture unless he had considered and rejected every alternative. Then General Lee lifted his hand in salutation; and he and Hill turned away, leaving to Longstreet the conduct of the day.

Longstreet felt the weight of responsibility press down upon him, felt for a moment hopelessly and dreadfully alone; so it was a relief when Sorrel approached. Sorrell's eyes were shining; he had a letter in his hand.

"General," he said proudly, "my commission as lieutenant colonel has just arrived."

"Is there mail from Richmond?"

"Yes sir."

Longstreet wished to ask whether there was a letter for him, some word of Louisa; but if there were, Sorrel would have told him. "Well,

Colonel, that commission was well-earned." He forced himself to concentrate on the problem here at hand. "Please ask General Pettigrew and General Trimble to spread their steps when they move. They must align with Pickett."

Sorrel cantered off to deliver this direction; and Alexander rode up to join Longstreet. They sat surveying the gentle valley across which fifteen thousand men presently must march into a blast of fire. "Well, Colonel," Longstreet asked, "any enemy activity?"

"They tried the range once or twice; but we were careful not to give them a worth-while target."

"How many guns have you in hand?"

"Seventy-five here, and eight off to the right to guard our flank; and General Pendleton offered me some of the Third Corps Howitzers to go forward with the infantry. I have them ready back behind the woods. They'll be useful at short range."

"I'll send you word when to open. You'd better arrange a signal to the guns."

When Alexander was gone, Longstreet dismounted. A courier from General Law reported that enemy cavalry had threatened his right rear, so that he had to swing his flank to face them. Longstreet thought Kershaw had better draw his men back a little to conform, and he sent the order to General McLaws. The adjutant of the Washington Artillery came to say they were ready to give the signal for the batteries to open.

"Tell Colonel Walton I will send him word," Longstreet directed, and he drew away to be alone. It was his responsibility now to give the order that would send many men to die. When death might clear a road to victory, he never hesitated; but he could see no path to victory today. Still vainly hoping that some alternative might be found, he wrote a note to Colonel Alexander, writing slowly, forming every word with a conscious effort.

Colonel: If the artillery fire does not have the effect to drive off the enemy or greatly demoralize him, so as to make our effort pretty certain, I would prefer that you should not advise Pickett to make the charge. I shall rely a great deal upon your judgment to determine the matter, and shall expect you to let General Pickett know when the moment offers.

He signed the note in due form, looked up, called the nearest courier. "Give this to Colonel Alexander with my compliments." When the note had gone, he who had never been tired in his life was terribly tired. He walked to a near-by tree, lay down and closed his eyes; he lay there trying to find some device that might at least reduce the losses of the attacking columns. Tears stung his closed eyes, and his thoughts blurred. It would be heaven to sleep and wake and find this moment gone. Why, he was crying like a child! The men must not see him. He turned on his side, buried his face in his arms, brushed his eyes on his sleeve.

A horseman approached and he sat up. Here was the reply from Colonel Alexander.

> General: I will only be able to judge the effect of our fire on the enemy by his return fire, as his infantry is little exposed to view and the smoke will obscure the field. If, as I infer from your note, there is any alternative to this attack, it should be carefully considered before opening our fire, for it will take all the artillery ammunition we have left to test this one, and if the result is unfavorable we will have none left for another effort. And even if this is entirely successful, it can only be so at a very bloody cost.

So Alexander too feared the results of this attack! A bloody cost? God Almighty, why should Alexander tell him that? Why not let him forget it? He wrote in harsh haste: "The intention is to advance the infantry if the artillery has the desired effect. . . . When that moment arrives, advise General Pickett . . ." He sent off the message, thinking that even this paltering exchange of meaningless notes used up a little time. Something might yet happen to avert the catastrophe into which this army was about to plunge. In a sudden concern for the safety of his right he decided that General McLaws had better withdraw Kershaw above the road to his original ground of yesterday, and he sent messengers to Kershaw and to McLaws.

The courier returned with a last note from Colonel Alexander. "When our fire is at its best," the Colonel wrote, "I will advise General Pickett to advance."

So there could be no more delay, no escape. Longstreet grimly accepted the inescapable. He wrote to Colonel Walton: "Let the batteries open." Let the guns go! Let them do their best! Let Pickett advance, God help him! God help them all!

After an interval when he thought his heart had stopped he heard the signal guns, one and then another! A moment more, and then the ground shook to the concussion of a hundred cannon, smoke blossomed from every muzzle, yonder against the sky appeared for an instant the speeding black dots that were shot and shell arcing toward the enemy. So! With the beginning of the cannonade, Longstreet's thoughts cleared. He considered once more the arrangement of the attacking columns. Heth's division, led today by Pettigrew, would be on the left of the front line; Pickett's on the right. Pickett was five thousand men; he might be not quite so many, but five thousand men was near enough. Pettigrew? Well, a month ago Heth had counted seventy-five hundred men; but he had fought a hard battle day before yesterday, had taken heavy losses. Pettigrew probably led a scant five thousand men today, with Pender's two brigades—commanded today by Trimble—to give him backing. Add Anderson for support in depth and you brought the count to twelve brigades, say fifteen thousand muskets.

And all these brigades would converge upon that clump of trees over on the opposite ridge, Pickett's division angling in from the right, while Pettigrew on the left advanced almost straight ahead. The pattern of attack was clear in Longstreet's mind. Pettigrew's four brigades and two of Pickett's in front, Trimble's brigades and Armistead to back them, Anderson ready to help where help was needed. The attacking front would be a flexible line of about nine thousand men, a line perhaps a mile in length; the second line would be more than half as long. When enemy fire thinned the front ranks, they would dress toward the center. At first the left would be weaker than the right; but the right had farther to go, and must by that much longer be under enemy fire. Longstreet had arranged his forces so that the right might accept heavy losses and still be strong enough to drive home the attack.

He tried to anticipate the development of this battle. Assume that of nine thousand men in the assaulting front, six thousand reached Meade's lines; assume that with four or five thousand comrades coming in support they pierced that line. Having accomplished that miracle, the ten thousand survivors would face on either flank enemy masses of twice or thrice their number, pressing in to squeeze them in a terrible vise. A year ago, if you cut a Yankee line, the fragments broke and fled; but these Northern men were better soldiers now than they had been a year ago. His First Corps had broken their line yesterday; but instead of turning tail as they would once have done, they had fought fiercely and well to mend the break; and for lack of support to the attackers, they had succeeded. Had General Lee made sure that support would be ready today? Had he given the orders necessary to exploit success if it were achieved, to reinforce the assaulting column and roll back the broken enemy to right and left? Ten thousand men —if that many lived to reach the goal over there across the valley— could accomplish nothing alone; but presumably General Lee would see to it that the Third Corps, the brigades not already involved, would rush to take a hand. And presumably Ewell had his orders.

Longstreet dismissed the question. His task was to break the enemy center. If that were done, it would remain for Lee to use to the utmost the advantage gained.

The guns were roaring, the Yankee guns were answering and there was as yet no slackening of the fire on either side. Longstreet judged that since this gigantic cannonade began, an hour had passed. A courier from General Law reported enemy cavalry on his right rear, and Longstreet called Captain Goree.

"Yankee cavalry are feeling Law," he said. "We've some troopers guarding the trains. Take them and any horse artillery you can find, and keep Law's flanks clear."

Goree galloped away, and Longstreet reflected that the assault here, when it opened, would relieve the pressure on Law. He mounted and rode to join Colonel Alexander near the guns; and from that new position he tried to appraise the effect of the cannonade. The fire from the rocky hill which Lieutenant Wentz called Little Round Top was light and inconsiderable, so apparently Colonel Long had been right about those guns. Elsewhere, hostile fire was slow; and once Longstreet was sure he saw a Yankee battery move to the rear. The time to attack was close at hand.

He rode back to where among the trees that crowned the ridge

Pickett and his men were waiting. Meade's cannon were searching the woods to find the assaulting column, and solid shot and bursting shell came hungrily seeking human flesh to tear. Longstreet saw a man sitting against a tree, staring at him with astonished eyes. The man had only half a face. A solid shot had struck away his jaws and the lower end of his nose; and in that huge torn wound white bone showed, and the stump of a tongue moved as though the man tried to speak, or to swallow, or to spit out the choking blood. The man wore a hat with no crown, and his red hair was enough to identify him as that soldier in the Virginia regiment whose jests amused Pickett's men: Red Wheatley, something of the sort, that was his name.

Well, Red Wheatley would never joke again, unless that writhing stump of a tongue sought even now to utter some jesting word. Longstreet felt a great and flooding sorrow for this man and for all the other men who would go valiantly out across those fields to death today. He swung his horse aside and at a little distance he dismounted and stood leaning against a fence. His downcast eyes filled and overflowed and he did not heed the tears.

General Pickett came to him and saw his distress, and asked quickly: "Are you all right, General?"

Longstreet spoke almost humbly. "All right? Why, Pickett, I am being crucified!" But that sort of talk would not do! He touched Pickett's shoulder in an affectionate gesture. "Yes, I'm all right! I've directed Alexander to tell you when to advance."

From the guns a courier galloped toward them. Longstreet thought the message might be for him, but the courier handed it to Pickett. Pickett read it, then gave it to Longstreet. The words blurred under his eyes.

General: If you are to advance at all, you must come at once or we cannot support you as we ought. But the enemy's fire has not slackened materially, and there are still 18 guns firing from the cemetery.

Pickett asked: "General, shall I advance?"

Longstreet's eyes drifted toward the men, waiting in what cover they could find, extending in an irregular line away from him through the woods. Red Wheatley with his jaw shot away was no longer propped against the tree. He had fallen over sidewise, but he was still alive. What had been his face was turned toward them; and that stump of a tongue still twitched from side to side.

Here came another note from Colonel Alexander. Again Pickett handed it to Longstreet.

> For God's sake come quick. The 18 guns have gone. Come quick or my ammunition will not let me support you properly.

Longstreet stared at the slip of paper for a long time, till Pickett said quietly: "I shall lead my men forward, sir." He waited a moment. Longstreet, unable to speak, extended his hand. Pickett clasped it, then saluted and turned toward his horse; but after a few paces he came back, drawing a letter from his pocket, smiling.

"General," he requested, "will you send this letter to Miss Sally?"

Longstreet nodded, tears streaming down his cheeks. He took the letter, and Pickett rode toward where his brigades were waiting. Longstreet heard his ringing cry: "Up, men!" Then, like a spur: "Don't forget today that you're from old Virginia!"

The regiments began to move out of the woods and down into the sheltering swale. There, the lines took shape, each regiment compact and three ranks deep. Longstreet watched them briefly; then he mounted and with a gesture summoned the men of his staff, waiting near-by.

"Sorrel," he said. "Stay with me. You too, Fairfax. Keep three or four couriers." His eye swept the others. "Gentlemen, some of General Pettigrew's brigades are under new leaders today. They may need guidance or direction. Three or four of you had better report to General Pettigrew."

Major Currain asked: "May I go to Colonel Marshall, General? I've friends in the Eleventh North Carolina, in his brigade. I'd like to be with them."

"If you desire," Longstreet agreed. He smiled grimly. "But leave that black horse of yours behind. He'll get you into hot water." He rode to find Colonel Alexander, Sorrel and Fairfax following him. "Colonel," he asked the artilleryman, "what's this about not enough ammunition? You should have sent for more."

"I did, General; but the ordnance train has been moved. My men couldn't find it."

"Then stop Pickett. Let him wait till you fill your limbers."

Alexander protested: "That would take God knows how long, General; it would give the enemy time to repair what damage we've done."

This was so obviously true that Longstreet nodded in sorrowful agreement. "I'd halt this charge if I could," he confessed. "But General Lee wants it. Have you those howitzers ready to go along with Pickett?"

"I sent for them some time ago, sir; but General Pendleton had moved them, presumably to get away from the enemy fire. I've sent twice without finding them."

Longstreet made an angry gesture. Mishaps and mistakes had trailed them day by day. "Pickett has a hard row to hoe, Colonel."

"General Wright says it's not hard to get there," Alexander replied. "Pickett will need reinforcements if he is to stay; but I understand General Lee is throwing the whole army in to support him." He added in a quickening tone, looking toward the ravine where Pickett's men were forming. "Here they come."

Longstreet turned to watch. Smoke from the enemy shells and from their own guns somewhat obscured the sun; but he could see regiments move up out of the swale. The line took shape. Kemper's brigade extended from the ravine to the right, Garnett's to the left; Armistead would follow close on their heels. Kemper was forming behind the screen of an orchard; he would have farther to go than Garnett or Armistead. This spot where Longstreet and Alexander sat their horses was in Kemper's line of march, for he would approach the road at a long diagonal, passing through the batteries, so Longstreet rode to one side to be out of Kemper's way.

Under red sunlight that came sickly through the canopy of smoke, the regiments, beginning now to move forward, were dark and gloomy masses. Over the clamor of the cannon Longstreet shouted to Alexander:

"Keep your guns firing till it's time to let them through. Then follow and guard their right."

Alexander nodded, but Longstreet's eyes never left the unfolding scene. As the nearer regiments came on, a faint west wind carried the smoke toward the enemy and caught the battle flags and fluttered them. Longstreet saw the pause here, the hurry there, which brought Kemper's front into alignment. On Kemper's left Garnett; and beyond Garnett all the rest of the assaulting force came into position. The gently rolling fields between the woods and the road, till a moment ago almost deserted, now suddenly were alive with men. Six brigades, say thirty regiments, say nine thousand men, formed the front of attack; six thousand more would press on their heels.

Longstreet from his position on the right flank could at first see across the gently undulating meadows the whole length of the front line, and the open ground between brigades and regiments as each unit preserved its individuality; but as the line came up abreast of him, it became increasingly foreshortened. The skirmishers moved in advance in many little files, four or five or six men in each file, so spaced as to cover and protect the whole front of the attack and to clear away enemy skirmishers before the main body came near enough to suffer from their fire. They went forward in short rushes, not running but moving at quickstep for a few paces and then taking cover while the main body came on. The skirmishers kept their formation, five paces apart, except when the order was to fire while advancing; then each leader halted and fired and waited to reload, the men behind proceeding a few paces beyond him, each in turn halting to let off his piece and load again. Thus the long front of the moving line was alive with single figures weaving an orderly pattern as they shuttled precisely to their tasks.

As the front of attack came abreast of Longstreet, his attention centered on the nearest regiments. Here was General Kemper, his brigade crossing a lane where two fences for a moment hindered. Kemper had resigned from Congress, had left the legislative labors for which he was preeminently fitted, to enter the army; but he should not be here today. In Congress, guiding the passage of needed legislation, he was infinitely more valuable to the Confederacy than on this deadly field. As an active force in the Confederate legislature he would be worth a division to this army; but here, any chance Yankee bullet might destroy him. But the South had little respect for politicians; it wanted its great men to fight. So Kemper had come perhaps to meet his death today.

The men marched at a steady battle step, slow enough so that none need lag and slow enough so that the lines could dress, yet fast enough to carry them steadily forward. Kemper's brigade had almost a mile to go, across those open fields and across the road and up to where the enemy awaited them; the other brigades not quite so far. When now they came abreast of Longstreet, they had covered perhaps a third of the way.

When the column of assault began to move, the enemy guns for a few moments held their fire. In this brief respite, Longstreet dismounted and seated himself on a fence clear of the right flank of the advance; but Kemper had scarce passed him before, from the hill by the cemetery, from the whole length of the ridge over there, from the rocky heights to the right, Meade's batteries let loose a cascade of shot and shell.

So Colonel Long was wrong; those guns on that lower hill to the right had not been silenced. They had simply withheld their fire to wait for a target. Well, they had their target now; but the men went on, unshaken. Longstreet found himself trembling with pride and with love for these brave men. He saw Kemper turn and shout something to Armistead behind him; heard a word or two. ". . . close up!" Armistead made an assenting sign. The regiments marched as if on parade. Pickett as he passed gave Longstreet a salute. His long curls hung to his shoulder, and Longstreet smiled in grim affection.

The fire from the hill to the right harassed this flank, and Longstreet bade Colonel Alexander give it his attention. Alexander said quietly: "I will move my guns forward, General, as soon as the men are past." Longstreet assented. Kemper and Garnett filed their brigades through the silent batteries, angling toward the road, and at once Alexander's guns whose fire was blanketed began to limber to the front. A signal brought their horses from the trees back on the ridge at full gallop to their work. Alexander explained: "I'm moving forward all guns that have enough shell to be of use, General. Most of them have nothing but canister left."

Longstreet made no comment, watching the advance. The long front of attack was far enough past him now so that he began again to see it in perspective, this time from the rear, sometimes as a whole, and sometimes in segments when the smoke of shell bursts for a moment obscured his view. Armistead's supporting brigade came on. There were brief clots of men here and there at a fence while the men tore rails away, or ripped off boards and crowded through the openings they had made. In one of these crowding groups Longstreet saw a shell burst, and another; and when that regiment paused to form again beyond the fence, half its strength was gone.

Kemper was across the road now, obliquing to the left toward where low ground behind a house and barn offered some shelter from enemy fire. That must be the Codori house of which Lieutenant Wentz had spoken; that was the swale where Ranse Wright had said they could correct their alignment and repair the ravages of enemy fire. Garnett was in the road beyond Kemper. Armistead, still on this side of the road, was approaching the knoll above the Codori house through a hollow twice as deep as a tall man, so his men were for the moment protected; but as they climbed the knoll and came again into enemy view Longstreet saw shells tear their solid ranks before they plunged down into the road.

Off to the north the regiments of Pettigrew's division were almost completely hidden by the smoke and dust; but they seemed to be maintaining their advance. Longstreet saw Kemper move up out of that hollow by the Codori house. Garnett was on his left, and in firm formation the brigades marched up the gentle slope toward the clump of trees where they must strike their blow. Armistead hurried to lend his weight to theirs. To reach the road they had advanced through steady punishment by solid shot and by shell; but beyond the road they came within musket range of Meade's line, and Longstreet saw the scythe of grapeshot and canister lay windrows of dead and wounded, as the mower's scythe lays ripe grain along the ground. He could not see clearly because of the smoke, but he could see enough. As Pickett's brigades emerged from the sheltering swale by the Codori house, the enemy cross fire caught them, and a blue column thrust out of some trees on their right to hit their flank; but Colonel Alexander opened on that column and Longstreet saw the Yankees break and scurry back to shelter. Alexander knew how to use those guns of his.

A courier galloped up to the fence where Longstreet sat with a message from Pickett. Pickett promised that the enemy's center would be pierced; but he said his right would need support. Longstreet, without taking his eyes off that smoking, fire-swept slope where the Virginians marched steadily toward the enemy, asked the messenger: "Where is General Pickett?"

The courier pointed: "At that barn."

"Tell him support is coming."

The courier raced away. Pickett was at the Codori barn, not two hundred yards short of the goal; but that last two hundred yards, every foot of it within musket range of the enemy, was a long road to travel. Yet Pickett's men went steadily into the storm of fire.

Longstreet turned to Moxley Sorrel. "Tell Anderson to keep the damned bluebellies off Pickett's flank. Tell him to hurry! Don't go yourself—send." He saw Sorrel's messenger start, saw the man's horse sheer from a shell burst and almost unseat the rider. Sometimes a courier's death or wounding lost a battle, changed the course of history; and also, Longstreet remembered that when Anderson's brigade commanders yesterday sent to him for help, Anderson had been hard to find. "Better go yourself, Colonel Sorrel," he decided. "If you don't see Anderson, direct Wilcox and Perry to support that flank."

When Sorrel was gone, his attention returned to Pickett's brigades. Those regiments, their ranks thrashed and thinned by cross fire, had not yet fired a shot; and Longstreet's heart lifted with pride. It needed brave men to march into the face of intolerable fire and never loose their pieces till the word of command. The slope they were climbing was not severe. From the Codori house up to the enemy position there was a rise of no more than twenty feet. But the men had no protection now, and the Yankee infantry had them in range; yet they went on at a steady pace. The line bent a little but it did not break. Longstreet thought that line of men was like a rug hung in the sun while the dust was beaten out. At every blow it yielded, it bellied backward; but after every blow it made firm front again.

A fierce impatience shook him. It seemed hours since those regiments had formed and begun their advance. Of course it had not been as long as it seemed; to march a mile, unfalteringly as these men had marched, was a matter of half an hour at most. But half an hour was a long time for men marching into death, and unable to strike their enemy a retaliatory blow.

Major Fairfax spoke to him. "General, Pettigrew's left is lagging. I think it's shaken."

Longstreet, his eyes on Pickett's brigades, had missed this. Smoke clouded the field, and Pettigrew's left was a mile to the north; but at first glance he saw Fairfax was right. "Send someone," he directed. "Have that corrected. And tell Anderson to move forward and support the assault."

As the couriers departed, his eyes remained fixed on the wavering left. Even from this distance, through the smoke of shell bursts and the hanging dust of battle, he saw men by ones and twos dropping behind their comrades. Those brigades had been badly hurt day before yesterday, and some of them today were in new hands. It was because he had feared some weakness there that he had sent Major Currain and others of his staff to that quarter of the field. They would do what they could; but Pettigrew's left was under close and heavy fire from batteries in the cemetery. Surely Hill would move help forward; and Anderson could throw some of his weight that way.

Then his attention was drawn back to Pickett's front; for from the ridge, even through the steady roar of battle, he heard the sudden shrill, yipping falsetto yell that had sounded on every field since First Manassas at the high moment when the Southern men drove in for the kill; and he heard a slatting blast of musketry. It was a little muffled. Those guns were pointed toward the enemy. Pickett's men had delivered their first volley.

So the charge had come to hand grips. This was the moment of decision, the climax of the charge, for which all else had been only preparation. His senses sharpened; he weighed every note in the clanging uproar; his eyes strove to pierce the heavy clouds of smoke; he summoned all his faculties to help him see what in fact could not be seen at all. He saw not with his eyes but with a sixth sense. He saw three or four or five thousand men smashing at the Yankee centre, saw as many more coming on to lend mass to that terrific impact.

This was the hour. It was for this moment they had marched the long way from their old lines at Fredericksburg. Now at last the question was put; in a moment more the answer would be given. The violence of that contention yonder could not long be maintained. Presently the scales must tip.

Longstreet could see nothing. All was hidden in that spreading, slowly rising smoke cloud on the ridge. But he could guess what was happening. Meade must have held reserves in hand for this moment. Meade knew tactics as well as any man. To defend against such an attack as this, the rule was standard: Let your guns weaken the attacking column; then at the moment of final impact batter its head with reserves, stab at its flanks, hack at its roots. So Longstreet knew that in this moment Meade would be sending a countercharge from the hill by the cemetery against Pettigrew's wavering left; he would throw a heavy stroke against Pickett's right. A momentary glimpse of a blue column coming down on Pickett was not needed to confirm that certainty.

Listening, watching, testing the pulse of this battle, he felt the issue hang in wavering balance for minutes that might have been seconds, might have been hours. He did not know; time had no meaning. As long as the attacking column moved forward even by inches, success was possible; but once Pickett was surely brought to a stand, his momentum spent, then he must in the end recoil.

When that moment came, when the attack was held, Longstreet knew it beyond any hopeful doubt. So the day was lost; the day that could never have been won was lost. He knew it certainly.

Well, they had failed. Now what could be salvaged must be. General Anderson came at a gallop, pulled up his horse, pointed down across the road toward a mass of men moving against the enemy force which threatened Pickett's flank.

"I've sent Lang to help Wilcox, General," he shouted.

Longstreet looked at him. "Lang? Who's Lang?"

"Colonel Lang's commanding Perry's brigade today."

Longstreet grunted. Another brigade in strange hands. But no matter now. "Halt them," he directed. "The assault has failed." Anderson looked at him in astonishment, for the battle on the ridge seemed at its keenest pitch; and Longstreet spoke in sharpened tones: "It's all over! Recall them! Place your brigades to rally the men." Anderson exclaimed in protest; but Longstreet pointed. "See for yourself."

Off to the north, soldiers of Pettigrew's division were streaming back across the death-strewn fields in confused disorder. Anderson saw. "I'll stop that!" he cried, and wheeled to race that way.

Longstreet glanced at the sun, still high. If Meade pressed them now, the danger would be great; but his jaw set. By God, if Meade tried a stroke, they would teach him a lesson to remember. Yet first Pickett must be extricated. Up on the ridge, the Virginians and some North Carolinians who on Pickett's left had pushed home their charge were trapped. The bluebellies would close in on them from each flank as they had closed in on Wright yesterday. Longstreet sent Sorrel to bid Pickett draw back his left and thus strengthen Pettigrew against a blow from the cemetery; he sent Fairfax to bid McLaws move forward and give Pickett's right what help he could.

The assault was broken; but Pickett's battle, though his flanks were crumbling, incredibly still held to hottest pitch as the men fought off the pressure on front and flank. Longstreet growled a curse. Were those Virginians going to stay there till the last of them died? A high admiration for their stubborn valor ran through him like wine; yet they must yield, they must withdraw while there were still a few of them alive!

Colonel Fremantle, afoot, came running toward him, panting with excitement. "General," he cried, "I wouldn't have missed this for anything!"

The contrast between the Englishman's words and his own thoughts was so absurd that Longstreet in a grim amusement laughed aloud. "The hell you wouldn't! I'd give a good deal to have missed it!"

The other stared. "Why? What?"

"Look!" Longstreet told him, sternly now. He pointed northward along the line of the road toward where men by twos and threes and half-dozens were trudging wearily to the rear, sullenly retreating.

Fremantle stared in astonishment. "Oh! I couldn't see that from the ridge, back there. What happened?"

"What happened?" Longstreet for a moment let his wrath loose. "Why, we threw fifteen thousand men against a hundred thousand. The God-damned Yankee guns made mincemeat of us, and Pettigrew's left broke, and if Pickett and his men had the brains God gave a rabbit they'd have broken too! But by God they didn't! They drove right into Meade's center and stayed there!" His voice changed, he spoke low and sadly. "But they're coming now. They're coming now. . . ."

What he said was true. Pickett's shattered regiments were sullenly withdrawing. They were not in flight, nor was there pursuit. It was rather as though two individual combatants, having met breast to breast in a storm and flurry of blows, now parted and stood breathless, with chests heaving and lungs sucking in great drafts of air. Up there two hundred yards from the road, the head of the attacking column had driven deep into the enemy lines; but then from the front and from both flanks men in blue converged, and the head of the column was crushed and obliterated, the supporting masses were pressed backward toward the road. The mêlée, in which all organization disappeared, rolled half way to the road, at first as a mass, then dissolving into groups. The enemy countercharge spent itself against the stubborn remnants of Pickett's division and of Pettigrew's. Meade's thrust could drive them no farther, but they were too exhausted and too few to attempt again to go ahead.

So on the gentle slope between the road and the stone wall that marked the enemy front, attackers and defenders separated. The men in blue withdrew toward the wall, gathering prisoners as they went; the Virginians and the North Carolinians, walking backward or looking over their shoulders toward the enemy, retreated toward the road. There was for the moment little firing on either side. The guns of the individual soldiers were empty; the men were too near exhaustion to reload. Even the Yankee batteries, until between Northerners and Southerners open ground appeared, were briefly silent; either they had no target where they could be sure not to hit their own men, or their ammunition was exhausted. When they opened fire again, it was to sweep the undulating levels beyond the road, across which by ones and twos and dozens the Confederates drifted toward the shelter of the woods.

Longstreet saw the contesting thousands cease to be one battling mob and separate into exhausted components. His eye swept the field. From the right, a few score men were falling back past Alexander's guns; and for a moment he did not identify them. A larger force was sidling off to the right, retreating toward the peach orchard; and they were commanded by a mounted man wearing a straw hat. That must be Wilcox! That must be his brigade. Then the torn regiments filtering through Alexander's guns were probably Perry's, led today by Lang. Longstreet had ordered Anderson to halt the supporting columns; but Anderson, intent on placing Ranse Wright to rally the broken left, must have forgotten these two brigades already advancing to guard Pickett's flank. Or perhaps Anderson sent a courier who was shot down before he could deliver the message of recall. So Wilcox and Lang had gone on to futile, costly failure.

That was a mistake, certainly; but if there was blame, it was not all Anderson's. He himself must share it. He should have made sure his orders reached those two brigades.

Pickett's men, what was left of them, were reaching the road. Longstreet went to meet them, walking along the road to intercept their heavy-footed withdrawal, heedless of the furious cannonade, ignoring the shell bursts from those unrelenting Yankee guns which took their heavy toll. General Lee was already among the retreating men, steadying them with firm words. Longstreet came to Ranse Wright's brigade, ready where Anderson had halted it. "You had better extend your lines, General," he suggested. "Give these men a reassuring word. We must rally them."

He himself went on into the trickling stream. The men were not running. They moved at a walk, ignoring the shells that sprinkled death among them as a man shakes salt on eggs. Some seemed half-asleep, their eyes dulled, their mouths blackened with powder from the cartridges they had ripped open with their teeth when they reloaded. Some weaved and wavered with the drunkenness of fatigue, with weariness more of the spirit than of the flesh. Many, weaponless, hugged blood-stained arms, or pressed their hands against dark spreading blots on their jackets; or their trousers were red streaked where blood had spilled from a wounded leg, or their feet left red prints on the ground. In some, anger found outlet in curses, in backward-shaken fists.

Longstreet spoke in easy tones. "Take your time, men. Keep your faces towards those people. You don't want to be shot in the back. Form among the trees up there on the ridge. They'll come over and give you a chance at them." Some heeded, some like deaf men pressed

by him and went on. He was a rock dividing the ebbing flood, talking steadily and calmly to the passing men; his throat was dry from
powder fumes and from the dust raised by scuffing feet. He said absently to Colonel Fremantle, still at his side: "I'd give a good deal for
a drink."

The Englishman produced a small silver flask. "There's a little rum
in this." Longstreet lifted it to his lips, then stoppered the flask to return it; but Fremantle said: "Won't you keep it, sir, as a remembrance?"

Longstreet smiled. "Remembrance? I'm not likely to forget today,
Colonel. But thank you." It occurred to him to warn McLaws to be
ready to hit Meade's flank if the Yankees advanced. He turned back
to where he had left his horse, retracing his steps to the fence above
the road where he had sat to watch the charge. As he arrived there,
so did Latrobe, with his saddle slung over his shoulder. Longstreet
asked: "Where's your horse, Latrobe?"

"I left him down by the barn yonder, went on with Garnett's brigade." Latrobe added in a low tone: "That was a slaughter house up
there, General. I could hear the bullets thudding into men's flesh all
around me, like hailstones on a roof. My horse was dead when I got
back to where I'd left him."

Sorrel joined them. He too was afoot. Longstreet bade him take a
courier's mount and carry the message to McLaws. Then he saw
Pickett walking toward him, and went to meet Pickett and threw his
arms around the man in a heartening embrace. Even in that moment
he was struck by the absurdity of Pickett's perfumed locks, their scent
heavy in his nostrils. With his arm across the other's shoulder, he
said:

"They're steadying now, General. It's all right now."

Pickett's lips were twisting like tortured snakes, his eyes blazing.
"Colonel Alexander promised to take some howitzers forward with
me! Why didn't he?"

Longstreet almost smiled. How often men desperate with grief thus
lashed out at some trifling annoyance! He said appeasingly: "Colonel
Alexander could not find the howitzers when they were needed, General. Someone had moved them to safety."

"Safety!" Pickett's voice rang. "General, we shattered two lines of

Federal infantry, took two lines of guns. But I had no support! Pettigrew's men broke! I sent my brother to try to rally them, but most of them ran away!"

Someone spoke beside them, and Longstreet saw Major Currain. "I was with Colonel Marshall's regiment, on your left, General Pickett," Trav said in a grating voice; and Longstreet saw the dregs of battle passion in his eyes. "Your words are unjustified!" Pickett stared at him in some astonishment, and Longstreet nodded in affectionate approval. Good for Currain! Let him stand up for his North Carolinians! Pickett was too ready with blame. Currain went on, speaking with a characteristic precision. "When we came under fire from the batteries in the cemetery, our artillery gave us no protection. I sent back to ask for help; but they were out of ammunition, had used it all this morning. So the guns in the cemetery cut us to pieces. I expected Pettigrew's men to break long before they did. I don't know how they went so far. But not all of them faltered, sir! I was with the Eleventh North Carolina. Some of us got into the Yankee lines, till a column coming down from the cemetery threatened to cut us off." His tone modified, lost its stern rasp. "Company C of our regiment went in with forty men and only three came back." Longstreet chuckled again. Trust Currain to think in figures. "We did all men could do, General!"

Pickett nodded. "Yes, yes," he assented, "I suppose you did, but so did we!" He turned to Longstreet. "Garnett is dead," he said. "Armistead too, I believe. Kemper's badly hurt. I don't think there's a field officer left in my division."

General Lee, unperceived, rode up to where they stood, and heard, and said gently: "This was all my fault, General Pickett." Longstreet looked at Lee in sudden surging tenderness for this brave man who spread his broad shoulders to receive the burden of blame. Today was General Lee's fault, yes; but it was also Stuart's fault, and Hill's, and Ewell's. Yes, and his own fault, too. This army was invincible unless its leaders failed. "It was all my fault," Lee repeated. "But now you must rally your division to meet those people."

Pickett, his voice hard with rage and sorrow, stiffly protested: "General Lee, I have no division!"

But Longstreet touched his arm, silenced him; and Lee repeated:

"This has been my fight, General; and the blame is mine. Your men did all men can do. The fault is entirely my own."

He rode away from them, and Pickett said, half-sobbing: "Armistead led his men right into them, his hat on his sword!"

Trav spoke. "Yes, I saw him! The sword had pierced his hat, and the hat slid down to the hilt. He had his hand on one of their guns when he fell."

Currain's face was smoke-blackened, and his garments were stained. "Are you hurt, Major?" Longstreet asked.

"No sir." Trav looked at blood on his sleeve. "I helped lead one of the men who had a broken arm."

Longstreet only half listened. West of the road there were steady men now, waiting for the attack that was sure to come. He said to Pickett as a quiet reminder: "Those are your men, General. Your place is with them." Pickett turned that way, and Longstreet rode down to where Colonel Alexander's guns were throwing canister to scatter some enemy skirmishers. Sorrel overtook him to report that cavalry had broken into Law's flank and rear.

"In force?"

"Two or three hundred."

"Law will destroy them," Longstreet said confidently. The skirmishers under Alexander's guns scattered and disappeared. Time was passing. Perhaps Meade would not attack, after all. He must be shaken by this day's work, and caution would restrain him. The afternoon was waning fast. Unless Meade struck quickly, night would come.

General Wilcox came to Longstreet, his face white under that old straw hat. "General," he said quietly, "you sent me in support, but when I got up to the Yankee front I could find no one to support."

"We've all done the best we could, General," Longstreet reminded him. He spoke to Alexander. "How's your ammunition?"

"I've a little."

"Use it sparingly. We must stay here and make a bold front for a while."

"We've no thought of withdrawing, General."

The retreating infantry reached the cover of the woods. Except for the thickly scattered forms of dead men and of wounded, and the litter-bearers at their work, and a few officers riding here and there, the fields and meadows across which the attacking columns had advanced were now almost deserted. General Lee rode down to join Longstreet here behind the guns, and they sat side by side, both of them studying the enemy position which so many men had died to reach. There was no stir of forming columns there; and Longstreet said quietly:

"I don't believe they're coming, General."

Lee did not at once reply. Longstreet looked toward him, then quickly away again. For that moment, since there were none to see, since he need not for the sake of his beaten army wear a firm demeanor, Lee's defenses were down, and his woeful grief was in his eyes. Longstreet felt shamed as though he had intruded upon another's prayers. Lee said half to himself: "It's all my fault. I thought my men were invincible."

A courier from General Law reported that the enemy cavalry which pierced his line had been destroyed. Longstreet nodded. "Please tell General Law and General McLaws that they had better resume the positions from which they attacked yesterday." The courier galloped away.

Over near the cemetery there was a sudden gust of cheers. That might be the signal for an enemy advance; but nothing happened. Colonel Alexander said the Yankees appeared to be cheering some officer riding along the ridge. "Probably General Meade," he said. Longstreet saw Lee's shoulders sag a little, and the commanding general rode slowly away.

Longstreet's thoughts turned to the hours ahead. He sent word to General Law to draw his right back far enough to protect the trains, then spoke to Colonel Alexander. "I think you might move your guns, one or two at a time. If they can find the caisson trains, they can fill their limbers."

Alexander signalled, and horses came cantering from the woods. The artilleryman said thoughtfully: "It was strange for General Lee to come down here alone, with none of his staff, not even couriers. I think Marse Robert was looking for a fight! I think he expected the enemy would charge these guns and wanted to be in it."

"Probably," Longstreet agreed. "I used to feel that way sometimes. That's why I no longer wear even a sword. Being unarmed keeps me out of temptation."

Two guns, the horses at a trot, moved off toward the shelter of the woods. Far away on Ewell's front, a few guns sounded. Longstreet, as the sun sank behind him, saw his shadow reach out toward the enemy. The day was spent. Alexander sent two more guns to safety, and Longstreet's thoughts went to dwell among the Yankees yonder. He imagined their jubilations, their loud exultant words. Victory there, defeat here; but both there and here, and all across these fields upon which presently night would lay its shades, dead men and wounded men, friend and enemy, were united in death or in the shared agony of dreadful hurt. Would the moon shine tonight upon this silent field? He thought not. There was some mackerel sky. If that meant rain tomorrow, retreat would be hindered; but pursuit would be hindered too.

The sun set and darker shadows shrouded the scene, where now the only sounds were far faint cries of wounded men beseeching easement of their pain. He raised his glasses to study in the failing light the ground Pickett's men had trod today. The slightly rising slope beyond the road was clotted with the bodies of the dead. They lay flattened like sacks from which the grain had spilled. He thought he could distinguish even at this distance a wounded man from a dead one. No matter how motionless a wounded man lay, life somehow gave his body form and composition. He was still visibly a man; the dead were just bodies. A body emptied of life ceased to look like a man.

Alexander's last guns were withdrawing. It was time to go. The protecting skirmishers would fall back with the guns till they were within reach of support from the woods where the army lay. As he rode slowly toward the peach orchard he heard, ahead of him and at some distance, a long scream, rattling and choking and terrible. The surgeons were at their work. In the deepening shadows among the peach trees he saw some howitzers, and called a question. "Whose guns are these?"

A man he knew stepped forward. "Mine, General."

"Ah, Captain Miller. What are you doing here?"

"Oh, I thought if the Yanks came out of their holes we'd have some fun."

These puny little howitzers against that victorious army yonder! In sudden ironic mirth at the valorous absurdity of man, Longstreet laughed aloud. "You damned old fool, Buck," he said, "get back where you belong."

That laugh had done him good. He rode up to the barn which last night furnished hay for his bed. He was not hungry; but when food was prepared he ate. General Lee sent word to prepare to retreat. The loaded ambulances and the trains would go by way of Cashtown and Chambersburg, the army by the road through Fairfield and over Monterey Pass and down to Hagerstown. Hill would lead, then the First Corps; Ewell would guard the rear.

Longstreet recalled to his mind the map, considered the necessary preparations. The lane past the school house, by which they had come forward yesterday, would be their best guide in withdrawing. He summoned his divisional commanders to tell them what they must do. Pickett was silent with sorrow. McLaws had little to report, but General Law had been kept all day on the alert by enemy cavalry.

At ten o'clock Colonel Alexander came to say his guns were all withdrawn behind the ridge and their ammunition replenished. "We'll get no more till we meet the reserve trains, but we have enough for an hour or two of careful work."

Longstreet, watching Pickett, thought it would do him good to talk to someone. "General," he said, "here's Colonel Alexander. Did his guns serve you well?" He wondered whether Pickett would repeat that complaint he had made when the charge failed.

Pickett looked up and seemed to collect his thoughts. "Why, yes, Colonel," he said. "The enemy batteries on our right and in our front did us very little harm. There was one gun off to the right that had us under enfilade. I saw one shell knock over eleven men. But aside from that, we weren't hit hard." He hesitated, his eyes clouding with memories. "We were all right till Garnett reached the wall," he said. "Kemper was fifty yards behind, and Armistead too; so Garnett's men took the first volley. It staggered them. Kemper was lapping

Garnett a little; so I swung him more to the right, and then Armistead came up, and we all went in together." Longstreet saw that to talk did seem to steady him. Pickett said to Alexander: "Your guns helped. Yes."

"We drew their fire, at least," Alexander remarked. "We had a hundred and forty men killed and wounded, lost about as many horses."

Pickett seemed to shudder. "I dread our next roll call. We must have lost fully half our strength, two or three thousand men."

When Colonel Alexander left them, Longstreet stayed with Pickett in slow talk with many silences. After a time General Imboden rode into the firelight and dismounted. Longstreet rose to greet him, and the cavalryman said: "General, I've just seen General Lee." They drew aside together, and Imboden explained: "I am to guard the trains on the retreat. General Lee wants all wagons and ambulances ready to start early in the morning."

"How is he?"

"Why—tired, of course." Imboden spoke slowly. "I ventured to say the day had been hard on him, and he said it was a sad, sad, day for all of us. Then he said he'd never seen troops behave as splendidly as Pickett's. He said it was too bad, said it two or three times: too bad, too bad, too bad."

Longstreet rubbed his hand across his beard. "You'll be taking the wounded," he remarked. "It will be a bitter journey for them."

"I'd rather be shot than have this duty."

"Yes, they'll have a hard time. If they had their choice, I think most of them would prefer to stay here, to die or get well in Yankee hands."

"I suppose so," Imboden assented. "But we can't leave them behind."

"My wagons will be ready," Longstreet promised; and he watched the other ride away. His thoughts were harsh with pity. No, we can't leave the wounded behind. We can't waste men, so we will gather up the poor broken fellows and haul them back to Virginia! Never mind their screams! Haul them back so the surgeons can patch them up! From now on we'll need every man who can fire a gun. We'll grow weaker now with every day; but we'll fight on, fight on, fight on as long as we've a finger to pull trigger. So dump the poor devils in the ambulances and trundle them back to Virginia. Bounce them over the mountain roads. Never mind their screams. Haul them home. Patch them up and thrust a gun into their hands.

They'll wish they were dead, before they get back across the mountains to the river. Many of them will die before they see Virginia again. Yes, a lot of them.

And the lucky ones will be the first to die.

III

Retreat to Appomattox
1863 - 1865

1

REDFORD STREEAN was worried about the price of nails; but the worry was rather a matter of sentiment than of cupidity. More than two years before, convinced that war with the North would provide many opportunities for profit, he had put what money and credit he could muster into commodities that seemed likely to advance in price. His first purchase was a hundred kegs of cut nails. There were only two nail factories in the Confederacy; and it seemed likely that not only would nails be in demand, but also, since metal would be directed to more warlike uses, they would be scarce. He had seen that original modest speculation show, at least on paper, a substantial profit; and when General Lee's northward-moving army invaded Pennsylvania, the market price of his little trove of nails was five or six times their original cost.

The amount involved was no longer of any real importance to Streean. By a discreet use of government funds diverted from the sums he handled in the Quartermaster's department, he had made so many and such substantial profits on salt and leather and flour and bacon, and through his partnership with Captain Pew in running the blockade, that he could give away that little lot of nails and laugh at the loss involved. But they were his first venture and as a matter of pride he wished to squeeze out of them the last possible penny.

The campaign of 1862, when Lee threw the Union armies back from Richmond and after a summer's fighting invaded Maryland, had caused him no concern. The men then were ill supplied; probably half the soldiers were barefoot—he himself was holding some leather for a rising market, so he kept a careful eye on such matters—and he had been sure Lee could accomplish nothing with the hungry, tired, ragged army he led across the Potomac. This year, however, Lee's army was fresh, inspired by a great victory at Chancellorsville, and more numerous and better equipped than ever before. Also, it was early summer and there were months of fighting weather ahead. Lee might quite possibly seize Baltimore and even Washington; for the army as it moved northward met no serious opposition anywhere. If the South held its own, or gained any real advantage, the peace party in the North would sweep Lincoln out of office at next year's election, though it was true that President Davis feared an invasion of the North would strengthen Lincoln's hand and had advised against this move. There were even some whispers that secret assurances from England promised that recognition of the Confederacy could be won by a successful summer campaign. Colonel Fremantle had been in Richmond a week or ten days ago; he had seen General Bragg in Chattanooga, he had visited Charlestown; and now he was gone to watch Lee's army. Conceivably he was sent by England to report what he saw and thus to guide her decision.

So if Lee's campaign proved to be a success, the war might come to a sudden end; and if that happened the price of nails would fall. But if he sold them now and Lee was beaten and the price continued to advance, his nails would feel he had betrayed them. They were his lucky nails; if he failed them, they might take his luck away. They were stored in the cellar of his home; he sometimes went down to touch the neatly piled kegs, as though to consult an oracle.

To sell or not to sell, that was his problem. He wavered in a long indecision. Panic in Pennsylvania? Perhaps he had better sell; but he waited through the late June days, postponing any action. Sunday, the twenty-eighth of June, there was a rumor that Lee had taken and destroyed Harrisburg, and he decided to sell; but before he could do so another rumor that Vicksburg had fallen made him change his mind and wait again. Wednesday, the first of July, the officer of the flag-of-truce boat at City Point said it was true that Harrisburg had fallen; but the Union army on the Peninsula had marched up close to the fortifications of Richmond. If Lee took Washington while Richmond fell, what then? On Thursday, President Davis was reported to be sick. That suggested he had heard bad news from Lee. Friday the Union force in front of Richmond withdrew. Had it gone to try to save Washington? Streean, weighing every fact and rumor, lost his appetite; but three men came offering him five hundred dollars apiece if he would see that they were detailed to government duties that would keep them out of the clutches of the conscription bureau till fall, and to pocket this money revived his confidence. He would wait a little longer.

Saturday was the Fourth, but it brought no news. Streean spent a profitable hour with Mr. Myers, the lawyer, who had clients willing to pay as much as a thousand dollars to anyone who could get them out of the army. Sunday evening came Northern papers reporting an indecisive battle at Gettysburg. If the North called the battle indecisive it was probably a victory for Lee. Monday, street rumor said that Lee had annihilated the enemy; and Streean would have sold his nails that day had not Captain Pew come from Wilmington with reports of a tremendously profitable voyage and with a cool certainty that any rumor of a victory for Lee must be false.

"He's two hundred miles from his base," Captain Pew pointed out. "He's grown weaker with every mile, and the army in front of him has grown stronger." He laughed confidently. "Don't draw such a long face, Streean. We can't beat the North, and we'll never admit we're beaten. This business will go on another two years, maybe more."

So Streean was heartened. Captain Pew gave some account of his trip. "I brought in one box of medicines," he said. "Just a little box, so small I stowed it in my cabin; but I charged them five hundred pounds sterling as freight on that alone. And I had a lot of stays that cost me a shilling and brought three dollars in Wilmington." But these were just odd items. He had taken out nine hundred bales of cotton, bought at eleven cents the pound and sold in Nassau for sixty; his return freight—cloth for uniforms, blankets, boots and shoes, boiler iron, copper, and zinc—was carried at eighty pounds sterling the ton. "And I brought enough light goods—silks, laces, linens—to pay all expenses of the voyage, so the rest is profit. We'll net half what the *Dragonfly* cost us." He grinned. "I brought a hundred barrels of beef. It was some condemned navy beef, billed out of New York to

Liverpool; but they carried it to Nassau, and the freight was right. We scraped off the 'condemned' marks. The army can eat it."

"Did you have any trouble coming in?"

"Well, we were chased. We had to run right in the breakers for two hours, with one of their steamers shooting at us; but at dark I stopped and she went on—she couldn't see me, but I could see her guns flash—and I put out to sea across her wake and she lost us."

"Did she hit you?"

"Twice. It will take a week or two to patch us up."

"I suppose you know," Streean remarked, "that the Government's planning to start a line of steamers."

Pew smiled. "They won't make more than a trip or two. The pilots would rather work for the trading companies. We pay better. They'll lose the Government ships, run them ashore."

Streean nodded. "Nassau as lively as ever?"

"More so," Pew assured him. "They're opening a fine hotel, the Royal Victoria, on the hill above the jail. The town built it and leased it to a man named Powell, to run. You can sit on the balconies and see all over the town and the harbor."

"Town built it?"

"Yes. Yes, they've money to burn. They've paid off the public debt from harbor fees. Imports and exports this year will run close to ten million pounds sterling, four or five times last year. There's cotton piled on every wharf, so much that when you get there with a cargo you have to wait till there's room to unload it." His tone stirred, half with mirth. "I tell you, Streean, it's one of the sights of the world. I like to sit on deck and watch the people on Bay Street, black and white, thousands of them, every one drunk either with rum or money. There are only a few buildings between Bay Street and the water, so you can see the whole show."

Streean wetted his lips. "Good harbor?"

"Good enough, long and narrow, with an entrance at either end. Hog Island lies across from the town. There's a thirteen foot channel, and fourteen or fifteen feet along the wharves. Channel's so narrow you can hardly turn around. I've known steamers to back out across the bar. The hurricanes hit it hard. There's a chain along the bottom of the harbor to catch dragging anchors. Yellow fever in the summer, and hurricanes summer and fall. All the houses have battens on the windows, shut them during a hurricane. But in winter it's a gay, pleasant place. Mrs. Bayley, the Governor's wife, and Mrs. Murray-Aynsley, and Mrs. Hobart give charming little dinners. Lodging ashore used to be filthy, but the new hotel is fine."

"Difficult to do business?"

"Oh no. Mr. Adderly's the consignee for most of the cargoes that come in, and he runs things. King Conch, they call him. He takes no nonsense."

Streean took Captain Pew home for supper, and Dolly gave him a pretty welcome, teasing like a lovely child. "What did you bring me, Captain?" A tiny flask of perfume and a bit of rare lace delighted her. Darrell had gone with Captain Pew on this voyage, and Dolly asked where he was. He had stayed in Nassau, Captain Pew explained, to watch for profitable cargoes for the *Mosquito* and the *Bumble Bee,* the other two blockade-runners which from the profits of their partnership they had acquired.

Dolly laughed lightly. "Cargoes? I don't believe that for a minute. You know he planned to go to Chimneys about the first of June, but he stayed on here till he went to Wilmington with you, and he wouldn't say why. If you ask me, I think he was flirting with someone, till he got tired of her; or else he ran away to Nassau to keep out of her husband's way."

"If he did, he didn't confide in me," Captain Pew assured her. "But I don't think Darrell's easily frightened by husbands."

Tilda was not at home when Streean and Captain Pew reached the house, but she came in time for supper. Since Mrs. Brownlaw decided that the starvation diet in Richmond was bad for her health and went to live with her daughter on a Georgia plantation where there was no shortage of good things to eat, Tilda had somehow stepped into her place, directing much of the volunteer work by the ladies of Richmond. Streean found this highly amusing. Arriving now she greeted Captain Pew and thanked him for the sacks of coffee and of sugar which he brought her. "I've had such a day," she sighed. "So much to be done, and so many ladies eager to help; but if someone didn't boss them around—" To imagine Tilda, who seemed to him so in-effectual, bossing anyone around made Streean chuckle.

At supper Captain Pew spoke again of the chase which might have turned out more seriously than it did, when for two hours or so the *Dragonfly* was under long-range fire; and Dolly cried: "Why didn't you shoot back and see how they liked that?"

He smiled. "We trust our wits and our heels, Miss Dolly; not our guns. In fact we don't carry any, no big guns. Blockaders would rather carry freight than the extra weight. There's more profit in it. Besides, if we fought back we'd be sunk—and maybe hung if we were caught."

"It must have been wonderfully exciting!"

"Why, not particularly, I should say. Except that our engineer was a coward. We took a shot through the bow and he came running on deck, scared white; so I stuck a Colt in his face and drove him below. I had to sit on the engine room ladder and keep an eye on him till we were clear."

"I wish I could go on a voyage with you some time," Dolly cried.

Tilda said: "Nonsense! Don't be ridiculous!"

"I don't see anything ridiculous about it!"

"It's too dangerous."

"Darrell goes."

"Well, Darrell's a man. It's no place for a young lady!" Tilda appealed to Captain Pew. "Is it, Captain?"

"Why, Miss Dolly would be safe enough aboard ship," Captain Pew declared. "But a lady might have some unpleasant experiences in Nassau. Yes, or in Wilmington. There are some rough men there."

"I could dress up like a boy," Dolly declared. "I could wear some of Darrell's clothes. You know I could, Mama. I could fool anybody. Couldn't I, Captain?"

"I doubt whether you could deceive anyone with an eye for beauty, ma'am."

"Maybe not you, but I wouldn't need to deceive you! Couldn't I go some time when Darrell's going, Mama?"

But Tilda, with authority in her voice, said simply: "No." Streean saw that even Dolly was learning a new respect for her mother; the girl pouted, but she did not argue.

Captain Pew lodged with them for a fortnight while the *Dragonfly* was being repaired. He spent as much of his time with Dolly as she would permit; but since she had many beaux, and divided her favors impartially among them, Captain Pew had no monopoly. She was as likely as not to go brightly off with some gallant young officer and leave him to his own devices. Streean sometimes wondered how long she could keep him dangling. He himself certainly would not have risked making Captain Pew as ridiculous as she did.

One evening after Streean had the reassuring news that Lee had retreated from Gettysburg to the Potomac, Enid came uninvited and stayed to have supper with them. Streean thought at first she must be ill. She had always seemed to him a casually pretty woman with a provocative suggestion of impropriety in her demeanor; but she was not pretty now. Her hair was in slovenly disorder; her color was bad, her eyes inflamed; and he saw for the first time pinched lines at either side of her nose. He was so struck by this that he spoke of it.

"Cousin Enid, what have you been doing to yourself? You look half-sick, tired."

"I?" She laughed nervously, protesting: "Heavens, you should never tell a lady she looks badly."

"Oh, you couldn't look badly if you tried; but you do look tired."

She made a careless gesture. "Don't let's talk about me. Captain Pew, I only just heard you were in town; and you hadn't come to pay your respects to me, so I had to come and see you!" Supper began to be served, and she cried: "Heavens, I must run! I had no idea it was so late." Tilda, of necessity, urged her to stay, and Captain Pew said courteously:

"Miss Dolly and I will see you home."

"I can't," Dolly told him. "Lieutenant Barwick just insisted that I go to Mrs. Marmont's with him to do charades. But Captain Pew will be your gallant, Aunt Enid."

Streean saw the Captain's jaw harden, but he said nothing; and Enid stayed, and when the waiters had been brought she asked: "Captain, didn't Darrell go to Nassau with you?" Captain Pew nodded, and Enid asked: "Where is he?"

"In Nassau. He had some business there."

Streean, watching Enid, thought she might have asked another question, but Tilda spoke. "Enid, have you heard from Trav since the battle?"

"Oh, I never get a word from him when he's away. I might as well be a widow."

"It's about time we had Lee's report," Pew remarked, and Streean said:

"The *Enquirer* claims President Davis had word that the invasion was successful and that we took eighteen thousand prisoners; but I don't believe it."

Enid agreed with him. "Neither do I. Trav says you can't ever believe General Lee's brags. He says we always lose more than we gain, every time we fight."

Tilda protested: "That doesn't sound like Trav."

"Oh he doesn't say it to everyone, just to me." Enid's tone was spiteful. "Of course, he's your brother, Tilda; but if you heard the way he talks when we're alone sometimes, you wouldn't believe your ears."

"Well," Streean commented, "we lost twenty-two thousand men when Pemberton surrendered Vicksburg; so even if we captured eighteen thousand at Gettysburg, the balance is against us." He was watching Enid, and with a certain anger, resenting her readiness to criticize Trav. Streean had always liked Trav better than the other Currains. This was partly because he could feel toward Trav, who seemed to him a dull and stupid man, a certain condescension; partly because Trav was less likely than the others to show open disapproval of his words or actions. The fact that to them he was always "Mister Streean," that sometimes as though sure he dared not resent it they let him see their dislike and their contempt, was too plain to be ignored.

He was handicapped too by a conviction of his own inferiority; yet he had good capacities, and once he had held ambitions of which he could be proud. If Brett and Faunt and Cinda had given him their friendship, he might have been much more than he was, and in worthier ways. If they had thought him admirable, he would have striven to become so; if they had liked him he would have labored to deserve their liking. Without pitying himself, nevertheless he sometimes thought that for his faults and his vices some of the blame was theirs.

Yet at the same time he accepted their unspoken verdict on himself, knowing that in their place his attitude would have been the same. In Virginia, when you asked who a man was, you meant who was his father, his grandfather; you looked first to the generations from which a man had sprung before you judged the man. A thousand, ten thousand times, Streean had heard conversations cut to the same pattern. "Mr. Cartwright Smith? Yes, his father was Judge Robert Smith, and his mother was Molly Case, and her father was Colonel Abernathy of King and Queen County. Her older sister married Jonathan Wright, and her brother married Sally Carter. Judge Smith's father was . . ." So on and on, through many ramifications. He could imagine someone asking Cinda: "Who is your sister's husband?" And he could imagine Cinda saying: "Mister Redford Streean. His father, Mister Tolbert Streean, is a farmer, a very respectable man." What more could she say and still speak the truth?

Streean accepted this tally of the generations as a proper test of a man's credentials, and he had hoped that marrying a Currain might somehow let him share their genealogical respectability; but Faunt and Cinda and even Tony had long ago made clear to him that it did not. Cinda's sharp tongue showed him no mercy, Tony sneered at him, Faunt was coldly courteous. Brett was friendly enough, but even Brett in the heat of discussion often let his dislike appear.

Of them all, Trav was the only one who seemed willing to accept him. Because this was true, Streean secretly thought there was a common streak in Trav; yet he was grateful, too.

So now he resented Enid's contemptuous tone. Certainly, her mother being what she was, Enid was in no position to be critical of anyone. He watched her with shrewd, hostile eyes. Tilda said the first of the wounded from Gettysburg had reached Richmond that day, that more would be coming; and then Lieutenant Barwick arrived and bore Dolly away, and after the brief confusion of their departure, Enid asked Captain Pew:

"Captain, how long is Darrell going to stay in Nassau?"

Streean thought she seemed almighty interested in Darrell. Captain Pew said he did not know, and Streean, his eye on Enid, inquired: "What's he up to, Captain? I supposed he'd come back with you."

"I don't think he needs a keeper," the blockader evaded. "He seemed happy where he was. He said he liked the climate there, said Richmond was too hot for him."

Enid's hand pressed her lips, and Streean half guessed the truth. By God, it was too bad of Darrell, even for a cruel jest, to involve himself with a woman old enough to be his mother; and it was worse of Darrell to injure Trav. Enid, as though suddenly conscious of his scrutiny, rose and said she must go; and Captain Pew dutifully went with her. Streean thought Darrell had probably found Enid easy game. Trav, for all his virtues, was not a sufficiently romantic figure to bind any woman in a long devotion. Enid had spoken of him tonight as venomously as though she hated him; and Streean with an enlightening memory, recalled the day he himself had begun to hate Tilda. It was after he wronged her by buying that wench, Sally, and bringing her home.

Thus now Enid hated Trav: Streean thought her hate was proof enough that his guess was true.

Streean soon forgot Enid in the contenting news of the next few days. Steady rain, which for a fortnight had drenched the city, continued; and up in Maryland Lee was backed against the river with an enemy in his front. A losing battle would mean disaster; and Vicksburg and Port Hudson and Gettysburg were disasters enough.

For Richmond knew now that Gettysburg had been a disaster. A dozen generals were killed and wounded, and hundreds or even thousands of lesser men had died. For a while, the defeat was not officially admitted; but Secretary Seddon, with heavy dark circles under his eyes, looking like a walking ghost, was unmistakably a man who had heard evil tidings. For further proof, President Davis on Thursday called all men between eighteen and forty-five into the army; and next day the announcement that Lee had crossed the Potomac back into Virginia was full confession.

Within a day or two, ten dollars Confederate would buy only one gold dollar; and Streean felt a cheerful satisfaction. As prices rose there was a rich harvest to be reaped; but so many others were bent like himself on profiting from the general distress that a man must be quick to seize the opportunity. Enid said one day that Trav had made money in tobacco, and Streean with a new respect for Trav considered investigating the possibilities of the tobacco market; but he decided against it. It was wiser to continue to deal in commodities with which he was familiar.

Captain Pew stayed two weeks in Richmond, taking what favors Dolly granted him. For the evening before he was to depart he counted on her company; but she came downstairs, so bewitchingly beautiful that even Streean chuckled in delight, to say she was away to a moonlight picnic at Drewry's Bluff.

"I declare, I just hate to go, your very last night here, Captain; but I've promised for simply weeks, and it's going to be wonderful fun, a band, and dancing, and marvelous things to eat. Sally Pickering has two turkeys from her father's plantation, and chickens and everything. If you liked, I'd take you too; but you just think we're silly children. Well, I suppose we are! So good-by, Captain. Some day maybe Mama'll let me go to Nassau with you! Won't that be wonderful? Come back soon, and bring me lots of pretties. Here's a good-luck kiss, if you really want it!"

She offered him her cheek like a ripe peach; but for once she had exasperated him beyond control. He took her face in his hands and kissed her lips with a rough violence; and she pushed free of him and protested: "Why, Captain Pew!" Her word was almost a sob, and Streean, watching with a secret amusement, saw reproachful tears in her eyes. "You hurt me!" she whispered; and when Captain Pew would have touched her hand, she cried: "No, no!"

Then she turned and fled. Captain Pew swung sharply toward her father, and Streean said dryly: "Why not play Dolly's game with her, Captain? Beau her to these shindigs!"

Pew was still angry. "If I do, she props me in a corner and goes gallivanting off with some sprig who's still wet behind the ears. Short of calling them out, there's nothing I can do."

"She'd probably relish it if you did just that. She collects scalps like an Indian."

"I don't bully children," Pew said curtly, and he added: "But I prefer not to be made publicly ridiculous, even by Miss Dolly." He grinned reluctantly at his own discomfiture. "Of course she enjoys tormenting me! If she ever did go on a voyage with me I'd have to put her in irons, or she'd whittle me in little pieces and feed me to the sharks."

"I thought a captain was absolute master on his own ship."

Pew's eyes changed in a way that made Streean wonder what he was thinking; but after an instant he said amiably: "Oh yes, but no man's master of a girl as bewitching as Miss Dolly."

Tilda did not come home for supper. Since wounded men from Gettysburg had flooded the hospitals she was absorbed in her work. So Streean and Captain Pew were alone, and they sat in talk a while. This had been a month of bad news for the Confederacy. Vicksburg was gone, and General Morgan's raid into Ohio had ended in disaster and in his capture, and Lee was back at Culpeper with his great venture lost. But the French had moved into Mexico and proposed to put an emperor on the throne there. "Plenty of Southerners would like to be included in that empire," Streean remarked.

Captain Pew nodded. "They'd snatch at even that straw; but sooner or later the South will be dragged back into the Union. The only question is how long will it take."

"Unless President Davis finds some way to feed and equip the army, they can't go on fighting. Quartermaster General Myers will soon be out of office. The public has been after his scalp ever since last November when he sent back General Wise's requisition for shoes for his barefoot soldiers and said to let them suffer. President Davis is so stubborn that the surest way to keep a man in a post is to urge Davis to kick him out; but Myers is going."

"Ah! Then I suppose you'll take his place?"

Streean laughed. "No. I don't want to operate in the—what's the phrase?—the fierce white light which beats upon the throne. I'll creep around in the shadows and pick up the crumbs." And he said: "By the way, speaking of crumbs, we can get its weight in gold for any railroad iron you bring in."

"It's heavy stuff to freight."

"The Government will pay any price for it. When the Yankees pulled back from the Rappahannock to go chasing Lee, we tried to gather up the rails as far as Acquia Creek; but we couldn't work without cavalry protection, and when the cavalry was available, we couldn't get men to do the work. But we've got to have rails. We're taking those on the York River line to build the Piedmont Railroad from Danville to Greensboro. If the Weldon Railroad is ever cut, that will be our only road south."

"They're not building that Greensboro road yet, are they?"

"Hell, no! Congress authorized it sixteen months ago, and North Carolina chartered the new road a year ago last May; but they've done nothing since then but make surveys and tie knots in red tape. They can't build it till they get rails."

Captain Pew was sure easier profits could be found in less weighty commodities, and Streean eventually accepted his opinion. "But we want to take our profits while we can," he urged. "By winter, Mississippi and Alabama will be in Yankee hands, and when we lost Vicksburg we lost everything west of the river. You've seen the crowds on the street here, heard the way men talk. A month ago everyone thought we'd won the war. Now everybody thinks we're licked, and they're trying to save something from the wreck."

"Talk won't bring peace," Pew reminded him. "All along the coast from Norfolk to Florida, outside of Wilmington and Charleston and Savannah, the country people are all for the Union; and Holden has a strong peace party in North Carolina, and there are peace societies all over the South. But Davis will hang on just as long as the army will stand by him."

"The women will stand by him." Streean thought of Tilda. He knew well enough her envious hatred of this world from which since she married him she had been excluded; but she was happy now in giving orders to these women who had ignored her, in seeing them grateful for being told what to do. Yes, Tilda was getting a lot of personal satisfaction out of the war; and you heard women every day insisting that the Confederacy would fight on and on. "But Davis will lose the army finally. The Yankees will kill them off, and the soldiers will desert every chance they get. They see a lot of the sons of the rich planters staying at home under the 'twenty slave' law, or getting some safe detail so they needn't fight; and they hear from their wives that their children are starving, and they hear all this talk about people getting rich out of the war. I had a letter from a Staunton man today. He said the roads down the Valley toward Winchester are full of deserters, most of them with their guns, so no one dares stop them. I heard in the War Department today that there've been close to forty thousand desertions this month."

"They'll shoot a few of them, put a stop to that."

Streean shook his head. "They can't afford to shoot them. They need them to do the fighting. Secretary Seddon's talking about an amnesty, to bring them back to duty."

Pew chuckled. "Tell 'em to be nice boys and come back and let the Yankees shoot them, eh?"

"But they won't come," Streean insisted. "I tell you, this war may end any time. The army's falling apart. There's even a rumor that General Lee has resigned."

"He won't resign as long as he's needed," Captain Pew said positively. "Don't count on that."

"I wasn't counting on it!" Streean retorted. "I was dreading it! Lee's worth an army by himself. If we lost him, we couldn't keep up the fight; so I don't want to lose him. I want to see us fight as long as we can." He added frankly: "The longer the war, the bigger the profits."

"Speaking of profits, is anyone trying to collect the taxes on incomes and profits under the April law?"

Streean laughed. "Not that I've heard. The tax on incomes isn't payable till January."

"There's a ten percent tax on profits made last year. That's due the first of the month."

"I haven't heard of anyone walking in and paying it," Streean assured him. "No, the only tax that's likely to be collected is the tax-in-kind, from the farmers. There's no way the Government can find out what profits were made, unless we tell them."

Pew chuckled and rose. "Well then, if my winnings won't be taxed, I think I'll drop in at Merrihay's for an hour or two. Come along?"

"No, gambling isn't one of my vices."

"You're the only man in Richmond who can say that. Except the ones who've no money to gamble with."

"Well, it keeps the criminals off the streets—and in good, respectable company." Streean smiled. "Have you seen that 'Stranger's Guide' someone wrote to the papers? I clipped it out. I've got it here somewhere." He went to his desk. "It's all aimed at General Winder and his Baltimore thugs." And he read aloud. " 'One: The very large number of houses on Main Street with large gilt numbers on the door are Faro Banks.' "

Pew drawled: "There's no number on Merrihay's door;" but Streean ignored him, continuing.

" 'Two: The very large numbers of flashily dressed young men with villainous faces who hang about the street corners are studying for the ministry and therefore exempt from military duty.' "

"That might be an idea for Darrell," Captain Pew remarked. "As a minister he'd please the ladies."

Streean read: " 'Three: The very large number of able-bodied, red-faced, beefy, brawny individuals mixing liquors in the very large number of bar-rooms in the city are not able to do military duty. They are consumptive invalids.

" 'Four: The very large number of men who frequent the very large number of bar-rooms and Faro——' "

Pew laughed. "Don't! You're breaking my heart. Besides, I've a little frequenting of Merrihay's to do, myself." He rose. "Whoever wrote that did us a service. As long as people swear at General Winder, they won't remember to swear at good patriotic blockade-runners who happen to make a little money out of the war."

"There'll be plenty to be made, as long as the war lasts."

"To be sure! And we'll make hay while the sun shines." Captain Pew lifted his hand in a cheerful gesture. "Good night. Leave the gas turned low, will you, so I won't stumble in the dark when I come in."

Alone, Streean went to his desk to consider some papers there and to study a letter from a man named Lenoir in New Orleans. Lenoir and Streean had had some profitable dealings, and Lenoir proposed now that Streean use his influence in the Quartermaster General's department to further a new venture. 'The Confederate Quartermaster in trans-Mississippi won't act without some sanction,' Lenoir wrote. 'But he's favorably inclined. I propose to buy two thousand bales in Arkansas and ship it here and trade it for supplies for the Confederate army, and then trade those supplies for more cotton and bring it to market here.' He went into details, and Streean checked the figures with care. If no hitch developed, there would be a profit of close to five million dollars, and those dollars would be greenbacks, not Confederate paper!

Streean had considered inviting Pew to participate; but he decided against it. Pew's share of their joint profits in their blockading venture, when you considered that he took out a bonus of five thousand dollars every voyage before any division was made, was scandalously large. A man who threw money away over the gambling table as Pew would do tonight, did not deserve to have it. Money was respectable! It should be kept in respectable hands.

2

FOR Cinda and Vesta those early July days when rumors filled the air but brought no certainty were hard and weary. Since Julian and Anne were living with Judge Tudor, they were, except for the servants, alone in the house on Fifth Street. Cinda's duty in the hospital gave her respite from her own anxieties; and Vesta, upon whom housekeeping cares descended, found in them distraction. Hard work was an anodyne; to go to bed exhausted was to sleep soundly. To be busy all day might keep concern for loved ones in the background of your thoughts.

But this was not always true. With the first trainload of wounded from the battle, Cinda's ward filled. Among the wounded was a boy whose shattered leg had to be taken off close to his body. A new supply of chloroform was hoped for, but the leg was already in such condition that amputation could not wait; so the boy screamed under knife and saw. Afterward when Cinda promised to write his mother in Raleigh, he said: "Please, ma'am, don't tell her I hollered."

She promised, and wrote the letter; but the leg did not readily heal. One day it began to bleed, and the surgeon who came to mend it said a small artery had sloughed off. He took up the artery and secured it; but on the second day afterward the youngster called Cinda to his side. His leg was bleeding again, this time with a hard steady pumping. She had learned by observation enough anatomy to press her thumb into his groin and stop the bleeding till a surgeon could be called; and the surgeon bade Cinda keep up the pressure and summoned Dr. McCaw.

The two agreed that the boy was lost. The main artery was gone, and there was no room to catch it except in the spot where Cinda's thumb was pressed. If she moved her thumb, the youngster's life would spill away before the artery could be secured.

When the boy knew the truth, he was the steadiest of them all. He spoke to Cinda. "Why, ma'am, I reckon you'll have to write another letter to Mama." She looked to the surgeons in helpless entreaty. "You tell her how it was," the boy said, "and tell her you was with me, and that I was all right." He smiled, and there was beauty in his eyes. "Tell her I wasn't skeered, ma'am." She nodded, careful not to weep, yet unable to speak. He spoke to the doctors. "Thank'ee kindly, gentlemen," he said. Then to Cinda: "Now ma'am, you been holding on a long time. I reckon you must be real tired. You just take your thumb away."

Her whole arm and side ached from the steady pressure she had maintained; yet she said to Dr. McCaw: "I can hold it." But he shook his head.

The boy smiled at her. "It's all right, ma'am," he murmured.

She met his eyes for a moment, bound he should not see tears nor hear a sob. Then with a swift movement she caught him up in her arms, held his head close against her breast. In a few seconds he was dead.

This boy might have been Burr; so it was wonderful to find when she came home an extraordinarily long letter from Burr, dated at Williamsport two weeks before.

Dear Mama and all—I've seen Papa and Uncle Trav since the battle. They were all right and so am I, but pretty tired. We've been on the go for over three weeks now, and from the twenty-fourth of June till the second of July we were between the Union army and Washington, making as much trouble for them as we could. We captured a wagon train right outside Washington, and some of the wagons tried to get away and we caught them on a hill and I could see all over Washington. The wagons were loaded with oats, and our horses needed grain, so that was good luck; but guarding the wagons slowed us down pretty badly, so we didn't join the army till they'd had two days' fighting at Gettysburg. Captain Blackford went to General Lee's headquarters that night and he says General Lee was sick with dysentery. We had a hard fight the next day, but the worst part of it for me came afterward. I was detached to come with General Imboden guarding the ambulances. It rained all the time. The whole trip was awful. The wounded were loaded in ambulances and on wagons; and the wagons, the canvas tops leaked, so the men were drenched all the time; and the rain and wind scared the horses and mules so they kept trying to run away, and wagons kept upsetting into the ditches, and we'd just leave them, because orders were not to stop for anything. There wasn't even straw in most of the wagons, so the wounded men bumped around on the rough road, screaming and crying and dying and you couldn't do anything to help them. Some of them kept begging us please God to kill them or to dump them out and leave them or anything. The road was jammed all the way from Gettysburg over the mountains and down the other side. As far as Cashtown it's fairly level, and that wasn't so bad. All the wounded men who could walk tramped along with the wagons. But climbing the pass above Cashtown was terrible. There must be four or five miles of steep climb along a winding road through a deep ravine and woods, a hard pull for the horses and worse for the men walking and worst of all for the men in the ambulances, jolting every which way, with their legs and arms shot to pieces, and the bones coming out through the skin, and rolling around like so many logs when the wagons jolted over the ruts.

I had to go on from Cashtown to the head of the column. You couldn't see anything, but you could hear the men crying and screaming and begging somebody to kill them. After we finished the climb, the down grade was almost worse. I'd have gone crazy but I sort of refused to listen, remembering other night marches we had made that were fun, if you weren't so tired you just went to sleep in the saddle. There'd always be somebody joking, making us laugh. One night on our way to Gettysburg it was pouring, and an old man in a house we passed opened his window and yelled to know who we were, and somebody yelled: 'Mister, you'd better take your chimney in! It's going to rain.' That kept us laughing till daylight.

But there wasn't any laughing on this ride. We didn't go through Chambersburg. Some country people showed us a short cut. I guess even the Pennsylvania farmers were sorry for our wounded. We took the Pine Stump Road—that's what they called it—through Walnut Bottom and New Guilford to Marion. You never heard of those little places, but I'll never forget them if I live to be a thousand. We came on here through Greencastle. The first ambulances got here day before yesterday, and the rest of them, those that didn't break down and have to be abandoned on the way, were still coming yesterday all day, so I guess the whole train of wounded must have been at least thirty miles long. There must have been eight or ten thousand walking, and thousands in the wagons. I don't suppose as many men as that ever suffered as much all at the same time before. Even not being wounded,

I was so tired I ached all over so badly that I wanted to just lie down and cry, so you can imagine what it must have been for them.

We were supposed to go right on to Winchester, but the Yankee cavalry had cut our pontoon bridge here the last day of the fighting at Gettysburg, and the river had been so high since that it hadn't been rebuilt. So we're still here; so the surgeons have had a chance to work on the ones that are still alive. We've been ferrying some men across, the ones that can walk. They'd all walk if they could. They fight to keep from being put back in the ambulances again.

Oh I ought not to write you about it, but I'll never forget it. It was the worst thing I ever saw.

But Papa and Uncle Trav are all right and so am I. I'm writing to Barbara too. Just a note. I couldn't tell her all this, but I had to tell someone. You write her that you've heard from me, in case my letter doesn't reach her. I haven't seen Uncle Faunt. He's probably on de-tached duty. He usually is. He's all right, I'm sure. I love you all.

Burr

We may have to fight here, if the Yankees can catch up with us through this mud. But I don't think they can.

Cinda had already heard something of the horrors of that march he described, for many of those wounded were here now in her care. Burr's letter made her live over that dreadful night with them. The letter had been written on the seventh of July, but next day they had another, written on the sixteenth and in better spirits; and at the month's end came a letter from Brett, brief but reassuring. He was back at Culpeper Court House. "We're camped two miles away, on the Sperryville pike," he wrote, and he said Trav was fine. "And I've seen Burr. He says he's written you. I saw Faunt yesterday. He's just skin and bones, but he says he's well."

Two weeks later, a warm Sunday evening toward sunset, Anne and Julian had come for supper; and they were all together on the veranda above the garden when Cinda heard the bell ring, heard Caesar go to answer, heard Brett's strong happy tones. Without knowing how she got there she was in his arms, hugging him and laughing and crying and pushing him away so that she could feast her eyes on this dear bronzed man, then snatching him close again; and then Vesta thrust her aside to have her turn with him, and Anne was next. Julian, last of all, came swinging expertly on his single crutch, and Brett kissed him too; and he said admiringly:

"Well, son, you're as spry on one leg as you ever were on two!"

"I'm all right for anything but riding," Julian agreed. "And I'll learn to do that before I'm through."

Cinda shivered with dread. If he could ride, would he wish to fight again? But this was not the hour for fears. "Come out where it's cool," she said. "We're going to have supper out there."

But Brett wished first to wash the grime of travel away, and she went up with him, clinging to his arm; and Vesta called after them: "Now don't you two talk about anything! Don't say a word till we can all hear."

They promised, and at first Cinda wanted nothing but Brett's arms around her; but when he came from the bathing room and began to put on fresh linen she asked quietly: "Was it as bad as we think, Brett Dewain?"

"It was bad enough."

"The newspapers had been promising us a great victory, and everybody believed them. Even the speculators. Prices went down."

"The papers print what people want to hear. You must expect that."

"We've stood so much; seen our homes ruined, seen our sons killed, seen speculators get rich and politicians squabble while things grow worse all the time. Politicians got us into this. Why don't they get us out?"

"Our best men aren't in politics, Cinda. We've let so many poor, shiftless, irresponsible people vote that good men can't be elected, and good men in office won't stay there. To be a politician is disreputable, so they go into the army. Men like General Kemper. In the Virginia legislature, he put through the bills to organize our state troops and to buy ammunition months before the war started, so we were at least partly ready to fight. If he were in Congress now, he'd see to it that the army was better supplied. We need such men there. But he resigned and went off to command a brigade at Gettysburg and got himself killed. Or at least badly wounded. I hear he's still alive, in Yankee hands."

"Were we badly whipped, Brett Dewain?"

Brett said thoughtfully: "I suppose so. Oh, we didn't run away. The soldiers fought magnificently."

"People are saying Ewell was to blame for not winning the first day.

And the same ones who said the invasion would win the war for us this summer are saying now Lee shouldn't have gone north at all."

"It's easy to be right afterward," Brett reminded her. "Ewell missed a chance the first day, of course. He did well at Winchester; but that first day at Gettysburg he hesitated. I doubt whether a man with only one leg is ever a good commanding officer." Cinda thought of Julian and her heart checked, but as though he read her mind Brett said quickly: "Julian's not a soldier, Cinda. He's all right." She nodded, and he said: "I wish after the first day we'd drawn back into the mountains, so they'd have had to attack us. To fight them at Gettysburg was a defeat before a gun was fired." He kissed her. "Come, let's go down to the children."

On the balcony Vesta and Anne were plaiting straw hats; the cheerful litter lay all around their chairs, and Brett asked a question.

"We're making ourselves new hats, Papa," Vesta said proudly, and perched the shapeless straw on her head. "Pretty, isn't it?" He laughed at her, and she explained: "It will look better when it's done. We get straw from the country and soak it in water all night, and plait it and sew the plaits together; and then we press them into shape and dye them pretty colors and put some feathers or flowers on them. They're lovely!"

Cinda saw, behind his amusement, tenderness and pride. "Hats are hard to come by, are they?"

"Hard?" Vesta laughed. "Oh no, this is easy, much better than paying blockade prices. Five hundred dollars is nothing for a really good hat, and I simply won't buy at the prices they charge. Why, merino is fifty dollars a yard, and even unbleached linen is twenty dollars. Everything has to come through the blockade, except Alamance plaid and things from the mills over in Manchester; so we just rummage in our trunks and take old things and make them over."

Cinda said quietly: "Sometimes we can buy dresses from our friends, when they go into mourning or when they have to sell things to buy food."

"I'm even learning to make my own shoes," Anne boasted, and Julian said smilingly:

"She doesn't have to, Papa. After all, we've plenty of money. But she thinks it's fun."

Cinda saw something stern in Brett's eye, the reflection of a thought unspoken; but he spoke lightly enough. "I'm about out of shoes myself," he declared. "I'll give you an order, Anne."

"Oh, I couldn't make men's shoes," the girl confessed. "I just take my old shoes for a pattern and make the tops out of some of Papa's old broadcloth suits; but I have to have them soled by a regular shoemaker."

Cinda had picked up her knitting. He asked her smilingly: "Have you turned cobbler too? Or milliner?"

"No, I just knit." She met his eyes. "It's something I can do without thinking."

After Caesar brought their suppers, Vesta had questions. Cinda thought Brett spoke evasively and only of nonessentials, relating small incidents that would amuse these young people. The prettiest girls, he declared, were at Winchester. "Along toward time to make camp I always kept my eye out for a pleasant smile; and then when we were settled I'd go back and invite myself to supper." They laughed at the picture of him playing the gallant, but he said with pretended complacency: "Well, I had mighty few failures. A neat compliment was always good for a meal." He chuckled. "And sometimes I sang for my supper." He looked at Vesta. "You get that lovely voice of yours from me, you know."

"How did you manage in Pennsylvania?" Vesta asked. "Play beau to the little Dutch girls?"

"Oh, we lived high," he assured them. "Cherries were ripe everywhere, and we could buy anything we wanted."

"Why didn't you just take things?"

Brett shook his head. "General Lee didn't allow any of that. No, the army paid for everything." He added, in a different tone: "Confederate money, of course."

"What's wrong with Confederate money?" Vesta protested.

Brett looked at Cinda and she felt again a thought in him which he did not utter. "Well, it takes fifteen of our dollars to buy one dollar gold, for one thing."

He had spoken only of trivial things, but now Julian asked:

"With all those pretty girls at Winchester, did you do any fighting there?"

"Not the Howitzers; no, we didn't fire a gun." He added: "We did some good work at Gettysburg, though. Not the first day. We were too late for that. But the second day and the third." He told Cinda: "My horse got away from me the second day, with everything I owned on his back."

"Did you catch him?"

"No." He smiled. "My big excitement came when one of their shells knocked over a tree right in front of my gun. I had to climb up on the tree and cut the top off, so we could fire. It wasn't any more dangerous up there than on the ground, but it seemed so. I felt almighty vulnerable, like one of those dreams when you think you're in a crowd with not enough clothes on. I chopped that tree in two with my eyes shut!"

Julian laughed with the others, but he asked: "Why didn't we beat them, Papa?"

Brett hesitated, his eyes sombre. "They were on a low ridge," he said. "Behind stone walls and with batteries set on high ground at either end of their line. We had no more chance to break them than the Yankees had to break us at Fredericksburg. We made a grand try, though. That charge on the last day—well, no one can imagine it unless they saw it." But as though reluctant to speak of the battle, he went on quickly, in a mirthful tone: "You should have seen us floundering through the mud afterward. I wished I was an alligator. Those miles back to Hagerstown were the longest, meanest, muddiest doggoned miles I ever saw. But we had a chance to rest while we were waiting for the river to fall. It was ten days before we got back into Virginia." He added cheerfully: "We've a pleasant camp now near Blue Run Church, with plenty of grazing, and clean drinking water, and a prayer meeting every night in the church. It's always crowded, too. The army's getting religion." His eyes met Cinda's. "They're so thankful to be home."

After supper, Rollin Lyle appeared. He too was on furlough, but only for a few days, with not time to go to South Carolina and return. Cinda had always been fond of Rollin, though the fact that despite a hundred open slights he humbly worshipped Dolly sometimes made her furious. She invited him to lodge with them, and he readily accepted.

When she and Brett at last went upstairs and were alone, they did not at once go to bed. He was in a mood for talk. "Well, I've told you all my news," he said. "What's been happening in Richmond?"

So she told him this and that, seeing him content to sit and smoke his cigar and listen, relaxed and at peace in this quiet place that was home. "I'm busy at the hospital, spending almost all day there; but I shall spend more time here, with you at home. They need me, but you need me too, Brett Dewain. There are wounds that don't show, but that need healing just the same."

He smiled, not speaking, and she talked on. The speculators, since Gettysburg, were worse than ever. Redford Streean, of course, was prosperous. "I don't see how any man in the commissary or the Quartermaster's department can look the rest of us in the face after this war is over." Some people thought that when that day came, everyone who was richer after the war than he had been before ought to be made to give up the difference. Brett said quietly that it would then be too late; and she nodded. "I suppose so, but we ought to do something."

Flour was fifty dollars a barrel, she said. "But the Warwick mills at least try to be decent. They sell one barrel to a customer for thirty-five dollars." There was talk that the Government might fix prices for everything.

"If they do, people won't sell," Brett predicted. "The farmers will stop bringing things to market. No one is going to sell anything unless what he gets is worth more to him than what he sells."

She nodded. This was probably true; but something in his tone frightened her a little and she spoke more quickly. General Hood was in Richmond, recovering from his wounds. His arm had been saved, but it was shrunken and of no use. Vesta had met him, thought him the gentlest, shyest man she had ever seen. Vesta was managing the house now, forever talking about making dyes out of herbs and alum and copperas and soda and such outlandish things, and planning to learn to use a spinning wheel and even a loom if they could find space to set one up. She was doing all the household shopping. Someone had said prices were so high that you took your money to market in a basket and brought home your purchases in your pocketbook; and everyone thought that so clever that now everyone was saying it. "If

I'm expected to laugh at that remark once more I shall throw a fit and kick and scream," Cinda declared. Richmond was full of refugees whose homes were in Yankee hands. Some of the finest people in Virginia were among them, ladies working as clerks in the government offices to earn a living, selling their jewelry and their books and even their clothes, sending their Negroes sometimes from door to door to peddle their pitiful treasures.

Brett's lids closed and she thought he might be asleep and hoped he was and kept her voice at a soothing monotone, letting her eyes have their fill of him, seeing the new lines in his face, the new gray at his temples, how thin he was. Some of the ladies were signing Mr. Memminger's currency. The notes were printed on big pink sheets, and they had to be cut apart and each note signed by two people. The cutting was done in one room, the signing in another, the numbering in a third. There were fifty women and girls in each room. Ladies signed their own names on the notes. Cinda's tone was like a lullaby, as though Brett were a baby in her arms; but suddenly he seemed to strangle. His head jerked up and his eyes opened, and she laughed and said:

"There, Mr. Dewain! I'm going to put you to bed before you choke yourself to death on your own collar!"

"Eh?" He rubbed his eyes. "I wasn't asleep!"

"Oh, you—" In tender amusement. "My dear, you were snoring like a furnace!"

He dropped his arm around her shoulders. "Just breathing heavily, that's all."

"You didn't hear a word I said. Why, you didn't even hear me read Jenny's letter!"

"Of course I did!"

She twisted away from him, twirling a teasing finger in his face. "Yah! Yah! Yah! I didn't read any letter from Jenny. I didn't even mention her. Liar, liar, liar! Brett Dewain's a li-ar!"

He cried in pretense of wrath: "Why, you infernal, contriving little trickster! Come here to me!" He sought to catch her hand, and she snatched it away and he caught her and with an arm around her waist swept her to him; and she whispered soft warning.

"H-sh! Don't, Mr. Dewain. The people will hear you!"

"Who cares?"

"Chasing me around the room like a greedy boy! Shame! What a way for a man in his fifties to behave!"

"I don't feel like a man in his fifties. Not when I'm with you, my darling!" He hushed her tenderly.

Next morning, laughingly remembering the night before, Brett asked: "Was there a letter from Jenny?" There had been two since he was last here, and she brought them from her desk and read them to him.

"She doesn't write often," she said, "but she gets an awful lot into a letter." And she read:

" 'Dear all: We're fine here. The people seem perfectly happy. They're mighty proud to be taking care of Little Missy. I suppose I'll always be Little Missy to them. They worship the children. Kyle and even Janet usually ride with me, and Clayton has a regular train of attendants everywhere he goes.

" 'I'm very much the planter now, in the saddle all day, watching everything. We'll have plenty of hogs and corn. The mill needs new mud-sills, and we're putting them in. We're raising hundreds of chickens and lots of turkeys, and I'm fattening ten steers in their stalls for beef. I'm having the people build a new church at South End, so they won't have to come so far to meetings. Old Barry makes very good work shoes for the men. We're raising enough cotton and wool for our own looms. Salt is our hardest problem. We've scraped up the smoke house floor and boiled all the salt out of it and we get some from the sea-water salt works. Our coffee is made out of potatoes, or corn; and we dry goobers and pound them up and mix them with milk and long sweetening and it's as good to drink as chocolate. The children love it. We can't get pins, of course; and you can see by these scraps of paper all written crosswise and up and down till you probably can't read it that we haven't much of that, and when we want buttons we make them out of gourd seeds, but the river's full of ducks and fish, so no one goes hungry.' "

There was more, about their friends and neighbors. Jenny said everyone resented the constant demands for soldiers to be sent to Virginia, when the Yankees were ready to gobble up Charleston any minute. Since the enemy forces had seized the islands along the coast, Camden and Columbia were full of refugees from the Low Country.

" 'Everybody hates the impressing officers taking our people to work on forts and things, and the Governor says he'll never sacrifice our rights just to please President Davis. He puts everybody into some office or other to exempt them from the conscription. Nobody has to go into the army unless he wants to, except of course the tackeys and the small farmers. Everybody with a few slaves is trying to buy more so he'll have twenty and not have to go and fight. A man named Matthewson over near Camden had nineteen and he was just desperate; but one of his women had a baby in the nick of time so he doesn't have to go. The poor women on the little farms around here have a hard time. They can't buy enough to keep them alive out of their husbands' pay in the army. Tell Rollin Lyle if you see him that I saw his father and mother in Camden a week ago, visiting the Warwicks, and they were all well. Tell Vesta Mrs. Cloyd is fine, although she just rages because so many rich young men are still at home, commanding militia companies, or safe on details, or something.' "

Cinda finished and gathered together the odd-sized sheets on which the letters were written, and Brett said cheerfully: "Well, she's all right."

"What if the Yankees take Charleston?"

"It won't matter to her. No Yankees will ever get as far as Columbia or Camden. Before that happens, the South will have been beaten."

"I think what scares me most is the inevitable way things keep happening. You see them coming dimly, through a cloud, like a herd of stampeding cattle, and you pretend you don't see them, and all of a sudden they're trampling you." Cinda pressed her hands to her eyes as though to shut out terror. "We're going to be beaten, aren't we, Brett Dewain?"

He came to put his arm around her and hold her hard against his side. "Not if your husband can help it," he said lightly, and she smiled; yet she knew the answer to her question.

The evening of Brett's second day at home, Rollin Lyle and Vesta went together to one of those "starvation parties" which began to be the fashion, and where the fact that no supper was served did not mar the fun. When they returned, Brett and Cinda were already abed; but as Vesta passed their door Cinda called: "Come in and say good night to us, darling." So Vesta came and sat on the foot of the bed in the darkness to talk a moment. "Nice party?" Cinda asked.

"Well, Dolly was there, so of course Rollin was miserable. He's such an idiot! But we sang and told conundrums, and talked. It was fun." Vesta laughed. "These 'starvation parties' may be all right, but I really am starved!"

"Go down and get a piece," Brett suggested. "There must be things in the pantry."

"Oh yes, dried apple pies, and molasses cookies, and cold pork and bread. Times have changed, Papa. But I guess I will go get something."

"Maybe Rollin's hungry too," Cinda suggested.

"No, I asked him. He says after living on what little they get in the army he feels stuffed here." She said good night and went downstairs, but a moment later she came racing up the stairs again and burst into the room and shut the door behind her. Brett called a question through the darkness, and she said breathlessly: "Oh I'm all right! I was silly to be scared!"

"What happened?" Brett was on his feet, going toward her.

"Why, I'd stepped out of my slippers so I wouldn't disturb Rollin, so I guess he didn't hear me——"

"Rollin?"

"No, no, the negro. When I drew a match and lighted the gas, the pantry window was open and there were two black hands holding onto the sill." The pantry was on the ground floor on the Franklin Street side, and the house on that side was flush with the street; but since the street descended steeply from the corner, the pantry windows were high above the sidewalk. "I slammed the window down on his fingers and locked it and ran!" Brett in his night shirt raced for the stairs, and Cinda came to take Vesta in her arms; but the girl said: "Oh I'm all right now! It startled me for a minute, that's all!"

"I should think it might, poor baby!"

"I'm silly to make a fuss."

Brett came back. "Gone," he said. "I turned out the gas." He asked gravely: "Cinda, does that sort of thing happen often?"

She nodded. "Richmond's full of half-starved negroes, of course. Not even rats and mice get enough to eat here now, you know."

"It isn't only negroes who're hungry," Vesta told him. "Of course people like us have plenty—not always what we want, but plenty of what there is; but the poor people are just starving. You'll see crowds of women standing outside the cartridge factories and the clothing bureau begging for work. They're there before daylight every day, and the police have to keep them from fighting for what few jobs there are. They have to work if they can, with their husbands in the army." She said in sudden anger: "Oh, it just makes me sick to see all the young men who've been exempted and who do nothing but speculate and gamble and spend a lot of money, when poor women have to see their husbands go off and get killed." She tried to laugh. "Heavens, I hate to get so worked up this time of night. Good night, dears."

When Vesta was gone, Brett asked: "Is it as bad as she says?"

"Yes," Cinda assented. "Yes." And she added grimly: " 'Rich man's war, poor man's fight.' There's more truth than poetry in that, Brett Dewain."

"I suppose you'd call us rich, but we've lost one son, and a son-in-law, and had another son maimed. We're fighting, Cinda."

"Oh yes. So are most of the people we know, our kind of people. But for every one like us there are twenty like Redford Streean. The poor people didn't want the war, but they're being made to fight it, while their wives and children starve." She came into his arms, sobbing on his shoulder, for a moment surrendering to bitter woe. "Oh, I hate it, Brett Dewain. I hate it, hate it, hate it! Oh, I hate it so!"

She did not again let her secret anguish mar the happiness of these fine days when she had him at home, but she realized more and more surely that there lay some trouble in his mind. After his breakfast with her, since even with him here she usually went to spend part of each day at the hospital, he was apt to walk down to the Spottswood, or to the Capitol, or to call upon some of his friends who were still in Richmond. But they had hours of quiet content, Cinda knitting, Brett talking with her or perhaps reading to himself or to her a passage from the papers. This might be a more or less covert criticism of Lee for his failure at Gettysburg, or for his strict orders against looting in Pennsylvania, or of the Government's failure to supply Lee with the ammunition so badly needed on the third day of the battle.

Once Brett read aloud to her passages from Lord Campbell's speech in the House of Lords, advocating England's recognition of the Confederacy.

"Listen to this, Cinda," he said half in amusement, half in anger. "He's arguing that slavery isn't really the issue, talking about 'the lingering idea that freedom is involved in the retention of the Union.' And he says: 'It is for a despotism that the people of the North are pouring out their blood and tarnishing their glory. Already it exists. It had its birth in war and it would take its immortality from conquest. Then would the Union be restored for the advantage of the world? What country would be safe? What country would be free? At first indeed the necessity of Southern garrisons might keep them in repose. But in a few years—and they do not labor to conceal it from us—a power more rapacious, more unprincipled, more arrogant, more selfish and encroaching would arise than has ever yet increased the outlay, multiplied the fears, and compromised the general tranquillity of Europe.'" Brett chuckled. "You'd think the United States was threatening to invade England, instead of Virginia! Why do politicians always talk like fools?"

"They fall in love with ideas," she suggested. "Or else surrender to selfishness." And she said thoughtfully: "Have you noticed that Mr. Rhett and Mr. Yancey, who talked us into this war, are never heard of now? States' rights, secession, coercion! Yes, and slavery, too! All of them put together aren't worth the sorrow and suffering just our family has had to endure, much less all the other families all over the South."

He nodded. "The trouble is, people believe what they hear. I suppose that's because they don't know any better. That's why I don't believe ignorant people ought to be allowed to vote."

"Do they have to be ignorant?"

"Well, we've made it a crime to teach a negro to read and write, and we've never had many schools, even for white people. I've sometimes thought that if we'd spent as much money in educating poor whites, these last fifty years, as we're spending now to send them off to kill and be killed, the South would be a wonderfully happy land today."

"Are poor people any better educated in the North?"

"I suppose not. I suppose the ruling class and the moneyed class there—people like us and our friends down here—think it isn't safe to teach them too much. The more they learn, the more they want. We think if negroes learn to read they'll want to be free, and Northern business men think if working people are educated they'll want higher pay." He was silent for a moment, said grimly: "I wonder if sometimes good business isn't bad business in the end."

Knowing him as she did, his tone caught her ear. She guessed that some matter of business filled his thoughts, so she was not surprised when one evening as his furlough neared its end, he told her he expected some gentlemen to call; Judge Tudor, Mr. Daniel of the Fredericksburg railroad, Mr. Harvie of the Danville line, Mr. Haxall and Mr. Crenshaw who were bankers. Cinda thought they would prefer to be left alone together; but Brett asked her to sit with them when they came.

"I want you to hear," he said. "I want you to help me decide something, Cinda."

She asked no question. When he was ready, he would tell her. When the gentlemen arrived, Judge Tudor first, the two railroad men together, and then the bankers singly, she greeted them; and while they talked, she sat a silent listener, her knitting needles clicking. She would find later many a dropped stitch in that knitting, and much that must be ravelled out and done again.

They spoke first of the wave of desertions from the army. President Davis had offered free pardon to all but second and third offenders; but none of these gentlemen believed the losses could be checked. Mr. Haxall said there were too many causes behind the desertions: "Poor food, inadequate clothing, defective ammunition, the sufferings of their families at home. And the men see too many exempts getting rich out of the war, too many rich young men hiring substitutes or bribing their way out of the army."

Mr. Harvie added a word. "The deserters are organizing. All through the mountain country, from southwest Virginia to the Gulf, they're gathering in armed bands to resist capture; and they're turning to robbery, to violence against their neighbors."

Brett asked: "Can't they be rounded up, forced back into the army?"

Judge Tudor answered him. "The state governments won't allow force to be made effective. Governor Brown of Georgia, Vance of North Carolina, none of them. When the conscript bureau catches a man, the state courts turn him loose under a writ of *habeas corpus*. Congress suspended the writ last fall; but the states refused to recognize the suspension, and Judge Pearson in North Carolina ruled that to suspend the writ was unconstitutional. I talked with Judge Halliburton last week—he was a Federal judge under the Union, in the United States District Court—and I've discussed it with Judge Meredith. They agree with Judge Pearson; and they say they will never refuse a writ of *habeas corpus* in their courts." He added strongly: "And if I were still on the bench, gentlemen, I should feel as they do. This war is being fought to defend rights which we hold to be fundamental in a free nation. Not even to win the war should those rights be impaired."

Mr. Crenshaw took issue with him. "Judge, you know as well as I do that if you want a thing, you have to pay for it. If you want a pair of shoes you have to give up some money. If you want to win this war, you have to give up something, even some rights. We've destroyed the Union by insisting on our right to secede; but the Confederacy cannot survive, any more than the Union did, unless the states surrender some of their rights." He added: "The North, the Northern states and the Northern people, are giving up treasured rights, and they're stronger for doing so."

Judge Tudor said stiffly: "It's a matter of conviction, with me, Mr. Crenshaw."

The banker lifted his shoulders. "It's a matter of expediency, with me."

For a moment no one spoke. Then Brett said: "Let's take it, then, that desertions will continue. Mr. Daniel, can the railroads carry their burden?"

"Well, we can try. We'll try our damnedest." He looked at Cinda. "Forgive me, Mrs. Dewain. We'll try our best, I should have said. But we're short of railroad iron and short of workmen and short of brains. We Southerners have never learned to take orders, and we're so used to having things done for us that we aren't ready to do them for ourselves. On our roads, trains are wrecked every day by carelessness and by inefficiency. Of course, if we could pick and choose, we could carry more private freight and make tremendous profits; but we've put ourselves at the service of the Government, and that means heavy wear and tear on cars and locomotives. We've had to raise wages, and the Government refuses to recognize the tax exemption in our charter, so we pay heavy taxes; but we're allowed to raise rates when necessary, so income stands up pretty well. But we're being ruined by loss and destruction of things we can't replace. If a bridge is burned, it takes us forever to repair it. Last May a year ago, the North rebuilt the bridge over Potomac Creek, four hundred feet long and eighty feet high, in nine days. That same month, some Yankee raiders destroyed our bridge over the South Anna and it was five months before we could put it in shape to use again. Nine days against five months. That gives you some idea of the North's advantage in labor and material and methods. I don't know how long we can keep on, but we'll do our best."

Brett nodded. "I've heard complaints that some railroads carry such heavy shipments of speculators' goods that corn and bacon and uniforms for the army lie for weeks in the freight houses, and the foodstuffs rot."

"Not on our road," Mr. Daniel insisted. "But it's hard to blame the railroads that do take that trade. It's at higher rates than government traffic, and the pay is prompt."

Mr. Harvie grimly echoed that word. "Prompt, yes! The Government doesn't know the meaning of that word. Half our troubles come from their unnecessary delays. If the Weldon Railroad is ever cut, Richmond's only rail line to the interior and the south will be through Danville. The Piedmont Railroad from Danville to Greensboro would let us reach the lower south. That's only fifty miles. Congress voted a loan to build that road over a year ago, and we agreed to take over all the Piedmont stock and do the work; but we can't get proper surveys, we can't get labor, we can't get iron, we can't do a lick. We can't get iron to repair our own road. We've five miles of line between here and Danville that you can't call a railroad at all, till we get new rails; and our rolling stock is wearing out. But of course, as Mr. Daniel says, we'll do our best."

There was nothing to be said to that. The picture was plain enough. Brett looked at Mr. Haxall. "I'm trying to get some idea of what's in the future," he explained. "Outside of this room, all of us curb our tongues; but here we can perhaps speak more frankly. I'm disturbed about the financial situation, the depreciated currency, the inadequate tax program, the steady borrowing. Funding the currency last June, forcing people to take bonds—that was repudiation. What do you gentlemen think of the government finances?"

"Why, they're in bad shape," the banker said honestly. "I'd rather see our bank buy state bonds, Virginia or Tennessee, than Confederates. Last March, Virginia bonds were at a hundred and fifteen, and we sold them and bought Confederate eight percents; but by Christmas the eight percents won't be worth fifty cents on the dollar." He shook his head. "Bad, yes. Bad and getting worse. Look at the Erlanger Loan. The Erlanger people took the bonds at seventy-seven, and put them on the European market at ninety. They were oversubscribed five times, sold up to ninety-five. Then they began to go down, and the Confederacy agreed to support them. Right now we're shipping gold to support those bonds. The Erlanger people will make more out of that loan than the Confederacy." After a moment he went on: "If we'd shipped cotton while we still could do so, and had held it abroad, we could have established a credit to last us five years. Cotton's worth seventy cents in London now, and every ship that takes a load through the blockade makes a fortune for its owners. North Carolina troops are the best clothed and the best equipped in the army, and North Carolina has largely financed that by buying cotton and sending it to market through the blockade. But Mr. Davis preferred to use cotton as a club, to try to bully England into recognizing us. Now it's too late. It takes fifteen or twenty of our dollars to buy a gold dollar today. It will take a thousand of our dollars before we're through. The Government's wasting money right and left, allowing a seventy-five percent profit on every contract for shoes or cloth or war supplies."

"And that isn't enough!" Mr. Crenshaw reminded him. "The speculators outbid the Government, so the Government has to threaten to conscript a firm's employees before it'll accept a contract at that figure."

"Oh I suppose seventy-five-percent profit isn't so bad," Mr. Haxall agreed. "If the work were done in a businesslike way. But under such an arrangement every contractor knows that the higher his costs, the bigger his profits. If he wastes a dollar, the Government pays him a dollar seventy-five." He made an angry gesture. "There's only one end to it, Mr. Dewain. Two years ago, our credit was better than the credit of the Washington Government. It was a strong cable. We've stretched it till it's thin as a string. It will snap by and by."

"And our private fortunes will go with it?" Brett suggested.

"We'll all be paupers," Mr. Crenshaw agreed. "And proud of it." His jaw set stubbornly.

Brett looked from man to man. "So our army is weaker every day, the states are insisting on their rights even if to do so means destroying the Confederacy, our railroads are breaking down, and our finances are collapsing. Is that a fair statement, gentlemen?"

He waited, but no one contradicted him.

When Brett returned from bidding them good-by at the door, Cinda kept her eyes on her knitting. Brett sat down, his legs extended, staring at his boots, and for a long time he did not speak at all; but at last his head lifted, and he looked at her and smiled. "How'd you like to be a pauper, Mrs. Dewain?" he asked.

"I don't think I'd like it very much." She finished one needle, turned the sock, began to throw stitches on the next needle. Her hands were trembling, but her voice was steady. "You were a clever man to put our money into Northern securities."

"Yes," he agreed. "Everything but some stock in the Wilmington bank. Yes, that was the prudent thing to do. Of course."

She looked at him sidewise. He resumed his scrutiny of his toes. "Don't be afraid of me, Mr. Dewain," she said softly.

His eyes rose and met hers for a moment, then returned to his boots again. "I think," he said in a dispassionate tone, "that the invasion of Pennsylvania was our last chance for victory. If we ever had a chance. I've never thought we had a chance, really. The odds were always too heavy." And he added: "I've even thought sometimes that the moral odds were too heavy. This is a war to defend slavery. Oh, I know we cloud the issue by talking about resisting coercion; but the Gulf States seceded to prevent the abolition of slavery. They admitted it, avowed it; the men they sent as emissaries to the Virginia Convention in 1861 said it over and over. Take them at their word. They seceded so they could continue to own slaves. They shouted about their right to own slaves and their right to secede; but by seceding they broke up the Union. I was always a Union man. I'm not sure the Union isn't more important than the rights of any of us. States or individuals. I've sometimes thought—" He hesitated, said reverently: "I've sometimes thought that God might one day have work for a strong United States to do in the world."

"I love you very much, you know," she told him.

He nodded, abstracted, only half hearing. "I suppose," he reflected, "that you and I don't matter to anyone but ourselves. I began by thinking first of us; by stocking the Plains against famine, by saving as much of our fortune as I could save to insure our future. But we're on the losing side, Cinda."

"What then?" she asked softly.

He almost smiled. "I suspect our side ought to lose," he said. "And yet, if our side is to lose, I'd rather lose too." The needles helped keep her fingers steady. After a moment he went on: "Our family finances, the Currain finances, are somewhat involved, as you know. Your father left everything to your mother, with power to dispose of it as she wished. Under her will, made ten years ago, she left Chimneys to Trav, Great Oak to Tony, Belle Vue to Faunt, the Plains to you."

"Not to me, to you," she reminded him. "When a woman marries, she and her husband become one person, and he is the person."

He nodded. "To us, then. She had made a gift to Redford Streean when he and Tilda married, so there was nothing for Tilda; but all of you, including Tilda, share equally in her monetary estate." He frowned at his own thoughts. "I haven't consulted Streean, but I've talked to Trav and Faunt, and I wrote Tony. Trav and Faunt leave the decision to me; and Tony writes that he will take a deed to Chimneys as his share."

"Just what is it you're going to do, Brett Dewain?"

"Why, write Mr. Gilby," he said. "I'll have him set apart Streean's share." He met her eyes. "If you agree, of course. Then I'll have him send the rest to London in sterling exchange, and buy Confederate bonds there."

She bit her lip. "Everything?"

"Yes, the Currain funds, and what I had from my father."

"If you do, and the Confederacy falls, we and our children won't have anything?"

"No honorable man in the Confederacy will have anything, Cinda; not when this war ends."

She tucked her knitting away. "I don't understand business," she said cheerfully. "But I understand you. I knew you'd get over being a business man some day. I'm very proud of you." She went to kiss him. "Proud and proud of you."

"We're probably damned fools!"

"Of course we are. I'm proud of that, too."

Brett laughed, lighthearted now in her approval. "When this is over, Jenny'll have to support the family; Jenny and the Plains."

Cinda tossed her head. "Why not?"

She kept, as long as he was in Richmond, a high heart; but when he was gone terror swept her like a strong wind. What would it be like to be poor, poor, poor?

3

To TRAV, the retreat from Gettysburg had the quality of a nightmare. On the afternoon of that terrible third day at Gettysburg, he marched with those simple friendly men from the mountain coves around Martinston through dreadful fire from the guns on Cemetery Hill and through a driving storm of musketry into the very lines of the Yankees. He met them breast to breast, emptying into their ranks every chamber of that huge revolving pistol von Borcke had given him, hurling the charge of slugs from the lower barrel into the face of a great bearded man with the insignia of rank on his shoulders. Then the pistol in his left hand served to parry the strokes of an enemy officer's sword, while he himself wielded that terrible long blade which had been his father's. He would find later, deep scars cut into the steel barrel of his pistol where the Yankee's slashes had been caught and turned aside; but at the moment he saw only the spilled dead sprawling, the wounded shocked and still in their first numbed hurt.

That was reality, but the days of retreat that followed were a bewildering dream. He had seen these men beaten, but they did not march like beaten men. Their heads were high; the rough jests that broke the tedium of any march ran along the files. Their manner was that of victims of a clever practical joke, at which even though they were its butt they could still be amused. He thought their cheerfulness might be half-hysterical relief to find themselves still alive; yet it had the ring of complete sincerity.

Some of the officers by their mien confessed defeat. Pickett, sent off with his shattered division to guard prisoners on the march to Richmond, raged at the assignment; but most officers shared or imitated the good humor of the men. When on the morning of the Fourth a flag of truce brought Meade's message that General Longstreet was wounded and a prisoner and receiving solicitous care, Longstreet laughed aloud.

"Thank your commanding officer," he directed the messenger. "But say you saw me neither wounded nor a prisoner, and quite able to continue to take care of myself."

His staff took their cue from him. They laughed at Major Moses because someone had stolen a small trunk in which he kept the First Corps' supply of currency; and they laughed when he had a lively argument with a gathering of women in a farm house. They laughed at the furious rain that began soon after noon on the Fourth and turned the roads over which they must retreat to muddy sluices; and they laughed when the dinner which General Longstreet had ordered to be ready for them at a tavern on the way was pre-empted and devoured by General McLaws and some companions, before they could arrive for the expected feast. They laughed at a proud Negro in Yankee uniform who marched two prisoners into camp. They laughed when a cry in the night that Yankee cavalry was coming caused a minor stampede in the darkness and the rain, till the Yankee cavalry turned out to be a carriageful of women. They laughed at rain and mud, at their own discomfort and their hunger and their pain.

Yet Trav noticed that it was only when there were a number of them together that they laughed so easily. If you were with one man or with two, you were serious enough.

Before the retreat began, in Longstreet's tent on the Fairfield road, while the rain slashed at the dripping canvas over their heads, Trav heard the General briefly discuss the battle with Colonel Fremantle. "What if Meade had attacked, after the repulse?" the Englishman inquired.

Longstreet spoke with certainty. "We would have smashed them. McLaws and Law would have crushed their flank, Alexander's guns would have shattered their front."

Fremantle remarked: "I've heard the opinion that the Second and Third Corps artillery, properly placed, could have taken the hill above the cemetery under enfilade. Colonel Alexander thinks so."

"If there was such an opportunity, General Pendleton would have seized it. After defeat, it is an evasion to seek scapegoats."

The big man spoke so sternly that his tone was a dismissal. Trav and Fremantle left the General's tent together; but the Englishman's curiosity was not satisfied. "You went with the assaulting troops, did you not, Major Currain?"

"Yes."

"What was it like?"

Trav said thoughtfully: "Well, it was like walking all by yourself for a mile across open ground and up to a stone wall, with two men behind the wall shooting at you, and three or four more shooting at you from the sides."

Fremantle nodded. "Did you not underrate the enemy?"

"I suppose so," Trav smiled mirthlessly. "No Southerner ever doubts that he's better than any two or three Yankees. Yes, I suppose we did."

"I'm told that General Longstreet argued against the attack."

"General Longstreet will always say what he thinks." He was glad to be rid of the other's persistent probings.

They began their retreat on the afternoon of the Fourth, and they marched that night a few slow miles, following Hill's corps. Ewell would bring up the rear and fight off any hard pursuit. The road beyond Fairfield wound to and fro like a snake's track in the dust, and it was flanked by friendly hills; but presently they turned off that road to ascend the valley of Miney Branch. In that narrow gorge the road at first climbed gradually and then became abruptly steep and arduous, with many hairpin turns and tortuous zigzags. It was scoured by steady rain, so that they waded in little casual torrents or plucked each foot painfully out of deep mud; and every upward step was a conscious effort.

At the summit of Monterey Pass there was the blessed relief of level going for a while, though they had to make a wide circuit around a green morass which rain had converted into a shallow lake. Beyond, the road descended through another ravine, following a waxing stream down into a valley that promised easy travel; but there was another hard short climb into Waynesboro, and the miles to Hagerstown were a wearying succession of heights from which they looked down into rain-shrouded valleys, and of valleys where they moved blindly through the pitiless rain.

That day in a village store someone chanced upon a heap of colored prints of President Lincoln; and as the pictures passed from hand to hand along the plodding files, every man had his own comment. "Turn around, Mister, so we can see your tail!" "You're wrong, thar; it's monkeys that have tails. This here's a baboon!" "Say, if that was all the face I had, I wouldn't have my picture took." "Hey, come down out of that hat. I know you're thar! I see yore laigs a-hanging down." "If I ever seed that phiz over my sights it'd skeer me so bad I'd run clear home to Mammy."

Trav, listening to their good-humored jests, realized with some surprise that they were actually all good-humored. No one cursed President Lincoln. No one damned him. He saw a sullen soldier tear one of the pictures across twice and trample it into the mud; but there was no other sign of anger. Abraham Lincoln seemed to command even from his enemies a jocular and tolerant affection.

It occurred to Trav that except for an occasional loose-tongued woman, he had not for a long time heard anyone speak bitterly of Lincoln. They damned Milroy, and Pope, and Butler most of all; but though they laughed at President Lincoln, it seemed to Trav most people no longer hated him. The politicians, of course, and some women, and the voluble bombproofs and skulkers loud for war who nevertheless took care to stay at a safe distance from the battle lines—they all hated him and cursed him; but these simple, hard-fighting, incredibly and recklessly valorous, patient, cheerful men did not hate him. Was it because fighting men learned to respect a stout enemy? Or was there in Lincoln some deep gentleness, some profound sorrow and compassion, some tremendous comprehension which they recognized, and which made them accept him as an honest, greatly troubled man not much different from themselves?

Trav's head lifted; he felt a slow stir of pride because in Lincoln's veins ran Currain blood. "I'd like to tell him, some day," he thought. "I wonder if he knows."

On the march they had heard occasional firing behind them, where enemy cavalry sought to find or to make an opportunity; but at Hagerstown a message from Stuart asked for infantry to help beat off a mass of Union horsemen threatening their flank; and Longstreet sent Trav to throw two brigades that way. Trav went with them, taking detachments from Semmes' brigade and from that of G. T. Anderson across Antietam Creek toward Funkstown. They did their work at cost of heavy punishment by the horse artillery, and when they fell back toward the river, they crossed the creek again near the battlefield of Sharpsburg. Riding through a field of corn, keeping between the rows with a farmer's instinct to avoid danger to the standing crop, Trav saw rain-washed bones under Nig's feet, and headboards tumbled down, and torn rags sodden in the mud. Some of the Sharpsburg dead had been buried here last fall in shallow graves, but all winter the hogs had had their way, and this spring the farmer here had run his plow. When Trav came to the fence, some rails had been replaced, but other rails and boards must have been here during the battle; for they were pierced by many bullet holes as close together as the holes in a sifter. He was glad to leave that field behind and come back to headquarters again, and to the ranks of living men.

The rain had raised the river, and till bridges could be built or till the flood subsided they could not hope to cross. Improvised ferries set the Yankee prisoners over to begin their march up the Valley toward captivity, and the bridge builders were put to work. Longstreet supervised the entrenching, and the arrangement of defensive lines which Meade might choose to test. From Williamsport the river ran southwest to Falling Waters, and curved back on itself. Longstreet drew a line between the river and Hagerstown which covered the ford at Williamsport and touched the river again beyond Downsville, two or three miles southeasterly. In the loop of the river thus enclosed the army was secure, able to throw its weight quickly to any threatened point. After these days of work Longstreet went to report to General Lee, and Trav rode with him; and he heard Lee greet Longstreet with that affectionate phrase he liked to use.

"Well, my old War Horse!"

Longstreet told him the army was ready to meet Meade's best work. The artillery had ammunition for one good day's fight, the men would do the rest.

General Imboden was there, and Lee told Longstreet: "Imboden reports all the wounded safely across the river and on the road to Winchester." He spoke to the cavalryman. "You know this region, General. Tell me the possible fords."

Imboden did so, the others listening, and Lee said at last, smiling: "One more question, General. Does it ever stop raining here?"

Behind that light question Trav read the commanding general's deep anxiety. When Imboden was gone, Trav left Lee and Longstreet together till Longstreet came to join him for the return ride. Trav said General Lee seemed tired, and Longstreet looked at him with stern eyes.

"He carries a burden that would crush ten men, Currain." Trav was silenced; but when they had gone a little farther, Longstreet said: "He was blaming himself for expecting too much of the army. I remarked that vain regrets were folly. He said that if he had foreseen the failure of the third day's attack he would have tried some other course."

"You foresaw the failure, General."

Longstreet spoke in sharp reminder. "What I foresaw is of no consequence! The penalty of successful generalship is increased responsibility; and in the hour of decision a man stands alone."

For a week they lay expecting attack. There were daily cavalry affairs, and Stuart's screen was driven in; but at last the bridge was repaired, the river fell a little, and on the morning of the thirteenth Lee decided to cross during the night.

"I suggested we wait one more day," Longstreet told his staff. "To let Meade try us. We'd teach him respect, and then cross without molestation. But General Lee has decided to cross tonight, asks me to oversee the work."

He gave his orders. The movement began at dusk. Trav would never forget the incessant labor of that night. The rain, as though furious at their imminent escape, came on again with such violence that torches were extinguished and great bonfires hissed and spluttered and but for constant attention would have been drowned. Wagons and guns churned the improvised road into a morass; and an ambulance loaded with wounded, the plunging horses out of control, lurched off the narrow bridge into three or four feet of water and a scouring current. Trav and twenty others waded in to save the wounded, to control the horses, to right the ambulance somehow and by brute strength get it back on the bridge and lift the hurt men in again. The poles laid like corduroy to make an approach to the bridge bent and broke and sprang out of position. Horses, their feet caught between these poles as though in a trap, fell; and sometimes in their struggles they broke a leg, and were shot, and the harness was stripped off them and their carcasses dragged aside while men took their places to haul the wagons or the guns. Longstreet's great roaring voice bellowed through the tumult of the long night. Every man felt that voice like a lash laid across his shoulders; and the General revealed an unsuspected gift of tongue, so that his profane vocabulary would become as much a legend among those who heard him that night as Ewell's had been before marriage and a new wife taught him self-control. Once when a mule team balked on the bridge itself, Longstreet's blast was like a lightning flame lancing through the darkness. Trav heard, and though he was at the moment waist-deep in the river, he laughed aloud. Major Fairfax called to him in a high amusement:

"Don't go near Old Pete tonight! He's so mad he'd kick a baby in the teeth."

"I know! I heard him start those mules."

"Start them?" Fairfax guffawed. "Start them? Why, when they heard him they lit out full gallop. I'll wager they're in Winchester by now."

The approach to the river was difficult, through mud so deep that wagons and batteries sometimes stalled even on the descent to the stream, and at the Virginia end of the bridge there was a steep climb up to level going, and here the laden wagons and the guns mired, and horses labored with cracking sinews, and men slipping and sliding in the mud lent their strength to help. Each delay there halted traffic on the bridge, and Longstreet sent Trav to spur the work on the Virginia side. Gray dawn broke through the plunging rain before Longstreet, relieved by General Lee, came to lead the First Corps on.

They lodged that night at Bunker Hill, a twenty-mile march from the crossing; and they learned there of the minor disaster that struck the rear of the column. General Pettigrew's division was the last of the infantry to cross. Through some error, the cavalry screen which should have protected their move allowed the Yankees to come down on them. Hundreds of Pettigrew's exhausted men were taken prisoner, and General Pettigrew himself was mortally wounded. He was brought to Bunker Hill and lodged in a hospitable house west of the road just south of town.

Trav heard from Ed Blandy the account of the affray. "It was about eleven o'clock," Ed said. "We were waiting our turn to cross, most of us wore out and half-asleep; and when their cavalry come up, we thought they were ours. They charged us, and we broke them; but the Major leading the charge, he shot the General."

"Where was our cavalry?" Trav asked. Ed did not know; and Trav, because he had marched with Pettigrew's division on that third day at Gettysburg, felt a personal loss in the General's approaching death and blamed Stuart. Next day while he was with Longstreet and others on a knoll above Mill Creek beside the road, he saw Stuart pass like a pageant. Two buglers rode ahead, sounding on their instruments the promise that Stuart was coming; his staff and the attendant couriers made an impressive cavalcade. Trav swore under his breath, and Longstreet, whose hearing was keen enough when he chose, heard.

"Grumbling, Currain?"

"I wish Stuart loved work as well as he loves making a show."

Longstreet said seriously: "Stuart has virtues to match his failings. No better cavalry leader ever lived, unless Forrest is better."

They stayed a few days at Bunker Hill, and General Pettigrew died; and then Stuart reported that Meade had passed the Potomac east of the Blue Ridge, so they marched again. Ten days after the crossing at Falling Waters, they lay once more behind the Rapidan, across Meade's road to Richmond. Their headquarters were near Erasmus Taylor's home, with good pasture for the weary horses, food enough, and friendliness and welcome at the big house. Moxley Sorrel and Peyton Manning and all the younger men of the staff, from the first evening, flocked that way; for every pretty girl in the neighborhood was there to laugh and dance with them.

While they lay there, Brett and Faunt came together to seek Trav, and he thought Faunt was wasted to a shadow, worn and ill; but Faunt said there was nothing wrong with him that a few days' rest would not cure. "The trouble is to get the rest," he admitted. "But I'll rejoin Mosby tomorrow behind Meade's lines, and take my ease."

"I shouldn't think that would be a place to rest."

Faunt laughed in a dry fashion. "Nothing rests me so much as inheriting a new horse from a Yankee who won't need it any more."

His tone chilled them both, and Trav saw that Brett felt as he did. Faunt was become a stranger, a cold and deadly man. Brett put to them his proposal to turn all the Currain funds into Confederate bonds; and they agreed. Trav said: "I've sent money to Enid to stock the house with flour and coal and bacon and sugar enough to last eighteen months, so she and the children are provided for. I've a twenty-five-percent profit on tobacco I bought in April, and I'll margin a new trade with that in next month's market."

Brett smiled. "You've done well. Then you both agree?" They nodded, and Brett said, "I'll write Tony. We'll see."

Faunt turned to his horse. "Do as you please," he said. They watched him ride away, and Trav shook his head.

"Faunt's not the same man, Brett, since those damned letters."

"Yes, he's taken that mighty hard."

"I did, at first. But I can't help seeing that in Lincoln's place I'd do as he has done." He spoke of those pictures of Lincoln which the men had found on the way to Hagerstown. "They laughed and made jokes; but it was the way you laugh at someone you like." He hesitated, said in a shy way: "I'm almost proud to be related to him."

Brett met his eyes. "Lincoln's life, the way he has been brought up from nowhere and put where he is—Trav, do you suppose that's just an accident? I've wondered sometimes whether God didn't decide Lincoln was a man He could use."

Trav said uneasily: "I've never thought much about—religious things."

"No, neither have I. Oh, I've gone to church with Cinda and the children, naturally. But without thinking. Now I'm beginning to."

During the quiet weeks that followed, since in these idle days most of the staff were much at Mr. Taylor's, Trav and Longstreet had many hours together. Once they spoke of the battle. Trav had remarked that the Richmond papers were blaming Ewell, were saying that Jackson in Ewell's place would have won the battle the first day, were even critical of General Lee; and Longstreet said angrily:

"After things go wrong, civilians are always ready to say what should have been done; but they don't get those brilliant ideas beforehand."

"You had some ideas beforehand," Trav recalled.

"I did, yes; and I thought it my duty to express my views. But General Lee considered and appraised every plan that offered any promise. We ought to believe that what he did was best. He drew the enemy out of Virginia long enough to make it impossible for them to launch any summer campaign against us." He smiled grimly. "He says Meade's army will be as mild as a brooding dove, for the next twelve months or so; and I agree with him. But in any case, to talk of what might have been done is folly."

"I heard you defend General Pendleton to Colonel Fremantle."

"Certainly! General Pendleton did his best. So did Ewell. So did General Heth. To criticize them now is to weaken their future usefulness." Longstreet moved his broad shoulders. "If these little editors want to blame someone, let them blame me! I'd rather take all the blame than have them yapping at Ewell's heels, or Heth's. General Lee selected them for the work. To criticize his subordinates is to criticize him; and our commanding general must never be undermined by criticism."

"What will we do now?" Trav asked. "Stand on the defensive?"

"There is one stroke we might try." Longstreet spoke thoughtfully. "I discussed it with Secretary Seddon last spring." He frowned. "My suggestions are badly timed, Currain. Perhaps I make them too soon. A year ago when McClellan was landing on the Peninsula, I suggested using the Valley as a sally port to threaten Washington, so Lincoln would call McClellan back. It was not done. We let McClellan come on. It's true General Lee drove him into the James. That was a splendid thing, but it was more risky than my plan." Trav did not speak, and Longstreet went on: "We've just one advantage over the North, Currain. The Confederacy has interior lines. You saw what that meant at Gettysburg, where the advantage was with them. They could reinforce any threatened spot by moving troops a mile or so; while for us to call troops from our left to our right meant a march of four or five miles. But in the war as a whole, that advantage of interior lines is ours. We can move divisions, yes and whole corps, by rail to any point we choose. We haven't used that advantage. Last spring I thought a sally into Tennessee might make Lincoln call Grant away from Vicksburg. If we'd put the First Corps on the cars and thrown them west to give Bragg enough strength for great work, we might have made Grant let go his grip on Vicksburg. We didn't do it then; but even now, a quick move into Tennessee might crush the Union army there and give us an open road to Cincinnati."

"Have you suggested that again?"

Longstreet shook his head. "Not yet. Best to wait a while, see what Meade means to do. The end of August will be time enough, if the move seems wise."

Sometimes they rode together, and they heard from the country folk echoes of last winter's battle at Fredericksburg, and of the victory at Chancellorsville. Some poor people were living by harvesting the bullets from those hard-fought fields; and one farmer said there would be a good yield of bones next summer, when the dead horses had had time to rot and the flesh to be picked clean off them. Trav wondered whether the bones of men would go into that ugly gleaning. There was a bone factory at Fredericksburg, the farmer said, which would pay a good price for all they could bring in.

"It's about the only crop a man can make around here these times," he declared. "With the cavalry letting their horses eat things up soon as a sprout shows above the ground." Bones were worth five or six dollars a hundred pounds. "And my old woman can pick up enough bullets in a day to pay for all the pork and meal we can eat in a week. They'll fetch two-three cents a pound; and it don't take many bullets to make a pound. Only trouble, it's quite a ways to where the fighting was." He cackled mirthfully. "Next time you have a battle, have it here on my place and I'll be obliged to you."

That month of August was a time of ferment in the camps. The soldiers got mail from home, and every letter was so full of discouragement that Longstreet thought mail should be opened and read before being delivered to the men. The Richmond papers were querulous; and in North Carolina, Mr. Holden openly declared in the *Standard* that it was time for peace negotiations. Early in August the North Carolina regiments sent delegates to a meeting at Orange Court House to denounce Holden's editorials and to urge the people of North Carolina to repudiate the editor and all his works. Moxley Sorrel and Major Fairfax joked Trav about his North Carolinians, but Longstreet came to his defense.

"Those North Carolina regiments that faltered at Gettysburg should never have been put into the assaulting column," he said firmly. "They had been cut to pieces two days before, and they had lost most of their officers, so they were under strange commanders. Outside of Pickett's division, half the men killed and wounded at Gettysburg were North Carolina men. There are no harder fighters in the army."

Nevertheless, especially among the North Carolina and the Georgia troops, there were through August many desertions. Trav thought idleness might be one of the causes. Men in camp with nothing to do were always likely to slip away to their homes. After Chancellorsville, General Lee had refused all furloughs, fearing that men who went home would not return; but now as many as could be spared were given leave. When Brett went to Richmond, Trav wished to go with him, but Longstreet said: "No, Currain. We may be moving soon. I'd like to go to Petersburg myself. Louisa writes me that she's more comfortable now, but it's a long time since I've seen her. But we may be needed here."

"If I'm needed, of course I don't want to go," Trav agreed. He asked: "What is the move to be?"

"Some force may be sent to strengthen Bragg. I've repeated my suggestion to the Secretary of War. If General Lee would go out there, he might do great things."

Trav did not repeat this confidence to anyone; but rumors of a possible venture into Tennessee began to spread. When, late in August, General Lee went to Richmond, leaving Longstreet in command, the air was full of guesses and conjectures. Then suddenly everyone seemed to know that two divisions of the First Corps would go to Tennessee, and Longstreet put his staff to work on preparations. "The essence is to move quickly," he told them. "The railroad from here through Cumberland Gap is in good order. We should be able to move the divisions there in two days at the best, four at the worst." When, early in September, word came that that route was in imminent danger of being cut by the Union forces, the first plan had to be changed; and the two or three or four days which the journey by that route would have taken became ten or twelve. But Longstreet, eager for this adventure in the field of his selection, brushed aside these delays as of no importance.

"We'll have to go south to Georgia and then north again," he told Trav. "And the railroads that way are in poor condition, with different gauges so we'll have to change cars at every junction point. But at least, Currain, you'll have a day or two at home, and I'll have a glimpse of Louisa."

The first trains loaded with troops left Orange Court House to begin that long journey; but Longstreet, with Trav and a part of the staff, stayed three days longer. The night before they were to leave for Richmond, Trav heard that ten North Carolina deserters, men from Steuart's brigade of Ewell's corps, had been sentenced to be shot at sunrise; and they were to be shot by firing squads drawn from North Carolina regiments. When next morning Longstreet rode to say goodby to General Lee, Trav went with him, and from a distance he heard the rattle of that fusillade. His lips were white with hurt and sorrow, and while he waited outside General Lee's tent for Longstreet to appear, his eyes were wet with tears.

Then the two generals came out together, and Trav heard a word or two. "Give my compliments to Mrs. Longstreet, General," Lee said courteously.

"May I tell her, sir, that if her baby is a boy he is to bear your name?"

"By all means," Lee assured him. "Now go, and finish quickly, and return to me."

Longstreet said frankly: "If I didn't think this move necessary, I would be disturbed at leaving you. All that this army has to be proud of has been accomplished under your eye and under your orders. And our affection for you is as strong as our admiration."

Trav saw that Lee was deeply moved. "You cannot return too soon to please me," he said. "Go beat those people out there."

"I will, if I live," Longstreet promised. "But any success must be driven home. I wouldn't give one man's life for an empty victory."

"Your success will be driven home," Lee replied. He raised his hand in a gesture of farewell. Longstreet saluted, and mounted, and he and Trav turned their horses to the waiting train.

At the cars, Trav went to see their mounts put aboard. Nig was restless, so he stayed to reassure the big horse. When the train was about to move, half a dozen soldiers, breathless from running, clambered aboard the car where Trav was, and one of them was Ed Blandy. Trav had meant as soon as Nig was quiet to join the General; but he saw Ed's cheeks streaked with tears, so he and Ed sat in the car door, their legs hanging down, as the heavy train jerked to a hiccoughing start.

"Furlough?" he asked, when the other's hard panting eased.

"Yes sir. They're letting some of us go home for a spell, let us borry a ride a ways."

"The cars are going through Raleigh, some of them. That will be handy for you."

Ed said grimly: "I aim to stop off there. I'd like to get my hands on that Mr. Holden." Trav felt the hard rage and grief in the man beside him; and Ed added: "He just now killed some good men, friends of mine."

Trav knew Ed meant the deserters executed that morning, whom Holden's editorials might have influenced. "That was a bad business." He spoke gently.

"They made us march out to watch it," Ed said, between tight teeth. "There was three of them I knew myself. They was men had volunteered, same as me; not conscripts. Ike Towner was one of 'em. Ike was always one to make a joke; and when they was marching along to where they was going to be shot, a wagonload of their coffins come along; and Ike yells: 'Hey, boys, there go our winter homes!' " Ed brushed his eyes with his knuckles, unashamed. "I don't blame General Lee, Major. He has to hold on to his army somehow. But that man Holden has started poison talk. He's got the home folks feeling sorry for theirselves, and they write letters to the boys to come on home. I'd like to handle him."

"I heard the volleys," Trav admitted.

"There'll be more shootings," Ed predicted. "You know the way men are, Major. Try to stop 'em doing something and they'll be dead set to do it. You can't scare a North Carolina man, Major; not by killing. We've got used to seeing men killed. Why, back there at Gettysburg, Company C in our regiment started out that last afternoon with three officers and thirty-four men; and only one officer and four men come back without a bullet or something had hit them some-where. Men like that don't scare, I tell you!"

"I was there that day."

"I seen you there." Memory of that shared experience drew them to-gether. Trav took out his tobacco, offered it to Ed, put a little in his own cheek. Ed spat at the ground that slid slowly past beneath their dangling feet. "Can't they get some of the skulkers and shoot a few of them?" he asked bitterly. "That might do some good. Men like us don't have any money to buy ourselves out of the army, so they shoot us."

"A lot of fine men who could buy their way out haven't done so."

Ed nodded in ungrudging assent. "There's good rich folks and good poor folks. I don't size a man by the money he's got in his pocket. But we-uns ain't fighting to hang onto our slaves, Major. We ain't fighting to do ourselves any good. We're fighting just because it looks like with things the way they are, fighting's what a man ought to do. You uns, you can come off to fight and leave your women folks with plenty of servants to take care of them; but when we uns fight, our women folks have to take care of theirselves any way they can." He added: "And there's a hundred of us, or a thousand maybe, for every one there is of you all." A moment later he said in a wretched tone: "Being in the army's bad for a man, Major; for a poor man, anyway. He gets to helping himself to other folks' chickens and hogs and things, and it's a joke and he brags about it. The boys tell me that all around home, some that have deserted or have hid out from the con-script officers have gone to thieving from their own neighbors. Yes, and shooting and burning too."

"I know that's true," Trav assented. "It's the same in Virginia, Ed; in all the mountain country. Deserters have burned some houses, whipped some men; yes, and killed some."

"Being in the army does hard things to a man," Ed repeated. "Worse than killing him, some ways."

Trav for a little did not speak. Most men, he suspected, were like Ed, and like himself, and Brett, and Burr, and Julian with only one leg, and Clayton now two years dead and in his grave. They fought not from devotion to those vague abstractions the politicians talked about, but simply because, under the circumstances of these terrible years, to fight was what a man should do. Even General Lee had been opposed to secession, opposed to this war; he fought because Virginia chose to fight and he was a Virginian. Longstreet fought not from any free choice or decision of his own but because Alabama was fighting. Oh, some men—Faunt for instance—were driven by a deadly and murderous hatred of the Yankees; but there were not many like Faunt. Of course, in battle, men fought by infection, their hearts forged by comradeship into a single sword; but battle was so small a part of war. "Why, if I were brave enough," he thought, "brave enough to face my own thoughts and the people I love, I too would desert. Perhaps deserters are in some ways the bravest of the brave." And he thought of Ike Towner this morning, flinging a laugh into the grinning face of shameful death; and he thought: "There was a braver man than I will ever be."

He sat with Ed as far as Ashland, the train jolting along no faster than a man could trot. At Ashland many kindly women came with pails of water for the thirsty men, and apologized because they had no greater gifts to bring; and there Trav said good-by to Ed, and their hands struck, and Trav went to find the General. Walking back along the cars, he surveyed them in a sorry wonder. They were a mixed lot. Some were designed to carry passengers, and one was a mail car; but most were built for freight—box cars, coal cars, platforms. Men were crowded aboard them everywhere, sprawling on the platform cars, perching on the roofs, breaking out the sides of the box cars for air and a chance to see. They would be a week or more in these cars and others like them, trundling south to Georgia and then north again into Tennessee, going hungry or thirsty when they must, sooted and cindered and begrimed, yet always ready to shout a greeting at every girl who waved to them along the way. And when they came to journey's end they would be ready to fight, and to die if they must. Had there ever been such soldiers in the world before? Not one in a hundred of these private soldiers had any personal stake in the war or could hope for any personal gain from victory. For a moment Trav had something like a vision of what the South might become, of what the United States might become, if some way could be found to use rather than to destroy such valiant men, Northerners and Southerners, as these.

Of what splendid generations still unborn might not these men who were dying now on bloody battlefields have been the seed? Could any nation thus spend its best and get value for the price it paid?

He found Longstreet with Moxley Sorrel and some others in a passenger car at the rear of the train, and Sorrel said laughingly: "Currain, I've just been telling the General; our old scout, Harrison, has turned actor. He's wagered he'll play Shakespeare in Richmond this week. We'll have to go and give him our applause."

The scout had stayed with them till a week or so ago. Trav knew Longstreet valued his services, but he himself had never trusted the man. Paid spies could be bought by anyone who met their price. "I expect I'll spend my time with my family," he said.

When the laboring engine dragged the long line of cars to a stop on Broad Street, Trav was surprised and disturbed to see a welcoming crowd waiting. If this move to help Bragg were to succeed, speed and secrecy were alike desirable; but the cutting of the Virginia and Tennessee Railroad had made speed impossible, and now it was clear that their plan was no secret. When Longstreet's burly figure appeared on the car steps, it was to meet a roar of affectionate welcome, clear voices of women mingling with the hoarser tones of men. General Hood, his arm still in a sling from the wound he had taken at Gettysburg, was here to greet his commander. Despite his wound he would go with them to Tennessee.

Longstreet for their brief days planned to make his headquarters at the Spottswood; but when he had seen to Nig, Trav would be free to go directly home. At the horse cars he found Big Mill, and he greeted the gigantic black man with a quick gladness. Then Lucy and Peter came pressing toward him. Mill would look out for Nig, so Trav went to meet the children; and his eyes filled with happy pride. Lucy in the four months since he saw her had blossomed into ripe young beauty. It was hard to believe that she was not yet fifteen. She had her mother's fair loveliness, her mother's slender grace. Fifteen? Why, Enid was only a year older than that when he and she were married.

Lucy was first to reach him, Peter lagging a little. Peter was a lank youngster. "He's more like me," Trav thought. "He'll never be handsome." Lucy would have thrown herself into his arms, but he held her off in laughing fondness.

"Wait a minute, young one! You'll get yourself all dirty."

"Oh, you always say that, Papa. I don't care!"

"Wait till I can get out of these clothes." Enid used to say that Trav was as finicky as a woman about keeping clean; but in camp this was not easy, and the train journey had been a sooty one. "Don't touch me, honey! And don't brush against anyone. Soldiers can't keep the fleas off themselves any more than a dog can, you know. How's Mama?"

"Oh, she's all right. She had a headache."

"You're fine, that's plain to see." And to his son: "Isn't she, Peter? Have you been taking good care of her and Mama?" They had left the crowd behind.

"I guess so," Peter said. "But Mama keeps nagging at me."

Trav laughed, and looked at Lucy to share his amusement; but Lucy was not laughing. She was staring straight ahead, with something in her young eyes mature and stern. Trav felt in each of them some constraint. "I hope you don't let her get lonesome," he suggested.

"Oh she's not lonesome!" Peter said sullenly. "I guess she is now, though."

Lucy spoke a warning word. "Peter!"

"Oh all right," the boy grumbled; but he was silenced, and Trav would not question them. When they came home, old April opened the door, beaming a welcome; but then she cried in tender scolding: "Now, Marse Trav, don' you come tromping in heah in dem ole boots and mess up de whole place! Go on 'roun' to de shed. I'll fill a tub and bring you some clean clo'es."

Trav laughed. "You make me feel about ten years old, April. Where's Mrs. Currain?"

"She done shet her doah!"

Lucy explained: "Mama said she'd lie down till supper time, Papa, to cure her headache."

Trav heard April's eloquent sniff; he felt in her as in these children something unspoken. "Why, that's fine," he agreed. "All right, get the tub ready."

While he bathed, he wondered what it was that the children knew and that April knew, yet which none of them would say; but he was too happy in being again at home to disturb himself with doubts.

When he was ready he shouted for April, and she handed in through the half-opened door fresh garments.

"I'll leave everything here," he told her.

"Yassuh. I'll clean 'em nice."

"Take a look at the seams, April. Might be some crawlers there."

"Doan try tuh tell me, Marse Trav! I be'n cleaning up yo' nastiness sence you was so high!"

When he went indoors, Lucy was waiting. "Now I'll take that hug, Honey," he said, and she clung to him, and he felt her near tears, and held her close and said: "There, there!" He tried to tease her into laughter. "What's there to cry about? Sorry I came home?"

"Oh, no, no! Oh, I wish you'd stay home, Papa. Can't you, please? I wish you'd stay."

"What's the matter, Honey?"

"It's so lonesome with you gone!"

"You and Mama——"

"Mama don't—" Lucy caught herself. "I'll be awful glad when you come home to stay."

There was again that shadow in her tones, but Enid could explain it. "I think I'll go wake Mama," he decided. "It's almost supper time. Where's Peter?"

"Oh I guess he's out with those boys he plays with." She said earnestly: "Papa, Peter needs you to make him behave. He's always around with horrid little boys."

He laughed reassuringly. "Young ladies your age think all little boys are horrid, Lucy."

But he was troubled. He went up to the bed room and knocked; and when there was no answer he went in. As he opened the door Enid whirled to face him. The shades were drawn, the room darkened; but he saw plainly enough the twist of terror in her, and heard fear in the forced anger of her word.

"Trav Currain, I've told you a thousand times not to come bursting in on me."

"Why—I'm sorry, Enid." This then was his welcome! "It's almost supper time." He tried to jest. "I had breakfast early, nothing since. I'm hungry!"

"Well, you didn't expect to eat me, did you!"

He chuckled teasingly. "Did you expect me to?" Her eyes widened, and he said soberly: "I believe you're scared!"

"Scared?" She laughed in a shrill scorn. "Why should I be scared of you?"

"Yes, why should you?" he echoed. She was half dressed, her hair in stringy disorder, her eyes red, her cheeks blotched. "You don't look well, Enid."

"I've a horrible headache. This is the third day of it. It's driving me crazy."

Tenderness for her softened his tones. "Then why don't you stay in bed? I'll have April bring your supper up to you."

"Oh I don't want any supper."

"April will fix you something nice."

"I don't want her coming near me!" Her tone was shrill again. "I want you to get rid of her, Trav! She's a suspicious, spying, lying, deceitful nigger! I want you to get rid of her."

Trav smiled, shook his head. "April brought me up, Enid. I'll never send her away."

"Oh, I suppose not. But for Heaven's sake get out and let me dress."

"Don't you want to stay in bed?"

"No. No. Go on downstairs. I'll be down."

He hesitated. The children ought not to see her so. "When you've freshened up a little, perhaps you'll feel better."

"If you don't like the way I look, you don't have to come home."

His shoulders sagged unhappily. He had hoped she would be glad to see him; but there could be no good in quarrelling. "We'll wait for you," he promised, and went out and closed the door. In the drawing room Lucy looked at him with a searching question in her eyes; and he tried to make his tone normal.

"Well, did Peter turn up?"

"Yes, he's washing his hands. How's Mama?"

"Coming right down. She'll be fine when she's had supper."

But supper proved to be a dreadful hour. Enid had masked herself with too much powder; and through this mask peered furtive, angry, frightened eyes. He saw lines about her mouth, and her lips were never still, and she licked them constantly with a restless tongue. Her hair needed brushing, and it had lost that alive quality which had been its beauty. It was a dull mat now upon her head. She talked constantly, as though afraid of what they might say if she gave them time to speak. Trav saw in Lucy and Peter no suggestion of surprise at her manner and her appearance. Was it possible that they were used to see her so, that this in so short a time had become her normal mien? What upheaval like an earthquake had produced this dreadful change?

When supper was done, Peter vanished; but Lucy stayed till Enid cried: "Oh, Lucy, don't sit there like a statue! Go on to bed."

Trav protested: "Now, now, Enid, it's early; and I haven't been home for a long time. Let her stay a while."

"I hate to have her always staring at me!"

Lucy with a quick movement rose and fled, and Trav did not call her back; but when he and Enid were alone he asked quietly:

"What is it, Enid? What has happened?"

"Nothing! What are you talking about!"

"I'm afraid you're sick!"

"I told you my head's ready to split!"

Perhaps that was all. Perhaps a night's rest would restore her. "A good night's sleep's what you need," he decided. "I'll take the other room tonight so you can have the bed to yourself. You're so used to sleeping alone now that I'd bother you."

Her eyes touched his, then turned away again. "All right, I'll go to bed now," she said, and rose.

He took her for a moment in his arms, wishing somehow to comfort and soothe her; but holding her thus close he felt in her passivity the tenseness of terror barely under control. Once when he was a boy he had found a rabbit in a Negro's box trap, and took it out, and mastered its frantic struggles till it lay for a moment motionless under his hands. Yet he had felt in that moment the rabbit's terror, so that he said to the little creature: "Don't be scared! I won't hurt you!" As he spoke, he relaxed his grip a little, and in a sudden violent convulsion the rabbit kicked free, one of its toenails gouging his hand so deeply that he still wore the scar.

Trav felt that same fright in Enid now, and he loosed the circle of his arms; she twisted away from him and with no backward glance went darting up the stairs. He was left to read the puzzle as he chose.

At headquarters next day he heard that a Georgia regiment of Long-street's men, halted for a few hours at Raleigh, had tried to capture Mr. Holden. Presumably they intended violence to the editor who had begun to shout so loudly for peace, and whose editorials contributed so largely to the wholesale desertions. When Mr. Holden fled to the sanctuary of the Governor's mansion, they broke into the office of the *Standard* and wrecked it before Governor Vance could persuade them to disperse. Trav remembered Ed Blandy's anger at Mr. Holden yesterday; but Ed could not yet have reached Raleigh. This had been done by other men.

He found Longstreet concerned for fear the Georgia and South Carolina regiments in his command, which on this roundabout journey to Tennessee would pass near their homes, would have many desertions. "They'll want to drop off the trains for a day or two with their families," he predicted. "And God knows I don't blame them; but if they get away from us, a lot of them won't come back. I've telegraphed orders to take precautions."

Trav thought most of the men were loyal, and said so. "You heard what they did to Holden. Or tried to."

Longstreet shook his head. "We can't risk it. Any man leaving the trains without permission will be instantly shot." He asked: "How did you find Mrs. Currain?"

"Why, very well," Trav said. He need not inflict his own concern on General Longstreet; but he suddenly began to dread seeing Enid alone, and he invited Longstreet to dine with them. Longstreet agreed, but business engaged them so continuously that this plan had to be abandoned. A note from Cinda suggested that they both come to supper and said Enid and the children were coming. Longstreet was to meet President Davis and could not accept, so Trav went to the house on Fifth Street alone.

When he arrived, Enid and Lucy were already there, with Anne and Julian, Cinda and Vesta. He saw gratefully that Enid was now completely herself. It was fine to be with Cinda again, fine to see Julian so happy with Anne, fine to see the friendship between Lucy and Anne and Vesta. They all had questions. What had he done? What would he do? Julian spoke of Gettysburg. "Papa says you were in the attack the last day, Uncle Trav. Was it wonderful?"

"I think General Longstreet has the right idea about battles, Julian," Trav suggested. "To forget them, once they're over, except to remember the lessons they taught."

"What lessons did Gettysburg teach?"

"Well, I haven't heard anyone else say so," Trav confessed, "but the lesson it taught me was that the Yankees can fight just as hard as we can."

"But their generals aren't as good as General Lee!"

Trav smiled. "General Longstreet says President Lincoln is our best general, because he keeps interfering with his commanding officers." His eyes met Cinda's, sharing the same thought; and then somewhere abovestairs a baby's cry sounded, and Vesta laughed in a rich happy way.

"That's my Tommy!" she said proudly. "Anybody want to see my wonderful son?" Lucy and Anne and Enid went with her; and Trav asked Cinda:

"How's Tilda?"

"She's taken over Mrs. Brownlaw's place, organizing the ladies to help take care of wounded and refugees." She added fairly: "She does it well, Travis."

"I suppose Mr. Streean's prospering."

"Oh yes."

"Dolly?"

"Just the same. Twenty beaux—and, whenever he's in town, Captain Pew."

"Is Darrell here much?"

"He was here for a while in May and June; but we saw little or nothing of him. Dolly says he's in Nassau now, went with Captain Pew on one of his voyages and stayed." Enid and Lucy came back downstairs, and Cinda added: "Jenny's managing the Plains, you know. Brett thinks she's rather wonderful."

He spoke of Burr and Brett and Faunt, and Enid said: "None of us ever see Faunt when he comes to Richmond."

"We saw him last spring," Julian reminded her.

"Heavens!" Enid laughed. "He's been here since then!"

Trav was struck by her tone, and Julian asked: "Has he? How do you know?"

"Oh, I—" Enid brushed the question aside. "He's been here. Take my word for that."

Yet she did not say she had seen him, and when they were at home and Lucy had gone to bed, Trav asked curiously: "Enid, what makes you think Faunt's been here?"

"Think? I don't think! I know he has!" She spoke with a spiteful emphasis.

"How do you know? If no one has seen him?"

Enid after a moment's hesitation said maliciously: "He comes to see Mama." Trav stared at her in complete astonishment, and she laughed. "Oh, you needn't look so surprised! You were crazy about her yourself once, you know."

He spoke at random. "I always thought she was very nice, but I'd forgotten she was in Richmond. Do you ever see her?"

"Why, Trav!" She spoke in a teasing drawl. "And me a respectable woman! How can you suggest such a thing?"

"Eh?" He was completely confused. "What? What do you mean?"

"Darling, don't you know?" Enid threw back her head, laughing in a fashion that was like a lash across his cheek. "You poor innocent man!" She explained, as one explains a mystery to a child: "You see, Honey, when I took you away from Mama, she had to get her hands on Currain money somehow, so she landed Tony; and when he was through with her she nabbed Faunt! She's a family pensioner!"

Anger swept him. "Enid, that just isn't true!"

"So I'm a liar!"

"Well, at least you're mistaken! Who told you?"

She laughed again. "Why, darling—if I needed to be told—Darrell did."

"Darrell's always been a liar."

"Tell him so to his face some day! I dare you!"

"Darrell's needed a lesson for a long time." Trav's throat was dry with rage. "I'll stop his slanderous tongue."

"Really? Do you think you can? Besides, it's the truth! Mama told me the same thing."

She spoke so positively that he began to believe her. "You really mean that, Enid?"

She rose, moving toward the stairs, smiling at him over her shoulder.

"You Currains with your heads in the clouds! Yes, darling, these brothers of yours have feet of clay. If you want it in plain words, Mama was Tony's mistress for ten years, and she's Faunt's now!" She started up the stairs. "But don't let it make you lose any sleep, Honey! I know you don't want any scandal in the family; but they're all ever so discreet. I don't suppose half of Richmond knows! Good night, my simple dear."

Trav when she was gone tried to tell himself that she was lying; but he was not sure. Like most men he had lived incuriously. Mrs. Albion when he last saw her four years ago at Chimneys had said she would go to live in Washington. If he had ever heard of her return to Richmond it had made no impression on him. But if she were here, then the fact that neither Cinda nor Tilda had welcomed her into the large circle of the family was proof enough that she was somehow outside the pale.

He took sick thoughts to bed with him, and they oppressed his mind next day. Sorrel and the others, when he joined them at the Spottswood, were laughing at their experience at the theatre the night before. Harrison the scout had won his wager, playing Cassio in a performance of *Othello*.

"He's an actor, all right," Sorrel declared. "You could tell he'd been on the stage before. But the whole thing was the damnedest shenanigan you ever saw, Currain. Harrison was drunk, and so was Othello, and I'd wager Desdemona had had more than a lady should!" He laughed at the memory, then added more seriously: "But I didn't like it. I asked some questions afterward. Harrison's not only been drunk for a week, but he's been gambling at every faro bank in town. The General agrees with me that he's not to be trusted, so we're not taking him to Tennessee."

"The New York papers knew almost as soon as we did about this move we're making," Trav remembered. "Harrison may have sold us out, may be working for both sides."

"Someone sold us out," Sorrel agreed. "The only thing they don't know is whether Pickett is going with us." He laughed. "And I don't know that myself. But we can't prove anything on Harrison. I just paid him off and let him go."

Longstreet finished on Saturday what military business kept him in Richmond and went to Petersburg to spend Sunday with Louisa. Sorrel would stay here till Alexander's artillery entrained; Trav would join Longstreet in Petersburg on Monday and go on with him from there. Tag ends of business, the procuring and loading of munitions and supplies and the endless problems involved in moving thirteen thousand fighting men over eight or nine hundred miles of inadequate railroad, kept him late Saturday night at the Spottswood. At home, except for a gas jet burning low in the hall, the house was dark; but Mill was waiting to let him in. Trav remembered that if Nig were loaded on the cars here in Richmond, he would have to be unloaded and led across Petersburg to be put aboard the Weldon train; so he told the Negro to ride the big horse to Petersburg tomorrow, taking an easy gait.

"He doesn't like the cars," he said. "You can help in putting him aboard."

"Y'all better tek me along, Marse Trav. You need me tuh tek keer o' you."

Trav shook his head. "I need you here, taking care of my son, my family. With you here, I don't have to worry about them." Mill hesitated, so that Trav thought there was some urgency he wished to try, but in the end he assented and said good night.

Trav slept late next morning. When he came downstairs Enid had gone to church, leaving word that Tilda had invited them all to dinner and that she and the children would meet him there; and he had a momentary sense of guilt because he had not called on Tilda before now.

Enid and the children were at Tilda's before him. Dolly was as lovely as ever. Streean had gained weight till he was as softly plump as a force-fed goose. But in Tilda, Trav saw something new, and he led her to talk about the work she did and the problems she had to meet and solve.

Any great battle filled the hospitals, she explained. There was always a shortage of blankets, linen, lint, bandages, food. "And when a man dies there's always someone waiting for his cot. They carry him off to the death house and change the sheets and put some other poor man in his place; and sometimes the bed's still warm."

Dolly shivered. "Oh, Mama, how disgusting!" And Streean grinned and said:

"Besides, Tilda, a dead man's cold!"

But Tilda ignored them. "What we do," she told Trav, "is to work with the hospitals, try to provide cots and bedding, and help them get food. We send trading scows and canal boats up as far as Lynchburg to buy things from the farmers, and we've put in soup houses. We used to just carry food from our own kitchens; but so many people now don't have anything to spare. And we run the hospital bakeries, and keep cows, and raise chickens."

Trav, who knew from his own experience the difficulties of finding rations for hungry men, was interested in what she said; but he was more interested in Tilda herself. She was like a stranger, someone he had never known before. She spoke of her work as General Longstreet spoke of his, with calm certainty and in accents of authority. He realized with a sudden surprise that he liked her! Till now she had been just someone to be tolerated because she was his sister and to be pitied because she was married to Redford Streean; but he liked her now.

He asked many questions, till the others, Enid and Dolly and Streean, protested that they were sick and tired of hearing about hospitals. Dolly brought for Enid to admire a bolt of silk which Captain Pew had given her after his recent return from Nassau, and Enid asked:

"Oh, did Dal come back with him this time?" There was a sharp insistence in the question which caught Trav's ear and puzzled him.

"No, Captain Pew was only here one day."

Streean said in a jocular tone: "I don't believe Darrell's coming back, Enid. I think he's afraid of the conscript officers; but Dolly says he's probably tired of some conquest he made here in Richmond and wants to keep out of the lady's way."

Enid tossed her head. "Conceit! Does he expect her to run after him?" She began to laugh and fell into a hard spasm of coughing, till Dolly clapped her on the back.

"Well!" Streean exclaimed. "I didn't know what I said was as funny as all that!" Trav felt the other's eye upon him and wondered why;

and he wondered why Enid's face, after that fit of choking, had sagged in haggard lines. There was some mystery here. He remembered Lucy's tone when she spoke of her mother, and the way she hushed Peter at the station, and April's sulky sniffing, and the shadow in Mill's loyal eyes, and Enid's own fright and her meaningless angers and malicious taunts. He sat in troubled silence, searching for some explanation, till dinner called them all.

After dinner he and Streean were left alone. He had never felt any positive dislike for Streean, and had sometimes been made uncomfortable by Cinda's open contempt and Faunt's cold courtesy. Streean so obviously wanted to please them that Trav was sympathetic, and a little sorry for the man. But of course no one could be sorry for Streean now.

When they were alone Streean seemed not to notice Trav's silence, delivering a complacent monologue reciting some of his profitable ventures. "You and I are both levelheaded men," he said, and Trav felt a faint irritation at this suggestion of a bond between them. "It's fortunate that there are men like us to keep our heads, or the Confederacy would have collapsed before now." He added, in a judicial tone: "Of course local government in most places has already collapsed. Everywhere away from the cities armed bands of deserters are the only law, and the army is the only police force. We men of business have bolstered up the Confederacy so far; but I don't know how long we can keep it going." Trav held his tongue and Streean said: "Your North Carolinians run your affairs with some intelligence. They buy cotton, ship it, bring in supplies, keep the state's regiments clothed and equipped. Jeff Davis could take a lesson from Governor Vance."

Trav thought this was true. "I know. The North Carolina uniforms are good enough so that after a battle our men strip the North Carolina dead just as they do the Yankees. But maybe if North Carolina put all her surplus uniforms into the general depots, there'd be enough to go around."

"She won't," Streean assured him. "Why should she? Every state has a right to take care of her own men." Trav thought there had been too much talk about a state's rights, but he did not say so; and Streean, eyeing his cigar, said: "I suppose you agree that our defeat is only a matter of time."

Trav felt his cheeks stiffen. "I haven't thought much about it." This was not true, but his thoughts were his own.

"High time you did," Streean assured him. "Yes, sir, we're licked. Of course, we never did have a chance unless we got European recognition." He laughed. "It's like a wife leaving her husband. Unless she can turn to some other man, she's lost."

There was something in the other's tone which made Trav uncomfortable. He said Longstreet thought something might be done in Tennessee, that victory there and a march to the Ohio might lead the northwestern states to demand peace. "There's a strong peace party in Ohio and Illinois—all through that region."

Streean said like an oracle: "There might be some hope if those states needed the Mississippi as an outlet for their produce. If we'd seceded ten or fifteen years ago, and held the river, we'd have had them by the throat; and self-interest would have brought them to our side. But Henry Clay and his compromises postponed this war and gave the North time to build railroads; and the railroads bind that northwestern country to the eastern seaboard, bind the North together. No, Trav, we're lost. It's just a question of time." He lighted a fresh cigar. "A wise man will face the fact and plan accordingly."

Trav, without knowing why, was uneasy and therefore angry. "You seem pleased with the idea."

Streean laughed. "God bless you, no! I make no bones about it, Trav; I'd be glad to see the war last forever. Every week is money in my pockets. No, I was thinking of you."

"I'm not looking for a profit!"

Streean smiled. "You're wiser than you admit, Trav. Enid tells me you're making money in tobacco."

Trav flushed, as much with surprise as with embarrassment. He had told Enid of his transactions, but his own habit of silence was so strong that it had not occurred to him she would speak of them. But also Streean had put him on the defensive. "I'm no damned speculator," he said angrily. "People don't have to have tobacco! That's not like dealing in—food!"

Streean's color rose, his eyes narrowed. "A nice point," he drawled. "If you're ashamed of being intelligent, you'd better bridle Enid's tongue." And he went on in an amused tone: "You Currains are a virtuous lot! Brett Dewain came to me a while ago with a proposal to donate everything in the family vaults to the cause. I told him I'd take Tilda's share in gold and the rest of you could do what you liked. I didn't know at the time that you were turning a penny where you could." He nodded admiringly. "Yes, sir, a high-minded lot of patriots, you Currains!"

Trav was confused and silenced. It was a relief to hear voices in the hall, and when Enid called that it was time to go he rose at once, eager to escape. But before he reached the door, Streean checked him. "Oh, Trav, just a minute." Trav turned and Streean said in a reassuring tone: "I just wanted to urge you not to let Enid's friendship with Darrell bother you. Darrell will always pay a compliment if he thinks it will be welcome; and of course Enid's a natural flirt. But I'm sure there's no harm in either of them."

Trav stared at him, feeling the slow pound of pulses in his throat. With the rushing of his blood his vision blurred, so that Streean's face went out of focus. He set a hard control upon himself, turned to join Enid and the children with Tilda and Dolly in the hall. He had Tilda's good-by kiss and Dolly's. Then they were out of the house, turning toward home.

He did not speak. Enid chattered pleasantly; the children walked in silence. But for Trav, Streean's word was a key that unlocked the door to understanding. Streean had meant him to understand, and absently he wondered why, and guessed that anger had prompted the other to this malicious revelation. But no matter. Streean had meant him to know the truth. Well, now he knew.

And he remembered that the children knew, as much as children could know, and April knew, and Mill knew. He remembered Lucy at the train. "Mama had a headache." Her young eyes mature and stern. Peter: "Oh, she's not lonesome. I guess she is now, though!" And Lucy's instant warning: "Peter!" that silenced him. Trav thought he could have forgiven Enid any crime but this, thrusting evil knowledge into Lucy's mind.

At home Enid went at once to her room, but Trav kept the children with him. "Lucy," he said, "you and Peter go to Aunt Cinda's. Tell her we're inviting ourselves to supper. Tell her Mama and I will be over pretty soon." He added, like an afterthought: "But tell her not to wait for us!" Lucy's eyes widened in surprise, and in alarm too; and he forced himself to smile, controlled his tones, spoke to Peter. "Like that, would you, son?"

Peter clearly sensed nothing wrong; Lucy yielded obedience without understanding. When they were gone, surely gone, out of sight and around the corner where they turned into Fifth Street, he went up to the bed room. He entered without knocking. Enid had removed her dress, her hair was down, she lay along the couch by the window. When he shut the door behind him she said angrily: "Must you always burst into my room?"

He said harshly: "Get up!" She did not move; and he caught her arm, jerked her to her feet, asked in a low tone: "What's between you and Darrell?"

She freed her arm. "You're hurting me!"

"Answer my question."

She hesitated, but only for an instant. "Between me and Darrell?" She looked up at him with mocking eyes, as angry now as he. "Don't you wish you knew?"

That was confession enough. Trav struck as a snake strikes, with an unleashed violence. By his blow she was swept against the couch and fell over it, rolling across the floor. She lay there unconscious, her eyes half-open, seeming not to breathe. Her petticoats were disordered, her corset cover was split across her breast, her legs sprawled.

In that moment, if she had moved or cried out he might have killed her, but since she lay senseless he let her lie. Yet to do so, to be passive, was a thwarting bafflement. He was trembling with passionate and terrible anger for which he had now no outlet. He sat down on the couch, head in his hands, elbows on his knees, watching her and hating her.

After a while his pulses slowed; and after a while she began to breathe, heavily at first, her breast heaving with her deep inhalations. Then that stertorous gasping eased, and her half-open eyes closed, and then they opened and fastened on him, and seemed to try to recognize him; and then into her blank eyes sense and remembrance came, and she sat up, pushing herself desperately away from him across the floor till she was backed against the wall. She crouched there, her cheek swollen and flaming red where his palm had struck, her face elsewhere white as ice, her mouth working soundlessly.

Trav watched her for a long moment; but—she had been his wife. He could not kill her. Without a word he rose and left the room. He found April. "I'm going to supper at Miss Cinda's," he said. "The children have gone." April's eyes turned questioningly toward the stairs, but he made no explanation. April was full of years and wisdom. He need tell her nothing.

At Cinda's he said Enid had decided not to come, that she was tired. He was sure not even Cinda guessed the turmoil in him. When he and the children walked home through the pleasant mid-September night, he made them laugh, telling them how soldiers on a weary march would trudge in sagging silence for a while, till someone wailed in exaggerated woe: "I'm tired of walking and I want to go ho-o-ome," and someone would answer: "I'm a sick little boy and I want my Ma-a-ma!" and the doleful wails would go on till the men forgot they were tired. He told them about the day General Longstreet tried to shame a soldier running away from a fight. "He said: 'You're acting like a baby,' and the soldier began to cry and said: 'I don't care, General, I wish I was a baby—and a gal baby at that!'" Dredging his memory for incidents that would amuse them, he went on: "One day one of the men tried to cook some rice for his mess. This fellow was a fast talker. They used to say he talked like molasses in July. He didn't know how much rice to cook, but he thought a gallon would be about right; so he put the rice to boil and it swelled till the kettle was full, and kept on swelling; and he kept dipping it out into tin cups and into his hat and every hat he could borrow, and the more the rice swelled the faster he talked, trying to explain what was wrong."

Their delighted laughter rang through the dark streets, and when they came home they sat together for a while and Trav strove to please them in every way he could, giving them a feast of himself upon which their memories might feed while he was away.

For he must leave them at dawn, leave them with Enid; he must leave them to face what new knowledge? What new shame? While he played his part with them, he sought alternatives. Take them to Cinda? To Tilda? No, there was no recourse but just to leave them here, no one in whom he could confide the truth, no one he could en-list as their protector. He even considered appealing to Mrs. Albion, but of course that was impossible.

No, they must stay and he must go. He would have said good-by to them tonight, but Lucy promised to breakfast with him. When they had bidden him good night and gone upstairs, he sat a longer while. If Enid were awake, she might come down. But she did not, and he did not go to her. He had no word to say to her. To depart without a word would be more eloquent than many words.

When he went upstairs he listened at her door and heard no sound; yet he thought she must have heard him. The silence had a listening quality. He went into the room beyond hers. There was a connecting door between. The children slept across the hall. He undressed and lay down, but he did not sleep. Through the long night he sometimes wondered whether, a few feet away in the other room, Enid lay wake-ful too.

At dawn old April tapped on the door to rouse him; not on the door of the room he and Enid shared but on this door behind which he lay. How did the servants always know so well what their white folks did? He heard her rouse Lucy, too; and before he himself was ready Lucy went downstairs.

Then the door between his room and Enid's opened. His back was turned that way when he heard the sound; he swung and saw her. The red morning sky threw a crimson radiance that touched her; and she had made herself beautiful, her hair smoothly brushed lay loose about her shoulders, her soft garment was fresh and delicate, her color was bright; even the swollen cheek was made inconspicuous with powder. He stared at her and felt his anger ebb, and then she was clinging to him, kissing him, sobbing with flowing tears, beseeching him.

"Don't go, Trav! Don't go! Don't leave me all alone, Honey. Please!"

He dared not speak. With a violence barely held in bounds, he thrust her away and hurriedly caught up his coat and opened the door into the hall. Her wailing cry made him look back; he saw her in a small woeful heap upon the floor. He turned and went quickly toward the stair.

After their quiet breakfast Lucy walked with Trav through the empty streets of early morning to the depot where he would board the cars. He did not speak to her of Enid, for what could he say? "See a lot of Anne, and Vesta, and Aunt Cinda, Lucy," he told her. "You and Peter both. I hope Peter and Julian get to be friends. If you ever wish you could talk to me, talk to Aunt Cinda. She and I are a lot alike, you know."

"I just love you both, Papa." He wondered how much a child could comprehend; but Lucy was no longer quite a child. "Take awful good care of yourself, Papa. I'd die if anything happened to you."

"No, you wouldn't, Honey." For something might happen to him, and she must be able to go on alone. "Everybody has to live his own life, her own life. Nothing that anyone else does, even if they do it to you, really matters; not as long as you go on being yourself." The train was about to start. "There, Honey!" Her warm arms were tight around his neck, her lips under his. "Good-by."

Thus he left all that bitter and all that sweet behind him. At the station in Pocahontas, Big Mill met him with news that General Longstreet's departure would be delayed till next day. Mill had put Nig in Ragland's Livery Stables, by Powell's Hotel on Sycamore Street. Trav nodded. "You stay with Nig and bring him to the Union Street depot tomorrow to put him on the train," he directed, and went to report to Longstreet. The General explained the delay.

"Pickett's division is not to go with us after all. It's still below strength, and short of officers." He smiled. "But when he expected to go, General Pickett persuaded Miss Sally to marry him before he left, and we'll wait to see the knot tied."

Trav tried to find something to say. "How's Mrs. Longstreet?"

"Why, real peart, Major." Trav saw a fine happiness in the big man. "Yes, she's comfortable, feeling fine. I'd like to stay a week or two, see the new recruit when he arrives; but we've got our work to do. We'll leave tomorrow."

The hours till they boarded the cars were a torment of churning thoughts, despair and shame and rage. There were moments when he wished to return to Richmond and set his hands on Enid's soft throat and rip the flesh away; and above all he wanted to lay his hands on Darrell. Some day he would.

But suppose Darrell came back to Richmond while he himself was away, for weeks or perhaps for months in Tennessee? Suppose Darrell came again to the house on Clay Street, and Enid welcomed him, and Lucy and Peter had again to hear them laughing together in the drawing room. He imagined Lucy in her bed, across the hall from her mother's room, lying awake in the listening night, hearing low laughing voices belowstairs, hearing stealthy footsteps on the stair and the soft click of a latch and then muffled whispers and half-smothered, breathless cries. To realize what Enid had already done to these children made him halfway mad. This that had happened in the past must not happen again.

But if he were far away, how prevent it? Brett, Burr, Faunt, they would not be here. Julian was a helpless cripple. Yet somehow, for Lucy's sake, a way must be found.

He found it, and finding no other, desperately bent on protecting the children from new shame, he accepted it. Next day when he came to the depot Big Mill was already there, gentling Nig in the car with Longstreet's Hero and the other horses belonging to the staff. He called the Negro aside and laid a charge upon the man.

"Mill," he said, "I want you to do something for me. You may get hurt in doing it, or afterward. After you've done it, come and find me. I'll protect you if I can." The Negro's eyes were calm and unafraid. No gray tint of terror touched his lips; and Trav said: "I want you to take care of—everything of mine. And Mill, if Mr. Darrell Streean comes to the house while I am gone, kill him."

He saw Mill's throat muscles work, saw the man's eyes set and burn, and he saw in them a sort of joy. Mill said gently: "I ain't nevah kilt a white man, Marse Trav; but I kin if you say so."

"I do say so." They were in this moment no longer master and man, but friends.

Big Mill nodded. "Yassuh, I will. I will, Marse Trav. You go on an' whup dem Yankees an' rest yo mind."

4

THROUGH that summer's heat, Faunt had been ridden hard by a persistent cough; by weakness and a treacherous lassitude and an alarming failure of his energies. Sometimes he knew that he was parched by fever; and more than once Major Mosby, as though hiding secret solicitude behind a jesting tone, told him his cheeks were pink as a girl's. Faunt was wise enough to suspect the truth, but he thrust it into the background of his mind.

Late in August he rode with Mosby and his men toward Annandale for a raid on some unguarded bridges. They saw an opportunity to cut off a herd of a hundred horses being taken forward on lead to Meade's army, and divided for the attack. At the last moment the guard on the horses was reinforced by the chance arrival of twenty or thirty Union cavalry, and the sharp fight that followed took an ill turn; for Major Mosby himself received a disabling bullet through the side.

The led horses were captured, the Yankees driven off, Mosby borne away to precarious hiding; but the sharp work of the day had been exhausting, and when Faunt began to cough uncontrollably there was suddenly a sweet taste in his mouth and bright arterial blood stained his handkerchief.

He turned off the road into a sheltering pine forest, and lay hidden for a day and a night, waiting for strength to come back to him. Clearly he must rest a while if he hoped to resume the violent exertions which his work as a scout involved; and he accepted this necessity. Moving slowly, conserving what strength he had, he came from behind Meade's lines and passed through Lee's army and rode slowly toward Richmond.

It was well past midnight when he reached Nell's door, tugging at the bell, holding to the door frame with both hands till Milly came to call: "Who dere?" A moment later she and Nell were helping him into the hall.

When they had bathed him and put him to bed, Milly brought warm milk fortified with wine and a beaten egg. He drank it slowly, and Nell said he must sleep and sleep; but he made her sit a while. "Just seeing you, hearing your voice, letting your hand touch mine is the medicine I need most. Stay, let me talk myself to sleep." So she stayed, stroking his hand between hers; and he told her of things done and seen in the weeks since they were last together. Lee's army was recruiting its strength after the invasion of Pennsylvania. "He had seventy thousand men of all arms on the first of June," he said. "By the time he got back into the Valley after Gettysburg, he was below forty thousand, not counting cavalry. Now he has close to sixty thousand again, feels strong enough to send Longstreet's best divisions to Tennessee and face Meade with Ewell and Hill."

"We've heard General Lee will go to Tennessee himself?" she suggested.

"No, Lee won't leave Virginia. Longstreet will go, with McLaws and Hood and probably Pickett. They'll join Bragg, hit Rosecrans hard." He smothered a cough, for he tried always not to cough. To do so might tear apart the fragile web in which his life was precariously hung.

"You'd better not talk," she said, and her lips touched his brow. Her lips seemed cool, so he knew fever was on him. Doubtless she too knew. She talked in low easy tones, monotonous and soothing. Everyone was depressed by the reverses of the summer. From the deep South—Alabama, Mississippi—letters to Mr. Davis were full of lament and the forewarning of disaster. The Yankees, having failed at Charleston, now meant to try Wilmington; for it was to and from these ports that the blockade-runners came and went. Governor Vance was threatening to call home all North Carolina troops to defend their own state. While she talked, sleep rose like a tide to drown his senses; her low voice faded from his consciousness.

When he woke it was full sun, and she was still sitting by his bed. He said she must be tired, but she would not let him talk. There was food, and milk to drink, and he slept again. For days, while she and Milly tended him, he seldom fully woke, sleeping as easily as a dog. It was a week or more before his wakeful intervals began to extend themselves into hours when he and Nell had the rich communion of long talk together.

When she feared this would tire him again he said: "No, I need it. Away from you, I'm a solitary person, Nell; seldom talk with anyone. I'm starved for it." He said slowly: "I'm surfeited with scouts and raids and dodging bullets and killing Yankees; but I'm starved for quietness and tenderness and—talk. I'm starved for you." He smiled. "I'm like a baby, wanting nothing but to be fed and loved and fondled."

Yet he was soon hungry too for news; so though most of all they talked of themselves, he made her tell him what was happening outside this secret, happy room. Longstreet was gone to Tennessee; but a general named Frazier had shamelessly surrendered Cumberland Gap to the Yankees, so Longstreet and his men had to go roundabout. "I never heard of General Frazier," Faunt commented; and she said no one had heard of him till this craven surrender. When word came of victory at Chickamauga, they exulted together; and she shared his dry rage because that victory, like so many others, was left, for lack of bold pursuit, a fruitless and an empty one. But she said that to be angry was bad for him; and she told him about the little kitchen garden which Rufus had made and strictly guarded, and from which came the fresh vegetables she gave him to eat from day to day. They had tomatoes in plenty, and lima beans. The cabbages were slow to head up, but Rufus picked the leaves to boil with bacon. Red peppers and okra gave a fine flavor to the rich soups Milly concocted, and Faunt gained strength every day.

"You don't know how lucky you are to have me taking care of you," she told him proudly. "Not many people in Richmond get such nice things nowadays. Prices are so high no one can buy what little the stores have to sell. A barrel of flour costs sixty dollars!"

Yet she gave him not only vegetables and bread but bacon and beef and everything he desired; and he told her she was a maker of miracles.

"They're very simple miracles," she assured him. "It's just the miracle of having money. I bought this beef today from Mr. Moffitt. He's one of Colonel Northrop's agents. He buys for the Government at twenty cents or less, and sells to the stores—and to people who keep on his good side, as I do—for fifty cents. Of course, the stores charge two or three times that."

Faunt frowned. "You're as conscienceless as any woman! I suppose he's making his fortune out of starving the army."

"I suppose so. Most of the commissary agents are getting rich."

"And you help him!"

She said quietly: "My dear, I'd become a partner in any crime to get the things you need. And after all, the one little roast of beef I bought for you wouldn't go far to feed the army."

"But a thousand roasts would go far, and ten thousand women like you would starve an army."

Nell smiled. "You needn't scold me. I shall still buy whatever you need." She said seriously: "It's the Government that should be blamed, darling, not the women. Women will always feed their men and their babies if they can. But the Government manages badly. Food collected under the tax-in-kind is stored here in Richmond and allowed to spoil. The army doesn't get it—it just spoils, with people begging a chance to buy some of it. I heard of a woman who tried to buy a barrel of flour, and the merchant wanted seventy dollars for it, and she said she couldn't pay such a price and that she had seven starving children. He told her if she was hungry she could eat her children."

He laughed. "That's made up. I don't believe it!"

"Neither do I," she admitted, smiling with him; yet she added: "But it might be true. Faunt, if the hungry women in Richmond ever get mad enough, they'll sweep the whole Government away." Then, sorrowfully: "There, I shouldn't tell you these things. They only anger you, and that's bad for you."

"No," he said. "No, it's good for me. When I was on duty I didn't think about how things were going here. I didn't think much about anything except the men I was trying to kill; but maybe it's not only Yankees that need killing." His own words, for some obscure reason, woke a sudden memory, and he added: "By the way, Nell, I've been in Washington since I saw you."

"Washington?" Her tone was startled.

"Yes." And he added: "I may go again, some day. It's very simple. There's a regular highway back and forth, you know." And to her sharp and anxious question, he explained: "Why, General Longstreet wanted to send a spy through the lines, and he asked Stuart's help, and General Stuart spoke to Major Mosby, and he turned the task over to me. The spy was a man named Harrison. I proposed to take him toward Leesburg, but he said the simplest way was across the Northern Neck to Port Tobacco." She was staring at him, her eyes wide with something like fear; and he asked: "What's the matter?"

"Nothing! Just—frightened for you! Oh Faunt, they'd have called you a spy!"

"Hard names break no bones."

"I know you're never afraid, my darling; though I die a thousand deaths with fear for you. But they hang spies, even here in Richmond."

"Someone said they'd caught a woman spy here."

"Yes, Mrs. Patterson Allan. When they went to arrest her, she was visiting Mrs. Hoge. Mrs. Hoge's son was dying, and Mrs. Allan was staying with her, and General Winder put a guard on the house till Lacy Hoge died, and then he arrested Mrs. Allan."

"But they didn't hang her."

"No, but they put her in the Asylum of St. Francis de Sales, out on Brooke Road; and the poor woman has come down with brain fever, and they've shaved her head! That's almost as bad."

He chuckled, touched her bright hair. "Don't ever turn spy, my dear. But if you do, and they shave this lovely head of yours, I'll scalp them all."

"I'm frightened for you," she repeated.

"Well, they didn't catch me," he reminded her. "We only saw two Yankees the whole way." No need to tell her how he had dealt with those two.

"But if Harrison knew the way, why did he need you?"

"He knew where to go, and who to ask for; but he'd never been that way himself," Faunt explained. "But of course Belle Vue was on the Northern Neck, and I knew every cow path in those woods. We rode down below Port Royal and found a negro to ferry us across to the Neck. We stayed that night in the pines near Belle Vue, and then went on to Mathias Point, to the farm of a man named Ben Grimes." He smiled at his own tone. "I enjoyed it, Nell; the secrecy and the mystery. It was like a romance."

"It might have been a tragedy, Faunt."

"I don't think so. They've never had any trouble. There's a regular signal station in the swamp back of the Grimes house. Lieutenant Caywood and Sergeant Brogden are in charge. Over on the Maryland shore there are two houses on a high bluff, and if it isn't safe for a boat to cross, a black signal is hung in the dormer window of one of the houses. A young lady, Miss Mary Watson, attends to that warning."

Nell smiled. "This begins to sound like a real romance, Faunt."

"I never encountered her," he admitted; "but she is highly spoken of." And he explained: "There was no warning signal that day. The boat put out just before sunset, because the shadows on the water help hide it then, and the pickets on the Maryland side don't come on duty till about dark. We landed at the foot of a high bluff, and a man met us there and led us up a steep, deep ravine all tangled with honeysuckle to his house on top of the bluff. His name was Jones, Thomas Jones. He handles all the mail. If he's not on the beach, they hide it in the fork of a dead tree and he comes to get it when he can; but Lieutenant Caywood had signalled him we were on the way, so he came down to meet us. His farm's just below a place called Pope's Creek; and there was a detachment of Yankee troops there, and another at Major Watson's, within two or three hundred yards of his farm in the other direction."

She said smilingly: "You enjoyed it, didn't you? You're like a boy, telling about it."

Faunt chuckled. "As a matter of fact, there was a boy helping Mr. Jones. Warren Dent, the son of a doctor. He wasn't more than ten years old. Doctor Dent used to call at Mr. Jones's house on his rounds, to carry the mail to Port Tobacco or to Bryantown; but if he couldn't come he sometimes sent his boy. It was the youngster who led us on, before daylight, toward a place called Allen's Fresh; and a man there let us have horses. Harrison had no more need of me, of course; but

I was interested and curious, so I rode on with him. We made a wide circuit through Bryantown to a place called Surrattsville, and put up at Mrs. Surratt's tavern there, and rode into Washington that night." He chuckled at the memory. "Harrison and I drank with more than one Yankee in the Washington barrooms before he and I parted."

"You reckless idiot!"

He laughed reassuringly. "It wasn't as bad as it sounds! Washington's full of Southern sympathizers; and of course Mosby's men don't wear any distinguishing uniform, so no one challenged me. But I didn't push my luck too far. I was out of Washington and back at Mrs. Surratt's before daylight, and back at Mr. Jones's home that night." He said in a different tone: "You can see for miles up and down river from his place, and that ravine with the trees all blanketed with honeysuckle is a natural covered way down to the beach. I could have disposed of every Yankee picket for a quarter-mile in each direction, but it would have made trouble for Mr. Jones."

"Bloodthirsty man!" Her tone was tenderly affectionate. "I can't imagine you killing Yankees. But Faunt, promise you'll never go again?"

"Oh I've no notion of trying it again. I didn't care for Washington, didn't like the company. It was interesting, though. Harrison said that route is used all the time, not only by the mail, but by spies and smugglers. That part of Maryland is all for the South, of course."

"Don't ever go again, Faunt. Promise me!"

Her concern for him was wine in his veins, but he made no promise. "I certainly don't expect to," he assured her. "But I can look out for myself, you know."

She came to kiss him, shaking his head fondly between her hands. "Oh I know, I know. I expect you're just as fierce as fierce can be; but I can't imagine it. I can't imagine you really being in a fight, a battle, shooting at anyone. You seem so gentle here with me."

He smiled up at her, wondering what she would think if she knew some of his deeds. How little even the wisest women really knew of man!

It was a full two months before Faunt left her. He might have gone before he did; but her persuasions and his own happiness held him for a while. Through her and through the Richmond papers Rufus brought, he began to see more clearly than before the weakness of the Confederacy. Because Bragg had failed to seize the ripe fruits of victory at Chickamauga, there was a cry for his removal so persistent that President Davis himself went to Tennessee; but there, he left Bragg still in command. Faunt and Nell agreed that the arrogant stubbornness which was so much a part of Davis could do disastrous harm. When the new wealth in the Cotton States seized political control of the South, the dominance of intellect and character was ended. "Even Virginia surrendered to mob rule in the convention of 1850," Faunt reminded her, "when they gave up homestead suffrage and let everybody vote. Before that, no one could vote in Richmond unless he owned land—lots in the city worth at least a hundred and fifty dollars. I don't suppose there were more than five or six hundred voters. There must be ten times that many now; and any loud-mouthed politician can tell them they're the backbone of the state and they'll elect him. Fifteen years ago it was the men who paid taxes who decided how tax money should be spent. Now the mob decides. They don't have to furnish the money, so they're all for spending it. So we're doomed to submit to the tyranny of the majority; and God knows the majority is just poor white trash, not fit to rule!"

There were rumors that President Davis and members of his cabinet—Mr. Memminger, the Secretary of the Treasury, was named as one of them—were selling their property and converting the money into gold and sterling exchange and sending it to England for security. To Faunt's question whether that was possible, Nell said passports could be bought, and permits to take tobacco out of the country and to sell cotton to the enemy.

"Anything you want in Richmond can be bought today," she assured him. "These speculators even bribe the railroads to work for them, while food for the army spoils because there are no cars to carry it."

"I can't believe it's as bad as you say," he protested; and to prove her point she found a month-old paper and read him a paragraph from a letter President Davis had written to an organization in Mississippi.

The passion for speculation has become a gigantic evil. It has seemed to take possession of the whole country, and has seduced citizens of all classes from a determined prosecution of the war to a sordid effort to amass money.

"But if he's right," Faunt protested, "why doesn't he do something about it?"

She shook her head. "What can he do, Faunt? Rich people won't let him tax land and slaves, even if he wanted to. They say the Constitution forbids it. The Congress passed a law last April to tax bankers and auctioneers and liquor dealers and store keepers and apothecaries and all sorts of people, lawyers and doctors and surgeons; but what little they pay doesn't amount to anything. Congress put a tax on incomes, but it doesn't have to be paid till January; and honest people haven't any incomes worth taxing, and dishonest people will say they haven't. There's a ten-percent tax on profits people made last year, but the speculators won't pay it. But Mr. Davis has to have money to pay for the war, so he has to borrow it or just print it. Up to this month, the Government has collected less than five million dollars in taxes; but they've spent six hundred millions, printed money! So money's worth less and less, so naturally people would rather have things than money, and prices go up and up."

"You make it sound as though everything in the Confederacy were rotten but the army." And he added in sudden challenge: "You sound as though you were glad of it, too!"

Her eyes met his honestly. "I've no reason to love the South, Faunt; none except that I was born here." She smiled a little. "It's my own fault, of course; but I'm outside the pale. I expect even you are sometimes ashamed of loving me." He did not speak. What she said was true, and he would not lie to her. "I have no illusions, you see. Perhaps that's why I treasure so deeply what you feel you can give me."

He rose with a swift movement, came to her. "Nell, will you marry me?"

She caught his hand, pressed it to her cheek. "Don't be silly! Of course not, my dear." Then, in tender teasing: "But don't let me see so plainly the relief you feel when I refuse."

He could not deny this. "Damn the whole damned world!" he said.

She laughed softly. "It's all right, darling. We couldn't possibly have anything richer or finer than we have."

He moved restlessly around the room. "Even the army—" he said, his thoughts reverting. "Even the army's rotten in spots. Men are deserting all the time. But that's because they're starving, or their families are. The men are all right." He came back to sit near her. "But we're not as good as we were, Nell. We used to be able to charge three or four times our numbers of Yankees and scatter them. They'd run away, fall off their horses like a lot of clowns, surrender by dozens. But now they fight back, and they've learned to ride, and their horses are better than ours. Ours are half-starved. We can't keep them properly shod, and we work them too hard, wear them out. Half the men in every cavalry regiment are in Company Q most of the time."

"Company Q? What's that?"

"Men whose horses are sick, or worn out, not fit to fight." He turned to her and said in flat tones: "Nell, we're going to be beaten in the end."

Her eyes searched his. "Will it hurt you so? I don't want you hurt, my dear."

"Oh, I won't be here!" She cried out in soft tender protest, and he said affectionately: "It's all right, Nell. I've had all the happiness a man's life can hold, since I knew you." Her heart, at his words, was cold with fear.

It was late August when he came to Richmond. Early in October, the news of Lee's move around Meade's flank made Faunt resentful of his own inaction here. But Lee's maneuver ended in futility, for Meade drew his army back so skillfully that his losses were slight, and he had not even to abandon any considerable stores. After a week of fruitless marching, General Hill fought and lost a costly skirmish at Bristoe Station, and Lee fell back to the defensive lines along the Rappahannock.

Thereafter Faunt was increasingly anxious to return to the field. Nell tried to dissuade him, arguing that Mosby and his handful of men could do no real hurt to the Yankees; but Faunt disagreed. "Fifty of us, free to hit his lines of supply where we choose, can tie down thousands of his men to guard duty. If he could get rid of us it would be worth an army corps to Meade."

She said with narrowed eyes: "I wish the Yankees would gobble up Mosby and all his men! Then you'd stay here with me!"

He smiled affectionately. "Don't talk nonsense, Nell!"

"I mean it!" she insisted; then, seeing his sombre eyes: "At least I think I do."

He chuckled, forgiving her. "Well, the Yankees won't get Major Mosby," he assured her. "But just to be sure—I'd better go back and take care of him."

Before October ended, he rode away. Nell gave him her farewell kiss, and her smile, and shed no tears. "Come when you need me, Faunt. Whenever you come, I will be here."

He left in the hour before dawn, and he took the journey easily, angry to find how soft he was become. He went at first toward Charlottesville and thence up the eastern flank of the mountains to Sperryville, hardening his horse and himself, relishing the crisp fall days. At Sperryville he heard that Mosby was recovered from his wound and that there was a rendezvous appointed at the crossing of Thumb Run, northwest of Warrenton. When Faunt reached the spot, he was fit and ready for any work in hand.

Mosby greeted him warmly, with many questions. "I thought we'd lost you for good and all, when you didn't come back from Annandale." Faunt confessed that he had been ill, and Mosby nodded in understanding sympathy. "You'll need to take better care of yourself," he said. "Try to sleep a little more often indoors." And then as though on sudden inspiration he said: "See here!"

Faunt waited, but Mosby was silent so long that he asked at last: "See what?"

"I was thinking. Speaking of taking care of yourself reminded me. You know we're short of medicines in the hospitals."

"I've heard so."

"Quinine's worth any price, a hundred dollars an ounce, perhaps more. Opium's just as scarce. Even blue mass costs twenty dollars an ounce."

Faunt smiled. "Without the one to counteract the other, the doctors must be hard put."

"Our laboratories try to make it," Major Mosby told him. "But the mercury seeps out of it. But the point is—we need all that sort of thing." Faunt waited curiously, and Mosby said: "You know the underground route to Washington."

"I've been there, yes."

"I've had word that one of our friends in the North has acquired a lot of quinine and opium and wants to give it to us. He seems to have heard of me, says some day he'd like to ride with us; and he offers this gift of medicines as an introduction, if we'll send and get it. I could hire someone to smuggle it through, but that would cost three or four times what it's worth; and I don't want to trust the ordinary blockade-runners anyway. Will you go?"

Faunt remembered Nell's pleading. "I don't object to—ordinary danger," he commented. "But this might be difficult." He asked: "Could your generous gentleman meet me, say, at Surrattsville? That's a few miles this side of Washington."

"He can't," Major Mosby explained. "He's an actor, playing at Ford's New Theatre there this week and next. He says he'd bring it himself if he could, but that he's too much in the public eye. I think actually he hopes I will come myself. It may be a trap, but I don't believe so. A Baltimore friend of mine brought me his letter, says he can be trusted." He chuckled. "Being an actor, he likes theatrical gestures, of course; so he's arranged a rigmarole. My messenger is to go to the stage door of the theatre and ask for peanuts, and say his own name is Shell."

Faunt smiled. "What's this actor's name?"

"Booth. J. W. Booth."

Faunt instantly remembered a ringing voice declaiming on a Richmond street, a man in a fur-collared coat somewhat too big for him, an actor from George Kunkel's theatre; and he remembered the strong impact of that man's eyes meeting his, the sense he had of something powerful and moving in the actor.

"J. W. Booth?" he echoed. "John Wilkes Booth?"

"Yes, that's the man."

"I met him once, at the time of the John Brown raid. He was acting at the Marshall Theatre in Richmond. He was a friend of the South, even then." And he said in quiet decision: "Yes, Major, I will go. I was much struck with that man."

5

WHEN Tony took Sapphira, he recognized that 'Phemy, Sapphira's mother, had contrived for him to do so; and he was amused at her cleverness. These niggers were as cute as a 'coon, shrewd and full of guile. Well, let them be; he could when he chose be rid of 'Phemy, and of Sapphira too. They were his property. He could sell them away, if they became a nuisance, as he had sold those others.

Tony was at that time seldom sober. The discovery that that ruffianly blackguard in Washington was the son of his father's bastard destroyed the new-won sense of responsibility which had come to be the precarious foundation of his life. If the father of whom he had always secretly been proud could let loose this nigger-loving, poorwhite backwoodsman to destroy the South, why then damn the name of Currain! He would drag it in the mire!

So to the bottle, to the easy black wenches, and finally to Sapphira. When he presented her to Trav as the mistress of Chimneys it was a gesture of defiance and derision, alike of Trav and of the name of Currain.

It was a long time before he began to realize that Sapphira and 'Phemy between them were changing him. What they did was done in little ways. When he rose in the morning he found fresh linen laid ready by his bed; a neatly pressed coat, trousers brushed and sponged, boots brightly shined. He was amused at these attentions. Why should a man trouble about his appearance when there was nobody to see him but a lot of niggers? Nevertheless he dressed in the garments they laid out for him, and with an instinctive distaste for putting clean clothes on a dirty body, he began by degrees to pay closer attention to his person. Trav in his days here had installed at Chimneys an outside shower for bathing; and Tony came to use it, at first occasionally and then with regularity.

Sapphira was always crisply immaculate. That first summer, if he had ridden in dust and sun and came home soiled and sweaty, it amused him to clip her and tumble her and paw at her fresh-laundered dress with his stained and grimy hands. But she never protested and never let him see any resentment she may have felt, and the game ceased to amuse him. He came in time to be as fastidious as she. The fact that when he drank heavily his hand shook, so that he spilled liquor on himself or at table, and spilled food on his garments or on the always spotless linen, led him to curtail his drinking. Because Sapphira always bore herself with a serene dignity, he learned to match his manner to hers, to play a decorous and gentle part.

Tony never replaced James Fiddler, for he discovered that there was no need. 'Phemy and Sapphira, and under their direction old Maria in the kitchen, acquired a mysterious dominance over the Negroes; Peg-leg as their lieutenant saw to it that the work was done in the fields, at the saw mill down by the branch, in the blacksmith shop, everywhere. When Tony realized this, he approved his own good judgment in leaving matters in their hands. He was so pleased with himself and with them that he went to Raleigh and eventually to Richmond to buy laces and linens and cashmeres and whatever finery the stores that handled blockade goods could offer; and it amused him to let Dolly try fabrics and colors for him. Back at Chimneys he told Sapphira:

"The prettiest girl in Richmond tried that on, and she couldn't hold a candle to you."

Sapphira made no comment. She was of silent habit, and Tony liked this. Most women, even Nell, talked too much, gave a man no chance to be with his thoughts alone.

Winter passed contentingly, and as spring ripened into summer the very look of the place testified to the good management of Sapphira and her mother. Everywhere within sight of the house trash had disappeared, the fences were in repair, paint had been used where it was needed, well-tended flower beds flourished. Tony had no need to use any supervision. Things were done before he realized they should be done. He admitted to himself one day that the place was better run than he could possibly have run it. These two women were smart. Maybe that bearded ape in Washington was right in standing up for the niggers!

But he could never forget that any white man who knew his way of life would damn him; and 'Phemy' and Sapphira understood this as well as he. That was why, whenever travellers stopped for a night's hospitality, Sapphira kept herself invisible. Once Tony assured her that she was mistress of the house, and that she should dine with them just as she dined with him when he was here alone.

But Sapphira would not do so. "That would insult any white gentleman," she reminded him. "I don't want to see any guest in your house insulted."

"Why, damn it, girl," he cried, "you're as white as any of them! And twice as smart! They ought to feel honored to make your acquaintance."

But she knew this was not true, and so did he. The attitude of the men of his old company, when he occasionally rode into Martinston, was a reminder. He knew their code. If he chose to dally with a Negro wench, that was his affair; but when he set Sapphira at his dinner table he affronted them all. In the past, these neighbors of his had sometimes ridden up to Chimneys to see him. They had always preferred not to come into the big house; but they had been till now ready enough to stay and talk on the veranda steps, or in that ground-floor room which Trav had used as an office. Now, however, none ever came; and if Tony appeared in Martinston, though they were carefully polite, they raised an invisible wall against him.

He damned them all for a lot of white trash; and he resented their attitude the more because he knew that behind them lay the united and inflexible opinion of the South. In time, his anger at them enlarged itself to embrace all who thought as they did. Lincoln was right: Southerners were a lot of stubborn fools; they deserved what they were getting!

Yet he felt his ostracism, and as one result he began to offer friendship to the deserters in the mountain country. Jeremy Blackstone had deserted after Sharpsburg, and Alex Spain and Joe Merritt and Nat Emerson. All except Alex Spain had families, and they lived at home except when word that the conscript officers were near sent them to hiding in the mountains till the danger passed. But Spain united with fifteen or twenty others in an armed band of bushwhackers who, though they never molested their old neighbors hereabouts, ranged into Southwest Virginia and into Tennessee and southward as far as Asheville. Alex and his fellows occasionally stopped at Chimneys, and they accepted food and drink if it were offered.

After Gettysburg, others of Tony's old company came back to Martinston. Not all were deserters. When Bob Grimm, who had lost one arm at Williamsburg and the other at Gettysburg came home from the hospital, Tony took him a side of bacon and a bag of corn. Bob accepted the gift because he must. His farm was poor, his family in distress, he himself helpless to do any real work; but he thanked Tony in a way which made it clear that only necessity compelled his acceptance. To Wick Temple, who had deserted, Tony sent a cow just coming fresh; but Wick returned the cow with an ill-written but politely phrased assurance that he could get along. Need Hayfurt, another homecomer whose nickname had been earned by a lifetime of suppliance, walked up to the big house one day to say he needed this and needed that. Tony gave him as much corn meal and sow belly as he could carry, but he despised Need as much as he resented Wick Temple's refusal of his beneficence.

Tony's increasing hatred of his neighbors and of the whole South of whose opinion they were representative colored all his thoughts. In the Richmond and the Raleigh papers he read greedily every criticism of President Davis. Mr. Holden's Raleigh *Standard* was his favorite paper. The Raleigh *State Journal* supported the administration, so Tony stopped reading it. Mr. Holden was right! This was a rich man's war and a poor man's fight. The rich man could stay at home while the poor man was dragged away to die, and his wife and children were left to starve. Taxes never touched the rich man; but the poor farmer had to pay the tax-in-kind. He had to see the things he had raised by his own hard sweating toil taken away from him, while the rich men on their plantations were left untouched. The brave men were those who stayed at home and took care of their families. President Davis wished to set himself up as a dictator. If he could, he would make slaves of them all, reduce the poor white farmer to the level of the blacks.

Thus said Mr. Holden, day by day; and Tony read and agreed with him. Sometimes he considered going to Raleigh to meet the editor and tell him so; but he was so comfortable in his smoothly ordered home and so calmly happy with Sapphira that he never reached the point of doing this. Instead, though it was by proxy, Mr. Holden came to him. Late in July, Tony heard that there was to be a "peace meeting" in Martinston; and he rode to town to attend. He went into the assemblage with a high head, long since accustomed to ignore the fact that even these humble men drew a little away from him as though he were tainted.

A man Tony had never seen before spoke to the meeting. He said it was high time to put an end to the war, to seek any peace that was not disgraceful and degrading. "The Federals are ready to be friendly with all good conservative men," he cried. "Let us unite together to show them our good will. Now that Federal victory and the restoration of the Union is sure, we who are friends of the Union should make ourselves known, stand and be counted for the right." He gave them a phrase: "Let's stand for the Constitution as it is, the Union as it was!"

Tony, watching the listening audience, thought the speaker won them. He waited afterward to introduce himself to this stranger.

"I'm Anthony Currain," he said. "I was late in arriving, did not hear your name."

"Dean, sir. Horace Dean," the other told him, mopping his brow.

"How did you happen to come here?"

"It was the suggestion of Mr. Holden of the *Standard.*"

"I follow Mr. Holden's editorials with full approval," Tony assured him; and he said: "My home is a few miles away. May I offer you some hospitality?"

The other hesitated, and Tony felt himself weighed and appraised; but then Mr. Dean spoke a word of acceptance and they rode out of town together. Over their juleps on the cool veranda and at supper and afterward they talked for hours; and Mr. Dean's tongue as he sipped his brandy loosened more and more.

"I see you're a man of proper feeling, a man to be trusted," he declared at last. "You should unite with us to work for peace."

"Who is 'us'?" Tony asked. "I'm remote here from affairs, know little of what goes on."

"Why, sir, we are a group, and there are thousands of us, who believe that the war should be ended by an honorable peace, and the Union be restored. You know Mr. Holden, at least by his works. He is one of us, and Henderson Adams, and others equally respectable. We number our thousands, in North Carolina and to the north and to the south, all bound together by a common desire to end this bloody, hopeless war. All through the South, for two years now, honest men have united secretly or openly to help restore the Union. The Peace Society in the Cotton States is a year old and stronger all the time. Our organization, growing every day, is the Order of the Heroes of America. Mr. Holden is its inspiration. Everywhere, men who agree with him are flocking to his standard."

Tony said warily: "I've been surprised the Government didn't take steps against Mr. Holden. Some of his editorials are pretty strong."

"The Government in Richmond cannot hurt him here," Mr. Dean declared. "North Carolina is still sovereign within her own borders, Mr. Currain. However," he admitted, "though the constitutional right of free speech protects Mr. Holden, we do use certain precautions for mutual recognition." He smiled flatteringly. "With you, sir, I know I can speak freely. You may, meeting a stranger, remark a bit of red string tied in his button hole. That will suggest to you that he is to be trusted; but in order to make sure, say to him: 'These are gloomy times.'"

Tony was enough the small boy to feel a lively interest in such mysteries. "'These are gloomy times,'" he repeated.

"Exactly. He will reply: 'Yes, but we are looking for better.' You ask: 'What are you looking for?' He says: 'A red and white cord.' You: 'Why a cord?' He: 'Because it is safe for us and our families.'" He rose and crossed to Tony with extended hand, stumbling a little on the way. "You then exchange the secret grip—thus." Their hands clasped. "You say 'Three' and he will answer 'Dogs.'" Mr. Dean hiccoughed faintly; he freed his hand. "So, sir, I greet you and welcome you to our great Order."

Tony was not ready to commit himself. "Is that all there is to it?"

"From ignorant men we require an oath," Mr. Dean admitted. "But that is unnecessary between gentlemen."

"But outside of talking, what do you do?"

"Encourage desertion, protect deserters, contribute in every way to Federal success."

"I'd prefer not to feel a rope around my neck!"

"Sir," said Mr. Dean, "as long as Judge Preston sits at Salisbury, the writ of *habeas corpus* will still operate in North Carolina for your protection. Yes, and if necessary, every North Carolina regiment will be recalled within the borders of the state to uphold our sovereign laws."

"Well, even if that's so, North Carolina can't stand alone!"

"She does not stand alone!" Mr. Dean assured him. "If you go into Virginia you will see the red string everywhere; and you will find judges who respect and uphold the Constitution. Tennessee, Alabama, Georgia, South Carolina—you will see the red string in thousands of button holes. Mr. Davis would like to make himself a dictator; but the sovereign states of the Confederacy say to him with one voice—'Nay! Thus far but no farther! For we are sovereign still!'"

Tony thought Mr. Dean sometimes seemed to forget he was not on the platform. He made no promises, but a day or two later he rode into Martinston, and again and again, tied into the buttonholes of men there, he marked a bit of red string. He himself wore no such sign. If he wished to do so, Sapphira would say a tag end of string was an unsuitable adornment; but it was heartening to think he could be one with all these men, bound by a common purpose and a common loyalty.

And to unite with them was the part of wisdom, too. When the North won, a heavy vengeance would descend on those who had been her enemies, on Richmond and Charleston and the seaboard cities that had resisted her. This was in his mind when Brett wrote proposing that all the Currain funds be put into Confederate bonds. Tony replied that the others could do as they chose, that if Trav would deed him Chimneys in return for a deed to Great Oak, he would make no other claim on the estate. Trav's assent pleased him. Here at Chimneys he would be safe, protected against the Yankees by the loyalty to the Union which his membership in Mr. Holden's order attested;

and when the Piedmont Railroad was completed from Greensboro to Danville, the markets in Lynchburg and in Petersburg and Richmond would be more easily reached, and Chimneys would be an increasingly valuable property!

Toward the end of September, passing the Blandy farm, Tony saw Ed in the door yard and pulled up his horse; and Ed came hesitantly to the gate to exchange a word or two. Behind him, Mrs. Blandy and one of the children appeared for a moment in the doorway, then disappeared again; and Tony felt a faint stir of anger at this mute evidence of her reprobation. The women were worse than the men.

"Well, Mr. Blandy," he said, "I'm glad to see you. Home to stay?"

"No, sir, I'm on furlough."

"Some of your neighbors make their furloughs long ones."

"A lot of that's Mr. Holden's doings, Captain Currain." Ed's tone was hard, but Tony heard with pleasure that title of which he had once been so proud.

"It's not all Mr. Holden," he remarked. "A soldier's pay for a month won't buy a good meal for his family, the way prices are. And he doesn't get his pay half the time."

"I reckon sometimes the Gov'ment has a hard time to find the money." There was a stubborn set to Ed's jaw. "No, I'm going back to duty. Mis' Blandy's made a good crop, and with the young ones to help she'll get along."

"All the same, I expect she'll be glad when this is over, so you can come home to take the hard work off her hands." Tony rode on, anger in him. Ed's words were like a rebuke. Damn the man! Damn that wife of his, too! A woman no better than a field hand, working the summer long, sweating like a nigger! What right had she to set herself above Sapphira? Why, Sapphira in beauty and intelligence was a match for any lady in the South, to say nothing of a poor farm drudge!

One day not long after this encounter with Ed, when Tony and Peg-leg returned from their morning survey of the place, Tony found a fat little man with something sleek about him sitting on the veranda drinking one of 'Phemy's juleps and smoking a cigar. "Thomas

Cosby, Mr. Currain," the stranger explained. "Commissary agent. Mr. Dean in Raleigh told me to make myself known to you."

Tony saw the red string in the other's lapel, and he wondered whether, if Mr. Cosby began that series of questions and answers that Mr. Dean had recited, he could remember the rejoinders; but since his visitor did not speak he said graciously: "Ah, Mr. Cosby. You're welcome. I see your wants have been attended to."

"Yes sir."

"Then if you will excuse me briefly, it will soon be the dinner hour."

At dinner, the commissary agent explained his errand. "I've come to impress supplies for General Lee's army," he told Tony. "My wagons will reach Martinston tomorrow." He looked a little smug. "A painful duty, Mr. Currain! If I were not allowed a military escort, my life would be in danger. These extortionate farmers yield only to compulsion, flatly refuse to sell at the government price unless they must. Why, sir, they would let the army starve!"

"I suppose government prices are below the market."

"To be sure, to be sure. Speculators have run market prices to the skies, five or six times the government price. But our orders are to take at the fixed price horses, wagons, hogs, cattle, everything; to leave only what is necessary to subsistence."

"Do I understand that you propose to empty my corn cribs, my smoke houses, my cattle pens?"

"My dear sir!" Mr. Cosby protested. "Don't imagine such a thing for a moment! Why, our depots are already full of provisions spoiling for lack of cars to move them to Richmond. It requires constant work to collect enough to take the place of what spoils. Sweet potatoes are particularly perishable. You'll hardly believe me, but there are thousands of bushels of sweet potatoes rotting in depots between Wilmington and Richmond right now for lack of transportation. Of course we must replace them, keep the depots supplied; but that does not compel us to harass gentlemen!" He laughed. "It's the little farmers who make the trouble."

"I know they resent the tax-in-kind," Tony agreed. "I suppose they resent impressment equally."

"Yes, yes! We could hardly accomplish anything if it weren't that so many men are away in the army. Women may scold and complain, but they're not so ready to resort to violence, though I could tell you some incredible stories." He added casually: "By the way, Mr. Currain, I'm commissioned by some gentlemen in Richmond to buy any surplus produce you may have for their personal account. At a fair price, of course. If you care to sell."

"A fair price? You mean the government prices?"

"Oh not at all, not at all. The price I can pay depends on the article." Mr. Cosby crossed his pudgy knees. "Take bacon, for instance. I'll be frank with you, Mr. Currain. If you wished to buy a pound of bacon in Richmond, it might cost you two dollars and a half. A bushel of meal? Say twenty dollars. I can offer you no such prices. Captain Warner, whose agent I am, has many expenses." He smiled. "My commission, for one; and then, he must lay out a little here and a little there to secure space on the cars to transport his purchases; and of course he must be generous to his friends. But I can pay you a dollar a pound for prime bacon, and for other things in proportion. That's only a fraction of the market price in Richmond, to be sure; yet it's three or four times the government maximum for what I impress." Tony did not speak. The price seemed to him, considering the difficulty of transporting anything over the long and roundabout way to Richmond, an astonishingly good one. As though reading his thought, Mr. Cosby added: "Frankly, Mr. Currain, I'm not always so openhanded; but—" He hesitated, looked at Tony's lapel, said in a questioning tone: "Three?"

Tony for a moment did not understand. "Eh?"

Mr. Cosby repeated, more sharply: "Three?"

So Tony remembered. "Oh, to be sure! Dogs," he replied.

The other man smiled with relief. "Exactly! As I was saying, I'm not always so openhanded; but I always pay liberally for anything that comes in a parcel tied up with red string!" He lifted his glass. "Your very good health, Mr. Currain."

Tony lifted his. "And yours, sir," he agreed.

The commissary agent was Tony's guest for several days, while the soldiers who served as escort for the wagons he brought and for those he seized camped by the branch below the mill. Mr. Cosby complained of the difficulties of his task. "This region's full of organized deserters, dangerous men," he declared. "The Government should send a regiment or two to teach them manners. I'm careful not to provoke them too far, though of course I must take what I need."

Tony felt no sympathy for these neighbors who suffered under Mr. Cosby's demands. If they were his friends, he might save them now; since they had elected to be his enemies, he would not lift his hand.

Two or three weeks after Mr. Cosby's departure, Tony was sitting on the veranda after dinner, Sapphira beside him in fresh-starched white, when they saw Mrs. Blandy trudging up the road. Sapphira went at once into the house. Tony called to her:

"No, no. Stay! You're mistress here!" But Sapphira only smiled and disappeared, and Tony admitted to himself that she was right. If she dared stay with him to receive a white woman as an equal, her own life might hang in the balance.

He himself, when Mrs. Blandy came near, rose and descended the wide steps to meet her with the utmost courtesy. He invited her to join him on the veranda; but she declined. "Thank you kindly, sir." In sunbonnet and worn and faded calico, dusty from the road, barefooted, she faced him doubtfully. "Mr. Currain, please, sir, could you sell me a bag of corn meal and maybe a piece of hog meat?"

Tony thought with a malicious satisfaction that she must be reduced to desperate straits. Before coming to appeal to him, she would have tried every other resource. Obviously she had tried and failed. Oh, these people who had treated him so scornfully would regret it! "But Mrs. Blandy," he said gravely, "Mr. Blandy told me you had made a good crop."

She nodded, and her lips were white. "Yes sir, we did, with the young ones and me all working at it. But now the impressment men done took our mule, and emptied our corn crib and our smoke house."

"Now surely not! Their orders were to leave you enough for your subsistence."

"I reckon they thought we didn't eat more than birds."

"But at least, they paid you," he insisted.

"They called it pay, but the gov'ment money ain't wuth anything. But that and what Mr. Blandy give me, all his pay he'd saved, has to git us through some way."

Tony made a sympathetic sound. "Dear, dear! I'm very sorry to hear of your distress." He said regretfully: "But they levied on me too, you know. They left me only enough for our needs. I can't starve my people."

In her eyes meeting his a slow flame burned. "White folks git as hungry as colored people."

"Yes. Yes, indeed. This war is hard on all of us. If we were sensible we'd end it."

Her head was high. She said proudly: "Mr. Blandy's doing his best to end it the way it'd ought to be ended."

"I know. I know. I honor him for it. Yet I sometimes think a man's first duty is to his family."

She held him with her eyes. "Mr. Blandy knows what's right to do. I didn't come to talk about it. I come to see if I could buy from you."

"Why, I've really nothing at all to spare," he assured her. "So many mouths to feed, you know. I might give you a——"

"I ain't asking anything to be give." Her tones were level. "I'm wanting to buy."

So she was not yet humbled! "Well, let me see. Meal, you say? And pork? The latest Richmond papers put fat shoulder at two dollars and a half a pound, and meal at twenty dollars a bushel. I might spare a little at those prices."

Her lips twitched and then were still again. "The commissary man paid me twenty cents for prime bacon. He give me six dollars for the meal in the chest, and there was all of four bushels."

"My dear Mrs. Blandy, I'm afraid he imposed on you. You should keep informed on Richmond prices."

"He said it was the gov'ment price. He said I could take it or not, but he was going to 'press what he wanted anyway."

"Ah yes. Well, too bad. But you say you don't want me to give you anything. It seems only fair, if you wish to buy, that you should pay the market price; don't you think so?" Her hard eyes on his were like a bruising blow; he smiled. "After all, this is a matter of business."

"We had enough put away to feed us all winter," she said evenly. "But all he give for it and all Mr. Blandy's back pay put together wouldn't buy enough to keep us a month from starving. Not paying your prices."

He said nothing, waiting. If she wanted charity, let her beg! But after a moment, with no other word, she turned away. He watched her, resisting the impulse to call her back. Let her go! When her children were hungry enough she would come again. She passed out of sight, and he returned to his comfortable chair, and Sapphira rejoined him. Wanting reassurance, he told her Mrs. Blandy's errand, using words to fan the flame of his own anger and thus burn away his guilty shame. "A fine piece of impudence! She's so hoity-toity she'd look down her nose at you, but she's not too high and mighty to want favors."

Sapphira gave him no comfort. "You could be generous, Mr. Currain."

"Generous, be damned! You're as good as she is."

She spoke without bitterness. "No, I'm not. She's white. I'm a colored person."

"Abe Lincoln says that makes no difference. And by God I believe he's right!"

"Mr. Lincoln is a great, good man," she said simply. "But he's wrong. He doesn't know. Colored people know." He felt the firm compulsion of her level intelligence, half understood the tragedy of life for such a woman. An almost impersonal tenderness awoke in him; her thoughts must often be such sad and hopeless ones.

November was well sped and winter near when into his existence here without forewarning Darrell suddenly intruded. The day was stormy with a cold drizzle falling; and Tony's first hint of Darrell's coming was his hail, calling for a boy to take his horse. At the moment, Sapphira was safely in the kitchen with 'Phemy, so no immediate harm was done. Tony opened the door and saw Darrell and another man dismounting at the steps, while a Negro on a mule, with four long-eared, sad-eyed dogs on leash, sat dejected at a little distance, drooping in the rain. As they came up the steps, Tony recognized the other man as Mr. Pudrick, the slave dealer whom Darrell had brought here a year ago last summer.

He gave them a grudging welcome; but Darrell made himself cheerfully at home, stripping off his cloak, warming himself before the roaring fire. Mr. Pudrick bowed and said politely: "Servant, sir!" 'Phemy brought them warming drinks, and a scuttling wench fed the fire, and Darrell gave 'Phemy orders. Bring in the saddlebags. Lay out some dry clothes. These they wore were to be cleaned and dried. Tony's anger, as he listened, left a bitter taste in his mouth. You might have thought Darrell, not he, was master here. But at least Sapphira would keep out of Darrell's sight. On such occasions as this she stayed invisible in 'Phemy's quarters.

'Phemy showed these unwelcome visitors to rooms upstairs, and Tony wondered why Darrell had come, and why was Pudrick here, and why had he brought those hounds. When they had changed to dry clothes, the explanation came.

"I suppose we surprised you, Uncle Tony," Darrell remarked. "Matter of fact, I meant to come in June and help you run the place. You seem to have managed without me."

His tone was a question. Tony said: "Yes, I get along very comfortably. Mr. Fiddler went into the army, but Peg-leg is my driver and I'm my own overseer."

"Well, I meant to come," Darrell repeated. "But an amusing matter detained me—till it ceased to be amusing. To escape called for drastic measures, so I went to Nassau on one of our blockaders, stayed there till a fortnight since. On my return I met Mr. Pudrick in Wilmington. One of the niggers you sold him ran away from the man to whom Mr. Pudrick sold him, a month or so ago. That's bad for Mr. Pudrick's business; when he sells a nigger, that nigger's expected to stay sold. He thinks the nigger might be here, and I suggested that we bring some dogs and run him down. Mr. Pudrick got a pair of the nigger's old shoes, so if the rascal's here we can have some sport."

"What makes you think he might be here?" Tony asked. The slaves he had sold were all from Great Oak or Belle Vue. Chimneys had only briefly been their home. Also, if there were a runaway on the place, Peg-leg or 'Phemy would surely have told him.

Mr. Pudrick said confidently: "Oh, I know niggers, Mr. Currain. They're my business. This scamp wouldn't eat, from the first; so I knew that either he was homesick, or else he had a wench back here. I always put a couple of my own niggers in with a new batch to listen to their talk. It turned out this one had his eye on a wench, a bright. So when I heard he'd run away—I guarantee every nigger I sell—I paid back his purchase price and headed this way."

A bright mulatto wench? Sapphira was the only bright at Chimneys. Tony felt new anger flood his throat. "What's his name?"

"Sam."

The name was meaningless, but what did a name matter? Why had not 'Phemy or Peg-leg reported the runaway's presence? Had the nigger seen Sapphira? By God, he himself would have some questions to ask 'Phemy; yes, and to ask Sapphira too.

"There's no bright here," he said harshly. "There are browns and yellows, but no true bright." He felt Darrell's eye upon him, carefully held his own on Mr. Pudrick. "And if your nigger was here, I'd have heard of it."

"Well, he may be hiding somewhere," the slave dealer suggested. "If he is, the sight of the dogs will flush him. We'll take the hounds for a stroll through the quarter tomorrow."

"You can't trail him in this rain."

Pudrick chuckled. "Mr. Currain, those hounds of mine could trail a fish downstream to the Yadkin!"

Tony fell into a stormy silence, and his thoughts were raging. Was it possible that Sapphira would take up with a black? Of course it was! To that nigger strain in her anything was possible. Then in sudden hopefulness he remembered that when Darrell and Mr. Pudrick came to buy those slaves, Sapphira had only that day been brought over from the Pettigrew place. Surely this Sam had had no chance to see her before he was herded away in the coffle with the others.

But during his stay here he might have discovered her, even over at the Pettigrew place. There were no patrollers hereabouts. Negroes could wander at night if they chose; and if Sapphira had ever let her hot black blood have its way, every buck nigger in twenty miles would have known it! They were as sharp as dogs in such matters.

When 'Phemy brought supper he glared at her with bloodshot eyes. She seemed not to see, but that was pretense. She saw, no doubt of that. Well, by and by, when these men were gone, he would deal with her; but first he must be rid of Darrell and Mr. Pudrick, and as quickly as possible.

After supper, stretching his feet before the fire, yawning comfortably, Darrell said: "By the way, Uncle Tony, our blockading venture is a great success. Captain Pew gets the lion's share, but there's plenty for all of us. Why don't you run over to Nassau and spend some of the money? You'd find a variety of pleasures there."

Tony floundered for words. "Have you had no trouble? I saw by the papers that some of the Government's steamers have been lost."

"Yes, yes, very sad. The *Hebe* and the *Venus,* and the *R. E. Lee,* and the *Lady Davis.* She used to be the *Cornubia.* Yes, the government pilots seem to lose vessels faster than Jeff Davis can buy them; but of course, the fewer steamers they operate, the more profits for the rest of us." He yawned again. "Uncle Tony, you're mighty comfortable here. I think I'll stay and be your overseer."

Darrell under the same roof with Sapphira? No sir! Tony meant to be rid of this whelp even if he had to shoot him. "Peg-leg does the work all right."

"All the same, I think I'll stay," Darrell repeated. "There's talk of a new conscription law, you know, to make up for desertions." He laughed. "They give a soldier a thirty-day furlough now for shooting a deserter; so half the army will shoot the other half and then go home. And the Government's going to stop substitutes. Wilmington's full of gentlemen who hired substitutes while they made their fortunes; but now they've bought passports and they're taking their gold out of the country before the conscript bureau knocks on their door. But I'll stay here and turn planter."

Tony bit his lip. "The conscript officers are busy here; and Salisbury prison is a mighty uncomfortable place. Ten thousand prisoners of war, there, and not room enough to lodge a thousand. You might not enjoy it."

Darrell looked at him with lifted brows. "I declare, Uncle Tony, your fears for me are touching. But you've slaves enough to count off twenty to exempt me; and even if the conscript men get me, Judge Preston will turn me loose." He called for 'Phemy. "Brandy," he said, when she appeared.

Tony thought brandy might make Darrell sleepy. His own room was on this floor, but Darrell and Mr. Pudrick would presently go upstairs. When they did, he could summon Sapphira, twist the truth out of her. He was by this time sure that Mr. Pudrick's nigger was here; yes, perhaps hidden away in that room behind the kitchen where Sapphira took refuge when Tony had visitors. He might even be there with Sapphira now. Tony twitched and twisted with the jealous rage in him, and longed for the hour when these others would retire.

But the liquor 'Phemy brought loosed Darrell's tongue. He talked of the easy pleasures of Nassau, and of men grown suddenly rich, and of the stupidity of any man who neglected those golden opportunities. "Why, there's money lying around loose for the trouble of picking it up," he declared. "I heard of a Baltimore man the other day, a clerk. He put three hundred dollars into merchandise and marked the box to be delivered to Yankee prisoners in Richmond and put it on the flag-of-truce boat. Then he slipped through the lines and met the boat in Richmond and carted off his box and made fifteen thousand dollars' profit on the deal."

Mr. Pudrick chuckled enviously. "I'm in the wrong line of business, gentlemen; but all I know is slaves."

Darrell grinned. "With prime niggers worth three or four thousand dollars, you make a living, my friend."

"That reminds me." Mr. Pudrick bestirred himself. "I think the rain has stopped. If my man is here, he saw the dogs, and he'll be off to the swamps by this time. Mr. Currain, may I let the hounds take a swing around?"

"Can they do anything in the dark?"

"They see with their noses," Mr. Pudrick assured him. "Let's have a look at the weather."

Tony came to his feet. By God, if that nigger was here, the sooner he was caught the better. From the veranda they saw that the west wind had freshened to blow rain clouds away, and stars were out. Tony bade 'Phemy summon Mr. Pudrick's Negro with the hounds; and Peg-leg brought men to carry lanterns.

When they were ready, they went afoot, the dogs loudly snuffling at the wet ground. Mr. Pudrick said the man they sought would make for the nearest running water to lose his scent. There was a branch, a tributary to the south fork of the Yadkin, which threaded its way through the hills northeast of the house and furnished power for the mill below the quarter before it crossed the Martinston road. Darrell remembered this stream, and spoke of it, and Mr. Pudrick agreed that it was a probability. Tony thought that if the fugitive had been hidden in the quarter they might pick up his scent among the cabins there, but Mr. Pudrick said this was unlikely.

"He'd have got some buck nigger to tote him to where he could put his feet in water," he predicted.

So they went down the driveway to the main road, and along the road to the ford. The Negro, if he were wading, might have gone toward the Yadkin. "They most generally head downstream," Mr. Pudrick admitted. "But this is a smart nigger. We'll try the other way tonight, and if we don't pick him up we'll go down the branch tomorrow."

So they turned up toward the mill. The Negroes with the lanterns were wall-eyed in the darkness, staring fearfully at the dogs, edging away from the mournful beasts. Mr. Pudrick's man who controlled the hounds held them on leash in couples, and he went afoot, his mule on lead. Now and then, to remind the dogs of their prey, he thrust under their noses a worn old shoe.

Tony watched them, and his pulse was pounding and his lips were dry, and there was a murderous impatience in him. "Suppose you find him?" he asked.

"I'll teach him not to run away again!"

"Kill him?"

"No, no. Sam's worth four thousand dollars in Alabama or Mississippi today. No, but I'll teach him some manners."

The slow search went on, and Tony began to think it would prove futile. They came up the branch past the saw mill; but a few yards above, the hounds gave tongue. Mr. Pudrick cried out in triumph; and Tony asked: "Have they got him?"

"Yes, got the smell of him. We'll need horses now."

Tony sent for mounts. While they waited, the hounds clamored to be gone; and there was a zealous haste in Tony too. The horses came, and Tony and Darrell and Mr. Pudrick mounted, and each took a lantern. The Negroes who had brought the horses faded away into darkness and at Mr. Pudrick's command the hounds were loosed, and the black man who handled them shouted some encouragement. Two of the hounds splashed across to the other bank of the little brook while the others stayed on this side. With the horsemen following, they began to move up the stream through the winding gorge.

The hounds, save for an occasional questing bay, were silent at their work. They tested every inch of the ground, considered every bush and tree, tried not only the ground scent but the air. They moved for a while so slowly that it was easy to keep upon their heels, and Tony sweated with the excitement of this man hunt. He forgot his personal animus against the fugitive in watching the dogs and in watching Mr. Pudrick's Negro, mounted on his old mule, as he directed them. This was for Tony a completely new experience. At Great Oak no slave ever ran away. As long as Negroes were decently treated, they were easily content. A man whose people ran away was subject to almost as much criticism, spoken or unspoken, as one who whipped his slaves. But Tony reminded himself that dealers like Mr. Pudrick were in a category by themselves. They were not masters of their slaves; they were simply owners, commanding from their human property neither affection nor slightest loyalty. A slave who had been sold away from home might run away if he saw his chance; so dealers had to be prepared to hunt them down.

Mr. Pudrick saw Tony's interest, and he explained: "Those dogs know he's gone to water, you see. Watch them look up at every tree to see if he's climbed it. See them stand up and smell the trunk and sniff the air. When he comes out of the water, they'll know it. They'll tell us."

This prediction proved a good one. A mile or two above their starting place, a smaller tributary stream threaded the laurel to enter the creek they were following. Tony saw one of the hounds wade up that lesser stream, scenting the banks, standing on its hind legs to sniff at the boughs on either side. Almost at once it uttered a long doleful cry that made Tony shiver. The other hounds answered and came that way.

"Got him!" Mr. Pudrick shouted; and he urged the dogs. "On, boys! On, on, on!"

The hounds broke into a loose-jointed lope that seemed slow; but it soon became impossible to keep up with them. They threaded their

way through the undergrowth faster than a horse in the darkness
could safely go. Tony forgot caution in his zeal, till a branch he did
not see twitched the lantern out of his hand and broke it and left him
in darkness. Thereafter he followed Mr. Pudrick and Darrell; and
for a while the mournful baying of the hounds drew farther and
farther away. The dogs reached the crest of this ridge well ahead of
the horses, and their cries were muffled as they went down the slope
beyond, to become clearer again when the riders topped the crest. Then
the tonguing faded and was almost lost before Tony heard, far away,
a sudden fiercer clamor.

"Treed," said Mr. Pudrick in calm satisfaction. "You can tell by
the sound. We'll take our time now, gentlemen. That nigger will
wait for us right where he is."

They were long in coming to him, picking their way through tall
pines and then through tangled scrub oak, descending steadily, the
baying of the hounds beckoning them on. But the end was sure. The
fugitive in his panic had allowed himself to be overtaken in a sparse-
grown old field where there were no big trees, and only a few young
pines offered brief security. The tree into which he had climbed was
hardly tall enough and stout enough to keep him above the reach of
the leaping hounds. In the light of the upheld lanterns Tony saw his
eyes burning red like those of a wild thing in the night. They were
red with a rim of white, and below him the hounds leaped sluggishly,
more from duty and from a sense of what was expected of them than
from any lust to kill. Between leaps they bayed, or in a bored way
scratched themselves.

Pudrick's Negro who was their warden and their master had outrun
the three white men. He sat his mule a little to one side, drooped and
still. "He'll tell around what we do to Sam," Pudrick explained. "It
makes the others slow to run away." He rode nearer the tree and
spoke in calm tones to the fugitive. "Sam," he said, "you might as well
come down."

Tony stared at that frightened thing, more animal than man, in the
tree above them; and his throat was hot with rage. That and Sapphira? He wished he had brought a pistol, one of those revolving
pistols that would ram slug after slug into the nigger. No man, white
or black, should touch Sapphira, should lay even a thought upon her.

He heard the click of a lock, and saw Pudrick with a pistol in his hand.

"Are you going to kill him?" he asked.

"No, no; just wing him, shoot him out of the tree, let the dogs tear him a little." And Mr. Pudrick said: "Here, take my lantern. Hold it so I can see." He spoke to Darrell. "Hold yours up too. I don't want to spoil him, break any bones." He gave Tony the lantern, urged his horse around the tree. "I'll get a side shot, burn his rump," he said.

The tree was small. Pudrick on his horse was only a few feet below the Negro. The fugitive had heard Pudrick's word. He tried to scramble around the slender trunk, to keep his face to the slave dealer; but the tree bowed under his weight. Then suddenly the Negro screamed and flung himself outward like a bat, arms and legs wide.

Pudrick, too late, tried to spur aside; Sam descended upon him, had his throat. They slid sidewise off the horse together. Mr. Pudrick's horse danced away from the rolling heap, white man and black, on the ground almost under his feet. The dogs with dutiful cries found black flesh and began to tear. The Negro was making a worrying, unearthly sound, but Mr. Pudrick was silent. Clearly, Sam had him by the throat.

Darrell laughed aloud. "Damnedest funniest thing I ever saw," he said; and he moved his horse in among the dogs, his pistol now in hand, the lantern in his other hand held low. The flash of the pistol for a moment blinded Tony; its smoke briefly blurred the scene. Then the dogs were worrying something under a screen of smoke that thinned and drifted away.

Pudrick yelled with pain and anger. He rolled Sam's body aside and kicked his way to his feet, kicked the dogs. "The God-damned hounds bit me!" he roared, shocked and scandalized. Darrell bowed in his saddle, weak with laughter; and Pudrick raged at him. "Your powder flash singed my ear!"

Darrell, his pistol lightly balanced, asked in icy tones: "Do you object, Mr. Pudrick?"

"Eh? No! Oh no, not at all!" Mr. Pudrick spoke in quick appeasement. His Negro came to pull the hounds away from dead Sam and put them on leash again. Pudrick counted rents in coat and trousers;

he inspected a gashed leg. "Bet I won't sit easy for a month," he grumbled.

"You'll be able to take nourishment, at least," Darrell reminded him. Pudrick touched his throat.

"I feel as though I'd been half-hanged!" He mounted, looked down at the dead Negro. "Four thousand dollars for the buzzards!" he said disgustedly. "Well, that's all there is to that." He kicked his horse and moved away.

Tony stayed a moment longer, looking at the Negro on the ground. That and Sapphira? That buzzard bait? Why, good enough. This was the due of any man who looked at her.

He rode after the others, and when he overtook them Darrell turned in his saddle with a question. "Uncle Tony, is there any better way up through these woods? They're thick riding in the dark."

"Wait for light," Tony suggested. "It won't be long. The night's nearly gone."

This seemed wise. They dismounted, and Mr. Pudrick found a little stream and bathed his wounds. "By God, Mr. Streean," he cried, "you've burned half my hair away, and blistered my ear. Can't you shoot straighter than that?"

Darrell turned toward him. "By daylight, yes, I think so, Mr. Pudrick," he said coldly. "If I see a target still at hand."

For a moment silence lay among them. "Eh?" said Mr. Pudrick. "What do you mean?"

"I mean," Darrell explained, "that the business that brought you here is done. Why should you stay?" Tony held his tongue. This might lead to something. Mr. Pudrick did not seem like a man who would submit to such dictation. Darrell, a chuckle in his tone, added: "Unless, of course, you wish to make a really extended stay."

There was a long silence, while Mr. Pudrick, pressing his handkerchief against his burned ear, seemed to consider. The handkerchief was in his right hand, while Darrell's hands were free; so he was at a disadvantage. This may have influenced him, for when he spoke it was peaceably enough. "Why, perhaps you're right," he agreed. "If Mr. Currain here will forgive my somewhat unceremonious departure, I have in fact affairs which require my prompt return." His Negro was near, with the leashed hounds sleeping about the feet of the mule he rode. Mr. Pudrick mounted his horse. There were no more words. The horse, the mule, the men, the dogs, receded into darkness. Hoof beats muffled on the sodden ground departed into silence and were gone.

Tony, his horse's reins knotted to a low-hanging bough, set his shoulders against a tree to wait for dawn. This hour had left him drained and very tired; but Darrell, sitting against another tree, talked casually of many things. He remarked that Tony seldom came to Richmond. "You should, you know. Things happen there. I sometimes think, for instance, that Aunt Enid has fallen out of love with Uncle Trav. Do you suppose that's true?" Tony did not reply, and Darrell asked: "And had you heard, Uncle Tony, that Uncle Faunt has taken up with your old light-o'-love?" Tony thought someone would throw a bullet into Darrell, one of these days. Pudrick, a while ago, had wanted to, had not dared. Tony wished Pudrick had dared. If Darrell stayed at Chimneys, how long would it be before he knew Sapphira was hidden there? Darrell's mocking voice went on and on.

When they came back to Chimneys, Peg-leg reported that someone in the night had tried to wrench the lock off the smoke house door, prying at the staples with an inexpert hand; that someone had loosened a board on the corn crib and laboriously extracted a few ears. Tony, listening abstractedly, thought that probably Sam, who now was buzzard bait over in the next valley, had tried before he fled to lay hand on some provisions. He decided not to ask Peg-leg or 'Phemy or Sapphira about Sam. If they had sheltered Sam, he did not want to know it. Besides, if they had hid his presence, they would lie now; and you couldn't make a nigger tell the truth unless he wanted to. Buzzards circling in the next valley, miles away, would not be noticed here; and a day or two would finish that. Let Sam be forgotten.

"Put on a stronger lock," he directed. "And nail up the corn cribs so they're tight."

Darrell said: "Wait a minute, Uncle Tony. Who'd be thieving here? Don't you feed your people?"

"Certainly. It might have been—" Better not speak of Sam at all, in Peg-leg's hearing. "It might have been some of these white trash farmers around here."

Darrell seemed pleased. "Why, that's mighty interesting. Maybe I can find a way to protect you, Uncle Tony. I don't like thieves."

Tony, moving toward the house in a fog of weariness, and hungry for sleep, hardly heard him. He went to his room and to bed, and he slept till dark, and to avoid seeing Darrell he kept his bed and let 'Phemy bring him supper. Perhaps Darrell would be gone tomorrow.

In the morning 'Phemy said Darrell had ridden off to Martinston. "Anyways, he say he do." Tony read the warning in her words, so he did not ask for Sapphira, and this was fortunate, for in midforenoon Darrell came casually down through the orchard behind the house and up the back steps and was in the house before 'Phemy knew he was near.

"Oh, I was in the mood for a stroll," he replied, to Tony's question. "Send someone to bring my horse. He's a mile or so away toward Martinston, tied in the edge of the woods."

Tony shivered to think what might have happened if Darrell had returned and found Sapphira with him here. For the week that followed he felt like a man besieged. Darrell made no move to depart, yet during the daylight hours he was seldom at the house. He disappeared without saying where he was going, returned without forewarning. Usually in the evening he insisted on cards, and Tony lost enormous sums, inattentive to the game, searching his wits for some way to be rid of this young man so that he and Sapphira could once more be at ease. He was sure by this time that Darrell suspected or knew she was somewhere here, but the young man asked no questions, never provoked an issue. Yet Tony felt the other's watchfulness. Even after he went to bed, Darrell was apt to sit for hours, perhaps idling over a book, before the fire in the big room across the hall from which he could see Tony's closed door; and Tony, though he sometimes tried to stay awake, inevitably fell asleep before he heard his unwelcome guest go upstairs.

Darrell was waiting to tire him out, waiting for Sapphira to appear, waiting for something; of this he was sure. Tony settled grimly to the necessity of patience. If Darrell could wait, then so could he.

On the eighth night, hard asleep, he was roused by the heavy roar of a gun. The sound was muffled, as though the explosion were somehow confined. Before he could move, he heard Darrell's window, in the room above his, flung open; and he heard Darrell's pistol speak twice, heard the young man's exultant cry. That first shot had come from the direction of the smoke house, beyond the kitchen wing. Tony scrambled to his window and looked out, but though the stars were shining he could see nothing clearly. He touched a spill to the coals on the hearth and lighted a candle, and as he did so he heard Darrell coming at a run down the stairs. He was pulling on his trousers over his night shirt when Darrell, without knocking, opened his door.

"Well, I got your thief, Uncle Tony!" the young man cried exultantly. "I rigged a set gun in the smoke house, just inside the door. When the gun went off just now I jumped to my window. The charge didn't catch him square, because he was trying to crawl away; so I put a bullet through him. Come on."

Tony, still dazed with sleep, drew on his boots. As they went out along the kitchen gallery, Peg-leg appeared from down toward the quarter with a pine torch flaring, hurrying toward them. In the torch light, Tony saw a shadow on the ground by the open smoke house door. As they approached, the shadow seemed to be the body of a small man, in clothes too big for him, sprawled on his face.

Darrell leaned down and caught one outflung hand to turn the dead man over; and then he checked, looking at the hand in his grasp, upon which now as Peg-leg stumped nearer the torch light began to play.

"By God, he's white, Uncle Tony," he exclaimed. "It's just a boy!" He twitched the body over; the hat fell off, a mass of long hair tumbled loosely free. "It's a woman!" Darrell Streean cried.

Tony saw that this was true. It was a woman. It was Mrs. Blandy.

6

CINDA, when she let herself, had dreaded this Christmas. It would be the first without her mother; and though Brett might come home, Trav was off in Tennessee with Longstreet, and she knew there was no likelihood that Faunt or Tony would appear. Jenny and the children were at the Plains, and Barbara and her babies—little Burr had been born in October—were in Raleigh, so if big Burr had a furlough he would certainly go to them. Christmas had always been a day for family gatherings and a crowded dinner table loaded with good things to eat, but this year it promised to be a dreary, empty time.

It proved to be not so bad as she had feared. A week beforehand Burr arrived, with his hair cut so short it might have been shaved and his uniform in tatters; and he spent two days with them while June cleaned and mended his coat and trousers, and Caesar found a shoemaker to patch the soles of his boots, worn completely through. He was on his way to Raleigh, and Vesta warned him Barbara would laugh at that shorn head.

"Can't help it," he said cheerfully. "This is what they call a 'horse thief cut'; keeps you from having too many extra boarders." He laughed. "You ought to see Tommy Waring. Joe Murr had the only pair of scissors in the regiment, so we kept him busy; and last Saturday he was cutting Tommy's hair and had one side of it pretty well off when a Yankee squadron came along, so we were busy for a while, and in the excitement Joe lost his scissors. Tommy's hair was still half on and half off when I left camp!"

They laughed at that and at many a tale he told, while Cinda watched this son of hers and saw small changes in him; the faint lines around his mouth and eyes, the sudden twist of his lips as though at some sharp pain, the wrinkling frown that sometimes came and went as quickly as a dimple appears and disappears when a pretty girl smiles. They all laughed when he described that September day when Stuart, attacked from two sides, had his cannon firing breech to breech in opposite directions; and Colonel Grenfell, the Englishman who had attached himself to Stuart's staff, was so confused by this unconventional warfare that he bolted through a thicket, swam the river, galloped to Orange Court House and reported that Stuart and all his men were lost.

"When we rode back safe and sound," Burr said, "he was so embarrassed that we haven't seen him since."

He described a night when Stuart and his whole command, surrounded by heavy Yankee forces, spent the hushed hours till dawn within hearing distance of marching columns of the enemy. "We could even hear the officers telling the men to close up," Burr declared. "We had a man at every mule's head to keep them from braying. That was the longest night I ever spent; but we pushed through them and came clear at dawn." He spoke of their work on the march that led to the costly repulse at Bristoe Station. "General Lee hoped to flank the Yankees and hurt them, but Meade slipped away so cleverly we didn't even get any booty. I found one oilcloth, and that was all. I tell you, we were a disappointed lot. The cavalry likes to make a haul now and then, you know, even if it's from our own folks. The farmers up that way say they'd as soon see the Yankees come along as us; that the Yankees don't steal any more than we do." He told them of that hilarious hour when Stuart and Fitz Lee's command trapped the Yankee cavalry and broke them and chased them for miles. "Near a little place called Bucklands," he said. "We call that day the Bucklands Races."

Vesta asked what General Stuart would do for Christmas; and Burr said: "Oh, Mrs. Stuart and General Jimmy Junior—he's only four— live near headquarters, so the General will be with them. He'll have a feast, too. Ladies have sent him everything from turkeys to oysters." He laughed. "He has a party or a ball or something every chance he gets, you know. He loves to sing as well as he loves dancing."

"General Lee's been here," Vesta told him. "Mrs. Lee and the girls came back from the Warm Springs in October and rented a little house on Leigh Street. It's just big enough for her and Agnes and Mildred, so they can't have Charlotte with them." Charlotte was Rooney Lee's wife, her husband a Yankee prisoner. "Mrs. Lee's been sick, you know, and Charlotte is ill, and General Lee looks terribly. His hair's just perfectly white, and his beard too."

"I know. I see him occasionally."

"He was in church last Sunday," Cinda said. "When the service was over we all stood in our pews while he walked out, to show him our—love."

"The girls thought surely he'd stay for Christmas," Vesta added. "But he's gone back to headquarters. Agnes told me yesterday they don't believe Charlotte will live till Rooney's exchanged; and she says her father has a terrible pain in his side all the time, and Rooney is in prison, and Mrs. Lee hardly ever gets out of her wheel chair. It just doesn't seem fair they should have so much trouble."

Cinda picked up her knitting. "We all do," she said quietly. "When I think of the promises Mr. Rhett and Mr. Yancey and Roger Pryor made us, how secession was going to bring us liberty and peace and prosperity and all sorts of good things, I'd like to kill them."

"Mr. Yancey's already dead, Mama," Vesta reminded her. "And nobody in South Carolina listens to Mr. Rhett now."

"I wish someone would shoot him!"

They laughed, as they were likely to laugh at Cinda's explosions; but she did not smile. While she knitted, her eyes searched every line of Burr's young countenance. She saw weariness in him, and a deep hurt; and she remembered the charming, gentle boy he had been, and thought that Burr would never take easily to the ruthless, rushing business of killing. In one of the pauses in this conversation, she said affectionately: "You know, Burr, I'm glad you're not an officer." He looked at her as though suspecting she sought to cover her disappointment at his failure to win promotion, but she said: "No, I mean it, Honey. You wouldn't like making other men do the things you have to do."

"That's right," he admitted. "No, I'd never make a good officer,

Mama. I can ride and holler and pop off my pistol as well as anyone; but that's all."

She knew proudly that this was true. He was too gentle and too kindly for the duties of command, too eager to please others. Why, even Barbara could twist him around her finger whenever she chose. If Barbara wasn't good to this darling boy, Cinda told herself she would —well, of course there was nothing she could do!

The night before Burr was to leave for Raleigh, Brett came home. Cinda, taking his first kiss, felt the weakness in him; and to her anxious question he said with a chuckle: "Why, I'm on sick leave, Honey, but don't look so scared! I'm about the healthiest sick man you ever saw. Ellis Bird says all I need is some home cooking. He told me to come home and get it, stay till I'd had enough."

"You look so thin and ill!"

"You should have seen me two or three days ago. I really felt sick then." He would not, as she urged, let her put him at once to bed. "Not yet. Can't spoil my first evening."

He and Burr came to quick talk, matching their experiences. Brett said the Howitzers had been kept on the move so much that they felt like cavalry. "Colonel Long's our commander now; and he's a West Pointer and never forgets it. In camp we're up at daylight for roll call, and it's hurry, hurry, hurry all day long. Curry horses for an hour, feed them, eat our own breakfast, if we have anything to eat; then put the horses out to grass, police camp, drill. Another roll call at noon. Another drill at three o'clock. Catch up the horses and water them and wish we had some grain for them. They're just walking skeletons. Another roll call at six, and another at eight." He laughed. "I tell you it's a relief to have a forced march now and then, to stop that program for a while."

Cinda asked: "Are you really short of food?"

He grinned. "Short? If one old cottontail hops through camp, every man in sight helps run him down and we stew him and have a feast. If it weren't for persimmons I don't know what we'd do."

"I'd hate to live on persimmons," Vesta protested, and he said smilingly:

"That's our favorite joke, Honey; we say they pucker us up so we're not hungry any more." And he added more seriously: "Yes, the men are half-starved. The ration's a pint of meal a day, and a quarter of a pound of pork—when you get it. And the meal's just ground-up corn cobs and dust, and so sour you can hardly eat it. Being hungry all the time makes the men look like animals after a while; hard greedy eyes, and cheeks so hollow their faces seem to come to a point, like a fox or a dog. Sometimes we don't get the pork. Once in a while we get a few dried peas, or a spoonful or two of sugar, and once we got coffee! I counted mine. Seventeen beans!" He laughed. "One of our games is to sit around and order imaginary dinners, but of course that just makes us hungrier! The queer thing is that we stay healthy. I'm the only man in our company who's been sick at all, this winter. And a lot of men are getting religion. Every camp has built at least one church, and when there's no chaplain, somebody reads the Bible and prays as well as he can. That's happening all through the army. Regular revivals whenever there's a real preacher, lots of men professing." He said gravely: "I think they're sincere; but some of the skeptics say they're just feeding their souls because they can't feed their stomachs."

For a moment no one spoke. Then Vesta said: "People are hungry in Richmond too, Papa. Can you imagine, a hundred and ten dollars a barrel for flour?"

He laughed. "I don't call that much! I've seen times when I'd give a thousand dollars for one good biscuit! A whole barrel of flour? Why, Vesta, that's worth ten thousand."

She came to her feet. "Are you hungry? I'll get you a piece right now!"

But Brett declined. "No, give me a good night's sleep first; then I'll be able to stand the shock of eating again!"

Alone with him at last Cinda asked: "Can you really stay a while?"

"I'm to stay till I'm well again," he assured her, and she felt the high happiness in him. "And I'm certainly going to make a mighty slow recovery, my dear." So, even though Burr must leave tomorrow morning, Christmas would be merry after all.

When they went upstairs, she had said Brett must go right to bed; but he protested: "No, no; not yet. Go on and tell me things."

"What things?"

"Anything but the war. We hear all that in camp." Yet he added gravely: "Do you realize, Cinda, that the fight on Missionary Ridge was the first big battle we've lost because our soldiers broke and ran?"

"They needed Cousin Jeems that day. He really won the battle at Chickamauga. But our western victories never seem to do us any good." He had said she must not talk about the war. "Cousin Louisa's baby's fine. They're naming it after General Lee. Cousin Jeems must have been simply wild, not being here with her."

"I suppose so. And probably he was furious at having to serve under Bragg. Longstreet's a fighting man, but Bragg's a fool. President Davis should have removed him long ago." Brett spoke with a slow sadness. "Cinda, our great weakness is at the top! We've mismanaged everything—finances, commissary, conscription, impressment. We've nursed treacherous delusions, that the North wouldn't fight, that we could whip them if they did, that England would let us lead her by the nose with a cotton string! It's a wonder we've held out so long!"

"Don't get excited! Please. Let's go to bed." He began to undress, and she saw a red patch on the seat of his trousers, neatly square; and tears stung her eyes. "Poor man," she laughed. "Has to mend his own britches!"

"Oh, that!" He chuckled. "You ought to see some of us. We cut up our drawers to patch our pants, and some men are pretty fancy about it. They cut the red flannel in patterns; a heart with an arrow through it, or a spread eagle, or a cow, or a horse. Colonel Long says we'll never dare turn our backs to the enemy. They couldn't miss such shining marks."

Even when they were abed he was wakeful; and he spoke again of the mismanagement on the part of Mr. Davis and his appointees, from which the army suffered so. "Why, half the men are barefoot, Cinda," he declared. "That's why General Lee had to stop trying to bring Meade to battle this fall. The men's feet gave out. They couldn't march." And he said: "I suppose part of the trouble is that everyone's money-mad. Even the bankers are speculating with the currency, selling Northern money at a thousand-percent premium, pushing the value of our own money down and down."

She saw he must talk himself to exhaustion. "I never did understand about money. I never had to, of course, when we had plenty."

"Probably I was a fool to put all ours into Confederate bonds," he reflected. "But I'm glad I did. I don't want to be one of those who make money out of this war! I don't even want to keep what we have. If the South is ruined—well, I want us to be ruined too."

"I'm not as brave as you; but I'll always want what you want, Brett Dewain. And we can get along, one way or another, even if we have to sell things. There are auctions all the time now, with everything imaginable being sold; rolls of ribbon and groceries and books and furniture and cavalry boots and rum and brandy and old wine and silver and jewels. Some of our friends have had to do that, sell things they've always treasured; but no one complains, and neither will we."

For a moment he did not speak. "We see newspapers in camp," he said then. "But they always make things either better or worse than they are. Do you get enough to eat? Is food as scarce as the papers say?"

She hesitated. "I suppose it is, for poor people. If you pay enough, you can buy most things." She added: "We have a windfall now and then. You remember Major Tarrington? He used to live in Columbia, and he's in the commissary now; and sometimes he lets Vesta buy things at the government price, and he sends us presents. He sent us a great cut of beef one day and wouldn't let us pay for it. He said his butcher had given him a whole quarter, more than he could use."

Brett said quickly: "Vesta mustn't deal with him. No man in the commissary department should take presents from butchers. That sounds too much like a bribe."

"Major Tarrington? Why, I always rather liked him."

"You wouldn't take a present from Redford Streean," he reminded her.

"Of course not! I know he's a rascal."

"Well, greed makes rascals out of good men sometimes, Cinda. Let's keep clear of taking favors."

She sighed. "Well, all right. But I declare, Brett Dewain, sometimes I hate your scruples as much as I admire them. That was such good beef!"

He laughed at her doleful tone. "Do you have trouble getting sugar?"

"We do without it," Cinda confessed. "We use molasses. Sugar costs two or three dollars a pound, if you can buy it." She smiled in the darkness. "They say General Green put a fortune into sugar at a dollar a pound, and Colonel Northrop impressed it all and won't even pay him what it cost. The poor old man is telling his woes to anyone who will listen."

"The papers say the Government can't impress things on their way to market; but I suppose that rule just protects the speculators."

"I don't know." She was silent for a moment, but he said drowsily: "Keep on talking, Honey."

So she talked, about the government clerks who were afraid they might have to go into the army, and about Cousin Jeems's report to the Government that half the men on his muster rolls in Tennessee were absent or had deserted and that half his soldiers had no shoes and none of them proper rations. She said there were always wild, ridiculous rumors in the air, and people would believe anything; and he said that was because Congress had so many secret sessions. "When no one knows the truth, anyone who pretends to have inside information is easily listened to. It makes him feel important, so he keeps making up more and more stories." She said lawyers and even some Congressmen were getting rich by finding ways to get men out of the army, hiring substitutes or arranging details; that some of the wealthiest men in Richmond were paying for jobs as mechanics or laborers because such jobs would exempt them from the conscription. She told him that Mrs. Allen, arrested last summer as a traitor, had been allowed to live in comfort in the infirmary of St. Francis de Sales till her recent trial and then released on bail when the jury disagreed, though everyone thought she should have been shot or sent North or something. She described the contrivances by which Anne and Vesta made new dresses out of old ones, or out of window curtains or anything else that was available; and she reminded him that General Lee said that but for the valor of the women, the South would have been vanquished long ago.

Brett's deep breathing seemed to mean he was asleep, but she dared not stop talking for fear silence would awaken him. General Hood was in Richmond with one leg gone. Dr. Darby had promised to buy him a new leg in Europe, with money the Texas Brigade had raised; and General Hood thought he could then ride well enough to return to duty. Julian, with no artificial leg, was trying to contrive some way to stay on a horse so he could join the cavalry; but a general riding at his own pace and a cavalryman in a charge were two very different things. Julian had talked to General Hood, and the General told him this, and bade him stay home with Anne. Anne was a sweet darling girl. Her baby was coming in April. Every girl in Richmond had set her cap for General Hood. It was said that little Fanny May actually proposed to him, and he told her he couldn't accept because he was already engaged to four other girls.

Brett turned on his side and she let her hand rest on his shoulder in the way he liked and felt him completely limp and relaxed and knew he would not wake; and sleep flowed over her and wrapped her in content. Christmas would be fine, now that he was here.

Burr took the five o'clock train for Petersburg on his way to Raleigh; and Cinda, leaving Brett asleep, went early to the hospital and made sure she could be spared a while. When she came home Brett was still abed, playing with little Tommy while Vesta watched them both with lively eyes. Cinda kept Brett in bed and they had their dinners together in his room, and from the gray sky as dusk came down snow began to fall. They were all together when belowstairs the door bell rang. Cinda heard Caesar go to open it, and happy young voices erupted into the house, and Cinda and Vesta ran to the stairhead; and Cinda after one instant's glimpse was blinded by laughing, drenching tears.

For that one glimpse had been enough to see Jenny in the gas-lit hall, shaking snow off her cape; and seven-year-old Kyle came racing up the stairs, and Janet with him. Even little Clayton, holding fast to the banisters and screaming "Gam-maw, Gam-maw!", hitched himself up toward her. Cinda's knees gave way, she sat down weakly on the top step to gather them all into her arms; and Vesta ran down to embrace Jenny, and Brett in dressing gown and slippers came to demand what was going on here, and there was a wonderful laughing-crying confusion for a while, till Jenny remembered to explain that old Banquo and Mr. Peters were at the station guarding many boxes of good things to eat which they had brought all the way from the Plains. Caesar hurried off to fetch these treasures, and somehow at length peace began to come. Little Clayton was hustled away in black arms to be put to bed. "You remember Anarchy, Mama," Jenny reminded Cinda, and Cinda said of course she remembered. Anarchy was one of Banquo's many children, a strapping wench as strong as a man.

"I brought Banquo and Mr. Peters to take care of the boxes," Jenny explained. "I was afraid of trouble on the trains."

"Well, the things you brought will be just manna from Heaven," Cinda assured her. "I won't feel secure till we have them under lock and key. Richmond's full of half-starved people, poor whites and negroes, who will steal anything they can get. Castle Thunder is so full of robbers there's no room for any more."

"I was certainly glad Mr. Peters and Banquo were with us," Jenny confessed. Vesta had gone to show Kyle where he would sleep; Janet was to sleep with her. "The trains just creep along now, and they're crowded with men, even in the ladies' car. We had three breakdowns, and we spent one whole night in a station somewhere, in a room full of soldiers, with a wretched fizzling fire that threw out no heat at all." She laughed at the memory. "It's funny now, but it wasn't then. Anarchy propped me up on two chairs and put the children to sleep in a ball like so many puppies, wrapped up in blankets on the floor beside me. Banquo and Mr. Peters worked all night patching up the boxes. They'd been smashed in the breakdown. A train ahead of us broke in two, and some of the cars rolled backward down a long grade and bumped into our engine with a frightful thump. The pile of boxes tipped over and some of them cracked open. Mr. Peters says there were turkeys and onions and sweet potatoes rolling all over the car."

Brett asked: "How long were you on the road?"

"Heavens," Jenny confessed, "it seems like weeks! We left Kingsville Friday, and it took us all that night and all the next day and half the next night to get to Wilmington. We left there Sunday and only got to Petersburg this morning; three nights on the way counting the night we were broken down. I think today in Petersburg was the longest I ever spent. It just seemed as if the Richmond train never would start."

Cinda said sympathetically: "Poor darlings!"

"Oh, it was fun, really; watching the soldiers, and a marvelous great giant of a woman who kept joking with them in the broadest Irish way of talking I ever heard, and a lady with a no-count nurse maid and the worst-spoiled young one!"

Vesta rejoined them, and she asked eagerly: "What did you bring us, Jenny?"

"Oh, some fine fat turkeys, and a dozen sides of bacon, and a great enormous piece of beef—a whole side except the foreshoulder—and a bushel of sweet potatoes, and a bag of onions, and—well, everything we could hope to manage."

Cinda, with this sudden wealth of provisions, invited Tilda and Dolly and Mr. Streean and Enid and the children for Christmas dinner. "There's no telling when we'll have such a nice Christmas again, so we'll make the most of it," she told Vesta. Brett sent Caesar to the country to cut a cedar that would serve as a Christmas tree; and Julian and Anne and Vesta took the carriage and brought back heaps of holly for greenery. Julian bought firecrackers with which Kyle and Peter could make the celebration a fittingly noisy one. Some rummaging in closets and forgotten hideaways furnished presents that would content the children; and Cinda in all these preparations was so happy that she accepted with good grace the gifts Redford Streean brought to be hung on the tree. There was a length of printed silk, a box of artificial flowers to grace feminine hats, a dozen bottles of fine brandy, a bag of coffee, and a canister of tea. They were blockade goods, to be sure; but for this one day, she would not think critically of anyone.

Christmas morning they all walked to church except Brett, whom Cinda would not permit to move out of doors, and Anne who no longer went abroad. When they came home, Rollin Lyle was at the house, smiling his crooked smile, saying in a shy way: "I hoped maybe you'd take me in for Christmas, ma'am. I've got a furlough and I'm going home, but I didn't get here in time for the morning train."

Cinda was delighted. "Of course, Rollin! We're just as pleased as we can be."

Jenny too was glad to see him, and Vesta; but when they had gone upstairs to lay aside their bonnets and coats, Tilda and Streean and Dolly arrived, and Dolly came running to protest: "Oh, Aunt Cinda, do you have to have Rollin? I declare it just makes me sick to look at him, just turns my stomach. I won't be able to eat a bite if he's here."

Cinda looked at her evenly. "Then why don't you go home?" she suggested; and in sudden anger: "Dolly Streean, you ought to be smacked! Rollin's a fine boy! And as for his looks, if you'd behaved yourself, that would never have happened! He's here and he's going to stay."

Dolly tossed her head. "Oh, I suppose I don't have to look at him."

Cinda said sharply: "You listen to me! If you make Rollin unhappy today I'll pack you out of the house so fast you'll think your back teeth are loose!"

The girl laughed teasingly. "O-o-oh, aren't you fierce!"

"I'll show you how fierce I am if you don't behave," Cinda promised her, and downstairs she kept a watchful eye on the girl. As a precaution she seated Dolly and Rollin on the same side of the table, and separated them so that they need neither face each other nor talk together. But Dolly was on her best behavior. Once or twice she even leaned forward to say some laughing word directly to Rollin, and Cinda saw his quick happiness. Dolly could be so charming when she chose.

That was a bountiful board at which they gathered, with a fragrant, beautifully brown turkey at either end, and a ham and some roasted ribs of beef, and huge platters of sweet potatoes cooked in molasses, and boiled onions, and sausage to fill any gaps in the fare, and mounds of corn pone, and biscuits steaming hot, and butter to perfect them; and there was mince pie, the mincemeat drawn from a husbanded reserve in the cellar; and there was a treasured bottle or two of old Madeira, and Brett called toasts for the absent ones.

"To Tony." He began with the eldest of the family. "Good cheer and a fine Christmas to him!" He rose with lifted glass; and Dolly as she came to her feet with the others cried excitedly:

"Oh, I forgot to tell you! I had a letter from Darrell and he says Uncle Tony's been shot." Their quick ejaculations checked her swift tongue not at all. "But he's going to be all right." She laughed. "It was some little poor white boy twelve or thirteen years old. Isn't that a joke on Uncle Tony?" And to their questions: "Why, someone had been robbing his smoke house, and he fixed a gun to shoot whoever it was and it turned out to be a woman, someone named Blandy——"

Enid cried: "Ed Blandy? Trav thought more of Ed Blandy than he did of his own family!"

"Well, anyway, the gun went off and it killed her." Dolly was bound to tell her story. "And when they took her home, her little boy ran into the house and got a gun and shot poor Uncle Tony and almost killed him too. Isn't that exciting? But I do think it's a joke on Uncle Tony, don't you?"

Cinda caught Brett's eye, knew their shared thought; but he said heartily: "Then all the more—here's a quick recovery and health to him!" They raised their glasses, and drank, and sat down again, and Tilda said:

"Dolly, I didn't know you'd had a letter from Darrell. Why didn't you tell me?"

"I've told you now!" Cinda heard a spiteful anger in Dolly's tone that surprised her, for Dolly and her mother had never been at odds. But there was petulant resentment in Dolly's manner, a surprising authority in Tilda's quiet retort.

"You should have told me. You can be very thoughtless, Dolly. You knew I would want to read it."

"It wasn't to you, it was to me." Dolly's color was high. "And you can't read it. I burned it up!"

There was a moment's uncomfortable silence, and Cinda saw Redford Streean hide a smile. Then Brett came to his feet again. "To Trav now!" he cried. "Lift your glasses all. To Trav, good man, good brother, good husband, good father!"

Cinda saw Enid hesitate, then rise with them and lift her glass; she heard Lucy's young voice, clear and tender:

"To my papa!"

So the roll of all the absent ones was called. "To Faunt! Wherever he is, God bless him!" And while Cinda's eyes held Brett's over the rim of her glass: "To Burr!" But it was Tilda who rose at last and said in a quiet tone, without reproach:

"Shall we drink to Darrell too?"

Because they had all forgotten Darrell, and were sorry, the response was the heartiest of all; but Cinda, looking along the board, saw Enid white with some mysterious anger, and it puzzled her. She wished she had not this habit of watching people, trying to read their thoughts and to appraise them.

They were replete at last, torpid with the rich delicious fare; and when they rose Cinda sighed and said: "There, I don't care if I never eat again! We ought to be ashamed, of course; but—wasn't it fun?"

After dinner the gentlemen sat over their brandy in the library; Cinda and Tilda and the younger folk stayed in the drawing room, while the children ranged out of doors to burn up their heavy dinner by an hour's romp in the fresh snow. Cinda had one ear for the talk in the library, one for the chatter here around her. Tilda was discussing hospital problems, asking Cinda's opinion, offering her own; and in the other room Streean spoke mirthfully of the fears of the government clerks, dreading that they would be deprived of their exemption and forced into the army. "Every member of the cabinet has put all his sons and nephews into a safe berth somewhere," he declared. Dolly here was talking about Captain Pew's exploits. His steamer had been damaged on his latest trip; he would not sail again till early January. Gold, said Judge Tudor in the other room, was at a premium; thirty-five Confederate dollars for one of gold. This talk of figures made Cinda think of Travis, and she asked Enid for news of him.

"Oh I never hear a word," Enid confessed. "Of course Trav doesn't mean to be thoughtless, but he doesn't realize how I worry."

Lucy protested: "Why, Mama, he writes to me! I had a letter only last week, but you wouldn't even read it."

"I'm too polite to read other people's letters, Honey. You and he have your own secrets."

"I expect he's having a lonely Christmas," Cinda commented, hiding her loyal resentment. In the yard there were the occasional reports of firecrackers as Kyle and Peter took their pleasure there. Dolly said it was wonderful that Jenny had been able to come to Richmond and bring all those goodies, and she asked:

"Are you going to stay a while?"

"Not very long," Jenny told her. "Someone has to be there to keep an eye on things. Mr. Peters starts back tomorrow, and I'll have to go soon."

"I don't blame you for wanting to go back," Dolly declared. "I certainly wouldn't stay in Richmond unless I had to. I just simply begged Mama to let me go to Nassau with Captain Pew, but she was scandalized! I think it would be perfectly respectable if Darrell went with me, and he's going with Captain Pew next voyage. He thinks Nassau is wonderful."

Tilda said quietly: "I can't control Darrell, but you certainly aren't going off to Nassau on a blockade-runner."

Dolly looked at her with angry eyes. "You've told me so, often enough. You don't have to keep saying it." She asked abruptly: "When are you leaving, really, Jenny?"

"A week from Monday, I think," Jenny told her; and Cinda felt a sorry pang because they would go so soon. As though answering her unspoken thought, catching her eyes, smiling apologetically, Jenny added: "I must, I'm afraid. There's so much sickness in cities. I want to get the children safe home."

Tilda asked: "Do you dare travel without an escort?"

Jenny smiled. "Oh, Banquo's dignity is ample protection; and if it weren't, Anarchy is an Amazon."

Dolly cried in sudden pretty pleading: "Jenny, why don't you invite me down? I wouldn't be much help running the plantation, but I'd be company; and I know Mama'd let me go to the Plains."

"Why, of course," Jenny assented, with only the faintest hesitation. "I wish you'd all come, as far as that goes. I'd love to have you, Dolly." Her glance touched Cinda. "All of you," she repeated.

Cinda smiled, shook her head. She would never leave Richmond; not as long as Brett was near, and Burr; not while Trav, yes and even Faunt, might at any moment tug the bellpull; not while Julian was here. Jenny of course knew that; she had not meant the suggestion seriously.

And neither, for that matter, did Dolly mean what she said. Dolly would never leave Richmond, where so many gallant youngsters were always ready to pay her attention, for the seclusion of the Plains. Yet she was pretending now an effusive eagerness, appealing to Tilda. "May I, Mama?" And Tilda was saying: "Why, if Jenny wants you, you may go," and Jenny repeated that Dolly would be welcome, and

Dolly declared she would certainly go. But of course she never would. Cinda was sure of that; and Vesta, when she and Cinda and Jenny had an hour together that evening, agreed.

"She's having too good a time in Richmond," Vesta declared. "There's so much going on, and of course the town's full of officers to beau her around." She laughed. "I don't think she enjoys the 'starvation parties' very much. She's a greedy little pig. But she loves the dancing, and of course with all the things Captain Pew brings her, she has the prettiest dresses in town."

"She wouldn't have much gaiety at the Plains," Jenny remarked. "Even in Camden everybody works with the Ladies' Aid Society at the Soldiers' Rest, or does something."

Brett had gone early to bed, but when Cinda went up stairs he was still awake, and while she was preparing for the night he said thoughtfully: "You know, Cinda, that dinner we had today would have been a treat for the men in camp."

"It was a treat for us!" She felt herself on the defensive.

He nodded, but he said: "I saw two men get killed for a turkey no bigger than those we had. The turkey was in a field between our skirmish lines. One of our skirmishers shot it and ran to pick it up, and a Yankee shot him and tried to get the turkey, and our men killed the Yankee. Two men and the turkey all dead." He added, half-laughing: "The worst of it was that we fell back and the Yankees got the turkey."

"Oh, don't feel so guilty, my dear. After all, it's Christmas."

"May I take a box of things back with me?"

"Of course."

He said after a moment: "By the way, we've had a windfall. A letter came today. I still hold a few shares of the Bank of Wilmington, and they're paying a dividend of over six thousand dollars, the first of the year."

She was puzzled by his tone. "Is that much?"

"Yes. Yes, they used to pay about fifty dollars, but they paid a thousand dollars for 1861, and almost twelve hundred for 1862, and now this. It's blockade money, of course." He said wearily: "But it won't do any good not to take it."

"That conscience of yours will be the death of me, Brett Dewain," she protested; but her tone was tender, and she came to kiss him where he lay.

They had all been certain Dolly had no real intention of going to the Plains; but during the week that followed she came every day to the house to talk with Jenny and to make a thousand plans. "I can't believe even now that she means it," Jenny admitted. "But she declares she's really going."

"I wish you'd stay here," Cinda told her. "Not go back at all."

Jenny smiled. "I think I'm getting to be like a man," she reflected. "I've been managing things there so long that I keep thinking all the time of work that should be under way, details I should be handling. And I'm uneasy here. Richmond's so different, so many rough men, such wretched-looking women on the streets." She laughed at herself. "I'm just plain homesick, I guess. I want to go home."

"I know how you feel," Cinda admitted. "About Richmond, I mean. There are so many people here now, so many strangers. It used to be that you knew everyone, but not now——"

When the day of Jenny's departure arrived, Dolly did go with her. Cinda saw in the girl a high excitement, a sharp anticipation, as though Dolly were embarking on an adventure not only attractive but dangerous. Certainly the prospect of a sojourn at the Plains in these times when there would be no gaiety, no young men in attendance, nothing to break the gentle routine of plantation days, was not enough to account for the girl's high color, her shining eyes. After the train pulled out, walking homeward with Vesta, Cinda confessed her mystification. "Did it seem so to you?" she asked.

"Yes," Vesta agreed. "Yes, it did."

"I hope she doesn't bother Jenny!" Cinda made an exasperated sound. "I'd like to know what that young minx is up to now!"

7

December, 1863

TRAV, even if he had wished to do so, could not have come home for Christmas. General Longstreet's command was by that time established on the railroad between Morristown and Bull's Gap, with headquarters at Russellville. The little army had a dangerous distinction. It was the only Confederate force in position to strike a useful blow. A thrust through Kentucky toward the Ohio would be troublesome to the North, and a day or two before Christmas the General told Trav: " 'Lys Grant knows that as well as I do. He won't rest till he's driven us out of East Tennessee."

It was three months since Longstreet brought his divisions west. Trav's duties threw him twenty-four hours behind the General on the journey. At the request of Dr. Dunn, at whose home in Petersburg Mrs. Longstreet was staying, Longstreet had arranged that the doctor's cousin, Lieutenant Andrew Dunn, should be assigned to his staff; and he and Trav travelled together. Lieutenant Dunn had been born in Ireland, and he was a lively and amusing individual. Trav found him good company.

The battle along Chickamauga Creek had been fought and won before they arrived. It was late evening of that great day when they reached Ringold Station, a long low-roofed stone structure on the eastern fringe of the little town; and once off the cars the clamor of the guns came to them across the hills that lay between Ringold and the battlefield. When their horses had been unloaded, they trotted across the level valley and followed a road that wound through low, forest-covered hills, climbing and then descending to cross Chickamauga Creek and go on up gently rising ground to the rolling woodlands in whose thickets the battle had been fought. Before they reached headquarters just beyond Jay's Mill, the fight was over, and Trav found Moxley Sorrel drunk with victory.

"We've smashed them, Currain," he cried. "They're on the dead run for Chattanooga. We'll be after them at daylight, gather them in as easily as shaking ripe plums off a tree." All about them in the forest there was jubilation as the victorious Confederates built their cooking fires; and triumphant voices drowned even the moaning cries of wounded men as stretcher bearers gathered them for the surgeons' bitter work. "General Hood's killed, mortally wounded. But we've smashed them today."

"Where's General Longstreet?"

"Trying to find General Bragg, to get orders for tomorrow; but there's only one thing to do, and we'll do it." Sorrel fell to laughing at his own thoughts. "Oh, we've had a day! We got to Catoosa Station about two o'clock yesterday, and there were no orders for us, so we started to hunt General Bragg. Down by the creek we rode right into a Yankee outpost. It was dark by then. They challenged us and I asked who they were and they told us, and I thought we were goners, but the General just said, loud enough for them to hear: 'We'd better ride down the creek a little, find a better crossing.' So we turned away and they didn't fire a shot."

"He never gets excited, does he?"

"Not in danger, no; but in action, yes! You should have heard him roar today!" Sorrel grinned affectionately. "The old Bull-of-the-Woods! And how the men love him! Yes, and civilians, too! In Atlanta, we put up at the Trout Hotel; and just about everyone in town came crowding around the hotel and yelling for him. When he showed himself they wanted a speech. He held up his hand and that quieted them down and he said: 'I came not to speak but to meet the enemy!' That touched them off again. I wish you could have seen him today."

"I can imagine it. Were any of the staff hurt?"

Sorrel laughed. "No, but we thought Colonel Manning was a gone goose at dinner. A shell fragment hit him and he was gasping and strangling and black in the face, but the General said: 'Get that sweet potato out of his mouth and he'll stop choking!' So we clapped him on the back, and up came the potato and he was all right."

But the first fine exhilaration of that great victory did not long endure Next morning, although the Yankees were in full flight for Chattanooga, Bragg refused to permit the swift pursuit that would have made victory complete. Longstreet and the whole army raged at this excess of caution; and an open demand arose for Bragg's removal, a demand so vehement that a petition went to Richmond. So two or three weeks after the battle, President Davis himself came to Bragg's headquarters. He called the higher-ranking officers into conference, and next day he and Longstreet spent hours together.

Trav saw, thereafter, Longstreet's profound depression; and one evening when they had ridden to the heights above Chattanooga to look down on the enemy far below, the General spoke of what had happened.

"President Davis knew that every general officer in the army desired Bragg's removal; but I suppose he wanted to outface us. He called a council, with Bragg present, and asked me to be the first to express myself." He laughed. "Perhaps he expected to abash me into silence. I told him that I had not been an hour with this army before I knew General Bragg was unfit to command. I said his intentions were good but his capabilities inadequate. I said that properly handled we could have chased Rosecrans into Kentucky; but that General Bragg made us sit still while Burnside made Chattanooga impregnable."

"General Bragg heard you?" Trav asked, imagining the scene.

"Yes, and when I was done all his other officers urged his removal, and he heard them too. I don't know how any man of spirit could accept such a humiliation. I expected him to resign, but he did not, and President Davis will not remove him." He added angrily: "But it's probably just as well. Our chance was lost when we made no pursuit after Chickamauga."

"You think we had a real chance then?"

"Yes. Oh, I suppose we're all optimists in the hot hours of victory; but I thought that next day we could open the road to the Ohio and push on." After a moment he added: "Mr. Davis spoke to me privately after our council. He had some thought of assigning me to command. I told him General Johnston was the proper choice; but he doesn't like General Johnston, and he rebuked me as though I were a presumptuous child. I asked permission to resign, and he said I could not be spared; that my men would not let me go. I asked leave of absence, proposed to withdraw to Texas and to send in a later resignation. He would have none of that." He laughed gruffly. "Then he began to complain of the way the politicians torment him, said he couldn't decide what to do. Taking thought is a vice with him. There are occasions when even a wrong decision is better than indecision!" He shook his head. "We do everything at the wrong time, Currain. If we had won that victory at Chickamauga Creek in May instead of September, and had followed it up, I believe we would have saved Vicksburg. We would have invaded Ohio last July, instead of Pennsylvania. But time is one opportunity that is never offered twice."

Trav suspected that a major part of the other's depression had its source in his anxiety for news from Mrs. Longstreet, and when late in October the word at last reached them that on the twentieth Robert Lee Longstreet had been born, he saw an immediate change in the big man. The General, his mind at ease, became mellow and tolerant and genial. One morning when they were at breakfast an old woman in a black silk dress and an extraordinary hat of ancient pattern timidly approached and asked if General Longstreet were among them.

"At your service, madam," the General assured her. "What can I do for you?"

She looked around uncertainly. "Any harm in me a-comin' heah?"

"None whatever, ma'am. In fact it would please me mightily if you would join us at breakfast."

The old woman hesitated. "Well, I done walked eight miles sence I et my breakfast, and we-uns don't have much up in our settlement, so I rightly believe I'll take a bite."

She ate with the headlong, furtive haste of one to whom a full meal was an event, and food loosened her tongue, and she and the General chatted comfortably. She confessed at last that her real errand was to replenish her supply of pipe tobacco, and they filled her pouch and General Longstreet ordered an ambulance to carry her to her distant mountain home.

They had other humble visitors, and Trav thought Longstreet knew how to reassure and to win them; but the big man's eagerness for some military activity persisted. The move against Knoxville, a hundred miles away, seemed to Trav hopeless of success. He thought that for

Bragg thus to divide his army invited disaster. But Longstreet welcomed the opportunity; and with an effective force of no more than fifteen thousand men, he set out to attack and disperse General Burnside's army, which was at least as numerous and on good defensive ground. On that tedious march through bottomless mud he wore from day to day a hearty cheerfulness, and he laughed away Trav's doubts. "Even if we don't take Knoxville, as long as we have an army so near Kentucky, the Yankees won't sleep of nights."

His good spirits were heightened by an affectionate letter from General Lee, which he proudly showed Trav. "I urged him to come out here and take command," he explained. "This is his reply."

Trav read the letter. "As regards your position as to myself," General Lee wrote, "I wish that I could feel that it was prompted by other reasons than kind feelings to myself. I think that you could do better than I could." Lee told the story of his unsuccessful move against Meade which ended at Bristoe Station, and he added: "I missed you dreadfully, you and your brave corps. Your cheerful face and strong arms would have been invaluable. I hope you will soon return to me. I trust we may soon be together again. May God preserve you and all with you."

Trav handed the letter back, understanding how much it must have encouraged Longstreet in this present venture; but his own misgivings persisted, and others shared them. When they faced the enemy in his works at Knoxville and prepared to attack, they heard a rumor that Bragg had been defeated at Chattanooga; and General McLaws in a written protest to Longstreet argued that under the circumstances an assault on Knoxville offered little hope of profit. Longstreet, furiously angry, showed Trav the communication. "With that lack of spirit in my commanding officers," he demanded, "how can the attack succeed?"

Trav said honestly: "Well, sir, General McLaws is a brave and skillful fighter. He conceives it his duty to offer these considerations, just as you conceived it your duty to advise General Lee against making battle at Gettysburg."

Longstreet scowled. "Nonsense! Even if Bragg has been defeated, our best course is to beat the enemy in front of us!"

"General Lee felt at Gettysburg that our best course was to attack, but you did not agree."

Trav knew that to speak thus straightforwardly might draw Longstreet's anger on himself, and he braced to meet the storm. But Longstreet, after a moment, said almost sadly:

"If General Lee believed it was right to attack at Gettysburg, and you see here a parallel, then I am the more convinced that we must attack the forts over there." He added half to himself: "General Lee may have been wrong, and I may now be wrong; yet I think that in my place here, he would do as I shall do. Certainly I must take the responsibility of decision."

The assault failed. Trav thought it might have succeeded if it had been pushed home, but on a report from one of General McLaws's staff of difficulties in the way, Longstreet himself recalled the attacking column. Yet he said that night to Trav: "We had them! Blame our repulse on me. I let myself be discouraged by another's doubts." And he said in stern self-reproach: "No man is fit for high command, nor fit to send other men into the front of battle, if as I did he allows his own heart to waver in the crucial hour."

As far as Trav knew, he made this admission to no one else; and Trav understood the big man too well to expect that he would. For the repulse at Gettysburg, General Lee had at once and publicly taken the responsibility; but it was not in Longstreet openly to admit he was wrong. Perhaps he was right in this attitude; perhaps to confess his fallibility might shake the confidence of his men. General Lee could admit his errors and still command the highest devotion; but there was no other like Lee.

Immediately after the repulse, the telegraph confirmed the rumor of Bragg's defeat. He had been beaten into hard retreat; and he sent orders for Longstreet's army to unite with his disorganized command. But before Longstreet began to move in that direction, communications were cut; and thus left to his own resources he led his men eastward to reopen direct communication with Virginia.

During those weeks of rain and mud and hunger and disease, and perhaps because he remembered his own lapse at Knoxville, Longstreet's temper became increasingly brittle. He asked for a courtmartial for General Robertson, of whom General Hood had complained at Chickamauga; he relieved General McLaws and ordered him to proceed to Augusta, charging him with "want of confidence in the plans of the commanding general"; and when General Law a day or two later presented his resignation with a request for leave of absence, Longstreet growled:

"General, your request is cheerfully granted."

Trav understood the other's harshness toward these men who had been so long his comrades. Longstreet's wrath was not at them but at himself. The General had once said of Stuart that the cavalryman had the weaknesses which matched his virtues; that his vanity and his love for the spectacular were a part of the dashing courage which made him a great commander. Something of the sort was true of Longstreet himself. It was confidence in his own rightness that made him the fine battle leader he was, and he knew this, and so would never, unless he must, admit that he had been wrong. But the failure at Knoxville was so clearly his failure that he recognized the fact; and the memory of it must be a torment to him now. During these weeks the General kept even Trav at a distance, forever finding fault with him in little ways; and Trav guessed that Longstreet regretted that confession of his fault, and blamed Trav for having heard it. Certainly it was to find a scapegoat for his own sins that the commanding general now disciplined his lieutenants.

But when the army crossed into the region where the French Broad and the Holston rivers join, the big man became more like himself. They came into a land of plenty, of fine farms where the crops were ready for the reaper or had just been harvested. Major Moses found himself in a commissary officer's heaven; for wagons sent to collect supplies could be filled within half a dozen miles of camp. Even in mid-December they discovered corn still standing, pumpkins just touched with frost, vegetables in the cellars and the bins, fat hogs and sheep and cattle. Blankets and uniforms and shoes were worn-out and hard to replace; so men chosen from the ranks must turn hides into leather, and leather into shoes. This took time, and when there was a march to be made, barefoot soldiers left bloody prints on the frozen ground; but at least food was plentiful, and wood for fires to fight back the harsh and bitter cold.

So the spirits of the men were high, and Longstreet's temper improved, not only because of this but because he now had regular letters from Mrs. Longstreet. She was well, the baby throve. He told Trav that she proposed to go presently to Augusta, to visit the Sibleys there.

"Two of my cousins, Emma Eve Longstreet and Elizabeth Eve Longstreet, of the Virginia branch of the family, married Augusta men," he explained. "Cousin Emma married a cotton merchant, Josiah Sibley. She's his second wife, and she had a son last August and wrote asking permission to name him after me. She and Louisa have kept up a correspondence, and she wants Louisa to come and stay with them; and Louisa thinks Augusta will be better for the baby than the cold weather in Petersburg. Augusta's warm and pleasant even in winter, I believe. I'll be relieved to have her there."

But if the General's mind was at ease, Trav's was not. The long days of inactivity gave him too much time for thought, and thoughts of Enid were sorry company. He had letters from Lucy and from Cinda, and since they did not mention Darrell, he assumed that Darrell had not returned to Richmond. Lucy's letters seemed to say that their life at home followed a normal and not unhappy course.

Lucy never failed to assure him that Peter and Mama sent him just loads of love; but Enid had never written, and did not now, and Trav found himself longing for some word of her. To remember that moment when he struck her senseless filled him with shame; and when he recalled how on the morning of his departure she came to make her peace and he gave her no word, he blamed himself for hard brutality.

For after all, she might be innocent. Weighed at this distance, the evidence against her was frail and unconvincing. Streean's insinuation? Well, Streean was a malicious man, with a base and scandalous mind. Lucy's manner? Peter's? The disapproval of old April and of Mill? Trav realized that his imagination might have magnified these things. Possibly the children and the servants resented Darrell's frequent presence at the house; but why should Darrell not occasionally call on Enid, and why should she not welcome him? She was lovely, and hungry for companionship, and Darrell could be amusing when he chose. Trav tried to buttress his condemnation, to persuade himself she had confessed; but she had not. When he flung at her a question which any loyal wife would rightfully resent, she angrily retorted:

"Don't you wish you knew?" But that was not confession; that might have been no more than sudden furious hurt and rage. If he had been a little kinder, if they had talked calmly together for a while, she might have reassured him. He imagined her teasing him because he was jealous, turning at last to a sweet tenderness, forgiving his question because it was prompted by his love for her.

But he had given her no chance to do so. He flung at her an angry question which was actually a brutal affront; and when her hurt resentment framed an angry retort he knocked her down! Next morning when she was ready to forgive him he rebuffed her. What insane passion had made him so ready to believe her guilty, whom he should have trusted utterly? Oh, he had been wrong, cruelly wrong, condemning her without hearing. It was he who had been at fault, not she. Would she ever forgive him?

These remorseful thoughts were Trav's Christmas companions in that winter of '63. Like an erring child, expecting chastisement yet hopeful of pardon, he at once longed and dreaded to see her again.

8

WHEN Tony, leaning down to stare at the figure on the ground in the light of Peg-leg's approaching torch, recognized Ed Blandy's wife, it was with an instant shock of dreadful terror. He was afraid for his life. This woman had come to him so short a time before, to buy food which she and her children must have unless they were to starve, and he had refused it; so for her death he would inevitably be blamed. His squirming thoughts sought to find a justification. It was certainly his right—a right that not even Ed Blandy could deny—to refuse to sell to her at a price that was no better than charity! How could he be expected to guess that she would turn thereafter to outright thievery? First to beg, and then to steal! Why, how shamed Ed would be when he knew his wife had descended so low!

But now here she lay, and she was dead; and Tony sweated with fear of Ed, and with anger at the dead woman. She had no right to put him in such a situation, to get herself killed and thus let loose Ed's wrath on him! She must have written Ed about that day when she came here to buy and Tony would not sell. What would Ed say? What would he do?

His own terror made Tony turn on Darrell in a shrill fury. "Set-gun? Who told you you could put a set-gun in my smoke house? I might have opened that door myself! It might have killed anybody— me or anyone!" Peg-leg came up to them; he lowered the torch enough to see the dead woman's face, stood silently. "Blast it, Darrell," Tony cried, "you had no right to do that!"

Even Darrell was for the moment shaken. "How did I know it was a woman? I supposed it was some nigger!"

"Supposed!" But Tony checked his retort. After all, Darrell was not a man who could safely be abused. He turned furiously on the Negro. "Peg-leg, did you know about this damned gun?"

"Nawsuh!" The man's eyeballs gleamed white. "Nawsuh, not me!"

The night was hushed and silent; yet Tony knew every Negro within sound of those shots was awake, cowering in his cabin. When white folks started shooting, Negroes kept out of the way. Tony could imagine all those listeners down in the quarter, or here near-by in the loom house and the blacksmith shop and the kitchen wing where 'Phemy and Sapphira slept. Darrell said: "Nobody knew anything about it, Uncle Tony. Nobody but me!" He spoke in low tones to the Negro. "And if anybody ever finds it out, Peg-leg, it will be from you; and I'll tie you up to the nearest tree and peel your hide off you without bothering to shoot you first. Understand?"

"Yas suh," Peg-leg assented; but Tony thought with faint envy that the Negro did not sound scared.

"Go get 'Phemy," he said. Her level head must help him now. Peg-leg stumped away.

"This is a clever rig, Uncle Tony, if I do say it," Darrell declared, his complacency returning. "See here!" He showed Tony his deadly device. Just inside the smoke house door, under a low shelf where even in full day it was unlikely to be seen, a wide-mouthed pistol had been wedged. Tony had never seen the weapon before and said so, and Darrell explained: "It's mine. I stick it inside my trousers, sometimes, when I'm going into tight places. It's no good except for close work; but at short range it will throw three or four slugs through an oak board." He pointed to a cord looped around the trigger and butt which passed through a crevice in the chinking of the log wall and descended to the ground. "I've been coming out to set it at night after you'd gone to your room," Darrell said. "I stretched the cord across the door, so anyone coming in was bound to trip on it, and the charge would get them belly-high; but I came out before day every morning to take it away. I'm always up at the crack of dawn."

"You know this is Mrs. Blandy. Ed Blandy's a friend of Trav's."

"I know. White trash."

"Their place is on the road to Martinston. I wish to God you hadn't killed her."

Darrell said boldly: "I didn't! She killed herself, trying to steal your pork!" Then Peg-leg returned and 'Phemy came with him. No one spoke; but as Peg-leg had done, so did 'Phemy now lean down to look into the face of the dead woman.

"She tried to break into the smoke house," Tony said lamely.

'Phemy gently touched the loosened hair, lifted the limp head, put the old hat back in place, tucked the hair under it, drew the shabby coat together across the flat chest, straightened the limbs, laid her fingertips on the half-open eyes. She stayed thus kneeling for a moment, and Tony thought she was praying. Then she stood up.

"She's mighty pore and thin," she said. "I'll tote her into the kitchen. Come mawnin', y'all kin ca'y her home."

"Can't you do that?" Tony had no wish to face this dead woman's children.

"Rack'n it'd be moah fitten ef you did it." 'Phemy gathered the small figure in strong arms, bore her toward the house.

Tony mopped his brow. "I'll take care of her children," he muttered. "I'll see they don't want for anything."

Darrell drawled: "Oh tender heart!"

"Damn it, Dal, this won't be taken well!" 'Phemy, with Peg-leg lighting the way, was gone out of hearing.

"A little frightened, Uncle Tony?"

"I wish to God you hadn't done it."

"Why, I was simply helping you protect your property!" The young man's tone was that of one whose intentions have been cruelly misread.

"I don't look forward to facing Ed Blandy. He was home last September."

"September?" Darrell echoed. "Well, then you needn't worry. They won't give him another furlough soon; and if he deserts and comes home you can shoot him, or turn him over to the conscript officers. And if he stays in the army, the Yankees may shoot him and save you the trouble."

It would save a lot of trouble, certainly, if something happened to Ed Blandy. "But the men around here are all his friends," Tony remembered.

Darrell touched his arm. "Calm those twittering nerves of yours,

Uncle Tony," he advised. "I'll stand by till the storm clouds roll away."

That was some comfort. Tony feared Darrell as much as he hated him; but the young man had a cold courage that made him a useful ally. If there were to be trouble, Darrell would be a good man to stand by his side.

Before that night was done, Tony more than once came to the edge of panic. He might take his horse and ride away, never to return; but Chimneys was his, he would not give it up. And also, Sapphira was here. He would not leave her, and he could not take her with him. Nowhere in the South could he and she together find any refuge. To leave her was to lose her; to lose her perhaps to Darrell, who would certainly not run away. And to leave her was to lose Chimneys too. So Tony stayed, and dawn came, and he must face the day.

'Phemy had bathed and cleaned the dead woman, and she set Peg-leg to the nightlong task of fashioning for her, out of clean-sawed oak boards from the mill, a coffin. She herself sat all night by Mrs. Blandy's body, till a little after sunrise she came to Tony, abed but not asleep, to say it was time to take the dead woman home to her children.

Tony could not bring himself to face that duty alone. "You'd better come with me," he decided. "Tell Peg-leg to bring a clean wagon, lay some hay in it, bring my horse and Mister Darrell's."

Darrell cheerfully agreed to ride with him. "But don't look so damned guilty, Uncle Tony," he protested. "You had a right to protect your property. She's just a common thief, you know, dead or alive."

They set out, Peg-leg driving the wagon, 'Phemy sitting in the back beside the neat coffin, Tony and Darrell riding behind. At Ed Blandy's cabin, a woman and two or three children appeared in the door; and the woman and Ed Blandy's son came doubtfully toward them. The boy's face was streaked with stale tears. Tony knew the youngster by sight, but not the woman. He swung to the ground and with his hat in his hand approached her.

"Ma'am," he said, "I'm Mr. Currain from Chimneys."

His tone was a question, and she answered: "Tom Shadd's my husband." Tom had been in that first Martinston company; he was Ed Blandy's nearest neighbor. Mrs. Shadd's eyes went past Tony toward the wagon. She saw the new boards of the coffin, and put her arm around the thin shoulders of the boy beside her. "Eddie here come after me in the night, a-crying. He'd woke up and his maw 'uz gone."

"There's been a sad accident." Tony choked on his own words and began to cough; and Mrs. Shadd went past him toward the wagon. Peg-leg had climbed down to hold the mule's head; 'Phemy slipped to the ground and stood aside. Mrs. Shadd looked at that box, its shape so eloquent; the boy, hiccoughing with dry sobs, held to the side of the wagon and stood on tiptoes to look in. Mrs. Shadd asked Tony in an even tone:

"Is this her?"

"Yes, ma'am."

"I sh'd jedge she's dead."

He nodded. "Someone had been stealing pork out of our smoke house," he said, his throat dry. "We had to put a stop to that." Darrell was near, so he dared not tell the truth. "We fixed it so that anyone who opened the door would touch off a gun inside. It caught her, ma'am." The boy at her side turned and ran toward the house. Mrs. Shadd struck the back of her hard, veined hand against her mouth; she bit at it as a man under the surgeon's knife bites the bullet to hold back his cries. She leaned against the wagon, staring at the box there; and Tony said miserably: "I wouldn't have had it happen for anything in the world."

He was facing Mrs. Shadd, his back toward the house. Darrell, still mounted, shouted a sudden warning. "Look out!" He lifted his horse over the fence, charging toward the cabin.

At Darrell's cry, Tony whirled. The boy was there in the door, resting a musket against the jamb. Tony when he turned looked squarely into the barrel. He tried to fling himself aside, and felt the heavy blow of the bullet. Great weakness flowed into him; and then he was down, his legs giving way, propping himself briefly on both hands, then sagging forward on his face in the roadside dust.

When his senses began to return it was to sickening pain. He could see at first nothing at all; but he felt an uneven jolting which he recognized. He was in the wagon, lying on the hay in the wagon bed. He drifted into insensibility again, and when he roused it was at the foot of the steps at Chimneys, and Darrell was saying in cheerful reassurance:

"There you are, Uncle Tony. We'll give you a hand You're not hurt. Just a scratch. Now come along."

Darrell and 'Phemy helped him slide out of the wagon, slide his feet to the ground. His head hung weakly; he saw his long legs under him and wondered how they managed to support him. With strong hands under his shoulders helping, he watched those legs lift his feet from step to step, and so came presently to his own room and his bed and felt the bed receive him like tender arms. He lay with his eyes closed under 'Phemy's ministrations, and he heard Darrell's voice, and felt the probing blade against his naked side, and cried out in a brief sharp anguish and heard Darrell laugh and say triumphantly:

"There it is! He was lucky, 'Phemy! Two inches to the left would have done it. He's born to be hung!"

It was days before Tony's fever passed and before his strength was sufficiently returned so that he could move across his room to sit in his big chair by the fire. When he began to be himself again, 'Phemy told him things he did not remember. In that moment at Ed Blandy's cabin, Darrell had moved fast, but not fast enough. He flung his horse across the bullet's path too late; but he leaped off and caught the boy by the collar and wrenched the discharged weapon from his hands. Then he and Peg-leg and 'Phemy and Mrs. Shadd carried the rude coffin into the cabin. Mrs. Shadd promised to take care of the children, and 'Phemy had since sent Peg-leg to them with a bushel of meal, pork and bacon and a ham. Everyone in Martinston had gone to Mrs. Blandy's funeral, even the deserters who for the most part stayed in hiding, and Alex Spain and his wild, reckless band; but no one had come to ask for Tony or to inquire how he fared. Folks said word had been sent to Ed Blandy; he was expected to come home. Mister Darrell had twice ridden into Martinston, and 'Phemy guessed he was looking for trouble, but nothing happened.

By the way she spoke of Darrell, Tony knew she hated that bold young man. So did Tony; and he remarked to Darrell one day: "I'm surprised you're still here."

Darrell shrugged. "Oh, I won't go away and leave you to the wolves, not till you're on your feet again. I took that young murderer's gun away from him, but he may try again. You'll have to keep your eyes open after I'm gone."

"You think of leaving?"

"Captain Pew expects to sail early in January. I'll join him." Darrell's eyes glowed. "The blockaders make a fortune every voyage, you know; and they spend it in Nassau, and when men with a lot of money want pleasure, any pleasure they want comes into the market." He grinned. "If you were thirty years younger, you'd enjoy a visit there, Uncle Tony."

"When will you leave?"

"As soon as you're on your feet. I'll spend Christmas in Wilmington."

Tony was divided between relief at this prospective departure and dread of being left alone. There was still Ed Blandy some day to be faced. "Better stay for Christmas," he urged. "We'll celebrate together."

Darrell shook his head. "Wilmington has more to offer in the way of celebration."

Tony as he grew stronger came to accept Darrell's decision with a certain relief. Since the young man's first coming he had not seen Sapphira at all. As patiently as an animal in its den, she kept to her room next to 'Phemy's in the kitchen wing. She was well, 'Phemy said, but she would be glad when she need not stay in hiding all day long. Sometimes on warm nights she ventured secretly out of doors. Tony warned her to be careful; for Darrell slept more by day than by night, was up till all hours wandering around indoors and out. 'Phemy assured him Sapphira would be on her guard.

He began to long to see her again. When at last Darrell rode away, Tony bade him good-by almost gratefully, standing on the high veranda to watch him out of sight. He turned back to 'Phemy with a deep gladness in him.

"Tell Sapphira he's gone," he said.

'Phemy shook her head. "He ain' gone twell he's plumb good and gone," she corrected. Tony laughed at her fears; but she would not be easy till Darrell had put Martinston behind him. So Tony yielded and let the long day pass, and ate a solitary dinner; and not till well after the early December dark did he see Sapphira. She came to join him for supper by the fire, and he had forgotten how beautiful she was. He bade 'Phemy bring the best of the Madeira, and 'Phemy went to the cellar to fetch it, and Tony said:

"I've been lonesome for you, Sapphira."

"It's been long for me."

He nodded, wondering as he so often did at her beauty, her steady eyes, her rich and warming tones. By God, there was no handsomer woman anywhere. But in that moment of his full content, he saw her eyes suddenly go wide with terror. She rose shrinkingly to her feet, looking past him toward the open door; and before he could turn, from behind him, as though his own thoughts of a moment ago found words, came Darrell's voice.

"By God, I never saw a finer wench!"

Tony turned slowly in his chair, and Sapphira with a quick movement came behind him, putting him between her and Darrell, and Darrell grinned. "Frightened?" he protested. "Don't be frightened, gal."

He came into the room, booted and muddy from the road, and approached the fire to warm himself; and Sapphira, waiting for her chance, thought she saw it. She tried to dart past him to the open door, but he was too quick. His hand caught her wrist; he swung her whirling into the hard circle of his arms, clipping her close, pinning with one hand her elbows in a lock behind her and with the other forcing her chin up and turning her face this way and that in deliberate inspection. In his hard grasp, terror left her helpless. Darrell laughed and slapped her lightly on the cheek with his open hand. Then with his clenched fist he struck her sharply in the mouth, and Tony saw the thin trickle of blood from cut lips. Darrell laughed again; and he let her go with a parting slap as one slaps a horse's rump to speed it to the pasture. She fled, and he called after her: "I'll send for you."

Then he came to sit facing Tony, and Tony felt anger in him like strangling fingers at his throat. "I thought you'd gone," he muttered.

Darrell nodded cheerfully. "Of course you did. I meant you should, so you'd think it safe to bring your pretty out of hiding." He chuckled.

"I'd heard rumors about her, knew she was here somewhere. Enid tells me even Uncle Trav fancied her, when she was still a child. When you didn't produce her, I thought Enid must be mistaken." His tone was mocking. "I couldn't believe you'd wish to treat me so inhospitably; but I thought it worth while to make sure, as you see." He shouted 'Phemy's name; and while he waited for her to appear he added: "You suggested I spend Christmas here, Uncle Tony. Well, I accept. We'll celebrate together." 'Phemy appeared in the door; and he said: " 'Phemy, tell Peg-leg he'll find my horse at the corner by the big road."

She turned away without speaking, and Darrell drawled: "Yes, Uncle Tony, she'll make my Christmas a merry one."

Tony, remembering how Sapphira had sought to shelter herself behind him, felt old and ashamed by this truculent and deadly youth. He had always been afraid of Darrell. But for that secret fear, he would have shot this young scoundrel long ago, on that day when the Martinston men came to ask him to lead them away to war and Darrell jeered at him, or on that other day when he knew Darrell had betrayed little Miss Mary Meynell.

Now Sapphira would turn to Darrell. Tony had no doubt of that. Niggers were all alike. If Darrell wanted her, she would quickly yield. For that matter, she could not help herself; she was a chattel, permitted no decisions.

So here in this boy facing him now Tony saw the end of all his orderly and well-contented life. Darrell's return was black disaster. These thoughts came not in sequence but in an illumined flash of understanding. "What made you come back?" he asked hoarsely.

Darrell grinned derisively. "Frog in your throat, Uncle Tony? You don't sound glad to see me!" And he said: "Perhaps I came back to protect you. I met Ed Blandy on the road, on his way home. When he comes for his accounting you'll want me by your side." He extended his legs toward the fire, inspected his muddy boots, shouted for 'Phemy, bade her pull off his boots and bring him supper.

"And a bottle of wine," he directed. "To celebrate my return."

Tony himself had sent 'Phemy to the cellar a while ago. It was the old Madeira she brought now; and Darrell insisted Tony share it. "Come, come, don't offend me by declining, Uncle Tony."

There was no talk in Tony; but Darrell's light tongue ran. He ate and drank and rose at last and stretched himself and yawned in Tony's face. "You're dull company, Uncle. I must seek better. So—good night and pleasant dreams to you." He stepped out into the hall, shouted: " 'Phemy! 'Phemy!"

Tony heard her quiet answer. "Yes, Marse Darrell."

"Send that wench to my room." They were in the hall, not far from where Tony sat; their voices plain.

"She done gone," said 'Phemy.

Tony heard the quick slap of a blow and Darrell's dry tone. "I said, send her to my room." Then, as though certain of obedience, Darrell went up the stairs.

Tony came softly to his feet. If Sapphira had fled, Darrell might be thwarted still. He crossed to his desk and took his pistol from the drawer and thrust it under his vest and into his trousers; but when he turned, 'Phemy was at his shoulder with extended hand, whispering: "Gimme dat, please, suh!" He stared at her, not understanding; and she said: "Ain' no call to go git youse'f kilt! He ain' gwine tetch Sapphira! Gimme dat pistol, please suh!"

He had a moment's leaping certainty that she meant to kill Darrell. Well, let her! He gave her the weapon.

But she replaced it in his desk, softly closed the drawer. "Leave it be," she warned him, her whisper soft and still, and so was gone.

Tony closed his door. In the room above his he heard Darrell singing softly, moving to and fro. Leave this night in 'Phemy's strong hands; yes, and the future too! He undressed and hurried into bed. Whatever Darrell's rage and bafflement, the young man would try no violence on an old man in a night shirt! Yet with the firelight the only illumination in the room, Tony lay trembling and afraid.

He heard Darrell come down the stairs and go toward the kitchen; heard his angry shouting there and his questing to and fro. 'Phemy as well as Sapphira must have found some hiding place; and Tony grinned, relishing Darrell's disappointment. In darkness there was nothing the young man could do. After a while Darrell went upstairs again. He would be in a fine rage tomorrow; but tomorrow was tomorrow. Time to meet it when it came.

In the morning Tony, for precaution, kept his bed. Darrell found him there, opening the door with no ceremony, looking at him across the room with narrowed, flickering eyes. "Indisposed, Uncle Tony?" he drawled.

"I've not yet fully recovered from my wound."

Darrell showed his teeth. "That is clear. Your niggers here are out of hand. I'll bring them to time. I'll send for Mr. Pudrick and his hounds." Tony said nothing. This was 'Phemy's problem now. Darrell watched him for a moment, then turned away. Tony slipped out of bed and crossed to the window, hiding behind the curtains to see Darrell go.

He saw not only Darrell but 'Phemy. 'Phemy was coming up from the quarter; Darrell put himself in her path, slapping his riding crop against his thigh. She came steadily on as though to pass him, and he struck her in the face with the heavy thong. She stopped and stood still, not flinching, and he struck her again. But not again. Tony thought it possible her steadiness daunted even Darrell. The young man said something, and she came on and went into the kitchen. Darrell watched her as though in doubt, then returned toward the house again. Tony crept back to bed, to sanctuary.

After a time he heard Darrell in the dining room; and a little later he heard the thud of a horse's feet at the front steps and then the quicker beats as Darrell rode away. He was still in bed when 'Phemy came to him with breakfast. There were dark welts on her brown cheek.

"He's gone to Martinston," he said, "to send for dogs. You must send Sapphira away."

"He ain' gwine lay eyes on her."

"He'll kill you, 'Phemy."

"You res' you'se'f, Marse Tony."

"He'll be back."

"I'll know de minute he comes on de place ag'in."

Tony trusted her intent but not her powers. Bed was the safest place for him. But before the morning was far spent, 'Phemy came to say that Ed Blandy, with his son behind him on the mule and with Alex Spain for company, was riding along the main road toward Chimneys.

Well, Ed must be faced. Tony, hurrying into his clothes, thought he feared Ed less and Darrell more. Ed at least was an honest and a decent man.

When the men rode up to the house Tony went out to greet them. His heart was pounding; for if Ed knew he had refused to sell provisions to Mrs. Blandy, this moment might be the end of him. He saw with some relief that though Alex had as usual a musket across his saddle and a heavy pistol in his saddle holster, Ed was unarmed. Tony said as steadily as possible: "Good morning, gentlemen."

Alex Spain lifted his hand; Ed said: "Morning, Captain Currain."

"Come in and warm yourselves," Tony invited. "It's a cold day."

Ed said: "Why, I just came to speak to you, Captain. Here will do."

Tony understood that Ed would be ill at ease in the drawing room. "Into my office then," he insisted. "There'll be a fire there." They alighted and secured their animals to the hitching rail, and Ed's son watched Tony with sullen eyes. Tony walked with them around the corner of the veranda to that pleasant room on the ground level, with its plastered walls and fine old timbers, where the plantation ledgers were kept. As they came in, 'Phemy set a fire going. The lightwood sticks and logs caught quickly, made a bright blaze.

"Now gentlemen, be comfortable," Tony said courteously. When they were seated, Ed turning his hat in his hand, his son standing stiff beside him, Alex Spain with his musket across his knee, Tony said: "If I'd known you were home, Mr. Blandy, I would have come to you."

Ed's lips were white with grief and pain. "Captain Currain, my boy here wants to tell you something," he said; and to his son: "Go on, Eddie." The boy licked his lips, and he looked pleadingly at his father; but Ed did not relent. "Go on, son," he repeated.

So the youngster, head high, obeyed. "I'm shore sorry I shot you, please sir, Captain Currain," he said; and then tears burst in his eyes and he flung himself into his father's arms, sobbing bitterly.

Tony said in reassuring gentleness: "I didn't blame you, son, feeling the way you did."

Ed Blandy asked: "Are you all right now, Captain?"

"Yes," Tony told him. "Yes, I'm all right now."

Ed said: "I'm sorry my wife set out to steal from you." His arm encircled his son. "I told Eddie if you'd knowed we-uns was hungry you'd have helped us get along."

Tony felt a deep spring of relief; for clearly Mrs. Blandy had never written Ed the truth. This understanding gave him courage. Alex Spain, though with some sardonic amusement in his eyes, said: "Captain Currain's been a good neighbor to some of us, to be sure." He added: "But I wouldn't look for you to set a spring gun, Captain."

Tony remembered Darrell. Here might be strong allies against that bold young man. "I didn't," he said. "My nephew set that trap gun in the smoke house. I didn't know it was there."

Ed Blandy said in honest relief: "I might have knowed that. Not but what you had a right to, if you wanted. But it didn't look to me you would." The boy's sobs had ceased; he lifted his stained face from his father's shoulder to look at Tony with the searching gaze of youth. Tony was glad he need not lie.

"Someone had tried to get into the smoke house a few nights before," he said. "I told Peg-leg to fix it so they couldn't, that was all. Darrell put the gun there, not telling me."

Alex Spain shifted his position; he spoke carefully: "Please sir, Captain Currain, Mrs. Shadd laid Mrs. Blandy out. When she came to wash her, there was a slug in her that had come from the side, and scraped across her front; but that wouldn't have killed her. What killed her was another bullet in her back, right between the shoulder blades. That didn't come from no set-gun."

Tony had not known about the other bullet; the information spurred his memory. That night when Mrs. Blandy died, he had been awakened by the muffled sound when the set-gun was discharged; and an instant later he heard Darrell's window open and heard Darrell fire two shots. So Darrell had killed her when she might have lived! Tony saw Alex and Ed waiting for him to speak, and his pulse began to pound. He himself, at the moment of Darrell's shots, had been still in bed; but no one knew that. If he now made the case as black as possible against Darrell, there was none to challenge his testimony.

"Why yes," he said carefully. "Darrell shot her. His room's above mine. I heard the gun go off, and I ran to my window and I heard Darrell in the room over mine running to his window. There was enough starlight so we could see her, stumbling and crawling along, trying to get away. He shot her and she went down." He knew these men. This would finish Darrell!

After a moment's grave silence, Alex Spain rose deliberately to his feet; but Ed Blandy said quickly: "Hold on, Alex. He didn't know it was a woman."

Tony added the easy lie. "Yes, he did. When the set-gun went off, she screamed. A woman's voice."

Alex said reassuringly: "Why, I wasn't going nowhere, Ed. Only to the kitchen to get a drink of water."

" 'Phemy'll bring it," Tony told him.

"I'll go get it," said Alex Spain, and he went out.

Ed Blandy asked in a low tone: "Where's Mister Darrell, Captain Currain?"

"Gone to Martinston. He'll be back soon."

"Don't let him come back. Send word to him to get away and stay away."

"He won't."

"He'd better." Ed rose. "I'll go myself. There's been blood enough. I'll tell him to go away."

Tony protested. "You'll get hurt. Someone will."

"I'll not lay a hand on him," Ed promised. "I'll let him go away." He looked at his son. "Eddie, you come on," he said.

The boy followed them toward the door. When they came out, Alex Spain was yonder by the kitchen steps, 'Phemy holding a pail while Alex dipped water and drank. Blandy hesitated.

"Alex, you coming?" he called.

Alex shook his head. "No, I'm riding on."

Ed's mule was at the hitch rail. He swung to its back and gave Eddie a hand to scramble up behind him. "I'll leave Eddie at home," he told Tony quietly. "Then I'll ride on to Martinston. If I miss seeing Mr. Darrell and he comes back here, you tell him to make hisself scarce."

He waited for no answer. The mule trotted down the hill toward the big road.

Tony went indoors. He was cold, with sweat upon his brow. When he heard Alex Spain canter away, he began to tremble and his teeth to chatter. After some time, 'Phemy came to him. He asked her what Alex Spain had wanted of her. To know where Mr. Darrell was, she said. He told her Ed Blandy had gone to warn Darrell away. She smiled, and those welts Darrell had laid across her cheek burned red.

When Darrell returned, the western sun was low. Tony had thought to stay abed, but he could not; so he was dressed and about when Darrell's horse, sweat-flecked and weary, came with hanging head to the steps. A boy took the horse, and Darrell strode into the hall, and Tony met him there. 'Phemy stood in the background.

"Well," said Darrell grimly, "I had a long ride. The stage had gone, so I went to the railroad." He looked at 'Phemy. "When Mr. Pudrick and his hounds get here, I'll give them a practice run on you."

She said humbly: "Please suh, Sapphira's so little. She cain't git away. Don' put de dogs on her. She cain't run away. She done racked her foot twell she cain't hardly walk."

Darrell grinned. "Well then, stop this nonsense! Where is she?"

To Tony's astonishment, 'Phemy who was always so composed seemed on the verge of frightened tears. "Please suh, don't ha'm mah baby!"

"Speak up. Where is she?"

The woman looked helplessly right and left. Tony gnawed at his mustache, half understanding. "I ca'n' he'p but tell him, Marse Tony," she pleaded, as though seeking his permission.

Darrell laughed at them both. "Of course you can't! Where is she?"

'Phemy wretchedly surrendered. "She hidin' in de sawdust pit down undeh de mill."

Darrell chuckled and swung toward the door; he ran down the steps and away. When he had disappeared, Tony turned to 'Phemy.

"Is she there?"

'Phemy shook her head. "She in her own room. I tolt Mister Spain I'd send him tuh de mill soon's he come home." There was content in her tone. "He ain' gwine pester us no moah."

Tony sat down, but he could not be still; he rose again and went out on the porch to listen for a rattle of shots from the direction of the mill. He heard no sound from that direction, but a rider in haste galloped up toward him from the road. This was Ed Blandy on his mule. Ed pulled up, the mule breathing hard.

"Is he here, Captain Currain? I couldn't find him in town. They said he'd started for Statesville, and I went all the way. He'd been there and left. Is he here?"

"He came back," Tony said through dry lips.

Then they both heard a sound down past the smoke house toward the mill. Tony turned to look. He saw a dozen mounted men coming at a fast walk up the slope toward the house. In the lead rode Alex Spain. Behind Alex, his hands bound, a rope from his neck to Alex's saddle, Darrell was at a jog trot to keep the noosed rope slack.

As they neared the smoke house, Alex kicked his horse; its leap jerked Darrell off his feet, and the noose dragged him strangling to the smoke house door.

Ed Blandy met them there; and as Alex checked, Darrell sprawled in the dust behind him. Ed leaped off his mule and eased the noose around Darrell's throat. Tony heard Darrell choking and coughing, heard his hoarse cry:

"God's sake! God's sake!"

Ed Blandy faced Alex and the others. "Boys, don't do this. Let him go."

Jeremy Blackstone, one of the old Martinston company who had deserted from the army and come home months ago, rode up beside Ed. Darrell scrambled to his knees, sobbed out entreaties.

"For God's sake, gentlemen! For God's sake!"

Ed laid his hand on Alex's bridle. "Don't, Alex," he urged again. "She was my woman. I'm the one to say. Let him go."

Jeremy Blackstone, behind Ed, swung his pistol like a cudgel. The heavy barrel clipped Ed above the ear, and he crumpled where he stood. Tony, at the end of the veranda, looking down upon them all, felt a retching nausea shake him; he put his arm around a pillar so that he would not fall. Jeremy Blackstone said evenly: "He ain't hurt, Alex. Be all right in a minute or two. We don't want him bothering."

Alex nodded; he said mildly to Darrell, still on his knees: "We're going a ways down the road, polecat. I sh'd guess't you c'n walk faster'n you c'n crawl, but suit yourself."

He turned his horse, and Darrell stumbled to his feet. The noose, though Ed had loosed it enough to let him breathe, was still around his neck. The men paid no heed to Tony on the veranda; but Darrell saw him and uttered a screaming cry, till Alex touched his horse to a fast walk that tightened the noose and hushed him.

Thus they passed the veranda steps, Darrell in dreadful silent effort trotting at the horse's heels to keep some life-saving slack in the rope. The little group of horsemen moved down the drive toward the road, and presently Alex put his horse to a jog so that Darrell had to run to keep up. The horsemen following sometimes hid Darrell, but Tony still caught glimpses of the running man.

When the driveway dipped down to the big road, they all passed out of sight, but if they turned away from Martinston they would be in Tony's sight as they crossed the level bottom lands. He watched where they would reappear, and after a moment saw them. Honeysuckle grew along the fences, and the thick twining vines screened the road. Above that screen Tony could see the riders, and the heads and backs of their horses; and he could see Darrell's head. Alex had checked his horse to a fast walk, so Darrell sometimes walked, sometimes trotted. They were already half a mile away, making toward the woods along the Yadkin.

Alex's horse quickened its pace a little, and then suddenly it was trotting; and a moment later Darrell either tripped or was jerked off his feet. Because of the screening vines Tony could no longer see him; but Alex's horse lifted to a canter and then to full gallop. Tony tried to shut his eyes, but he could not. He watched Alex ride at a dead run for another long half-mile, the others keeping their distance behind him; till beyond the bottom lands where the road dipped to the ford, they pelted in among the trees and disappeared.

Tony held hard to the pillar, and his stomach seemed to turn over and he was sick; but beside him 'Phemy said calmly, as she had said before:

"He ain' gwine tuh pester us no moah."

From the distant mountains, shadow flowed across the land as in the west the sun went down.

9

DOLLY'S decision to go for a visit with Jenny at the Plains was a relief to Tilda. Perhaps because of her own new taste of responsibility and of authority, the girl's waywardness which she had used to think so charming now seemed to her dangerously frivolous. After all, Dolly was no longer a child in her 'teens; she was twenty. She had as many beaux as ever; but except for Rollin Lyle and his unwelcome devotion, and for Captain Pew, who was certainly no beau, the others sooner or later turned from her to someone else. Tilda thought Dolly should marry and settle down to a demure and decorous life. It was high time she ceased coquetting with every man she saw. Perhaps at the Plains, where there would not be so many charming young men, she might decide on one.

Till Dolly departed, Tilda was uneasy for fear the girl might change her mind. The day after Christmas, Captain Pew arrived in Richmond; and though he did not lodge with them, he was often at the house. He and Redford Streean one night entertained a company of gentlemen at the Spottswood. Tilda was still awake when Streean came late home. He was in a loquacious mood, and he told her, hiccoughing slightly, that the dinner had been a rousing success. "Champagne at a hundred dollars the bottle; sherry and Madeira at almost as much. That dinner will cost us fully three thousand dollars —Confederate." He laughed triumphantly. "Think of me spending half of three thousand dollars on a dinner! My dear, your husband is a rich man! The *Dragonfly's* last voyage showed a profit of over two hundred thousand dollars—and she'll sail again within the week. Yes, a rich man; a rich man!"

Tilda had not lost her relish for his success, and long after he was asleep she lay awake with her thoughts. Why, her husband was probably one of the richest men in Richmond! As his wife, she had a certain position to maintain; and since Dolly's madcap ways might at any time cause some scandal or other, it was a very good thing that the girl was going off to the Plains for a while. The fact that the night before Dolly's departure Captain Pew came to supper and said he himself would leave for Wilmington on the same train gave Tilda no uneasiness. He might be of use on the journey as far as Wilmington, and Dolly would see the last of him there.

Captain Pew said that Darrell would go with him on the *Dragonfly* to Nassau. "At least, he plans to. He's meeting me in Wilmington. But he may change his mind. A group of young Englishmen have taken a big yellow house up on Market Street. They're agents for the English companies that are running the blockade; half-pay naval officers, younger sons, a wild lot. It's the liveliest house in Wilmington, with cocking mains even on Sundays, nigger minstrels, balls, gaming. Darrell finds their company to his taste, and he may prefer it to Nassau for a while."

Dolly cried: "Oh, could you take me to a cockfight, Captain? We'll probably stay overnight in Wilmington anyway, between trains."

"Ladies don't attend cockfights, Miss Dolly."

"I could wear some of Darrell's clothes and no one would know."

Tilda said sharply: "Dolly, behave yourself!"

"But, Mama, if no one knew it was me——"

"Hush!" Tilda could silence Dolly when she must. "Captain Pew, I'm glad you and Darrell will be there to see Dolly and Jenny and the children on the train for Camden."

After Dolly's departure, Tilda had much to do. General Morgan, the heroic Kentuckian who when he and his raiders were captured in Ohio had been imprisoned in Columbus and treated shamefully till his audacious escape, was now expected in Richmond; and the city had voted him the honors that were his due. Tilda arranged that a throng should be at the station when he and Mrs. Morgan and his staff arrived, and she had overseen the preparation of the rooms at the Ballard which they would occupy. The reception at City Hall was managed by Mayor Mayo; but there was to be a great ball in the General's honor at the Ballard Saturday night, and that needed her feminine hand.

She went to ask Vesta and Cinda to help. Cinda was at Chimborazo Hospital when Tilda reached the house; but Brett and Vesta were there. When Tilda spoke of her errand Brett said, half-seriously:

"Pshaw, Tilda! Why make such a hero of General Morgan, just because the Yankees cut off his hair! If he'd been with the army where he should have been, instead of rampaging around Ohio and getting himself captured, Bragg needn't have been beaten at Chattanooga."

"Oh, Cousin Brett, you're as bad as Trav! Enid says he always finds fault when she admires any of our heroes."

"Too much admiration's bad for them," Brett retorted. "We think they're irresistible; but General Grant out West doesn't seem to agree, no matter how many receptions and balls we give them. Let General Morgan go teach Grant to admire him."

"Oh, you're just teasing," she protested. "Vesta, make him come to the ball! And I'm counting on you, of course."

Vesta shook her head. "I've promised to go to Mrs. Semmes's for the charades tonight, and they say General Morgan will be there; but even if he isn't, one party a week is enough for me. I'm housekeeper, you know. With flour two hundred dollars a barrel, I haven't time for balls."

"You're silly to pay those robber prices. Let Mr. Streean buy for you from the commissary. Why, two weeks ago he sent home a barrel of flour and some potatoes and rice and salt beef and a peck of salt, and all that only cost sixty dollars."

Brett said laughingly: "If it's flour you want, Vesta, I'll buy you a few barrels! I'm rich now, you know. Soldiers' pay has been raised to eighteen dollars a month."

Vesta did not smile. "That's not so funny for poor people, Papa! Eighteen dollars won't buy three needles, these days, much less three square meals."

Tilda protested: "Cousin Brett, you should have made them give you a commission long ago."

"We have to have some privates.'

"That's ridiculous! And besides, when you have friends it's silly not to let them help you. Everyone else does!" Feeling Brett's unspoken criticism, she struck out blindly: "And as far as food is concerned, I didn't see that you starved yourselves on Christmas! If you feel so bad about the poor hungry soldiers, why didn't you turn all the food Jenny brought right over to the commissary?"

"Giving food to the commissary doesn't mean it reaches the army," Brett reminded her. "The department has too many friends to feed." He added warningly: "You know, Tilda, the poor people here in Richmond won't go hungry forever. Captain Warner told me today that we're likely to see another food riot, and that if the mob catches Colonel Northrop they'll hang him!"

"Nonsense!" Yet Tilda felt a cold touch of fear. Mr. Streean might be wise to resign his government post. He was making so much money in so many other ways that he could do so as well as not. "People willing to work have plenty to eat," she declared. "It's just the lazy ones that stir up trouble."

But Vesta made an angry sound, and Brett smiled without mirth, and she knew they blamed her. Walking homeward she tried to tell herself that she did not care! When the war was over and Mr. Streean was rich and they were poor, they would not be so high and mighty. Yet she did want their good opinion. So many people hated Redford, hated everyone who made money out of the war. That was one reason why he and she had not been invited to Mrs. Semmes's charades to-night. Probably Dolly too would have been left out, even if she had been here. They were all tainted with the Streean name. But perhaps at the Plains some fine young man would love Dolly for herself alone, would woo and win and marry her and take her away from Richmond —and from the shadows of her father's disrepute.

The ball for General Morgan was a fine success; and at church on Sunday one or two of the ladies congratulated Tilda on her part in the arrangements, and she treasured their kindly words. But next day a letter from Jenny brought disturbing news.

Dear Aunt Tilda—I must let you know that Dolly changed her mind about coming to the Plains. Probably she has written you, but in case she hasn't, I don't want you to be worried. I enclose her note to me . . .

Tilda hastily picked up the enclosure, in Dolly's sprawling hand.

There were only a few lines, scribbled straight away with no punctuation, badly blotted.

> Dear Jenny Darling Captain Pew and I met Darrell at the theatre and Darrell wants me to go to Nassau with them and the Dragonfly is all ready to sail and come back in two or three weeks and maybe land in Charleston and Ill come right straight to the Plains so don't worry because Darrell will take care of me and Ive always been simply crazy to go to Nassau and Darrells gone with a boy to get my boxes so please forgive me but dont tell mama but its going to be such fun and Ill be at the Plains in no time. Much love.
>
> Dolly

Tilda uttered an exasperated sound and turned back to Jenny's letter.

> . . . I enclose her note to me. She says not to tell you but of course I must. We reached Wilmington too late for the Wednesday train. There was horrible sleet and snow all the way from Petersburg and we were a day and a half behindhand. We were supposed to get in at 4½ in the morning, but it was evening when we got here. Captain Pew got rooms for us at the Carolina Hotel on Market street. His ship was at a dock only about two blocks away. He invited us to go to the theatre. It was Douglas Jerrold's nautical drama—I'm copying off the advertisement—'Black-Eyed Susan with Miss Katie Estelle and Mr. James Harrison', and the advertisement says 'singing and dancing and the conjugal lesson, conjugal lesson, conjugal lesson'. Three times. I might have gone, though it didn't sound very nice, but Janet had eaten something that disagreed with her, and Clayton was upset, so Anarchy and I had our hands full. But Dolly went. Her room was across the hall from mine, but I must have been asleep when her note came, because it was just pushed under my door and I didn't see it till Janet woke in the morning with a stomach ache. I sent Banquo, first thing, to find Dolly, but the Dragonfly had sailed.
>
> Please don't worry. Banquo says the Dragonfly got through the blockading steamers all right, and I'm sure Dolly will have an exciting time; and of course she has Darrell to protect her.

Tilda took some reassurance from that fact, but she was furious with Dolly for this escapade. If it were ever known, it would ruin the child's chances to make a good marriage! Ladies did not go off through the blockade just for adventure.

But perhaps no one need ever know. She wrote to Jenny: "Dolly's always so headstrong. She'd begged to go on one of those dreadful voyages and I had told her she mustn't. Of course she's with her brother, so I suppose it's all right; but I hope no one knows but you and me. So many people would not understand." Jenny would keep a discreetly silent tongue; but Tilda thought she would not have a moment's peace till Dolly was safely at the Plains. In fact, she would never have an easy mind till the child was married.

During the days that followed she almost forgot Dolly in the pleasant gaieties contrived in General Morgan's honor, of which for once she found herself a part. Mrs. Randolph, with whom her work brought her in contact, invited her and Streean to an evening of charades. She thought he would refuse to go, but to her surprise he consented. President and Mrs. Davis were there, and most of the members of the Cabinet. Tilda watched the charades in happy delight, and guessed "Penitent", though she had not courage to say so, long before anyone else. She thought she was stupid not to guess "Matrimony" too, and might have done so if in the "Money" scene the turnstile on which Miss Cary was sitting had not collapsed and thrown them all into a hilarious amusement. General Stuart, in some way Tilda did not quite understand, was responsible for that mishap. Before the evening was over, Tilda had the tremulous honor of meeting the great cavalryman, and the happiness of receiving one of the gracious compliments that he was always so ready to bestow.

She went with Mr. Streean to the President's reception the night after someone, presumably bribed by Yankees, made a stupid attempt to set fire to the White House of the Confederacy. Everybody was thankful that the fire was discovered in time so that no one was hurt and little damage done. Richmond during these winter months was very gay, and someone suggested the fire might have been set by poor people resenting the many dances and parties; but General Lee himself had approved the dancing, declaring that when his officers had a chance to enjoy themselves, young ladies were quite right to entertain them.

Tilda enjoyed the reception. She saw in the throng many acquaintances, and felt a deep pleasure when ladies nodded or spoke to her and sometimes even engaged her in conversation. Why, they seemed to respect and to like her; and it was a part of her small triumph to see that Streean was left very much to himself, standing for most of the evening with two or three intimates in a corner of the room. Mrs. Grant, who had been a Crenshaw before her marriage and had converted her handsome home next door to the White House into a House of Mercy for wounded soldiers, herself presented Tilda to Mrs. Davis, and spoke of the useful work Tilda had done; and Mrs. Davis was pleasantly gracious. Tilda was left swimming in a sea of happy pride.

Judge Tudor spoke to her. His home was diagonally across Twelfth Street, only a few steps away. She asked why Julian and Anne had not come, and he said Julian kept away from crowds. "He and Anne are at home." He added, with a smile: "Anne was reading aloud to Julian out of Blackstone's *Commentaries* when I left them." Tilda had never heard of Blackstone's *Commentaries,* so she said hurriedly that this was a beautiful house, wasn't it, and Judge Tudor agreed. "Dr. Brockenbrough built it, forty or fifty years ago," he said. "There weren't any railroad tracks down in the ravine then, so the lot was more attractive than it is now. Mrs. Brockenbrough laid out a beautiful garden on the slope on that side. She had been Mrs. Randolph of Tuckahoe. When Dr. Brockenbrough retired, he sold the house to Mr. Morson; but Mr. Morson sold it to Miss Bruce—she was Mrs. Morson's sister, and a great belle before she married Mr. Seddon." Tilda listened blissfully to these great names. "Mr. Seddon added the third story, and then he sold it to Mr. Crenshaw, and the city bought it from him, and the Confederacy rented it as a residence for Mr. Davis." He added with a chuckle: "Mrs. Davis thinks it too small, but she keeps filling it with children."

Brett and Cinda joined them; and when to Judge Tudor's question Brett said he would return to duty on Monday, Tilda suggested to Cinda that they all come to Sunday dinner.

"We don't see each other as much as I wish we did," she pointed out. "I think families ought to be together more than ever now, don't you?"

Cinda readily agreed. "Only, don't try to have too much, Tilda. Starvation parties are the thing now, you know. Even on Sunday!"

Tilda promised, but Redford Streean when he heard they were coming said no one would go hungry in his house unless it were from choice, and took the matter out of Tilda's hands. She was disturbed, fearing Cinda's opinion and Brett's if Redford were too lavish; and before Sunday came she wished it were possible to withdraw her invitation, for she had a second letter from Jenny.

"I'm awfully sorry, Aunt Tilda," Jenny wrote. "But before your letter came I'd already written Mama that Dolly didn't come on with me. And I told Rollin Lyle. He had heard she was coming and he was visiting in Columbia and rode over to call on her and I had to explain to him."

If Cinda knew of Dolly's headstrong folly she would have told Brett, and probably Vesta too; so Tilda dreaded what she would see in their eyes, and prepared a defiant answer to any spoken criticism. After all, there was no reason why Dolly should not go to Nassau with Darrell if she wanted to.

But when they appeared at the house on Sunday there was nothing in their manner to suggest that they knew. Julian and Anne, since Anne's baby would be born in April, did not come, nor did Judge Tudor; but Tilda had invited Enid and the children as well as Brett and Cinda and Vesta. They sat down to a lavish board: oysters, a haunch of venison, a platter of partridges, hot biscuits of white flour, rice, salad, ices for dessert. Enid was exclamatory with delight.

"I declare, Cousin Redford, I think you're wonderful to find all these lovely good things."

"It only needs a little management." Streean turned to Brett. "There's more wild game in the markets than I've ever seen. The shop keeper who furnished this venison had eight deer hanging up; and wild turkeys, wild geese, ducks, fish, everything."

"The prices scare me," Vesta confessed. "Even venison is three dollars a pound."

Streean smiled. "That sounds like a high price, but you have to remember that Confederate money isn't worth what it used to be." His eye met Brett's again. "Congress has passed a law to stop your banker friends speculating in Federal money. They've been making some enormous profits, but of course they hurt our currency in doing so."

Tilda saw Brett's face harden, but he only said mildly that money had no heart. "It's always greedy. Money loves nothing but money."

"Well, in the long run that's true of everything," Streean remarked. "The instinct to survive includes the instinct to perpetuate, and at no matter what cost to others. Right now, for instance, each state is trying to take care of itself, even if that means ruining us all. Governor Vance has exempted twenty-five thousand men from service in the army, and keeps them at home to defend North Carolina; and Georgia and South Carolina and the other states are almost as bad. And Vance keeps a huge supply of uniforms and coats and shoes on hand, and lets the rest of the army go barefoot."

Lucy said: "I had a letter from Papa, and he says Governor Vance sent them fourteen thousand uniforms. But the soldiers in Tennessee have to make their own shoes out of the skins of the cattle they slaughter."

Streean chuckled. "Your friend Longstreet's turning his army into cobblers, Brett. Probably that's why they don't do more fighting. People are calling him 'Slow Pete.' "

Tilda stirred uneasily, feeling Brett's anger; and Vesta may have felt this too, for she said with a quick laugh: "Making shoes is fun! All you need is some old canvas and a strong needle, and then ask a shoemaker to put soles on them. The ones I make aren't very handsome, but it's better than paying a hundred dollars a pair."

Tilda thought they were on safer ground, but Streean persisted. "It's all right for North Carolina to send things to her men, but the states can't all do that. Texas can't send anything this far, so her men are ragged and barefoot, while North Carolina men have more than they need. All that ought to be handled by the Quartermaster's department."

"I suppose it's possible," Brett commented in a flat tone, "that the states feel the Quartermaster General doesn't do a good job."

"Oh, we hear that all the time, but our agents have to compete with the states for everything they buy or impress." Streean met Brett's eye, said in a resigned tone: "The quartermasters can't win the war, you know, Brett. Our only chance to win is European recognition, and the only way to get that is to free our slaves and convince England and France that we're fighting only for independence. But you slave holders will never agree to that; so we'll lose."

For a moment there was a tight silence, and Tilda tried desperately to think of something to say. This time Cinda came to her rescue. "How's Travis, Enid?"

"Oh, full of complaints!" Enid added lightly: "But then he always is! He thinks General Longstreet is perfect, so to hear him talk everyone else is plotting against his wonderful General, and the Quartermaster General ought to be shot, and General McLaws and everybody."

Tilda wished Enid would not talk so about Trav. It only made Cinda angry. Lucy protested: "Oh, Mama, Papa didn't mean that. He was just joking, the way he always does with me, making fun of the way grown men argue about things."

Streean asked, with a glance at Enid: "His letter was to you then, Lucy?"

Enid herself answered him. "Heavens, yes! Trav never bothers to write to me."

Lucy said defensively: "Well, you don't ever write to him!"

"Oh, I never write letters."

Streean watched Enid with a faint smile, and after a moment Brett spoke again. "Mister Streean, I judge you've no confidence in Southern success."

Tilda always felt a dull hurt when the others addressed Redford thus formally, but Streean moved his hand in a casual gesture. "Every Congressman I know has sold his Confederate bonds, and is advising his friends to do the same." He looked at Brett with a lifted eyebrow. "Might not be a bad idea for you to sell those Confederates you bought with the Currain funds last summer, if that's what's on your mind."

Brett shook his head. "We didn't buy them to sell. Tilda's share is set aside, as you desired. But these Congressmen—" He hesitated. "I believe they'll pass the new conscription bill."

"Oh, yes, I suppose they will," Streean agreed. "Of course, the newspapers are against it, because it will force a lot of their men to fight. And it abolishes substitutions, so the seventy or eighty thousand men who have hired substitutes are shouting that it annuls their contracts with the Government, and that they'll sue! And everyone liable to service who can afford to do so is turning his property into cash and buying a passport to leave the country. Yes, I think it will pass."

"I see a lot of talk in the papers about rich men trying to get posts in the Navy Department, or looking for safe details for themselves and their sons."

"Yes, and they'll get them," Streean said confidently. He chuckled. "Secretary Seddon exempted one fellow to write a history of the war. It's safe to say the Secretary will have only the kindest mentions in that history. And Mr. Memminger has found places for all his relatives. But people without influence will just have to skedaddle. The children of Israel are going by the hundreds, turning back to the fleshpots of Egypt, running away from the fiery serpent of the conscription officers." He laughed. "I heard an amusing tale yesterday; an embalmer named McClure has given up his regular business and is smuggling Jews through the lines in coffins."

"Is there as much of a flight as the papers say?"

"Oh yes. That's why you see so many auctions. Jews who've hired substitutes and stayed here and made fortunes are selling their household goods and paying any price for passports to Europe. But most of them will go North."

"It's not only the Jews who've made money during these years," Brett suggested, and Tilda wished they would keep away from such ugly topics. "But it's the fashion to speak of Jews and speculators as though the words were synonyms."

"It's the fashion among those who have not made money to throw hard names at those who have," Streean assented, not at all offended, and he smiled. "But it's not too high a price to pay."

"Speaking of prices and speculators, I wonder how much the Government collects out of the tax on profits," Brett remarked. "Mr. Hartshorn tells me he paid thirty-five hundred dollars, and his whole income was only ten thousand, including a hundred-percent dividend on some stock he owns in the Citizens' Savings Bank in Lynchburg."

"Well, the new tax bill adds ten percent to the fifteen percent already levied," Streean told him, "if anyone chooses to report his profits and pay it. But a sensible man can make it up easily enough, with this new currency bill. Putting a thirty-three-percent tax on everything bigger than a five-dollar note unless it's invested in four percents is just plain repudiation, so prices will go sky-high." He added calmly: "But of course, if he doesn't report his profits, who's to know that he made any? I don't know anyone innocent enough to report to the collector." Brett made a sudden movement, and Streean said dryly: "Mr. Green is the collector in your district, if you're interested, Brett; and William

Johnson's the assessor. Every registered business is supposed to report profits at three-month intervals, and farmers have to report what crops they make, and the value of their cattle as of November first. And anyone who made a profit last year by investing money or goods or even his abilities was supposed to report on the first of January." He lighted a cigar, repeated: "If you're interested."

His tone was a challenge, and Tilda saw Brett was blackly angry; so she rose, giving the signal to leave the table. Why need Redford go out of his way to be offensive to Brett and to them all? There had been a time when she exulted in his success; and she still tried to tell herself that people who did not like him were really just jealous of his shrewdness. But those very people, by the ready willingness with which they yielded to her direction, and the friendly gratitude they gave her because she told them how they could be most useful, made her feel for them a wistful liking. There were actually moments when she regretted Redford's fine achievements. That night, abed, thinking of Darrell and Dolly gone heedlessly off to Nassau, thinking of Redford noisily asleep beside her, Tilda found herself crying in the silent dark, gulping down her sobs, letting her eyes drain tears into her pillow. Oh, why could she not have had fine children like Cinda's? She wept not with envy, nor in self-pity, but in longing so hopeless it was like despair.

She had not told Redford of Dolly's escapade; but as January ended she began to regret her silence. The *Dragonfly* must soon return to Wilmington, and Captain Pew would surely come here, and then Redford would hear the truth. When on the second day of February he remarked that Captain Pew was in town, she was full of questions she dared not ask. "Is he going to stay with us?"

"No, he's only in Richmond for a day or two." Streean added in an amused tone: "We're going into the passenger business this trip. Mr. Hyman, the jeweler, has auctioned off everything he owns so he can get out of the country before the conscript officers grab him. He's bought a passport, and wants passage to Nassau for himself and his whole family, his wife and his mother and three or four others. He'll pay through the nose before we're done with him. He's made two or three hundred thousand dollars since the war started, and we'll make him give up most of it. And Colonel Northrop wants us to make a voyage for the Government, and he'll guarantee us a three-hundred-percent profit on any provisions and meat we'll bring in. Captain Pew says he can buy New York beef and Nassau bacon at a bargain, and get a bill at double the actual price to show Northrop. So he'll hurry off and sail as soon as his cotton's loaded."

Tilda was not interested in these transactions, but she wished to see Captain Pew. "You must bring him to supper, at least. Tell him he mustn't neglect us just because Dolly's not here." If Dolly had returned on the *Dragonfly* and gone directly on to the Plains as she had said she would, Captain Pew must have told Redford; and she watched his expression for any change.

But clearly he knew nothing of Dolly. "I doubt if he'll come. He likes a session at Mr. Merrihay's gaming tables." His eyes shadowed thoughtfully. "Gambling will be the ruin of the good Captain some day."

One question at least she could ask. "Did Darrell stay on in Nassau?"

"Oh Darrell didn't go to Nassau," Streean said casually. "I suppose he's still at Chimneys. Captain Pew hasn't seen him."

That word was like a blow, stopping Tilda's breath; for if Darrell had not gone to Nassau on the *Dragonfly* with Dolly, then Dolly had lied to Jenny. But why had Dolly lied? Where was she now? Questions like missiles pelted Tilda hard.

She slipped away upstairs to be alone, to try to guess the truth, to think what she must do. But what could she do, without risking harm to Dolly? It must be that Dolly had not gone to Nassau; for if she had, Captain Pew would have told Redford. Perhaps Dolly had met Darrell, and had been enticed by him into some adventure that she wished to conceal.

No, that guess was obviously wrong; for Dolly must have known her lie to Jenny would be discovered, so she must have expected to be by this time at the Plains. Perhaps in fact she was there now; but if she were, why had no word come? Tilda was frantic with terror deeper than anything she had ever known. Dolly had all her life gone her pretty, capricious way; no one had ever hurt or harmed her; she knew no more of danger than a child. Tilda's thoughts conjured up a thousand dreadful specters.

Thinking that Captain Pew might know more than he had told Redford, she tried next morning to see him, asking for him at the Spottswood and the Ballard; but she did not find him. She wrote Jenny to inquire whether Dolly had arrived at the Plains, and as an afterthought she wrote Tony at Chimneys for news of Darrell. Redford Streean told her that evening that Captain Pew had returned to Wilmington. She wished, too late, that she had gone with him to try to find Dolly.

She had long waiting for any answer to either of her letters. February brought a new pressure of hunger everywhere. Tilda heard spiteful talk about Mrs. Davis's luncheon for ladies when she served roast ducks, jellied chicken, oysters, a lavish meal; while at the same time the army was on such short rations that General Lee had to appeal to his soldiers for patience and endurance. On every street corner in Richmond there were muttering groups of poor women, each with a train of hungry children. Some thought that Lee might have to send a few regiments to keep down the unrest in the city.

Redford Streean told her that General Lee had asked President Davis to prevent commissary agents buying government supplies for their families and their friends. "He claims that it takes food out of the mouths of the army," he said resentfully. "If they want rations, why not capture them from the enemy? General Lee complains like an old woman. We have as much right to be fed as the soldiers, I suppose."

Tilda nodded indifferent agreement. He was right, of course. Everyone who could buy government beef and flour did so; and certainly there seemed to be plenty. Richmond had never been more gay than it was just now. Tilda had hoped she and Redford would be invited to Mrs. Ives's for the performance of *The Rivals,* an event for which rehearsals had been weeks in progress. They were not invited, but when the time came she no longer cared. Nothing else mattered till she knew where Dolly was.

The first answer to her letters came from Tony. "Darrell left here two or three days before Christmas," he wrote. "He expected to go to

Wilmington and on to Nassau." His letter was short, but Tony never wrote at length. Tilda found in what he said some reassurance. If Darrell had set out for Wilmington before Christmas, he must surely have reached there before Dolly did; so perhaps Dolly had not lied after all. She must have met Darrell and planned to go with him on the *Dragonfly,* and then they changed their plans and Dolly did not trouble to write Jenny again. Probably, Tilda told herself, snatching at any straw of hope, they had met friends and gone to visit on some plantation near Wilmington; and surely Dolly had joined Jenny at the Plains by now.

But the day after Tilda heard from Tony, Jenny wrote that Dolly was not at the Plains; so Tilda was distracted, nursing her terror in silence, confiding in no one, till on the eleventh of February Dolly's breathless letter came.

> Dear mama—I declare you must be just wild not hearing from me but I've been just simply too happy to write any old letters to anybody because mama youll never believe it but Im married to the very dar-lingest boy his names Bruce Kenyon and hes a lieutenant in the garri-son at Fort Fisher and the minute I laid eyes on him it was all over with me just like that and he was just going home on furlough and he lives in Charlotte and it was the same with both of us so we didn't waste a minute can you imagine mama Id known him less than a whole day before we were married hes only nineteen but he's the handsomest thing you ever saw and his papa and mama are darling and we have to go back to Wilmington next Monday because he only had two weeks at home and you must pack up all my prettiest clothes and send them on because Wilmingtons ever so gay and were going to live there and you must come and visit us as soon as ever you can probably you think Im just crazy and I am really but isnt it wonderful and please dont be mad at me for not waiting to tell you but Colonel Lamb and General Whiting say the Yankees are apt to attack Wil-mington just any time and I couldnt bear to think of waiting even a minute when Bruce might be killed or something and arent you glad mama because I know you worried about me and said you never would feel safe till I was married and settled down so now you wont worry any more Bruce sends loads and loads of love to his new mama and hes crazy to have you come and visit us real soon he has to be at the fort but he can come home lots of times and Im just the happiest girl in the world.
>
> Your loving daughter,
> Dolly

Tilda read the letter once and then twice, at first with surprise and with a great relief; but then questions came to trouble her. Dolly and her new husband, according to the letter, must have been married about the first of February. But Dolly had reached Wilmington on the sixth of January! Where had she been for those three weeks of which she now gave no accounting? If she had been with Darrell, why did she not speak of him? If she had gone to Nassau? Tilda shook her head. If Dolly had gone to Nassau, Captain Pew would have said so.

She showed Redford the letter and he read it with an amused chuckle. "Well, it's high time," he commented. "But young Kenyon has my sympathy. She'll lead him a dance."

Tilda tried to protest. "Why, Redford, Dolly'll make a real sweet wife! You know she will."

Streean laughed. "I wouldn't want to risk anything on it. She's a spoiled hussy, Tilda. No one man will ever be enough for her. She'll want a regiment." He looked at the letter again. "See here, where did she meet him, if she was at the Plains? Fort Fisher's in Wilmington."

"Maybe she met Darrell in Wilmington and stayed there a few days with him."

"I don't think so. Captain Pew didn't see Darrell, and he went to Wilmington on the same train with Dolly." Tilda had no answer, and he said: "I'll ask Pew about it, next time he comes to Richmond." He grinned. "Tilda, I'll bet that little lady never went to the Plains at all. She just made the trip an excuse to get out from under your wing. Well, at least she's married. Let her husband worry about her from now on."

Tilda wrote to Dolly, but that letter was hard to phrase. Your children had you always at a disadvantage. You loved them so much more than they loved you. If you sought to guide or to control them, they thought you a tiresome nuisance, or a tyrant; and in the long run they would always go their own way. If you tried too stubbornly to hold them fast, you lost them. No mother could ever win a battle with her daughter; for victory was itself defeat. Children were so much a part of you that to hurt them was to hurt yourself—and to lose them.

And Dolly was a grown woman. Scolding was emptiness. Whatever had been done was done, irrevocably. She must keep as much of Dolly's trust and of Dolly's love as the girl would grant her.

So she wrote carefully, trying not to sound querulous. "I was mighty glad to have your letter, darling, with your happy news. I'd been a little worried, of course, because Jenny wrote me that you'd met Darrell and gone off to Nassau on the Dragonfly. That sounded so dangerous. I know the Yankee cruisers shoot at the blockade-runners, and I couldn't bear to think of cannon balls rattling around your head. Captain Pew was here two weeks ago and he didn't mention your having gone, but I knew you were with Darrell, and so of course you were all right. I hadn't told your father what Jenny wrote me." That silence on her part might be a bond between her and Dolly. "Lieutenant Kenyon must be charming, if you love him so. Is he one of Darrell's friends? I haven't heard from Darrell for months. Tell him he ought to write me a nice letter some day. You and your Lieutenant must come for a visit when you can. I'll send your things as soon as you tell me where to direct them."

She made more than one draft of this letter, writing and rewriting it, careful to exclude from it everything but tenderness and affection. One wrong word now might create a rift between her and Dolly that could never be mended. Having written the letter she wondered where to send it, and added a postscript. "You don't give me your address so I'll send this to your nice husband to give to you." And she enclosed it in a note to Lieutenant Kenyon and addressed it to Fort Fisher

At once, to protect Dolly, she went to tell Cinda of Dolly's marriage. She tried to pretend a delight she did not feel, and Cinda joined in that pretense; but when Tilda said good-by, Cinda caught her and kissed her, and Tilda to her own dismay burst into tears.

"Oh, Cinda," she sobbed, "I'm so desperately unhappy. I hate this getting married in such a hurry. People's tongues!"

Cinda held her close, patted her shoulder. "There, dear; there!" And she said reassuringly: "Things happen more quickly in these times, darling. Dolly's all right." She laughed a little. "She ought to be smacked, of course, but she'll be all right. And she's a grown woman, you know."

"I hate it," Tilda insisted. "But if I scold her, she'll just hate me!"

"Why not go visit her? Go see this young man. I expect he's just as nice as he can be."

"You always make things seem all right, somehow." Tilda's tears came in a flood. "Oh, Cinda, I love you so! I wish we could be together more. I need someone to talk to. I'm so lonesome, sometimes."

"You can always talk to me."

"Do you think I ought to tell people about Dolly?"

"Of course! Don't go out of your way, but tell all your friends."

"I haven't any friends."

"Nonsense!"

"I haven't!" Tilda insisted. "People don't like Mr. Streean." In a burst of helpless confession she cried: "Oh, I wish I'd never married him, Cinda. Sometimes I wish I'd never been born."

"There—now you've got that off your mind you'll feel better."

"You all just despise him. And so do I."

"People don't despise you, though," Cinda assured her. "You've made a place for yourself. I'm real proud of you."

Tilda's tears no longer flowed. "I know I've tried awful hard," she admitted. "Sometimes I do feel as if I amounted to something." And she said in a low tone: "Cinda, when I first knew that about Papa and President Lincoln, I thought it was pretty awful; but now I'm sort of proud he's related to us. It's just simply crazy, I suppose; but after all, he's President. I sort of feel as though I wanted to live up to him."

Cinda said quietly: "I've been proud ever since I saw him in Washington."

Tilda kissed her again. "And I want to live up to you, Cinda," she said softly. "I'm awful proud that you're my sister."

When Captain Pew next came to Richmond, Streean brought him to the house. "He knows Dolly's husband," he told Tilda. "So you'll want to ask him a lot of questions."

He left them together while he went to his room, but Tilda's question was not about Lieutenant Kenyon. "Captain Pew," she asked in a low tone, "did Dolly go with you and Darrell to Nassau?"

She saw in his eyes what might have been uneasiness, but he evaded her question. "Oh, I haven't seen Darrell for several months."

She brushed that aside. "Then did Dolly go with you?" And when he hesitated, she said: "I'm not blaming you if she did. She's head-strong and impetuous, and she'll do anything to get her own way. I know she wanted to. Did she?"

He said, after a moment: "Well, yes ma'am, she did." She saw in him a deep embarrassment, and some sullen anger; and an apologetic desire to justify himself was plain in his next words. "On the train, on the way down there, she teased me to take her along. You know she can drive a man crazy with her teasing. But I told her no. Then she managed to come aboard, the night of our farewell supper. We always invite everyone in town, and she just mixed in with the crowd. She wore Darrell's clothes, ma'am." There was no question of the anger in him now. "She told me afterward she'd brought them along on purpose. She pretended to be going to the Plains just to get away from Richmond, but all the time she meant to make me take her to Nassau."

"Couldn't you have put her ashore?"

"She hid in my locker, ma'am. I was on deck till after we slipped through the blockading steamers, about daylight next morning. Then I went below and there she was, rolled up in one of my coats, asleep on my bunk! It was too late to put back."

Tilda, thinking of Dolly's shameful masquerade, remembered a night long ago when the child had dressed in Darrell's things and slipped out of the house to mingle with a celebrating throng on Richmond's streets. It was a long time now since Richmond had had anything to celebrate. "But you did bring her back to Wilmington?"

"Yes, ma'am," he said. "I kept her on shipboard in Nassau. We anchored in the harbor and lightered off our cotton, and she didn't leave the ship. And I brought her back. She wanted to go ashore at Nassau, but I wouldn't let her; so we didn't part on very good terms."

Tilda heard Redford Streean descending the stairs. She whispered: "Don't tell Mr. Streean, please." And then, aloud, as Streean appeared in the door: "Lieutenant Kenyon sounds perfectly charming."

"He's a fine young fellow," Captain Pew agreed.

Tilda wanted to be alone, but she was afraid that if she tried to walk her trembling knees would not support her; so she sat quietly while the two men fell at once into talk of business. Streean said: "Our venture into the passenger trade fell through."

Captain Pew nodded. He said that Mr. Hyman, when he came aboard the *Dragonfly* at Wilmington, balked at the sum demanded for transporting him and his family to Nassau.

"I was moderate enough," the Captain explained. "Ten thousand dollars per passenger, and there were only six of them. But our friend burst into a harangue, and I tossed him off the ship." He added frankly: "I thought he'd pay, once he saw I meant it; but he called down a thousand curses on my head and led his party away."

Streean laughed. "He wishes by now he'd paid your price. He came back to Richmond and they went from here to Staunton and tried to go down the Valley and through the lines that way; but some bushwhackers stopped them and took everything he had, a lot of jewelry and gold, over two hundred thousand dollars altogether."

"He'd have had a cheaper trip with me," Captain Pew commented. He said that the cargo which the *Dragonfly* brought in for Colonel Northrop showed a profit beyond their best expectations. The two discussed new ventures. With gold at thirty for one, and prices rising every day, it was impossible to go far wrong. Anything you bought would presently show a profit. Streean said a ham had sold at auction that day for three hundred and fifty dollars, and sugar was ten dollars a pound.

"And if Sherman takes Mobile, the price will go up like a skyrocket," he predicted.

Captain Pew said the trade with Nassau was at a peak. "The Governor has begun to enforce the Queen's proclamation, so blockading cruisers can't anchor in British waters unless they're in distress. They chased the *Hansa* from Stirrup's Cay till she jettisoned seventy bales of cotton and ran inside the reef at Six Shilling Channel. Three blockaderunners made Nassau the day they chased the *Hansa,* and twelve of us in January. The *Fannie* and the *Wild Dayrell* made two trips. And eight more came through in February. The *Pet* was captured off Wilmington, but the others all got through." He added, smiling: "The big sensation in Nassau now is the Governor wants an investigation of the way Mr. Powell is running the hotel." He hesitated, looking at Tilda, and Streean asked:

"What's wrong with it?"

"Oh, there've been complaints." Captain Pew spoke evasively.

Clearly, her presence put a curb upon his tongue; and Tilda, hoping she could walk steadily, left them.

Next day, seeking any comforting, she went to tell Cinda Dolly's escapade; and as she repeated some of the things Captain Pew had said, she remembered his manner and spoke of it. "I never saw him like that before," she said. "He's usually so—well, so sure of himself. I can't describe it, but it was as though he expected to be accused of something, and was ready to—well, to deny it, I suppose!" Cinda nodded, and Tilda added: "I suppose he knows he should have brought her right back, but probably he couldn't do it in broad daylight with the Yankee steamers there, and he thinks we're blaming him. But he acted —Cinda, if I didn't know nothing ever scared him, I'd think he was scared!"

"I can't think of anything, except perhaps his own conscience, which would frighten the bold Captain Pew."

"I don't think he has much conscience," Tilda confessed; and her own words frightened her. Dolly had been for days alone with him aboard the *Dragonfly*.

Before February ended she had another letter from Dolly, and she opened it with eager fingers; but it was brief and hurtful as a blow.

> Dear Mama, I had your letter but you dont need to be so mealy mouthed and hypocritical because you know perfectly well I wouldn't have married Bruce unless I thought I had to marry somebody but I didn't and Im simply furious and you dont need to ask me about Darrell because I havent the faintest idea where he is and I dont care, and as for Captain Pew I dont ever want to hear his name again as long as I live you dont need to worry about me Im a respectable married woman now and I can take care of myself perfectly well.
>
> Dolly

That letter was like a thunderstroke crashing in Tilda's ears, mercifully rendering her for a while insensible to pain. From any thought of Dolly she took refuge in anxiety for her son. Tony did not know where Darrell was, nor did Captain Pew, nor Dolly. Dolly was lost; but where was Darrell? Where was Darrell now?

10

SADNESS had never left any visible mark on Vesta, and if sometimes she still wept for Tommy it was secretly. There were tears enough in the world; she would not add her own. Rich hours with her baby were a sweet delight; the household responsibilities that Cinda put in her hands gave her no leisure for wistful sighs; she was busy, and she was young, and healthy active youth laughs easily. Through this winter and early spring she began more and more to enter into the social gaiety, a little forced, with something desperate about it, which Richmond people would always remember as the last brightness of a dying flame. Gentlemen competed for first honors for hospitality. Mr. Trenholm, who was said to own more blockade-runners than any man in the Confederacy, and to be one of the wealthiest men in the South, kept open house every Saturday evening. His old Madeira was the best in Richmond, and no one ever declined an invitation to his dinners. Mr. Benjamin, the Secretary of State, was always a guest; and most people believed Mr. Trenholm would soon replace Mr. Memminger as Secretary of the Treasury. Mr. Macfarland, the president of the Farmers' Bank, was another who gave lavish entertainments. He had been politically ambitious till Mr. Tyler defeated him for Congress; but he could still plan delightful balls and socials.

And hostesses won an equal fame. Cinda seldom attended any elaborate entertainments, but she had planned to go to see the performance of *The Rivals* at the home of Mrs. Ives, early in February. When the time came, however, she had a wretched cold; and though Vesta urged her to ignore it, Cinda said:

"No, Honey. When I have a cold, people can't hear themselves think in the same room with me. Sneezing and coughing, I'd be the real Mrs. Malaprop. You come home and tell me all about it."

Vesta had contrived for the occasion a new dress, put together out of odds and ends of resurrected finery. The skirt was of white-barred organdy with a flounce of black lace around the bottom, and a wide black sash with a bow in the back; the waist was charmingly puffed, and trimmed with lace-edged ruching.

"And a flounced muslin petticoat, Mama! See!" She made Cinda admire her ingenuity. "And all out of scraps. I just threw all the old rags I own in a heap and took things at random and put them together any old way. Tell me how clever I am!"

She departed in a happy excitement, and after the performance she went with the others to Mrs. Ould's to a midnight supper, so it was late when she came home. Old Caesar, bearing a candle, since gas was short and people used no more than they must, sleepily admitted her. When the door opened Vesta saw a scrap of paper on the floor and picked it up. It was a note from Rollin.

> Wanted to see you, but the house is dark, so I know you're all asleep, and I must take the morning train. Sorry.
>
>   Rollin.

Vesta was sorry too. She and Rollin had been friends so long. He must be just returning from his furlough. She tiptoed upstairs, but Cinda was awake and heard her and called her in. Vesta protested: "Heavens, Mama, you ought to have been asleep hours ago. How do you feel?"

"Oh, I'm lots better," Cinda assured her. "June rubbed my chest with hot mutton tallow mixed with sassafras and turpentine till I thought I was afire, and then made me drink a glass of hot lemonade and brandy, and pinned a cold compress around my neck and tucked me in. I got rid of the clammy thing as soon as she was out of the room, but I wasn't sleepy. I've been watching the moonlight." The night was bright outside her windows. "Was it fun, darling?"

"Wonderful!" Vesta lighted Cinda's candle, using three matches before one burned long enough to touch the wick. "We still haven't learned how to make matches," she said laughingly. "I'd almost forgive the Yankees everything else if they'd send us some good matches again. Mama, Rollin was here tonight." She showed Cinda his note. "This was tucked under the front door. I wish I'd been here."

"He didn't ring or I'd have heard him and kept him till you came. I like Rollin."

"So do I." Thinking of Rollin made her remember Dolly. "I wonder if Dolly's back from Nassau."

"Oh, bother Dolly! Tell me about tonight," Cinda urged. "Unless you're sleepy."

"Heavens, I'm too excited to be sleepy. It was such fun, Mama." The embers on the hearth were still warm. "Here, help me out of this dress; I mustn't muss it, even if it is a hodgepodge." In her petticoat, a quilt around her shoulders, she sat cross-legged on the foot of the bed, her tongue rattling. "Mrs. Clay kept us all just screaming, and Connie Cary was the loveliest thing you ever saw. Mr. Harrison just simply gawped at her!"

"Was he in it?"

"No. Connie was Lydia, and Mrs. Clay was Mrs. Malaprop, of course; and Lee Tucker was Captain Absolute, and Mr. John Randolph was Sir Anthony. Oh and Major Brown was Sir Lucius. He had the most marvellous brogue! Connie's brother was Fag."

"I suppose everyone was there."

"Oh yes, from President Davis down. The house was jammed. The stage was at the end of the parlors. Secretary Mallory says they did it as well as Drury Lane or any real theatre, and he's seen it dozens of times. Mrs. Drew said Mrs. Clay was as good as any Mrs. Malaprop she'd ever seen. Mrs. Ives filled in, in the afterpiece, and she borrowed Ruby Mallory's new hat that came through the blockade from Paris only last week, a huge black leghorn with black plumes. That hat just made everybody gasp. Connie had the most perfect dresses you can imagine. Mrs. Clay had on a brocade, and she was just simply festooned with lace, and jewels and plumes in her hair." Vesta doubled over with laughter at the memory. "Her hair was piled mountain-high, and she told us between the acts that to get it high enough she'd rolled up a pair of her black satin boots and then pinned her own hair on top of them. Oh, and the funniest thing was when Bob Acres—Major Ward was wonderful—was getting ready for the duel, and General Hood said, loud enough for everyone near him to hear: 'I believe that fellow's a coward.' I guess he'd never seen *The Rivals* before."

"Sam Hood's a nice boy," Cinda declared. "I hope nobody laughed."

"Oh no, but it was really the hit of the evening." Vesta smiled. "General Hood attracted attention again, later on, after the performance. Mr. Blanding from Lynchburg said General Pendleton had told him that the Yankees lost forty-eight thousand men at Chancellorsville, and fifty thousand at Gettysburg. General Hood said it wasn't true; Mr. Blanding said General Pendleton had it from General Lee, and that General Lee knew it from secret official Yankee reports; and General Hood said the statement was as unreliable as General Pendleton's reconnaissance at Gettysburg. He was angry, but I suppose you can't blame the poor man. After all, he was wounded there."

"They shouldn't talk war at a party."

"They didn't mean to be heard, I'm sure," Vesta explained. "But their voices rose."

Cinda said: "I was sure Mrs. Clay would be good in her part. I've heard she went to a costume party in Washington before the war as Mrs. Partington, and made a sensation; and of course Mrs. Malaprop's the same sort of thing."

"It was loads of fun," Vesta said happily. "But I do wish I'd seen Rollin. It would almost have been worth missing it."

"What did Connie wear?"

"Why, one dress was a white muslin, with a lace cap and blue ribbons, just as sweet as could be. But the prettiest was a pale blue brocade petticoat and bodice with a train of pink moiré and a fichu of Mechlin lace and a wreath of pink roses. She looked good enough to eat—and Mr. Harrison looked as though he'd like to eat her." She laughed again. "She told me her shoulder will be black and blue for days where Mrs. Malaprop pinched her! And 'Lissa Temple had her hair done a new way—three rolls on each side of her head running from the front to the back, big ones on top, and then smaller ones, and then little ones over her ears. 'Cats, rats, and mice' we called it, teasing her; but it looked ever so stylish. But of course Hetty Cary carried off all the honors, even without being in the performance. The gentlemen were just standing on their heads! Honestly, Mama, she's so lovely it's sinful, and so nice you can't possibly envy her. She wore a dotted

Swiss blouse with perfectly enormous puff sleeves, all caught in by a black velvet bodice laced across here—" Her rapid gesture with her fingertips made her meaning plain. "And a thin black ribbon like the lacing, tied in long bows at her throat, and tiny black lace across the top of the bodice. And her skirt was dark brown, with a brocaded panel in front, and she wore a perfectly lovely black lace shawl. Really, she was a picture!" She sighed and said again: "But I'm sorry I missed Rollin. Do you suppose he saw Jenny?"

"You like Rollin pretty well, don't you, Vesta?"

"Of course!" Vesta lay down, her head pillowed beside her mother's. "He and Tommy were such good friends, Mama." Her voice was soft.

"I know."

"I think Tommy'd be glad I like Rollin."

"I know he would."

Vesta turned to meet Cinda's eyes in a long questioning. "Is it all right, Mama?"

"It's all right, my dear," Cinda assured her. "Anything that makes you happy is all right." And she added: "Tommy'd say so too, darling."

Vesta smiled and stirred and sat up. "If I don't go to bed, I'll be asleep right here. Good night, Mama." She kissed Cinda, and went to her own room.

The day Tilda came to tell them Dolly was married, Vesta was not at home. When she returned and heard the news, her first thought was of Rollin, and her first word too. "Mama, do you suppose Rollin knew, that night he was here?"

"How could he, darling?"

"Well, he may have come through Wilmington, so he might have seen her. Do you suppose he's perfectly miserable?"

"If he is, he'll get over it."

"What did Aunt Tilda think about it?"

"She was wretched, though of course she tried not to show it." Cinda added in a thoughtful tone: "I never used to like Tilda, but I'm beginning to. I was so sorry for her."

Vesta murmured: "I wonder if Dolly's—in a scrape." But Cinda would not conjecture.

In spite of dancing and charades and theatricals and many valorous gaieties, that was a sober month in Richmond. With the passage of the new currency bill, prices soared. Sugar rose to twenty dollars a pound. One morning somebody had written on the walls of houses along Main Street threats of riot and violence unless the famine was relieved, and someone set fire to the government bakery on Clay Street, and there were other suspicious conflagrations. They were blamed on Yankee agents, but Vesta thought they might have been started by poor desperate folk who thus sought revenge for their helpless suffering. Only the wealthy and those whose influence allowed them to buy from the government commissary had enough to eat.

There were other complaints. The new conscription law had provoked an epidemic of evasion, and lawyers and unscrupulous physicians reaped a harvest. Judge Tudor told them of a lawyer in Lexington who handled sixty-odd cases in a month, at fat fees. "And every second-rate doctor is selling certificates of ill health. Rheumatism used to be a curse, but now men pay big fees to be told they have it. Gout too, but poor people can't afford gout! Men who used to shave their gray beards so they'd look young are letting them grow now to prove how old they are; and men as spry as boys a year ago are hobbling around on canes."

Julian, fretting at his own helplessness to serve, damned these malingerers; and when General Bragg, as though to reward him for his disgraceful failures in Tennessee, was assigned to serve under President Davis as directing head of all the armies of the Confederacy, Julian was white with indignation. "It's typical of President Davis to do a thing like that. From now on every soldier in the army knows that if the Yankees lick him he'll be promoted! You can imagine how General Lee feels, and General Longstreet, and Johnston, and Beauregard. They win battles, so President Davis hates them; but General Bragg loses battles, so President Davis promotes him! It makes me sick!"

Cinda laughed at his rage and accused him of reading the editorials in the *Examiner;* but Vesta saw Anne's distress and advised Julian to be careful. "It bothers her to see you angry, you know; and you don't want anything to bother her now."

"I know," he admitted. "But I get so mad! I suppose the reason I get so worked up is because I can't do anything."

"You've plenty to do, keeping Anne happy." She kissed him. "And I'm very glad you can't go off and fight any more. It's nice for Anne and for Mama and me to have one of our men at home."

On the last day of February a cold rain came to end the long spell of bright weather, and Vesta welcomed relief from the dust that for weeks had been stirred up by every passing horse or cart or carriage, sifting into the house through every crevice. Next morning was dark with low clouds emptying themselves of rain; but before noon there was a sudden rumble of guns north of the city. Julian brought Anne in the carriage to leave her with Vesta and his mother; and he said enemy cavalry, a force of several thousand sabres, was reported approaching Richmond, and the local militia had been called out.

"And even on crutches I can help man the fortifications," he told them. "So I'm going. You keep Anne here."

Vesta would have protested; but since Anne did not, she and Cinda held their tongues. Julian returned before dinner time to say the enemy had fled, but that night they heard again the guns and musketry at some distance. The *Dispatch* reported that the raiders had come within three miles of the city, but the danger was now past.

In the same paper Vesta's eye lighted on a paragraph of praise of General Longstreet, which she read aloud to Cinda. "It calls him 'one of the most sagacious and indefatigable of our military leaders,' and it says: 'His fame grows with a steady light, and the wider the field of action, the more are his rare qualities developed and demonstrated. It was always known that in battle his presence, like the white plume of Harry of Navarre, announced the post of honor and danger; but it remained for his management of a separate command to exhibit those faculties which constitute the great military leader.' There, isn't that nice? We must save it to show Uncle Trav. He thinks General Longstreet is so wonderful."

Cinda nodded. "I will." She added honestly: "Yet—well, I'm fond of Cousin Jeems, but I can't see that he's accomplished very much in Tennessee."

"Papa said he was being an awful nuisance to the Yankees," Vesta reminded her. "Just by staying where he is. They don't dare let him stay there for fear he'll march into Kentucky, and they can't drive him out. And Congress gave him a vote of thanks two weeks ago!"

"I suppose he's doing some good, or he wouldn't be there," Cinda assented. "I'll send the paper to Cousin Louisa to keep for him. I had a letter from her two or three weeks ago. It's too bad, when she's so near, that we can't see each other more often. She says the baby is thriving. You know they've named it after General Lee."

"General Longstreet hasn't even seen it yet, has he?"

"No, it was born after he went west."

"I'll bet he's crazy to. He loves his children so."

Rain had given way during the night to snow, but when the sun broke through clouds the snow soon disappeared. Tilda came that morning with Dolly's bitter letter. She was weak with tears, and they gave her what comfort they could; but when she was gone Vesta met her mother's eye in a long glance.

"Well!"

Cinda bit her lip. "I ought to be ashamed of myself for feeling the way I do about that child!"

"Do you suppose it was Captain Pew——"

"For Heaven's sake, Vesta, we've better things to think about, and talk about, than Dolly and Captain Pew."

"Aunt Tilda's desperately worried about Darrell, too, isn't she?"

Cinda said sharply: "Good riddance to both of them!" She added apologetically: "Oh, Dolly may have some good in her, but I'm certainly not ashamed of despising Darrell!"

By nightfall that day the Yankee raiders were surely gone; but everyone seemed to know that the enemy had meant to release the thousands of Yankees in Libby Prison; and the thought of what that might have meant was as frightening as the almost forgotten dread of a slave insurrection which had for generations haunted the South. Vesta remembered the thousands of hungry women, poor women with half-starved children clinging to their skirts, who tramped the streets. If the prisoners had been turned loose, these women might have joined them to loot and burn and kill. Enid came to tell them that hundreds of pounds of gunpowder had been placed under the prison to blow it and the prisoners to the skies at the first move to set them free; but Cinda refused to believe this.

"We're all just frightened into silliness," she declared. "People are never so credulous—and never so cruel—as when they're scared."

"But it's true, Cousin Cinda!" Enid insisted. Vesta thought Aunt Enid began to look like an old woman, with her lifeless hair and the thin little lines around her mouth and the faint pouchiness of her throat. "I heard it from a dozen people this morning. I'm simply terrified, with no one in the house but Lucy and Peter and me."

"Big Mill will take care of you."

"Weren't you scared at all, honestly?"

"Not for myself," Cinda said. "It's a long time since I've taken time to think much about myself."

Her dislike of Enid was so plain that Vesta thought Enid must see and resent it. When the other was gone, she asked: "Mama, does Aunt Enid look old to you? She looks older than you do!"

Cinda nodded. "Enid has always whined and complained and moaned and groaned," she said. "After a while those things show in a woman's face."

The clear cool weather held. Thursday there was another alarm, when General Butler was reported advancing up the Peninsula to attack the city; but nothing came of that. Then suddenly everyone knew that a detachment of the raiders had been ambushed at a ford near Walkerton in King and Queen County. Their leader, Colonel Dahlgren, was killed; and there was a rumor that he had meant to burn the city and kill President Davis. The *Dispatch* Saturday morning reported that an address to his command, found in Colonel Dahlgren's pocket, ordered his men to "destroy and burn the hateful city, and do not allow the rebel leader, Davis, and his traitorous crew to escape." It printed the address in full, and the detailed orders to burn mills with oakum and turpentine, to blow up bridges, to destroy the canal; and the repeated insistence: "The city must be destroyed, and Jeff Davis and Cabinet killed." The Cabinet was sitting to decide whether the ninety prisoners from Colonel Dahlgren's command should be hanged, and Secretary Seddon had written General Lee asking his opinion.

Vesta, going with Caesar to buy provisions, heard furious voices raised in black anger at the infamous purpose of the raiders. When she came home Cinda had chanced to meet Mrs. Davis. "She remembers Colonel Dahlgren when he was a little boy," she said. "Admiral

Dahlgren, his father, brought him to call on her once in Washington. She says he was a charming little fellow, in a velvet suit with a lace collar. She just can't believe the stories."

"Well, everyone else in Richmond believes them," Vesta assured her. "They're bringing his body to Richmond, and I heard one woman say when they do she's going to go and spit on it!"

Cinda pressed her hands to her temples, and she said wearily: "I think the worst thing about war is the way it makes credulous idiots out of silly women, and out of the men who stay at home and do no fighting. Mrs. Davis says Colonel Dahlgren and his men called at Secretary Seddon's home on the way to Richmond; and Mrs. Seddon gave him a glass of blackberry wine and reminded him that she and his mother were schoolmates, and that his father was one of her old beaux. Yet if those silly orders are genuine, Secretary Seddon was one of those they meant to kill."

"Don't you believe they're genuine?"

"Oh I don't know. You can be sure of one thing, the South will always believe they are. Even if they are genuine, we're at war, and I suppose they had a right to burn Richmond and kill Mr. Davis if they could; but I can't believe even a stupid Yankee would be silly enough to carry papers like that when he knew he might be captured."

Colonel Dahlgren's body came to Richmond Sunday afternoon by the York River Railroad. It lay in a baggage car till Wednesday before being secretly buried in an unmarked grave in Hollywood, and scores and hundreds crowded to see it, and for those three days every tongue was busy with the dead man and his deeds. At the hospital Cinda tended a wounded man who had been taken prisoner by Dahlgren's troops and who later escaped.

"He says they made a poor negro guide them, in Goochland," she told Vesta. "And when the river was so high they couldn't cross at the ford to which he led them, Colonel Dahlgren gave his own bridle rein to hang the negro with. Or so this man told me."

Vesta shivered. "They've put Colonel Dahlgren's crutch and his wooden leg on exhibition at the *Whig* office!"

Cinda cried: "Oh surely not!"

"Yes." Vesta said in a lower tone: "And Mama, the men who killed him stripped off his clothes, and they cut off one of his fingers to get a ring he was wearing. Aunt Tilda told me. Mr. Streean saw the body."

"That might have been done by any blackguard, North or South," Cinda commented. "That's not so horrible, somehow, as keeping his wooden leg on show. And there'll be people who will go to see it!"

The hubbub of these happenings had begun to die down before at the week's end Trav came home. He stopped at the house on Fifth Street, and Vesta and Cinda welcomed him with a surge of happiness and with eager questions.

"I'm just off the train," he said. "General Longstreet came to consult with General Lee and wanted my company."

"Oh, bring him for dinner tomorrow," Cinda urged. "All of you come."

"I'll tell him." Trav hesitated. "I haven't seen Enid yet. Are they all well?"

"Just as you left them."

Vesta thought her mother might have been intentionally evasive, for Aunt Enid certainly was changed. She said quickly: "All but Lucy, Uncle Trav! She's lovelier every day!"

He smiled. "How's Tilda—and her family?" Vesta told him of Dolly's marriage as though it were happy news, and Cinda added an affectionate word about Tilda, but he was not satisfied. "See anything of Darrell?" he asked.

The question surprised Vesta, but Cinda seemed unconscious of any strangeness in it. "No. He was at Chimneys for a while, but I don't think he's been in Richmond."

Vesta added: "He was at Chimneys when Uncle Tony was shot."

"Shot?" Trav was startled.

"Yes. He's all right now, though."

"Who shot him?"

"It was a boy." Vesta explained: "Someone had been stealing out of the smoke house, and Uncle Tony set a trap gun, and it was a woman named Mrs. Blandy, and it killed her."

"Ed Blandy's wife?" Trav came strongly to his feet.

"Why, I think so."

"My God!" Then in quick apology. "I'm sorry. But—Ed's my good friend. I wouldn't have had that happen. I'd rather be shot myself! Who shot Tony?"

"Why, her little boy, when Uncle Tony took her body home."

Trav nodded sorrowfully. "That must have been Eddie. He isn't as old as Lucy. I wonder who's taking care of those children. Ed's in the army." He shook his head. "Oh, that's too bad. I wish I could go down there."

He asked more questions, till they had told him the little they knew. They agreed, after he was gone on to Clay Street, that he looked well; but Vesta commented: "It's funny he came to see us before he went home."

"Well, after all, Enid's there." Cinda's tone was dry with dislike, and Vesta laughed.

"Now, Mama, you say too many cutting things just to be clever. Aunt Enid's all right! Shame on you!"

"I despise her."

"Maybe if you didn't she'd be nicer! Everybody's nicer if you like them and tell them so." And next day when they met Trav and Enid and the children on Grace Street on the way to church, Vesta put her own precept into practice, insisting they must come to dinner after the service. Enid eagerly agreed.

Vesta counted fourteen generals in the congregation that morning, and General Longstreet was among them, so he too came to dinner. Cinda spoke of Cousin Louisa, and of the baby General Longstreet had not yet seen.

"But I mean to, before I return to East Tennessee," he assured them. "Louisa intended to go to Augusta for the cold weather. I've some cousins there. But she wasn't well enough to travel, so she's still in Petersburg; but I shall send her off to Augusta. The fighting this summer will come nearer Richmond, make living harder here; but the war hasn't touched them down in Georgia."

"I've wanted to see her," Cinda said. "But even Petersburg seems a long journey now. I can understand her dreading a trip all the way to Georgia." And she asked: "You think things will be hard this summer?"

He nodded. "We can't keep all the holes stopped, and the Yankees are pressing in everywhere. Down in Mississippi, the little town where my sisters live is the state capital now. The legislature, the Governor, the state archives, everything has been moved from Jackson to Macon." He added thoughtfully: "It might be wisdom if Richmond too were given up, if we drew our armies nearer together so they could support one another."

Vesta saw her mother's eyes shadow, and she urged: "But, General, you've done some good in East Tennessee, haven't you?"

Longstreet chuckled. "Oh yes, we've been in General Grant's beard. He hated to waste the time and effort necessary to crush us, but we've kept three times our number of Yankees occupied."

"Was the winter hard?"

"No. No, we had a secure position at Bull's Gap, and a rich countryside to draw on. General Lee tells me his army has been on short rations all winter; but since we didn't have to depend on Colonel Northrop, we were well fed. And we've burned just enough powder to keep the men interested."

He left at once after dinner, but when he had gone they heard from Trav that these months had not been so idyllic as the General suggested. "He's tried two or three times to resign," he said, and to Cinda's question: "Why, mostly disgust with General Bragg. Bragg would have lost Chickamauga if General Longstreet hadn't driven ahead on his own responsibility. He was great, that day. Some of the European officers with the army thought his tactical formations were wonderful."

Cinda smiled. "What do you know about tactical formations?" Her tone was affectionate.

"Not much," he confessed. "I'm just telling you what others said. But after the battle President Davis came out there and called all the generals into council and asked General Longstreet to say what he thought of General Bragg."

"Right in front of General Bragg?"

Trav nodded. "I suppose Mr. Davis thought no one would dare criticize General Bragg to his face, but General Longstreet doesn't scare easily. He said he thought General Bragg would be a lot more useful somewhere else."

"Good for him!" Vesta cried, but Cinda asked:

"Hasn't Cousin Jeems had some trouble with his own generals?"

"Yes," Trav admitted, and he added honestly: "General Longstreet didn't agree with General Lee at Gettysburg, but he hasn't much patience when his own subordinates disagree with him."

Enid laughed. "I'm surprised you admit he has any faults at all."

Trav looked at her briefly. "Why, I think everyone has faults, but I think he has fewer than most men."

Lucy said happily: "Well, I just love him! He always makes me feel he likes me lots. I suppose that's why."

Cinda asked their errand in Richmond, and Trav said the General had come to discuss with General Lee plans for the spring campaign. "He's urging that we strengthen the western armies and march into Kentucky. I believe he's right. We might do something there."

Vesta, listening, thought men never wearied of warfare and of war talk. Last summer, after the fierce shock at Gettysburg had left both armies so dazed that there had been since then no major action in the East, she had been secretly sure the war was lost; but now Uncle Trav seemed to look forward to new conflicts with confidence as high as ever. She remembered three years ago, and two years ago, and last year, when each success seemed to promise final victory till news from the West, or from Sharpsburg, or from Pennsylvania, shattered hope again. Uncle Trav was hopeful now; but hope was so easy—and so vain.

Trav stayed in Richmond till the midweek following. Longstreet, after his business here was done, went to Petersburg to see Mrs. Longstreet and his new son and Garland before returning to Tennessee; and Trav waited to go back with him. He told Cinda and Vesta that Longstreet's proposals for a spring campaign toward Kentucky had been negatived.

"I suppose President Davis will never agree to anything if Longstreet favors it; so probably we'll be back in Virginia with General Lee pretty soon. If we are, I ought to be here again before long."

"I hope so," Vesta told him affectionately. She felt that he hated to leave, and wishing to please him she said: "I like Lucy so much, Uncle Trav. She's a darling girl."

His eyes lighted. "She seems wonderful to me." He spoke to Cinda:

"Enid's pretty lonesome. I wish you'd see as much of her as you can, sort of keep her contented."

Cinda hesitated. "Enid's hard to—content, Trav."

"Well, she thinks a lot of you. And she doesn't seem to have any special friends."

"Does she see anything of her mother?"

Vesta saw him color with slow anger. "No! I should hope not!" He hesitated, and looked at Vesta, and she suspected her presence prevented his saying what he might have said. "No, they don't see each other."

When he was gone it occurred to Vesta that he had not asked for any news of Faunt. "Did you notice, Mama?"

"I didn't, no," Cinda confessed. "It's so long since any of us have seen Faunt, he might as well be dead."

"We used to be such a close-together family," Vesta remembered wistfully. "All of us together for Christmas, and for Grandma's birthdays, and at every excuse we could find. We're pretty badly separated now. Is it just the war, Mama?"

Cinda looked at her for a hesitant moment, and Vesta had again, as she had had with Uncle Trav, the feeling that there was something she was not to be told; but the older woman said wearily: "I suppose everything that happens nowadays comes one way or another from the war." She leaned back in her chair. Her eyes closed, and her voice was low. "War's a madness. It drives men to self-destruction, like the Gadarene swine in the Bible. But war's only the beginning of misery, Vesta. This war will leave sores that will not heal in your lifetime, or your children's. When boys fight, they're often better friends afterward; but it's not so with nations." She said in a dull voice: "You see, when boys fight it's just in sudden anger. But when nations go to war, everyone has to be taught to hate, so they will kill and kill and kill."

"Like Tommy," Vesta murmured. "But he never learned to hate. He wasn't even carrying a gun when they killed him. He never killed anyone."

"Men don't like to hate," Cinda assented. "I think men are naturally friendly. But women have a gift for hating. All of us women in the South are proud to hate the North, and I suppose it's the same in the North, with the Northern women. They tell us lies about the Yankees, and they tell the Yankees lies about us, and we believe the lies." She shook her head. "Some blackguard cut off Colonel Dahlgren's finger, so Northern women will be told that all Southern soldiers mutilate dead Yankees—and they'll believe it. When one Yankee bullies a Southern woman, we're told that all Yankees are cruel monsters, and we believe it. So they hate us and we hate them. Of course, when we're conquered they'll stop hating us; but we'll go on hating them. North and South will be one country, but we'll hate the North and do all we can to hurt her, even though it hurts us too, as long as I live and as long as you live and as long as your children live."

Vesta thought of little Tommy, and she thought of other children who would one day be born to her. "Does it have to be so, Mama?"

Cinda for a moment did not speak. Then her eyes opened. "There is one man who will make the hating end with the war, if he can. I pray to God he can."

"Who?"

"President Lincoln."

Vesta felt a deep astonishment. "Why, Mama, you sound as though you—liked him. You used to abuse him terribly!"

Cinda's eyes held hers for a long time, as though in deep reflection; but she only said at last: "I've felt differently since I saw him. He's a great, good, compassionate, tender man."

While March drifted away, their days were filled with little things. Barbara wrote from Raleigh that people in North Carolina wanted to make peace. "Mr. Holden, the editor of the paper here, is running for Governor against Mr. Vance on a peace platform, and Governor Vance wants President Davis to try to make up with the North." She said the North Carolina mountains were full of deserters. "They caught twenty-two deserters in Yankee uniforms in a fight at Kinston last month, and they hanged them all before Judge Preston could turn them loose. Governor Vance says President Davis sha'n't suspend *habeas corpus* here as long as Judge Preston says he mustn't. I don't know what *habeas corpus* is, but there's lots of talk about it."

The babies, she said, were thriving. Virgil, though he was not yet two years old, was a perfect chatterbox, and little Burr was a buster. She hated to think of them all in Richmond with nothing to eat. Why didn't they come to Raleigh? "Governor Vance won't let the impress-ment men seize things here. He says North Carolina has a right to take care of herself."

The papers day by day reported from all over the South a like re-sistance to impressment, refusal to recognize the suspension of the writ of *habeas corpus,* anger at the more rigorous conscription law. Each state, jealous of its own rights, hindered or obstructed the central Gov-ernment, and Vesta cried indignantly:

"But, Mama, how do they think we can ever win the war unless we all work together?"

"Oh, the South has always believed in states' rights," Cinda re-minded her. "But unless the states give up some of their rights, there won't be any South by and by."

Late that month a thousand Southern soldiers returned from North-ern prisons. They arrived on Monday. The day before, at St. Paul's and in the other churches, the ministers asked everyone who could do so to send provisions to Capitol Square to feed them. Cinda and Vesta, enlisted by Tilda, helped manage that welcome. President Davis made a speech to the returned men and promised they would soon be with their old comrades in the army; and Vesta, seeing among them many who were no more than boys, wondered whether they were as glad of this as they dutifully pretended to be. When in the confusion after-ward she came near Mr. Davis and he bowed to her, she asked his opinion.

"Do they want to go back in the army, do you think?"

"They must go back," the President said coldly. "We need every man."

"Can you feed them? The army's hungry all the time, even now."

He smiled bitterly. "My dear young lady, it's easy to feed hungry men. They'd as soon eat rats as squirrels. At Vicksburg, mules were considered first-rate fare. Of course we can't spare our mules now; but our soldiers will be fed!"

She was furious at his heartlessness and thought General Longstreet was right in hating him; but when she repeated this conversation to her mother, Cinda said: "He's desperate, you know, Vesta. He knows we're lost. Be a little patient with the wretched man."

"Wretched!" Vesta protested. "The poor prisoners were the wretched ones, so hungry and weak and dazed. I don't think they ought to be made to fight again. They've done their share."

"I suppose no man's done his share as long as he's still alive," Cinda said in a low tone. "There's no end to it, you know."

They had that week a long letter from Jenny. Affairs at the Plains went well, she said, except that it was hard to find clothes for the people. "The neighbors tell me you can buy silks and laces at the Bee sales in Charleston when the blockaders come in, but the blockaders don't bring calico and linsey-woolsey and things fit for work clothes. We get some cotton from the Macon Mills, and we've put spinning wheels and hand looms to work; but they're too slow to keep everyone supplied." Needles were scarce, she said; and buttons too, though gourd seeds were a useful substitute.

"I can send her some needles," Vesta declared. "I've seven· and I only need a big one and a middle-sized and a little one."

Jenny told them the news of Columbia and of Camden. "There's a great to-do because General Lee wants our cavalry to go to Virginia," she wrote. "Charleston's getting up a petition of protest to send to Porcher Miles. They say if the cavalry goes, the Yankees will sail right into the harbor, as though the cavalry would be of any use against the Yankee fleet. Or for anything else, for that matter, as long as our bold young cavaliers insist on staying here. They spend their days riding around the country, and every farmer hates to see them come along, because they always want his likely horses. They wear their own horses out, they're always in such a hurry to get nowhere. Of course none of them has ever been within miles of any Yankee, except Yankee prisoners. They call themselves our protectors, but they're furious at the notion of going off to Virginia where they might have to do some real protecting. I hope General Lee insists. We'll be well rid of them."

She asked for news of Dolly, and Vesta said in surprise: "Why, I wrote her about Dolly's being married."

"So did I," Cinda assented. "But you never know what will happen to a letter in the mails nowadays. We don't seem able to manage so simple a thing as a post office, much less a war."

They were to hear more about that matter of the South Carolina cavalry. On the last Tuesday in March, when an easterly gale drove sheets of rain blindingly through the streets, Rollin Lyle appeared at the house. He was soaked through, and Vesta and Cinda made him change into some of Brett's clothes while old June took his uniform to dry. Then there was time for talk, and he said he was going to Charleston, where the Seventh South Carolina Cavalry was assembling to come to Virginia.

"I've transferred to the cavalry," he explained. "And I'll be in Major Trenholm's squadron, with some of my friends from the coast toward Savannah. I've always wanted to be in the cavalry. I've carried a pair of spurs in my knapsack for three years now. So when this chance came, I asked for it."

"I'm so glad you got it, if you want it." Vesta thought there was something new in Rollin. Perhaps Dolly's marriage had released him from long bondage. He was his own man now, with a high head.

"Why, I was lucky. I got mad at the right time." And he explained: "I was riding one day with some cavalry officers, and we took a few fences and came to a bad one, on a hillside, with slippery mud for the approach. It was pretty high, and they decided not to take it. I suppose I wanted to show off. Anyway, I tried it, but my mare slipped in the mud. She made the fence all right, but she came down so hard the girth broke, and the saddle and I went over her head." He grinned. "It must have knocked me senseless, or made me too mad to be sensible, because I didn't even notice her saddle was gone. I vaulted on her back and took the fence without any saddle at all; and they were all laughing, and that made me angrier than ever. They said they were laughing to see a man jump better without a saddle than with one; so I threw the saddle on her back without any girth and took the fence twice. They said the cavalry needed men who could ride like me." He colored. "Guess I'm bragging!"

"I like your brags," Vesta told him affectionately. "You've never bragged enough to suit me, Rollin."

He would stay the night, take the early train. When Cinda left these two together, Vesta to her own surprise found herself a little ill at ease, groped for any word at all. "I'm sorry I wasn't here that night you left the note, Rollin. Did you find everyone well at home?" Her own carefully polite tone amused her. How ridiculous, to make conversation as though they were strangers!

"Why, they've had some trouble," he said, yet so abstractedly that she knew he was thinking of something else; but he went on: "Papa's had a hard time keeping them from conscripting his overseers. Last year he sold about a thousand tierces of rice to the Government or to North Carolina or South Carolina, and five hundred more in January, and he's made four or five hundred bushels of salt. His taxes were over five thousand dollars. But even if the Yankees let him alone, he can't keep it up without overseers."

"I shouldn't think so," Vesta agreed.

"And of course negroes keep running off to the Yankees," Rollin told her. "And he can't work the swamps along the coast. He's working too hard. Mama's worried about him." He said without a pause: "I wanted to see you that night too." He looked toward the hall as though to be sure they were alone. "I was pretty excited, Vesta." He hesitated, his color high. "I'd seen Dolly in Wilmington."

"Oh?" She had not expected this. "In Wilmington?" How stupid I sound, she thought; repeating things like a ninny.

"Have you seen her?"

"No. She's married, you know. She's living down there."

"I know. Bruce Kenyon. Julian knew him when they were cadets at the Institute in Charlotte."

"Yes, he told us." Julian had said Kenyon was a tall, easily embarrassed youngster. "He just couldn't believe Dolly'd marry him, after all the beaux she's had. Julian says he's years younger than Dolly."

"A year or two." There was something guarded in Rollin's tone; and she prompted him.

"How did you happen to see her?"

Slowly he found words. "Well, I was on my way back to duty." He grinned. "You see, I had mumps while I was at home, so I was late starting back; and our train kept breaking down, so I stayed in Wilmington over Sunday."

"They say it's exciting there."

"I guess it is. The town's full of blockade-runners and speculators and English officers and thieves and gamblers, and everybody has his pockets full of money. I went to the Corner Celler and gave two months' pay for a dozen oysters. Prices are worse there than they are here. Gold's four hundred for one; but everybody seems to have plenty of money. There'd been two big auctions there that week. One was to sell the cargoes of three ships, the *Pet* and the *Lucy* and the *Wild Dayrell.*" His tone hardened. "I saw the lists of things to be sold. Nothing the army needs—just luxury goods. Reading the lists made me so mad I added up some of the figures. Ninety-one bales of prints; and I don't know how many of broadcloth and alpaca and cassimere and mohair and flannel and satinet. And clothes: shirts, handkerchiefs, thread, buttons, pins, needles, shawls, gloves, ribbons. There were eighty-seven cases of shoes. And hogsheads of crushed sugar and coffee and tea and vinegar and oil and soap and candles and salt; and a whole shipload of liquor. Six casks of brandy, and eighty casks of Bourbon, and ten half-pipes besides, and eight pipes of gin, and eight hundred cases of wine and ale. And drugs, of course. But not a gun, or a pound of lead, or a blanket, or anything for the army! The blockaders can make more money bringing in luxury goods."

She said gently. "You were telling me about Dolly, Rollin."

"Oh, yes! I got so mad I forgot. Well, I ate my oysters and read the paper, and I'd about decided to go see Miss Eliza Vane in *Lucretia Borgia* when Bevin Ross came in. He said the play was pretty unpleasant and the afterpiece, *Nan the Good-for-nothing,* wasn't as spicy as it sounded, and I'd better come down to Fort Fisher with him. He's an aide to Colonel Lamb.

"So we started, but we had a time getting there. It was a fine warm day in Wilmington and we had a fair breeze most of the way, but there was a hard blow coming up and I thought we'd swamp before we got to the Fort."

He hesitated, but Vesta did not prompt him. "Some of the blockaders had anchored in the lee of the Fort to ride out the storm," he said at last. "Colonel Lamb always entertains the captains when they can come ashore, and some of them were there for dinner. Colonel Lamb's a mighty handsome man. He wears a little chin whisker and a mustache, and he has big dark eyes and a slender, long face. He's as beautiful as a woman."

He paused again, and Vesta saw his color rise. He looked at her appealingly. "I probably ought not to tell you. I haven't told anyone else."

"You can tell me," she said, and wondered why she was trembling.

"It's you I want to tell," he said; and his tone made her pulse quicken. "You know how I've always been about Dolly? In love with her. Or thinking I was." She did not trust herself to speak; and he said, almost hurriedly: "Well, she was there, at the Fort, with a captain named Pew."

"Yes, I've met him."

"There were two other ladies," he explained. "Mrs. Tonne of New Orleans, and an English lady who had come to Wilmington to join her son. Dolly was ever so gay, more so than I've ever seen her. She told me that when she got to Wilmington with Jenny, on the way to the Plains, Darrell and Captain Pew took her to the theatre, and then Darrell persuaded her to go to Nassau with them——"

Vesta asked quietly: "Was Darrell there that night, at the Fort?"

"No, she said he'd gone up to Wilmington in a little sailing boat. Dolly had refused to go with him. She said she wouldn't risk anything smaller than the *Dragonfly*. That's Captain Pew's ship." Rollin met her eyes. "And Vesta, she told me she was going to marry Captain Pew."

Vesta was about to exclaim: "Captain Pew!" But she caught herself in time. No matter how astonished you were, you need not turn into an echo! "Really?" she said instead. That was stupid enough; but she could think of nothing else to say.

He nodded. "Yes. That was after dinner. She and I were talking, and he came to join us; and she put her hand on his arm and said they were going to be married." He hesitated. "So I said he was to be congratulated, and he bowed; but I thought he was surprised and angry. Then he said they must bid us goodnight and go aboard the *Dragonfly* so they'd be ready to catch the morning tide if the wind moderated, and Dolly said she hadn't half finished her visit with me, and couldn't I come with them; and he said there wasn't a vacant cabin, but that I could join them next morning for the trip up river."

He drew a deep breath, and Vesta felt her pulse thud in her throat as he went on.

"So at first light I got a boatman to take me out to the *Dragonfly*." He held her eyes. "I'd already realized something, Vesta. I'd realized that I was glad Dolly was going to be married. I'd always sort of imagined I was wild about her; but now I was glad she was going to marry someone else."

He waited as though expecting her to speak, but she only nodded, as though this were a matter of course, and he said hastily: "Well, Bruce Kenyon was at dinner at the Fort that night, and he was going home on furlough, so next morning when he heard I was going up river on the *Dragonfly* he went out with me to ask if he could go along, and Captain Pew said certainly."

"Did Dolly know him?"

"He'd never seen her till the night before, but she bowled him over. You could see that." She nodded, and he went on. "Crossing the bar was pretty exciting. There was a line of waves and foam, and it looked as though we'd surely sink or something. We did scrape the bottom once, between waves; but then we were over, and we just whizzed up the river." In a graver tone he continued: "But I could see that Dolly and Captain Pew had had a quarrel about something; and on the way up the river she led me off to the back end of the ship, and Bruce Kenyon came after us, and she laughed at him in her prettiest way, and told him to let us be alone."

Vesta watched him, intent on every word, half-guessing what he would say. He blurted it out at last. "Vesta—she wanted me to marry her."

Vesta found herself folding and refolding a pleat of her skirt. She watched her hands, drawing the fabric between her fingers, trying to control the great confusion in her mind. "But she'd said she was going to marry Captain Pew?"

"That's what I told her," Rollin agreed. "But she said I surely couldn't believe she would marry a blackguard." He spoke heavily, slowly. "I think she wanted me to call Captain Pew out. I'm sure she did. But I didn't do it. I wasn't afraid—that wasn't it."

"I know, Rollin."

"I just never wanted to see her again! I wanted to jump overboard, or run, or anything to get away from her. I'm ashamed of myself;

but—well, that was the way I felt." And he added miserably: "I didn't say anything, but I guess she knew."

"Did she really come straight out and ask you, Rollin?"

"Yes. Oh, she did it in a way that she could pretend was just a joke. After she sent Kenyon off she said: 'You know what I wish, Rollin?' And I said: 'What?' And she said: 'I wish you and I were going to be married in Wilmington this morning!'" He colored. "And then she waited, and all I could think of was to laugh and ask her what about Captain Pew."

"Did she seem frightened?"

"No, just sort of joking, but furious underneath." He added: "But I've thought since then that maybe she really was frightened."

"What happened?"

"Why, she said he was a blackguard, and waited, and I didn't say anything; and she laughed and said she had always thought I was crazy about her! I still didn't say anything, and then she said: 'Well, you can never say you didn't have your chance, Rollin!'

"And then she went away along the deck and I just stood there, and when we docked she took Bruce Kenyon's arm and walked off along Front Street with her head in the air. I was behind them. There are houses and yards and picket fences and trees along Front Street, and she and Mr. Kenyon were holding hands and she was laughing up at him. I turned off up Market and I didn't see her again."

"Did they get married right away?"

"I don't know. I tried to find Darrell. He wasn't at the Carolina Hotel, or at the old Purcell House; and no one had seen him. I didn't know about her being married till somebody brought the news to camp here. Everyone knew Dolly, of course."

Vesta bit her lip. "No one knows where Darrell is," she murmured.

"Was it all right for me to tell you?"

"Of course, Rollin."

He asked in a hushed voice: "Vesta—do you know why I wanted to tell you?"

She knew; yet there was in this moment soft panic in her, and she was not ready to let him know how much she knew. She rose, suddenly poised and mature and infinitely older than he. "It's time we retired," she said. "Don't be worried, Rollin. Not about anything. Come."

He followed her in silence. She turned out the gas and they went up the stairs together; and she felt him silent and shamed behind her, like a guilty boy. So at the stair head she relented a little.

"Don't blame yourself, Rollin," she said. "If Dolly is in trouble, she made it for herself." And she smiled at him and said: "And I'm ever so glad you don't think you're in love with her any more."

Thus, for then, they parted.

11

TRAV through the dreary winter in Tennessee never long freed himself from the shamed memory of his violence to Enid; and he came to Richmond in March not as a stern and unforgiving husband but hungry to be forgiven. Lucy's rapturous welcome and Peter's proud gladness warmed and comforted him; old April laughed through tears to see him again; but when Enid came downstairs and he turned to face her, it was like a small boy expecting punishment.

She met him with a confusing, humble sweetness; with a cheek for him to kiss; with a gentle word. "Why, Trav, how nice! We didn't expect you." Trav was grateful to her for making this reunion so easy. As long as the children were with them, asking many questions, eager for his answers, he was safe; but to put off the inevitable hour when he and she would be alone, he made the stories he told the children as long and as exciting as possible. There was little to tell except of cold and snow, but when Peter said in some disappointment that being a soldier didn't sound very exciting, Trav spoke of the guerrilla bands active in Tennessee.

"A lot of people there are for the Union, of course; and deserters from both armies hide in the mountains, and there are gangs of Yankees and Southerners all mixed together, and they go around robbing and burning and killing."

"Why didn't you just hang them?" Peter demanded.

"Well, sometimes we tried to catch them. Once we found a woman and her children crying in the snow by the ashes of her house. That gang had what the leader called a 'cash rope.' They hung her husband up by the neck to make him tell where his money was; but he didn't have any money, so he couldn't tell; so they bored a hole in his skull with a gimlet, trying to make him tell. When that killed him, they burned the house."

"Did you catch them?"

"Matter of fact, we did," Trav said, and he laughed. "That was funny, in one way. We found out where the leader lived, and sent some soldiers to surround the house and search it. We didn't catch him in the house, but one of the soldiers was sitting on a box out in the yard and he heard a noise underneath the box; so he got up off it, and the box moved. The man had a tunnel from inside his cabin so he could crawl out and get away, and the box covered the end of the tunnel. So we got him."

"Well, did you hang him?" Peter urged. Enid protested that Peter should go to bed, that he would not sleep a wink after such stories; but Peter pleaded till Trav assured him that that particular bushwhacker was well and duly hanged.

When Trav and Enid were at last alone, Trav thought they were like strangers newly met who seek to discover shared interests, mutual acquaintances, anything that will serve as foundation for commonplaces. They talked for a long time; and he found himself protracting this conversation, needlessly elaborating every incident.

For when this polite talk ended, they would go upstairs. What then? He could not answer this question, but at last it grew so late that to sit here longer was absurd. Enid was the first to rise; he followed her without a word. But in the upper hall, when they reached the door of their room and she laid her hand on the knob, he surrendered to his longing for confession and for absolution.

"Enid," he said humbly, "I've damned myself a thousand times for striking you."

When he spoke, her back was toward him; she was just opening her door. For a moment she did not move. It was as though she were still listening to the words he had spoken. But then she turned, at first slowly and finally with an eager, hungry haste; and she threw herself into his arms and her lips pressed his in a fierce, demanding rapture. "I loved it," she told him, in a husky whisper. "I loved it, Trav. I always love you most when you're mad!" Lips hot on his, eyes laughing up at him. "That's why I torment you, darling! To make you mad! I hate you when you're calm!"

When Trav set out on the return to Tennessee, he was ready to believe that his life with Enid would be hereafter untroubled and serene. He joined General Longstreet in Petersburg, and they went by the South Side Railroad to Lynchburg, and by the Virginia and Tennessee to Greenville and Longstreet's headquarters. Trav wished he might break the journey long enough to ride across the mountains to Martinston ·and Chimneys; and he confessed this desire to General Longstreet, telling him the sorry story of Mrs. Blandy's death. "Her husband's my good friend. I'd like to see if there's—anything I can do for them."

But Longstreet shook his head. "It would take several days, and you might have trouble. The mountains are full of bushwhackers." He chuckled. "A whacker behind every bush. No, I can't spare you, Currain. I expect we'll be moving back into Virginia presently."

"I suppose so. As soon as the roads are dry." Trav gave up thought of Martinston.

"Yes. And 'Lys Grant won't wait longer than he must before putting his army on the move. If we sent a force toward Kentucky, we might break up his plans for the summer; and if we could make Grant waste the summer, Lincoln might be defeated in the fall elections. I proposed this, but the decision is against me."

"You think a move into Kentucky would give us hope of winning?"

"I don't think it with my head, no," the big man admitted. "If we could concentrate our forces, much might be done; but our armies are scattered. Each state insists that its own borders be defended, so we have to keep an army in South Carolina, and another in Georgia, and another in North Carolina. We waste our strength by companies and regiments. There's no victory in such a course. So my head says there's no chance remaining." His voice sang. "But, Currain, my heart doesn't agree! The spring of the year always stirs my blood. There are battles ahead, and there's always hope in battle."

At headquarters they found that during their absence the condition of the little army, as far as clothing and shoes were concerned, was much improved; but now rations were short. Hunger meant desertions. The day after his return, riding to inspect the works on the heights above Bull's Gap, Trav saw in the valley below him men drawn up in a hollow square, and he heard the rattle of the volley as some culprit died.

He rode on, saddened by the sight, toward a shoulder of the hills whence he could look far across the rolling countryside. The day was fine and clear and deceptively warm; one of those spring days which tempt fruit trees into premature blossoming, just as a coquette's smiles invite advances which a moment later she repels. Off to the east, the mass of the Great Smokies notched the sky, and north and northeastward the rampart of Clinch Mountain marched into Virginia. General Lee and the Army of Northern Virginia lay far away in that direction in their camps along the Rapidan; and presently Longstreet's First Corps would move to the railroad and go to join Lee for the summer campaign.

Trav returned to headquarters still thinking of the poor fellow who had been shot that morning for his crime against the laws of war. In the two or three weeks that followed he had twice to serve on courts-martial; but the charges were minor ones; disobedience, theft and pilfering, insubordination, drunkenness, sleeping on the post. So the penalties imposed were trivial; confinement, ball and chain, the barrel shirt, bucking. The punishment might fit the crime. For insubordination, one culprit had to stand on the head of a barrel an hour a day for a week, reading aloud the Articles of War. For drunkenness another was required to ride a rail without a saddle while he was drummed three times around camp. A man who slept on post was ordered to wear day and night for a month an iron collar with spikes sharp enough to deny him any but the sleep of complete exhaustion.

Longstreet himself this winter and spring had been diligent to keep up the morale of the army. Once when they captured a train at Bean's Station and found a car loaded with coffee, he directed that after fifteen hundred pounds had been set aside for the sick, all the rest be distributed among the private soldiers, with none for the staff mess or the officers. He made regular visits to the hospitals and to the regimental bivouacs, doing whatever was possible for the greater comfort of the men. When the ground began to dry, he instituted drills by company and regiment and brigade and by division. Captain Black-ford's charming young wife had come on from Lynchburg to spend these winter months with her husband here; and when Longstreet one day ordered a march-past she sat with him to receive the salutes of the regiments; and she was so lovely that every man braced his shoulders as he came under her eye. Other wives were here for short stays or for long, so headquarters was pleasantly gay. As the time drew near when the army would have work to do, Trav thought the First Corps was at fighting pitch again.

Late in March came the expected orders to prepare to join Lee's army; and as though the orders were a signal, the weather took a turn for the worse. They marched through mud and a pelting snow to Zollicoffer, to wait there for the cars; and on the seventh of April the brigades began to entrain. But there were delays, for cars were scarce and the railroad was in precarious condition. Not till the thir-teenth did Longstreet and the staff reach Lynchburg.

There Captain Blackford had the ill news of his father's death, and he asked permission to stay a few days and wind up Mr. Blackford's affairs. "He worked himself to death," he told Trav. "He was in charge of funding all the currency under the new law; and trying to satisfy people, and explaining the law, and telling them why they couldn't buy six percents after the law went into effect, and making them take four percents, and keeping all the figures straight was more than he could stand. And he was handling money for a lot of his friends, so he had to watch the tobacco market, too."

Trav remembered regretfully that Mr. Blackford had managed some of his own transactions; so he had contributed to the burden the old man bore.

Captain Blackford stayed behind, but Longstreet and Trav and the others of the staff boarded the cars to go on to Charlottesville; and on the twenty-second they proceeded to Gordonsville, and the First Corps established itself at Cobham Station. Sunday, Brett rode over the few miles from Barboursville, where the Third Howitzers were in camp, to hear from Trav the latest news of loved ones in Richmond and to ask many questions about the winter in Tennessee.

Trav said that once Longstreet's little army was settled for the winter the men were able to be comfortable. "But the retreat from in front of Knoxville was a hard business. We were short of everything. The beef we got was so poor that there wasn't any grease left on top of the water you boiled it in. We had to take the shoes and the nails off dead horses to shoe the ones still alive, and we killed our own worn-out animals to get their shoes. The Yankees threw their dead horses into the river, and we'd watch for the carcasses coming down and drag them ashore and rip off their shoes. That was our worst pinch."

Brett nodded understandingly. "We can't get along without horses, but they're a lot of trouble."

"It was better after we went into winter quarters," Trav said. "Major Moses found plenty to feed us. He seized the account books of the mills and traced out the wheat that way; and he got bacon by seizing flocks of sheep and trading two pounds of mutton that wasn't fit to eat for one pound of bacon that was."

"That shouldn't have been necessary. You were in friendly country."

"We were supposed to be, but it didn't work out that way." Trav added thoughtfully: "We're going to miss Major Moses. He's gone to Georgia to see if he can get supplies for the army."

"The Georgia regiments say there's plenty there."

"Major Moses will get whatever there is," Trav predicted. "He knew of one district commissary who runs a distillery in Macon and seizes corn in the name of the Government and uses it to make whiskey and sells it for his own profit; and he impresses wheat or flour or tobacco at Government prices and ships it to Mobile and sells it for his own account. Major Moses plans to seize his shipments in transit."

"The Major sounds like a good man."

"He is. I wish we had more like him. They'd keep this army fed." Trav smiled. "You look as though you needed a square meal yourself, Brett."

"I was sick in December," Brett admitted. "But a month at home straightened me out." He said the Howitzers, except for an encounter with Dahlgren's Yankee horsemen on their way to Richmond, had had a quiet spring. "We're shorthanded, though. A lot of men are away on recruit furloughs."

Trav had not heard the phrase. "Recruit furloughs?"

"Yes, we're desperate for men, so up to a month ago, if a man brought in a recruit, General Lee gave him thirty days furlough as a reward."

"I see. We're short too. The First Corps had twenty thousand men at Gettysburg last summer; but with Pickett still in North Carolina, we haven't half that, now. And Hood's gone, and McLaws; and Law's brigade was left in Tennessee." He added: "They've been ordered back to us with Law in command; but the General says he'll arrest General Law again if he comes, threatens to resign if Richmond insists on sending him."

"Lee will support Longstreet, won't he?"

"Yes, they can't spare Longstreet."

Brett made sure they were not overheard. "How does he feel about things?"

"He's all right now, thinks we'll do good work this summer. But he was discouraged last winter. He opened a correspondence with General Schofield; thought they might initiate something that would lead toward honorable peace. He still thinks the armies will have to make the peace, that the politicians got us into war and now don't know how to get us out."

Brett nodded. "I suppose the soldiers will have to keep on dying till the politicians are satisfied."

"I wonder why they don't all desert, Brett. Not five men out of a hundred have anything to gain, even if we win."

"Oh, some of them enjoy the excitement. What would they be doing if they weren't in the army?"

"Working on their farms. Happy with their families."

Brett said thoughtfully: "Well, I suppose that's true of any war. The men who do the fighting have nothing to gain."

"How's Burr?"

"Oh, he's well. But he's ashamed to call himself a South Carolinian since the South Carolina cavalry regiments tried to avoid coming to this army. He was raging at them for cowards and renegades, last time I saw him."

"But he's well? That's the main thing."

"Yes. He's drawn fine by hard work, but he's well. Stuart's headquarters are at Orange Court House; and when Burr can he rides over to see me. But Stuart keeps his men pretty busy watching Meade's army."

"It's Grant's army now," Trav reminded him, and Brett asked:

"What does General Longstreet think of Grant?"

"Why, he says Grant will be hard to stop. He thinks we can beat him, but he says beating Grant won't stop him."

"Mosby's raising Cain behind Grant's lines," Brett reported. "I saw Faunt two weeks ago." Trav's jaw set. He could not forget what Enid had told him about Faunt and Mrs. Albion. For Faunt, who had always been the pattern of gentleness and valor, to involve himself in a shabby affair was base and shameful. Brett went on: "Mosby's handful of partisans manages to keep four or five thousand of the Yankee cavalry tied down to guarding their lines." He chuckled. "Faunt says he and Mosby are planning to go to Washington some time this month. Mosby sent Lincoln a lock of his hair and promised to call in person."

Trav grinned. "I expect Lincoln would be glad to see him; but what can Mosby do in Washington?"

"He has a friend there, an actor named Booth. Remember him? He was in Richmond at the time of the John Brown business."

Trav shook his head. "I was at Great Oak, didn't come to Richmond."

Brett nodded. "Well, anyway, Booth's hot for the South, sends morphine and medicines through the lines; and he wants to ride with Mosby on one of his raids." He spoke in dry distaste: "That's an ugly game they play, Trav; not much decency on either side. At Dranesville, a Yankee captain named Reed surrendered to Baron von Massow; but the Prussian neglected to disarm him, and the Yank shot him in the back. The Yankees consider Mosby's men guerrillas, and Faunt says he personally never takes prisoners." Trav met his eye, not speaking, and Brett said absently: "Faunt's not well, you know; he has lung trouble. He was sick last winter for weeks, stayed with friends."

"Where?"

"He didn't say."

Trav thought he could guess, but he did not speak his thought.

General Longstreet had his way about General Law. Lee supported Longstreet against the authorities in Richmond; and as a further mark of his esteem he came on the twenty-ninth to review the First Corps.

That day stirred Trav profoundly. The review was held in a broad and level valley along the South Anna river, near Green Springs; and the day was fine. Peters Mountain rose boldly a few miles to the westward, and through the gaps west of Gordonsville the summits of the Blue Ridge were pale against the distant sky. Before General Lee arrived, Longstreet's two divisions of infantry and General Alexander's battalion of artillery took formation. The fences had long since gone to feed campfires, so there were no obstacles to interfere with movement. The waiting lines faced a wood through which a country road approached the reviewing ground from the highway that led to Boswell Tavern; and Trav, in the interval after they were ready, watching them, felt his eyes sting and smart. There was in those silent ranks an expectancy that seemed to sing in the warm spring air.

He heard hoofbeats as General Lee at the head of his staff rode through the woodland toward where the road debouched on a knoll above the field. When the commanding general emerged from the wood, the bugles sounded, the cannons roared their salute. A light breeze bore the smoke away, and General Lee bared his head; and from the long lines of ragged men arose one hoarse glad shout, and then the shrill yipping yell that had been heard upon so many glorious battlefields. General Lee sat his horse and waited for a moment; and as he rode down toward his men a sudden silence swept them all, and silence lay across the sunny levels so that even on the heavy turf the hoofs were loud.

General Lee rode slowly the long length of the lines, so close that every man could see him plain and he could see every man; and the soft whipping of battle flags and the muffled thudding of hoofbeats were only an accent in the silence like a sacrament. Trav thought of Hill's corps and of Ewell's, waiting along the Rapidan; he thought of Grant's hosts poised upon the northern banks. Soon now these men here must dam with their bodies that oncoming flood of enemies: these tattered, bearded, grimed, half-starved thousands; these planters and small farmers and poor whites welded together into a flaming sword; these valiant ones, these loyal ones. This hour was like an absolution before the terrible affray.

He fell to wondering about the individuals in the ranks. Before they lost their identity, what was their way of life? This was a question the answer to which might be expressed in figures; and when after the review the men were dispersed to their camps again, Trav spent two or three days going from one company commander to another, checking muster rolls and questioning individuals. Before he was done he came to some conclusions; they might be faulty, but they were suggestive. At least six men out of ten called themselves farmers; but Trav, talking with them, guessed that fully half of these professed farmers were indolent men whose wives did most of the work upon the worthless acres where they made their slovenly homes. The rest were like his neighbors in Martinston; hard-working and self-respecting, but only one step above abject poverty. Of the men who were not farmers, most called themselves clerks or mechanics, and a few were students who had left the class room for the army. Companies like the Third Howitzers had doctors, teachers, lawyers; but Trav calculated that not five percent of this army were men of a station in life that matched his own. Certainly not five percent of them were of families that had ever owned a slave, or that would gain any fruits from victory.

The thought made his heart beat the more strongly, and intensified his pride in those thousands he had seen on parade, their worn gear polished, their uniforms as clean and as nearly whole as it was possible to make them, standing to be inspected by the commanding general. If this war bore no other fruit, certainly it had proved the dignity and the nobility of the ordinary man.

Yet he himself had in the past agreed with those who felt that the reins of government could only be trusted to aristocratic hands. He too had believed that wealth was a measure of a man's fitness for a voice in politics. In 1850, when the Virginia convention fought out the question of manhood suffrage as opposed to suffrage based on the ownership of property, Trav had been unquestioningly sure that unless a man owned land or slaves he had no right to vote; but during his years at Chimneys, though even among his neighbors at Martinston there were only a few whose political judgment he would trust, he had begun to suspect that he was wrong.

Now he was sure of it. The very men whom he had considered unfit to have a voice in public affairs were the backbone of the army now; and if this army was—as he believed—the finest group of soldiers ever brought together, it was these men who made it so.

Did this mean that he was coming to believe in the rule of the majority? No man in public life in the South trusted the majority; and the fact that President Lincoln had faith in the united wisdom of the common man, and said so, was one of the unadmitted reasons why Southern leaders hated him and refused allegiance to the nation that had elected him its head.

Yet Trav's own half-acceptance of this belief was now astonishingly comforting, giving him a peace of mind which for a long time he had not known. For if ordinary men could be trusted, then it did not greatly matter if their governments were overthrown; they would in time make better ones.

His thoughts turned to Ed Blandy. Ed's regiment, the Eleventh North Carolina, was in camp beyond Orange Court House; and Trav found time to ride that way. Lieutenant Colonel Martin, who had come into the command of the regiment, was a Virginian by birth; but he had before the war been a professor of mineralogy at the University of North Carolina. He was a bearded man who made Trav think of Stonewall Jackson, of grave demeanor with a frowning eye. His regiment, he told Trav, was far below its fighting strength; he himself was the only field officer left. "The Pennsylvania campaign weakened us so much we never recovered, and we were badly shot up at Bristoe Station last fall. We attacked what we thought was one Union corps and found two in front of us." He told Trav where to find J Company. "But I doubt if your friend is there. We've had a lot of men slip away and go home."

Trav found this prediction true. Tom Shadd and Lonn Tyler were the only ones remaining of those he had known. "And if us-uns wasn't plain damn fools," Lonn Tyler said cheerfully, "we wouldn't be here ourselves. My belly's been flapping agin' my backbone all winter, till the spring sprouts come; and there ain't nothing in me now only pokeberry shoots and wild onions. Yes sir, of all the wars I ever fit, this here's the damnedest. Legging it all over the country just to git ourselves an empty gut and a bullet into us!" He grinned, demanded: "What are you doing in it, Major? The rich men ain't supposed to do this fighting."

Trav smiled. "I'm as poor as anyone now; but I'm not much of a fighter." He asked the question he had come to ask.

"Ed Blandy?" Lonn tossed his head. "Ed had some sense. He's went along home."

Trav looked inquiringly at Tom Shadd. You could never be sure how much truth lay behind Lonn's fooling, but Tom spoke simple facts in simple words. Tom said slowly: "Ed got word Mrs. Blandy was dead." His eyes fell, and Trav suspected he knew how Mrs. Blandy died. "They give him a furlough to go see about it," Tom said. "But he ain't come back."

"When did he go?"

"Way back before Christmas."

So Ed was a deserter. Probably he had stayed at home to take care of the farm and the children, dodging into hiding whenever men from the conscript bureau came into the neighborhood; and Ed would hate that furtive life. For Mrs. Blandy's death, and so for Ed's shame, Tony was responsible. Trav promised himself that some day he would have a reckoning with Tony.

He stayed awhile, asking news of other men he once had known; and some were dead, and some had deserted, and some like Bob Grimm had gone home so maimed that they could fight no more. Riding back to headquarters he thought again that such men as Tom and Lonn were what made this army great; simple men who scratched a bare living out of the soil, watering their fields with their own sweat. Of course, yeomen farmers and poor whites fought no harder, fought perhaps not so hard nor so well, as the sons of wealth. But there were so many more of them.

If many of them deserted, it was hard to blame them. To desert was their only recourse. Richmond was full of able-bodied men in easy positions in the Government; clerks complaining when they were mustered to defend Richmond against raiding Yankees, and forever demanding higher pay, and living secure and safe. But men like these soldiers, and their sons, could not arrange to be detailed to safe work far behind the lines. Their only escape from battle and death was to desert, to run away, to hide in the forests and the mountains like so many animals. It was a proud and splendid thing that for a cause in which they had no selfish interest at all, they stayed and fought and died.

As presently, when Grant's army began to move, more of them would fight, and more of them would die.

Clark's Mountain, four or five miles beyond Rapidan Station toward Raccoon Ford, overlooked all the rolling plain toward Brandy Station where Grant's army was encamped. After that review of Longstreet's First Corps, the signal station on the summit was manned by night as well as by day; and on Monday, the second of May, the watchers there reported the smoke of an abnormally large number of fires rising from the enemy camps. That, since it meant the Yankees were cooking rations for three or four days, was a sign every private in the ranks could recognize. Grant was about to move.

Till his march began, it was impossible to be sure in which direction he would strike. If he came up river toward Liberty Mills, the First Corps would receive the first shock of his advance. Tuesday, dust clouds along distant roads marked troops making toward the upper fords; but this proved to be no more than a feint, for next daylight revealed the whole army of the enemy on the march down river toward the Confederate right.

General Longstreet set the men to cook rations, to break camp, and to discard all unnecessary burdens. The headquarters tents were struck and cut up into pieces, and the tents of officers, too; and the fragments of canvas distributed to the nearest men for use as bed or shelter in the days that were to come. Before Lee's orders reached them, they were almost ready; and at four o'clock in the afternoon the head of the column began to move.

While Lee awaited Grant's advance, Ewell's corps had formed the Confederate right, Hill's the center, Longstreet's the left. Now they must regroup. Two roads served them. Ewell's corps would follow the northernmost, the turnpike that ran from Orange Court House to Fredericksburg. Hill, using the Orange Plank Road, would cross Ewell's rear and come into position on his right. Longstreet and the First Corps must pass behind them by whatever highways and byways were available, and come into battle as the right flank of the Confederate line.

The orders were to march all night, with only brief rests. Colonel Taylor of Longstreet's staff rode ahead to find a guide for them. His home at Meadow Farm, beyond Orange Court House toward the tangled tract of second growth and scrub called the Wilderness, had been their rendezvous after their return from Gettysburg. He promised to meet them at Brock's Bridge.

"We'll come into action somewhere near the Brock Road," he predicted. "That's the road Jackson took to flank Hooker at Chancellorsville, so we'll be on ground that brings us success. Call it a good omen."

To the bridge where they would meet him was about twenty miles. When night forced a halt they were well on the way; and the head of the column reached Negro Run next day to find Colonel Taylor and Mr. Robinson, who had for years been sheriff of the county, ready to lead them on.

That evening they heard the guns; and when they came upon some skirmishing Yankee troopers who scattered before them, Longstreet halted the men for a rest and sent Trav and Captain Goree to discover and report back to him the results of the first clash.

"General Lee's orders to the others are to avoid battle till we are up," he said. "But if 'Lys Grant finds us, he will strike without waiting our pleasure."

Trav returned to him late that night, with a guide sent by General Lee to lead the First Corps through the forest to the plank road. "There's been hard fighting, General," he said. "They hit General Ewell, and then struck General Hill's advance on the plank road. Heth and Wilcox had hard work. They'll need you as quickly as you can get there."

Trav spoke urgently, for he had seen that need. Black Nig, as always when he heard the song of battle, had fretted at the bit; and Trav felt in himself that dry-throated wrath which he had learned to recognize. He spoke more strongly than he knew, and Longstreet smiled and said:

"Gently, Major. We'll want fresh men for the work. They must rest an hour or two."

It was not till after midnight that Longstreet gave the order to go on. The road through the forest was dim and overgrown. The moon was almost at the full, but among the trees lay darkness, and horses and men felt their way, guiding by the ruts under their feet and by the beaten trough between the ruts where years of occasional use had marked a shallow trail. When the trees thinned, the road became difficult to follow; but in this more open ground it was no longer necessary to move in single columns, so they came on more quickly and on a broader front.

At first daylight they heard raging musketry ahead and hurried their pace. When they reached the plank road, the two divisions in a doubled column filled it, eight men abreast. McLaws's division, now under Kershaw, was on the right-hand side; Hood's under Field on the left. They drove forward so briskly that some of the smaller men were forced to an occasional jog trot to keep their places.

The sun, obscured by smoke rising from the joined battle, rose red above the trees. They saw where a field hospital had been the day before, saw the dead bodies of men whom the surgeons had been unable to help. An aide on some urgent errand galloped across their front, and they saw more mounted men, couriers or officers. Ambulances met them, and there were stragglers in the scrub fields on either side, and litter-bearers left the road to let them pass.

Upon the head of their advancing column broke the rout of two divisions. The enemy attack, begun before sunrise, had shattered the Confederate right. The first men they met were single fugitives, and Trav recognized among them Lonn Tyler, and he shouted:

"Where you going, Lonn?"

Tyler waved his hand. "Home, b'God! I'll be there tonight, if my stren'th holds out." He darted into the trees. The fugitives became more numerous; and behind their straggling lines came a solid mass of men as orderly as a marching column, yet in full and hard retreat. The head of Longstreet's column was a rock on which they split, pouring into the woods and fields on either side, harangued by their desperate officers and pursued by the jeers of Longstreet's men, but stubbornly intent on making their way to safety.

Trav and the others riding in advance came to the crest of a gentle rise beyond which the ground sloped gradually downward. For two or three hundred yards there were old fields grown to brush head-high; and beyond that lay the tangled wood from which the song of battle came. Behind them, the doubled column of the First Corps halted; and Longstreet after one glance at the scene ahead deployed the men, throwing out three brigades on each side of the road. He rode along the forming lines, speaking in reassuring tones.

"Time enough, men. Do no firing till you've formed. Break your ranks to let these others through. They'll rally behind you. Time enough. Be easy. Dress your lines."

Trav had to repeat that admonition to himself. Time enough! Time enough! But it was hard to wait; to see emerging from the woods ahead gray-clad men in broken retreat, to see blue uniforms as the Yankees pressed them hard. He could see individual puffs of smoke as single muskets fired; he heard the thud of balls striking trees and men about him here.

General Lee joined Longstreet, and Trav had never seen the commanding general so obviously excited. Beside him, Longstreet seemed a monument of calm. Trav could not hear, over the steady drumming of musketry, what they said; but he heard Lee's voice shake as though the man were near tears. Then Lee rode to where the Texans under General Bragg were forming, while Trav followed Longstreet to the south side of the plank road. There Colonel Venable of Lee's staff came hurriedly to them.

"Sir," he said, "General Lee is over there insisting he will lead the Texans forward. He refuses to go to the rear."

Longstreet grunted. "Give General Lee my compliments, Colonel. Tell him if he will permit me to handle the affair, we will restore the situation in an hour." Colonel Venable hesitated; and Longstreet added dryly: "Say to him that if I am not needed, I ask permission to withdraw to some place of greater safety. It's not comfortable here."

Venable smiled and turned his horse, and Longstreet spoke to Trav. "Currain, tell General Field to advance his men as soon as they are formed. Tell him to use heavy skirmish lines with close support in strength." And as Trav whirled he added in a jocular tone: "And Major, you come back to me. Don't let that big horse of yours get his head. I want you in hand."

Trav gave Longstreet's orders to General Field, and he saw the skirmish lines move forward and heard their first careful, steady fire. His ear had learned to interpret battle sounds; he listened, and he began to think the enemy was checked. Then Colonel Venable and another officer rode up to him, and the Colonel said:

"Major, take General Smith to General Longstreet. General Lee thinks he may be useful."

Trav as he obeyed saw the sun already high, and he felt a familiar wonder at the way time during a battle seemed to speed. Only a moment ago they had been groping through the darkness of the forest; now it must be seven or eight o'clock. Before they crossed the road he heard Longstreet's great voice, audible even above the steady fire, as he shouted orders. Behind Longstreet's battle line, the best men from the two divisions which had broken under the Yankee attack were already rallying. They would presently be a fighting force again.

General Smith and Longstreet met like old friends; and Trav saw them talk together for a moment, saw Longstreet point to the right, saw General Smith ride away. Before them in the forest the hard battle rose in pitch, the firing so steady it seemed one continuous sound. The enemy, yielding a little at first, had stiffened and now held his ground. Trav had learned to distinguish between the muffled reports of their own muskets and the sharper note of guns fired in their direction. The volume of Yankee fire was rising; the enemy had been reinforced. If they were further strengthened they would be able to come on.

General Lee came to join Longstreet, and while they were together General Smith returned and made report. Longstreet listened, and spoke, and Trav saw Lee nod as though assenting. General Smith rode rapidly away, and Longstreet turned and called Moxley Sorrel. They met close enough to where Trav waited so that he heard the General's words.

"Colonel, this is a chance for good work. Their flank's loose. Collect some of the brigades behind us here in support and take them off to the right through the woods. Thrust your right forward, be sure you're ready before you strike, then hit their flank and drive them across our front. We'll move when we hear your guns."

They rode past Trav, Longstreet still speaking, till Sorrel turned his horse to thread his way at a smart trot through the scrub and brush. Longstreet watched him go and then came back, pausing by Trav. "Sorrel's gone to strike their flank. That should break them before they can be further reinforced."

He sat listening to the battle, and Trav stayed beside him, trying to estimate the passing time. What troops would Sorrel use? Anderson's division was in position as support, and two or three brigades of the First Corps were held on the flank. How long for Sorrel to reach them? How far must they march to strike their blow? How long before they would attack? The clamor of gunfire in the forest was a steady ringing like a smith's hammer on his anvil; it came in volume like the robust voices of a massed choir. Trav let his thoughts dwell on figures: so many minutes, so many men, so many fractions of miles that must be marched.

Before he arrived at any answer to the sum he set himself, the rhythm of the battle clamor changed. From the right came the strong staccato of firm fire from well-aimed guns.

That was Sorrel! Those were the guns of his brigades. The pulse beating in Trav's throat made it hard for him to hear. There was a sudden stir among the officers here around him, and Nig for a moment got his head, till Trav reined him under hard control. As his ears cleared they brought him the story of what was happening on the flank. He heard—he had no need to see—the enemy line waver and stagger, stumble and break. The sudden shrill yells from behind the screening forest were eloquent of victory.

Longstreet rode down toward the plank road, and Trav and the others of the staff came after him, and Longstreet shouted orders. Let Field's men and Kershaw's press the shaken enemy, while those three brigades Sorrel had led into position rolled them up from the flank. Longstreet himself crossed the plank road to speak to General Field. As he returned, General Smith came through the woods from the right to report an even greater opportunity: the whole Yankee flank was hanging in the air.

"Very well, sir. Take the force still in reserve and drive that flank in." There was a strong jubilance in Longstreet's voice, and as General Smith rode away the big man spoke to Captain Goree.

"Bring General Jenkins up to co-operate with Kershaw." And when Goree was gone, to Trav and the others while they waited: "Here's Second Manassas all over again; yes and Chancellorsville. We've thrown them in utter rout, and we've force in hand to press them. We'll sweep them clear across our front."

Colonel Taylor pointed east along the road: "General, the woods are on fire."

They saw creeping flames running through the carpet of dead leaves along the ground; smoke touched their nostrils, and Trav heard a man scream, and then another. There must be scores of wounded helpless in the path of those little running flames that spread like water over sand. Trav thought of the tide rising over the flats below Great Oak; and in a sudden flashing memory he saw the big house once so familiar, last seen two years ago almost to the day. It too had died in flames, as these wounded men in the forest here would die.

From behind them came General Jenkins at a smart trot; and beyond him the head of the column of his men, coming at the double, filled the road. Longstreet greeted him exultantly; in three swift sentences he explained the situation. "Three or four of our brigades have routed two full corps of Yankees," he said. "We hit their flank and hustled them across the road ahead of us. We've five fresh brigades now to keep them running!"

General Jenkins's eyes shone. "We'll throw them back across the river before night!" He turned and shouted so that every man in the column of his men could hear. "The Yanks are broken, boys! We'll finish them! Three cheers for General Longstreet!"

The full-throated answer ended in a chorus of shrill yipping yells that made Trav's pulses race. Moxley Sorrel returned to say the flanking troops were already across the road in front of them. With the advancing files of Jenkins's eager men close upon their heels, they rode on.

Smoke was heavy in the woods and across the road; and the cries of hurt men rang in their ears. Trav left the road and forced Nig through the trees toward the creeping fire. There were wounded scattered all about, most of them helpless; but a man with a shattered leg dragged himself like a snake with a broken back, trying to keep ahead of the spreading flames. Trav saw a file of men ahead, and he called to them: "Carry some of these poor fellows clear of the fire."

But the man with the broken leg swore at him furiously. "Git the hell away from here! Git them Yanks! Us-uns can crawl! Git on!"

Trav hesitated, abashed by this fierce urgency. A volley sounded close along the road ahead and he heard a desperate cry. "Friends!" There was terror like panic in that cry. He swung Nig back to the road and saw Jenkins's men dropping in their tracks, hugging the ground. A little way ahead there was confusion among the horsemen of the staff, and cries, and someone shouted for Dr. Cullen.

Then Trav's heart turned sick with sorrow, for he saw Longstreet's bulk sway in the saddle, and lean slowly sidewise, and he saw a dozen men run to ease the General to the ground.

He dismounted, passed Nig's reins to a soldier, pressed to Longstreet's side, saw a fountain of blood surging from the big man's throat. Dr. Cullen was already busy with the wound.

Longstreet's eyes were open; he weakly blew the blood out of his mouth. "Tell General Field to take command." He had to spit to clear his mouth again. "Press them!" he whispered.

General Field reached his side, uttering a sorrowing word; but Longstreet made a fierce gesture, laboring to speak. "Press them. Don't let them rally."

There was urgency in voice and eyes. General Field stood up to obey; and Longstreet spoke Lee's name. Moxley Sorrel came to hear his labored words. "Tell—situation. Tell General Lee—we have them!"

Sorrel rode to find the commanding general. After a little, Dr. Cullen staunched the hemorrhage and looked up and met Trav's eyes. "He can be moved," he said.

Trav called men; he sent Lieutenant Dunn to bring a stretcher. He heard someone say that General Jenkins was dead from the same volley that had struck Longstreet. Captain Manning came to help him; Trav asked some desperate question, and Manning told him what had happened. In the smoke and the confusion, the men of the Twelfth Virginia were mistaken for Yankees; shots and then a volley were exchanged.

"We rode right into the cross fire," Manning said. "We barely prevented a second volley."

General Anderson came to Longstreet's side, and painfully Longstreet explained to him the waiting opportunity, the position of the battle. "Press them hard," he urged. "Hard. Quick. No pause." He choked, his voice failed.

The stretcher was ready. Trav helped lift him on it; he placed the General's hat over his face to shield his eyes from the sun. They began to carry him to the rear, past Jenkins's men moving into the action; and a man here and there called a question.

"Is he dead?"

Trav answered them. "No, just wounded."

Someone muttered doubt, and Longstreet seemed to hear, for he lifted his hat from his face and dropped it. "Let them see me alive," he muttered. The nearest men saw the movement and raised a shout of gladness. Trav, walking behind the stretcher, heard the affection in those shouting voices and his eyes filled with proud tears.

He saw General Lee coming with Moxley Sorrel from the woods on one side, and he spoke to Longstreet. "General Lee's there! He'll drive them." Longstreet's lips moved contentedly.

Behind him Trav heard Captain Manning, choked with sorrow and with rage, cry: "Shot by our own men! Just like Jackson!"

Colonel Taylor answered him. "And within a few miles of the same spot, and just a year later. And—like Jackson—just when he had the winning hand."

A soldier touched Trav's arm. The man led Nig. Trav had forgotten the great horse. He mounted and overtook the others. Colonel Taylor spoke in a low tone: "We'll take him straight to Meadow Farm. Dr. Cullen says he can stand it." And he said admiringly, "Did you hear him? No thought for himself; just urging us to press on, drive them."

They reached the ambulance. Trav dismounted to help lift Longstreet in, and to make the big man more comfortable he took off the General's boots and his coat. His socks were white. Trav himself had put on fresh socks and underwear while the men rested at midnight last night, and he thought Longstreet must have done the same. Under his coat Longstreet wore only a thin undervest, darkly stained now with blood that had spilled from that wound in his throat. His eyes opened; he saw Trav and smiled faintly under his heavy beard and muttered a request.

"Stay near me, Currain."

"I will, General," Trav promised; and when the other had been lifted into the ambulance, he gave Nig to a courier to lead and stood upon the rear step of the vehicle. Longstreet was very pale, his high forehead white as snow. He lay motionless, but once with his hand he lifted the blood-sticky undershirt off the wound for a moment, filled his great lungs, lay still again with eyes not quite closed.

The ambulance moved on, ringed by the cluster of horsemen. Behind them the din of battle began to fade. Trav, listening, thought there was a lull in the staccato of the muskets. Perhaps the Yankees were being driven beyond easy hearing. He wished to go back, to take his part in that fine triumph; but Longstreet had bidden him stay near, so he would not leave the man he loved who lay helpless now.

Near Parker's Store a messenger from General Lee brought word of continued gains, and asked for a report on Longstreet's wound. Lieutenant Dunn wrote the reply: the surgeons agreed that the hurt was serious but not necessarily fatal. The brief delay had given Longstreet some rest and relief from the torment of the journey; but when they reached Meadow Farm the big man was exhausted. Mrs. Taylor was there to take him in charge.

A night's rest brought strength back to him; but the news from the battle he had fought so well was disappointing. He had left the enemy broken and in flight, but after he was wounded there had been too much delay in aligning the formations, a long and costly pause. Not till late afternoon were the brigades thrown forward, and by that time the Yankees had rallied and entrenched. They beat back the assaulting troops and held their ground.

By way of compensation, the surgeons said General Longstreet's wound promised well. The bullet had smashed through his throat and right shoulder, and he had lost much blood; but unless there were complications, he would recover.

In the meantime he must be removed to some place of greater safety, and Longstreet himself suggested Lynchburg. "I'll go to Mrs. Longstreet's kinfolks there," he said. "She's in Augusta, but she can join me." It was decided that Trav and Captain Goree would go with him.

Toward dusk, word came that Grant, after two or three days of heavy punishment, now lay inactive; and Colonel Taylor thought he would withdraw across the Rapidan as Hooker had done a year before. But Longstreet shook his heavy head. "Not 'Lys Grant." He spoke harshly, wincing with pain. "He won't retreat as long as he has a regiment that he can order forward. He'll march around our right for Richmond."

His prediction proved a true one. Next morning when they rode toward Orange Court House to put him aboard the Lynchburg train, they heard far away to the east the guns opening at Spottsylvania.

12

CINDA would all her life remember the month of April in 1864 as a peaceful interlude, the happier by contrast with the bloodstained summer of darkening despair that was to follow. In April Julian and Anne were radiant with expectation; and Vesta too was shining with an inner content, dwelling on the threshold of realization. So April was a happy time, and Anne's baby boy was born on the last day of the month, and named for Brett Dewain.

But that same day came a foreshadowing of greater griefs when little Joe Davis, the President's son, left for a moment unattended by his nurse, fell from the low balcony of the White House and was killed. All Richmond shared that sorrow, and it came close to Cinda. She liked Mrs. Davis, and if they were not intimates yet they were friends; and she knew the Davis children, rioting and handsome and lively youngsters. Cinda and Vesta went together to the White House to offer sympathy; and the day the baby was buried Cinda wept to see the President and Mrs. Davis standing erect and steadfast beside the open grave.

There was a great crowd; it seemed that everyone in Richmond, and certainly every child in Richmond, was there. "And everybody so sorry for them," Cinda said to Vesta afterward. "But a week from now they'll turn on Mr. Davis again, blame him for all our troubles."

"Well, of course, everyone loves babies, and everyone's sorry for people who lose them; but just because his baby died doesn't make Mr. Davis a good president!" Vesta spoke strongly. "Hungry people have to blame somebody, when flour costs three or four hundred dollars a barrel!"

"Oh I know! And of course it's silly to be sad over just one little baby being killed, when the armies will soon be killing each other again."

Vesta tucked her hand through her mother's arm. "We can't stop them, Mama."

"Can't anyone stop them?" Cinda cried, but she answered her own question. "No. I know. . . ."

On the Wednesday following they heard the first rumble of the coming storm. Tilda stopped at the house on Fifth Street to say there was a dispatch from General Lee, that Grant's army was moving. "And that means work for all of us," Tilda pointed out. "The trains of wounded will be coming."

"We'll be as ready as we can be," Cinda promised. "As long as men are bound to fight, that's all women can do."

That day too they heard gunfire toward York River, and next day Yankee troops were landing on the Peninsula; and the day after, two or three score enemy vessels put men ashore by the thousands at Bermuda Hundred. There was skirmishing along the Chickahominy, and the local militia marched to the defenses; but the peril at Richmond's very door was averted, and Saturday's dispatches from Lee reported successful battle against Grant's tremendous army.

At the hospital Cinda heard that Longstreet had been wounded. "Badly, they say," she told Vesta, when she brought the news home. Vesta wished to cheer her.

"Pooh! The Yankees can't really hurt that big man!"

Cinda herself had had that same unreasonable certainty that Cousin Jeems was invulnerable; so to know that he had been shot was a shaking thing. If he could be hurt, then no one was safe. She tried not to think of Brett and Burr; yet they too must have faced the Yankee fire.

At church on Sunday they heard that Grant's first advance had been thrown back with heavy loss; but that evening the wounded came in a thickening flood. Some of the hurt men were not only wounded but terribly burned, and the wards were pitiful with their groans. From those who were able to talk Cinda heard of the fire that swept the battlefield, when helpless men could only lie and watch the greedy little flames run among the dried leaves to gnaw at them. There was one boy, a Texan, a fair-haired child still in his 'teens, with a mercifully broken back so that though his feet and legs were charred like dead sticks he felt no pain.

"The woods were all smoke," he said. "You couldn't see what you were doing. That's how it happened Old Pete was shot. The old Bull-of-the-Woods rode into a cross fire from our own men." Cinda, listening to this boy, thought of his mother, his father; of what his home must be. They were fine people certainly to have so fine a son. She knew by his unnatural loquacity that he would not live the night, so since he was full of talk she stayed with him. "Bullets flying everywhere," he said with shining eyes. "I guess half the men in the Texas brigade were hit, but we smashed them, drove them back. I was lucky. Some of us couldn't get away from the fire, but my arms were all right, so I dragged myself over to the road." His quick tongue ran a while, till she saw his feverish color fade and his lips pale. When his words began to lag, she touched his head, said he must sleep; and he smiled and promised and closed his eyes. She turned to leave him, but as she did so his mouth opened in a strained stiff way, as though he wished to speak, or as though something choked him. His jaw locked with a little click; and while she stood beside him his closed eyes half opened. He was a slender, bright-haired youngster, very much like Julian; but she turned away. Living men needed her now.

She became inured to hideous sights and sounds and smells; and she had long ago learned to do tasks of which she would once have been incapable. These helpless men were as dependent as babies. To make them as clean and as comfortable as possible was no harder than to do the same for a baby, once you set your heart to the task. It was your heart, not your physical body, which gave you the needed strength. There were nights when she did not go home at all. She had a room, no more than a closet, where she had sometimes slept; but so many wounded needed beds that she gave up her cot to them. There was always a chair, or perhaps a bed from which some poor body had just been borne to the death house, where she could drop down for a moment's rest and rise again.

Wounded from the Wilderness were still arriving when a new host came from the first clash at Spottsylvania. Since there was no room for them indoors they were lifted out and laid on the ground while the ambulances departed for a fresh load. Tilda and the ladies she mustered were busy at the depot where, when a train arrived, the wounded men were unloaded and left on the pavement to await transportation to the hospitals, while the emptied cars rattled away to the northward to bring back another load. Day and night the trains came, and while the hurt men waited, ladies gave them what comforts were possible, working under broiling sun or by the smoky glare of pine-knot torches held high in dark hands, providing blankets against the night cold, shade against the sun, some fashion of pillow for the weary heads, and always water, water, water for the parched and thirst-burned throats. There was need for such attendance at the hospitals, too; for when the wards were full, men must wait again, in the hot sun under clouds of ravenous flies or in merciful night that made the flies sluggish with cold. Sometimes the surgeons worked among them where they lay. Once Cinda, stepping out of her ward for a moment's breath, saw Tilda with a severed arm and an amputated leg hugged like babies to her bosom as she trudged toward the refuse trench; and Cinda had an insane desire to laugh at this obscene horror. Tilda was so awkward, and so smeared with blood and grime, and so absorbed in her efforts not to trip over the helpless men among whom she picked her way. God bless her!

There was so much to do: keep the flies away; see to it that water dripped steadily upon the bandages; go constantly from man to man to watch for those in need of sudden care. Vesta, though Cinda wished her to stay at home where she might be sheltered from these terrors, came to help as she could.

"But I'm not much good," she told Cinda, smiling through tears. "I just blunder along. They're very patient with us, aren't they?—the men, I mean. I wanted to do something for one of them and he said he was all right, and I said: 'Let me wash your face. You'll be so much cooler,' and he grinned and said: 'Why, all right, ma'am; but you'll be the ninth lady that's washed my face today.' "

Once Cinda saw the girl kneeling beside a pallet on the floor where a man lay dying; and Cinda went to her and Vesta whispered: "He's French, Mama; talking French. I don't know enough French even to comfort him."

Cinda leaned nearer the man tossing restlessly in burning fever; she murmured uncertainly: *"Notre père, qui est en ciel—"* The man instantly was motionless, seeming to listen, his lips soundlessly following the words to the end: *"A toi soit la pouvoir, la gloire à jamais."* With the last words his lips were still, and a little parted. Cinda waited, Vesta standing beside her, till after a moment she was sure. She stood up, pressing her hands to her temples; but you must not let yourself feel anything. She called the nearest orderly.

"Take him to the death house," she said.

Vesta cried in an anguished protest: "Oh, Mama!"

"Hush, Honey," Cinda warned her. "There are seventeen men lying on the ground outside waiting for a bed."

The day after, Cinda persuaded the girl to stay at home; but toward sunset she saw Vesta in the doorway, some warning in her eyes, and went quickly toward her. Vesta tried to smile reassurance.

"It's all right, Mama. I'm sure it's all right. But Burr's home."

Cinda crossed her arms, wiping her hands on her sleeves. "He is hurt?"

"Yes. But not badly. But I thought maybe one of the surgeons—thought maybe you could come."

Burr was more than all these others. "What is his hurt?"

"Why, both his hands." Vesta spoke uncertainly. "He says some of his fingers are gone."

Cinda nodded, cold and calm. A surgeon would be needed. Dr. Mason, chief surgeon of the Department of Richmond, happened at the moment to be in her ward. She appealed to him, and he said he would come when he could. His office was in Belvin's Block on Twelfth Street, opposite the end of Bank Street; to stop would not take him out of his way. Cinda thanked him. Vesta had brought the carriage, Diamond held the reins. "We'll have to give up the carriage," Cinda thought, as she climbed in. "We mustn't keep horses when they're needed so." She said: "Diamond, hurry."

At home she found Burr lying on the sofa in her room, and he was white with pain. Cinda knew that a wound in the hand meant a peak of anguish; yet she faced him smiling. He was her son, but she could do as much for him as she had done for the sons of other women. She kissed him, carefully casual. To be casual was to be strong.

"Now let me look at them, Sonny."

His hands were bundles of twisted, filthy rags; he himself was dirty, worn, gaunt, his eyes red with sleeplessness. She would not let herself see this. His hands first. When the soiled bandage came stickily away, color drained out of his cheeks.

"June gave me brandy, Mama," he said carefully. "Can I have some more?"

"Of course, all you like." Brandy was the next best thing to chloroform.

Vesta held the glass to his lips while Cinda plucked the last wrapping off his right hand. The thumb was cleanly gone, the forefinger shattered and dangling by a thread. She felt a moment's gratitude; such a wound might make it impossible for him to fight again. He could never hold a sabre, or pull a trigger; she was sure of that. Under her quiet direction, old June brought hot water, castile soap, scissors, clean linen. Vesta began to scrape lint.

The oozing blood would do no harm. Cut away the proud flesh; then fresh bandages. Cinda worked in a steady concentration. There, that hand would do till Dr. Mason came. Now the other.

"More, Vesta," Burr whispered, and gulped the brandy she gave him.

On the left hand, thumb and forefinger were untouched, but the other fingers were shattered. "Well," Cinda commented, "put both hands together and you've a whole one, Burr."

The brandy loosed his tongue. "One bullet did it all," he said. "It just happened to catch both my hands in line. It tore my reins out of this one and my pistol out of the other. I wrapped them up as well as I could and came home."

"Where were you?"

"Out at Yellow Tavern, not far from here. Their cavalry rode around us and headed for Richmond, and we had to race to catch them. General Stuart's wounded, Mama."

Fresh bandages were in place. "There! Dr. Mason will come as soon as he can. Now we'll give you a bath, put you to bed."

"I can sleep for a week." On the way to his room, their hands under his arms, he talked in volleys. That was the brandy. Good. Morphine was better, but brandy would help. While he lay half-asleep, Cinda and June undressed him and bathed him from head to foot; and Cinda yearned over his lean young body, the ribs stretching the skin. When they were done he slept as quickly as a tired dog.

Downstairs, Vesta asked: "Mama, did you hear him say General Stuart's hurt?" But Cinda only nodded. Burr was more than Jeb Stuart with his laughter and his fine uniforms and his flowing plumes. Every woman in the South loved Jeb Stuart, but Burr was Cinda's own.

Dr. Mason was cheerfully reassuring. "As good as ever in a week or two," he promised. Not quite, Cinda thought; not with those maimed hands. Yet it was true that his hurts were mercifully slight. Anguish of torn nerves and smashed bone could be endured if life were safe. Dr. Mason spoke gravely of Stuart's hurt. "The Yankee cavalry were heading for Richmond," he said. "He held them long enough to give time to man our defenses toward Ashland. They're bringing him to Dr. Brewer's home." That was almost in the country, half a mile out Grace Street.

Vesta asked: "Is he badly hurt?"

"Fatally, I fear."

In the morning Burr made light of his own injuries. "I can still handle reins and sabre, or at least a pistol." He said that in the Wilderness the cavalry was not heavily engaged. "But then we had to hold Grant's advance at Spottsylvania till the First Corps could come up."

"Longstreet's men?"

"Yes, General Anderson commanding. Then after the First Corps was up, we heard that Sheridan had gone around our right toward Richmond, so we rode to catch them. We were in the saddle most of the time from Sunday afternoon till today—most of three days and nights. We got in front of them at Yellow Tavern. They hit us about noon yesterday. That was when I got this."

Cinda bade him rest. Burr wished to know how Stuart did, and Vesta volunteered to go and ask. Stuart died that night. The rumble of guns a few miles away, where his men still fought Sheridan's, tolled the hours of the death watch till dawn. Next day word came that the Yankees had withdrawn.

"They might as well," Burr said sorrowfully. "Short of capturing Richmond, killing General Stuart is the greatest victory they could hope to win."

He insisted on going to the funeral services in St. James's Church, and on following his old commander's body to Hollywood. All Richmond mourned, that day; and Cinda, thinking of the hundreds of others dying or dead in the hospitals, and on the battlefields to the northward, wondered that any one man's death could summon from eyes drained dry by grief so many tears.

Yet Stuart was more than a man. Yes, he was more than a thousand men. Jackson was gone, and Cousin Jeems was wounded, and Stuart was dead. Of the great men only Lee remained. For these who were gone, where would a worthy substitute be found?

It was from an officer with an amputated leg that she heard how Longstreet had been wounded, shot by his own men just as Jackson had been, and not far from the same spot. "The woods were full of smoke," the officer explained. "He and some others rode right across the front of our advance and our men gave them a volley. Before that, he had flanked the Union line and broken it. If he hadn't been hurt I think we'd have driven them back across the Rapidan that night."

So this was another of those mischances which sometimes made it seem that God Himself did not intend the Confederacy to win! It was bitter to come again and again to the very threshold of victory, only to be turned back; bitter and terrible to feel that they must go wearily on into the black valley of despair.

Sunday she was too tired to go to church; but Anne and Julian, Anne still pale but very lovely, came to dinner and brought the baby; and before Vesta and Burr returned from church, Rollin Lyle rang the bell. He had come north with Trenholm's squadron of the Seventh South Carolina Cavalry, assigned to Hampton's Division.

"We're in camp on the Chickahominy, with headquarters at Drewry's Bluff," he said. "We've been busy picketing, and scouting Butler's Yankees. We gave them a licking last Monday, just for practice."

Julian said an exultant word, but Cinda heard the heaviness in Rollin's tones. "Is something wrong?"

"Why—my father's dead," he said reluctantly.

"Oh, Rollin!"

"He'd been working too hard, Mama thinks. He died in his sleep." He hesitated. "I had a chance to go home. She was glad to see me."

Cinda knew Mrs. Lyle from occasional meetings in Charleston; a delicate little woman, seeming as utterly helpless as she was charming. "Where is she?"

"At Fallow Fields. That's up on the Peedee, in North Carolina. We've had to give up the plantations nearer the coast."

"What will she do?"

"Manage Fallow Fields." He added proudly: "Mama's strong, you know. She's little, but nothing can beat her down."

Before they could say more, Vesta appeared; and his eyes turned to her and never left her. Cinda decided it was for him to tell Vesta of his father's death, and she was glad when Julian and Anne did not speak of it at dinner. Afterward, to give Rollin and Vesta a chance to be together, she sent Vesta on an unnecessary errand to Tilda, sent Rollin to keep her company. When they were gone, Burr looked at her with a smile.

"That looked like some of your managing, Mama."

"Why not?" she demanded. Anne laughed softly and asked whether Burr was blind, and he said in a puzzled tone:

"I thought Rollin never looked at anyone but Dolly!"

"But Dolly's married, Burr!"

He had not known that, so Cinda told him what there was to tell, and Julian said Bruce Kenyon was a fine boy, and Burr said that if that was true he was much too good for Dolly. He asked where Darrell was.

"No one seems to know," Julian said, and Cinda added:

"And except Tilda, I don't suppose anyone cares."

When Vesta and Rollin returned, Rollin's quiet sadness was gone. These two wore happiness so openly that the others caught the infection, and they were all ridiculously jolly, laughing easily at nothing. Cinda thought how young they were, and how fine it was to be young and to be able to turn to laughter for a while. They could even laugh at the stories that began to be told about Butcher Grant, who seemed ready to give the lives of five of his soldiers to kill one Southerner.

"In the fight at the Wilderness," Julian told them, "they say he just sat under a tree smoking a cigar, and whenever the couriers told him a lot of his men were being killed he'd just say: 'Put in another regiment!' "

They laughed at that, and Burr had a tale to match it. "After he crossed the Rapidan we captured his pontoons, but he said: 'That's all right. If I beat General Lee I won't need them, and if he beats me, I can take all the men I'll have left by that time back across the river on a log!' "

Cinda could not share their relish for these jests at death. There was something inexorable and frightening about General Grant; and besides, she had seen the wounded. But let these youngsters laugh! If Julian could laugh, maimed as he was, and if Burr could laugh and forget his mutilated hands, why, so much the better! Her thoughts turned to Brett. Somewhere in the north he and his fellows still faced Butcher Grant day by day. "Send in another regiment." Brett must meet those fresh regiments, coming on in an endless procession, new ones to take the place of those destroyed. General Grant could afford to pay five lives for one; but Lee dared not accept the bargain. Lee— thank God for it!—Lee must be frugal of his men. Of men like Brett.

Burr, his hands well healed, went off to Raleigh to join Barbara; and for Cinda the days ran together. Talk touched her, but she heard without attention. Mr. Memminger had shipped the women clerks who signed the new currency as fast as it was printed off to Columbia to do their work there. Perhaps he expected Richmond's fall. Flour was five hundred dollars the barrel. A wounded man with a bullet through his shoulder and a bayonet wound in his chest swore to her that a Yankee had given him that bayonet thrust while he lay helpless from the bullet wound. Pyaemia struck the officers' hospital in the Baptist Female College and so many died that the wounded there had to be removed to the Almshouse; but Chimborazo Hospital was not affected. Butler's troops on the Peninsula and at Bermuda Hundred made it impossible for fishermen to bring their catch to Richmond, and Sheridan's cavalry cut off the flow of provisions from the farms, so food was increasingly expensive and hard to find at any price. Of the drugs needed at the hospital there was never enough, so the agony of hurt men could not always be eased. General Lee was ill. General Grant's hosts, checked again and again, nevertheless forever sought new avenues of approach and drew steadily nearer.

One day she was watching an ambulance being unloaded at the door of her ward when, among the wounded laid upon the ground where the grass was long since matted with dried brown blood, Cinda saw Rollin Lyle. His eyes were closed, and he was white as marble; but when she knelt and spoke to him he answered. She called the driver of the ambulance and bade him take Rollin to Fifth Street.

"Tell my daughter I'll find a doctor as soon as I can," she directed. "Where did you get him?"

"Freight cars brought a load of them from the Chickahominy."

She nodded. "He's a friend of ours. Take him to our house," she repeated. The pain of being moved again drove Rollin senseless. Cinda, ruthlessly releasing herself from her work here, found Dr. Mc-Caw and insisted that he come home with her.

When they arrived, Vesta and June had laid Rollin on the bed in the room that had been Mrs. Currain's, and had bathed him and pressed a pad of lint upon the small empurpled wound. Vesta stood by, unflinching while the surgeon's probe slipped into Rollin's body so far that even Cinda thought it must come out through his back. The probe touched the bullet, but could not move it. Dr. McCaw, when he had done what he could, drew Cinda from the room.

"I'm afraid bladder and kidney are pierced," he confessed. "I see little chance for him. There's nothing to do but let the wound suppurate and heal if it will."

"What was that smoky-smelling stuff you washed the wound with?"

"Creosote."

"Of course. That sooty smell. But for goodness' sake, why?" It was a relief to fasten one's thoughts on things that didn't matter.

"Why, Dr. Dunn of Petersburg suggested it. Dr. Spencer always used it when he operated for stone in the bladder. He's dead now, but he was marvelously successful, probably operated for stone as often as any man in the United States. He was a great believer in soap and

water first, and then creosote dissolved in alcohol. I'm sure there's no
harm in it. The boy really has very little chance anyway."

Cinda nodded. "I will stay with him," she said.

"Of course, Mrs. Dewain. Of course. And I will come when I can,
if only to ease him a little."

Vesta, with a decision Cinda could not shake, kept uninterrupted
watch by Rollin's side, never leaving him for more than a moment,
day or night. When Cinda pleaded with her to rest, to spare herself,
Vesta smiled and shook her head.

"No, Mama," she said. "No. I'm going to get him well. I'm not
going to let him die."

So she kept her post. Dr. McCaw returned late that first night and
again in the morning, and the next day and the next. On that third
day he was ready to smile.

"It's amazing what a healthy young warrior's body will endure," he
said. "There's no suppuration. The wound has healed as neatly as a
cut with a sharp knife. I'll keep drawing off blood and water every
day, but I'll be much surprised if a week from now this young man
isn't walking around."

At that incredible deliverance from dread, Cinda herself, to her own
disgust, took to her bed. Her thankfulness was more than she could
bear. Friday at dawn they heard for an hour or two the roar of massed
guns not far away; and that night came word of Grant's bloody repulse at Cold Harbor. Saturday and again on Sunday, while rain
swept the city, Cinda slept the day away. Julian came after church to
say that on the field of Cold Harbor there was a truce to bury the
Union dead. "The wounded had all died since the battle," he reported.
"The slopes in front of our entrenchments were crawling with them,
but Butcher Grant wouldn't ask for a truce till yesterday. One of their
deserters said Grant had threatened to let the wounded die and rot to
stink us out of our lines."

Rollin was strong enough that day to talk a little. He had been
wounded in a fight with Custer's cavalry, a few companies of South
Carolinians throwing themselves against overwhelming force to hold
open Lee's road to Cold Harbor. "After I was hurt, my horse didn't
want to carry me," he told Julian. "He threw me off; but they caught
him and twisted his ear and that quieted him enough so they could

make him carry me to Deep Bottom Bridge. There were a lot of us there. I think we were there all night before they loaded us on the train to bring us to Richmond. After that I don't remember much."

Vesta said in a low tone: "You were lucky, Rollin. One bullet nicked your cheek, and one smashed itself on your sword, and there were two or three bullet holes in your clothes, besides the one that hit you."

"It was pretty hot," he admitted. "I guess there's not much left of our squadron."

Cinda saw his lip begin to pale with fatigue, and she led Julian away; but Vesta stayed. In the hall Julian said in affectionate amusement: "Mama, those two don't know there's anyone else in the room, do they?" She smiled contentedly.

The day when Rollin for the first time put on his uniform, he and Vesta came to Cinda together. "I guess you'll be pretty surprised at what I'm going to say, Mrs. Dewain," he began, and Cinda laughed and kissed him.

"Do you think I'm blind?"

So they all laughed together; and Vesta said happily: "Well then, that's all right! But, Mama, I want us to be married before Rollin goes back to duty."

Cinda remembered Tommy Cloyd, who so soon after he and Vesta were married had ridden away never to return. Must Vesta face that bitter sorrow again? But her courage returned. No, Vesta's love had saved this boy and it would shield him now. Vesta deserved a bountiful happiness. If there were justice in the world, and there must be, then she should have it.

"That won't be soon," she suggested. "It will be a long time before he's well; weeks perhaps. Will you wait a while? With the armies so near Richmond, Papa's sure to come soon. He'd want to be here."

They would wait, but that waiting was not to be long. After Cold Harbor, Grant, like McClellan two years ago, moved toward the river and crossed to face Petersburg; and in mid-June Brett came home for two or three days.

Cinda was at the hospital when he arrived. Vesta sent Diamond to fetch her, and she came in flushed haste. Brett was in the hall to meet her; and she clung to him, pressing in his arms, smelling the strong man smell of garments long unchanged, of grime and sweat and powder smoke, of stress and weariness and strain. Her arms encircling him told her he was thin; but they told her too that he was all bone and sinew with no waste flesh at all. She made inarticulate sounds of joy and love, and wept her tears and swallowed her sobs and looked up into his loved and smiling eyes, touching his lined cheeks, touching his temples where the hair had thinned and was turning gray, pressing her lips to his. Even his beard now was gray. Oh, he was changed, changed, changed; but he was whole, and strong with health, and above all, he was alive.

She swept him away upstairs. "Let me get him clean, Vesta! He's not fit to be seen! I won't have such a tramp of a man in my drawing room." But when they were alone she held fast to him again, whispering his loved name. "Brett Dewain! Oh Brett Dewain!"

While he bathed, she gave his garments to June, who sniffed and said of rights they should go into the fire; but Brett called a warning: nothing must be destroyed. "There's no way to replace anything," he told Cinda. "Except off a dead Yankee."

They had had time before Cinda came to tell him of Burr's hurt, and now he spoke of it. "Vesta says he thinks he can fight again."

"I don't know. I suppose he can if he's bound to. Even Julian has tried to help in the home defense. Rollin will be as well as ever, in time. Did he and Vesta tell you about themselves?"

"Yes. I'm mighty glad, aren't you?"

"Of course. I love Rollin. And Vesta deserves so much. Oh, did she tell you Dolly's married?"

"Yes." He said: "Honey, Vesta and Rollin want to be married at once; and he wants to take her to Fallow Fields to see his mother. You might go with them, go to the Plains, have a visit with Jenny."

"No, I'll stay in Richmond. Unless Grant is going to drive us out?"

Brett shook his head. "We've beaten Grant to a standstill. He's lost seventy-five thousand men since he crossed the Rapidan, more men than General Lee has ever had to fight against him." His tone was not exultant; rather it was sober with a sort of wonder. "The Northern papers printed Grant's dispatch where he said he'd fight it out on that line if it took all summer; but he's had to eat his words. He didn't fight it out on that line. Every time we beat him, he tried a new line." He was dressed now, in old familiar garments. "It's been one long slaughter, Cinda. At Pole Green Church they came up within twenty yards of our gun in a solid column before we let loose at them with double charges of canister. The flames from the muzzle burned the men at the head of that column, they were so close. We fired seventeen rounds of canister into them, eleven rounds in one minute, at point-blank range. The ground where they'd been looked as though a giant had swung a scythe through the column."

"I'd rather not hear about it," she confessed. "I see enough men in the hospital, see what happens to them."

But when they went downstairs, Julian and Anne were there, and Julian and Rollin asked many questions which Brett must answer. He said the fighting in the tangle of the Wilderness gave little chance for artillery, but at Spottsylvania they had a hard and bitter day. "We opened fire about nine in the morning, and they worked on us with muskets and then with artillery till along in the afternoon." Cinda's eyes closed as though to banish a vision of the perils he had survived. "Then they charged us. A lot of our infantry ran over to their lines and surrendered, so there was nothing left in front of us to stop them; and they broke in on our right and rear and took three of our guns and scattered the whole company. We ran like good ones, I can tell you!" He laughed. "I tripped, getting over our breastworks, and came down so hard it knocked the breath out of me. I thought I'd been hit, but I tried to run and found I could—so I did!"

He was smiling, and so were they. "I found a soldier hiding behind a tree. It was a question whether I'd take his tree or his gun, but he was hugging that tree as though it were his sweetheart, so I took his gun. Then General Ewell came along. That one-legged man has just one idea in a fight, and that is to charge; so five companies of us charged five thousand Yankees. We got as far as the caissons they'd taken; but by that time there weren't many of us left, so we scuttled back; but we met our brigades coming up, and Ewell sent us in again." He chuckled. "There was a boy with him, not over twelve years old, riding a pony, and the pony was rearing and pawing, and the boy was shooting a little pistol at the Yankees. It was a sight, I tell you!"

Their breathless laughter, half mirth and half tears, made him pause a moment. "Well, we got the guns, finally," he said. "We'd taken all the implements from each gun, so the Yankees hadn't been able to use them; and we worked them till we hadn't enough men left to keep them going. But that was long enough. By dark, things quieted down, and next morning we pulled back."

He paused, and Julian said quickly: "Go on, Papa."

"Well," Brett continued, "Thursday was the bloody day. God knows how many men Grant threw at us, and how many we killed. I saw one tree almost two feet thick that had been cut down by musket balls. I walked down afterward to where the Yankees had been, and there must have been hundreds of dead men. It was artillery that stopped them. I don't suppose there was a man left all in one piece. That discouraged Grant. He moved off, and we didn't have much to do till the fight at Pole Green Church." He looked at Cinda. "I told you about that."

"Don't tell it again, please."

He nodded. "Well, that's about all. We were in reserve for a while; and now Grant's stopped in front of Petersburg, fought to a standstill, bled white; so we'll have some rest." He said in sober satisfaction: "If he'd come around by water, Grant could have put his army where it is now without losing a man. It's cost him close to a hundred thousand men to come the way he did."

Cinda spoke quietly. "Figures don't mean anything. At the hospital we see men die one at a time. I wonder if generals would go on fighting if they saw men die one at a time, instead of by the thousands."

"The generals are as helpless as any of us, Cinda. We're all just—grains of wheat in the hopper. The stones keep on grinding till there's no more wheat for them to grind."

She shook her head as though to shake away her own thoughts. "For Heaven's sake let's talk about something else for a while." Then suddenly she smiled. "Vesta, can't you and Rollin think of something we might be discussing?"

That made them all laugh together, and they turned to wedding plans. Brett could only stay till Monday. "And I won't be married unless Papa's here," Vesta declared. "So we must hurry." Cinda protested that this left only tomorrow to get ready, but Vesta said it need not take long. "I shall wear the dress I wore to *The Rivals,*" she decided. "Nothing we could possibly manage would be any prettier!"

But the dress was not all; for Rollin and Vesta would leave at once to spend his wound-leave at home. The Yankee cavalry, now at Petersburg, threatened every day to cut the Weldon Railroad, so travel to Wilmington might be interrupted; but the Piedmont from Danville to Greensboro had at last been completed, giving Richmond another direct communication with the lower South; so they could go that way. This meant taking the half-past-seven train for Danville, and couples planning to depart by that early train sometimes elected to be married at six in the morning.

But Vesta brushed aside this suggestion. "That's no time of day to be married! Goodness knows I'm homely enough anyway, but at the crack of dawn—br-r-r!"

She chose to have an evening wedding and an all-night party afterward; so they would be married Sunday evening. "It must be after supper," Cinda decided. "With everything that's fit to eat so scarce, we couldn't feed a crowd, so we'll have to make it a 'starvation party,' Vesta; but perhaps we can have a waffle-worry for early breakfast."

Vesta protested that they could surely manage supper for Julian and Anne and Judge Tudor, for Aunt Enid and the children, for Aunt Tilda and Mr. Streean. "And we can invite the others for afterward." So they settled on this compromise. In spite of the fact that there was little to do by way of preparation, Saturday and Sunday were so crowded with activity that when supper-time came, Cinda was glad to sit a passive listener for a while. They made that supper hour briefly gay, and then Vesta and Anne and Lucy fled away upstairs, and Rollin and Julian too. The others waited in the drawing room, and Enid complained because Trav stayed in Lynchburg, where General Longstreet had been taken after he was wounded, when he might quite as well be here with her. Streean remarked that some wives found they had more freedom when their husbands were not at home; and to Cinda's surprise that silenced Enid. Then Streean turned to Brett, saying that many believed Lee had failed at the Wilderness; that when Longstreet had Grant whipped, Lee let the enemy escape.

"Oh, I know Lee does the best he can," he admitted. "But he's a sick man."

Brett smiled. "If he's sick, I expect Grant wishes he'd get well—or that we'd put some of our healthy generals in his place."

"If Beauregard were in command you'd see the difference."

"We haven't heard much of Beauregard since First Manassas."

"He's the only one of our generals who has never lost a battle," Streean asserted. Cinda pressed her fingertips to her eyes. Could they not forget war for this last hour before Vesta's wedding? "And of course it was Beauregard, not Lee, who saved Richmond. If it hadn't been for Beauregard, Petersburg would have been lost a week after Cold Harbor; and Petersburg means Richmond. Beauregard had only two thousand troops to hold a four-mile line against the first attack, and next day he had about eight thousand against forty thousand; and the day after that, he had to hold off sixty-five thousand men. But he did it. Lee was at Drewry's Bluff, wouldn't believe that Grant had crossed the river. Beauregard had been telling him so for three days; but Lee's an old man, and his mind's no longer resilient."

Cinda watched Brett, uneasily fearing an explosion; but Brett said mildly: "Lee's army's not very resilient, either. Grant couldn't move us out of his way, no matter how many men he threw against us."

"Grant has men to spare," Streean reminded him. "He can afford to waste them. An officer told me yesterday that at Cold Harbor there was a line of dead Yankees two miles long, lying so close together you might have walked the whole distance and never set foot on the ground; and at Spottsylvania there were breastworks so full of bodies that wounded were smothered under them. You could see hands sticking up where wounded men had tried to push the dead men away so they could breathe."

Cinda thought if Streean went on much longer she would scream. Brett was about to speak, but she caught his eyes with a glance so angry that he held his tongue. But Enid said with a fluttering laugh: "I declare, I just get all mixed up about things. Ever since the war started the Yankees have been yelling 'On to Richmond!' and we've been saying we had to hold on to Richmond, and no one ever mentioned Petersburg, but now it's all we hear about."

Streean nodded pompously. "Captain Pew was the first man of my acquaintance to say that Petersburg was the key to Richmond. Lee didn't realize it, and I don't believe the Yankees did, or they'd have taken it when they could."

Cinda seized any pretext to turn the talk away from battles. "How is Captain Pew?" She wished the wedding guests would begin to come.

"Busy, and profitably so," Streean assured her; and he spoke to Brett again. "You know, Brett, speaking of profits, you're missing many opportunities."

Brett met Cinda's eyes. "I haven't given much thought to business recently."

Streean smiled. "I suppose you mean you've been too busy fighting the war. Well, so has the Government; but even the Government finds time to turn a penny now and then. They're selling meal to the public at twelve dollars a peck, meal that they've impressed at the set price. That gives them a profit of forty-five' dollars a bushel. And they're making money in cotton, too. Thousands of bales go out through Wilmington, bought with Confederate bonds and sold for sterling or for gold." He said in what sounded like friendly urgency: "In times like these, Brett, to insure against loss is just common sense. I understand that Mr. Anderson, and Mr. Arnshaw, and Mr. Haxall and many other gentlemen have already arranged with Grant that when Richmond falls, their mills and factories won't be harmed. That's just ordinary business precaution."

Brett said abruptly: "Richmond will not fall."

"Not yet, to be sure." Streean shrugged. "Not as long as we hold Petersburg. And certainly Grant has had his fill for a while."

The door bell rang, the first of their friends began to arrive. There had been a question whether to invite many or few; but though Cinda and Vesta agreed that a few would be better than many, the number somehow grew; and when Vesta and Rollin faced Dr. Minnigerode together, the drawing room and the wide hall and the library were crowded. Vesta was radiant, Rollin's scarred face transfigured. Cinda, while she listened to Doctor Minnigerode's familiar voice with the heavy German accent which in church she seldom noticed, thought even Dolly would think Rollin handsome if she could see him now.

Afterward there was for a while a pleasant turbulence of many voices before the guests began to say good night. President and Mrs. Davis were the first to go, and to Cinda's satisfaction Redford Streean and Tilda did not long remain. Enid, who had few intimates in this company, took Peter home early; but at Vesta's affectionate insistence, Lucy was allowed to stay. General and Mrs. Ould and General and Mrs. Randolph had come together and departed together; but Mattie Ould, who although she was a year or two the younger was Lucy's closest friend, stayed to share with Lucy in the nightlong merry-making.

When the older people were gone there were still Rollin's friends and Vesta's, Anne's and Julian's. Vesta slipped away to change into travelling garb, and someone begged Hetty Cary to sing, and she agreed on condition that they all sing with her. When Vesta reappeared they began to organize charades, and there was a great deal of moving of furniture to arrange settings, and every wardrobe in the house was searched to provide costumes. Cinda had dreaded that long night, sure that sooner or later even the young people would begin to be sleepy, and the hours would drag, and a certain grim determination would creep into the protracted gaiety; and she had promised Brett that, if he chose, he and she would quietly slip away and go to bed till time for Vesta and Rollin to depart. But actually the hours sped, and she forgot to notice whether she was sleepy or not; and when Caesar and June at the appointed hour brought in great platters of waffles, and jugs of molasses, and a hot beverage that would pass for coffee, she was astonished to find the night so quickly gone.

There would be young folk enough to see Vesta and Rollin aboard the cars; so Cinda and Brett said their good-bys at home, and Vesta's warm hug and her grateful kiss told Cinda many happy things. Then they were away.

When they were gone, and Brett was gone, the big house was left an echoing emptiness. Cinda, except for Vesta's little Tommy and the servants, was alone; and life took hold of her and bound her to her tasks again. Now she must do what buying had to be done; and till she went to market she had not realized the prices she must pay. The wave of optimism after Grant gave up a direct assault on Richmond had cut the price of flour from five hundred dollars a barrel to half that, but sugar was still ten dollars a pound.

"Don't give me coffee any more," she told June, on the second morning. "As near as I can reckon, it costs us a dollar a cup, if we put sugar and cream in it."

But June said no matter what it cost, if there was coffee in the house Cinda should have it. "Ain' no good tuh save hit," she said scornfully. "Hit don't git no cheaper, settin' in de can."

In mid-July, Trav came for a Sunday in Richmond, and he and Enid took Cinda home from church to dine with them, and Cinda made him tell her all the news of General Longstreet and of Cousin Louisa. He and the General, Trav said, had come now from Augusta to Petersburg to see General Lee.

"Augusta? I thought he was in Lynchburg," Cinda protested.

"No, only at first. We took him to Colonel Taylor's, and then on to Lynchburg on the cars." Trav said in a nostalgic tone: "You know, that's beautiful country all the way from Orange Court House, not touched by the war. A broad, rolling, fertile valley, and big places as far as Charlottesville; and after you're through the mountains, there are some fine orchards around Amherst."

"Oh, Travis, stop talking like a farmer! Tell me about Cousin Jeems. Where did he stay in Lynchburg?"

"With General Garland's mother. 'Sister Caroline,' they call her."

"I remember her at his wedding. She lives just a block or two from Judge Garland's, where Cousin Jeems and Louisa were married. Mrs. Samuel Garland?"

"No." Trav shook his head. "No, Mrs. Samuel Garland is 'Sister Mary,' 'Sister Caroline' is Mrs. Maurice Garland." With that careful precision which was his habit, he explained: "Judge Garland's house is at the head of Madison Street, with that steep hill running down to Blackwater Creek behind the house. Then on one side of Madison Street there's Grandma Slaughter's house, and then a steep field they call Aunt Mary's cow lot; and on the other side Charles Slaughter's lot runs from First to Second Street. Mr. Slaughter married Mary Garland. Major Latrobe was wounded in the thigh the day before Longstreet was hurt, and we took him to Lynchburg, too. He was at Mr. Jack Slaughter's. Then Dr. Murrell lives at the corner of Second and Madison, and 'Sister Mary' on the corner of Third and Madison. But 'Sister Caroline' lives further along, between Third and Fourth."

Cinda laughed. "No wonder it's hard to keep them straight! Was Cousin Louisa there when Cousin Jeems got there?"

"No, she was in Augusta when she heard he was wounded. She left Garland and the baby in Augusta and started for Lynchburg. The cars were so crowded and so slow that she came all the way by horse and buggy, travelling day and night, never knowing whether he was still alive."

"Poor thing!"

"She had a hard time," he agreed. "But by the time she got to Lynchburg, the General was out of danger."

"Why did she take the General all the way down to Augusta?"

"Oh, that was our idea, Captain Goree's and mine. Even before General Hunter's raid, we'd decided General Longstreet needed more quiet. He was pretty miserable, lots of pain, and mighty nervous. The first two or three weeks after he was hurt, he could hardly talk without having tears come into his eyes. He said to me one day: 'Damn it, Currain, why should a bullet through a man make a baby of him?' But you know everybody on Garland Hill is kinfolks—cousins and aunts and uncles and in-laws."

"I know."

"Well, then you can imagine all the visiting back and forth; and of course everyone wanted to pay their respects to the General; and we finally decided he'd be better off in the country, so we took him out to Colonel Jack Alexander's."

"In Rustburg?"

"Yes, out ten or twelve miles. Locust Grove, his place is called. He has about a thousand acres of land. The house is on a knoll beside the road just before you come to the Campbell County Court House. It's brick, two stories and a full basement and a full attic. The walls are a foot and a half thick, so it's always cool; and there are four windows in each room, so you always get a breeze. You look across the valley toward Lynchburg and the mountains; and the valley's level and all under the plow. There's a summer dining room in the basement, with soapstone tiles for a floor that make it seem cool on the hottest day. General Longstreet had a bed room in the house; but Goree and I had a room in a building in the front yard that used to be the County Clerk's office. It was a mighty comfortable home; plenty of servants, three children, fine gardens and fruit trees and stables." He smiled. "They named a colt after Longstreet while we were there. The General was a lot more comfortable, with not so many callers. But then General Hunter headed toward Lynchburg, and we thought he might send some cavalry to seize the General, so we decided he'd be safer in Lynchburg, especially if no one knew where he was. So Mrs. Olivia Page, Colonel Alexander's sister——"

"I thought it was Octavia who married Edwin Page."

"No, Olivia. She drove out to Rustburg as if she were just paying a call, and while she was indoors I sent her coachman on an errand, and Captain Goree and I helped the General into the carriage. He got down between the seats with a shawl thrown over him——"

Enid and the children had been listening in silent attention, but Lucy laughed at the picture Trav's words evoked. "Papa, I can't imagine General Longstreet hiding under a shawl. That big man!"

"Well, he did," Trav smilingly assured her. "Not even the coachman knew he was there. Then Mrs. Page came out of the house and got in and drove back to Lynchburg and smuggled the General into her home."

"Did Cousin Louisa go with him?" Cinda asked.

"No, she stayed with us at Colonel Alexander's, letting on the General was still there."

"That must have been an exciting adventure for Mrs. Page," Cinda commented.

"I reckon it didn't worry her."

Enid said: "Oh Trav, tell Cinda what General Lee said to her." Cinda was surprised. Enid often belittled Trav, or sought to silence him, but Cinda had never heard her thus prompt him while he held the centre of the stage. Perhaps the little idiot was coming to her senses. Trav at the suggestion chuckled and said:

"Why, General Lee told Mrs. Page it needed three salvos of Yankee artillery fire to rouse General Longstreet, but that once roused he was terrible."

Cinda colored with loyal resentment. "Nonsense! Do you think General Lee really said that, Travis?"

"I wouldn't be surprised. It's certainly true. General Longstreet is slow getting started, but once in a fight no one fights harder."

Cinda made an impatient gesture. "But Travis, after General Hunter was driven off, you didn't have to leave Lynchburg, did you? Or are they as pinched for food as we are?"

"No, there's food enough; but of course prices are high. Sister Caroline's son, General Garland, the one who was killed at South Mountain, left his mother a hundred and fifty thousand dollars; but his estate has shrunk so much that her income last year was only about two thousand."

Cinda smiled. "I think it's about time you stopped being so interested in figures, Travis. They're mighty depressing, nowadays."

Trav grinned awkwardly. "I suppose so, but I always think that way. No, she wanted the General and Mrs. Longstreet to stay. You know her son commanded the Eleventh Virginia in Longstreet's brigade at Manassas three years ago, and she and Longstreet talked about him for hours on end. But Mrs. Longstreet wanted to get back to the children, and after General Hunter was driven off, we thought the General would be safer farther south; so he asked Secretary Seddon's permission to go to Georgia. He was still pretty weak, but we stopped over at Danville with Mr. Estes and let the General rest a day or two. Augusta's a beautiful town; wide streets with rows of trees down each side, and a double row down the middle, and flowers everywhere, and no signs of war, except that the arsenal is busy and the powder mills. But there are lots of fine carriages on the streets, and the ladies' dresses are mighty handsome."

"Who is Cousin Jeems visiting there?"

"At first he stayed at Sunnyside, the Carmichael plantation, about six miles out along the Savannah road. His cousin Elizabeth Eve Longstreet from Richmond County married Anderson Carmichael. Dr. Eve took care of the General, and Mrs. Carmichael and Mrs. Longstreet nursed him. But now he's with another cousin, Mrs. Sibley. She was Emma Eve Longstreet. She had a son born last summer, and she named the baby after the General."

"Is he getting along all right?"

"Slowly, yes. The bullet paralyzed his right arm, so he can't use it; but he's learning to write with his left hand, and the doctor told him to keep pulling at his right arm to give it exercise. Yes, he's getting better, but he worries. That's why he came to talk with General Lee. He says Grant has Richmond under siege, and that there can be only one end to that."

"We hear no such talk in Richmond," Cinda declared. "Everybody thinks Grant is whipped, just the way McClellan was two years ago."

"Grant's not McClellan. Longstreet says Grant will never retreat, and that every move he makes will bring nearer the day Richmond has to be given up."

Cinda said in a dry tone: "Richmond doesn't seem to think so. Life here is just one long celebration; parties, dances, the streets full of able-bodied young clerks in clothes much too good for their salaries. I'm not sure whether people are lost in a fools' paradise, or just recklessly ready for any extravagance."

Enid said, with an echo of her familiar querulous tone: "I declare, Travis, if you think Richmond's in danger, I should think you'd want to take Lucy and Peter and me somewhere where we'd be safe."

Lucy urged: "Now Mama, Papa will take care of us. He always does."

Enid shrugged. "Leaving us here where we can't even get enough to eat? He says there's plenty to eat in Georgia."

Trav said soberly: "I thought you'd rather stay here, Enid; be in your own home."

"It's not much of a home with no husband! You know I'd rather be with you, Trav." Her tone, to Cinda's astonishment, was almost tender.

"Why—if you want to go, I'll take you to Augusta." But he spoke so reluctantly that even Cinda thought him unkind, and Enid colored resentfully.

"Oh, I certainly don't want to traipse around all over creation after you if you don't want me!"

Cinda took a hand. "Why don't you go, Enid? I expect you'd be a lot more comfortable there, and you'd see more of Travis."

"Oh, if I were there he'd probably spend all his time somewhere else."

Trav said uncertainly: "Well—I'm leaving in the morning."

"You know perfectly well I can't get ready so soon!"

Lucy cried: "Oh, Mama, yes we can. I'll help!" But Enid waited for Trav to speak again, and when he did not do so, she said:

"I wouldn't know a soul in Augusta. I'd probably be miserable there. Unless you want me, Trav."

"Of course he wants you!" Cinda assured her. "Don't you, Travis?" She said impatiently: "Speak up, for once, can't you?"

"Why, yes," he said. "Yes, Enid, I hope you'll come."

When this was settled, Enid called old April and she and Lucy went to begin the pleasant flurry of packing. Trav walked back to Fifth Street with Cinda. He was so abstracted that she supposed he had misgivings about this removal to Augusta, and she sought to beguile him to talk. "Is Cousin Jeems really discouraged? They say General Early's marching down the Valley now to invade the North. Won't that do some good?"

"Well, Longstreet thinks if we can hold out till November, President Lincoln may be defeated." But he spoke so absently that Cinda looked at him in sudden foreboding; and he said: "I wanted to tell you, Cinda. I didn't tell Enid; but I've been to Martinston. I went really to see Ed Blandy, but I saw Tony too. Cinda, Darrell's dead."

She thought her heart missed its beat. "Oh, Trav! Really?"

"Yes. But Tilda had better not know."

"Why not, Travis?"

"Well, it was pretty ugly. Some bushwhackers killed him for shooting Mrs. Blandy." She could not speak, holding to his arm, supporting herself; and he told her he had gone to Martinston from Augusta. Ed Blandy, except for an unnatural cheerfulness, had at first seemed to be all right; but after telling Trav about Darrell's death, he began to cackle with hysterical mirth. "Then his little boy, Eddie, the one who shot Tony, said I'd better leave him alone," Trav explained. "He said if Ed gets too excited he's that way for days, just crazy."

"Oh, Travis, I'm so sorry. That was hard for you! But if Mr. Blandy is that way, perhaps it isn't true about Darrell."

"Yes, it's true. Tony told me the whole thing. Ed tried to save Darrell, and Jeremy Blackstone hit him on the head, and Ed's never been himself since."

"But couldn't Tony do something? I despised Darrell, but—couldn't Tony stop them?"

Trav shook his head. "He was still weak from his wound, and there were a dozen of these men."

She nodded. "I hope Tilda never knows."

"Tony won't tell her." He added: "You wouldn't know **Tony**, Cinda."

"Why not, for Heaven's sake?"

Trav seemed uncertain whether to smile or frown. "Well, he's dyed his hair and his beard, dyed them black; and he shaves his mustache and his lower lip, and lets his beard grow on his cheeks and under his chin."

She tried to picture Tony thus disguised; and she said in sudden understanding, "Why, Travis, he must look like President Lincoln."

Trav nodded. "That's the first thing I thought, when I saw him. He was on the veranda as I rode up to the house. But when you're close to him, he just looks like an old man with dyed hair."

"He always did look a little like Mr. Lincoln, Travis. I've told Brett so. Except his expression, and his eyes; and of course he's not as tall. Did you say anything about it?" He shook his head, and she asked: "Do you suppose he does it on purpose?"

He looked at her in astonishment. "Why should he?"

"Did he say anything about—our being kin?"

"No. I didn't stay long, just long enough to ask him about **Darrell**. I didn't even go indoors."

She guessed there was something he had not told her; but clearly, whatever it was, he did not mean to tell. They were at her door. "Come in?" she suggested.

"No, I'll have to help Enid get ready for an early start tomorrow." He bade her good-by.

Trav and Enid and the children departed, and at that week's end Burr came back from Raleigh. His hands were stumps that made Cinda's heart ache; but he was sure he could handle reins and weapons well enough to return to duty. If that was what he wished, she would not oppose him. She asked many questions about Barbara and the babies, and he answered happily; but when he spoke of affairs in Raleigh, there was hard anger in eyes and voice.

"Everybody down there seems to think we ought to give in to the Yankees. Mr. Holden, the editor of the *Standard,* says North Carolina ought to secede from the Confederacy."

"Well, we all seceded from the Union. I suppose she thinks she has a right to!"

"She'd better not try it!" Burr retorted. "This Mr. Holden is just a traitor. They've proved that he organized a society called the Heroes of America, to try to help the North. They say President Lincoln's a member, and that there are thousands of members in North Carolina and all through the mountains, even in Virginia. There's a judge in Salisbury who turns deserters loose as fast as the conscript bureau catches them. I suppose he's a member."

Cinda nodded wearily. "Anne's father said the other day that in Southwest Virginia just about everybody's for giving up."

"Nobody but the white trash!"

"Well, he spoke of several lawyers, and county officers; Mr. Hoge in Montgomery County, and Mr. Camper in Botetourt, and a sheriff, and some men in Pulaski. He says they're talking of organizing a new state out there, to make peace with the North. So it isn't just North Carolina, Burr. It's Virginia too, and all over the South."

Burr said stubbornly: "Well, anyway, I think they ought to hang Holden! But he's actually running for Governor!"

"They don't hang politicians, Burr. It's a pity, too—they talk so much. I sometimes think talking too much is the worst of all crimes. It was all the talking and calling names in the North and in the South ever since I was a girl that finally started this war. And of course the ones who talked aren't doing the fighting, except Roger Pryor and a few others like him." She laughed. "We're talking too much ourselves, right now, and about the wrong things. Tell me more about Barbara and the babies."

She had a long happy evening with Burr, and even after he was gone some of his youthful optimism remained in her. But Brett when he next came home was uneasy about General Johnston, facing Sherman north of Atlanta. "Sherman keeps edging him back," he said. "If we lose Atlanta, that's the end of us."

"Oh, Atlanta isn't so much." She wished to hearten him. "I heard at the hospital today that General Early has captured Baltimore! Wouldn't you trade Atlanta for Baltimore?"

He shook his head. "Don't believe all you hear, Cinda. Early hasn't more than a few thousand men. He couldn't hold Baltimore if he took it. But if Sherman takes Atlanta, he'll set his teeth and hang on."

She learned next day that the rumor of the taking of Baltimore was false; and at church on Sunday Mrs. Davis told her that Early, after going within sight of Washington, had crossed the Potomac back into Virginia. Monday, General Johnston was removed from command of the army facing Sherman, and General Hood was put in his place. The *Examiner* said Johnston was a victim of spite on the part of President Davis, but Cinda was sure that if he had been doing well Mr. Davis would have kept him in command.

The summer days droned on; the sound of guns toward Petersburg became a commonplace, no longer heeded. General Hood reported successful battle against the Yankees, but Sherman somehow still held his ground outside Atlanta. Vesta and Rollin came back from South Carolina, Vesta serenely happy, Rollin hale and well. They had stopped for a few days at the Plains, and Cinda could never hear enough of Jenny and of her grandchildren there. They were all perfection, Vesta assured her. "But Jenny's worried for fear Atlanta will be captured, and maybe Mobile." Cinda in a sudden surge of weariness pressed her hands to her temples. Must she now begin to worry about Mobile? Where was Mobile anyway, and why should anyone worry about it? She shut her eyes, as though thus to shut away her own thoughts. "People down there say General Hood was wrong to fight," Vesta told her. "That he just lost a lot of men for nothing."

"Tell me more about the children," Cinda suggested. "I'm sick to death of hearing about generals." What bliss it would be to escape for a while from these thoughts of death, of coming defeat, of hopeless doom. What would it be like to be free again from the sight and sound and smell of hurt and dying men, and the sound of distant guns, and the talk, talk, talk that filled the air? Would she live long enough to see that day? When it rained, you felt it would never stop raining; when it was cold you thought you would never be warm again. Thus now, though she tried, she could not picture to herself a peaceful world.

Not even Brett in his occasional hours at home brought her comfort. He said the army was being whittled away by steady losses. "Not only men but guns. Losing men is bad enough, but losing guns is worse; and one way and another we've lost twenty-four guns in our corps alone since May." And the men, he said, were weary of spending day on day in the entrenchments. "They're safe enough, if they're careful," he said. "But they get bored. They hold their hands up over the breastworks, hoping they'll be wounded. 'Feeling for a furlough' they call it. And they desert at every chance. Even some officers are deserting now. The only excitement they get is wondering when the Yankees will spring their mine. They can hear the digging." Petersburg was having a hard time, he said; the Yankees dropped shells into the town right along.

"We've escaped that, at least so far," Cinda reminded him. "And we haven't had any raiders actually in Richmond." She tried to laugh. "So we haven't had to bury our silver. I heard of one lady in Petersburg who put everything in a pit in her garden and covered it with boards and then with dirt, and planted cabbages all over it. But the refugees have horrible stories to tell. General Hunter will be hated in the Valley for a hundred years. You know he burned V.M.I., and Governor Letcher's home too, for no reason at all."

"I heard so, yes."

"And the refugees say that even if they don't burn your house, they take everything they can find, from hams out of the smoke house to gold watches out of your pockets. But of course I don't believe all the tales."

"They're true," Brett admitted. "Too many of them, anyway. I've seen houses where they'd cut pictures out of their frames, split up pianos and doors and furniture just for the fun of smashing things, dumped books off the shelves and torn them apart and poured vinegar or molasses or any sort of mess over them. They take what they want and ruin what they don't take. They even shoot the cows and pigs and leave them to rot."

She asked hopelessly: "What do they expect to accomplish, Brett Dewain? Our soldiers didn't do such things in Pennsylvania. Even if the Yankees beat us, we'll always hate them. After the things the Yankee soldiers have done, the North and the South can't ever be friends again; not for generations, anyway. What will the rest of our lives be like?"

He shook his head. "I don't know. I've stopped trying to guess the future, Cinda. I just know that whatever happens to the South, I want the same thing to happen to us, to you and me."

"Haven't we a right to think of ourselves at all; of our family, of our homes?"

"A right, yes, I suppose," he admitted. "But we've thought too much about our rights, all of us. Each state's so busy standing up for its rights that they haven't time to fight for the Confederacy. When sovereign states confederate for a common purpose, they have to give up some of their sovereignty, or they'll fail. But it's a lesson we take a long time to learn."

When that famous Yankee mine at Petersburg, so long preparing, was finally exploded, a few hundred men died; but that was all. The monotonous days went on, and each day a few more men were killed, and a steady trickle of wounded came into the hospitals, and those hopes which in June and July had flickered for a while began to fade and die, subsiding into ashes under the summer heat as flames die in sunlight. Prices began to rise again. Vesta told Cinda one night:

"Mama, I went shopping today. I spent fifteen hundred dollars in an hour." She laughed. "It was so outrageous it was funny. I paid five dollars for a paper of pins, and five dollars apiece for three spools of thread. Cotton thread, too."

"You might as well spend what we have," Cinda reminded her. "Money buys less every day." A helpless submission weighed her down, physical weariness and vanishing hope left her dull and spiritless. She could not share the indignation everyone felt at General Grant's flat refusal to exchange prisoners. Tilda thought it heartless.

"But Redford says," she admitted, "that if they send back our prisoners, we put them to fighting again; and Grant knows it, and taking our prisoners and keeping them is as good from his point of view as killing them. Redford thinks that's good business." She added in a lower tone: "I should think he'd get tired, sometimes, of always being such a good business man."

A faint stir of curiosity, inspired by her tone, a desire to see Tilda and Streean together, led Cinda to invite them to dinner and with an eye on Tilda to lead Streean into talk. "I know so little of what is going on," she told him. "But of course you're so well-informed."

"I make it my business to be," he assured her. "Brett feels bound to shut his eyes, but I don't. The time is coming when a man must decide what's the wisest thing for him to do, and the only way he can decide is to watch events from one day to the next. It's just a question of time before Lee will have lost so many men that he can't hold his lines. That will be the end of Richmond. I mean to know beforehand when that's going to happen." He added thoughtfully: "In fact, I think I shall begin to take proper measures when Atlanta falls."

"Do you think Atlanta will fall? People say General Sherman's army is doomed if we just cut the railroad behind him."

Streean smiled. "The optimism of fools is the wise man's opportunity," he assured her. "Flour went down to two hundred dollars a barrel this summer, just because with Richmond safe for a while people thought the war was won. I bought all I could find at that price and stored it with what I already had in the warehouse on Cary Street. I'll sell that flour for a thousand dollars a barrel, before very many months." And he said: "Sherman will take Atlanta. Hood's no match for him. The only chance we have left is that Lincoln may be beaten in November."

"Do you think he will be?"

"If they nominate General McClellan against him, he may be."

Tilda said quietly: "I don't believe it. I think he's a great man. People love him."

Streean smiled in amused derision. "It isn't people who win elections, my dear—it's politicians pulling the strings, making the people dance."

Tilda met his eyes. "You used to be a politician, Redford, but you didn't seem to play the right tunes."

He chuckled, undisturbed by her open contempt. "I gave up politics a long time ago."

After that day, Cinda never thought of Tilda without a faint secret excitement, an unformed expectation. She made opportunities to see her sister, and once she spoke of what Tilda had said about Lincoln. "I know you didn't always feel so."

"None of us did," Tilda reminded her. "But Cinda, the war's going to be over some day. I hope he's still President when that happens. He doesn't hate us."

"Most of us hate him."

"I think we're wrong." Tilda's head lifted. "Sometimes I'm sort of proud of being related to him. Aren't you?"

"I don't know," Cinda admitted. "But I'm not ashamed of it. He's a good man."

August dragged itself away in a succession of sweltering days when the pitilessly blazing sun seemed to sear everything it touched, and the air quivered and trembled so that objects at a little distance might be blurred and distorted. Except for the ambulances forever coming and returning, there were few vehicles upon the streets; for even the cavalry were short of horses, and there was not feed enough to cover the ribs of the animals men rode. Not only men and women and children but the dumb things went on short rations; yet in this starved and hopeless time, the women Cinda met still pursued vain hopes. If Atlanta were mentioned, it was always with a surface confidence that Hood would keep Sherman at bay. Even Cinda sometimes, since no disaster struck, put despairing thoughts away, till one night Brett came home and said Grant had cut the Weldon Railroad beyond Petersburg.

"That's bad news, isn't it?" she asked.

"Yes," he admitted. "Yes, that's bad. The army has to be fed, and all our supplies now will have to come in wagons, or by the Danville road."

"Why can't General Lee beat them again? He's done it over and over."

"His army's shrinking away. The Conscription Bureau doesn't furnish enough men to make up our losses and our deserters." He said in hard tones: "Too many rich men and too many of the big planters have bought exemptions. Even now, the Governor is exempting fifty or sixty men a day." His lips twisted in anger. "Any rich man who wants to can buy his way out. Most of the men in the ranks are poor devils without a dollar to their name." His eyes abruptly filled. "And by God, Cinda, they're wonderful! They don't get enough to eat, and they live on nothing, and laugh at their troubles and fight like wildcats. There never were such men!"

"Lots of our friends are still fighting," she reminded him. "But I'm about ready to call quits. I don't hesitate to urge Julian to stay at home, and I'd beg you and Burr to get out of it somehow, if I thought you'd listen to me." Brett smiled, but she insisted. "I mean it, Brett Dewain. If there's any way for you to get out, I wish you would. I don't blame poor women who write begging their husbands to desert, and I don't blame the men who do it!"

He said gently: "I know, Cinda. But I'll keep on. There weren't many people like us in the South to begin with, and so there weren't many in the army. But a lot of us have been killed; and a lot of us, people who call themselves gentry, have dodged out of fighting. Mr. Haxall's a millionaire, but he got an appointment as an assistant assessor at nothing a year so he wouldn't be conscripted; and there are plenty like him. Half the men who are still fighting are what we used to call poor white trash! God bless them, they're grand! I'm proud to be in the same army with them."

He stayed over Sunday, the last Sunday in that dreary August of fading hope and mounting dread. She told him Streean's certainty that Atlanta could not stand.

"I hope he's wrong," he said. "If Sherman takes Atlanta, he'll cut the spinal column of the South. There won't be any hope at all after that."

At church a week later, on the fourth of September, she heard the news of Atlanta's fall.

13

Mosby's men, although the prospects of rich booty attracted to his ranks many who were bent on loot alone, had nevertheless a lively appreciation of the humorous aspects of their adventures. Joe Blackwell's lonely farm near Piedmont, which came to be known as "Mosby's Headquarters," was a jolly place, where men laughed equally at their own mishaps and at the discomfiture of the Yankees. "Chief" Blackwell himself was a robust giant whose slaves, except for feminine house servants, had run away long since to become camp followers of the Yankees. His farm hand was an Irishman named Lot Ryan, who because he lacked teeth with which to bite cartridges was unfit for military service. The Chief's house was small, and there were only eight chairs at his table; but a second table and a third and even a fourth could always be set if hungry Rangers must be fed.

Blackwell, a voluble braggart who liked to talk of his exploits but never risked his skin on a raid, was a natural butt for jokes. He swaggered in a gray uniform, with enormous spurs and pistols in his belt; and he was always ready on a moment's notice to harangue an audience on any subject under the sun, from the science of war to the art of making love. At night, strutting to and fro by the dying coals of a bonfire in the farm yard, he would deliver himself of endless dogmatic disquisitions, while his listeners chuckled with quiet mirth or guffawed in louder laughter.

Faunt thought him vulgar and tiresome, and the fact that the Chief amused the others reminded him that though he rode with these men and fought with them, he was not one with them in their careless fellowship. They paid him perfect courtesy, they never questioned his actions or his manner, but they never sought his company. He knew himself set apart by the fact that alone among them he never brought in prisoners. They were as deadly as he in the rushing scurry of combat, the shock of a charge well driven home, the blood-stirring pursuit; but if a man threw up his hands in surrender to them, he was spared. Of Faunt this was not true—and they knew it, and he knew they knew.

Once Colonel Mosby himself spoke of this to Faunt, not chidingly but in quiet curiosity. Mosby had sent the word abroad for a rendezvous at Upperville. On the way, Faunt encountered a regiment of Yankee cavalry. He whirled his horse, and the whole regiment came thundering after him. While he rode, he fitted to one of his pistols the adjustable stock which made it more accurate at long range; and he chose a spot where the road crossed a rise of ground, and wheeled his horse and opened fire. Even at seventy yards, he threw the head of the column into a delaying confusion that let him turn unseen into a byway and thread a path through the woodlands and leap his horse over a rail fence into another road.

But he found himself there confronting two bluecoats as surprised as he. Before they could lift their weapons he lifted his, and remembered as he did so that he had not reloaded the empty cylinder. The mate to that pistol was in his saddle holster, and there was a Colt Navy of somewhat lighter caliber in his belt, under his coat on the left-hand side. But the saddle holster was buckled and the Yankees' carbines were in their hands, so there was no time to arm himself. Instantly he levelled the useless weapon, made his horse bound toward the Yankees, and called for their surrender.

They were no more than boys, too young for quick decision. They dropped their pieces, and he drove the men ahead of him. But he must be at Upperville that night, and he had twenty miles or more to go; so it was necessary to dispose of these prisoners. He might have shot them out of hand, but Faunt had a sardonic sense of humor. As though absent-mindedly, he pushed his horse between them, leaving one of them on either side and a little behind.

They took the chance he seemed to give them. The boy on the left threw his arms around Faunt's body to pin him; the other snatched the stocked pistol, and wrenched the loaded weapon from the saddle holster. They fell back in triumph, thinking the tables turned; and Faunt drew the Navy from his belt and shot one and then the other.

As the riders fell, one horse pranced aside and then stood snorting. Faunt pursued and caught the other, and led it back. He dismounted to recover his heavy pistols, and removed the adjustable stock and secured it to the cantle of his saddle; and he was charging the empty chambers in the cylinders when Colonel Mosby and two of his men, drawn by the shots, leaped the fence and pulled up beside him.

"What happened?" Mosby asked, looking at the blue-clad bodies in the road.

"They tried to escape," Faunt explained. "You'll find their carbines back down the road."

Mosby's companions dismounted to search the dead boys, to take their money and watches, to strip off their boots and to halter their horses for leading. While they went to recover the carbines, Mosby and Faunt rode ahead, and Colonel Mosby remarked: "You seldom take prisoners, Mr. Currain."

His tone was neither criticism nor question, but Faunt for once was in a mood for speech. "I once lived down on the Northern Neck," he said quietly. "My wife and baby died there, and I built a chapel over their graves. Yankee patrols have stabled their horses in that chapel, befouled it, trampled those graves."

Mosby nodded in quiet understanding. "I suppose a personal hatred is as good as any other reason for killing Yankees."

The other Rangers rode up on their heels. "At least, Colonel," Faunt remarked, "I don't fight for a chance to rob the dead."

"The hope of gain is what holds us together."

"It's not your motive," Faunt retorted. Mosby himself never took a share of any booty. "Nor mine." He felt a flame of anger, never long subdued. "I'd like to kill every man in blue, from the least one of them up to—" He caught himself. "Up to Abraham Lincoln." He felt Mosby's glance, and he said harshly: "No, I don't take prisoners." And after a few paces, in a more controlled tone, he added: "The Yankees have ravaged Virginia from the Potomac to the Rappahannock. They've destroyed the finest, gentlest way of life men ever succeeded in creating on this earth. Lincoln's men!" He spat the name, said again: "No, I don't take prisoners, Colonel."

Mosby touched his horse. "We've far to go," he remarked; and for an hour, without speech, they held a faster pace. Faunt, hearing his own words over again in his thoughts, remembered another man who sometimes rolled forth execrations against the North; that little actor whom he had first seen long ago in Richmond, after John Brown's insane attack on Harper's Ferry. Wilkes Booth's first generous gift of morphine, which Faunt had gone to fetch through the lines, was not the last; nor was it the last time Faunt did a similar errand. The secret route through Maryland to Washington was familiar to him now. There were men along the way, Thomas Jones whose farm topped the high bluff below Pope's Creek and who received mail and travellers from the South and sent them safely northward; George Atzerodt who made wagons at Port Tobacco and had a barge that could set two men and their horses across the Potomac; John Surratt who kept the tavern at Surrattsville and was the Federal postmaster there and ran mail for the Confederates as well; Sam Arnold who could always be found at Barnum's City Hotel in Baltimore or at his brother's home in Hoffstown; "Peanuts" Burroughs who kept the stage door at Ford's Theatre in Washington. Any one of these men would help him or hide him according to his needs. Booth had vouched for him to them all; and Faunt had spent more than one hour with that little man who never forgot he was an actor, who sought always the center of the stage. Some day, Booth had said more than once, he would come and ride with Mosby's men; and Faunt had promised him a welcome.

When they slackened their pace, Mosby told Faunt the purpose of this gathering tonight. "General Sheridan has been put in command in the Valley," he said. "We'll give him an early lesson." They found scores of men at the rendezvous before them, and next day three hundred Rangers climbed the easy road toward Snicker's Gap. When they paused to breathe their horses, Faunt looked back across the wide and lovely sweep of Loudoun County, wooded hills and pleasant valleys and the wall of the Bull Run Mountains beyond. From this distance no scars of war were visible. Loudoun and Fauquier were the heart of "Mosby's Confederacy," that region behind the Yankee lines where a handful of partisans kept all Grant's communications in daily, nightly peril. When the men moved on again, Faunt thought that beautiful reach of country was well worth fighting for.

The Gap was unguarded. They descended steeply to the levels and forded the Shenandoah and hid themselves in the low wooded hills east of Berryville. Their scouts presently reported a cavalcade of five or six hundred wagons coming from Harper's Ferry toward Berryville; and although the train was guarded by almost ten times their own number, the Rangers in a surprise attack scattered the escorting brigade, burned seventy-five wagons, and drove back up the road through Snicker's Gap two hundred prisoners, six or seven hundred horses and mules, and more than two hundred head of beef cattle.

They rode in a high and laughing exultation, for this had been their greatest deed; but Mosby expected Sheridan's swift counter attack, so he left Captain Chapman with a company of Rangers to watch the Valley. Faunt stayed with them. Sheridan, since the raid had interrupted his communications, fell back to Halltown; but he burned barns and corn cribs and killed or drove off livestock from the farms, and Captain Chapman fretted for a chance at him. When a brigade of Custer's cavalry went into bivouac at dusk one day near Berryville, Faunt undertook to spy out the camp and estimate the chances for a night attack.

Since he must wait for darkness, he returned to a house near Castleman's Ferry, a quarter-mile north of the spot where the Rangers had crossed on their successful foray. The householder was a gentleman named Province McCormick. He and his wife greeted Faunt hospitably, they gave him supper, they exulted in Mosby's fine stroke at Sheridan's wagon train. Mr. McCormick's daughter and her baby were at home, his son-in-law was here ill and unable to leave his bed.

When night came, Faunt delayed till the enemy cavalry encampment was surely asleep. Then he proceeded cautiously upon his mission, flanking the road that climbed from the river toward Berryville and avoiding the town itself. When he approached the camp, he left his horse and went afoot, secret in the darkness. He discovered a picket watching the road and crept near the man; but a shot would alarm the Yankees, so he summoned the sentry to surrender.

"I'll be damned if I will!" the Yankee retorted, and fired; but he missed, and Faunt put a bullet precisely through his forehead. Then, since a surprise attack was now impossible, he rode back to the river and crossed and reported his failure.

Next morning they had begun the ascent to the Gap when, looking back, they saw a house burning in the Valley below them. Faunt recognized it as Province McCormick's home by the Ferry; and he and Captain Chapman rode full pitch that way, the other Rangers hard on their heels. When they came there, the house was already beyond saving; but Faunt saw Mr. McCormick, and his daughter, with her baby in her arms, under the trees by the gate. The sick man, Mr. McCormick's son-in-law, lay wrapped in blankets on the ground beside them.

Faunt and Captain Chapman reached the gate and pulled up their horses, the Rangers clustering around. Faunt lifted his hat; he said to his commanding officer: "Captain, this is Mrs. Brown. And Mr. McCormick. And Mr. Brown. They gave me supper last night." He asked Mr. McCormick: "Sir, where is Mrs. McCormick?"

The old gentleman seemed half-dazed. "Why, after you were gone, a messenger brought a note to tell Mrs. McCormick that her sister was dead. She left at dawn to go to her sister's home. Then an hour ago Captain Drake of the Fifth Michigan cavalry rode up and accused us of signalling to your men. We did light a lamp last night, but it was just to read the note about Mrs. McCormick's sister; and I told him that, but he said I was a liar and that the light was a signal to the assassins who killed one of his pickets. He said he was going to burn my house."

Mrs. Brown spoke in sobbing rage. "Two of them caught me and stripped my ring off my hand and dropped me over the banisters. I ran back upstairs to save what I could, and they set fire to the house under me." Her voice rang with scorn. "I saw even their chaplain steal a paper of pins out of Mother's bureau drawer! My baby was asleep, and when I went to get him, one of them said: 'Let the damned little rebel burn!' But I got my baby!"

Captain Chapman asked crisply: "Which way did they go?"

Mr. McCormick said: "Down the lane toward Mr. Sowers's house." He turned to point, and uttered an exclamation; and they saw in that direction a smoke column billowing above the trees.

Faunt instantly flung his horse to a gallop, Captain Chapman came beside him, and the others pressed on their heels. When they reached the Sowers house it could not be saved, and the Yankees were gone; but they saw another smoke column a short half-mile beyond. Faunt spurred his horse, and he called to Captain Chapman:

"No quarter today, Captain!"

The other nodded; he shouted over his shoulder: "No quarter today!" The order ran from man to man.

They burst from the woods below the burning house at full gallop; and before the Yankees could form, the Rangers were upon them. Many of the enemy, with no time to reach their horses, squandered like quail from a flushed covey; and those already in the saddle, after an instant's milling confusion, broke in headlong flight.

Faunt, hot after them, firing carefully in deadly rage, liked the hard jar of the heavy pistol in his hand. There was a Yankee crouching in a fence corner, cowering helplessly. Faunt saw him at close range, and since his pistols were sighted for fifty yards he remembered to aim low. With the shot, he moved clear of the smoke and saw the man sliding helplessly sidewise and saw the dark hole in the Yankee's cheekbone where the heavy bullet entered. Another bluecoat tried to swing his horse into the woods, but a low branch swept him from the saddle. While the Yankee lay on his back upon the ground, the breath jarred out of him, Faunt checked his horse long enough to make that bullet sure. A third, on a good mount, raced ahead. Faunt nursed his horse in relentless chase; but this man had too great a start, so Faunt at last turned back toward the burning house.

Rangers were searching the woods, and he saw more than one of them stop to kill a wounded Yankee. They left no living man behind; but when the troop was reassembled, Faunt discovered an unharmed prisoner among them. Hard rage still on him, he spoke to Captain Chapman.

"The orders were no quarter, sir."

Chapman hesitated, but two or three men muttered in stern agreement, and the Captain swore. "Damn them, house-burners, abusing women, yes! Take him into the woods!"

Faunt and three others, their pistols drawn, rode with the prisoner a little off the road. Faunt asked: "Are you ready?"

The young man smiled faintly. "Why, I'd like a moment."

Faunt nodded, and the Yankee swung to the ground. He knelt with his back toward them, as serenely as though he were alone, and he bowed his head for a time that seemed long. Then he rose, and turned to face them, holding his coat open, baring his breast. Faunt shot him through the heart.

Next day they rejoined Colonel Mosby, and Faunt heard Captain Chapman's report. "Thirty horses, no prisoners."

Mosby made no comment, but that evening he called Faunt to him. "Mr. Currain," he said gravely, "our operations have taken on a new character. General Grant has given orders to hang our men whenever they are captured." Faunt's lips set; but Mosby added: "However, that may only be meant to frighten us. I can't yet believe General Grant means what he says. We will wait and see. In the meantime, I wish you to take some dispatches to General Lee."

"I can be useful here."

Mosby smiled faintly. "This is a time to walk softly, to avoid excess," he suggested. "Since March, with a loss of only about twenty men, we have killed or wounded or captured twelve hundred Yankees, plus sixteen hundred horses and mules and a lot of beef cattle. We have done all this, till yesterday, within the rules and customs of war. Now they threaten to hang us as guerrillas. My opinion is that if they carry out the threat, we must retaliate, teach them a little decency; but first I wish to report to General Lee and have his orders. Come back to me with his reply."

So Faunt, the dispatches buttoned inside his coat, began the journey to Richmond. Since there were everywhere in his way scattered detachments of the enemy, he spent the daylight hours in secret places, travelled at night. He had found that his health was better if he slept in the open air, taking shelter only from snow or rain; and since that first severe hemorrhage he had had no serious ill turn. Hard riding wearied him, or any sustained exertion; so he saved himself for the hot moments of combat and the headlong chase.

Lee would surely be near Petersburg, but Richmond was on Faunt's road, and Nell, and it was long since he had seen her. He waited till nightfall to ride into the city, submitted to the picket's challenge,

showed Colonel Mosby's pass. The officer commanding, when he read
that pass, cried:

"Are you one of Mosby's men?"

"I am, as you see."

"Does he want recruits?"

Faunt said drily: "I suppose any officer wants men."

"Then take me back with you! I'll serve in the ranks anywhere."

Faunt recognized the greed in the other's tone. "I'm not recruiting,"
he said coldly. "I've dispatches for General Lee. May I pass?"

He went directly to Nell's house. Except for occasional hours with
Burr or Brett while Lee's army wintered around Orange Court House,
he had not seen any of his family for months; nor did he now wish to
do so. Since that day when he met Anne and Julian and mocked at
Julian's crutches, the boy must hate him. Good enough! Anne was
Julian's wife now. Brett said she had a baby. Good again! If he himself had played a fine and honorable part that day he taunted Julian,
no one need ever know. Certainly it was the last credit entry on the
ledger of his life. Now he was an outcast, coming back to one as base
as he. To Nell.

But though when he was away from her he despised Mrs. Albion,
that feeling vanished when they were together. If she was what respectable folk called a fallen woman, she was no lower than he, whose
father's vices had let Abraham Lincoln loose upon the world. But also,
she was gentle and wise and full of understanding. She gave him
much more than tenderness, much more than physical content, much
more than empty caresses. Tonight when Milly answered his ring Nell
was at the stair head in the darkness; and when she heard his voice
she came swooping like an angel to embrace him.

"Oh, Faunt, Faunt, when I heard the bell I knew! Faunt, my
darling, how did I know it was you?"

He laughed teasingly, already released from loneliness. "Who else
would ring your bell at such an hour?"

"Who else, to be sure," she agreed. "So I wasn't so clever, was I?
Yet I was asleep; and even in my sleep I knew!" Milly would rouse
Rufus to put his horse away. Let him rid himself of travel stains,
while she found a wrapper. In the pleasant upper room he knew so

well, they talked till dawn. He had to tell her of that great stroke at Berryville.

"It was a near thing to a failure," he confessed, able to laugh now as he had not laughed at the time. "We'd divided our force, planned to hit all at once; and three shots from our howitzer were to be the signal. But they unlimbered the gun right on top of a nest of yellow jackets, and the yellow jackets fairly captured the gun, drove the men away. There we were, three squadrons waiting for the signal and no gun to signal with, and the Yankee train in plain sight on the pike. The men would have faced a swarm of Yankees readily enough, but there wasn't a man willing to face those yellow jackets, till Sergeant Babcock risked the stings and dragged the gun far enough down hill so the gunners could get at it."

"And then you hit them?"

"Three hundred of us, against a whole brigade of them; and we got safely away with all we could drive or lead or carry."

She asked wonderingly: "Is Colonel Mosby really as successful as the stories we hear?"

"Yes," he said. "Yes, perhaps more so. In these last few months, he's taken three or four hundred beef cattle and about sixteen hundred horses and mules, and hundreds of prisoners—not counting those we've killed and wounded—and Heaven knows how much miscellaneous plunder; and he's lost only twenty men." He added, a laughing pride in his voice: "Last month at Point of Rocks he scattered a Federal battalion with only a hundred and fifty men; and a day or two later with ninety men he smashed a hundred and fifty Yankees."

"How does he do it?"

Faunt chuckled. "Why, that day they blazed away at us with their new Spencer repeating rifles, and that frightened their horses; so they tried to dismount and fight on foot, and while they were shifting their formation we charged them. We broke them and chased them five miles and killed and wounded and captured seventy of them; and we lost one man killed and six wounded."

"I know it's true," she said wonderingly, "but I still don't understand it."

"Well, it's partly that we're better horsemen," he said. "When we charge, their horses wheel and run; and when you're chasing a man whose horse is running away with him, he's helpless. Then another thing, they use their sabres, but we use pistols. One man with pistols can beat half a dozen men with sabres, if he's a steady shot." He added: "And of course we usually catch them off guard, surprise them."

"How can Colonel Mosby keep so many men together, up there with Yankees all around him?"

"Oh, he doesn't. After a raid we scatter. Then when he decides where to hit next, he sends out word. There are always men at headquarters to act as messengers."

"Does he actually have headquarters?"

Faunt smiled. "Oh, certainly. Chief Blackwell's farm near Piedmont."

She said happily how well he was. "I've worried so, but you do seem well, darling. Are you?"

"Fine," he said. "I cough a little, but I haven't had a bit of trouble since I was last here." She in her turn must answer questions. "How do Richmond people feel about the war?"

She hesitated. "A dispatch came tonight," she said soberly. "General Hood's given up Atlanta."

The news was shocking, but he was a Virginian, Atlanta far away. "They can't beat us till they beat Lee."

"Virginia's the head," she admitted. "But a head can't fight on without a body." She spoke in grave tones. "And the army is falling apart, Faunt. There are more deserters outside the army than there are soldiers in it."

"I met two deserters recently in Baltimore," he told her. "A man named Sam Arnold and an Irishman named O'Laughlin. Marylanders. They served with us for a while and then went back North and took the oath."

"Faunt! Baltimore? Again?" Her tone accused him. He said in light reassurance:

"Oh, I take a ride that way now and then; yes, even into Washington. Washington's full of our friends, and Baltimore, too. They send drugs south to our hospitals. I've brought some useful parcels home." He said: "You know, Nell, I expect some of those deserters you talk about are riding with Mosby now. The hope of loot attracts them."

"A few perhaps," she assented. "But thousands have deserted, Faunt. Some say a hundred thousand, some say more. It keeps whole regiments busy trying to catch them. The states won't help. North Carolina and Georgia and even Virginia protect them." She added: "And in Mississippi and Alabama, people are too busy making money by selling their cotton to the Yankees to care about fighting to beat the North."

Faunt nodded. "Mosby's men would kill a lot more Yankees if they didn't stop to search the dead ones for watches and money." He added contemptuously: "Yankee money, at that!"

"No one would bother to steal our money," she reminded him. "It's almost worthless."

"I believe you think we're beaten."

"I think we're beating ourselves," she admitted. "General Johnston might have held Atlanta. He fought Sherman as skilfully as Lee fought Grant. But President Davis put Sam Hood in his place, and Hood divided his forces and let them be beaten in sections, and he's lost Atlanta. People here in Richmond won't know that till tomorrow; but when they do they'll lose all faith in President Davis. And sooner or later our lines from here to Petersburg will stretch too thin. When General Lee loses a man, killed or wounded or deserting, that man can't be replaced."

He asked curiously: "How do you happen to know about Atlanta before the rest of Richmond knows?"

"Men tell me things," she reminded him.

"I suppose you still see a great many men." His tone was dry.

She smiled at him, her head on one side; and she tapped her teeth with her fingernail, making a little ticking sound. "Why yes, to be sure," she said. "I always have, you know. They like to come here, because when they want to talk I listen to them. Most men enjoy being listened to. But that doesn't mean they want a mistress!" She smiled. "Probably no one, much less you, would believe how rarely anyone tries to—make love to me. They come to talk, to pay little compliments, to spend an hour with a handsome and intelligent woman who enjoys their company and lets them see it." She nodded, teasing him fondly. "Yes, my dear, I'd never be lonely—if I didn't miss you so sorely."

He smiled, relaxed and at ease. "Do these talkative callers of yours feel as you do about the war?"

She nodded, grave again. "Yes, Faunt. Oh, if you were here, you would see for yourself. President Davis is bombarded with angry letters: people who demanded that he remove General Johnston and now blame him for doing so, speculators wanting licenses to export cotton and tobacco, Governor Vance threatening to call home his soldiers, Governor Brown threatening to arrest the impressment officers, South Carolina planters furious because their slaves are impressed to work on fortifications, people damning Colonel Northrop or General Bragg. Everyone's thinking of himself; his profits, or his rights, or how he can avoid going into the army. Even Vice President Stephens wants to take Georgia out of the Confederacy. The South is falling apart." She broke out in a sudden pleading urgency: "Oh, Faunt, how long will you go on fighting in this hopeless struggle?"

"Till I die," he said in a low tone. She bit her lip, and her eyes filled; and he felt her love like a warm cloak enfolding him, and asked more gently: "What would you have me do?"

She shook her head, smiling again. "You know, ordinarily I'm a sensible woman, Faunt; but not when I'm with you. With you, having you here with me, I think how wonderful it would be if you and I could be always together, could put everything behind us but each other." She shook her head. "Of course I know it's impossible. I'm as silly as any other woman in love, you see."

So for a while they spoke no more of great affairs, but of themselves.

He stayed with her till Monday morning. Sunday afternoon, when they had been a while silent together, she asked: "Faunt, why don't you go to see your kinfolks?" And since he did not speak, she said: "You could be proud of them. Your sister, Mrs. Streean, does more than anyone outside the hospitals to help not only the wounded men but the poor people. Richmond's full of hungry women and children, ladies from Loudoun and Fauquier and all the northern counties who have had to leave their homes and have lost everything. They live in attics and in damp cellars and in broken-down railroad cars along the tracks.

"But I don't mean them. Their friends help them. It's the ones who were always poor, and whose friends have nothing, who suffer most. The Council has voted thousands of dollars to keep them from starving. Mrs. Streean was one of the ladies who organized the Soup Association. She's a fine woman, Faunt. You should be proud of her."

"I was always a little sorry for Tilda," he admitted in slow surprise. "But it never occurred to me to be proud of her."

"She's highly respected," Nell assured him. "She knows how to plan things, how to tell other ladies what to do. And she'd like to see you, Faunt."

His eyes hardened. "I'm afraid not," he said. "Tilda and I were never close."

"Then Mrs. Dewain?" she urged. "Burr lost some fingers in the fight at Yellow Tavern, the day General Stuart was killed; but he's returned to duty. Oh, and Miss Vesta is married again." He did not know this, and looked at her in quick gladness. "To a boy named Lyle," she said. "He's a Lieutenant in the Seventh South Carolina Cavalry."

"I remember him."

She nodded. "And Julian married Anne Tudor, and they have a fine baby. Go see them, Faunt. They'd be so happy!" And she said gently: "I sometimes think you'd be happier yourself if you went to your own people instead of coming here to me."

He asked, deliberately cruel: "Are you giving me my *congé?*"

If his word left a wound she did not betray her hurt. "I think you might be happier if we had never met." She added honestly: "You must always feel a secret shame in loving me."

He hesitated, then answered her without evasion. "That is true, Nell. I can't help it. I suppose it comes from—what my life used to be." And he explained: "The night I met you, there were reasons outside myself to make me feel shamed and debased. I turned to you as a man in disgrace turns to the bottle, defiantly, flouting the world. But that was only at first. Very quickly—I—loved you. Yes and held you high. If you yourself would consent, I would marry you."

"Yet always, in your heart, you'd be ashamed of me." There was nothing but affectionate understanding in her tone or in her eyes.

"Yes," he admitted. "Yes, that is true."

"Then I've done you great harm, my dear."

"You've done me great good, in a thousand ways."

"Go back to your kinfolks, Faunt. Forget me."

He came near her, standing in front of her, taking her hands. "No," he said. "No, I'll never leave you." He kissed her gravely. "We will keep what we have, Nell. I'll not risk losing it by reaching out for more."

He went next day to deliver Colonel Mosby's dispatch. Nell was able to direct him to General Lee's headquarters, at Violet Bank, the Shippen home, just east of the Petersburg pike and a little north of the town. "He's been there since the middle of July," she said. The commanding general wished to communicate with Richmond before drafting his reply, so Faunt had days to wait. He took the opportunity to see the miles of breastworks and entrenchments where Lee's army stubbornly fought off Grant's wary thrusts. He saw men living like rats in ditches and caves and tunnels, starving on rations so short that they were always hungry, yet ready at a moment's warning to spring to battle; and he met men he knew and talked with them.

"A week of this would drive me mad," he said, and the men to whom he spoke agreed that the combination of monotony and physical discomfort was hard. Soldiers grew careless, indifferent even to death itself, exposing themselves to the fire of enemy sharpshooters simply because they would not trouble to stoop in passing a spot where the parapet was low. So losses were steady, and even minor wounds sometimes meant death; for men were so badly nourished that their resistance was low.

And the men made friends with the enemy, crawling out at night to trade tobacco for sugar or coffee. Some of the Petersburg hospitals sent secretly through the lines to exchange tobacco and cotton for needed drugs. This was still war, and many were killed; but there were intervals when the soldiers arranged an informal suspension of firing. After a few days of rain you might see men on both sides taking advantage of the first sun to spread blankets and clothes to dry in full sight of the enemy. Sometimes ladies came sight-seeing from Richmond and climbed on the parapets and strolled to and fro in perfect security.

When Lee's dispatch was ready, Faunt was glad to turn his back on this war that was not war, upon this rabbit warren where men lived in a fashion that animals could not have endured. He had another Sunday with Nell in Richmond, but when he took his careful way northward, an encounter with a Yankee patrol cost him his horse and set him afoot, till he found loyal men who even in that stricken land were able to provide him with a new mount. At Centerville he heard that Colonel Mosby had been gravely wounded the day before and was lying helpless at the home of Major Foster; but he found Mosby cheerfully amused at his own mishap.

"Tom Love and Guy Broadwaters and I were too ambitious," he confessed. "We met a regiment of bluebellies with an advance guard of seven men; and since the seven had a regiment to back them, we thought it not unfair for three of us to charge them. But one of them could shoot. He got a bullet into me and I won't be able to ride again for a week."

Faunt helped move him by easy stages to his father's home near Lynchburg. There they had news that Chief Blackwell's farm had been raided by the Yankees, the house searched, hidden letters and papers found, the house burned. Colonel Mosby was disturbed by this mischance. "No great harm was done, of course; but how did they know our headquarters? Someone has talked when he should have been silent." He stirred restlessly. "Treachery makes me uneasy. I'll be glad to get into the saddle again!"

But he was still on crutches; and since he must be inactive he decided to go to Petersburg to confer with General Lee, and took Faunt with him. They travelled by the South Side Railroad, and at Petersburg Faunt found an ambulance to carry them to Violet Bank. When they turned off the pike, Faunt saw Trav; and beyond him in the shade of a great tree, General Longstreet was talking with General Lee. Faunt helped Colonel Mosby out of the ambulance, and as the Colonel adjusted his crutches General Lee came toward them.

"Ah, Colonel," he said in smiling sympathy. "The only fault I ever find with you is that you are always getting wounded."

"This is nothing," Mosby assured him. "I could ride even now if it were necessary."

As they fell into talk, Faunt went to join Trav and General Longstreet. He spoke first, in due respect, to Longstreet. "You may not remember me, sir. Major Currain's brother."

Longstreet said cordially: "I remember you perfectly, Mr. Currain. You took my scout, Harrison, across the Potomac for me, June a year ago."

"I'm glad to see you recovered."

"Not completely," the big man admitted. "I'm not yet able to ride comfortably, but a little more practice will remedy that." His arm was carried in a sling, so no doubt it still troubled him.

Faunt turned to Trav, extending his hand. "You look well, Trav."

"Why, I'm well," Trav agreed. "How are you?"

"All right." There was some restraint in Trav's tones; and Faunt felt a deep sadness in himself, and old memories. "I'm all right," he repeated. "I'm very well." He was not well, would never be, and he knew this; but question and answer were only words.

"We're just going to take the train back to Danville." Trav spoke like an embarrassed hostess making conversation.

"Have you been to Richmond?" Faunt asked, for the sake of saying something.

"No, Enid's in Augusta. The General and I are on our way to Lynchburg with Mrs. Longstreet and her children."

"Enid's well, I hope?" This empty talk hurt like an aching tooth. He wanted Trav's old affection, wanted some kindly word.

"Why, yes," said Trav.

"We haven't seen each other for a long time, you and I."

"No." Trav hesitated. "I've missed you, Faunt," he confessed, his tone softer. "I always—" He shook his head. "Everything's changed," he said heavily. "All of us are changed."

Men found it hard to put their hearts in words. Faunt thought if he and Trav were women they would be by this time weeping happily in each other's arms. "If I were Nell, now," he told himself, "or if Trav were Nell, I could tell him I love him. Perhaps he knows about me and Nell. Enid's her daughter; perhaps she knew, has told him." Defiant anger woke in him. "Colonel Mosby may want me," he said stiffly. "And General Longstreet is waiting for you."

Trav nodded. "Yes." He extended his hand; and then suddenly his arm was around Faunt's shoulders in an awkward embrace. "Take care of yourself," he said huskily.

Faunt freed himself, smiling in a deep content at that caress. "Bad advice to give a soldier, Trav. Good-by." He watched Trav join the General and they drove away.

The encounter left a lonely longing in him; Nell in Richmond was not far away. He sought Colonel Mosby's permission, borrowed a horse, took the Richmond pike and found her glad welcome waiting.

He told her what news there was; and he spoke of the burning of Chief Blackwell's little farm which had been their headquarters. Would that hinder them, she asked; but he said there were other places they could use. "Glen Welby, for instance; Major Carter's home near Rectortown. We'll still give them trouble enough."

"Will you go back there soon?"

"Not for a week or two, certainly."

She told him what was happening in Richmond. He had heard of General Morgan's death, and when she spoke of it he commented: "They say he was betrayed by a woman." He had a momentary feeling that the word startled her, but she smiled, said teasingly:

"You poor men! Adam, and Samson, and now General Morgan. What treacherous creatures we are." And she said: "But perhaps he deserved it. Even his own officers accused him of robbing the bank at Mount Sterling. Of course he's a hero, now he's dead, so the charges against him will be dropped." His elaborate funeral here in Richmond was spoiled, she said, because the military escort had to hurry away to help repulse a Yankee attack at Chaffin's Farm. She went on to other gossip. The Secretary of War was the latest target for abuse, because he had allowed some of his friends to use the burdened railroads to bring flour from the Valley for their own use while the army was on short rations. Mr. Northrop had ordered the impressment of all wheat and meat in Virginia, and when someone protested that civilians would starve, he said, "Let them." Sheridan had beaten Early in the Valley and captured Winchester.

Everything she told him was so dreary that Faunt at last protested, half-smiling. "I declare, Nell, isn't there any sunshine anywhere?"

"I don't know where, Faunt," she declared. "Grant has two men to

Lee's one; Sherman has two men to Hood's one; Sheridan has two men to Early's one. Oh, I wish you were out of it! I worry so for you. Suppose you'd been there when Mr. Blackwell's house was burned. You'd have been taken."

He said mildly: "I think not. I don't expect to be captured, Nell." Then, seeing her lips whiten with pain at his words he rose and went to touch her bent head. "Let's be a little more cheerful, shall we?" She looked up at him and smiled; and he said in tender chiding: "You know I came here for happiness, my dear."

He had Sunday with her, and on Monday he and Colonel Mosby began their return journey. Mosby since his wound had not shaved, and Faunt spoke of this. "I'm not sure your new beard doesn't become you, Colonel."

"I think I shall keep it," Mosby confessed with a chuckle. "Close-shaven, I am too easily mistaken for a boy; but the Yankees will not take liberties with a bearded man."

"The liberties taken have been the other way around," Faunt suggested.

Mosby nodded thoughtfully. "But we've busy days ahead," he remarked. "The Federals are trying to rebuild the Manassas Gap Railroad. General Lee wants us to discourage them."

"What does General Lee think about Hangman Grant?"

Mosby said quietly: "So far, no one has carried out the orders to hang us whenever we are caught. We have always operated within the rules and customs of war. I hope we won't be driven into a contest of assassination."

But when they came to Gordonsville they heard that at least one of Grant's subordinate commanders had taken him at his word. A force of Rangers under Captain Chapman had attacked, a week before, an ambulance train near Front Royal, and found themselves trapped between two regiments of Custer's cavalry. They shot their way clear; but they left six prisoners behind. General Custer ordered the prisoners executed. He paraded a band through Front Royal playing the Dead March; but except for this, there was no ceremony. A disorganized crowd of soldiers shot David Jones and Lucien Love in front of the church. Some others thrust Tom Anderson against an elm tree south of town and riddled him with bullets. A Front Royal boy named Henry Rhodes, who that day served for the first time with Mosby's men, was hustled to an open field at the other end of town and there, although his mother clung to him till he was dragged away, one of Custer's men emptied his pistol into the boy's body. Tom Overby and young Carter were hanged.

Frank Angela met them in Gordonsville with the news. "I rode into Front Royal that night," he said. "The folks there say General Custer rode by, about the time they was hung, all dressed up in a velvet uniform with his yellow hair a-shining down his shoulders, eating plums off a branch he'd broke off someone's tree."

Faunt turned without a word toward the door, but Mosby called him back. "Wait a moment, Mr. Currain."

Faunt said tightly: "I'm riding toward Front Royal, Colonel."

Mosby shook his head. "Wait a little, if you please," he said sternly. "What we do must be done with a decent deliberation." Faunt hesitated, and Mosby insisted: "Be easy, Mr. Currain. My men are dead. I won't forget, but haste will not help them."

Faunt's first rage cooled to a still ferocity. Mosby next day, though he still used crutches to walk, was able to sit his horse; and he sent men ahead to watch the workmen busy on the Manassas Gap Railroad, while he and Faunt and a troop of Rangers followed more slowly. Within a fortnight, harassing the construction crews by day and by night, he put an end to that enterprise. The task was ridiculously easy, since an army would have been needed to guard the sixty miles of track against surprise that might strike anywhere. This done, Mosby led a force into the Valley and wrecked a train and found a Federal paymaster among the passengers with a hundred and seventy thousand dollars in good Yankee currency in his strongbox; and every raider had better than two thousand dollars as his share.

But there was bad news too. Sheridan had driven Early up the Valley; and while Mosby's men were gathering greenbacks, the enemy cavalry found four guns that Mosby had hidden in the forest on Cobbler Mountain and carried them away. Soon afterward, Yankee horsemen had appeared at Glen Welby with orders to burn Major Carter's home. Mrs. Scott, the Major's daughter, seated herself in the parlor with her son on her knee and declared that if the house were burned so would she be, so the house was saved; but the bluecoats told Mrs. Carter they knew the house was regularly used by Colonel Mosby, and the officer commanding said firmly:

"And if I ever hear of your welcoming that murderous guerrilla here again, I will not spare the house a second time."

When this was reported to him, Mosby said harshly: "They knew we used Chief Blackwell's farm; they knew we used Glen Welby." Faunt was with him. "They know too much about us, Mr. Currain."

Faunt spoke in open challenge. "They're overbold, Colonel. It's six weeks since they hanged your men. Perhaps they take courage from long impunity."

Mosby looked at him with blazing eyes. "I have a good memory, Mr. Currain. You need not remind me." He smiled grimly. "Meanwhile, since our return from Petersburg, we have killed or captured six hundred bluecoats, with a loss of thirty men. I don't think our enemies hold us too lightly."

But there was still no formal retaliation for the butchery at Front Royal. Faunt took his own revenges when the opportunity came; but they did not content him. Then at last, early in November and for the first time since Front Royal, twenty-seven of Custer's men were captured by the Rangers.

Mosby ordered them brought to Rectortown, and he summoned the whole battalion of the Rangers to assemble there. When Faunt reported to him, Mosby said in sombre tones: "Well, Mr. Currain, you will presently be satisfied. I have General Lee's orders, approved by Secretary Seddon; and I have twenty-seven prisoners from Custer's command. A certain Colonel Powell has hung another of us, so there will be seven executions."

"It's full time," Faunt said firmly.

Colonel Mosby called Lieutenant Thomson. "Put seven marked slips in a hat, Mr. Thomson," he directed. "Seven marked slips and twenty blanks. Take the men who draw the marked slips into the Valley as near Winchester as is safe. Hang them and placard the bodies."

Lieutenant Thomson hesitated. "Is it possible to assign someone else to this duty, Colonel?"

Mosby shook his head. "It is as painful for me as for you, sir; but it is necessary."

Faunt, sitting his horse near by, moved nearer. "I am willing to undertake it, Colonel."

Mosby's eyes met his. "No, Mr. Currain. Lieutenant Thomson is too good a soldier to evade even this task." He added: "And I have another duty for you, Mr. Currain. Come with me."

He turned his horse to depart. Faunt, looking back as they rode away, saw the twenty-seven prisoners lined up for the drawing of the lots, and he watched with a grim satisfaction till a bend of the road put the scene behind them.

When they had ridden for some distance, a horseman at a canter overtook them. It was Lieutenant Thomson. "Colonel," he said apologetically, "one of the marked slips was drawn by a drummer boy. I thought you might wish to spare him."

Mosby said instantly, with a sort of relief: "Yes. I never hated anything worse than this, yet we must curb Custer's insane ferocity." Then in a low tone: "But a substitute must be drawn in the boy's place, Lieutenant. Seven of them must die." As the other turned away, Mosby called him back. "However, Lieutenant, only three of our men were hanged, two by Custer, one by Powell. You must hang three of these; but I have no objection if you prefer to shoot the others."

The Lieutenant, white and still, saluted and rode away. Faunt and Mosby went slowly on; and at last, in a new tone, Mosby said:

"Well, that is done. Mr. Currain, I said I had work for you. You remember our friend Mr. Booth?"

"Yes, sir."

"I have a letter from him. He wishes to ride with us for a week or two. He has done the South good service, and I'm glad to oblige him. He asks that one of us—and he suggested you, Mr. Currain—meet him in Port Tobacco, at the home of a wagon maker with a German name. Perhaps you know the man?"

"George Atzerodt, yes," Faunt agreed. "And of course I'll be glad to go."

So when as dusk came down and a cold rain began to fall, Lieutenant Thomson and a detail of Rangers rode with Custer's doomed men toward Ashby's Gap, Faunt was travelling in the opposite direction. He looked forward to seeing Wilkes Booth again. The little actor had an overpowering quality not easy to define. By the very exuberance of his nature, by his tremendous loquacity, by his freedom from every restraint, he overpowered the senses. A year ago, on that journey to Washington to receive Booth's contribution of needed drugs, Faunt had seen the man in action on the stage. Booth then was playing in *The Marble Heart,* and when Faunt presented himself at the stage door the actor welcomed him and smuggled him into a box where, although the performance was just beginning, there was an extra chair.

"And this is a gala night," Booth assured him. "The President and Mrs. Lincoln will be in the State Box." He smiled. "So the audience will have no eyes for me."

It was a measure of Booth's genius that from the moment he stepped upon the stage even Faunt forgot the shadowed figure of the President in a box near his own. His eyes turned that way only in the intervals of the play. Afterward Booth again absorbed him, so that not until he was on the return journey did his thoughts dwell long upon the man whom he abhorred. Even at a distance, Faunt had felt something still and sad and brooding in the other, had felt himself shrink to unimportance; and thereafter he refused to remember those half-caught glimpses. In the months since that day, he had thought more often of Wilkes Booth than of the President. Twice since then he and Booth had met, once in Baltimore, and once at the Surratt tavern. As he rode now toward the Northern Neck, he looked forward to this next encounter.

At the signal station on Ben Grimes's farm at Mathias Point, Lieutenant Caywood advised against his crossing to Pope's Creek. Since Wat Bowie led a party of Mosby's men into Charles County a few weeks before, and mounted them at the expense of the provost guard in the court house, the Yankees in southern Maryland sometimes made unexpected visitations upon even the most innocent. Bowie himself was killed opposite Leesburg on his way back to "Mosby's Confederacy"; but his raid had put the enemy on the alert, and several times a black signal in Major Watson's dormer window had warned the mail boat not to cross.

But when at dusk that day the signs were fair, Faunt made the venture. There was no one to meet him on the bank, so he left the mail packet in the usual place in the dead tree on the beach and himself made a cautious way up that tangled ravine which the road descended. He halted once when half a dozen horsemen, Yankee cavalry by the sound, passed down the road on the other side of the ravine and not fifty feet from where he stood hidden; and even when they were surely gone he waited a longer while before continuing the ascent.

There was a light in Mr. Jones's house, and Faunt went near enough to listen and be sure there were no enemies within before he knocked. Mr. Jones opened the door, but when Faunt identified himself, the other came out and closed the door behind him.

"I can't take you in," he said. "I had callers not an hour ago, some troopers."

"They've gone on beyond the landing."

"They may return. You wait in the pines behind my barn and I'll come to you in an hour or two. We can't talk now."

Faunt respected the other's precautions, and Mr. Jones eventually joined him with a message. "Wilkes Booth was here last week, Mr. Currain. He's living in the National Hotel in Washington; but he's promised to join those brothers of his and play *Julius Caesar* in New York the last of this month, and he said to tell whoever came that he wouldn't miss that chance to show his brothers who's the best actor, even to ride with Mosby."

Faunt was disappointed, but he said: "Well, he can come another time."

"That man will give up anything to make a show of himself in a theatre," Mr. Jones commented. "He's got a crazy idea in his head now, came down here to see if it could be worked."

"What is it?"

"Why, he's talking about kidnapping Lincoln and shipping him to Richmond. His notion is he'll wait till some night when the President comes to the theatre, and jump up into his box and knock him senseless and swing him down to the stage and out into the alley. Then he'll have a carriage and some relays of horses ready, and haul him down here, and get George Atzerodt to ferry him across the river." Mr. Jones seemed to suspect he had talked too much. "I wouldn't be telling you this if there was any chance he'd try it."

Faunt smiled. "It's a harebrained scheme, certainly," he agreed; yet his blood stirred. Audacity sometimes worked miracles.

"He went to Bryantown to see Dr. Green and Dr. Mudd," Mr. Jones explained. "But he didn't tell them what he was up to, just let on he was looking for a farm to buy. George Atzerodt brought him to see me. I told him he was crazy and to go back to Washington and forget it."

Faunt thought of riding on toward Washington in the hope of seeing Booth, and he might have gone at least as far as Surrattsville; but Mr. Jones said the Surratts had moved to Washington the month before, had opened a boarding house. "It's on H Street," he said. "Five-forty-one, if you ever want to put up there. But you wouldn't find Booth. He's already gone on to New York to get ready for that play they're going to do."

When Faunt rejoined Mosby and reported the failure of his errand, he found the Colonel in ill humor, with a persistent cold.

"I'm not used to being laid up with anything less than a Yankee bullet," Mosby remarked. "And this is no time for me to be sick. All the news from Richmond is bad, Currain. When Hood marched north into Tennessee, Sherman burned Atlanta and headed for the sea and there's no one to stop him. And Early has been driven up the Valley, so we have to cover a lot of territory."

"Did you hang those men?" Faunt asked.

"Three of them," Mosby assured him. "Two got away. We shot the others." He added regretfully: "We're getting into the habit of shooting prisoners. I sent Captain Richards to dispose of Blazer the other day." Captain Blazer with a hundred picked men had been assigned to special duty against the Rangers some weeks before, had had some success. "They polished him off, captured Blazer, killed or captured most of his men. But John Puryear shot the Yankee lieutenant after he'd been disarmed and was a prisoner."

Faunt knew Puryear, a young man and a hard fighter but a fair one. "Why?"

"Oh, he had provocation," Mosby admitted. "Blazer had captured him the day before; and this lieutenant tried to make him talk, put a rope around his neck and hauled him up clear of the ground two or three times. Puryear was still a prisoner when Captain Richards hit them, and he knocked one of them off his horse and grabbed the fellow's guns and took a hand in the fight."

"Good!"

"Oh, that was all right; but after the fight the lieutenant was disarmed, dismounted, standing with the other prisoners, and Puryear just plain shot him." Mosby said soberly: "When we go outside the rules and customs of war, Mr. Currain, we forfeit the respect of friends as well as enemies." He shook his head. "Well, it's done. I'm glad you're back. Sheridan is bound to make a big strike at us now. He can't go after Early and leave us in his rear. So we'll need every man."

Before the month ended, Mosby's prediction was fulfilled. Sheridan sent five thousand men across the Blue Ridge into Loudoun Valley, and the Yankees, extended in a line miles long, swept the countryside. They burned every mill and barn and smoke house, and every wheat stack; they destroyed every pound of ham or pork or bacon and every grain of wheat or corn; they drove away or shot and left to rot every horse and every head of beef cattle and every cow and every hog. They killed chickens and ducks and geese and turkeys and even dogs and cats.

And to every plea for mercy and forbearance the answer was the same: "You've given too many meals to Mosby's cutthroats. You'd better be glad we don't burn your houses too."

For five days the systematic destruction continued. It ended only when in the whole valley there was nothing left except the smouldering embers of barns and corn cribs and farm buildings, the untouched houses which alone had been spared, and the hungry women and children and helpless old men who went plucking at charred carcasses or digging in the hot ashes of their smoke houses for a morsel of food.

In the face of this host, Mosby's men could only scatter and watch their chance to strike and kill and ride away. In front of the advancing cordon they fell back, and when its work was done and the bluecoats withdrew toward the Valley, they followed, watching for stragglers, killing without mercy every man they found.

Through that five days of Hell, days when a smoke pall lay heavy across Loudoun Valley and the nights were illumined in all directions by hungry, high-leaping flames, Faunt did not spare himself. From the cover of forest by day or from the shadows of night he watched for opportunity and seized it when it came. Half a dozen times he charged through Yankee detachments with his pistols blazing, leaving dead and wounded behind, and heedless of the wild shots flung too hastily after him. Twenty times, from cover where he was secure against blundering pursuit, and using the stock that could be fitted to his pistols or taking rest on fence or boulder to make sure of his aim, he sent bullets toward their mark. He forgot food and drink and sleep, and he did not know his own exhaustion till at last a spasm of coughing swept him from his horse and red blood bubbled from his lips to stain the grass where he fell.

Mosby's men found him and carried him to the nearest house, and Colonel Mosby himself came to offer his services. "I must go again to Richmond," he explained. "But I will see you cared for first."

Faunt, weak and weary, smiled a little. "Colonel, do you remember where we met?"

Mosby hesitated. "I'm not sure."

"In Richmond," Faunt reminded him. "At the home of a lady, Mrs. Albion."

"I remember now."

"Take me to her."

The other hesitated. "I'm afraid you're too ill to be moved, Mr. Currain."

"I will live," Faunt promised. "I will live to come to her."

14

Trav's stay in Augusta, while General Longstreet was there or at Hawthorne Heights, the Hart home in Union Point halfway to Atlanta, was a pleasant interlude; and particularly when, after that visit to General Lee in July, Longstreet's anxieties began to ease. Grant seemed, at least for the time, securely held. Early's little army marching boldly toward Washington would draw off some of the Union forces in front of Petersburg; and the Confederate lines were strong and defensible. There was little Grant could hope to do.

So, having brought Enid and the children to Augusta, Trav had weeks of relative repose. General Longstreet had stayed at first with the Anderson Carmichaels, six or seven miles out on the Savannah road. Mr. Carmichael farmed the fertile bottom lands in the bend of the river, where a shallow dry ditch marked the course of the old canal down which cargoes of tobacco had used to start their river journey to the Savannah market. The house was in a grove at the foot of the hills around which the river here had to make a detour; and across the tilled lands the mass of the Sand Hills west of Augusta was bold against the sky. Till he brought his family from Richmond, Trav, as well as the Longstreets, lodged there; but on the return from Petersburg the hot weather became unendurable, so the Longstreets went to live with Josiah Sibley. His big house was on Bay Street, not far down the river from the bridge, and so near the water and so vulnerable to spring floods that living quarters were all above the first-floor level. Josiah Sibley, who had married as his second wife Longstreet's cousin, was now in his middle fifties and with a lifetime of success behind him. He had come from Massachusetts while still in his teens, to work for his brothers who were already established in the cotton business. Before he was twenty he and his brother Amory were in partnership, with their offices in Hamburg just across the river in South Carolina. When Amory Sibley died in 1853, Hamburg was losing its importance as a business center, so in 1855 Josiah Sibley shifted his headquarters to Augusta. Three sons in succession as they reached maturity became members of the firm.

Robert, the youngest son by Mr. Sibley's first wife, was this summer sixteen; and he and Garland Longstreet and Trav's Lucy were from the first good companions. Trav enjoyed long hours with Mr. Sibley. The cotton merchant had not outlived his New England inheritance of sagacity and acumen, even though old thrifty ways had surrendered to the generous seductions of his adopted habitat; and he like Trav thought in figures. A neat sum in addition or in subtraction was beautiful, regardless of its meaning. They matched Northern resources in men and money and materials against those of the South, and in spite of the tragic significance of their results, they found in these elaborate calculations an almost sensuous content.

Through Mr. Sibley, Trav was able to rent for his family five rooms in a house in the Sand Hills where two ladies, Mrs. Sibley's distant relatives, lived alone. Enid made many friends in these new surroundings; and when Trav one day remarked on this she said:

"Why, of course! I'm really lots nicer than you think, Trav!" She spoke teasingly. "You hid me away in the country for years, and at Great Oak your mother kept me in the background, and in Richmond Cinda prejudiced everyone else against me." Though he himself had sometimes resented Cinda's attitude, Trav protested that this was not true; and Enid tossed her head. "Oh, naturally you'll stand up for your own family against me! The Currains are something pretty special, of course; and I know they feel you married beneath you. But people here don't know I'm the skeleton in the closet, so they like me."

In these days when she was more contented, they had reached an easy footing; and he said quizzically that she was a pretty well-nourished skeleton, and she laughed and retorted:

"Well, Honey, I may be a little plump, but I'm awfully comfortable." Her kiss was affectionate, and he caught her close, grateful for a happiness which he had once thought would never again be his.

He was happy with Enid, and happy with Peter and Lucy. They liked to ride together, rising early to escape the heat of the day. Trav bought at an absurdly high price a mare for Lucy, and borrowed a mount for Peter. Nig, here where the sound of battle never touched his ears, was as docile as a kitten. His smooth single-foot stretched the other horses to a half-gallop; and they might ride swift and far, and then while the horses cooled come more decorously home. Trav's only regret was that on these fine excursions Enid would never join them. To ride in hot weather produced on her fair skin an ugly rash; and she thought it was caused by the heat from the horses, and preferred to amuse herself in other ways. To Trav's satisfaction she even helped in the hospitals, as crowded here as they were everywhere in the South. Lucy answered the call for help in making cartridges at the Arsenal on the Sand Hills near where they lived; and when she came home after her first day at this work she had to describe to Peter how a cartridge was made.

"Why, you just roll a strip of paper around a piece of stick that's the right size," she explained. "And you paste it so it won't come unrolled, and tie one end with a string the way you would a bag. Then you put in the bullet, and a wad, and just the right amount of powder; and then you twist the paper at the other end, with some paste so it will stay—and that's all there is to it."

She made some cartridges for him, using a stick for a mold, and pebbles for bullets and sand for powder; and Peter said they looked like so many mice with their tails tucked along their sides. "I bet I could do that," he declared. "Do they pay you for doing it?"

"Of course not! Oh, they would; but I do it to help our soldiers."

"Well, they'd have to pay me!" Peter declared; and Trav, listening, suggested that Peter try the work. The boy thereafter earned at first fifty cents and presently a dollar a day. "I'm going to save up till I'm big enough to go and be a soldier," he announced.

But Peter was only twelve. Before he could achieve that ambition, the fighting would be done. "Better spend it, son," Trav advised. "Those shinplasters they pay you will buy a lot of butterscotch, even at twenty-five cents a piece." Nevertheless the youngster zealously treasured his little hoard.

Trav rode with the children almost every morning, but after dinner he went to be with the General. Longstreet's arm was still paralyzed, and Trav wrote at his dictation many letters. For the rest, Longstreet liked to talk of what had been and of what would be. The news of Stuart's death, soon after his own hurt, had saddened him, and he often spoke of the young cavalryman. "I first met him in the Indian country," he remembered. "He was the best young officer in the army at getting guns through hard country, lowering them down precipices or hauling them up, manhandling them if there was no other way, getting them to the spot where they were needed. That first summer of the war—is it only three years ago, Currain?"

"After First Manassas? Only three years, yes sir."

"It seems a lifetime," Longstreet commented. "Yes, that summer, when we were on the outpost, Stuart was splendid. I think I was the first to recommend him for promotion." And he said sorrowfully: "A gallant and a bold and yet a discreet and careful man. His only mistakes arose from his high qualities. When he failed, it was his own audacity that betrayed him."

When General Hood superseded General Johnston in command of the army defending Atlanta, Secretary Seddon wrote suggesting that Longstreet take over Hood's corps. Longstreet replied that he would prefer to wait till he was fully recovered, and Mr. Seddon agreed that until his strength was restored he should remain inactive. Longstreet thought putting Hood in Johnston's place was a mistake.

"I've always rated General Johnston high," he told Trav. "His strategy against Sherman has been as splendid as Lee's against 'Lys Grant. Johnston would have played a waiting game to baffle Sherman at Atlanta; but I'm afraid Sam Hood will be too ready to fight."

"Isn't General Hood's name 'John'?"

"Yes, but everyone calls him 'Sam.'" Longstreet chuckled. "Just as the men call me 'Old Pete' when my name is 'James.' But by either name, Hood is no match for Sherman. Putting him in command is another of Mr. Davis's mistakes."

He added harshly: "President Davis has an extraordinary aptitude for doing the wrong thing, in small matters and in great ones." And he referred to an incident of the previous fall. "Remember after Chickamauga I sent those captured flags back to Richmond with a guard of honor selected from men who had specially distinguished themselves? In Washington, Union soldiers on such an errand would have been given a fine reception; yes, and promotions. But my men were met by an old negro with a cart to haul the flags to the Capitol, and the only reward they got was transportation back to the army. President Davis seems to go out of his way to affront the men who are fighting this war for him."

Through the weeks that followed, the General's anxieties persisted; and when Atlanta fell he was more depressed than Trav had ever seen him. Sherman's action a few days later in expelling from Atlanta all the civilian residents, sending old men and women and children through the Confederate lines as homeless wanderers, made him hot with rage.

"I regret now our forbearance in Pennsylvania," he commented. "Hunter's outrages in the Valley, and Sheridan's burning and stealing, and now Sherman's prodding ladies and children out of their homes at the point of a bayonet! There you have three crimes no decent men, North or South, will condone."

Yet he was even more angered when President Davis on his way to General Hood's army spoke in Macon and announced, in terms so plain that no one could doubt his meaning, that Hood would move to get in Sherman's rear.

"That delivers us into the hands of the enemy," Longstreet declared. "Sherman is forewarned, so he will know exactly what to expect, and what to do." He decided to take Mrs. Longstreet and the children back to Lynchburg. "For I am almost ready to return to duty, and I can't leave them here in Sherman's path."

Trav echoed: "In his path? You think Sherman will try to move south?"

"Of course! As soon as Hood moves around him to the north, there'll be nothing to stop him. He can go where he pleases; and though Sherman is a brutal ruffian, he's soldier enough to seize the opportunity. Georgia is hardly touched by the war, so Sherman can live off the country; and he'll rip the heart out of the South." He added bitterly: "Georgia may even welcome him! She's been full of peace talk for months. But if she throws any garlands in Sherman's path she'll regret it. He'll strip her to the bone." And he added: "Yes, we must get back to Lynchburg before Hood opens the door and lets Sherman come this way."

Trav told Enid the General's decision, and he said she and the children had better return to Richmond; but she refused to leave Augusta. "I don't believe him," she declared. "He's just scared! We're ever so much better off here. There's plenty of food in the stores, and it's not too expensive, and I have so many friends. No, indeed, the children and I will stay right here."

"The General will want me with him," Trav reminded her.

"Well, for that matter, Lucy and Peter and I want you with us," Enid retorted. "But of course what we want doesn't matter."

So they would stay, but Trav must go; and in late September he bade them good-by. He and the General left Mrs. Longstreet and the children at the Estes home in Danville long enough to go to Petersburg to see General Lee. When he met Faunt there, Trav's disgust at the other's intimacy with Mrs. Albion gave way to the old affection; but he took away with him memory of his brother's wasted body, his haggard eyes and flaming cheeks. That Faunt was ill, perhaps beyond recovery, was unmistakable.

General Longstreet was equally concerned for General Lee. "He's worn to death," he said, when they were on the cars again.

"His hair has grown almost completely white since I saw him."

Longstreet nodded. "He's been ill ever since May, and that damned pain in his back torments him steadily. And he has too many burdens to bear. The commissary has completely broken down, so he has to feed the army as well as fight it. I told him supplies were plentiful in Georgia, but apparently the speculators monopolize the railroads so there aren't enough cars to carry what the army needs." Anger stirred in his heavy tones. "He tells me that in Mississippi and Alabama everyone's selling cotton to the Yankees, trading it for bacon pound for pound; but the bacon never reaches the army. And he's desperate for men. Governor Brown of Georgia not only refuses to let the state militia join General Lee; he wants the Georgia troops now in the army sent home. General Lee says half to two-thirds of the paper strength of his army is absent without leave. Of course, hungry men are easily persuaded to desert, but General Lee can't face Grant alone."

He was eager for duty. His arm was still useless, but in Lynchburg he began to ride every day, testing his strength. In mid-October he and Trav returned to Richmond, and Longstreet dictated a letter to Colonel Taylor, Lee's adjutant general. "I doubt the propriety of being assigned in my crippled condition to positions now filled by officers of vigorous health," he confessed; but he added that if he could be used anywhere, even west of the Mississippi, without displacing an efficient officer, he would welcome the assignment.

Trav, writing at the other's dictation, felt his throat filled with sympathy, thinking this humility in one who had always been profoundly self-confident infinitely touching. Trav found most people perplexing; they did inexplicable things. Cinda and Brett, Tony, Tilda, Faunt; Enid most of all: each sometimes reacted to life in ways he could not comprehend. He had sometimes thought, watching them, listening to them, that they were as mysterious as chemicals in an opaque bottle. Until the cork was removed you never knew what they would do. The way of a seed in the ground, of a beast in the field, of a fish in the water or a wild animal in the forest—these were all predictable; but not the ways of man and woman.

Yet he did not have this sense of mystification where General Longstreet was concerned, and he was rarely surprised at the other's deeds or words. Everything about the General seemed to Trav consistent, all of a part, cut off the same piece. Thus now he understood that Longstreet's lifetime of vigorous health made him feel the more keenly his present handicaps; and he looked for and saw, with gladness for the other's sake, the lift in spirits when orders came assigning him to command the left wing of Lee's army, holding the line from Chapin's Bluff to the Chickahominy at New Bridge.

They were near Richmond, so Trav asked Cinda to send servants to open the house on Clay Street; and he and the General made it their Richmond headquarters, and when the lines were quiet they frequently spent the night there. It was good to see Cinda again. She had a new and warming quality. Her tart tongue, since sadness came to dull the bite of her sardonic humor, had long since lost its edge; but now sadness too was gone, and all bitterness and anger. Trav felt in her a strong serenity, and a gentleness that matched her strength. She smiled easily, and her eyes when they rested upon those she loved held a peace which Trav himself, in this collapsing world, had not achieved. When the house on Clay Street was ready she took him to see it, and she said laughingly:

"And I'll have no complaints out of you, Travis. You're lucky to have a roof of your own, with Richmond full of refugees. There are four families living in a house not so large as ours, two or three blocks away from us on Franklin Street; two old gentlemen, six ladies, eight children. Every basement room in Richmond that hasn't water actually standing on the floor has a lady and a child or two in it. I'm ashamed not to have taken someone in, but I like to keep room for Brett and Burr and Rollin, now they're so near. People keep pouring into Richmond. They seem to think they're safe here. There are even a few ladies from Atlanta. General Sherman drove them out as a man drives scratching chickens out of his garden. The poor things seem to get some sort of comfort out of telling their experiences. They seem to make themselves feel better off by remembering the bitter times they've had. But then women always like to talk. The soldiers aren't like that, the wounded. They don't talk about their wounds."

"Do you still go to the hospital every day?"

"Almost. Of course we've let the carriage go, and it's a long walk on a rainy day. It's been good for me, though. I haven't felt so well in years." She laughed. "That's probably because I don't overeat. No one does in Richmond now. Come to dinner tomorrow, you and Cousin Jeems. We'll give you bacon and Italian peas and sorghum and cornbread, and expect you to like it."

Trav and General Longstreet accepted that invitation, and Brett was there, and they spoke of General Early's defeat in the Valley. He was beaten because after driving the Yankees into headlong flight his men stopped to plunder the captured camp; and Brett commented:

"I suppose it's not surprising the army should prefer looting to fighting. Everyone's money-grabbing these days."

Trav felt a faint guilt, for his ventures in tobacco were steadily profitable. Captain Blackford was on Richmond duty now, had been here since September; and Trav had confessed his uneasiness about these transactions, but the Captain reminded him that other officers in the army bought and sold. Now that prices rose every day, speculation had become a game any novice could play successfully. Trav continued his dealings, but his conscience still troubled him.

So now he shut his ears to Brett's remark, watching the young people here at Cinda's dinner table. His eyes turned from Vesta to Anne and back again. Vesta's Tommy had been killed within a few days of their wedding; her Rollin even before they were married had been wounded near death. Anne's Julian would always go on crutches. Yet in their faces there was a happy radiance, and no shadow dwelt in their eyes. They were young; and young people were resilient, bending to the storms of life without breaking. Vesta's loss had enriched her, had bestowed upon her a rare spiritual beauty; Anne probably loved Julian maimed more tenderly than she would have loved him whole. Older people, facing like hurts, took more lasting bruises and deeper scars. He himself, and Brett, and even Cinda, had lost some deep part of themselves which they could never recover; but Anne and Julian and Vesta had for their loss some intangible gain.

Why was it that young folk could face the future with more serenity? Was it because they knew the future was theirs, while even middle-aged people like Cinda and Brett and General Longstreet and himself unconsciously came to feel that they had no future, that life was behind them? A moment later he was sure this was true; for Judge Tudor was there that day, and he was the oldest of them all, and now when he spoke it was in a hard and fretful bitterness, in the querulous tones of age.

"That is true, Mr. Dewain. There's greed and corruption everywhere, high and low. Mr. Peck, whom the clerks sent to North Carolina to get supplies, bought and shipped back here at government expense wheat and bacon for himself and his friends, for Judge Campbell and for Mr. Kean—all. at government expense! Why, he bought ten barrels of flour and four hundred pounds of bacon for himself! Yet he told the clerks who sent him that he could get nothing for them. And it's been proved in court that General Winder sold passports at two thousand dollars apiece. The rottenness runs from top to bottom of society, and government officials are the worst offenders!"

Vesta said cheerfully that prices were not so high as they had been. "Why, flour's only three hundred dollars a barrel!" She smiled. "But of course not everyone's lucky enough to have jewelry and things that they can sell, to get the money to buy even at that price."

General Longstreet said: "Judge Tudor, we in the army are more interested in getting men than in making money. I see there is a widening of conscription."

The older man shook his head. "Most of it is much ado about nothing, I'm afraid; though it's true any man on the streets without a pass is hustled off to the depots."

Julian laughed. "Why, General, they even grabbed Judge Reagan and Judge Davis, last month; because neither one is fifty years old."

"But they were released, Julian," Judge Tudor reminded him. He turned to General Longstreet. "No one with any influence needs serve unless he wants to. The medical boards pass any man physically able to endure ten days of army life; but Governor Smith is dealing out certificates of exemption wholesale, three or four hundred every week, to perfectly healthy rich young men, appointing them revenue commissioners, justices of the peace, clerks, constables, anything." He added harshly: "For that matter, there are enough conscription officers walking the streets of Richmond to make two or three divisions of able-bodied soldiers for Lee, husky loafers with muskets in their hands, challenging even soldiers and officers on the streets!"

"They've stopped me a dozen times," Julian said. "I carry no pass, and I wish they'd take me; but the medical boards say I'm no good." Trav saw Anne at Julian's side catch his hand and press it in strong tenderness.

"Of course you're not!" the Judge said angrily. "Yet these bombproofs hide behind any ridiculous pretext to save their skins. Every government official puts his sons and nephews and his cousins and their nephews—yes, and all the friends of their nephews, and the nephews of his own friends—into safe berths. The conscript men go out and drag the farmers off their farms so we'll all starve this winter for lack of farm produce; but it takes half a dozen of them two days to go out and conscript one man!" He said sadly: "The glory has gone out of war, General! The young beaux who rushed into it in 'sixty-one are either dead or maimed or they've had their fill of it. The only ones still in the army are a few fine men and a lot of poor devils with neither influence nor money, nor the courage to desert."

Cinda spoke quietly: "I've heard women say they wish all the soldiers would desert and end it. Three years ago we were all telling our sons to return with their shields or on them! Now, we just want them to return, and as long as they come home alive, that's all we ask."

During the weeks that followed, Trav came to realize that not only in Richmond but at the front the war now wore a different aspect. Battle was no longer a question of march and countermarch, of feeling for an undefended flank, of solid ranks of infantry standing to face the enemy at twenty yards' range for minutes at a time, loading and firing till one line or the other recoiled or was shot to shreds. Now the Confederates fought behind breastworks, and the Yankees likewise kept under shelter, except when Grant ordered here or there a probing thrust at the defensive lines. It seemed to Trav that nothing was accomplished by these spurts of small activity, but Longstreet set him right.

"Much is accomplished, Currain, and to our disadvantage. When we lose a man, his place can't be filled; and 'Lys Grant kills a few of us every day, and he keeps stretching our lines thinner and thinner. By and by, when we can stretch no farther, he'll overlap our right and hit for the Danville road; and then it will be a race to see if this army can get away before he cuts our only escape."

Trav had not looked so far ahead, and this word was like a revelation. "But can't we do anything?" he protested.

Longstreet shook his head. "No. No, we can't give up Richmond, and we can't hold it." He added simply: "We can do nothing but surrender, return to the Union, take up our lives again no longer as Confederates, but as Americans."

"We won't do that."

"Currain, the test of any idea is its ability to get itself accepted. We've put our belief in the right of secession to the test of war, and by that test we have failed."

"Not yet, sir! We're not beaten. We still whip them in every engagement." Trav was a little surprised to hear himself dissent, but he persisted. "Until the Yankees begin to outfight us, I won't accept the idea of defeat."

"You can't avoid accepting it, unless you shut your eyes."

Trav said incredulously: "You don't act like a man who expects defeat."

"Of course not." Longstreet half smiled. "I believe it is time to end this war, yes; but—whatever I believe—I will go on fighting."

"We certainly won't give in till we must!"

"No. No, before we give in, I suppose a few thousands more of us must die."

Trav after that day discovered all around him signs enough to foreshadow the coming collapse. Richmond was become a nest of crime. Hunger drove the poor to petty theft, to burglary, to murder; there was again an epidemic of incendiary fires; Castle Thunder was crowded with wrongdoers. In three months that fall, the army lost ten thousand men by desertion, and public executions became so frequent that they ceased to attract throngs of morbid spectators.

Not only in the army and in Richmond but throughout the South there was demoralization. Tony wrote in early December that he had decided to abandon Chimneys. "There are so many deserters around here that they rule the countryside," he said. "By yielding to their demands I've so far avoided any trouble; but to do so has reduced our supplies till now we can't feed the people on the place through the winter. I don't intend to starve myself to fill the mouths of a lot of lazy niggers, so I'm leaving. I'm going to New Orleans. Chimneys will probably be looted by the local desperadoes, unless you care to resume possession. A few of the people have run away, but you're welcome to take title to those still here; and you may consider this letter a deed of gift to you of the niggers and the place, with my blessing! Don't feel any obligation to repay me. I've dabbled in blockading and in the cotton trade and I shall be able to live quite comfortably on my credits in New Orleans."

Trav on Sunday, when they were alone together, showed Brett and Cinda the letter, and Brett read it thoughtfully. "Tony sounds scared," he commented.

"I thought so," Trav assented. "Of course people around there remember Mrs. Blandy; and Tony remembers what happened to Darrell."

"I suppose the bushwhackers rule the roost. Civil law must be pretty well broken down everywhere outside the cities."

"The states can't enforce their own laws," Trav agreed, "and their courts nullify the laws Congress makes."

"States' rights," Brett said dryly. "Sacred states' rights!" Already they had forgotten Tony.

"Well, that's what the Confederacy set out to defend," Cinda reminded him.

"States' rights can't be maintained, not against a central government," Brett said strongly. "Not if the central government is to survive. When the South seceded, that was proof enough that no union from which the members could withdraw at will had any permanence; but we in the South tried to make the Confederacy and states' rights work together. And we've failed. You can't drive even two horses in a team, unless you harness them and bridle them so they'll do what you want. Then imagine trying to make a dozen horses pull usefully together when you have no harness on them, no reins."

"Nor a whip," said Trav.

Cinda spoke quietly. "That's what President Lincoln is doing, laying the whip across our backs to make us come back and pull together." There was suddenly passion in her tones. "But oh, it's such a pity! For the whip makes a brute of the man who wields it, and leaves a lasting scar on the man who feels its lash." And she said: "These years will leave a stain on the souls of all of us, North and South, that our children and our grandchildren and our great-grandchildren will still be trying to scrub away." She pressed her hands to her eyes, and after a moment, since they did not speak, she went on: "A man came into the hospital Thursday night from Petersburg. His name was Captain Martin. Both his legs had been shot away below the knee. He died that night and he was buried Friday afternoon. Next morning his wife came asking for him. She had had a telegram that he was wounded. He had been in my ward; the office knew that, so they sent her there. I was at the other end of the ward when I saw her at the door. She was a tall and lovely lady, smiling the brave smile people muster to meet their loved ones who have been hurt. She asked the nearest nurse, in a glorious, eager voice: 'Where is Captain Martin?' The nurse was a poor ignorant man not wise enough to understand, and he blurted out the truth. 'Captain Martin, ma'am? Why, he's dead and buried yesterday!' Then she went insane for a while; and she screamed and sobbed and told us over and over how the message came to her and how she'd hurried to reach his side. Grief crucified her!" Cinda looked from one of them to the other. "What have such things to do with states' rights, or Confederacies, or Unions, or teams of horses, Brett Dewain?"

Brett came to touch her shoulder, and Trav asked: "What did you do?"

"I? I could not even weep with her. It was Tilda who gave her something to do, sent her to have his body dug up again so she could take the poor legless thing home to her children. Just planning that seemed to comfort her—perhaps even saved her reason."

"I haven't seen Tilda," Trav said guiltily. "Not since I came back." He dreaded facing her, for she might ask whether he had any word of Darrell. He was a poor liar, and he knew it. It was better not to see her at all than to risk telling her the truth about her son. "I suppose you've told Brett about Darrell?"

Cinda shook her head. "No, I hadn't thought to do so. I'd almost forgotten. It's not easy to remember one death among so many." So Trav gave Brett the ugly story, and when he was done, Cinda said: "But, Travis, you needn't avoid Tilda. She never speaks of him. I think in her heart she knows he's dead."

Before he returned to headquarters Trav did go to see Tilda; but they had no moment alone, for Redford Streean was at home and full of talk. He too had heard from Tony.

"Too bad for him to abandon Chimneys," he commented. "But of course land has no value now. I don't suppose the place could be sold today for enough to buy a good horse. An acquaintance of mine, Mr. Thorofare, the acting adjutant general, paid twenty-seven thousand dollars for a horse last week. Probably he thought he might need it when Richmond is abandoned. Chimneys wouldn't bring a third of that, if it could be sold at all."

Trav remarked that Tony seemed to have prospered, and Streean nodded. "Yes. We were associated in some blockade ventures which turned out well for both of us." He added, as though to turn aside possible criticism: "And for the Confederacy, too! If it hadn't been for the gunpowder we blockade-runners have brought in, and the blankets, and the material for uniforms, and the food, the South could never have fought so bravely and so long. The Confederacy owes a great debt to the men who risked their lives in that traffic."

Trav was often surprised by the things people said and did, and he was surprised now to see Streean assume the defensive, and wondered why. Tilda was knitting and she did not raise her eyes, but she said in a dry voice: "Wilmington is full of men who've grown rich while they 'risked their lives' so bravely. I went to visit Dolly last summer, Trav. It's a very gay town."

"How is Dolly?" He asked, not with any real curiosity. He was still puzzled by Streean, and even more by Tilda's remark. That hint of sarcasm sounded like Cinda; but Tilda had never criticized her husband.

"Dolly's quite well. She has rooms in a very nice house on Front Street. Lieutenant Kenyon is often able to be with her; and Captain Pew knows everyone in Wilmington, and he's there between his voyages. I think she finds life pleasantly exciting."

"I suppose Wilmington is pretty lively."

"In a fashion," Tilda assented. "Of course when the yellow fever was so bad two years ago, the gentlefolk went to their country places; and the town is so changed that many of them have not returned, and those who have returned live in retirement and see no one except their friends."

Her quiet words were eloquent, and there was a moment's silence before Streean spoke. "Yes, Wilmington has prospered." Trav was wondering why Tilda had referred to Dolly in a tone so completely without inflection or emphasis. "War disturbs the economic balance of society," Streean went on. "Business is a weed that thrives on war." He seemed to deplore this. "And of course that leads to corruption everywhere. Many bonded officers of the Government have grown rich through the sale of privilege. Even clerks are now paid four and five thousand dollars a year, and yet they take every opportunity for private profit." Trav thought Streean had acquired virtue somewhat belatedly, till the other added: "But of course, when we're beaten, these poor fools won't have a dollar they can call their own. The wise rats are already leaving the sinking ship. George Randolph has taken his family to Europe." Trav remembered seeing Major Randolph fire the first shot at Bethel, long ago. "After he resigned as Secretary of War, he and Mr. Myers made a fortune by arranging exemptions from army service for their clients."

Tilda, not lifting her head, said: "Mr. Randolph's health failed. It was for his health's sake he went abroad; but his funds were all put into Confederate bonds before he left."

This again was astonishingly like a reproof, but Streean said generously: "I should be glad to believe so. But other government officials have gone of whom that was not true, who had fortunes waiting in Europe or elsewhere." He added: "Like Tony, skedaddling off to New Orleans to live on his gains."

"You seem to think we're beaten," Trav hazarded.

"I think we must face it, yes. Our army might hold its own against theirs, but now instead of fighting our army they turn their strength against helpless women and children. Sheridan at this very moment is ravaging Loudoun Valley, putting all Northern Virginia to the torch; and Sherman is destroying every house in his path through Georgia."

Tilda asked: "Trav, is Enid still in Augusta?"

"Yes. General Bragg's headquarters are there, and he reports that Sherman is passing south of him. She and the children are safe enough, I'm sure."

Streean shook his head. "Don't be too sure, Trav. There's no safety anywhere. Gold is forty or fifty for one. That's proof enough of what's coming. The army's leaking away. Conscription can't find men fast enough to make up the desertions."

Trav knew this was true. "General Pickett has a hundred deserters under arrest right now," he admitted. "General Longstreet thinks the only way to stop desertion is by severe penalties; but if deserters are sentenced, President Davis remits the sentences. So any man who thinks of deserting knows he has everything to gain and nothing to lose."

Streean said scornfully: "President Davis is losing what wit and sense he had. He even talks now of making an army of negroes! No, Trav, we're lost. Hood's army has been destroyed in Tennessee, and

Early's is gone. There's nothing but defeat ahead, nothing we can do but face it like men."

Trav rode back to Longstreet's headquarters troubled not so much by what Streean had said as by the way he said it. Streean talked almost like a devoted and honorable man, which he was not; and this, because he could not understand it, made Trav obscurely uneasy.

But Monday night he forgot Streean, for Big Mill, whom he had left in Augusta with April to watch over Enid and the children, came to tell him they were at home. As he and Mill rode toward the city, the giant Negro said the journey, in spite of all he and April could do, had been a hard one. They were more than a week upon the way, cold most of the time, and always hungry.

Mill added another bit of news. Faunt too was in Richmond; and he was sick, or hurt. Old Caesar had recognized him as he was lifted off the train and into an ambulance. Caesar followed the ambulance and saw Faunt carried to the home of Mrs. Albion.

15

TILDA could have told Trav the reason for the change in her husband. He had played his game to the utmost; now to continue was to risk losing all his gains. He was planning to collect his winnings and depart before the final catastrophe.

Tilda knew Streean's decision almost before he did. She had been married to this man for twenty-seven years and she had long since learned to recognize his humors and his purposes. When he began to frequent the auctions and to buy table silver and jewelry, she guessed the direction his thoughts had taken. The day he sold the flour he had bought during the summer, he came home to boast to her.

"Six hundred dollars the barrel, Tilda; and some of it I bought as low as a hundred and fifty. It will go higher. Like as not I could get seven hundred, before the year's end; but it doesn't pay to be too greedy."

"I suppose not, Redford."

"And I got payment in gold, at forty-five for one." He stood on the hearth, his hands clasped behind him, facing her proudly. "By the way, my dear," he remarked. "A friend of mine, an auctioneer, says your mother's old silver has been coming on the market in steady driblets. Brett must be bankrupt, or Cinda would never let it go."

She thought she had never seen him so jubilant. Teetering on his toes, his back to the fire, he made her think of a rooster beating its breast and about to crow, or of a hen that has laid an egg and must express to the world its delight in its own achievement. He seemed to expect an answer, so she said something meaningless. "I suppose that's so."

"Yes, all the old high-and-mightys are crawling mighty low." His eyes became thoughtful, and he sat down and fell into a long abstraction. She guessed what he was thinking, and when a few days later wagons came to haul away those kegs of nails in the cellar, she knew her guess was a true one. The nails had been so long a symbol of his success, they had come to hold for him an almost mystical significance. He had liked to talk about them, to tell Captain Pew—or anyone whom he trusted—the date of their purchase, the price paid, the price at which he could if he chose sell them now. They were tangible evidence of his foresight and his wisdom. When he spoke of them, no matter how modestly, it was as if he said: "I am a clever man; and if you don't believe me, consider these nails."

But now he had not mentioned them for weeks, and she knew the meaning of that silence. As long as a husband speaks in open admiration of a pretty woman, there is no need for his wife to worry. It is when he seems to ignore the charmer, or even to affect indifference, that she should feel concern. When Streean no longer bragged about his nails, Tilda guessed he was on the point of selling them. When he sold them, she knew he had decided on departure.

She had long ago accepted the fact that she held no place in his life, so she expected him to go alone and without warning, but he surprised her. One day in mid-December she returned from her day's activity to find him already at home; and he called her in from the hall.

"We must make some plans, Tilda," he said. "It's time for you and me to remove ourselves from the Richmond scene." She looked at him in blank surprise. It had never occurred to her that he would wish to take her with him in his flight. "Captain Pew and the *Dragonfly* will be in Wilmington for Christmas," he continued. "When he sails for Nassau again, we'll be aboard." He chuckled, patted his stomach comfortably. "I saw a letter in the paper somewhere, two or three days ago. The writer said it was time the South repealed the Declaration of Independence and went back to our old sovereigns, to England, or even France, or Spain. I like the notion. We'll go to London, Tilda; kiss the Queen's hand and declare ourselves her loyal subjects."

Tilda sat down, her eyes meeting his. "I suppose you're a rich man, Redford."

He laughed. "Rich enough. Yes, my dear. Yes, you'll be rich, Mrs. Streean!"

She shook her head. "No, not I."

"What? What's that?"

Tilda crossed her hands in her lap, looking down at them. "I'm not going with you."

"Eh?" A sharp astonishment edged his exclamation. "Not going? For God's sake, why not? What's got into you?"

Tilda folded her thin arms across her flat bosom. She echoed his words. "What's got into me? Why, Redford, I don't know. Some sort of happiness, something I've never had in my life before. I'm a little surprised, myself. But I'm not going. I'll stay here."

"You're out of your mind!"

"I think perhaps I'm—in my mind," she corrected. "Perhaps I've come to myself." She half smiled at her own words. "It's curious the way people use that phrase. When a person turns over a new leaf, reforms, we say he's come to himself! But if he turns from good to bad we say he's gone to the dogs, something like that. As though it were natural for men to be good; and when they aren't, they're not themselves."

"What are you trying to do? Preach a sermon?"

She met his startled eyes. "Oh, no. I was just thinking aloud. I've always kept my thoughts to myself. You see, Mr. Streean, I've always despised you. You were the only man who ever paid me any attention, so I married you; but I've been sorry I did, through all these years."

He laughed at her in a scornful mirth. "Why, you poor faded old— I don't know what!" Laughter turned to anger. "Shut your silly mouth!"

"You're a bad man, you know," Tilda told him, ignoring his command. "Oh, you're not bad in any big, bold, dashing way; just in small, sneaking, sly, cowardly ways. Your blood is bad, Mr. Streean."

He came to stand over her. "I ought to smash you in the face!" He was hoarse with rage.

"It would be like you," she agreed. "Yes, you've bad blood in you, certainly. I know that even a thin strain of good blood may work miracles in a man, or in a woman. But you're bad, and you've fathered bad children, Mr. Streean." In humble confession she added: "Probably, if I were fine enough they'd have been better than they are, in spite of you; but I don't amount to much. I'm—well, nothing to brag about, myself."

He laughed, in angry scorn. "That's true, anyway!"

"Your son's a scoundrel," she reminded him. "He's a better man than you, perhaps, but he's a scoundrel all the same. I hope he's dead. I hope he never passes on to some little baby the heritage of your blood which I gave him. I hope no man with any of you in him is ever born into the world again."

"Listen," he challenged. "Do you think for a minute that I want you to go with me?"

"No, I know you don't."

"I suppose you think I'm going to buy you off?"

She smiled. "Heavens, no, Mr. Streean. I know you'd never part with a dollar."

"Not to you, by God! If you want to stay here, you can stay and welcome. I meant to take you along just out of politeness; but any yellow wench is more to a man than you ever knew how to be. Stay here and be damned to you, for all I care! I promise you I won't have to travel alone."

"Your bad blood went into poor Dolly, too," she said quietly. "If I could help Darrell, or Dolly, by going with you, I'd go."

"The devil you would! I wouldn't have you."

"Oh yes you would, if I wished to go." Her tones were mild, but they silenced him. "You're a coward, Mr. Streean. In a pinch you're even afraid of me." She shook her head. "But for me to go with you wouldn't help the children. I sometimes think Darrell is dead, and of course Dolly is lost."

"Lost! She's a married woman!"

"She made a fool of herself with Captain Pew, thinking he'd marry her; but he wouldn't, and she was afraid she'd have a baby. That's the only reason she married poor Lieutenant Kenyon. She would have married anyone."

"You're crazy!"

"Ask her."

"I will, by God! I'll see her in Wilmington!"

"You won't dare ask her," she predicted. "If you did, she might tell Captain Pew; and you'd never risk offending him. I know you, Mr. Streean. You're a bad, mean, greedy, scheming, pompous little coward. Don't ever forget I told you so; and remember, no one else in the world knows you as well as I." She rose firmly. "Goodby, Mr. Streean. Please go soon."

She turned to the door, and he let her go, and she went blindly up the stairs. Facing him, she had been strong and sure; but once she was out of his sight her knees began to tremble, and she held to the banister for fear of falling. She heard him, in the drawing room, begin to laugh; and that laughter frightened her more than any anger to which he might have given rein. It pursued her, a maniacal din of mirth, eloquent of all the fury and the emptiness, all the rage and the terror, all the incredulity mixed with inescapable humiliation which she had waked in him. In the room they for so many years had shared, staring at the wardrobe, the chairs, the bed, panic caught hold on her; and she wished to secure the door against him, but there was no way to do so. Through the closed door she could hear him still laughing; and she slipped out and up to the attic, crouching there in darkness, shaken by waves of trembling.

But after a time she heard the crash of the front door closing and knew he had gone out. He must not return and find her here. She raced down the stairs and caught up cloak and bonnet and bolted into the early December dusk; but she was uncertain where to turn. He would look for her at Cinda's, or at Trav's. She moved aimlessly away, the strength all gone out of her; and it was more chance than plan that guided her till she saw the dim-lit windows of the scores of rough white buildings that were the hospital on Chimborazo Hill.

There was safety, there she was known, there she could find endless tasks to do. She stayed at the hospital all that night, sitting by the bedside of a man in delirium whose gangrenous leg emitted a horrible odor, whose fevered and profane mutterings never ceased. Obviously he was a countryman, rude and ribald, ridden all his days by hopeless poverty. He was dying now, in torment unspeakable, far from the rough acres that had been his home; dying for a cause that for such as he had never held any selfish appeal, dying because no matter how many of his comrades deserted, some deep loyalty made him stay and meet his duty and his death. Tilda was proud to share with such a man this that was his highest hour.

In the dull dawn he died, and she called someone and saw him borne away. Redford Streean had grown rich through the war such men had fought. Her head rose, and strength came into her again; she knew no more fear.

She walked the long way home, expecting to find Streean waiting, and ready to confront him. Yesterday had been warm for December, with a promise, not yet fulfilled, of rain. In this early morning not many people were as yet abroad, but on Bank Street below the Capitol there were scattering groups, and she heard someone say that General Sherman was at Savannah; that if he had not yet taken the city he was about to. She came to her own door, but Streean was not at home. Fat old Emma answered her ring; and she said he had come home late, in a hackney cab, and stayed an hour or two and then gone out again. In their room Tilda found disorder, his wardrobe emptied.

So he was gone. Perhaps she need not see him again. Relief and sleeplessness overcame her. She kept her bed that day, and Sunday too, drained and empty, all emotion gone out of her, her strength gone with it. She scarce knew when over that Sunday of steady rain night drew a curtain.

Monday, dawn was not dawn. Night ended, but day did not come. Black fog rose from the river, and earth and sky were lost in it till rain thinned the mists away. Toward noon Tilda was still abed when Emma announced a caller. "Kunnel suthin'r udder," Emma reported. "A right nice gemmun. He say if it don' suit tuh see him now he come again."

Tilda sent word to him to wait, and she dressed and descended, wondering what his errand might be. He told her he was Colonel Gruber, of Kershaw's division, back from the Valley where he had served under Early, and about to rejoin the First Corps. "Your husband told you to expect me?" he suggested.

Tilda hesitated, unwilling to betray herself. "Yes?" The word was half assent, half question.

"I was fortunate to meet him at the moment you and he had decided to leave Richmond," Colonel Gruber explained. "Mrs. Gruber and our children will arrive this evening. Your husband said we could take possession of the house at once." He said gratefully: "Mrs. Gruber will be delighted. We'd heard so much about the difficulty of finding even rooms in Richmond. I telegraphed her Saturday, as soon as Mr. Streean and I struck a bargain."

Tilda held herself under firm control. She must know a little more. "We had a hard time deciding whether to rent or to sell," she said tentatively.

He smiled. "Rents are almost as high as selling prices," he commented. "I was glad to be able to buy." He looked around, in some uncertainty. "If you wish to stay a few days longer, and will permit us to come in with you——"

So this was Redford Streean's revenge, to sell the house over her head and leave her homeless. It was like him, she thought; but she felt more relief than pain. Her mother had given her this house when she was married, but it was always his. It stank of him now; of the perfume of his hair, of his cigars, of his mean craven soul.

"Not at all," she said calmly. "I am going to my sister's for a few days. I may want to come in for some of my personal things; but most of my packing is already done."

She saw him to the door, and closed it behind him and stood a moment in the empty hall of this house that had so long been her home. She would be glad to leave it, glad never to enter its door again. She had a vague impression that Streean lacked the legal right to sell it without her assent; but no matter. Let it go. She would never seek to keep it. She had told Colonel Gruber that her personal things were already packed. This was of course not true, but there was so little here that she had any reason to treasure and to cherish. Yet garments of any kind were in these times hard to come by. She must at least have her clothes.

But she would not stay long enough to collect them. She called Emma. "You and Sally get trunks from the attic and pack all my clothes, shoes, everything," she said. "I'll send for them later." Her cape and bonnet were hanging here in the hall; while she spoke, she put them on. Emma demanded in suspicious protest:

"Whah you gwine, Missy?"

Tilda, her hand on the knob, hesitated. "I'll send for them," she repeated, and went out and drew the door to behind her. She could not answer Emma's question, not now.

Yet there was no doubt in her mind where she would go. She walked along Franklin Street, walked so rapidly that the slight ascent made her pant, to Fifth Street, to Cinda's. Vesta was there when she arrived, Cinda still at the hospital.

"Oh, Aunt Tilda, how nice to see you!" the girl cried. "Did you ever know such a wretched, black, foggy, miserable day? I had to go down to Main Street, and I fairly groped my way. And everyone wearing such a long face! I'm so glad you came! Be a little bit cheerful with me, won't you, please? I'm so tired of gloomy people."

Tilda smiled. "Nobody can help being cheerful when you're around, Honey." She wondered how she could ever have thought Vesta was anything but beautiful. It was like stepping from shadow into sunlight to come near her. "How's that Tommy?" she asked smilingly. It amused Vesta when people spoke so of her baby. Brett had set the fashion; the youngster was always "that Tommy" now.

"He's a little monster!" Vesta said proudly. "I don't see how he manages to stay so fat on what we get to eat. But I did get a turkey today! Only I'll never dare tell Mama what I paid for it! You must have Christmas dinner with us."

Tilda almost smiled, thinking that now she would probably have not only Christmas dinner with them, but every other dinner, and breakfast and supper too. Where else could she go? Not to Enid certainly. She was half-minded to tell Vesta what had happened, but she decided to wait till Cinda came. Meanwhile, it was comfort and contenting to feel around her the warmth and love and courage which were a part of Cinda's home.

She had supposed that when Cinda came she would be able to tell them what had happened; but while Cinda in the hall laid aside her cloak and bonnet, Tilda began to tremble terribly, and her teeth to chatter, and she knew she could not speak in Vesta's presence. Vesta had gone to greet her mother in the hall. Now they reappeared together, and Tilda came uncontrollably to her feet, stammered her appeal.

"Vesta, d-darling, leave us alone a minute, will you, p-please? Something I must tell your mother."

Vesta's quick glance was keen, and Tilda tried to smile and could not. The girl said affectionately: "Of course! Have your secrets, you two!" She drew the sliding doors together behind her, and Tilda heard her light feet on the stair.

"She's happy, isn't she, Cinda?"

Cinda sat down, weary from her day. "Yes, Vesta's very happy. What's happened, Tilda?"

Speech was empty, yet words must be found. "Why, Cinda—" Tilda's throat, to her astonishment, filled with choking sobs. "Oh, Cinda——"

Cinda, as though forgetting her own fatigue, rose and came swiftly to touch Tilda's shoulder; and Tilda bowed forward, her face in her hands, and Cinda said: "There, there, dear! Tell me." And she asked in a tone that even in that moment seemed to Tilda strange: "Is it Darrell?"

Tilda looked up, eyes streaming. "Why did you ask that?"

Cinda did not reply. "What is it, darling?"

"It's Redford." Tilda lifted her head, fought back sobs. "He's going to England. I refused to go with him."

She saw Cinda's shoulders straighten as though suddenly free from some burden. "Oh, Tilda, I'm so glad!"

"He's sold the house." Tilda steadied her voice.

"What of it? You can stay here."

"Please may I? Till I don't feel quite so alone?"

Cinda said briskly. "Alone, fiddlesticks! You have all of us." She hesitated. "Do you want to tell me about it, Tilda?"

"I think so," Tilda admitted, still tremulous with the overpowering relief of sharing her tragedy. "Oh, I've expected it. Lately he's been buying jewelry, and gold; and he came home Friday and said we were going to Wilmington and on to Nassau and to England and be rich. He's leaving because he thinks the South's beaten. I told him I wouldn't go. I told him what I thought of him. I said some terrible things to him, Cinda!"

"I wish I'd been there!"

"I've hated him so!"

"Of course. Everybody has. Never mind him. You say he sold the house?"

Tilda nodded, and she told of Colonel Gruber's call. "I had to guess at what had happened. I suppose that was Redford's way of getting even. But I didn't let Colonel Gruber see, I'm sure. But—oh, Cinda, I dread answering questions. People will want to know where Redford is."

Cinda laughed cheerfully. "I doubt it. No one will miss him. If anyone does ask about him it will be just politeness, not because they care. Tell them the truth; that he's gone to England, that you preferred to stay. They'll love you for it!"

"I don't see how I can face it. I'm such a coward."

"A coward! I wish I had your courage, darling."

Tilda looked at her in an astonishment so great she began to forget her own woe. "I can't imagine you being afraid of anything."

Cinda shrugged. "I've been playing the coward for two weeks," she confessed. "Did you know Faunt is in Richmond?"

"No! Where? In the hospital, Cinda?"

"He's wounded, or sick, I don't know which," Cinda said. "But he isn't in the hospital. He's at Mrs. Albion's."

"Mrs. Albion? Why? I see her sometimes at the Soup Association, but of course I don't know her. Did she take Faunt in? Why didn't he come to us?"

Cinda said flatly: "He's her lover."

"Cinda!" Tilda's cry was half terror, half refusal to believe. "Faunt?"

Cinda nodded. "Yes. Travis told me." And she added: "For almost two weeks now, I've known he was there, and I haven't had the courage to go to her house."

Strength flowed into Tilda, to meet Cinda's need. Through these months she had become strong through serving others and forgetting herself, and she forgot herself for Cinda now. "It can't be, Cinda! I know Tony kept her for years; but Faunt is a gentleman."

Vesta tapped on the door. "Aren't you two almost through? Dinner's ready."

"In a minute, darling," Cinda called. She said thoughtfully: "You know, Tilda, those letters knocked Faunt off his feet. Of course he was always pitying himself, always weak; but the feeling that he was wellborn propped him up as a stick props up the scarecrow in a negro's corn patch." She said in steady appraisal: "I don't think those letters did the rest of us any harm. Tony was always a rascal, and I expect he still is. Travis is even finer than he was, and so are you; and I haven't been unhappy about all that, except just at first. But it ruined Faunt, Tilda."

"But he's our brother, Cinda. And he's sick, or hurt." Tilda smiled, remembering her own estate. "A deserted wife is almost as easily despised as a—woman of that sort. I don't feel too superior. I shall go see him."

"Stop it! Stop thinking you're disgraced!"

Tilda laughed. "I don't really think so! You know, Cinda, I really enjoyed telling Redford what I thought of him. I wasn't a bit scared till afterward!"

Cinda said again: "I'd have given a pretty penny to be there and cheer! Oh, Honey, I've been so proud of you, all the work you've done. But I'm prouder than ever now."

"I haven't done as much as you."

"Yes, you have! And you've done things I could never do, managing people, keeping them busy. I don't see how you do it."

Tilda said thoughtfully: "I don't know myself. Except that if you start people off a little at a time, they seem to accomplish a lot before they're through."

"I never can be patient enough for that. I either want to do things quick, or I can't bring myself to do them at all. Like going to see Faunt."

"I'll go. It won't bother me."

"Well, maybe I'll go with you," Cinda said. "Maybe eating dinner will give me courage."

They did not go that day. Cinda said it was absurd to walk so far through fog and spitting rain; but next morning was fine. Mrs. Albion received them composedly, and she remarked that a day like this, clear and cold, was a relief after the bad weather; and Cinda said yes, it was a shame to have bad weather when all the news was so distressing; Sherman near Savannah, General Hood beaten in Tennessee.

Mrs. Albion nodded. "Yes, Hood's army is destroyed."

Cinda said: "I like Sam Hood; but I wonder whether a man who has lost a leg is ever a good commander again. It must do something to his soul. Like General Ewell. He wasted great opportunities at Gettysburg, and again at the Wilderness, just by not making up his mind."

The other assented. "General Ewell fights too little, and General Hood is so anxious to prove he is as good as a whole man that he fights too much."

"He's so handsome, such sad eyes."

"There's sadness in most of our eyes these days," Mrs. Albion suggested; and Tilda stirred in a faint impatience. It was not for such empty talk as this that they were here. If Cinda would not come to the point, someone must.

"You're very good to see us, Mrs. Albion," she said. "You must guess why we have called." She added simply: "If Faunt doesn't want to see us, I hope you will at least tell us how he is."

Mrs. Albion offered no evasion. "He's been very ill. His lungs are weak. When the Yankees were devastating Loudoun Valley, he overtaxed his strength, had a severe hemorrhage."

"May we see him?"

The other woman rose. "I'll ask him." She faced them serenely. "I love him, you know. Of course, if he lives, there is no place in his life for me; and in the past I've sometimes urged him to go to you. But that was when he was well. If he is to die, I will never let him go." She added simply: "But if he wishes, you may see him, certainly."

She left the room and they did not speak for the long minutes till she returned. Then in her eyes Tilda read their answer; and she rose, and Cinda too.

"I'm sorry. I'm really sorry," Mrs. Albion assured them. "If I thought seeing you would help him, I would insist, but—it would do him harm. It would. I'm sure of that. Please."

"Is there anything he needs?"

"If there were, I would get it for him."

Tilda said sincerely: "I'm glad he has you."

"You're generous and kind. If there is any change——" Mrs. Albion's voice seemed to catch, and she repeated that word. "Change for the worse, or if he wishes to see you, I will send word."

On the homeward way, they had passed Adams Street before Tilda spoke. "You didn't say a word, Cinda, except just at first."

"I couldn't. I felt so silly, talking about General Hood, and the weather. It was a relief when you came to the point. You were wonderful." And after a moment: "You know, she's a remarkable woman. And she's really beautiful. How old do you suppose she is?"

They turned in relief to this absorbing question. "Enid's thirty-two or -three, so Mrs. Albion must be fifty if she's a day. She doesn't look it, does she?"

"She does, and yet she doesn't." Cinda tried to put her thoughts in words. "She seems—mature. I feel like a silly child beside her, and like an old hag, too. Her cheeks are as smooth as a girl's."

"She made me think of a bride. Why wouldn't Faunt see us, do you suppose?"

"Ashamed, perhaps. I suppose he should be, but I declare I can't blame him. She certainly loves him. I'm not sure he isn't a lucky man." Cinda laughed. "How did such a woman tolerate Tony all those years?" And she said reflectively: "Tony's gone, and Faunt has shut us out. There's just you and me and Travis left, Tilda." So they came home.

Next day there was disturbing news. A Yankee fleet had arrived off Wilmington; and that port was the artery through which came supplies General Lee must have in order to fight on. But to Tilda the attack on Wilmington was chiefly important because if the *Dragonfly* could not run through the Yankee squadrons, Redford might return to Richmond. That terror made her tremble, but she fought it down.

Anne and Julian and Judge Tudor would come for Christmas dinner, and Enid and her children; and there was always the hope that some of the menfolk might appear. Julian and Judge Tudor drove into the country the day before to cut holly and arbor vitae and cedar for greenery, and a Christmas tree so tremendous that it rode atop the carriage. Cinda and Tilda spent that day in the hospitals, but Anne and Vesta turned the drawing room and the dining room into bowers of beauty. Tilda went to Chimborazo Hospital last of all, and she and Cinda walked home together through the clear cold light of early dusk. Cinda was so silent that Tilda asked whether she was tired.

"Oh, yes, I'm always tired at day's end," Cinda admitted. "But I'm worrying about Jenny, alone way off down there at the Plains. If Sherman takes Savannah, there's nothing to prevent his marching north, even as far as the Plains. I wish Jenny were here."

"They wouldn't harm her."

"I don't know. They might. Sheridan left the people in Northern Virginia nothing but their homes to live in; nothing to eat, no horses, livestock, nothing. Now he's begun to do the same things in the Valley. And Sherman's army either stole or ruined everything in their way from Atlanta to Savannah." She said in bitter sadness: "General Lee said two years ago we were all in this war, so perhaps you can't blame the Yankees for taking him at his word. Turning us out of house and home will do more to make us beg for peace than anything they can do to the army. But I don't want anything to happen to Jenny and those babies."

"Nothing will," Tilda urged, and she said hopefully: "Maybe Savannah will hold out. And the paper today says they've had a storm at Wilmington that drove the blockaders away, and we're sending some soldiers there. Things may get better, Cinda."

"They can't get much worse." Cinda tried to banish her own fears. "Heavens, what a way to talk on Christmas Eve! Let's make a rule no one's to mention the war all day tomorrow."

When they reached home gladness greeted them, for Brett was there. He and Trav had ridden in together, and he was sure Rollin and possibly Burr would appear either tonight or tomorrow. So that evening was a happy one, and Cinda imposed upon them her rule of silence about the war, and they kept it fairly well. Vesta had heard on her shopping expedition the fabulous stories about the wedding of Mr. Hill's daughter. "He's just nobody," she declared. "He keeps a little food store, and his prices are outrageous, but they say he was so proud of the wedding, bragged that he spent thirty thousand dollars on it."

Anne said stoutly: "Well, I'm glad Miss Hill had a nice wedding. Weddings ought to be just as grand as you can possibly make them. Besides, it's not fair to criticize him, when everyone else is having parties all the time."

"Starvation parties," Vesta reminded her.

"Oh, you know perfectly well Richmond's ever so gay this winter."

"It's bound to be," Vesta argued. "The army is so near that the officers can ride into town any time they want to, and they're all hungry for fun, and who's to say they shan't have anything they want! There never were such flirtations, and so many people getting married; and there's a dancing party somewhere every night. Of course no one ever serves refreshments; but someone with a fiddle, and plenty of pretty girls to dance with, is the only refreshment the soldiers want."

Brett said dryly: "It's about all they get. There was no meat ration at all, last Wednesday." Tilda saw Cinda look at him reproachfully; and he laughed. "Sorry. I'm on forbidden ground!"

"Some of the ladies are scandalized by the cotillion," Tilda told them. "They declare it's disgraceful to dance like that."

"Well, if I wanted to try one I certainly wouldn't care what anyone said," Vesta declared. "Nobody's ever the worse for being as happy as they can be."

They went to bed to the sound of sharp explosions in the street and the shrill cries of boys celebrating in the immemorial fashion. Probably they were shooting off cartridges, Tilda reflected, for there were no fireworks to be had. From some house near-by she heard music and the occasional sound of singing, and bursts of laughter. Vesta was right: it was surely brave and wonderful to find happiness in song and in dancing when Grant's hordes lay in the beleaguering trenches not a dozen miles away, when at any hour Lee's thinned lines might break and let the enemy in upon the city. She felt a great love for these people of the South, for this land of which she was a part, where men and women could face ruin and death with a laugh and a gallant song.

Christmas morning was clear and frosty; and St. Paul's was decorated for the morning service, the fragrant greenery as bright as though there were no sadness anywhere. When they came back to the house Burr had not appeared; but Rollin was there with a treasure, a Christmas box sent from some Northern home, and which he himself had captured in a cavalry foray against the enemy the day before. It was filled with jellies, preserved blueberries, strawberry jam, sweet pickles and sour; and best of all, there was a jar of white sugar.

"Nobody's to open that!" Vesta declared. "We'll just put it on the table and look at it and let our mouths water!"

They laughed at her, but Rollin protested. "Not a bit of it! I'm going to eat my fill, even if I have to spread it on bread!"

"Bread?" Vesta tossed her head. "Where do you expect to get any bread? Flour is seven hundred dollars a barrel, I'll have you know!" She kissed him. "But there, darling, you shall have your sugar. You can just eat it with a spoon!"

The turkey was none too plump a bird. "But it was the very biggest I could find," Vesta assured them. "The other one didn't compare with it!" They laughed with her at the picture of two forlorn birds hanging on the butcher's hook, and when a roast of beef appeared to supplement the turkey, Brett said she worked miracles; but Enid protested:

"If you think this is a feast, you should have been in Augusta. There's plenty of everything there. You wouldn't suppose they'd ever heard of the war."

In spite of Enid's complaint, no one went hungry. When they returned to the drawing room, Caesar had deposited a tremendous old trunk in the middle of the floor, and everyone asked questions at once, till Cinda hushed them.

"This is my Christmas surprise," she declared. "I found it way back in the attic, but the key's lost. It's heavy, so it isn't empty; but I haven't the faintest idea what's in it. Brett, break it open and we'll let everyone pick and choose."

Brett and Rollin, using a poker from the hearth, cracked the lock; but before they raised the lid Vesta cried: "Wait a minute. Let's make a game out of it. Papa, swing the trunk around facing the wall, with the lid toward us so we can't see into it, and then we'll take turns, and whosever turn it is can be blindfolded and reach in and take the first thing he touches!"

They made that game last till dusk, till they were weak with laughter. Cinda decided that not chance but seniority should determine the order in which they approached the trunk; so Judge Tudor was the first. To their hilarious delight he gingerly lifted into view a chemise!

When Brett drew another like it, and Trav too, Cinda protested:

"No fair! The men are getting them all, and Heaven knows I need one!"

But she was reconciled when she picked up a petticoat. Tilda's hand fell upon a lace collar, and Enid to her open disappointment got an absurd and useless little basket woven of reeds with a faded ribbon on the handle.

Rollin's prize was a stocking. He argued that he was entitled to its mate, and Vesta told him not to be ridiculous. "What do you want a stocking for anyway?" she demanded. "You can just give that to me."

"I need it," he insisted. "A nice long stocking's ever so much better than a sock to keep my knees warm these cold days, riding in the rain." And when she in her turn drew its mate, he snatched it away from her; and they tussled for it happily, till he kissed her and she lay content and breathless in his arms.

The old trunk for a while seemed bottomless. The treasures they unearthed made them laugh, and sometimes made their eyes sting even while they laughed. "I must have packed all these things in it before we went to Europe six years ago," Cinda decided. "Heavens, how long ago that seems! Just look at that!" Vesta had lifted out a white muslin dress flounced with yards of Valenciennes. "You had that when you were fourteen, darling!"

"I can sell it tomorrow," Vesta declared. "It will bring as much as I paid for our turkey. Yes, maybe more!"

Brett laughed. "You needn't be quite so thrifty, Vesta." He looked at Cinda. "The Wilmington bank dividend is thirty-eight thousand dollars this year." Tilda remembered Redford had some shares in that bank, so he was richer than ever.

"Oh, you can buy some Confederate bonds with that, Papa," Vesta retorted. "There are enough treasures right here to take care of us. From now on I'm going to claim everything in the trunk that can be sold; yes, and impress the things we've already found."

"Do you really think this trash is worth anything?"

Vesta smiled. "Papa darling, I can see you haven't paid any bills lately. Just an ordinary calico that used to cost twelve and a half cents a yard is thirty dollars a yard now—if you can get it. Fifty dollars for chintz, a thousand dollars for a good merino, two thousand dollars for a cloak." She dived into the trunk with exploring hands. "Why, Papa, there's a fortune here! Look!" She produced an evening gown, and then another and a third. They were out of fashion now, but worth a fortune for their materials alone. One was of green silk with gold embroidery, one was of silver brocade, one of bayadere silk trimmed with lace; and she found boxes of artificial flowers and of accessories appropriate to the stately gowns. Of two velvet cloaks, one was beyond use; but the other was trimmed with fur that had escaped the moths. A great store of sky-blue yarn was priceless, and a bolt of Brussels lace. "Why, I can buy enough with all this to keep the pantry stocked for months!" Vesta promised.

Beneath these treasures, many odd objects were valueless except for the memories they evoked; half a dozen pairs of worn slippers, a few books, an assortment of toys most of which were broken. "You children played with them when you were babies," Cinda told Vesta and Julian. There were lace bonnets made for small heads, and three pairs of dilapidated baby shoes. "Those were Clayton's," Cinda said, and pressed her hands to her eyes.

But Vesta would not let any sadness mar this evening, and she swept them all into merriment again. Tilda laughed with them, but this was her bitter hour. How different her life had been from Cinda's. Brett was here by Cinda's side, but Redford must be by this time on the seas, bound for Nassau and oblivion. Julian was here, and Vesta; and Burr was near, and his name was often on their lips. But Dolly was lost and gone, and Darrell was gone. Tilda did not even know whether Darrell was alive, and almost she hoped he was not. They were Streeans, all of them; Redford and Darrell and Dolly. To Darrell and Dolly she had given life, but it would have been better for the world if they had never been born.

The trunk at last was empty. Brett would stay till tomorrow night, but Rollin must ride back to camp. Trav took Enid and the children home; Julian and Anne departed with Judge Tudor. Vesta and Tilda, to let Brett and Cinda be alone together, went upstairs; and so the day was done. It had been happy and tender and fine; but Tilda, lying long awake, knew that tomorrow she must face reality again.

In the morning while she was dressing she heard the bell, heard

Caesar go to answer and then come to Cinda's room, heard a moment later Cinda's delighted summons. "Vesta, Tilda, here's a letter from Jenny!"

That letter had come by the hand of young Tommy Izard, just back from a furlough in Camden and in such a hurry to rejoin his command that he could not wait for thanks. To hear it, they gathered by Cinda's bed, Vesta lovely in her lacy wrapper, Brett sitting beside Cinda while she read the letter aloud.

Dearest Everybody—I must just dash this off because I have a chance to send it straight to you and goodness knows when that will happen again.

Well, the children are perfect. Kyle rides as well as Clayton used to, and Janet is almost as good. I caught Kyle trying to make her jump the hedge yesterday and switched him soundly, but she says she's going to do it today. Even little Clayton would like to. They're as busy as puppies. As for me, I feel like a fighting cock; but of course my complexion is ruined, being out of doors so much. The people work hard, and they take good care of me. Banquo damns the Yankees with the best of them. I could go on for hours, but it would just be the same thing over and over, how well and how busy we all are.

Brett said in surprise: "That doesn't sound like Jenny. She's never so exuberant."

Cinda nodded. "Either she's trying to reassure us or the child's in love."

Vesta cried: "Oh, I hope it's that, Mama! She's so wonderful."

Cinda smiled and read on. " 'Everybody's expecting to hear any day that Sherman's been cut off and whipped.' " She paused, looked at Brett. "She's trying to reassure us," she said, and he agreed, and she began to read again.

And everybody's furious at President Davis for trying to impress slaves. They say the Government hasn't any right to do it. Mr. Rhett says if the Government's going to destroy the rights of the states, what are we fighting for? I think that's silly. Even if the states have to give up their rights to win they ought to be glad to do it; but they say the Legislature is going to refuse to let the slaves be impressed, and tell President Davis to mind his own business; and the Governor says he won't allow any more conscription in South Carolina, even if he has to exempt every able-bodied man in the state. I guess he already has. If they're firemen or policemen or bank clerks or school teachers or judges or state officers or secretaries or aides or tax collectors—tell Papa I paid our taxes. I thought he'd want me to. Mr. McKeen's the assessor here, and Mr. Kennedy is the collector—or if they work in factories or anything, he exempts them; and of course everybody's something! General Preston says South Carolina's the first state to commit treason against the Confederacy. If they do take our people, I don't see how we can plant anything, but probably it won't be as bad as it sounds.

Lots of refugees are here from Beaufort and the Low Country, and of course from Charleston now. They say the whole lower end of Charleston is deserted for fifteen blocks or so, for fear of the shells. Oh, did you know old Mrs. Chesnut is dead? I wrote you last spring, but perhaps my letters don't reach you. The poor Colonel was heartbroken, but his head's still high. He strides along, striking out with his cane—and he doesn't see at all, of course—and if he hears footsteps he calls 'Who's there?' and if a lady answers, he bows so grandly. Scipio goes with him everywhere.

But Heavens, I must stop and let this go. There's nothing to say anyway, except that we're all simply wonderful, and we love you heaps, and everything's fine.

Dearest love,
Jenny

For a moment after Cinda finished, no one spoke. Then she said, half to herself: "Yes, she's lonely and frightened." She looked at Brett. "I suppose the trains to Wilmington don't run now."

He met her eyes, completely understanding; but he shook his head. "The Weldon road was lost last summer," he reminded her. "And the Piedmont, from Danville to Greensboro, keeps breaking down."

"I see. But I can't help it." She spoke to Tilda. "I'm glad you can be here with Vesta."

Tilda did not understand. "Why, Cinda?"

It was Brett who answered. "She's going to Jenny." Vesta squeezed her mother's hand, not dissenting; but Tilda cried in astonishment and concern:

"Oh, Cinda, you can't possibly, can you?"

Brett chuckled. "If anyone can, she can."

Cinda kissed him as tenderly as though they were alone. "You're my dear husband. Brett Dewain," she said.

16

TRAV would remember that last winter in front of Richmond as a time when he longed to do something, and do it quickly, but could not know what to do. He had moments of ravening hunger to strike the enemy while he was still strong enough to do so; to strike them in his own person, with his own hand. He regularly wore that long sword which his father once had borne; and to supplement the LeMat which Von Borcke had given him, he belted on a heavy revolving pistol patterned on the Colt Navy model and made by Griswold and Grier at their Georgia armory. Except that the frame was of brass—for iron was scarce in the Confederacy—it was a duplicate of the Colt. Trav gave his weapons solicitous care, drawing the charges and renewing them every damp or rainy day. He was a little self-conscious about his warlike gear, but not even General Longstreet seemed to find it amusing.

"We're going to need every man before we're through," he said. "And every bullet."

But that hour of need was to be a long time coming. Too weak to attack, they could only wait for the enemy's move. In late autumn, in order to secure his flank, Longstreet set his men to strengthening the works toward White Oak Swamp; and at Trav's suggestion every road that might be useful to the enemy was broken up with heavy plows, so each rain left them bottomless pits of mud, and bad weather presently put an end to effective movement.

Thereafter, between their forces and the regiments on their front something like a truce was reached. The scattered firing by the pickets ceased, and on occasion the men bartered with the enemy for small luxuries. Trav resented this. To wait the winter through, with sure defeat coming nearer every day, preyed on him and drew his temper short; he said explosively one day to Longstreet: "They make friends too damned quickly, General. Can't we stop that?"

Longstreet smiled. "Man was designed to be a peaceable animal, Currain; to live in trees and to survive by avoiding danger, rather than by fighting. His natural weapons aren't strong enough to protect him against even small wild creatures. A few rats, if they work together, can kill and devour the strongest man; yes, even a few ants can do it. But man was ambitious to be the master, so he invented weapons. He learned to make nooses, to strike with clubs, to stab, to hurl projectiles. He learned how to kill, so that he could come down out of his tree. He's taught himself to kill; but it's a lesson he has learned, not his natural bent. And it's a lesson he easily forgets. We make men into soldiers, killers; but as soon as we leave them to themselves, they stop fighting and become men again."

But though he did not interfere with this friendliness between the lines, Longstreet kept his men at work, digging bombproofs, building entrenchments, opening fields of fire, strengthening in every way the defenses they must hold. He wished for cavalry, but the horses were worn out after months of heavy work and scant feed, and General Lee had found it necessary to let many cavalry units withdraw from the front to rest and recuperate their mounts. A day or two before Christmas, Longstreet told Trav that he had suggested to General Lee that the cavalry be mounted on mules.

"Though probably if we tried it, the men would desert in a body, with a few hot remarks about tradition. We're all thinking too much of the past, Currain, and not enough of the future. I'd like to hear some fine word from General Lee that would turn our minds in that direction."

The General declined Cinda's invitation to share their Christmas. "That's just the day 'Lys Grant might try to take us off guard." Trav reminded him that at the request of Dr. Platt, the rector of St. Paul's in Petersburg, General Grant had stopped all bombardment of the city on Sunday, so that worshippers might attend church undisturbed; but Longstreet said: "That doesn't prevent his attacking our lines, Sunday or Christmas or any other day. No, I'll stay here. Tell Cousin Cinda to ask me another time."

His headquarters were in a house on the Williamsburg road, a short hour's ride outside the city. Not infrequently he and Trav spent the night at the house on Clay Street, and between Longstreet and Lucy a pleasant fondness grew. The bearded man teased her about Garland. What would she say to his bringing Garland to Richmond, instead of leaving him to pine in Lynchburg with his mother? A pity, surely, to keep young hearts so far apart! Lucy, at first confused and hot with pretty blushes at his jesting, learned to answer him in kind. She might coquet with him, declaring that she could not be really fond of Garland when she knew an older man who was so wonderful and for whom—since, alas, he was already wed—her heart was breaking. Playing this comedy with him she passed more and more quickly into young womanhood.

Trav envied the General his ability, during these interludes in Richmond, to put aside his cares. At headquarters there was no respite. Each day's reports from divisional and brigade commanders brought new anxieties. Too many soldiers were applying for sick leave without sufficient cause; and the daily losses, a man here and a man there killed by enemy sharpshooters, provoked gloomy thoughts. To die in the heat of battle might serve some purpose; but to die from a random shell or a casual bullet, though it did no good, left you just as dead. On the South Side there was more activity, but in Longstreet's lines north of the river there was little to do except listen to disturbing news and read desperate letters addressed to the soldiers by wives at home who were half-crazed with weariness and with worry for their hungry children. Each morning brought reports of fresh desertions; the numbers began to run to scores.

But Longstreet and his divisional commanders held their men better than the generals on the Petersburg front. "We're more comfortable here, for one thing," Longstreet explained when Trav spoke of this. "And also, we've not so many conscripts. Pickett on the South Side has ten deserters to Kershaw's one here; five hundred and twelve desertions in one ten-day period to Kershaw's forty-one. That is to Kershaw's credit, but it's no discredit to Pickett."

Trav knew that Longstreet's affection for Pickett—an affection which Trav had never shared—might color his words; but he did not speak; and Longstreet went on: "The men can't be blamed. We can shoot them—or at least we could if President Davis would let us—but we can't blame them. They're ill-fed; they know there's no longer hope of victory, and they know that the faint hearts in high places who can escape are doing so. The men stand to it better than their officers. Too many of our soft-fingered Richmond dandies plead sick to dodge duty in the winter mud; and the men see these officers take sick leave and fail to recover from their trumped-up ailments. Right now, in my thirteen brigades, I have a major general and seven brigadiers absent. With faltering at the top, Currain, it's a wonder the ranks are as steady as they are."

The number of desertions steadily increased, particularly after the failure of the Hampton Roads conference, when Confederate commissioners proposed peace and President Lincoln replied that a return to the Union was his only condition. The whisper went through the ranks that this was no longer a fight for freedom, but only to save Jeff Davis's skin. Trav had from Captain Blackford a hint of the despair in high government circles. Mrs. Blackford had come to be with her husband, and they had rooms in the home of Dr. George, at the corner of Grace and Jefferson. The house was one of a row, and Mr. Hunter, the Secretary of State, lived at Mr. Stegar's, next door.

"The walls are thin," Captain Blackford said. "And after the commissioners returned from Hampton Roads we could hear him sigh, all night long, and groan, and pace up and down."

It had not occurred to Trav that men like the Secretary of State had their hours of solitary torment and despair. Trav rarely tried to put himself in another's place; but Captain Blackford's word made him wonder. Did President Davis sometimes in lonely darkness sigh and groan and wring his hands and pace the floor? Did Mr. Benjamin? General Lee? General Longstreet?

Not General Longstreet, no; Trav was sure of that. Others might falter and despair, but not Longstreet; no, nor the officers nearest him, who took from him their inspiration. General Field and General Kershaw were as steadfast as ever. Since Kershaw became a divisional commander, he had fought with Early in the Valley and shared the humiliation of defeat at Cedar Creek; yet when he brought his division back to its work in the First Corps the men were disciplined and reliable. Because General Kershaw was a Camden man, and he and Brett and Cinda were old friends, Trav had some personal acquaintance with him. He wore a heavy mustache so low that it was like a beard; his upper lip appeared to be clean-shaven while his chin was almost concealed by that remarkable mustache. But though it was easy to smile at the visage he chose to present to the world, he was a steady and a competent divisional commander.

Trav believed the First Corps would hold its fighting strength as long as Longstreet himself survived, and one day he said so. Longstreet's eyes lighted with pride.

"But the Yankees have ripped the entrails out of the Confederacy, Currain," he said. "I talked with Admiral Semmes a day or two ago. Instead of ranging the seven seas in the *Alabama,* he's now commanding a few anchored gunboats here in the river. But when he was making his way back to Richmond, he travelled from Mexico clear across the South; and he saw collapse and destruction everywhere. Plantations ravaged, houses burned, every sugar mill and saw mill and grist mill put to the torch; homeless slaves wandering through the country, stealing, living any way they can. He saw our own soldiers, deserters or disorganized units, drunken, plundering, doing as much harm as Sherman did in his worst fury." And he repeated: "The body of the South has been eviscerated, Currain. Nothing but head and heart and hands remains."

Trav was slowly beaten into despair. By the first of February Longstreet's artillery had not enough horses to move the guns, and one section of his lines had only two small regiments facing seven of the enemy's. A few days after that peace conference on a Yankee steamer in Hampton Roads, President Davis in a public speech predicted that before summer ended the North would sue for peace. He said Sherman, who had begun to march northward, was hastening to his ruin; said Lincoln would find that when he met the Confederate peace commissioners he had been talking to his masters. Davis's predictions were so absurd that no one took them seriously, and in the army Longstreet's comment seemed to Trav a just one.

"I've thought for a long time that Mr. Davis was a rascal," the General said. "But he's worse: he's a fool."

Yet Trav found some Richmond people thought President Davis was right, and were confident of eventual independence, and predicted that England and France would realize that if the North conquered the South she would turn her strength against them. These optimists were vocal; the pessimists kept their opinions to themselves. But if Trav stayed at home over night, when he rode out to headquarters in the early morning he sometimes saw the words "Vae Victis" chalked upon walls; and once on Purcell and Ladd's drug store on Main Street someone had written in huge letters: "The Lord is on our side, but in consequence of pressing engagements elsewhere He could not attend at Fisher's Creek, Winchester, and Atlanta." More than once Trav saw the police erasing these signs, but they reappeared.

In mid-February, Longstreet said he had written General Lee urging a surprise seizure of gold, to be used to buy supplies with which to feed the army. "The farmers won't take Confederate money," he pointed out. "But they'll rush to sell their produce for gold."

"We can't do that legally, can we?" Trav asked.

"Necessity's our law. If we stop to make a law about it, the gold will disappear. No, I'd send men with an armed guard simultaneously to every vault in Richmond and take possession."

Trav wondered whether such a measure would be worth the indignation it would cause. "Most of the gold in the country is in private hands. I knew a lady in Augusta who buried nineteen thousand dollars in gold in the cellar under a sawdust pile. Some of it was hers, the rest belonged to her relatives."

"I know who you mean," Longstreet agreed. "Mrs. Morgan. She also confided in me." He added honestly: "And I suppose there are many like her. But that nineteen thousand dollars would give a good many soldiers some substantial meals." He banged his fist on his knee. "Why, Currain, hundreds of these poor fellows are so nearly starved that they're going blind. They can't see a thing at night, and they can't see well even in daylight."

Trav knew that many men suffered from this affliction. "They'll get better when the spring sprouts come, when they can eat some green things."

"A great deal can happen before that," Longstreet reminded him.

One day the General showed him a note from General Ord, commanding the Union army whose lines faced theirs. "What do you read in that, Currain?"

The note asked for a meeting to discuss measures to end the friendly exchanges between pickets. "Why, General Ord can stop these exchanges whenever he chooses," Trav pointed out.

"Exactly. So he has some other purpose. We will meet him, hear what it is."

On the return from that rendezvous between the lines, Longstreet at first was silent. "General Ord thinks it is time to make peace," he said at last. "He suggests certain amenities, informal, unofficial, which might have good result."

"What amenities, General?"

"He would have the ladies begin it." Trav understood from Longstreet's tone that the proposal appealed to him. "You know Louisa and Mrs. Grant are old friends. He suggests they exchange calls. Mrs. Longstreet would go into the Union lines under a flag and pay her respects to Mrs. Grant, and then Mrs. Grant would come into Richmond and return the courtesy. He thinks that might lead to a meeting between 'Lys Grant and General Lee; and that five minutes' frank private talk between them would find a formula for ending all this." He was briefly silent. "I suppose it will be necessary to consider Mr. Davis and his feelings," he reflected, and touched his horse. "I think we must ride into Richmond, Currain."

In Richmond, Longstreet lodged at the Spottswood, but Trav went home. Enid was fuming at the high prices and the impossibility of getting enough to eat, and she was sure that as soon as spring dried the roads Grant would capture Richmond. Wasn't it time Trav did something about taking care of his family? Did he propose to leave her and Lucy and Peter here till the Yankees came? Did he want the same terrible things to happen to them that had happened to ladies when Sherman's men caught them?

Trav said Richmond was as safe as any place, and seeking to appease her he added affectionately: "It means a lot to me to have you here, where I can see you often. And you're all right here for the present, Enid."

"Oh, really!" Her tone was scornful. "Well, other husbands don't think so. Captain Blackford's sending his wife to Charlottesville; and I notice General Longstreet keeps his wife safe in Lynchburg!"

Before he returned to headquarters Trav was able to tell her that she could no longer complain of this. On Longstreet's report of his talk with General Ord, General Lee was summoned from Petersburg to confer with President Davis; and after hours of discussion it was agreed that a meeting of the two commanders might have a useful outcome. Secretary Breckenridge particularly approved the suggestion that the opening moves be made by the ladies; so Longstreet telegraphed Mrs. Longstreet asking her to come to Richmond.

"So you see, Enid," Trav assured her, "the General thinks Richmond is quite as safe as Lynchburg, or he wouldn't let her come. She's going to have another baby the end of May."

"Really? You never told me." She shrugged. "Poor thing! But if she does come, she certainly won't stay long!"

Back at headquarters, Longstreet was in a hopeful humor; but next day he showed Trav a letter from General Lee. Lee said it might be necessary to abandon their position on the James River. The commanding general directed Longstreet to be prepared to withdraw through Richmond to some point on the Danville road, and to accumulate wagons and supplies in readiness.

"But he hasn't given up," Trav urged, when he had read the letter. "He only says withdrawal may become necessary if Sherman joins Grant."

"Grant won't wait for Sherman."

"How long will he wait?"

"Depends on the weather."

Trav made an angry movement. "Well, so can we wait."

Longstreet smiled grimly. "Yet for us to wait is destruction." He added after a moment: "To act may only hasten that destruction, but it's better than waiting. If Ewell can raise a few regiments and take over our lines here, the First Corps can move and make our right strong enough to interpose between Grant and Sherman and unite with Johnston. And if we impress gold we can supply this army and feed the men and give them strength for work." Then he shook his head. "But General Lee will not agree to seizing the gold. He says, as you do, that it's largely in the hands of individuals. So I'm afraid we'll—just go on waiting, till Grant moves."

"How soon will that be?"

"Say the first of April."

Trav looked at the date on General Lee's letter. February twenty-second. This was the twenty-third. The first of April was five weeks away.

17

VESTA readily accepted Cinda's decision to go to the Plains.
Tilda said the journey would be hazardous and tiring, but Cinda
laughed at her. "Tiresome? With my grandchildren waiting at the
other end? Nonsense! And as for danger, there's danger everywhere!"

Old June would go with her mistress; and she packed an enormous
hamper with food for the journey. "Take plenty," Cinda warned her.
"The trains may break down or something, and there may be hungry
wounded men aboard, and no knowing how long we'll be on the
way." Her own necessities she reduced to a minimum; and before
that week's end they departed.

The day after Cinda took the train, Tilda heard that stormy weather
had scattered the enemy fleet off Wilmington. "Mr. Streean planned
to sail from there," she remarked to Vesta, and she asked: "Did Cinda
tell you? He's gone to Europe."

"Mama told me, yes. And she told me you wouldn't go with him."
Vesta said affectionately: "And I love you very much, Aunt Tilda."

"Probably I was foolish."

The girl smiled. "It's mighty sensible to be foolish sometimes."

Tilda returned to the routine of her days. The flow of wounded
from Petersburg and from the defenses north of the river was not
heavy, but there were thousands of hungry people in Richmond who
must be fed by public relief or by the Soup Association; so Tilda's
hands were full. Vesta had her problems too. After Cinda was gone,
Brett asked her:

"Were you serious, Honey, in saying we don't need that money
from the Wilmington bank?"

"Of course I was! Why, just the things in that old trunk will buy all we can eat for months." She kissed him quickly. "There, Mister Brett Dewain, you leave running the house to me."

He smiled and obeyed her; and Vesta began at once to convert those miscellaneous treasures into Confederate currency. She had had for months now an ally in Mr. Lehman, the auctioneer. When in her role of housekeeper she first felt the pinch, her mother was busy in the hospitals, and Brett was fighting somewhere toward the Wilderness, and Vesta confided her perplexities to Anne. "I don't want to bother Papa and Mama, but we've lots of old silver and things we could sell and not miss them, if I only knew who to go to."

Anne sent her to Mr. Lehman. "Mrs. Harrison, who used to live near Papa and me up on the Northern Neck, told Julian and me about him last year. She says he's been awfully good to her, and sold lots of things for her, and got wonderful prices."

Vesta took this advice, and she had never regretted it. Mr. Lehman was a round, olive-skinned, gray-haired little man in whom she at once discovered a warm and helpful heart. All this ruin and hurt and death was bad, bad, bad, he said. For fine ladies and gentlemen like her papa and mama it was terrible. But he could help, because there were so many people who had money for the first time in their lives and who were hungry to buy nice fine things. Vesta saw that it was a joy to him to make them pay dearly for the treasures they coveted. When something desirable was put up for sale, his agents bid it to a figure far above its worth before they let it be sold to one of those greedy purchasers. Vesta had heard Mr. Lehman's race damned so violently that "Jew" and "speculator" and "extortioner" were become synonymous; but Mr. Lehman was certainly not an extortioner. She asked him one day:

"Why do you go to so much trouble to help me?"

His eyes beamed. "I tell you a secret, ma'am. For ladies and gentlemen, I do the best I can. This war is over some day. I do not go away. I am here since I was a little boy, and I will be here when I die, and my children and their children. Then people remember: 'When I am in trouble, old Lehman don't try to rob me!'" He smiled through gentle tears. "I am a poor man, mustn't waste money, so I tell myself it is good business to do this for you. So if it is good business for me it is all right, and I can do it and not lie awake nights oy-oying on account of the money I don't make that day! Good business is good business, ma'am, even if the profit don't come today or tomorrow or maybe for five-ten years. So when you need money, you bring me some little thing you can spare and I do the best I can for you."

The gray-haired auctioneer was Vesta's secret, a secret she shared only with Anne and Julian. She doubted whether her father and mother would approve, as Caesar certainly did not, of her visits to the small office behind the auction rooms. "You let you'self down, Miss Vesta," the old Negro said reproachfully, but he would not betray her.

Vesta was fond of Mr. Lehman, and she might stay for an hour of talk with him. His father had come into the South with a pack on his back, and had saved enough to establish here a little store, and died. Mr. Lehman was then a boy of seven; but he and his mother carried on the store. Mr. Lehman's second son fell at First Manassas. There was an older boy who before the war had settled in New Orleans. "A fine boy, in the banking business and does good, but now he rides in Forrest's cavalry and no more bank." Of four daughters, three were married: of their husbands, one, having left an arm at Chancellorsville, now helped Mr. Lehman; one was in the artillery; one with Mosby. "That's a good business, too," Mr. Lehman remarked, in full approval of Colonel Mosby's methods.

He despised speculators. "When people are in trouble, fools can make money," he declared. "Then they think they are good business men, and as soon as they think that, then I begin to take money away from them." He was well-informed. It was he who first told Vesta that General Hood had been relieved of command, and he who knew the day Congress in secret session created the office of General-in-chief for General Lee. "But that is too late, three years too late," he said sorrowfully. "Everything is done too late. Cotton ought to be shipped to England four years ago. They do it now, too late. Every man ought to be a soldier three years ago. Now they try to get all the men out of the departments and the exempt places into the army. Too late! They go to teach negroes to fight. Too late! They say they will turn the slaves free. Too late! They talk about make peace on good terms, but after you have lost a war to make a bargain it is too late. All is too late." He said reassuringly: "But one day all this foolishness end. Then we begin to fix things right again. Not me, maybe. But you do it, you and your husband and your babies when they grow up. Lose a war is like to go bankrupt. If you learn something out of it, is good business after a while."

She asked what could be learned from defeat. "Why, it is plain," he told her. "One man is strong as one strong man. Two men work together, they are strong as three strong men. But three strong men that don't work together are not so strong as one strong man." He made an impatient gesture. "All the talk is states. The states do this; they won't let the Government do that. So nobody does anything. That is bad business, and bad business is bad everything. Business is just be sensible, give the penny to get the dollar. Men and states is no difference. They make more if they work all together, give up little to get much. That is what to learn in this war."

"I've heard Papa say almost the same thing."

"Your papa is good business man. He knows when it is smart not to make money. Profit is not just money. If a man burns up all his money and feels good doing it, that is profit. Just do what makes you feel good and glad and never sorry you did it. That is good business."

"Papa would like you, Mr. Lehman," she said warmly.

"I know all about him. He is good man." Vesta was surprised at the depth of her own pleasure in that word.

Rollin came home in time to take Vesta to the Wellfords' ball, and she danced her stockings to shreds. She would remember that evening as the last bright flame of the old beautiful life that was ending. Not till they came back to the house on Fifth Street did Rollin show her a sad letter from his mother. All Mrs. Lyle's efforts to keep the plantation on the Peedee in profitable operation had proved vain; and their rice swamps on the coast would soon be overrun with weeds and shoots. Dams and sluices were gone, there had been no ditching for six years. Her friends refugeeing from the Low Country painted a hopeless picture. When white folks left, the Negroes moved into the big houses and turned them into pig sties or, because they were too lazy to cut firewood, burned them piecemeal. If a white man tried to control them, they complained to the Yankee provosts and their masters were arrested and often imprisoned. Some of the Negroes were enlisting in Yankee regiments and lording it over their former masters. Provisions were stolen and wasted. The Yankees said that owners who left their plantations forfeited their ownership. The Negroes had not yet harmed any white folks, but no one knew when outrages would begin. Fallow Fields thus far was peaceful, except that the Negroes could not be made to work; but all the Low Country was becoming a lawless desolation and a waste.

Vesta wept as she read. When she handed the letter back to him, he said: "So I expect you've married a pauper, darling."

She pressed her fingers to his lips. "Sh-h-h! You're never a pauper while you have me; nor I while I have you."

He swept her close, laughing in her ear. "Papa made a fortune in thirty years," he said. "If he could do it, so can I."

"And we've thirty years, and thirty years more on top of that, Rollin. You and I are young! And we love each other. That's being just as rich as I ever want to be." So he forgot his griefs and they spoke of love and of bright dreams.

When Hetty Cary and General Pegram were married at St. Paul's, Vesta insisted that Aunt Tilda go with her to the wedding; and she refused to be frightened by the long tally of mischances and ill omens which marked the occasion. "So many bad luck signs will cancel each other out," she predicted. "Nothing really bad can happen to anyone as beautiful and sweet and dear as Hetty. Besides, I'm not superstitious anyway."

The days slipped away, sometimes warm, sometimes cold, sometimes wretched with drizzling rain that turned the skies into a smothering canopy of gloom. Coal was a hundred dollars a load if you could get it, and a stick of firewood of any size cost five dollars. Indoors, Vesta and Tilda huddled in capes and comforters, and Caesar and the servants bundled themselves like mummies.

One day at dusk a man rang the bell. He brought a letter from Redford Streean. "I saw him in Wilmington," he explained. "I'm Mr. Peck. The letter, I regret to say, is almost a month old."

Tilda turned the sealed packet in her hands. "Mr. Peck?" she echoed. "Yes, I remember. You were in the Post Office Department.

You sent Mr. Streean some barrels of flour from North Carolina. Didn't the lady clerks in the department raise a fund and give it to you to buy foodstuffs for them?"

Mr. Peck seemed faintly confused. "Why, yes, but I was able to do very little."

"But you sent Mr. Streean flour and bacon."

"Only a small quantity, ma'am. The condition of the railroads——"

"You had the money the ladies raised."

Mr. Peck fingered his hat. "I must of course reimburse them." He said hurriedly: "You must understand that all North Carolina is confusion now. Refugees are thronging toward Richmond; swarms of them, literally swarms, ma'am, at every station. Railroads in collapse. Corn, bacon, foods of all kinds piled up at every station and rotting in mud and rain for lack of cars to move it to the army."

Vesta thought of her mother. "Were you in Columbia?" she asked.

"Ten days ago." He threw up his hands. "Insane throngs waiting to board every train. Sherman's name on every lip. Only my acquaintance with the express agents made it possible for me to hold my place on the train." He mopped his brow. "Well, ladies, I must bid you good day."

Vesta rang for Caesar to show him to the door, and she almost smiled at Caesar's august disapproval. When Mr. Peck was gone, Tilda made no move to open Streean's letter. She turned it idly in her hands, till Vesta asked: "Aren't you going to read it?"

Tilda extended it to her. "No," she decided. "Burn it, Vesta. I don't even want to hear from him again."

Vesta, without taking the letter, lighted the gas; and she said hesitantly: "But—maybe he's seen Dolly."

So Tilda opened the letter. She began to read it to herself, and Vesta left her alone and went upstairs to see Tommy put to bed. When she came down again, Tilda was sitting as though she had not moved. Gas was expensive now, fifty dollars per thousand feet; but the jet was still burning brightly. When Vesta came in, their eyes met and held, and after a moment Tilda extended the letter.

"You'd better read it, before you burn it," she said.

So Vesta, wondering where Mr. Streean had found such a fine sheet of paper, since to write even a short letter nowadays you might have to tear a little paper off the wall of some dark closet, went near the gas and read.

My dear Tilda—The Dragonfly sails on tonight's tide, Captain Pew, Dolly and I. Lieutenant Kenyon has been fool enough to get himself killed. After the storm scattered the Yankee fleet, the young idiot came home unexpectedly; and because he found Captain Pew and Dolly alone, he chose to think the worst. Not that Captain Pew isn't a gallant man, to be sure; but you know your daughter too well to credit all the idle gossip on Wilmington tongues. Kenyon hurried back to the Fort and chose to make an ugly scandal by leading an unauthorized sally against the Yankees, and naturally he was riddled for his pains. Captain Pew did what he could to hush the talk and protect Dolly. He even called out and shot one or two of Kenyon's friends whom he was able to lead into excessive loquacity. But I fear those meetings only increased the talk; so it seems best to remove Dolly from possible criticism, and we sail tonight for Nassau. Dolly seems enchanted with the prospect. I scent a romance between her and Captain Pew. You always wanted her married, but I'm not sure Dolly contemplates marriage. It might be a mistake for one so lovely to commit herself to just one man. I suspect you were right in thinking she was more my child than yours. Certainly I would never suspect you of betraying me. Not while men have eyes, ma'am.

My most profound devotions, etcetera, etcetera, etcetera.

Your admirer,
Redford Streean.

I regret I can give you no equally explicit news of Darrell.

Vesta as she read felt a shivering cold along her spine. When she had finished she looked toward Tilda, but Tilda's eyes were closed. There was the smallest possible fire upon the hearth, a few red coals and charred ends. She twisted the sheet of paper into a spill and held it against the coals till it caught, then allowed the paper to unroll and laid it on the embers. When it was all consumed, she stirred black fragments into the ashes till they were indistinguishable. Then she rose and put the poker by and brushed her hands together and came back to Tilda. She took Tilda's face in her hands, and Tilda's eyes opened, and Vesta kissed her on the lips.

"There! Now we're all clean," she said.

Tilda spoke pleadingly. "Vesta, would you mind not telling anyone? Except of course Cinda."

Vesta smiled in fond tenderness. "Tell anyone?" she echoed. "Why, Aunt Tilda, I don't know what you're talking about! I haven't the least idea!"

Tilda nodded. "You're darling, Vesta! But—tell your Mama. Tell Cinda. I could never do it, but I want her to know. And of course I know you'll tell Rollin. But no one else, please."

Before Vesta could answer, the door bell rang, startling them both. Tilda rose hurriedly to escape upstairs, so Vesta was alone when Caesar announced Mrs. Albion.

Mrs. Albion's name was at first meaningless to Vesta; the attractive woman whom Caesar ushered into the room was a stranger. Mrs. Albion, seeing no one here but Vesta, said doubtfully: "I asked for Mrs. Dewain."

"Mama is away," Vesta told her. "I'm Mrs. Lyle." She added: "But Aunt Tilda, Mrs. Streean, is here."

"May I see her?"

Vesta suddenly remembered. This was Aunt Enid's mother, who had been Uncle Tony's mistress for so long. She felt a lively interest. "I think Aunt Tilda has retired," she explained, and smiled. "But I'm the lady of the house, I suppose, with Mama away. If there's anything I can do . . . ?"

The other hesitated, shook her head. "I'd really like to speak to Mrs. Streean." She bit her lip, studying the girl; then nodded her head. "But you're not a child," she said, assenting. "And he must like you. He might listen to you."

"Who?"

"Your Uncle Faunt."

Vesta's head lifted; she put on a steady dignity. "You had better tell me what you are talking about," she said coldly.

"May I sit down?" Vesta nodded, and Mrs. Albion did so. "I came on foot," she explained. "And I hurried, told him I would not be long away." She looked at Vesta, still hesitant. "Well, I must," she said, half to herself; and then to Vesta: "He's at my home. He's been there almost two months. He's extremely ill. Lung trouble. But now he is well enough, or thinks he is well enough, to go."

Mrs. Albion clearly was mistaken. Uncle Faunt could have nothing to do with this woman. "You mean Uncle Tony?" Vesta protested.

"I do not. I mean your Uncle Faunt. He insists on leaving Richmond in the morning."

Vesta stared at her, still incredulous. Yet there could be no mistake. What this woman said so positively must be true.

"Then why doesn't he go?" She spoke in hard challenge.

Mrs. Albion hesitated, she seemed to choose her words. "Mrs. Lyle, you're a young woman," she said. "I'm—not. You're a good woman and I'm not. But you and I have one thing in common: we have the capacity to love. I know a great deal about you, you see; and I suppose you know a little about me. I love your Uncle Faunt. He loves me. I know this should not be true, but it is." She sighed, as though to speak these words had been a hard task. "I've—asked him to come back to you all."

"You knew he wouldn't!" Vesta's tones were level, but her heart was pounding.

"Yes," Mrs. Albion agreed. "Yes, I knew he wouldn't. I prayed he wouldn't. But all the same, I urged him to."

"Why did you come here?"

"He's really very ill," Mrs. Albion told her. "Your mother and Mrs. Streean know he is at my house. They've known almost from the first. They came to see him, but he refused to see them; but because they knew he was there, he has wanted to leave; and now he thinks he is well enough to do so."

"And you don't want him to?"

"I do want him to," Mrs. Albion corrected. "But I don't want him to go back to Colonel Mosby. To do so will kill him." She shivered suddenly, and pressed her hands to her eyes. "I'd do anything, anything at all, to keep him from going back. I have done—— Oh, I've tried!" She said icily: "Mrs. Lyle, can you understand that rather than let him go back to duty, I would gladly see Mosby and all his men shot, or hanged? If I could have brought that about. But I couldn't!" She shook her head, said in level tones: "No, I don't want him to return to duty. I want him to come here to you, to let his lungs heal, to grow strong again."

"So you can whistle him back, I suppose." Vesta felt no relenting.

Mrs. Albion smiled sadly. "I know what you think about me, Mrs. Lyle. I agree with you, you know. And I make no excuses." She spoke remotely. "I was a greedy and a selfish young woman. When Mr. Albion died, he left me penniless. I tried to make a rich marriage. I tried to marry your Uncle Trav. Probably you didn't know that. I failed because Enid took him away from me. She's a stupid woman, but as a girl she had a malicious cleverness.

"She married your Uncle Trav, and I was getting old. I was older then than I am now, Mrs. Lyle, although that was sixteen years ago. And just then I met your Uncle Tony, and he was dissolute and weak, but he was rich. He wouldn't marry me, so I got what I could from him. I'm making no excuses at all, you see.

"But during the years with Tony I learned a great deal about men; not much about women, perhaps, but a great deal about men." She hesitated, tapping her teeth with a fingernail. "Mrs. Lyle, don't ever misunderstand men," she said quietly. "Most women imagine that men are all gallants, that they seek feminine companionship for only one reason. I assure you that is not true. A woman can be a man's completely contenting mistress without ever spending a moment alone with him. It isn't the wives who know how to make pretty love whose husbands adore them; it's the wives with whom a man can sit down and talk and be listened to, can sorrow and be comforted, can worry and be eased. I assure you, my dear, men want to be told where they left their socks, or where they can find their fresh linen, or that they may stay quietly at home when they don't wish to go out, or that they're intelligent and interesting and wise and brave and clever. They want these things much more often than they want—love."

She hesitated, and Vesta realized in a slow surprise that she liked this woman, and Mrs. Albion went on:

"Yes, I learned that men would give me things, or put me in the way of making money, and ask of me nothing in return except amiable and flattering companionship." She smiled briefly, not with mirth. "If you asked the question in your thoughts"—Vesta's cheek crimsoned—"and I answered you truthfully, you wouldn't believe me. No matter."

Her eyes sobered. "But now I love a man," she said. "Now I'd do anything. I have done desperate things to keep him away from the war.

I would do more. I'd never see him again, I'd insult him, I'd flout him, yes, I'd kill myself, if by doing so I could be sure he would come back to this house and stay here and grow well again and—live, not die." She pressed her handkerchief to her lips. "I wish your mother were here," she said wretchedly. "She would believe me."

Vesta said at once: "I believe you. I probably don't understand half you said, but I believe you. What can I do?"

"Go to my house, get him, bring him here."

"Will you come with me?"

"To the door, if you like; but I'll not go in, not unless you call me. You go to him alone."

Vesta rose. "May I take Caesar?"

"Of course."

"We don't have a carriage now."

"We can walk there in twenty minutes. It's cold, but the night's fine."

Vesta would always remember that walk through Richmond's darkened streets. Mrs. Albion in her haste kept a few paces ahead; and Caesar, audibly muttering his disapproval of such goings on, came a little behind. They talked not at all, for the confusion in Vesta's thoughts would not shape itself into the questions she wished to ask. At the gate, Mrs. Albion stopped.

"There," she said. "Tell Milly I sent you. I'll keep out of sight."

So Vesta went bravely to the door and tugged at the bell. The door was snatched open so quickly it startled her. A cringing Negro woman swallowed sobs of fright and stared at her and cried:

"Who you?"

"Mrs. Albion sent me to——"

"Whah she?" Milly, in panic fear, slipped past Vesta to the open door; she called despairingly into the outer darkness: "He gone, ma'am! He done tuk his hoss and gone!"

Mrs. Albion, swift as vengeance, came sweeping up the walk. Milly collapsed in abject tears; but her mistress said reassuringly: "All right, Milly. I know you couldn't help it. Go now."

She watched Milly shuffle away, and turned; and Vesta saw under the gaslight the deep lines which sorrow drew upon her countenance.

"He knew I wanted him to stay," she said in a hushed, broken voice. "So he slipped away, to avoid any arguing. We never argued."

"Perhaps he's still——"

Vesta did not finish the sentence; for Mrs. Albion shook her head. "No, he would ride off quickly. I suppose he's well out the Brooke Turnpike before this." And she said to herself: "I'll never see him again."

Vesta felt herself an intruder in an abyss of grief; yet she was uncertain what to do, till Mrs. Albion turned and, as though forgetful of the girl's presence, climbed the stairs. Vesta after a moment went out and softly closed the door behind her. With Caesar two paces behind, she walked slowly home.

The door of Tilda's room was open; and this news of Faunt might help her forget Dolly for a while. So Vesta went in and sat on Tilda's bed in the half-dark and told the story; and Tilda held her hand and said when she was done:

"That was hard for you, darling."

"It didn't seem real," Vesta confessed. "None of it seemed real. It was like a dream."

"Sleep and forget it, then. Remember it that way, just as a dream."

Early in February, Rollin came home for a night; a Rollin lean and haggard with fatigue, but with spirits high. He had news of Cinda. "Colonel Haskell's just returned to duty," he said. "He saw her and Jenny and the children in Columbia, says they were fine, says they were just waiting to see what Sherman would do. They were going to come north if Sherman headed that way; but the railroads are all broken down. It took Colonel Haskell from the fifteenth to get here."

"If it took him two weeks, it will take them a month," Vesta reflected. "But if Mama makes up her mind to get here, she will, somehow!"

She was richly happy in these hours with Rollin; and in the whispering night she told him Dolly's shame. She told him too of Mrs. Albion's call, and he held her close and protectingly. "I wish that hadn't happened to you, Vesta."

"I think I grew up a little," she confessed. "I hated her at first. But she—well, I almost liked her in the end."

"I wish you didn't."

"Oh, you'd like her!" she said. "I guess any man would." And she quoted to him, teasingly, some of Mrs. Albion's wisdoms, till he gravely declared Mrs. Albion was a wonderful woman, and Vesta told him he was a beast to say so, and they quarrelled in whispers and were reconciled again.

Rollin left next day, and thereafter Vesta watched for every crumb of news from Columbia, and she and Tilda tried to guess where Cinda was. General Pegram was killed a short three weeks after that wedding which so many omens marred, and Hetty and her mother brought his body home in a freight car. Vesta saw his coffin set on the same spot in the chancel where he had taken his bride; and she wept as she had never wept for any sadness of her own. Then in mid-February Brett came home, his face a mask of weariness; and she told him Rollin's news of Cinda, and he said that to carry troops for the defense of Wilmington the Government had impressed the Piedmont Railroad from Danville to Greensboro. "So there's no knowing how Mama'll get back when she's ready to come," he said.

Vesta wanted to laugh aside his anxiety. "Trust her to manage, when the time comes." And to distract him: "We've enough to worry about without her, Brett Dewain! Flour's fifteen hundred dollars a barrel! What do you propose to do about that?"

He chuckled. "You sound like your mother, calling me by my name!"

"I want to sound just like her, so you won't be so lonesome for her."

"You're mighty sweet, Vesta." He added soberly: "But the Yankees are trying Fort Fisher again. If they take the fort, seal off Wilmington, we'll all starve!"

"Why not capture flour from the Yankees, the way you do guns?"

He shook his head. "It's working the other way around, now. They're capturing things from us."

Trav was in town that day, and after dinner he came to be with them, and he and Brett talked of the steady losses which wore away the army. Since Sherman burned their homes and scattered their families, Georgia men were deserting at every chance; and each new report of pillaging and torture and destruction increased the toll.

"He's costing us as many men as if he were beating us in battle," Trav declared.

"I see only one chance," Brett confessed. "I respect President Davis, but his stubbornness will ruin us, if we're not already ruined."

Vesta said crisply: "Brett Dewain, Mr. Davis has had nothing but criticism and reproach for four years. I've never heard anyone say: 'There's a fine thing he did!' Praise never hurt anyone. A little praise and approval might do wonders for him."

Brett smiled. "There you go again, talking like your mother."

"Well, I think so myself too, Papa," she assured him. "Mr. Davis is blamed for everything that goes wrong; but when anything goes right, General Lee or someone gets the credit."

Trav said: "There's a lot of talk in Congress and in the papers about making Lee General-in-chief; but he can't command all our armies unless they're concentrated."

"They never will be," Brett reminded him. "Every state wants to call its own troops home. To read Governor Brown's letters you'd think Georgia could have whipped Sherman if all her soldiers had been at home instead of in Lee's army. And Mr. DeSaussure sent a petition from Columbia the other day, asking Lee to send a corps down there to defend South Carolina." He added: "I almost wish he would, since Cinda's there."

Trav said gravely: "Brett, we lost seventy thousand bushels of badly needed grain in that fire in Charlotte, and a lot of sugar, too."

"I wouldn't be surprised if Mama's in Charlotte," Vesta suggested. "I think she'd bring Jenny and the children as far north as she could."

"Columbia won't be defended," Brett said surely. "So they'd be safe there. Sherman won't have any excuse to loot the town, or harm anyone."

Brett went back to duty, and there was a rumor that Columbia had fallen and no one doubted it. When on Sunday he came home again, he said the city had been burned. "I hope Cinda and the others got away all right. I'd give a good deal to know where they are."

Vesta saw his desperate anxiety. Cinda sometimes made him forget his concerns by absurd questions or by pretended ignorance that made him storm at her; and Vesta tried the same device. Did he suppose

Mama would go Charleston? He explained that to do that, Cinda would have to go through Sherman's army. Besides, Charleston was already evacuated, no doubt of that; though of course Beauregard might somehow work a miracle. Vesta said brightly that four years ago, after Manassas, people thought General Beauregard could just do anything, but Brett did not comment, and she asked: "What do they mean, Papa, when they say gold is a hundred for one?"

He laughed and told her not to pretend to be stupid. "You don't fool me, you know." He came and kissed her. "Trying to take my mind off Mama, Honey? I know your tricks."

"But what do they mean, Papa?" she persisted.

"Why, a hundred Confederate dollars for one gold dollar." His eyes shadowed. "Evans and Cogswell in Columbia printed most of our currency, but with Sherman there we can't print any more. I hear we have several millions in specie in Charlotte, right in his path. Probably he'll get that too."

"Would that be bad?" He made an angry gesture, and she said apologetically: "But Papa, I get so confused! People say so many things I just don't know what to believe. They say Mr. Davis is going crazy, or that he already is, something about a pain in his head; and all this talk about evacuating Richmond. Surely they won't, will they?"

So she brought him to the point where he needed no more distraction. "Oh, we won't till we must, of course. When we do, that will be the end of us, Vesta." And he said thoughtfully: "This is all part of the end; the end of the whole madness of states' rights." He swung to face her. "We even make more states, as if there weren't too many already! Western Virginia seceded and joined the North, and last fall some cowardly rascals organized the 'State of Southwest Virginia' and elected a governor and a full slate of officers. And the Yankees have organized their own Virginia state government up in Alexandria, to take control of the conquered counties. So what used to be one Virginia is three or four states now. And all the Confederate states are babbling about their rights! Georgia says she has a right to make a separate peace with the North, and North Carolina's threatening to, and some Virginians talk about it." And he said: "The Confederacy's trying to dodge out of what's coming, trying to bribe the North, offering Lincoln to become his allies against European powers if he'll grant us independence. I'd rather see us fight and lose and take our whipping without so much whining."

He tramped across the room and back again. "The army knows we're beaten," he said. "The men are making their own separate peace, deserting to the Yankees or slipping away to their homes. Mr. Wigfall wanted General Lee to let the Texas brigade go home to recruit; but if they went, they'd never come back! There are only four hundred of them left, but even four hundred soldiers can't be spared. Men whose homes are near-by go without permission. General Wilcox says he's losing three hundred deserters a week. The army loses hundreds every night! I don't blame them, the poor devils. Too many of the gentry—" He spat the word. "The big planters and their sons, the slave owners, have got out of the army, set the example."

He sat down, looking at her under lowered brows, and there was a profound sadness in his tones. "The best men in the South joined the army in 'sixty-one," he said. "But most of them are dead. The best blood of the South is dead, Vesta. Your little Tommy, and other babies like him who never knew their fathers; they'll have to carry on the fine old strains. They'll have to breed a new race to take the place of the dead; your grandchildren and their grandchildren. Most of our best young men are dead, or will be, if this rotten business goes on."

She said in a low tone: "Like General Pegram, Papa. I went to their wedding. You know Hetty broke her mirror, two days before. She was showing Connie her bridal veil and dropped the mirror. Then they were to ride to the church in Mr. Davis's carriage, but the horses reared up and acted so badly that General Pegram and Hetty had to come in an old broken-down hack. Then Hetty tore her veil, coming into the church. Everybody said they didn't believe in signs; but he's dead."

"How's she standing it?"

"She's wonderful, Papa."

He kissed her gently. "No man was ever as valiant as you women."

She said with a faint smile: "But I cry pretty easily now. I cried awfully at General Pegram's funeral."

It may have been long weariness—the weariness of waiting on the torturingly slow approach of the inevitable end—or it may have been the anxiety for her mother which she would not admit even to herself;

but what she had said was true. She did cry easily. When fire broke out in a store on Main Street, and a family named Stebbins who lived on an upper floor, a father and mother and grown daughter and two youngsters and a Negro servant, all were burned to death, she wept for them as though her heart were bursting. It was somehow sweet and comforting to weep for strangers.

There was a monotony about the sluggish days, and no spark of hope to lighten them. Wilmington and Charleston and Columbia, all were gone. The deep South cried that Virginia should be abandoned, that Lee should turn and crush Sherman and gather all the scattered Confederate forces and retreat to the mountains to fight on till the North was wearied of the struggle. People whispered that even General Lee was traitorously ready to agree to the emancipation of slaves, and recalled the damning fact that he had freed his own, long before the war began. If Lee could not be trusted, then who could? Colonel Northrop had been the target for criticism and abuse since the first summer of the war. Men said that a dyspeptic who lived on rice and milk and water could not be expected to understand that healthy soldiers needed food. Now he was at last removed, and Mr. St. John took up the task of supply which had long since become hopeless. Nine leading citizens of Richmond issued an appeal to everyone to give food out of his own pantry and cellar to feed the army; but everyone whispered that these nine men and their families were still well-fed. Suspicion and envy and hatred walked the streets.

February was on the ebb, and with spring and the drying of the roads Grant would strike. Terror came to dwell in every mind. Toward the end of February, Rollin and a squad of men went south to try to find recruits for his regiment; but Vesta forgot all else when on the last day of the month, a warm day with streaming rain, Cinda at last came home.

18

FAUNT, seizing the hour when Nell left him briefly alone, rode out of Richmond like a fugitive. Since that December day when Cinda and Tilda tried to see him, he had felt himself debased and shamed. That they knew he was here made blacker his crime in being here. As long as they were ignorant of the truth he had found happy hours and days with Nell; but now that was no longer true. Still too weak and ill to move, he fretted for the day when he would be well enough, at any cost, to get away.

When the Richmond papers reported that Mosby had died of wounds at Charlottesville, Nell tried to persuade him to surrender to inactivity. "I suppose there's no one to take his place, is there?" she asked.

"No," Faunt agreed. "No, without him the Rangers will break up into guerrilla bands." But one man alone could still accomplish much, and Faunt had as often as not worked alone; so Mosby's death made him the more eager to go back into the field. When word came that Mosby instead of being dead was recovering, Faunt's impatience increased; but he hid from Nell his returning strength, and seized secret opportunities to exercise his weak and shrunken muscles.

From mid-January on, he was stronger than Nell suspected; and the day she went to appeal to Cinda and Tilda, and so brought Vesta to the house, he was ready to act. Milly tried to detain him; and he was still so weak that Rufus had to help him into the saddle; but once seated, though his horse after weeks of rest and good feed was lively, he knew himself secure.

His own determination and the luck that kept him clear of roving

Yankee troopers brought him after days and nights of wary riding into Mosby's country. There he met Pete Madison, an old comrade in the Rangers, and heard the story of Mosby's wound. While the Colonel was at supper at Lud Lake's, a troop of Yankees crept near enough to see Mosby through a window. Knowing by his uniform that he was a Confederate officer, and without any challenge to surrender, they shot him.

But before they broke into the house, Mosby got out of his coat and into another, stuffing under the bed his own coat and the plumed hat which they would surely have recognized. "Time they got to him," Madison explained, "he was bleeding like a stuck pig, and he looked to be dying. They asked who he was and he said his name was Johnson or Wilson or something. The Yankee major was drunk, and he decided the Colonel was done for; so they took his boots, and stripped off the old coat and a hat he'd grabbed up, and left him there."

"Shot him without warning?" Faunt's voice was mild.

"Yup!" Pete went on: "They thought they'd killed him; but after they was gone, Lud Lake got him into an oxcart and hauled him off into the woods and hid him in a pile of leaves. The Yanks found out by'n'by who he was, and they come back and searched every hen coop in twenty miles. That was when they put out word that he was dead; but he'll turn out to be about the liveliest dead man they ever did see. He'll come back r'aring to go, head up and tail erect. Them Yankees better look out!"

"Where is he?"

"At McIvor, nigh Lynchburg, at his Pa's place, and ready to ride again any day."

But at Glen Welby Faunt learned that Mosby, as soon as he could stand, had gone from his father's place to Lynchburg and then to Richmond; and at Glen Welby he met Dr. Monteiro, who had seen the Colonel through the later stages of his convalescence. "He'll be as good as ever," the doctor said. "Any other man would be dead, but not John Mosby. I knew him when we were boys at the University. There was a town constable named George Slaughter who tried to arrest John for whistling on the streets, and John took his club away from him and made George yell for help. George was twice his size, too. No, the Yankees haven't yet run the bullet that will kill John."

Mosby's men, even in his absence, were active; but Faunt, tired from his journey, was glad to rest for a few days at Major Carter's home. Willie Mosby was there, and Charlie Grogan, bed-bound from a recent wound; and a man named Lomas, a Marylander for whom Willie Mosby vouched. Faunt noticed that Lomas did more listening than talking; but Willie Mosby as usual talked enough for all of them. He was just then engaged in filling Dr. Monteiro's ears with tales of Ranger exploits; and as silent listeners, Faunt and the man named Lomas insensibly drew together.

"I take to you," Lomas one day remarked. "You don't talk as much as some."

"Willie fights as hard as he talks," Faunt said guardedly.

"There's times," Lomas suggested, "when not talking does more good than talking or fighting either."

Faunt thought the other's tones invited questions, and when presently to be idle here began to fret him, he led Lomas to say more. The Marylander proved to be, under a little encouragement, as vocal as Willie Mosby. There were all sorts of ways of hurting the Yankees, he said. One good way was to make them think you were helping them. Thus he came to the point.

"F'r instance, General Sheridan sent me to find out all I could about Mosby and his men," he said. "That's why I'm here."

Faunt stared at him, his lips tightening. "To spy on us?"

Lomas nodded. "Least, that's what Sheridan thinks. Secretary Stanton recommended me to him. But Colonel Mosby knows me, and Willie told you I'm all right. They give me what to tell Sheridan, things that won't do any hurt for him to know; and I fetch them news about him and what he's up to."

Faunt watched him narrowly. The man was a confessed double-dealer, and therefore not to be trusted. "Why confide in me?" he asked, in a neutral tone.

"Well," Lomas explained, "in my line of work, two men can do more than one." He cleared his throat as though in apology for what he was about to say. "They tell me you're one that likes to do the Yankees all the harm you can, and that you go off and run a one-man war a good part of the time. It looked to me you might want to hook up with me." He added: "You'd get your bellyful of fun, and you wouldn't be wasting your time."

"Just what is your idea?"

"Well, I was thinking. Everybody knows how Colonel Mosby is about his men, sharing every haul they make, dividing everything up. Sheridan knows some of the men don't like that. If you go along with me, I'll tell him you and the Colonel had a falling out about dividing up some plunder, and that he threw you out of the Rangers, and that you're looking for a chance to get even. General Sheridan'd be real glad to see you, I reckon."

The prospect of meeting General Sheridan face to face attracted Faunt. He knew he was not strong enough for the scurry and race of raid and battle. The first violent exertion would be his end; but this that Lomas suggested he could do. He agreed, and when their plans were made, they crossed into the Valley and rode toward Winchester to find Sheridan's headquarters.

"You'd better have a different name," Lomas suggested on the way.

Faunt hesitated at the thought of wearing false colors; but then he remembered that even princes travelled incognito. The Prince of Wales had been Mr. Renfrew in Richmond, on that visit before the war began. He smiled in a saturnine amusement at the thought.

"Call me Renfrew," he directed. If the name was good enough for a prince, it was good enough for him. Still weak, knowing he would never be strong again, he despised his own weakness and himself too. If on this enterprise he were caught and hanged as a spy, what did it matter? He was already the paramour of a notorious woman; there was no deeper shame.

The enemy cavalry had gone into winter quarters near Winchester. Lomas left Faunt well outside the picket line to stay hidden in a thick bit of woodland till he returned. "I'll want to make sure of your welcome first," he explained. "I don't want to run you into a trap."

"Do you expect to take me to Sheridan himself?"

"Of course."

Faunt nodded, and Lomas rode away, and Faunt was left with his thoughts. It was this Sheridan who had given the orders which last fall laid waste all Loudoun Valley. It was this man's orders, passed on by him from Grant to Custer, which had directed the hanging, the murder of those men at Front Royal. Lomas was gone all day, and long before he returned, Faunt's throat was dry with rage and abhorrence and with deadly hate of the man he was to see. Would it not be best service to the South, yes and to the world, to shoot Sheridan down like the dog he was, the moment they were first confronted? He longed to do so; but if Sheridan were dead another would instantly take his place. Better to speak softly, to watch and wait, to strike at last a more damaging blow than the death of just one man.

So when Lomas came back to fetch him, he submitted completely to the other's guidance. "The General likes mysteries," Lomas assured him. "So we'll dress you up a bit." He swathed Faunt's head in a handkerchief till none of his hair showed; he bound another handkerchief over Faunt's nose and chin. "Take them off when he questions you," he directed. "But be careful to put them on again before you leave him. Make a fuss about it. He'll like that."

They waited till darkness fell, then rode together through the lines, Lomas satisfying every picket and sentry with the General's pass, and went direct to headquarters. Faunt judged it to be near midnight; but Sheridan was waiting. When they faced him, Faunt saw a lean man with prominent cheekbones and narrowed eyes, at the outer corners of which drooping lids etched cruel lines. A mustache in need of trimming and a wisp of whisker almost concealed his mouth. Lomas said a word of introduction.

"Well, Mr. Renfrew," Sheridan directed. "Take off all those bandages and let's have a look at you." Faunt, obeying, faced a disturbingly keen inspection and a swift, searching interrogation. "So, you're one of Mosby's cutthroats?"

"I have been one of his Rangers."

"You have the voice and bearing of a gentleman."

"Colonel Mosby would call himself a gentleman. Certainly there are gentlemen in his battalion."

"Yet gentlemen do not quarrel over a share of plunder." Sheridan spoke in dry scorn, and Faunt remembered just in time the story Lomas had planned to tell to account for his presence here.

"Even gentlemen, if they are hungry enough, will quarrel over a loaf of bread."

Sheridan chuckled. "Hungry? Nonsense! You're a pack of rascals underneath your fine manners, all of you. Tell me a little more about that quarrel, Mr. Renfrew."

Faunt held his temper under hard control; and though he was not practiced in deception, he remembered a scene that could be adapted to his present need. "Colonel Mosby himself never takes a share of any loot," he explained. "And his orders are that his men shall rob none but Yankees. But a damned Tory farmer refused me a meal one day, and I put a pistol under his ear and helped myself to a few things. Mosby dared to reprove me for doing so." He let the rage in him find outlet in his voice. "I called him to account; but he had his men around him, and he refused to meet me, ordered me out of his company."

"He gives himself some excessively fine airs," Sheridan commented. He began to ask questions, casually phrased yet shrewdly searching, about some of Mosby's operations; and Faunt, understanding that he was being tested, and sure that nothing he might say of past activities could handicap Colonel Mosby in the future, answered them explicitly. So General Sheridan at last was satisfied.

"Very well," he said. "I can use you both. I want you to go destroy the railroad bridges east of Lynchburg." His mouth twisted in a faint smile. "I understand, Mr. Renfrew, that you expect to be paid; but payment will follow on performance. You may have a modest sum for expenses, of course; but beyond that, only what you earn. Say a thousand dollars to be divided between you for every bridge you destroy."

Faunt played his part. "In gold, General?"

"In greenbacks," General Sheridan retorted. "They're as good as gold."

Faunt looked at Lomas; Lomas said: "Very well, greenbacks."

"When will you start?"

"Tomorrow night," Lomas told him; and Sheridan nodded dismissal. Faunt, remembering the advice Lomas had given him, began to bundle up his head again; and Sheridan challenged: "What's that for?"

"Mosby has his men all around you, General," Faunt assured him. "Even here in your camp. I don't wish to risk recognition."

"Ha! Point a few of those men out to me. I'll see to it they have no chance to betray you!"

"We'll be away from your lines before daylight."

"All right. Good night."

When they were safely beyond the lines, Lomas said a word of approval. "Well played, Mr. Currain!"

"I'll burn no bridges."

"Certainly not. But if Sheridan wants bridges burned, he evidently plans to move on Lynchburg as soon as weather lets him. We'll send that word to Colonel Mosby. General Lee will be glad to know it, and Colonel Mosby can be ready to harry them on their way. As for the bridges, we'll just report they were so well guarded that we could do nothing."

Faunt and Lomas went only as far as Strasburg. They sent a message to Mosby, and in mid-February they returned to Winchester to report failure at every attempt upon the bridges. Lomas embroidered that report with narratives of half a dozen narrow escapes, and Sheridan seemed deceived.

"Well, well, you can try it again presently," he suggested. "Report to me daily, gentlemen."

During the ten days that followed, they watched for any sign that Sheridan planned an early movement; but his officers seemed more interested in fox hunting than in warlike pursuits. "They've collected some trapped foxes, and a pack of hounds," Lomas told Faunt. "They're planning a big hunt for the end of the month."

"That sounds like a Yankee's idea of sport, to run tame foxes."

Lomas said thoughtfully: "I don't know. It sounds to me like an excuse to get this army together and steal a march on General Early. I'll look for a chance to warn him."

The chance came when Sheridan directed another attempt against those bridges on the railroad from Lynchburg. They rode to the home of a man whom Lomas knew to be friendly, and who furnished a trustworthy Negro to carry their message through Ashby's Gap to Mosby.

Then they proceeded toward Newtown; but on the road a detachment of Sheridan's cavalry met them. Before Faunt guessed what was coming, he and Lomas faced so many levelled carbines that not even his reckless courage ventured any resistance. Disarmed, they were escorted to Colonel Young, who was in charge of Sheridan's scouts.

"Well, gentlemen," the Colonel said mildly, "I do regret that you submitted so peacefully." His easy tone did not blind Faunt to the hard glint in the other's eye. "You see, I've been watching you. You spent a night at the house of Warren Hutley, and next morning his Negro took a mule and started east. It's true we could get nothing out of him. If he carried a written message he swallowed it. If he did, that was your great good fortune." He added: "That and the fact that at least one of you is a *protégé* of Mr. Stanton. So there will be no court martial, and no sentence; but you'll be our guests at Fort Warren for a while."

Faunt bit his lip in a dark frustrated wrath; but Lomas said easily: "You are mistaken in your suspicions, Colonel; yet I can see your point of view, and of course it's much better for you to make a safe mistake than one that might have bad results." He smiled. "I've been so active in the field for months now that a few weeks' rest will be welcome."

He saluted briskly, and the Colonel grinned. "I'd like to hang you. I think you'd look well on a rope."

"I'm glad General Sheridan isn't quite so ready to forget past services."

Lomas was soon on good terms with the guards who escorted them toward the railroad; but not till they were on the cars bound for Harper's Ferry did he and Faunt have a chance to speak together. Then, the noise of the train covering his words, Faunt said furiously:

"I didn't contract for a stay in a Yankee prison."

Lomas whispered: "We'll be free in Baltimore."

"How?"

Lomas shook his head for silence, but his prediction was fulfilled. In the Baltimore station, an uproar distracted their guards; and when the confusion reached its height, a sudden jostling crowd swept the two prisoners away. Lomas gripped Faunt's arm and led him quickly out into the security of darkness; and he whispered a question:

"Do you know Baltimore?"

"Yes, I've been here."

"Meet me in an hour at the corner of Fayette and Calvert, outside Guy's Monument House. Don't speak to me till I'm alone." He darted off.

Faunt took an opposite direction. Lomas must somehow have arranged that factitious disturbance at the station, and Faunt's respect for the man's capacities increased. Conceivably the guards were bribed; there were enough Confederate sympathizers in Baltimore so that if they were forewarned, to stage that small riot would not have been difficult. Lomas must have found a way to communicate with them.

Faunt delayed his approach to the rendezvous till the appointed time. Lomas was there before him, talking with a man of nondescript appearance. When this man departed, Faunt approached; and at Lomas's word they walked along Fayette Street together. Lomas handed him a sheaf of greenbacks and a key.

"That's the key to a room in Barnum's City Hotel," he explained. "The room's on the fourth floor, toward the back of the house. Find it yourself. Don't speak to the clerk. I must go to Washington tonight, but I'll meet you in Guy's restaurant between six and seven o'clock tomorrow evening."

"I'd feel more comfortable if I were armed."

"Here's a Deringer, then; but if you stay in your room you'll not be disturbed."

Faunt did not relish the prospect of hiding away for the twenty-four hours of waiting. There was a reckless mood upon him, and also he began to be hungry. He walked back to Guy's restaurant, taking a precautionary survey before venturing in; but when he did step through the door he felt a quick satisfaction. At a table by the wall a man sat half facing him, leaning to talk in low tones to his companion. Faunt recognized Wilkes Booth; and after a moment's hesitation he went boldly that way.

When Faunt approached the table, Booth looked up, and instantly he smiled and rose with extended hand. "Mr. Currain? Sir, I'm delighted to see you." He indicated his companion. "You remember Sam Arnold, Mr. Currain."

Faunt had met Arnold on one of his former trips to Baltimore. Arnold and Booth were boyhood friends; and the packets of drugs which Booth sent South had once or twice come through Arnold's hands. Faunt sat down with them, and Booth said: "I was sorry not to meet you last month, during my visit in Mosby's Confederacy, Mr. Currain."

"Were you there?"

"For ten fine days, yes."

"Then you relished your adventures?"

"Never in my life have I been so drunk with delicious terror." Booth chuckled, his eyes glowing. "Colonel Mosby had not returned from Richmond, but I was with Captain Richards at Mount Carmel. We killed thirteen of them there, took sixty-three prisoners and ninety horses, lost one man. Oh, it was glorious! I'll be forever grateful for that experience."

"The gratitude is on our side," Faunt assured him. "You've been a good friend of the South."

Booth said strongly: "Sir, my possessions, my life, yes, my very soul, are committed to your cause!" He looked at Sam Arnold, then back at Faunt with brooding eyes. "Day before yesterday, I could have delivered a mighty stroke for the Confederacy. At the moment of his inauguration I was as near the tyrant as I am to you; near enough to—" His voice sank to a deeper register—"'with a blow strike life out from his heart.' But the opportunity caught me unawares, and I faltered and paltered in the pinch. 'The fault is not in our stars, but in ourselves . . .' Yet to resolve on such a course takes time. 'Between the acting of a dreadful thing and the first motion, all the interim is like a phantasma, or a hideous dream.' But I will act!" His eyes flashed, he leaned nearer. "I will, sir! It's true that a dead man's place is soon filled; but not the place of a living man! I have before this done for the South what I could, but by the Eternal I will do more! I project, sir, an exploit worthy of Mosby himself, or of his men!" Faunt felt his temple pulses pound, and Booth said in measured tones: "Mr. Currain, I have in mind a blow that may well change the course and channels of the war."

"Then it's high time the blow were struck. The tide's running out. But to turn the tide calls for a miracle."

"Miracles can be worked. 'I can call spirits from the vasty deep,' my friend."

Faunt smiled faintly. "What's the next line: 'Yes, but will they come?'"

The actor's voice sank to a whisper. "Mr. Currain, suppose Mr. Lincoln were delivered in handcuffs to Libby Prison?" Faunt saw Arnold turn to look uneasily around. His own heart leaped like a spurred horse; but then it slowed again and he shook his head.

"That can't be done."

Booth flung up his hand. "I do not know that word, sir! To audacity, anything is possible." He spoke to Arnold, as though seeing the other's alarm. "Be easy, Sam. Mr. Currain is a bold and a discreet man." Faunt's eye fell upon the brandy bottle half empty here between them, and Booth saw the glance and said strongly: "This is no drunken dream, Mr. Currain! I have had it in mind for months to seize the President and thrust him into a carriage, with relays of fresh horses ready. Two hours would bring him to Port Tobacco ahead of any pursuit, while confusion covered the trail behind us. Then into a boat with him; and once in Virginia the rest would be easy."

Faunt considered. "Well, not easy; but possible, yes. Anything is possible, once he's in your hands. The difficulty, I should think, lies there." He tried to speak calmly, but he began to take fire. This scheme of course was folly. If he helped put Abe Lincoln in Libby Prison, that would not make the Northern armies drop their weapons. But let him once come within pistol range of that hedge-bred monster from Illinois and the Currain blood would at last be purged.

"There is no difficulty," Booth assured him. "Come, Mr. Currain; we need a man like you to play this scene." Faunt did not speak, and Booth urged persuasively: "We have considered every detail, sir. Mr. Lincoln sometimes drives without escort. We weighed the chance of seizing him on such an occasion; but to do so required foreknowledge of his movements, not easily to be had. He sometimes comes to the Theatre. He might be mastered in his box, swung down to the stage and out to a waiting carriage and away. Or we might take him when he walks alone at night along a dim-lit path from the White House to the War Department. There's an empty house near the river where he could be securely hidden till the hue and cry was past."

Faunt shook his head. These were absurd and hopeless dreams. "You would surely fail."

Booth nodded cheerfully. "We might," he agreed. "Planning thus in the dark we might fail. But now luck deals us a winning hand." He leaned forward, speaking earnestly. "On the seventeenth," he said, "there will be a performance of *Still Waters Run Deep* for the pleasure of the wounded at the Soldiers' Home. Lincoln will drive out to grace the occasion with his presence. He will go unguarded, and a little troop of us will meet his carriage on the road." He snapped his fingers jubilantly. "So!"

Faunt's blood at the word ran hot again. To kidnap Lincoln and escape was certainly impossible. Too many long miles of road lay between Washington and any Southern refuge. But a pistol shot, in the flurry by the carriage, was feasible enough. That would not save the South, true; but Faunt, already seeing a bearded face along his pistol barrel, already feeling the jump of the weapon as he fired, shook with a deep contentment. Let him live long enough for that moment; then what matter if he died?

"It might be done," he said carefully. "But the seventeenth is almost two weeks away."

"You're with us?"

"How many of you?"

"Seven. Eight with you. Sam here. Mike O'Laughlin. George Atzerodt. You know him at Port Tobacco. John Surratt. You've lodged with him in Surrattsville. He has a boarding house now on H Street, in Washington. And you know Lew Powell. Till six weeks ago, he was one of Mosby's men. He's our newest recruit. He calls himself Paine now; and he's big enough to carry the tyrant like a baby in his arms. Then David Herold—I doubt you know him—and I." He leaned back in his chair. "We've enough without you, Mr. Currain; but with you the thing's a certainty!"

"Suppose there's some change in his plans."

"If so, we shall know it in full time. Meet us in Washington, Mr. Currain, two days beforehand. Go to Maggie Branson's, on North Eutaw Street." He looked at Sam Arnold. "Or go back to Washington with Sam tomorrow. He and O'Laughlin live at Mrs. Van Tine's, on D Street."

Arnold spoke sullenly. "Three of us is too many there. Let him stay here."

Faunt said: "I have the key to a safe room in Barnum's."

"As you please," Booth assented. "But if you choose to come to Washington I can find you lodging there. Do you know Gautier's?" Faunt shook his head. "Pennsylvania Avenue, near Twelfth Street. A restaurant. There are private rooms. Ask for me." And he challenged: "Are you with us, Mr. Currain?"

Faunt's doubts gave way. "If I'm alive, I'll be there."

Booth, with an exultant word, reached for the bottle. They finished it and another before Faunt, unused to heavy potations, felt his senses blur. When he rose to take his leave, he knew that Sam Arnold crossed the street with him to the hotel and guided him to the room to which he had a key; but once abed he slept senselessly till far into the day.

His sleep was disturbed at last by the sound of a bell ringing somewhere; and he came slowly back to consciousness to the tune of these repeated peals. Barnum's was always full of the sound of bells, guests ringing to summon the carefully disciplined servants, or the head waiter ringing his huge bell to announce that dinner was ready. Faunt on former occasions had dined in the public room. There a long central table was heaped with the rich and elaborate fare for which Zenas Barnum had made his hostelry famous, and attentive waiters bustled to and fro to bring each guest what he desired; but today Faunt had no desire for food, and the bells made his head ache, and he wished they would be still.

He kept his room till dusk, and these hours alone were heavy with the burden of his thoughts. He lay most of the time with his eyes closed; and against his translucent lids he watched the passing panorama of his years, from laughing youth to love and then to tragic loss and grief past any healing. He had dwelt in loneliness, yet his days were not all darkness; and his ways were gracious with an enriching pride and self-respect till that night at Great Oak left him to choke forever upon unconquerable shame.

Since then? Well, there was one credit on his score, for he had cleansed Anne Tudor's heart of any secret tenderness for him, and she was happy now. But the rest was ruthless killing, and the degradation of his hours with Nell.

Now there was one more killing to be done. What then? He felt within his breast the gnawing mice of death. Perhaps a bullet flung at random in the pitch and pinch of the affray this little actor planned might give him quick release. If not, why then he would go back to Nell. Whatever she was, she gave him happiness. Whatever she was, she loved him; and he would never be completely lost so long as he had her sure and loyal love.

To wait a while; to ride out one day along the road to the Soldiers' Home and meet a carriage in which rode a certain apelike man; then if he lived, to return to Nell again. If it were for the last time, let it be so. Life was a weary business and he was sick of it.

Lomas would be at Guy's tonight. At first dark Faunt went to await him there. It was no long time before the other appeared; but Lomas said they must ride at once for Port Tobacco, must find Tom Jones to set them across to the Northern Neck, and make haste to Richmond.

"I've horses waiting," he explained. "I should have gone directly, but I didn't want to leave you here."

"I shall stay here," Faunt said. "I have some business to attend."

"Then I've wasted precious time." Faunt saw the haste in him.

"Why?" he asked. "What has happened?"

The other had already risen, but he hesitated. "I play a double game, you know," he said, and sat down again. "I'm trusted in Washington as well as in Richmond. For four years now, every scrap of information from Richmond has been forwarded to Washington or to Grant. Grant knows our decisions as soon as they are reached. Did you ever hear the name of Miss Van Lew?"

"Of course. Everyone in Richmond knows she's a Union agent."

Lomas nodded. "Yes. So she has been watched for years; but we've found no proof against her, apart from her admitted and open partisanship for the North. But Lee's plans, every movement of his forces, every shift in his lines is reported instantly to Grant; so someone in Richmond is the center of the web of conspiracy against us. We've known that for a long time; we've even known her nickname. She is always referred to as 'The Quaker.' Today in Washington I learned her real name."

"Her name?" Faunt emphasized the pronoun. "A woman?"

"Yes. Till now she's never been suspected, yet if what I hear of her is true she should have been suspect long ago, for a thousand reasons."

Faunt looked at his hand limp upon the table; he wondered why his fingers were not shaking. His voice was steady enough. "You know her name, you say?"

"Yes, Albion. Mrs. Albion."

Faunt felt no surprise, he was at once sure that what Lomas said was true. He remembered that man he met outside Nell's house the day he started with Stuart for the ride around McClellan's army, and whom he had seen hanged as a confessed spy on the way to Second Manassas. When he questioned Nell, she admitted the acquaintance, relying on his love for her to blind his eyes. He remembered other matters. When he himself told her where Mosby's headquarters were, at the Chief's, and then at Glen Welby, each time the Yankees struck within the month! Faunt even remembered that she had first questioned him about his plans and thus assured herself he would not be caught in the traps she set.

She had cozened him with tenderness and listened to his wagging tongue and sent the information she seduced from him straightway to her masters! There was a curdling bitterness in his throat, the burning taste of bile. He rose, Wilkes Booth and his mad project all forgotten. He spoke with a cold precision.

"You're right, Mr. Lomas. You should make haste to report this. And it occurs to me that I too have pressing business in Richmond. Let us take the road."

19

CINDA came home to Richmond in time to share with the capital city the last agony of the Confederacy. Dusk was already the early darkness of a stormy evening when the train on which she and Jenny and the children and the servants had made the last stage of their journey splashed lamely into the depot and to a weary stop. The cars were packed with refugees like themselves, flowing north before Sherman's advance, and equally exhausted by days and nights of insufficient sleep and rest and food. This driven, homeless host had kindness in it still, and a readiness to share what comfort could be had; yet Cinda was glad, as she descended to the platform and the crowd thinned, to feel no longer so many bodies pressing close around her and be able to fill her lungs with clean, untainted air.

Even the warm drenching rain was grateful, like happy tears or welcome; for though it might wet them through, it seemed to wash away long-accumulated grime. She had been unable to send word ahead, so there was no one to meet them, and no conveyance. They set out to walk through the pelting downpour. The way up Fourteenth Street and Main was increasingly steep, with a last hard pitch up Fifth Street to the house. Jenny carried little Clayton, too sleepy to move his feet; Cinda led Kyle with one hand and Janet with the other; and behind them June and Anarchy and old Banquo bore heavy burdens.

There were no gas lights burning in the streets, but even in the darkness Cinda detected a difference in the scene and in the tone of people's voices. The voices were higher pitched than she remembered, almost shrill; and there was an unnatural amount of laughter in the air. She wondered how much little Clayton would remember of this night, of these years. He was almost exactly as old as the war, born soon after Trav brought Clayton's body home from Manassas. Thinking of Clayton who was dead made Cinda wonder whether Burr still lived, and Trav, and Vesta's Rollin. She had had no word of any of them for so long. Eagerness hurried her steps, and they came to the familiar doorway, and Caesar heard the bell.

The bright confusion of that hour made them for a while forget, in happiness and sparkling questions, that they were wet and tired and hungry. Burr? Travis? Yes, they were safe; and so was Rollin, and so was Brett. Cinda laughed. "I've worried about the others, but not about him," she confessed. "It never entered my head that anything could happen to Brett Dewain."

Everyone talked at once, and Tilda took little Clayton in her arms; but he began a fretful whimpering, so Anarchy bore him away to bed. Vesta sent word to Julian and Anne, but Cinda warned her to tell them not to come tonight. "None of us are fit to talk," she declared. "We're wet through, for one thing. Bath and bed and a bowl of soup, that's all I can stand; that and a good night's sleep. We'll talk tomorrow. We're here, and you're here, and everyone's well. Nothing else matters for now."

Next morning she slept late, refusing to wake till at last she heard young Clayton's cheerful voice upraised, and his scampering feet along the hall outside her door; and she heard Anarchy catch him up and hush him, so she called: "It's all right. I'm awake. Let him make all the noise he wants to. Bring him in."

Vesta appeared with them; but Clayton, having dutifully submitted to be kissed, raced away. Cinda smiled fondly. "How wonderful to be that age! He's forgotten he was ever tired. I don't think my old bones will ever stop aching."

Vesta said Jenny was still asleep, and the older children; and Tilda had gone to work at the Soup Association. June brought breakfast, and it was a delight to have this hour with Vesta alone. "Tell me things," Cinda bade, busy with cornbread and bacon and coffee. "Wherever did you get this coffee, Vesta?"

"Some I'd saved for an occasion. This is the occasion." And while

Cinda dallied happily over the first hot breakfast she had eaten in days, Vesta told her of their loved menfolk, and of the weary waiting for the inevitable end. "But now we're together, so we can face anything, Mama."

"After the last few weeks, anything will be a relief!"

Vesta took the waiter away and came back to curl up on the foot of the bed. "I expect you've had a terrible time, but don't talk about it unless you want to."

"Oh, maybe I can talk it out of my mind and forget it," Cinda declared. "I'd like to. The trip down was easy enough." She amended that. "At least it seems so now. Of course at the time it was exasperating. There was a ladies' car as far as Danville, but it was full of soldiers on their way to Wilmington. The new railroad from Danville to Greensboro is just simply ramshackle, and terribly rough. I expected the train to jump the track any minute, and we rattled around like dried peas in a bladder; but we were only four nights and five days to Columbia."

She paused, pressing her hands to her eyes as though thus easily she could banish memory. "We began to hear the Sherman stories there, Vesta. Columbia was full of refugees. You know the first thing Sherman did was to drive out of Atlanta all the civilians except negroes; almost a thousand ladies, and men too old to fight, and more than a thousand children. He just sent them to General Hood's lines. I saw Sam Hood in Columbia. His eyes are sadder than ever, now. He said that was the most horrible thing he ever saw, hundreds of women and little children homeless, with no shelter and no food and nowhere to go."

"What did they do, Mama?"

"Oh, some of them died, and some of them lived. People took them in till every house was filled. But of course when General Sherman started for Savannah he burned almost every house, and destroyed all the grain, and killed or drove off the cattle and horses and hogs. I met a young lady, Miss Cuyler of Social Circle, who had come from Americus after his army passed, right across its track. She said for fifty miles there were hardly any houses left, just the chimneys. 'Sherman's Sentinels,' people call those blackened chimneys. There were so many dead animals killed and left to rot that the smell was sickening. Every farm building had been burned, except a few houses; all the gins and packing screws, and hay ricks and corn cribs and stacks of fodder. She said there weren't even any chickens left to eat the corn Sherman's cavalry horses spilled along their picket lines; and people picked up the corn and parched it and ate it, or pulled turnips in the fields, anything they could get."

"Why didn't she stay in Americus? Didn't they have anything to eat?"

"Yes, there's plenty of food in southwest Georgia; but her father, Colonel Cuyler, was afraid Sherman would send raiders to release the Yankee prisoners of war at Andersonville and that they'd murder everyone, so he was bringing her to Danville, to his sister's."

"Why do people scare so easily, Mama? The prisoners wouldn't murder them!"

"They might have," Cinda confessed. "They've been starving to death. In December there were already over thirteen thousand graves in the prison cemetery. Miss Cuyler met Father Hamilton, from Macon, and he had worked there. He told her the prisoners lived in holes in the ground, and some of them hadn't even any clothes, and sometimes as many as a hundred and fifty of them died in a day."

"Do you believe it?" Vesta challenged.

"Miss Cuyler says it's true. She kept insisting that the prisoners had as much to eat as our own soldiers; but our soldiers here are hungry because we can't bring food to them over the wretched railroads. There wasn't that excuse for not feeding the prisoners, because even Miss Cuyler says there's plenty to eat all around Americus, and they could surely send some to Andersonville." Cinda added soberly: "But of course people are hungry everywhere else. I talked with a Mrs. McDonald who had refugeed from Atlanta. She kept her family alive by picking up bullets on the battlefield and taking them to the Yankee commissary and trading them for food. Wherever there'd been battles, there were lots of bullets, and the lead was worth its weight in sugar and coffee and flour and meal and lard and even meat." She tried to laugh. "It made my mouth water to hear her! I was hungry myself, often enough. But then the commissary moved on, following Sherman's army, so Mrs. McDonald had to go somewhere or starve. She brought her children to Columbia." Cinda added thoughtfully: "Georgia has suffered more than any other state, now, except possibly Virginia; and yet Georgia people have wanted for a long time to go back into the Union. It's a joke on them, in a way. But not a very funny joke."

Vesta, to turn her thoughts in a happier direction, said: "But, Mama, you're way ahead of yourself. You haven't told about getting to the Plains or anything!"

Cinda smiled gratefully. "To be sure. Well, so June and I got to Columbia, and they said Sherman was at Hardieville. We stayed in Columbia overnight and Mr. DeSaussure sent us on to the Plains in his carriage." Her tone was lively now. "And what a welcome I got, Vesta! It was worth all the trouble, just as getting home again now is worth all we've had to endure."

"Hush! Stop skipping around! You're at the Plains. Go on and tell about that!"

Cinda nodded, laughing. "All right, then, I got to the Plains; and just in time, too, because next day it began to rain as though it would never stop. Then we heard Sherman was at Branchville. Most people said we'd be safe at the Plains, but I didn't believe them; so I decided we'd all better go to Columbia where we'd at least be on the railroad. Jenny had plenty of Confederate money, but people were beginning to refuse to take it, so I went to Camden to the branch bank. Mr. Shannon wasn't there, but Mr. Doby——"

"Who's Mr. Doby?"

"He's the cashier. He changed about twenty thousand dollars of ours for three hundred and fifty dollars in gold. Everyone will take gold, of course.

"Then we buried all the silver at the Plains; Banquo and June and Jenny and I. We did it in the middle of the night, down below the garden toward the creek. Heaven knows whether we'll ever find it again, but Banquo was sure no Yankee would ever find it, and that's the main thing. Banquo hitched a team of mules to the wagon to carry us to Columbia. The horses are all gone. Our cavalry took some, and some were just stolen. Jenny had the children's ponies stabled right under the side piazza, because she thought they'd be safer near the house; and Kyle and Janet wanted to ride them to Columbia, but we decided to leave them behind."

"Poor ponies! Poor Kyle!"

"He was brave about it. We left them with Mrs. Nickerson. I suppose Sherman's men will kill them. They kill everything they don't steal, and they steal anything they can carry. People say Sherman brags that he stole twenty million dollars' worth of things between Atlanta and Savannah, and wasted and destroyed eighty million more."

"We've heard terrible stories, even here."

"You'll be hearing them the rest of your life, Vesta; you and your children. Yes, and their children. This will never be a united country again, not as long as women have memories. Men are not so apt to hold grudges, but Southern women will tell these tales for generations. Yet with all the terrible things that were happening, Columbia was gayer than I've ever seen it."

"It's that way here," Vesta agreed. "Just as gay as it was last winter, Mama. There's a dancing party somewhere almost every night. But people aren't so gay in the daytime."

Cinda nodded. "I suppose it's the same everywhere. In Columbia they were having a bazaar in the State House. They'd been getting ready for weeks, making things, and collecting things to be sold, to raise money for sick and wounded soldiers; and each state had a booth, and the sale went on for days. Heaven knows how much money they made. People would buy anything, because of course no one had anything. Even at the Plains we had no candles, just terebene lamps, and you know how terribly they smoke. But everyone had plenty of Confederate money, so they'd pay any price at all."

"It's the same everywhere. I've sold those things out of the Christmas trunk for thousands of dollars, actually."

"I suppose we're all crazy, Vesta. Delirious. Columbia turned into an insane asylum, just in the few days I was at the Plains. Thousands of new people had come, refugees from Sherman, so it was hard to find any place to stay, but Colonel Trenholm took us in. De Greffin never looked so lovely; and of course the Colonel had everything in the way of luxuries. I suppose he gets the pick of whatever his blockade-runners bring in. He even had horses! General Hampton was in Columbia with his cavalry, but he hadn't enough horses to mount all his men."

"Rollin has gone to South Carolina to try to get some horses for his regiment."

"He won't be able to find any, I'm afraid. General Hampton couldn't, to save his soul; and if he couldn't, nobody can. Everyone loves him, poor man. Preston killed, and Wade hurt, and the General had to just kiss his dead son good-by and go on fighting. And I told you General Hood was there. He seldom speaks, just sits and sweats at his own thoughts."

"He must be heartbroken, losing his whole army."

"It made me weep to see him. But I soon saw we'd better get out of Columbia. I wanted to come home, and if we waited till the last minute there'd be such a mob we couldn't possibly get into the cars. Colonel Johnson, the president of the railroad, helped us, and Mr. Hayne. Sherman was already at Orangeburg, so the cars were so crowded none of us could sit down. We had to stand all the way to Charlotte, and then we couldn't go any farther, so we took the train to Lincolnton, because everyone said Sherman would go toward Fayetteville and that Lincolnton would be safe."

"I thought you might go to Raleigh, to Barbara and Mr. and Mrs. Pierce."

"We couldn't get beyond Charlotte, but I don't think I'd have done that anyway. Of course it's my fault, but I just can't seem to love Barbara, or her family either, running off down there and living comfortably all this time."

Vesta laughed at her. "Idiot! It wouldn't have made things any easier for us, having them miserable here."

"Well, at least Burr could have seen her oftener! But anyway, we went to Lincolnton and thought ourselves clever; but we found that others had had the same idea. The town was crowded; but I got two rooms, bare floors, feather beds but no bedsteads, a few chairs." She hesitated, and after a moment went on. "We were there when Sherman burned Columbia. People kept coming to Lincolnton, each with a new story worse than the last. Some of them sounded like the truth, and some sounded like hysteria." She smiled weakly. "But I was beginning to be a little hysterical myself. I had what seemed like a brilliant idea, to get a wagon and go north to Chimneys. Chimneys would surely be out of the way, and Tony wasn't there, so we could make ourselves at home." She filled her lungs with a deep breath. "Well, Banquo got a wagon with two mules. I don't know how, and I didn't ask questions. That old man could always work miracles. I gave him a hundred dollars in gold and told him what I wanted, and that night he walked us all out of town into the blackest woods I ever saw, and there was the wagon and a man. I didn't even see the man, it was so dark; but his voice was white. He put us on what he said was the right road, and said we were to turn north after we crossed the Catawba River and that would bring us to Statesville. So we went on all night, up hill and down, mud and cold and woods. Anarchy and June and Jenny mostly walked. I couldn't. The mud was full of sharp rocks that hurt my feet. Walking was easier than riding, though. The wagon had no springs, so it almost shook our teeth out; and not even Banquo and his miracles could make the mules hurry. June somehow had filled a hamper, of course; so we didn't starve, but it seemed to me it was either pouring rain or freezing cold all the time. I don't know why we didn't all die. I know I wanted to."

Vesta laughed affectionately. "Poor Mama. I'll bet you were mad!"

"Oh, I was! And no way to blow off steam! You can't quarrel with Jenny, or the children; and when I scolded June or Banquo they just said 'Yas'm' in that miserable way a half-frozen negro talks. Then at daylight we came to the river; and the mud in the bottoms was knee-deep, so we all tried to ride; but the wagon bogged down and we had to get out and push. Luckily the ford had a hard bottom; but I thought we were lost! I'd have given my eyeteeth for a man to take charge, even a Yankee! Yes, even Redford Streean!"

"That reminds me." Vesta told her mother about Streean's letter, and Dolly's shameful widowhood, and her departure from Wilmington with Captain Pew.

Cinda listened almost absently. "That poor, lost young one!" For a moment she forgot all else in memories of Dolly, so lovely and so gay. "She's on my conscience, Vesta! I've always been ashamed of despising her as I did. Do you suppose if we'd been nicer to her she'd have turned out better, somehow?"

"I always liked her."

"Oh, you like everyone!"

The girl laughed. "Heavens, Mama, you make me sound awfully wishy-washy. Go on. You were all in the wagon."

"Oh bother! I hoped you'd let me forget that. Well, let me see. I think we were three days in that accursed wagon, plodding on and on. The roads are all red clay, and the houses all that graceless sort, two stories high, no veranda, one room deep from front to back, and a kitchen wing behind. And every one was full of refugees, or else deserted and empty. There were roads leading in all directions, and Banquo got lost. He finally brought us into Salisbury, instead of Statesville.

"But that was really lucky, because when we drove into town, there was a train for Greensboro puffing away to get up its courage to start. Jenny and I each grabbed one of the children and made for the cars, and June and Banquo and Anarchy and Kyle came racing after us, and by the grace of pushing and fighting we got on!"

Vesta drew a deep breath. "And here you are!"

Cinda laughed. "It wasn't as simple as that, my dear! The Piedmont Railroad must be a thousand miles long. Actually, we were three full days on their miserable train, while it wandered across fields and through woods and up and down hills and everywhere but on the tracks. It did every conceivable thing trains shouldn't do!"

"Papa says all the food the army gets has to come by that road."

"I know! We gave a man forty dollars in gold to let us ride in a car full of barrels of flour; and once a snakehead came up——"

"What's a snakehead?"

"A broken rail, I think. Anyway, that's what the men called it. It came up through the bottom of our car and burst a barrel open and stopped us so short the barrels were all toppling over and rolling around and bursting open. I was afraid for our lives. Banquo managed to keep the barrels from crushing us; but I've breathed in so much flour—the air was full of it—I never want to taste bread again as long as I live!"

Vesta laughed in a swift amusement. "I'm glad to hear it. You've come to a flourless household. There are some prices I simply refuse to pay!"

"I don't care if I starve, now that I'm home." Memories suddenly flooded Cinda's eyes with tears. "Oh, Vesta, Vesta, the things Sherman and his men have done to us! I think he's just decided to destroy everything we own, houses, food, everything."

"Sheridan's done the same thing in the Valley, and in Northern Virginia."

Cinda nodded. "I suppose they've decided that's the only way to beat us. Ladies told me of nights when they could see houses burning in all directions around them while they hid in the woods with their children. Mr. Hayne said the night they burned Columbia he was at Meek's Mill and he could see the fire from there, the whole city burning. Mrs. Poppenheim at Liberty Hill says they poured into her house and took all her silver and smashed everything, even the furniture, looking for money. If ladies pleaded with them, they were sworn at. The Yankees all said the same thing, as if they'd been taught. They said it was the ladies who egged the men on to keep fighting. You know they burned the Ursuline Convent school at Columbia; and before they did it, the soldiers played the piano and danced, and they broke into the nuns' rooms and smashed open their trunks and searched everything. Twenty women must have told me about soldiers stripping rings off their fingers. One girl had some money in a belt around her waist, and when they burned her father's ears with spills she told them, and they cut off her stays to get at it." She said honestly: "Some of our own men in Wheeler's cavalry were almost as bad, stealing everything. I suppose they learned it from Sherman's men. Sherman's soldiers hung old men to make them tell where their money was. They'd pull them up off the floor till they were choking, and keep doing it till they told, or till they died. On his line of march from Atlanta to Savannah there are just the chimneys standing, no houses at all, for a path fifty miles wide. Sometimes they'd send spies ahead, men pretending to be hungry Confederate soldiers, and people would feed them and get their help in hiding things and then when the soldiers came, the spies would know where everything was. They drank all the liquor they found. At the Clifford place near Walhalla they drank up dozens of bottles of Ayer's Cherry Pectoral, and all got sick." Vesta smiled faintly, and Cinda said: "Oh, yes, there've been some funny things. Remember poor dear old Miss Cartin in Columbia? She put on all her dresses, one on top of the other, and packed her silver in her bustle, and it made her so heavy she couldn't climb on the cars, and when she was lifted on, she couldn't sit down because the forks and knives hurt her." Vesta laughed aloud, and Cinda went on in an even tone: "But it wasn't funny very often. At Mrs. Parremore's, the Yankees saw some fresh-dug earth and thought they'd find silver buried there. Actually it was a grave, a little negro baby, the grandson of Mrs. Parremore's cook. They dug him up, and threw him to one side,—I suppose they thought there might be some silver buried under him—and hogs ate him. But of course even human beings will eat anything if they're hungry enough." She saw Vesta's lips white with pain and came back from hideous memories. "Forgive me, Honey. I shouldn't tell you all these things. You're going to have to live in the same nation with these people till you die."

"Oh, Mama, why do they do it?"

Cinda shrugged. "Why, to make us love them, Vesta!" She spoke in a weary sarcasm. "To make us want to come back into the Union. Yet I suppose they'll wonder, by and by, why we're slow to make friends with them again."

That long spate of talk eased her, yet Cinda for a few days was content to stay quietly at home, to spend long mornings abed. She held a sort of court there, and after the first day Tilda came every morning before leaving the house; and Julian came, and Anne, and Enid and her children. The first Sunday after her return, Trav stopped in. She thought he had grown older in the weeks since she saw him. His shoulders were as broad, but they stooped more than she remembered; and his cheeks were hollowed, and deep lines framed his mouth, and hair and beard showed a sprinkling of gray. She told him he looked fine, and he said he was well. "Most people are," he remarked. "Maybe short rations are good for us."

"How's Cousin Jeems?"

"He still carries his arm in a sling, but he can write a little now." He added: "He's sent for Cousin Louisa. She'd have been here before this if Sheridan weren't so near Lynchburg." Sheridan at Waynesboro had scattered General Early's little army that not so long ago had been strong enough to march to the outer defenses of Washington itself. "She's going to have another baby this summer."

"Really? Is that why he sent for her?"

"Partly, I think. But there was a plan for her to go see Mrs. Grant, to see if that wouldn't lead to a meeting between General Grant and General Lee. The whole thing fell through. General Lee asked Grant for an interview to discuss peace; but Grant said he couldn't discuss anything but a military surrender."

"Are we as near as that to giving up?"

Trav said honestly: "Yes. Some of us have given up already. Major Walton—he's on the staff—has taken a transfer to Mississippi, so when the end comes he'll be that much nearer his home."

"Why is it so hopeless, Trav? Oh I know it is, but why?"

"Well, for one thing, General Lee hasn't forty-five thousand men in his army, and Grant has a hundred thousand. Then our men get at most one square meal a week and Grant's get three every day. We haven't enough horses to move our guns, nor to mount our cavalry, but Grant has more horses than he can use. And Grant can collect an army of two hundred and fifty thousand men this summer, and General Lee will do well to get together fifty thousand, even including General Johnston's army."

She almost smiled. "You and your figures."

"I've got so I hate figures. I wish I didn't know two plus two. But I can't get away from them."

"You say Cousin Jeems has sent for Cousin Louisa?"

"Yes. As soon as it's safe to travel. He wants her here if she can come. The river's high, so Sheridan probably can't cross; but north of the river there's nothing to stop him between Lynchburg and our defenses here."

From Trav, from Vesta and Tilda and Julian, from the testimony of her own eyes, Cinda had evidence enough that the end was near. Richmond was beleaguered, the city and her defenders were half-starved. There was provision enough in North Carolina, but the broken-down railroad could not move it fast enough to feed the army, much less the hundred thousand people in the city. Civilians who could do so were leaving Richmond as eagerly as deserters left the army. There were daily rumors that Mr. Davis's family and General Lee's had gone or were preparing to go. Cinda, a little ashamed of wishing to make sure this was not so, walked down Franklin Street to call on Mrs. Lee, living now with her daughters in the narrow brick house only two or three blocks away. General Lee had had his Richmond office there since the first year of the war, and Custis Lee and some of his friends had used the house when they were on duty in Richmond; till Mrs. Lee came last fall to live there with the girls. Cinda found the General's wife in her wheel chair on the second floor veranda, enjoying the warm spring day. As usual, she was knitting. May and Agnes were with her and as busy as she; and she was so serenely cheerful that Cinda as they chatted began to be ashamed of her own fears.

"This has been good for me, Mrs. Lee," she said when she rose to go. "May I make a confession? I'd heard that you were leaving Richmond, and I came to see for myself."

"It has been decided to defend Richmond, Mrs. Dewain. Why should I leave?"

"Do you think it can be defended?"

Mrs. Lee's eyes were stern. "I have never been so presumptuous as to doubt the mercy of God!"

But though Mrs. Lee would stay, there were many who departed; and the talk was that every government official kept a horse saddled ready for instant flight. Rumors of a treaty with France or with England that might yet bring salvation gave the witless a breath of hope; and some thought enough Negroes might still be recruited to make an army strong enough to crush Grant. Why, three hundred thousand Negro soldiers could destroy the Yankee armies, march on Washington, bring the North to its knees!

But Cinda was sickened by these childish follies. "We might save at least our dignity," she told Julian. "To lose everything, even our lives, is better than this whining chatter." She was weary of inaction and thought there might be work for her in the hospital, so she walked out to Chimborazo. Some impulse made her follow Main Street. The iron fence and low arches of the Farmers' Bank always seemed to her to have a hint of the Oriental. Main Street was the financial center, the heart of the city. She wondered how long that heart would continue to beat. There were already visible symptoms of inanition and of decay. At the landings where Main Street crossed Shockoe Creek, a few barges lay idle and deserted; and a fisherman's small sailboat was

awash, hanging sluggish in her slack moorings. The creek was roofed
over from Main Street upstream as far as Broad, and since it served as
a sewer, its waters were noisome and repulsive. She turned up to
Grace Street, wishing Richmond had not so many hills. She had never
realized how numerous they were until she gave up the carriage and
began to go afoot. She passed Miss Van Lew's, fronting on Grace
Street and with gardens and servants' quarters extending down to Main.
That extraordinary woman through these terrible years had openly
avowed her loyalty to the Union. Probably she was happy now in the
certainty that the end for which she had prayed was near.

At the hospital Cinda found her old ward almost empty. The
soldiers were so sadly undernourished that even a slight wound often
proved fatal, and most of those who came to the hospital soon died,
and there was not much hard fighting in early March to fill the empty
beds. So, finding nothing here for her to do, Cinda turned homeward,
following Broad Street. When she crossed the creek, she saw on the
slopes of the ravine toward the White House young grass and new
green; but it was still too early for the Scotch broom to clothe those
slopes in bright golden blossoms. At Fourteenth Street she waited for
a brigade of soldiers to pass. The marching men were thin and weary,
gaunt shadows shambling through the city to strengthen some threatened point in the long defensive lines.

At home she found Julian just arrived with news that Fitz Lee's
men were marching through the city to meet Sheridan; and he and
Cinda and Vesta hurried to see them pass and to watch for Burr. At
their call, Burr swung his skeleton of a horse to where they stood, and
dismounted for a swift embrace and a moment's breathless talk. When
he was gone Vesta wept with pity for him.

"Oh, Mama, he's just a shadow," she cried. "Just skin and bones!"

Cinda nodded. "So is his horse," she commented. "I wonder what
the horses think about this war. I'm sorrier for them, sometimes, than
I am for the men. The men at least know what they're doing, and
why."

Sheridan's horsemen passed north of Richmond, and after he was
gone across the Pamunkey, a new trickle of refugees from Ashland
and from as far as Gordonsville brought the familiar stories of Yankee

thievery and waste: of earrings, brooches, rings, snatched from their wearers; of barns and smoke houses and storage bins and houses burned; of cattle killed and left to rot. To hear of these new depredations awoke in many sympathetic listeners a hysterical mania for sacrifice; and Tilda reported that ladies were begging the privilege of giving anything that might help feed the army and thus defeat the brutal enemy. "They even talk of cutting off their hair and selling it to the wig makers in Paris to buy bread," she said. "As if a suit of hair in Paris, even if you could get it there, would make a soldier in the trenches at Petersburg any less hungry."

"They're trying to ease their own heartbreak a little by parading it in public," Cinda commented. "I'm as sad as any of them, I suppose; but there's a line in the Bible, a good rule for anyone who is grieving: 'Rend your hearts and not your garments.'"

Vesta, who kept her spirits high, laughed. "Well, that's mighty good advice," she declared. "I've only about two dresses to my name. If I start rending my garments where will I be?"

In mid-March the weather turned bright and fair, and occasional frosty mornings accented the beauty of the fine warm days. Brett came for dear and heartening hours at home. "But I shouldn't have come," he confessed. "We've so few men left that the breastworks in front of us are just held by a skirmish line. The Yankees can march through us any time." He added: "And I should have walked instead of riding. Our horses are too worn out to carry us to town and back unless it's absolutely necessary."

"Not enough men, not enough horses, not enough food!" Cinda spoke in dull sorrow.

"Not enough anything," Brett assented. "Not even enough bullets, Cinda. General Lee sent word to Colonel Mosby the other day to pick up all the lead he can find on the old battlefields in Northern Virginia. We work every day cutting down trees along our lines and burning them and then sifting the melted bullets out of the ashes."

"The Yankees need lead, too," she remembered, and she told him of those Atlanta ladies who lived by collecting bullets and trading them for food at Sherman's commissary.

"Well, they've enough to finish us with," he said.

Next day Mrs. Longstreet came to call. She was just from Lynchburg; and since so many had already fled from Richmond, the General had been able to find her a room at the Spottswood. She told them of Lynchburg's perils now past. "When Sheridan came, General Early's cavalry had mostly deserted," she said. "And at Waynesboro, General Early was just about the only one in his army who got away. Sheridan wrecked the railroad all the way to Amherst, and the canal locks at Duguidsville; but the river was so high he couldn't cross, and the next thing we knew he'd gone away toward Richmond." She tossed her head. "So I came to be with Jeems."

Cinda smiled, knowing the tender bond between these two. "Cousin Jeems can whip Grant's whole army by himself, with you here," she declared. "Trav says he's miserable away from you."

Mrs. Longstreet's eyes were warm. "That big husband of mine is a very dear man."

On the nineteenth, Judge Tudor and Anne and Julian came to Sunday dinner; and afterward, when the young people trooped away to the upper balcony where the children were at play, Cinda and the Judge stayed for a while in the drawing room alone. Congress had adjourned the day before, having refused to pass any of the measures President Davis urged on them. "None so poor to do him reverence," the Judge commented with a faint relish. "Once they called him a giant; but now they say he was never anything but a straw man puffed up to greatness by his brother's money."

She wondered absently how old Judge Tudor was. Just now his voice held an almost senile petulance. But of course, he had always resented every move by the administration to suppress those civil rights which in their exercise were such a hindrance to the prosecution of the war; so naturally he would have no sympathy for Mr. Davis.

"I suppose the losing side always turns against its leaders," she suggested.

He nodded. "Yes. And we're lost. The collapse is complete. The Government's bankrupt. It no longer even respects itself. Since farmers began to refuse to take Confederate money for impressed goods, the agents have seized what they wanted and given paper promises to pay; and over five hundred millions of those promises are outstanding. That's not only bankruptcy, it's plain fraud. I don't suppose a thousand Confederate dollars would buy a dollar gold today. The end is near."

The end? Defeat? Yes, but also—peace! "What will peace be, Judge Tudor? What form will it take?"

"President Lincoln said at Hampton Roads his only requirement is restoration of the Union. I believe he may be our best friend, presently."

"Will we ever want any Northern man for a friend? Sherman and Sheridan have made no friends among us. Their outrages were planned and ordered and deliberately carried out."

"That's true." He nodded. "They were policy, not accident. But remember, General Lee said long ago that we were all in the war; the North has taken him at his word, that's all."

"You men are so ready to excuse your enemies," she commented. "But what General Lee said was that every man should either fight or work to help the fighting men. He didn't say anything about women and children."

Judge Tudor said gallantly: "It is you noble women who have kept our fighting spirits alive. To crush the South, it was necessary to crush you; to make you ladies cry for peace." She was about to protest, but he checked her. "That is not my opinion, of course; but it is what the Yankees would say. Sherman has said publicly that he believes in terrible war and kindly peace."

"Well, he has lived by at least one of his beliefs!" Cinda spoke in angry scorn. "But, Judge Tudor, as long as any woman now alive in the South keeps her memory, and her tongue to tell the stories to her children, the South will hate Sherman. And it will hate the North. So how can there ever be union again? How can there be peace?" He did not reply, and after a moment she asked: "Did the Confederacy ever have any real hope of victory?"

He said reflectively: "Well, I'm an old man, Mrs. Dewain; and it's natural for old men to criticize the mistakes, or what seem to be the mistakes, of younger men. But I think so, yes." He went on, in thoughtful summary. "We've lost because we've never done our level best. Lack of money has wrecked us; but a wise use of our surplus cotton in 1861 would have financed the war. Then our lack of an intelligent working class has wrecked us. Before this war, very few white men in the South worked for hire. Labor was the lot of slaves, so white men considered labor demeaning. Therefore we had almost no men who knew how to do such simple things as run an engine, repair a railroad track or a locomotive, keep our trains operating; and now for lack of cars to bring the plentiful supplies from a region not a hundred miles away, we're starving. Ignorance about finances wrecked us, ignorance of the mechanic arts wrecked us, and the lack of real ability in the higher circles of the Government wrecked us. Before the war began, the Cotton States had seized control of the South; but their leaders were politicians, not statesmen. When great men were needed, we had only politicians. We had a surfeit of them, each one more concerned with the power he could seize and the prestige he could command than with the good work he could do."

"Yet at first everyone liked Mr. Davis."

"It is not enough for a politician to be liked to make him a statesman," he reminded her. "Great men are not 'liked' any more than great books are 'liked.' The quality of greatness commands respect, and even fear; but it quite often inspires hatred. General Lee's weakness is that he is too likable, too kindly, too gentle, too forgiving, too modest. To be likable is not an attribute of greatness. To be loved, yes; or to be hated. But to be liked, no!"

She did not speak, and he continued: "Yes, we might have won the war. In 1861, the states of the Confederacy had a respectable supply of small arms, but they would not throw them into the general pool. The Confederate armies, if those weapons had been available, might have been strengthened by a quarter of a million men. Such an army could have marched through Washington and Baltimore to Philadelphia; could have won the war then and there. Again, in 1862, at least a hundred thousand men were kept at home by the several states, when with that added strength our armies could have gone where they chose.

"And the states have continued to think first of themselves. Why, within the fortnight, when Sherman marched north out of South Carolina toward Fayetteville, the South Carolina militia in Beauregard's command stayed on their own side of the state line, and Beauregard's little army was reduced to uselessness."

"It was too late then," Cinda urged.

"It was not too late in 1861, when Maxcy Gregg's regiment insisted on going home even before Manassas was fought. It was not too late in 1862, or even in 1863, if the militia of all the states had been used for the common good. But now—" He smiled grimly. "Well, since we would not hang together, we will all hang separately. To accomplish any great work requires not confederation—a loose and precarious association—but a firm and indissoluble union."

"Mr. Lincoln wants union," she reflected.

"I believe he is right," the Judge admitted. "The United States, if they are really united, will be the greatest force for good in the world that is to come. But without union they can accomplish nothing." And he said reverently: "I have learned to pray to God to give that man strength and long life to finish the work he has begun."

Far away, dimly, she heard the murmur of guns; and she shivered and said no more. This was one of those perfect days which come only in spring, warm and fine, the pulse of new birth and waking life in the soft air. But it was not too fine a day for men to die in the entrenchments around Petersburg, where Grant only waited till the roads were firm to begin the westward thrust that would destroy them all.

20

WHEN Sheridan passed north of Richmond, moving toward the Pamunkey to cross it and turn southward and unite with Grant's army, he wasted all the country from Ashland to the Rappahannock, burned the four principal bridges on the Fredericksburg railroad, and incidentally intercepted Lomas and Faunt on their way to Richmond. Three times the two men were chased by Yankee cavalry; the third time Lomas was shot off his horse and Faunt took a bullet through his shoulder which fractured the bone in his upper arm. He was able to stick his horse and to escape, leaving Lomas in enemy hands. If Lomas were still alive, he would probably be recognized and hanged; but Faunt did not wait to investigate. At the moment when he was struck, the Deringer Lomas had given him in Baltimore was in his hand ready for use; but the blow of the bullet left his right arm nerveless, and he dropped the pistol and went on unarmed.

He might have found some friendly household and attendance for his wound; but he was no longer wholly rational. The journey from Washington had been exhausting, bringing on one slight hemorrhage even before they began to encounter Sheridan's scouts; the final chase and the labors of his escape produced another, of which he was not aware. The agony of the splintered bone in his arm served as a stimulant and a spur, keeping him back from the abyss of complete delirium; but when on the third evening he reached the outskirts of Richmond, inflammation had set in, his fever was high, and he had lost any sense of pain. He was no longer a sentient individual but a deadly purpose in the shape of a man, an automaton, a physical engine in which power has expired and which continues to move only on the dregs of its own momentum.

He came to Nell's house late at night, slid off his almost foundered horse at her gate, and reached her door so nearly insensible that only the expiring flame of his implacable determination gave him strength to tug at the bell. Milly and Rufus bore him upstairs, and Nell undressed him. They tended his wound and cleansed it; and Nell thought of a surgeon, but no surgeon could help Faunt now. True, his arm was mortified and should be amputated; but amputation would not save him. Telltale streaks ran from the wound up to his shoulder and across his chest. She knew their significance.

And even if his hurts could be mended, he was dying. This too she knew.

Yet from the lip of death itself he had held back to come to her; and this knowledge gave her a fierce triumphant happiness. He had returned to her arms to die. He was her love and she was his, and while he lived no surgeon's knife should take any part of him. She was fiercely jealous of these their last hours together. She remembered his sisters and his brothers, and thought of summoning Mrs. Dewain and Mrs. Streean; but it was to her he had turned, not to them. She put the thought away.

She felt not so much sadness, or rending grief, as a triumphant rapture of complete possession. She did not pray Faunt might recover, for she knew he could not. Her only entreaty was that he might once more smile in the way she loved, and speak her name. She fed him warm milk touched with brandy, thin broth, egg whipped in cream; she cooled his brow with damp cloths, and sponged his throat and breast to ease the fever; and she asked only that he might have one moment of recognition, one moment when he knew her, before he died.

If such a moment came, none must share it; so she kept his side, and after the first hour she never again admitted Milly to the room where he lay. Night melted into day, day turned to dark again. If she slept it was for no more than seconds at a time. She felt no weariness, nor any need for sleep. If there was need, it was his need of her. That need had brought him to her door. That need she would not deny. As long as he lived she was his. Beyond that moment when his life should end she did not think at all.

She had at last what she had wished for. Toward dark of the third day she rose to light the candle and draw the heavy curtains; and when having done so she turned again, his eyes were open. She went to him quickly, dropping on her knees.

"Darling, darling," she whispered. "It's Nell."

"Nell." His word was so softly spoken she scarcely heard it. She leaned nearer, pressing her cheek to his.

"Yes, Nell. Oh, Faunt, my darling!"

His left hand, weak and fluttering, came up to touch her arm. Her arms cradled him, and his hand crawled up her arm like a bat creeping awkwardly against the walls of a cave. He spoke her name again. "Nell." His hand was so feeble. She drew his arm around her neck and held him close, looking down into his eyes. His hand was still moving, unsatisfied; his shoulder stirred as he tried to raise his right arm, too. His hand touched her neck, found her throat which he had used to caress so tenderly.

Then in sudden access of strength his fingers and thumb gripped her throat, bedding in the soft flesh. She thought him still delirious, thought he did not know her. Making no effort to release herself, she said tenderly:

"It's Nell, darling. It's Nell, Faunt. You're in Nell's arms."

In a last spasm of strength, his fingers dug deep and made her choke and cough. He said clearly: "I know you!" In his eyes close to hers she saw that this was true, and as she saw this, he spoke again in stern damnation. "I know you, Nell. You spy. I came to kill you! So!"

His fingers set hard on her throat, but that was nothing; for his words tightened a vise upon her heart, and it seemed to burst in her breast. She let her head fall, let her throat relax in his clasp, thrust herself down against his hand; and she was hungry for the death he wished to deal her. His body arched; he tried to pull her down, to lift himself.

Then like a man struck through the lungs he collapsed in every muscle, and a gush of blood came out of his mouth. She felt the blood against her cheek pressed hard to his, felt the thin fingers let go her throat. She lay across his breast, and his body under hers seemed to shrink and grow less.

And she knew that he was dead.

He had come back to her not in love but in ferocious judgment; he had come not to die in the cradle of her love, but to kill.

She freed herself and stood looking down at him. He had come to kill her. Well, she had never denied him anything; she would not deny him her life. But first she bathed him and composed his limbs; and she bathed herself. Her thoughts were orderly and calm; she was in this hour completely practical. Rufus slept above the stable, apart from the house; but Milly's room was behind the kitchen, connected with the house by the gallery, and she might not wake in time to escape. After some consideration, Nell folded and sealed a blank sheet of paper and went downstairs and called Milly. The Negro woman asked at once:

"How is he?"

"He's better, Milly," Nell assured her. "But he needs a doctor. Take this note to Chimborazo Hospital." Milly would need almost two hours to go and come. "Ask someone to give it to Dr. McCaw. Don't bother to see him; don't say anything; just leave the note for him."

"Yas'm."

"Go right along."

"Yas'm. I'se gone."

When Nell had heard the door close, she worked swiftly for a while. The house was of heart pine, richly resinous; it would burn like a torch. There was lightwood in a closet near the fireplace in the drawing room, a further supply in the closet under the stairs. She tore pages out of books till she had sufficient paper, and stuffed it into the closets, against the logs. She touched the paper with the candle flame and watched the logs catch; and through their thick and choking smoke, with the fire crackling hungrily under her feet, she went quickly up the stairs.

Her Deringer was in the drawer of the table by her bed. She took it in her hand. She went to the door of the room where Faunt lay, and stood for a moment looking at him there.

Then she returned to her own room and made sure the pistol was charged and capped, and then she lay down upon her bed.

21

THE fire which destroyed Mrs. Albion's attractive little house out in the country west of town made no great stir in Richmond; but April, when she took breakfast to Enid's room, had heard, and spoke of it. "All burned up," she said. "De lady lived dere, she said. Name Mis' Albion."

"Mrs. Albion?" Enid sat bolt upright, tipping the waiter so that dishes slid and makeshift coffee spilled.

"Yas'm. Dey say dere was a gemmun. He daid too." April began hurriedly to clean the saucer, mop up the coffee. Enid understood that April knew, as no doubt every house servant in Richmond knew, that Mrs. Albion was her mother; but the old Negro woman would of course never avow this knowledge. A gentleman? That was certainly Faunt. Enid's pulse was racing, but not with grief nor with any sense of loss. She had not seen her mother or Faunt for months, and if she had thought of them at all it was resentfully.

But she must hurry to tell Cinda. "I'll dress, April. The waiter's all a mess. Give me breakfast downstairs." The prospect of being the first to bring this news to Cinda and to Tilda, to tell them Faunt was dead, was so exciting that it made her for the moment forget her mother. She made haste, and neither Lucy nor Peter had wakened when she left the house.

Cinda and Vesta were just coming downstairs for the day when Caesar admitted her. Without waiting for any greeting, Enid cried: "Cinda, Cinda, the most terrible thing!" She looked at Vesta, hesitated, then said breathlessly: "Mama's house burned down last night, and she's dead!" Her eyes touched Vesta again, but she did not pause. "And Cousin Faunt too!"

For a moment Cinda did not speak. She looked at Vesta, and Enid guessed she was thinking to send Vesta away; but the girl said quietly: "I know all about them, Mama. Mrs. Albion came here while you were away."

Enid asked: "Has Tilda gone?" Cinda nodded, moving into the drawing room, and Enid followed her, saying rapidly: "Isn't it terrible? April told me. Of course she knew who Mrs. Albion was, but she pretended not to. I wanted to go right out there; but probably I shouldn't!" To her own surprise she began to cry. "Oh what are we going to do?" Cinda shook her head, and Enid urged: "We've got to do something, Cousin Cinda!"

"There's nothing to do. Nothing we can do. If they're alive, they're all right; and there's certainly nothing we can do if they're dead."

"We can go see! Can't we? Please?"

"Why?" Cinda sat down, and she spoke as one speaks to a bewildered child. "Very few people knew much about your mother, Enid; and those who knew her were mostly men who won't—talk about it. After all, with our whole world in flames, she will be forgotten. Why not let her be?"

"But she was my mother!"

"Oh don't be so self-righteous! You didn't care a fig for her!"

Enid, suddenly convinced of her own filial grief, sobbed: "You're just afraid to talk about her and Cousin Faunt!"

Cinda pressed her hands to her eyes. "Yes, I suppose I am. So should you be!"

"Well, I'm not! I declare, I believe Cousin Faunt killed her or something!" Her own words frightened her, but she defiantly insisted: "Well, I don't care! I do!" Cinda was looking toward the tall mirror between the two windows across the room. Enid glanced that way and saw herself, and she had that familiar feeling that she was looking at a stranger which is so often provoked by a recognition of one's own image. She was a sight, her eyes streaming, her nose red; and she mopped her eyes, and repeated: "I declare I do, Cousin Cinda! He must have! The house wouldn't just catch fire and burn her up and Mama not know it, unless she was dead!"

"He may have," Cinda assented. "All of us Currains have high tempers, even Travis. We're quite capable of killing, if we're angry enough." She turned to meet Enid's eyes. "Yes, Faunt may have killed her. But if he did, she's dead, and talk will do no good. I'm sure I don't want it. And I'm sure Travis wouldn't want you to make a spectacle of yourself."

"Well, I don't care! I want to know what happened to my mother! I'm going to find out, too!"

"I won't try to stop you, Enid. Do whatever you choose."

Enid turned to the door. "I'm going out there right now!" Cinda did not move, and Enid hesitated. "Won't you come, please?" Cinda shook her head. "Vesta, won't you?" And she began to weep again. "Oh, you've never cared anything about me, any of you! You're always so mean! But now my mama's dead, I should think——"

Vesta interrupted. "I'll go with you, Aunt Enid, but I don't see the good of it."

Enid drooped miserably. "I don't know what to do."

"Let me walk home with you," Vesta suggested. "We'll talk it over, and perhaps we can think of something."

"No, you're just being sorry for me! I hate people being sorry for me! All right, Cousin Cinda, I'll go home!" Spite edged her tones. "I won't disgrace you wonderful Currains."

But in the hall she lingered wretchedly, feeling helpless and alone, till Vesta came after her. "Don't go, Aunt Enid. Wait. We'll send someone. This—well, we feel badly too, you know." Enid went gratefully back with her into the drawing room, and Vesta spoke to Cinda. "Mama, can't we find out a little more about it?"

"I'll speak to June," Cinda decided. "She can send someone, or go. Mrs. Albion had a servant. Perhaps June can find her, if she's alive."

Enid stayed with Vesta, trembling with an emotion so near grief that her eyes filled easily, wondering why she wept. "I declare I don't know why I'm such a ninny," she confessed. "Mama and I never had anything to do with each other. Why should I keep crying?"

Vesta said affectionately: "I don't think we ever get over loving our mothers, really. Mrs. Albion came here when Uncle Faunt was sick at her house, and I liked her. She wanted me to persuade him to come here; but he had gone before we reached her house."

Cinda returned to say June would go find out what she could. Then Tilda came home, having heard of the fire and guessed it was

Mrs. Albion's house which had been burned. "I thought of going out there," she admitted, "but I didn't know what to do."

They waited till at last June returned. She had found Milly weeping in the curious throng around the still smouldering ashes of the house, and heard her story. Mister Faunt had come to the house Saturday night—this was Tuesday—badly hurt and sick and so nearly dead that Milly thought he was; but Mrs. Albion had nursed him ever since, and last night she told Milly he was better and sent her to the hospital with a letter to the doctor; and when Milly started back she saw the far glare of flames and hurried all the way. But when she got to the house the roof and walls had already fallen. Rufus, who slept in the stable, was gone. Milly knew no more than this.

"Probably Rufus was afraid he'd be blamed," Tilda suggested, and the others nodded, agreeing.

"I suppose he died," Cinda hazarded.

Enid's tears flowed again, but Vesta spoke in comfort. "Then he didn't—hurt her, Aunt Enid."

"But—what happened?" Enid pleaded. "What happened to her?" No one spoke, and she sobbed: "I declare, I'll go crazy, not knowing!"

"He was dead, I'm sure." Cinda nodded at her own certainty. "And —she loved him, you know! Let them rest, Enid. Let them be."

"You mean Mama killed herself because she loved him?"

"I think so, yes." And Cinda said in a low tone: "She was a fine woman. You can be proud of her."

Enid felt a deep wonder, as though she looked on beauty never seen before. Obscurely, she wished for Trav. When that evening he came home, she clung to him, and told herself she loved him as greatly as her mother had loved Uncle Faunt; that if he died, then so would she!

"But Cinda thought we shouldn't do anything, Trav, or say anything," she wailed, sobbing in his arms.

"Cinda's wrong." He spoke firmly. "She was your mother. I'll take care of things, Honey."

His plain common sense which had sometimes seemed to her so dull gave her comfort now. The charred bodies, one to be forever nameless, were buried side by side in Hollywood; and the brief sensation was forgotten. Richmond in that third week of March had larger matters on her mind.

22

March–April, 1865

CINDA found that she too could forget Faunt in these speeding days when fine spring weather held, and flowering fruit trees made the city bright with beauty as it waited for the end. She wished for Brett, for Burr, for Rollin; and she and Vesta went often to be with Julian and Anne. Along the way, they saw here and there the red flag of the auctioneer, as house owners preparing to take flight put up their property for sale at any price at all; and once they watched some of the hurriedly recruited Negro troops parade on Main Street. The Negroes had no uniforms, but they were as delighted as children with this new game; and in the faces of the onlookers, Cinda saw a desperate hope appear. To such frail straws the hopeless now would cling.

Famine was at their elbow, and even Vesta half despaired. "I don't mind so much for us grownups, Mama; but Tommy's such a glutton, and Kyle and Janet and Clayton. I hate not having enough for them. Caesar caught some eels and catfish this morning or I don't know what we'd do."

"Well, there's nothing better than a fish fry," Cinda reminded her. "Tell him tó go catch some more for Sunday dinner."

"I've enough meal to last us maybe two weeks," Vesta said. "And a little pork. Lucky it's well salted."

"Lots of people haven't that."

"Other people being hungry doesn't make us—or the children—any less so. Mama, if we do give up Richmond, do you suppose the Yankees will feed us?"

"They'd better!" Cinda declared. "Or I'll give them a piece of my mind!" They laughed together at that familiar phrase that was an echo out of the past; but laughter was so near to tears. "Oh, Vesta," she said wearily, "I wouldn't mind so much if I could just see Brett Dewain!"

Saturday they heard Lee had attacked the enemy lines at Petersburg and had taken prisoners by the hundreds; but next day at church the word went around that the attack was a costly failure, wasting many lives. The starved soldiers had fought like raging tigers, driving home their charge with as much vigor as in the first years of the war; but Grant easily restored his lines. Monday the *Dispatch* said France and the United States were about to go to war, and that the Confederacy need only hold out a little longer; but next day Tilda brought news that Mrs. Davis and her children had left for Charlotte.

"But we needn't tell Vesta and Jenny," she suggested, and Cinda indifferently agreed. They would know soon enough whatever there was to know.

Tuesday Vesta paid fifty dollars for a pair of roe shad and they had a feast. The children had the roe, and for the grownups the shad were planked, and every bone was picked clean. "I never tasted nicer shad," Vesta declared. "And they were dirt-cheap, too; but of course this is the real beginning of the run."

They were still at table when Julian came in. A dispatch from General Lee reported that Grant had thrown a heavy force toward Dinwiddie Court House, beyond Lee's left flank. "Infantry and cavalry," Julian said. "Fitz Lee has gone to stop them, or they'll cut the Danville road."

Fitz Lee meant Burr. Cinda closed her eyes. Burr four years ago had been such a handsome, slender boy. Now he was rail-thin, with yellow unhealthy skin and red-lidded eyes, and poor fumbling things for hands. But he would have to help meet that new move by the enemy. Fitz Lee had not many men left; less than fifteen hundred, or so Burr said when she and Vesta had that brief word with him two weeks ago. Yet even a few brave men might yet do some great deed.

"Have you thought of leaving, Mama?" Julian asked. "Mrs. Davis has gone."

She smiled lightly, spoke lightly. "Leave Richmond? Leave you and Anne? Leave Vesta and Jenny and the children? Don't be silly, Son."

"You could all go."

"No, thank you. I've had my fill of travelling." No, she would stay; here in her own home she would face whatever was to come.

Thursday, rain fell. Let it rain hard enough and Grant might be bogged down. It rained all day and all that night, and Cinda welcomed every drop, happy to hear it beat against the windows. Yet all day Thursday and again on Friday the guns were rumbling far away, audible even through the slashing rain.

"So March is going out like a lion, instead of a lamb," Cinda told Vesta when they said good night.

"Yes, and tomorrow's April Fool's Day, Mama. Watch out the children don't fool you. I heard Kyle and Janet whispering about something, and giggling together before they went to bed."

Next morning the rain was gone, the skies clear. The boiled egg on Cinda's waiter at breakfast proved when she cracked it to be an empty shell; and at her exclamation of astonishment Kyle and Janet, listening at the door, came charging in with shouts of glee at her befoolment, and she called them a pair of scamps, and thus delighted them the more. Tilda came home with bits of news. Mr. Daniel, the editor of the *Examiner,* was dead. General Preston said that when the Conscript Bureau was abolished, sixty thousand Virginians were listed as deserters or absent without leave. At dusk soldiers marched past the house, stumbling like leg-weary ghosts; and a few minutes later Julian and Anne appeared, and Julian said the soldiers were some of Longstreet's men of Field's division, marching to the station to take the cars for Petersburg. "So I guess we must have been beaten somewhere down there today."

"I've heard guns all afternoon," Cinda assented. She felt in him a boy's prayer for comfort, and she thought: Why, he's still my little baby wanting his mama to tell him what to do. She looked at Anne and smiled reassuringly, and at something in the girl's eyes she thought: I believe she's going to have another, she has that look; they haven't told me, but I suppose the darlings didn't want to worry me.

Aloud she said with hardly a pause: "I suppose so; but I for one shall get a good night's sleep if I can. No matter what happened, there's nothing we can do."

She kept them for supper, and they found pretexts for laughter. That happy hour together would be a source of strength in the days to come.

At daybreak Sunday morning Cinda was waked by alarm bells calling the militia to man the defenses. She supposed they would take the place of Field's division, gone off to Petersburg. June brought her breakfast and news of defeat suffered the day before by Pickett's men somewhere near Dinwiddie Court House; and the old woman's eyes rolled as she told the tale.

But the day was so fair and fine, with fruit trees in bloom and spring flowers in every garden, that fears vanished in the smiling sun; and a few minutes before they were to start for church, the morning suddenly was glorious, for Brett appeared. The Howitzers had been drawn back a mile or so from the front, he said, and smiled. "So I took my foot in my hand and walked in to go to church with you. It's communion Sunday. And besides, I'm hungry for one of Vesta's dinners." The lines were quiet, he said; no sign of action near.

Walking leisurely along Grace Street toward St. Paul's, Cinda on Brett's arm, Vesta and Jenny and Tilda at their heels, they met many friends; but except for churchgoers the streets were almost deserted as on a Sunday morning they were apt to be. It was so quiet they could hear the soft murmur of the rapids in the river below the city. In the church they saw Mrs. Longstreet already seated, and it was reassuring to discover President Davis in his pew, even though since Mrs. Davis and the children were gone away to Charlotte he sat alone.

Cinda heard Vesta's lovely voice join in the opening hymn. She herself, though she followed the words with her lips, made no sound. She was always a little surprised to find that the music in her heart came so discordantly from her throat; but it was happiness enough to hear Vesta, and to hear Jenny's softer tones, and to feel Brett close beside her. When the hymn was done Doctor Minnigerode read:

"'The Lord is in his holy temple; let all the earth keep silence before him.'" And after an instant: "Let us pray." Cinda was more than usually conscious of his heavy accent. "Let us bray" was what he said, actually; and as she murmured the Lord's Prayer she thought "bray" was an ugly word. It meant to crush and grind as in a mortar. It had a frightening sound.

Footsteps whispered in the aisle beside her. Who would come in during the prayer? She opened her eyes and raised her head a little and saw a messenger stop by Mr. Davis and hand him something, a folded paper or an envelope. There was a rustle across the kneeling congregation. Between two heads, Cinda could see the President's cheek, the side of his face. She saw, as he read the message, his color drain away and leave only grayness behind; and he rose and walked quietly toward the door.

At once, others here and there about the church moved to follow him; but Cinda bowed her head, pressing back the tears. When the prayer was done her eyes were clear again; but her hand clasped Brett's by her side.

He leaned to whisper to her. "That must be important, Cinda. I'll have to go." There were men rising all around, quietly departing. She nodded her assent. Yes, he must go.

Doctor Minnigerode came to the altar rail to bid those whose duties did not call them away stay and finish the service. Brett was gone; and Cinda dared not trust herself to look after him, dared not see him go. She could hold herself outwardly passive, but her body seemed to be a boiling vessel in which her heart pounded hard and her lungs strained and her bowels writhed like snakes caught in a grass fire and helpless to escape. Doctor Minnigerode's voice seemed far away; she only half heard what he said, till presently responses all around drew her to join in their murmuring. "Have mercy upon us." "Spare us, good Lord." "Good Lord, deliver us." "We beseech thee to hear us, good Lord." "Son of God, we beseech thee to hear us." "Grant us thy peace." Peace. Peace. Peace. "Lord have mercy upon us." Were ever responses drawn up from so deep a well of grief and longing and humble supplication? The whispered words went on. "Lord have mercy upon us and incline our hearts to keep this law."

From turbulence of mind and heart came quiet and serenity. When the service ended Doctor Minnigerode made an announcement. The local militia were summoned for three o'clock that afternoon. Cinda knew the meaning of that: Longstreet's men must be withdrawing from the defenses east of the city. Richmond would be abandoned; the army was in flight; Lee's thin lines at last had given way.

When they walked down the aisle it was as parts of a sluggish stream; but outside the church the stream became an eddying throng, and sharp questions flew. "What is it?" "What's happened?" As if they did not know! As if pretending ignorance would somehow thrust aside the bitter truth! Cinda did not pause; the others came with her. Grace Street was crowded. The congregations from St. James's and St. Peter's and the United Presbyterian Church, all dismissed together, met there in a medley of many voices. Cinda nodded to friends, and they spoke to these friends, but not to each other; not till they were at home and the door had closed behind them.

Then Cinda turned to Tilda. "I don't suppose we can be of any use at the hospitals?" Her voice, even to her own ears, was that of a stranger.

"I'll go see." Tilda was in some ways the strongest of them all. She went out at once. None of them pretended not to understand what had happened.

"We must bring Anne here," Cinda decided. "We had better be all together. Vesta, shall we go fetch her?"

"Of course, Mama."

"Enid and her children too. There may be a tumult in the city tonight."

They went at first to Enid's, but she would not come to be with them. "Indeed I won't," she cried. "Trav's got to take care of us! He promised he would. He was home for a minute night before last, but he refused to stay. I could have killed him! I'm perfectly sure he knew what was going to happen!"

"We'd like to have you with us," Cinda assured her. "We could all be together."

"I sha'n't budge an inch! You're just wasting your breath!"

Cinda was really relieved at this refusal. "She'd be a nuisance," she told Vesta, as they walked along Clay toward Twelfth. President Davis's mansion, at the corner where they turned, showed no outward sign that this day differed from any other. Judge Tudor was at home when they arrived. He had attended Dr. Hoge's church on Fifth Street, in the block below Cinda's home, and he said:

"Dr. Hoge made the announcement, told us General Lee had been forced to retreat and that Richmond was to be evacuated."

"Vesta and I thought you'd better all come to our house," Cinda suggested.

The Judge agreed, and they walked back to Fifth Street together. Julian, having seen Anne safely there, proposed to go for news, but Cinda dissuaded him; and before dinner Tilda returned. To their questioning eyes she said at once:

"Yes, our lines were broken this morning; the army will retreat. Everyone in the hospitals is going, Cinda; everyone who can walk. Mrs. Pember says she never saw sick men get well so fast. All the hospital rats who've been insisting they were helpless, making any excuse not to go back into the army, are as spry as crickets now."

"I'm glad I don't have to do anything," Cinda confessed. "My bones have just turned to water."

"I feel better keeping busy," Tilda said. "I walked down Main Street to see what's happening. They're loading all the government papers into wagons, taking them to the depot, sending them away. Everybody who can is leaving, walking or riding or in carriages or wagons or on the canal boats, and carrying everything they own. The banks are open, and people who have any money are drawing it out. They're burning all the paper money in Capitol Square."

Vesta suddenly laughed. "Well, at least we don't have to worry about that. We haven't any money in their old banks."

After dinner Judge Tudor said he would go to the War Department to ask whether he could be of any use; and Tilda went with him. "I may see something that needs doing," she explained. They watched from the windows the hurry and movement on Franklin Street, recognized passing friends, saw wagons driven by with the mules at a fast trot and sometimes at a gallop. Horsemen raced past, and even people afoot moved in desperate haste. Time lost any meaning, till Cinda realized that the light was failing, that day was nearly done, night near. Night? What would this night bring?

Toward sunset Trav rode up to the door and had their eager welcome and Cinda's instant question. Where was Brett?

"His company will pass through Richmond some time tonight," he said. "He can probably stop to see you." He told Vesta: "Rollin too, I think."

"You're so tired, Uncle Trav." Vesta touched his arm. "Rest a while."

"I didn't sleep last night," he admitted. "But I must hurry to rejoin General Longstreet. He went to Petersburg last night."

Cinda asked: "You've seen Enid?"

"Yes. Yes, I put her and the children and Mrs. Longstreet on the cars." He said: "If you want to go, I can probably get you away."

"No, we'll stay here."

"I thought you would."

"What's going to happen, Travis?"

"Why, the army is retreating," he said. "But we'll try to meet Johnston and make a fight somewhere. I suppose we'll get into the mountains, perhaps split up into partisan bands. I don't know. There's some talk of scattering and uniting again in Texas, or even in Mexico. We can fight for years, they say. I don't see how we can, but that's what they say."

Cinda folded her arms because her fingers would not be still. "Why don't we surrender?"

"Oh, I don't think Mr. Davis would ever surrender." He said heavily: "I might lie down for a minute. I told Big Mill to come here. I'm going to let him stay with you. He's a good man, Cinda. Wake me when he comes, won't you?"

He had slept only a few minutes when Caesar came to say Big Mill "He'll stay here," he promised. "Now I'll have to go."

"I suppose there's no telling when we'll see you again, Travis."

"No, no telling, I guess. Good-by."

Dusk was falling as he rode away, and soon afterward Judge Tudor returned to tell them as much as he had learned. He had seen General Breckenridge, who had recently replaced Mr. Seddon as Secretary of War. "He's managing what there is left to manage," he said. "The bullion—what we had, half a million or so—has gone; and what government papers could be saved. Mayor Mayo and the City Council are planning to surrender the city when the time comes. They'll have two regiments of militia to keep order till the Yankees come in. They plan to destroy all the liquor in the city to avoid trouble. There's some scattered looting already, and a mob in the lower part of town."

Cinda asked: "Where's Mr. Davis?"

"I didn't see him. No one's seen him, as far as I know. They say he's hiding in Manchester till time to get away."

"I should think he'd be—managing things," she protested. "Or showing himself to people, telling them what's happening, doing something."

He repeated that President Davis seemed to have vanished, and as he spoke Tilda returned with news worth hearing. "As soon as all the army wagons are loaded, and the soldiers have taken all they can carry, the government stores are going to be distributed to the people in the streets," she said. "But that won't be right away, and I thought if someone could come back with me now we might stock up."

Vesta said quickly: "I'll go. We've hardly anything in the house."

"We'll both go," Jenny agreed.

Cinda was about to protest; but Vesta met her glance. "It's all right, Mama. We'll be all right! After all, it's still my job to keep the kitchen supplied."

"You two children can't go alone!"

Jenny said gently: "I've been alone at the Plains for a long time, Mama."

Vesta added: "And we'll take Big Mill."

"And I'll escort them," Judge Tudor said reassuringly; and Tilda would return with them and stay to help in distributing the stores to the people when the time came. So Cinda yielded.

She had at first no real misgivings. After all, ladies were safe from molestation anywhere. But when they were gone it seemed to her that the stir and murmur in the city increased. She and Anne and Julian stood in the open windows with the room dark behind them; and she heard down toward Main Street and Cary a louder hum of voices and an occasional hoarse shout and sometimes an angry cry. It was hard to wait passive here.

But Vesta and Jenny returned triumphant. "We got two whole hams, Mama," Vesta told her. "And a bag of dried apples, and a side of bacon, and a bag of coffee. Real coffee! June's making some now. And a barrel of flour and some meal and a jug of sorghum." She laughed in a nervous excitement. "It's lucky we had Big Mill. We couldn't possibly have carried everything!"

"Didn't you get more than our share?"

"If we did, we can divide with our friends."

Coffee heartened them, and Vesta insisted on a lavish supper. Judge Tudor and Tilda had not returned. "The wagons are still loading," Vesta explained. "Aunt Tilda has some ladies helping her, and they're getting ready so they can pass out things quickly when the time comes. There was already a perfect mob in the streets, men and women, cursing and yelling while they waited. We went in through an alley and the back door." And she said: "Mama, the warehouse we were in was just full of things. I don't see why they didn't give them to the soldiers to eat up long ago."

Cinda smiled faintly. "Men are stupid, darling. They'll always save and save for fear they won't have enough, instead of using what they have while they still can."

A little after midnight the door bell rang and it was Brett, Brett Dewain whom Cinda had thought she might never see again. Vesta scurried to bid June be sure he was well fed, and he told them while he waited and while he ate what he had done in the hours since he followed President Davis out of church that morning.

"I made sure what was happening first, and then jog trotted back to camp," he said. "They hadn't heard anything, and the men all thought it was just another Sunday rumor, till some more of us got back from Richmond. There weren't any orders, but we began to get ready to move. We were short of horses. Our Napoleons each need six-horse teams, but we could only put four horses to a gun, and we could only move two caissons. The orders came about ten o'clock; and we started. Then most of the men hurried ahead to say good-by to their families, so I decided to come on myself." He laughed suddenly. "What do you think? I met Colonel Taylor of General Lee's staff outside. He'd just been getting married; had ridden up from Petersburg on purpose. But he said General Lee has ordered a rendezvous at Amelia Court-House; so he had to bid a quick good-by to his bride—and so must I."

"Will you be back soon?"

"Well, we've got to join forces with General Johnston and give those bluebellies a licking first."

His tone was confident, but Cinda said: "You don't expect us to believe you, do you?"

He met her eyes, spoke slowly. "I expect to go on fighting as long as the South fights, Cinda. I'm sorry to leave you, but you'll be all right if you just stay indoors. The Yankees will be here tomorrow to keep order."

A moment's silence lay upon them all. Then Cinda said: "They didn't keep very good order in Columbia."

"You'll be all right," he insisted. "I'm sure you will. You've got to be. Only for Heaven's sake stay in the house. I came in past Rockett's, and the streets were jammed; men and women loaded down with things from the commissary stores. Stolen, I suppose."

"No," Cinda explained. "Whatever the army can't use is being given away. Vesta and Jenny got all we'll need." At his sharp ejaculation she added quickly: "Oh, Big Mill was with them. Trav left him here to take care of us. Tilda's down there now, helping distribute the food."

He was eating hurriedly. "Well, stay in the house from now on," he insisted. "Someone's dumping all the liquor, pouring it out of the warehouse windows. I saw people scooping it up in their hands and drinking it. Every blackguard in town will be drunk before morning." He finished and rose. "I'll have to go. I want to meet our guns at Mayo's Bridge."

Cinda in that last moment was weak as any woman. Clinging to him she pleaded: "Don't go! Oh, Brett Dewain, don't go!"

He kissed her, but he put her arms aside. "I started the race, Cinda. I'll finish it. But I'll send you word, first chance I can." He kissed Vesta and Jenny and Anne, and Julian too. "Take care of Mama, young'uns," he said cheerfully. "And here's another kiss for my Cinda."

"I'm sorry, Brett Dewain," she whispered, lips on his. "I just had to let go for a minute. Good-by, my dear."

Brett had been gone only a moment when Tilda appeared. She was half-weeping with fatigue. "Oh it's awful, Cinda," she said, dropping helplessly into the nearest chair. "Everyone's insane! We tried to parcel out the stores, but we were just overwhelmed by women and children and horrible men like things out of the sewers. They swarmed everywhere and helped themselves, swearing and fighting and wasting more than they took. And coming home—oh, it seems as though I'd been hours on the way—I saw women and even children, and men of course, drinking liquor out of the gutters and dipping it up in cups and pails."

"I'm glad you're home," Cinda assured her. "It will be worse before daylight. You must be starved, but we'll take care of that." She sent Vesta to bring hot coffee and biscuits and molasses, and she bade Julian take Anne upstairs and put her to bed. "Stay with her, Son," she said. "I expect we'll all go to bed pretty soon."

"I wish Papa were here," Anne confessed.

"He'll be here when you wake in the morning, darling."

So Anne let herself be led away, and Tilda too, but Vesta would not go. "Rollin may come," she reminded Cinda. "I want to be awake so I won't miss a minute." Cinda had no sleep in her, and Jenny stayed with them. They drew the curtains and sat in candlelight, talking in snatches; but a little after two o'clock Tilda called from the upper hall:

"Cinda! Cinda, there's a building on fire down near the river. I think it's Shockoe's Warehouse."

They parted the draperies and saw that dawning redness above the lower city; and then Cinda heard Julian's crutch and he came down to them. He could see three fires from his window, he said; and when he showed them where to look, they saw the mounting glare. But Cinda sent him back to Anne. "She might wake and be frightened, Son," she reminded him. As he went upstairs, Tilda in a wrapper descended; and they stood in the windows, too numb to be afraid, watching as below them the several fires merged into one, and the conflagration spread.

The door bell rang, and Vesta thought this might be Rollin and ran to open to him; but it was Judge Tudor, as haggard and tired as Tilda had been. He told them the fires had been set by General Ewell's men. "The gunboats on the river are to be burned, and the Armory and the machine shops and the tobacco warehouses," he explained. "Army orders. Mayor Mayo tried to persuade them not to do it, but they did. He's going out to the Yankee lines to surrender the city. The last of our soldiers will be gone by daylight." He asked: "Is Anne all right?"

"Fine," Cinda told him. "Julian's with her. I sent her to bed, and she's asleep. She was the bravest of us all."

"General Breckenridge has gone," he said. "President Davis, all the Government." He added: "General Hill was killed yesterday. They say he seemed to invite death, showed himself to the Yankees when he needn't."

"What will happen now, Judge Tudor? After the city is surrendered?"

He shook his head. "God knows."

Jenny said sensibly: "If I rest tonight, I can be more useful tomorrow, Mama." At Cinda's advice Judge Tudor also consented to go to bed; but though Vesta dozed in a chair, she would not go upstairs lest Rollin come. Tilda stayed too; and neither she nor Cinda slept that night at all. Toward the river the whole city seemed to be afire. The burning buildings threw up agonized arms of flame, and bright embers sailed like shooting stars across the sky. Canal Street, and Clay and Main must be all ablaze, and there were buildings burning as close at hand as Eighth Street. The wind bore embers this way. Cinda heard some sound overhead, and called Caesar to question him; and he said Big Mill was on the roof with pails of water to watch for burning brands. What went on in the hearts behind these black faces? Why were they loyal without bidding, even now, to those who had fought for four years to keep them enslaved? Did they welcome their coming freedom? Were their dark passions merely held in check, awaiting the hour of release? What horrors would Richmond see tomorrow when the Yankees came?

The fire crawled nearer, a sluggish patient beast that made no haste, devouring and digesting as it came. Before dawn Cinda heard a tremendous explosion, and then another and another, each seeming worse than the last; and the concussions shattered several panes of glass in the windows on the Franklin Street side. Cinda even in that moment noticed with a dull surprise that the broken glass had fallen out, not in. She called Caesar to bring something to stop the windows, to replace the broken panes. "We can't have all outdoors blowing in. Suppose it rained all over my beautiful carpet!" Vesta and Tilda laughed with her, and they all admired the ingenuity with which Caesar mended the damage. The explosions had waked Judge Tudor and he came down to join them; and Caesar finished, and silence was suddenly as awkward as an unwanted hush at a dinner table. Cinda made polite conversation.

"What do you suppose those explosions were?" She dropped the question at random, for anyone to pick up who chose.

Judge Tudor hazarded an answer. "I expect it was the ironclads in the river. I know they were to be set on fire. Probably the fire reached the magazines. And one of the blasts may have been the Armory. That's just down at the foot of Fifth Street."

Cinda nodded absently. How difficult it was to sit here and make conversation, with the end of the world going on outside! With Vesta and Tilda she could have been silent, but Judge Tudor had to be kept in play.

"I suppose no one was really surprised when the news came."

"The Government perhaps." He spoke resentfully. "You'd have thought evacuation was entirely unforeseen. No preparations had been made, no plans drawn. I believe a few boxes of records had been sent away, but that was all. Everything had to be improvised helterskelter, confusion thrice confounded. And of course after dark there was not even a pretense of keeping order. The mob took charge. The prisoners from the penitentiary got loose to lead them, and they broke into the stores, took everything they could carry away."

Tilda came into the conversation, reciting her experiences; she and the old man talked on and on. Vesta stayed near the front windows, watching always for Rollin to appear. Cinda sat limply, her head resting against the back of her tall chair, her eyes turning sometimes to Vesta, or to Tilda and Judge Tudor, but always swinging back to the windows against which the red smoky glare seemed to press close. At first dawn they heard another explosion at some distance, off toward the upper ravine of Shockoe Creek. That was probably the arsenal, the Judge suggested.

Day paled the fire's brightness, but a vast column of black smoke rising into the sky and mushrooming there spread a continuing canopy of darkness, spilling a rain of soot and sparks and burning embers, drifting on the light dawn wind. When the sun rose, Cinda saw it as a red disk through the curtain of smoke and flame that boiled upward from the conflagration only a few blocks away. Big Mill was still on the roof and she could sometimes hear him moving there; but if this southerly wind held, or freshened at all, the fire would inevitably come at full race toward them. They must be ready to escape if it were necessary, and standing at the window she began to think of waking the children, of giving them their breakfast, of preparing to hurry them away. Franklin Street was sprinkled with people, little knots of Negroes and of ragged whites scudding to and fro. People came up Fifth Street laden with loot. Now and then a horseman passed, or a wagon or a carriage, the vehicles always loaded. A rider came at a gallop up the steep ascent of Franklin Street, and as he passed her window Cinda recognized him.

"Here's Rollin, Vesta!" she called. Vesta raced to the door and they pressed after her. Rollin swung off his sweating horse to catch Vesta in the tight circle of his arm; and Cinda went out to where they stood in close embracing.

"Come in," she urged. "Long enough for coffee and a piece."

Rollin shook his head, never releasing his clasp on Vesta. "Can't," he said, panting with haste and with the heat of the fire so near. "I just came to see if you're all right. Yankees right behind us. We're about the last ones through town." He kissed Vesta, lifting her clear off the ground in that swift hard clipping. Then he leaped into the saddle; but Vesta still clung to his leg.

"Where will you go, Rollin?"

He laughed, with an upflung hand. "To the mountains!" It was like a battle cry. "You'll know where we are by hearing of the things we do!" He blew her a last kiss and spurred his horse away.

Instinctively Vesta followed him, running a few paces to the corner, pausing there; and Cinda came to her side. The smoke-shadowed dawn made all this familiar scene seem strange, unreal; yet it was the same. Down Franklin Street, with its graceful sycamores and elms, there was a confusion of shuttling figures and a din of hoarse shouts; and down Fifth Street, spurts of flame flashed through the smoke-fog toward the river. But here close by there was no smoke, and the trees were as graceful, the houses as substantial and secure, as in the past. Mr. Bransford's house diagonally opposite, where Dr. Hoge had lived till he moved down beyond the church; Mr. Ender's home, and Mr. Palmer's with its curious bay windows; down across Main Street Mr. Hobson's mansion almost concealed by trees, with its twin chimneys rising from the middle of the almost flat roof in dim silhouette against the smoke: all these Cinda had seen a thousand times, yet she saw them now as something never seen before.

Perhaps, if the fire swept this way, never to be seen again . . .

Rollin was gone; and suddenly a great throng of Negroes, drunk with liquor or with the first savor of freedom, came surging up Fifth Street from Main. Cinda drew Vesta indoors. "There, Honey. Now we'll think about breakfast." She closed the door, shut out the tumult in the street. "Then we'll see what comes next."

"Why, the Yankees come next." Vesta spoke serenely. "Rollin said they were right behind him. After breakfast I shall go to the commanding officer and ask for a guard for the house."

Cinda wondered at resilient youth. All their world, it seemed to her, was gone; but already Vesta began to think of salvaging what remained, already she began to build anew. Yet to be sure, this was as it should be, as it must be. Youth must build the future, build a new world upon the ruins of the old. She and her generation had destroyed that fine world that now was gone. By what faults and errors? By what deeds done or neglected? No one could surely answer. Most men did, in a given hour, that which seemed to them their honorable best to do. Yet, if the result of their deeds were now to be taken as the test, how unutterably wrong they had been! Youth might be wiser. Age was apt to chide youth for its follies, but surely there could be no more fatal folly than this of which mature men—yes, and women—had in these years been guilty. It was time for age to give youth full rein; time to give into youth's clean and valorous and eager hands the building of the years that were to come.

They breakfasted all together except Anne. June took a waiter up to her. The smoke made day so dark that they lighted candles. More explosions, some distant and some close at hand, woke cries and shouts in the street outside. Judge Tudor went out, but presently returned to say there were Yankee soldiers in Capitol Square, Negro cavalry.

"I went to ask for a guard for the house," he told them. "But they say one of you will have to go. The Provost Marshal is Colonel Manning, and his office is at City Hall; but he will not receive any petitions for guards except from ladies." Vesta was already on her feet as he added: "I think they mean to be courteous and helpful. They've put their own soldiers to try to stop the fire; and there are orders against disorder or pillage or insult. The sentries would not admit me, but there are already many ladies there."

Cinda went with Vesta on that errand, unwilling to stay longer hidden away indoors like a blindfolded criminal awaiting the deadly volley. They started down Franklin Street, where in the yards the flowers bloomed as brightly as ever, and they saw a guard of soldiers in blue in the yard of General Lee's house; but beyond, toward the Square, the street was littered with smouldering, half-burned papers; and other blue-clad men rummaged curiously in the rubbish, picking up fragments still legible, reading them aloud with shouts of laughter.

So these were the Yankee conquerors! Cinda shut her eyes tight, pressing back the tears. Looking down Seventh Street, she saw that toward the river the flames were not yet checked, and even at this distance heat touched her cheeks. The fire had reached up the hill to cross Franklin Street between General Lee's home and the Square, and the United Presbyterian Church seemed to have been burned. They turned up Seventh Street, Cinda blindly following Vesta's guidance, and came along Grace and up Ninth and along the head of the Square.

A throng filled the street and clustered in the shade of the tall trees that marked the front of the City Hall. Cinda had always thought this graceful building with its tall Doric columns and its wide steps the most beautiful in Richmond; but today there were blue uniforms on the steps and on the portico, the mounts of Yankee officers fast to the hitch rail under the trees. Yet though her eyes were blurred, she saw familiar faces in the throng, ladies here on errands like their own. Vesta spoke to a sentry; and Cinda saw with some faint stir of hope that the answers, though brief, were readily and courteously given.

Following the man's instructions, they made themselves part of a stream of petitioners, moving up the broad steps of the south portico and along a wide corridor with offices on either hand till they came into the circular central hall. Sometimes Cinda's eyes met those of ladies who were her friends; but their eyes like hers were blank with grief, and they exchanged not even a nod. When they faced a dozen uniformed Yankees seated at a long table, her ears were ringing so that she heard nothing that passed; and she stood in a trembling paralysis till Vesta touched her arm.

"It's all right, Mama. The Lieutenant is going home with us, to place our guard."

Cinda had to make an effort before she could clearly see the young man here at Vesta's side. She tried to speak to him but could not; yet she heard Vesta's voice, and his. They went along Broad Street, and he said something about avoiding danger from shells still bursting in the Armory. Negro soldiers in blue uniforms marched past them, and Cinda shivered; and then they were at their own door, and the young officer disappeared, and she and Vesta came into the hall together, and her senses began to clear.

"The guards will stay in the basement," Vesta explained. "The Lieutenant says we won't be disturbed. He says there'll be only white troops in the city tonight."

"Are we prisoners?"

"We can go anywhere we choose until nine o'clock, but after that we must be indoors."

To lose even this much liberty made Cinda treasure what was left; and after dinner she and Tilda walked along Grace Street toward Capitol Square till they could see the Stars and Stripes flying on the staff. The lower end of the Square was surrounded by burned and still smouldering buildings; and the Square itself was full of homeless people and heaps of salvaged furniture. They turned toward Broad Street and saw a troop of Negro cavalry. The men were singing as they rode, the rich voices blending in a jubilant harmony:

"John Brown's body lies a-mouldering in the grave."

John Brown? Cinda remembered that day at Great Oak so long

ago, when they heard the first news of the mad murderer's butcheries at Harper's Ferry. After that day, when loose-lipped orators in many a Northern pulpit canonized the maniac, men like Brett and Trav and Faunt first began to comprehend the storm of passion which the abolitionists had raised against the South. John Brown, the lunatic who dragged helpless men out of their beds and without even an accusation hacked them to death with sabres; John Brown more than any one man had let loose the forces which since then had slain how many thousands! General Lee and young Jeb Stuart captured John Brown, and judge and jury hanged him till he was dead, dead, dead; yet these Negroes sang the truth! His body for long years now had lain mouldering in the grave, but his blood-stained soul went marching on.

How long? How much longer? Clayton was dead, and Tommy, and Faunt; and Julian was maimed, and Burr's hands were things like claws. Brett was still whole and sound, yet how long would he go untouched? How long would he escape the blood bath with which John Brown's soul had sprinkled all her world?

The Negro soldiers sang, and the Negro mobs in the streets were singing. Well, let them sing, since they were free. She would never begrudge them their songs. It was not to keep them bound that Brett had fought. How few in the South had fought to keep their slaves! General Lee had freed his before the war. General Jackson had never owned but one, and he bought that one at the boy's own pleading. General Longstreet had inherited half a dozen, but he gave them away. For that matter, not one in ten of the men who fought these four years for the Southern land they loved had ever owned a slave or hoped to own one.

Why then had they fought so long and hard and wearily? She shook her head. What did it matter now?

In her abstraction, she and Tilda had become separated, and she came to her own door alone; but she heard behind her the cheering and the shouts, and the hard hoof beats of the horses and the singing of the Negro soldiers as they rode on toward Camp Lee.

The children were wide-eyed when they greeted her, and she mustered smiles to answer their many questions, and asked where Jenny was. Their mother was on the roof, they said, helping Big Mill put out the sparks that still landed there. Jenny presently came down, sooty but cheerful, to say the wind had changed and now swept the smoke the other way. "And the fire's burning out, I'm sure," she said.

They had early supper, and Vesta went out with Judge Tudor for the brief time permitted before nine o'clock; but sleeplessness and fatigue drove Cinda to her bed. Yet she did not sleep. From the direction of the Capitol she heard a band playing, heard the strains of *Annie Laurie* and then of the *Star Spangled Banner*. Vesta came to kiss her goodnight. "And everything is quieting down, Mama," she said reassuringly. "The Yankees stopped the fire from spreading. All the banks and newspaper offices and stores and hotels in that part of town are gone; but we'll soon build it up again." The young were so confident and sure.

Cinda fell asleep to the light touch of Vesta's caressing hand upon her hair. She woke early and surprisingly refreshed, and was dressed before June brought her breakfast. Judge Tudor wished to go to his own home to see that all was in order there, and Anne asked that some of her things be brought; so Julian and Judge Tudor and Cinda went to do that errand together. Before they started, they heard cannon firing at regular intervals somewhere toward Rockett's, and they hesitated, wondering what that meant; but when the guns fell silent they set out.

Fifth Street was almost deserted, but they had to pick their way through a throng on Broad. They turned along Marshall to Twelfth, and saw shuttered houses and drawn curtains. When they reached Twelfth, there was some tumult toward Capitol Square; and the street by the Governor's mansion, down the hill below their line of vision, seemed to be thronged, Negroes running that way. Before they reached Judge Tudor's house, halfway along the block toward the White House where President Davis had lived for these four years, a solid mass of Negroes came swirling past the Governor's mansion a short two blocks away, filling the street from side to side, flowing slowly toward them.

They went quickly indoors, but they waited to watch from the windows. The Negroes drew nearer, and Cinda heard their shouts and cries and snatches of song. Trees that lined the street made it impossible to see anything till the front of the throng was close at hand.

Then with a swifter-beating heart Cinda saw among them a figure easily recognized, an immensely tall, bearded man in a high hat, leading by the hand a boy.

Julian, in an incredulous astonishment, as though he knew the truth, asked: "Who's that?"

Cinda answered: "It's President Lincoln, Julian."

"Lincoln? But Mama, he hasn't any escort!"

Judge Tudor said quietly: "He has a thousand negroes; maybe five thousand. No one will harm him, not in their company."

Cinda wetted dry lips. Mr. Lincoln and the youngster whom he led by the hand walked in a little circle of emptiness; but all around him, in front and on either side and behind, the Negroes sang and prayed and shouted. They backed away before him; some, like toys actuated by a hidden spring, revolved in a slow, whirling dance; they came beside him, walking crab-fashion, their eyes never leaving him; they trooped like devoted dogs hard on his heels.

Directly in front of the window where Cinda stood, a woman ran to fall on her knees in his path; and Cinda recognized June! Old June bowed low before him, her palms on the ground, her forehead in the dust; yet she did not stay to impede his passing, but still on her knees shuffled to one side out of his path. Cinda saw her kiss, after he had gone, the ground where he had trod.

Mr. Lincoln went on to the corner of Clay Street and turned toward the entrance to the White House and disappeared; but the Negroes stayed in an increasing throng. Cinda's thoughts ran slowly. Those Negroes had worshipped Abraham Lincoln as thought he were God. Was that just hysteria? Through these four years, while their masters fought for a victory that would keep them slaves, the Negroes had shown no least desire to break their bonds. To be sure, a few rascally individuals had run away, a few had turned to thievery; but Cinda had heard never a rumor of any violence of slave against master, of Negro against white.

A thousand times and ten thousand she had heard Southerners assert that the slaves were the happiest people on the face of the earth. She herself had said it more than once, and had believed it true. But if they had been happy in servitude, why should they worship Lincoln now? Through the street outside the house, scores and hundreds of them, drawn by the rumor of his presence, were hurrying to do him homage, and lingering in the hope of catching a glimpse of that tall, ugly man.

Was it possible that the Negroes had always wanted to be free? Had June? June here had bowed down with the rest. Cinda had sometimes wondered about Negro men, trying to guess their thoughts, trying to read their dark and secret minds; but it had never occurred to her that June wanted to be free!

Would there be a change in June when they met again? Or would she ever see June again? After a time, a carriage and a military escort threaded the packed mob in the street, and she had another glimpse of Mr. Lincoln as he was driven away; and when he was gone the Negroes departed. Abstractedly she helped Julian select and pack what Anne would need; but she was still thinking of June. Why, she had loved that old woman! What right or reason had June to go bowing and scraping to Abraham Lincoln? Well, if June wished to be free, let her go. "I can do without her if she can do without me," Cinda thought, and found herself near tears. "She ought to be ashamed!"

At home she went at once to her room. To do so had in it something of a challenge; for June always came to help her get ready for dinner. Would she come today?

June did come, exactly as usual. Cinda was lying on the couch by the window. The old woman said, as she had said a thousand times in the past: "Set up heah, Missy, an' let me bresh out yo' hair."

Cinda obeyed, taking the stool in front of her mirror, watching June in the glass. June drew the pins and loosed Cinda's hair and took the brush; and Cinda said in a flat tone:

"You don't have to do that, you know! Mr. Lincoln's come."

"Bress Gawd! He sho is!"

"So now you're free," Cinda insisted. "So now I suppose you'll go along about your business!"

"Huh-uh!" June chuckled comfortably. "You ain' gwine git shet o' me, long as I got mah stren'th." She nodded, vigorously wielding the brush. "I tuk keer o' you befoah you uz dry behind de ears, Missy. Old Missy say I had tuh, and my mammy say I had tuh, so I had tuh! So I done it!" She looked at Cinda in the mirror. "But I don' have tuh tek keer o' you no moah, Missy. I does it kaze I wants tuh, now."

Cinda held June's eyes till her heart and her eyes filled and overflowed; and she laughed in rich content. "Well, you· don't have to pull my hair out by the roots, you clumsy old cow!"

June cackled with delight. "Yes, ma'am," she cried. "Clumsy cow I sho is. You b'en saying so twell it mus' be true. Neveh breshed you' hair sence you uz a baby dat you didn't fuss an' ca'y on! Ol' Miss Fussbudget, da's you!" She brushed harder, and they laughed together, two women, lifelong friends.

When Cinda came down to dinner the others knew that Mr. Lincoln was here. Tilda had brought home a copy of the *Whig*. "The Yankees are publishing it now. I thought you might like to see it."

Cinda shook her head. "No, thank you. I don't think I ever want to see a newspaper again as long as I live."

But Vesta took the diminutive paper, two pages of four columns each, and read a fragment here and there aloud. " 'The publication of the *Whig* is resumed with the consent of the military authorities. The editor and all who heretofore controlled its columns have taken their departure. The proprietor and one *attaché* of the editorial corps remain.' " And a moment later she said eagerly: "Listen! 'Several days will elapse, we suppose, before business is actively resumed. Still, there are stocks of goods in the city, and others will be introduced by loyal persons who may be authorized to carry on trade in Richmond.' So, Mama, we'll be able to buy things presently."

"Does it say anything about General Lee?" Cinda asked, but Vesta could discover nothing.

Cinda was to find the keenest agony of the days that followed lay in the fact that from Lee's army they had no news. Whispered rumors spoke of battle at Amelia Court House, and said Grant's hosts had been scattered in flight; but that was nonsense, not to be believed. A rumor equally incredible said President Davis had been captured and would be marched in chains through Capitol Square. They heard that when the shells in the magazine behind the Almshouse exploded, some of them hit the Almshouse and killed twelve of the poor people in it and injured many others. That might be true, but of the world outside, they heard nothing that could be believed at all.

Cinda seldom left the house. Tilda heard that many of their friends had nothing to eat; and from their own relative abundance they sent old Caesar with baskets to those whose need was great. Yankee sutlers had pitched their tents in Capitol Square with tempting wares displayed; but they would only accept greenbacks or gold. Vesta, hearing this, set the kitchen to making pies out of those dried apples they had brought home Sunday; and the soldiers who guarded the house readily paid for them a dollar apiece in greenbacks. Vesta gave the money to Julian to buy what he could.

Northerners were pouring into the city, doubtful womenfolk, and small traders who quickly reopened stores the fire had not destroyed, and stocked the empty shelves. Thursday, driven by hunger, some Richmond people were forced to appeal to the conquerors for food. They were given corn meal and salt fish, and were promised better fare as soon as it could be provided; and there would be ration tickets to be issued to those in need.

Friday a soft shower fell across the city, damping out the last smouldering embers in the burnt district to leave it a black and sodden waste; but Saturday was fine again, and Sunday was as beautiful as that other Sunday a week ago, which seemed now to belong to some long-forgotten age. They went to church; but the service, so long familiar, had one change: the prayer, instead of naming President Davis, was for all those having authority. Doubtless, the conquerors had required this. Cinda was glad after church to be once more at home, the door closed against the city that was no longer Richmond but a Yankee town.

Late that night they heard a sudden cannonade, the roar of many guns; but it was against the military regulation to leave the house after nine, so they could only guess the meaning of that uproar which went on for long. At dawn next morning the guns began again. This time they sounded at regular intervals, like tolling bells; but Cinda heard the bands playing, and shouting in the streets, and June brought her the explanation. General Lee had surrendered, with all his army.

After the first dreadful thrust of pain, Cinda's eyes filled with a gush of gladness. Now at last there would be a merciful end to battle and to starvation and to mutilation and to death; now Brett Dewain would come home, would come home to stay. Nations made wars and came to victory or to defeat; but it was men, dear beloved men, who fought those wars, and lived or died. That the Confederacy had lost was nothing to her now. For these four years she—or Brett—would have given life itself for victory; but that was a part of war's madness. Now she saw more clearly: Victory was nothing, defeat was nothing, as long as Brett lived and came safely home.

23

TRAV when the war began saw no possibility of Southern victory. There were six million white people in the South, twenty million in the North; say a million soldiers against three million. To boast that one Southerner could whip half a dozen Yankees sounded well, but of course it was not true; and even if it were true, the North could always draw new soldiers from Europe—thousands and tens of thousands—and the South could not. Figures, if you added them correctly, did not lie. The South could never hope to win.

But as the months passed, facts confounded figures. McClellan marched a hundred and twenty-five thousand men to the gates of Richmond, and Lee with little more than half that many drove McClellan in headlong flight. Pope had a hundred thousand men in Northern Virginia, and Lee with scarce fifty thousand shattered Pope. McClellan brought a hundred thousand men to Sharpsburg, but Lee with thirty-five thousand stood them off. At Fredericksburg a few thousand of Lee's men drenched the slopes in front of their position with Yankee blood. At Chancellorsville the odds were surely three to one against Lee, but look at the result!

Perhaps figures did lie! That grand march into Pennsylvania was a triumphant parade. At Gettysburg, it was true, Lee failed to win; but it was not a beaten army which returned to Virginia. Rather it was the Yankees who, after the punishment they took in those three days, for ten long months refused every offer of battle. When at last they did advance, Lee in the thirty days of the campaign from the Rapidan to the James killed or wounded or captured more of Grant's men than he had at any one time in his own command. Figures meant nothing, they could be ignored!

Trav did not finally accept the certainty of eventual defeat until one March day in this spring of 1865. When the swollen river forced Sheridan to march eastward north of the James, Fitz Lee came to strengthen the Richmond defenses; but after Sheridan was no longer immediately dangerous, the cavalry was ordered back to Petersburg. At the same time, Longstreet sent Trav with a dispatch for the commanding general; and on the way Trav encountered Fitz Lee's force, and he rode a while with Burr.

Burr was no longer a boy, but a haggard man with seldom smiling eyes; and he saw Trav's glance touch the gaunt horses and the worn-out riders. "There aren't many of us left, Uncle Trav." His voice was hoarse with dust and fatigue. "Hardly fifteen hundred. We were six thousand once."

Such figures, at least, were facts. "There were five thousand Texas cavalry in Virginia a year or two ago," Trav commented. "They're down to a hundred and eighty men now."

"If we had the riders, we couldn't mount them." Burr stroked his horse's neck. "This poor beast is so thin I hate to make him carry me."

"Longstreet thinks infantry might work with cavalry as they do with the guns, protect the horsemen till they're needed."

Burr's voice had no mirth in it. "Infantry protecting cavalry! General Stuart would laugh if he could hear that!"

"But Stuart's gone."

"Yes, he's gone. When Grant moves, we'll miss him."

Trav tried to speak cheerfully. "Perhaps we can keep Grant where he is, not let him move." But there was no conviction in his words, and Burr did not reply.

The cavalry was worn out, horses and men; but Trav before he found General Lee saw enough to realize that the infantry was worse. Longstreet's front was inactive, and the men there found some rest and food and modest comfort; but the Petersburg front was a rabbit warren inhabited by starved men apathetic with exhaustion. Trav went directly to General Lee's headquarters at Edge Hill, the Turnbull home on the plank road west of Petersburg. Lee had moved there late last November from the Beasley mansion on High Street in Petersburg. Before that, his headquarters had been north of the town, and Trav thought these removals told the story of the siege, for Lee moved always to confront his adversary. Each change resulted from some western extension of Grant's lines; each such extension meant that the dwindling Confederate army had a few more yards or a few more miles of front to cover.

At Edge Hill, Trav learned that General Lee had ridden to inspect the lines, and General Longstreet wanted an answer to his message, so Trav must find the commanding general. Thus he rode along the rear lines, and he saw to what straits the army was reduced. Soldiers sat like clods by the roadside; and many of them did not even lift their eyes to watch him pass. When they did look up, their faces were shrunken till the bones seemed about to break through the tight-drawn yellow skin, and their eyeballs were inflamed, and sometimes their lower lids sagged like the eyelids of very old men, revealing not a healthy pink but a faintly greenish hue on the inner membranes. Sometimes Trav saw them cooking their ration, a scant handful of meal and water mixed to a stiff consistency and laid on a board or a flat stone before the fire long enough to warm it through before it was gulped down. He saw men lying as though they were dead, looking like dead men since their bodies were shrunk to skin and bones and no longer filled out their ragged garments. Surely these soldiers could never muster strength to stand on their feet again.

That day at last Trav's heart surrendered. These men had done their utmost. It was not the Yankees who had beaten them. They were starved to the point of death. The end waited only till Grant chose his hour.

A few days later they had intelligence that Grant was withdrawing some of the force here in front of them on the north side of the James. "He will use them to overreach our right," Longstreet commented. "He's preparing to strike."

Trav's jaw set. "What then?"

"Why, if he shifts away from our front, we too can move, to meet his move."

"Leave this road to Richmond open?"

Longstreet nodded calmly. "Leave Richmond, yes. It's been a burden on our backs long enough." He was almost cheerful. "An army that travels light travels fast."

"Will you send Mrs. Longstreet back to Lynchburg? Mrs. Currain wants to go when Mrs. Longstreet goes."

"General Lee will give us due warning. They can go together when the time comes."

The hours were breathless waiting. Pickett's division was ordered to Petersburg, to extend the Confederate right and meet Grant's maneuver. They heard of Gordon's assault on Fort Steadman and its good early promise and its eventual collapse; but Trav felt no longer any emotion, either hope or fear. When on Thursday rain fell in a warm deluge, he heard men say this might clog Grant's movements; but the rain would not last forever.

Friday, since it was still raining, he rode into the city; and Enid told him that Mrs. Davis had fled away to safety, and asked when she and the children would go. Did he mean to leave them helpless here?

"Mrs. Longstreet is still here. You can go when she does."

Lucy said steadily: "I'm not afraid to stay here, Papa. Don't worry about us."

But Enid hushed her. "Don't talk nonsense, Lucy! We should have gone long ago."

Trav said: "I'll get you away if I can; but if I can't, you'll just have to stay."

Back at headquarters he learned that Pickett had driven the Yankee cavalry toward Dinwiddie Court House. That night Trav heard the rain slack and cease. The dawn was cloudy, but sun drove clouds and mist away. Toward seven o'clock in the evening, Trav and the others were with Longstreet when a telegram came from General Lee.

The big man read it with no change of expression. "General Lee wishes one of our divisions to report to him at Petersburg," he said calmly, and at once gave his orders. Field's division would march into Richmond; the quartermaster would ride ahead and have trains ready for them. To leave as many cars as possible at their disposal, he and those of the staff who had no other duties would ride direct to Petersburg, crossing by the pontoon bridge. When this had been explained, he called Trav aside.

"I think it likely," he explained, "that Richmond will be evacuated tomorrow. However, General Lee's dispatch goes no further than to summon one division. Will you, if you please, stay here and receive and execute any further orders from him or from me?" He hesitated. "I desire that you attend to orders first of all; but if you can then do so without neglect of greater things, you may be able to assist Mrs. Longstreet and your own family to a place on one of the departing trains."

So when Longstreet and the others of the staff rode away, Trav stayed behind. At full dark, Field's division began their march into the city, moving quietly so that the enemy might not discover their withdrawal. Off toward Petersburg there was the mutter of guns in a heavy night bombardment. Trav remembered that there were government stores in Richmond; and if the regiments still here were tomorrow to withdraw through the city to join the army in retreat, they could start with loaded wagons. He roused some of the quartermaster's men and directed them to harness their animals and take the wagons toward Richmond where they would be ready if the need arose.

Through that long night he slept little. Sunday morning was as serene as the fine Saturday had been, but still the empty hours marched slowly by. The enemy showed no activity; and Trav thought to have a word with Brett, and rode to where the Howitzer company was withdrawn behind the lines. Brett had gone into Richmond. The chaplain, Mr. White, was about to begin the morning service, and Trav wanted to stay, for surely this was an hour for prayer; but his place was at headquarters. On his return he found General Kershaw there; and General Ewell who commanded the Richmond defenses came in his carriage to join them. The loss of his leg at Second Manassas had not damped Ewell's fighting ardor; but in such hours as this when they could only wait, his lisp became more pronounced, he fretted, and mopped his high, bald brow; and his side whiskers and the heavy tuft upon his chin were kept in constant agitation by the movement of his jaws. In the first year of the war he had earned a reputation for picturesque profanity, but despite his restless anxiety his speech was mild today.

The morning was almost gone when at last the order came. Kershaw's division was to march as soon as possible, passing through Richmond; the cavalry and guns would follow at dark, using the pontoon bridge for the artillery and letting the cavalry retire by the most convenient way. Militiamen from the city would cover their withdrawal. The army would rendezvous at Amelia Court House.

Trav saw the generals depart to give their orders. Then, since he was no longer needed here he rode toward Richmond. He came into the city past Rockett's and up Main Street. A stir and tumult everywhere made it clear that the rumor of evacuation was already abroad. He made sure the wagons he had sent ahead were loading. A close-packed throng of ragged men and women were already gathering outside the storehouses, watching these proceedings with starved eyes and angry shouts. He spoke to the young officer in charge, asked how matters went.

"Why, well enough so far," the lieutenant assured him. "But I've had respectable gentlemen here offering me gold by the handful for a wagon and team. I think they did bribe some of my men, for we've lost a few wagons. That crowd's ready to rush us any minute. I can't do anything short of shooting, and I won't do that. Too many poor old hags in the mob. Look at their eyes, the way they watch the food."

The press of people jostled closer, and one woman shrilled an entreaty. "Throw me one of them hams, Mister, will ye?"

Trav spoke to them, loudly enough so that the nearest could hear. "We're taking these things to feed your soldiers. They can't fight on empty stomachs, you know."

The woman laughed in harsh derision. "Who's a-fightin'? The lot of them're running away." And a man shouted: "Leave 'em starve! They kin run faster with holler bellies!" Cries of angry laughter mocked Trav and the young lieutenant; and Nig fretted nervously among these seething people. Trav said in a low tone:

"Do what you can, Lieutenant. Get your wagons loaded and away. Make for Amelia Court House. And use your muskets if you have to. The men will need every ration we can give them."

He eased Nig through the crowd, holding the big horse steady against the hungry mob, and made his way to the Danville station. Soldiers were there, and he asked a question and was reassured. Yes, there would be cars to take the members of the Government away, and to transport what papers must be saved. There would be room for ladies, though within limits. Mrs. Longstreet? Certainly, and Mrs. Currain too; but they had better come and take their places as soon as possible.

Trav rode up Fourteenth Street and turned along Main. Mrs. Longstreet would be at the Spottswood. Main Street was packed with people, white and black, men and women and children. If he left Nig tied to the hitch rail, someone might try to steal him; but Trav saw an officer he knew, Captain Meriden of Hood's old brigade, with a wooden leg to replace one lost at the Wilderness, and explained his difficulty. The Captain said easily: "Certainly, Major. I'll hold a horse to help Old Pete's lady any time."

The colonnade along the front of the hotel was crowded, but Trav forced his way through. He found Mrs. Longstreet with other ladies in the hotel parlors; and he recognized familiar faces, the wives of cabinet members and officers of the Government. Mrs. Longstreet came to meet him smilingly.

"Well, Major?" She seemed completely calm.

"The army is to leave Richmond tonight," he told her. "The enemy will be here, I suppose, tomorrow. The General rode to Petersburg last night. I came to put you on the cars for Lynchburg."

"I'm quite willing to stay, if I'm a bother."

"No, there will be room on the cars, but you should go aboard as soon as you're ready."

Her eyes for a moment shadowed. "I was in church when Mr. Davis received the news. I suppose this begins the end." He did not speak, and she said, "My packing won't take long, Major Currain."

"I'll arrange some transportation, come as soon as I can."

"Why don't you go fetch Mrs. Currain and the children? Then we'll go together."

He was grateful for that permission. Nig was safe, though made nervous by the crowd. At home Big Mill met him. The Negro's eyes were rolling, but his voice was steady. Trav had given him instructions two or three days before, so Mill had a cart and two mules ready in the stable. Trav spoke a word of praise. In the house he found Enid pacing up and down among many bags and boxes, some closed and secured, some gaping open. Lucy and Peter were quiet, watching her; and Lucy smiled when he came in.

"Well!" Enid cried. "You finally got here! It's high time!"

"I'll put you on the cars," he said. "But not all this gear. You'll have to carry anything you take." That precipitated nervous tears, and a rising hysteria, but Trav silenced her. "You must come now, or else stay here."

Big Mill with the cart was at the door; Trav on Nig rode beside them. When they came down Eighth Street through the milling crowd, Enid was hushed with terror; but Trav found Mrs. Longstreet steady and quite composed. He and Nig opened the way for the cart down Main toward Fourteenth; and a man he had never seen before, dressed with a certain elegance, caught at his stirrup.

"I'll give you a thousand dollars gold for that cart, sir!"

Trav looked at him with contemptuous eyes. Probably this was a rascal like Redford Streean, who had made his fortune but whose greed had kept him here too long. Without a word he thrust Nig forward and the big horse shouldered the suppliant aside.

"Two thousand!" the other cried. "Three thousand, gold!" Trav did not turn his head. "Gold, man! Gold!" But the way was clear of him, the cart moved on. Trav saw Enid huddle closer to Mrs. Longstreet, staring at the famine-ridden throng through which they made their way; but Lucy's head was as high as Mrs. Longstreet's, her lovely face equally composed.

At the station Enid without a word scuttled into one of the cars, but Mrs. Longstreet thanked Trav graciously. "Tell the General not to be concerned for me. I will be in Lynchburg. I'll take care of Mrs. Currain." Then smiling at Lucy and Peter, she added: "The children and I."

Trav nodded, and Lucy hugged him close and kissed him fondly. "We'll be all right, Papa. You take care of yourself, won't you?" He helped them into the car, then turned back to Big Mill, who still guarded the cart and held Nig.

"You'll find soldiers loading rations at the store house," Trav said. "Give the cart to them. They can use it. Then come to Mr. Dewain's."

"Yas suh."

Trav's place now was with General Longstreet; but he went first to Cinda's and stayed till Mill came. When he rode down through town the sun had set and night was near. The crowd in the streets eddied and swirled, grudgingly making way for him. As he passed the station, a train was just departing. Perhaps Enid and the children were in those cars. Riding across Mayo's Bridge, moving slowly in the press of men and wagons, he watched the train crawl away up river and disappear in darkness. Some day, perhaps, they would all be together again. It was on Lucy his thoughts dwelt most of all.

In Manchester he saw some of General Ewell's regiments in motion. When he rode out along the Petersburg Turnpike he began to hear ahead of him, still miles away, the thunder of the guns; and occasionally he saw a flicker of light as in the gathering dusk a shell burst too high. The turnpike was crowded with a moving stream of refugees; carts and wagons and men and women and children riding and walking in a general frantic rush to escape from the doomed city, hurrying blindly anywhere at all, panting and stumbling through the darkness. Richmond tonight would be humming like a hive of disturbed bees.

He rode on toward Petersburg till about ten miles from Richmond he came to an artillery battalion crossing the turnpike and marching westward, under command of Major Stiles. The Major told him Mahone's division was ordered to Chesterfield Court House to cover the withdrawal of Kershaw and the others from the North Side, that Longstreet was marching westward from Petersburg by the Hickory Road.

If that were true, as it must be, there was no need to go to Petersburg; so Trav turned toward Chesterfield Court House. The night was dark and this countryside was strange to him, but the road seemed to ascend slightly over gently rolling ground, winding through woodland. After a few miles, he saw lighted windows in a large house to the right of the road, and turned aside to ask how he might best intercept Longstreet. The house was a miniature of Great Oak, wings a story and a half high connected by enclosed passages with the main central structure. He found frightened ladies there bravely pretending courage, and at his request they summoned an old Negro and bade him go with Trav and put him on the way.

With the Negro for a guide, Trav rode through the Court House and then took a byroad; and the Negro, trotting at his stirrup, kept him company while they crossed a wide level grown to pine and scrub oak and dipped into a ravine and splashed through a shallow brook. But Trav, in a hurry to rejoin his command, fretted at their slow pace. Could he not just follow this byway and surely come to the Hickory Road? The Negro assented so eagerly that Trav guessed the man had already reached the limits of the region he knew. Trav rode on alone, and the road wound its way across a rolling plateau and descended after two or three miles into a ravine where a larger creek was deep enough to splash his feet in the stirrups. Beyond, he came to a fork, and took the road that seemed most travelled, and this road descended into swampy ground and met another road at an angle. Many cart tracks and side roads confused his progress, and he sweated with weariness and bewilderment and haste. When at last he came to a highway filled with men and wagons and guns, he knew a vast relief.

To his question, a mounted officer told him this was Hill's corps. "Or what's left of it. General Hill's dead." He added grimly: "He had to relieve himself, turned into a patch of woods, ran into the Yanks. We're part of Longstreet's command now."

"Where is he?"

"Up ahead."

Trav rode on, thinking absently of Powell Hill who had done great deeds and now was dead. A halt came down the marching column, and the men fell out to rest; but Trav pushed ahead. At first dawn he saw a great leaping fire beside the road, and men sitting around it, and tethered horses among the trees near-by. He turned Nig that way and recognized Longstreet and secured Nig and went forward.

Longstreet greeted him cheerfully. "Well, Major, I think I would know the hoof beats of that black beast of yours, even in the dark. Glad you're with us again."

"I saw Mrs. Longstreet on the cars, General; saw the train start for Danville."

"Thank you. And Mrs. Currain?"

"Yes, sir."

"Was Kershaw on the move?"

"Yes, sir, and General Ewell too."

"Mahone's division has gone to Chesterfield Court House to cover them."

"I met them. They said that you were on this road. How far back is Petersburg?"

"We've done fifteen or sixteen miles since dark, in spite of the mud."

"I left Richmond at dark. I must have ridden twenty-five or thirty miles." Trav added in half question: "It seems a long time since you started for Petersburg Saturday."

Longstreet nodded. "Yes. We reached General Lee's headquarters before day. His rheumatism is severe again; he had not risen. I reported to his bedside. He said our right, Pickett and Fitz Lee, had been crushed. He at first directed me to march to bolster the right; but while I was still with him, word came that our lines in his immediate front were broken. By that time it was light enough so that from his front door we could see the Yankee skirmishers moving across the open toward us." The bearded man hesitated, said sadly: "He asked me to stop them; but the trains bringing Field's division had not yet reached the Petersburg station. Luckily, Benning came up with his Rock Brigade. He had only six hundred men, but they checked the Yankee skirmishers; and at Fort Gregg it cost 'Lys Grant seven or eight hundred casualties to overcome our handful in the Fort. That gave us delay till night, saved us from being broken into fragments then and there."

"What now?"

"Why, a race to round their left and turn south and unite with General Johnston. We marched all night on empty stomachs, and we've nothing for breakfast, so this will be a hungry day; but General Lee has ordered a trainload of supplies to meet us at Amelia Court House. Thinking about that will help." He rose. "It's time to take the road."

Their orders were to cross the Appomattox at Bevill's Bridge, and they pressed on at the best pace the half-starved men could muster. The winding road was all up and down, the hills neither long nor arduous yet by their monotonous persistence wearisome. When after a ten-mile march the head of the column descended toward the river, they saw flooded lowlands. The water was across the road; and the picket riding in advance came splashing back to report the bridge impassable.

"Impassable?" Longstreet demanded. "It's there, isn't it?"

"Yes, General; but a horse would have to swim to reach the nigh end of it."

Longstreet grunted angrily. "Well then, we'll have to go up river to Goode's." It was impossible to march the men through the tangled bottoms along the river, so the column doubled on itself, a courier bore orders to the rear, and they returned a mile or two to the first fork and took the road, deep with mud, that paralleled the river.

When at dusk they reached Goode's Bridge, Gordon's brigades and trains were already crossing there, and they must wait their turn. All that night the bridge creaked and bobbed under men and guns; but Tuesday morning, with Yankee horsemen on their left keeping the column in view, so that the men had to be constantly alert against a sudden thrust, they pushed on.

Longstreet raged at the delay. "A few more such disasters and we'll lose the race. If Grant guesses what we're up to, he has the shortest road to cut us off. We got a day's start yesterday, but we must hold it to get through Burkville before he can intercept us there."

Trav knew Burkville, the junction of the South Side and the Danville railroads. "We'll be in Amelia Court House this afternoon. That's halfway there."

Longstreet muttered something Trav could not hear. The march that day was easier, and he thought this was fortunate. Few of the men had eaten anything since Sunday morning, and they were weak with hunger, and lagged easily. But there would be rations waiting at Amelia Court House, and once their stomachs were full they would be fit for anything.

When they rode into the Court House, General Lee was there before them, and Trav saw Longstreet meet him and heard Lee's word.

"The rations are not here, General," Lee said. His head twitched sidewise in the way he had when he was angry. "The train came here as ordered, and it was fully loaded; but it was summoned to Richmond to bring off the personnel and records of the Government and did not wait to unload the cars." He added gravely: "But the men can do no more without food, so we must stop and collect what provisions there are in the neighborhood."

The commanding general spoke no word of blame for that error; but General Longstreet, when he turned back to give orders for foraging, was not so restrained, and his anger infected them all. Grant's men would have moved at once in hard pursuit to make up the lead which the hard-marching Confederates had won, but now that lead would be lost while every horse and every wagon and every available man was put to the task of gathering food from the nearest farms.

They worked in a hard rage, damning the delay; and Trav heard from angry men a dozen stories to account for the failure of supply. No one knew who gave those orders for the train to go on to Richmond, but Trav felt that he must share the guilt. Perhaps this was the very train upon which Enid and the children had escaped. Probably the rations had been dumped off the cars at Richmond and abandoned there, to make room for fleeing refugees. He worked in a passionate zeal, to atone for as much of the fault as he must share; but he heard Mr. Davis damned on every side by famished soldiers, and by sweating muleteers who cursed their animals and the President of the Confederacy with an equal eloquence. To save his own neck from a stretching, they said, old Jeff Davis would let the men who for four years had fought for him starve on their feet, while he scuttled like a scared hen to the safety they could never hope to reach.

Trav did not seek to silence them. Rage might make them forget their hunger. Most of the foragers returned empty-handed, since this countryside had long since been combed clean to supply the lines around Petersburg. The corn cribs offered the only substantial contribution. The lucky regiments received an issue of two ears of dry corn on the cob per man. They parched it, and added salt if they had salt, and put it in their pockets to chew as they went on.

They were almost twenty-four hours at Amelia Court House. A little after noon on Wednesday, they marched toward Burkville in a doubled column. The road was muddy, but the railroad right of way was seductively level, with cuts through the low hills, and fills to cross the swampy bottoms; and the men, seeking the least arduous footing, abandoned the highway for the railroad. Trav saw where here and there wooden beams faced with strap iron had been used to replace wornout rails. Even the railroad was starved!

They pushed on toward Jetersville, till the advance reported that enemy skirmishers barred the way; and the columns halted while General Lee rode to survey the situation. Since the region was strange to them all, and no maps were available, Longstreet set Trav and others to find someone who knew the countryside and the available near-by roads; but beyond their own door yards and their immediate surroundings, none of the men and women to whom Trav talked knew more than he. By the time he reported this to General Longstreet, Lee's decision had been made. Rather than risk an attack on the enemy in their front they would seek a way around.

As Longstreet countermarched, rain began to fall. They turned off by the road to Amelia Springs. Longstreet had said they must reach Burkville before Grant barred the way; but now, miles short of Burkville, Grant had forced them to another northerly detour. Presently a word from Longstreet let Trav understand that this same thought was in the other's mind.

" 'Lys Grant has moved fast. He's a better guesser than I thought, unless he's heard somehow what we meant to do."

"He's across our road to Burkville," Trav agreed.

Longstreet looked at him with hard eyes. "No matter," he said gruffly. "Farmville will do as well." But Trav knew this was not so. Farmville was on the road to Lynchburg, and that road led west, not south to General Johnston.

They found Flat Creek at a flood stage, with water out over the road on either side of the creek itself; and the bridge was shaky. Infantry could use it, or could wade the creek; but wagons and artillery must wait till the bridge was strengthened. Trav was left to see to this while the leading divisions pushed ahead.

It was dark and the rain had ceased when Trav rode through Amelia Springs. Once, long ago, he had come here with his mother, when she desired to take the waters. In those days, Otterbein Lithia Water was famous, bottled and shipped all over the world; but the Springs were no longer a resort, the hotel was abandoned, even brick buildings were falling into ruin.

At the Springs and beyond, Trav found dangerous congestion. The army's trains, almost a thousand wagons, had left Amelia Court House with orders for Burkville, and using every available road. But since Grant forced a change of plan, Farmville was now the goal; and this meant confusion. Worse, Yankee cavalry had caught some wagons in the swampy ground along the creek on the road to Painesville, and burned them and blocked that road for hours. Now, guns and wagons marching by the route Trav followed encountered another column entering the same road short of Deatonville; and a mass of men and mules and horses shouldered each other along the narrow way.

The mud was deep and the night was raw with the threat of rain to come. The wagons moved slowly with many halts, the men stumbled wearily in the blackness. Trav, to give them room, kept Nig off the road, picking his way through the fields and woods; and the big horse was nervous, catching by infection the tension of haste and fear and weariness and hunger and bewilderment which bound the trudging men. Trav, himself blinded by the darkness, gave Nig his head; for there were flankers out against any sudden rush of enemy cavalry, and when the column halted for even a moment, worn-out men moved off the road and dropped in their tracks. Nig could be trusted not to step on them.

Trav heard officers shouting to awaken these sleepers, and he thought some would be hard to wake, would need to be shaken, or dragged to their feet. He knew that if he surrendered to slumber, no ordinary outcry would rouse him. Even Nig was tremulous, as much with fatigue as with tight nerves.

Into that dreadful plodding, that sleep-walking nightmare, burst sudden tragedy. A man lying in exhausted sleep a little off the road, his dreams disturbed by Nig's passing, uttered a terrible strangled cry and let off his gun. At that flash almost under his nose, the great horse bounded to one side so violently that Trav was almost unseated. Nig crashed into a fence; and even in the darkness Trav saw another horse, tied to the fence, rear high with a scream of terror and the splintering of breaking wood, and then plunge full gallop along the road jammed with men.

Trav brought Nig under control, but ahead of him the other horse was running through the scattering soldiers, the fragment of rail to which his reins had been secured flailing against his heels; and there was a clamor of shouts, and then screams of pain, and then sudden bursts of musketry. Instantly, in the black confusion, guns were going everywhere, in disorderly but deadly volleys. Nig was wild, and Trav fought to control him, and felt the twitch of a bullet pluck his sleeve, and knew himself the target of some of that fire. He swung Nig away into the cover of the trees and brought him to a halt and heard along the road behind him rapid firing still continue, and the shouts of officers trying to steady the men. There came a brief hush, and he could hear the voices, the excited harangues; and then at some new alarm the men along the road broke down the fence with a universal rush and came running toward the wood where he was, firing back toward the road as they ran.

It was dread of enemy cavalry which had wrought them to this pitch. Sight of Trav and Nig would fan them to a higher frenzy; so Trav guided Nig straight away from the road, and risked a gallop through the scrub oak and dwarf pines, till behind him the firing dwindled and died down and silence came again. He rode on in bitter grief. Not all those bullets could have gone astray. Many must have found human flesh; more than one man must have died in that medley, friend killing friend with no enemy near. But night was a time for panic. Even strong men knew in darkness fears which daylight banished. How much more easily, then, would phantom fears infect these starved skeletons of men whose valor for four years had shone so bright! They could be forgiven. Whatever errors they might now commit could not wipe out the great deeds they had done.

Trav came up with the advance and reported to the General. Approaching dawn brought a new sprinkle of rain that retarded coming day and shrouded everything in a gray veil. It fretted them all, as strands of spiderweb may fret one who walks through an untrodden wood, wetting them a little and a little more, forming drops on cheek and beard. Longstreet called a halt. Rest must take the place of food, yet they could not rest for long.

With first light, the General and Trav and a few others, leaving orders for the men presently to follow, rode on toward Rice's Station. They came to a considerable creek, now at the flood and out of its banks. The road crossed by a rattling bridge of poles and then climbed steeply, circling the heads of deep ravines where little streams were born to work their devious way northward to the Appomattox, keeping to high ground where in the forest dogwoods were showing their first bloom.

When they reached the crest above the valley in which the railroad ran, the drizzle had ceased and the skies began to clear. Longstreet waited there for Field's division to come up, and they rode with the head of the column down the long hill. At the Station, the advance encountered a light force of enemy infantry and scattered them; but a householder reported that several hundred Yankees had gone toward Farmville. They might burn the bridges which the army must use, so Longstreet sent Rosser's cavalry to overtake those Yankees and destroy them. He put his arriving divisions into position to meet any threat from the south, and waited for word from General Lee.

General Rosser returned to report the enemy scattered, the bridge at Farmville safely held; and Trav recognized Burr among the troopers and had brief word with him. "All right, Burr?"

Burr nodded. "But I could sleep a week." His tones were dull. "Have you seen Papa? Or Rollin?"

"No. I saw your mother in Richmond. They're all right. At least, they were then."

"Has Sherman taken Raleigh?"

Trav guessed Burr's thought, for Barbara was in Raleigh. "I don't know." Burr moved on, trotting his tired horse to overtake his comrades.

Before that day ended, Longstreet's divisions, with screening cavalry watching the growing enemy strength on the road from Burkville, were well concentrated; but there were no rations for the men. Trav heard that General Lee, having stayed the night before at Amelia Springs, had come up with them; but he did not see the commanding general. He was with Latrobe when a little after dark on Thursday Longstreet summoned them to say they must move on.

"There was some hope of turning south from here," he said. "But enemy columns are coming up the Burkville road." He directed Latrobe to draft the orders: trains and batteries to start at once for

Farmville; Field, Heth, Wilcox to follow in that order; the skirmish lines to give the last division an hour's start; Rosser's horsemen to protect the rear. "And every effort must be made to bring along stragglers, and to wake every man who may have fallen asleep."

Latrobe asked: "Where is Anderson? He should have been up hours ago."

"General Lee has taken Mahone's division back to find him. They will march to High Bridge while we move to Farmville. Give the orders; then we will ride ahead with the trains."

A little after ten o'clock they mounted; but they found the road jammed with halted wagons and guns, and rode along the column through the darkness to find where the trouble lay. The bridge over Sandy Run had proved too weak to support a heavy load; and Longstreet set men to unload ammunition wagons and limbers and thus lighten them so they could cross. The ammunition must be carried over and reloaded on the other side. Trav and the others of the staff shared in that work, wading the shallow river to their boot tops; and Trav thought his arms would crack under the heavy burdens, yet found resolution to keep on. Longstreet damned the useless arm that prevented him from working as hard as they; and he damned the bridge and the river and the toiling men, lashing them all alike with a steady and picturesque profanity which made them grin, even while they winced under his bruising tongue.

Not till near dawn was that hard task done. When at last they rode on toward Farmville and came to another bridge and to a third a mile beyond, Trav was profoundly grateful that these bridges were equal to the tasks imposed, so those hours of toil need not be again endured.

In Friday's first daylight, they rode through Farmville and across the Appomattox, and they found wagons loaded with rations which had been brought by the South Side Railroad from Lynchburg. The starving men swarmed around the wagons, and little cooking fires sent smoke banners drifting gently upward toward the threatening sky; but Trav, more tired than hungry, sought a patch of new-springing grass where Nig could graze, and himself lay flat along the ground and was instantly asleep.

Yet not for long. A sudden stir waked him, and he saw General Lee ride at a trot to where Longstreet was standing. Trav rose and led Nig, reluctant to leave the good grass, plucking a last mouthful as he yielded to the tug of the reins, toward the group surrounding the commanding general; and he heard General Lee's words. There had been disaster yesterday at Sayler's Creek, back beyond Rice's Station. Trav thought that must be the creek which they had crossed on the pole bridge, before they climbed to the ridge where dogwoods were in bloom. General Lee was saying that there or thereabouts, the rear under Ewell and Kershaw had been cut off and captured; seven or eight thousand men were lost. Worse, the enemy cavalry was now across the Appomattox at High Bridge, and coming up on their flank.

"So you had better not let your men wait to eat their rations," General Lee directed. "We must move toward Cumberland Church, and at once."

Trav had never heard of Cumberland Church, but the guns were going behind them, south of Farmville, and there was firing off to the east; so once more the enemy was edging them north again, away from the course they wished to take. He was dumb with weariness and hopelessness; but if Longstreet was shaken by this new blow the big man gave no sign. At his orders the hungry men fell in, gnawing at raw pork and gobbling meal mush which there had not been time to cook. Everything else was thrown into the wagons any way at all; the teamsters caught the infection of haste and whipped their teams away; the columns formed and began to move. From the Farmville bridge, the protecting screen of horsemen came pell-mell toward them before a thrust of blue cavalry; and Longstreet's great voice boomed above the sound of musketry, the cracking whips and the rumble of the wagons.

"Quick—march!" he ordered. Trav saw Lee speak to him; and though the men struck off as briskly as tired men could, he roared a new command. "Double quick—march!" The men obediently began to jog.

Longstreet sent Heth to support the cavalry. General Lee rode on at a canter to the head of the column; but Longstreet waited till the rear was moving, then followed at a walk. Trav, half asleep in his saddle, heard in remote indifference the steady chatter of Heth's musketry diminishing behind them. From a hilltop a mile north of the river there was a distant view to the eastward, back toward Petersburg; and to the northwest he saw a little group of bold heights not far away, and he glimpsed the distant mountains. When they had gone two or three miles, there was another halt to meet a Yankee thrust against their flank along a crossroad that came in past some coal pits. Mahone's division went that way, with cavalry to help him meet the danger; the infantry halted to be ready for any need while the trains went on.

The long day was for Trav a troubled dream. Without the relief of action, he could only wait. That pressure against their flank held them here till dark; then they took up their march and pushed on for hours. At the halt, Trav slept without waking till sun burned away the morning mists. When its full rays struck across his eyes and he roused, the weary men were already on the move; but he saw General Longstreet and Colonel Latrobe and two or three others at breakfast, sitting around a fire by the roadside. He stopped to get a bit of salt pork and a slab of corn bread, and then joined them. General Longstreet said, speaking so quietly that none but the immediate group could hear:

"I've been telling these gentlemen, Major, that 'Lys Grant sent in a flag last night, inviting surrender." Trav, his mouth full, stopped chewing; then began again. "The commanding general asked my opinion. I said the time had not yet come."

Trav found that he was trembling, not with fear but with fatigue. His weakness was a hateful thing, and he hid it as he could. He watched Longstreet, and wondered that any man in such an hour could appear so steady and unshaken. He himself felt old and broken and no longer capable of anything. He saw the same dark weariness in the others of the staff, in the soldiers, in the very horses cropping sparse grass and too weak to move from one tuft to the next without a pause and an obviously painful effort.

His breakfast done, he found Nig and took a handful of last year's dead broom sedge and wiped the caked mud and sweat off the big horse's flanks; and Nig nuzzled him affectionately. Trav returned to General Longstreet. Colonel Latrobe, who was Chief of Staff since Moxley Sorrel had been promoted to become a brigadier and to take an almost fatal wound in front of Petersburg, departed on some business of command; and Longstreet said affectionately:

"Well, Currain, you look better since your breakfast."

"I'm ashamed to be so worn-out," Trav confessed. "I'm beaten down, no more strength left in me."

Longstreet spoke in an impersonal, reflective tone. "I'm rarely tired."

"You never seem tired," Trav agreed. Then he turned at the sound of an approaching horseman; and General Pendleton rode near, dismounted, dropped the reins over his arm and approached them.

Longstreet greeted him courteously, and Trav rose and moved aside. Beyond hearing, he watched them speak briefly together; but General Pendleton did not sit down, and General Longstreet did not rise. When Pendleton rode away, Trav returned; but at once he felt a surging anger in the big man; and after a moment, thinking the other might prefer to be alone, he was about to leave him. But Longstreet said gruffly: "Sit down! Sit down!" Trav obeyed; and after a moment Longstreet seemed to laugh to himself, and without looking at Trav he said: "If I hadn't other business in hand I should have called him to account."

He seemed to invite a question. Trav asked: "What was it, sir?"

"Why, if you please," said Longstreet scornfully, "some of our general officers believe we should surrender this army, and Pendleton came to ask me to convey their opinion to the commanding general!" He added: "I assured him that if General Lee didn't know when to surrender without my volunteering the information, he would never know. Pendleton said he would go to General Lee himself; and I told him that if I were in command and he brought me such a message I would invoke the Articles of War and have him shot!"

Trav did not speak, for he knew guiltily that he too believed the hour for surrender had come. Longstreet after a moment reflected: "I was perhaps too blunt; so doubtless I have made an enemy of General Pendleton—as if we hadn't, all of us, enough enemies on our hands just now. But such men as he are good haters. If the chance ever comes, he will do me an injury one day."

Latrobe returned. "The road will soon be open for us, General," he reported.

The march that day was along a road deep in mud, and through a forest of pines with rare small openings on either side, and past shabby cabins where fields had been worked to exhaustion and abandoned. Everywhere along the road they saw silent evidence that this mass of men was no longer an army. They passed wagons broken down and abandoned, guns mired and left hub deep in mud, muskets and cartridge boxes thrown aside by men too tired to carry them further. They passed human debris, too: men who had marched a hundred miles in these six days with no more than an occasional handful of corn to eat, till they fell in their tracks and could only drag themselves to the roadside and lie helpless there. Trav remembered that for almost a year, in the trenches in front of Petersburg, these men had been on short rations. There had rarely been even one day when they could eat their fill, through all the weary winter that was done. It was little wonder that after a week of marching and fighting, marching through mud ankle-deep and which clung to their broken shoes so stubbornly that even with a stick it was hard to scrape it away, they should at last collapse. Many of them lay like dead men, and half a dozen times Trav saw men who surely were dead; and once he dismounted to examine a gaunt boy with long, fair hair, whose open eyes stared upward at the sky. The boy was dead, though with no wound on him; dead of hunger and fatigue, dead of a broken heart.

He was not the only one. Trav counted a dozen along that dreadful road where the abandoned wreckage of the army, as explicitly as a white flag, confessed defeat.

That day the enemy pressed them hardly at all. The column moved slowly, for worn-out horses were barely able to drag wagons through the stiffening mud of drying roads. The eternal trees that walled the road, shutting out any distant view, seemed to Trav to make the ordeal even more terrible. Once from a gentle rise beyond New Store they saw, through the notch which the road cut in the woods ahead, distant mountains far away; and sometimes they caught glimpses of three low wooded peaks rising against the sky a few miles to the right. But for the most part they might as well have been making a night march, trudging blindly on. There were no crossroads. The Yankees were coming on behind them in countless hosts. None knew what force might wait to bar their way ahead.

Their thinned ranks, before night, were somewhat recruited. The woods were full of stragglers from the head of the column whom exhaustion had forced to drop behind, or of men from units which had been crushed and scattered. All the long day these men came out of the fringing forests, some with muskets and some without, begging for any scrap of food. Promises, or the gift of a bit of bacon or a crust of corn bread, drew them into the column; so that at dusk Trav thought the First Corps was by hundreds stronger than when the day's march began.

A little before sunset, they overtook an artillery battalion which had drawn off the road, and the commanding officer came to speak to them. "I'm Colonel Hardaway, General," he reported. "I regret, sir, that we can go no farther. Horses and men are exhausted."

"All your horses, Colonel? All your men?"

"Most of them."

Longstreet said gently: "Very well. Abandon the guns you cannot move. Bury them and cover their graves with leaves, so those people won't find them and use them against us. Bring on what you can."

Before Colonel Hardaway turned aside, Trav asked: "Aren't the Third Richmond Howitzers in your battalion, Colonel?" And when the other said yes, Trav asked Longstreet's permission to delay a moment here. "Brett Dewain is with the Howitzers," he explained.

Trav found Brett slumped beside his gun, and they had a few minutes together. Brett said Cinda and the others were still safe when he left Richmond. "But I don't know what's happened to them since. We saw a great glare in the sky, toward morning; and some refugees said the whole city was on fire. The Yankees weren't there, not then. I suppose General Ewell burned the warehouses, and the fire spread."

Trav nodded. Richmond was in another world. "Are you all right?" he asked.

Brett laughed feebly. "My jaws and gums and teeth are sore from chewing parched corn. It's all we've had since Tuesday, and damned little of that. And my feet are blistered raw. We marched to Branch's Church Sunday night; walked, for fear we'd break down the horses. It seems to me we've done nothing since then but march—or run. Cavalry began to cut at us as soon as we passed Amelia Court House.

Day before yesterday they really scattered us. Then yesterday we got into a hellhole of a swamp, and the drivers cut the traces and galloped away." He added grimly: "Oh, not all of them of course. We saved some guns, to lug them this far and bury them here."

"It's almost over, I suppose."

Brett nodded. "I suppose so. It's hard to see how we can go on."

Trav said: "I saw Burr at Rice's Station. He is—tired, of course, and worried about Barbara, with Sherman so near Raleigh."

The sun was low; the day had been gentle and cool, with a fine soft breeze. "They've let us alone today," Brett said.

"They're just herding us north, keeping us away from Johnston's army. That's all they have to do." Brett did not speak, and Trav looked all around. The oak trees were in tassel, spring was on the flood. "I saw a wild turkey in the woods a while ago," Trav remarked; and he rose stiffly, sore muscles lame and aching. "Well, I'll have to go," he said. They clasped hands and he climbed into the saddle and rode away.

The sun was near its setting. Trav passed a roadside church and went on, and the western sky burned red with bright glory and then paled as night came down. When Trav overtook Longstreet, the General asked: "Well, did you see Mr. Dewain?"

"Yes, sir."

"Good!" Longstreet fell into abstracted silence, their horses plodded wearily through the night. Trav mustered strength to speak.

"They haven't hit us today."

Longstreet made a half-mirthful sound. " 'Lys Grant's giving us a chance to think things over."

"Did we burn the bridges at Farmville? That would slow them."

"Alexander burned them, yes. A little too soon. Fitz Lee wasn't across, but he found a ford upstream."

"I don't see how the men keep going."

"Every man has untapped powers. No one knows what he can do till he's tried to the uttermost. There's an exhilaration in doing something you didn't know you could do. A horse will founder itself. Once a man is tired enough, his own exhaustion feeds his spirit, and he will march himself to death."

"Some of the men have done it today, and before today."

Longstreet did not speak. After a long time, trains at a halt clogged the road ahead, and Longstreet said: "Well, it's eleven o'clock. We might as well bivouac here. The men had better be prepared to meet some pressure from the enemy at dawn. I'll ride on and find the commanding general."

Trav and the others stayed behind. When Longstreet returned, the headquarters tents were pitched, the fires burning, pork broiling over the flames. No one questioned him, but after he had eaten he spoke to them.

"Well, gentlemen, our advance is near Appomattox Station, five or six miles ahead." He reflected, half to himself: "Two years ago this army with its trains would have made a column sixty miles long. Now, from front to rear, we're strung along a scant six miles of the Lynchburg pike." No one spoke, and he said: "General Lee's headquarters are a mile or two ahead, and General Gordon is close to Appomattox Station. He thought there was no one in front of him; but some Yankee cavalry hit Walker's guns about nine o'clock, and captured some of them and drove them back on Gordon. Gordon says he has only some two thousand men in hand. His stragglers have been falling back all day, some of them to join us. We're the body of the army now."

Trav asked: "What will we do?"

Longstreet said calmly: "Why, bivouac, sleep, wake tomorrow, and march on."

"To what?" Trav persisted, in dull rebellion at this long futile folly.

"To whatever waits, Major. We will march till we find some barrier we cannot break." The big man's tone hardened. "And then we'll break it, if our orders so direct."

Trav nodded, moving wearily aside. He led Nig to a patch of new grass to let the big horse crop what he could. Away from the fire, darkness settled smotheringly down, and Trav hated the night. They had been groping in the dark for days, plodding along unfamiliar roads where the mud was churned deep under their laboring feet, threading their way among monotonously similar hills and valleys, seeking always to turn southward but finding always those blue-clad men across their path. This army was like a penned animal running along beside a fence in search of any opening and finding none. It was breathless with its own haste to be free, and exhausted by its many failures.

He could not rest; and at last he mounted and went slowly toward the front. The road he followed was a congestion of wagons halted either in the road itself or in park just off the highway; and soldiers slept or sprawled in limp exhaustion or sat in muttering groups among the trees on either side.

He came after a little to a clearing, and saw in the moonlight a building beside the road, and heard men's voices and a word or two. Half a dozen men were sitting in talk on the steps of the building. He thought it a church and asked a question. Yes, this was New Hope Church, they said. He caught a sardonic amusement in the voice of the man who spoke; and he remembered with a curious pang that there was a New Hope Church not far from Chimneys, on the road to Martinston.

"Where is the advance?" he asked.

"Two or three miles ahead."

Trav moved on. After a mile or so the road descended steeply and then climbed to the crest of a low ridge and then descended gradually into more open land. He saw scattered campfires in the valley below him; and he saw other campfires burning on the opposite heights. A group of horsemen came up the road toward him, and he spoke to one of them.

The officer was of Gordon's staff. He said those fires yonder on the heights were Gordon's men. "But if you were there, you could see Yankee fires beyond." General Lee had summoned General Gordon; they were riding back in obedience to that summons.

The officer went on to overtake the others, but Trav rode slowly down the hill. Nig's hoofs woke hollow echoes from a bridge across a little stream. Up the hill beyond lay a village, with a courthouse around which the road divided and then united to become one road again and to go on toward the west. Gordon's men were there; and beyond, at no great distance, fires marked the enemy lines.

Trav needed to ask no questions. Their situation was clear enough. With the enemy across their front, and the enemy pressing their rear, they were hopelessly penned. Lee's great Army of Northern Virginia, that army which for almost a year had manned forty miles of defenses against all the force Grant could bring to bear, was now just a weary huddle of exhausted, hungry men.

Trav rode slowly back toward Longstreet's bivouac, scarce heeding his surroundings; but half a mile or so beyond the stream, and a little off the road to the right, he saw a small fire burning. Beside it stood General Lee; and Longstreet, puffing at his pipe, sat on a log across the fire. Trav recognized Gordon and Fitz Lee. Peyton Manning and Colonel Latrobe were at the roadside, too far away to overhear the group in council there, and Trav paused with them.

After a time, Gordon and Fitz Lee departed, and Longstreet came to where Trav and the others waited. Manning had the General's horse; and Longstreet mounted before speaking. "There is cavalry, and possibly infantry, across our road ahead," he explained, as casually as though he spoke of posting sentries. "Gordon and Fitz Lee will brush them aside, as soon as it is light enough for work; and we'll march east by Campbell Court House. We'll close up the rear before daybreak, bring our men on as far as New Hope Church. See to it, gentlemen."

Latrobe nodded. Back at their bivouac, Longstreet turned to his tent, and Trav led Nig through the wood into a moonlit field where the grass seemed good, and he lay down with the rein looped over his wrist. He tried to imagine what had passed in the council of the commanding generals tonight. Faced with the almost inevitable surrender, what were the thoughts of those men? What would surrender mean to them? Arrest? Trial? The traitor's noose? Fitz Lee and Gordon would presumably take flight to escape prosecution, but General Lee was too old and frail, yes and too valorous, to accept the part of a hunted fugitive; and certainly Longstreet would face a Yankee judge or a Yankee firing squad or even a Yankee hangman as steadily as he faced Yankee batteries. Yet surely, unless they fled, surrender would mean the arrest of all the higher officers of this army as traitors and felons. That was inevitable, at least for all who had been officers of the old army; and the knowledge must tonight have been in all their minds. They could foresee martial law, trials at the drumhead, quick execution of the fatal sentences. Trav was not a man of acute sensibilities, but he could understand the bitterness of that dreadful hour when they knew themselves helpless, when abject submission seemed the only open road.

Trav's own thoughts bludgeoned him into an uneasy sleep. When the sound of firing roused him, the skies were gray. The early airs were damp. He got stiffly to his feet and saw with dull interest how close Nig had cropped the grass all about him as he lay. He had sprawled on his face with his head in his arms, and even between his spread legs and all around his elbows and his head the grass was eaten short. He must have slept soundly indeed, not to be waked by those grinding teeth so near his ears. The simple incident touched him profoundly, and he patted the big horse and stroked its muzzle and caressed it before he tightened the girth again.

When he came back to the road, the last regiments of the First Corps were moving on toward New Hope Church, and at the church he found line of battle being formed across the road. Colonel Latrobe explained the situation. "General Longstreet rode to the front at daylight," he said. "He and General Lee wanted to see what Gordon and Fitz Lee might accomplish. This ridge seems to be a divide. There's a creek a little to the northwest that runs north and empties into the James, and there's another east of us that flows into Appomattox waters. We're extending our line each way to anchor it on those creeks."

West of the church the road ran level through heavy woods. Trav looked that way, listening to the sounds of distant battle. "They're at it now. Over beyond the Court House."

"Yes; but the firing doesn't move. If anything, it's coming this way."

They both knew what that meant. Gordon and Fitz Lee had been unable to clear the road for the advance. After a time, the sounds of distant conflict slowed and ceased; but presently there were scattered shots in the woods east of the church, close on their rear. The enemy skirmishers must be feeling their line.

Colonel Latrobe said: "Well, Major, you had better find the General and tell him we are about to be under some pressure here."

So Trav rode toward the front. After a mile or so, when byways turned off to right and left, the road dropped into a valley; and he saw an old brick mansion masked by trees a little off to his right, and cultivated fields. He climbed out of that valley and topped a lesser ridge and came down to Lee's headquarters where last night he had seen the commanding generals in council.

Lee's tent was pitched under a towering white oak. Longstreet was there, standing beside a smoky fire. General Lee in a spotless uniform, wearing sword and sash, his boots high-polished and his spurs of gold, stood beyond the fire, talking with General Mahone. Mahone was a small man, thin and frail and with a long beard. There was a story in the army that when a messenger reported to Mrs. Mahone that he had a slight flesh wound, she retorted: "Slight? That must be serious, for the General has no flesh whatever!" Small though he was, the excellence of Mahone's mess was famous, and whenever possible he had not only a cow but a few laying hens near his headquarters; but in the fighting of these last months no one had done better work than he.

Trav had never seen General Lee so carefully dressed; and his heart rather than his mind understood. The commanding general was prepared to surrender. How long had this new uniform, that splendid sword and sash, those golden spurs been carried in his baggage? How long ago had General Lee first known certainly that some day this hour would come? How long ago had he thus prepared to go in seemly garb to the hour that would be like crucifixion? Trav, granted this glimpse into the great man's secret soul, felt his eyes sting with poignant understanding; he forgot his errand here, till General Longstreet came near and spoke.

"Well, Currain?"

Trav delivered Colonel Latrobe's message. As he finished, General Lee called Longstreet to him; and after a moment Longstreet returned. Since his useless arm made him awkward, Trav helped him mount and they rode toward the rear together. Longstreet spoke only once. "The commanding general asked my opinion, Currain. The question is of surrender. Gordon could not move the force in our front, and now Latrobe says the Yankees are feeling our rear. I asked if the sacrifice of this army would help our forces elsewhere in the

South. General Lee said it would not. I told him the situation spoke for itself, and Mahone agreed. So General Lee will go to call upon 'Lys Grant."

Trav felt a great surge of relief. Surrender meant they could rest at last. To sleep, to lie down to untroubled slumber, even though it were with hunger for a bedfellow, would be bliss unspeakable. When they reached the church, Latrobe said the enemy appeared to be deploying to attack; and General Longstreet directed General Alexander to place his guns to meet the assault preparing.

Trav wished to cry out to them to stop! With the end so near, must still more blood be spilled upon last year's dried leaves, matted by winter's snow and rain, now lying sodden in the forest lanes? He might have yielded to that impulse of protest, but the hoof beats of horsemen caught his ear, and he turned and saw General Lee approaching. The commanding general seemed not to observe the battle deployment here across the road beside the church. Preceded by a flag, he rode at a foot pace through the thin ranks and on toward the Union front. The flag told his errand plain; and behind him silence lay.

Trav went toward where Longstreet, a little off the road, directed Field's men in strengthening their defensive lines. As he approached, a messenger came at a gallop to speak to Longstreet; and the General called Colonel Haskell and said a word to him. Haskell raced away, his mare at full stretch of utmost speed, along the road Lee had taken. There was a time of waiting when General Longstreet's steady voice as he gave directions was the only spoken sound. Then Colonel Haskell returned to report that Lee wished General Gordon to arrange for a truce on his front. Longstreet sent a messenger to Gordon, and he dismounted, and the slow minutes ticked away.

General Lee's flag had called a temporary truce here; the Union skirmishers drew no nearer. Trav's throat was dry with waiting. Messengers came and went, and at length an officer in a blue uniform, accompanied by two Confederates, rode full pelt to where Longstreet stood. The Yankee pulled his panting horse to its haunches with a flourish, and he swung to the ground. His long yellow hair was loose upon his shoulders, his shoulder straps were enormous, his red scarf was secured with a broad gold pin. Even before he spoke, Trav hated this Yankee with an abysmal hatred; he hated him worse when the officer strode abruptly to face General Longstreet and cried in dramatic tones:

"In the name of General Sheridan, I demand the unconditional surrender of this army!"

General Longstreet surveyed the gorgeous individual from head to toe. "And who are you, sir?" he inquired, in dry wrath.

"General Custer."

Longstreet stared at him under lowered brows, and he spoke more loudly. "Custer! Ah, yes! The hangman of Front Royal?" His voice rose another note, ringing in the silence. "Young man, you are within our lines without a shadow of authority——"

Custer cried furiously: "There is authority enough behind me! General Sheridan is in position to——"

Longstreet—and Trav almost smiled, remembering how often the big man was deaf when he did not wish to hear—proceeded as though the other had not spoken—"and subject to be shot at sight," he said. He spoke in harsh contempt. "You are rash and ignorant and discourteous not only to me, your superior in rank, but to your own commander." His voice rose higher still. "I am not the commanding general, my young friend; but if I were, I would receive no communication from you, nor from General Sheridan, nor from any other—" He growled the word, in a lower tone, like a blow. "From any other underling!"

The other flushed; he said in some embarrassment: "I thought only to prevent the spilling of more blood." He glanced uneasily around the circle of angry eyes.

Longstreet said scornfully: "To spill blood, whether their own or the enemy's, is the business of soldiers, young man. You should not shrink at it, like some lily-fingered civilian! However, since you now moderate your tone, I will say to you that General Lee has ridden to meet your commanding officer."

Custer bowed low; and thus dismissed, he turned away. There was a smile and a stir behind him, and when he was out of hearing, Longstreet chuckled. "Well, gentlemen," he told them, "that did me a world of good!"

Trav saw Custer pause by his horse, which was still badly blown;

and with a sharp pleasure he recognized Rollin Lyle in the group there. Custer spoke to Colonel Haskell and they stood for a moment in conversation before Custer mounted. At a sign from Haskell, a trooper kept the Yankee company as he rode away.

Trav went to speak to Rollin, and the boy's scarred face lighted with pleasure. Trav said he had seen Vesta in Richmond, and Rollin nodded.

"Yes sir, I had a moment with her."

"Then you came through Richmond?"

"Yes sir. You know we were between the Williamsburg Turnpike and the Nine-Mile Road, quartered there all winter. But after dark Sunday we moved down to the Charles City Road and made a demonstration and held on there till sunrise before returning to the River Road and falling back to Richmond."

"That made it pretty close work, didn't it?"

Rollin said soberly: "Yes, sir, it did. We could see the glare of the fire even before we started for Richmond. We were under pressure by their pickets when we rode in past Rockett's, and the whole city from the Capitol to the river seemed to be on fire, and the damnedest mob of hideous human beings you can imagine was in the streets, drinking, yelling, fighting. Lots of men in the mob. They say there were at least five thousand deserters hiding in the city, but they came out of hiding that morning." And he said: "The fire was on both sides of Main Street, so we turned up Twentieth Street to Franklin, and I raced ahead through Capitol Square to the house." He grinned. "I was almost cut off. The Yankees came in by Main Street, so I had to go down Fifth and along the river bank to the bridge."

"How bad was the fire?"

"Why, everything between the river and Capitol Square was burning," Rollin told him. "And as far west as Gamble's Hill, I guess. We stopped on the hill in Manchester after we got across the river, and we could look right down into it."

Trav nodded. "Hard work since?"

Rollin's lips twisted in a grin. "Some, yes sir. Some funny things, too. A grass fire burned us out of our blankets one night at Amelia Court House, but we found a barrel of apple brandy and filled our canteens, so we didn't mind that very much. We had some fighting at Amelia Springs and at Farmville, and again around the Court House ahead, last night." He pointed along the road. "And when that Yankee show-off headed this way I came along to see what he was up to."

"What did he have to say after General Longstreet dismissed him, here just now?"

Rollin laughed. "He wanted to buy Colonel Haskell's mare," he explained. "That crow bait of his was all but foundered. Colonel Haskell said he could neither buy the mare nor steal it; and then the Colonel asked whether Frank Huger was alive, and he said: 'I notice you're wearing his spurs.' So General Custer reddened up and said he was saving the spurs for Colonel Huger; and he asked for an escort back to his lines and rode away."

Someone spoke sharply: "Here's General Lee!" That silenced them all. The commanding general acknowledged their salutes, and he said:

"Gentlemen, General Grant has gone to Appomattox Court House; so I did not meet him. He left orders to attack our lines here; but if those people advance against you, I hope you will hold your fire as long as you can. There will be a truce presently."

Even as he spoke, a flag from General Meade said he had ordered a truce for long enough to allow the commanding generals to meet. Lee thanked the messenger; he called Longstreet and they rode toward the advance together.

Trav and Latrobe followed at a respectful distance. When they emerged from the forest below Lee's headquarters, they pulled up to survey the scene. Below them, the valley sloped down to the north branch of the Appomattox; and along the willow-fringed stream and across the road, Gordon's men, drawn back from the village yonder after their repulse this morning, were extended in a disorganized and ragged line. The slopes were a scrambled litter of wagons and ambulances, some with horses, some without. Exhausted men sprawled at random everywhere, except where General Alexander's guns, thrown into position as a rallying point for the forces beaten back in the morning fight, still held an ordered line on the left and right of the road. Beyond the stream the road ascended, curving slightly to the right around a bold shoulder of the hill; and through the trees they could see the tops of houses and of the court house in the village there.

They followed the commanding generals down the slope. Lee and Longstreet, comrades through these years now ending, dismounted in an apple orchard in the curve of the road and a little short of the stream and sat down on a pile of fence rails there, speaking quietly together with intervals of silence. Their words could not be heard, except once when Longstreet's voice was a little raised in strong emphasis.

"Unless he offers honorable terms, General, return and let us fight it to the end!"

Presently a horseman trotted down the steep descent from the village and crossed the stream and approached them. General Lee listened to him, then called for his secretary and a courier and rode up toward the court house to meet his adversary. When he had disappeared, General Longstreet walked slowly to where Trav and the others waited. He mounted without assistance, using his weak arm, then slipping it back into the sling and holding the reins in his left hand; and they returned in silence the long three miles to where the First Corps stood in unshaken line of battle, ready for whatever was to come.

At sight of those orderly ranks Longstreet pulled up his horse, and Trav beside him saw sudden tears in the big man's eyes, and a high pride. "Well, Currain," he said, "the First Corps is still ready for a fight. There were never better men."

General Field approached to ask what was happening. Longstreet hesitated. "Surrender, I believe," he said. "Unless 'Lys Grant is less reasonable than he used to be."

Field protested: "There is still fight in my men, General! We're as strong today as we were a week ago."

Longstreet nodded. "That is true. But we've had the easy part, no hard contention; and aside from your men here, there is not much left of the army." He looked toward the ranks. Every man was watching him. "Perhaps they had better be kept busy till the business is settled, General," he suggested. So the men were put to work improving their position here, till a Union officer came to announce a general truce and even this activity was halted.

Longstreet, as composed during this long waiting as in the flush of battle, sat under a tree with Trav and others of the staff, puffing hard at his pipe; and the fine Sunday afternoon droned away. Trav thought there was an unearthly stillness in the forest and along the roadside. His ears had for so long been tuned to the crackle of musketry that the silence made him restless. There had been some action at dawn when Gordon tried the enemy in their front, but now for hours hardly a shot had sounded. What would life be when the staccato of musket fire and the occasional single shots of skirmishers and sharpshooters were no longer a commonplace of every daylight hour; when the sound of a distant shot meant only that a rabbit, or a duck, or possibly a deer had been killed, and not a man? He sat leaning against a tree, Nig cropping grass near-by with a grinding sound; and he felt a heavy beating in his blood, and his thoughts went wandering. Presently there would be surrender and an end to all this. What then?

He groped back toward contact with the peaceful world as it had been; but that world was gone; for now the Negroes were no longer "our people." They were no longer men and women with whom you worked in a sort of partnership, and toward whom you had a duty of which you were much more conscious than you were of your authority over them. There would be no more slaves.

But—what would become of them? They would not disappear; they would not vanish off the face of the earth. They would still be here, as liable to hunger and to sickness and to cold as they had ever been. Who would feed them, warm them, cure them when they were ill, shelter them when they were feeble and old?

Why, that was a task which the South must accept. Now the slaves were free, but not the masters. As a matter of self-interest, if for no other reason, you had always taken solicitous care of your people. They had been yours, but also you were theirs. Now they were no longer yours; but you were still as surely theirs. They would forever be a part of your world, a part of your community. If a Negro were sick or hungry, it was as necessary as it had ever been to provide in some way for his healing and his sustenance. If you did not, then all around you and your family there would be pestilence and famine; and to live in the South would be like dwelling in a wilderness where roamed bands of starved and rabid wolves.

Clearly, the Negroes were destined, at least in the beginning, to work the land. This was a task they knew; it would serve as a stop-gap until somehow they developed new capacities. Thus thinking, Trav remembered Great Oak and the labors which had absorbed him there. But the house was gone, and to make Great Oak again a healthy and a fruitful property would require years. Not for a long time could those fields be restored to productivity.

But Chimneys now was his, tossed back to him by Tony. War had not ravaged that region; he might return there. Enid would hate it, but she would have to accept his decision. Certainly he must some-how provide for her and for Lucy and Peter a living and a home. In a South where no one had anything, they were as well off as anyone; but when peace came, from the dead level of impoverishment, here and there an individual would presently emerge. Every man with an aptitude would seek a way to use it. Trav knew his only aptitude was for husbandry; but how could anyone work land without black hands to help him? His own thoughts brought him to a stop; against this blank wall he could make no forward progress.

He was too tired to think, too hungry to think. For a week now, since that other Sunday which seemed so long ago when he rode out of Richmond, there had been short rations or none at all even for Longstreet and the officers of the staff. They were better off than the men, but not much. Trav was hungry for food, and hungry for sleep. He shook his head, brushed his hands across his eyes. General Lee had gone to meet Longstreet's friend, 'Lys Grant, and to surrender this army. Beyond that no man could see.

This waiting was hard. Even Longstreet, as though unable to en-dure it, at last rose and called for his horse; and they returned with him toward the front. He pulled up on the heights above the valley, looking across toward the Court House. This morning there had been cavalry in the valley to the right, but Trav did not see them now. He spoke of this to Longstreet, and the big man nodded.

"Yes, Fitz Lee last night asked permission to ride away before any surrender and try to join General Johnston."

Then Burr was gone, with Rosser's division of Fitz Lee's command. So Burr was not yet done with the hard gallop, the weary days, the *mêlée* of the charge, the pistol shot, the thrust, the wounds and death. Yet if Lee surrendered, what could Johnston do?

On the heights across the stream where the court house stood, they heard a sudden distant clamor of cheering, quickly silenced. The Yankees up there in Appomattox Court House had learned something which pleased them. It was not long after that cheering before Trav saw General Lee, with two or three companions, ride down the hill and cross the little stream that threaded the valley between them and the village and come slowly toward them. Gordon's men gave him a cheer, but the cheer was broken off in a clamor of many voices as the men rushed to meet him with questions.

As General Lee approached, Trav and the others had no need to question. The commanding general rode with his hat in his hands, his hands resting on the pommel; they saw him nod to those urgent questioners, nod and nod with a heavy head; but his eyes were fixed between Traveller's ears. Behind him, when he had passed, the men halted and stood still. They looked after him, they answered the questions asked by others who came running up to them, they dropped to the ground or wandered off by ones or twos, or they went alone; and Trav saw grown men crying without shame, crying openly and with a dreadful violence, beating their fists together, shaking with sobs. They were like children after a harsh whipping, convulsed with the bruising sting of the lash, helpless to control themselves. He saw a man throw himself flat on the ground and lie on his back and cry aloud, howling like a lost dog in an intolerable grief and woe. He saw men with blank faces from whose red, haggard eyes tears streamed unheeded, like water from a leaky cup. He saw men draw together in groups, not speaking, staring at one another as though at strangers. He heard curses and monstrous obscenities, and he saw men everywhere frankly kneel and pray. General Lee's passage left these valiants in collapse behind him as a tornado leaves broken trees in its path through what was a noble forest.

The commanding general turned off the road at the orchard and dismounted and withdrew among the apple trees. There, alone, he paced slowly up and down; and Trav in his own heart shared the lonely man's solitary Golgotha. Surrounded at a respectful distance by the circle of these men who loved him, General Lee moved like an animal in a cage.

To that circle newcomers constantly were added. After a time, two or three Yankee officers came to speak to members of his staff, and someone took them to General Lee for introductions; and at that Longstreet turned his horse.

"I'll not watch that lion-baiting," he said through grating teeth; and Trav heard the furious anger in him. "Let us ride into the enemy lines." He added sternly: "If they have rations to spare, they must share with our hungry men. We can see to that!"

This sharing, as it proved, had already been arranged. Before they reached the bridge at the foot of the hill, they saw laden wagons coming down the road from the village. General Longstreet, riding on up the hill, left Trav and the others to see to the distribution. There was bread in some wagons, meat in others; but the men were too nearly famished to make selection. Those who got bread ate it, and those to whose lot fell the meat scarce waited to start their cooking fires and scorch it a little before it was hungrily devoured.

During the afternoon, the terms of the surrender were reported by word of mouth from man to man; and Trav shared the surprised gratefulness at General Grant's generosity. The men would be paroled; those who owned horses would retain them; the officers would keep their side arms; the railroads would, so far as their capacities permitted, help the infantrymen to distant homes.

Of the surrender itself, Trav heard the details from General Alexander. "They met in Major McLean's house," he said. "Wilmer McLean. It's just beyond the court house." And Alexander added: "Major McLean owned the farm at Blackburn's Ford, where Longstreet threw back the first Yankee thrust, a day or two before Manassas, four years ago. You might say the war began and ended on his farm." The artilleryman confessed that he himself had begged General Lee not to surrender. "My men had saved their ammunition, still had a good supply, hated to give up without using it. I thought we might scatter and find our separate ways to join General Johnston; but probably General Lee is right."

Darkness came, and the night air held a threat of rain. General Lee had named Longstreet and Gordon and Pendleton to arrange the details of the surrender; so Monday morning Trav and the other staff officers turned to long dull drudgery of paper work, tallying the names of men to be paroled. That day, while rain fell softly as tears upon them all, Trav found solace in totting up long columns, checking his results. The regimental reports as of Sunday morning showed only a scant eight thousand infantry in those units which still retained their organization. Seven thousand, eight hundred and ninety-two. But that figure met continual modification, for all day Monday, hundreds of stragglers rejoined their commands. They were usually weaponless. It would be a proud man who could say in the years to come: "I surrendered my musket at Appomattox." No more than a few thousand would be able to rank themselves in that category. Trav suspected that many of the stragglers were actually deserters who came now to secure the protection of parole. Hour by hour the totals grew, and once he thought with grim amusement: Why, if this keeps on, we'll have a sizeable army to surrender before we're through!

All day, that first pleasantly precise figure—seven thousand, eight hundred and ninety-two organized infantry with seventy-five rounds of ammunition, and sixty-three guns with ninety-three rounds—grew and grew. That night Trav copied off the tally:

General Lee and his staff	15
Longstreet's corps	14,833
Gordon's corps	7,200
Ewell's corps	287
Cavalry	1,786
Artillery	2,586
Detachments	1,649
	28,356

He took these totals to General Longstreet, and the big man scanned them thoughtfully. "The First Corps had accretions, Currain," he remarked. "Part of Hill's corps, and those who escaped the shambles at Sayler's Creek, have come into our ranks. But of the force committed to me by General Lee at Petersburg, we've lost hardly two hundred men, including stragglers. Yet we've marched a hundred miles, and eaten little, and had a dozen skirmishes. The First Corps is a fighting weapon still."

Trav said honestly: "You've reason to be proud of them, General." He added: "Gordon's corps was fought to a shadow. His figures there include about five thousand fragments and stragglers."

"Twenty-eight thousand altogether," Longstreet reflected. "No doubt 'Lys Grant could count a hundred thousand men, in hand or within call."

Trav asked: "Have you seen him?"

"Briefly, yes." Longstreet and the others had done their work as commissioners for the surrender in a room in the McLean house. "Yes, as I passed his door he called me in for a friendly word."

"Will he receive the surrender?"

"No, he and Meade and Sheridan have already gone." His voice checked in his throat; and Trav understood and turned away.

Since the capitulation, Lee's army had contracted, the First Corps moving up from New Hope Church, where they had drawn that last defensive line across the road, to make themselves as comfortable as was possible in the woods on the upper slopes no more than a mile from the Appomattox. Tuesday morning, General Alexander put his guns in single column along the road and delivered them where they stood to the Federal officers appointed to receive them. Trav, from the slopes above, watched that formality; and he waited to see the guns file away down to the bridge and up the hill to the village. But they did not move, and after a time the men grouped around them began to drift back up the road again, and Trav saw Brett and joined him, walking Nig by Brett's side.

"Why didn't they take the guns?" he asked.

Brett said in a hoarse voice, his eyes on the road: "They're too deep in mud. Our horses can't move them. We had to manhandle every gun to get them into line. The Yankees haven't any horses to spare. They haven't decided what to do." His tone was heavy with stale fatigue, and Trav did not speak. Brett said absently: "General Alexander plans to leave the country, go to Brazil, or anywhere there's work for a good artilleryman."

"West Point men have no other trade but war," Trav reflected. "But I suppose they can never have an army command again, not Confederate officers." He added: "Latrobe is planning to go to England."

Brett plodded through the mud. "Fitz Lee took his men away before the surrender. Burr and Rollin are gone. I don't hear any more talk about taking to the mountains, guerrilla war."

"No, this will end it all. Will you go back to Richmond?"

"Yes, at first. I think we may all go to the Plains when we can. If we can. Probably Richmond will be garrisoned."

"General Longstreet and I will go to Lynchburg," Trav told him. "Enid's there, and Mrs. Longstreet."

After a few paces Brett said: "Trav, I have some news of Tony." Trav looked at him in surprise, and Brett explained: "From Mr. Owen, of the Washington Artillery. He had a letter from a friend in New Orleans, describing conditions there. Mr. Owen did not know there was any relationship between Anthony Currain and me, and I did not inform him."

"What was it he said?"

"Why, that Tony has set up an establishment there." Brett did not meet Trav's eyes. "His wife is a very beautiful—Creole. Every Yankee in New Orleans knows Miss Sapphira." Trav felt his spine prick, and Brett went on: "According to Mr. Owen's correspondent, Tony is in politics. There have always been free negroes in New Orleans, and now Tony is on familiar political—and social—terms with their leaders. He seems to have a financial interest in a Republican newspaper there, run by some San Domingan negroes." Trav could not speak, and after a moment Brett added: "You see, New Orleans has been a Northern city for three years now. I suppose it's a sample of what will happen in the whole South. Mr. Owen is afraid that when civil government is re-established, negroes may get the suffrage. Apparently, if that happens, Tony will control a good many votes."

Trav felt anger like a sickness in him. He would not look at Brett, trudging with downcast head beside him; and when someone called his name—"Mornin', Major Currain!"—he welcomed the interruption. He turned and saw, lounging among the trees with half a dozen others whose faces were familiar, Lonn Tyler. Here were the fragments of the Eleventh North Carolina, the regiment with which he had faced those flaming guns at Gettysburg. When he pulled up his horse, Brett went on; and Trav after a moment's hesitation let him go. Of Tony, there was no more to be said. Let him be forgotten.

So he stayed, sitting his horse with these simple men grouped around him. Lonn offered him a canteen, and more from politeness than desire Trav lifted it to his lips. Some fiery liquid with a bitter flavor burned his throat, and he stifled a cough. "God Almighty, what's that?"

"Pine-top whiskey, Major. They make it around here. A farmer back along give us a jug of it. You got to say for it, it warms you!"

Trav wiped his streaming eyes. "Well, gentlemen; we'll all soon be starting home."

Lonn said cheerfully: "If I had the sense God give a chipmunk I'd have started four years ago. Yes, and got there and stayed there, too!"

"Your soldiering's almost done." Trav spoke at random, any words at all. "One more march, to lay down your guns and cartridge boxes, and your flag."

Lonn grinned and looked around and saw an officer near-by and called to him. "Cap'n, the Major here says we-uns got to lay down our flag." The officer approached and Trav recognized Captain Outlaw of C Company.

"Why, no, Major," the Captain said mildly. "Not our regiment. Last Friday night we all saw this coming, and we decided no Yankee was ever going to touch our flag. The legislature gave it to the Bethel Regiment, and the Bethel Regiment passed it on to us; so we decided it was too good for the Yankees. We took it off the staff and carried the staff with the cover on it all day Saturday, so no one could tell the flag wasn't there; and Sunday morning when we saw General Lee all dressed up and riding to meet Grant, we took the flag off in the woods and burned it."

Lonn Tyler said dryly: "So, Major, if you look to see us lay down our flag you're due to be some supprised."

Trav was astonished at his own fierce rush of gladness at this incident. A flag was such a little thing; yet how many men North and South—rude, untutored men like Lonn Tyler in whom you would not readily suspect fine sensibilities and spiritual loyalties—had died in these four years for just such draggled, shot-torn banners as the one these men had consecrated in the flames! In any combat, the battle flags were focus of the fiercest fighting. Men did not, in the heat of action, fight for their families, or their homes, or their possessions, or their states, or the cause to which they adhered; they fought for their flags, to protect their own, to seize the enemy's. Trifles meant in the end so much more, moved men's hearts so much more deeply, than the great things. Perhaps it was because they were trifles, and so within reach of every comprehension.

All that day, General Alexander's guns remained in the road where they had been surrendered, the column extending from the bridge up the slope for almost a mile. The exhausted horses stood patiently in the rain; and dusk came down and found them there. At dawn Wednesday, when Trav went to look, the guns had not been moved, but many of the horses were down. They had fallen from exhaustion and were too nearly starved to scramble to their feet again.

There were other gaps in the bogged column too; for horses with any work left in them had been cut from their traces during the night and spirited away. Trav guessed that the Yankee guards had shut their eyes to this. "Let the men keep their horses," Grant had said. Well, many a man, when the time came to depart, would have a horse to ride who had had none before.

The final act of the tragedy was played out under skies that had been wept dry by two days' rain, under a gloomy canopy of lowering clouds. There were no bands to set the rhythm of the last march, and no drums to beat. If the sun rose that day, no man saw it. Dawn came gray through the cloud scud.

The formal laying down of arms would follow a pattern prearranged. For the march down to the stream, and up the road along which the victors would await their coming, General Gordon and his Second Corps would lead, the First Corps bring up the rear. Till time for the First Corps to fall in, Trav had no duties; so he watched from the heights half a mile short of the bridge as Gordon's men began to form in the field beside the road still clogged with Alexander's guns. Beyond the stream he saw, through the gray light of that dull morning, files of Union soldiers march down toward the bridge and form facing the road, two lines on one side, one on the other. He remembered old tales of prisoners taken captive by Indians and required to run a gant-let. Yonder was the gantlet which this army presently must run.

Some of Gordon's regiments now taking position yonder were so reduced in numbers that only a color guard remained. Except for an occasional low word of command, a hush lay across that gentle valley. Men moved in silence to their places and stood waiting; and some were proudly erect and some hung their heads.

Trav watched till at last General Gordon led his van down toward the stream. In addition to the Stars and Bars which most regiments displayed, there were so many battle flags that the moving files of men seemed to be crowned with red, and Trav had a sudden vision of what those flags meant, of the many regiments which once in full strength had marched under those colors. How many thousands of brave men had followed these torn and tattered flags into the bloody battles of the years now ending here! How few of those fine men of valor were alive today! Their blood, blood of the bravest and the best, was long since spilled; their bodies, often left unburied, had rotted or had been devoured by hogs and vermin. Their bones lay bleaching in the new green grass of this month of April, all across those southern fields.

They were dead, and the sons they might have sired would never be born. The South, yes, and the nation, had lost not those fine men alone, but the generations of their sons who now would never be. The nation and the world would be poorer for that loss, poorer forever-more.

Trav's eyes blurred, and he turned back to be ready to take his place when the First Corps should move. Behind him, across the river to-ward the village, he heard a bugle blow; but he did not look that way. When he rejoined the staff, the men of the First Corps were already in formation, but they would not tread too close on the heels of those in front; and whenever the head of the column halted, so must they all.

Thus on that last march there were many halts, and many brief for-ward movements. At the halts even Nig stood patiently; when they moved on, the horse showed no eagerness or haste. Trav with his comrades of the staff—Manning, Latrobe, all the others—came a little behind Longstreet, letting the General have the road to himself. Trav wondered why he had followed that big man so far. Except for brief moments when battle frenzy spurred him into explosive action, he had never been at heart the warrior. He wondered, too, why grief now tortured him. He was glad the war was done; yet the gloomy pageantry of this hour, the set faces all around him, the silent men and the sluggish beat of weary feet in the churned mud of the road, combined to wring his very vitals, as though all his organs were caught in a twisted rope and squeezed to agonizing pain.

When the road dipped more steeply toward the bridge, the whole scene lay under his eye. The gray-clad column flowed past the abandoned guns down to the stream; it climbed the hill between those ranks of men in blue and disappeared over the crest. Beyond the bridge he saw a group of mounted Union officers. Doubtless they were the ones chosen to receive this surrender.

He heard suddenly a bugle blow, and along the ranks of the enemy a ripple ran. Their pieces moved smartly and were still. Trav looked at Longstreet. The big man, since his wound paralyzed the nerves, had carried his right arm in a sling; but he who rarely or never wore any weapon today had belted on a sword. Trav saw him now remove the sling and stuff it into the pocket of his uniform, leaving his right arm free.

They came near the stream and halted again, and again went on. As Nig crossed the bridge, Trav held his eyes straight ahead, feeling upon him the steady eyes of the ranked soldiers in blue who walled the road. A moment later he heard again the bugle sound, and every Yankee musket came to Carry Arms, in courteous salute to the vanquished. Longstreet at the column's head swept his sword up and down in signal for response; and Trav heard the men behind him shift their pieces in acknowledgment of the victor's gesture. He understood then why Longstreet a while ago had freed his sword arm; and this proof of the General's unshaken mastery of himself made Trav's eyes burn with proud tears.

They had to halt once more, just short of the crest of the rise, while Gordon's last division laid down its arms. When the road was clear they moved again, and at command halted and left-faced. Longstreet and his staff wheeled into position behind their men. Trav saw the shabby lines dress ranks; he heard the scrape of steel as bayonets were fixed and arms were stacked. At the word, the men stripped off their cartridge boxes and hung them on the muskets; the color-bearers rolled the flags and laid them on the ground with lingering, tender hands.

The leading division stood at attention while Yankee wagons came to collect the stacked muskets, to empty the cartridge boxes, to gather the battle flags. When the surrendered weapons and the trophies had been removed, this division marched on, and another took its place; and again there was that pattern of relinquishment, and again and again. Trav did not know how long he sat there; the solemn pageant of surrender beat upon him blow by blow.

After the last man had made his gesture and the long ordeal ended, there was some mingling with blue-clad officers. Small fires began to burn along the street where the cartridges which had been emptied from the boxes lay in a windrow, and now spent their strength in futile spurts among the crawling flames. Trav was not of that fraternity of West Point men who now renewed old acquaintances, so he took no part in this exchange of polite words; and he was relieved when Longstreet presently drew apart, gathering the officers of his staff around him, all of them for the last time together.

There were no long farewells. "Well, gentlemen," the General said, his voice harsh to mask his deep emotion, "the war is ended. It is time for us to ride to our homes and take up the harder tasks of peace."

They talked a moment quietly; they exchanged hand clasps, and Trav was surprised at his own sense of loss in saying these good-bys. Little Peyton Manning, so small he might have been a boy, a Mississippi man from Aberdeen, would ride first to Richmond. "I'll stay there till things are more settled before I start for home." Manning, always considerate and kind, had a thousand times led them all to laughter; but there was never any sting in his jests. Latrobe was equally kindly; and Fairfax, for all his addiction to his cups and his clumsy buffoonery, had a heart big enough to love all the world—and to make you love him. Young Dunn, and Frank Potts, and Goree, and Major Otey who would ride with them to Lynchburg; yes, Trav loved them all.

Four of them took the Lynchburg road; Longstreet and Trav, and Captain Goree who had been at Longstreet's side since the beginning, and Major Otey. The Lynchburg pike led them with many meanderings through pines and scrub oak and past small farms; and they crossed and recrossed the railroad right of way. Silence for the most part kept them company, but once Longstreet spoke.

"I've wondered ever since Grant cut our road at Jetersville how he knew exactly what we meant to do. I learned the answer yesterday. Some weeks ago, the Legislature required General Lee to disclose his plans for our retreat, if retreat became necessary; and when President Davis skedaddled out of Richmond he threw Lee's letter into his wastebasket. The Yankees found it. 'Lys Grant had a copy of it Monday night a week ago; so by the kindness of Mr. Davis the enemy always knew what we intended."

There was no heat in his voice, and they made no comment. The past was past. But Trav remembered that President Davis had summoned on to Richmond that train loaded with supplies which was waiting for the army at Amelia Court House. There were many crimes to be laid at the President's door; but Mr. Davis was a fugitive, and probably with a noose waiting for him if he were caught. It was a time for pity, not for empty blame.

Longstreet lifted their pace. After a few miles they crossed the railroad again, and rode for a quarter of a mile through swampy ground, and came up past a cemetery on their left to the outskirts of the little town of Concord Depot, twenty or thirty houses scattered along the highways that converged at the railroad station. The first house on the right of the road, set among chestnut trees, with a big black gum opposite the front door between the driveway and the road, had a substantial and hospitable aspect. The house itself was two stories high, with square pillars in front rising to the roof of the second floor veranda. Trav saw a separate kitchen and a smoke house in the yard, thinly shaded by the first pricking green of the unfolding leaves of the chestnut trees. There was a white fence of crisscrossed boards, with a rounded board atop; and as they approached the house three small children, two boys and a girl of about five, scrambled up to stand precariously atop this fence to watch them.

Longstreet spoke to the oldest youngster. "Son, do you think your mother could find dinner for four hungry men?"

The boy scuttled toward the house, and a woman met him in the doorway. The General led the way along the drive; and she said hospitably:

"Light and come in, sirs."

"We don't wish to burden you, ma'am."

"There's aplenty," she assured him. Trav saw her eyes red with weeping. The boys took their horses. The little girl had disappeared. The woman led them through a hall with a room on either side and into a dining room beyond. "My husband's in a Yankee prison somewheres, but I can always rustle up a meal for soldiers."

"We are no longer soldiers. General Lee's army is surrendered."

"I heard so. I guess you all did as much as flesh and blood could do."

"What is your husband's name, ma'am?"

"J. J. Landrum." Her hands twisted in her apron. "He's b'en a long time gone, but me and the young'uns git along. They set out to conscript my oldest, but I said they'd have to conscript me first. He's sixteen, and he worked in the station store till the Yankees burned it down. They like to burned him too. He hid in the closet under the stairs in the store, and they yelled for anyone that was inside to come out because they was going to burn the place; but he didn't dast come out till he heard the crackling. Then he scuttered up here to the house. With him to do the heavy work, we git along. You all rest you'selves and dinner'll be ready right soon."

There were windows in both sides of this large pleasant room, the fireplace at the end farthest from the road. They laid their swords on a small table near the door and turned to the dinner table. Longstreet sat with his back to the hearth, the others flanking him; and they fell into quiet talk. Where will you go? What will you do? And you? And you?

After a time, and some silence, Longstreet said reflectively: "I wonder if any other great nation has ever had so short a history as the Confederacy. Born at Sumter four years ago almost to the day, died at Appomattox Court House today."

The Confederacy dead? Yes. To each of them Lee's Army of Northern Virginia was the Confederacy; with Lee's surrender, the Confederacy was gone.

"Four years," the General repeated. "Four years from founding to dissolution. Old Egypt, Greece, Rome, France, Spain; they have had their centuries. We had four years."

"Four crowded years, General." It was Goree who spoke. "They will be remembered."

Longstreet nodded. "Four years, the entire lifetime of a nation, and every day of it devoted to war. And war captures man's imagination; so yes, these years will be remembered." After a moment he added gravely: "Remembered perhaps too long."

He was thinking aloud, and he continued to speak, but Trav's attention suddenly was drawn away. The door of one of the front rooms was open a crack, open wide enough so that through the crack he could see a bed beyond. In this slightly open door a small head appeared. That little girl who had watched them arrive, and who fled when General Longstreet spoke to her brother, peered in through the crack of the door.

Trav, lest he frighten her to flight, was ready to avert his eyes if she looked toward him; but she did not. She slipped into the room and like a fascinated bird sidled to where on the table against the wall they had laid down their swords. Her small hand reached up to touch the weapons, to move caressingly along the length of one scabbard and another, to stroke this hilt and that with little loving gestures. The setting sun struck through the window into her face and Trav saw her tears, and his throat filled.

The warriors' swords were now forever sheathed; but even this child wept for those who had fought and died, for those who had fought and failed. Well, there would be many tears to mingle with hers. She need not weep alone.

24

THE news that General Lee had surrendered his fragment of an army at first brought Cinda not only sadness but comfort too; for this was peace, and Brett would come home! But then the courage which for four years had helped her to composure gave way to a hysteria of unreasoning fears. Suppose Brett did not come! Suppose he never came! There must have been hard, desperate fighting through the week since she last held him in her arms; for nothing less than great defeats and dreadful losses could have brought Lee's hosts to helplessness. So perhaps Brett was dead; or perhaps he lay wounded somewhere along the path the army in retreat had followed; or perhaps he was a captive, already hurried away to one of the dreadful Northern prisons.

Cinda had seen Southern men, just back from those death camps. There was food enough everywhere in the North, but released prisoners came home no longer men but the skeletons of men. Their legs were pipe stems, their arms as frail as those of a sick child, their skin yellow Below their sunken eyes, in the pits above the cheekbones, the skin was black like the mark of a deep bruise, with jaundiced edges; sagging eyelids revealed inner membranes of a greenish blue, and yellow-veined eyeballs. So shrunken were their muscles that their joints seemed enlarged; great knobby knees, elbows like knots in a rope. Their lips, pale and with a bluish tinge, twisted at any kindness in a shamed, frightened grimace meant for a smile. If they were fed very gently and a few crumbs at a time with bread soaked in wine, some of them recovered; but many who were brought to the hospitals lay almost inanimate, with blankly staring eyes that never closed, and with their knees drawn up in a terrible contortion so that they were like corpses which had been allowed to stiffen in death's rigor, till they mercifully died.

To think that Brett might be on his way to one of those Yankee torture camps was a nightmare. When Cinda confessed her weak despair, Vesta protested: "But, Mama, the war's over, so they won't take any more prisoners."

"The whole army surrendered! They're all prisoners!"

"Why, no, they'll be paroled."

But Cinda perversely clung to terror, almost resenting Vesta's reassurances. The girl tried to make her smile, telling her about the Yankee band concerts in Capitol Square, so near the big house on Fifth Street that from the balcony they could hear the strains of music. "All last week, no one went to hear them except the negroes," she said. "So this week they're not letting any negroes come into the Square at all—but of course no white people go near the place, and the band just sits there and plays and plays all by itself."

Cinda would not be diverted. "Oh, Vesta, he'll never come home!"

"Hush! I'll begin to be provoked with you! Papa's all right! Wait and see!"

"I'm tired of waiting!"

"Well, then, come take a walk with me, get a little fresh air."

"Walk the streets? With Yankee soldiers staring?"

"You can't always stay indoors! It's going to be like this for goodness knows how long. You might as well get used to it!" Vesta's tone quickened. "Put on your bonnet and we'll walk down the hill and call on Mrs. Lee."

Cinda would not go even that short distance, but Vesta did. "And Mrs. Lee hasn't given up!" she reported when she returned. "She says General Lee isn't the whole Confederacy! The brave old thing says the Yankees have never captured any Southern city except Vicksburg, except places we'd already given up!"

"Has she heard from General Lee?"

"No." Vesta added persuasively: "And if he hasn't come home yet, you couldn't expect Papa to be here this soon!"

Cinda shook her head, refusing comfort. General Lee was nothing now, but Brett was everything. The days dragged wearily. Wednesday, General Weitzel, the Federal Commandant, issued an order that the prayer for the President of the United States must be included in religious services; so on Good Friday St. Paul's did not open its doors for the usual observances. Brett did not come and did not come; but Saturday they began to see from the windows an occasional haggard man in a gray uniform; and toward dusk they heard voices and some confusion down Franklin Street, and people hurried past the house in that direction. From the upper balcony, through an opening among the branches of the big magnolia, they saw a crowd collected in front of the Lee house, and a little knot of horsemen for whom the throng made way. Despite the dusk and the gloom of a rainy evening they saw enough to guess the truth. General Lee had come home.

Tilda suggested that evening that since there would be no Easter service at St. Paul's, they go tomorrow to Dr. Hoge's church, a few steps down Fifth Street from the house. Dr. Hoge had left the city when Richmond was evacuated, but Dr. Reed, whose church had burned, would preach in his place. But Cinda had no desire to hear Dr. Reed. "I don't want to hear any voice but Brett's," she confessed. "I know I ought to be ashamed of myself. I wasn't ever as bad as this, not even when Clayton was killed; but I can't help it, Tilda! There's just nothing but water in my bones."

"You're acting like an idiot! I've a mind to box your ears."

Cinda smiled weakly. "Why, Tilda, you sound the way I used to talk to you! Go on, do it! It might be good for me."

"If I thought so, I would," Tilda retorted, and stormed away.

Next morning Cinda lay late, her curtains drawn, wishing for sleep. When her door opened, softly and without any warning knock, she sat up in quick rapture, certain this was Brett; but it was Tilda, and in exasperated disappointment, Cinda cried: "I declare, Tilda, it's too bad of you to wake me! I didn't get to sleep at all till daylight."

Tilda came in and closed the door. "I had to, Cinda." Her voice was low. "Cinda, Lincoln's dead!"

Cinda at first did not comprehend. "Well, waking me up won't bring him back to life again!" But then she realized what Tilda had said. "Lincoln! Dead?"

"They say someone shot him."

"Shot him!" Cinda's throat contracted. "Oh, Tilda, I don't believe it! It's just another Sunday rumor!"

"Julian says it's true. He's just come." Julian and Anne and Judge Tudor had returned to the Twelfth Street house when order in the city was restored. "Mr. Grant told Judge Tudor. They shot Lincoln, and killed Mr. Seward and his whole family, and tried to kill all the cabinet officers."

Cinda, with a confused feeling that she must do something, began to dress. "Call June," she said absently. "I want my breakfast." She felt in Tilda a need for words; but what was there to say? Their own father was Abraham Lincoln's grandfather, but it was Lincoln who had made this war, and Lincoln's fleets had starved the South, and Lincoln's armies had stolen and burned and destroyed everything they could lay their hands on, and Lincoln's soldiers had killed Clayton and maimed Julian. If Lincoln were dead, she was glad of it! It was high time for him to die!

But Tilda might read her thoughts. "Don't stand there gawking at me! Call June, do!" Tilda went out on the balcony to summon June from the kitchen in the back yard; and when the shutters were opened Cinda saw sun glint on the leaves of the magnolia. Tilda returned. "She's coming, Cinda." She hesitated. "What are you thinking?"

"About Lincoln! I think it serves him right! After all the things he's done to us!"

"You don't mean that!"

"Oh, I suppose I don't."

"I wish I'd known him," Tilda confessed. "Or at least seen him. They say he called on Mrs. Pickett while he was in Richmond. He knew the General, or something." She wrung her hands. "I suppose the Yankees will do all sorts of terrible things, to get even. Julian said we'd better close the shutters, but Vesta wouldn't let him. She said it would just be acting guilty."

Cinda was already half dressed. "Tell Julian I'll be right down," she said. "Don't let him go."

As Tilda departed, June came with breakfast; and Cinda heard her swallow hard, and she thought the old woman had been crying. She spoke quietly.

"He was a good man, June."

"Yas'm." There was a faint, wailing overtone in June's voice. "But he done de wuk de good Lawd set him tuh do. He gone to rest in Jesus' bosom now." That simple faith released Cinda's own tears, and to weep brought her some easement.

They were all together, the children with them, when Brett appeared. They had no warning that he was near. He came in through the basement door and up the stairs; and the sound of his step was enough for Cinda. She flew to meet him, too nearly breathless to speak, and her streaming tears wetted the lips she lifted to his kiss. The others pressed about them, laughing and crying together, and they led him into the drawing room, and Cinda demanded—as though it mattered—why he came in by the back door; and he said in weary amusement:

"Well, I was afraid my mare would play out before I got to the front door, so I took her through the alley right to the stable. I'd have been here yesterday, but she went dead lame and I had to walk and lead her the last twenty or thirty miles." He turned to a chair. "Let's sit down. I'm tired."

Julian asked: "Did you know Lincoln's dead?"

"Yes, we heard it as we came up from the bridge."

Vesta cried: "Who's 'we,' Papa? Is Rollin with you?"

"No, Honey; Fitz Lee and Rosser didn't surrender. They're trying to get to General Johnston; and of course Burr and Rollin went with them." He spoke to Cinda. "Trav planned to go to Lynchburg, to Enid."

She saw how tired he was, drained equally of strength and spirit; and his need of her now made her stronger. "It's all over, darling," she said gently.

He nodded, slumped in his chair. "Yes, all over." He fumbled in his pocket, found a slip of paper, held it out. Cinda read the printed lines.

Appomattox Court House,
Virginia
April 10, 1865

The bearer, Private—Brett Dewain—Third Company Howitzers, Hardaway's Battalion, a paroled prisoner of the Army of Northern

Virginia, has permission to go to his home and remain there undisturbed with one horse.

B. H. Smith, Jr.
Captain Commanding Third
Company Howitzers

Cinda passed the parole to Vesta, it went from hand to hand. "I got that on the eleventh," Brett explained in dull tones. "But we couldn't leave till Wednesday. A dozen of us started together, but some of the horses were better than others, so we soon separated. We made Buckingham Court House that night. Confederate money was no good, so we couldn't buy anything, but some people gave us supper." His voice was empty and spiritless. "There were only three of us, by that time. We decided the farmers on that road would have too many soldiers to feed; so we went to Cartersville and ferried across the river." Julian was looking at the parole, and Brett said: "Better give that back to me, son, so I can show it to the Yankee sentries and prove I'm an honest man."

Cinda thought with pitying tenderness and love: Why, he's beaten, he's given up, he's worn to death; but I will make him whole again. Brett droned on. He had lodged in Manikin Town last night, and made an early start this morning, walking, leading his limping horse. His voice trailed into silence. Cinda rose.

"Brett Dewain, I'm going to put you to bed."

He nodded. "I'd like to go to bed. I'd like to sleep a year." Vesta came to help him up the stairs, and feeling his weakness Cinda wondered whether he would ever be strong again. She helped him out of his clothes while June in the bathing room filled the tub. The old woman took his worn, stained garments away to wash and clean them, and Cinda helped him bathe, and when he was in bed she sat beside him. He fell instantly asleep, and when she stole from the room he did not wake; nor did he wake that day at all. Lest she disturb him, she slept that night on a pallet by his bed. Let him sleep; let him rest; at least now and forever he was at home.

Monday the newspapers, in black-bordered columns, told the story of Lincoln's assassination; and at dinner Cinda asked: "What do the soldiers think? About his being dead."

Brett said honestly: "Why, they hope he'll roast in hell! We used to laugh at him, when he was alive; but we've had four years of blood and death and starvation and general misery, and blamed him for it." He added: "But of course we'll keep our tongues between our teeth!"

"He's brought death to plenty of others. I can't really feel sad about it. And yet . . ."

Cinda left the sentence unfinished, and Vesta said: "I've never thought he was as bad as people said, Mama. Not since he let you bring Julian home."

Brett spoke thoughtfully. "I remember this actor who killed him. He was in Richmond at the time of the John Brown business." He shook his head in slow amazement. "My, but that was a long time ago. In another world."

Cinda nodded; yes, a long time ago. The day they heard of John Brown's deed, she and Brett had just returned from England, with the shipload of beautiful things which made this great house still so lovely and contenting. Mama was alive, spry as a cricket, as gay as any of them; and the big old house at Great Oak with its floors of heart pine as enduring as marble and its panelled walls and all its spacious beauty was still standing; and Trav was bringing the fields back to good culture, and the people were happy, and life was leisured and gracious and friendly. Vesta was a child just coming to womanhood, with her first love in her eyes, and Clayton was alive, and Burr's hands were whole and beautiful, and Julian's legs were strong.

Cinda shook her head, putting thoughts away. To remember was to weep, and she must dry her eyes of tears.

They heard that day that Roger Pryor had called a meeting of Petersburg ladies to mourn President Lincoln; and Cinda remembered Mr. Pryor speaking from the balcony at the hotel in Charleston, his long hair flying as he urged the attack on Sumter which ushered in these years of grief and suffering and terror and despair. Rhett, Yancey, Pryor, old Mr. Ruffin—these men more than any others had led the South on the dreadful road to war. They promised secession would bring liberty and peace and prosperity. Well, they had lied; and Mr. Yancey was dead, and Mr. Rhett had been repudiated even by his own state, and Roger Pryor who had called Mr. Lincoln every name in the calendar now hypocritically summoned ladies to pay the dead man homage. Old Mr. Ruffin? Cinda remembered that Mrs. Lee and her daughters had visited him at Marlbourne, out on the Pamunkey three years ago, during those months when after the Yankees seized Arlington Mrs. Lee was a homeless wanderer; but McClellan's army came so near Marlbourne that she removed to Richmond, and probably Mr. Ruffin left his home at the same time. That old man had fired the first shot at Sumter; he had even touched off one cannon at First Manassas. Where was he now? Let him, too, answer for his sins!

Through that week, people flocked into Richmond: soldiers coming home, refugees returning, freed Negroes guzzling freedom. Crowds were forbidden to gather on the streets, or people to assemble; and any public gathering of more than two people was held to be an assembly. "So if I'm with a friend and we meet a mutual friend, we cannot pause to speak to him," Brett explained, mocking his own helplessness. The Yankees openly accused President Davis and the leading figures in the Confederate government of complicity in the assassination. Mr. Davis and his cabinet were gone none knew where, and Cinda prayed for Mr. Davis to escape; since if he were caught the Yankees would surely hang him, and once the hanging began, no neck would be safe. For four years now they had been proud to call themselves rebels; but rebels, if rebellion failed, were hanged. It was true that General Ord, who had taken over from General Weitzel the command of the city, seemed to be a considerate and courteous gentleman; but probably he and all the Yankees were just waiting for President Davis to be captured before setting up a gallows at every street corner!

To be sure, they would presumably hang only the great men, the leaders; so Brett was safe. But he was changed, something gone out of him. He seemed to feel most deeply the fact that they were completely impoverished. Confederate money would buy nothing; gold or the Yankee greenbacks were the only acceptable currency. Once Cinda found him tearing up and burning the Confederate bonds into which he had converted their fortune. It had been easy enough to say at that time: "If everybody in the South is to lose everything, so will we." But no one then really believed in the possibility of this complete disaster. She asked in an empty wonder:

"Brett Dewain, how rich were we?"

He did not look up, continuing to feed the flames. "Well, most of our wealth was in slaves, Cinda. Slaves and land. In money at interest, and securities, all the Currain funds together amounted to about three hundred thousand dollars." He added with a sound vaguely mirthful: "And now Julian—I saw him this morning, sitting on a pile of rubbish —is cleaning bricks down on Main Street at five Yankee dollars a week, knocking the mortar off them with a trowel."

"Vesta sells pies to Yankee soldiers."

He nodded. "Caesar brought me three dollars in Yankee scrip today; three dollars and two bits. He earned it helping clean up the fire wreckage." He smiled mirthlessly. "As soon as my mare gets over her limp, I'll take the carriage and go into the hackney cab business and help support the family." The last flame died, and he rose, brushing his hands. "Well, that's done. The slate is clean." He frowned in a puzzled way. "Cinda, I feel as though I were dead." She could offer him no comfort but her arms.

On the twenty-eighth, Rollin returned. It was dusk when he arrived; and clinging to him, heedless of his dusty garments, Vesta in laughing gladness pulled down his face to hers and kissed and kissed him and plucked at his ears and his nose and pulled his hair till he protested happily: "Hey, what are you trying to do to me, Honey?"

"Seeing if you're all here! Oh, darling, it's wonderful just to feel you!"

Brett and Tilda were not at home when Rollin arrived, but Vesta and Jenny and Cinda were hungry to hear all he could tell. He had ridden off from Appomattox on the ninth with General Rosser's command. They went to Lynchburg and decided to disband. "But some of us thought we could do something with General Johnston's army. So——"

Cinda interrupted breathlessly. "Rollin, did you see Burr?"

"Yes, he was with us. About two hundred of us started for Greensboro." Rollin added honestly: "But some dropped out on the way; went home, I suppose. President Davis was in Greensboro. He and his family were living in a box car at the station. Nobody offered them hospitality."

Vesta cried: "Oh how cruel! Letting them live like beggars!"

"I suppose people were afraid to take them in." Rollin went on: "Then we heard General Johnston was going to surrender, so three or four of us started back here." He laughed. "We got a scare near Danville; saw a picket of Union cavalry come over the top of the hill and ride toward us. We held our breath, expecting them to charge us. It turned out they didn't; but I'll never forget seeing them silhouetted against the sky ahead. They told us we could get our paroles in Danville, and we did."

Cinda asked: "But, Rollin, didn't Burr come with you?"

"No, he went to Raleigh to find Barbara."

She bit her lip. Barbara and her father and mother had gone off to Raleigh long ago, escaping all the misery of these last years, living in ease and comfort; and Cinda hated her. Burr was not Barbara's; he was hers! Yet now he had gone to Barbara, and the thought was bitter in her throat. She asked Rollin: "Isn't Sherman in Raleigh?"

"I suppose so. He was almost there before we left Greensboro. But they say that as soon as General Lee surrendered, Sherman stopped his men from doing any more damage; so Burr will be all right."

Since it was almost supper time, Vesta led him away upstairs to rid himself of travel stains; but at supper and afterward, all of them together, there was more long talk; and before they went up to bed, Jenny asked a question.

"Rollin, how did you get home? Are the cars running?"

"I rode," he said. "I came slowly, to let Prince get some strength back."

Jenny repeated her unanswered question. "Are the cars running, Rollin? Or the stages?"

"Some, I think," he said. "But of course the tracks are torn up wherever the Yankees got at them. Why?"

"I was—wondering," Jenny said, and said no more that night; but next day she spoke to Cinda alone. "Mama, as soon as I can, I'm going back to the Plains. Do you think Papa might want to go? He needs something to do."

Cinda started to protest, for of course Jenny could not go back to the

Plains. Yet Brett might go. If he were busy, he would presently be happy too.

"But what can he do there, Jenny?" she asked.

"Make a crop."

"With no negroes?"

"I expect most of them are still there, unless Sherman's men burned the house. And even if they did, Banquo wouldn't run away, nor old James, nor—well, lots of them; and I know Mr. Peters would keep them all at work if he could." She added, with a shy pride: "We made some cotton last summer, and Mr. Peters had the people gin it with the old treadle gins, and pressed it in our own screw and baled it and hid it in the deep woods away from the house. If the Yankees didn't find it, Papa could sell it now."

"I suppose he might go," Cinda reflected. "But of course you couldn't."

Jenny answered quickly: "Yes, I could. You and Aunt Tilda stay here and keep the children, and Papa and I will go."

Cinda shivered in sudden fear. "Oh no! I'll never let Brett Dewain out of my sight again!"

"You will if it's the best thing to do."

"He'll soon be all right here," Cinda argued, trying to persuade her-self. "He goes to see his business friends, and they talk about reopen-ing the banks and starting to run the railroads." But she knew Jenny was right. It would do Brett good to go back to the Plains; and she found herself longing for the old fine years of quiet peace and deep contenting there.

On the Sunday after Rollin's return the vanguard of Grant's vic-torious army marched through Richmond, crossing the pontoon bridge at Seventeenth Street and passing in review before General Meade and General Halleck at City Hall. Rollin and Julian went to see that spectacle, but Brett stayed indoors.

"They say there were fifty thousand of them," Rollin reported when he came home. "It was a sight."

Brett said thoughtfully: "Lee hadn't that many men in his whole army, not after the first of January; and this was less than half of

Grant's army. But we kept them busy for a while, all the same."
Cinda heard something new in his tone, an awakening pride; and
when next day a reward of one hundred thousand dollars was offered
for the capture of President Davis, and twenty-five thousand dollars
for each of a considerable list of Confederate leaders, Brett said
jocosely: "Now there's a real business opportunity, Cinda! I think I'll
go win that reward and restore our fallen fortunes."

She laughed with him, happy that now at last he began to be able
to jest; and the day after, when he decided to stroll as far as Capitol
Square, she kept him company.

She and Brett walked down Franklin Street and entered the Square
at the gate by the Bell Tower. She kept her eyes straight ahead, pretending not to see the blue uniforms everywhere; but there were men
in gray too, and to each she gave an eager smile. Negroes by ones and
twos and dozens sat in the sun or swarmed across the sidewalks; the
shrill laughter of the wenches and the hoarse mirth of the men filled
the air. But the Square was alien ground, with Yankee sentries at the
Governor's mansion, and around the Capitol and across in front of the
City Hall; so Cinda suggested they walk out Twelfth Street and call
on Anne and the baby. Brett agreed, and she told him about seeing
President Lincoln pass this way.

"And thousands of negroes following him. June was here. I saw
her kneel in front of him; and after he passed, she kissed the ground
he stepped on." Brett did not speak, and she said: "Brett Dewain, I
never believed before that day that our people wanted to be free."

"I suppose we never let ourselves believe it. We couldn't very well
believe it and keep our self-respect, so we pretended it wasn't true."
He met her eyes. "But June has stayed with you," he reminded her.

"She says there's a difference between having to take care of me, and
wanting to."

When they reached the house they found only Anne at home.
"Julian's working," she said proudly. "And Papa's taken the carriage
and driven out to the country to buy vegetables."

"Vegetables!" Cinda echoed. "Whatever for?"

"Why, to eat, of course. But he buys all he can, and what we don't
need he sells to the market men!" She laughed at her own words. "I
really think he enjoys it! He makes fun of himself for turning huck-

ster; but he loves to get out in the country, and he's so proud to be earning some money."

Brett nodded. "I know how he feels."

"As soon as things settle down, he's going to open an office again," Anne told them. "And Julian's going to read law with him. Papa says Julian will be a fine lawyer." She went to bring the baby for them to admire. "Molly's left," she explained. "So I take care of him now, and I love it."

Molly, granddaughter of old Sal who presided over the Judge's kitchen, had been the baby's nurse. "Where's Molly gone?"

"She decided she was free." Anne smiled. "Aunty Sal told her never to show her face around here again!"

"Sal hasn't left?"

"Heavens, no! Papa told her she'd better, because we can't pay her anything; but she told him to hush his mouth!" Brett laughed aloud, the first full-throated laughter Cinda had heard since he came home; and Anne said with twinkling eyes: "She told Papa she'd helped bring him into the world and she intended to be here to bury him!"

The baby, just a few days more than a year old, bounced on Cinda's knee; and Brett said: "Here, give that young one to me!" Cinda watched him in a rising happiness.

When they started home, they walked along Clay Street to Ninth, and then along Marshall to Seventh, and so to Broad before turning into Fifth; and Cinda saw everywhere garbage and refuse in the gutters and the alleys and the streets. "I declare, Brett Dewain," she cried, "we need a good housecleaning. I wouldn't have believed so much filth could accumulate in a month. Where does it come from?"

"Richmond's full of negroes," he reminded her. "The Yankees are feeding twenty thousand of them, men and women and children." And he said: "That will be worse before it's better, too. The negroes don't know what to do with freedom. They don't know anything at all." His tone was grave, but it was no longer dull and hopeless. "We've kept them ignorant and dependent. Whatever they are now is what we've made them. If they don't know how to use their freedom, it's our fault. And we'll pay for it. They'll always be here. Somehow we have to live with them."

"The Yankees might at least make them clean up the streets!"

"The negroes shouldn't be in Richmond. They ought to be working the farms."

She hesitated, seized the moment. "Jenny thinks someone ought to go back to the Plains. She thinks if our people there are kept busy, they'll stay on the place."

He did not speak till they had crossed Broad Street and turned toward Fifth. "Yes, I've been thinking something of the kind," he agreed. She waited, but he said no more.

At home Vesta declared their walk had done them good. "You both look like new people. Mama, your cheeks are as pink as a girl's."

Cinda smiled. "That's temper! It made me mad to see the nastiness in the streets everywhere!"

Vesta laughed. "Did you go by the Old Market? You can hardly get near it for the piles of fish heads and entrails and all sorts of garbage, and the swarms of flies. I hold my handkerchief over my nose."

"Something ought to be done about it!"

"Oh, everybody's too busy cleaning up after the fire, pulling down the old walls and cleaning bricks and laying foundations for new buildings. I like to walk along Main Street. You see so many gentlemen you know, scraping bricks like Julian, or mixing mortar, or learning how to be carpenters." Vesta smiled. "Why, Mama, it's as sociable as an evening promenade out to Gamble's Hill used to be. You ought to come with me some time."

But Cinda shook her head, and it was long before she again ventured out. Tilda and Vesta went somewhere almost every day. Tilda was busy. The Yankee commissary issued rations to indigent white women as well as to Negroes; but they must present certificates from a doctor or a minister, attesting that they were at once too poor to buy food, and too ill to work. Tilda and the ladies she directed spent their days marshalling these necessary proofs of need; and Vesta too seemed to have many matters to which she must attend. But Cinda stayed indoors. Thus at least she need not see all the tragedy which in Richmond now was a commonplace.

Brett began to wear a new abstraction, and Cinda knew that once or twice he had long conversations with Jenny. He, like Tilda, usually left the house for a while every morning; and one day when he returned he said he had called on Mr. Daniel, the president of the Fredericksburg railroad.

"He's hopeful," he told her. "But of course the road is a ruin. Most of the bridges have been burned, tracks torn up, engines and cars worn out. And they've nothing in the treasury but Confederate bonds and Confederate money. But he believes they can sell their bonds in Philadelphia and New York to finance rebuilding."

"I should think he'd hate asking Northerners for money."

"Well, of course no Southerners have any credit now. Technically we're all outlaws, so we can't sell anything, can't give good title; and naturally we can't borrow, not while all our property is still liable to confiscation. There've been confiscations in Louisiana." His lips twisted in a mirthless smile. "And the confiscated lands have been sold or leased to negroes, forty acres to a man. I suppose that's what will happen to the Plains." He added: "Mr. Daniel hears from Charleston that the rice swamps are all ruined, dams and levees broken, the swamps grown up to brush and weeds. I don't suppose anyone will ever raise rice again down there; not without slaves. The negroes always dreaded working in the swamps because so many of them sickened and died. They certainly won't do it now when they no longer have to."

"That means Rollin's family is ruined, doesn't it?"

"Yes. I believe since his father died his mother has tried to keep things going; but it's hopeless. The rice planters are even worse off than we. We at least have land that can be used to make a crop; and Mr. Daniel thinks if we can raise cotton it will bring tremendous prices." She guessed he was about decided to return to the Plains, but he went on to speak of a projected trip to Great Oak. "Rollin wants to go down," he explained. "He and Vesta plan to try to farm there. Vesta says Rooney Lee and his cousin John are going back to White House, build a cabin, make a home. Rollin wants to live in Virginia, bring his mother here."

Cinda felt a sudden homesick longing. "Great Oak seems a thousand miles away."

"We can take the carriage. My mare and Rollin's horse will have to get used to working in harness. We'll go through New Market, cross at Barrett's Ferry." He added, watching her: "Vesta says she's going."

She nodded. "So am I."

Cinda would regret that decision, and not only because the journey was hard and wearying. Along the way to New Market, she caught glimpses of the fortifications which here on the North Side Longstreet and his men had held so long; and she saw broken guns and wagons, and sometimes the smell of carrion lay sickly sweet upon the morning air. Beyond New Market, across the Strawberry Plains, the marks of battle were not so numerous; but at Turkey Creek the bridge was broken, and they had to retrace their way and take the Quaker Road and then climb the gentle slopes of Malvern Hill, where three years ago so many Southern men had died under McClellan's guns. Cinda saw bleached bones half-hidden in the new grass; and she took refuge from sick grief in empty questions.

"Brett Dewain, I always supposed Malvern Hill was steep and terrible; but I don't think we've climbed fifty feet in half a mile. Why was it so hard?"

"Our men had no cover." Brett spoke half to himself. "The Yankee guns were massed along the crest here, and our men had to come across open fields all the way from the woods back there." And he said: "Steep slopes are easier to attack than gentle ones, Cinda. If they're steep enough, the guns can't point down at the men. At Fredericksburg, and at Gettysburg there was no real climb, nothing you'd notice if you were just taking a stroll. But it's different when you're marching into cannon fire, with not even a ditch or a tree where you can hide for a minute from the bullets and the shells."

She was glad when the road dipped down into deep woods toward the river; and weariness helped her sleep the slow miles away. She woke at Barrett's Ferry and her heart quickened, for their goal was near.

But to arrive was worse than the journey. When they came to where the big house had been, the chimneys were standing; but that was all. The Yankees—McClellan's men or Butler's—had had a depot here; and they had left their mark. The fences were gone, and every outside building had been wrecked and ravaged by soldiers seeking wood for their fires. The tremendous oak which gave the place its name stood unharmed; but all around it, wagons crossing the lawns toward the river had rutted the deep sod, and a road had been cut at an angle down the bluff to the landing. Garbage and filth were scattered everywhere. The largest accumulations were marked by clumps of weeds; and the air was sour with a stale smell of men and of rotten meat and of decay. The gardens were trampled, and even the lovely clumps of bush box were hacked and torn, or scorched by campfires built heedlessly near. From the top of the bluff, thousands of bottles had been thrown down toward the river, and an enormous confusion of rubbish dumped atop them. The heap of bottles and of broken glass and of worn out harnesses and old newspapers and rusted muskets and rotting garbage was higher than a man's head. Cinda saw rats appear and disappear from every cranny in the pile, loping sluggishly away to hide at their approach, peering out at them with beady eyes. When the Union soldiers departed they had set fire to a mountain of stores not worth removal; and in the ash heap that remained rats had tunnelled to reach the barrels and boxes charred but not consumed. Even the wells had been made useless. In one the swollen carcass of a pig still floated. Where the house had stood and for a quarter-mile on either side, every yard of ground was desolated and defiled.

But away from the house lay a promise and a challenge; for though the fields were grown to weeds among which pine saplings already began to lift their heads, Brett thought they could be brought back. "Trav can give you good advice on that, Rollin. He's a real farmer."

Vesta was eager, but Rollin had his doubts. "It would be hard for you, Honey."

"I'll love it!" She smiled at him and kissed him. "Don't try to pack me up in cotton and put me on a shelf, Rollin! I'm as strong as a horse really. You'll get lots of good hard work out of me."

"We've no place to live! There's not a roof that will keep out the rain."

"We'll build one! It doesn't have to be a big one, not at first." Cinda, listening, loved this dear daughter of hers; she saw Rollin begin to catch fire. Oh, they were young, young, young; and she and Brett were old. But perhaps she and Brett could borrow strength from them.

When the others returned to Richmond, Rollin stayed behind to make a place ready for Vesta's coming. The third day after they came home again, Sherman's army marched through Richmond, northward bound; and for Cinda that departure was a lifting of old burdens. Sherman had left bitterness in every Southern heart, to persist long after the ashes and destruction which marked his path were covered and hidden by healing time. Homes burned, women insulted, old men tortured, houses pillaged, money and jewels as well as worthless knick-knacks stolen—these things would be remembered and reported to generations yet unborn. But at least now his army of robbers and torturers was gone out of the land they had looted and laid waste, and their bloodstained boots no longer defiled the beloved Southern soil.

Sunday morning, boys came racing through the streets selling extra editions of the new paper, the *Republic,* which had been allowed to begin publication the Wednesday before. The news they cried seemed to Cinda somehow to draw a curtain across the past, for President Davis was captured. This was the real end, even more definite than the surrender of the armies. So long as Mr. Davis was free, he in his person was still the Confederacy.

But now he was a prisoner, so now the hanging would begin. She was fiercely anxious for Brett to leave Richmond, to go to the Plains or somewhere far away; for here the Terror would have its center. She urged him to go at once; but Brett refused to believe that there would be the wholesale arrests which she expected.

"Because after all, there are some sensible people in the North," he argued. "President Johnson is a rascally renegade, a turncoat Democrat, beneath contempt; but he will be controlled by wiser heads."

"He says they'll hang Mr. Davis," Cinda reminded him.

"I doubt it." Brett added, half-smiling: "In fact I suspect they're already wishing they hadn't caught him. President Davis had come to be the most hated man in the Confederacy. He bore the blame for all our failures. If he had escaped, like the scapegoat the Hebrews used to chase away into the wilderness, he'd have taken our sins with him and we'd have felt ourselves absolved; but now we'll make a martyr out of him, or at least the Yankees will. If they hang him, he'll be deified by the South, to be worshipped in our secret hearts forever. So they won't. Some of them are wise enough to know that."

Wednesday the *Republic* printed an account of the capture. Mr. Davis had been taken at Irwinsville, Georgia; and in an attempt to escape he had disguised himself in woman's clothes. Cinda refused to believe that. "Mr. Davis wouldn't humiliate himself!"

Vesta had brought the *Republic* home, and she urged: "It's right here in the paper, Mama!"

"Newspapers have printed so many lies these four years, I'll never believe them again."

Vesta laughed. "Well, you can read for yourself."

Cinda could not resist doing so. She still held to her disbelief; but apart from the lies about Mr. Davis, there were things in the paper worth reading, and believing. Yankee patrols, finding idle Negroes pitching pennies in Third Street, where young people used to walk out to Gamble's Hill, had marched them away and put them to work at cleaning streets. A good thing! She saw an advertisement which said that Stone and Rosston's circus was performing in a rain-proof pavilion at Main and Third. Probably the circus had attracted the Negroes to the neighborhood. There were other advertisements eloquent and sad. People sought to sell watches or jewelry, or they offered extravagant security to borrow money; a hundred dollars or a thousand or ten thousand. She thought she could guess the identity of some of the advertisers, and wished to weep for them. There were columns of testimony from the trial of Mrs. Surratt and those men who had conspired to kill Mr. Lincoln. It would be like the Yankees to hang a woman! The paper said carts and wagons were dumping garbage into the ravine at Fourth and Leigh, and the foul odor made noisome the whole neighborhood. Portable houses two stories high, which could be erected in a few hours, were being put up in the burned district. There were many burglaries reported, and a man named William Tyree saw a Negro in a Second Street market selling onions, and complained to the Provost Marshal that the onions had been stolen from his garden, and positively identified them as his. The Provost Marshal gave Mr. Tyree back his onions; but Cinda thought the Yankee officer would enjoy telling his friends in the North about the Virginia man who could identify his own onions! Probably when the story came to be told, Mr. Tyree would be described as a Southern gentleman, an FFV at the very least. Cinda went to tell the others this jest, finding herself moved to a mirth almost hysterical. She could not remember when she had laughed so hard and so long.

That laughter marked for her the return of a more buoyant heart. After all, life seemed to go on. They had little or no money, but the big house, except that it was impossible to get glass to repair the broken windows, was as cool and comfortable and beautiful as ever. People had used to predict that when the Yankees came no one would be safe; they would all be murdered in their beds, and robbery, arson, insult would be commonplace. But none of these predictions proved true. Probably not even the prophets of woe had believed **their own** predictions.

She could laugh now at things that a month ago would have made her hot with anger. Richmond was full of gaping, vulgar Yankees come to peer and pry and wander through the city and gloat over the marks of suffering. Tilda every day brought stories of these visitors and their ape-like behavior; and once she spoke of a group from some little town in New York State.

"Six men and two ladies," she said. "They stayed at the Spottswood, and they went to the Capitol, and one of them sat in the Speaker's chair and pulled out some hair from the seat and took it as a souvenir!"

Cinda smiled. "Mercy! Are we so wonderful they worship what we sit on?"

"Oh, they were crazy for souvenirs. They split pieces off doorways, and whittled walls. They went to the White House and tried all the chairs and sofas; and everywhere they went, they gloated over the ruins, and kept saying at the tops of their voices that we got what we deserved. Even the Yankee officers who had to escort them were ashamed. One of the officers told Mr. Harrison—I saw Mrs. Harrison today—that at Brandon they stole handfuls of letters out of desks in the house, and they broke whole branches off the magnolia trees, and trampled the strawberry beds. In Mrs. Harrison's place I'd have been furious, but she said she didn't blame them any more than she'd have blamed so many hogs; said they didn't know any better."

Cinda nodded understandingly. Small wrongs were forgotten in the shadow of greater sorrow. Then too it was reassuring to be reminded that Yankees, despite their numbers and their wealth and now their victory, were a poking, thieving lot, no better than so many meddlesome monkeys. Let them take their stolen souvenirs and go home!

Brett was planning departure to the Plains. He had consulted the Yankee officers at the Freedmen's Bureau, and he reported to Cinda what they told him. "We're expected to make contracts with our people. The negroes agree to go on working just as they always have, and we agree to feed them and house them and take care of them. The only difference is that after the crop is made they get a third of it. I suggested that negroes don't know what a contract is, and of course they can't read or write; but the Bureau says they can make their mark, and if any of them don't do their work we can take them to the Provost Court and have them punished."

She laughed with him at the absurdity of imagining that Negroes would pay any attention to a contract. "But at least they'll work as long as you feed them, and as long as they haven't any money."

"Well, they will if the Yankees make them," he agreed. He meant to try it, but there was a rumor that President Johnson would presently issue an amnesty proclamation; and Brett waited to hear its terms. While he waited, the new Governor of Virginia came to Richmond. Mr. Pierpont had been a Union man, and President Lincoln had set him up last February as Governor of as much of Virginia as was held by Union armies. Now he moved his capital from Alexandria to Richmond; and Richmond men anxious to see orderly government reestablished arranged a reception, and Mr. Macfarland and Mr. Haxall and Mr. Goddin were chosen to assure Mr. Pierpont that Richmond and all Virginia were prepared to work with him for the restoration of good order.

He was expected on Thursday, but his steamer was delayed till the next day; and a deluge of rain thinned the procession which to the accompaniment of a salute of thirty-six guns at Rockett's and of fifteen at Capitol Square escorted him to the Capitol. Neither Cinda nor any of the household went to witness his arrival, but the *Republic* gave a detailed account of the occasion. Governor Pierpont in his speech referred to the days when war came, and to his efforts to hold Virginia in the Union; and he said proudly:

"We did save a large part of West Virginia, and were fast embracing the eastern portion also, but those who commenced this rebellion were bent on vile, needless, cruel destruction; and the charred ruins of Richmond attest how well they accomplished their nefarious design."

Vesta was reading the speech aloud to them. Cinda said, half amused: "I don't think we'll ever really love Mr. Pierpont, not if he talks like that!"

"Well, he was speaking to Northerners, mostly," Vesta explained. "Or to men from Western Virginia." She added, smiling at something she read: "The reception was very stiff and formal at first, but then they served refreshments, solid and liquid. Listen to this: 'In a short time the best feeling and cheer prevailed in the assembly. Conspicuous among them—' I suppose because they were more intoxicated than the others. 'Conspicuous among them were Senator Lane from Kansas, and the Honorable Mr. Norton from Illinois.'"

"Well, let Mr. Pierpont go ahead and govern, for all of me," Cinda commented. "I expect we'll get along in spite of him."

And in fact Richmond every day seemed to draw nearer to normal ways. Sometimes she thought the process too rapid. There was a May Festival out on Church Hill, in which a number of young ladies took part, and Miss Julia Picot was named Queen of the Festival and there were refreshments afterward at Mrs. Parkinson's home; and the band and the glee club of the Twenty-Fourth Massachusetts regiment provided music for the occasion. "But it's curious." Cinda spoke in a sarcastic tone. "It's curious that we don't know any of the young ladies who took part; at least none of those whose names are in the paper."

Yet the Yankees were certainly trying to restore good order. The idle Negroes were the greatest problem. General Patrick, the Provost Marshal, addressed a mass meeting at the African Church and urged them all to leave Richmond and return to the farms and go to work, or to find jobs in the city; but Brett said next day:

"If any of them took his advice it doesn't show! There must be thirty or forty thousand of them still here."

The soldiers patrolling the streets became increasingly stern in smothering any disturbance. When a battle of sticks and stones and fists broke out on Fifteenth Street between Negroes on one side and worthless white men on the other, scores of combatants were hustled away to prison. There were still many thefts and robberies and even burglaries, but a hundred or more of the prisoners released from Castle Thunder during the fire were still at large; so not all those crimes could be blamed on the Negroes.

On the last Monday in May—the day the slander that President Davis wore woman's clothes in trying to escape his captors was admitted by the Yankees to have been a lie—Trav and Enid came from Lynchburg. They travelled by the Central, since not for another ten days would the Danville road be ready to renew operations. When they reached the house, Brett had gone to investigate a report that President Johnson had at last issued the proclamation of amnesty; but Cinda and the others were at home, and to see Trav again was great happiness. Cinda laughed at her own tears. "I declare, Travis, I don't know why I should be sniffling; but you always were my favorite brother."

Her gladness embraced Enid, too; but she thought that even in the short weeks since they last saw each other, Enid had grown older. There were lines at the corners of her eyes, and something bruised and hopeless in her expression. Cinda felt a sympathy for her which she had rarely felt before. Enid was so much younger than Travis; and no matter how dearly you loved him, Travis had never any gaiety in him, nor any youthfulness. She decided Enid was overtired, and took her away upstairs and bade June bring supper to her there; and she stayed while Enid undressed and made herself comfortable, asking her many questions. Lucy? Peter?

Lucy was grown up, Enid told her, trying to smile. "She makes me feel like an old woman, she's so much the young lady. I know now how Mama must have felt, with me for a grown daughter when she was no older than I am now." Lucy even had a beau, a most devoted beau. "Tom Buford. He was in one of those terrible Yankee prisons, at Elmira in New York State. He's only just come home. They starved him till some of his teeth actually fell out. He says thousands of our soldiers died there, of smallpox or pneumonia, or from not having enough to eat."

"I know. In the hospital I used to see our men come home so nearly starved that they just died."

"I wish the Yankees would get into a war with someone else, so we could fight against them and get even for all the things they did to us!"

"A good many Northerners died in our prisons, too."

Enid nodded. "I guess so. Trav says our prison at Salisbury was terrible. It was so crowded that lots of the prisoners had to dig caves to live in, or crawl under the buildings, even in the winter; and they all had pneumonia or dysentery or something, and they never got enough to eat."

"I always supposed there was plenty of food in that part of North Carolina."

"Well, there's plenty of it up North, too; but the Yankees starved our men!" Enid's tone was defiant. "So naturally we starved theirs! Trav says as many as fifty died sometimes in a day, at Salisbury. The carts would haul them away, piled up like logs. If they had any clothes on when they died, somebody stripped them. They hauled the bodies out and dumped them in a gully and sometimes didn't bother to throw any dirt over them. Trav says even Salisbury people thought it was terrible to treat them so; but it certainly was no worse than what the Yankees did to our boys. Like Tom Buford."

Cinda said sadly: "I think if people would remember the awful things in war—the things both sides do—there wouldn't be any more wars, ever."

She asked how the Longstreets were; and Enid said Mrs. Longstreet was about to have another baby. "Any day now. The General's as proud as if it was their first." She added: "He and Judge Garland have terrible arguments."

"What about?"

"Oh, about what we ought to do, now the war's over. General Longstreet thinks we ought to be good little boys!" Enid's tone was scornful. "For once, even Trav disagrees with him."

"General Lee says the same thing," Cinda suggested.

"Oh, I suppose they all have to say it; but General Longstreet seems really to believe it."

"Is he afraid of being arrested?"

"No, he says General Grant won't let any paroled men be bothered as long as they behave themselves."

Cinda presently heard Brett's voice belowstairs, and she left Enid to sleep. "Get a good night's rest, dear," she said affectionately. "Sleep as late as you can."

Jenny and Vesta were putting the children to bed, so she found Brett and Trav alone; and Brett had news.

"Burr and Mr. Pierce just arrived, Cinda. I saw them at the Spottswood. Burr's coming right up, as soon as they're settled." Cinda, quick with happiness, declared they must both come here; but Brett said Mr. Pierce was worn out by the trip. "And Burr promised Barbara to take care of him." Poor Burr was so gentle and so kind that he would always let Barbara impose on him. "Mr. Pierce wants to move back to Richmond," Brett explained. "He's come house hunting. He'll find prices pretty high. Houses couldn't cost more if there were a gold mine on every lot."

Trav said: "I'd sell the Clay Street house back to him." Cinda looked at him in surprise, and he explained: "That's why I came to Richmond, to sell the house."

"But, Travis, where will you live?"

"We're going back to Chimneys. I've been down there." Cinda thought it must have been on his way that he heard those hideous tales of the horror of Salisbury. "Mr. Fiddler, my old overseer, is there." Trav spoke to Brett. "He was with Hood in Tennessee, in the fighting at Franklin; but he's all right, and Pegleg has kept the people together, kept them working."

"Have you told Enid, Travis?" If he had, this might explain Enid's haggard eyes, her look of despair; for Enid had been wretched at Chimneys.

"Yes."

"She was never happy there."

He said in hard tones: "We're going back." Cinda knew nothing would shake him. Enid might batter as she chose against the stone wall of his decision and get only bruises for her pains.

"There must be bushwhackers in the mountains around there," Brett suggested. "Is it safe?" Cinda suspected that he too felt sympathy for Enid.

"They won't bother us," Trav said positively. "A man named Alex Spain led a band that made the Martinston region their headquarters; but he lives near there and his men too, and now they've gone back to farming and they're really a protection. They chased one gang clear back to Tennessee, killed two of them and caught another and strung him up to a beam in his own barn; and they helped round up the Wade gang, up near Holman's Ford on the Yadkin; gave four of them a trial and shot them. No, we won't be bothered at Chimneys." He added: "The wheat's badly rusted, and rains have beaten it down, so we can't hope for much of a crop; but I made some money trading in tobacco, so we'll be all right till next year's crop comes in."

Brett said approvingly: "Well! You're the business man of the family, Trav. I've nothing left except a reputation."

"I can help you. I sold my tobacco for almost five thousand dollars —in greenbacks—and when I sell the house——"

"You can't sell the house," Brett told him. "Not under the terms of the amnesty proclamation." Cinda had been only half listening, waiting for Burr's step at the door; but she forgot Burr now as Brett explained: "We're excluded from amnesty; all general officers and public officials, and every one worth twenty thousand dollars who voluntarily aided the Confederacy. So you and I can't sell anything."

Cinda protested. "Why not, for Heaven's sake?"

"Because we're outlaws! Everything we have is liable to confiscation, so we can't give good title to anything we—think we own."

"You mean to say they can take our house?"

"Well, they took Senator Semmes's house in New Orleans, and a lot of plantations in Louisiana." Brett looked at Trav. "Sold them, or leased them to free negroes, in forty acre lots."

"That's the most outrageous—" Cinda began, but then here was Burr; and in the bliss of holding him again in her arms, every trouble was for a while forgotten. He was thin, but he was alive and well after years of deadly danger; and he was here! Now for a while at least she need not share him with Barbara. She was sorry even to share him with Vesta and Jenny, who when they heard her call his name came running down the stairs; and she was furious when after half an hour Burr said he must go back to Mr. Pierce.

"He's nervous, and he gets excited," he explained. "I left him asleep, but he wakes up and worries."

"Worries? What has he to worry about?"

Burr grinned in an embarrassed way. "Oh he's got into the habit." And he said, like a confession: "You see, he put everything he had into gold and buried it in the cellar; and he worried about that. Of course by the time Sherman got to Raleigh the war was as good as over, so Sherman kept his men on their good behavior, didn't let them bother anyone."

Cinda thought spitefully that it would have served Mr. Pierce right if Sherman's thieves had stolen his miserly hoard. Anyone who had saved anything out of the past ought to be ashamed of himself! She said in dry contempt: "Why, wasn't Mr. Pierce clever? Brett was so stupid. He put all our money into Confederate bonds, so of course we're just paupers now!"

Brett said in a tone he seldom used to her: "Cinda!"

She bit her lip, and Burr tried to laugh. "It's all right, Papa! I know the way Mama talks." He kissed Cinda and she clung to him as though she would never let him go.

When Burr left, and Vesta and Jenny had gone upstairs, Cinda stayed with Brett and Trav, listening to their talk together. Brett, as soon as the cars were running to Danville, would start for the Plains. "Beyond Greensboro, I'll have to travel any way I can, but I'll get there." He meant to contract with the Negroes who had been his slaves. "The price of cotton won't break much this year, and Jenny says they baled last year's crop and hid it in the woods, and she's sure Sherman's men wouldn't find it. If I can get it to Charleston and ship it to New York, I ought to get fifty or seventy-five cents the pound."

"The railroads can't carry it, can they?"

"I'll put it on barges and take it down river. Jenny says there are three hundred and seven bales. If the price holds up, that will bring forty or fifty thousand dollars."

But shipment, until the railroads were restored, would surely be difficult; and they agreed that the railroads could not operate till some sort of civil government was re-established. Cinda was reminded of

General Longstreet's arguments with Judge Garland. "Travis," she asked, "what does Cousin Jeems think is going to happen?"

"Well, he's afraid the South will make trouble for itself. He says too many politicians, and preachers, and ladies, and men who got safe details and stayed out of the army, are going around saying we weren't beaten."

Brett laughed grimly. "I was beaten," he said. Cinda remembered him as he had been when he came home to her, utterly exhausted, worn in mind and body and spirit.

"So was I," Trav agreed. "I was ready to give in, and I was glad when we did. The trouble with wars is, politicians start them, but armies have to fight them. It's the armies that get beaten. The people who don't fight don't take the beating." Cinda thought those who stayed at home during these years had suffered to the limit of endurance; yet she knew what Travis meant. "Longstreet says we ought to admit we're licked," Trav explained. "He believes we should accept what he calls the verdict of the sword. He says we'll talk ourselves into trouble."

Brett nodded. "I know what he means. I hear men bragging that we'll never do this, and we'll never submit to that. Of course, in the end we'll have to do what we're told; but if we stop boasting about what we won't do, maybe the Yankees won't make us do it."

"Well," Trav explained, "Longstreet's point isn't so much that submission is expedient, but that it's right!" He smiled at a sudden memory. "One day I was with him and Judge Garland, and Longstreet said that what the South needed was for some of her best men to turn Republican. I thought the Judge would explode! He said Longstreet was as bad as Jack Slaughter."

Cinda asked: "What's Mr. Slaughter done?"

"Oh, he's the skeleton in the Garland closet. He hired substitutes, never went into the army. Two of the substitutes he hired were killed, and he jokes about it, says he was killed twice! Judge Garland won't speak to him."

Brett said doubtfully: "Longstreet goes pretty far. It will be a long time before any Southern man will dare admit he's a Republican. Unless of course he's a negro."

"I know," Trav assented. "But I think the General just said it for the sake of emphasis. When anyone disagrees with him, that makes him sure he's right. And he is right about some things. New England in the North and the Gulf States in the South pushed us into the war. They were so far apart that they didn't know the truth about each other; so when Yancey and Rhett told us all Northerners were cowards we believed it; and when Beecher and Emerson and Mrs. Stowe told the North that Southerners spent every fine day slicing the skin off a negro's back with a rawhide whip, the Northerners believed that. Longstreet says when you begin to think you're better than other people, you're heading for trouble. And with nations, trouble means war."

"He's right, of course," Brett agreed. "I doubt if any Southerner who really knew the North wanted secession."

"The General said something, the day we rode away from Appomattox Court House." Trav looked at Cinda, then at Brett again. "I've thought a lot about it. He said no nation as powerful as the Confederacy ever had as short a history."

For a moment they were silent, till Brett nodded. "I suppose that's true."

Trav said, pride in his eyes: "He's really a great man, Brett. Oh, he's stubborn, and sometimes he's wrong; but he'll always stand up for what he believes." He added uneasily: "The thing that bothers me, I think he's glad we were beaten."

Brett said thoughtfully. "I'm not sure I don't agree with him. God knows I fought as hard as I could, and I know we had a right to secede; but the Union would never be a great nation as long as any state could drop out whenever she chose. When men or states agree to work together, they have to give up something. We've proved that, in the South; proved it by not doing it. Our belief in states' rights would have destroyed the Union, if the Northern states hadn't given up their rights in order to beat us; and even then we'd have beaten them if each Southern state hadn't kept insisting on her rights. We fought it out our way, and they fought it out their way; and the war settled it."

Cinda protested: "But does force ever settle anything?"

"When it settles things right, yes," Brett declared. "And this question of secession has been settled right! The United States are really united now. I think that's a good thing even for us in the South. Some day it may prove to be a good thing for the world."

"I'm woman enough to keep remembering we had a right to do what we did."

"This was once when to be right was wrong."

Cinda laughed and rose. "When we start talking in riddles it's time to go to bed. For Heaven's sake don't say such things to anyone else, Mr. Dewain. It will be a long time before the South can forgive the man who tells her she was wrong!"

Next morning, June said Big Mill was in the kitchen. Cinda when she came downstairs asked Trav where Mill had been. "You left him here to take care of us; but after things settled down here, he disappeared. I thought he had run away."

"No, he came to Lynchburg to find me. He said you were all right, didn't need him. I took him with me to Chimneys, thought he might stay there; but he wants to go back to Great Oak."

"Oh, I'm glad. You know, Rollin and Vesta are going to farm the place. Rollin's there now, building them a cabin."

Trav had not heard this. "They'll have a hard time."

"They won't mind. They're young." And she said: "If you don't need Big Mill, send him to help Rollin. If he'd like to, that is. I keep forgetting they're not slaves now."

"He's already gone," Trav said. "Started this morning." He smiled. "Mill says his feet are all wore out from trompin' furrin ground. He says the old fields at Great Oak are as lonesome for him as he is for them. He said to me: 'I got deep roots in dem fiel's, Marse Trav. I'm gwine plant mah feets again an' let 'em grow.'"

Cinda nodded, feeling her eyes sting. Brett joined them, and she said: "The negroes are wonderful, aren't they? Has anyone heard of a single negro who made trouble for his white folks while the men were off to war?" Neither Trav nor Brett spoke, and she said softly: "Loyal, devoted, protecting Missy and the children while the men were fighting to keep them slaves. Did that ever happen in the world before?"

"I never heard of it," Trav admitted.

"What will become of them now? What will they do without us?"

His eyes shadowed. "God knows! They'll be some trouble, probably. We'll have to have laws to—control them."

Brett said dryly: "I've already heard some talk about those laws. The politicians plan to extend the vagrancy acts to cover all negroes. As if the North would let us make them slaves again under another name!"

Cinda asked: "Why do we need special laws for them?"

"For their own good," Trav said. "I learned something in the army, Cinda. I found out that to obey orders, to do what you're told, never having to make decisions, is a mighty restful thing. When the negroes were slaves, we took care of them and did their thinking for them. Sometimes I believe it was really we who were bound; it was really they who were free. Now they think they're free, but really, as their own masters, they're more truly slaves than they ever were before."

Brett added a word. "There's no freedom except in doing your duty, accepting your responsibilities. The only way to achieve freedom is to surrender it."

Cinda was puzzled. "I suppose you mean that now they're free they'll have to take care of themselves and their families?"

Trav said, half laughing: "Ask any married man about freedom. He knows!"

Resentfully she thought of Enid, and wished to retort that wives were the real slaves; but no word from her could help Enid. Travis would never change. She rose and left them, putting their conversation out of her mind. There were so many things she must learn to forget. The old years were gone, and already they seemed infinitely far away. When the newspapers reported that General Kirby Smith, away off yonder in Texas, had surrendered the remnant of the last Confederate army and fled to Mexico, it was like an echo from an empty room.

Thursday morning, St. Paul's and the other churches held a service of mourning and prayer for President Lincoln. The military authorities had ordered that these services be held, that flags should hang at half-mast, that public buildings were to be draped and all places of business closed; but there was no compulsion on anyone to attend.

Cinda went without compulsion; and when they heard her intention, the others except Enid decided to go with her.

"I wouldn't think of going," Enid said with a certain violence. "Pray for him? What I'd pray wouldn't do him much good!"

But the others went with Cinda, and she found it fine to walk along Grace Street to St. Paul's; it was heartening to enter these familiar doors, to turn to their own pew where even the red upholstery was like a friend's smile; it was peace to sit in this holy place and let her thoughts drift where they chose.

The service began, mourning and prayer for dead Abraham Lincoln. Her own father had been that dead man's grandfather. She remembered Tilda running down the stairs that night long ago at Great Oak with those letters in her hands. How different their lives since then might have been if Tilda had not found those letters! Travis of course would always be the same. He would take Enid back to Chimneys to live out her days an unwilling captive there; but doubtless he would have done that anyway. Cinda thought she herself had acquired a clearer vision, the ability to see weakness and folly here among her own people and to see some virtue in the North. Tilda certainly was changed, and for the better. From the wreckage of her life she had emerged with strength and resolution and—of all incredible things—a capacity for leadership and even for command. And of course that revelation had changed poor Faunt; or perhaps it had merely stripped off the handsome mask which for so long had deceived even Faunt himself. Tony? All his life Tony had followed shameful ways. If the knowledge that Abraham Lincoln and he were kin had made a difference in him, he could hardly have become worse than he was before.

Yet even without the knowledge of that kinship, these four years would have changed them all. Four years. What was it Cousin Jeems had said: That no great nation had ever had so short a history? Four years, and every day of those four years devoted to war.

Why had they fought? She tried to remember. For slavery? Yes, the Cotton States seceded because they wished to prevent the abolition of slavery. They announced that purpose openly, when their delegates came to urge Virginia to secede. But was that the only reason? She had heard men blame the tariff, which made Southern purchasers pay tribute to Northern manufacturers. Was that the reason? Brett Dewain had told her that some politicians in the Gulf States fomented war because they wished to set up a new nation for their own aggrandizement; and Trav had once suggested that secession was part of a design to stop the steady increase in the political power of the common man.

Yet certainly Virginia had not fought for slavery, nor against the tariff, nor for any other reason except the necessity of fighting either with the Cotton States or against them. Standing between North and South, she was compelled to turn one way or the other; and in that dilemma, only one choice was possible to her.

So they had plunged into four years of pitiful, needless folly. But at least those four years were done, and they should be forgotten. Cousin Jeems was right. The South should accept defeat, forget the past. He had said to Judge Garland that it would be a good thing if some of the best men in the South turned Republican; and it would be like the big, stubborn man to do exactly that. Of course, if he did, the South would cast him out; for it would be generations before the South could hear that accursed word without a bitter rage. The South would never forgive, and never follow him.

But if Cousin Jeems thought he ought to turn Republican, he would do so, and accept the consequences; and that would be a grand and valiant deed to do.

A word from the pulpit caught her ear, the name of the man they were here today to mourn. She put her thoughts aside, content at last to listen; and listening, she came to a deep certainty that in that dead kinsman whom so many hundreds and thousands and millions of people mourned today, there had dwelt a greatness which to serve God's plan would forever leave its mark upon the world.

Walking home afterward they were all silent till they came to their own door; but there Cinda paused, looking down Fifth Street toward the river, looking all around; and she stood thus for so long that Vesta asked softly:

"What is it, Mama?"

Cinda turned to face them all. "Why—I'm just saying good-by," she said. "Good-by to the past. I made up my mind, during the service. I'm not going to think any more—if I can help it—about what used to be." She had for a moment a prophetic vision. "If the South isn't careful, it's going to start feeling sorry for itself, and being proud and wistful, and boasting how brave our men were, and how beautiful our women, and what charming lives we led till the Yankees spoiled it all.

"But as long as we keep looking back over our shoulders, we'll be forever stumbling. When we learn to forget, then we will go ahead."

THE END

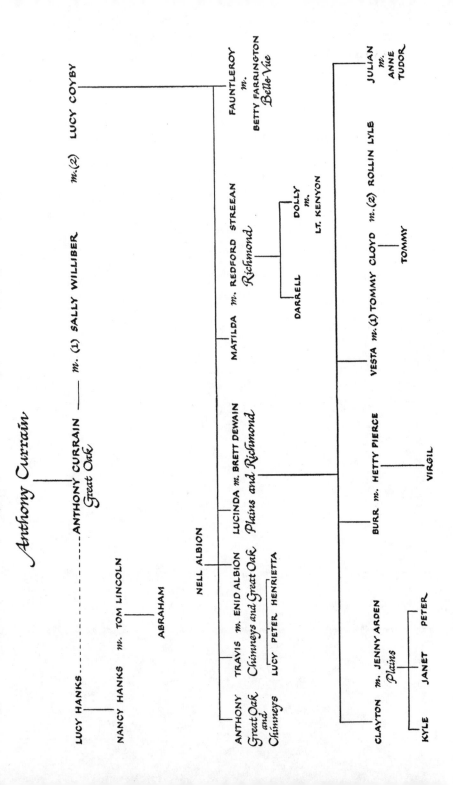